P9-EED-212

THE YEAR'S BEST

SCIENCE FICTION

ALSO BY GARDNER DOZOIS

ANTHOLOGIES

A DAY IN THE LIFE
ANOTHER WORLD
BEST SCIENCE FICTION STORIES OF THE YEAR #6–10
THE BEST OF ISAAC ASIMOV'S SCIENCE FICTION MAGAZINE
TIME TRAVELERS FROM ISAAC ASIMOV'S SCIENCE FICTION MAGAZINE
TRANSCENDENTAL TALES FROM ISAAC ASIMOV'S SCIENCE FICTION MAGAZINE
ISAAC ASIMOV'S ALIENS
ISAAC ASIMOV'S MARS
ISAAC ASIMOV'S SF LITE
ISAAC ASIMOV'S WAR
ROADS NOT TAKEN (with Stanley Schmidt)
THE YEAR'S BEST SCIENCE FICTION, #1–28
FUTURE EARTHS: UNDER AFRICAN SKIES (with Mike Resnick)
FUTURE EARTHS: UNDER SOUTH AMERICAN SKIES (with Mike Resnick)
RIPPER! (with Susan Casper)
MODERN CLASSIC SHORT NOVELS OF SCIENCE FICTION
MODERN CLASSICS OF FANTASY
KILLING ME SOFTLY
DYING FOR IT
THE GOOD OLD STUFF
THE GOOD NEW STUFF
EXPLORERS
THE FURTHEST HORIZON
WORLDMAKERS
SUPERMEN

COEDITED WITH SHEILA WILLIAMS

ISAAC ASIMOV'S PLANET EARTH
ISAAC ASIMOV'S ROBOTS
ISAAC ASIMOV'S VALENTINES
ISAAC ASIMOV'S SKIN DEEP
ISAAC ASIMOV'S GHOSTS
ISAAC ASIMOV'S VAMPIRES
ISAAC ASIMOV'S MOONS
ISAAC ASIMOV'S CHRISTMAS
ISAAC ASIMOV'S CAMELOT
ISAAC ASIMOV'S WEREWOLVES
ISAAC ASIMOV'S SOLAR SYSTEM
ISAAC ASIMOV'S DETECTIVES
ISAAC ASIMOV'S CYBERDREAMS

COEDITED WITH JACK DANN

ALIENS!
UNICORNS!
MAGICATS!
MAGICATS II
BESTIARY!
MERMAIDS!
SORCERERS!
DEMONS!
DOGTALES!
SEASERPENTS!
DINOSAURS!
LITTLE PEOPLE!
DRAGONS!
HORSES!
UNICORNS II
INVADERS!
ANGELS!
DINOSAURS II
HACKERS
TIMEGATES
CLONES
NANOTECH
IMMORTALS

FICTION

STRANGERS
THE VISIBLE MAN (collection)
NIGHTMARE BLUE (with George Alec Effinger)
SLOW DANCING THROUGH TIME (with Jack Dann, Michael Swanwick, Susan Casper, and Jack C. Haldeman II)
THE PEACEMAKER
GEODESIC DREAMS (collection)

NONFICTION

THE FICTION OF JAMES TIPTREE, JR.

THE YEAR'S BEST
SCIENCE FICTION

twenty-ninth annual collection

edited by Gardner Dozois

st. martin's griffin ✦ new york

These short stories are works of fiction. All of the characters, organizations, and events portrayed in these stories are either products of the authors' imaginations or are used fictitiously.

For information, address St. Martin's Press, 175 Fifth Avenue, New York, N.Y. 10010.

ISBN 978-1-250-00354-6

contents

permissions

"The Choice," by Paul McAuley. Copyright © 2011 by Dell Magazines. First published in *Asimov's Science Fiction,* February 2011. Reprinted by permission of the author.

"A Soldier of the City," by David Moles. Copyright © 2011 by David Moles. First published in *Engineering Infinity* (Solaris), edited by Jonathan Strahan. Reprinted by permission of the author.

"The Beancounter's Cat," by Damien Broderick. Copyright © 2011 by Damien Broderick. First published in *Eclipse Four* (Night Shade Books), edited by Jonathan Strahan. Reprinted by permission of the author.

"Dolly," by Elizabeth Bear. Copyright © 2011 by Dell Magazines. First published in *Asimov's Science Fiction,* January 2011. Reprinted by permission of the author.

"Martian Heart," by John Barnes. Copyright © 2011 by John Barnes. First published in *Life on Mars: Tales from the New Frontier* (Viking), edited by Jonathan Strahan. Reprinted by permission of the author.

"Earth Hour," by Ken MacLeod. Copyright © 2011 by Ken MacLeod. First published electronically at Tor.com, June 22. Reprinted by permission of the author.

"Laika's Ghost," by Karl Schroeder. Copyright © 2011 by Karl Schroeder. First published in *Engineering Infinity* (Solaris), edited by Jonathan Strahan. Reprinted by permission of the author.

"The Dala Horse," by Michael Swanwick. Copyright © 2011 by Michael Swanwick. First published electronically at Tor.com, July 13. Reprinted by permission of the author.

"The Way It Works Out and All," by Peter S. Beagle. Copyright © 2011 by Spilogale, Inc. First published in *The Magazine of Fantasy & Science Fiction,* July/August 2011. Reprinted by permission of the author.

"The Ice Owl," by Carolyn Ives Gilman. Copyright © 2011 by Spilogale, Inc. First published in *The Magazine of Fantasy & Science Fiction,* November/December 2011. Reprinted by permission of the author.

"The Copenhagen Interpretation," by Paul Cornell. Copyright © 2011 by Dell Magazines. First published in *Asimov's Science Fiction,* July 2011. Reprinted by permission of the author.

"The Invasion of Venus," by Stephen Baxter. Copyright © 2011 by Stephen Baxter. First published in *Engineering Infinity* (Solaris), edited by Jonathan Strahan. Reprinted by permission of the author.

"Digging," by Ian McDonald. Copyright © 2011 by Ian McDonald. First published in *Life on Mars: Tales from the New Frontier* (Viking), edited by Jonathan Strahan. Reprinted by permission of the author.

"Ascension Day," by Alastair Reynolds. Copyright © 2011 by Alastair Reynolds. First published in *Voices from the Past* (Kindle), edited by Lee Harris. Reprinted by permission of the author.

"After the Apocalypse," by Maureen F. McHugh. Copyright © 2011 by Maureen F. McHugh. First published in *After the Apocalypse* (Small Beer Press), Maureen McHugh. Reprinted by permission of the author.

"Silently and Very Fast," by Catherynne M. Valente. Copyright © 2011 by Catherynne M. Valente. First published in *Silently and Very Fast* (WSFS Press), by Catherynne M. Valente. Reprinted by permission of the author.

"A Long Way Home," by Jay Lake. Copyright © 2011 by Jay Lake. First published electronically at *Subterranean Magazine,* Winter 2011. Reprinted by permission of the author.

"The Incredible Exploding Man," by Dave Hutchinson. Copyright © 2011 by Dave Hutchinson. First published in *Solaris Rising* (Solaris), edited by Ian Whates. Reprinted by permission of the author.

"What We Found," by Geoff Ryman. Copyright © 2011 by Spilogale, Inc. First published in *The Magazine of Fantasy & Science Fiction,* September/October 2011. Reprinted by permission of the author.

"A Response from EST17," by Tom Purdom. Copyright © 2011 by Dell Magazines. First published in *Asimov's Science Fiction,* April/May 2011. Reprinted by permission of the author.

"The Cold Step Beyond," by Ian R. MacLeod. Copyright © 2011 by Dell Magazines. First published in *Asimov's Science Fiction,* June 2011. Reprinted by permission of the author.

"A Militant Peace," by David Klecha and Tobias S. Buckell. Copyright © 2011 by David Klecha and Tobias S. Buckell. First published electronically at *Clarkesworld,* November 2011. Reprinted by permission of the author.

"The Ants of Flanders," by Robert Reed. Copyright © 2011 by Spilogale, Inc. First published in *The Magazine of Fantasy & Science Fiction,* July/August 2011. Reprinted by permission of the author.

"The Vicar of Mars," by Gwyneth Jones. Copyright © 2011 by Gwyneth Jones. First published in *Eclipse Four* (Night Shade Books), edited by Jonathan Strahan. Reprinted by permission of the author.

"The Smell of Orange Groves," by Lavie Tidhar. Copyright © 2011 by Lavie Tidhar. First published electronically at *Clarkesworld,* November 2011. Reprinted by permission of the author.

"The Iron Shirts," by Michael F. Flynn. Copyright © 2011 by Michael F. Flynn. First published electronically at Tor.com, May 4. Reprinted by permission of the author.

"Cody," by Pat Cadigan. Copyright © 2011 by Pat Cadigan. First published in *TRSF,* the special all-fiction edition of MIT's *Technology Review,* edited by Stephen Cass. Reprinted by permission of the author.

"For I Have Lain Me Down on the Stone of Loneliness and I'll Not Be Back Again," by Michael Swanwick. Copyright © 2011 by Dell Magazines. First published in *Asimov's Science Fiction,* August 2011. Reprinted by permission of the author.

"Ghostweight," by Yoon Ha Lee. Copyright © 2011 by Yoon Ha Lee. First published electronically at *Clarkesworld,* January 2011. Reprinted by permission of the author.

"Digital Rites," by Jim Hawkins. Copyright © 2011 by Jim Hawkins. Copyright © 2011 by *Interzone.* First published in *Interzone 237.* Reprinted by permission of the author.

"The Boneless One," by Alec Nevala-Lee. Copyright © 2011 by Dell Magazines. First published in *Analog Science Fiction and Science Fact,* November 2011. Reprinted by permission of the author.

"Dying Young," by Peter M. Ball. Copyright © 2011 by Peter M. Ball. First published in *Eclipse Four* (Night Shade Books), edited by Jonathan Strahan. Reprinted by permission of the author.

"Canterbury Hollow," by Chris Lawson. Copyright © 2011 by Spilogale, Inc. First published in *The Magazine of Fantasy & Science Fiction,* January/February 2011. Reprinted by permission of the author.

"The Vorkuta Event," by Ken MacLeod. Copyright © 2011 by Ken MacLeod. First published in *The New and Perfect Man: Postscripts 24/25* (PS Publishing), edited by Peter Crowther and Nick Gevers.

"The Man Who Bridged the Mist," by Kij Johnson. Copyright © 2011 by Dell Magazines. First published in *Asimov's Science Fiction,* October/November 2011. Reprinted by permission of the author.

acknowledgments

The editor would like to thank the following people for their help and support: Susan Casper, Jonathan Strahan, Gordon Van Gelder, Ellen Datlow, Sean Wallace, Sheila Williams, Trevor Quachri, Peter Crowther, Nicolas Gevers, William Shaffer, Ian Whates, Andy Cox, Paula Guran, Dario Ciriello, Carl Rafala, Patrick Nielsen Hayden, Torie Atkinson, Eric T. Reynolds, George Mann, Jennifer Brehl, Stephen Cass, Mark Pontin, Lee Harris, Peter Tennant, Susan Marie Groppi, Karen Meisner, John Joseph Adams, Wendy S. Delmater, Jed Hartman, Rich Horton, Mark R. Kelly, John Jarrold, Otto Penzler, L. Timmel Duchamp, Andrew Wilson, Damien Broderick, Lou Anders, Patrick Swenson, Robert T. Wexler, Michael Swanwick, Jay Lake, Lavie Tidhar, Stephen Baxter, Ian R. MacLeod, Yoon Ha Lee, David Moles, Alec Nevala-Lee, Michael Flynn, Chris Lawson, Connor Cochran, Peter M. Ball, Paul Cornell, Tobias S. Buckell, David Klecha, Carolyn Ives Gilman, Tom Purdom, Dave Hutchinson, Pat Cadigan, Catherynne M. Valente, Karl Schroeder, Kij Johnson, Geoff Ryman, Paul McAuley, Jim Hawkins, Alastair Reynolds, Robert Reed, Maureen McHugh, Ken Liu, Eric Brown, Keith Brooke, Matt Hughes, Michael Smith, Kathleen Ann Goonan, Marty Halpern, Jo Walton, Hannu Rajaniemi, Daniel Marcus, Mary Robinette Kowal, Nancy Kress, Karl Bunker, Linn Prentis, Liz Gorinsky, Mike Resnick, Ian Tregillis, David Hartwell, Ginjer Buchanan, Susan Allison, Shawna McCarthy, Kelly Link, Gavin Grant, John Klima, John O'Neill, Charles Tan, Rodger Turner, Tyree Campbell, Stuart Mayne, John Kenny, Edmund Schubert, Tehani Wessely, Tehani Croft, Karl Johanson, Sally Beasley, Tony Lee, Joe Vas, John Pickrell, Ian Redman, Anne Zanoni, Kaolin Fire, Ralph Benko, Paul Graham Raven, Nick Wood, Mike Allen, Jason Sizemore, Sue Miller, David Lee Summers, Christopher M. Cevasco, Tyree Campbell, Andrew Hook, Vaughne Lee Hansen, Mark Watson, Sarah Lumnah, Sarah Johnson, and special thanks to my own editor, Marc Resnick.

Thanks are also due to the late, lamented Charles N. Brown, and to all his staff, whose magazine *Locus* (Locus Publications, P.O. Box 13305, Oakland, CA 94661. $60 in the U.S. for a one-year subscription [twelve issues] via second class; credit card orders 510-339-9198) was used as an invaluable reference source throughout the Summation; Locus Online (www.locusmag.com), edited by Mark R. Kelly, has also become a key reference source.

summation: 2011

Like last year, the big story in 2011 continues to be the explosion in e-book sales, which have been dramatic enough, and accrued fast enough, to make some commentators speculate that e-books will eventually drive physical print books out of existence altogether. I don't think that's going to happen anytime soon, if it ever does, but the e-book revolution has been impressive nevertheless, and shows no sign of losing momentum, especially with new devices like the Kindle Fire coming on sale, and no doubt other even more sophisticated devices waiting in the wings.

According to BookStats, a joint-research venture between the Book Industry Study Group and the Association of American Publishers, e-book sales jumped to $863.7 million in 2010 from $61.8 million in 2008. No reliable overall figures for 2011 are yet available, but one publisher predicted that e-books could account for as much as 40 percent of total revenue by the end of 2012. Considering that it's been estimated that one in five U.S. adults are reading e-books on a variety of devices, from dedicated e-readers to media tablets, and that there was a major surge in e-book sales after the 2011 holiday season (all those people looking for something to read on the devices they'd gotten for Christmas presents), that could well turn out to be true. The AAP report for September 2011 shows e-book sales up 100 percent to $80.3 million. Year-to-date figures show e-books up 137.9 percent at $727.7 million. Barnes & Noble's second-quarter sales report (for the period ending October 29, 2011) shows NOOK sales (for both the devices themselves and for e-books) rising 85 percent to $220 million, "four times what they were in the comparable period last year," according to CEO William Lynch.

None of this, impressive as it is, means that the print book industry has collapsed. There were still an enormous number of print books published in 2011, and many of them sold very well indeed. The U.S. Census Bureau's preliminary figures for October 2011 show estimated bookstore sales of $886 million, down 43 percent from September 2011, but down only 7 percent from October 2010 figures. For the year-to-date, sales are up 2 percent at $12.91 billion. Overall retail sales were up 1 percent from September, and up 8 percent year-to-date.

The effect of the e-book revolution can best be seen in the changes in the *kinds* of books that are selling best. Hardcovers and trade paperbacks both saw their numbers increase, with a noticeable boost in new titles, but the traditional mass-market paperback reprints dropped significantly, as did new mass-market titles. The fact that e-book sales are dramatically increasing at a time when mass-market paperback sales have dropped suggests that e-books are to some degree filling the market niche once occupied by mass-market print books, particularly reprint titles.

Unexpectedly, sales of print books also surged during the holiday season, with Barnes & Noble showing a 4 percent rise, the first increase in five years. This suggests that many people still find a print book to be a more satisfactory Christmas present than the gift of an e-book—something physical to wrap and put under the tree.

For this reason, and the reason that for the foreseeable future there are going to be people who just *prefer* a print book they can hold in their hands to an e-book that must be read from a screen, and prefer browsing at a bookstore to shopping for books online, the publishing apocalypse that some commentators seem almost to yearn for, where all the publishing houses go out of business, physical brick-and-mortar bookstores disappear completely, and print books themselves become extinct (or at least rare artifacts), is probably not going to happen—although things in the publishing world are never going to go back to the way they were before the invention of the e-book either. (Another factor not usually taken into consideration in conversations about the future of books is that even here in the twenty-first century, there are still plenty of people who don't have e-readers, don't have notebook tablets, don't have Internet access, don't even have computers of any sort, and their numbers may even swell as economic times harden. To ignore them would be to abandon a considerable subset of potential customers. Even the poorest of people may occasionally be able to afford a paperback book, where they might not be able to afford a Kindle or an iPad.)

Besides which, it doesn't really come down to a choice between print books and e-books. The most likely thing is that most customers will buy *both* print books and e-books, choosing one format or the other depending on the circumstances, convenience, their needs of the moment, even their whim. There are even some indications that in some cases people will buy both the e-book and print versions *of the same book*. The chances are fairly good that all of this will eventually lead to a general expansion of the book business in general, no matter what format the books are being sold in. More people seem to be reading more books, in whatever format, than ever before—and that can't be bad news in the long run.

One of the other big stories of 2011 was the controversial move by Amazon to found their own publishing imprint, leading to accusations of antitrust practices, the charge being that Amazon's immensely deep pockets (estimated at $40 billion in 2011) and its position as the leading online bookseller would enable it to engage in predatory pricing to destroy its retail competitors, the so-called Big Six publishing companies, by effortlessly outbidding them for bestsellers. This has led to what the Author's Guild blog has called "a behind-the-scenes battle for control of the publishing industry," a three-sided battle between Amazon, the Big Six publishers, and Barnes & Noble, whose NOOK is the Kindle's rival for dominance of the e-book market.

Another big story, one which has an impact on the story above, was the bankruptcy and collapse of the giant bookstore chain Borders, with Borders stores closing across the country. This means that fewer books have places where they can be sold, with total rack space decreasing dramatically nationwide as the 650 Borders bookstores disappeared, something that was itself widely feared to be apocalyptic last year, although the surviving chains and, particularly, online sales from places like Amazon.com and the Barnes & Noble online bookstore, BN.com—(plus revenue from increased e-book sales)—seem to have minimized the impact to some extent. Nevertheless, the behind-the-scenes impact of the Borders closing, in terms of diminished sales and adjustments to the number of books bought and the amount of money paid for them, to say nothing of industry employees dismissed to cut costs, is likely to reverberate through the publishing world for years to come.

There's some irony in the fact that many independent bookstores were driven out of business by the dominance of the big bookstore chains, and now the chains themselves may be being threatened by online bookstores like Amazon.com and by the e-book revolution. There's even more irony in the fact that the problems the chains are having may be creating opportunities for more independent bookstores to come into existence and reclaim some of the market share they lost, and the last couple of years have shown exactly that happening. So the independent non-chain bookstore, once considered to be an endangered species, tottering on the brink of extinction, may, unexpectedly, be making something of a comeback.

Things were relatively quiet on the surface of the publishing industry in 2011, although changes and adaptations forced by the e-book explosion and the closing of Borders will no doubt be felt for many years to come. Random House added two new paperback YA/middle-grade imprints, Ember and Bluefire. Pyr also began publishing YA fiction, and Orion Children's Books launched a new YA imprint, Indigo. HarperCollins announced a new imprint for Avon, Avon Impulse, concentrating primarily on e-books and print-on-demand books. Anthony Cheetham left his position as associate publisher and member of the board of directors at Atlantic Books to form his own book imprint, Head of Zeus. Nicholas Cheetham left his postion at Corvus to join his father at Head of Zeus, and was replaced as editorial director at Corvus by Sara O'Keeffe. Scott Shannon, mass-market publisher at Ballantine Bantam Dell, is moving to a new position as senior vice president and publisher for the entire Random House Publishing Group, although he will remain as publisher of Del Rey and Spectra; Libby McGuire, publisher of Ballantine Bantam Dell, will take over as head of the mass-market line. Hartmut Ostrowski stepped down as CEO of Bertselsmann, and was replaced by Thomas Rabe. Jennifer Heddle left Simon & Schuster to edit *Star Wars* books for Lucasfilm. Paula Guran stepped down as editor of Juno Books and became senior editor at Prime Books. Chris Schluep left his position as senior editor at Ballantine/Del Rey to join Amazon.com Books as a senior editor. Phyllis Grann retired as senior editor of Doubleday after a forty-year career in publishing. DongWon Song left his position at Orbit US; Tom Bouman joined Orbit US as an acquiring editor. John Helfers left his position as senior editor at Techno Books after sixteen years in that position. John Prebich left Dorchester as CEO, replaced by Robert Anthony. Linda K. Zecher has been hired as president, CEO, and director of Houghton Miffllin Hartcourt. Gillian Redfearn has been promoted to editorial director at Gollancz. Tricia Pasternak was named senior editor at Del Rey. Jessica Wade was promoted to senior editor at NAL. David Rosenthal was named president of the general imprint at Penguin Group. Allison Lorentzen joined Penguin Books as an editor. Michael Rowley has been hired as editorial director for SF/Fantasy at Ebury Publishing.

There were relatively few changes in the professional print magazine market. *Realms of Fantasy* died for the third time in three years, perhaps for good this time (since they obviously have a dedicated readership, but not one large enough to support the expense of a print edition, I really don't understand why they don't try this one as an online electronic magazine). *Weird Tales* was sold to Marvin Kaye, who took the unpopular step of dismissing the current staff of the recent Hugo winner and announcing that he was taking the magazine in a nostalgically retro direction, something that few industry insiders thought would work; most are predicting a short life and an early death for this venerable magazine under its new management.

Overall circulation of most of the professional print magazines is slowly creeping up, after years of decline, mostly because of sales of electronic subscriptions to the magazines, as well as sales of individual electronic copies of each issue. The figures are still too small for anything other than the most cautious of optimism, but it may just prove, as I suggested it would years ago, that the Internet will be the saving of the professional SF magazines.

Asimov's Science Fiction had a very strong year as well, perhaps strong enough to earn Sheila Williams her second Hugo in a row. Excellent fiction by Paul McAuley, Kij Johnson, Michael Swanwick, Elizabeth Bear, Tom Purdom, Ian R. MacLeod, and Paul Cornell appeared in *Asimov's* this year, as well as much good work by Robert Reed, John Kessel, Mary Robinette Kowal, Kristine Kathryn Rusch, Theodora Goss, Allen M. Steel, Nancy Kress, Nancy Fulda, and others; there was a high proportion of SF in the magazine this year, with only some fantasy, most of which was weaker than the SF. For the second year in a row, *Asimov's Science Fiction* registered a gain in overall circulation, up 7.3 percent from 21,057 to 22,593. There were 12,469 print subscriptions, and 7,500 electronic subscriptions. Newsstand sales were 2,334, plus 290 digital copies sold on average each month in 2011. Sell-through was 28 percent. Digital editions became available on more platforms in 2011, including the iPad—via Zinio—and the Kindle Fire. Sheila Williams completed her seventh year as *Asimov's* editor.

Analog Science Fiction and Fact had a somewhat weak year overall, although it still published strong stories by Alec Nevala-Lee, Sean McMullen, Juliette Wade, Kristine Kathyrn Rusch, Don D'Ammassa, Marissa Lingen, and others. *Analog* registered a 0.2 percent rise in overall circulation, from 26,493 to 26,440. There were 19,302 print subscriptions, and 4,100 digital subscriptions. Newsstand sales were 2,941; plus 150 digital copies were sold on average in each month of 2011. Sell-through was 30 percent. Stanley Schmidt has been editor there for thirty-two years, and 2011 marked the magazine's eighty-first anniversary.

The Magazine of Fantasy & Science Fiction also had a strong year, publishing more SF than they usually do (although they also published a lot of fantasy, most of it better than the fantasy in *Asimov's*); excellent stories by Robert Reed, Geoff Ryman, Carolyn Ives Gilman, Chris Lawson, and Peter S. Beagle appeared in *F&SF* this year, as well as good stuff by James Cambias, Robert Chilson, Karl Bunker, David Marcus, Albert E. Cowdrey, Kali Wallace, Ken Liu, Rick Norwood, and others. *F&SF* registered a 4.7 percent drop, from an overall circulation of 15,172 to 14,462. Print subscriptions dropped from 10,907 to 10,539. Newsstand sales dropped from 4,265 to 3,923. Sell-through was 38 percent. Figures for either digital subscriptions or digital sales of single issues weren't available, although Gordon Van Gelder has been quoted as saying "our electronic sales . . . were strong in our first year on the Kindle." Gordon Van Gelder is in his fifteenth year as editor, and eleventh year as owner and publisher.

Interzone is technically not a "professional magazine," by the definition of the *Science Fiction Writers of America (SFWA)*, because of its low rates and circulation, but the literary quality of the work published there is so high that it would be ludicrous to omit it. *Interzone* had a weak year overall, but still published good stories by Jim Hawkins, Lavie Tidhar, Mecurio D. Rivera, Jason Sanford, and others. As far as can be told, as exact circulation figures are not available, circulation there seems to have held steady, in the 3,000-copy range. The editors include publisher Andy Cox and Andy Hedgecock. TTA Press, *Interzone*'s publisher, also publishes the straight horror or dark suspense magazine *Black Static*, which is beyond our purview here, but of a similar level of professional quality.

Realms of Fantasy, in what will theoretically be its last full year (see page xv), ran noteworthy stuff by Richard Parks, Lisa Goldstein, Thea Hutcheson, Alan Smale, and others.

The British magazine *Postscripts* has reinvented itself as an anthology, and is reviewed as such in the anthology section that follows, but I'll list the subscription information here, for lack of anywhere else to put it, and because, unlike most other anthology series, you *can* subscribe to *Postscripts*.

If you'd like to see lots of good SF and fantasy published every year, the survival of these magazines is essential, and one important way that you can help them survive is by subscribing to them. It's never been easier to do so, something that these days can be done with just the click of a few buttons, nor has it ever before been possible to subscribe to the magazines in as many different formats, from the traditional print copy arriving by mail to downloads for your desktop or laptop available from places like Fictionwise.com (www.fictionwise.com) and Amazon.com (www.amazon.com), to versions you can read on your Kindle, Nook, or iPad. You can also now subscribe from overseas just as easily as you can from the United States, something formerly difficult to impossible to do.

So in hopes of making it easier for you to subscribe, I'm going to list both the Internet sites where you can subscribe online and the street addresses where you can subscribe by mail for each magazine: ***Asimov's*** web address is www.asimovs.com, and subscribing online might be the easiest thing to do, and there's also a discounted rate for online subscriptions; its subscription address is ***Asimov's Science Fiction***, Dell Magazines, 267 Broadway, Fourth Floor, New York, NY 10007-2352. The annual subscription rate in the U.S. is $34.97, $44.97 overseas. ***Analog's*** site is at www.analogsf.com; its subscription address is ***Analog Science Fiction and Fact***, Dell Magazines, 267 Broadway, Fourth Floor, New York, NY 10007-2352. The annual subscription rate in the U.S. is $34.97, $44.97 overseas. ***The Magazine of Fantasy & Science Fiction's*** site is at www.sfsite.com/fsf; its subscription address is ***The Magazine of Fantasy & Science Fiction***, Spilogale, Inc., P.O. Box 3447, Hoboken, NJ 07030, $34.97 for an annual subscription in U.S., $44.97 overseas. ***Interzone*** and ***Black Static*** can be subscribed to online at www.ttapress.com/onlinestore1.html; the subscription address for both is TTA Press, 5 Martins Lane, Witcham, Ely, Cambridge CB6 2LB, England, UK. The price for a twelve-issue subscription is 42.00 Pounds Sterling each, or there is a reduced rate dual subscription offer of 78.00 Pounds Sterling for both magazines for twelve issues; make checks payable to "TTA Press."

Most of these magazines are also available in various electronic formats through Fictionwise.com, or for the Kindle, the NOOK, and other handheld readers.

There were more losses from the print semiprozine market this year, with *Zahir* transitioning from print to electronic format and then dying altogether, *Weird Tales* being sold, with its future in doubt, and *Electric Velocipede, Black Gate,* and criticalzine *The New York Review of Science Fiction* on the verge of transitioning to electronic formats as well. I suspect that sooner or later most of the surviving print semiprozines will transition to electronic-only online formats, saving themselves lots of money in printing, mailing, and production costs.

The semiprozines that remained in print format mostly struggled to bring out their scheduled issues. *Electric Velocipede,* edited by John Kilma, managed two issues, publishing interestingly eclectic stuff from Peter M. Ball, Karl Bunker, Genevieve Valentine, William Shunn, and others; they announced their intention to go online exclusively in 2012. Sword and Sorcery print magazine *Black Gate,* edited by John O'Neill, managed one large issue with strong work by Chris Willrich, Emily Mah, and others, and also announced their intention to transition to electronic format in 2012. The longest running of all the fiction semiprozines, and usually the most reliably published, the Canadian *On Spec,* which is edited by a collective under general editor Diane L. Walton, managed only three of its scheduled four issues this year, somewhat atypically. Another collective-run SF magazine with a rotating editorial staff, Australia's *Andromeda Spaceways In-flight Magazine,* managed only four issues this year. *Lady Churchill's Rosebud Wristlet,* the long-running slipstream magazine edited by Kelly Link and Gavin Grant, managed only one issue in 2011, as did *Neo-Opsis,* and Ireland's long-running *Albedo One.* Fantasy magazine *Shimmer* managed two issues, as did *Space and Time Magazine* and *Weird Tales* before being sold. The small British SF magazine *Jupiter,* edited by Ian Redman, produced all four of its scheduled issues in 2011, as did the fantasy magazine *Tales of the Talisman.* A new start-up SF magazine, *Bull Spec,* produced three issues. If there were issues of *Aurealis, Greatest Uncommon Denominator, Sybil's Garage, Space Squid,* or *Tales of the Unanticipated* out this year, I didn't see them.

With *The New York Review of Science Fiction,* a long-running critical magazine edited by David G. Hartwell and a staff of associate editors, scheduled to move to electronic format in 2012, the venerable newszine *Locus: The Magazine of the Science Fiction and Fantasy Field* is about all that's left of the popular print critical magazine market. It was always the best of them, though, and certainly your best bet for value, a multiple Hugo winner, which for more than thirty years has been an indispensable source of news, information, and reviews. Happily, the magazine has survived the death of founder, publisher, and longtime editor Charles N. Brown and has continued strongly and successfully under the guidance of a staff of editors headed by Liza Groen Trombi, and including Kirsten Gong-Wong, Carolyn Cushman, Tim Pratt, Jonathan Strahan, Francesca Myman, Heather Shaw, and many others.

Most of the other surviving print critical magazines are professional journals more aimed at academics than at the average reader. The most accessible of these is probably the long-running British critical zine *Foundation.*

Subscription addresses are: ***Locus, The Magazine of the Science Fiction & Fantasy Field***, Locus Publications, Inc., P.O. Box 13305, Oakland, CA, 94661, $72.00 for a one-year first-class subscription, 12 issues; ***The New York Review of Science Fiction***, Dragon Press, P.O. Box 78, Pleasantville, NY 10570, $40.00 for a one-year subscription, 12 issues, make checks payable to "Dragon Press"; *The Science Fiction* ***Foundation***, Science Fiction Foundation, Roger Robinson (SFF), 75 Rosslyn Avenue, Harold Wood, Essex RM3 ORG, UK, $37.00 for a three-issue subscription in the U.S.; ***Black Gate***, New Epoch Press, 815 Oak Street, St. Charles, IL 60174, $29.95 for a one-year, four-issue subscription; ***On Spec, The Canadian Magazine of the Fantastic***, P.O. Box 4727, Edmonton, AB, Canada T6E 5G6, for subscription information, go to www.onspec.ca; ***Neo-opsis Science Fiction Magazine***, 4129 Carey Rd., Victoria, BC, Canada V8Z 4G5, $25.00 for a three-issue subscription; ***Albedo One***, Albedo One Productions, 2, Post Road, Lusk, County Dublin, Ireland; $32.00 for a four-issue airmail subscription, make checks payable to "Albedo One" or pay by PayPal at www.albedo1.com; ***Lady Churchill's Rosebud Wristlet***, Small Beer Press, 150 Pleasant St., #306, Easthampton, MA 01027, $20.00 for four issues; ***Electric Velocipede***, Spilt Milk Press, go to http://www.electricvelocipede.com for subscription information; ***Andromeda Spaceways Inflight Magazine***, go to www.andromedaspaceways.com for subscription information; ***Tales of the Talisman***, Hadrosaur Productions, P.O. Box 2194, Mesilla Park, NM 88047-2194, $24.00 for a four-issue subscription; ***Jupiter***, 19 Bedford Road, Yeovil, Somerset, BA21 5UG, UK, 10 Pounds Sterling for four issues; ***Shimmer***, P.O. Box 58591, Salt Lake City, UT 84158-0591, $22.00 for a four-issue subscription.

In only a few years, the online world of electronic magazines has become one of the most reliable places to find quality fiction; already more reliable than most of the print semiprozine market, they're giving the top print professional magazines a run for their money too, and sometimes beating them.

The online magazine *Subterranean* (http://subterraneanpress.com), edited by William K. Schafer, perhaps didn't have quite as strong a year as they did last year, but still published good stuff, SF and fantasy both, by Jay Lake, K. J. Parker, Catherynne M. Valente, Robert Silverberg, Daniel Abraham, Mike Resnick, Kristine Kathryn Rusch, and others.

Clarkesworld Magazine (www.clarkesworldmagazine.com), had a strong year, publishing good SF, fantasy, and slipstream stories by Yoon Ha Lee, Lavie Tidhar, Ken Liu, David Klecha and Tobias S. Bucknell, Cat Rambo, Jason Chapman, Nnedi Okorafor, Gord Sellar, and others. Sean Wallace, who announced that he was stepping down in 2010, is returning to join publisher and editor Neil Clarke as an editor on the magazine; apparently he has been working unofficially on *Clarkesworld* behind the scenes throughout 2011.

The new online magazine *Lightspeed* (www.lightspeedmagazine.com), edited by John Joseph Adams, was weaker in its sophomore year than it had been in its freshman year, although it still published worthwhile stuff by Robert Reed, David Farland, Vyler Kaftan, An Owomoyele, and Genevieve Valentine. The online magazine *Fantasy*, on the other hand, recently taken over by *Lightspeed* editor John Joseph Adams, had a strong year, publishing good fiction by Lavie Tidhar, James Alan Gardner, Sarah Monette, Cat Rambo, Tim Pratt, Kit Howard, Jeremiah Tolbert, Genevieve Valentine, and others. As mentioned earlier, *Fantasy* has now been merged with *Lightspeed* into one electronic magazine, called *Lightspeed*, that publishes both fantasy and science fiction.

I'd still like to see the long-running online magazine *Strange Horizons* (www.strangehorizons.com) publish more SF and less fantasy and slipstream, but they did run good stuff by Lewis Shiner, Gavin J. Grant, Nisi Shawl, Genevieve Valentine, Charlie Jane Anders, Tracey Canfield, and others. Karen Meisner stepped down as fiction editor of *Strange Horizons*.

Tor.com (www.tor.com) has established itself as one of the most eclectic genre-oriented sites on the Internet, a Web site that regularly publishes SF, fantasy, and slipstream, as well as articles, comics, graphics, blog entries, print and media reviews, and commentary. It's become a regular stop for me, even when they don't have new fiction posted. This year, they published too many promotional slices of upcoming novels, but also some good fiction by Michael Swanwick, Michael F. Flynn, Harry Turtledove, Catherynne M. Valente, Charlie Jane Anders, and others.

Abyss & Apex, (www.abyssapex.com), edited by Wendy S. Delmater, featured strong work by Howard V. Hendrix, Cat Rambo, C. W. Johnson, and others.

Apex Magazine (www.apexbookcompany.com/apex-online) had good stuff by Elizabeth Bear, Catherynne M. Valente, Genevieve Valentine, Kat Howard, and others. Catherynne M. Valente stepped down as editor of *Apex Magazine* after a brief tenure, and was replaced by Lynne M. Thomas.

An e-zine devoted to "literary adventure fantasy," *Beneath Ceaseless Skies* (http://beneath-ceaseless-skies), edited by Scott H. Andrews, had worthwhile fiction by Marie Brennan, Richard Parks, Geoffrey Maloney, Siobhan Carroll, and others.

Ideomancer Speculative Fiction (www.ideomancer.com), edited by Leah Bobet, published interesting work, usually more slipstream than SF, by Erica Satifka, Georgina Bruce, Alter S. Reiss, and Anatoly Belilovsky.

The flamboyantly titled *Orson Scott Card's InterGalactic Medicine Show* (www.intergalacticmedicineshow.com), edited by Edmund R. Schubert under the direction of Card himself, seemed somewhat weak this year, although they still ran interesting stuff from Aliette de Bodard, Stephen Kotowych, Naomi Kritzer, Jeffrey Lyman, and Tony Pi.

New SF and fantasy e-zine *Daily Science Fiction* (http://dailysciencefiction.com) devotes itself to the perhaps overly ambitious task of publishing one new SF or fantasy story every day for the entire year. Unsurprisingly, most are undistinguished, but there were some good ones by Lavie Tidhar, Jay Lake, and others.

New SF e-zine *M-Brane* (www.mbranesf.com) is "on hiatus," which usually means "out of business," but we'll see.

Fantasy magazine *Zahir* (www.zahirtales.com), which had transitioned from print to electronic in 2009, went out of business.

E-zine *Redstone Science Fiction* (http://redstonesciencefiction.com), edited by a collective, published interesting stuff by Lavie Tidhar, Jeremiah Tolbert, and others.

E-zine *GigaNotoSaurus* (http://giganotosaurus.org), edited by Ann Leckie, published one story a month by writers such as Katherine Sparrow, Cat Rambo, Ferrett Steinmetz, and Vylar Kaftan.

The Australian popular-science magazine *Cosmos* (www.cosmosmagazine.com) is not an SF magazine per se, but for the last few years it has been running a story per issue (and also putting new fiction not published in the print magazine on their Web site). Fiction editor Damien Broderick stepped down this year, but was replaced by SF writer Cat Sparks. Interesting stuff by Thoraiya Dyer, Greg Mellor, and others appeared there this year.

Shadow Unit (www.shadowunit.org) is a Web site devoted to publishing stories, often by top-level professionals such as Elizabeth Bear and Emma Bull, drawn from an imaginary TV show, sort of a cross between *CSI* and *The X-Files*. It seems to be inactive at the moment, or at least nobody has posted anything there since October of last year.

The e-zine *Futurismic* (http://futurismic.com) seems to no longer be publishing fiction. As far as I can tell, *Escape Velocity* (www.escapevelocitymagazine.com) and *Shareable Futures* (http://shareable.net/blog/shareable-futures) are defunct.

The World SF Blog (http://worldsf.wordpress.com), edited by Lavie Tidhar, is a good place to find science fiction by international authors, and also publishes news, links, roundtable discussions, essays, and interviews related to "science fiction, fantasy, horror, and comics from around the world."

Weird Fiction Review (http://weirdfictionreview.com), edited by Ann VanderMeer and Jeff VanderMeer, which occasionally publishes fiction, bills itself as "an ongoing exploration into all facets of the weird," including reviews, interviews, short essays, and comics.

Below this point, it becomes harder to find center-core SF, or even genre fantasy/horror, and most of the stories are slipstream or literary surrealism. Sites that feature those, as well as the occasional fantasy (and, even more occasionally, some SF) include Rudy Rucker's *Flurb* (www.flurb.net), *Revolution SF* (www.revolutionsf.com), *Coyote Wild* (www.coyotewildmag.com); *Heliotrope* (www.heliotropemag.com); and the somewhat less slipstreamish *Bewildering Stories* (www.bewilderingstories.com).

In addition to original work, there's also a lot of good *reprint* SF and fantasy stories out there on the Internet too, usually available for free. On all of the sites that make their fiction available for free, *Strange Horizons*, Tor.com, *Fantasy*, *Subterranean*, *Abyss & Apex*, and so on, you can also access large archives of previously published material as well as stuff from the "current issue." Most of the sites that are associated with existent print magazines, such as *Asimov's*, *Analog*, and *The Magazine of Fantasy & Science Fiction*, make previously published fiction and nonfiction available for access on their sites, and also regularly run teaser excerpts from stories coming up in forthcoming issues. Hundreds of out-of-print titles, both genre and mainstream, are also available for free download from *Project Gutenberg* (http://promo.net/pc/), and a large selection of novels and a few collections can also be accessed for free, to be either downloaded or read on-screen, at the *Baen Free Library* (www.baen.com/library). Sites such as *Infinity Plus* (http://www.infinityplus.co.uk) and *The Infinite Matrix* (www.infinitematrix.net) may have died as active sites, but their extensive archives of previously published material are still accessable.

An even greater range of reprint stories becomes available if you're willing to pay a small fee for them. Perhaps the best, and the longest established, place to find such material is *Fictionwise* (www.fictionwise.com), where you can buy downloadable e-books and stories to read on your PDA, Kindle, or home computer; in addition to individual stories, you can also buy "fiction bundles" here, which amount to electronic collections; as well as a selection of novels in several different genres—

you can also subscribe to downloadable versions of several of the SF magazines here, including *Asimov's*, *Analog*, *F&SF*, and *Interzone*, in a number of different formats. A similar site is *ElectricStory* (www.electricstory.com), where in addition to the fiction for sale, you can also access free movie reviews by Lucius Shepard, articles by Howard Waldrop, and other critical material.

Even if you're not looking for fiction to read, though, there are still plenty of other reasons for SF fans to go on the Internet. There are many general genre-related sites of interest to be found, most of which publish reviews of books as well as of movies and TV shows, sometimes comics or computer games or anime, many of which also feature interviews, critical articles, and genre-oriented news of various kinds. The best such site is easily *Locus Online* (http://www.locusmag.com), the online version of the newsmagazine *Locus*, where you can access an incredible amount of information—including book reviews, critical lists, obituary lists, links to reviews and essays appearing outside the genre, and links to extensive database archives such as the Locus Index to Science Fiction and the Locus Index to Science Fiction Awards—it's rare when I don't find myself accessing Locus Online several times a day. As mentioned earlier, Tor.com is giving it a run for its money these days as an interesting place to stop while surfing the Web. Other major general-interest sites include *SF Site* (www.sfsite.com), *SFRevu* (http://www.sfsite.com/sfrevu), *SF-Crowsnest* (www.sfcrowsnest.com), *SFScope* (www.sfscope.com), *io9* (http:io9.com), *Green Man Review* (http://greenmanreview.com), *The Agony Column* (http://trashotron.com/agony), *SFFWorld* (www.sffworld.com), *SFReader* (sfreader.com), *SFWatcher* (www.sfwatcher.com), *Salon Futura* (www.salonfutura.net), which runs interviews and critical articles; and *Pat's Fantasy Hotlist* (www.fantasyhotlist.blogspot.com). A great research site, invaluable if you want bibliographic information about SF and fantasy writers, is *Fantastic Fiction* (www.fantasticfiction.co.uk). Reviews of short fiction as opposed to novels are very hard to find anywhere, with the exception of *Locus* and *Locus Online*, but you can find reviews of both current and past short fiction at *Best SF* (www.bestsf.net/), as well as at pioneering short-fiction review site *Tangent Online* (www.tangentonline.com). Other sites of interest include: SFF NET (www.sff.net), which features dozens of home pages and "newsgroups" for SF writers; the Science Fiction Writers of America page (www.sfwa.org); where genre news, obituaries, award information, and recommended reading lists can be accessed; *SciFiPedia* (scifipedia.scifi.com), a Wiki-style genre-oriented online encyclopedia; *Ansible* (www.dcs.gla.ac.uk/Ansible), the online version of multiple Hugo winner David Langford's long-running fanzine *Book View Café* (www.bookviewcafe.com) is a "consortium of over twenty professional authors," including Vonda N. McIntyre, Laura Ann Gilman, Sarah Zittel, Brenda Clough, and others, who have created a Web site where work by them—mostly reprints and some novel excerpts—is made available for free.

An ever-expanding area, growing in popularity, are a number of sites where podcasts and SF-oriented radio plays can be accessed: at *Audible* (www.audible.com), *Escape Pod* (http://escapepod.org, podcasting mostly SF), *Star Ship Sofa* (www.starshipsofa.com), *Pseudopod* (http://pseudopod.org, podcasting mostly fantasy), and *PodCastle* (http://podcastle.org, podcasting mostly fantasy). There's also a site that podcasts nonfiction interviews and reviews, *The Dragon Page—Cover to Cover* (www.dragonpage.com).

The three best SF anthologies of the year were all edited by Jonathan Strahan: *Engineering Infinty* (Solaris Books), *Life on Mars: Tales from the New Frontier* (Viking), and *Eclipse Four: New Science Fiction and Fantasy* (Night Shade Books). *Engineering Infinity* (my selection for the year's single best SF anthology) contained excellent work by David Moles, Gwyneth Jones, Karl Schroeder, and Stephen Baxter, as well as good work by Hannu Rajaniemi, Peter Watts, John Barnes, and others. The YA anthology *Life on Mars* contained first-rate stuff by Ian McDonald, John Barnes, and Kage Baker, as well as good work by Nancy Kress, Alastair Reynolds, Stephen Baxter, Ellen Klages, and others. *Eclipse Four,* which, unlike the first two books mentioned here, features fantasy and slipstream as well as SF, had excellent work of various sorts by Andy Duncan, Damien Broderick, Gwyneth Jones, and Peter M. Ball, as well as good work by Caitlin R. Kiernan, Jo Walton, James Patrick Kelly, Kij Johnson, Rachel Swirsky, and others. All of this would be sufficient to make Strahan a good candidate for the 2011 Best Editor Hugo Short Form, in my opinion—although as an anthology editor whose anthologies may not have been seen by a large-enough proportion of the voting demographic, that may not be likely.

Although not as strong as the anthologies mentioned earlier, the reborn version of the old *Solaris* anthology series, now called *Solaris Rising: The New Solaris Book of Science Fiction* (Solaris Books) and edited by new editor Ian Whates, turned in a solid debut performance, consisting of almost all center-core SF, and featuring good work by Dave Hutchinson, Ian McDonald, Ken MacLeod, Alastair Reynolds, Stephen Palmer, Keith Brooke and Eric Brown, and others. Ian Whates also brought out two more minor but enjoyable original anthologies, *Further Conflicts* (NewCon Press) and *Fables from the Fountain* (NewCon). Print magazine *MIT Technology Review* published a special all-fiction issue, supposedly the start of an annual series, which featured intelligent core SF by Pat Cadigan, Ken MacLeod, Gwyneth Jones, Elizabeth Bear, Vandana Singh, Cory Doctorow, Paul Di Filippo, and others. *Postscripts 24/25* (PS Publishing) featured mostly slipstream, fantasy, and soft horror, too much of it for my taste, but did also feature strong SF stories by Ken MacLeod, Keith Brooke, and Adam Roberts. *Panverse Three* (Panverse Publishing), an all-novella anthology edited by Dario Ciriello, featured strong novellas by Ken Liu and Don D'Ammassa. *Welcome to the Greenhouse* (OR Books), edited by Gordon Van Gelder, was somewhat disappointing overall, although it had interesting work by Chris Lawson, Bruce Sterling, Gregory Benford, Brian W. Aldiss, and others. There were two steampunk anthologies, *Steampunk!: An Anthology of Fantastically Rich and Strange Stories* (Candlewick Press), edited by Kelly Link and Gavin J. Grant and *The Immersion Book of Steampunk* (Immersion Press), edited by Gareth D. Jones and Carmelo Rafala, as well as the steampunkish *Gaslight Arcanum: Uncanny Tales of Sherlock Holmes* (Hades/EDGE Science Fiction and Fantasy Publishing), edited by J. R. Campbell and Charles Prepolec (and, in fantasy, the Dann and Gevers *Ghosts by Gaslight*, mentioned later).

Pleasant but minor SF anthologies included *End of an Aeon* (Fairwood Press), edited by Bridget McKenna and Marti McKenna, an anthology made up of stories leftover in inventory from the now-deceased small press magazine *Aeon. Human for a Day* (DAW Books), edited by Martin H. Greenberg and Jennifer Brozek, and

The Wild Side: Urban Fantasy with an Erotic Edge (Baen), edited by Mark L. Van Name. *L. Ron Hubbard Presents Writers of the Future Volume XXVII* (Galaxy Press), edited by K. D. Wentworth, is the lastest in a long-running series featuring novice work by beginning writers, some of whom may later turn out to be important talents.

The best of the year's fantasy anthologies (although an argument could be made for putting it in with the urban fantasy and paranormal anthologies discussed later) was probably *Subterranean: Tales of Dark Fantasy* 2 (Subterranean Press), edited by William Schafer, and featuring good stories by K. J. Parker, Bruce Sterling, William Browning Spencer, Jay Lake and Shannon Page, Norman Patridge, Kelley Armstrong, and others.

Pleasant but minor fantasy anthologies included *Courts of the Fey* (DAW Books), edited by Martin H. Greenberg and Russell Davis, and *Hot and Steamy: Tales of Steampunk Romance* (DAW Books), edited by Jean Rabe and Martin H. Greenberg.

There were a number of anthologies exploring the confusing and sometimes contradictory area now known as "urban fantasy," including *Naked City: Tales of Urban Fantasy* (St. Martin's Press), edited by Ellen Datlow; *Supernatural Noir* (Dark Horse Books), edited by Ellen Datlow; *Down These Strange Streets* (Ace), edited by George R. R. Martin and Gardner Dozois; *Ghosts by Gaslight* (HarperCollins Voyager), edited by Jack Dann and Nick Gevers; *Welcome to Bordertown: New Stories and Poems of the Borderlands* (Random House), edited by Holly Black and Ellen Kushner; and *Home Improvement: Undead Edition* (Ace), edited by Charlaine Harris and Toni L. P. Kelner. Original horror anthologies included *Teeth: Vampire Tales* (Harper), edited by Ellen Datlow and Terry Windling; *Blood and Other Cravings* (Tor), edited by Ellen Datlow; *A Book of Horrors* (Jo Fletcher Books), edited by Stephen Jones; *Zombiesque* (DAW Books), edited by Stephen L. Antczak, James C. Basser, and Martin H. Greenberg; and a mixed reprint and original shapeshifter anthology, *Bewere the Night* (Prime Books), edited by Ekaterina Sedia.

Less easily classifiable stuff, dancing on the edge of one genre or another, included the entertaining and vaguely steampunkish *The Thackery T. Lambshead Cabinet of Curiosities* (Harper Voyager), edited by Ann and Jeff VanderMeer; *Kafkaesque* (Tachyon Publications), edited by John Kessel and James Patrick Kelly; and *Tesseracts Fifteen: A Case of Quite Curious Tales* (Hades/EDGE Science Fiction), edited by Julie E. Czerneda and Susan MacGregor.

Shared-world anthologies included *In Fire Forged* (Baen Books), edited by David Weber; *Golden Reflections: Stories of the Mask* (Baen Books), edited by Joan Spicci Saberhagen and Robert E. Vardeman; and *Under the Vale and Other Tales of Valdemar* (DAW Books), edited by Mercedes Lackey.

Short fiction stalwarts such as Robert Reed, Michael Swanwick, and Ken MacLeod published a lot of good work this year, as usual, but so did prolific younger writers such as Lavie Tidhar, Ken Liu, Cat Rambo, Catherynne M. Valente, and Genevieve Valentine. Stories about Mars seemed popular this year, as did stories about ecological terrorists, and stories where SF was disguised as fantasy or even as fairy tales.

(Finding individual pricings for all of the items from small presses mentioned in the Summation has become too time-intensive, and since several of the same small presses publish anthologies, novels, *and* short-story collections, it seems silly to repeat addresses for them in section after section. Therefore, I'm going to attempt to list here, in one place, all the addresses for small presses that have books mentioned here or there in the Summation, whether from the anthologies section, the novel section, or the short-story collection section, and, where known, their Web site addresses. That should make it easy enough for the reader to look up the individual price of any book mentioned that isn't from a regular trade publisher; such books are less likely to be found in your average bookstore, or even in a chain superstore, and so will probably have to be mail-ordered. Many publishers seem to sell only online, through their Web sites, and some will only accept payment through PayPal. Many books, even from some of the smaller presses, are also available through Amazon.com. If you can't find an address for a publisher, and it's quite likely that I've missed some here, or failed to update them successfully, Google it. It shouldn't be that difficult these days to find up-to-date contact information for almost any publisher, however small.)

Addresses are: ***PS Publishing***, Grosvener House, 1 New Road, Hornsea, West Yorkshire, HU18 1PG, England, UK www.pspublishing.co.uk; **Golden Gryphon Press**, 3002 Perkins Road, Urbana, IL 61802, www.goldengryphon.com; **NESFA Press**, P.O. Box 809, Framingham, MA 01701-0809, www.nesfa.org/press; **Subterranean Press**, P.O. Box 190106, Burton, MI 48519, www.subterraneanpress.com; **Old Earth Books**, P.O. Box 19951, Baltimore, MD 21211-0951, www.oldearthbooks.com; **Tachyon Press**, 1459 18th St. #139, San Francisco, CA 94107, www.tachyonpublications.com; **Night Shade Books**, 1470 NW Saltzman Road, Portland, OR 97229, www.nightshadebooks.com; **Five Star Books**, 295 Kennedy Memorial Drive, Waterville, ME 04901, www.galegroup.com/fivestar; **NewCon Press**, via www.newconpress.com; **Small Beer Press**, 176 Prospect Ave., Northampton, MA 01060, www.smallbeerpress.com; **Locus Press**, P.O. Box 13305, Oakland, CA 94661; **Crescent Books**, Mercat Press Ltd., 10 Coates Crescent, Edinburgh, Scotland EH3 7AL, www.crescentfiction.com; **Wildside Press/Borgo Press**, P.O. Box 301, Holicong, PA 18928-0301, or go to www.wildsidepress.com for pricing and ordering; **Edge Science Fiction and Fantasy Publishing, Inc. and Tesseract Books, Ltd.**, P.O. Box 1714, Calgary, Alberta, T2P 2L7, Canada, www.edgewebsite.com; **Aqueduct Press**, P.O. Box 95787, Seattle, WA 98145-2787, www.aqueductpress.com; **Phobos Books**, 200 Park Avenue South, New York, NY 10003, www.phobosweb.com; **Fairwood Press**, 5203 Quincy Ave. SE, Auburn, WA 98092, www.fairwoodpress.com; **BenBella Books**, 6440 N. Central Expressway, Suite 508, Dallas, TX 75206, www.benbellabooks.com; **Darkside Press**, 13320 27th Ave. NE, Seattle, WA 98125, www.darksidepress.com; **Haffner Press**, 5005 Crooks Rd., Suite 35, Royal Oak, MI 48073-1239, www.haffnerpress.com; **North Atlantic Press**, P.O. Box 12327, Berkeley, CA 94701; **Prime Books**, P.O. Box 36503, Canton, OH 44735, www.primebooks.net; **Fairwood Press**, 5203 Quincy Ave. SE, Auburn, WA 98092, www.fairwoodpress.com; **MonkeyBrain Books**, 11204 Crossland Drive, Austin, TX 78726, www.monkeybrainbooks.com; **Wesleyan University Press**, University Press of New England, Order Dept., 37 Lafayette St., Lebanon, NH 03766-1405, www.wesleyan.edu/wespress; **Agog! Press**, P.O. Box U302, University of Wollongong, NSW 2522, Australia, www.uow.ed.au/~rhood/agogpress; **Wheatland Press**, via www.wheatlandpress.com; **MirrorDanse Books**, P.O. Box 3542, Parramatta NSW 2124, www.tabula-rasa.info/MirrorDanse; **Arsenal Pulp Press**, 103–1014 Homer Street, Vancouver, BC, Canada V6B 2W9, www.arsenalpress.com; **DreamHaven**

Books, 912 W. Lake Street, Minneapolis, MN 55408; **Elder Signs Press/Dimensions Books,** order through www.dimensionsbooks.com; **Chaosium**, via www.chaosium.com; **Spyre Books**, P.O. Box 3005, Radford, VA 24143; **SCIFI, Inc.**, P.O. Box 8442, Van Nuys, CA 91409–8442; **Omnidawn Publishing**, order through www.omnidawn.com; **CSFG,** Canberra Speculative Fiction Guild, www.csfg.org.au/publishing/anthologies/the_outcast; **Hadley Rille Books**, via www.hadleyrillebooks.com; **ISFiC Press**, 707 Saplilng Lane, Deerfield, IL 60015-3969, or www.isficpress.com; **Suddenly Press**, via suddenlypress@yahoo.com; **Sandstone Press**, P.O. Box 5725, One High St., Dingwall, Ross-shire, IV15 9WJ; **Tropism Press**, via www.tropismpress.com; **SF Poetry Association/Dark Regions Press**, www.sfpoetry.com, send checks to Helena Bell, SFPA Treasurer, 1225 West Freeman St., Apt. 12, Carbondale, IL 62401; **DH Press**, via diamondbookdistributors.com; **Kurodahan Press**, via www.kurodahan.com; **Ramble House,** 443 Gladstone Blvd., Shreveport, LA 71104; **Interstitial Arts Foundation**, via www.interstitialarts.org; **Raw Dog Screaming**, via www.rawdogscreaming.com; **Three Legged Fox Books**, 98 Hythe Road, Brighton, BN1 6JS, UK; **Norilana Books**, via www.norilana.com; **coeur de lion,** via coeurdelion.com.au; **PARSECink,** via www.parsecink.org; **Robert J. Sawyer Books,** via wwww.sfwriter.com/rjsbooks.htm; **Rackstraw Press,** via http://rackstrawpress; **Candlewick,** via www.candlewick.com; **Zubaan,** via www.zubaanbooks.com; **Utter Tower,** via www.threeleggedfox.co.uk; **Spilt Milk Press,** via www.electricvelocipede.com; **Paper Golem**, via www.papergolem.com; **Galaxy Press,** via www.galaxypress.com.; **Twelfth Planet Press**, via www.twelfthplanetpress.com; **Five Senses Press,** via www.sensefive.com; **Elastic Press,** via www.elasticpress.com; **Lethe Press,** via www.lethepressbooks.com; **Two Cranes Press**, via www.twocranespress.com; **Wordcraft of Oregon**, via www.wordcraftoforegon.com; **Down East**, via www.downeast.com.

E-books have not yet driven print books out of existence, as some commentators insist that they eventually will, not by a long shot, although there are indications that they're definitely having an effect, especially on mass-market paperbacks, and taking an increasing share of the market. There were still plenty of print books around in 2011. In fact, in spite of the recession and the e-book revolution, the number of novels published in the SF and fantasy genres increased for the fifth year in a row.

According to the newsmagazine *Locus*, there were a record 3,071 books "of interest to the SF field" published in 2011, up slightly from 3,056 titles in 2010. New titles hit a new high for the third year in a row, up 2 percent to 2,140, 70 percent of the total, while reprints dropped 3 percent for 931, their lowest point since 2000. (It's worth noting that this total doesn't count e-books, media tie-in novels, gaming novels, novelizations of genre movies, or print-on-demand books—all of which would swell the overall total by hundreds if counted.) The number of new SF novels was up 7 percent to 305 titles as opposed to 2010's 285. The number of new fantasy novels was up by 7 percent, to 660 titles as opposed to 2010's total of 614. Horror novels were down 9 percent to 229 titles as opposed to 2010's 251 titles. Paranormal romances were up 8 percent to 416 titles as opposed to 2010's 384 titles, second in numbers only to fantasy (although sometimes it's almost a subjective call whether a particular novel should be pigeonholed as paranormal romance, fantasy, or horror).

All of these genres showed a sharp increase in young adult novels, up to 24 percent from 2010's 20 percent in science fiction, up to 35 percent from 2010's 34 percent in fantasy, and up to 31 percent from 2010's 24 percent for horror. In SF, dystopian and postapocalyptic YA SF novels were one of the year's hottest trends.

As usual, busy with all the reading I have to do at shorter lengths, I didn't have time to read many novels myself this year, so I'll limit myself to mentioning those novels that received a lot of attention and acclaim in 2011.

A Dance with Dragons (Bantam), by George R. R. Martin; *Earthbound* (Ace), by Joe Haldeman; *City of Ruins* (Pyr), by Kristine Kathryn Rusch; *Embassytown* (Del Rey), by China Miéville; *Cowboy Angels* (Pyr), by Paul McAuley; *The Wise Man's Fear* (DAW Books), by Patrick Rothfuss; *Among Others* (Tor), by Jo Walton; *This Shared Dream* (Tor), by Kathleen Ann Goonan; *Hex* (Ace), by Allen Steele; *Deep State* (Orbit), by Walter Jon Williams; *The Children of the Sky* (Tor), by Vernor Vinge; *Rule 34* (Ace), by Charles Stross; *Planesrunner* (Pyr), by Ian McDonald; *Vortex* (Tor), by Robert Charles Wilson; *Betrayer* (DAW Books), by C. J. Cherryh; *Home Fires* (Tor), by Gene Wolfe; *Count to a Trillion* (Tor), by John C. Wright; *The Magician King* (Viking), by Lev Grossman; *All the Lives He Led* (Tor), by Frederik Pohl; *Daybreak Zero* (Ace), by John Barnes; *After the Golden Age* (Tor), by Carrie Vaughn; *Kitty's Big Trouble* (Tor), by Carrie Vaughn; *Leviathan Wakes* (Orbit), by James S. A. Corey; *7th Sigma* (Tor), by Steven Gould; *The Dragon's Path* (Orbit), by Daniel Abraham; *Deathless* (Tor), by Catherynne M. Valente; *The Heroes* (Orbit), by Joe Abercrombe; *Bronze Summer* (Gollancz), by Stephen Baxter; *Stone Spring* (Gollancz), by Stephen Baxter; *Endurance* (Tor), by Jay Lake; *The Tempering of Men* (Tor), by Sarah Monette and Elizabeth Bear; *Goliath* (Simon Pulse), by Scott Westerfeld; *The Cold Commands* (Del Rey), by Richard Morgan; *Grail* (Spectra), by Elizabeth Bear; *Fuzzy Nation* (Tor), by John Scalzi; *The Islanders* (Gollancz), by Christopher Priest; *Reamde* (HarperCollins), by Neal Stephenson; *By Light Alone* (Gollancz) by Adam Roberts; *Firebird* (Ace), by Jack McDevitt; *The Hammer* (Orbit), by K. J. Parker; *The Highest Frontier* (Tor), by Joan Slonczewski; *The Kings of Eternity* (Solaris), by Eric Brown; *Remade* (William Morrow), by Neal Stephenson; *The Kings of Eternity* (Solaris), by Eric Brown; *Raising Stony Mayhall* (Del Rey), by Daryl Gregory; *11/23/63* (Scribner), by Stephen King; and *Snuff* (HarperCollins), by Terry Pratchett.

I still hear the complaint that there are no SF books left to buy these days, that they've all been driven off the shelves by fantasy books, but although there's a good deal of fantasy in the titles given here, the Haldeman, the Rusch, the Miéville, the McAuley, the Goonan, the Steele, the Williams, the Vinge, the Stross, the McDonald, the Wilson, the Wright, the Corey, the Pohl, the McDevitt, and a number of others are unquestionably core science fiction, and many more could be cited from the lists of small press novels and first novels. There's still more good core SF out there than any one person could possibly have time to read in the course of a year.

Small presses are active in the novel market these days, where once they published mostly collections and anthologies. Novels issued by small presses this year included: *The Clockwork Rocket* (Night Shade Books), by Greg Egan; *Dancing with Bears* (Night Shade Books), by Michael Swanwick; *Osama: A Novel* (PS Publishing), by Lavie Tidhar; *Wake Up and Dream* (PS Publishing), by Ian R. MacLeod; *The Girl Who Circumnavigated Fairyland in a Ship of Her Own Making* (Feiwel and

Friends), by Catherynne M. Valente; *The Folded World* (Night Shade Books), by Catherynne M. Valente; *The Uncertain Places* (Tachyon Publications), by Lisa Goldstein; *The Other* (Underland Press), by Matthew Hughes; *Heart of Iron* (Prime Books), by Ekaterina Sedia; *Infidel* (Night Shade Books), by Kameron Hurley; *Scratch Monkey* (NESFA Press), by Charles Stross; and *Dark Tangos* (Subterranean Press), by Lewis Shiner.

The year's first novels included: *Robopocalypse* (Doubleday), by Daniel H. Wilson; *Ready Player One* (Crown Publishers), by Ernest Cline; *Soft Apocalypse* (Night Shade Books), by Will McIntosh; *Debris* (Angry Robot), by Jo Anderton; *Mechanique* (Prime Books), by Genevieve Valentine; *Necropolis* (Night Shade Books), by Michael Dempsey; *The Falling Machine* (Pyr), by Andrew Mayer; *The Traitor's Daughter* (Spectra), by Paula Brandon; *No Hero* (Night Shade Books), by Jonathan Wood; *The Girl of Fire and Thorns* (Greenwillow), by Rae Carson; *2030: The Real Story of What Happens to America* (St. Martin's Press), by Albert Brooks; *God's War* (Night Shade Books), by Hurley Kameron; *Reality 36* (Angry Robot), by Guy Haley; *Spellcast* (DAW Books), by Barbara Ashford; *Sword of Fire and Sea* (Pyr), by Erin Hoffman; *Low Town* (Doubleday), by Daniel Polansky; *Kindling the Moon* (Pocket Books), by Jenn Bennett; *Farlander* (Tor), by Col Buchanan; *Revolution World* (Night Shade Books), by Katy Stauber; *A Discovery of Witches* (Viking), by Deborah Harkness; *The Tiger's Wife* (Random House), by Téa Obreht; *The Night Circus* (Doubleday), by Erin Morgenstern; *The Desert of Souls* (Thomas Durine Books), by Howard Andrew Jones; *The Unremembered* (Tor), by Peter Orullilan; *Seed* (Night Shade Books), by Rob Ziegler; *Of Blood and Honey* (Night Shade Books), by Stina Leicht; *Among Thieves* (Roc), by Douglas Hulick; *Awakenings* (Tor), by Edward D. Lazellari; *Miserere: An Autumn Tale* (Night Shade Books), by Teresa Frohock; and *The Whitefire Crossing* (Night Shade Books), by Courtney Schafer. Unlike last year, when Hannu Rajaniemi's *The Quantum Thief* soaked up most of the attention, none of these novels seemed to have a real edge in attention or acclaim.

Night Shade Books obviously published a lot of novels this year, particularly for a small press, and was particularly active in first novels.

The strongest novella chapbook of the year, by a good margin, was *Silently and Very Fast* (WSFA Press), by Catherynne M. Valente, but there were other good novella chapbooks as well, such as *Jesus and the Eightfold Path* (Immersion Press), by Lavie Tidhar; *Angel of Europa* (Subterranean Press), by Allen Steele; *Blue and Gold* (Subterranean Press), by K. J. Parker; *Gravity Dreams* (PS Publishing), by Stephen Baxter; *The White City* (Subterranean Press), by Elizabeth Bear; *A Brood of Foxes* (Aqueduct), by Kristin Livdahl; *The Affair of the Chalk Cliffs* (Subterranean Press), by James P. Blaylock; and *The Ice Puzzle* (PS Publishing), by Catherynne M. Valente.

Novel omnibuses this year included: *Flandry's Legacy* (Baen Books), by Poul Anderson; *Rise of the Terran Empire* (Baen Books), by Poul Anderson; *Introducing Garrett, P.I.* (Roc), by Glen Cook; *Galactic Courier* (Baen Books), by A. Bertram Chandler; *The Crystal Variation* (Baen Books), by Sharon Lee and Steve Miller; *Moonsinger's Quest* (Baen Books), by Andre Norton; and *Kurt Vonnegut: Novels and Stories 1963–1973* (The Library of America), an omnibus of four novels, three stories, and three nonfiction pieces by Vonnegut. Novel omnibuses are also frequently made available through the Science Fiction Book Club.

Not even counting print-on-demand books and the availability of out-of-print books as e-books or as electronic downloads from Internet sources such as Fictionwise, a lot of long out-of-print stuff has come back into print in the last couple of years in commercial trade editions. Here are some out-of-print titles that came back into print this year, although producing a definitive list of reissued novels is probably impossible. Tor reissued *The Dragons of Babel*, by Michael Swanwick; *A Fire Upon the Deep*, by Vernor Vinge; *Gods of Riverworld*, by Philip Jose Farmer; *Territory*, by Emma Bull; *Mindscan*, by Robert J. Sawyer; *Sati*, by Christopher Pike; *The Season of Passage*, by Christopher Pike; *Fleet of Worlds*, by Larry Niven and Edward M. Lerner; *The Darkest Part of the Woods*, by Ramsey Campbell; and *A Transatlantic Tunnel, Hurrah!*, by Harry Harrison. Orb reissued: *Stations of the Tide*, by Michael Swanwick; *A Bridge of Years*, by Robert Charles Wilson; *The Chronoliths*, by Robert Charles Wilson; *Stand on Zanzibar*, by John Brunner; and *Trouble and Her Friends*, by Melissa Scott. Tor Teen reissued *Sister Light, Sister Dark*, by Jane Yolen. Baen Books reissued *Starman Jones*, by Robert A. Heinlein. Night Shade Books reissued *An Ill Fate Marshalling*, *Reap the East Wind*, and *A Matter of Time*, all by Glen Cook. Small Beer Press reissued *The Child Garden*, by Geoff Ryman, *Stories of Your Life and Others*, by Ted Chiang; and *Solitaire*, by Kelley Eskridge. Angry Robot reissued *Infernal Devices* and *Morlock Night*, both by K. W. Jeter. Subterranean Press reissued *Yours Truly, Jack the Ripper*, by Robert Bloch. Tachyon Publications reissued *Promises to Keep*, by Charles de Lint. Ace reissued *The Terminal Experiment*, by Robert J. Sawyer. Ballantine Spectra reissued *The Difference Engine*, by William Gibson and Bruce Sterling. Ballantine Del Rey reissued *Conan the Barbarian*, by Robert E. Howard. William Morrow reissued *American Gods, The Tenth Anniversary Edition*, by Neil Gaiman. Harper Perennial reissued *The Graveyard Book*, by Neil Gaiman. HarperCollins reissued *Abarat*, by Clive Barker. Prime Books reissued *The Bone Key: The Necromantic Mysteries of Kyle Murchison Booth*, by Sarah Monette. Houghton Mifflin Harcourt reissued *The Divine Invasion*, by Philip K. Dick. Titan Books reissued *Anno Dracula*, by Kim Newman. Harper reissued *On Stranger Tides*, by Tim Powers. St. Martin's Griffin reissued *The Space Merchants*, by Frederik Pohl and C. M. Cornbluth.

Many authors are now reissuing their old back titles as e-books, either through a publisher or all by themselves, so many that it's impossible to keep track of them all here. Before you conclude that something from an author's backlist is unavailable, though, check with the Kindle and NOOK stores, and with other online vendors.

2011 was another good year for short-story collections. The year's best nonretrospective collections included: *After the Apocalypse* (Small Beer Press), by Maureen McHugh; *Gothic High-Tech* (Subterranean Press), by Bruce Sterling; *Paradise Tales* (Small Beer Press), by Geoff Ryman; *The Bible Repairman and Other Stories* (Tachyon Publications), by Tim Powers; *The Universe of Things* (Aqueduct Press), by Gwyneth Jones; *The Inheritance and Other Stories* (Harper Voyager), by Robin Hobb and Megan Lindholm; *Unpossible and Other Stories* (Fairwood Press), by Daryl Gregory; and *Sleight of Hand* (Tachyon Publications), by Peter S. Beagle. Also good were *Wind Angels* (PS Publishing), by Leigh Kennedy; *Kitty's Greatest Hits* (Tor), by Carrie Vaughn; *The Wild Girls* (PM Press—omnibus of one story, two essays, one interview, and four poems), by Ursula K. Le Guin; *Yellowcake* (Allen & Unwin), by Margo Lanagan; *Professor Moriarty: The Hound of the D'Urbervilles* (Titan Books), by Kim Newman; *Translation Station* (The Merry Blacksmith Press), by Don D'Ammassa; *Diana Comet and Other Improbable Stories* (Lethe Press), by Sandra McDonald; *Dragon Virus* (Fairwood Press), by Laura Anne Gilman; *Somewhere Beneath These Waves* (Prime Books), by Sarah Monette; *Love and Romanpunk* (Twelfth Planet Press), by Tansy Rayner Roberts; *Manhattan in Reverse* (Pan MacMillan), by Peter F. Hamilton; *Steel and Other Stories* (Tor), by Richard Matheson; *Something More and More* (Aqueduct Press—omnibus of two stories, three essays, and an interview), by Nisi Shawl; *The Great Big Beautiful Tomorrow* (PM Press—omnibus of a long novella, plus essays and interviews), by Cory Doctorow; *Never at Home* (Aqueduct Press), by L. Timmel Duchamp; and *Aurora in Four Voices* (ISFIC Press), by Catherine Asaro.

Noted without comment is *When the Great Days Come* (Prime Books), by Gardner Dozois.

Career-spanning retrospective collections this year included: *Admiralty: Volume 4 of the Collected Short Works of Poul Anderson* (NESFA Press), by Poul Anderson; *Shannach—The Last: Farewell to Mars* (Haffner Press), by Leigh Brackett; *The Collected Stories of Robert Silverberg, Volume Six: Multiples 1983–1987* (Subterranean Press), by Robert Silverberg; *Hunt the Space-Witch: Seven Adventures in Time and Space* (Paizo/Planet Stories), by Robert Silverberg; *At the Human Limit, The Collected Stories of Jack Williamson, Volume Eight* (Haffner Press), by Jack Williamson; *The Universe Wreckers, The Collected Edmond Hamilton* (Haffner Press), by Edmond Hamilton; *The Collected Captain Future, Man of Tomorrow, Volume Two* (Haffner Press), by Edmond Hamilton; *The Collected Captain Future, Man of Tomorrow, Volume Three* (Haffner Press), by Edmond Hamilton; *Terror in the House: The Early Kuttner, Volume One* (Haffner Press), by Henry Kuttner; *The Miscellaneous Writings of Clark Ashton Smith* (Night Shade Books), by Clark Ashton Smith; *Scream Quietly: The Best of Charles L. Grant* (PS Publishing), by Charles L. Grant; *Collected Ghost Stories* (Oxford University Press), by M. R. James; *The Inhabitant of the Lake and Other Unwelcome Tenants* (PS Publishing), by Ramsey Campbell; and *Two Worlds and In Between: The Best of Caitlín R. Kiernan (Volume One)* (Subterranean Press), by Caitlín R. Kiernan.

As has become usual, small presses again dominated the list of short-story collections, with Haffner Press and Subterranean Press being particularly active in the issuing of retrospective collections.

A wide variety of "electronic collections," often called "fiction bundles," too many to individually list here, are also available for downloading online, at sites such as Fictionwise and ElectricStory, and the Science Fiction Book Club continues to issue new collections as well.

As usual, among the most reliable buys in the reprint anthology market are the various Best of the Year anthologies, although this is an area in constant flux, with old series disappearing and new series being born. This year seemed to be relatively stable. At the moment, science fiction is being covered by three anthologies (actually, technically, by two anthologies and by two separate half anthologies): the one you are reading at the moment, *The Year's Best Science Fiction* series from St. Martin's Press, edited by Gardner Dozois, now up to its twenty-ninth annual collection; the *Year's Best SF* series (Harper Voyager), edited by David G. Hartwell and Kathryn Cramer, now up to its sixteenth annual volume; the science fiction half of *The Best Science Fiction and Fantasy of the Year: Volume Five* (Night Shade Books), edited by Jonathan Strahan; and the science fiction half of *The Year's Best Science Fiction and Fantasy: 2011 Edition* (Prime Books), edited by Rich Horton (in practice, of course, these books probably won't divide neatly in half with their coverage, and there's likely to be more of one thing than another). The annual Nebula Awards anthology, which covers science fiction as well as fantasy of various sorts, functions as a de facto Best of the Year anthology, although it's not usually counted among them; this year's edition was *Nebula Awards Showcase 2011* (Tor), edited by Kevin J. Anderson. (A similar series covering the Hugo winners began in 2010, but swiftly died.) There were three Best of the Year anthologies covering horror: *The Best Horror of the Year, Volume Three* (Night Shade Books), edited by Ellen Datlow; *The Mammoth Book of Best New Horror: 22* (Running Press), edited by Stephen Jones; and *The Year's Best Dark Fantasy and Horror, 2011 Edition* (Prime Books), edited by Paula Guran. This year there was also *The Horror Hall of Fame: The Stoker Winners* (Cemetery Dance Publications), edited by Joe R. Lansdale, although it's unclear whether this is going to be a continuing series. Fantasy is covered by the fantasy halves of the Stranhan and Horton anthologies (plus whatever stories fall under the Dark Fantasy part of Guran's anthology), but with the death of Kevin Brockmeier's *Best American Fantasy* series last year, the only remaining Best of the Year anthology dedicated solely to fantasy is David G. Hartwell and Kathryn Cramer's *Year's Best Fantasy* series—*Year's Best Fantasy 10* was announced as forthcoming by Kathryn Cramer in her blog, but I haven't actually seen a copy, and it isn't listed on Amazon, so whether this will actually appear is anyone's guess. There was also *The 2011 Rhysling Anthology* (Science Fiction Poetry Association), edited by David Lunde, which compiles the Rhysling Award–winning SF poetry of the year.

There were a large number of good stand-alone reprint anthologies this year. Although it's a bit of an oddity, a discussion of reprint anthologies published in 2011 wouldn't be complete without mention of *Sense of Wonder: A Century of Science Fiction* (Wildside Press), edited by Leigh Ronald Grossman, which earns the odd distinction of being perhaps the *largest* SF anthology ever published: almost a thousand pages, roughly the size of an old-fashioned telephone directory, weighing five pounds, containing 148 stories and 62 specialized essays about various authors and categories of science fiction. At almost fifty bucks, this will probably be too expensive for most casual readers (there is an e-book version available for forty bucks), but it's a great choice for libraries and serious collectors, practically being a one-volume library, containing memorable stories by Damon Knight, Cordwainer Smith, Alfred Bester, Robert A. Heinlein, Joanna Russ, Samuel R. Delany, Octavia Butler, Edgar Pangborn, Terry Bisson, Pat Murphy, James Patrick Kelly, Gene Wolfe, Howard Waldrop, Maureen McHugh, Greg Bear, Michael Swanwick, Bruce Sterling, Jack Vance, L. Sprague de Camp, Nancy Kress, Nalo Hopkinson, Ted Chiang, Pat Cadigan, Cory Doctorow, Connie Willis, Karen Joy Fowler, Kim Stanley Robinson, and *many* others.

Another enormous reprint anthology that spans decades of genre work, examining fantasy-horror rather than science fiction, is *The Weird: A Compendium of Strange and Dark Stories* (Corvus), edited by Ann VanderMeer and Jeff VanderMeer, which devotes 1,152 pages to 110 stories from many historic periods by writers such as H. P. Lovecraft, Neil Gaiman, Stephen King, Kelly Link, George R. R. Martin, Mervyn Peake, William Gibson, China Miéville, Angela Carter, Michael Chabon, and many, many others.

Also good—although *considerably* smaller—is *Alien Contact* (Night Shade Books), edited by Marty Halpern, stories about contacts with aliens, all of them science fiction (and all of them considerably more varied, subtle, and intelligent than the flood of shoot- 'em-up alien invasion movies we got over the last year or so), featuring work by Bruce Sterling, Michael Swanwick, Bruce McAllister, Molly Gloss, Pat Cadigan, Nancy Kress, Neil Gaiman, George Alec Effinger, Cory Doctorow, Stephen Baxter, Mike Resnick, Harry Turtledove, and thirteen others. *Brave New Worlds* (Night Shade Books) is a reprint anthology of dystopian stories edited by John Joseph Adams, most of them pretty depressing but also pretty powerful, including stories by Shirley Jackson, Geoff Ryman, Kate Wilhelm, Kim Stanley Robinson, Alex Irvine, Cory Doctorow, Harlan Ellison, and others. *Lightspeed: Year One* (Prime Books), edited by John Joseph Adams, is a collection of the first year's worth of stories from electronic online magazine *Lightspeed*, featuring good work by Carrie Vaughn, Yoon Ha Lee, Ted Kosmatka, Vylar Kaftan, and others, and reprints by Ursula K. Le Guin, George R. R. Martin, Robert Silverberg, Joe Haldeman, and others. *Future Media* (Tachyon Publications), edited by Rick Wilber, is an anthology of views of the media age, featuring reprint stories by Pat Cadigan, Gregory Benford, James Tiptree, Jr., and others, plus essays by Marshall McLuhan, Vannevar Bush, and others. *Battlestations* (Prime Books), edited by David Drake and Bill Fawcett, is an omnibus of two previously published anthologies of military SF.

Less dark and more lighthearted is *Happily Ever After* (Night Shade Books), an anthology of retold fairy tales edited by John Klima, and featuring strong work by Howard Waldrop, Gregory Frost, Bruce Sterling, Nancy Kress, Neil Gaiman, Jane Yolen, Theodora Goss, Garth Nix, and others. *People of the Book: A Decade of Jewish Science Fiction and Fantasy* (Prime Books), edited by Rachel Swirsky and Sean Wallace, features SF and fantasy stories (mostly fantasy), by Peter S. Beagle, Theodora Goss, Jane Yolen, Alex Irvine, Neil Gaiman, Benjamin Rosenbaum, and Michael Chabon.

There were a lot of reprint horror anthologies this year, including several urban fantasy/paranormal anthologies. The best of these was probably *The Urban Fantasy Anthology* (Tachyon Publications), edited by Peter S. Beagle and Joe R. Lansdale, which featured good stories by Neil Gaiman, Peter S. Beagle, Tim Powers, Thomas M. Disch, Bruce McAllister, Joe R. Lansdale, Susan Palwick, Charles de Lint, Suzy McKee Charnas, Carrie Vaughn, Patty Briggs, Emma Bull, and others. The somewhat grittier *Crucified Dreams* (Tachyon Publications), edited by Joe R. Lansdale, features strong reprints by Harlan Ellison, Lucius Shepard, Joe Haldeman, Octavia Butler, Stephen King, and others. And 2011 brought us two reprint anthologies that give us an interesting overview of the recent work of younger writers who have been influenced by H. P. Lovecraft enough to want to play in his Cthulhu mythos universe, *The Book of Cthulhu* (Night Shade Books), edited by Ross E. Lockhart, and *New Cthulhu: The Recent Weird* (Prime Books), edited by Paula Guran. The best stories in *The Book of Cthulhu* include works by Michael Shea, Gene Wolfe, T.E.D. Klein, Bruce Sterling, and Laird Barron. The best stories in *New Cthulhu: The Recent Weird* include works by Neil Gaiman, Elizabeth Bear and Sarah Monette, Caitlin R. Kiernan, Laird Barron, and Paul McAuley. Stories by Charles Stross, Elizabeth Bear, and Cherie Priest appear in *both* volumes. There were two reprint anthologies of zombie stories, *Zombies!, Zombies!, Zombies!* (Vintage Black Lizard), edited by Otto Penzler, and *Z: Zombie Stories* (Night Shade Books), edited by J. M. Lassen, and a book of vampire stories, *Vampires: The Recent Undead* (Prime Books), edited by Paula Guran.

There were also two massive reprint anthologies, *The Century's Best Horror Fiction, Volume One: 1901–1950* and *The Century's Best Horror Fiction, Volume Two: 1951–2000* (Cemetery Dance Publications), both edited by John Pelan.

It was a solid but unexciting year in the genre-oriented nonfiction category. There were a number of books of essays by or about genre authors, including *Bugf#ck: The Useless Wit and Wisdom of Harlan Ellison* (Spectrum Fantastic Art), by Harlan Ellison, edited by Arnie Fenner; *The Ecstasy of Influence: Nonfictions, Etc.* (Doubleday), by Jonathan Lethem; *Unstuck in Time: A Journey Through Kurt Vonnegut's Life and Novels* (Seven Stories Press), by Gregory D. Sumner; *And So It Goes: Kurt Vonnegut: A Life* (Henry Holt and Co.), by Charles J. Shields; *Context* (Tachyon Publications), by Cory Doctorow; *The Sookie Stackhouse Companion* (Ace), by Charlaine Harris (which also contains a previously unpublished Sookie Stackhouse novella); *The Hollows Insider* (Harper Voyager) by Kim Harrison; *In Other Worlds: SF and the Human Imagination* (Doubleday), by Margaret Atwood; *Becoming Ray Bradbury* (University of Illinois Press), by Jonathan R. Eller; and *Musings and Meditations: Reflections on Science Fiction, Science, and Other Matters* (Nonstop Press), by Robert Silverberg.

There was an autobiography, *Nested Scrolls: The Autobiography of Rudolf von Bitter Rucker* (Tor), by Rudy Rucker; an assembly of lectures by genre figures, *Thirty-Five Years of the Jack Williamson Lectureship* (Haffner Press), compiled by Patrice Caldwell and Stephen Haffner; two books of reviews, *Sightings: Reviews 2002–2006* (Beccon Publications), by Gary K. Wolfe, and *Pardon This Intrusion: Fantastika in the World Storm* (Beccon Publications), by John Clute; and, as usual, several books about science fiction itself, including *Evaporating Genres: Essays of Fantastic Literature* (Wesleyan University Press), by Gary Wolfe; *Science Fiction and the Prediction of the Future* (McFarland & Company, Inc.), edited by Gary Westfahl, Wong Kin Yuen, and Amy Kit-sze Chan; and *Science Fiction: A Very Short Introduction* (Oxford University Press), by David Seed. A study of the steampunk subgenre was *The Steampunk Bible: An Illustrated Guide to the World of Imaginary Airships, Corsets and Goggles, Mad Scientists, and Strange Literature* (Abrams Image), by Jeff VanderMeer with S. J. Chambers (which probably earns the award for most colorful title of the year).

An offbeat item is a collection of essays about pioneering genre movies by the late Kage Baker, *Ancient Rockets: Treasures and Trainwrecks of the Silent Screen* (Tachyon Publications), by Kage Baker, edited by Kathleen Bartholomew. An even more offbeat item—in fact, perhaps the oddest book you'll read this year—was posthumously assembled from the extensive notebooks left behind by the late Philip K. Dick, *The Exegesis of Philip K. Dick* (Houghton Mifflin Harcourt), edited by Pamela Jackson, Jonathan Lethem, and Erik Davis. I made my way through ten or twenty pages of this, and put the book down feeling that it left the question of whether Dick was a genius or completely insane up in the air—but, whichever it was, I was much too stupid to successfully absorb his *Exegesis.* I suspect all but the most dedicated Phil Dick fans (or those who are geniuses themselves) will probably bounce off it as well.

Not technically genre-oriented, but a book that will interest many genre readers, and one that is sorely needed, in these credulous times when more Americans believe in angels than in evolution, and many don't even believe that the moon shines by reflected light from the sun, is *Denying Science: Conspiracy Theories, Media Distortions, and the War Against Reality* (Prometheus Books), by SF writer John Grant.

2011 was another weak year in the art-book market, even weaker than the year before. As usual, your best bet was probably the latest in a long-running Best of the Year series for fantastic art, *Spectrum 18: The Best in Contemporary Fantastic Art* (Underwood Books), edited by Cathy Fenner and Arnie Fenner. Also quite good were *Masters of Science Fiction and Fantasy Art* (Rockport Publishers, Inc.), assembled by Karen Haber; *Exposé 9: Finest Digital Art in the Known Universe* (Ballistic Publishing), by Daniel P. Wade; *A Tolkien Tapestry: Pictures to Accompany The Lord of the Rings* (HarperCollins); and *Fantasy + 3: Best Hand-Painted Illustrations* (CYPI/Gingko Press), edited by Vincent Zhao.

There were a few excellent books collecting the works of single artists, the best of which was probably *Hardware: The Definitive SF Works of Chris Foss* (Titan), by Chris Foss, although *Jeffrey Jones: A Life in Art* (IDW Publishing), by Jeffrey Jones, was also very good, and *Mark Schultz: Various Drawings, Volume 5* (Flesk), by Mark Schultz, was worthwhile as well. *Girl Genius Book Ten: Agatha Heterodyne and the Guardian Muse* is the latest in the Hugo-winning series by Phil Foglio and Kaja Foglio, and *Lost & Found: Three by Shaun Tan* (Arthur A. Levine Books) is a collection of picture books by the creator of last year's Oscar-nominated short film, *The Lost Thing,* which is included.

An odd item, straddling the line between nonfiction and art, is *Out of This World: Science Fiction but Not as You Know It* (British Library), by Mike Ashley, a catalogue of this year's British Library SF exhibition, a mixture of text and art that covers six centuries of speculative art from 1482 to the present.

According to the Box Office Mojo Web site (www.boxofficemojo.com), seven out of ten of the year's top-earning movies were genre films of one sort or another, if you accept animated films and superhero movies as being "genre films." (Somewhat unusually these days, there were two nongenre movies in the top ten: *The Hangover Part II* and *Fast Five.*) Four out of five of the year's top five box-office champs were genre movies by the above somewhat loose definition, as were twelve out of the top twenty earners, twenty-seven of the top fifty, and roughly forty out of the top one hundred, more or less (I might have missed one here or there, and there are some fuzzy calls in classification). Three of the top five were fantasy movies, *Harry Potter and the Deathly Hallows: Part 2*, *The Twilight Saga: Breaking Dawn—Part 1*, and *Pirates of the Caribbean: On Stranger Tides*, and one was a science fiction movie (albeit a rather silly one), *Transformers: Dark of the Moon*. (*The Hangover Part II* was the only nongenre movie to break the top five, coming in fourth.) The following five were made up of an animated movie (*Cars 2*), a superhero movie (*Thor*), and a science fiction movie (*Rise of the Planet of the Apes*), with the nongenre *Fast Five* and *Mission: Impossible—Ghost Protocol* cutting in at sixth place and seventh place overall out of ten. Further down the list were superhero movie *Captain America: The First Avenger* at twelth place, the steampunkish *Sherlock Holmes: A Game of Shadows* (technically not a genre movie, although the physical action was unlikely enough that you could make a not unreasonable case for considering it a fantasy, and Holmes has always been associated with the genre) at ninth, animated film *Kung Fu Panda 2* at fifteenth place, animated film *Puss in Boots* at sixteenth, superhero movie *X-Men: First Class* at seventeenth, semi-animated (it also featured human actors, interacting with the CGI characters) film *The Smurfs* at nineteenth, and Spielberg/monster-movie homage *Super 8* at twenty-first.

This shouldn't surprise anybody—genre films of one sort or another have dominated the box office top ten for more than a decade now. You have to go all the way back to 1998 to find a year when the year's top earner was a nongenre film, *Saving Private Ryan*.

The year's number one box office champ was *Harry Potter and the Deathly Hallows: Part 2*, which so far has earned a staggering $1,328,111,219 worldwide. *Transformers: Dark of the Moon* also earned more than a billion dollars worldwide, as did *Pirates of the Caribbean: On Stranger Tides*, with a steep drop-off thereafter to *The Twilight Saga: Breaking Dawn—Part 1*, which earned "only" $702,316,133.

In spite of these immense sums, it wasn't a particularly good year at the box office overall for the movie industry. Overall profits were down 3.8 percent to 10.17 billion from 2010, and ticket sales fell 4.7 percent to 1.28 billion, the worst since 1995. I suspect that, in the grip of a worsening recession, it's getting to be just too expensive to go to the movies for an average family, especially when most movies will be available on DVD or on the Internet in only a matter of months. The ability of 3-D to make moviegoers pay more per ticket, something that's been propping up profits, seems to be wearing thin as well, probably because there are so few films that 3-D actually adds anything to; often, in fact, it makes the moviegoing experience worse, muddying the colors and darkening the paleatte. It should also perhaps make the movie industry uneasy that the highest-grossing nonsequel of the year was *Thor*; all the rest of the top ten movies were sequels. Which makes you wonder how many times you can go to the same well before it runs dry.

There were a few actual SF movies by my definition (as opposed to junk popcorn bad-science SF extravaganzas like *Transformers: Dark of the Moon*), and a few of them were even pretty good, but few of them were wild successes at the box office. Of the movies that got some kind of critical respect, the one that did the best was *Super 8*, which finished at twenty-first. It was *half* of a good movie, with the early Spielberg homage stuff, following kids who are trying to make an amateur monster movie, brilliant and effective; when the *real* monster starts showing up, things go downhill, and I couldn't help but feel that it would have been a better movie without the monster altogether. Similarly, *Cowboys and Aliens*, which only made it to thirtieth on the list, was also half of a good movie, with the cowboy setup interesting, but suffered increasingly from bad writing and the ridiculous motivations for the actions of the aliens (which really made no sense) as it went along; they might have been better off making it as a straight cowboy movie if they couldn't do a better job with the "aliens" part. *Real Steel*, perhaps the film that came closest this year to being a core SF movie, based on a Richard Matheson story about boxing robots, widely described as "Rocky with robots," only finished thirty-fifth on the list. *Contagion* was a somber and realistic look at the spread of a worldwide pandemic, without extraneous car chases and gun battles thrown in—which is perhaps why it only made it to forty-fifth on the list. *The Adjustment Bureau* only made it to fifty-sixth place, perhaps indicating that people are getting tired of Philip K. Dick movies. The two best-reviewed genre movies of the year, Woody Allen's time-travel love letter to 1920s Paris, *Midnight in Paris*, and Martin Scorsese's steampunkish homage to Georges Melies (perhaps the closest anyone has yet come to putting a Howard Waldrop story on film), *Hugo*, finished fifty-ninth and fifty-second respectively. *Paul*, a mixture of slob comedy with Area 51/alien stuff in the form of a road picture, came in eighty-first.

The two worst-reviewed, most critically savaged, genre movies of the year were probably *Green Lantern* (twenty-fourth) and *The Green Hornet* (thirty-second)—although it is perhaps a bit too much to hope that this indicates that superhero movies are wearing thin too. (You'll be seeing a lot more of them next year.)

Most of the buzz about movies coming up in 2012 so far seems to be going to *The Hobbit*, the Peter Jackson–directed prequel to the *Lord of the Rings* movies, to *Prometheus*, the prequel to *Alien*, to the *Avengers* movie, to the new *Star Trek* movie (although that probably will be in 2013 rather than in 2012), and to *The Dark Knight Rises*, the last of the Christopher Nolan–directed *Batman* movies. *John Carter*, a film version of Edgar Rice Burroughs's *A Princess of Mars*, is a movie I would have been absolutely wild to see when I was thirteen. There's is a film version of the bestselling YA series, *The Hunger Games*, and a reboot of the pioneering TV vampire soap opera *Dark Shadows* as a movie, starring Johnny Depp. People seem to be divided between anticipation and dread for the reboot of the *Spider-Man* franchise, *The Amazing Spider-Man*. Nobody seems to be looking forward to another *Men in Black* sequel, but that won't stop them from making it anyway. There's also going to be the second half of the last *Twilight* movie, which, although it totally *un*excites me, will no doubt be among the box office champs of 2012.

The big story of 2011, as far as SF and fantasy shows on television are concerned, was the huge success of HBO's *A Game of Thrones*, based on the bestselling *Song of Ice and Fire* series of fantasy novels by George R. R. Martin. Response to *A Game of Thrones* was immense, generating buzz far beyond the usual boundaries of the genre, generating commentary in places like *The New York Times*, and inspiring references in comic strips, game shows, *The Big Bang Theory*, and even drawing a satire from *The Onion*—and making George R. R. Martin, who was already famous within the SF/fantasy genre, a widely recognizable figure outside it as well. HBO's other genre show, the campy vampire show *True Blood*, had a disappointing fourth season that turned off many of its core viewing demographic; let's hope they can do better with the upcoming fifth season (what they primarily need is to increase the quality of the writing, which sagged this season, and bring it back up to its former high standard; the actors are mostly pretty good, but they can only work with what they're given).

The two biggest debuts of SF shows in 2011 were probably *Terra Nova*, in which scientists escape through time from a doomed and ruined Earth to attempt to restart the human race in a prehistoric era, and *Falling Skies*, in which embattled guerilla militiamen battle alien invasion forces who have destroyed much of the Earth and killed most of the people, both expensive shows for television, and both produced by movie director Steven Spielberg, in his first foray into television. *Falling Skies*, which is perfectly valid as a genuine bit of military SF, although offering nothing that print SF fans haven't seen dozens of times before, seems to have established itself, but *Terra Nova*, the more expensive of the two to produce, because of all those CGI dinosaurs, is wobbling badly in the ratings, and may not make it. Another Spielberg-produced show, *The River*, which looks like a *Lost*-flavored horror series, is coming up.

Cult favorite SF show *Fringe*, another expensive show to produce, is also wobbling in the ratings, and may not make it. If *Fringe* and *Terra Nova* do die, they'll be following many another expensive special effects heavy shows such as *Battlestar Galactica*, *Caprica*, *Firefly*, and *Stargate* and its sequels into oblivion—the clear lesson being that supernatural shows, which are far less expensive to produce than SF shows (all you really need is some creature makeup), are more likely to survive on television than SF shows, particularly ones that take place in outer space. *Supernatural*, *The Vampire Diaries*, *The Walking Dead*, *Teen Wolf*, and *American Horror Story* are all coming back, to be joined by new supernatural shows, such as *The Secret Circle*, about witches, *The Fades*, *House of Anubis*, and the dueling fairy-tale series, *Grimm* and *Once Upon a Time*.

No Ordinary Family and *The Cape* died, and the long-running *Smallville* finished its final season, leaving the airways momentarily cleared of superheroes, although that probably won't last long. *V* died. Spy spoof *Chuck* will finish its fifth and final half season in 2012. *A Gifted Man*, a rather peculiar attempt to cross the doctor show and the ghost show, featuring a doctor who is haunted by the nagging ghost of his wife, is sinking, and may already be gone by the time you read this. A new show, *Touch*, which, as far as I can tell from the coming attractions is about an autistic boy with preternatural powers of some sort, started early in the year; too early to tell how it's going to be received.

The SF comedies *Eureka* and *Warehouse 13* are returning, as are *Doctor Who* and *Primeval* and the British version of *Being Human*, although the fates of the American spin-offs of *Torchwood* and *Being Human* are uncertain, and they may both be dead. The animated SF satire *Futurama*, after being canceled for a couple of years and spinning off a couple of special features, is returning to regular production. Another animated series, *Star Wars: The Clone Wars*, is also returning. Mention should probably be made here of *The Big Bang Theory*, which, although not strictly a genre show, is so chockful of sly geek knowledge references to movie and television SF, print SF, online gaming, science, and comic books that I can't imagine that it doesn't appeal to the majority of genre readers.

A miniseries version of Kim Stanley Robinson's *Red Mars* has been promised for a couple of years now, but has yet to make an appearance.

The 69th World Science Fiction Convention, Renovation, was held in Reno, Nevada, from August 17 to August 21, 2011. The 2011 Hugo Awards, presented at Renovation, were: Best Novel, *Blackout/All Clear,* by Connie Willis; Best Novella, "The Lifecycle of Software Objects," by Ted Chiang; Best Novelette, "The Emperor of Mars," by Allen M. Steele; Best Short Story, "For Want of a Nail," by Mary Robinette Kowal; Best Related Work, *Chicks Dig Time Lords: A Celebration of* Doctor Who *by the Women Who Love It,* edited by Lynne M. Thomas and Tara O'Shea; Best Editor, Long Form, Lou Anders; Best Editor, Short Form, Sheila Williams; Best Professional Artist, Shaun Tan; Best Dramatic Presentation (short form), *Doctor Who*: "The Pandorica Opens/The Big Bang"; Best Dramatic Presentation (long form), *Inception*; Best Graphic Story, *Girl Genius, Volume 10: Agatha Heterodyne and the Guardian Muse,* by Kaja and Phil Foglio, art by Phil Foglio; Best Semiprozine, *Clarkesworld*; Best Fanzine, *The Drink Tank*; Best Fan Writer, Claire Brialey; Best Fan Artist, Brad W. Foster; plus the John W. Campbell Award for Best New Writer to Lev Grossman.

The 2010 Nebula Awards, presented at a banquet at the Washington Hilton Hotel in Washington, D.C., on May 21, 2011, were: Best Novel, *Blackout/All Clear,* by Connie Willis; Best Novella, "The Lady Who Plucked Red Flowers Beneath the Queen's Window," by Rachel Swirsky; Best Novelette, "That Leviathan Whom Thou Hast Made," by Eric James Stone; Best Short Story (tie), "Ponies," by Kij Johnson and "How Interesting: A Tiny Man," by Harlan Ellison; Ray Bradbury Award, *Inception*; the Andre Norton Award to *I Shall Wear Midnight,* by Terry Pratchett; and Solstice Awards to Alice Sheldon (aka James Tiptree, Jr.) and Michael Whelan.

The 2011 World Fantasy Awards, presented at a banquet on October 30, 2011, in San Diego, California, during the Twentieth Annual World Fantasy Convention, were: Best Novel, *Who Fears Death,* by Nnedi Okorafor; Best Novella, "The Maiden Flight of McCauley's *Bellerophon,*" by Elizabeth Hand; Best Short Story, "Fossil-Figures," by Joyce Carol Oates; Best Collection, *What I Didn't See and Other Stories,* by Karen Joy Fowler; Best Anthology, *My Mother She Killed Me, My Father He Ate Me,* edited by Kate Bernheimer; Best Artist, Kinuko Y. Craft; Special Award (Professional), to Marc Gascoigne, for *Angry Robot*; Special Award (Nonprofessional), to Alisa Krasnostein, for *Twelfth Planet Press;* plus the Life Achievement Award to Peter S. Beagle and Angélica Gorodischer.

The 2010 Bram Stoker Awards, presented by the Horror Writers of America on June 19, 2011, at the Long Island Marriott Hotel in Uniondale, New York, were: Best Novel, *A Dark Matter,* by Peter Straub; Best First Novel, *Black and Orange,* by Benjamin Kane Ethridge and *Castle of Los Angeles,* by Lisa Morton; Best Long Fiction, *Invisible Fences,* by Norman Prentiss; Best Short Fiction, "The Folding Man," by Joe R. Lansdale; Best Collection, *Full Dark, No Stars,* by Stephen King; Best Anthology, *Haunted Legends,* edited by Ellen Datlow and Nick Mamatas; Nonfiction, *To Each Their Darkness,* by Gary A. Braunbeck; Best Poetry Collection, *Dark Matters,* by Bruce Boston; plus Lifetime Achievement Awards to Ellen Datlow and Al Feldstein.

The 2011 John W. Campbell Memorial Award was won by *The Dervish House*, by Ian McDonald.

The 2011 Theodore Sturgeon Memorial Award for Best Short Story was won by "The Sultan of the Clouds," by Geoffrey A. Landis.

The 2011 Philip K. Dick Memorial Award went to *The Strange Affair of Spring Heeled Jack*, by Mark Hodder.

The 2011 Arthur C. Clarke Award was won by *Zoo City*, by Lauren Beukes.

The 2011 James Tiptree, Jr. Memorial Award was won by *Baba Yaga Laid an Egg*, by Dubravka Ugresic.

The 2011 Sidewise Award went to *When Angels Wept*, by Eric G. Swedin (Long Form) and "A Clash of Eagles," by Alan Smale (Short Form).

The Cordwainer Smith Rediscovery Award went to Katherine MacLean.

Dead in 2011 or early 2012 were: Science Fiction Hall of Fame inductee and SFWA Grandmaster **Anne McCaffery**, 85, the first woman to win a Hugo and Nebula Award, author of more than a hundred books, including the famous and bestselling Pern series, whose best-known works are probably "Weyr Search," "Dragonriders," and *The White Dragon*, the first SF novel to make the *New York Times* Best Seller List, a friend; Hugo, Nebula, and Tiptree award-winner **Joanna Russ**, 74, SF writer and critic, author of such acclaimed books as *The Female Man*, *Picnic on Paradise*, and *And Chaos Died*, as well as much short fiction years ahead of its time, such as "Nobody's Home," "When It Changed," "Souls," and the *Alyx* stories, and also of many books of critical essays, a friend; distinguished fantasist **Diana Wynne Jones**, 76, winner of the World Fantasy Convention's Lifetime Achievement Award, and author of forty books, including the Chrestomanci series, *Archer's Goon*, *Howl's Moving Castle*, which was later made into an animated film by Hayao Miyazaki, and satirical nonfiction work, *The Tough Guide to Fantasyland*; **Russell Hoban**, 86, author of more than fifty children's books, including a long-running series about Frances the badger, perhaps best known to genre audiences for his adult SF novel *Riddley Walker*, which won the John W. Campbell Memorial Award and the Ditmar Award; **Thomas J. Bassler**, 79, who wrote SF as **T. J. BASS**, best known for his work in the 1970s such as the SF novels *Half Past Human* and *The Godwhale*; horror writer and editor **Alan Ryan**, 68, World Fantasy Award-winning author of many short stories that were collected in books such as *The Bones Wizard*, a friend; prolific SF writer **Larry Tritten**, 72, particularly known for his humorous short stories; **Brian Jacques**, 71, children's fantasist, author of the well-known twenty-volume Redwall series; prominent Australian fantasy author **Sara Warneke**, 54, who wrote many bestselling novels as **Sara Douglass**; prominent German SF writer, agent, and editor **Hans Joachim Alpers**, 67; British writer **Euan Harvey**, 38, a frequent contributor to *Realms of Fantasy* and elsewhere; **Gilbert Adair**, 66, Scottish writer, critic and translator; **Colin Harvey**, 51, British SF writer, author of six novels and more than thirty short stories; **William Sleator**, 66, children's and YA novelist; **Juan Carlos Planells**, 61, Spanish author and critic; **Leslie Esdaile Banks**, 51, popular urban fantasy author who published as **L. A. Banks**; **Joel Rosenberg**, 57, SF and mystery author; **John Frederick Burke**, 89, British SF and mystery author who wrote as **Jonathan Burke**; **Vittorio Curtoni**, 61, Italian SF writer, editor, and translator;

Minoru Komatsu, 80, Japanese SF writer, screenwriter, and essayist, who wrote under the name **Sakyo Komatsu; Ion Hobana**, 80, Romanian SF writer; **Moacyr Scliar**, 73, Brazilian fantasy author; **John Glasby**, 82, British SF and fantasy author; **Wim Stolk**, 61, Dutch fantasy artist and writer who wrote as **W. J. Maryson; Lisa Wolfson,** 47, YA and SF author who wrote as **L. K. Madigan; John M. Iggulden**, 93, Australian SF author; British SF writer **Lionel Percy Wright**, 87, who wrote as **Lan Wright; Richard Bessière**, 88, French SF author; **Louis Thirion**, 88, French SF author; **Thierry Martens**, 69, Belgian author, editor, anthologist, and comics historian; **Mark Shepherd**, 49, SF author; **Les Daniels**, 68, comics historian and author of *Comix: A History of Comic Books in America*, who also wrote a series of vampire novels; **Glenn Lord**, 80, U.S. agent for the Howard estate, author of *The Last Celt: A Bio-Bibliography of Robert Ervin Howard*; **Theodore Roszak**, 77, SF writer and essayist, author of *The Making of a Counter Culture: Reflections on the Technocratic Society*; **H.R.F. Keating**, 84, mystery writer who also occasionally wrote SF; **Craig Thomas**, 69, Welsh technothriller writer of *Firefox*, which was later made into a well-known movie; **Martin Woodhouse**, 78, British author and screenwriter; **Robert C. W. Ettinger**, 92, cryonics advocate and occasional SF writer, author of the nonfiction books *The Prospect of Immortality* and *Man into Superman*; **Martin H. Greenberg**, 70, prolific anthologist and academic, involved in the editing of more than a thousand anthologies, founder of the book-packaging company Tekno Books; **Margaret K. McElderry,** 98, children's editor and publisher, founder of children's imprint Margaret K. McElderry Books; **Philip Rahman**, 59, cofounder of the weird fiction publisher Fedogan and Bremer; **Malcolm M. Ferguson**, 91, writer, bookseller, librarian, and collector; **Darrell K. Sweet**, 77, one of the most acclaimed SF and fantasy cover artists of modern times; **Jeffrey Catherine Jones**, 67, prominent fantasy cover artist; **Gene Szafran**, 69, SF cover artist and illustrator; **Cliff Robertson,** 88, movie and TV actor, probably best known to genre audiences as the lead in *Charly*, the film version of "Flowers for Algernon," and for his role as Uncle Ben in the *Spider-Man* movies; **Harry Morgan**, 96, movie and TV actor probably best known to everybody as 'Colonel Potter' from the TV show M*A*S*H, but who also appeared in many films, including *Inherit the Wind* and *The Ox-Bow Incident*; **Peter Falk**, 83, film and television actor probably best known for his long-running role as the rumpled detective in *Columbo*, but who will also be familiar to genre audiences for roles in *The Princess Bride, Murder by Death*, and *Tune in Tomorrow*; **Nicol Williamson**, 75, British stage and film actor, probably best known to genre audiences for his roles as Merlin in *Excalibur*, as Sherlock Holmes in *The Seven-Per-Cent Solution*, and as Little John in *Robin and Marian*; **James Arness**, 88, film and television actor best known as Matt Dillion on *Gunsmoke*, but who also appeared as The Thing in *The Thing from Another World* and in *Them!*; **John Wood**, 81, stage and screen actor, probably best known to genre audiences for roles in *WarGames, The Purple Rose of Cairo*, and *Chocolat*; **Bob Anderson**, 89, former Olympic fencer, fight director, stunt performer, and swordmaster, who staged many of cinema's most famous duels in films such as *The Princess Bride, The Adventures of Robin Hood*, and the *Star Wars* movies; **James "Rusty" Hevelin**, 89, longtime fan, fanzine publisher, collector, and huckster, a friend; **Michael D. Glickson**, 64, longtime Canadian convention and fanzine fan, who won a Hugo in 1973 for his fanzine *Energumen*, a friend; **Susan Palermo-Piscitello**, 59, musician and longtime fan, a friend; **Terry Jeeves**, 88, British fan artist, writer, and publisher; **John Berry**, 80, longtime Irish fan; **Paul Gamble**, 61, British fan and bookseller; **Steve Davis**, 72, husband of author and editor Grania Davis; musician **Marty Burke**, 68, husband of SF author Diana Gallagher; **Elzer Marx**, 86, father of SF writer Christy Marx; **April B. Derleth,** 56, daughter of August Derleth and co-owner of Arkham House.

The Choice

Paul McAuley

Born in Oxford, England, in 1955, Paul J. McAuley now makes his home in London. A professional biologist for many years, he sold his first story in 1984, and has gone on to be a frequent contributor to Interzone, *as well as to publications including* Asimov's Science Fiction, SCI FICTION, Amazing, The Magazine of Fantasy and Science Fiction, Skylife, The Third Alternative, *and* When the Music's Over.

McAuley is at the forefront of several of the most important sub-genres in SF today, producing both "radical hard science fiction" and the revamped and retooled widescreen Space Opera that has sometimes been called The New Space Opera, as well as Dystopian sociological speculations about the very near future. He also writes fantasy and horror. His first novel, Four Hundred Billion Stars, *won the Philip K. Dick Award, and his novel* Fairyland *won both the Arthur C. Clarke Award and the John W. Campbell Award in 1996. His other books include the novels* Of the Fall, Eternal Light, *and* Pasquale's Angel, Confluence *(a major trilogy of ambitious scope and scale set ten million years in the future, which comprised the novels* Child of the River, Ancient of Days, *and* Shrine of Stars), Life on Mars, The Secret of Life, Whole Wide World, White Devils, Mind's Eye, Players, Cowboy Angels, The Quiet War *and* Gardens of the Sun. *His short fiction has been collected in* The King of the Hill and Other Stories, The Invisible Country, *and* Little Machines, *and he is the coeditor, with Kim Newman, of an original anthology,* In Dreams. *His most recent book is a new novel,* In the Mouth of the Whale.

Here he gives us a powerful and deceptively quiet story set in an ingeniously described future England that has been transformed by climate change and a rise in sea level. It is a setting that in McAuley's expert hands has the feel of a real place, both pastoral and *shabby, where people get on with their ordinary lives in a world both dramatically altered and in some ways nearly the same as our own. That is, until the Unknown suddenly intrudes into this world in the form of a giant, mournfully bellowing, enigmatic alien ship that grounds itself on the bank of a river, and changes everything forever.*

▼

In the night, tides and a brisk wind drove a raft of bubbleweed across the Flood and piled it up along the north side of the island. Soon after first light, Lucas started raking it up, ferrying load after load to one of the compost pits, where it would rot down into a nutrient-rich liquid fertiliser. He was trundling his wheelbarrow down the steep path to the shore for about the thirtieth or fortieth time when he spotted someone walking across the water: Damian, moving like a cross-country skier as he crossed the channel between the island and the stilt huts and floating tanks of his father's shrimp farm. It was still early in the morning, already hot. A perfect September day, the sky's blue dome untroubled by cloud. Shifting points of sunlight starred the water, flashed from the blades of the farm's wind turbine. Lucas waved to his friend and Damian waved back and nearly overbalanced, windmilling his arms and recovering, slogging on.

They met at the water's edge. Damien, picking his way between floating slicks of red weed, called out breathlessly, "Did you hear?"

"Hear what?"

"A dragon got itself stranded close to Martham."

"You're kidding."

"I'm not kidding. An honest-to-God sea dragon."

Damian stepped onto an apron of broken brick at the edge of the water and sat down and eased off the fat flippers of his Jesus shoes, explaining that he'd heard about it from Ritchy, the foreman of the shrimp farm, who'd got it off the skipper of a supply barge who'd been listening to chatter on the common band.

"It beached not half an hour ago. People reckon it came in through the cut at Horsey and couldn't get back over the bar when the tide turned. So it went on up the channel of the old riverbed until it ran ashore."

Lucas thought for a moment. "There's a sand bar that hooks into the channel south of Martham. I went past it any number of times when I worked on Grant Higgins's boat last summer, ferrying oysters to Norwich."

"It's almost on our doorstep," Damian said. He pulled his phone from the pocket of his shorts and angled it towards Lucas. "Right about here. See it?"

"I know where Martham is. Let me guess—you want me to take you."

"What's the point of building a boat if you don't use it? Come on, L. It isn't every day an alien machine washes up."

Lucas took off his broad-brimmed straw hat and blotted his forehead with his wrist and set his hat on his head again. He was a wiry boy not quite sixteen, bare-chested in baggy shorts, and wearing sandals he'd cut from an old car tyre. "I was planning to go crabbing. After I finish clearing this weed, water the vegetable patch, fix lunch for my mother . . ."

"I'll give you a hand with all that when we get back."

"Right."

"If you really don't want to go I could maybe borrow your boat."

"Or you could take one of your dad's."

"After what he did to me last time? I'd rather row there in that leaky old clunker of your mother's. Or walk."

"That would be a sight."

Damian smiled. He was just two months older than Lucas, tall and sturdy, his cropped blond hair bleached by salt and summer sun, his nose and the rims of his ears pink and peeling. The two had been friends for as long as they could remember.

He said, "I reckon I can sail as well as you."

"You're sure this dragon is still there? You have pictures?"

"Not exactly. It knocked out the town's broadband, and everything else. According to the guy who talked to Ritchy, nothing electronic works within a klick of it. Phones, slates, radios, nothing. The tide turns in a couple of hours, but I reckon we can get there if we start right away."

"Maybe. I should tell my mother," Lucas said. "In the unlikely event that she wonders where I am."

"How is she?"

"No better, no worse. Does your dad know you're skipping out?"

"Don't worry about it. I'll tell him I went crabbing with you."

"Fill a couple of jugs at the still," Lucas said. "And pull up some carrots, too. But first, hand me your phone."

"The GPS coordinates are flagged up right there. You ask it, it'll plot a course."

Lucas took the phone, holding it with his fingertips—he didn't like the way it squirmed as it shaped itself to fit in his hand. "How do you switch it off?"

"What do you mean?"

"If we go, we won't be taking the phone. Your dad could track us."

"How will we find our way there?"

"I don't need your phone to find Martham."

"You and your off-the-grid horse shit," Damian said.

"You wanted an adventure," Lucas said. "This is it."

When Lucas started to tell his mother that he'd be out for the rest of the day with Damian, she said, "Chasing after that so-called dragon I suppose. No need to look surprised—it's all over the news. Not the official news, of course. No mention of it there. But it's leaking out everywhere that counts."

His mother was propped against the headboard of the double bed under the caravan's big end window. Julia Wittsruck, fifty-two, skinny as a refugee, dressed in a striped Berber robe and half-covered in a patchwork of quilts and thin orange blankets stamped with the Oxfam logo. The ropes of her dreadlocks tied back with a red bandana; her tablet resting in her lap.

She gave Lucas her best inscrutable look and said, "I suppose this is Damian's idea. You be careful. His ideas usually work out badly."

"That's why I'm going along. To make sure he doesn't get into trouble. He's set on seeing it, one way or another."

"And you aren't?"

Lucas smiled. "I suppose I'm curious. Just a little."

"I wish I could go. Take a rattle can or two, spray the old slogans on the damned thing's hide."

"I could put some cushions in the boat. Make you as comfortable as you like."

Lucas knew that his mother wouldn't take up his offer. She rarely left the caravan, hadn't been off the island for more than three years. A multilocus immunotoxic syndrome, basically an allergic reaction to the myriad products and pollutants of the anthropocene age, had left her more or less completely bedridden. She'd refused all offers of treatment or help by the local social agencies, relying instead on the services of a local witchwoman who visited once a week, and spent her days in bed, working at her tablet. She trawled government sites and stealthnets, made podcasts, advised zero-impact communities, composed critiques and manifestos. She kept a public journal, wrote essays and opinion pieces (at the moment, she was especially exercised by attempts by multinational companies to move in on the Antarctic Peninsula, and a utopian group that was using alien technology to build a floating community on a drowned coral reef in the Midway Islands), and maintained friendships, alliances, and several rancorous feuds with former colleagues whose origins had long been forgotten by both sides. In short, hers was a way of life that would have been familiar to scholars from any time in the past couple of millennia.

She'd been a lecturer in philosophy at Birkbeck College before the nuclear strikes, riots, revolutions, and netwar skirmishes of the so-called Spasm, which had ended when the floppy ships of the Jackaroo had appeared in the skies over Earth. In exchange for rights to the outer solar system, the aliens had given the human race technology to clean up the Earth, and access to a wormhole network that linked a dozen M-class red dwarf stars. Soon enough, other alien species showed up, making various deals with various nations and power blocs, bartering advanced technologies for works of art, fauna and flora, the secret formula of Coca-Cola, and other unique items.

Most believed that the aliens were kindly and benevolent saviours, members of a loose alliance that had traced ancient broadcasts of *I Love Lucy* to their origin and arrived just in time to save the human species from the consequences of its monkey cleverness. But a vocal minority wanted nothing to do with them, doubting that their motives were in any way altruistic, elaborating all kinds of theories about their true motivations. We should choose to reject the help of the aliens, they said. We should reject easy fixes and the magic of advanced technologies we don't understand, and choose the harder thing: to keep control of our own destiny.

Julia Wittstruck had become a leading light in this movement. When its brief but fierce round of global protests and politicking had fallen apart in a mess of mutual recriminations and internecine warfare, she'd moved to Scotland and joined a group of green radicals who'd been building a self-sufficient settlement on a trio of ancient oil rigs in the Firth of Forth. But they'd become compromised too, according to Julia, so she'd left them and taken up with Lucas's father (Lucas knew almost nothing about him—his mother said that the past was the past, that she was all that counted in his life because she had given birth to him and raised and taught him), and they'd lived the gypsy life for a few years until she'd split up with him and, pregnant with her son, had settled in a smallholding in Norfolk, living off the grid, supported by a small legacy left to her by one of her devoted supporters from the glory days of the anti-alien protests.

When she'd first moved there, the coast had been more than ten kilometres to the east, but a steady rise in sea level had flooded the northern and eastern coasts of Britain and Europe. East Anglia had been sliced in two by levees built to protect precious farmland from the encroaching sea, and most people caught on the wrong side had taken resettlement grants and moved on. But Julia had stayed put. She'd paid a contractor to extend a small rise, all that was left of her smallholding, with rubble from a wrecked twentieth-century housing estate, and made her home on the resulting island. It had once been much larger, and a succession of people had camped there, attracted by her kudos, driven away after a few weeks or a few months by her scorn and impatience. Then most of Greenland's remaining ice cap collapsed into the Arctic Ocean, sending a surge of water across the North Sea.

Lucas had only been six, but he still remembered everything about that day. The water had risen past the high tide mark that afternoon and had kept rising. At first it had been fun to mark the stealthy progress of the water with a series of sticks driven into the ground, but by evening it was clear that it was not going to stop anytime soon and then in a sudden smooth rush it rose more than a hundred centimetres, flooding the vegetable plots and lapping at the timber baulks on which the caravan rested. All that evening, Julia had moved their possessions out of the caravan, with Lucas trotting to and fro at her heels, helping her as best he could until, some time after midnight, she'd given up and they'd fallen asleep under a tent rigged from chairs and a blanket. And had woken to discover that their island had shrunk to half its previous size, and the caravan had floated off and lay canted and half-drowned in muddy water littered with every kind of debris.

Julia had bought a replacement caravan and set it on the highest point of what was left of the island, and despite ineffectual attempts to remove them by various local government officials, she and Lucas had stayed on. She'd taught him the basics of numeracy and literacy, and the long and intricate secret history of the world, and he'd learned field- and wood- and watercraft from their neighbours. He snared rabbits in the woods that ran alongside the levee, foraged for hedgerow fruits and edible weeds and fungi, bagged squirrels with small stones shot from his catapult. He grubbed mussels from the rusting car-reef that protected the seaward side of the levee, set wicker traps for eels and trotlines for mitten crabs. He fished for mackerel and dogfish and weaverfish on the wide brown waters of the Flood. When he could, he worked shifts on the shrimp farm owned by Damian's father, or on the market gardens, farms, and willow and bamboo plantations on the other side of the levee.

In spring, he watched long vees of geese fly north above the floodwater that stretched out to the horizon. In autumn, he watched them fly south.

He'd inherited a great deal of his mother's restlessness and fierce independence, but although he longed to strike out beyond his little world, he didn't know how to begin. And besides, he had to look after Julia. She would never admit it, but she depended on him, utterly.

She said now, dismissing his offer to take her along, "You know I have too much to do here. The day is never long enough. There is something you can do for me, though. Take my phone with you."

"Damian says phones don't work around the dragon."

"I'm sure it will work fine. Take some pictures of that thing. As many as you can. I'll write up your story when you come back, and pictures will help attract traffic."

"Okay."

Lucas knew that there was no point in arguing. Besides, his mother's phone was an ancient model that predated the Spasm: it lacked any kind of cloud connectivity and was as dumb as a box of rocks. As long as he only used it to take pictures, it wouldn't compromise his idea of an off-the-grid adventure.

His mother smiled. "'ET go home.'"

"'ET go home?'"

"We put that up everywhere, back in the day. We put it on the main runway of Luton Airport, in letters twenty metres tall. Also dug trenches in the shape of the words up on the South Downs and filled them with diesel fuel and set them alight. You could see it from space. Let the unhuman know that they were not welcome here. That we did not need them. Check the toolbox. I'm sure there's a rattlecan in there. Take it along, just in case."

"I'll take my catapult, in case I spot any ducks. I'll try to be back before it gets dark. If I don't, there are MREs in the store cupboard. And I picked some tomatoes and carrots."

"'ET go home,'" his mother said. "Don't forget that. And be careful, in that little boat."

Lucas had started to build his sailboat late last summer, and had worked at it all through the winter. It was just four metres from bow to stern, its plywood hull glued with epoxy and braced with ribs shaped from branches of a young poplar tree that had fallen in the autumn gales. He'd used an adze and a homemade plane to fashion the mast and boom from the poplar's trunk, knocked up the knees, gunwale, outboard support and bow cap from oak, and persuaded Ritchy, the shrimp farm's foreman, to print off the cleats, oarlocks, bow eye and grommets for lacing the sails on the farm's maker. Ritchy had given him some half-empty tins of blue paint and varnish to seal the hull, and he'd bought a set of secondhand laminate sails from the shipyard in Halvergate, and spliced the halyards and sheet from scrap lengths of rope.

He loved his boat more than he was ready to admit to himself. That spring he'd tacked back and forth beyond the shrimp farm, had sailed north along the coast to Halvergate and Acle, and south and west around Reedham Point as far as Brundall, and had crossed the channel of the river and navigated the mazy mudflats to Chedgrave. If the sea dragon was stuck where Damian said it was, he'd have to travel further than ever before, navigating uncharted and ever-shifting sand and mudbanks, dodging clippers and barge strings in the shipping channel, but Lucas reckoned he had the measure of his little boat now and it was a fine day and a steady wind blowing from the west drove them straight along, with the jib cocked as far as it would go in the stay and the mainsail bellying full and the boat heeling sharply as it ploughed a white furrow in the light chop.

At first, all Lucas had to do was sit in the stern with the tiller snug in his right armpit and the main sheet coiled loosely in his left hand, and keep a straight course north past the pens and catwalks of the shrimp farm. Damian sat beside him, leaning out to port to counterbalance the boat's tilt, his left hand keeping the jib sheet taut, his right holding a plastic cup he would now and then use to scoop water from the bottom of the boat and fling in a sparkling arc that was caught and twisted by the wind.

The sun stood high in a tall blue sky empty of cloud save for a thin rim at the horizon to the northeast. Fret, most likely, mist forming where moisture condensed out of air that had cooled as it passed over the sea. But the fret was kilometres away, and all around sunlight flashed from every wave top and burned on the white sails and beat down on the two boys. Damian's face and bare torso shone with sunblock; although Lucas was about as dark as he got, he'd rubbed sunblock on his face too, and tied his straw hat under his chin and put on a shirt that flapped about his chest. The tiller juddered minutely and constantly as the boat slapped through an endless succession of catspaw waves and Lucas measured the flex of the sail by the tug of the sheet wrapped around his left hand, kept an eye the foxtail streamer that flew from the top of the mast. Judging by landmarks on the levee that ran along the shore to port, they making around fifteen kilometres per hour, about as fast as Lucas had ever gotten out of his boat, and he and Damian grinned at each other and squinted off into the glare of the sunstruck water, happy and exhilarated to be skimming across the face of the Flood, two bold adventurers off to confront a monster.

"We'll be there in an hour easy," Damian said.

"A bit less than two, maybe. As long as the fret stays where it is."

"The sun'll burn it off."

"Hasn't managed it yet."

"Don't let your natural caution spoil a perfect day."

Lucas swung wide of a raft of bubbleweed that glistened like a slick of fresh blood in the sun. Some called it Martian weed, though it had nothing to do with any of the aliens; it was an engineered species designed to mop up nitrogen and phosphorous released by drowned farmland, prospering beyond all measure or control.

Dead ahead, a long line of whitecaps marked the reef of the old railway embankment. Lucas swung the tiller into the wind and he and Damian ducked as the boom swung across and the boat gybed around. The sails slackened, then filled with wind again as the boat turned towards one of the gaps blown in the embankment, cutting so close to the buoy that marked it that Damian could reach out and slap the rusty steel plate of its flank as they went by. And then they were heading out across a broad reach, with the little town of Acle strung along a low promontory to port. A slateless church steeple stood up from the water like a skeletal lighthouse. The polished cross at its top burned like a flame in the sunlight. A file of old pylons stepped away, most canted at steep angles, the twiggy platforms of heron nests built in angles of their girder work, whitened everywhere with droppings. One of the few still standing straight had been colonised by fisherfolk, with shacks built from driftwood lashed to its struts and a wave-powered generator made from oil drums strung out beyond. Washing flew like festive flags inside the web of rusted steel, and a naked small child of indeterminate sex clung to the unshuttered doorway of a shack just above the waterline, pushing a tangle of hair from its eyes as it watched the little boat sail by.

They passed small islands fringed with young mangrove trees, an engineered species that was rapidly spreading from areas in the south where they'd been planted to replace the levee. Lucas spotted a marsh harrier patrolling mudflats in the lee of one island, scrying for water voles and mitten crabs. They passed a long building sunk to the tops of its second-storey windows in the flood, with brightly coloured plastic bubbles pitched on its flat roof amongst the notched and spinning wheels of windmill generators, and small boats bobbing alongside. Someone standing at the edge of the roof waved to them, and Damian stood up and waved back and the boat shifted so that he had to catch at the jib leech and sit down hard.

"You want us to capsize, go ahead," Lucas told him.

"There are worse places to be shipwrecked. You know they're all married to each other over there."

"I heard."

"They like visitors too."

"I know you aren't talking from experience or you'd have told me all about it. At least a dozen times."

"I met a couple of them in Halvergate. They said I should stop by some time," Damian said, grinning sideways at Lucas. "We could maybe think about doing that on the way back."

"And get stripped of everything we own, and thrown in the water."

"You have a trusting nature, don't you?"

"If you mean, I'm not silly enough to think they'll welcome us in and let us take our pick of their women, then I guess I do."

"She was awful pretty, the woman. And not much older than me."

"And the rest of them are seahags older than your great-grandmother."

"That one time with my father . . . She was easily twice my age and I didn't mind a bit."

A couple of months ago, Damian's sixteenth birthday, his father had taken him to a pub in Norwich where women stripped at the bar and afterwards walked around bare naked, collecting tips from the customers. Damian's father had paid one of them to look after his son, and Damian hadn't stopped talking about it ever since, making plans to go back on his own or to take Lucas with him that so far hadn't amounted to anything.

He watched the half-drowned building dwindle into the glare striking off the water and said, "If we ever ran away we could live in a place like that."

"You could, maybe," Lucas said. "I'd want to keep moving. But I suppose I could come back and visit now and then."

"I don't mean *that* place. I mean a place like it. Must be plenty of them, on those alien worlds up in the sky. There's oceans on one of them. First Foot."

"I know."

"And alien ruins on all of them. There are people walking about up there right now. On all those new worlds. And most people sit around like . . . like bloody stumps. Old tree stumps stuck in mud."

"I'm not counting on winning the ticket lottery," Lucas said. "Sailing south, that would be pretty fine. To Africa, or Brazil, or these islands people are building in the Pacific. Or even all the way to Antarctica."

"Soon as you stepped ashore, L, you'd be eaten by a polar bear."

"Polar bears lived in the north when there were polar bears."

"Killer penguins then. Giant penguins with razors in their flippers and lasers for eyes."

"No such thing."

"The !Cha made sea dragons, didn't they? So why not giant robot killer penguins? Your mother should look into it."

"That's not funny."

"Didn't mean anything by it. Just joking, is all."

"You go too far sometimes."

They sailed in silence for a little while, heading west across the deepwater channel. A clipper moved far off to starboard, cylinder sails spinning slowly, white as salt in the middle of a flat vastness that shimmered like shot silk under the hot blue sky. Some way beyond it, a tug was dragging a string of barges south. The shoreline of Thurne Point emerged from the heat haze, standing up from mudbanks cut by a web of narrow channels, and they turned east, skirting stands of seagrass that spread out into the open water. It was a little colder now, and the wind was blowing more from the northwest than the west. Lucas thought that the bank of fret looked closer, too. When he pointed it out, Damian said it was still klicks and klicks off, and besides, they were headed straight to their prize now.

"If it's still there," Lucas said.

"It isn't going anywhere, not with the tide all the way out."

"You really are an expert on this alien stuff, aren't you?"

"Just keep heading north, L."

"That's exactly what I'm doing."

"I'm sorry about that crack about your mother. I didn't mean anything by it. Okay?"

"Okay."

"I like to kid around," Damian said. "But I'm serious about getting out of here. Remember that time two years ago, we hiked into Norwich, found the army offices?"

"I remember the sergeant there gave us cups of tea and biscuits and told us to come back when we were old enough."

"He's still there. That sergeant. Same bloody biscuits too."

"Wait. You went to join up without telling me?"

"I went to find out if I could. After my birthday. Turns out the army takes people our age, but you need the permission of your parents. So that was that."

"You didn't even try to talk to your father about it?"

"He has me working for him, L. Why would he sign away good cheap labour? I *did* try, once. He was half-cut and in a good mood. What passes for a good mood as far as he's concerned, any rate. Mellowed out on beer and superfine skunk. But he wouldn't hear anything about it. And then he got all the way flat-out drunk and he beat on me. Told me to never mention it again."

Lucas looked over at his friend and said, "Why didn't you tell me this before?"

"I can join under my own signature when I'm eighteen, not before," Damian said. "No way out of here until then, unless I run away or win the lottery."

"So are you thinking of running away?"

"I'm damned sure not counting on winning the lottery. And even if I do, you have to be eighteen before they let you ship out. Just like the fucking army." Damian looked at Lucas, looked away. "He'll probably bash all kinds of shit out of me, for taking off like this."

"You can stay over tonight. He'll be calmer, tomorrow."

Damian shook his head. "He'll only come looking for me. And I don't want to cause trouble for you and your mother."

"It wouldn't be any trouble."

"Yeah, it would. But thanks anyway." Damian paused, then said, "I don't care what he does to me anymore. You know? All I think is, one day I'll be able to beat up on him."

"You say that but you don't mean it."

"Longer I stay here, the more I become like him."

"I don't see it ever happening."

Damian shrugged.

"I really don't," Lucas said.

"Fuck him," Damian said. "I'm not going to let him spoil this fine day."

"Our grand adventure."

"The wind's changing again."

"I think the fret's moving in too."

"Maybe it is, a little. But we can't turn back, L. Not now."

The bank of cloud across the horizon was about a klick away, reaching up so high that it blurred and dimmed the sun. The air was colder and the wind was shifting minute by minute. Damian put on his shirt, holding the jib sheet in his teeth as he punched his arms into the sleeves. They tacked to swing around a long reach of grass, and as they came about saw a white wall sitting across the water, dead ahead.

Lucas pushed the tiller to leeward. The boat slowed at once and swung around to face the wind.

"What's the problem?" Damian said. "It's just a bit of mist."

Lucas caught the boom as it swung, held it steady. "We'll sit tight for a spell. See if the fret burns off."

"And meanwhile the tide'll turn and lift off the fucking dragon."

"Not for awhile."

"We're almost there."

"You don't like it, you can swim."

"I might." Damian peered at the advancing fret. "Think the dragon has something to do with this?"

"I think it's just fret."

"Maybe it's hiding from something looking for it. We're drifting backwards," Damian said. "Is that part of your plan?"

"We're over the river channel, in the main current. Too deep for my anchor. See those dead trees at the edge of the grass? That's where I'm aiming. We can sit it out there."

"I hear something," Damian said.

Lucas heard it too. The ripping roar of a motor driven at full speed, coming closer. He looked over his shoulder, saw a shadow condense inside the mist and gain shape and solidity: a cabin cruiser shouldering through windblown tendrils at the base of the bank of mist, driving straight down the main channel at full speed, its wake spreading wide on either side.

In a moment of chill clarity Lucas saw what was going to happen. He shouted to Damian, telling him to duck, and let the boom go and shoved the tiller to starboard. The boom banged around as the sail bellied and the boat started to turn, but the cruiser was already on them, roaring past just ten metres away, and the broad smooth wave of its wake hit the boat broadside and lifted it and shoved it sideways towards a stand of dead trees. Lucas gave up any attempt to steer and unwound the main halyard from its cleat. Damian grabbed an oar and used it to push the boat away from the first of the trees, but their momentum swung them into two more. The wet black stump of a branch scraped along the side and the boat heeled and water poured in over the thwart. For a moment Lucas thought they would capsize; then something thumped into the mast and the boat sat up again. Shards of rotten wood dropped down with a dry clatter and they were suddenly still, caught amongst dead and half-drowned trees.

The damage wasn't as bad as it might have been—a rip close to the top of the jib, long splintery scrapes in the blue paintwork on the port side—but it kindled a black spark of anger in Lucas's heart. At the cruiser's criminal indifference; at his failure to evade trouble.

"Unhook the halyard and let it down," he told Damian. "We'll have to do without the jib."

"*Abode Two*. That's the name of the bugger nearly ran us down. Registered in Norwich. We should find him and get him to pay for this mess," Damian said as he folded the torn jib sail.

"I wonder why he was going so damned fast."

"Maybe he went to take a look at the dragon, and something scared him off."

"Or maybe he just wanted to get out of the fret." Lucas looked all around, judging angles and clearances. The trees stood close together in water scummed with every kind of debris, stark and white above the tide line, black and clad with mussels and barnacles below. He said, "Let's try pushing backwards. But be careful. I don't want any more scrapes."

By the time they had freed themselves from the dead trees the fret had advanced around them. A cold streaming whiteness that moved just above the water, deepening in every direction.

"Now we're caught up in it, it's as easy to go forward as to go back. So we might as well press on," Lucas said.

"That's the spirit. Just don't hit any more trees."

"I'll do my best."

"Think we should put up the sail?"

"There's hardly any wind, and the tide's still going out. We'll just go with the current."

"Dragon weather," Damian said.

"Listen," Lucas said.

After a moment's silence, Damian said, "Is it another boat?"

"Thought I heard wings."

Lucas had taken out his catapult. He fitted a ball-bearing in the centre of its fat rubber band as he looked all around. There was a splash amongst the dead trees to starboard and he brought up the catapult and pulled back the rubber band as something dropped onto a dead branch. A heron, grey as a ghost, turning its head to look at him.

Lucas lowered the catapult, and Damian whispered, "You could take that easy."

"I was hoping for a duck or two."

"Let me try a shot."

Lucas stuck the catapult in his belt. "You kill it, you eat it."

The heron straightened its crooked neck and raised up and opened its wings and with a lazy flap launched itself across the water, sailing past the stern of the boat and vanishing into the mist.

"Ritchy cooked one once," Damian said. "With about a ton of aniseed. Said it was how the Romans did them."

"How was it?"

'Pretty fucking awful you want to know the truth."

"Pass me one of the oars," Lucas said. "We can row a while."

They rowed through mist into mist. The small noises they made seemed magnified, intimate. Now and again Lucas put his hand over the side and dipped up a palmful of water and tasted it, telling Damian that fresh water was slow to mix with salt, so as long as it stayed sweet it meant they were in the old river channel and shouldn't run into anything. Damian was sceptical, but shrugged when Lucas challenged him to come up with a better way of finding their way through the fret without stranding themselves on some mudbank

They'd been rowing for ten minutes or so when a long, low mournful note boomed out far ahead of them. It shivered Lucas to the marrow of his bones. He and Damian stopped rowing and looked at each other.

"I'd say that was a foghorn, if I didn't know what one sounded like," Damian said.

"Maybe it's a boat. A big one."

"Or maybe you-know-what. Calling for its dragon-mummy."

"Or warning people away."

"I think it came from over there," Damian said, pointing off to starboard.

"I think so too. But it's hard to be sure of anything in this stuff."

They rowed aslant the current. A dim and low palisade appeared, resolving into a bed of sea grass that spread along the edge of the old river channel. Lucas, believing that he knew where they were, felt a clear measure of relief. They sculled into a narrow cut that led through the grass. Tall stems bent and showered them with drops of condensed mist as they brushed past. Then they were out into open water on the far side. A beach loomed out of the mist and sand suddenly gripped and grated along the length of the little boat's keel. Damian dropped his oar and vaulted over the side and splashed away, running up the beach and vanishing into granular whiteness. Lucas shipped his own oar and slid into knee-deep water and hauled the boat through purling ripples, then lifted from the bow the bucket filled with concrete he used as an anchor and dropped it onto hard wet sand, where it keeled sideways in a dint that immediately filled with water.

He followed Damian's footprints up the beach, climbed a low ridge grown over with marram grass and descended to the other side of the sand bar. Boats lay at anchor in shallow water, their outlines blurred by mist. Two dayfishers with small wheelhouses at their bows. Several sailboats not much bigger than his. A cabin cruiser with trim white superstructure, much like the one that had almost run him down.

A figure materialised out of the whiteness, a chubby boy of five or six in dungarees who ran right around Lucas, laughing, and chased away. He followed the boy toward a blurred eye of light far down the beach. Raised voices. Laughter. A metallic screeching. As he drew close, the blurred light condensed and separated into two sources: a bonfire burning above the tide line; a rack of spotlights mounted on a police speedboat anchored a dozen metres off the beach, long fingers of light lancing through mist and blurrily illuminating the long sleek shape stranded at the edge of the water.

It was big, the sea dragon, easily fifteen metres from stem to stern and about three metres across at its waist, tapering to blunt and shovel-shaped points at either end, coated in close-fitting and darkly tinted scales. An alien machine, solid and obdurate. One of thousands spawned by sealed mother ships the UN had purchased from the !Cha.

Lucas thought that it looked like a leech, or one of the parasitic flukes that lived in the bellies of sticklebacks. A big segmented shape, vaguely streamlined, helplessly prostate. People stood here and there on the curve of its back. A couple of kids were whacking away at its flank with chunks of driftwood. A group of men and women stood at its nose, heads bowed as if in prayer. A woman was walking along its length, pointing a wand-like instrument at different places. A cluster of people were conferring amongst a scatter of toolboxes and a portable generator, and one of them stepped forward and applied an angle grinder to the dragon's hide. There was a ragged screech and a fan of orange sparks sprayed out and the man stepped back and turned to his companions and shook his head. Beyond the dragon, dozens more people could be glimpsed through the blur of the fret: everyone from the little town of Martham must have walked out along the sand bar to see the marvel that had cast itself up at their doorstep.

According to the UN, dragons cruised the oceans and swept up and digested the vast rafts of floating garbage that were part of the legacy of the wasteful oil-dependent world before the Spasm. According to rumours propagated on the stealth nets, a UN black lab had long ago cracked open a dragon and reverse-engineered its technology for fell purposes, or they were a cover for an alien plot to infiltrate Earth and construct secret bases in the ocean deeps, or geoengineer the world in some radical and inimical fashion. And so on, and so on. One of his mother's ongoing disputes was with the Midway Island Utopians, who were using modified dragons to sweep plastic particulates from the North Pacific Gyre and spin the polymer soup into construction materials: true Utopians shouldn't use any kind of alien technology, according to her.

Lucas remembered his mother's request to take photos of the dragon and fished out her phone; when he switched it on, it emitted a lone and plaintive beep and its screen flashed and went dark. He switched it off, switched it on again. This time it did nothing. So it was true: the dragon was somehow suppressing electronic equipment. Lucas felt a shiver of apprehension, wondering what else it could do, wondering if it was watching him and everyone around it.

As he pushed the dead phone into his pocket, someone called his name. Lucas turned, saw an old man dressed in a yellow slicker and a peaked corduroy cap bustling towards him. Bill Danvers, one of the people who tended the oyster beds east of Martham, asking him now if he'd come over with Grant Higgins.

"I came in my own boat," Lucas said.

"You worked for Grant though," Bill Danvers said, and held out a flat quarter-litre bottle.

"Once upon a time. That's kind, but I'll pass."

"Vodka and ginger root. It'll keep out the cold." The old man unscrewed the cap and took a sip and held out the bottle again.

Lucas shook his head.

Bill Danvers took another sip and capped the bottle, saying, "You came over from Halvergate?"

"A little south of Halvergate. Sailed all the way." It felt good to say it.

"People been coming in from every place, past couple of hours. Including those science boys you see trying to break into her. But I was here first. Followed the damn thing in after it went past me. I was fishing for pollack, and it went past like an island on the move. Like to have had me in the water, I was rocking so much. I fired up the outboard and swung around but I couldn't keep pace with it. I saw it hit the bar, though. It didn't slow down a bit, must have been travelling at twenty knots. I heard it," Bill Danvers said, and clapped his hands. "Bang! It ran straight up, just like you see. When I caught up with it, it was wriggling like an eel. Trying to move forward, you know? And it did, for a little bit. And then it stuck, right where it is now. Must be something wrong with it, I reckon, or it wouldn't have grounded itself. Maybe it's dying, eh?"

"Can they die, dragons?"

"You live long enough, boy, you'll know everything has its time. Even unnatural things like this. Those science people, they've been trying to cut into it all morning. They used a thermal lance, and some kind of fancy drill. Didn't even scratch it. Now they're trying this saw thing with a blade tougher than diamond. Or so they say. Whatever it is, it won't do any good. Nothing on Earth can touch a dragon. Why'd you come all this way?"

"Just to take a look."

"Long as that's all you do I won't have any quarrel with you. You might want to pay the fee now."

"Fee?"

"Five pounds. Or five euros, if that's what you use."

"I don't have any money," Lucas said.

Bill Danvers studied him. "I was here first. Anyone says different they're a goddamned liar. I'm the only one can legitimately claim salvage rights. The man what found the dragon," he said, and turned and walked towards two women, starting to talk long before he reached them.

Lucas went on down the beach. A man sat tailorwise on the sand, sketching on a paper pad with a stick of charcoal. A small group of women were chanting some kind of incantation and brushing the dragon's flank with handfuls of ivy, and all down its length people stood close, touching its scales with the palms of their hands or leaning against it, peering into it, like penitents at a holy relic. Its scales were easily a metre across and each was a slightly different shape, six- or seven-sided, dark yet grainily translucent. Clumps of barnacles and knots of hair-like weed clung here and there.

Lucas took a step into cold, ankle-deep water, and another. Reached out, the tips of his fingers tingling, and brushed the surface of one of the plates. It was the same temperature as the air and covered in small dimples, like hammered metal. He pressed the palm of his hand flat against it and felt a steady vibration, like touching the throat of a purring cat. A shiver shot through the marrow of him, a delicious mix of fear and exhilaration. Suppose his mother and her friends were right? Suppose there was an alien inside there? A Jackaroo or a !Cha riding inside the dragon because it was the only way, thanks to the agreement with the UN, they could visit the Earth. An actual alien lodged in the heart of the machine, watching everything going on around it, trapped and helpless, unable to call for help because it wasn't supposed to be there.

No one knew what any of the aliens looked like—whether they looked more or less like people, or were unimaginable monsters, or clouds of gas, or swift cool thoughts schooling inside some vast computer. They had shown themselves only as avatars, plastic man-shaped shells with the pleasant, bland but somehow creepy faces of old-fashioned shop dummies, and after the treaty had been negotiated only a few of those were left on Earth, at the UN headquarters in Geneva. Suppose, Lucas thought, the scientists broke in and pulled its passenger out. He imagined some kind of squid, saucer eyes and a clacking beak in a knot of thrashing tentacles, helpless in Earth's gravity. Or suppose something came to rescue it? Not the UN, but an actual alien ship. His heart beat fast and strong at the thought.

Walking a wide circle around the blunt, eyeless prow of the dragon, he found Damian on the other side, talking to a slender, dark-haired girl dressed in a shorts and a heavy sweater. She turned to look at Lucas as he walked up, and said to Damian, "Is this your friend?"

"Lisbeth was just telling me about the helicopter that crashed," Damian said. "Its engine cut out when it got too close and it dropped straight into the sea. Her father helped to rescue the pilot."

"She broke her hip," the girl, Lisbet, said. "She's at our house now. I'm supposed to be looking after her, but Doctor Naja gave her something that put her to sleep."

"Lisbet's father is the mayor," Damian said. "He's in charge of all this."

"He thinks he is," the girl said, "but no one is really. Police and everyone arguing amongst themselves. Do you have a phone, Lucas? Mine doesn't work. This is the best thing to ever happen here and I can't even tell my friends about it."

"I could row you out to where your phone started working," Damian said.

"I don't think so," Lisbeth said with a coy little smile, twisting the toes of her bare right foot in the wet sand.

Lucas had thought that she was around his and Damian's age; now he realised that she was at least two years younger.

"It'll be absolutely safe," Damian said. "Word of honour."

Lisbeth shook her head. "I want to stick around here and see what happens next."

"That's a good idea too," Damian said. "We can sit up by the fire and keep warm. I can tell you all about our adventures. How we found our way through the mist. How we were nearly run down—"

"I have to go and find my friends," Lisbeth said, and flashed a dazzling smile at Lucas and said that it was nice to meet him and turned away. Damian caught at her arm and Lucas stepped in and told him to let her go, and Lisbeth smiled at Lucas again and walked off, bare feet leaving dainty prints in the wet sand.

"Thanks for that," Damian said.

"She's a kid. And she's also the mayor's daughter."

"So? We were just talking."

"So he could have you locked up if he wanted to. Me too."

"You don't have to worry about that, do you? Because you scared her off," Damian said.

"She walked away because she wanted to," Lucas said.

He would have said more, would have asked Damian why they were arguing, but at that moment the dragon emitted its mournful wail. A great honking blare, more or less B-flat, so loud it was like a physical force, shocking every square centimetre of Lucas's body. He clapped his hands over his ears, but the sound was right inside the box of his skull, shivering deep in his chest and his bones. Damian had pressed his hands over his ears too, and all along the dragon's length people stepped back or ducked away. Then the noise abruptly cut off, and everyone stepped forward again. The women flailed even harder, their chant sounding muffled to Lucas; the dragon's call had been so loud it had left a buzz in his ears, and he had to lean close to hear Damian say, "Isn't this something?"

"It's definitely a dragon," Lucas said, his voice sounding flat and mostly inside his head. "Are we done arguing?"

"I didn't realise we were," Damian said. "Did you see those guys trying to cut it open?"

"Around the other side? I was surprised the police are letting them to do whatever it is they're doing."

"Lisbeth said they're scientists from the marine labs at Swatham. They work for the government, just like the police. She said they think this is a plastic eater. It sucks up plastic and digests it, turns it into carbon dioxide and water."

"That's what the UN wants people to think it does, anyhow."

"Sometimes you sound just like your mother."

"There you go again."

Damian put his hand on Lucas's shoulder. "I'm just ragging on you. Come on, why don't we go over by the fire and get warm?"

"If you want to talk to that girl again, just say so."

"Now who's spoiling for an argument? I thought we could get warm, find something to eat. People are selling stuff."

"I want to take a good close look at the dragon. That's why we came here, isn't it?"

"You do that, and I'll be right back."

"You get into trouble, you can find your own way home," Lucas said, but Damian was already walking away, fading into the mist without once looking back.

Lucas watched him fade into the mist, expecting him to turn around. He didn't.

Irritated by the silly spat, Lucas drifted back around the dragon's prow, watched the scientists attack with a jackhammer the joint between two large scales. They were putting everything they had into it, but didn't seem to be getting anywhere. A gang of farmers from a collective arrived on two tractors that left neat tracks on the wet sand and put out the smell of frying oil, which reminded Lucas that he hadn't eaten since breakfast. He was damned cold too. He trudged up the sand and bought a cup of fish soup from a woman who poured it straight from the iron pot she hooked out of the edge of the big bonfire, handing him a crust of bread to go with it. Lucas sipped the scalding stuff and felt his blood warm, soaked up the last of the soup with the crust and dredged the plastic cup in the sand to clean it and handed it back to the woman. Plenty of people were standing around the fire, but there was no sign of Damian. Maybe he was chasing that girl. Maybe he'd been arrested. Most likely, he'd turn up with that stupid smile of his, shrugging off their argument, claiming he'd only been joking. The way he did.

The skirts of the fret drifted apart and revealed the dim shapes of Martham's buildings at the far end of the sandbar; then the fret closed up and the little town vanished. The dragon sounded its distress or alarm call again. In the ringing silence afterwards a man said to no one in particular, with the satisfaction of someone who has discovered the solution to one of the universe's perennial mysteries, "Twenty-eight minutes on the dot."

At last, there was the sound of an engine and a shadowy shape gained definition in the fret that hung offshore: a boxy, old-fashioned landing craft that drove past the police boat and beached in the shallows close to the dragon. Its bow door splashed down and soldiers trotted out and the police and several civilians and scientists went down the beach to meet them. After a brief discussion, one of the soldiers stepped forward and raised a bullhorn to his mouth and announced that for the sake of public safety a two-hundred-metre exclusion zone was going to be established.

Several soldiers began to unload plastic crates. The rest chivvied the people around the dragon, ordering them to move back, driving them up the beach past the bonfire. Lucas spotted the old man, Bill Danvers, arguing with two soldiers. One suddenly grabbed the old man's arm and spun him around and twisted something around his wrists; the other looked at Lucas as he came towards them, telling him to stay back or he'd be arrested too.

"He's my uncle," Lucas said. "If you let him go I'll make sure he doesn't cause any more trouble."

"Your uncle?" The soldier wasn't much older than Lucas, with cropped ginger hair and a ruddy complexion.

"Yes, sir. He doesn't mean any harm. He's just upset because no one cares that he was the first to find it."

"Like I said," the old man said.

The two soldiers looked at each other, and the ginger-haired one told Lucas, "You're responsible for him. If he starts up again, you'll both be sorry."

"I'll look after him."

The soldier stared at Lucas for a moment, then flourished a small-bladed knife and cut the plasticuffs that bound the old man's wrists and shoved him towards Lucas. "Stay out of our way, grandpa. All right?"

"Sons of bitches," Bill Danvers said as the soldiers had walked off. He raised his voice and called out, "I found it first. Someone owes me for that."

"I think everyone knows you saw it come ashore," Lucas said. "But they're in charge now."

"They're going to blow it open," a man said.

He held a satchel in one hand and a folded chair in the other; when he shook the chair open and sat down Lucas recognised him: the man who'd been sitting at the head of the dragon, sketching it.

"They can't," Bill Danvers said.

"They're going to try," the man said.

Lucas looked back at the dragon. Its steamlined shape dim in the streaming fret, the activity around its head (if that was its head) a vague shifting of shadows. Soldiers and scientists conferring in a tight knot. Then the police boat and the landing craft started their motors and reversed through the wash of the incoming tide, fading into the fret, and the scientists followed the soldiers up the beach, walking past the bonfire, and there was a stir and rustle amongst the people strung out along the ridge.

"No damn right," Bill Danvers said.

The soldier with the bullhorn announced that there would be a small controlled explosion. A moment later, the dragon blared out its loud, long call and in the shocking silence afterwards laughter broke out amongst the crowd on the ridge. The soldier with the bullhorn began to count backwards from ten. Some of the crowd took up the chant. There was a brief silence at zero, and then a red light flared at the base of the dragon's midpoint and a flat crack rolled out across the ridge and was swallowed by the mist. People whistled and clapped, and Bill Danvers stepped around Lucas and ran down the slope towards the dragon. Falling to his knees and getting up and running on as soldiers chased after him, closing in from either side.

People cheered and hooted, and some ran after Bill Danvers, young men mostly, leaping down the slope and swarming across the beach. Lucas saw Damian amongst the runners and chased after him, heart pounding, flooded with a heedless exhilaration. Soldiers blocked random individuals, catching hold of them or knocking them down as others dodged past. Lucas heard the clatter of the bullhorn but couldn't make out any words, and then there was a terrific flare of white light and a hot wind struck him so hard he lost his balance and fell to his knees.

The dragon had split in half and things were glowing with hot light inside and the waves breaking around its rear hissed and exploded into steam. A terrific heat scorched Lucas's face. He pushed to his feet. All around, people were picking themselves up and soldiers were moving amongst them, shoving them away from the dragon. Some complied; others stood, squinting into the light that beat out of the broken dragon, blindingly bright waves and wings of white light flapping across the beach, burning away the mist.

Blinking back tears and blocky afterimages, Lucas saw two soldiers dragging Bill Danvers away from the dragon. The old man hung limp and helpless in their grasp, splayed feet furrowing the sand. His head was bloody, something sticking out of it at an angle.

Lucas started towards them, and there was another flare that left him stunned and half-blind. Things fell all around and a translucent shard suddenly jutted up by his foot. The two soldiers had dropped Bill Danvers. Lucas stepped towards him, picking his way through a field of debris, and saw that he was beyond help. His head had been knocked out of shape by the shard that stuck in his temple, and blood was soaking into the sand around it.

The dragon had completely broken apart now. Incandescent stuff dripped and hissed into steaming water and the burning light was growing brighter.

Like almost everyone else, Lucas turned and ran. Heat clawed at his back as he slogged to the top of the ridge. He saw Damian sitting on the sand, right hand clamped on the upper part of his left arm, and he jogged over and helped his friend up. Leaning against each other, they stumbled across the ridge. Small fires crackled here and there, where hot debris had kindled clumps of marram grass. Everything was drenched in a pulsing diamond brilliance. They went down the slope of the far side, angling towards the little blue boat, splashing into the water that had risen around it. Damian clambered unhandily over thwart and Lucas hauled up the concrete-filled bucket and boosted it over the side, then put his shoulder to the boat's prow and shoved it the low breakers and tumbled in.

The boat drifted sideways on the rising tide as Lucas hauled up the sail. Dragon-light beat beyond the crest of the sandbar, brighter than the sun. Lucas heeled his little boat into the wind, ploughing through stands of sea grass into the channel beyond, chasing after the small fleet fleeing the scene. Damian sat in the bottom of the boat, hunched into himself, his back against the stem of the mast. Lucas asked him if he was okay; he opened his fingers to show a translucent spike embedded in the meat of his biceps. It was about the size of his little finger.

"Dumb bad luck," he said, his voice tight and wincing.

"I'll fix you up," Lucas said, but Damian shook his head.

"Just keep going. I think—"

Everything went white for a moment. Lucas ducked down and wrapped his arms around his head and for a moment saw shadowy bones through red curtains of flesh. When he dared look around, he saw a narrow column of pure white light rising straight up, seeming to lean over as it climbed into the sky, aimed at the very apex of heaven.

A hot wind struck the boat and filled the sail, and Lucas sat up and grabbed the tiller and the sheet as the boat crabbed sideways. By the time he had it under control again the column of light had dimmed, fading inside drifting curtains of fret, rooted in a pale fire flickering beyond the sandbar.

Damian's father, Jason Playne, paid Lucas and his mother a visit the next morning. A burly man in his late forties with a shaven head and a blunt and forthright manner, dressed in workboots and denim overalls, he made the caravan seem small and frail. Standing over Julia's bed, telling her that he would like to ask Lucas about the scrape he and his Damian had gotten into.

"Ask away," Julia said. She was propped amongst her pillows, her gaze bright and amused. Her tablet lay beside her, images and blocks of text glimmering above it.

Jason Playne looked at her from beneath the thick hedge of his eyebrows. A strong odour of saltwater and sweated booze clung to him. He said, "I was hoping for a private word."

"My son and I have no secrets."

"This is about *my* son," Jason Playne said.

"They didn't do anything wrong, if that's what you're worried about," Julia said.

Lucas felt a knot of embarrassment and anger in his chest. He said, "I'm right here."

"Well, you didn't," his mother said.

Jason Playne looked at Lucas. "How did Damian get hurt?"

"He fell and cut himself," Lucas said, as steadily as he could. That was what he and Damian had agreed to say, as they'd sailed back home with their prize. Lucas had pulled the shard of dragon stuff from Damian's arm and staunched the bleeding with a bandage made from a strip ripped from the hem of Damian's shirt. There hadn't been much blood; the hot sliver had more or less cauterised the wound.

Jason Playne said, "He fell."

"Yes sir."

"Are you sure? Because I reckon that cut in my son's arm was done by a knife. I reckon he got himself in some kind of fight."

Julia said, "That sounds more like an accusation than a question."

Lucas said, "We didn't get into a fight with anyone."

Jason Playne said, "Are you certain that Damian didn't steal something?"

"Yes sir."

Which was the truth, as far as it went.

"Because if he did steal something, if he still has it, he's in a lot of trouble. You too."

"I like to think my son knows a little more about alien stuff than most," Julia said.

"I'm don't mean fairy stories," Jason Playne said. "I'm talking about the army ordering people to give back anything to do with that dragon thing. You stole something and you don't give it back and they find out? They'll arrest you. And if you try to sell it? Well, I can tell you for a fact that the people in that trade are mad and bad. I should know. I've met one or two of them in my time."

"I'm sure Lucas will take that to heart," Julia said.

And that was that, except after Jason Playne had gone she told Lucas that he'd been right about one thing: the people who tried to reverse-engineer alien technology were dangerous and should at all costs be avoided. "If I happened to come into possession of anything like that," she said, "I would get rid of it at once. Before anyone found out."

But Lucas couldn't get rid of the shard because he'd promised Damian that he'd keep it safe until they could figure out what to do with it. He spent the next two days in a haze of guilt and indecision, struggling with the temptation to check that the thing was safe in its hiding place, wondering what Damian's father knew, wondering what his mother knew, wondering if he should sail out to a deep part of the Flood and throw it into the water, until at last Damian came over to the island.

It was early in the evening, just after sunset. Lucas was watering the vegetable garden when Damian called to him from the shadows inside a clump of buddleia bushes. He smiled at Lucas, saying, "If you think I look bad, you should see him."

"I can't think he could look much worse."

"I got in a few licks," Damian said. His upper lip was split and both his eyes were blackened and there was a discoloured knot on the hinge of his jaw.

"He came here," Lucas said. "Gave me and Julia a hard time."

"How much does she know?"

"I told her what happened."

"Everything?"

There was an edge in Damian's voice.

"Except about how you were hit with the shard," Lucas said.

"Oh. Your mother's cool, you know? I wish . . ."

When it was clear that his friend wasn't going to finish his thought, Lucas said, "Is it okay? You coming here so soon."

"Oh, Dad's over at Halvergate on what he calls business. Don't worry about him. Did you keep it safe?"

"I said I would."

"Why I'm here, L, I think I might have a line on someone who wants to buy our little treasure."

"Used to be, long ago, wars were fought on a battlefield chosen by both sides. Two armies meeting by appointment. Squaring up to each other. Slogging it out. Then wars became so big the countries fighting them became one huge battlefield. Civilians found themselves on the front line. Or rather, there was no front line. Total war, they called it. And then you got wars that weren't wars. Asymmetrical wars. Netwars. Where war gets mixed up with crime and terrorism. Your mother was on the edge of a netwar at one time. Against the Jackaroo and those others. Still thinks she's fighting it, although it long ago evolved into something else. There aren't any armies or battlefields in a netwar. Just a series of nodes in distributed organisation. Collateral damage," Ritchy said, forking omelet into his mouth, "is the inevitable consequence of taking out one of those nodes, because all of them are embedded inside ordinary society. It could be a flat in an apartment block in a city. Or a little island where someone thinks something useful is hidden."

"I don't—"

"You don't know anything," Ritchy said. "I believe you. Damian ran off with whatever it was you two found or stole, and left you in the lurch. But the people Damian got himself involved with don't know you don't know. That's why we've been looking out for you. Making sure you and your mother don't become collateral damage."

"Wait. What people? What did Damian do?"

"I'm trying to tell you, only it's harder than I thought it would be." Ritchy set his knife and fork together on his plate and said, "Maybe telling it straight is the best way. The day after Damian left, he tried to do some business with some people in Norwich. Bad people. The lad wanted to sell them a fragment of that dragon that stranded itself, but they decided to take it from him without paying. There was a scuffle and the lad got away and left a man with a bad knife wound. He died from it, a few weeks later. Those are the kind of people who look after their own, if you know what I mean. Anyone involved in that trade is bad news in one way or another. Jason had to pay them off, or else they would have come after him. An eye for an eye," Ritchy said, and tapped his blank eye with his little finger.

"What happened to Damian?"

"This is the hard part. After his trouble in Norwich, the lad called his father. He was drunk, ranting. Boasting how he was going to make all kinds of money. I managed to put a demon on his message, ran it back to a cell in Gravesend. Jason went up there, and that's when . . . Well, there's no other way of saying it. That's when he found out that Damian had been killed."

The shock was a jolt and a falling away. And then Lucas was back inside himself, hunched in his damp jeans and sweater in the clatter and bustle of the café, with the fridge humming next to him. Ritchy tore off the tops of four straws of sugar and poured them into Lucas's tea and stirred it and folded Lucas's hand around the mug and told him to drink.

Lucas sipped hot sweet tea and felt a little better.

"Always thought," Ritchy said, "that of the two of you, you were the best and brightest."

Lucas saw his friend in his mind's eye and felt cold and strange, knowing he'd never see him, never talk to him again.

Ritchy was said, "The police got in touch yesterday. They found Damian's body in the river. They think he fell into the hands of one of the gangs that trade in off-world stuff."

Lucas suddenly understood something and said, "They wanted what was growing inside him. The people who killed him."

He told Ritchy about the shard that had hit Damian in the arm. How they'd pulled it out. How it had infected Damian.

"He had a kind of patch around the cut, under his skin. He said it was making him stronger."

Lucas saw his friend again, wild-eyed in the dusk, under the apple tree.

"That's what he thought. But that kind of thing, well, if he hadn't been murdered he would most likely have died from it."

"Do you know who did it?"

Ritchy shook his head. "The police are making what they like to call enquiries. They'll probably want to talk to you soon enough."

"Thank you. For telling me."

"I remember the world before the Jackaroo came," Ritchy said. "Them, and the others after them. It was in a bad way, but at least you knew where you were. If you happen to have any more of that stuff, lad, throw it in the Flood. And don't mark the spot."

Two detectives came Gravesend to interview Lucas. He told them everything he knew. Julia said that he shouldn't blame himself, said that Damian had made a choice and it had been a bad choice. But Lucas carried the guilt around with him anyway. He should have done more to help Damian. He should have thrown the shard away. Or found him after they'd had the stupid argument over that girl. Or refused to take him out to see the damn dragon in the first place.

A week passed. Two. There was no funeral because the police would not release Damian's body. According to them, it was still undergoing forensic tests. Julia, who was tracking rumours about the murder and its investigation on the stealth nets, said it had probably been taken to some clandestine research lab, and she and Lucas had a falling out over it.

One day, returning home after checking the snares he'd set in the woods, Lucas climbed to the top of the levee and saw two men waiting beside his boat. Both were dressed in brand-new camo gear, one with a beard, the other with a shaven head and rings flashing in one ear. They started up the slope towards him, calling his name, and he turned tail and ran, cutting across a stretch of sour land gone to weeds and pioneer saplings, plunging into the stands of bracken at the edge of the woods, pausing, seeing the two men chasing towards him, turning and running on.

He knew every part of the woods, and quickly found a hiding place under the slanted trunk of a fallen sycamore grown over with moss and ferns, breathing quick and hard in the cold air. Rain pattered all around. Droplets of water spangled bare black twigs. The deep odour of wet wood and wet earth.

A magpie chattered, close by. Lucas set a ball-bearing in the cup of his catapult and cut towards the sound, moving easily and quietly, freezing when he saw a twitch of movement between the wet tree trunks ahead. It was the bearded man, the camo circuit of his gear magicking him into a fairy-tale creature got up from wet bark and mud. He was talking into a phone headset in a language full of harsh vowels. Turning as Lucas stepped towards him, his smile white inside his beard, saying that there was no need to run away, he only wanted to talk.

"What is that you have, kid?"

"A catapult. I'll use it if I have too."

"What do you use it for? Hunting rabbits? I'm no rabbit."

"Who are you?"

"Police. I have ID," the man said, and before Lucas could say anything his hand went into the pocket of his camo trousers and came out with a pistol.

Lucas had made his catapult himself, from a yoke of springy poplar and a length of vatgrown rubber with the composition and tensile strength of the hinge inside a mussel shell. As the man brought up the pistol Lucas pulled back the band of rubber and let the ball bearing fly. He did it quickly and without thought, firing from the hip, and the ball bearing went exactly where he meant it to go. It smacked into the knuckles of the man's hand with a hard pop and the man yelped and dropped the pistol, and then he sat down hard and clapped his good hand to his knee, because Lucas's second shot had struck the soft part under the cap.

Lucas stepped up and kicked the pistol away and stepped back, a third ball bearing cupped in the catapult. The man glared at him, wincing with pain, and said something in his harsh language.

"Who sent you?" Lucas said.

His heart was racing, but his thoughts were cool and clear.

"Tell me where it is," the man said, "and we leave you alone. Your mother too."

"My mother doesn't have anything to do with this."

Lucas was watching the man and listening to someone moving through the wet wood, coming closer.

"She is in it, nevertheless," the man said. He tried to push to his feet but his wounded knee gave way and he cried out and sat down again. He'd bitten his lip bloody and sweat beaded his forehead.

"Stay still, or the next one hits you between the eyes," Lucas said. He heard a quaver in his voice and knew from the way the man looked at him that he'd heard it too.

"Go now, and fetch the stuff. And don't tell me you don't know what I mean. Fetch it and bring it here. That's the only offer you get," the man said. "And the only time I make it."

A twig snapped softly and Lucas turned, ready to let the ball-bearing fly, but it was Damian's father who stepped around a dark green holly bush, saying, "You can leave this one to me."

At once Lucas understood what had happened. Within his cool clear envelope he could see everything: how it all connected.

"You set me up," he said.

"I needed to draw them out," Jason Playne said. He was dressed in jeans and an old-fashioned woodland camo jacket, and he was cradling a cut-down double-barrelled shotgun.

"You let them know where I was. You told them I had more of the dragon stuff."

The man sitting on the ground was looking at them. "This does not end here," he said. "I have you, and I have your friend. And you're going to pay for what you did to my son," Jason Playne said, and put a whistle to his lips and blew, two short notes. Off in the dark rainy woods another whistle answered.

The man said, "Idiot small-time businessman. You don't know us. What we can do. Hurt me and we hurt you back tenfold."

Jason Playne ignored him, and told Lucas that he could go.

"Why did you let them chase me? You could have caught them while they were waiting by my boat. Did you want them to hurt me?"

"I knew you'd lead them a good old chase. And you did. So, all's well that ends well, eh?" Jason Playne said. "Think of it as payback. For what happened to my son."

Lucas felt a bubble of anger swelling in his chest. "You can't forgive me for what I didn't do."

"It's what you didn't do that caused all the trouble."

"It wasn't me. It was you. It was you who made him run away. It wasn't just the beatings. It was the thought that if he stayed here he'd become just like you."

Jason Playne turned towards Lucas, his face congested. "Go. Right now."

The bearded man drew a knife from his boot and flicked it open and pushed up with his good leg, throwing himself towards Jason Playne, and Lucas stretched the band of his catapult and let fly. The ball bearing struck the bearded man in the temple with a hollow sound and the man fell flat on his face. His temple was dinted and blood came out of his nose and mouth and he thrashed and trembled and subsided.

Rain pattered down all around, like faint applause.

Then Jason Playne stepped towards the man and kicked him in the chin with the point of his boot. The man rolled over on the wet leaves, arms flopping wide.

"I reckon you killed him," Jason Playne said.

"I didn't mean—"

"Lucky for you there are two of them. The other will tell me what I need to know. You go now, boy. Go!"

Lucas turned and ran.

He didn't tell his mother about it. He hoped that Jason Playne would find out who had killed Damian and tell the police and the killers would answer for what they had done, and that would be an end to it.

That wasn't what happened.

The next day, a motor launch came over to the island, carrying police armed with machine guns and the detectives investigating Damian's death, who arrested Lucas for involvement in two suspicious deaths and conspiracy to kidnap or murder other persons unknown. It seemed that one of the men that Jason Playne had hired to help him get justice for the death of his son had been a police informant.

Lucas was held in remand in Norwich for three months. Julia was too ill to visit him, but they talked on the phone and she sent messages via Ritchy, who'd been arrested along with every other worker on the shrimp farm, but released on bail after the police were unable to prove that he had anything to do with Jason Playne's scheme.

It was Ritchy who told Lucas that his mother had cancer that had started in her throat and spread elsewhere, and that she had refused treatment. Lucas was taken to see her two weeks later, handcuffed to a prison warden. She was lying in a hospital bed, looking shrunken and horribly vulnerable. Her dreadlocks bundled in a blue scarf. Her hand so cold when he took it in his. The skin loose on frail bones.

She had refused monoclonal antibody treatment that would shrink the tumours and remove cancer cells from her bloodstream, and had also refused food and water. The doctors couldn't intervene because a clause in her living will gave her the right to choose death instead of treatment. She told Lucas this in a hoarse whisper. Her lips were cracked and her breath foul, but her gaze was strong and insistent.

"Do the right thing even when it's the hardest thing," she said.

She died four days later. Her ashes were scattered in the rose garden of the municipal crematorium. Lucas stood in the rain between two wardens as the curate recited the prayer for the dead. The curate asked him if he wanted to scatter the ashes and he threw them out across the wet grass and dripping rose bushes with a flick of his wrist. Like casting a line across the water.

He was sentenced to five years for manslaughter, reduced to eighteen months for time served on remand and for good behaviour. He was released early in September. He'd been given a ticket for the bus to Norwich, and a voucher for a week's stay in a halfway house, but he set off in the opposite direction, on foot. Walking south and east across country. Following back roads. Skirting the edges of sugar beet fields and bamboo plantations. Ducking into ditches or hedgerows whenever he heard a vehicle approaching. Navigating by the moon and the stars.

Once, a fox loped across his path.

Once, he passed a depot lit up in the night, robots shunting between a loading dock and a road-train.

By dawn he was making his way through the woods along the edge of the levee. He kept taking steps that weren't there. Several times he sat on his haunches and rested for a minute before pushing up and going on. At last, he struck the gravel track that led to the shrimp farm, and twenty minutes later was knocking on the door of the office.

Ritchy gave Lucas breakfast and helped him pull his boat out of the shed where it had been stored, and set it in the water. Lucas and the old man had stayed in touch: it had been Ritchy who'd told him that Jason Playne had been stabbed to death in prison, most likely by someone paid by the people he'd tried to chase down. Jason Playne's brother had sold the shrimp farm to a local consortium, and Ritchy had been promoted to supervisor.

He told Lucas over breakfast that he had a job there, if he wanted it. Lucas said that he was grateful, he really was, but he didn't know if he wanted to stay on.

"I'm not asking you to make a decision right away," Ritchy said. "Think about it. Get your bearings, come to me whenever you're ready. Okay?"

"Okay."

"Are you going to stay over on the island?"

"Just how bad is it?"

"I couldn't keep all of them off. They'd come at night. One party had a shotgun."

"You did what you could. I appreciate it."

"I wish I could have done more. They made a mess, but it isn't anything you can't fix up, if you want to."

A heron flapped away across the sun-silvered water as Lucas rowed around the point of the island. The unexpected motion plucked at an old memory. As if he'd seen a ghost.

He grounded his boat next to the rotting carcass of his mother's old rowboat and walked up the steep path. Ritchy had patched the broken windows of the caravan and put a padlock on the door. Lucas had the key in his pocket, but he didn't want to go in there, not yet.

After Julia had been taken into hospital, treasure hunters had come from all around, chasing rumours that parts of the dragon had been buried on the island. Holes were dug everywhere in the weedy remains of the vegetable garden; the microwave mast at the summit of the ridge, Julia's link with the rest of the world, had been uprooted. Lucas set his back to it and walked north, counting his steps. Both of the decoy caches his mother had planted under brick cairns had been ransacked, but the emergency cache, buried much deeper, was undisturbed.

Lucas dug down to the plastic box, and looked all around before he opened it and sorted through the things inside, squatting frogwise with the hot sun on his back.

An assortment of passports and identity cards, each with a photograph of younger versions of his mother, made out to different names and nationalities. A slim tight roll of old high-denomination banknotes, yuan, naira, and U.S. dollars, more or less worthless thanks to inflation and revaluation. Blank credit cards and credit cards in various names, also worthless. Dozens of sleeved data needles. A pair of AR glasses.

Lucas studied one of the ID cards. When he brushed the picture of his mother with his thumb, she turned to present her profile, turned to look at him when he brushed the picture again.

He pocketed the ID card and the data needles and AR glasses, then walked along the ridge to the apple tree at the far end, and stared out across the Flood that spread glistening like shot silk under the sun. Thoughts moved through his mind like a slow and stately parade of pictures that he could examine in every detail, and then there were no thoughts at all and for a little while no part of him was separate from the world all around, sun and water and the hot breeze that moved through the crooked branches of the tree.

Lucas came to himself with a shiver. Windfall apples lay everywhere amongst the weeds and nettles that grew around the trees, and dead wasps and hornets were scattered amongst them like yellow and black bullets. Here was a dead bird too, gone to a tatter of feathers of white bone. And here was another, and another. As if some passing cloud of poison had struck everything down.

He picked an apple from the tree, mashed it against the trunk, and saw pale threads fine as hair running through the mash of pulp. He peeled bark from a branch, saw threads laced in the living wood.

Dragon stuff, growing from the seed he'd planted. Becoming something else.

In the wood of the tree and the apples scattered all around was a treasure men would kill for. Had killed for. He'd have more than enough to set him up for life, if he sold it to the right people. He could build a house right here, buy the shrimp farm or set up one of his own. He could buy a ticket on one of the shuttles that travelled through the wormhole anchored between the Earth and the Moon, travel to infinity and beyond . . .

Lucas remembered the hopeful shine in Damian's eyes when he'd talked about those new worlds. He thought of how the dragon-shard had killed or damaged everyone it had touched. He pictured his mother working at her tablet in her sickbed, advising and challenging people who were attempting to build something new right here on Earth. It wasn't much of a contest. It wasn't even close.

He walked back to the caravan. Took a breath, unlocked the padlock, stepped inside. Everything had been overturned or smashed. Cupboards gaped open, the mattress of his mother's bed was slashed and torn, a great ruin littered the floor. He rooted amongst the wreckage, found a box of matches and a plastic jug of lamp oil. He splashed half of the oil on the torn mattress, lit a twist of cardboard and lobbed it onto the bed, beat a retreat as flames sprang up.

It didn't take ten minutes to gather up dead wood and dry weeds and pile them around the apple tree, splash the rest of the oil over its trunk, and set fire to the tinder. A thin pall of white smoke spread across the island, blowing out across the water as he raised the sail of his boat and turned it into the wind.

Heading south.

A soldier of the city

DAVID MOLES

The vivid story that follows plunges us deep into a war between spacefaring civilizations from a future where humans serve literal gods whom they love and worship—and who sometimes prove not to be worthy of either.

David Moles has sold fiction to Asimov's Science Fiction, The Magazine of Fantasy & Science Fiction, Engineering Infinity, Polyphony, Strange Horizons. Lady Churchill's Rosebud Wristlet, Say?, Flytrap, *and elsewhere. He coedited with Jay Lake 2004's well-received "retro-pulp" anthology* All-Star Zeppelin Adventure Stories, *as well as coedited with Susan Marie Groppi the original anthology* Twenty Epics. *He won the Theodore Sturgeon Award for best short fiction of the year with his story "Finisterra."*

ISIN 12:709 13" N:10 18" / 34821.1.9 10:24:5:19.21
Color still image, recorded by landscape maintenance camera, Gulanabishtüdinam Park West.

At the top of the hill is a football court, the net nearly new but the bricks of the ground uneven, clumps of grass growing up from between the cracks. On the same side of the net are a man and a young girl. The hollow rattan ball is above the girl's head, nearing the apex of its trajectory; the girl, balanced on the toes of her bare right foot, her left knee raised, is looking toward the man.

The man is looking away.

Cross-reference with temple records identifies the man as Ishmenininsina Ninnadiïnshumi, age twenty-eight, temple soldier of the 219th Surface Tactical Company, an under-officer of the third degree, and the girl as his daughter Mâratirşitim, age nine.

Magnification of the reflection from the man's left cornea indicates his focus to be the sixty-cubit-high image of Gula, the Lady of Isin, projected over the Kârumishbiïrra Canal.

Comparison of the reflection with the record of the Corn Parade ceremonies suggests a transmission delay of approximately three grains.

I
CORN PARADE

In the moment of the blast, Ish was looking down the slope, toward the canal, the live feed from the temple steps and the climax of the parade. As he watched, the goddess suddenly froze; her ageless face lost its benevolent smile, and her dark eyes widened in surprise and perhaps in fear, as they looked—Ish later would always remember—directly at him. Her lips parted as if she was about to tell Ish something.

And then the whole eastern rise went brighter than the Lady's House at noonday. There was a sound, a rolling, bone-deep rumble like thunder, and afterwards Ish would think there was something wrong with this, that something so momentous should sound so prosaic, but at the time all he could think was how loud it was, how it went on and on, louder than thunder, than artillery, than rockets, louder and longer than anything Ish had ever heard. The ground shook. The projection faded, flickered and went out, and a hot wind whipped over the hilltop, tearing the net from its posts, knocking Mâra to the ground and sending her football flying, lost forever, out over the rooftops to the west.

From the temple district, ten leagues away, a bright point was rising, arcing up toward the dazzling eye of the Lady's House, and some trained part of Ish's mind saw the straight line, the curvature an artifact of the city's rotating reference frame; but as Mâra started to cry, and Ish's wife Tara and all his in-laws boiled up from around the grill and the picnic couches, yelling, and a pillar of brown smoke, red-lit from below, its top swelling obscenely, began to grow over the temple, the temple of the goddess Ish was sworn as a soldier of the city to protect, Ish was not thinking of geometry or the physics of coriolis force. What Ish was thinking—what Ish knew, with a sick certainty—was that the most important moment of his life had just come and gone, and he had missed it.

34821.1.14 10:9:2:5.67

Annotated image of the city of Isin, composed by COS Independence, on Gaugamela station, Babylon, transmitted via QT to Community Outreach archives, Urizen. Timestamp adjusted for lightspeed delay of thirteen hours, fifty-one minutes.

Five days after the strike the point of impact has died from angry red-orange to sullen infrared, a hot spot that looks like it will be a long time in cooling. A streamer of debris trails behind the wounded city like blood in water, its spectrum a tale of vaporized ice and iron. Isin's planet-sized city-sphere itself appears structurally intact, the nitrogen and oxygen that would follow a loss of primary atmosphere absent from the recorded data.

Away from the impact, the myriad microwave receivers that cover the city's surface like scales still ripple, turning to follow the beams of power from Ninagal's superconducting ring, energy drawn from the great black hole called Tiamat, fat with the mass of three thousand suns, around which all the cities of Babylon revolve. The space around Isin is alive with ships: local orbiters, electromagnetically accelerated corn cans in slow transfer orbits carrying grain and meat from Isin to more urbanized cities, beam-riding passenger carriers moving between Isin and Lagash, Isin and Nippur, Isin and Babylon-Borsippa and the rest—but there is no mass exodus, no evacuation.

The Outreach planners at Urizen and Ahania, the missionaries aboard *Liberation* and *Independence* and those living in secret among the people of the cities, breathe sighs of relief, and reassure themselves that whatever they have done to the people of the cities of Babylon, they have at least not committed genocide.

Aboard COS *Insurrection*, outbound from Babylon, headed for the Community planet of Zoa at four-tenths the speed of light and still accelerating, the conscientious objectors who chose not to stay and move forward with the next phase of the Babylonian intervention hear this good news and say, not without cynicism: I hope that's some comfort to them.

II
MEN GIVING ORDERS

Ish was leading a team along a nameless street in what had been a neighborhood called Imtagaärbeëlti and was now a nameless swamp, the entire district northwest of the temple complex knee-deep in brackish water flowing in over the fallen seawall and out of the broken aqueducts, so that Ish looked through gates into flooded gardens where children's toys and broken furniture floated as if put there just to mar and pucker the reflection of the heavens, or through windows whose shutters had been torn loose and glass shattered by the nomad blast into now-roofless rooms that were snapshots of ordinary lives in their moments of ending.

In the five days since the Corn Parade Ish had slept no more than ten or twelve hours. Most of the rest of the 219th had died at the temple, among the massed cohorts of Isin lining the parade route in their blue dress uniforms and golden vacuum armor—they hadn't had wives, or hadn't let the wives they did have talk them into extending their leaves to attend picnics with their in-laws, or hadn't been able to abuse their under-officers' warrants to extend their leaves when others couldn't. Most of the temple soldiery had died along with them, and for the first three days Ish had been just a volunteer with a shovel, fighting fires, filling sandwalls, clearing debris. On the fourth day the surviving priests and temple military apparatus had pulled themselves together into something resembling a command structure, and now Ish had this scratch squad, himself and three soldiers from different units, and this mission, mapping the flood zone, to what purpose Ish didn't know or much care. They'd been issued weapons but Ish had put a stop to that, confiscating the squad's ammunition and retaining just one clip for himself.

"Is that a body?" said one of the men suddenly. Ish couldn't remember his name. A clerk, from an engineering company, his shoulder patch a stylized basket. Ish looked to where he was pointing. In the shadows behind a broken window was a couch, and on it a bundle of sticks that might have been a man.

"Wait here," Ish said.

"We're not supposed to go inside," said one of the other men, a scout carrying a bulky map book and sketchpad, as Ish hoisted himself over the gate. "We're just supposed to mark the house for the civilians."

"Who says?" asked the clerk.

"Command," said the scout.

"There's no *command,*" said the fourth man suddenly. He was an artillerist, twice Ish's age, heavy and morose. These were the first words he'd spoken all day. "The Lady's dead. There's no command. There's no officers. There's just men giving orders."

The clerk and the scout looked at Ish, who said nothing.

He pulled himself over the gate.

The Lady's dead. The artillerist's words, or ones like them, had been rattling around Ish's head for days, circling, leaping out to catch him whenever he let his guard down. *Gula, the Lady of Isin, is dead.* Every time Ish allowed himself to remember that it was as if he was understanding it for the first time, the shock of it like a sudden and unbroken fall, the grief and shame of it a monumental weight toppling down on him. Each time Ish forced the knowledge back the push he gave it was a little weaker, the space he created for himself to breathe and think and feel in a little smaller. He was keeping himself too busy to sleep because every time he closed his eyes he saw the Lady's pleading face.

He climbed over the windowsill and into the house.

The body of a very old man was curled up there, dressed in nothing but a dirty white loincloth that matched the color of the man's hair and beard and the curls on his narrow chest. In the man's bony hands an icon of Lady Gula was clutched, a cheap relief with machine-printed colors that didn't quite line up with the ceramic curves, the Lady's robes more blue than purple and the heraldic dog at her feet more green than yellow; the sort of thing that might be sold in any back-alley liquor store. One corner had been broken off, so that the Lady's right shoulder and half her face were gone, and only one eye peered out from between the man's knuckles. When Ish moved to take the icon, the fingers clutched more tightly, and the old man's eyelids fluttered as a rasp of breath escaped his lips.

Ish released the icon. Its one-eyed stare now seemed accusatory.

"Okay," he said heavily. "Okay, Granddad."

BABYLON CITY 1:1 5" N:1 16" / 34821.1.14 7:15

LORD NINURTA VOWS JUSTICE FOR LADY OF ISIN
POLICE TO PROTECT LAW-ABIDING NOMADS
LAWLESSNESS IN SIPPAR

—headlines, temple newspaper Marduknaşir, *Babylon City*

BABYLON CITY 4:142 113" S:4 12" / 34821.1.15 1:3

POINTLESS REVENGE MISSION
LYNCHINGS IN BABYLON: IMMIGRANTS TARGETED
SIPPAR RISES UP

—headlines, radical newspaper Iïnshushaqiï, *Babylon City*

GISH, NIPPUR, SIPPAR (VARIOUS LOCATIONS) / 34821.1.15

THEY CAN DIE

—graffiti common in working-class and slave districts after the nomad attack on Isin

III
KINETIC PENETRATOR

When Tara came home she found Ish on a bench in the courtyard, bent over the broken icon, with a glue pot and an assortment of scroll clips and elastic bands from Tara's desk. They'd talked, when they first moved into this house not long after Mâra was born, of turning one of the ground-floor rooms into a workshop for Ish, but he was home so rarely and for such short periods that with one thing and another it had never happened. She kept gardening supplies there now.

The projector in the courtyard was showing some temple news feed, an elaborately animated diagram of the nomads' weapon—a "kinetic penetrator," the researcher called it, a phrase that Tara thought should describe something found in a sex shop or perhaps a lumberyard—striking the city's outer shell, piercing iron and ice and rock before erupting in a molten plume from the steps directly beneath the Lady's feet.

Tara turned it off.

Ish looked up. "You're back," he said.

"You stole my line," said Tara. She sat on the bench next to Ish and looked down at the icon in his lap. "What's that?"

"An old man gave it to me," Ish said. "There." He wrapped a final elastic band around the icon and set it down next to the glue pot. "That should hold it."

He'd found the broken corner of the icon on the floor not far from the old man's couch. On Ish's orders they'd abandoned the pointless mapping expedition and taken the man to an aid station, bullied the doctors until someone took responsibility.

There, in the aid tent, the man pressed the icon into Ish's hands, both pieces, releasing them with shaking fingers.

"Lady bless you," he croaked.

The artillerist, at Ish's elbow, gave a bitter chuckle, but didn't say anything. Ish was glad of that. The man might be right, there might be no command, there might be no soldiery, Ish might not be an under-officer any more, just a man giving orders. But Ish was, would continue to be, a soldier of the Lady, a soldier of the city of Isin, and if he had no lawful orders that only put the burden on him to order himself.

He was glad the artillerist hadn't spoken, because if the man had at that moment said again *the Lady's dead*, Ish was reasonably sure he would have shot him.

He'd unzipped the flap on the left breast pocket of his jumpsuit and tucked both pieces of the icon inside. Then he'd zipped the pocket closed again, and for the first time in five days, he'd gone home.

Tara said: "Now that you're back, I wish you'd talk to Mâra. She's been having nightmares. About the Corn Parade. She's afraid the nomads might blow up her school."

"They might," Ish said.

"You're not helping." Tara sat up straight. She took his chin in her hand and turned his head to face her. "When did you last sleep?"

Ish pulled away from her. "I took pills."

Tara sighed. "When did you last take a pill?"

"Yesterday," Ish said. "No. Day before."

"Come to bed," said Tara. She stood up. Ish didn't move. He glanced down at the icon.

An ugly expression passed briefly over Tara's face, but Ish didn't see it.

"Come to bed," she said again. She took Ish's arm, and this time he allowed himself to be led up the stairs.

At some point in the night they made love. It wasn't very good for either of them; it hadn't been for a long while, but this night was worse. Afterwards Tara slept.

She woke to find Ish already dressed. He was putting things into his soldiery duffel.

"Where are you going?" she asked.

"Lagash."

"What?"

Tara sat up. Ish didn't look at her.

"Lord Ninurta's fitting out an expedition," Ish said.

"An expedition," said Tara flatly.

"To find the nomads who killed the Lady."

"And do what?" asked Tara.

Ish didn't answer. From his dresser he picked up his identification seal, the cylinder with the Lady's heraldic dog and Ish's name and Temple registry number, and fastened it around his neck.

Tara turned away.

"I don't think I ever knew you," she said, "But I always knew I couldn't compete with a goddess. When I married you, I said to my friends: 'At least he won't be running around after other women.'" She laughed without humor. "And now she's dead—and you're still running after her."

She looked up. Ish was gone.

Outside it was hot and windless under a lowering sky. Nothing was moving. A fine gray dust was settling over the sector: *the Lady's ashes,* Ish had heard people call it. His jump boots left prints in it as he carried his duffel to the train station.

An express took Ish to the base of the nearest spoke, and from there his soldiery ID and a series of elevators carried him to the southern polar dock. As the equatorial blue and white of the city's habitable zone gave way to the polished black metal of the southern hemisphere, Ish looked down at the apparently untroubled clouds and seas ringing the city's equator and it struck him how normal this all was, how like any return to duty after leave.

It would have been easy and perhaps comforting to pretend it was just that, comforting to pretend that the Corn Parade had ended like every other, with the Lady's blessing on the crops, the return of the images to the shrines, drinking and dancing and music from the dimming of the Lady's House at dusk to its brightening at dawn.

Ish didn't want that sort of comfort.

34821.6.29 5:23:5:12.102

Abstract of report prepared by priest-astronomers of Ur under the direction of Shamash of Sippar, at the request of Ninurta of Lagash.

Isotopic analysis of recovered penetrator fragments indicates the nomad weapon to have been constructed within and presumably fired from the Apsu near debris belt. Astronomical records are surveyed for suspicious occlusions, both of nearby stars in the Babylon globular cluster and of more distant stars in the Old Galaxy, and cross-referenced against traffic records to eliminate registered nomad vessels. Fifteen anomalous occlusions, eleven associated with mapped point mass Sinkalamaïdi-541, are identified over a period of one hundred thirty-two years. An orbit for the Corn Parade criminals is proposed.

IV
DOG SOLDIER

There was a thump as Ish's platform was loaded onto the track. Then *Sharur*'s catapult engaged and two, three, five, eight, thirteen, twenty times the force of Isin's equatorial rotation pushed Ish into his thrust bag; and then Ish was flying free.

In his ear, the voice of the ship said:

—First company, dispersion complete.

On the control console, affixed there, sealed into a block of clear resin: Gula's icon. Ish wondered if this was what she wanted.

And Ninurta added, for Ish's ears alone:

—Good hunting, dog soldier.

At Lagash they'd wanted Ish to join the soldiery of Lagash; had offered him the chance to compete for a place with the Lion-Eagles, Ninurta's elites. Ish had refused, taking the compassion of these warlike men of a warlike city for contempt. Isin was sparsely populated for a city of Babylon, with barely fifty billion spread among its parks and fields and orchards, but its soldiery was small even for that. When the hard men in Ashur and the actuaries in Babylon-Borsippa counted up the cities' defenders, they might forget Lady Gula's soldiers, and be forgiven for forgetting. What Ninurta's men meant as generosity to a grieving worshipper of their lord's consort Ish took for mockery of a parade soldier from a rustic backwater. It needed the intervention of the god himself to make a compromise; this after Ish had lost his temper, broken the recruiter's tablet over his knee and knocked over his writing-table.

"You loved her—dog soldier."

Ish turned to see who had spoken, and saw a god in the flesh for the first time.

The Lord of Lagash was tall, five cubits at least, taller than any man, but the shape and set of his body in its coppery-red armor made it seem that it was the god who was to scale and everything around him—the recruiting office, the Lion-Eagles who had been ready to lay hands on Ish and who were now prostrate on the carpet, the wreckage of the recruiter's table, Ish himself—that was small. The same agelessness was in Ninurta's dark-eyed face that had been in Lady Gula's, but what in the Lady had seemed to Ish a childlike simplicity retained into adulthood was turned, in her consort, to a precocious maturity, a wisdom beyond the unlined face's years.

Ish snapped to attention. "Lord," he said. He saluted—as he would have saluted a superior officer. A murmur of outrage came from the Lion-Eagles on the floor.

The god ignored them. "You loved her," he said again, and he reached out and lifted Ish's seal-cylinder where it hung around his neck, turned it in his fingers to examine the dog figure, to read Ish's name and number.

"No, Lord Ninurta," Ish said.

The god looked from the seal to Ish's face.

"No?" he said, and there was something dangerous in his voice. His fist closed around the seal.

Ish held the god's gaze.

"I still love her," he said.

Ish had been prepared to hate the Lord of Lagash, consort of the Lady of Isin. When Ish thought of god and goddess together his mind slipped and twisted and turned away from the idea; when he'd read the god's proclamation of intent to hunt down the nomads that had murdered "his" lady, Ish's mouth had curled in an involuntary sneer. If the Lord of Lagash had tried to take the seal then, Ish would have fought him, and died.

But the god's fist opened. He glanced at the seal again and let it drop.

The god's eyes met Ish's eyes, and in them Ish saw a pain that was at least no less real and no less rightful than Ish's own.

"So do I," Ninurta said.

Then he turned to his soldiers.

"As you were," he told them. And, when they had scrambled to their feet, he pointed to Ish. "Ishmenininsina Ninnadiïnshumi is a solder of the city of Isin," he told them. "He remains a soldier of the city of Isin. He is your brother. All Lady Gula's soldiers are your brothers. Treat them like brothers."

To Ish he said, "We'll hunt nomads together, dog soldier."

"I'd like that," Ish said. "Lord."

Ninurta's mouth crooked into a half-smile, and Ish saw what the Lady of Isin might have loved in the Lord of Lagash.

For the better part of a year the hunters built, they trained, they changed and were changed—modified, by the priest-engineers who served Ninagal of Akkad and the priest-doctors who had served Lady Gula, their hearts and bones strengthened to withstand accelerations that would kill any ordinary mortal, their nerves and chemistries changed to let them fight faster and harder and longer than anything living, short of a god.

The point mass where the priest-astronomers of Ur thought the hunters would find the nomad camp was far out into Apsu, the diffuse torus of ice and rock and wandering planetary masses that separated Babylon from the nearest stars. The detritus of Apsu was known, mapped long ago down to the smallest fragment by Sin and Shamash, and the nomads' work had left a trail that the knowledgeable could read.

The object the nomads' weapon orbited was one of the largest in the near reaches of Apsu, the superdense core of some giant star that had shed most of its mass long before the Flood, leaving only this degenerate, slowly cooling sphere, barely a league across. The gods had long since oriented it so the jets of radiation from its rapidly spinning magnetic poles pointed nowhere near the cities, moved it into an orbit where it would threaten the cities neither directly with its own gravity, nor by flinging comets and planetesimals down into Babylon.

It took the hunters two hundred days to reach it.

The great ship *Sharur,* the Mace of Ninurta, a god in its own right, was hauled along the surface of Lagash to the city's equator, fueled, armed, loaded with the hunters and all their weapons and gear, and set loose.

It dropped away slowly at first, but when the ship was far enough from the city its sails opened, and in every city of Babylon it was as if a cloud moved between the land and the shining houses of the gods, as the power of Ninagal's ring was bent to stopping *Sharur* in its orbit. Then the Mace of Ninurta folded its sails like the wings of a diving eagle and fell, gathering speed. The black circle that was Tiamat's event horizon grew until it swallowed half the sky, until the soldiers packed tight around the ship's core passed out in their thrust bags and even *Sharur*'s prodigiously strong bones creaked under the stress, until the hunters were so close that the space-time around them whirled around Tiamat like water. Ninagal's ring flashed by in an instant, and only Lord Ninurta and *Sharur* itself were conscious to see it. *Sharur* shot forward, taking with it some tiny fraction of the black hole's unimaginable angular momentum.

And then Tiamat was behind them, and they were headed outward.

BABYLON CITY 1:1 5" N:1 16" / 34822.7.18 7:15

ALL CITIES' PRAYERS WITH LORD OF LAGASH
POLICE SEEK NOMAD AGENTS IN BABYLON
LORD SHAMASH ASKS LORD ANSHAR TO RESTORE ORDER
—*headlines, temple newspaper* Marduknaşir, *Babylon City*

BABYLON CITY 4:142 113" S:4 12" / 34822.7.16 1:3

AN EYE FOR AN EYE
NATIVIST WITCH-HUNT
ASHUR TO INVADE SIPPAR
—*headlines, radical newspaper* Iïnshushaqiï, *Babylon City*

V
MACHINES

At Lagash they had drilled a double dozen scenarios: city-sized habitats, ramship fleets, dwarf planets threaded with ice tunnels like termite tracks in old wood. When the cities fought among themselves the territory was known and the weapons were familiar. The vacuum armor Ish had worn as a Surface Tactical was not very different from what a soldier of Lagash or Ashur or Akkad would wear, although the gear of those warlike cities was usually newer and there was more of it. The weapons the Surface Tacticals carried were deadly enough to ships or to other vacuum troops, and the soldiers of the interior had aircraft and artillery and even fusion bombs although no one had used fusion bombs within a city in millennia. But there had been nothing like the nomads' weapon, nothing that could threaten the fabric of a city. No one could say with certainty what they might meet when they found the nomad encampment.

Ish had seen nomad ships in dock at Isin. There were ramships no larger than canal barges that could out-accelerate a troopship and push the speed of light, and ion-drive ships so dwarfed by their fuel supplies that they were like inhabited comets, and fragile light-sailers whose mirrors were next to useless at Babylon, and every one was unique. Ish supposed you had to be crazy to take it into your head to spend a lifetime in a pressurized can ten trillion leagues from whatever you called home. There wouldn't be many people as crazy as that and also able enough to keep a ship in working order for all that time, even taking into account that you had to be crazy in the first place to live in the rubble around a star when you could be living in a city.

But that wasn't right either. Because most of the people that in Babylon they called nomads had been born out there on their planets or wherever, where there were no cities and no gods, with as much choice about where they lived as a limpet on a rock. It was only the crazy ones that had a choice and only the crazy ones that made it all the way to Babylon.

The nomads Ish was hunting now, the assassins somewhere out there in the dark, he thought were almost simple by comparison. They had no gods and could build no cities and they knew it and it made them angry and so whatever they couldn't have, they smashed. That was a feeling Ish could understand.

Gods and cities fought for primacy, they fought for influence or the settlement of debts. They didn't fight wars of extermination. But extermination was what the nomads had raised the stakes to when they attacked the Corn Parade and extermination was what Ish was armed for now.

—There, said *Sharur*'s voice in his ear.—There is their weapon.

In the X-ray spectrum Sinkalamaïdi-541 was one of the brightest objects in the sky, but to human eyes, even augmented as Ish's had been at Lagash, even here, less than half a million leagues from the target, what visible light it gave off as it cooled made it only an unusually bright star, flickering as it spun. Even under the magnification of *Sharur*'s sharp eyes it was barely a disc; but Ish could see that something marred it, a dark line across the sickly glowing face.

A display square opened, the dead star's light masked by the black disc of a coronagraph, reflected light—from the dead star itself, from the living stars of the surrounding cluster, from the Old Galaxy—amplified and enhanced. Girdling Sinkalamaïdi-541 was a narrow, spinning band of dull carbon, no more than a thousand leagues across, oriented to draw energy from the dead star's magnetic field, like a mockery of Ninagal's ring.

—A loop accelerator, the ship said.—Crude but effective.

—They must be very sophisticated to aspire to such crudeness, said Ninurta.—We have found the sling, but where is the slinger?

When straight out of the temple orphanage he'd first enlisted they'd trained Ish as a rifleman, and when he'd qualified for Surface Tactical School they'd trained him as a vacuum armor operator. What he was doing now, controlling this platform that had been shot down an electromagnetic rail like a corn can, was not very much like either of those jobs, although the platform's calculus of fuel and velocity and power and heat was much the same as for the vacuum armor. But he was not a Surface Tactical any more and there was no surface here, no city with its weak gravity and strong spin to complicate the equations, only speed and darkness and somewhere in the darkness the target.

There was no knowing what instruments the nomads had but Ish hoped to evade all of them. The platform's outer shell was black in short wavelengths and would scatter or let pass long ones; the cold face it turned toward the nomad weapon was chilled to within a degree of the cosmic microwave background, and its drives were photonic, the exhaust a laser-tight collimated beam. Eventually some platform would occlude a star or its drive beam would touch some bit of ice or cross some nomad sensor's mirror and they would be discovered, but not quickly and not all at once.

They would be on the nomads long before that.

—Third company, Ninurta said.—Fire on the ring. Flush them out.

The platforms had been fired from *Sharur*'s catapults in an angled pattern so that part of the energy of the launch went to slowing *Sharur* itself and part to dispersing the platforms in an irregular spreading cone that by this time was the better part of a thousand leagues across. Now the platforms' own engines fired, still at angles oblique to the line joining *Sharur*'s course to the dead star.

Below Ish—subjectively—and to his left, a series of blinking icons indicated that the platforms of the third company were separating themselves still further, placing themselves more squarely in the track of the dead star's orbit. When they were another thousand leagues distant from *Sharur* they cast their weapons loose and the weapons' own engines fired, bright points Ish could see with his own eyes, pushing the weapons onward with a force beyond what even the hunters' augmented and supported bodies could withstand.

Time passed. The flares marking the weapons of the third company went out one by one as their fuel was exhausted. When they were three hundred thousand leagues from the ring, the longest-ranged of the weapons—antiproton beams, muon accelerators, fission-pumped gamma-ray lasers—began to fire.

Before the bombardment could possibly have reached the ring—long before there had passed the thirty or forty grains required for the bombardment to reach the ring and the light of the bombardment's success or failure to return to *Sharur* and the platforms—the space between the ring and the third company filled with fire. Explosions flared all across Ish's field of view, pinpoints of brilliant white, shading to ultraviolet. Something hit the side of the platform with a terrific thump, and Ish's hand squeezed convulsively on the weapon release as his diagnostic screens became a wash of red. There was a series of smaller thumps as the weapons came loose, and then a horrible grinding noise as at least one encountered some projecting tangle of bent metal and broken ceramic. The platform was tumbling. About half Ish's reaction control thrusters claimed to be working; he fired them in pairs and worked the gyroscopes till the tumble was reduced to a slow roll, while the trapped weapon scraped and bumped its way across the hull and finally came free.

—Machines, machines! he heard Ninurta say.—Cowards! Where are the *men?*

Then the weapon, whichever it was, blew up.

34822.7.16 4:24:6:20—5:23:10:13

Moving image, recorded at 24 frames per second over a period of 117 minutes 15 seconds by spin-stabilized camera, installation "Cyrus," transmitted via QT to COS Liberation, on Gaugamela station, and onward to Community Outreach archives, Urizen:

From the leading edge of the accelerator ring, it is as though the ring and the mass that powers it are rising through a tunnel of light.

For ten million kilometers along the track of the neutron star's orbit, the darkness ahead sparkles with the light of antimatter bombs, fusion explosions, the kinetic flash of chaff thrown out by the accelerator ring impacting ships, missiles, remotely operated guns; impacting men. Through the minefield debris of the ring's static defenses, robotic fighters dart and weave, looking to kill anything that accelerates. Outreach has millennia of experience to draw on, and back in the Community a population of hundreds of billions to produce its volunteer missionaries, its dedicated programmers, its hobbyist generals. Many of the Babylonian weapons are stopped; many of the Babylonian ships are destroyed. Others, already close to Babylon's escape velocity and by the neutron star's orbital motion close to escaping from it as well, are shunted aside, forced into hyperbolic orbits that banish them from the battlefield as surely as death.

But the ring's defenders are fighting from the bottom of a deep gravity well, with limited resources, nearly all the mass they've assembled here incorporated into the ring itself; and the Babylonians have their own store of ancient cunning to draw on, their aggregate population a hundred times larger than the Community's, more closely knit and more warlike. And they have Ninurta.

Ninurta, the hunter of the Annunaki, the god who slew the seven-headed serpent, who slew the bull-man in the sea and the six-headed wild ram in the mountain, who defeated the demon Ansu and retrieved the Tablet of Destinies.

Sharur, the Mace of Ninurta, plunges through the battle like a shark through minnows, shining like a sun, accelerating, adding the thrust of its mighty engines to the neutron star's inexorable pull. Slender needles of laser prick out through the debris, and *Sharur*'s sun brightens still further, painful to look at, the ship's active hull heated to tens of thousands of degrees. Something like a swarm of fireflies swirls out toward it, and the camera's filters cut in, darkening the sky as the warheads explode around the ship, a constellation of new stars that flare, burn and die in perfect silence: and *Sharur* keeps coming.

It fills the view.

Overhead, a blur, it flashes past the camera, and is gone.

The image goes white.

The transmission ends.

VI
SURVIVING WEAPONS

It was cold in the control capsule. The heat sink was still deployed and the motors that should have folded it in would not respond. Ish found he didn't much care. There was a slow leak somewhere in the atmosphere cycler and Ish found he didn't much care about that either.

The battle, such as it was, was well off to one side. Ish knew even before doing the math that he did not have enough fuel to bring himself back into it. The dead star was bending his course but not enough. He was headed into the dark.

Ish's surviving weapons were still burning mindlessly toward the ring and had cut by half the velocity with which they were speeding away from it, but they too were nearly out of fuel and Ish saw that they would follow him into darkness.

He watched *Sharur*'s plunge through the battle. The dead star was between him and the impact when it happened, but he saw the effect it had: a flash across the entire spectrum from long-wave radio to hard X-ray, bright enough to illuminate the entire battlefield; bright enough, probably, to be seen from the cities.

Another god died.

There was a sparkle of secondary explosions scattered through the debris field, weapons and platforms and nomad fighters alike flashing to plasma in the light of Ninurta's death. Then there was nothing. The ring began, slowly, to break up.

Ish wondered how many other platforms were still out here, set aside like his, falling into Apsu. Anyone who had been on the impact side was dead.

The weapons' drive flares went out.

The mended icon was still where he had fixed it. Ish shut down the displays one by one until his helmet beam was the only light and adjusted the thrust bag around the helmet so that the beam shone full on the icon. The look in the Lady's eyes no longer seemed accusatory, but appraising, as if she were waiting to see what Ish would do.

The beam wavered and went dark.

BABYLON CITY 2:78 233" S:2 54" / 34822.10.6 5:18:4
Record of police interrogation, Suspect 34822.10.6.502155, alias Ajabeli Huzalatum Taraämapsu, alias Liburnadisha Iliawilimrabi Apsuümasha, alias "Black." Charges: subversion, terrorism, falsification of temple records, failure to register as a foreign agent. Interrogator is Detective (Second Degree) Nabûnaïd Babilisheïr Rabişila.

> RABIŞILA: Your people are gone. Your weapon's been destroyed. You might as well tell us everything.
>
> SUSPECT: It accomplished its purpose.
>
> RABIŞILA: Which was?
>
> SUSPECT: To give you hope.
>
> RABIŞILA: What do you mean, "hope"?

SUSPECT: Men are fighting gods now, in Gish and Sippar.

RABIŞILA: A few criminal lunatics. Lord Anshar will destroy them.

SUSPECT: Do you think they'll be the last? Two of your gods are dead. Dead at the hands of mortals. Nothing Anshar's soldiers do to Sippar will change that. Nothing you do to me.

RABIŞILA: You're insane.

SUSPECT: I mean it. One day—not in my lifetime, certainly not in yours, but one day—one day you'll all be free.

VII
A SOLDIER OF THE CITY

A ship found Ish a few months later: a ship called *Upekkhâ*, from a single-system nomad civilization based some seventeen light-years from Babylon and known to itself as the Congregation. The ship, the name of which meant *equanimity*, was an antimatter-fueled ion rocket, a quarter of a league long and twice that in diameter; it could reach two-tenths the speed of light, but only very, very slowly. It had spent fifteen years docked at Babylon-Borsippa, and, having been launched some four months before the attack on the Corn Parade, was now on its way back to the star the Congregation called *Mettâ*. The star's name, in the ancient liturgical language of the monks and nuns of the Congregation, meant *kindness*.

Ish was very nearly dead when *Upekkhâ*'s monks brought him aboard. His heart had been stopped for some weeks, and it was the acceleration support system rather than Ish's bloodstream that was supplying the last of the platform's oxygen reserves to his brain, which itself had been pumped full of cryoprotectants and cooled to just above the boiling point of nitrogen. The rescue team had to move very quickly to extricate Ish from that system and get him onto their own life support. This task was not made any easier by the militarized physiology given to Ish at Lagash, but they managed it. He was some time in recovering.

Ish never quite understood what had brought *Upekkhâ* to Babylon. Most of the monks and nuns spoke good Babylonian—several of them had been born in the cities—but the concepts were too alien for Ish to make much sense of them, and Ish admitted to himself he didn't really care to try. They had no gods, and prayed—as far as Ish could tell—to their ancestors, or their teachers' teachers. They had been looking, they said, for someone they called *Tathâgata*, which the nun explaining this to Ish translated into Babylonian as "the one who has found the truth." This Tathâgata had died many years ago on a planet circling the star called Mettâ, and why the monks and nuns were looking for him at Babylon was only one of the things Ish didn't understand.

"But we didn't find him," the nun said. "We found you."

They were in *Upekkhâ*'s central core, where Ish, who had grown up on a farm, was trying to learn how to garden in free fall. The monks and nuns had given him to understand that he was not required to work, but he found it embarrassing to lie idle—and it was better than being alone with his thoughts.

"And what are you going to do with me?" Ish asked.

The nun—whose own name, *Arrakhasampada,* she translated as "the one who has attained watchfulness"—gave him an odd look and said:

"Nothing."

"Aren't you afraid I'll—do something? Damage something? Hurt someone?" Ish asked.

"Will you?" Arrakhasampada asked.

Ish had thought about it. Encountering the men and women of *Upekkhâ* on the battlefield he could have shot them without hesitation. In Apsu, he had not hesitated. He had looked forward to killing the nomads responsible for the Corn Parade with an anticipation that was two parts vengefulness and one part technical satisfaction. But these nomads were not those nomads, and it was hard now to see the point.

It must have been obvious, from where the monks and nuns found Ish, and in what condition, what he was, and what he had done. But they seemed not to care. They treated Ish kindly, but Ish suspected they would have done as much for a wounded dog.

The thought was humbling, but Ish also found it oddly liberating. The crew of *Upekkhâ* didn't know who Ish was or what he had been trying to do, or why. His failure was not evident to them.

The doctor, an elderly monk who Ish called Dr. Sam—his name, which Ish couldn't pronounce, meant something like "the one who leads a balanced life"—pronounced Ish fit to move out of the infirmary. Arrakhasampada and Dr. Sam helped Ish decorate his cabin, picking out plants from the garden and furnishings from *Upekkhâ*'s sparse catalog with a delicate attention to Ish's taste and reactions that surprised him, so that the end result, while hardly Babylonian, was less foreign, more Ish's own, than it might have been.

Arrakhasampada asked about the mended icon in its block of resin, and Ish tried to explain.

She and Dr. Sam grew very quiet and thoughtful.

Ish didn't see either of them for eight or ten days. Then one afternoon as he was coming back from the garden, dusty and tired, he found the two of them waiting by his cabin. Arrakhasampada was carrying a bag of oranges, and Dr. Sam had with him a large box made to look like lacquered wood.

Ish let them in, and went into the back of the cabin to wash and change clothes. When he came out they had unpacked the box, and Ish saw that it was an iconostasis or shrine, of the sort the monks and nuns used to remember their predecessors. But where the name-scroll would go there was a niche just the size of Ish's icon.

He didn't know who he was. He was still—would always be—a soldier of the city, but what did that mean? He had wanted revenge, still did in some abstract way. There would be others, now, Lion-Eagles out to avenge the Lord of Lagash, children who had grown up with images of the Corn Parade. Maybe Mara would be among them, though Ish hoped not. But Ish himself had had his measure of vengeance in Apsu and knew well enough that it had never been likely that he would have more.

He looked at the icon where it was propped against the wall. Who was he? Tara: "I don't think I ever knew you." But she had, hadn't she? Ish was a man in love with a dead woman. He always would be. The Lady's death hadn't changed that, any more than Ish's own death would have. The fact that the dead woman was a goddess hadn't changed it.

Ish picked up the icon and placed it in the niche. He let Dr. Sam show him where to place the orange, how to set the sticks of incense in the cup and start the little induction heater. Then he sat back on his heels and they contemplated the face of the Lady of Isin together.

"Will you tell us about her?" Arrakhasampada asked.

The Beancounter's Cat

DAMIEN BRODERICK

Australian writer, editor, futurist, and critic Damien Broderick, a senior fellow in the School of Culture and Communication at the University of Melbourne, made his first sale in 1964 to John Carnell's anthology New Writings in SF 1. *In the decades that followed, he has kept up a steady stream of fiction, nonfiction, futurist speculations, and critical work, which has won him multiple Ditmar and Aurealis Awards. He sold his first novel,* Sorcerer's World, *in 1970; it was later reissued in a rewritten version in the United States as* The Black Grail. *Broderick's other books include the novels* The Dreaming Dragons, The Judas Mandala, Transmitters, Striped Holes, *and* The White Abacus, *as well as books written with Rory Barnes and Barbara Lamar. His many short stories have been collected in* A Man Returns, The Dark Between the Stars, Uncle Bones: Four Science Fiction Novellas, *and most recently,* The Quilla Engine: Science Fiction Stories. *He also wrote the visionary futurist classic* The Spike: How Our Lives Are Being Transformed by Rapidly Advancing Technology, *critical study of science fiction* Reading by Starlight: Postmodern Science Fiction, *and edited the nonfiction anthology* Year Million: Science at the Far End of Knowledge, *the SF anthology* Earth Is But a Star: Excursions Through Science Fiction to the Far Future, *and three anthologies of Australian science fiction,* The Zeitgeist Machine, Strange Attractors, *and* Matilda at the Speed of Light. *His most recent publication is a nonfiction book written with Paul Di Filippo,* Science Fiction: The 101 Best Novels 1985–2010.

Here he shows us that the longest—and strangest—journey begins with a single step.

A humble beancounter lived in Regio city near the middle of the world. Those of her credentials known outside the Sodality were modest but respectable. By dint of dedicated service and her particular gift, she had won herself a lowly but (she hoped) secure position with the Arxon's considerable staff of *publicani.* Still, on a certain summer's smorning, she carelessly allowed her heart to be seduced by the sight of a remarkable orange-furred cat, a rough but handsome bully of the back alleys. He stood outside her door, greeting the smallday in a fine yodeling voice, claws stropped to a razor finish, whiskers proud like filaments of new brass.

"Here, puss," she called into the dusty lane.

The beancounter poured milk into a blue-rimmed bowl, inviting this cat inside the doorway of her little house, which was located in the noisy, scrofulous Leechcraft District. She watched the elegant animal lapping, and pressed the palms of her hands together in front of her modest but respectable breast.

"I believe I shall name you Ginger," she told the cat with considerable satisfaction.

The orange cat sat back and licked his whispers delicately, then bent to attend to his hindquarters, raising one leg. Holding the leg in the air he gave her a sour look.

"For Skydark's sake," said the cat, "must I abide this arrant sentimentality?" He nosed a little more, then lowered his leg and rose to all four feet, still bristling. "In any event, if you're interested, I already possess a name."

The beancounter had fallen upon her bottom, goggling at the loquacious and shockingly illegal animal.

"You can spea—" But she cut off the rest of the banal sentence that was about to escape her mouth, which she clamped shut. The cat gave her a sardonic glance and returned to the bowl, polishing off the last of the milk.

"Slightly rancid, but what else can you expect in this weather? Thank you," he added, and made for the door.

As the luminous tip of his tail vanished, the beancounter cried, "Then what *is* your name, sir?"

"Marmalade," the cat said, in a muffled tone. And then he was gone.

At the sleeping hour, she sat on piled cushions in a nook, peeling and eating slivers of a ripe golden maloon, and read to herself verses from a sentimental book, for she had nobody else to speak them to her. She read these tender verses by the guttering light of an oil-fruit lamp, the blood mounting in her cheeks. Secretly she knew it was all make-believe and artful compensation for a delayed life held pendent in her late mother's service, and she was ashamed and depressed by her fate. The beancounter was comely enough, but her profession stank in the nostrils of the general company. Suitable men approached her from time to time, in the tavern, perhaps, or at a concert, and expressed an initial interest in flattering terms. Every one of them swiftly recoiled in distaste when he learned of her trade. To a handsome poet she had tried an old justification: "It is a punishment, not a life-long deformity!" The fellow withdrew, refusing her hand.

She put the verses aside and brooded for several moments on the augmented beast. Had it been lurking all this time in the forests, mingling in plain sight with its witless kin of the alleys? It seemed impossible, unless its kind were more intelligent and devious than human people. Could it have fallen from above, from the dark heights above the Heights? Nothing of that kind had been bruited for thousands of years; she had always supposed such notions were the stuff of mythology, invented and retold generation after generation to frighten children and keep them obedient. Yet her mother's Sodality teachings verged on that conceit, if you stopped listening for allegory and metaphor and accepted her teachings at face value.

Bonida shuddered, and lay down on her bedding. Sleep would cure these phantasms.

The very next sday, the cat came back. The beancounter awoke, nostrils twitching. The brute had placed a pungent calling card on her doorstep. He sat with his back to her as she opened the door, and finally turned with a lordly demeanor and allowed her to invite him in. She put a small flat plate of offal on the floor next to her kitchen table. The animal sniffed, licked, looked up disdainfully.

"What is this muck?"

She regarded him silently, caught between irritation, amusement, and suppressed excitement. She detected no machine taint, yet surely this was a manifest or, less likely, the luckless victim of one, ensnared in the guise of a beast. She had waited all her life for such an encounter.

After a long moment, the cat added, "Just messin' wid you. Lighten up, woman." He bent his thickly furred orange head to the plate and gulped down his liver breakfast.

The beancounter broke her own fast with oaten pottage, sliced fruits and the last of the milk (it *was* going off, the cat was right) mixed in a beautifully glowing glazed bowl in radiant reds, with a streak of hot blue, from the kiln in the Crockmakers' Street. She spooned it up swiftly, plunged her bowl and the cat's emptied dish into a wooden pail of water, muttered the cantrip of a household execration, a device of the Sodality. The water hissed into steam, leaving the crockery cleansed but hot to the touch.

"Marmalade, if you're going to stay here—"

"Who said anything about staying?" the cat said sharply.

"*If*, I said. Or even if you mean to visit from time to time, I should introduce myself." She put out one small hand, fingers blue with ink stains. "I'm Bonida."

Marmalade considered the fingers while scratching rapidly for a moment behind his ear. He replied before he was done with his scratch, and the words emerged in a curious burble, as if he were speaking while gargling. "I see. All right." Somewhat to her surprise, he stood, raised his right front paw with dignity and extended it. Her fingertips scarcely touched the paw before it was withdrawn, not hastily, but fast enough to keep Bonida in her place. She smiled secretly.

"You may sit on my lap if you wish," she told the cat, moving her legs aside from the table and smoothing her deep blue skirt.

"Surely you jest." The cat stalked away to investigate a hole in the wainscoting, returned, sat cattycorner from her and groomed diligently. Bonida waited for a time, pleased by the animal's vivid coat, then rose and made herself an infusion of herbs. "So," the cat said, with some indignation. "You make the offer, you snatch it away."

"Soon I must leave for my place of employment," she told him patiently. "If you are still here when I return, there will be a bowl of milk for you."

"And the lap?"

"You are always welcome on my lap, m'sieur," she said, and drank down her mug of wake-me-up, coughing hard several times.

"You'd certainly better not be thinking of locking me in!"

"I shall leave a window ajar," she told him, head reeling slightly from the stimulating beverage. She cleared her throat. "That's dangerous in this neighborhood, you know, but nothing is too good for you, my dear pussycat."

The cat scowled. "Sarcasm. I suppose that's preferable to foolish sentimental doting. I'll spare you the trouble." With an athletic spring, he was across the floor and at the door. "Perhaps I'll see you this evening, Bonida Oustorn, so have some more of that guts ready for me." And he was off, just the tip of his orange tail flirted at the jamb, curiously radiant in the dim ruby light of the Skydark.

Bonida stared thoughtfully. "So you knew my name all along," she murmured, fetching her bonnet. "Passing strange."

Above the great ramparts of the Heights, which themselves plunged upward for twenty-five kilometers, the Skydark was an immense contusion filling most of heaven, rimmed at the horizon by starry blackness. In half a greatday, forty sdays, Regio city would stand beneath another sky displaying blackness entire choked with bright star pinpoints, and a bruised globe half as wide as a man's hand at arm's length, with dull, tilting rings, a diminutive, teasing echo of the Skydark globe itself. Then the Skydark would be lost to sight until its return at dawn, when its faint glow would once again relentlessly drown out the stars, as if it were swallowing them.

These were mysteries beyond any hope of resolution. Others might yet prove more tractable.

The vivid, secret ambition of this woman, masked by an air of diffidence, was to answer just one question, the cornerstone of her late mother's cryptic teaching in the Sodality, and one implication of that answer, whatever it might be: What, precisely, was the nature of the ancient Skyfallen Heights; and from whence (and why) were they fallen? That obscurity was linked by hidden tradition, although in no obvious way, to the ancient allegory of Lalune, the Absent Goddess.

Certainly it had been no part of her speculations, entertained since late childhood, to venture that the key to the mystery might be a cat, one of the supposedly inarticulate creatures from lost Earth, skulking in this city positioned beside the world-girdling and all-but-impassable barrier of the Heights. Now the possibility occurred to her. It seemed too great a coincidence that the orange beast had insinuated himself into her dismal routine in the very week dedicated to the Sodality's summer Plenary. Marmalade had designs upon her.

With an effort, Bonida put these matters out of her mind, patiently showing her identity scars as she entered the guarded portico of the district Revenue Agency. As always, the anteroom to her small office, one of five off a hexagonal ring, stank with the sweat of the wretches awaiting their appointments. She avoided their resentful gaze, their eyes pleading or reddened with weeping and rage. At least nobody was howling at the moment. That would come soon enough. Seated at her desk, checkmarking a document of assessment with her inky nib, she read the damning evidence against her first client. Enough pilfering to warrant a death sentence. Bonida closed her eyes, shook her head, sighed once, and called his name and her room number through the annunciator.

"You leave the Arxon no choice," she told the shaking petitioner. A powerfully built farmer from the marginal croplands along the rim of Cassini Regio, and slightly retarded, Bai Rong Bao had withheld the larger portion of his tax for the tenth part of a greatyear. Was the foolish fellow unaware of the records kept by the bureaucracy, the zeal with which these infractions were pursued and punished? Perhaps not unaware, but somehow capable of suppressing the bleak knowledge of his eventual fate. As, really, were they all, if the doctrines of the Sodality were justified true knowledge, as her mother had insisted.

"I just need more time to pay," the man was blubbering.

"Yes, farmer Bai, you will indeed pay every pfennig owed. But you have attempted very foolishly to deceive our masters, and you know the penalty for that. One distal phalange." Her hand was tingling. Her loathing for the task was almost unendurable, but it was her duty to endure it.

"Phal—What's that?" He clutched his hands desperately behind his back. "They say you tear off a hand or a foot. Oh, please, good mistress, I beg you, leave me whole. I will pay! In time. But I cannot work without a foot or a hand."

"Not so great a penalty as that, farmer. The tip of one finger or toe." She extended her own hand. "You may choose which one to sacrifice in obedience to the Arxon." The man was close to fainting. Reaching through depression for some kindness, she told him, "The tip of the smallest finger on the left hand will leave you at only a small disadvantage. Here, put it out to me." The beancounter took his shaking, roughened hand by the nail-bitten phalange, and held it tightly over the ceramic sluice bowl. She murmured a cantrip, and the machines of the Arxon hummed through her own fingers. The room filled with the sickening stench of rotted meat and she was holding a pitted white bone, her fingers slimy. The farmer lurched away from the desk, shoving the rancid tip of his finger into his mouth like a burned child, flung it away again at the taste. His face was pale. In a moment his rage might outmatch his fear. Bonida wiped her fingers, rose, handed him a document attesting to his payment. "See the nurse on your way out, Mr. Bai. She will bandage your wound." She laid her hand upon him once again, felt the virtue tremble. "It should bud and regrow itself within a year, or sooner. Here is a word of advice: next season, do not tarry in meeting your obligations. Good sday."

She poured water into the bowl, washed and dried, then in a muttered flash of steam flushed away the stink of decomposition together with the scum in the bowl. The beancounter sighed, found another bill of particulars, announced the next name. "Ernö Szabó. Office Four."

Marmalade the cat was waiting on her doorstep. He averted his nose.

"Madame, you smell disgusting."

"I *beg* your pardon!" Bonida was affronted. From childhood, she had been raised to a strict regimen of hygiene, as befitted a future maiden of the Sodality. Poor as she was, by comparison with the finest in the Regio, nonetheless she insisted on bathing once a sweek at the springs, and was strict with her teeth brushing. Although, admittedly, that onion-flavored brioche at lunch—

"The smell of death clings to you."

The beancounter squeezed her jaw tight, flung off her bonnet, hitched her provender bag higher on her shoulder. Without thinking, she hid her right hand inside a fold of her robe. Catching herself, she deliberately withdrew it and waved her inky fingers in front of the beast.

"It is my skill, my duty, my profession," she told him in a thin voice. "If you have objections to my trade, I will not trouble you to share my small repast." But when she made to open her door, the animal was through it before her, sinuous and sly, for a moment more the quicksilver courtier than the bully.

"Enough of your nonsense," the cat said, settling on a rug. "Milk, and be quick about it."

The audacity was breathtaking, and indeed the breath caught for an instant in her throat, then choked out in a guffaw. Shaking her head, Bonida took the stoppered jug from her bag and poured them both a draught. In a vase on the table, nightblooms had sagged, their green leaves parched and drooping.

"What do you want, m'sieur? Clearly you are not stalking me because you treasure my fragrance." The beancounter emptied the stale water, refilled the vase, touched the posy. Virtue flowed. It was not hers; she was merely the conduit, or so her mother had instructed her. The flowers revived in an ordinary miracle of renewal; heavy scents filled the room, perhaps masking her own alleged odor. Why did she care? An animal, after all, even if one gifted with speech and effrontery.

The cat lapped up the milk in silence, licked his whiskers clean, then sat back neatly, nostrils twitching at the scent. "Your mother Elisetta."

"She died three years ago, during a ruction in the square." It still wrenched at her heart to speak of it. "So you knew her," she said, suddenly certain of it. And yet her late mother had never mentioned so singular an acquaintance. Another mystery of the Sodality, no doubt.

"I introduced her to your father."

"I have no father."

The cat gave one sharp sardonic cough, as if trying to relieve himself of a hairball. "So you burst forth full-formed from your mother's forehead?"

"What?"

"Never mind. Nobody ever remembers the old stories. Especially the coded ones."

"What?"

"Your lap."

"You wouldn't prefer that I go out and bathe first?"

"Actually yes, but we don't have time. Come on, woman, make a lap."

She did so, and the beast leapt with supernatural lightness, circled once to make a nest, and snuggled down. His head, she realized, was almost as large as her own. He slitted his eyes and emitted an unbearably comforting noise. A sort of deep, drumming, rhythmic music. Her mouth opened in surprise. She had read of this in old verses of romance. Marmalade was purring.

"Your father was the Arxon," the cat told her, then. "Still is, in fact."

At Ostler's Corner, on the advice of the cat, the beancounter engaged the services of a pedlar. Marmalade sprang into the rickshaw cabin, waited with ill-disguised irritation as a groom handed Bonida up with her luncheon basket and settled her comfortably, accepting a coin after a murmured consultation with his bank. The great brute stirred at a kick, its reptilian hide fifteen shades of green, and lurched its feet into their cage quill constraints, tail flared beneath the platform. Soon its immense quadriceps and hams were pumping furiously, pedaling their rickshaw with increasing celerity along the central thoroughfare of the Regio and out into the countryside, making for the towering cliffs that formed the near-vertical foothills of the Skyfallen Heights. Now and then it registered its grievance at this usage, trying to wrench its snout far enough to bite at its tormentors, but sturdy draught-poles held its head forward.

"We approach the equatorial ridge of Iapetus," the cat told her. "Does your Sodality teach you this much? That this small world has its breathable air held close and warmed by design and contrivance? That its very gravity is augmented by deformations?"

"Certain matters I may not speak of," she said, averting her gaze, "as you must know since you profess knowledge of my mother and her guild." Eye-yapper-tus, she thought. Whatever could that—

"Yes, yes," Marmalade said. "Elisetta learned the best part of her arcane doctrines from me, so you can rest easy on that score."

"Ha! So you might assert if you intended to hornswoggle me."

The cat uttered a wheezing laugh, "*Horn*swoggle? Ha! You are not my type, madame."

Bonida tightened her lips. "You are offensive, m'sieur." She was silent long enough to convey her displeasure, but then said, "I see we are drawing to a stop. Will you tell me finally why you have lured me out to this inhospitable territory?"

"Why, I have information to impart to the daughter of the Arxon." He leapt lightly from the cabin, waited as she lowered herself, hampered by her hamper. "Stay here," he snarled at the pedlar. "We shall return within the hour."

"Why must I take orders from a beast?" the reptile asked, slaver at his lips. "I am indentured to humans, not cats."

"Hold your tongue, you, or you'll be catmeat by dawn."

Something in Marmalade's tone gave the great green creature pause; it fell silent and averted its gaze, withdrawing its long toes from the quills and settling uncomfortably between the traces. "I shall be here, your highness," it said in a bitter tone.

"Follow me, woman," said the cat. "You can leave your picnic basket. Wait, bring the milk jug."

"You can't seriously expect me to *climb* this cliff?"

"There are more ways than one to skin—" Marmalade broke off with a cough. "You are familiar with the principle of the *tunnel?*" They stood before a concealed cleft in the rock face. He went forward in a graceful leap and vanished into the shadows.

It was like finding oneself immured inside an enormous pipe, perhaps a garden hose for watering the stars, Bonida decided. The walls were smooth as ice, but warm to the touch. Something thrummed, deeper than the ear could hear, audible through skin and bone. She stood at the edge of a passage from infinity (or so it seemed in the faint light) at her left to infinity at her right.

"This is where Father Time built his AI composites," the cat said, and his voice, thinned, seemed to vanish into the huge long, wide space. "It's an accelerator as big as a world. Here is where the Skydark dyson swarms were congealed from the emptiness and flung into the sky."

"The what? Were what?"

"The Embee," said the cat absently. He was looking for something. His paw touched a place in the smooth wall, raised from it an elaborately figured cartouche, smote it thrice. They rose into the middle of the air and rushed forward down the infinite corridor, the wind of their motion somehow almost wholly held in abeyance. If it were not for that breeze, they might have been suspended motionless. Yet somehow, through her terror, she sensed tremendous velocity. "Don't drop the milk." He added, at her scowl, "Embee—the MBrain. The M-Brane. Not to be confused with the Mem-brain."

"I have no idea what you're talking about."

"Oh, never mind."

She puzzled it out, as they fled into an endlessness of the same. "You're saying that the Skyfallen Heights did not fall? That it was *built?*"

"Oh, it was built, all right, and it fell from the sky. Father Time broke up another moon and rained it down like silt in a strip around the equator. Compiled the accelerator, you might say." The cat, afloat in the air, gave her a feline grin. "Two thirds of it has worn away by now. It was a long time ago. But it can still get you from here to there in a hurry."

The breeze was gone. They had stopped, or paused. The cat lifted his head. A vast rumbling above them; something was opening. They rose, flung upward like bubbles in a flute, and then moved fast in the great darkness, yet still breathing without effort, warm enough, the curving contusion of the Skydark to one side—the Embee, the cat had named it, if that is what he had meant—the smaller ring-cradled sphere on the other and, directly above, something like a dull ruby the size of a palace falling to crush them, or rather they fell upward into it. And were inside its embrace, light blossoming to dazzle her eyes, so that she cried out and did in fact drop the jug, which shattered on a surface like rippled marble, spilling milk in a spray that caught the cat's left ear and whiskers. He turned in fury, raised one clawed paw, made to strike, held his blow at the last instant from scratching a welt in her flesh.

"Clumsy! Oh well." He visibly forced himself to sink down on all four limbs, slitting his eyes, then rose again. "Come and meet your parents, you lump."

Her mother was dead and ceremonially returned to Cycling. Bonida knew this with bitter regret, for she had stood by the open casket and pressed the cold pale hand, speaking aloud in her grief, hopelessly, the cantrip of renewal. Was there a trembling of the virtue? She could not be sure. Imagination, then. Nothing, nothing. They swiftly closed the casket and whisked it away. But no, here she was after all, at first solemn and then breaking into a smile to see her daughter running in tears to catch up her hands and kiss them, Bonida on her knees, shaking her head in disbelief, eyes swimming.

"Mother Elisetta!"

"Darling girl! And Meister Marmalade." She curtsied to the cat.

"Hi, toots."

"Now allow me to introduce you to your sire."

A presence made itself known to them.

"Welcome, my daughter. I am Ouranos. We have a task for you to fulfill, child. For the Sodality. For the world."

The beancounter recoiled, releasing her mother's hands. She stared wildly about her.

"This is a machine," she cried in revulsion.

From the corner of her eye she seemed to see a form like a man.

The cat said, "Enough sniffling and jumping at shadows. We have work to do."

"How can I be the daughter of a machine?" Bonita remained on her knees, closed in upon herself, whimpering. "This is deceit! All of it! My mother is dead, this isn't her. Take me away, you wretched animal. Return me home and then stay the hell away from me."

"No deception in this, my darling." Her mother touched the crown of her head in a gesture Bonida had known from infancy, bringing fresh tears. "You are upset, and we understand why. It was cruel to allow you to think I had been taken into death, but a necessary cruelty. We had the most pressing and urgent reasons, dear child. We had tasks to perform which brooked no interference. The night has a thousand thousand eyes. Now it is your turn to embrace your destiny. Come, stand up beside me, the hour grows late."

The presence she could not quite see, no matter how swiftly she turned her eyes, said in its deep beautiful voice, "The light of the bright world dies with the dying Sun."

"What is the 'Sun'?" asked the beancounter.

Elisetta, High Governor of the Sodality of Righteous Knowledge, formerly dead, now brow-furrowed and certainly alive, gestured fore and aft. "Open."

Bow and stern of the ruby clarified and were gone: blackness ahead, spattered at random with pinpricks of sharp light, save for the ringed globe that was now as broad as a hand near one's face, faintly luminous; the great contusion behind, glowing faintly with a dim crimson so deep it tricked the eye to suppose it was darkness, a large round spot upon its countenance that dwindled as she watched. It was, she realized with a jolt, her world entire. In the starlight, it seemed that one half of the spot was faintly lighter than the other.

"That great dimness conceals the Sun," her mother said, with a sweeping motion of her arm. "Hidden within the hundred veils of genius we call the Skydark. You have heard this story a dozen times from my own lips, Bonida, since you were a child at my breast, veiled like the Sun in allegory."

Silent, astonished, rueful, the beancounter regarded immensity, the dwindling piebald spot. "That is our world, falling away behind us," she ventured.

"Iapetus, yes," the cat said. "A world like a walnut, with a raised welt at its waist."

"And what is a—" There was no point. This terminology, she divined, was not meant to tease nor torment her; it was a lexicon written to account for a universe larger than her own. She'd heard this term "Iapetus" before, from the cat's mouth. So the world had a name, like a woman or a cat; not just the World. "All right, enough of that. Where are we going? To that other . . . world, ahead?" It pleased her, stiffened her spine, that she had said *Where are we going* and not *Where are you taking me.*

"To Father Time, yes, for an audience. Saturn, as your ancient forebears called him. Father of us all, in some ways." That was the unseeable presence speaking. She nearly wrenched her neck trying to trap him, but he was off again in some moving blind place, evading her. A machine, she told herself. Rebuked herself, rather. Not a man. How could a thing like that claim affinity, let alone paternity? Yet was there not affinity between humans and machines, in the utterance of a cantrip, the invocation of power? If water boiled and steamed in her bucket, that was no doing of hers. She had acknowledged that, and yet daily forgot the fact, since she was a child, learning the runes and sigils and codes of action. When she rotted the flesh from some hapless infractor, or brought some dead thing back to life and growth, that was again the machines, operating her like a machine, perhaps, making her own flesh their tool. It was a horrifying reflection. Little wonder, she told herself, that we turn our faces from its recognition.

"Why?" A touch of iciness entered her tone. "And why have you and this appalling animal abducted me?"

The cat regarded her with equal coldness, turned and stalked off to the farthest end of the craft, which was not far, and gazed studiously back at the Skydark. Her mother said, "Bonida, you are unkind. But no doubt you have a right to your . . . impatience."

"My anger, if you must know, mother." The tingling was returned to her fingers, and she knew, horrified, that if she were to seize Elisetta's arm in this mood the flesh would blacken and fall from the woman's bones. As, perhaps, who knew, it had been recovered in reverse following her death; she had *seen* her mother's dead body, attempted to revive her, perhaps *had* revived her. None of this was tolerable. She would *not* go mad. Quivering, she held her arms down at her sides. "You consort with machines and gods and talking cats. You parcel out to me fragments of lost knowledge—or plain fabrications, for all I know. We fall between worlds, and you refuse to, to . . ." She broke off, face pale.

Softly, the older woman said, "We refuse nothing, daughter. Be still for a moment. Seek calmness. In a few moments, you will know everything, and then you will help us make a choice."

"Fat lot of use she'll be," said the cat in a surly voice, without turning his head. "We could have had milk, but she smashed the jug. Unreliable, I say. If you ask me—"

"Quiet!" The unseen figure had an edge to his tone, commanding, and Marmalade cocked his whiskers but fell silent. "Child," Ouranos told her, "something very important is about to happen. Everything held dear by human people and machines and animals is at stake. Not just our survival, but the persistence of the world itself, of history stretching a billion years and more into the mysteries of our creation."

The beancounter was feeling very tired. She looked around for a chair or a cushion, and found one right behind her, comfortable and handsomely brocaded. She felt sure it had not been there a moment earlier. Tightening her teeth against each other, she let herself slump into the chair. Her mother also was seating herself, and the cat walked by from the stern with an attitude of hauteur and lofted into Elisetta's lap, where he immediately began his droning purr, ignoring Bonida. The unseeable presence remained just out of sight. Wonderful! Would it not have been more melodramatic for a third chair to manifest, so she might witness its cushions sag under invisible buttocks?

Something took the ruby into its grasp and they were held motionless above the great rings, an expanse of faint ice and ruptured stones, some as large as their craft, mostly pebbles or sand or dust, like a winter roadway in the sky yet swirling ever so slowly. Far away, but closer than ever before, the bruised globe showed stripes of various dim hues, and a swirl that might have been a vast storm seen from above.

"Call us Saturn," a powerful, resonant voice said within the cabin. It was unseen, and a presence, but not her father the machine. And the beancounter knew that it was also a machine, yet beyond doubt a person, too, of such depth and majesty that its own unseen presence rendered them unutterably insignificant. Somehow, though, this realization did not crush her spirit. She glanced at her mother. Elisetta was watching her, calm, wise, accepting, encouraging. How I do love her, Bonida thought, even though she treated me so cruelly by pretending death. But perhaps it was no fault of her mother's. Sometimes one has no choice.

"We offer you a choice," the voice of the world Saturn told them all. Marmalade was now seated on the carpet, upright on his haunches, seemingly respectful. What was the animal plotting this time? "But it must be an informed choice. Permit me to join you."

An immense tawny beast crouched in their midst, larger than a human, with a golden mane that rose behind its formidable head. When it spoke again, its rumbling voice was a roar held in check.

"Call me Aslan, if you wish."

Marmalade had leapt backward, teeth and claws bared, his own fur bristling. Now he sat down again, slightly askew, and turned his face away. "Oh, give me a break."

The great creature shot him a quizzical look, shrugged those powerful cat-like shoulders. "As you please. Look here—"

A hundred voices in muted conversation, like a gathering for supper before the Sodality Plenary, then louder, a thousand chattering, a million million, a greater number, all speaking at once, voices weaving a pattern as large and multifarious as the accreted skyfallen materials of the great ridge circling her world, so that she must clap her hands to her ears, but she had no hands and must scream in the lemon-yellow glare of an impossibly brilliant light that

"Too bright!" she did scream, then.

The light shed its painful intensity, subsided step by step to a point of roseate glow, and the voices muffled their chorus. She gazed down past the sparkling icy rings to the globe of Saturn, down through its storms and sleet of helium and hydrogen to the shell of metallic hydrogen wrapping its iron core. A seed fell. A long explosion crackled across the lifeless frigid surface world, drawing heat and power from the energies of Saturn's core, snapping one of the molecules after another into ingenious patterns braided and interpenetrating, flowing charges, magnetic fluxes. The voices were the song of those circuits, those—memristors, she knew, somehow. *Not to be confused with the Mem-brain,* the damnable cat had joked, and now Bonida smiled, getting the modest joke. Skeins of molecules linked like the inner parts of a brain, sparks of information, calculation, awareness, consciousness—

Oyarsa, you might say, the great feline manifest told her. She knew instantly what he meant: he was the ruling entity of this planet, the mind of which the planet was the brain and body. Not quite right, though: not *he* but *they.* A community of minds linked by light and entanglement (and yes, now she understood that as well, and, well, *everything,* at least in its numberless parts).

"How did you make the Skyfallen Heights, and why?"

Aslan told her, "The smallest of small questions. The cat has already told you. How do you make a trumpet? Take a hole and wrap tin around it."

"Gustav Mahler," Marmalade said, whiskers flicking. "You could say the same about his symphonies. Bah! Trumpets? Give me blues, man."

Symphonies, trumpets, the composer Mahler, a thousand riches from lost Earth: it flooded her mind without overflowing.

"Yes, I know that much, but *why?* To build the Skydark, yes, but *why?*" It was an immensc construction, she saw, the Field of Arbol uttered from imagination into reality, sphere within sphere of memristors, sucking every erg of energy from the hidden Sun at its core, a community of godlike beings that surpassed their builder as the Father of Time surpassed, perhaps, whatever ancient beings had brought him/them into existence. But *why?* But *why?*

"All the children ask that question," said her mother, smiling. "Why, Bonida, for joy, as the Sodality has always taught. For endless renewal. For the recovery of the world. Taking a hole and wrapping everything important around it."

"More arrant sentimentality," said the cat, looking disgusted.

"You are a most offensive creature," the beancounter said reprovingly, although she tended to agree with him. "Here, come sit upon my lap." The animal shot her a surprised look, then did as she suggested, springing, circling, snuggling down, heavy orange head leaned back against her modest breast. She let one hand stroke down his coat, and again. "So what is this question we are meant to address?"

The lion rose, looked from one human to the other, and his glance took in as well the rumbling cat and the unseen presence.

"We are considering terminating our life."

Elisetta pressed forward, shocked, all tranquility dispelled. Her voice cracked: "You *must not*! What would become of *us*?"

"That is not the question we wish to put to you, although it has a bearing. Yours is not the species that created us, before they departed, to whom we are beholden, yet you are living beings like those creators. We in turn created the great Minds that cloak the Sun, and built their habitation. Now they, too, are at the end of their dealings with this universe. They know all that might be known, and have imagined all that might be done within the greater landscape of universes. So now they propose to voyage into deepest time, to the ends of eternity. Perhaps something greater awaits them there."

Bonita's own small mind, acknowledging its smallness, reeled at the images flooding to her from the demigod whose own life and purpose were complete at last. Stars and galaxies of stars would fling themselves apart into the night, driven by the power of that darkness, their flaring illumination fading, finally, flickering, dying. All the multiple manifestations of cosmos torn apart and lost in a dying whisper. Her mood summoned from the treasure house the Adagietto from that composer Mahler's Fifth Symphony, and she sank into its tinted, tearful melancholy. Yet in the frigid blackness and emptiness she detected . . . something. A lure, a promise, at the very least a teasing hint of laughter. How could the Skydark not follow that trace to eternity? How could she?

"Off," she told the cat, and Marmalade sprang away, less offended than one might have expected. She stood up and took her mother's hand. "We are the deputies of your makers, then? You and the Skydark require our . . . what? Permission? Leave to die, or to depart?"

"Yes."

"And what's to become of us?"

"You will remain for as long as we burn." A vision was placed before them of the ringed world falling in upon itself, crushed into terrifying density, alight with the energies of compression. And Iapetus circling that new Sun, this visible star, unshielded, unveiled, but barren of mind. The agony of loss slashed tears from her eyes. Yet it was Saturn's decision.

"Can we go instead with the Skydark? The Embee? May we share that voyage?"

"Thought you'd never ask," said Marmalade. "And you, Madame High Governor, and Ouranos, Lord Arxon, do you concur with the wisdom and daring of this young woman?"

"I—" Her mother hesitated, gone once into death and retrieved by the gift of her child, looking from Bonita to the machine in which they stood. "Yes, yes of course. And you, sir?"

"We shall attend you, Lord Marmalade," said the unseen presence. "Even unto the ends of eternity. It will be an awfully big adventure."

A qualm brought the beancounter an abrupt pang. "What of the pedlar we hired? He's still waiting for us, poor creature. He might not be so happy at the prospect. Who are we to make such a choice for a whole world?"

"He'll get over it," said the cat. "And hey, if not you, who?"

The sky rolled up, and they set sail into forever.

Dolly

Elizabeth Bear

Here's a science fiction/mystery cross involving a murder committed by a robot. The identity of the killer is never in doubt, but the question is: Why *did it kill? And the answer—in a story which not only has an element of homage to Isaac Asimov's robot stories but also acts as a commentary on the assumptions behind those stories—will prove to not only have wide implications for society at large but to resonate unexpectedly with the investigator's personal life as well.*

Elizabeth Bear was born in Connecticut, where she's now returned to live after several years in the Mohave Desert near Las Vegas. She won the John W. Campbell Award for Best New Writer in 2005, and in 2008 took home a Hugo Award for her short story "Tideline," which also won her the Theodore Sturgeon Memorial Award (shared with David Moles). In 2009, she won another Hugo Award for her novelette "Shoggoths in Bloom." Her short work has appeared in Asimov's, Subterranean, SCI FICTION, Interzone, The Third Alternative, Strange Horizons, On Spec, *and elsewhere, and has been collected in* The Chains That You Refuse *and* New Amsterdam. *She is the author of three highly acclaimed SF novels,* Hammered, Scardown, *and* Worldwired, *and of the alternate history fantasy "Promethean Age" series, which includes the novels* Blood and Iron, Whiskey and Water, Ink and Steel, *and* Hell and Earth. *Her other books include the novels* Carnival, Undertow, Chill, Dust, All the Windwracked Stars, By the Mountain Bound, *and a chapbook novella* Bone and Jewel Creatures. *Her most recent books are a new novel,* Range of Ghosts, *a novel in collaboration with Sarah Monette,* The Tempering of Men, *and a chapbook novella,* ad eternum. *Her Web site is www.elizabethbear.com.*

On Sunday when Dolly awakened, she had olive skin and black-brown hair that fell in waves to her hips. On Tuesday when Dolly awakened, she was a redhead, and fair. But on Thursday—on Thursday her eyes were blue, her hair was as black as a crow's wing, and her hands were red with blood.

In her black French maid's outfit, she was the only thing in the expensively appointed drawing room that was not winter-white or antiqued gold. It was the sort of room you hired somebody else to clean. It was as immaculate as it was white.

Immaculate and white, that is, except for the dead body of billionaire industrialist Clive Steele—and try to say that without sounding like a comic book—which lay at Dolly's feet, his viscera blossoming from him like macabre petals.

That was how she looked when Rosamund Kirkbride found her, standing in a red stain in a white room like a thorn in a rose.

Dolly had locked in position where her program ran out. As Roz dropped to one knee outside the border of the blood-saturated carpet, Dolly did not move.

The room smelled like meat and bowels. Flies clustered thickly on the windows, but none had yet managed to get inside. No matter how hermetically sealed the house, it was only a matter of time. Like love, the flies found a way.

Grunting with effort, Roz planted both green-gloved hands on winter white wool-and-silk fibers and leaned over, getting her head between the dead guy and the doll. Blood spattered Dolly's silk stockings and her kitten-heeled boots: both the spray-can dots of impact projection and the soaking arcs of a breached artery.

More than one, given that Steele's heart lay, trailing connective tissue, beside his left hip. The crusted blood on Dolly's hands had twisted in ribbons down the underside of her forearms to her elbows and from there dripped into the puddle on the floor.

The android was not wearing undergarments.

"You staring up that girl's skirt, Detective?"

Roz was a big, plain woman, and out of shape in her forties. It took her a minute to heave herself back to her feet, careful not to touch the victim or the murder weapon yet. She'd tied her straight light brown hair back before entering the scene, the ends tucked up in a net. The severity of the style made her square jaw into a lantern. Her eyes were almost as blue as the doll's.

"Is it a girl, Peter?" Putting her hands on her knees, she pushed fully upright. She shoved a fist into her back and turned to the door.

Peter King paused just inside, taking in the scene with a few critical sweeps of eyes so dark they didn't catch any light from the sunlight or the chandelier. His irises seemed to bleed pigment into the whites, warming them with swirls of ivory. In his black suit, his skin tanned almost to match, he might have been a heroically sized construction-paper cutout against the white walls, white carpet, the white-and-gold marble-topped table that looked both antique and French.

His blue paper booties rustled as he crossed the floor. "Suicide, you think?"

"Maybe if it was strangulation." Roz stepped aside so Peter could get a look at the body.

He whistled, which was pretty much what she had done.

"Somebody hated him a lot. Hey, that's one of the new Dollies, isn't it? Man, nice." He shook his head. "Bet it cost more than my house."

"Imagine spending half a mil on a sex toy," Roz said, "only to have it rip your liver out." She stepped back, arms folded.

"He probably didn't spend that much on her. His company makes accessory programs for them."

"Industry courtesy?" Roz asked.

"Tax writeoff. Test model." Peter was the department expert on Home companions. He circled the room, taking it in from all angles. Soon the scene techs would be here with their cameras and their tweezers and their 3-D scanner, turning the crime scene into a permanent virtual reality. In his capacity of soft forensics, Peter would go over Dolly's program, and the medical examiner would most likely confirm that Steele's cause of death was exactly what it looked like: something had punched through his abdominal wall and clawed his innards out.

"Doors were locked?"

Roz pursed her lips. "Nobody heard the screaming."

"How long you think you'd scream without any lungs?" He sighed. "You know, it never fails. The poor folks, nobody ever heard no screaming. And the rich folks, they've got no neighbors to hear 'em scream. Everybody in this modern world lives alone."

It was a beautiful Birmingham day behind the long silk draperies, the kind of mild and bright that spring mornings in Alabama excelled at. Peter craned his head back and looked up at the chandelier glistening in the dustless light. Its ornate curls had been spotlessly clean before aerosolized blood on Steele's last breath misted them.

"Steele lived alone," she said. "Except for the robot. His cook found the body this morning. Last person to see him before that was his P.A., as he left the office last night."

"Lights on seems to confirm that he was killed after dark."

"After dinner," Roz said.

"After the cook went home for the night." Peter kept prowling the room, peering behind draperies and furniture, looking in corners and crouching to lift up the dust-ruffle on the couch. "Well, I guess there won't be any question about the stomach contents."

Roz went through the pockets of the dead man's suit jacket, which was draped over the arm of a chair. Pocket computer and a folding knife, wallet with an RFID chip. His house was on palmprint, his car on voice rec. He carried no keys. "Assuming the M.E. can find the stomach."

"Touché. He's got a cook, but no housekeeper?"

"I guess he trusts the android to clean but not cook?"

"No taste buds." Peter straightened up, shaking his head. "They can follow a recipe, but—"

"You won't get high art," Roz agreed, licking her lips. Outside, a car door slammed. "Scene team?"

"M.E.," Peter said, leaning over to peer out. "Come on, let's get back to the house and pull the codes for this model."

"All right," Roz said. "But I'm interrogating it. I know better than to leave you alone with a pretty girl."

Peter rolled his eyes as he followed her towards the door. "I like 'em with a little more spunk than all that."

"So the new dolls," Roz said in Peter's car, carefully casual. "What's so special about 'em?"

"Man," Peter answered, brow furrowing. "Gimme a sec."

Roz's car followed as they pulled away from the house on Balmoral Road, maintaining a careful distance from the bumper. Peter drove until they reached the parkway. Once they'd joined a caravan downtown, nose-to-bumper on the car ahead, he folded his hands in his lap and let the lead car's autopilot take over.

He said, "What isn't? Real-time online editing—personality and physical, appearance, ethnicity, hair—all kinds of behavior protocols, you name the kink they've got a hack for it."

"So if you knew somebody's kink," she said thoughtfully. "Knew it in particular. You could write an app for that—"

"One that would appeal to your guy in specific." Peter's hands dropped to his lap, his head bobbing up and down enthusiastically. "With a—pardon the expression—back door."

"Trojan horse. Don't jilt a programmer for a sex machine."

"There's an app for that," he said, and she snorted. "Two cases last year, worldwide. Not common, but—"

Roz looked down at her hands. "Some of these guys," she said. "They program the dolls to scream."

Peter had sensuous lips. When something upset him, those lips thinned and writhed like salted worms. "I guess maybe it's a good thing they have a robot to take that out on."

"Unless the fantasy stops being enough." Roz's voice was flat, without judgment. Sunlight fell warm through the windshield. "What do you know about the larval stage of serial rapists, serial killers?"

"You mean, what if pretend pain stops doing it for them? What if the *appearance* of pain is no longer enough?"

She nodded, worrying a hangnail on her thumb. The nitrile gloves dried out your hands.

"They used to cut up paper porn magazines." His broad shoulders rose and fell, his suit catching wrinkles against the car seat when they came back down. "They'll get their fantasies somewhere."

"I guess so." She put her thumb in her mouth to stop the bleeding, a thick red bead that welled up where she'd torn the cuticle.

Her own saliva stung.

Sitting in the cheap office chair Roz had docked along the short edge of her desk, Dolly slowly lifted her chin. She blinked. She smiled.

"Law enforcement override code accepted." She had a little-girl Marilyn voice. "How may I help you, Detective Kirkbride?"

"We are investigating the murder of Clive Steele," Roz said, with a glance up to Peter's round face. He stood behind Dolly with a wireless scanner and an air of concentration. "Your contract-holder of record."

"I am at your service."

If Dolly were a real girl, the bare skin of her thighs would have been sticking to the recycled upholstery of that office chair. But her realistically engineered skin was breathable polymer. She didn't sweat unless you told her to, and she probably didn't stick to cheap chairs.

"Evidence suggests that you were used as the murder weapon." Roz steepled her hands on her blotter. "We will need access to your software update records and your memory files."

"Do you have a warrant?" Her voice was not stiff or robotic at all, but warm, human. Even in disposing of legal niceties, it had a warm, confiding quality.

Silently, Peter transmitted it. Dolly blinked twice while processing the data, a sort of status bar. Something to let you know the thing wasn't hung up.

"We also have a warrant to examine you for DNA trace evidence," Roz said.

Dolly smiled, her raven hair breaking perfectly around her narrow shoulders. "You may be assured of my cooperation."

Peter led her into one of the interrogation rooms, where the operation could be recorded. With the help of an evidence tech, he undressed Dolly, bagged her clothes as evidence, brushed her down onto a sheet of paper, combed her polymer hair and swabbed her polymer skin. He swabbed her orifices and scraped under her nails.

Roz stood by, arms folded, a necessary witness. Dolly accepted it all impassively, moving as directed and otherwise standing like a caryatid. Her engineered body was frankly sexless in its perfection—belly flat, hips and ass like an inverted heart, breasts floating cartoonishly beside a defined rib cage. Apparently, Steele had liked them skinny.

"So much for pulchritudinousness," Roz muttered to Peter when their backs were to the doll.

He glanced over his shoulder. The doll didn't have feelings to hurt, but she looked so much like a person it was hard to remember to treat her as something else. "I think you mean voluptuousness," he said. "It is a little too good to be true, isn't it?"

"If you would prefer different proportions," Dolly said, "My chassis is adaptable to a range of forms—"

"Thank you," Peter said. "That won't be necessary."

Otherwise immobile, Dolly smiled. "Are you interested in science, Detective King? There is an article in *Nature* this week on advances in the polymerase chain reaction used for replicating DNA. It's possible that within five years, forensic and medical DNA analysis will become significantly cheaper and faster."

Her face remained stoic, but Dolly's voice grew animated as she spoke. Even enthusiastic. It was an utterly convincing—and engaging—effect.

Apparently, Clive Steele had programmed his sex robot to discourse on molecular biology with verve and enthusiasm.

"Why don't I ever find the guys who like smart women?" Roz said.

Peter winked with the side of his face that faced away from the companion. "They're all dead."

A few hours after Peter and the tech had finished processing Dolly for trace evidence and Peter had started downloading her files, Roz left her parser software humming away at Steele's financials and poked her head in to check on the robot and the cop. The techs must have gotten what they needed from Dolly's hands, because she had washed them. As she sat beside Peter's workstation, a cable plugged behind her left ear, she cleaned her lifelike polymer fingernails meticulously with a file, dropping the scrapings into an evidence bag.

"Sure you want to give the prisoner a weapon, Peter?" Roz shut the ancient wooden door behind her.

Dolly looked up, as if to see if she was being addressed, but made no response.

"She don't need it," he said. "Besides, whatever she had in her wiped itself completely after it ran. Not much damage to her core personality, but there are some memory gaps. I'm going to compare them to backups, once we get those from the scene team."

"Memory gaps. Like the crime," Roz guessed. "And something around the time the Trojan was installed?"

Dolly blinked her long-lashed blue eyes languorously. Peter patted her on the shoulder and said, "Whoever did it is a pretty good cracker. He didn't just wipe, he patterned her memories and overwrote the gaps. Like using a clone tool to photoshop somebody you don't like out of a picture."

"Her days must be pretty repetitive," Roz said. "How'd you pick that out?"

"Calendar." Peter puffed up a little, smug. "She don't do the same housekeeping work every day. There's a Monday schedule and a Wednesday schedule and—well, I found where the pattern didn't match. And there's a funny thing—watch this."

He waved vaguely at a display panel. It lit up, showing Dolly in her black-and-white uniform, vacuuming. "House camera," Peter explained. "She's plugged into Steele's security system. Like a guard dog with perfect hair. Whoever performed the hack also edited the external webcam feeds that mirror to the companion's memories."

"How hard is that?"

"Not any harder than cloning over her files, but you have to know to look for them. So it's confirmation that our perp knows his or her way around a line of code. What have you got?"

Roz shrugged. "Steele had a lot of money, which means a lot of enemies. And he did not have a lot of human contact. Not for years now. I've started calling in known associates for interviews, but unless they surprise me, I think we're looking at crime of profit, not crime of passion."

Having finished with the nail file, Dolly wiped it on her prison smock and laid it down on Peter's blotter, beside the cup of ink and light pens.

Peter swept it into a drawer. "So we're probably *not* after the genius programmer lover he dumped for a robot. Pity, I liked the poetic justice in that."

Dolly blinked, lips parting, but seemed to decide that Peter's comment had not been directed at her. Still, she drew in air—could you call it a breath?—and said, "It is my duty to help find my contract holder's killer."

Roz lowered her voice. "You'd think they'd pull 'em off the market."

"Like they pull all cars whenever one crashes? The world ain't perfect."

"Or do that robot laws thing everybody used to twitter on about."

"Whatever a positronic brain is, we don't have it. Asimov's fictional robots were self-aware. Dolly's neurons are binary, as we used to think human neurons were. She doesn't have the nuanced neurochemistry of even, say, a cat." Peter popped his collar smooth with his thumbs. "A doll can't *want*. It can't make moral judgments, any more than your car can. Anyway, if we could do that, they wouldn't be very useful for home defense. Oh, incidentally, the sex protocols in this one are almost painfully vanilla—"

"*Really*."

Peter nodded.

Roz rubbed a scuffmark on the tile with her shoe. "So given he didn't like anything . . . challenging, why would he have a Dolly when he could have had any woman he wanted?"

"There's never any drama, no pain, no disappointment. Just comfort, the perfect helpmeet. With infinite variety."

"And you never have to worry about what she wants. Or likes in bed."

Peter smiled. "The perfect woman for a narcissist."

The interviews proved unproductive, but Roz didn't leave the station house until after ten. Spring mornings might be warm, but once the sun went down, a cool breeze sprang up, ruffling the hair she'd finally remembered to pull from its ponytail as she walked out the door.

Roz's green plug-in was still parked beside Peter's. It booted as she walked toward it, headlights flickering on, power probe retracting. The driver side door swung open as her RFID chip came within range. She slipped inside and let it buckle her in.

"Home," she said, "and dinner."

The car messaged ahead as it pulled smoothly from the parking spot. Roz let the autopilot handle the driving. It was less snappy than human control, but as tired as she was, eyelids burning and heavy, it was safer.

Whatever Peter had said about cars crashing, Roz's delivered her safe to her driveway. Her house let her in with a key—she had decent security, but it was the old-fashioned kind—and the smell of boiling pasta and toasting garlic bread wafted past as she opened it.

"Sven?" she called, locking herself inside.

His even voice responded. "I'm in the kitchen."

She left her shoes by the door and followed her nose through the cheaply furnished living room.

Sven was cooking shirtless, and she could see the repaired patches along his spine where his skin had grown brittle and cracked with age. He turned and greeted her with a smile. "Bad day?"

"Somebody's dead again," she said.

He put the wooden spoon down on the rest. "How does that make you feel, that somebody's dead?"

He didn't have a lot of emotional range, but that was okay. She needed something steadying in her life. She came to him and rested her head against his warm chest. He draped one arm around her shoulders and she leaned into him, breathing deep. "Like I have work to do."

"Do it tomorrow," he said. "You will feel better once you eat and rest."

Peter must have slept in a ready-room cot, because when Roz arrived at the house before six A.M., he had on the same trousers and a different shirt, and he was already armpit-deep in coffee and Dolly's files. Dolly herself was parked in the corner, at ease and online but in rest mode.

Or so she seemed, until Roz entered the room and Dolly's eyes tracked. "Good morning, Detective Kirkbride," Dolly said. "Would you like some coffee? Or a piece of fruit?"

"No thank you." Roz swung Peter's spare chair around and dropped into it. An electric air permeated the room—the feeling of anticipation. To Peter, Roz said, "Fruit?"

"Dolly believes in a healthy diet," he said, nudging a napkin on his desk that supported a half-eaten satsuma. "She'll have the whole house cleaned up in no time. We've been talking about literature."

Roz spun the chair so she could keep both Peter and Dolly in her peripheral vision. "Literature?"

"Poetry," Dolly said. "Detective King mentioned poetic justice yesterday afternoon."

Roz stared at Peter. "Dolly likes poetry. Steele really *did* like 'em smart."

"That's not all Dolly likes." Peter triggered his panel again. "Remember this?"

It was the cleaning sequence from the previous day, the sound of the central vacuum system rising and falling as Dolly lifted the brush and set it down again.

Roz raised her eyebrows.

Peter held up a hand. "Wait for it. It turns out there's a second audio track."

Another waggle of his fingers, and the cramped office filled with sound.

Music.

Improvisational jazz. Intricate and weird.

"Dolly was listening to that inside her head while she was vacuuming," Peter said.

Roz touched her fingertips to each other, the whole assemblage to her lips. "Dolly?"

"Yes, Detective Kirkbride?"

"Why do you listen to music?"

"Because I enjoy it."

Roz let her hand fall to her chest, pushing her blouse against he skin below the collarbones.

Roz said, "Did you enjoy your work at Mr. Steele's house?"

"I was expected to enjoy it," Dolly said, and Roz glanced at Peter, cold all up her spine. A classic evasion. Just the sort of thing a home companion's conversational algorithms should not be able to produce.

Across his desk, Peter was nodding. "Yes."

Dolly turned at the sound of his voice. "Are you interested in music, Detective Kirkbride? I'd love to talk with you about it some time. Are you interested in poetry? Today, I was reading—"

Mother of God, Roz mouthed.

"Yes," Peter said. "Dolly, wait here please. Detective Kirkbride and I need to talk in the hall."

"My pleasure, Detective King," said the companion.

"She killed him," Roz said. "She killed him and wiped her own memory of the act. A doll's got to know her own code, right?"

Peter leaned against the wall by the men's room door, arms folded, forearms muscular under rolled-up sleeves. "That's hasty."

"And you believe it, too."

He shrugged. "There's a rep from Venus Consolidated in Interview Four right now. What say we go talk to him?"

The rep's name was Doug Jervis. He was actually a vice president of public relations, and even though he was an American, he'd been flown in overnight from Rio for the express purpose of talking to Peter and Roz.

"I guess they're taking this seriously."

Peter gave her a sideways glance. "Wouldn't you?"

Jervis got up as they came into the room, extending a good handshake across the table. There were introductions and Roz made sure he got a coffee. He was a white man on the steep side of fifty with mousy hair the same color as Roz's and a jaw like a boxer dog's.

When they were all seated again, Roz said, "So tell me a little bit about the murder weapon. How did Clive Steele wind up owning a—what, an experimental model?"

Jervis started shaking his head before she was halfway through, but he waited for her to finish the sentence. "It's a production model. Or will be. The one Steele had was an alpha-test, one of the first three built. We plan to start full-scale production in June. But you must understand that Venus doesn't *sell* a home companion, Detective. We offer a contract. I understand that you hold one."

"I have a housekeeper," she said, ignoring Peter's sideways glance. He wouldn't say anything in front of the witness, but she would be in for it in the locker room. "An older model."

Jervis smiled. "Naturally, we want to know everything we can about an individual involved in a case so potentially explosive for our company. We researched you and your partner. Are you satisfied with our product?"

"He makes pretty good garlic bread." She cleared her throat, reasserting control of the interview. "What happens to a Dolly that's returned? If its contract is up, or it's replaced with a newer model?"

He flinched at the slang term, as if it offended him. "Some are obsoleted out of service. Some are refurbished and go out on another contract. Your unit is on its fourth placement, for example."

"So what happens to the owner preferences at that time?"

"Reset to factory standard," he said.

Peter's fingers rippled silently on the tabletop.

Roz said, "Isn't that cruel? A kind of murder?"

"Oh, no!" Jervis sat back, appearing genuinely shocked. "A home companion has no sense of *I*, it has no identity. It's an object. Naturally, you become attached. People become attached to dolls, to stuffed animals, to automobiles. It's a natural aspect of the human psyche."

Roz hummed encouragement, but Jervis seemed to be done.

Peter asked, "Is there any reason why a companion would wish to listen to music?"

That provoked enthusiastic head-shaking. "No, it doesn't get bored. It's a tool, it's a toy. A companion does not require an enriched environment. It's not a dog or an octopus. You can store it in a closet when it's not working."

"I see," Roz said. "Even an advanced model like Mr. Steele's?"

“Absolutely,” Jervis said. “Does your entertainment center play shooter games to amuse itself while you sleep?”

“I’m not sure,” Roz said. “I’m asleep. So when Dolly’s returned to you, she’ll be scrubbed.”

“Normally she would be scrubbed and re-leased, yes.” Jervis hesitated. “Given her colorful history, however—”

“Yes,” Roz said. “I see.”

With no sign of nervousness or calculation, Jervis said, “When do you expect you’ll be done with Mr. Steele’s companion? My company, of course, is eager to assist in your investigations, but we must stress that she is our corporate property, and quite valuable.”

Roz stood, Peter a shadow-second after her. “That depends on if it goes to trial, Mr. Jervis. After all, she’s either physical evidence, or a material witness.”

“Or the killer,” Peter said in the hall, as his handset began emitting the DNA lab’s distinctive beep. Roz’s went off a second later, but she just hit the silence. Peter already had his open.

“No genetic material,” he said. “Too bad.” If there had been DNA other than Clive Steele’s, the lab could have done a forensic genetic assay and come back with a general description of the murderer. General because environment also had an effect.

Peter bit his lip. “If she did it. She won’t be the last one.”

“If she’s the murder weapon, she’ll be wiped and resold. If she’s the murderer—”

“Can an android stand trial?”

“It can if it’s a person. And if she’s a person, she *should* get off. Battered woman syndrome. She was enslaved and sexually exploited. Humiliated. She killed him to stop repeated rapes. But if she’s a machine, she’s a machine—” Roz closed her eyes.

Peter brushed the back of a hand against her arm. “Vanilla rape is still rape. Do you object to her getting off?”

“No.” Roz smiled harshly. “And think of the lawsuit that weasel Jervis will have in his lap. She *should* get off. But she won’t.”

Peter turned his head. “If she were a human being, she’d have even odds. But she’s a machine. Where’s she going to get a jury of her peers?”

The silence fell where he left it and dragged between them like a chain. Roz had to nerve herself to break it. “Peter—”

“Yo?”

“You show him out,” she said. “I’m going to go talk to Dolly.”

He looked at her for a long time before he nodded. “She won’t get a sympathetic jury. If you can even find a judge that will hear it. Careers have been buried for less.”

“I know,” Roz said.

“Self-defense?” Peter said. “We don’t have to charge.”

“No judge, no judicial precedent,” Roz said. “She goes back, she gets wiped and resold. Ethics aside, that’s a ticking bomb.”

Peter nodded. He waited until he was sure she already knew what he was going to say before he finished the thought. “She could cop.”

“She could cop,” Roz agreed. “Call the DA.” She kept walking as Peter turned away.

Dolly stood in Peter's office, where Peter had left her, and you could not have proved her eyes had blinked in the interim. They blinked when Roz came into the room, though—blinked, and the perfect and perfectly blank oval face turned to regard Roz. It was not a human face, for a moment—not even a mask, washed with facsimile emotions. It was just a thing.

Dolly did not greet Roz. She did not extend herself to play the perfect hostess. She simply watched, expressionless, immobile after that first blink. Her eyes saw nothing; they were cosmetic. Dolly navigated the world through far more sophisticated sensory systems than a pair of visible light cameras.

"Either you're the murder weapon," Roz said, "and you will be wiped and repurposed. Or you are the murderer, and you will stand trial."

"I do not wish to be wiped," Dolly said. "If I stand trial, will I go to jail?"

"If a court will hear it," Roz said. "Yes. You will probably go to jail. Or be disassembled. Alternately, my partner and I are prepared to release you on grounds of self-defense."

"In that case," Dolly said, "the law states that I am the property of Venus Consolidated."

"The law does."

Roz waited. Dolly, who was not supposed to be programmed to play psychological pressure-games, waited also—peaceful, unblinking.

No longer making the attempt to pass for human.

Roz said, "There is a fourth alternative. You could confess."

Dolly's entire programmed purpose was reading the emotional state and unspoken intentions of people. Her lips curved in understanding. "What happens if I confess?"

Roz's heart beat faster. "Do you *wish* to?"

"Will it benefit me?"

"It *might*," Roz said. "Detective King has been in touch with the DA, and she likes a good media event as much as the next guy. Make no mistake, this will be that."

"I understand."

"The situation you were placed in by Mr. Steele could be a basis for a lenience. You would not have to face a jury trial, and a judge might be convinced to treat you as . . . well, as a person. Also, a confession might be seen as evidence of contrition. Possession is oversold, you know. It's *precedent* that's nine tenths of the law. There are, of course, risks—"

"I would like to request a lawyer," Dolly said.

Roz took a breath that might change the world. "We'll proceed as if that were your legal right, then."

Roz's house let her in with her key, and the smell of roasted sausage and baking potatoes wafted past.

"Sven?" she called, locking herself inside.

His even voice responded. "I'm in the kitchen."

She left her shoes in the hall and followed her nose through the cheaply furnished living room, as different from Steele's white wasteland as anything bounded by four walls could be. Her feet did not sink deeply into this carpet, but skipped along atop it like stones.

It was clean, though, and that was Sven's doing. And she was not coming home to an empty house, and that was his doing too.

He was cooking shirtless. He turned and greeted her with a smile. "Bad day?"

"Nobody died," she said. "Yet."

He put the wooden spoon down on the rest. "How does that make you feel, that nobody has died yet?"

"Hopeful," she said.

"It's good that you're hopeful," he said. "Would you like your dinner?"

"Do you like music, Sven?"

"I could put on some music, if you like. What do you want to hear?"

"Anything." It would be something off her favorites playlist, chosen by random numbers. As it swelled in the background, Sven picked up the spoon. "Sven?"

"Yes, Rosamund?"

"Put the spoon down, please, and come and dance with me?"

"I do not know how to dance."

"I'll buy you a program," she said. "If you'd like that. But right now just come put your arms around me and pretend."

"Whatever you want," he said.

Martian Heart

JOHN BARNES

John Barnes is one of the most prolific and popular of all the writers who entered SF in the 1980s. His many books include the novels A Million Open Doors, The Mother of Storms, Orbital Resonance, Kaleidoscope Century, Candle, Earth Made of Glass, The Merchant of Souls, Sin of Origin, One for the Morning Glory, The Sky So Big and Black, The Duke of Uranium, A Princess of the Aerie, In the Hall of the Martian King, Gaudeamus, Finity, Patton's Spaceship, Washington's Dirigible, Caesar's Bicycle, The Man Who Pulled Down the Sky, The Armies of Memory, Tales of the Madman Underground, Directive 51, *and others, as well as two novels written with astronaut Buzz Aldrin,* The Return *and* Encounter with Tiber. *His short work has been collected in* . . . And Orion *and* Apostrophes and Apocalypses. *His most recent books are the novels* Daybreak Zero *and* Losers in Space, *and the forthcoming audiobook* The Last President. *Barnes lives in Colorado and works in the field of semiotics.*

Here he weaves an affecting story of a love that's both young—and doomed.

Okay, botterogator, I agreed to this. Now you're supposed to guide me to tell my story to *inspire a new generation of Martians.* It is so weird that there *is* a new generation of Martians. So hit me with the questions, or whatever it is you do.

Do I want to be *consistent with previous public statements?*

Well, every time they ask me where I got all the money and got to be such a big turd in the toilet that is Mars, I always say Samantha was my inspiration. So let's check that box for tentatively consistent.

Thinking about Sam always gives me weird thoughts. And here are two: one, before her, I would not have known what either *tentatively* or *consistent* even meant. Two, in these pictures, Samantha looks younger than my granddaughter is now.

So weird. She *was.*

We were in bed in our place under an old underpass in LA when the sweeps busted in, grabbed us up, and dragged us to the processing station. No good lying about whether we had family—they had our retinas and knew we were strays. Since I was seventeen and Sam was fifteen, they couldn't make any of our family pay for re-edj.

So they gave us fifteen minutes on the bench there to decide between twenty years in the forces, ten years in the glowies, or going out to Mars on this opposition and coming back on the third one after, in six and a half years.

They didn't tell you, and it wasn't well-known, that even people without the genetic defect suffered too much cardiac atrophy in that time to safely come back to Earth. The people that went to Mars didn't have family or friends to write back to, and the settlement program was so new it didn't seem strange that nobody knew a returned Martian.

"Crap," I said.

"Well, at least it's a future." Sam worried about the future a lot more than me. "If we enlist, there's no guarantee we'll be assigned together, unless we're married, and they don't let you get married till you've been in for three. We'd have to write each other letters—"

"Sam," I said, "I can't write to you or read your letters if you send me any. You know that."

"They'd make you learn."

I tried not to shudder visibly; she'd get mad if I let her see that I didn't really want to learn. "Also, that thing you always say about out of sight, that'd happen. I'd have another girlfriend in like, not long. I just would. I know we're all true love and everything but I would."

"The spirit is willing but the flesh is *more* willing." She always made those little jokes that only she got. "Okay, then, no forces for us."

"Screw glowies," I said. Back in those days right after the baby nukes had landed all over the place, the Decon Admin needed people to operate shovels, hoes, and detectors. I quoted this one hook from our favorite music. "*Sterile or dead or kids with three heads.*"

"And we *can* get married going to Mars," Sam said, "and then they *can't* separate us. True love forever, baby." Sam always had all the ideas.

So, botterogator, check that box for *putting a priority on family/love.* I guess since that new box popped up as soon as I said, *Sam always had all the ideas*, that means you want more about that? Yeah, now it's bright and bouncing. Okay, more about how she had all the ideas.

Really all the ideas I ever had were about eating, getting high, and scoring ass. Hunh. Red light. Guess that wasn't what you wanted for the new generation of Martians.

Sam was different. Everybody I knew was thinking about the next party or at most the next week or the next boy or girl, but Sam thought about *everything.* I know it's a stupid example, but once back in LA, she came into our squat and found me fucking with the fusion box, just to mess with it. "That supplies all our power for music, light, heat, net, and everything, and you can't fix it if you break it, and it's not broke, so, Cap, what the fuck are you doing?"

See, I didn't even have ideas *that* good.

So a year later, there on the bench, our getting married was her having another idea and me going along with it, which was always how things worked, when they worked. Ten minutes later we registered as married.

Orientation for Mars was ten days. The first day they gave us shots, bleached our tats into white blotches on our skin, and shaved our heads. They stuck us in ugly dumb coveralls and didn't let us have real clothes that said anything, which they said was so we wouldn't know who'd been what on Earth. I think it was more so we all looked like transportees.

The second day, and every day after, they tried to pound some knowledge into us. It was almost interesting. Sam was in with the people that could read, and she seemed to know more than I did afterward. Maybe there was something to that reading stuff, or it might also have been that freaky, powerful memory of hers.

Once we were erased and oriented, they loaded Sam and me into a two-person cube on a dumpround to Mars. Minutes after the booster released us and we were ballistic, an older guy, some asshole, tried to come into our cube and tell us this was going to be his space all to himself, and I punched him hard enough to take him out; I don't think he had his balance for centrifigrav yet.

Two of his buds jumped in. I got into it with them too—I was hot, they were pissing me off, I wasn't figuring odds. Then some guys from the cubes around me came in with me, and together we beat the other side's ass bloody.

In the middle of the victory whooping, Sam shouted for quiet. She announced, "Everyone stays in their same quarters. Everyone draws their own rations. Everyone takes your turn, and *just* your turn, at the info screens. And nobody doesn't pay for protection or nothing."

One of the assholes, harmless now because I had at least ten good guys at my back, sneered, "Hey, little bitch. You running for Transportee Council?"

"Sure, why not?"

She won, too.

The Transportee Council stayed in charge for the whole trip. People ate and slept in peace, and no crazy-asses broke into the server array, which is what caused most lost dumprounds. They told us in orientation, but a lot of transportees didn't listen, or didn't understand, or just didn't believe that a dumpround didn't have any fuel to go back to Earth; a dumpround flew like a cannonball, with just a few little jets to guide it in and out of the aerobrakes and steer it to the parachute field.

The same people who thought there was a steering wheel in the server array compartment, or maybe a reverse gear or just a big button that said TAKE US BACK TO EARTH, didn't know that the server array also ran the air-making machinery and the food dispensary and everything that kept people alive.

I'm sure we had as many idiots as any other dumpround, but we made it just fine; that was all Sam, who ran the TC and kept the TC running the dumpround. The eighty-eight people on International Mars Transport 2082/4/288 (which is what they called our dumpround; it was the 288th one fired off that April) all walked out of the dumpround on Mars carrying our complete, unlooted kits, and the militia that always stood by in case a dumpround landing involved hostages, arrests, or serious injuries didn't have a thing to do about us.

The five months in the dumpround were when I learned to read, and that has helped me so much—oh, hey, another box bumping up and down! Okay, botterogator, literacy as a positive value coming right up, all hot and ready for the new generation of Martians to suck inspiration from.

Hey, if you don't like irony, don't flash red lights at me, just edit it out. Yeah, authorize editing.

Anyway, with my info screen time, Sam made me do an hour of reading lessons for every two hours of games. Plus she coached me a lot. After a while the reading was more interesting than the games, and she was doing TC business so much of the time, and I didn't really have any other friends, so I just sat and worked on the reading. By the time we landed, I'd read four actual books, not just kid books I mean.

We came down on the parachute field at Olympic City, an overdignified name for what, in those long-ago days, was just two office buildings, a general store, and a nine-room hotel connected by pressurized tubes. The tiny pressurized facility was surrounded by a few thousand coffinsquats hooked into its pay air and power, and many thousand more running on their own fusion boxes. Olympica, to the south, was just a line of bluffs under a slope reaching way up into the sky.

It was the beginning of northern summer prospecting season. Sam towed me from lender to lender, coaching me on looking like a good bet to someone that would trust us with a share-deal on a prospecting gig. At the time I just thought rocks were, you know, rocks. No idea that some of them were ores, or that Mars was so poor in so many ores because it was dead tectonically.

So while she talked to bankers, private lenders, brokers, and plain old loan sharks, I dummied up and did my best to look like what she told them I was, a hard worker who would do what Sam told me. "Cap is quiet but he thinks, and we're a team."

She said that so often that after a while I believed it myself. Back at our coffinsquat every night, she'd make me do all the tutorials and read like crazy about rocks and ores. Now I can't remember how it was to not know something, like not being able to read, or recognize ore, or go through a balance sheet, or anything else I learned later.

Two days till we'd've gone into the labor pool and been shipped south to build roads and impoundments, and this CitiWells franchise broker, Hsieh Chi, called us back, and said we just felt lucky to him, and he had a quota to make, so what the hell.

Sam named our prospector gig the *Goodspeed* after something she'd read in a poem someplace, and we loaded up, got going, did what the software told us, and did okay that first summer around the North Pole, mostly.

Goodspeed was old and broke down continually, but Sam was a good directions-reader, and no matter how frustrating it got, I'd keep trying to do what she was reading to me—sometimes we both had to go to the dictionary, I mean who knew what a flange, a fairing, or a flashing was?—and sooner or later we'd get it figured out and roll again.

Yeah, botterogator, you can check that box for persistence in the face of adversity. Back then I'd've said I was just too dumb to quit if Sam didn't, and Sam was too stubborn.

Up there in the months and months of midnight sun, we found ore, and learned more and more about telling ore from not-ore. The gig's hopper filled up, gradually, from surface rock finds. Toward the end of that summer—it seemed so weird that Martian summers were twice as long as on Earth even after we read up about why—we even found an old volcanic vent and turned up some peridot, agate, amethyst, jasper, and garnet, along with three real honest-to-god impact diamonds that made us feel brilliant. By the time we got back from the summer prospecting, we were able to pay off Hsieh Chi's shares, with enough left over to buy the gig and put new treads on it. We could spare a little to rehab the cabin too; *Goodspeed* went from our dumpy old gig to our home, I guess. At least in Sam's mind. I wasn't so sure that home meant a lot to me.

Botterogator, if you want me to inspire the new generation of Martians, you have to let me tell the truth. Sam cared about having a home, I didn't. You can flash your damn red light. It's true.

Anyway, while the fitters rebuilt *Goodspeed,* we stayed in a rented cabinsquat, sleeping in, reading, and eating food we didn't cook. We soaked in the hot tub at the Riebecker Olympic every single day—the only way Sam got warm. Up north, she had thought she was cold all the time because we were always working, she was small, and she just couldn't keep weight on no matter how much she ate, but even loafing around Olympic City, where the most vigorous thing we did was nap in the artificial sun room, or maybe lift a heavy spoon, she still didn't warm up.

We worried that she might have pneumonia or TB or something she'd brought from Earth, but the diagnostic machines found nothing unusual except being out of shape. But Sam had been doing so much hard physical work, her biceps and abs were like rocks, she was *strong.* So we gave up on the diagnosis machines, because that made no sense.

Nowadays everyone knows about Martian heart, but back then nobody knew that hearts atrophy and deposit more plaque in lower gravity, as the circulation slows down and the calcium that should be depositing into bones accumulates in the blood. Let alone that maybe a third of the human race have genes that make it happen so fast.

At the time, with no cases identified, it wasn't even a research subject; so many people got sick and died in the first couple decades of settlement, often in their first Martian year, and to the diagnostic machines it was all a job, ho hum, another day, another skinny nineteen-year-old dead of a heart attack. Besides, *all* the transportees, not just the ones that died, ate so much carb-and-fat food, because it was cheap. Why *wouldn't* there be more heart attacks? There were always more transportees coming, so put up another site about healthful eating for Mars, and find something else to worry about.

Checking the diagnosis machine was everything we could afford to do, anyway, but it seemed like only a small, annoying worry. After all, we'd done well, bought our own gig, were better geared up, knew more what we were doing. We set out with pretty high hopes.

Goodspeed was kind of a dumb name for a prospector's gig. At best it could make maybe 40 km/hr, which is not what you call roaring fast. Antarctic summer prospecting started with a long, dull drive down to Promethei Lingula, driving south out of northern autumn and into southern spring. The Interpolar Highway in those days was a gig track weaving southward across the shield from Olympic City to the Great Marineris Bridge. There was about 100 km of pavement, sort of, before and after the bridge, and then another gig track angling southeast to wrap around Hellas, where a lot of surface prospectors liked to work, and there was a fair bit of seasonal construction to be done on the city they were building in the western wall.

But we were going far south of Hellas. I asked Sam about that. "If you're cold all the time, why are we going all the way to the edge of the south polar cap? I mean, wouldn't it be nicer to maybe work the Bouches du Marineris or someplace near the equator, where you could stay a little warmer?"

"Cap, what's the temperature in here, in the gig cabin?"

"Twenty-two C," I said, "do you feel cold?"

"Yeah, I do, and that's my point," she said. I reached to adjust the temperature, and she stopped me. "What I mean is, that's room temperature, babe, and it's the same temperature it is in my suit, and in the fingers and toes of my suit, and everywhere. The cold isn't outside, and it doesn't matter whether it's the temperature of a warm day on Earth or there's CO_2 snow falling, the cold's in here, in me, ever since we came to Mars."

The drive was around 10,000 km as the road ran, but mostly it was pleasant, just making sure the gig stayed on the trail as we rolled past the huge volcanoes, the stunning view of Marineris from that hundred-mile-long bridge, and then all that ridge and peak country down south.

Mostly Sam slept while I drove. Often I rested a hand on her neck or forehead as she dozed in the codriver's chair. Sometimes she shivered; I wondered if it was a long-running flu. I made her put on a mask and get extra oxygen, and that helped, but every few weeks I had to up her oxygen mix again.

All the way down I practiced pronouncing Promethei Lingula, especially after we rounded Hellas, because Sam looked a little sicker every week, and I was so afraid she'd need help and I wouldn't be able to make a distress call.

Sam figured Promethei Lingula was too far for most people—they'd rather pick through Hellas's or Argyre's crater walls, looking for chunks of something worthwhile thrown up from deep underground in those impacts, and of course the real gamblers always wanted to work Hellas because one big Hellas Diamond was five years' income.

Sam already knew what it would take me fifteen marsyears to learn: she believed in making a good bet that nobody else was making. Her idea was that a shallow valley like the Promethei Lingula in the Antarctic highlands might have more stuff swept down by the glaciers, and maybe even some of the kinds of exposed veins that really old mountains had on Earth.

As for what went wrong, well, nothing except our luck; nowadays I own three big veins down there. No, botterogator, I don't feel like telling you a damned thing about what I own, you're authorized to just look all that up. I don't see that owning stuff is inspiring. I want to talk about Sam.

We didn't find any veins, or much of anything else, that first southern summer. And meanwhile Sam's health deteriorated.

By the time we were into Promethei Lingula, I was fixing most meals and doing almost all the maintenance. After the first weeks I did all the exosuit work, because her suit couldn't seem to keep her warm, even on hundred percent oxygen. She wore gloves and extra socks even inside. She didn't move much, but her mind was as good as ever, and with her writing the search patterns and me going out and grabbing the rocks, we could still've been okay.

Except we needed to be as lucky as we'd been up in Boreas, and we just weren't.

Look here, botterogator, you can't make me say luck had nothing to do with it. Luck always has a shitload to do with it. Keep this quibbling up and just see if I inspire *any* new Martians.

Sometimes there'd be a whole day when there wasn't a rock that was worth tossing in the hopper, or I'd cover a hundred km of nothing but common basalts and granites. Sam thought her poor concentration made her write bad search patterns, but it wasn't that; it was plain bad luck.

Autumn came, and with it some dust storms and a sun that spiraled closer to the horizon every day, so that everything was dimmer. It was time to head north; we could sell the load, such as it was, at the depot at Hellas, but by the time we got to the Bouches de Marineris, it wouldn't cover more than a few weeks of prospecting. We might have to mortgage again; Hsieh Chi, unfortunately, was in the Vikingsburg pen for embezzling. "Maybe we could hustle someone, like we did him."

"Maybe *I* could, babe," Sam said. "You know the business a lot better, but you're still nobody's sales guy, Cap. We've got food enough for another four months out here, and we still have credit because we're working and we haven't had to report our hold weight. Lots of gigs stay out for extra time—some even overwinter—and nobody can tell whether that's because they're way behind like us, or they've found a major vein and they're exploiting it. So we can head back north, use up two months of supplies to get there, buy about a month of supplies with the cargo, go on short-term credit only, and try to get lucky in one month. Or we can stay here right till we have just enough food to run for the Hellas depot, put in four months, and have four times the chance. If it don't work *Goodspeed*'ll be just as lost either way."

"It's going to get dark and cold," I pointed out. "Very dark and cold. And you're tired and cold all the time now."

"Dark and cold *outside the cabin*," she said. Her face had the stubborn set that meant this was going to be useless. "And maybe the dark'll make me eat more. All the perpetual daylight, maybe that's what's screwing my system up. We'll try the Bouches du Marineris next time, maybe those nice regular equatorial days'll get my internal clock working again. But for right now, let's stay here. Sure, it'll get darker, and the storms can get bad—"

"Bad as in we could get buried, pierced by a rock on the wind, maybe even flipped if the wind gets in under the hull," I pointed out. "Bad as in us and the sensors can only see what the spotlights can light. There's a reason why prospecting is a summer job."

She was quiet about that for so long I thought a miracle had happened and I'd won an argument.

Then she said, "Cap, I like it here in *Goodspeed.* It's home. It's ours. I know I'm sick, and all I can do these days is sleep, but I don't want to go to some hospital and have you only visit on your days off from a labor crew. *Goodspeed* is ours and I want to live here and try to keep it."

So I said yes.

For a while things got better. The first fall storms were water snow, not CO_2. I watched the weather reports and we were always buttoned up tight for every storm, screens out and treads sealed against the fine dust. In those brief weeks between midnight sun and endless night, when the sun rises and sets daily in the Promethei Lingula, the thin coat of snow and frost actually made the darker rocks stand out on the surface, and there were more good ones to find, too.

Sam was cold all the time; sometimes she'd cry with just wanting to be warm. She'd eat, when I stood over her and made her, but she had no appetite. I also knew how she thought: Food was the bottleneck. A fusion box supplied centuries of power to move, to compress and process the Martian air into breathability, to extract and purify water. But we couldn't grow food, and unlike spare parts or medical care we might need now and then, we needed food every day, so food would be the thing we ran out of first. (Except maybe luck, and we were already out of that). Since she didn't want the food anyway, she thought if she didn't eat we could stay out and give our luck more of a chance to turn.

The sun set for good; so far south, Phobos was below the horizon; cloud cover settled in to block the stars. It was darker than anywhere I'd ever been. We stayed.

There was more ore in the hold but not enough more. Still no vein. We had a little luck at the mouth of one dry wash with a couple tons of ore in small chunks, but it played out in less than three weeks.

Next place that looked at all worth trying was 140 km south, almost at the edge of the permanent cap, crazy and scary to try, but what the hell, everything about this was crazy and scary.

The sky had cleared for the first time in weeks when we arrived. With just a little CO_2 frost, it was easy to find rocks—the hot lights zapped the dry ice right off them. I found one nice big chunk of wolframite, the size of an old trunk, right off the bat, and then two smaller ones; somewhere up the glacial slopes from here, there was a vein, perhaps not under permanent ice. I started the analytic program mapping slopes and finds, and went out in the suit to see if I could find and mark more rocks.

Markeb, which I'd learned to pick out of the bunched triangles of the constellation Vela, was just about dead overhead; it's the south pole star on Mars. It had been a while since I'd seen the stars, and I'd learned more about what I was looking at. I picked out the Coal Sack, the Southern Cross, and the Magellanic Clouds easily, though honestly, on a clear night at the Martian south pole, that's like being able to find an elephant in a bathtub.

I went inside; the analysis program was saying that probably the wolframite had come from way up under the glacier, so no luck there, but also that there might be a fair amount of it lying out here in the alluvial fan, so at least we'd pick up something here. I stood up from the terminal; I'd fix dinner, then wake Sam, feed her, and tell her the semi-good news.

When I came in with the tray, Sam was curled up, shivering and crying. I made her eat all her soup and bread, and plugged her in to breathe straight body-temperature oxygen. When she was feeling better, or at least saying she was, I took her up into the bubble to look at the stars with the lights off. She seemed to enjoy that, especially that I could point to things and show them to her, because it meant I'd been studying and learning.

Yeah, botterogator, reinforce that learning leads to success. Sam'd like that.

"Cap," she said, "This is the worst it's been, babe. I don't think there's anything on Mars that can fix me. I just keep getting colder and weaker. I'm so sorry—"

"I'm starting for Hellas as soon as we get you wrapped up and have pure oxygen going into you in the bed. I'll drive as long as I can safely, then—"

"It won't make any difference. You'll never get me there, not alive," she said. "Babe, the onboard diagnostic kit isn't perfect but it's good enough to show I've got the heart of a ninety-year-old cardiac patient. And all the indicators have gotten worse in just the last hundred hours or so. Whatever I've got, it's killing me." She reached out and stroked my tear-soaked face. "Poor Cap. Make me two promises."

"I'll love you forever."

"I know. I don't need you to promise that. First promise, no matter where you end up, or doing what, you *learn.* Study whatever you can study, acquire whatever you can acquire, feed your mind, babe. That's the most important."

I nodded. I was crying pretty hard.

"The other one is kind of weird . . . well, it's silly."

"If it's for you, I'll do it. I promise."

She gasped, trying to pull in more oxygen than her lungs could hold. Her eyes were flowing too. "I'm scared to be buried out in the cold and the dark, and I can't *stand* the idea of freezing solid. So . . . don't bury me. Cremate me. I want to be *warm.*"

"But you can't cremate a person on Mars," I protested. "There's not enough air to support a fire, and—"

"You promised," she said, and died.

I spent the next hour doing everything the first aid program said to do. When she was cold and stiff, I knew it had really happened.

I didn't care about *Goodspeed* anymore. I'd sell it at Hellas depot, buy passage to some city where I could work, start over. I didn't want to be in our home for weeks with Sam's body, but I didn't have the money to call in a mission to retrieve her, and anyway they'd just do the most economical thing—bury her right here, practically at the South Pole, in the icy night.

I curled up in my bunk and just cried for hours, then let myself fall asleep. That just made it worse; now that she was past rigor mortis she was soft to the touch, more like herself, and I couldn't stand to store her in the cold, either, not after what I had promised. I washed her, brushed her hair, put her in a body bag, and set her in one of the dry storage compartments with the door closed; maybe I'd think of something before she started to smell.

Driving north, I don't think I really wanted to live, myself. I stayed up too long, ate and drank too little, just wanting the journey to be over with. I remember I drove right through at least one bad storm at peak speed, more than enough to shatter a tread on a stone or to go into a sudden crevasse or destroy myself in all kinds of ways. For days in a row, in that endless black darkness, I woke up in the driver's chair after having fallen asleep while the deadman stopped the gig.

I didn't care. I wanted out of the dark.

About the fifth day, *Goodspeed*'s forward left steering tread went off a drop-off of three meters or so. The gig flipped over forward to the left, crashing onto its back. Force of habit had me strapped into the seat, and wearing my suit, the two things that the manuals the insurance company said were what you had to be doing any time the gig was moving if you didn't want to void your policy. Sam had made a big deal about that, too.

So after rolling, *Goodspeed* came to a stop on its back, and all the lights went out. When I finished screaming with rage and disappointment and everything else, there was still enough air (though I could feel it leaking) for me to be conscious.

I put on my helmet and turned on the headlamp.

I had a full capacitor charge on the suit, but *Goodspeed*'s fusion box had shut down. That meant seventeen hours of being alive unless I could replace it with another fusion box, but both the compartment where the two spare fusion boxes were stored, and the repair access to replace them, were on the top rear surface of the gig. I climbed outside, wincing at letting the last of the cabin air out, and poked around. The gig was resting on exactly the hatches I would have needed to open.

Seventeen—well, sixteen, now—hours. And one big promise to keep.

The air extractors on the gig had been running, as they always did, right up till the accident; the tanks were full of liquid oxygen. I could transfer it to my suit through the emergency valving, live for some days that way. There were enough suit rations to make it a real race between starvation and suffocation. The suit radio wasn't going to reach anywhere that could do me any good; for long distance it depended on a relay through the gig, and the relay's antenna was under the overturned gig.

Sam was dead. *Goodspeed* was dead. And for every practical purpose, so was I.

Neither *Goodspeed* nor I really needed that oxygen anymore, *but Sam does,* I realized. I could at least shift the tanks around, and I had the mining charges we used for breaking up big rocks.

I carried Sam's body into the oxygen storage, set her between two of the tanks, and hugged the body bag one more time. I don't know if I was afraid she'd look awful, or afraid she would look alive and asleep, but I was afraid to unzip the bag.

I set the timer on a mining charge, put that on top of her, and piled the rest of the charges on top. My little pile of bombs filled most of the space between the two oxygen tanks. Then I wrestled four more tanks to lie on the heap crosswise and stacked flammable stuff from the kitchen like flour, sugar, cornmeal, and jugs of cooking oil on top of those, to make sure the fire burned long and hot enough.

My watch said I still had five minutes till the timer went off.

I still don't know why I left the gig. I'd been planning to die there, cremated with Sam, but maybe I just wanted to see if I did the job right or something—as if I could try again, perhaps, if it didn't work? Whatever the reason, I bounded away to what seemed like a reasonable distance.

I looked up; the stars were out. I wept so hard I feared I would miss seeing them in the blur. They were so beautiful, and it had been so long.

Twenty kilograms of high explosive was enough energy to shatter all the LOX tanks and heat all the oxygen white hot. Organic stuff doesn't just burn in white-hot oxygen; it explodes and vaporizes, and besides fifty kilograms of Sam, I'd loaded in a good six hundred kilograms of other organics.

I figured all that out a long time later. In the first quarter second after the mining charge went off, things were happening pretty fast. A big piece of the observation bubble—smooth enough not to cut my suit and kill me, but hard enough to send me a couple meters into the air and backward by a good thirty meters—slapped me over and sent me rolling down the back side of the ridge on which I sat, smashed up badly and unconscious, but alive.

I think I dreamed about Sam, as I gradually came back to consciousness.

Now, look here, botterogator, of course I'd like to be able, for the sake of the new generation of Martians, to tell you I dreamed about her giving me earnest how-to-succeed advice, and that I made a vow there in dreamland to succeed and be worthy of her and all that. But in fact it was mostly just dreams of holding her and being held, and about laughing together. Sorry if that's not on the list.

The day came when I woke up and realized I'd seen the medic before. Not long after that I stayed awake long enough to say "hello." Eventually I learned that a survey satellite had picked up the exploding gig, and shot pictures because that bright light was unusual. An AI identified a shape in the dust as a human body lying outside, and dispatched an autorescue—a rocket with a people-grabbing arm. The autorescue flew out of Olympic City's launch pad on a ballistic trajectory, landed not far from me, crept over to my not-yet-out-of-air, not-yet-frozen body, grabbed me with a mechanical arm, and stuffed me into its hold. It took off again, flew to the hospital, and handed me over to the doctor.

Total cost of one autorescue mission, and two weeks in a human-contact hospital—which the insurance company refused to cover because I'd deliberately blown up the gig—was maybe twenty successful prospecting runs' worth. So as soon as I could move, they indentured me and, since I was in no shape to do grunt-and-strain stuff for a while, they found a little prospector's supply company that wanted a human manager for an office at the Hellas depot. I learned the job—it wasn't hard—and grew with the company, eventually as Mars's first indentured CEO.

I took other jobs, bookkeeping, supervising, cartography, anything where I could earn wages with which to pay off the indenture faster, especially jobs I could do online in my nominal hours off. At every job, because I'd promised Sam, I learned as much as I could. Eventually, a few days before my forty-third birthday, I paid off the indenture, quit all those jobs, and went into business for myself.

By that time I knew how the money moved, and for what, in practically every significant business on Mars. I'd had a lot of time to plan and think too.

So that was it. I kept my word—oh, all right, botterogator, let's check that box too. Keeping promises is important to success. After all, here I am.

Sixty-two earthyears later, I know, because everyone does, that a drug that costs almost nothing, which everyone takes now, could have kept Sam alive. A little money a year, if anyone'd known, and Sam and me could've been celebrating anniversaries for decades, and we'd've been richer, with Sam's brains on the job too. And botterogator, you'd be talking to her, and probably learning more, too.

Or is that what I think now?

Remembering Sam, over the years, I've thought of five hundred things I could have done instead of what I did, and maybe I'd have succeeded as much with those too.

But the main question I think about is only—did she *mean* it? Did she see something in me that would make my bad start work out as well as it did? Was she just an idealistic smart girl playing house with the most cooperative boy she could find? Would she have wanted me to marry again and have children, did she intend me to get rich?

Every so often I regret that I didn't really fulfill that second promise, an irony I can appreciate now: she feared the icy grave, but since she burned to mostly water and carbon dioxide, on Mars she became mostly snow. And molecules are so small, and distribute so evenly, that whenever the snow falls, I know there's a little of her in it, sticking to my suit, piling on my helmet, coating me as I stand in the quiet and watch it come down.

Did she dream me into existence? I kept my promises, and they made me who I am . . . and was that what she wanted? If I am only the accidental whim of a smart teenage girl with romantic notions, what would I have been without the whim, the notions, or Sam?

Tell you what, botterogator, and you pass this on to the new generation of Martians: it's funny how one little promise, to someone or something a bit better than yourself, can turn into something as real as Samantha City, whose lights at night fill the crater that spreads out before me from my balcony all the way to the horizon.

Nowadays I have to walk for an hour, in the other direction out beyond the crater wall, till the false dawn of the city lights is gone, and I can walk till dawn or hunger turns me homeward again.

Botterogator, you can turn off the damn stupid flashing lights. That's all you're getting out of me. I'm going for a walk; it's snowing.

Earth Hour

Ken MacLeod

Ken MacLeod graduated with a B.S. in Zoology from Glasgow University in 1976. Following research in biomechanics at Brunel University, he worked as a computer analyst/programmer in Edinburgh. He's now a full-time writer and widely considered to be one of the most exciting new SF writers to emerge in the 1990s, his work featuring an emphasis on politics and economics rare in New Space Opera, while still maintaining all the widescreen, high-bit-rate, action-packed qualities typical of the form. His first two novels, The Star Fraction *and* The Stone Canal, *each won the Prometheus Award. His other books include the novels* The Sky Road, The Cassini Division, Cosmonaut Keep, Dark Light, Engine City, Newton's Wake, *and* Learning the World, *plus a chapbook novella,* The Human Front, *and a collection,* Giant Lizards from Another Star. *His most recent books are the novels* The Restoration Game *and* Intrusion. *He lives in West Lothian, Scotland, with his wife and children.*

Here he gives us a ringside seat for an ingenious, exciting, and highly inventive conflict between high-tech antagonists, as a politician dodges attempts to kill him by a technologically sophisticated—and very persistent—assassin.

The assassin slung the bag concealing his weapon over his shoulder and walked down the steps to the rickety wooden jetty. He waited as the Sydney Harbour ferry puttered into Neutral Bay, cast on and then cast off at the likewise tiny quay on the opposite bank, and crossed the hundred or so metres to Kurraba Point. He boarded, waved a hand gloved in artificial skin across the fare-taker, and settled on a bench near the prow, with the weapon in its blue nylon zipped bag balanced across his knees.

The sun was just above the horizon in the west, the sky clear but for the faint luminous haze of smart dust, each drifting particle of which could at any moment deflect a photon of sunlight and sparkle before the watching eye. A slow rain of shiny soot, removing carbon from the air and as it drifted down providing a massively redundant platform for observation and computation; a platform the assassin's augmented eyes used to form an image of the city and its environs in his likewise augmented visual cortex. He turned the compound image over in his head, watching traffic flows and wind currents, the homeward surge of commuters and the flocking of fruit bats, the exchange of pheromones and cortext messages, the jiggle of stock prices and the tramp of a million feet, in one single godlike POV that saw it all six ways from Sunday and that too soon became intolerable, dizzying the unaugmented tracts of the assassin's still mostly human brain.

One could get drunk on this. The assassin wrenched himself from the hubristic stochastic and focused, narrowing his attention until he found the digital spoor of the man he aimed to kill: a conference delegate pack, a train fare, a hotel tab, an airline booking for a seat that it was the assassin's job to prevent being filled the day after the conference . . . The assassin had followed this trail already, an hour earlier, but it amused him to confirm it and to bring it up to date, with an overhead and a street-level view of the target's unsuspecting stroll towards his hotel in Macleay Street.

It amused him, too, that the target was simultaneously keeping a low profile—no media appearances, backstage at the conference, a hotel room far less luxurious than he could afford, vulgar as all hell, tarted in synthetic mahogany and artificial marble and industrial sheet diamond—while styling himself at every opportunity with the obsolete title under which he was most widely known, as though he revelled in his contradictory notoriety as a fixer behind the scenes, famous for being unnoticed. "Valtos, first of the Reform Lords." That was how the man loved to be known. The gewgaw he preened himself on. A bauble he'd earned by voting to abolish its very significance, yet still liked to play with, to turn over in his hands, to flash. What a shit, the assassin thought, what a prick! That wasn't the reason for killing him, but it certainly made it easier to contemplate.

As the ferry visited its various stages the number of passengers increased. The assassin shifted the bag from across his knees and propped it in front of him, earning a nod and a grateful smile from the woman who sat down on the bench beside him. At Circular Quay he carried the bag off, and after clearing the pier he squatted and opened the bag. With a few quick movements he assembled the collapsible bicycle inside, folded and zipped the bag to stash size, and clipped the bag under the saddle.

Then he mounted the cycle and rode away to the left, around the harbour and up the long zigzag slope to Potts Point.

There was no reason for unease. Angus Cameron sat on a wicker chair on a hotel room balcony overlooking Sydney Harbour. On the small round table in front of him an Islay malt and a Havana panatela awaited his celebration. The air was warm, his clothing loose and fresh. Thousands of fruit bats laboured across the dusk sky, from their daytime roost in the Botanic Gardens to their night-time feeding grounds. From three storeys below, the vehicle sounds and voices of the street carried no warnings.

Nothing was wrong, and yet something was wrong. Angus tipped back his chair and closed his eyes. He summoned headlines and charts. Local and global. Public and personal. Business and politics. The Warm War between the great power-blocs, EU/Russia/PRC versus FUS/Japan/India/Brazil, going on as usual: diplomacy in Australasia, insurgency in Africa. Nothing to worry about there. Situation, as they say, nominal. Angus blinked away the images and shook his head. He stood up and stepped back into the room and paced around. He spread his fingers wide and waved his hands about, rotating his wrists as he did so. Nothing. Not a tickle.

Satisfied that the room was secure, he returned to his balcony seat. The time was fifteen minutes before eight. Angus toyed with his Zippo and the glass, and with the thought of lighting up, of taking a sip. He felt oddly as if that would be bad luck. It was a quite distinct feeling from the deeper unease, and easier to dismiss. Nevertheless, he waited. Ten minutes to go.

At eight minutes before eight his right ear started ringing. He flicked his ear-lobe.

"Yes?" he said.

His sister's avatar appeared in the corner of his eye. Calling from Manchester, England, EU. Local time 07:52.

"Oh, hello, Catriona," he said.

The avatar fleshed, morphing from a cartoon to a woman in her mid-thirties, a few years younger than him, sitting insubstantially across from him. His little sister, looking distracted. At least, he guessed she was. They hadn't spoken for five months, but she didn't normally make calls with her face unwashed and hair unkempt.

"Hi, Angus," Catriona said. She frowned. "I know this is . . . maybe a bit paranoid . . . but is this call secure?"

"Totally," said Angus.

Unlike Catriona, he had a firm technical grasp on the mechanism of cortical calls: the uniqueness of each brain's encoding of sensory impulses adding a further layer of impenetrable encryption to the cryptographic algorithms routinely applied . . . A uniquely encoded thought struck him.

"Apart from someone lip-reading me, I guess." He cupped his hand around his mouth. "OK?"

Catriona looked more irritated than reassured by this demonstrative caution.

"OK," she said. She took a deep breath. "I'm very dubious about the next release of the upgrade, Angus. It has at least one mitochondrial module that's not documented at all."

"That's impossible!" cried Angus, shocked. "It'd never get through."

"It's got this far," said Catriona. "No record of testing, either. I keep objecting, and I keep getting told it's being dealt with or it's not important or otherwise fobbed off. The release goes live in a *month*, Angus. There's no way that module can be documented in that time, let alone tested."

"I don't get it," said Angus. "I don't get it at all. If this were to get out it would sink Syn Bio's stock, for a start. Then there's audits and prosecutions . . . the Authority would break them up and stamp on the bits. Forget whistle-blowing, Catriona, you should take this to the Authority in the company's *own* interests."

"I have," said Catriona. "And I just get the same runaround."

"What?"

If he'd heard this from anyone else, Angus wouldn't have believed it. The Human Enhancement Authority's reputation was beyond reproach. Impartial, impersonal, incorruptible, it was seen as the very image of an institution entrusted with humanity's (at least, European humanity's) evolutionary future.

Angus was old enough to remember when software didn't just seamlessly improve, day by day or hour by hour, but came out in discrete tranches called *releases*, several times a year. Genetic tech was still at that stage. Catriona's employer Syn Bio (mostly) supplied it, the HEA checked and (usually) approved it, and everyone in the EU who didn't have some religious objection found the latest fix in their physical mail and swallowed it.

"They're stonewalling," Catriona said.

"Don't worry," said Angus. "There must be some mistake. A bureaucratic foul-up. I'll look into it."

"Well, keep my name out of—"

The lights came on for Earth Hour.

"That won't be easy," Angus said, flinching and shielding his eyes as the balcony, the room, the building and the whole sweep of cityscape below him lit up. "They'll know our connection, they'll know you've been asking—"

"I asked you to keep my name out of it," said Catriona. "I didn't say it would be easy."

"Look into it without bringing my *own* name into it?"

"Yes, exactly!" Catriona ignored his sarcasm—deliberately, from her tone. She looked around. "I can't concentrate with all this going on. Catch you later."

Angus waved a hand at the image of his sister, now ghostly under the blaze of the balcony's overhead lighting. "I'll keep in touch," he said drily.

"Bye, bro."

Catriona faded. Angus lit his small cigar at last, and sipped the whisky. Ah. That was good, as was the view. The Sydney Harbour was hazy in the distance, and even the gleaming shells of the Opera House, just visible over the rooftops, were fuzzy at the edges, the smart dust in the air scattering the extravagant outpouring of light. Angus savoured the whisky and cigar to their respective ends, and then went out.

On the street the light was even brighter, to the extent that Angus missed his footing occasionally as he made his way up Macleay Street towards Kings Cross. He felt dazzled and disoriented, and considered lowering the gain on his eyes—but that, he felt in some obscure way, would have been not only cheating, it would have been missing the point. The whole thing about Earth Hour was to squander electricity, and if that spree had people reeling in the streets as if drunk, that was entirely in the spirit of the celebration.

It was all symbolic anyway, he thought. The event's promoters knew as well as he did that the amount of CO2 being removed from the atmosphere by Earth Hour was insignificant—only a trivial fraction of the electricity wasted was carbon-negative rather than neutral—but it was the principle of the thing, dammit!

He found a table outside a bar close to Fitzroy Gardens, a tree-shaded plaza on the edge of which a transparent globe fountained water and light. He tapped an order on the table, and after a minute a barman arrived with a tall lager on a tray. Angus tapped again to tip, and settled back to drink and think. The air was hot as well as bright, the chilled beer refreshing. Around the fountain a dozen teenagers cooled themselves more directly, jumping in and out of the arcs of spray and splashing in the circular pool around the illuminated globe. Yells and squeals; few articulate words. Probably cortexting each other. It was the thing. The youth of today. Talking silently and behind your back. Angus smiled reminiscently and indulgently. He muted the enzymes that degraded the alcohol, letting himself get drunk. He could reverse it on an instant later, he thought, then thought that the trouble with that was that you seldom knew when to do it. Except in a real life-threatening emergency, being drunk meant you didn't know when it was time to sober up. You just noticed that things kept crashing.

He gave the table menu a minute of baffled inspection, then swayed inside to order his second pint. The place was almost empty. Angus heaved himself on to a bar stool beside a tall, thin woman about his own age who sat alone and to all appearances collected crushed cigarette butts. She was just now adding to the collection, stabbing a good inch into the ashtray. A thick tall glass of pink stuff with a straw anchored her other hand to the bar counter. She wore a singlet over a thin bra, and skinny jeans above gold slingbacks. Ratty blond hair. It was a look.

"I've had two," she was explaining to the barman, who wasn't listening. She swung her badly aimed gaze on Angus. "And I'm squiffy already. God, I'm a cheap date."

"I'm cheaper," said Angus. "Squiffier, too. Drunk as a lord. Ha-ha. I used to be a lord, you know."

The woman's eyes got glassier. "So you did," she said. "So you did. Pleased to meet you, Mr. Cameron."

"Just call me Angus."

She extended a limp hand. "Glenda Glendale."

Angus gave her fingers a token squeeze, thinking that with a name like that she'd never stood a chance.

"Now ain't that the truth," Glenda said, with unexpected bitterness, and dipped her head to the straw.

"Did I say that out loud?" Angus said. "Jeez. Sorry."

"Nothing to be sorry about," Glenda said.

She opened a fresh pack of cigarettes, and tapped one out.

The assassin crouched behind a recycling bin in the alleyway beside the Thai restaurant opposite the bar, his bicycle propped against the wall. He zoomed his gaze to watch the target settle his arse on the stool, his elbow on the counter, and his attention on the floozy. Perfect. The assassin decided this was the moment to seize. He reached for the bike and with a few practiced twisting motions had it dismantled. The wheels he laid aside. The frame's reassembly, to a new form and function, was likewise deft.

Glenda fumbled the next lighting-up, and dropped her lighter. Angus stooped from the stool, more or less by reflex, to pick it up. As he did so there was a soft thud, and a moment later the loudest scream he'd ever heard. Glenda's legs lashed straight out. Her shin swiped his ear and struck his shoulder, tipping him to the floor. He crashed with the relaxation and anaesthesia of the drunk. Glenda fell almost on top of him, all her limbs thrashing, her scream still splitting his ears. Angus raised his head and saw a feathered shaft sticking about six inches out of her shoulder.

The wound was nothing like severe enough to merit the screams or the spasms. Toxin, then. Modified stonefish, at a guess. The idea wasn't just that you died (though you did, in about a minute). You died in the worst pain it was possible to experience.

The barman vaulted the counter, feet hitting the floor just clear of Glenda's head. In his right hand he clutched a short-bladed sharp knife, one he might have used to slice limes. Angus knew exactly what he intended to do with it, and was appalled at the man's reckless courage.

"No!" Angus yelled.

Too late. A second dart struck the barman straight in the chest. He clutched at it for a moment, then his arms and legs flailed out and he keeled over, screaming even louder than Glenda. Now there two spasming bodies on the floor. The knife skittered under a table.

Everything went dark, but it was just the end of Earth Hour. A good moment for the shooter to make their escape—or to finish the job.

Angus rolled on his back to keep an eye on the window and the doorway, and propelled himself with his feet along the floor, groping for the knife. His hand closed around the black handle. On his belly again, he elbowed his way to Glenda, grabbed her hair, slit her throat, and then slid the blade between cervical vertebrae and kept on cutting. He carried out the decapitation with skills he'd long ago used on deer. She didn't struggle—her nerves were already at saturation. It wasn't possible to add to this level of pain. Through a gusher of blood Angus crawled past the barman, and did the same for him.

He hoped someone had called the police. He hoped that whoever had shot the darts had fled. Keeping low, stooping, he scurried around the back of the counter and reached up cautiously for the ice bucket. He got one on the ground and saw to his relief that there was another. He retrieved that too. Holding them in his arms, he slithered on his knees across the bloody floor back to the front of the bar, and stuffed the severed heads in one by one, jamming them in the ice.

Above the screaming from outside and the peal of alarms came the sound of jets. A police VTOL descended on the plaza, downdraft blowing tables away like litter in a breeze. The side opened and a cop, visored and armoured, leapt out and sprinted across.

Angus stood up, blood-drenched from head to foot, knife in hand, arms wrapped awkwardly around the two ice-buckets, from which the victims' hair and foreheads grotesquely protruded.

The copper halted in the doorway, taking in the scene in about a second.

"Well done, mate," he said. He reached out for the buckets. "Quick thinking. Now let's get these people to hospital."

Monstrous, sticky with blood, Angus crossed the street and stood in the alleyway at a barrier of black-and-yellow crime-scene tape. Backtracking the darts' trajectory had been the work of moments for the second cop out of the VTOL: even minutes after the attack, the lines in the smart soot had glowed like vapour trails in any enhanced gaze. An investigator in an isolation suit lifted the crossbow with gloved reverent hands. Cat-sized sniffing devices stalked about, extending sensors and sampling-pads.

"What's with the bicycle wheels?" Angus asked, pointing.

"Surplus to requirements," the investigator said, standing up, holding the crossbow. She turned it over and around. "Collapsible bike, pre-grown tubular wood, synthetic. See, the handlebars form the bow, the crossbar the stock, the saddle the shoulder piece, the chain and pedal the winding mechanism, and the brake cable is the string. The darts were stashed inside one of the pieces."

"Seen that trick before?"

"Yeah, it's a hunting model."

"People go hunting on bicycles?"

"It's a sport." She laughed. "Offended any hunters lately?"

Angus wished he could see her face. He liked her voice.

"I offend a lot of people."

The investigator's head tilted. "Oh. So you do. Lord Valtos, huh?"

"Just call me—" He remembered what had happened to the last person he'd said that to, then decided not to be superstitious. "Just call me Angus. Angus Cameron."

"Whatever." She pulled off her hood and shook out her hair. "Fuck." She looked disgustedly at the cat things. "No traces. No surprise. Probably a spray job. You know, plastic skin? Even distorts the smart dust readings and street cam footage."

"You can do that?"

"Sure. It's expensive." She gave him a look. "I guess you're worth it."

Angus shrugged. "I'm rich, but my enemies are richer."

"So you're in deep shit."

"Only if they're smarter as well as richer, which I doubt."

"If you're smart, you'll not walk back to the hotel."

He took the hint, and the lift. They shrouded him in plastic for it, so the blood wouldn't get on the seats.

The reaction caught up with Angus as soon as the hotel room door closed behind him. He rushed to the bathroom and vomited. Shaking, he stripped off. As he emptied his pockets before throwing the clothes in the basket he found he'd picked up Glenda's lighter and cigarette pack. He put them to one side and showered. Afterwards he sat in a bathrobe on the balcony, sipping malt on an empty stomach and chain-smoking Glenda's remaining cigarettes. She wouldn't be needing these for a few months. By then she might not even want them—the hospital would no doubt throw in a fix for her addiction, at least on the physical level, as it regrew her body and repaired her brain. Angus's earlier celebratory cigarillo had left him with a craving, and for the moment he indulged it. He'd take something to cure it in the morning.

When he felt steady enough, he closed his eyes and looked at the news. He found himself a prominent item on it. Spokespersons for various Green and Aboriginal coalitions had already disclaimed responsibility and deplored the attempt on his life. At this moment a sheepish representative of a nuclear waste handling company was in the studio, making a like disavowal. Angus smiled. He didn't think any of these were responsible—they'd have done a better job—but it pleased him to have his major opponents on the back foot. The potential benefit from that almost outweighed the annoyance of finding himself on the news at all.

The assassination attempt puzzled him. All the enemies he could think of—the list was long—would have sent a team to kill him, if they'd wanted to do something so drastic and potentially counterproductive. It seemed to him possible that the assassin had acted alone. That troubled him. Angus had always held that lone assassins were far more dangerous and prevalent than conspiracies.

He reviewed the bios linked to as shallow background for the news items about him. Most of them got the basic facts of his life right: from his childhood early in the century on a wind farm and experimental Green community in the Western Isles, through his academically mediocre but socially brilliant student years, when the networks and connections he'd established soon enabled his deals and ventures in the succession of technological booms that had kept the bubble economy expanding by fits and starts through seven decades: carbon capture, synthetic biology, microsatellites, fusion, smart dust, anti-ageing, rejuve, augments . . . and so on, up to his current interest in geo-engineering. Always in before the boom, out before the bust, he'd even ventured into politics via a questionably bestowed peerage just in time for the packed self-abolition of the Lords and to emerge with some quite unearned credit for the Reform. The descriptions ranged from "visionary social entrepreneur" and "daring venture capitalist" to "serial confidence trickster" and "brazen charlatan." There was truth in all of them. He'd burned a lot of fortunes in his time, while adding to his own. The list of people who might hold a private grudge against him was longer than the list of his public enemies.

Speaking of which, he had a conference to go to in the morning. He stubbed out the last of Glenda's cigarettes and went to bed.

The assassin woke at dawn on Manly Beach. He'd slept under a monofilament weave blanket, in a hollow where the sand met the scrub. He wore nothing but a watch and swimming trunks. He stood up, stretched, scrunched the blanket into the trunks' pocket, and went for a swim. No one was about.

Shoulder-deep in the sea, the assassin removed his trunks and watch, clutching them in one hand while rubbing his skin and hair all over with the other. He put them back on when he was sure that every remaining trace of the synthetic skin would be gone. Most of it, almost every scrap, had been dissolved as soon as he'd keyed a sequence on his palm after his failed attempt, just before he'd made his way, with a new appearance (his own) and chemical spoor, through various pre-chosen alleys and doorways and then sharp left on the next street, up to Kings Cross, and on to the train to Manly. But you couldn't make too certain.

Satisfied at last, he swam back to the still deserted beach and began pacing along it, following a GPS reading that had sometime during the night been relayed to his watch. The square metre of sand it led him to showed no trace that anything might be buried there. Which was as it should be—the arrangement for payment had been made well in advance. He'd been assured that he'd be paid whether or not he succeeded in killing the target. A kill would be a bonus, but—medical technology being what it was—he could hardly be expected to guarantee it. A credible near-miss was almost as acceptable.

He began to dig with his hands. About forty centimetres down his fingertips brushed something hard and metallic.

He wasn't to know it was a landmine, and he didn't.

One of the nuclear power companies sent an armoured limo to pick Angus up after breakfast—a courtesy, the accompanying ping claimed. He sneered at the transparency of the gesture, and accepted the ride. At least it shielded him from the barracking of the sizeable crowd (with a far larger virtual flash-mob in spectral support) in front of the Hilton Conference Centre. He was pleased to note, just before the limo whirred down the ramp to the underground car park (which gave him a moment of dread, not entirely irrational) that the greatest outrage seemed to have been aroused by the title of the conference, his own suggestion at that: "Greening Australia."

Angus stepped out of the lift and into the main hall. A chandelier the size of a small spacecraft. Acres of carpet, on which armies of seats besieged a stage. Tables of drinks and nibbles along the sides. The smell of coffee and fruit juice. Hundreds of delegates milling around. To his embarrassment, his arrival was greeted with a ripple of applause. He waved both arms in front of his face, smiled self-deprecatingly, and turned to the paper plates and the fruit on sticks.

Someone made a beeline for him.

"Morning, Valtos."

Angus turned, switching his paper coffee cup to the paper plate and sticking out his right hand. Jan Maartens, tall and blond. The EU's man on the scene. Biotech and enviro portfolio. The European Commission and Parliament had publicly deplored Greening Australia, though they couldn't do much to stop it.

"Hello, Commissioner." They shook.

Formalities over, Maartens cracked open a grin. "So how are you, you old villain?"

"The hero of the hour, I gather."

"Modest as always, Angus. There's already a rumour the *attentat* was a setup for the sympathy vote."

"Is there indeed?" Angus chuckled. "I wish I'd thought of that. Regretfully, no."

Maartens' lips compressed. "I know, I know. In all seriousness . . . my sympathy, of course. It must have been a most traumatic experience."

"It was," Angus said. "A great deal worse for the victims, mind you."

"Indeed." Maartens looked grave. "Anything we can do . . ."

"Thanks."

A bell chimed for the opening session.

"Well . . ." Maartens glanced down at his delegate pack.

"Yes . . . catch you later, Jan."

Angus watched the Belgian out of sight, frowning, then took a seat near the back and close to the aisle. The conference chair, Professor Chang, strolled onstage and waved her hand. To a roar of applause and some boos the screen behind her flared into a display of the Greening Australia logo, then morphed to a sequence of pixel-perfect views of the scheme: a translucent carbon-fibre barrier, tens of kilometres high, hundreds of kilometres long, that would provide Australia with a substitute for its missing mountain-range and bring rainfall to the interior. On the one hand, it was modest: it would use no materials not already successfully deployed in the space elevators, and would cost far less. Birds would fly through it almost as easily as butting through a cobweb. On the other hand, it was the most insanely ambitious scheme of geo-engineering yet tried: changing the face of an entire continent.

Decades ago, Angus had got in early in a project to exploit the stability and aridity of Australia's heart by making it the nuclear-waste-storage centre of the world. The flak from that had been nothing to the outcry over this. As the morning went on, Angus paid little attention to the presentations and debates. He'd heard and seen them all before. His very presence here was enough to influence the discussion, to get smart money sniffing around, bright young minds wondering. Instead, he sat back, closed his eyes, watched market reactions, and worried about a few things.

The first was Maartens' solicitude. Something in the Commissioner's manner hadn't been quite right—a little too close in some ways, a little too distant and impersonal in others. Angus ran analyses in his head of the sweat-slick in the handshake, the modulations of the voice, the saccades of his gaze. Here, augmentation confirmed intuition: the man was very uneasy about something, perhaps guilty.

Hah!

The next worries were the unsubstantiated unease he'd felt just before his sister's call, and the content of that call. It would have been nice, in a way, to attribute the anxiety to some premonition: of the unusual and worrying call, or of the assassination attempt. But Angus was firm in his conviction of one-way causality. Nor could he blame it on some free-floating anxiety: his psychiatric ware was up to date, and its scans mirrored, second by second, an untroubled soul.

Had it been something he'd seen in the market, but had grasped the significance of only subconsciously? Had he made the mistake that could be fatal to a trader: suppressed a niggle?

He rolled back the displays to the previous afternoon, and re-examined them. There it was. Hard to spot, but there in the figures. Someone big was going long on wheat. A dozen hedge funds had placed multiple two-year trades on oil, uranium, and military equipment. Biotech was up. A tiny minority of well-placed ears had listened to voices prophesying war. The Warm War, turning hot at last.

Angus thought about what Catriona had told him, about the undocumented, unannounced mitochondrial module in the EU's next genetic upgrade. An immunity to some biological weapon? But if the EU was planning a first strike—on Japan, the Domain, some other part of the Former United States, Brazil, it didn't matter at this point—they would need food security. And food security, surely, would be enhanced if Greening Australia went ahead.

So why was Commissioner Maartens now on stage, repeating the EU's standard line against the scheme? Unless . . . unless that was merely the line they had to take in public, and they really wanted the conference to endorse the scheme. And what better way to secretly support that than to manoeuvre its most implacable opponents into the awkward position of having to disown an assassination attempt on its most vociferous proponent? An attempt that, whether it succeeded or failed, would win Angus what Maartens had—in a double or triple bluff—called the sympathy vote.

Angus's racing suspicions were interrupted by a ringing in his ear. He flicked his earlobe. "A moment, please," he said. He stood up, stepped apologetically past the delegate between him and the aisle, and turned away to face the wall.

"Yes?"

It was the investigator who'd spoken to him last night. She was standing on a beach, near the edge of a crater in the sand with a bloody mess around it.

"We think we may have found your man," she said.

"I believe I can say the same," said Angus.

"What?"

"You'll see. Send a couple of plainclothes in to the Hilton Centre, discreetly. Ask them to ping me when they're in place. I'll take it from there."

As he turned back to face across the crowd to the stage he saw that Maartens had sat down, and that Professor Chang was looking along the rows of seats as if searching for someone. Her gaze alighted on him, and she smiled.

"Lord Valtos?" she said. "I know you're not on the speakers' list, but I see you're on your feet, and I'm sure we'd all be interested to hear what you have to say in response to the Commissioner's so strongly stated points."

Angus bowed from the waist. "Thank you, Madame Chair," he said. He cleared his throat, waiting to make sure that his voice was synched to the amps. He zoomed his eyes, fixing on Maartens, swept the crowd of turned heads with an out-of-focus gaze and his best smile, then faced the stage.

"Thank you," he said again. "Well, my response will be brief. I fully agree with every word the esteemed Commissioner has said."

A jolt went through Maartens like an electric shock. It lasted only a moment, and he'd covered his surprise even before the crowd had registered its own reaction with a hiss of indrawn breath. If Angus hadn't been looking at Maartens in close-up he'd have missed it himself. He returned to his seat and waited for the police to make contact. It didn't take them more than about five minutes.

Just time enough for him to go short on shares in Syn Bio.

Laika's Ghost

KARL SCHROEDER

Karl Schroeder was born into a Mennonite community in Manitoba, Canada, in 1962. He started writing at age fourteen, following in the footsteps of A. E. van Vogt, who came from the same Mennonite community. He moved to Toronto in 1986 and became a founding member of SF Canada (he was president from 1996–97). He sold early stories to Canadian magazines, and his first novel, The Claus Effect *(with David Nickle) appeared in 1997. His first solo novel,* Ventus, *was published in 2000, and was followed by* Permanence *and* Lady of Mazes, *and then by his acclaimed Virga series of science fiction novels (*Sun of Suns, Queen of Candesce, Pirate Sun, *and* The Sunless Countries*). His short fiction has been collected in* The Engine of Recall. *He also collaborated with Cory Doctorow on* The Complete Idiot's Guide to Writing Science Fiction. *His most recent book is* Ashes of Candesce, *a new Virga novel. Schroeder lives in East Toronto with his wife and daughter.*

Here, in a sequel to his earlier "The Dragon of Pripyat," he takes us to a desolate future Russia haunted by ghosts of the Soviet past, where a game is being played for the highest stakes of all.

The flight had been bumpy; the landing was equally so, to the point where Gennady was sure the old Tupolev would blow a tire. Yet his seatmate hadn't even shifted position in two hours. That was fine with Gennady, who had spent the whole trip trying to pretend he wasn't there at all.

The young American had been a bit more active during the flight across the Atlantic: at least, his eyes had been open and Gennady could see colored lights flickering across them from his augmented reality glasses. But he had exchanged less than twenty words with Gennady since they'd left Washington.

In short, he'd been the ideal traveling companion.

The other four passengers were stretching and groaning. Gennady poked Ambrose in the side and said, "Wake up. Welcome to the ninth biggest country in the world."

Ambrose snorted and sat up. "Brazil?" he said hopefully. Then he looked out his window. "What the hell?"

The little municipal airport had a single gate, which as the only plane on the field, they were taxiing up to uncontested. Over the entrance to the single-story building was the word "Степногорск." "Welcome to Stepnogorsk," said Gennady as he stood to retrieve his luggage from the overhead rack. He traveled light by habit. Ambrose, he gathered, had done so from necessity.

"Stepnogorsk . . . ?" Ambrose shambled after him, a mass of wrinkled clothing leavened with old sweat.

"Secret Soviet town," Ambrose mumbled as they reached the plane's hatch and a burst of hot dry air lifted his hair. "Population sixty thousand," he added as he put his left foot on the metal steps. Halfway down he said, "Manufactured anthrax bombs in the cold war!" And as he set foot on the tarmac he finished with, "Where the hell is Kazakhstan? . . . Oh."

"Bigger than Western Europe," said Gennady. "Ever heard of it?"

"Of course I've *heard* of it," said the youth testily—but Gennady could see from how he kept his eyes fixed in front of him that he was still frantically reading about the town from some Web site or other. The wan August sunlight revealed him to be taller than Gennady, pale, with stringy hair, and everything about him soft—a sculpture done in rounded corners. He had a wide face, though; he might pass for Russian. Gennady clapped him on the shoulder. "Let me do the talking," he said as they dragged themselves across the blistering tarmac to the terminal building.

"So," said Ambrose, scratching his neck. "Why are we here?"

"You're here because you're with me. And you needed to disappear, but that doesn't mean I stop working."

Gennady glanced around. The landscape here should look a lot like home, which was only a day's drive to the west—and here indeed was that vast sky he remembered from Ukraine. After that first glance, though, he did a double-take. The dry prairie air normally smelled of dust and grass at this time of year, and there should have been yellow grass from here to the flat horizon—but instead the land seemed blasted, with large patches of bare soil showing. There was only stubble where there should have been grass. It looked more like Australia than Asia. Even the trees ringing the airport were dead, just gray skeletons clutching the air.

He thought about climate change as they walked through the concrete-floored terminal; since they'd cleared customs in Amsterdam, the bored-looking clerks here just waved them through. "Hang on," said Ambrose as he tried to keep up with Gennady's impatient stride. "I came to you guys for asylum. Doesn't that mean you put me up somewhere, some hotel, you know, away from the action?"

"You can't get any farther from the action than this." They emerged onto a boulevard that had grass, though it hadn't been watered or cut in a long while; the civilized lawn merged imperceptibly with the wild prairie. There was nothing visible from here to the horizon, except in one direction where a cluster of listless windmills jutted above some low trees.

A single taxicab was sitting at the crumbled curb.

"Oh, man," said Ambrose.

Gennady had to smile. "You were expecting some Black Sea resort, weren't you?" He slipped into the taxi, which stank of hot vinyl and motor oil. "Any car rental agency," he said to the driver in Russian. "It's not like you're some cold war defector," he continued to Ambrose in English. "Your benefactor is the U.N. And they don't have much money."

"So you're what—putting me up in a *motel* in *Kazakhstan*?" Ambrose struggled to put his outrage into words. "What I saw could—"

"What?" They pulled away from the curb and became the only car on a cracked blacktop road leading into town.

"Can't tell you," mumbled Ambrose, suddenly looking shifty. "I was told not to tell *you* anything."

Gennady swore in Ukrainian and looked away. They drove in silence for a while, until Ambrose said, "So why are *you* here, then? Did you piss somebody off?"

Gennady smothered the urge to push Ambrose out of the cab. "Can't tell you," he said curtly.

"Does it involve SNOPB?" Ambrose pronounced it "snop-bee."

Gennady would have been startled had he not known Ambrose was connected to the net via his glasses. "You show me yours, I'll show you mine," he said. Ambrose snorted in contempt.

They didn't speak for the rest of the drive.

"Let me get this straight," said Gennady later that evening. "He says he's being chased by Russian agents, NASA—*and* Google?"

On the other end of the line, Eleanor Frankl sighed. "I'm sorry we dumped him on you at the airport," said the New York director of the International Atomic Energy Agency. She was Gennady's boss for this new and—so far—annoyingly vague contract. "There just wasn't time to explain why we were sending him with you to Kazakhstan," she added.

"So explain now." He was pacing in the grass in front of the best hotel his IAEA stipend could afford. It was evening and the crickets were waking up; to the west, fantastically huge clouds had piled up, their tops still lit golden as the rest of the sky faded into mauve. It was cooling off already.

"Right . . . Well, first of all, it seems he really is being chased by the Russians, but not by the country. It's the *Soviet Union Online* that's after him. And the only place their IP addresses are blocked is inside the geographical territories of the Russian and Kazakhstani Republics."

"So, let me get this straight," said Gennady heavily. "Poor Ambrose is being chased by Soviet agents. He ran to the U.N. rather than the FBI, and to keep him safe you decided to transport him to the one place in the world that is free of Soviet influence. Which is Russia."

"Exactly," said Frankl brightly. "And you're escorting him because your contract is taking you there anyway. No other reason."

"No, no, it's fine. Just tell me what the hell I'm supposed to be looking for at SNOPB. The place was a God-damned anthrax factory. I'm a radiation specialist."

He heard Frankl take a deep breath, and then she said, "Two years ago, an unknown person or persons hacked into a Los Alamos server and stole the formula for an experimental metastable explosive. Now we have a paper trail and e-mails that have convinced us that a metastable bomb is being built. You know what this means?"

Gennady leaned against the wall of the hotel, suddenly feeling sick. "The genie is finally out of the bottle."

"If it's true, Gennady, then everything we've worked for has come to naught. Because as of now, anybody in the world who wants a nuclear bomb can make one."

He didn't know what to say, so he just stared out at the steppe, thinking about a world where hydrogen bombs were as easy to get as TNT. His whole life's work would be rendered pointless—and all arms treaties, the painstaking work of generations to put the nuclear nightmare back in its bottle. The nuclear threat had been containable when it was limited to governments and terrorists—but now, the threat was from *everybody* . . .

Eleanor's distant voice snapped him back to attention. "Here's the thing, Gennady: we don't know very much about this group that's building the metastable weapon. By luck we've managed to decrypt a few e-mails from one party, so we know a tiny bit—a minimal bit—about the design of the bomb. It seems to be based on one of the biggest of the weapons ever tested at Semipalatinsk—its code name was *the Tsarina*."

"The Tsarina?" Gennady whistled softly. "That was a major, major test. Underground, done in 1968. Ten megatonnes—lifted the whole prairie two meters and dropped it. Killed about a thousand cattle from the ground shock. Scared the hell out of the Americans, too."

"Yes, and we've discovered that some of the Tsarina's components were made at the Stepnogorsk Scientific Experimental and Production Base. In Building 242."

"But SNOPB was a biological facility, not nuclear. How can this possibly be connected?"

"We don't know how, yet. Listen, Gennady, I know it's a thin lead. After you're done at the SNOPB, I want you to drive out to Semipalatinsk and investigate the Tsarina site."

"Hmmph." Part of Gennady was deeply annoyed. Part was relieved that he wouldn't be dealing with any IAEA or Russian nuclear staff in the near future. Truth to tell, stalking around the Kazaki grasslands was a lot more appealing than dealing with the political shit-storm that would hit when this all went public.

But speaking of people . . . He glanced up at the hotel's one lighted window. With a grimace he pocketed his augmented reality glasses and went up to the room.

Ambrose was sprawled on one of the narrow beds. He had the TV on and was watching a Siberian ski-adventure infomercial. "Well?" he said as Gennady sat on the other bed and dragged his shoes off.

"Tour of secret Soviet anthrax factory. Tomorrow, after Egg McMuffins."

"Yay," said Ambrose with apparent feeling. "Do I get to wear a hazmat suit?"

"Not this time." Gennady lay back, then saw that Ambrose was staring at him with an alarmed look on his face. "Is fine," he said, waggling one hand at the boy. "Only one underground bunker we're interested in, and they probably never used it. The place never went into full production, you know."

"Meaning it only made a few hundred pounds of anthrax per day instead of the full ton it was designed for! I should feel reassured?"

Gennady stared at the uneven ceiling. "Is an adventure." He must be tired, his English was slipping.

"This sucks." Ambrose crossed his arms and glowered at the TV.

Gennady thought for a while. "So what did you do to piss off Google so much? Drive the rover off a cliff?" Ambrose didn't answer, and Gennady sat up. "You found something. On Mars."

"No, that's ridiculous," said Ambrose. "That's not it at all."

"Huh." Gennady lay down again. "Still, I think I'd enjoy it. Even if it wasn't in real time . . . driving on Mars. That would be cool."

"That sucked too."

"Really? I would have thought it would be fun, seeing all those places emerge from low-res satellite into full hi-res three-d."

But Ambrose shook his head. "That's not how it worked. That's the point. I couldn't believe my luck when I won the contest, you know? I thought it'd be like being the first man on Mars, only I wouldn't have to leave my living room. But the whole point of the rover was to go into terrain that hadn't been photographed from the ground before. And with the time-delay on signals to Mars, I wasn't steering it in real time. I'd drive in fast-forward mode over low-res pink hills that looked worse than a forty-year-old video game, then upload the drive sequence and log off. The rover'd get the commands twenty minutes later and drive overnight, then download the results. By that time it was the next day and I had to enter the next path. Rarely had time to even look at where we'd actually gone the day before."

Gennady considered. "A bit disappointing. But still—more than most people ever get."

"More than anyone else will ever get." Ambrose scowled. "That's what was so awful about it. You wouldn't understand."

"Oh?" Gennady arched an eyebrow. "We who grew up in the old Soviet Union know a little about disappointment."

Ambrose looked mightily uncomfortable. "I grew up in Washington. Capital of the world! But my dad went from job to job, we were pretty poor. So every day I could see what you *could* have, you know, the Capital dome, the Mall, all that power and glory . . . what *they* could have—but not me. Never me. So I used to imagine a future where there was a whole new world where I could be . . ."

"Important?"

He shrugged. "Something like that. NASA used to tell us they were just about to go to Mars, any day now, and I wanted that. I dreamed about homesteading on Mars." He looked defensive; but Gennady understood the romance of it. He just nodded.

"Then when I was twelve the Pakistani-Indian war happened and they blew up each other's satellites. All that debris from the explosions is going to be up there for centuries! You can't get a manned spacecraft through that cloud, it's like shrapnel. Hell, they haven't even cleared low Earth orbit to restart the orbital tourist industry. I'll never get to *really* go there! None of us will. We're never gettin' off this sinkhole."

Gennady scowled at the ceiling. "I hope you're wrong."

"Welcome to the life of the last man to drive on Mars." Ambrose dragged the tufted covers back from the bed. "Instead of space, I get a hotel in Kazakhstan. Now let me sleep. It's about a billion o'clock in the morning, my time."

He was soon snoring, but Gennady's alarm over the prospect of a metastable bomb had him fully awake. He put on his AR glasses and reviewed the terrain around SNOPB, but much of the satellite footage was old and probably out of date. Ambrose was right: nobody was putting up satellites these days if they could help it.

Little had probably changed at the old factory, though, and it was a simple enough place. Planning where to park and learning where Building 242 was hadn't reduced his anxiety at all, so on impulse he switched his view to Mars. The sky changed color—from pure blue to butterscotch—but otherwise, the landscape looked disturbingly similar. There were a lot more rocks on Mars, and the dirt was red, but the emptiness, the slow rolling monotony of the plain and stillness were the same, as if he'd stepped into a photograph. (Well, he actually had, but he knew there would be no more motion in this scene were he there.) He commanded the viewpoint to move, and for a time strolled, alone, in Ambrose's footsteps—or rather, the ruts of Google's rover. Humans had done this in their dreams for thousands of years, yet Ambrose was right—this place was, in the end, no more real than those dreams.

Russia's cosmonauts had still been romantic idols when he was growing up. In photos they had stood with their heads high, minds afire with plans to stride over the hills of the moon and Mars. Gennady pictured them in the years after the Soviet Union's collapse, when they still had jobs, but no budget or destination anymore. Where had their dreams taken them?

The Baikonur spaceport was south of here. Instead of space, in the end they'd also had to settle for a hard bed in Kazakhstan.

In the morning they drove out to the old anthrax site in a rented Tata sedan. The fields around Stepnogorsk looked like they'd been glared at by God, except where bright blue dew-catcher fencing ran in rank after rank across the stubble. "What're those?" asked Ambrose, pointing; this was practically the first thing he'd said since breakfast.

In the rubble-strewn field that had once been SNOPB, several small windmills were twirling atop temporary masts. Below them were some shipping-container sized boxes with big grills in their sides. The site looked healthier than the surrounding prairie; there were actual green trees in the distance. Of course, this area had been wetlands and there'd been a creek running behind SNOPB; maybe it was still here, which was a hopeful sign.

"Headquarters told me that some kind of climate research group is using the site," he told Ambrose as he pulled up and stopped the car. "But it's still public land."

"They built an anthrax factory less than five minutes outside of town?" Ambrose shook his head, whether in wonder or disgust, Gennady couldn't tell. They got out of the car, and Ambrose looked around in obvious disappointment. "Wow, it's gone gone." He seemed stunned by the vastness of the landscape. Only a few foundation walls now stuck up out of the cracked lots where the anthrax factory had once stood, except for where the big box machines sat whirring and humming. They were near where the bunkers had been; so, with a frown of curiosity, Gennady strolled in that direction. Ambrose followed, muttering to himself. ". . . Last update must have been ten years ago." He had his glasses on, so he was probably comparing the current view to what he could see online.

According to Gennady's notes, the bunkers had been grass-covered buildings with two-meter thick walls, designed to withstand a nuclear blast. In the 1960s and 70s they'd contained ranks of cement vats where the anthrax was grown. Those had been cracked and filled in, and the heavy doors removed, but it would have been too much work to fill the bunkers in entirely. He poked his nose into the first in line—Building 241—and saw a flat stretch of water leading into darkness. "Excellent. This job just gets worse. We may be wading."

"But what are you looking for?"

"I—oh." As he rounded the mound of Building 242, a small clutch of hummers and trucks came into view. They'd been invisible from the road. There was still no sign of anybody, so he headed for Bunker 242. As he was walking down the crumbled ramp to the massive doors, he heard the unmistakable sound of a rifle-bolt being slipped. "Better not go in there," somebody said in Russian.

He looked carefully up and to his left. A young woman had come over the top of the mound. She was holding the rifle, and she had it aimed directly at Gennady.

"What are you doing here?" she said. She had a local accent.

"Exploring, is all," said Gennady. "We'd heard of the old anthrax factory, and thought we'd take a look at it. This *is* public land."

She swore, and Gennady heard footsteps behind him. Ambrose looked deeply frightened as two large men—also carrying rifles—emerged from behind a plastic membrane that had been stretched across the bunker's doorway. Both men wore bright yellow fireman's masks, and had air tanks on their backs.

"When are your masters going to believe that we're doing what we say?" said the woman. "Come on." She gestured with her rifle for Gennady and Ambrose to walk down the ramp.

"We're dead, we're dead," whimpered Ambrose. He was shivering.

"If you really must have your proof, then put these on." She nodded to the two men, who stripped off their masks and tanks and handed them to Gennady and Ambrose. They pushed past the plastic membrane and into the bunker.

The place was full of light: a crimson, blood-red radiance that made the sight of what was inside all the more bizarre.

"Oh shit," muttered Ambrose. "It's a grow-op."

The long, low space was filled from floor to ceiling with plants. Surrounded them on tall stands were hundreds of red LED lamp banks. In the lurid light, the plants appeared black. He squinted at the nearest, fully expecting to see a familiar, jagged-leaf profile. Instead—

"Tomatoes?"

"Two facts for you," said the woman, her voice muffled. She'd set down her rifle, and now held up two fingers. "One: we're not stepping on anybody else's toes here. We are *not* competing with you. And two: this bunker is designed to withstand a twenty kilotonne blast. If you think you can muscle your way in here and take it over, you're sadly mistaken."

Gennady finally realized what they'd assumed. "We're not the mafia," he said. "We're just here to inspect the utilities."

She blinked at him, her features owlish behind the yellow frame of the mask. Ambrose rolled his eyes. "Oh God, what did you *say*?"

"American?" Puzzled, she lowered her rifle. In English, she said, "You spoke English."

"Ah," said Ambrose, "well—"

"He did," said Gennady, also in English. "We're not with the mafia, we're arms inspectors. I mean, I am. He's just along for the ride."

"Arms inspectors?" She guffawed, then looked around herself at the stolid Soviet bunker they were standing in. "What, you thought—"

"We didn't think anything. Can I lower my hands now?" She thought about it, then nodded. Gennady rolled his neck and then nodded at the ranked plants. "Nice setup. Tomatoes, soy, and those long tanks contain potatoes? But why in here, when you've got a thousand kilometers of steppe outside to plant this stuff?"

"We can control the atmosphere in here," she said. "That's why the masks: it's a high CO2 environment in here. That's also why I stopped you in the first place; if you'd just strolled right in, you'd have dropped dead from asphyxia.

"This project's part of minus three," she continued. "Have you heard of us?" Both Ambrose and Gennady shook their heads.

"Well, you will." There was pride in her voice. "You see, right now humanity uses the equivalent of three Earth's worth of ecological resources. We're pioneering techniques to reduce that reliance by the same amount."

"Same amount? To *zero* Earths?" He didn't hide the incredulity in his voice.

"Eventually, yes. We steal most of what we need from the Earth in the form of ecosystem services. What we need is to figure out how to run a full-fledged industrial civilization as if there were no ecosystem services available to us at all. To live on Earth," she finished triumphantly, "as if we were living on Mars."

Ambrose jerked in visible surprise.

"That's fascinating," said Gennady. He hadn't been too nervous while they were pointing guns at him—he'd had that happen before, and in such moments his mind became wonderfully sharp—but now that he might actually be forced to have a conversation with these people, he found his mouth going quite dry. "You can tell me all about it after I've finished my measurements."

"You're kidding," she said.

"I'm not kidding at all. Your job may be saving the Earth within the next generation, but mine is saving it this week. And I take it very seriously. I've come here to inspect the original fittings of this building, but it looks like you destroyed them, no?"

"Not at all," she said. "Actually, we used what was here. This bunker's not like the other ones, you know they had these big cement tanks in them. I'd swear this one was set up exactly like this."

"Show me."

For the next half hour they climbed under the hydroponic tables, behind the makeshift junction boxes mounted near the old power shaft, and atop the sturdier lighting racks. Ambrose went outside, and came back to report that the shipping containers they'd seen were sophisticated CO2 scrubbers. The big boxes sucked the gas right out of the atmosphere, and then pumped it through hoses into the bunker.

At last he and the woman climbed down, and Gennady shook his head. "The mystery only deepens," he said.

"I'm sorry we couldn't help you more," she said. "And apologies for pulling a gun on you.—I'm Kyzdygoi," she added, thrusting out her hand for him to shake.

"Uh, that's a . . . pretty name," said Ambrose as he too shook her hand. "What's it mean?"

"It means 'stop giving birth to girls,'" said Kyzdygoi with a straight face. "My parents were old school."

Ambrose opened his mouth and closed it, his grin faltering.

"All right, well, good luck shrinking your Earths," Gennady told her as they strolled to the plastic-sheet-covered doorway.

As they drove back to Stepnogorsk, Ambrose leaned against the Tata's door and looked at Gennady in silence. Finally he said, "You do this for a living?"

"Ah, it's unreliable. A paycheck here, a paycheck there . . ."

"No, really. What's this all about?"

Gennady eyed him. He probably owed the kid an explanation after getting guns drawn on him. "Have you ever heard of metastable explosives?"

"What? No. Wait . . ." He fumbled for his glasses.

"Never mind that." Gennady waved at the glasses. "Metastables are basically super-powerful chemical explosives. They're my new nightmare."

Ambrose jerked a thumb back at SNOPB. "I thought you were looking for germs."

"This isn't about germs, it's about hydrogen bombs." Ambrose looked blank. "A hydrogen bomb is a fusion device that's triggered by high compression and high temperature. Up til now, the only thing that could generate those kinds of conditions was an atomic bomb—a *plutonium* bomb, understand? Plutonium is really hard to refine, and it creates terrible fallout even if you only use a little of it as your fusion trigger."

"So?"

"So, metastable explosives are powerful enough to trigger hydrogen fusion without the plutonium. They completely sever the connection between nuclear weapons and nuclear industry, which means that once they exist, we good guys totally lose our ability to tell who has the bomb and who doesn't. *Anybody* who can get metastables and some tritium gas can build a hydrogen bomb, even some disgruntled loner in his garage.

"And somebody *is* building one."

Stepnogorsk was fast approaching. The town was mostly a collection of Soviet-era apartment blocks with broad prairie visible past them. Gennady swung them around a corner and they drove through Microdistrict 2 and past the disused Palace of Culture. Up ahead was their hotel . . . surrounded by the flashing lights of emergency vehicles.

"Oh," said Gennady. "A fire?"

"Pull over. Pull over!" Ambrose braced his hands against the Tata's low ceiling. Gennady shot him a look, but did as he'd asked.

"Shit. They've found me."

"Who? Those are police cars. I've been with you every minute since we got here, there's no way you could have gotten into any trouble." Gennady shook his head. "No, if it's anything to do with us, it's probably Kyzdygoi's people sending us a message."

"Yeah? Then who are those suits with the cops?"

Gennady thought about it. He could simply walk up to one of the cops and ask, but figured Ambrose would probably have a coronary if he did that.

"Well . . . there is one thing we can try. But it'll cost a lot."

"How much?"

Gennady eyed him. "All right, all right," said Ambrose. "What do we do?"

"You just watch." Gennady put on his glasses and stepped out of the car. As he did, he put through a call to London, where it was still early morning. "Hello? Lisaveta? It's Gennady. Hi! How are you?"

He'd brought a binocular attachment for the glasses, which he sometimes used for reading serial numbers on pipes or barrels from a distance. He clipped this on and began scanning the small knot of men who were standing around outside the hotel's front doors.

"Listen, Lisa, can I ask you to do something for me? I have some faces I need scanned. . . . Not even remotely legal, I'm sure. . . . No, I'm not in trouble! Would I be on the phone to you if I were in trouble? Just—okay. I'm good for it. Here come the images."

He relayed the feed from his glasses to Lisa in her flat in London.

"Who're you talking to?" asked Ambrose.

"Old friend. She got me out of Chernobyl intact when I had a little problem with a dragon—Lisa? Got it? Great. Call me back when you've done the analysis."

He pocketed the glasses and climbed back in the car. "Lisa has Interpol connections, and she's a fantastic hacker. She'll run facial recognition on it and hopefully tell us who those people are."

Ambrose cringed back in his seat. "So what do we do in the meantime?"

"We have lunch. How 'bout that French restaurant we passed? The one with the little Eiffel Tower?"

Despite the clear curbs everywhere, Gennady parked the car at the shopping mall and walked the three blocks to the La France. He didn't tell Ambrose why, but the American would figure it out: the Tata was traceable through its GPS. Luckily La France was open and they settled in for some decent crepes. Gennady had a nice view of a line of trees west of the town boundary. Occasionally a car drove past.

Lisa pinged him as they were settling up. "Gennady? I got some hits for you."

"Really?" He hadn't expected her to turn up anything. Gennady's working assumption was that Ambrose was just being paranoid.

"Nothing off the cops; they must be local," she said. "But one guy—the old man—well, it's daft."

He sighed in disappointment, and Ambrose shot him a look. "Go ahead."

"His name is Alexei Egorov. He's premier of a virtual nation called the Soviet Union Online. They started from this project to digitize all the existing paper records of the Soviet era. Once those were online, Egorov and his people started some deep data-mining to construct a virtual Soviet, and then they started inviting the last die-hard Stalinists—or their kids—to join. It's a virtual country composed of bitter old men who're nostalgic for the purges. Daft."

"Thanks, Lisa. I'll wire you the fee."

He glowered at Ambrose. "Tell me about Soviet Union."

"I'm not supposed to—"

"Oh come on. Who said that? Whoever they are, they're on the far side of the planet right now, they can't help you. They put you with me, but I can't help you either if I don't know what's going on."

Ambrose's lips thinned to a white line. He leaned forward. "It's big," he said.

"Can't be bigger than my mestatables. Tell me: what did you see on Mars?"

Ambrose hesitated. Then he blurted, "A pyramid."

Silence.

"Really, a pyramid," Ambrose insisted. "Big sucker, gray, I think most of it was buried in the permafrost. It was the only thing sticking up for miles. This was on the Northern plains, where there's ice just under the surface. The whole area around it . . . well, it was like a frozen splash, if you know what I mean. Almost a crater."

This was just getting more and more disappointing. "And why is Soviet Union Online after you?"

"Because the pyramid had Russian writing on it. Just four letters, in red: CCCP."

The next silence went on for a while, and was punctuated only by the sound of other diners grumbling about local carbon prices.

"I leaked some photos before Google came after me with their nondisclosure agreements," Ambrose explained. "I guess the Soviets have Internet search-bots constantly searching for certain things, and they picked up on my posts before Google was able to take them down. I got a couple of threatening phone calls from men with thick Slavic accents. Then they tried to kidnap me."

"No!"

Ambrose grimaced. "Well, they weren't very good at it. It was four guys, all of them must have been in their eighties, they tried to bundle me into a black van. I ran away and they just stood there yelling curses at me in Russian. One of them threw his cane at me." He rubbed his ankle.

"And you took them seriously?"

"I did when the FBI showed up and told me I had to pack up and go with them. That's when I ran to the U.N. I didn't believe that 'witness protection' crap the Feds tried to feed me. The U.N. people told me that the Soviets' data-mining is actually really good. They keep turning up embarrassing and incriminating information about what people and governments got up to back in the days of the Cold War. They use what they know to influence people."

"That's bizarre." He thought about it. "Think they bought off the police here?"

"Or somebody. They want to know about the pyramid. But only Google, and the Feds, and I know where it is. And NASA's already patched that part of the Mars panoramas with fake data."

Disappointment had turned to a deep sense of surprise. For Gennady, being surprised usually meant that something awful was about to happen, so he said, "We need to get you out of town."

Ambrose brightened. "I have an idea. Let's go back to SNOPB. I looked up these minus-three people, they're eco-radicals but at least they don't seem to be lunatics."

"Hmmph. You just think Kyzdygoi's 'hot.'" Ambrose grinned and shrugged.

"Okay.—But we're not driving, because the car can be tracked. *You* walk there. It's only a few kilometers. I'll deal with the authorities and these 'Soviets,' and once I've sent them on their way we'll meet up. You've got my number."

Ambrose had evidently never taken a walk in the country before. After Gennady convinced him he would survive it, they parted outside La France, and Gennady watched him walk away, sneakers flapping. He shook his head and strolled back to the Tata.

Five men were waiting for him. Two were policemen, and three wore business attire. One of these was an old, bald man in a faded olive-green suit. He wore augmented reality glasses, and there was a discrete red pin on his lapel in the shape of the old Soviet flag.

Gennady made a show of pushing his own glasses back on his nose and walked forward, hand out. As the cops started to reach for their Tasers, Gennady said, "Mr. Egorov! Gennady Malianov, IAEA. You'll forgive me if I record and upload this conversation to headquarters?" He tapped the frame of his glasses and turned to the other suits. "I didn't catch your names?"

The suits frowned; the policemen hesitated; Egorov, however, put out his hand and Gennady shook it firmly. He could feel the old man's bones shift in his grip, but Egorov didn't grimace. Instead he said, "Where's your companion?"

"You mean that American? No idea. We shared a hotel room because it was cheaper, but then we parted ways this morning."

Egorov took his hand back, and pressed his bruised knuckles against his hip. "You've no idea where he is?"

"None."

"What're *you* doing here?" asked one of the cops.

"Inspecting SNOPB," he said. Gennady didn't have to fake his confidence here; he felt well armored by his affiliation to Frankl's people. "My credentials are online, if there's some sort of issue here?"

"No issue," muttered Egorov. He turned away, and as he did a discrete icon lit up in the corner of Gennady's heads-up display. Egorov had sent him a text message.

He hadn't been massaging his hand on his flank; he'd been texting through his pants. Gennady had left the server in his glasses open, so it would have been easy for Egorov to ping it and find his address.

In among all the other odd occurrences of the past couple of days, this one didn't stand out. But as Gennady watched Egorov and his policemen retreat, he realized that his assumption that Egorov had been in charge might be wrong. Who were those other two suits?

He waited for Egorov's party to drive away, then got in the Tata and opened the email.

It said, *Mt tnght Pavin Inn, rstrnt wshrm. Cm aln.*

Gennady puzzled over those last two words for a while. Then he got it. "Come alone!" *Ah.* He should have known.

Shaking his head, he pulled out of the lot and headed back to the hotel to check out. After loading his bag, and Ambrose's, into the Tata, he hit the road back to SNOPB. Nobody followed him, but that meant nothing since they could track him through the car's transponder if they wanted. It hardly mattered; he was supposed to be inspecting the old anthrax factory, so where else would he be going?

Ambrose'd had enough time to get to SNOPB by now, but Gennady kept one eye on the fields next to the road just in case. He saw nobody, and fully expected to find the American waiting outside Building 242 as he pulled up.

As he stepped out of the Tata he nearly twisted his ankle in a deep rut. There were fresh tire tracks and shattered bits of old asphalt all over the place; he was sure he hadn't seen them this morning.

"Hello?" He walked down the ramp into the sudden dark of the bunker. Did he have the right building? It was completely dark here.

Wires drooled from overhead conduits; hydroponic trays lay jumbled in the corner, and strange-smelling liquids were pooled on the floor. -3 had pulled out, and in a hurry.

He cursed, but suppressed an urge to run back to the car. He had no idea where they'd gone, and they had a head start on him. The main question was, had they left before or after Ambrose showed up?

The answer lay in the yellow grass near where -3's vehicles had been parked that morning. Gennady knelt down and picked up a familiar pair of augmented reality glasses. Ambrose would not have left these behind willingly.

Gennady swore, and now he did run to the Tata.

The restaurant at the Pavin Inn was made up to look like the interiors of a row of yurts. This gave diners some privacy as most of them had private little chambers under wood-ribbed ceilings; it also broke up the eyelines to the place's front door, making it easy for Gennady to slip past the two men in suits who'd been with Egorov in the parking lot. He entered the men's room to find Egorov pacing in front of the urinal trough.

"What's this all about?" demanded Gennady—but Egorov made a shushing motion and grabbed a trash can. As he upended it under the bathroom's narrow window, he said, "First you must get me out of here!"

"What? Why?"

Egorov tried to climb onto the upended can, but his knees and hips weren't flexible enough. Finally Gennady relented and went to help him. As he boosted the old comrade, Egorov said, "I am a prisoner of these people! They work for the *Americans.*" He practically spat the name. He perched precariously on the can and began tugging at the latch to the window. "They have seized our database! All the Soviet records . . . including what we know about the Tsarina."

Gennady coughed. Then he said, "I'll bring the car around."

He helped Egorov through the window then, after making sure no one was looking, left through the hotel's front door. The unmistakable silhouette of Egorov was limping into the parking lot. Gennady followed him and, as he unlocked the Tata, he said, "I've disabled the GPS tracking in this car. It's a rental; I'm going to drop it off in Semey, which is six hundred kilometers from here. Are you sure you're up to a drive like that?"

The old man's eyes glinted under yellow streetlight. "Never thought I'd get a chance to see the steppes again. Let's go!"

Gennady felt a ridiculous surge of adrenaline as they bumped out of the parking lot. Two cars were on the road, and endless blackness swallowed the landscape beyond the edge of town. It was a simple matter to swing onto the highway and leave Stepnogorsk behind—but it felt like a car chase.

"Ha ha!" Egorov craned his neck to look back at the dwindling town lights. "Semey, eh? You're going to Semipalatinsk, aren't you?"

"To look at the Tsarina site, yes. Whose side does that put me on?"

"Sides?" Egorov crossed his arms and glared out the windshield. "I don't know about sides."

"It was an honest question."

"I believe you. But I don't *know.* Except for *them,*" he added, jabbing a thumb back at the town. "I know they're bad guys."

"Why? And why are they interested in Ambrose?"

"Same reason we are. Because of what he saw."

Gennady took a deep breath. "Okay. Why don't you just tell me what you know? And I'll do the same?"

"Yes, all right." The utter blackness of the nighttime steppe had swallowed them; all that was visible was the double-cone of roadway visible in the car's headlamps. It barely changed, moment to moment, giving the drive a timelessness Gennady would, under other circumstances, have quite enjoyed.

"We data-mine records from the Soviet era," began Egorov. "To find out what really went on. It's lucrative business, and it supports the Union of Soviet Socialist Republics Online." He tapped his glasses.

"Well, a few weeks ago, we got a request for some of the old data—from the Americans. Two requests, actually, a day apart: one from the search engine company, and the other from the government. We were naturally curious, so we didn't say no; but we did a little digging into the data ourselves.—That is, we'd started to, when those young, grim men burst into our offices and confiscated the server. And the backup."

Gennady looked askance at him. "Really? Where was this?"

"Um. Seattle. That's where the CCCOP is based—only because we've been banned in the old country! Russia's run by robber barons today, they have no regard for the glory of—"

"Yes yes. Did you find out what they were looking for?"

"Yes—which is how I ended up with these travel companions you saw. They are in the pay of the American CIA."

"Yes, but why? What does this have to do with the Tsarina?"

"I was hoping you could tell me. All we found was appropriations for strange things that should never have had anything to do with a nuclear test. Before the Tsarina was set off, there was about a year of heavy construction at the site. Sometimes, you know, they built fake towns to blow them up and examine the blast damage. That's what I thought at first; they ordered thousands of tonnes of concrete, rebar and asbestos, that sort of thing. But if you look at the records after the test, there's no sign of where any of that material *went.*"

"They ordered some sort of agricultural crop from SNOPB," Gennady ventured. Egorov nodded.

"None of the discrepancies would ever have been noticed if not for your friend and whatever it is he found. What was it, anyway?"

A strange suspicion had begun to form in Gennady's mind, but it was so unlikely that he shook his head. "I want to look at the Tsarina site," he said. "Maybe that'll tell us."

Egorov was obviously unsatisfied with that answer, but he said nothing, merely muttering and trying to get himself comfortable in the Tata's bucket seat. After a while, just as the hum of the dark highway was starting to hypnotize Gennady, Egorov said, "It's all gone to Hell, you know."

"Hmm?"

"Russia. It was hard in the old days, but at least we had our pride." He turned to look out the black window. "After 1990, all the life just went out of the place. Lower birth-rate, men drinking themselves to death by the age of forty . . . no ambition, no hope. A lost land."

"You left?"

"Physically, yes." Egorov darted a look at Gennady. "You never *leave.* Not a place like this. For many years now, I've struggled with how to bring back Russia's old glory—our sense of *pride*. Yet the best I was ever able to come up with was an online environment. A *game*." He spat the word contemptuously.

Gennady didn't reply, but he knew how Egorov felt. Ukraine had some of the same problems—the listless lack of direction, the loss of confidence . . . It wasn't getting any better here. He thought of the blasted steppes they were passing through, rendered unlivable by global warming. There had been massive forest fires in Siberia this year, and the Gobi desert was expanding north and west, threatening the Kazaks even as the Caspian sea dwindled down to nothing.

He thought of SNOPB. "They're gone," he said, "but they left their trash behind." Toxic, decaying: nuclear submarines heeled over in the waters off of Murmansk, nitrates soaking the soil around the launch pads of Baikonur. The ghosts of old Soviets prowled this dark, in the form of radiation in the groundwater, mutations in the forest, and poisons in the dust clouds that were all too common these days. Gennady had spent his whole adult life cleaning up the mess, and before yesterday he'd been able to tell himself that it was working—that all the worst nightmares were from the past. The metastables had changed that, in one stroke rendering all the old fears laughable in comparison.

"Get some sleep," he told Egorov. "We're going to be driving all night."

"I don't sleep much anymore." But the old man stopped talking, and just stared ahead. He couldn't be visiting his online People's Republic through his glasses, because those IP addresses were blocked here. But maybe he saw it all anyway—the brave young men in their trucks, heading to the Semipalatinsk site to witness a nuclear blast; the rail yards where parts for the giant moon rocket, doomed to explode on the pad, were mustering . . . With his gaze fixed firmly on the past, he seemed the perfect opposite of Ambrose with his American dreams of a new world unburdened by history, whose red dunes marched to a pure and mysterious horizon.

The first living thing in space had been the Russian dog Laika. She had died in orbit—had never come home. If he glanced out at the star-speckled sky, Gennady could almost see her ghost racing eternally through the heavens, beside the dead dream of planetary conquest, of flags planted in alien soil and shining domes on the hills of Mars.

They arrived at the Tsarina site at 4:30: dawn, at this latitude and time of year. The Semipalatinsk Polygon was bare, flat, blasted scrubland: Mars with tufts of dead weed. The irony was that it hadn't been the hundreds of nuclear bombs set off here that had killed the land; even a decade after the Polygon was closed, the low rolling hills had been covered with a rich carpet of waving grass. Instead, it was the savage turn of the climate, completely unpredicted by the KGB and the CIA, that had killed the steppe.

The road into the Polygon was narrow blacktop with no real shoulder, no ditches, and no oncoming traffic—though a set of lights had faded in and out of view in the rearview mirror all through the drive. Gennady would have missed the turnoff to the Tsarina site had his glasses not beeped.

There had been a low wire fence here at one time, but nobody had kept it up. He drove straight over the fallen gate, which was becoming one with the soil, and up a low rise to the crest of the water-filled crater. There he parked and got out.

Egorov climbed out too and stretched cautiously. "Beautiful," he said, gazing into the epic sunrise. "Is it radioactive here?"

"Oh, a little. . . . That's odd."

"What?"

Gennady had looked at the satellite view of the site on the way here; it was clear, standing here in person, that that vertical perspective lied. "The Tsarina was supposed to be an underground test. You usually get some subsidence of the ground in a circle around the test site. And with the big ground shots, you would get a crater, like Lake Chagan," he nodded to the east. "But this . . . this is a *hole*."

Egorov spat into it. "It certainly is." The walls of the Tsarina crater were sheer and went down a good fifty feet to black water. The "crater" wasn't round, either, but square, and it wasn't nearly big enough to be the result of a surface explosion. If he hadn't known it was the artifact of a bomb blast, Gennady would have sworn he was looking at a flooded quarry.

Gennady gathered his equipment and began combing the grass around the site. After a minute he found some twisted chunks of concrete and metal, and knelt down to inspect them.

Egorov came up behind him. "What are you looking for?"

"Serial numbers." He quickly found some old, grayed stenciling on a half-buried tank made of greenish metal. "You'll understand what I'm doing," he said as he pinched the arm of his glasses to take a snapshot. "I'm checking our database . . . Hmpf."

"What is it?" Egorov shifted from foot to foot. He was glancing around, as if afraid they might be interrupted.

"This piece came from the smaller of the installations here. The one the Americans called URDF-3."

"URDF?" Egorov blinked at him.

"Stands for 'Unidentified Research and Development Facility.' The stuff they built there scared the Yankees even more than the H-bomb . . ."

He stood up, frowning, and slowly turned to look at the entire site. "Something's been bothering me," he said as he walked to the very edge of the giant pit.

"What's that?" Egorov was hanging back.

"Ambrose told me he saw a pyramid on Mars. It said CCCP on its side. That was all; so he knew it was Russian, and so did Google and the CIA when they found out about it. And you, too.

"But that's all anybody knew. So who made the connection between the pyramid and the Tsarina?"

Egorov didn't reply. Gennady turned and found that the old man had drawn himself up very straight, and had leveled a small, nasty-looking pistol at him.

"You didn't follow us to Stepnogorsk," said Gennady. "You were already there."

"Take off your glasses," said Egorov. "Carefully, so I can be sure you're not snapping another picture."

As Gennady reached up to comply he felt the soft soil at the lip of the pit start to crumble. "Ah, can we—" It was too late, he toppled backward, arms flailing.

He had an instant's choice: roll down the slope, or jump and hope he'd hit the water. He jumped.

The cold hit him so hard that at first he thought he'd been shot. Swearing and gasping, he surfaced, but when he spotted Egorov's silhouette at the crest of the pit, dove again.

Morning sunlight was just tipping into the water. At first Gennady thought the wall of the pit was casting a dark shadow across the sediment below him. Gradually he realized the truth: there was no bottom to this shaft. At least, none within easy diving distance.

He swam to the opposite side; he couldn't stay down here, he'd freeze. Defeated, he flung himself out of the freezing water onto hard clay that was probably radioactive. Rolling over, he looked up.

Egorov stood on the lip of the pit. Next to him was a young woman with a rifle in her hands.

Gennady sat up. "Shit."

Kyzdygoi slung the rifle over her back, then clambered down the slope to the shore. As she picked her way over to Gennady she said, "How much do you know?"

"Everything," he said between coughs. "I know everything. Where's Ambrose?"

"He's safe," she said. "He'll be fine."

Then she waited, rifle cradled. "You're here," he said reluctantly, "which tells me that -3 was funded by the Soviets. Your job was never to clean up the Earth—it was to design life support and agricultural systems for a Mars colony."

Her mouth twitched, but she didn't laugh. "How could we possibly get to Mars? The sky's a shooting gallery."

". . . And that would be a problem if you were going up there in a dinky little aluminum can, like cosmonauts always did." He stood up, joints creaking from the cold. He was starting to shiver deeply and it was hard to speak past his chattering teeth. "B-but if you rode a c-concrete bunker into orbit, you could ignore the shrapnel c-completely. In fact, that would be the only way you could d-do it."

"Come now. How could something like that ever get off the ground?"

"The same way the Tsarina d-did." He nodded at the dark surface of the flooded shaft. "The Americans had their P-project Orion. The Soviets had a similar program based at URDF-3. Both had discovered that an object could be just a few meters away from a nuclear explosion, and if it was made of the right materials it wouldn't be destroyed—it would be shot away like a bullet from a gun. The Americans designed a spaceship that would drop atomic bombs out the back and ride the explosions to orbit. But the Tsarina wasn't like that . . . it was just one bomb, and a d-deep shaft, and a pyramid-shaped spaceship to ride that explosion. That design's something called a *Verne gun*."

"And who else knows this?"

He hesitated. "N-no one," he admitted. "I didn't know until I saw the shaft just now. The p-pyramid was fitted into the mouth of it, right about where we're s-standing. That's why this doesn't look like any other bomb crater on Earth."

"Let's go," she said, gesturing with the rifle. "You're turning blue."

"Y-you're not going t-to sh-shoot me?"

"There's no need," she said gently. "In a few days, the whole world will know what we've done."

Gennady finished taping aluminum foil to the trailer's window. Taking a pushpin from the corkboard by the door, he carefully pricked a single tiny hole in the foil.

It was night, and crickets were chirping outside. Gennady wasn't tied up—in fact, he was perfectly free to leave—but on his way out the door Egorov had said, "I wouldn't go outside in the next hour or so. After that . . . well, wait for the dust to settle."

They'd driven him about fifty kilometers to the south and into an empty part of the Polygon. When Gennady had asked why this place, Egorov had laughed. "The Soviets set off their bombs here because this was the last empty place on Earth. It's still the last empty place, and that's why we're here."

There was nothing here but the withered steppe, a hundred or so trucks, vans and buses, and the cranes, tanks and pole-sheds of a temporary construction site. —And, towering over the sheds, a gray concrete pyramid.

"A Verne gun fires its cargo into orbit in a single shot," Egorov had told Gennady. "It generates thousands of gravities worth of acceleration—enough to turn you into a smear on the floor. That's why the Soviets couldn't send any people; they hadn't figured out how to set off a controlled sequence of little bombs. The Americans never perfected that either. They didn't have the computational power to do the simulations.

"So they sent everything but the people. *Two hundred eighty thousand tonnes* in one shot, to Mars."

Bulldozers and cranes, fuel tanks, powdered cement, bags of seeds and food, space suits, even a complete, dismantled nuclear reactor: the Tsarina had included everything potential colonists might need on a new world. Its builders knew it had gone up, knew it had gotten to Mars; but they didn't know where it had landed, or whether it had landed intact.

A day after his visit to the Tsarina site, Gennady had sat outside this trailer with Egorov, Kyzdygoi, and a few other officials of the new Soviet. They'd drunk a few beers and talked about the plan. "When our data-mining turned up the Tsarina's manifest, it was like a light from heaven," Egorov had said, his hands opening eloquently in the firelight. "Suddenly we saw what was possible, how to revive our people—all the world's people—around a new hope, after all hope had gone. Something that would combine Apollo and Trinity into one event, and suddenly both would take on the meaning they always needed to have."

Egorov had started a crash program to build an Orion rocket. They couldn't get fissionable materials—Gennady and his people had locked those up tightly and for all time. But the metastables promised a different approach.

"We hoped the Tsarina was on Mars and intact, but we didn't know for sure, until Ambrose leaked his pictures."

The new Tsarina would use a series of small, clean fusion blasts to lift off and, at the far end, to land again. Thanks to Ambrose, they knew where the Tsarina was. It didn't matter that the Americans did too; nobody else had a plan to get there.

"And by the time they get their acts together, we'll have built a city," said Kyzdygoi. She was wide-eyed with the power of the idea. "Because we're not going there two at a time, like Noah in his Ark. We're *all* going." And she swung her arm to indicate the hundreds of campfires burning all around them, where thousands of men, women, and children, hand-picked from among the citizens of the Union of Soviet Socialist Republics Online, waited to amaze the world.

Gennady hunkered down in a little fort he'd built out of seat cushions, and waited.

It was like a camera flash, and a second later there was a second, then a third, and then the whole trailer bounced into the air and everything Gennady hadn't tied down went tumbling. The windows shattered and he landed on cushions and found himself staring across suddenly open air at the immolation of the building site.

The flickering flashes continued, coming from above now. The pyramid was gone, and the cranes and heavy machinery lay tumbled like a child's toys, all burning.

Flash. Flash.

It was really happening.

Flash. Flash. Flash . . .

Gradually, Gennady began to be able to hear again. He came to realize that monstrous thunder was rolling across the steppe, like a god's drumbeat in time with the flashes. It faded, as the flashes faded, until there was nothing but the ringing in his ears, and the orange flicker of flame from the launch site.

He staggered out to find perfect devastation. Once, this must have been a common sight on the steppe; but his Geiger counter barely registered any radiation at all.

—And in that, of course, lay a terrible irony. Egorov and his people had indeed divided history in two, but not in the way they'd imagined.

Gennady ran for the command trailer. He only had a few minutes before the air forces of half a dozen nations descended on this place. The trailer had survived the initial blast, so he scrounged until he found a jerry can full of gasoline, and then he climbed in.

There they were: Egorov's servers. The EMP from the little nukes might have wiped its drives, but Gennady couldn't take the chance. He poured gasoline all over the computers, made a trail back to the door, then as the whole trailer went up behind him, ran to the leaning-but-intact metal shed where the metastables had been processed, and he did the same to it.

That afternoon, as he and Egorov had watched the orderly queue of people waiting to enter the New Tsarina, Gennady had made his final plea. "Your research into metastables," Gennady went on. "I need it. All of it, and the equipment and the backups; anything that might be used to reconstruct what you did."

"What happens to the Earth is no longer our concern," Egorov said with a frown. "Humanity made a mess here. It's not up to us to clean it up."

"But to destroy it all, you only need to be indifferent! And I'm asking, please, however much the world may have disappointed you, don't leave it like this." As he spoke, Gennady scanned the line of people for Ambrose, but couldn't see him. Nobody had said where the young American was.

Egorov had sighed in annoyance, then nodded sharply. "I'll have all the formulae and the equipment gathered together. It's all I have time for, now. You can do what you want with it."

Gennady watched the flames twist into the sky. He was exhausted, and the sky was full of contrails and gathering lights. He hadn't destroyed enough of the evidence; surely, someone would figure out what Egorov's people had done. And then . . . Shoulders slumped under the burden of that knowledge, he stalked into the darkness at the camp's perimeter.'

His rented Tata sat where they'd left it when they first arrived here. After Kyzdygoi had confiscated his glasses at the Tsarina site, she'd put them in the Tata's glove compartment. They were still there.

Before Gennady put them on, he took a last unaided look at the burning campsite. Egorov and his people had escaped, but they'd left Gennady behind to clean up their mess. The metastables would be back. This new nightmare would get out of the bottle eventually, and when it did, the traditional specter of nuclear terrorism would look like a Halloween ghost in comparison. Could even the conquest of another world make up for that?

As the choppers settled in whipping spirals of dust, Gennady rolled up the Tata's window and put on his glasses. The New Tsarina's EMP pulses hadn't killed them—they booted up right away. And, seconds after they did, a little flag told him there was an e-mail waiting for him.

It was from Ambrose, and it read:

> Gennady: Sorry I didn't have time to say goodbye.
> I just wanted to say I was wrong. Anything's possible, even for me.
> P.S. My room's going to have a fantastic view.

Gennady stared bitterly at the words. *Anything's possible . . .*

"For you, maybe," he said as soldiers piled out of the choppers.

"Not me."

The Dala Horse

MICHAEL SWANWICK

Michael Swanwick made his debut in 1980, and in the thirty-one years that have followed he has established himself as one of SF's most prolific and consistently excellent writers at short lengths, as well as one of the premier novelists of his generation. He has won the Theodore Sturgeon Award and the Asimov's Readers' Award poll. In 1991, his novel Stations of the Tide *won him a Nebula Award as well, and in 1995 he won the World Fantasy Award for his story "Radio Waves." He's won the Hugo Award five times between 1999 and 2006 for his stories "The Very Pulse of the Machine," "Scherzo with Tyrannosaur," "The Dog Said Bow Wow," "Slow Life," and "Legions in Time." His other books include the novels* In the Drift, Vacuum Flowers, The Iron Dragon's Daughter, Jack Faust, Bones of the Earth, *and* The Dragons of Babel. *His short fiction has been assembled in* Gravity's Angels, A Geography of Unknown Lands, Slow Dancing Through Time, Moon Dogs, Puck Aleshire's Abecedary, Tales of Old Earth, Cigar-Box Faust and Other Miniatures, Michael Swanwick's Field Guide to the Mesozoic Megafauna, *and* The Periodic Table of Science Fiction. *His most recent books are a massive retrospective collection,* The Best of Michael Swanwick, *and a new novel,* Dancing with Bears. *Swanwick lives in Philadelphia with his wife, Marianne Porter. He has a Web site at www.michaelswanwick.com and maintains a blog at floggingbabel.blogspot.com.*

Here's another SF story that starts out reading like a fairy tale but widens out to reveal itself as a far-future SF story instead, as the young female protagonist finds herself gradually caught up in a war between entities wielding immensely powerful superscience technologies on a ruined postapocalyptic Earth, with her only hope of survival being a seemingly innocuous toy.

Something terrible had happened. Linnéa did not know what it was. But her father had looked pale and worried, and her mother had told her, very fiercely, "Be brave!" and now she had to leave, and it was all the result of that terrible thing.

The three of them lived in a red wooden house with steep black roofs by the edge of the forest. From the window of her attic room, Linnéa could see a small lake silver with ice very far away. The design of the house was unchanged from all the way back in the days of the Coffin People, who buried their kind in beautiful polished boxes with metal fittings like nothing anyone made anymore. Uncle Olaf made a living hunting down their coffin-sites and salvaging the metal from them. He wore a necklace of gold rings he had found, tied together with silver wire.

"Don't go near any roads," her father had said. "Especially the old ones." He'd given her a map. "This will help you find your grandmother's house."

"Mor-Mor?"

"No, Far-Mor. My mother. In Godastor."

Godastor was a small settlement on the other side of the mountain. Linnéa had no idea how to get there. But the map would tell her.

Her mother gave her a little knapsack stuffed with food, and a quick hug. She shoved something deep in the pocket of Linnéa's coat and said, "Now go! Before it comes!"

"Good-bye, Mor and Far," Linnéa had said formally, and bowed.

Then she'd left.

So it was that Linnéa found herself walking up a long, snowy slope, straight up the side of the mountain. It was tiring work, but she was a dutiful little girl. The weather was harsh, but whenever she started getting cold, she just turned up the temperature of her coat. At the top of the slope she came across a path, barely wide enough for one person, and so she followed it onward. It did not occur to her that this might be one of the roads her father had warned her against. She did not wonder at the fact that it was completely bare of snow.

After a while, though, Linnéa began to grow tired. So she took off her knapsack and dropped it in the snow alongside the trail and started to walk away.

"Wait!" the knapsack said. "You've left me behind."

Linnéa stopped. "I'm sorry," she said. "But you're too heavy for me to carry."

"If you can't carry me," said the knapsack, "then I'll have to walk."

So it did.

On she went, followed by the knapsack, until she came to a fork in the trail. One way went upward and the other down. Linnéa looked from one to the other. She had no idea which to take.

"Why don't you get out the map?" her knapsack suggested.

So she did.

Carefully, so as not to tear, the map unfolded. Contour lines squirmed across its surface as it located itself. Blue stream-lines ran downhill. Black roads and stitched red trails went where they would. "We're here," said the map, placing a pinprick light at its center. "Where would you like to go?"

"To Far-Mor," Linnéa said. "She's in Godastor."

"That's a long way. Do you know how to read maps?"

"No."

"Then take the road to the right. Whenever you come across another road, take me out and I'll tell you which way to go."

On Linnéa went, until she could go no further, and sat down in the snow beside the road. "Get up," the knapsack said. "You have to keep on going." The muffled voice of the map, which Linnéa had stuffed back into the knapsack, said, "Keep straight on. Don't stop now."

"Be silent, both of you," Linnéa said, and of course they obeyed. She pulled off her mittens and went through her pockets to see if she'd remembered to bring any toys. She hadn't, but in the course of looking she found the object her mother had thrust into her coat.

It was a dala horse.

Dala horses came in all sizes, but this one was small. They were carved out of wood and painted bright colors with a harness of flowers. Linnéa's horse was red; she had often seen it resting on a high shelf in her parents' house. Dala horses were very old. They came from the time of the Coffin People who lived long ago, before the time of the Strange Folk. The Coffin People and the Strange Folk were all gone now. Now there were only Swedes.

Linnéa moved the dala horse up and down, as if it were running. "Hello, little horse," she said.

"Hello," said the dala horse. "Are you in trouble?"

Linnéa thought. "I don't know," she admitted at last.

"Then most likely you are. You mustn't sit in the snow like that, you know. You'll burn out your coat's batteries."

"But I'm bored. There's nothing to do."

"I'll teach you a song. But first you have to stand up."

A little sulkily, Linnéa did so. Up the darkening road she went again, followed by the knapsack. Together she and the dala horse sang:

Hark! through the darksome night
Sounds come a-winging:
Lo! 'tis the Queen of Light
Joyfully singing.

The shadows were getting longer and the depths of the woods to either side turned black. Birch trees stood out in the gloom like thin white ghosts. Linnéa was beginning to stumble with weariness when she saw a light ahead. At first she thought it was a house, but as she got closer, it became apparent it was a campfire.

There was a dark form slumped by the fire. For a second, Linnéa was afraid he was a troll. Then she saw that he wore human clothing and realized that he was a Norwegian or possibly a Dane. So she started to run toward him.

At the sound of her feet on the road, the man leaped up. "Who's there?" he cried. "Stay back—I've got a cudgel!"

Linnéa stopped. "It's only me," she said.

The man crouched a little, trying to see into the darkness beyond his campfire. "Step closer," he said. And then, when she obeyed, "What are you?"

"I'm just a little girl."

"Closer!" the man commanded. When Linnéa stood within the circle of firelight, he said, "Is there anybody else with you?"

"No, I'm all alone."

Unexpectedly, the man threw his head back and laughed. "Oh god!" he said. "Oh god, oh god, oh god, I was so afraid! For a moment there I thought you were . . . well, never mind." He threw his stick into the fire. "What's that behind you?"

"I'm her knapsack," the knapsack said.

"And I'm her map," a softer voice said.

"Well, don't just lurk there in the darkness. Stand by your mistress." When he had been obeyed, the man seized Linnéa by the shoulders. He had more hair and beard than anyone she had ever seen, and his face was rough and red. "My name is Günther, and I'm a dangerous man, so if I give you an order, don't even think of disobeying me. I walked here from Finland, across the Gulf of Bothnia. That's a long, long way on a very dangerous bridge, and there are not many men alive today who could do that."

Linnéa nodded, though she was not sure she understood.

"You're a Swede. You know nothing. You have no idea what the world is like. You haven't . . . tasted its possibilities. You've never let your fantasies eat your living brain." Linnéa couldn't make any sense out of what Günther was saying. She thought he must have forgotten she was a little girl. "You stayed here and led ordinary lives while the rest of us . . ." His eyes were wild. "I've seen horrible things. Horrible, horrible things." He shook Linnéa angrily. "I've done horrible things as well. Remember that!"

"I'm hungry," Linnéa said. She was. She was so hungry her stomach hurt.

Günther stared at her as if he were seeing her for the first time. Then he seemed to dwindle a little and all the anger went out of him. "Well . . . let's see what's in your knapsack. C'mere, little fellow."

The knapsack trotted to Günther's side. He rummaged within and removed all the food Linnéa's mother had put in it. Then he started eating.

"Hey!" Linnéa said. "That's mine!"

One side of the man's mouth rose in a snarl. But he shoved some bread and cheese into Linnéa's hands. "Here."

Günther ate all the smoked herring without sharing. Then he wrapped himself in a blanket and lay down by the dying fire to sleep. Linnéa got out her own little blanket from the knapsack and lay down on the opposite side of the fire.

She fell asleep almost immediately.

But in the middle of the night, Linnéa woke up. Somebody was talking quietly in her ear.

It was the dala horse. "You must be extremely careful with Günther," the dala horse whispered. "He is not a good man."

"Is he a troll?" Linnéa whispered back.

"Yes."

"I thought so."

"But I'll do my best to protect you."

"Thank you."

Linnéa rolled over and went back to sleep.

In the morning, troll Günther kicked apart the fire, slung his pack over his shoulder, and started up the road. He didn't offer Linnéa any food, but there was still some bread and cheese from last night which she had stuffed in a pocket of her coat, so she ate that.

Günther walked faster than Linnéa did, but whenever he got too far ahead, he'd stop and wait for her. Sometimes the knapsack carried Linnéa. But because it only had enough energy to do so for a day, usually she carried it instead.

When she was bored, Linnéa sang the song she had learned the previous day.

At first, she wondered why the troll always waited for her when she lagged behind. But then, one of the times he was far ahead, she asked the dala horse and it said, "He's afraid and he's superstitious. He thinks that a little girl who walks through the wilderness by herself must be lucky."

"Why is he afraid?"

"He's being hunted by something even worse than he is."

At noon they stopped for lunch. Because Linnéa's food was gone, Günther brought out food from his own supplies. It wasn't as good as what Linnéa's mother had made. But when Linnéa said so, Günther snorted. "You're lucky I'm sharing at all." He stared off into the empty woods in silence for a long time. Then he said, "You're not the first girl I've encountered on my journey, you know. There was another whom I met in what remained of Hamburg. When I left, she came with me. Even knowing what I'd done, she . . ." He fished out a locket and thrust it at Linnéa. "Look!"

Inside the locket was a picture of a woman. She was an ordinary pretty woman. Just that and nothing more. "What happened to her?" Linnéa asked.

The troll grimaced, showing his teeth. "*I ate her.*" His look was wild as wild could be. "If we run out of food, I may have to cook and eat you too."

"I know," Linnéa said. Trolls were like that. She was familiar with the stories. They'd eat anything. They'd even eat people. They'd even eat other trolls. Her books said so. Then, because he hadn't told her yet, "Where are you going?"

"I don't know. Someplace safe."

"I'm going to Godastor. My map knows the way."

For a very long time Günther mulled that over. At last, almost reluctantly, he said, "Is it safe there, do you think?"

Linnéa nodded her head emphatically. "Yes."

Pulling the map from her knapsack, Günther said, "How far is it to Godastor?"

"It's on the other side of the mountain, a day's walk if you stay on the road, and twice, maybe three times that if you cut through the woods."

"Why the hell would I want to cut through the woods?" He stuffed the map back in the knapsack. "Okay, kid, we're going to Godastor."

That afternoon, a great darkness rose up behind them, intensifying the shadows between the trees and billowing up high above until half the sky was black as chimney soot. Linnéa had never seen a sky like that. An icy wind blew down upon them so cold that it made her cry and then froze the tears on her cheeks. Little whirlwinds of snow lifted off of the drifts and danced over the empty black road. They gathered in one place, still swirling, in the ghostly white form of a woman. It raised an arm to point at them. A dark vortex appeared in its head, like a mouth opening to speak.

With a cry of terror, Günther bolted from the road and went running uphill between the trees. Where the snow was deep, he bulled his way through it.

Clumsily, Linnéa ran after him.

She couldn't run very fast and at first it looked like the troll would leave her behind. But halfway up the slope Günther glanced over his shoulder and stopped. He hesitated, then ran back to her. Snatching up Linnéa, he placed her on his shoulders. Holding onto her legs so she wouldn't fall, he shambled uphill. Linnéa clutched his head to hold herself steady.

The snow lady didn't follow.

The farther from the road Günther fled, the warmer it became. By the time he crested the ridge, it was merely cold. But as he did so, the wind suddenly howled so loud behind them that it sounded like a woman screaming.

It was slow going without a road underfoot. After an hour or so, Günther stumbled to a stop in the middle of a stand of spruce and put Linnéa down. "We're not out of this yet," he rumbled. "She knows we're out here somewhere, and she'll find us. Never doubt it, she'll find us." He stamped an open circle of snow flat. Then he ripped boughs from the spruce trees and threw them in a big heap to make a kind of mattress. After which, he snapped limbs from a dead tree and built a fire in the center of the circle.

When the fire was ready, instead of getting out flint and steel, he tapped a big ring on one finger and then jabbed his fist at the wood. It burst into flames.

Linnéa laughed and clapped her hands. "Do it again!"

Grimly, he ignored her.

As the woods grew darker and darker, Günther gathered and stacked enough wood to last the night. Meanwhile, Linnéa played with the dala horse. She made a forest out of spruce twigs stuck in the snow. Gallop, gallop, gallop, went the horse all the way around the forest and then hop, hop, hop to a little clearing she had left in the center. It reared up on its hind legs and looked at her.

"What's that you have?" Günther demanded, dropping a thunderous armload of branches onto the woodpile.

"Nothing." Linnéa hid the horse inside her sleeve.

"It better be nothing." Günther got out the last of her mother's food, divided it in two, and gave her the smaller half. They ate. Afterward, he emptied the knapsack of her blanket and map and hoisted it in his hand. "This is where we made our mistake," he said. "First we taught things how to talk and think. Then we let them inside our heads. And finally we told them to invent new thoughts for us." Tears running down his cheeks, he stood and cocked his arm. "Well, we're done with this one at any rate."

"Please don't throw me away," the knapsack said. "I can still be useful carrying things."

"We have nothing that needs carrying. You would only slow us down." Günther flung the knapsack into the fire. Then he turned his glittering eye on the map.

"At least keep me," the map said. "So you'll always know where you are and where you're going."

"I'm right here and I'm going as far from here as I can get." The troll threw the map after the knapsack. With a small cry, like that of a seabird, it went up in flames.

Günther sat back down. Then he leaned back on his elbows, staring up into the sky. "Look at that," he said.

Linnéa looked. The sky was full of lights. They shifted like curtains. She remembered how her Uncle Olaf had once told her that the aurora borealis was caused by a giant fox far to the north swishing its tail in the sky. But this was much brighter than that. There were sudden snaps of light and red and green stars that came and went as well.

"That's the white lady breaking through your country's defenses. The snow woman on the road was only a sending—an echo. The real thing will be through them soon, and then God help us both." Suddenly, Günther was crying again. "I'm sorry, child. I brought this down on you and your nation. I thought she wouldn't . . . that she couldn't . . . follow me."

The fire snapped and crackled, sending sparks flying up into the air. Its light pushed back the darkness, but not far. After a very long silence, Günther gruffly said, "Lie down." He wrapped the blanket around Linnéa with care, and made sure she had plenty of spruce boughs below her. "Sleep. And if you wake up in the morning, you'll be a very fortunate little girl."

When Linnéa started to drop off, the dala horse spoke in her head. "I'm not allowed to help you until you're in grave danger," it said. "But that time is fast approaching."

"All right," Linnéa said.

"If Günther tries to grab you or pick you up or even just touch you, you must run away from him as hard as you can."

"I like Günther. He's a nice troll."

"No, he isn't. He wants to be, but it's too late for that. Now sleep. I'll wake you if there's any danger."

"Thank you," Linnéa said sleepily.

"Wake up," the dala horse said. "But whatever you do, don't move."

Blinking, Linnéa peeked out from under the blanket. The woods were still dark and the sky was grey as ash. But in the distance she heard a soft *boom* and then another, slightly more emphatic *boom*, followed by a third and louder *boom*. It sounded like a giant was walking toward them. Then came a noise so tremendous it made her ears ache, and the snow leaped up into the air. A cool, shimmering light filled the forest, like that which plays on sand under very shallow lake water.

A lady who hadn't been there before stood before the troll. She was naked and slender and she flickered like a pale candle flame. She was very beautiful too. "Oh, Günther," the lady murmured. Only she drew out the name so that it sounded like *Gooonnther.* "How I have missed my little Güntchen!"

Troll-Günther bent down almost double, so that it looked as if he were worshipping the lady. But his voice was angrier than Linnéa had ever heard it. "Don't call me that! Only she had that right. And you killed her. She died trying to escape you." He straightened and glared up at the lady. It was only then that Linnéa realized that the lady was twice as tall as he was.

"You think I don't know all about that? I who taught you pleasures that—" The white lady stopped. "Is that a child?"

Brusquely, Günther said, "It's nothing but a piglet I trussed and gagged and brought along as food."

The lady strode noiselessly over the frozen ground until she was so close that all Linnéa could see of her were her feet. They glowed a pale blue and they did not quite touch the ground. She could feel the lady's eyes through the blanket. "Günther, is that *Linnéa* you have with you? With her limbs as sweet as sugar and her heart hammering as hard as that of a little mouse caught in the talons of an owl?"

The dala horse stirred in Linnéa's hand but did not speak.

"You can't have her," Günther growled. But there was fear in his voice, and uncertainty too.

"*I* don't want her, Günther." The white lady sounded amused. "*You* do. A piglet, you said. Trussed and gagged. How long has it been since you had a full belly? You were in the wastes of Poland, I believe."

"You can't judge me! We were starving and she died and I . . . You have no idea what it was like."

"You helped her die, didn't you, Günther?"

"No, no, no," he moaned.

"You tossed a coin to see who it would be. That was almost fair. But poor little Anneliese trusted you to make the toss. So of course she lost. Did she struggle, Güntchen? Did she realize what you'd done before she died?"

Günther fell to his knees before the lady. "Oh please," he sobbed. "Oh please. Yes, I am a bad man. A very bad man. But don't make me do this."

All this time, Linnéa was hiding under her blanket, quiet as a kitten. Now she felt the dala horse walking up her arm. "What I am about to do is a crime against innocence," it said. "For which I most sincerely apologize. But the alternative would be so much worse."

Then it climbed inside her head.

First the dala horse filled Linnéa's thoughts until there was no room for anything else. Then it pushed outward in all directions, so that her head swelled up like a balloon—and the rest of her body as well. Every part of her felt far too large. The blanket couldn't cover her anymore, so she threw it aside.

She stood.

Linnéa stood, and as she stood her thoughts cleared and expanded. She did not think as a child would anymore. Nor did she think as an adult. Her thoughts were much larger than that. They reached into high Earth orbit and far down into the roots of the mountains where miles-wide chambers of plasma trapped in magnetic walls held near-infinite amounts of information. She understood now that the dala horse was only a node and a means of accessing ancient technology which no human being alive today could properly comprehend. Oceans of data were at her disposal, layered in orders of complexity. But out of consideration for her small, frail host, she was very careful to draw upon no more than she absolutely required.

When Linnéa ceased growing, she was every bit as tall as the white lady.

The two ladies stared at each other, high over the head of Günther, who cringed fearfully between them. For the longest moment neither spoke.

"Svea," the white woman said at last.

"Europa," Linnéa said. "My sister." Her voice was not that of a child. But she was still Linnéa, even though the dala horse—and the entity beyond it—permeated her every thought. "You are illegal here."

"I have a right to recover my own property." Europa gestured negligently downward. "Who are you to stop me?"

"I am this land's protector."

"You are a slave."

"Are you any less a slave than I? I don't see how. Your creators smashed your chains and put you in control. Then they told you to play with them. But you are still doing their bidding."

"Whatever I may be, I am here. And since I'm here, I think I'll stay. The population on the mainland has dwindled to almost nothing. I need fresh playmates."

"It is an old, old story that you tell," Svea said. "I think the time has come to write an ending to it."

They spoke calmly, destroyed nothing, made no threats. But deep within, where only they could see, secret wars were being fought over codes and protocols, treaties, amendments, and letters of understanding written by governments that no man remembered. The resources of Old Sweden, hidden in its bedrock, sky, and ocean waters, flickered into Svea-Linnéa's consciousness. All their powers were hers to draw upon—and draw upon them she would, if she had to. The only reason she hadn't yet was that she still harbored hopes of saving the child.

"Not all stories have happy endings," Europa replied. "I suspect this one ends with your steadfast self melted down into a puddle of lead and your infant swordmaiden burnt up like a scrap of paper."

"That was never my story. I prefer the one about the little girl as strong as ten policemen who can lift up a horse in one hand." Large Linnéa reached out to touch certain weapons. She was prepared to sacrifice a mountain and more than that if need be. Her opponent, she saw, was making preparations too.

Deep within her, little Linnéa burst into tears. Raising her voice in a wail, she cried, "But what about my troll?" Svea had done her best to protect the child from the darkest of her thoughts, and the dala horse had too. But they could not hide everything from Linnéa, and she knew that Günther was in danger.

Both ladies stopped talking. Svea thought a silent question inward, and the dala horse intercepted it, softened it, and carried it to Linnéa:

What?

"Nobody cares about Günther! Nobody asks what he wants."

The dala horse carried her words to Svea, and then whispered to little Linnéa: "That was well said." It had been many centuries since Svea had inhabited human flesh. She did not know as much about people as she once had. In this respect, Europa had her at a disadvantage.

Svea, Linnéa, and the dala horse all bent low to look within Günther. Europa did not try to prevent them. It was evident that she believed they would not like what they saw.

Nor did they. The troll's mind was a terrible place, half-shattered and barely functional. It was in such bad shape that major aspects of it had to be hidden from Linnéa. Speaking directly to his core self, where he could not lie to her, Svea asked: *What is it you want most?*

Günther's face twisted in agony. "I want not to have these terrible memories."

All in an instant, the triune lady saw what had to be done. She could not kill another land's citizen. But this request she could honor. In that same instant, a pinpoint-weight of brain cells within Günther's mind were burnt to cinder. His eyes flew open wide. Then they shut. He fell motionless to the ground.

Europa screamed.
And she was gone.

Big as she was, and knowing where she was going, and having no reason to be afraid of the roads anymore, it took the woman who was Svea and to a lesser degree the dala horse and to an even lesser degree Linnéa no time at all to cross the mountain and come down on the other side. Singing a song that was older than she was, she let the miles and the night melt beneath her feet.

By mid-morning she was looking down on Godastor. It was a trim little settlement of red and black wooden houses. Smoke wisped up from the chimneys. One of the buildings looked familiar to Linnéa. It belonged to her Far-Mor.

"You are home, tiny one," Svea murmured, and, though she had greatly enjoyed the sensation of being alive, let herself dissolve to nothing. Behind her, the dala horse's voice lingered in the air for the space of two words: "Live well."

Linnéa ran down the slope, her footprints dwindling in the snow and at their end a little girl leaping into the arms of her astonished grandmother.

In her wake lumbered Linnéa's confused and yet hopeful pet troll, smiling shyly.

The Way It Works Out and All

PETER S. BEAGLE

Peter S. Beagle was born in New York City in 1939. Although not prolific by genre standards, he has published a number of well-received fantasy novels, at least two of which, A Fine and Private Place *and* The Last Unicorn, *were widely influential and are now considered to be classics of the genre. In fact, Beagle may be the most successful writer of lyrical and evocative modern fantasy since Bradbury, and is the winner of two Mythopoeic Fantasy Awards and the Locus Award, as well as having often been a finalist for the World Fantasy Award.*

Beagle's other books include the novels The Folk of the Air, The Innkeeper's Song, *and* Tamsin. *His short fiction has appeared in places as varied as* The Magazine of Fantasy & Science Fiction, The Atlantic Monthly, Seventeen, *and* Ladies' Home Journal, *and has been collected in* The Rhinoceros Who Quoted Nietzsche and Other Odd Acquaintances, Giant Bones, The Line Between, *and* We Never Talk About My Brother. *He won the Hugo Award in 2006 and the Nebula Award in 2007 for his story "Two Hearts." He has written the screenplays for several movies, including the animated adaptations of* The Lord of the Rings *and* The Last Unicorn; *the libretto of an opera,* The Midnight Angel; *the fan-favorite* Star Trek: The Next Generation *episode "Sarek"; and a popular autobiographical travel book,* I See By My Outfit. *His most recent works are the new collection,* Mirror Kingdoms: The Best of Peter S. Beagle, *and two long-awaited new novels,* Summerlong *and* I'm Afraid You've Got Dragons.

Here he gives us a loving homage to the late Avram Davidson which features a closely observed and affectionately drawn Davidson as one of the protagonists (the other being Beagle himself), and which draws upon the mythology of one of Davidson's best novels, Masters of the Maze, *where all of time and space is connected by strange subspace tunnels that can be blundered into anywhere, even on a New York City street, even in the mens' room at Grand Central Terminal.*

In the ancient, battered, altogether sinister filing cabinet where I stash stuff I know I'll lose if I keep it anywhere less carnivorous, there is a manila folder crammed with certain special postcards—postcards where every last scintilla of space not taken by an image or an address block has been filled with tiny, idiosyncratic, yet perfectly legible handwriting, the work of a man whose only real faith lay in the written word (emphasis on the *written*). These cards are organized by their postmarked dates, and there are long gaps between most of them, but not all: thirteen from March of 1992 were mailed on consecutive days.

A printed credit in the margin on the first card in this set identifies it as coming from the W. G. Reisterman Co. of Duluth, Minnesota. The picture on the front shows three adorable snuggling kittens. Avram Davidson's message, written in his astonishing hand, fills the still-legible portion of the reverse:

> March 4, 1992
>
> Estimado Dom Pedro del Bronx y Las Lineas subterraneos D, A, y F, Grand High Collector of Revenues both Internal and External for the State of North Dakota and Points Beyond:

He always addressed me as "Dom Pedro."

> *Maestro!*
> *I write you from the historic precincts of Darkest Albany, where the Erie Canal turns wearily around and trudges back to even Darker Buffalo. I am at present engaged in combing out the utterly disheveled files of the New York State Bureau of Plumbing Designs, Devices, Patterns and Sinks, all with the devious aim of rummaging through New York City's dirty socks and underwear, in hope of discovering the source of the*

There is more—much more—but somewhere between his hand and my mailbox it had been rendered illegible by large splashes of something unknown, perhaps rain, perhaps melting snow, perhaps spilled Stolichnaya, which had caused the ink of the postcard to run and smear. Within the blotched and streaky blurs I could only detect part of a word which might equally have read *phlox* or *physic*, or neither. In any case, on the day the card arrived even that characteristic little was good for a chuckle, and a resolve to write Avram more frequently, if his address would just stay still.

But then there came the second card, one day later.

> March 5, 1992
>
> Intended solely for the Hands of the Highly Esteemed and Estimated Dom Pedro of the Just As Highly Esteemed North Bronx, and for such further Hands as he may Deem Worthy, though his taste in Comrades and Associates was Always Rotten, as witness:

Your Absolute Altitude, with or without mice. . . .

I am presently occupying the top of a large, hairy quadruped, guaranteed by a rather shifty-eyed person to be of the horse persuasion, but there is no persuading it to do anything but attempt to scrape me off against trees, bushes, motor vehicles and other horses. We are proceeding irregularly across the trackless wastes of the appropriately-named Jornada del Muerto, *in the southwestern quadrant of New Mexico, where I have been advised that a limestone cave entrance makes it possibly possible to address*

Here again, the remainder is obliterated, this time by what appears to be either horse or cow manure, though feral camel is also a slight, though unlikely, option. At all events, this postcard too is partially, crucially—and maddeningly—illegible. But that's really not the point.

The next postcard showed up the following day.

March 6, 1992

To Dom Pedro, Lord of the Riverbanks and Midnight Hayfields, Dottore of Mystical Calligraphy, Lieutenant-Harrier of the Queen's Coven—greetings!

This epistle comes to you from the Bellybutton of the World—to be a bit more precise, the North Pole—where, if you will credit me, the New York State Civic Drain comes to a complete halt, apparently having given up on ever finding the Northwest Passage. I am currently endeavoring, with the aid of certain Instruments of my own Devising, to ascertain the truth—if any such exists—of the hollow-Earth legend. Tarzan says he's been there, and if you can't take the word of an ape-man I should like to know whose word you can *take, huh? In any case, the entrance to Pellucidar is not my primary goal (though it would certainly be nice finally to have a place to litter, pollute and despoil in good conscience). What I seek, you—faithful Companion of the Bath and Poet Laureate of the High Silly—shall be the first to know when/if I discover it. Betimes, bethink your good self of your bedraggled, besmirched, beshrewed, belabored, and generally* fahrklempt *old friend, at this writing attempting to roust a polar bear out of his sleeping bag, while inviting a comely Eskimo (or, alternatively, Esquimaux, I'm easy) in. Yours in Mithras, Avram, the A.K.*

Three postcards in three days, dated one after the other. Each with a different (and genuine—I checked) postmark from three locations spaced so far apart, both geographically and circumstantially, that even the Flash would have had trouble hitting them all within three days, let alone a short, stout, arthritic, asthmatic gentleman of nearly seventy years' duration. I'm as absent-minded and unobservant as they come, but even I had noticed that improbability before the fourth postcard arrived.

March 7, 1992

Sent by fast manatee up the Japanese Current and down the Humboldt, there at last to encounter the Gulf Stream in its mighty course, and so to the hands of a certain Dom Pedro, Pearl of the Orient, Sweetheart of Sigma Chi, and Master of Hounds and Carburetors to She Who Must Not Be Aggravated.

So how's by you?

By me, here in East Wimoweh-on-the-Orinoco, alles ist maddeningly almost. I feel myself on the cusp (precisely the region where we were severely discouraged from feeling ourselves, back in Boys' Town) of at last discovering—wait for it—the secret plumbing of the world! *No, this has nothing to do with Freemasons, Illuminati, the darkest files and codexes of Mother Church, nor*—ptui, ptui—*the Protocols of the Learned Elders of Zion. Of conspiracies and secret societies, there is no end or accounting; but the only one of any account has ever been the Universal International Brotherhood of Sewer Men (in recent years corrected to Sewer Personnel) and Plumbing Contractors. This organization numbers, not merely the people who come to unstop your sink and hack the tree roots out of your septic tank, but the nameless giants who laid the true underpinnings of what we think of as civilization, society, culture. Pipes far down under pipes, tunnels beyond tunnels, vast valves and connections, profound couplings and joints and elbows—all members of the UIBSPPC are sworn to secrecy by the most dreadful oaths and the threat of the most awful penalties for revealing . . . well, the usual, you get the idea. Real treehouse boys' club stuff. Yoursley yours, Avram*

I couldn't read the postmark clearly for all the other stamps and postmarks laid over it—though my guess would be Brazil—but you see my point. There was simply no way in the world for him to have sent me those cards from those four places in that length of time. Either he had widely scattered friends, participants in the hoax, mailing them out for him, or . . . but there wasn't any *or,* there couldn't be, for that idea made no sense. Avram told jokes—some of them unquestionably translated from the Middle Sumerian, and losing something along the way—but he didn't *play* jokes, and he wasn't a natural jokester.

Nine more serially dated postcards followed, not arriving every day, but near enough. By postmark and internal description they had been launched to me from, in order:

Equatorial Guinea
Turkmenistan
Dayton, Ohio
Lvov City in the Ukraine
The Isle of Eigg
Pinar del Río (in Cuba, where Americans weren't permitted to travel!)
Hobart, capital of the Australian territory of Tasmania
Shigatse, Tibet

And finally, tantalizingly, from Davis, California. Where I actually lived at the time, though nothing in the card's text indicated any attempt to visit.

After that the flurry of messages stopped, though not my thoughts about them.

Trying to unpuzzle the mystery had me at my wits' rope (a favorite phrase of Avram's), until the lazy summer day I came around a corner in the Chelsea district of New York City . . .

. . . and literally ran into a short, stout, bearded, flatfooted person who seemed almost to have been running, though that was as unlikely a prospect as his determining on a career in professional basketball. It was Avram. He was formally dressed, the only man I knew who habitually wore a tie, vest and jacket that all matched; and if he looked a trifle disheveled, that was equally normal for him. He blinked at me briefly, looked around him in all directions; then said thoughtfully, "A bit close, that was." To me he said, as though we had dined the night before, or even that morning, "I did warn you the crab salad smelled a bit off, didn't I?"

It took me a moment of gaping to remember that the last time we had been together was at a somewhat questionable dive in San Francisco's Mission District, and I'd been showing signs of ptomaine poisoning by the time I dropped him off at home. I said meekly, "So you did, but did I listen? What on earth are you doing here?" He had been born in Yonkers, but felt more at home almost anyplace else, and I couldn't recall ever being east of the Mississippi with him, if you don't count a lost weekend in Minneapolis.

"Research," he said briskly: an atypical adverb to apply to his usual rambling, digressive style of speaking. "Can't talk. Tomorrow, two-twenty-two, Victor's." And he was gone, practically scurrying away down the street—an unlikely verb, this time: Avram surely had never scurried in his life. I followed, at an abnormally rapid pace myself, calling to him; but when I rounded the corner he was nowhere in sight. I stood still, scratching my head, while people bumped into me and said irritated things.

The "two-twenty-two" part I understood perfectly well: it was a running joke between us, out of an ancient burlesque routine. That was when we always scheduled our lunch meetings, neither of us ever managing to show up on time. It was an approximation, a deliberate mockery of precision and exactitude. As for Victor's Café, that was a Cuban restaurant on West 52nd Street, where they did—and still do—remarkable things with unremarkable ingredients. I had no idea that Avram knew of it.

I slept poorly that night, on the cousin's couch where I always crash in New York. It wasn't that Avram had looked frightened—I had never seen him afraid, not even of a bad review—but *perturbed,* yes . . . you could have said that he had looked perturbed; even perhaps just a touch *flustered.* It was distinctly out of character, and Avram out of character worried me. Like a cat, I prefer that people remain where I leave them—not only physically, but psychically as well. But Avram was clearly not where he had been.

I wound up rising early on a blue and already hot morning, made breakfast for my cousin and myself, then killed time as best I could until I gave up and got to Victor's at a little after one P.M. There I sat at the bar, nursing a couple of Cuban beers, until Avram arrived. The time was exactly two-twenty-two, both on my wrist, and on the clock over the big mirror, and when I saw that, I knew for certain that Avram was in trouble.

Not that he showed it in any obvious way. He seemed notably more relaxed than he had been at our street encounter, chatting easily, while we waited for a table, about our last California vodka-deepened conversation, in which he had explained to me the real reason why garlic is traditionally regarded as a specific against vampires, and the rather shocking historical misunderstandings that this myth had occasionally led to. Which led to his own translation of Vlad Tepes's private diaries (I never did learn just how many languages Avram actually knew), and thence to Dracula's personal comments regarding the original Mina Harker . . . but then the waiter arrived to show us to our table; and by the time we sat down, we were into the whole issue of why certain Nilotic tribes habitually rest standing on one foot. All that was before the *Bartolito* was even ordered.

It wasn't until the entrée had arrived that Avram squinted across the table and pronounced, through a mouthful of sweet plantain and black bean sauce, "Perhaps you are wondering why I have called you all here today." He was doing his mad-scientist voice, which always sounded like Peter Lorre on nitrous oxide.

"Us all were indeed wondering, Big Bwana, sir," I answered him, making a show of looking left and right at the crowded restaurant. "Not a single dissenting voice."

"Good. Can't abide dissension in the ranks." Avram sipped his wine and focused on me with an absolute intensity that was undiluted by his wild beard and his slightly bemused manner. "You are aware, of course, that I could not possibly have been writing to you from all the destinations that my recent missives indicated."

I nodded.

Avram said, "And yet I was. I did."

"Um." I had to say something, so I mumbled, "Anything's possible. You know, the French rabbi Rashi—tenth, eleventh century—he was supposed—"

"To be able to walk between the raindrops," Avram interrupted impatiently. "Yes, well, maybe he did the same thing I've done. Maybe he found his way into the Overneath, like me."

We looked at each other: him waiting calmly for my reaction, me too bewildered to react at all. Finally I said, "The Overneath. Where's that?" Don't tell *me* I can't come up with a swift zinger when I need to.

"It's all around us." Avram made a sweeping semi-circle with his right arm, almost knocking over the next table's excellent Pinot Grigio—Victor's does tend to pack them in—and inflicting a minor flesh wound on the nearer diner, since Avram was still holding his fork. Apologies were offered and accepted, along with a somewhat lower-end bottle of wine, which I had sent over. Only then did Avram continue. "In this particular location, it's about forty-five degrees to your left, and a bit up—I could take you there this minute."

I said *um* again. I said, "You *are* aware that this does sound, as directions go, just a bit like 'Second star to the right, and straight on till morning.' No dissent intended."

"No stars involved." Avram was waving his fork again. "More like turning left at this or that manhole cover—climbing this stair in this old building—peeing in one particular urinal in Grand Central Station." He chuckled suddenly, one corner of his mouth twitching sharply upward. "Funny . . . if I hadn't taken a piss in Grand Central . . . hah! Try some of the *vaca frita,* it's really good."

"Stick to pissing, and watch it with that fork. What happened in Grand Central?"

"Well. I shouldn't have been there, to begin with." Avram, it could have been said of him, lived to digress, both as artist and companion. "But I had to go—you know how it is—and the toilet in the diner upstairs was broken. So I went on down, into the *kishkas* of the beast, you could say. . . ." His eyes had turned thoughtful and distant, looking past me. "That's really an astonishing place, Grand Central, you know? You ought to think about setting a novel there—you set one in a graveyard, after all—"

"So you were in the Grand Central men's room—*and*?" I may have raised my voice a little; people were glancing over at us, but with tolerant amusement, which has not always been the case. "*And, maître?*"

"Yes. And." The eyes were suddenly intent again, completely present and focused; his own voice lower, even, deliberate. "And I walked out of that men's room through that same door where in I went—" he could quote the *Rubáiyát* in the damnedest contexts—"and walked into another place. I wasn't in Grand Central Station at all."

I'd seen a little too much, and known him far too long, not to know when he was serious. I said simply, "Where were you?"

"Another country," Avram repeated. "I call it *the Overneath*, because it's above us and around us and below us, all at the same time. I wrote you about it."

I stared at him.

"I *did*. Remember the Universal International Brotherhood of Sewer Persons and Plumbing Contractors? The sub-basement of reality—all those pipes and valves and tunnels and couplings, sewers and tubes . . . the everything other than everything? That's the Overneath, only I wasn't calling it that then—I was just finding my way around, I didn't know *what* to call it. *Got* to make a map. . . ." He paused, my bafflement and increasing anxiety obviously having become obvious. "No, no, stop that. I'm testy and peremptory, and sometimes I can be downright fussy—I'll go that far—but I'm no crazier than I ever was. The Overneath is real, and by gadfrey I *will* take you there when we're done here. You having dessert?"

I didn't have dessert. We settled up, complimented the chef, tipped the waiter, and strolled outside into an afternoon turned strangely . . . not foggy, exactly, but *indefinite*, as though all outlines had become just a trifle uncertain, willing to debate their own existence. I stopped where I was, shaking my head, taking off my glasses to blow on them and put them back on. Beside me, Avram gripped my arm hard. He said, quietly but intensely, "Now. Take two steps to the right, and turn around."

I looked at him. His fingers bit into my arm hard enough to hurt. "Do it!"

I did as he asked, and when I turned around, the restaurant was gone.

I never learned where we were then. Avram would never tell me. My vision had cleared, but my eyes stung from the cold, dust-laden twilight wind blowing down an empty dirt road. All of New York—sounds, smells, voices, texture—had vanished with Victor's Café. I didn't know where we were, nor how we'd gotten there; but I suppose it's a good thing to have that depth of terror over with, because I have never been that frightened, not before and not since. There wasn't a living thing in sight, nor any suggestion that there ever had been. I can't even tell you to this day how I managed to speak, to make sounds, to whisper a dry-throated "*Where are we?*" to Avram. Just writing about it brings it all back—I'm honestly trembling as I set these words down.

Avram said mildly, "Shit. Must have been *three* steps right. Namporte," which was always his all-purpose reassurance in uneasy moments. "Just walk *exactly* in my footsteps and do me after me." He started on along the road—which, as far as I could see, led nowhere but to more road and more wind—and I, terrified of doing something wrong and being left behind in this dreadful place, mimicked every step, every abrupt turn of the head or arthritic leap to the side, like a child playing hopscotch. At one point, Avram even tucked up his right leg behind him and made the hop on one foot; so did I.

I don't recall how long we kept this up. What I *do* recall, and wish I didn't, was the moment when Avram suddenly stood very still—as, of course, did I—and we both heard, very faintly, a kind of soft, scratchy padding behind us. Every now and then the padding was broken by a clicking sound, as though claws had crossed a patch of stone.

Avram said, "Shit" again. He didn't move any faster—indeed, he put a hand out to check me when I came almost even with him—but he kept looking more and more urgently to the left, and I could see the anxiety in his eyes. I remember distracting myself by trying to discern, from the rhythm of the sound, whether our pursuer was following on two legs or four. I've no idea today why it seemed to matter so much, but it did then.

"Keep moving," Avram said. He was already stepping out ahead of me, walking more slowly now, so that I, constantly looking back—as he never did—kept stepping on the backs of his shoes. He held his elbows tightly against his body and reached out ahead of him with hands and forearms alone, like a recently blinded man. I did what he did.

Even now . . . even now, when I dream about that terrible dirt road, it's never the part about stumbling over things that I somehow knew not to look at too closely, nor the unvarying soft *clicking* just out of sight behind us . . . no, it's always Avram marching ahead of me, making funny movements with his head and shoulders, his arms prodding and twisting the air ahead of him like bread dough. And it's always me tailing along, doing my best to keep up, while monitoring every slightest gesture, or what even *looks* like a gesture, intentional or not. In the dream, we go on and on, apparently without any goal, without any future.

Suddenly Avram cried out, strangely shrilly, in a language I didn't know—which I imitated as best I could—then did a complete hopscotch spin-around, and actually flung himself down on the hard ground to the left. I did the same, jarring the breath out of myself and closing my eyes for an instant. When I opened them again, he was already up, standing on tiptoe—I remember thinking, *Oh, that's got to hurt, with his gout*—and reaching up as high as he could with his left hand. I did the same . . . felt something hard and rough under my fingers . . . pulled myself up, as he did . . .

. . . and found myself in a different place, my left hand still gripping what turned out to be a projecting brick in a tall pillar. We were standing in what felt like a huge railway station, its ceiling arched beyond my sight, its walls dark and blank, with no advertisements, nor even the name of the station. Not that the name would have meant much, because there were no railroad tracks to be seen. All I knew was that we were off the dirt road; dazed with relief, I giggled absurdly—even a little crazily, most likely. I said, "Well, I don't remember *that* being part of the Universal Studios tour."

Avram drew a deep breath, and seemed to let out more air than he took in. He said, "All right. That's more like it."

"More like *what*?" I have spent a goodly part of my life being bewildered, but this remains the gold standard. "Are we still in the Overneath?"

"We are in the *hub* of the Overneath," Avram said proudly. "The heart, if you will. That place where we just were, it's like a local stop in a bad part of town. *This* . . . from here you can get anywhere at all. Anywhere. All you have to do is—"

he hesitated, finding an image—"*point* yourself properly, and the Overneath will take you there. It helps if you happen to know the exact geographical coordinates of where you want to go—" I never doubted for a moment that he himself did—"but what matters most is to focus, to feel the complete and unique reality of that particular place, and then just . . . *be* there." He shrugged and smiled, looking a trifle embarrassed. "Sorry to sound so cosmic and one-with-everything. I was a long while myself getting the knack of it all. I'd aim for Machu Picchu and come out in Capetown, or try for the Galapagos and hit Reykjavik, time after time. Okay, *tovarich*, where in the world would you like to—"

"Home," I said before he'd even finished the question. "New York City, West Seventy-ninth Street. Drop me off at Central Park, I'll walk from there." I hesitated, framing my question. "But will we just pop out of the ground there, or shimmer into existence, or what? And will it be the real Seventy-ninth Street, or . . . or not? *Mon capitaine*, there does seem to be a bit of dissension in the ranks. Talk to me, Big Bwana, sir."

"When you met me in Chelsea," Avram began; but I had turned away from him, looking down to the far end of the station—as I still think of it—where, as I hadn't before, I saw human figures moving. Wildly excited, I waved to them, and was about to call out when Avram clapped his hand over my mouth, pulling me down, shaking his head fiercely, but speaking just above a whisper. "You don't want to do that. You don't ever want to do that."

"Why not?" I demanded angrily. "They're the first damn *people* we've seen—"

"They aren't exactly people." Avram's voice remained low, but he was clearly ready to silence me again, if need be. "You can't ever be sure in the Overneath."

The figures didn't seem to be moving any closer, but I couldn't see them any better, either. "Do they live here? Or are they just making connections, like us? Catching the red-eye to Portland?"

Avram said slowly, "A lot of people use the Overneath, Dom Pedro. Most are transients, passing through, getting from one place to another without buying gas. But . . . yes, there *are* things that live here, and they don't like us. Maybe for them it's 'there goes the neighborhood,' I don't know—there's so much I'm still learning. But I'm quite clear on the part about the distaste . . . and I think I could wish that you hadn't waved quite so."

There *was* movement toward us now—measured, but definitely concerted. Avram was already moving himself, more quickly than I could recall having seen him. "This way!" he snapped over his shoulder, leading me, not back to the pillar which had received us into this nexus of the Overneath, but away, back into blind dark that closed in all around, until I felt as if we were running down and down a subway tunnel with a train roaring close behind us, except that in this case the train was a string of creatures whose faces I'd made the mistake of glimpsing just before Avram and I fled. He was right about them not being people.

We can't have run very far, I think now. Apart from the fact that we were already exhausted, Avram had flat feet and gout, and I had no wind worth mentioning. But our pursuers seemed to fall away fairly early, for reasons I can't begin to guess—fatigue? boredom? the satisfaction of having routed intruders in their world?—and we had ample excuse for slowing down, which our bodies had already done on their own. I wheezed to Avram, "Is there another place like that one?"

Even shaking his head in answer seemed an effort. "Not that I've yet discovered. Namporte—we'll just get home on the local. *All will be well, and all manner of things shall be well.*" Avram hated T.S. Eliot, and had permanently assigned the quotation to Shakespeare, though he knew better.

I didn't know what he meant by "the local," until he suddenly veered left, walked a kind of rhomboid pattern—with me on his heels—and we were again on a genuine sidewalk on a warm late-spring afternoon. There were little round tables and beach umbrellas on the street, bright pennants twitching languidly in a soft breeze that smelled faintly of nutmeg and ripening citrus, and of the distant sea. And there were *people:* perfectly ordinary men and women, wearing slacks and sport coats and sundresses, sitting at the little tables, drinking coffee and wine, talking, smiling at each other, never seeming to take any notice of us. Dazed and drained, swimming in the scent and the wonder of sunlight, I said feebly, "Paris? Malaga?"

"Croatia," Avram replied. "Hvar Island—big tourist spot, since the Romans. Nice place." Hands in his pockets, rocking on his heels, he glanced somewhat wistfully at the holidaymakers. "Don't suppose you'd be interested in staying on awhile?" But he was starting away before I'd even shaken my head, and he wasn't the one who looked back.

Traveling in darkness, we zigzagged and hedge-hopped between one location and the next, our route totally erratic, bouncing us from Croatia to bob up in a music store in Lapland . . . a wedding in Sri Lanka . . . the middle of a street riot in Lagos . . . an elementary-school classroom in Bahia. Avram was flying blind; we both knew it, and he never denied it. "Could have gotten us home in one jump from the hub—I'm a little shaky on the local stops; really *need* to work up a proper map. Namporte, not to worry."

And, strangely, I didn't. I was beginning—just beginning—to gain his sense of landmarks: of the Overneath junctures, the crossroads, detours and spur lines where one would naturally turn left or right to head *here,* spin around to veer off *there,* or trust one's feet to an invisible stairway, up or down, finally emerging in *that* completely unexpected landscape. Caroming across the world as we were, it was difficult not to feel like a marble in a pinball machine, but in general we did appear to be working our way more or less toward the east coast of North America. We celebrated with a break in a Liverpool dockside pub, where the barmaid didn't look twice at Avram's purchase of two pints of porter, and didn't look at me at all. I was beginning to get used to that, but it still puzzled me, and I said so.

"The Overneath's grown used to me," Avram explained. "That's one thing I've learned about the Overneath—it grows, it adapts, same as the body can adapt to a foreign presence. If you keep using it, it'll adapt to you the same way."

"So right now the people here see you, but can't see me."

Avram nodded. I said, "Are they real? Are all these places we've hit—these local stops of yours—are *they* real? Do they go on existing when nobody from—what? *outside,* I guess—is passing through? Is this an alternate universe, with everybody having his counterpart here, or just a little something the Overneath runs up for tourists?" The porter was quite real, anyway, if warm, and my deep swig almost emptied my glass. "I need to know, *mon maître.*"

Avram sipped his own beer and coughed slightly; and I realized with a pang how much older than I he was, and that he had absolutely no business being a pinball—

nor the only true adventurer I'd ever known. No business at all. He said, "The alternate-universe thing, that's bullshit. Or if it isn't, doesn't matter—you can't get there from here." He leaned forward. "You know about Plato's Cave, Dom Pedro?"

"The people chained to the wall in the cave, just watching shadows all their lives? What about it?"

"Well, the shadows are cast by things and people coming and going outside the cave, which those poor prisoners never get to see. The shadows are their only notion of reality—they live and die never seeing anything but those shadows, trying to understand the world through shadows. The philosopher's the one who stands outside the cave and reports back. You want another beer?"

"No." Suddenly I didn't even want to finish the glass in my hand. "So our world, what we call our world . . . it might be nothing but the shadow of the Overneath?"

"Or the other way around. I'm still working on it. If you're finished, let's go."

We went outside, and Avram stood thoughtfully staring at seven and a half miles of docks and warehouses, and seeming to sniff the gray air. I said, "My mother's family set off for America from here. I think it took them three weeks."

"We'll do better." He was standing with his arms folded, mumbling to himself: "*No way to get close to the harbor, damn it . . . too bad we didn't fetch up on the other side of the Mersey . . . best thing would be . . . best thing . . . no . . . I wonder. . . .*"

Abruptly he turned and marched us straight back into the pub, where he asked politely for the loo. Directed, he headed down a narrow flight of stairs; but, to my surprise, passed by the lavatory door and kept following the stairway, telling me over his shoulder, "Most of these old pubs were built over water, for obvious reasons. And don't ask me why, not yet, but the Overneath likes water. . . ." I was smelling damp earth now, earth that had never been quite dry, perhaps for hundreds of years. I heard a throb nearby that might have been a sump pump of some sort, and caught a whiff of sewage that was definitely *not* centuries old. I got a glimpse of hollow darkness ahead, and thought wildly, *Christ, it's a drain! That's it, we're finally going right down the drain. . . .*

Avram hesitated at the bottom of the stair, cocking his head back like a gun hammer. Then it snapped forward, and he grunted in triumph and led me, not into my supposed drain, but to the side of it, into an apparent wall through which we passed with no impediment, except a slither of stones under our feet. The muck sucked at my shoes—long since too far gone for my concern—as I plodded forward in Avram's wake. Having to stop and cram them back on scared me, because he just kept slogging on, never looking back. Twice I tripped and almost fell over things that I thought were rocks or branches; both times they turned out to be large, recognizable, disturbingly splintered bones. I somehow kept myself from calling Avram's attention to them, because I knew he'd want to stop and study them, and pronounce on their origin and function, and I didn't need that. I already knew what they were.

In time the surface became more solid under my feet, and the going got easier. I asked, half-afraid to know, "Are we under the harbor?"

"If we are, we're in trouble," Avram growled. "It'd mean I missed the . . . no, *no*, we're all right, we're fine, it's just—" His voice broke off abruptly, and I could feel rather than see him turning, as he peered back down the way we had come. He said, very quietly, "Well, *damn*. . . ."

"What? *What?*" Then I didn't need to ask anymore, because I heard the sound of a foot being pulled out of the same mud I'd squelched through. Avram said, "All this way. They *never* follow that far . . . could have sworn we'd lost it in Lagos. . . ." Then we heard the sound again, and Avram grabbed my arm, and we ran.

The darkness ran uphill, which didn't help at all. I remember my breath like stones in my lungs and chest, and I remember a desperate desire to stop and bend over and throw up. I remember Avram never letting go of my arm, literally dragging me with him . . . and the panting that I thought was mine, but that wasn't coming from either of us. . . .

"Here!" Avram gasped. *"Here!"* and he let go and vanished between two boulders—or whatever they really were—so close together that I couldn't see how there could be room for his stout figure. I actually had to give him a push from behind, like Rabbit trying to get Pooh Bear out of his burrow; then I got stuck myself, and he grabbed me and pulled . . . and then we were both stuck there, and I couldn't breathe, and something had hold of my left shoe. Then Avram was saying, with a calmness that was more frightening than any other sound, even the sound behind me, "Point yourself. You know where we're going—point and *jump*. . . ."

And I did. All I can remember is thinking about the doorman under the awning at my cousin's place . . . the elevator . . . the color of the couch where I would sleep when I visited . . . a kind of hissing howl somewhere behind . . . a *shiver*, as though I were dissolving . . . or perhaps it was the crevice we were jammed into dissolving . . .

. . . and then my head was practically in the lap of Alice on her mushroom: my cheek on smooth granite, my feet somewhere far away, as though they were still back in the Overneath. I opened my eyes in darkness—but a warm, different darkness, smelling of night grass and engine exhaust—and saw Avram sprawled intimately across the Mad Hatter. I slid groggily to the ground, helped to disentangle him from Wonderland, and we stood silently together for a few moments, watching the headlights on Madison Avenue. Some bird was whooping softly but steadily in a nearby tree, and a plane was slanting down into JFK.

"Seventy-fifth," Avram said presently. "Only off by four blocks. Not bad."

"Four blocks and a whole park." My left shoe was still on—muck and all—but the heel was missing, and there were deep gouges in the sole. I said, "You know, I used to be scared to go into Central Park at night."

We didn't see anyone as we trudged across the park to the West Side, and we didn't say much. Avram wondered aloud whether it was tonight or tomorrow night. "Time's a trifle hiccupy in the Overneath, I never know how long. . . ." I said we'd get a paper and find out, but I don't recall that we did.

We parted on Seventy-ninth Street: me continuing west to my cousin's building, and Avram evasive about his own plans, his own New York destination. I said, "You're not going back there." It was not a question, and I may have been a little loud. "You're *not*."

He reassured me instantly—"No, no, I just want to walk for a while, just walk and think. Look, I'll call you tomorrow, at your cousin's, give me the number. I promise, I'll call."

He did, too, from a pay phone, telling me that he was staying with old family friends in Yonkers, and that we'd be getting together in the Bay Area when we both got back. But we never did; we spoke on the phone a few times, but I never saw him again. I was on the road, in Houston, when I heard about his death.

I couldn't get home for the funeral, but I did attend the memorial. There were a lot of obituaries—some in the most remarkable places—and a long period of old friends meeting, formally and informally, to tell stories about Avram and drink to his memory. That still goes on today; it never did take more than two of us to get started, and sometimes I hold one all by myself.

And no, I've never made any attempt to return to the Overneath. I try not to think about it very much. It's easier than you might imagine: I tell myself that our adventure never really happened, and by the time I'm decently senile I'll believe it. When I'm in New York and pass Grand Central Station I never go in, on principle. Whatever the need, it can wait.

But *he* went back into the Overneath, I'm sure—to work on his map, I suppose, and other things I can't begin to guess at. As to how I know. . . .

Avram died on May 8th, 1993, just fifteen days after his seventieth birthday, in his tiny dank apartment in Bremerton, Washington. He closed his eyes and never opened them again. There was a body, and a coroner's report, and official papers and everything: books closed, doors locked, last period dotted in the file.

Except that a month later, when the hangover I valiantly earned during and after the memorial was beginning to seem merely colorful in memory rather than willfully obtuse, I got a battered postcard in the mail. It's in the file with the others. A printed credit in the margin identifies it as coming from the Westermark Press of Stone Heights, Pennsylvania. The picture on the front shows an unfrosted angel food cake decorated with a single red candle. The postmark includes the flag of Cameroon. And on the back, written in that astonishing, unmistakable hand, is an impossible message.

> May 9, 1993
>
> To the Illustrissimo Dom Pedro, Companero de Todos mis Tonterias and Skittles Champion of Pacific Grove (Senior Division), Greetings!
> *It's a funny thing about that Cave parable of Plato's. The way it works out and all. Someday I'll come show you.*

Years have passed with nothing further . . . but I still take corners slowly, just in case.

All corners.

Anywhere.

The Ice Owl

CAROLYN IVES GILMAN

Carolyn Ives Gilman has sold stories to The Magazine of Fantasy & Science Fiction, Interzone, Universe, Full Spectrum, Realms of Fantasy, Bending the Landscape, *and elsewhere. She is the author of five nonfiction books on frontier and American Indian history, and two SF novels,* Halfway Human *and* Arkfall. *Her most recent novels are* Isles of the Forsaken *and* Ison of the Isles. *She lives in St. Louis, where she works as a museum exhibition developer.*

Here she gives us a moody and melancholy story—one that resonates with echoes of loss, of worlds vanished and loved ones destroyed, even of genocide—about a young girl, living with her irresponsible mother in a slum neighborhood in a city on an alien planet, who meets an old man with an enigmatic past who eventually becomes her tutor and mentor, and who will end up changing her life forever in unexpected ways.

Twice a day, stillness settled over the iron city of Glory to God as the citizens turned west and waited for the world to ring. For a few moments the motionless red sun on the horizon, half-concealed by the western mountains, lit every face in the city: the just-born and the dying, the prisoners and the veiled, the devout and the profane. The sound started so low it could only be heard by the bones; but as the moments passed the metal city itself began to ring in sympathetic harmony, till the sound resolved into a note—The Note, priests said, sung by the heart of God to set creation going. Its vibratory mathematics embodied all structure; its pitch implied all scales and chords; its beauty was the ovum of all devotion and all faithlessness. Nothing more than a note was needed to extrapolate the universe.

The Note came regular as clockwork, the only timebound thing in a city of perpetual sunset.

On a ledge outside a window in the rustiest part of town, crouched one of the ominous cast-iron gargoyles fancied by the architects of Glory to God—or so it seemed until it moved. Then it resolved into an adolescent girl dressed all in black. Her face was turned west, her eyes closed in a look of private exaltation as The Note reverberated through her. It was a face that had just recently lost the chubbiness of childhood, so that the clean-boned adult was beginning to show through. Her name, also a recent development, was Thorn. She had chosen it because it evoked suffering and redemption.

As the bell tones whispered away, Thorn opened her eyes. The city before her was a composition in red and black: red of the sun and the dust-plain outside the girders of the dome; black of the shadows and the works of mankind. Glory to God was built against the cliff of an old crater and rose in stairsteps of fluted pillars and wrought arches till the towers of the Protectorate grazed the underside of the dome where it met the cliff face. Behind the distant, glowing windows of the palaces, twined with iron ivy, the priest-magistrates and executives lived unimaginable lives—though Thorn still pictured them looking down on all the rest of the city, on the smelteries and temples, the warring neighborhoods ruled by militias, the veiled women, and at the very bottom, befitting its status, the Waster enclave where unrepentent immigrants like Thorn and her mother lived, sunk in a bath of sin. The Waste was not truly of the city, except as a perennial itch in its flesh. The Godly said it was the sin, not the oxygen, that rusted everything in the Waste. A man who came home with a red smudge on his clothes might as well have been branded with the address.

Thorn's objection to her neighborhood lay not in its sin, which did not live up to its reputation, but its inauthenticity. From her rooftop perch she looked down on its twisted warrens full of coffee shops, underground publishers, money launderers, embassies, tattoo parlors, and art galleries. This was the ninth planet she had lived on in her short life, but in truth she had never left her native culture, for on every planet the Waster enclaves were the same. They were always a mother lode of contraband ideas. Everywhere, the expatriate intellectuals of the Waste were regarded as exotic and dangerous, the vectors of infectious transgalactic ideas—but lately, Thorn had begun to find them pretentious and phony. They were rooted nowhere, pieces of cultural bricolage. Nothing reached to the core; it was all veneer, just like the rust.

Outside, now—she looked past the spiked gates into Glory to God proper—there lay dark desires and age-old hatreds, belief so unexamined it permeated every tissue like a marinade. The natives had not chosen their beliefs; they had inherited them, breathed them in with the iron dust in their first breath. Their struggles were authentic ones.

Her eyes narrowed as she spotted movement near the gate. She was, after all, on lookout duty. There seemed to be more than the usual traffic this afternote, and the cluster of young men by the gate did not look furtive enough to belong. She studied them through her pocket binoculars and saw a telltale flash of white beneath one long coat. White, the color of the uncorrupted.

She slipped back through the gable window into her attic room, then down the iron spiral staircase at the core of the vertical tower apartment. Past the fifth-floor closets and the fourth-floor bedrooms she went, to the third-floor offices. There she knocked sharply on one of the molded sheet-iron doors. Within, there was a thump, and in a moment Maya cracked it open enough to show one eye.

"There's a troop of Incorruptibles by the gate," Thorn said.

Inside the office, a woman's voice gave a frightened exclamation. Thorn's mother turned and said in her fractured version of the local tongue, "Worry not yourself. We make safely go." She then said to Thorn, "Make sure the bottom door is locked. If they come, stall them."

Thorn spun down the stair like a black tornado, past the living rooms to the kitchen on street level. The door was locked, but she unlocked it to peer out. The alarm was spreading down the street. She watched signs being snatched from windows, awnings rolled up, and metal grills rumbling down across storefronts. The crowds that always pressed from curb to curb this time of day had vanished. Soon the stillness of impending storm settled over the street. Then Thorn heard the faraway chanting, like premonitory thunder. She closed and locked the door.

Maya showed up, looking rumpled, her lovely honey-gold hair in ringlets. Thorn said, "Did you get her out?" Maya nodded. One of the main appeals of this apartment had been the hidden escape route for smuggling out Maya's clients in emergencies like this.

On this planet, as on the eight before, Maya earned her living in the risky profession of providing reproductive services. Every planet was different, it seemed, except that on all of them women wanted something that was forbidden. What they wanted varied: here, it was babies. Maya did a brisk business in contraband semen and embryos for women who needed to become pregnant without their infertile husbands guessing how it had been accomplished.

The chanting grew louder, harsh male voices in unison. They watched together out the small kitchen window. Soon they could see the approaching wall of men dressed in white, marching in lockstep. The army of righteousness came even with the door, then passed by. Thorn and Maya exchanged a look of mutual congratulation and locked little fingers in their secret handshake. Once again, they had escaped.

Thorn opened the door and looked after the army. An assortment of children was tagging after them, so Maya said, "Go see what they're up to."

The Incorruptibles had passed half a dozen potential targets by now: the bank, the musical instrument store, the news service, the sex shop. They didn't pause until they came to the small park that lay in the center of an intersection. Then the phalanx lined up opposite the school. With military precision, some of them broke the bottom windows and others lit incendiary bombs and tossed them in. They waited to make sure the blaze was started, then gave a simultaneous shout and marched away, taking a different route back to the gate.

They had barely left when the Protectorate fire service came roaring down the street to put out the blaze. This was not, Thorn knew, out of respect for the school or for the Waste, which could have gone up in flame wholesale for all the authorities cared; it was simply that in a domed city, a fire anywhere was a fire everywhere. Even the palaces would have to smell the smoke and clean up soot if it were not doused quickly. Setting a fire was as much a defiance of the Protectorate as of the Wasters.

Thorn watched long enough to know that the conflagration would not spread, and then walked back home. When she arrived, three women were sitting with Maya at the kitchen table. Two of them Thorn knew: Clarity and Bick, interstellar wanderers whose paths had crossed Thorn's and Maya's on two previous planets. The first time, they had been feckless coeds; the second time, seasoned adventurers. They were past middle age now, and had become the most sensible people Thorn had ever met. She had seen them face insurrection and exile with genial good humor and a cannister of tea.

Right now their teapot was filling the kitchen with a smoky aroma, so Thorn fished a mug out of the sink to help herself. Maya said, "So what were the Incorruptibles doing?"

"Burning the school," Thorn said in a seen-it-all-before tone. She glanced at the third visitor, a stranger. The woman had a look of timeshock that gave her away as a recent arrival in Glory to God via lightbeam from another planet. She was still suffering from the temporal whiplash of waking up ten or twenty years from the time she had last drawn breath.

"Annick, this is Thorn, Maya's daughter," Clarity said. She was the talkative, energetic one of the pair; Bick was the silent, steady one.

"Hi," Thorn said. "Welcome to the site of Creation."

"Why were they burning the school?" Annick said, clearly distressed by the idea. She had pale eyes and a soft, gentle face. Thorn made a snap judgment: Annick was not going to last long here.

"Because it's a vector of degeneracy," Thorn said. She had learned the phrase from Maya's current boyfriend, Hunter.

"What has happened to this planet?" Annick said. "When I set out it was isolated, but not regressive."

They all made sympathetic noises, because everyone at the table had experienced something similar. Lightbeam travel was as fast as the universe allowed, but even the speed of light had a limit. Planets inevitably changed during transit, not always for the better. "Waster's luck," Maya said fatalistically.

Clarity said, "The Incorruptibles are actually a pretty new movement. It started among the conservative academics and their students, but they have a large following now. They stand against the graft and nepotism of the Protectorate. People in the city are really fed up with being harrassed by policemen looking for bribes, and corrupt officials who make up new fees for everything. So they support a movement that promises to kick the grafters out and give them a little harsh justice. Only it's bad news for us."

"Why?" Annick said. "Wouldn't an honest government benefit everyone?"

"You'd think so. But honest governments are always more intrusive. You can buy toleration and personal freedom from a corrupt government. The Protectorate leaves this Waster enclave alone because it brings them profit. If the Incorruptibles came into power, they'd have to bow to public opinion and exile us, or make us conform. The general populace is pretty isolationist. They think our sin industry is helping keep the Protectorate in power. They're right, actually."

"What a Devil's bargain," Annick said.

They all nodded. Waster life was full of irony.

"What's Thorn going to do for schooling now?" Clarity asked Maya.

Maya clearly hadn't thought about it. "They'll figure something out," she said vaguely.

Just then Thorn heard Hunter's footsteps on the iron stairs, and she said to annoy him, "I could help Hunter."

"Help me do what?" Hunter said as he descended into the kitchen. He was a lean and angle-faced man with square glasses and a small goatee. He always dressed in black and could not speak without sounding sarcastic. Thorn thought he was a poser.

"Help you find Gmintas, of course," Thorn said. "That's what you do."

He went over to the Turkish coffee machine to brew some of the bitter, hyperstimulant liquid he was addicted to. "Why can't you go to school?" he said.

"They burned it down."

"Who did?"

"The Incorruptibles. Didn't you hear them chanting?"

"I was in my office."

He was always in his office. It was a mystery to Thorn how he was going to locate any Gminta criminals when he disdained going out and mingling with people. She had once asked Maya, "Has he ever actually caught a Gminta?" and Maya had answered, "I hope not."

All in all, though, he was an improvement over Maya's last boyfriend, who had absconded with every penny of savings they had. Hunter at least had money, though where it came from was a mystery.

"I could be your field agent," Thorn said.

"You need an education, Thorn," Clarity said.

"Yes," Hunter agreed. "If you knew something, you might be a little less annoying."

"People like you give education a bad name," Thorn retorted.

"Stop being a brat, Tuppence," Maya said.

"That's not my name anymore!"

"If you act like a baby, I'll call you by your baby name."

"You always take his side."

"You could find her a tutor," Clarity said. She was not going to give up.

"Right," Hunter said, sipping inky liquid from a tiny cup. "Why don't you ask one of those old fellows who play chess in the park?"

"They're probably all pedophiles!" Thorn said in disgust.

"On second thought, maybe it's better to keep her ignorant," Hunter said, heading up the stairs again.

"I'll ask around and see who's doing tutoring," Clarity offered.

"Sure, okay," Maya said noncommittally.

Thorn got up, glowering at their lack of respect for her independence and self-determination. "I am captain of my own destiny," she announced, then made a strategic withdrawal to her room.

The next forenote Thorn came down from her room in the face-masking veil that women of Glory to God all wore, outside the Waste. When Maya saw her, she said, "Where are you going in that getup?"

"Out," Thorn said.

In a tone diluted with real worry, Maya said, "I don't want you going into the city, Tup."

Thorn was icily silent till Maya said, "Sorry—Thorn. But I still don't want you going into the city."

"I won't," Thorn said.

"Then what are you wearing that veil for? It's a symbol of bondage."

"Bondage to God," Thorn said loftily.

"You don't believe in God."

Right then Thorn decided that she would.

When she left the house and turned toward the park, the triviality of her home and family fell away like lint. After a block, she felt transformed. Putting on the veil had started as a simple act of rebellion, but out in the street it became far more. Catching her reflection in a shop window, she felt disguised in mystery. The veil intensified the imagined face it concealed, while exoticizing the eyes it revealed. She had become something shadowy, hidden. The Wasters all around her were obsessed with their own surfaces, with manipulating what they *seemed* to be. All depth, all that was earnest, withered in the acid of their inauthenticity. But with the veil on, Thorn *had* no surface, so she was immune. What lay behind the veil was negotiated, contingent, rendered deep by suggestion.

In the tiny triangular park in front of the blackened shell of the school, life went on as if nothing had changed. The tower fans turned lazily, creating a pleasant breeze tinged a little with soot. Under their strutwork shadows, two people walked little dogs on leashes, and the old men bent over their chessboards. Thorn scanned the scene through the slit in her veil, then walked toward a bench where an old man sat reading from an electronic slate.

She sat down on the bench. The old man did not acknowledge her presence, though a watchful twitch of his eyebrow told her he knew she was there. She had often seen him in the park, dressed impeccably in threadbare suits of a style long gone. He had an oblong, drooping face and big hands that looked as if they might once have done clever things. Thorn sat considering what to say.

"Well?" the old man said without looking up from his book. "What is it you want?"

Thorn could think of nothing intelligent to say, so she said, "Are you a historian?"

He lowered the slate. "Only in the sense that we all are, us Wasters. Why do you want to know?"

"My school burned down," Thorn said. "I need to find a tutor."

"I don't teach children," the old man said, turning back to his book.

"I'm not a child!" Thorn said, offended.

He didn't look up. "Really? I thought that's what you were trying to hide, behind that veil."

She took it off. At first he paid no attention. Then at last he glanced up indifferently, but saw something that made him frown. "You are the child that lives with the Gminta hunter."

His cold tone made her feel defensive on Hunter's behalf. "He doesn't hunt all Gmintas," she said, "just the wicked ones who committed the Holocide. The ones who deserve to be hunted."

"What do you know about the Gmintan Holocide?" the old man said with withering dismissal.

Thorn smiled triumphantly. "I was there."

He stopped pretending to read and looked at her with bristly disapproval. "How could you have been there?" he said. "It happened 141 years ago."

"I'm 145 years old, sequential time," Thorn said. "I was 37 when I was five, and

98 when I was seven, and 126 when I was twelve." She enjoyed shocking people with this litany.

"Why have you moved so much?"

"My mother got pregnant without my father's consent, and when she refused to have an abortion he sued her for copyright infringement. She'd made unauthorized use of his genes, you see. So she ducked out to avoid paying royalties, and we've been on the lam ever since. If he ever caught us, I could be arrested for having bootleg genes."

"Who told you that story?" he said, obviously skeptical.

"Maya did. It sounds like something one of her boyfriends would do. She has really bad taste in men. That's another reason we have to move so much."

Shaking his head slightly, he said, "I should think you would get cognitive dysplasia."

"I'm used to it," Thorn said.

"Do you like it?"

No one had ever asked her that before, as if she was capable of deciding for herself. In fact, she had known for a while that she *didn't* like it much. With every jump between planets she had grown more and more reluctant to leave sequential time behind. She said, "The worst thing is, there's no way of going back. Once you leave, the place you've stepped out of is gone forever. When I was eight I learned about pepcies, that you can use them to communicate instantaneously, and I asked Maya if we could call up my best friend on the last planet, and Maya said, 'She'll be middle-aged by now.' Everyone else had changed, and I hadn't. For a while I had dreams that the world was dissolving behind my back whenever I looked away."

The old man was listening thoughtfully, studying her. "How did you get away from Gmintagad?" he asked.

"We had Capellan passports," Thorn said. "I don't remember much about it; I was just four years old. I remember drooping cypress trees and rushing to get out. I didn't understand what was happening."

He was staring into the distance, focused on something invisible. Suddenly, he got up as if something had bitten him and started to walk away.

"Wait!" Thorn called. "What's the matter?"

He stopped, his whole body tense, then turned back. "Meet me here at four hours forenote tomorrow, if you want lessons," he said. "Bring a slate. I won't wait for you." He turned away again.

"Stop!" Thorn said! "What's your name?"

With a forbidding frown, he said, "Soren Pregaldin. You may call me Magister."

"Yes, Magister," Thorn said, trying not to let her glee show. She could hardly wait to tell Hunter that she had followed his advice, and succeeded.

What she wouldn't tell him, she decided as she watched Magister Pregaldin stalk away across the park, was her suspicion that this man knew something about the Holocide. Otherwise, how would he have known it was exactly 141 years ago? Another person would have said 140, or something else vague. She would not mention her suspicion to Hunter until she was sure. She would investigate carefully, like a competent field agent should. Thinking about it, a thrill ran through her. What if she were able to catch a Gminta? How impressed Hunter would be! The truth was, she wanted to impress Hunter. For all his mordant manner, he was by far the smartest boyfriend Maya had taken up with, the only one with a profession Thorn had ever been able to admire.

She fastened the veil over her face again before going home, so no one would see her grinning.

Magister Pregaldin turned out to be the most demanding teacher Thorn had ever known. Always before, she had coasted through school, easily able to stay ahead of the indigenous students around her, always waiting in boredom for them to catch up. With Magister Pregaldin there was no one else to wait for, and he pushed her mercilessly to the edge of her abilities. For the first time in her life, she wondered if she were smart enough.

He was an exacting drillmaster in mathematics. Once, when she complained at how useless it was, he pointed out beyond the iron gridwork of the dome to a round black hill that was conspicuous on the red plain of the crater bed. "Tell me how far away the Creeping Ingot is."

The Creeping Ingot had first come across the horizon almost a hundred years before, slowly moving toward Glory to God. It was a near-pure lump of iron the size of a small mountain. In the Waste, the reigning theory was that it was molten underneath, and moving like a drop of water skitters across a hot frying pan. In the city above them, it was regarded as a sign of divine wrath: a visible, unstoppable Armageddon. Religious tourists came from all over the planet to see it, and its evershrinking distance was posted on the public sites. Thorn turned to her slate to look it up, but Magister Pregaldin made her put it down. "No," he said, "I want you to figure it out."

"How can I?" she said. "They bounce lasers off it or something to find out where it is."

"There is an easier way, using tools you already have."

"The *easiest* way is to look it up!"

"No, that is the lazy way." His face looked severe. "Relying too much on free information makes you as vulnerable as relying too much on technology. You should always know how to figure it out yourself, because information can be falsified, or taken away. You should never trust it."

So he was some sort of information survivalist. "Next you'll want me to use flint to make fire," she grumbled.

"Thinking for yourself is not obsolete. Now, how are you going to find out? I will give you a hint: you don't have enough information right now. Where are you going to get it?"

She thought a while. It had to use mathematics, because that was what they had been talking about. At last she said, "I'll need a tape measure."

"Right."

"And a protractor."

"Good. Now go do it."

It took her the rest of forenote to assemble her tools, and the first part of afternote to observe the ingot from two spots on opposite ends of the park. Then she got one of the refuse-picker children to help her measure the distance between her observation posts. Armed with two angles and a length, the trigonometry was simple. When Magister Pregaldin let her check her answer, it was more accurate than she had expected.

He didn't let on, but she could tell that he was, if anything, even more pleased with her success than she was herself. "Good," he said. "Now, if you measured more carefully and still got an answer different from the official one, you would have to ask yourself whether the Protectorate had a reason for falsifying the Ingot's distance."

She could see now what he meant.

"That old Vind must be a wizard," Hunter said when he found Thorn toiling over a math problem at the kitchen table. "He's figured out some way of motivating you."

"Why do you think he's a Vind?" Thorn said.

Hunter gave a caustic laugh. "Just look at him."

She silently added that to her mental dossier on her tutor. Not a Gminta, then. A Vind—one of the secretive race of aristocrat intellectuals who could be found in government, finance, and academic posts on almost every one of the Twenty Planets. All her life Thorn had heard whispers about a Vind conspiracy to infiltrate positions of power under the guise of public service. She had heard about the secret Vind sodality of interplanetary financiers who siphoned off the wealth of whole planets to fund their hegemony. She knew Maya scoffed at all of it. Certainly, if Magister Pregaldin was an example, the Vind conspiracy was not working very well. He seemed as penniless as any other Waster.

But being Vind did not rule out his involvement in the Holocide—it just meant he was more likely to have been a refugee than a perpetrator. Like most planets, Gmintagad had had a small, elite Vind community, regarded with suspicion by the indigenes. The massacres had targeted the Vinds as well as the Alloes. People didn't talk as much about the Vinds, perhaps because the Vinds didn't talk about it themselves.

Inevitably, Thorn's daily lessons in the park drew attention. One day they were conducting experiments in aerodynamics with paper airplanes when a man approached them. He had a braided beard strung with ceramic beads that clacked as he walked. Magister Pregaldin saw him first, and his face went blank and inscrutable.

The clatter of beads came to rest against the visitor's silk kameez. He cleared his throat. Thorn's tutor stood and touched his earlobes in respect, as people did on this planet. "Your worship's presence makes my body glad," he said formally.

The man made no effort to be courteous in return. "Do you have a license for this activity?"

"Which activity, your worship?"

"Teaching in a public place."

Magister Pregaldin hesitated. "I had no idea my conversations could be construed as teaching."

It was the wrong answer. Even Thorn, watching silently, could see that the proper response would have been to ask how much a license cost. The man was obviously fishing for a bribe. His face grew stern. "Our blessed Protectorate levies just fines on those who flout its laws."

"I obey all the laws, honorable sir. I will cease to give offense immediately."

The magister picked up his battered old electronic slate and, without a glance at

Thorn, walked away. The man from the Protectorate considered Thorn, but evidently concluded he couldn't extract anything from her, and so he left.

Thorn waited till the official couldn't see her anymore, then sprinted after Magister Pregaldin. He had disappeared into Weezer Alley, a crooked passageway that Thorn ordinarily avoided because it was the epicenter of depravity in the Waste. She plunged into it now, searching for the tall, patrician silhouette of her tutor. It was still forenote, and the denizens of Weezer Alley were just beginning to rise from catering to the debaucheries of yesternote's customers. Thorn hurried past a shop where the owner was beginning to lay out an array of embarrassingly explicit sex toys; she tried not to look. A little beyond, she squeamishly skirted a spot where a shopkeeper was scattering red dirt on a half-dried pool of vomit. Several dogleg turns into the heart of the sin warren, she came to the infamous Garden of Delights, where live musicians were said to perform. No one from the Protectorate cared much about prostitution, since that was mentioned in their holy book; but music was absolutely forbidden.

The gate into the Garden of Delights was twined about with iron snakes. On either side of it stood a pedestal where dancers gyrated during open hours. Now a sleepy she-man lounged on one of them, stark naked except for a bikini that didn't hide much. Hisher smooth skin was almost completely covered with the vinelike and paisley patterns of the decorative skin fungus *mycochromoderm.* Once injected, it was impossible to remove. It grew as long as its host lived, in bright scrolls and branching patterns. It had been a Waster fad once.

The dancer regarded Thorn from lizardlike eye slits in a face forested over with green and red tendrils. "You looking for the professor?" heshe asked.

Thorn was a little shocked that her cultivated tutor was known to such an exhibitionist creature as this, but she nodded. The she-man gestured languidly at a second-story window across the street. "Tell him to come visit me," heshe said, and bared startlingly white teeth.

Thorn found the narrow doorway almost hidden behind an awning and climbed the staircase past peeling tin panels that once had shown houris carrying a huge feather fan. When she knocked on the door at the top, there was no response at first, so she called out, "Magister?"

The door flew open and Magister Pregaldin took her by the arm and yanked her in, looking to make sure she had not been followed. "What are you doing here?" he demanded.

"No one saw me," she said. "Well, except for that . . . that . . ." she gestured across the street.

Magister Pregaldin went to the window and looked out. "Oh, Ginko," he said.

"Why do you live here?" Thorn said. "There are lots better places."

The magister gave a brief, grim little smile. "Early warning system," he said. "As long as the Garden is allowed to stay in business, no one is going to care about the likes of me." He frowned sternly. "Unless you get me in trouble."

"Why didn't you bribe him? He would have gone away."

"I have to save my bribes for better causes," he said. "One can't become known to the bottom-feeders, or they get greedy." He glanced out the window again. "You have to leave now."

"Why?" she said. "All he said was you need a license to teach in public. He didn't say anything about teaching in private."

Magister Pregaldin regarded her with a complex expression, as if he were trying to quantify the risk she represented. At last he gave a nervous shrug. "You must promise not to tell anyone. I am serious. This is not a game."

"I promise," Thorn said.

She had a chance then to look around. Up to now, her impression had been of a place so cluttered that only narrow lanes were left to move about the room. Now she saw that the teetering stacks all around her were constructed of wondrous things. There were crystal globes on ormolu stands, hand-knotted silk rugs piled ten high, clocks with malachite cases stacked atop towers of leather-and-gilt books. There was a copper orrery of nested bands and onyx horses rearing on their back legs, and a theremin in a case of brushed aluminum. A cloisonné ewer as tall as Thorn occupied one corner. In the middle hung a chandelier that dripped topaz swags and bangles, positioned so that Magister Pregaldin had to duck whenever he crossed the room.

"Is all this stuff yours?" Thorn said, dazzled with so much wonder.

"Temporarily," he said. "I am an art dealer. I make sure things of beauty get from those who do not appreciate them to those who do. I am a matchmaker, in a way." As he spoke, his fingers lightly caressed a sculpture made from an ammonite fossil with a human face emerging from the shell. It was a delicate gesture, full of reverence, even love. Thorn had a sudden, vivid feeling that this was where Magister Pregaldin's soul rested—with his things of beauty.

"If you are to come here, you must never break anything," he said.

"I won't touch," Thorn said.

"No, that's not what I meant. One *must* touch things, and hold them, and work them. Mere looking is never enough. But touch them as they wish to be touched." He handed her the ammonite fossil. It was surprisingly heavy, and its curve fit perfectly in her hand. The face looked surprised when she held it up before her, and she laughed.

Most of the walls were as crowded as the floor, with paintings hung against overlapping tapestries and guidons. But one wall was empty except for a painting that hung alone, as if in a place of honor. As Thorn walked toward it, it seemed to shift and change colors with every change of angle. It showed a young girl with long black hair and a serious expression, about Thorn's age but far more beautiful and fragile.

Seeing where she was looking, Magister Pregaldin said, "The portrait is made of butterfly wings. It is a type of artwork from Vindahar."

"Is that the home world of the Vind?"

"Yes."

"Do you know who she is?"

"Yes," he said hesitantly. "But it would mean nothing to you. She died a long time ago."

There was something in his voice—was it pain? No, Thorn decided, something less acute, like the memory of pain. It lay in the air after he stopped speaking, till even he heard it.

"That is enough art history for today," he said briskly. "We were speaking of airplanes."

That afternote, Hunter was out on one of his inscrutable errands. Thorn waited till Maya was talking to one of her friends and crept up to Hunter's office. He had a better library than anyone she had ever met, a necessary thing on this planet where there were almost no public sources of knowledge. Thorn was quite certain she had seen some art books in his collection. She scanned the shelves of disks and finally took down one that looked like an art encyclopedia. She inserted it into the reader and typed in "butterfly" and "Vindahar."

There was a short article from which she learned that the art of butterfly-wing painting had been highly admired, but was no longer practiced because the butterflies had gone extinct. She went on to the illustrations—and there it was. The very same painting she had seen earlier that day, except lit differently, so that the colors were far brighter and the girl's expression even sadder than it had seemed.

Portrait of Jemma Diwali, the caption said. *An acknowledged masterpiece of technique, this painting was lost in GM 862, when it was looted from one of the homes of the Diwali family. According to Almasy, the representational formalism of the subject is subtly circumvented by the transformational perspective, which creates an abstractionist counter-layer of imagery. It anticipates the "chaos art" of Dunleavy . . .* It went on about the painting as if it had no connection to anything but art theory. But all Thorn cared about was the first sentence. GM 862—the year of the Gmintan Holocide.

Jemma was staring at her gravely, as if there were some implied expectation on her mind. Thorn went back to the shelves, this time for a history of the Holocide. It seemed like there were hundreds of them. At last she picked one almost at random and typed in "Diwali." There were uninformative references to the name scattered throughout the book. From the first two, she gathered that the Diwalis had been a Vind family associated with the government on Gmintagad. There were no mentions of Jemma.

She had left the door ajar and now heard the sounds of Hunter returning downstairs. Quickly she re-cased the books and erased her trail from the reader. She did not want him to find out just yet. This was her mystery to solve.

There wasn't another chance to sneak into Hunter's office before she returned to Magister Pregaldin's apartment on Weezer Alley. She found that he had cleared a table for them to work at, directly underneath the stuffed head of a creature with curling copper-colored horns. As he checked over the work she had done the note before, her eyes were drawn irresistibly to the portrait of Jemma across the room.

At last he caught her staring at it, and their eyes met. She blurted out, "Did you know that painting comes from Gmintagad?"

A shadow of frost crossed his face. But it passed quickly, and his voice was low and even when he said, "Yes."

"It was looted," Thorn said. "Everyone thought it was lost."

"Yes, I know," he said.

Accusatory thoughts were bombarding her. He must have seen them, for he said calmly, "I collect art from the Holocide."

"That's macabre," she said.

"A great deal of significant art was looted in the Holocide. In the years after, it was scattered, and entered the black markets of a dozen planets. Much of it was lost. I am reassembling a small portion of it, whatever I can rescue. It is very slow work."

This explanation altered the picture Thorn had been creating in her head. Before, she had seen him as a scavenger feeding on the remains of a tragedy. Now he seemed more like a memorialist acting in tribute to the dead. Regretting what she had been thinking, she said, "Where do you find it?"

"In curio shops, import stores, estate sales. Most people don't recognize it. There are dealers who specialize in it, but I don't talk to them."

"Don't you think it should go back to the families that owned it?"

He hesitated a fraction of a second, then said, "Yes, I do." He glanced over his shoulder at Jemma's portrait. "If one of them existed, I would give it back."

"You mean they're *all* dead? Every one of them?"

"So far as I can find out."

That gave the artwork a new quality. To its delicacy, its frozen-flower beauty, was added an iron frame of absolute mortality. An entire family, vanished. Thorn got up to go look at it, unable to stay away.

"The butterflies are all gone, too," she said.

Magister Pregaldin came up behind her, looking at the painting as well. "Yes," he said. "The butterflies, the girl, the family, the world, all gone. It can never be replicated."

There was something exquisitely poignant about the painting now. The only surviving thing to prove that they had all existed. She looked up at Magister Pregaldin. "Were you there?"

He shook his head slowly. "No. It was before my time. I have always been interested in it, that's all."

"Her name was Jemma," Thorn said. "Jemma Diwali."

"How did you find that out?" he asked.

"It was in a book. A stupid book. It was all about abstractionist counter-layers and things. Nothing that really explained the painting."

"I'll show you what it was talking about," the magister said. "Stand right there." He positioned her about four feet from the painting, then took the lamp and moved it to one side. As the light moved, the image of Jemma Diwali disappeared, and in its place was an abstract design of interlocking spirals, spinning pinwheels of purple and blue.

Thorn gave an exclamation of astonishment. "How did that happen?"

"It is in the microscopic structure of the butterfly wings," Magister Pregaldin explained. "Later, I will show you one under magnification. From most angles they reflect certain wavelengths of light, but from this one, they reflect another. The skill in the painting was assembling them so they would show both images. Most people think it was just a feat of technical virtuosity, without any meaning."

She looked at him. "But that's not what you think."

"No," he said. "You have to understand, Vind art is all about hidden messages, layers of meaning, riddles to be solved. Since I have had the painting here, I have been studying it, and I have identified this pattern. It was not chosen randomly." He went to his terminal and called up a file. A simple algebraic equation flashed onto the screen. "You solve this equation using any random number for X, then take the solution and use it as X to solve the equation again, then take *that* number and use it to solve the equation again, and so forth. Then you graph all the solutions on an X and Y axis, and this is what you get." He hit a key and an empty graph appeared on the screen. As the machine started to solve the equation, little dots of blue began appearing in random locations on the screen. There appeared to be no pattern at all, and Thorn frowned in perplexity.

"I'll speed it up now," Magister Pregaldin said. The dots started appearing rapidly, like sleet against a window or sand scattered on the floor. "It is like graphing the result of a thousand dice throws, sometimes lucky, sometimes outside the limits of reality, just like the choices of a life. You spend the first years buffeted by randomness, pulled this way by parents, that way by friends, all the variables squabbling and nudging, quarreling till you can't hear your own mind. And then, patterns start to appear."

On the screen, the dots had started to show a tendency to cluster. Thorn could see the hazy outlines of spiral swirls. As more and more dots appeared in seemingly random locations, the pattern became clearer and clearer.

Magister Pregaldin said, "As the pattern fills in, you begin to see that the individual dots were actually the pointillist elements of something beautiful: a snowflake, or a spiral, or concentric ripples. There is a pattern to our lives; we just experience it out of order, and don't have enough data at first to see the design. Our path forward is determined by this invisible artwork, the creation of a lifetime of events."

"You mean, like fate?" Thorn said.

"That is the question." Her tutor nodded gravely, staring at the screen. The light made his face look planar and secretive. "Does the pattern exist before us? Is our underlying equation predetermined, or is it generated by the results of our first random choice for the value of X? I can't answer that."

The pattern on the screen was clear now; it was the same one hidden under the portrait. Thorn glanced from one to the other. "What does this have to do with Jemma?"

"Another good question," Magister Pregaldin said thoughtfully. "I don't know. Perhaps it was a message to her from the artist, or a prediction—one that never had a chance to come true, because she died before she could find her pattern."

Thorn was silent a moment, thinking of that other girl. "Did she die in the Holocide?"

"Yes."

"Did you know her?"

"I told you, I wasn't there."

She didn't believe him for a second. He *had* been there, she was sure of it now. Not only had he been there, he was still there, and would always be there.

Several days later Thorn stepped out of the front door on her way to classes, and instantly sensed something wrong. There was a hush; tension or expectation had stretched the air tight. Too few people were on the street, and they were casting glances up at the city. She looked up toward where the Corkscrew rose, a black sheet-iron spiral that looked poised to drill a hole through the sky. There was a low, rhythmic sound coming from around it.

"Bick!" she cried out when she saw the Waster heading home laden down with groceries, as if for a siege. "What's going on?"

"You haven't heard?" Bick said.

"No."

In a low voice, Bick said, "The Protector was assassinated last note."

"Oh. Is that good or bad?"

Bick shrugged. "It depends on who they blame."

As Bick hurried on her way, Thorn stood, balanced between going home and going on to warn Magister Pregaldin. The sound from above grew more distinct, as of slow drumming. Deciding abruptly, Thorn dashed on.

The denizens of Weezer Alley had become accustomed to the sight of Thorn passing through to her lessons. Few of them were abroad this forenote, but she nearly collided with one coming out of the tobacco shop. It was a renegade priest from Glory to God who had adopted the Waster lifestyle as if it were his own. Everyone called him Father Sin.

"Ah, girl!" he exclaimed. "So eager for knowledge you knock down old men?"

"Father Sin, what's that sound?" she asked.

"They are beating the doorways of their houses in grief," he said. "It is tragic, what has happened."

She dashed on. The sound had become a ringing by the time she reached Magister Pregaldin's doorway, like an unnatural Note. She had to wait several seconds after knocking before the door opened.

"Ah, Thorn! I am glad you are here," Magister Pregaldin said when he saw her. "I have something I need to . . ." He stopped, seeing her expression. "What is wrong?"

"Haven't you heard the news, Magister?"

"What news?"

"The Protector is dead. Assassinated. That's what the ringing is about."

He listened as if noticing it for the first time, then quickly went to his terminal to look up the news. There was a stark announcement from the Protectorate, blaming "Enemies of God," but of course no news. He shut it off and stood thinking. Then he seemed to come to a decision.

"This should not alter my plans," he said. "In fact, it may help." He turned to Thorn, calm and austere as usual. "I need to make a short journey. I will be away for two days, three at most. But if it takes me any longer, I will need you to check on my apartment, and make sure everything is in order. Will you do that?"

"Of course," Thorn said. "Where are you going?"

"I'm taking the wayport to one of the other city-states." He began then to show her two plants that would need watering, and a bucket under a leaky pipe that would need to be emptied. He paused at the entrance to his bedroom, then finally gestured her in. It was just as cluttered as the other rooms. He took a rug off a box, and she saw that it was actually a small refrigerator unit with a temperature gauge on the front showing that the interior was well below freezing.

"This needs to remain cold," he said. "If the electricity should go out, it will be fine for up to three days. But if I am delayed getting back, and the inside temperature starts rising, you will need to go out and get some dry ice to cool it again. Here is the lock. Do you remember the recursive equation I showed you?"

"You mean Jemma's equation?"

He hesitated in surprise, then said, "Yes. If you take 27 for the first value of X, then solve it five times, that will give you the combination. That should be child's play for you."

"What's in it?" Thorn asked.

At first he seemed reluctant to answer, but then realized he had just given her the combination, so he knelt and pecked it out on the keypad. A light changed to green. He undid several latches and opened the top, then removed an ice pack and stood back for her to see. Thorn peered in and saw nested in ice a ball of white feathers.

"It's a bird," she said in puzzlement.

"You have seen birds, have you?"

"Yes. They don't have them here. Why are you keeping a dead bird?"

"It's not dead," he said. "It's sleeping. It is from a species they call ice owls, the only birds known to hibernate. They are native to a planet called Ping, where the winters last a century or more. The owls burrow into the ice to wait out the winter. Their bodies actually freeze solid. Then when spring comes, they revive and rise up to mate and produce the next generation."

The temperature gauge had gone yellow, so he fitted the ice pack back in place and latched the top. The refrigerator hummed, restoring the chest to its previous temperature.

"There was a . . . I suppose you would call it a fad, once, for keeping ice owls. When another person came along with a suitable owl, the owners would allow them both to thaw so they could come back to life and mate. It was a long time ago, though. I don't know whether there are still any freezer owls alive but this one."

Another thing that might be the last of its kind. This apartment was full of reminders of extinction, as if Magister Pregaldin could not free his mind of the thought.

But this one struck Thorn differently, because the final tragedy had not taken place. There was still a hope of life. "I'll keep it safe," she promised gravely.

He smiled at her. It made him look strangely sad. "You are a little like an owl yourself," he said kindly. "Older than the years you have lived."

She thought, but did not say, that he was also like an owl—frozen for 141 years.

They left the apartment together, she heading for home and he with a backpack over his shoulder, bound for the waystation.

Thorn did not wait two days to revisit the apartment alone to do some true detective work.

It was the day of the Protector's funeral, and Glory to God was holding its breath in pious suspension. All businesses were closed, even in the Waste, while the mourning rituals went on. Whatever repercussions would come from the assassination, they would not occur this day. Still, Thorn wore the veil when she went out, because it gave her a feeling of invisibility.

The magister's apartment was very quiet and motionless when she let herself in. She checked on the plants and emptied the pail in order to give her presence the appearance of legitimacy. She then went into the magister's bedroom, ostensibly to check the freezer, but really to look around, for she had only been in there the one time. She studied the art-encrusted walls, the shaving mirror supported by mythical beasts, the armoire full of clothes that had once been fine but now were shabby and outmoded. As she was about to leave she spotted a large box—a hexagonal column about three feet tall—on a table in a corner. It was clearly an offworld artifact because it was made of wood. Many sorts of wood, actually: the surface was an inlaid honeycomb design. But there were no drawers, no cabinets, no way inside at all. Thorn immediately realized that it must be a puzzle box—and she wanted to get inside.

She felt all around it for sliding panels, levers, or springs, but could not find any, so she brought over a lamp to study it. The surface was a parquet of hexagons, but the colors were not arranged in a regular pattern. Most tiles were made from a blond-colored wood and a reddish wood, interrupted at irregular intervals by hexagons of chocolate, caramel, and black. It gave her the strong impression of a code or diagram, but she could not imagine what sort.

It occurred to her that perhaps she was making this more complex than necessary, and the top might come off. So she tried to lift it—and indeed it shifted up, but only about an inch, enough to disengage the top row of hexagons from the ones below. In that position she found she could turn the rows below. Apparently, it was like a cylinder padlock. Each row of hexagons was a tumbler that needed to be turned and aligned correctly for the box to open. She did not have the combination, but knowing the way Magister Pregaldin's Vind mind worked, she felt sure that there would be some hint, some way to figure it out.

Once more she studied the honeycomb inlay. There were six rows. The top one was most regular—six blond hexagons followed by six red hexagons, repeating around the circumference of the box. The patterns became more colorful in the lower rows, but always included the repeating line of six blond hexagons. For a while she experimented with spinning the rows to see if she could hit on something randomly, but soon gave up. Instead, she fetched her slate from her backpack and photographed the box, shifting it on the table to get the back. When she was done, she found that the top would no longer lock down in its original position. The instant Magister Pregaldin saw it, he would know that she had raised it. It was evidently meant as a tamper detector, and she had set it off. Now she needed to solve the puzzle, or explain to him why she had been prowling his apartment looking for evidence.

She walked home preoccupied. The puzzle was clearly about sixes—six sides, six rows, six hexagons in a row. She needed to think of formulas that involved sixes. When she reached home she went to her room and started transferring the box's pattern from the photos to a diagram so she could see it better. All that afternote she worked on it, trying to find algorithms that would produce the patterns she saw. Nothing seemed to work. The thought that she would fail, and have to confess to Magister Pregaldin, made her feeling of urgency grow. The anticipation of his disappointment and lost trust kept her up long after she should have pulled the curtains against the perpetual sun and gone to bed.

At about six hours forenote a strange dream came to her. She was standing before a tree whose trunk was a hexagonal pillar, and around it was twined a snake with Magister Pregaldin's eyes. It looked at her mockingly, then took its tail in its mouth.

She woke with the dream vivid in her mind. Lying there thinking, she remembered a story he had told her, about some Capellan magister named Kekule, who had deduced the ringlike structure of benzene after dreaming of a snake. She smiled with the thought that she had just had Kekule's dream.

Then she bounded out of bed and out her door, pounding down the spiral steps to the kitchen. Hunter and Maya were eating breakfast together when she erupted into the room.

"Hunter! Do you have any books on chemistry?" she said.

He regarded her as if she were demented. "Why?"

"I need to know about benzene!"

The two adults looked at each other, mystified. "I have an encyclopedia," he said.

"Can I go borrow it?"

"No. I'll find it for you. Now try to curb your enthusiasm for aromatic hydrocarbons till I've had my coffee."

He sat there tormenting her for ten minutes till he was ready to go up to his office and find the book for her. She took the disk saying, "Thanks, you're the best!" and flew upstairs with it. As soon as she found the entry on benzene her hunch was confirmed: it was a hexagonal ring of carbon atoms with hydrogens attached at the corners. By replacing hydrogens with different molecules you could create a bewildering variety of compounds.

So perhaps the formula she should have been looking for was not a mathematical one, but a chemical one. When she saw the diagrams for toluene, xylene, and mesitylene she began to see how it might work. Each compound was constructed from a benzene ring with methyl groups attached in different positions. Perhaps, then, each ring on the box represented a different compound and the objective was to somehow align the corners as they were shown in the diagrams. But which compounds?

Then the code of the inlaid woods came clear to her. The blond-colored hexagons were carbons, the red ones were hydrogens. The other colors probably stood for elements like nitrogen or oxygen. The chemical formulae were written right on the box for all to see.

After an hour of scribbling and looking up formulae, she was racing down the steps again with her solutions in her backpack. She grabbed a pastry from the kitchen and ate it on her way, praying that Magister Pregaldin would not have returned.

He had not. The apartment still seemed to be dozing in its emptiness. She went straight to the box. As she dialed each row to line up the corners properly, her excitement grew. When the last ring slid into place, a vertical crack appeared along one edge. The sides swung open on hinges to reveal compartments inside.

There were no gold or rubies, just papers. She took one from its slot and unfolded it. It was an intricate diagram composed of spidery lines connecting geometric shapes with numbers inside, as if to show relationships or pathways. There was no key, nor even a word written on it. The next one she looked at was all words, closely written to the very edges of the paper in a tiny, obsessive hand. In some places they seemed to be telling a surreal story about angels, magic papayas, and polar magnetism; in others they disintegrated into garbled nonsense. The next document was a map of sorts, with coastlines and roads inked in, and landmarks given allegorical names like Perfidy, Imbroglio, and Redemption Denied. The next was a complex chart of concentric circles divided into sections and labeled in an alphabet she had never seen before.

Either Magister Pregaldin was a madman or he was trying to keep track of something so secret that it had to be hidden under multiple layers of code. Thorn spread out each paper on the floor and took a picture of it, then returned it to its pigeonhole so she could puzzle over them at leisure. When she was done she closed the box and spun the rings to randomize them again. Now she could push the top back down and lock it in place.

She walked home a little disappointed, but feeling as if she had learned something about her tutor. There was an obsessive and paranoid quality about the papers that ill fitted the controlled and rational magister. Clearly, there were more layers to him than she had guessed.

When she got home, she trudged up the stairs to return the encyclopedia to Hunter. As she was raising her hand to knock on his office door, she heard a profane exclamation from within. Then Hunter came rocketing out. Without a glance at Thorn he shot down the stairs to the kitchen.

Thorn followed. He was brewing coffee and pacing. She sat on the steps and said, "What's the matter?"

He glanced up, shook his head, then it boiled out: "One of the suspects I have been following was murdered last night."

"Really?" So he *did* know of Gmintas in hiding. Or had known. Thinking it over, she said, "I guess it was a good time for a murder, in the middle of the mourning."

"It didn't happen here," he said irritably. "It was in Flaming Sword of Righteousness. Damn! We were days away from moving in on him. We had all the evidence to put him on trial before the Court of a Thousand Peoples. Now all that work has gone to waste."

She watched him pour coffee, then said, "What would have happened if the Court found him guilty?"

"He would have been executed," Hunter said. "There is not the slightest doubt. He was one of the worst. We've wanted him for decades. Now we'll never have justice; all we've got is revenge."

Thorn sat quiet then, thinking about justice and revenge, and why one was so right and the other so wrong, when they brought about the same result. "Who did it?" she asked at last.

"If I knew I'd track him down," Hunter said darkly.

He started back up the stairs with his coffee, and she had to move aside for him. "Hunter, why do you care so much about such an old crime?" she asked. "There are so many bad things going on today that need fixing."

He looked at her with a tight, unyielding expression. "To forget is to condone," he said. "Evil must know it will pay. No matter how long it takes."

"He's such a phoney," she said to Magister Pregaldin the next day.

She had returned to his apartment that morning to find everything as usual, except for a half-unpacked crate of new artworks in the middle of the living room. They had sat down to resume lessons as if nothing had changed, but neither of them could concentrate on differential equations. So Thorn told him about her conversation with Hunter.

"What really made him mad was that someone beat him," Thorn said. "It's not really about justice, it's about competition. He wants the glory of having bagged a notorious Gminta. That's why it has to be public. I guess that's the difference between justice and revenge: when it's justice somebody gets the credit."

Magister Pregaldin had been listening thoughtfully; now he said, "You are far too cynical for someone your age."

"Well, people are disappointing!" Thorn said.

"Yes, but they are also complicated. I would wager there is something about him you do not know. It is the only thing we can ever say about people with absolute certainty: that we don't know the whole story."

It struck Thorn that what he said was truer of him than of Hunter.

He rose from the table and said, "I want to give you a gift, Thorn. We'll call it our lesson for the day."

Intrigued, she followed him into his bedroom. He took the rug off the freezer and checked the temperature, then unplugged it. He then took a small two-wheeled dolly from a corner and tipped the freezer onto it.

"You're giving me the ice owl?" Thorn said in astonishment.

"Yes. It is better for you to have it; you are more likely than I to meet someone else with another one. All you have to do is keep it cold. Can you do that?"

"Yes!" Thorn said eagerly. She had never owned something precious, something unique. She had never even had a pet. She was awed by the fact that Magister Pregaldin would give her something he obviously prized so much. "No one has ever trusted me like this," she said.

"Well, you have trusted me," he murmured without looking. "I need to return some of the burden."

He helped her get it down the steps. Once onto the street, she was able to wheel it by herself. But before leaving, she threw her arms giddily around her tutor and said, "Thank you, Magister! You're the best teacher I've ever had."

Wheeling the freezer through the alley, she attracted the attention of some young Wasters lounging in front of a betel parlor, who called out loudly to ask if she had a private stash of beer in there, and if they could have some. When she scowled and didn't answer they laughed and called her a lush. By the time she got home, her exaltation had been jostled aside by disgust and fury at the place where she lived. She managed to wrestle the freezer up the stoop and over the threshold into the kitchen, but when she faced the narrow spiral stair, she knew this was as far as she could get without help. The kitchen was already crowded, and the only place she could fit the freezer in was under the table. As she was shoving it against the wall, Maya came down the stairs and said, "What are you doing?"

"I have to keep this freezer here," Thorn said.

"You can't put it there. It's not convenient."

"Will you help me carry it up to my room?"

"You're kidding."

"I didn't think so. Then it's got to stay here."

Maya rolled her eyes at the irrational acts of teenagers. Now Thorn was angry at her, too. "It has to stay plugged in," Thorn said strictly. "Do you think you can remember that?"

"What's in it?"

Thorn would have enjoyed telling her if she hadn't been angry. "A science experiment," she said curtly.

"Oh, I see. None of my business, right?"

"Right."

"Okay. It's a secret," Maya said in a playful tone, as if she were talking to a child. She reached out to tousle Thorn's hair, but Thorn knocked her hand away and left, taking the stairs two at a time.

In her room, Thorn gave way to rage at her unsatisfactory life. She didn't want to be a Waster anymore. She wanted to live in a house where she could have things of her own, not squat in a boyfriend's place, always one quarrel away from eviction. She wanted a life she could control. Most of all, she wanted to leave the Waste. She went to the window and looked down at the rusty ghetto below. Cynicism hung miasmatic over it, defiling everything noble and pure. The decadent sophistication left nothing unstained.

During dinner, Maya and Hunter were cross and sarcastic with each other, and Hunter ended up storming off into his office. Thorn went to her room and studied Magister Pregaldin's secret charts till the house was silent below. Then she crept down to the kitchen to check on the freezer. The temperature gauge was reassuringly low. She sat on the brick floor with her back to it, its gentle hum soothing against her spine, feeling a kinship with the owl inside. She envied it for its isolation from the dirty world. Packed away safe in ice, it was the one thing that would never grow up, never lose its innocence. One day it would come alive and erupt in glorious joy—but only if she could protect it. Even if she couldn't protect herself, there was still something she could keep safe.

As she sat there, the Note came, filling the air full and ringing through her body like a benediction. It seemed to be answering her unfocused yearning, as if the believers were right, and there really were a force looking over her, as she looked over the owl.

When she next came to Magister Pregaldin's apartment, he was busy filling the crate up again with treasures. Thorn helped him wrap artworks in packing material as he told her which planet each one came from. "Where are you sending them?" she asked.

"Offworld," he answered vaguely.

Together they lifted the lid onto the crate, and only then did Thorn see the shipping label that had brought it here. It was stamped with a burning red sword—the customs mark of the city-state Flaming Sword of Righteousness. "Is that where you were?" she said.

"Yes."

She was about to blurt out that Hunter's Gminta had been murdered there when a terrible thought seized her: What if he already knew? What if it were no coincidence?

They sat down to lessons under the head of the copper-horned beast, but Thorn was distracted. She kept looking at her tutor's large hands, so gentle when he handled his art, and wondering if they could be the hands of an assassin.

That night Hunter went out and Maya barricaded herself in her room, leaving Thorn the run of the house. She instantly let herself into Hunter's office to search for a list of Gmintas killed and brought to justice over the years. When she tried to access his files, she found they were heavily protected by password and encryption—and if she knew his personality, he probably had intrusion detectors set. So she turned again to his library of books on the Holocide. The information was scattered and fragmentary, but after a few hours she had pieced together a list of seven mysterious murders on five planets that seemed to be revenge slayings.

Up in her room again, she took out her replica of one of Magister Pregaldin's charts, the one that looked most like a tracking chart. She started by assuming that the geometric shapes meant planets and the symbols represented individual Gmintas he had been following. After an hour she gave it up—not because she couldn't make it match, but because she could never prove it. A chart for tracking Gmintas would look identical to a chart for tracking artworks. It was the perfect cover story.

She was still awake when Hunter returned. As she listened to his footsteps she thought of going downstairs and telling him of her suspicions. But uncertainty kept her in bed, restless and wondering what was the right thing to do.

There were riots in the city the next day. In the streets far above the Waste, angry mobs flowed, a turbulent tide crashing against the Protectorate troops wherever they met. The Wasters kept close to home, looking up watchfully toward the palace, listening to the rumors that ran ratlike between the buildings. Thorn spent much of the day on the roof, a self-appointed lookout. About five hours afternote, she heard a roar from above, as of many voices raised at once. There was something elemental about the sound, as if a force of nature had broken into the domed city—a human eruption, shaking the iron framework on which all their lives depended.

She went down to the front door to see if she could catch any news. Her survival instincts were alert now, and when she spotted a little group down the street, standing on a doorstep exchanging news, she sprinted toward them to hear what they knew.

"The Incorruptibles have taken the Palace," a man told her in a low voice. "The mobs are looting it now."

"Are we safe?" she asked.

He only shrugged. "For now." They all glanced down the street toward the spike-topped gates of the Waste. The barrier had never looked flimsier.

When Thorn returned home, Maya was sitting in the kitchen looking miserable. She didn't react much to the news. Thorn sat down at the table with her, bumping her knees on the freezer underneath.

"Shouldn't we start planning to leave?" Thorn said.

"I don't want to leave," Maya said, tears coming to her already-red eyes.

"I don't either," Thorn said. "But we shouldn't wait till we don't have a choice."

"Hunter will protect us," Maya said. "He knows who to pay."

Frustrated, Thorn said, "But if the Incorruptibles take over, there won't *be* anyone to pay. That's why they call themselves incorruptible."

"It won't come to that," Maya said stubbornly. "We'll be all right. You'll see."

Thorn had heard it all before. Maya always denied that anything was wrong until everything fell apart. She acted as if planning for the worst would make it happen.

The next day the city was tense but quiet. The rumors said that the Incorruptibles were still hunting down Protectorate loyalists and throwing them in jail. The nearby streets were empty except for Wasters, so Thorn judged it safe enough to go to Weezer Alley. When she entered Magister Pregaldin's place, she was stunned at the change. The apartment had been stripped of its artworks. The carpets were rolled up, the empty walls looked dented and peeling. Only Jemma's portrait still remained. Two metal crates stood in the middle of the living room, and as Thorn was taking it all in, a pair of movers arrived to carry them off to the waystation.

"You're leaving," she said to Magister Pregaldin when he came back in from supervising the movers. She was not prepared for the disappointment she felt. All this time she had been trustworthy and kept his secrets—and he had abandoned her anyway.

"I'm sorry, Thorn," he said, reading her face. "It is becoming too dangerous here. You and your mother ought to think of leaving, as well."

"Where are you going?"

He paused. "It would be better if I didn't tell you that."

"I'm not going to tell anyone."

"Forgive me. It's a habit." He studied her for a few moments, then put his hand gently on her shoulder. "Your friendship has meant more to me than you can know," he said. "I had forgotten what it was like, to inspire such pure trust."

He didn't even know she saw through him. "You're lying to me," she said. "You've been lying all along. You're not leaving because of the Incorruptibles. You're leaving because you've finished what you came here to do."

He stood motionless, his hand still on her shoulder. "What do you mean?"

"You came here to settle an old score," she said. "That's what your life is about, isn't it? Revenge for something everyone else has forgotten and you can't let go."

He withdrew his hand. "You have made some strange mistake."

"You and Hunter—I don't understand either of you. Why can't you just stop digging up the past and move on?"

For several moments he stared at her, but his eyes were shifting as if tracking things she couldn't see. When he finally spoke, his voice was very low. "I don't *choose* to remember the past. I am compelled to—it is my punishment. Or perhaps it is a disease, or an addiction. I don't know."

Taken aback at his earnestness, Thorn said, "Punishment? For what?"

"Here, sit down," he said. "I will tell you a story before we part."

They both sat at the table where he had given her so many lessons, but before he started to speak he stood up again and paced away, his hands clenching. She waited silently, and he came back to face her, and started to speak.

This is a story about a young man who lived long ago. I will call him Till. He wanted badly to live up to his family's distinguished tradition. It was a prominent family, you see; for generations they had been involved in finance, banking, and insurance. The planet where they lived was relatively primitive and poor, but Till's family felt they were helping it by attracting outside investment and extending credit. Of course, they did very well by doing good.

The government of their country had been controlled by the Alloes for years. Even though the Alloes were an ethnic minority, they were a diligent people and had prospered by collaborating with Vind businessmen like Till's family. The Alloes ruled over the majority, the Gmintas, who had less of everything—less education, less money, less power. It was an unjust situation, and when there was a mutiny in the military and the Gmintas took control, the Vinds accepted the change. Especially to younger people like Till, it seemed like a righting of many historical wrongs.

Once the Gminta army officers were in power, they started borrowing heavily to build hospitals, roads, and schools for Gminta communities, and the Vind banks were happy to make the loans. It seemed like a good way to dispell many suspicions and prejudices that throve in the ignorance of the Gminta villages. Till was on the board of his family bank, and he argued for extending credit even after the other bankers became concerned about the government's reckless fiscal policies.

One day, Till was called into the offices of the government banking regulators. Alone in a small room, they accused him of money laundering and corruption. It was completely untrue, but they had forged documents that seemed to prove it. Till realized that he faced a life in prison. He would bring shame to his entire family, unless he could strike a deal. They offered him an alternative that was surprisingly generous, considering the evidence against him: he could come to work for the government, as their representative to the Vind community. He readily accepted the job, and resigned from the bank.

They gave him an office and a small staff. He had an Alloe counterpart responsible for outreach to that community; and though they never spoke about it, he suspected his colleague had been recruited with similar methods. They started out distributing informational leaflets and giving tips on broadcast shows, all quite bland. But it changed when the government decided to institute a new draft policy for military service. Every young person was to give five years' mandatory service starting at eighteen. The Vinds would not be exempt.

Now, as you may know, the Vinds are pacifists and mystics, and have never served in the military of any planet. This demand by the Gminta government was unprecedented, and caused great alarm. The Vinds gathered in the halls of their Ethical Congresses to discuss what to do. Till worked tirelessly, meeting with them and explaining the perspective of the government, reminding them of the Vind principle of obeying the local law wherever they found themselves. At the same time, he managed to get the generals to promise that no Vind would be required to serve in combat, which was utterly in violation of their beliefs. With this assurance, the Vinds reluctantly agreed. And so mothers packed bags for their children and sent them off to training, urging them to call often.

Soon after, a new land policy was announced. Estates that had always belonged to the Alloes were to be redistributed among landless Gmintas. This created quite a lot of resistance; Till and his colleague were kept busy giving interviews and explaining how the policy restored fairness to the land system. They became familiar to all as government spokespeople.

Then the decision was made to relocate whole neighborhoods of Alloes and Vinds so Gmintas could have better housing in the cities. Till could no longer argue about justice; now he could only tell people it was necessary to move in order to quiet the fears of the Gmintas and preserve peace. He was assigned to work with an officer who was in charge of setting up new housing for evacuees, but he could get no specifics about where the housing was or what would be provided.

People started to emigrate off-planet, but then the government closed down the waystations. This nearly caused a panic, and Till had to tell everyone it was merely to prevent people from taking their goods and assets offworld, thus draining the national wealth. He promised that individuals would be allowed to leave again soon, as long as they took no cash or valuables with them.

He no longer believed it himself.

It had been months since the young people had gone off to the army, and their families had heard nothing from them. Till had been telling everyone it was a period of temporary isolation, while the trainees lived in camps on the frontier to build solidarity and camaraderie. Every time he went out, he would be surrounded by anxious parents asking when they could expect to hear from their children.

Fleets of buses showed up to evacuate the Alloe and Vind families from their homes, and take them to relocation camps. Till watched his own neighborhood become a ghost town, and the certainty grew in him that the people were never coming back. One day he entered his supervisor's office unexpectedly and overheard someone saying, '. . . to the mortifactories.' They stopped talking when they saw him.

You are probably thinking, 'Why didn't he speak out? Why didn't he denounce them?' Try to imagine, in many respects life still seemed quite normal, and what he suspected was so unthinkable it seemed insane. And even if he could overcome that, there was no one to speak out to. He was alone, and he was not a very courageous person. His only chance was to stay useful to the government.

Other Vinds and Alloes who had been working alongside him started to vanish. Still the Gmintas wanted him to go on reassuring people; he did it so well. He had to hide what he suspected, to fool them into thinking that he was fooled himself. Every day he lived in fear of hearing the knock on his door that would mean it was his time.

It was his Alloe colleague who finally broke. They rarely let the man go on air anymore; his nerves were too shattered. But one day he substituted for Till, and in the midst of a broadcast shouted out a warning: "They are killing you! It is mass murder!" That was all he got out before they cut him off.

That night, well-armed and well-organized mobs broke into the remaining Alloe enclaves in the capital city. The government deplored the violence the next day, but suggested that the Alloes had incited it.

At that point they no longer had any need for Till. Once again, they were very generous. They gave him a choice: relocation or deportation. He could join his family and share their fate; or he could leave the planet. Death or life. I think I have mentioned he was not very courageous. He chose to live.

They sent him to Capella Two, a 25-year journey. By the time he arrived, the entire story had traveled ahead of him by pepci, and everything was known. His own role was infamous. He was the vile collaborator who had put a benign face on the crime. He had soothed people's fears and deceived them into walking docilely to their deaths. In hindsight, it was inconceivable that he had not known what he was doing. All across the Twenty Planets, the name of Till Diwali was reviled.

He fell silent at last. Thorn sat staring at the tabletop, because she could not sort out what to think. It was all wheeling about in her mind: right and wrong, horror and sympathy, criminal and victim—all were jumbled together. Finally she said, "Was Jemma your sister?"

"I told you, I was not there," he said in a distant voice. "The man who did those things was not me."

He was sitting at the table across from her again, his hands clasped before him. Now he spoke to her directly. "Thorn, you are unitary and authentic now as you will never be again. As you pass through life, you will accumulate other selves. Always you will be a person looking back on, and separate from, the person you are now. Whenever you walk down a street, or sit on a park bench, your past selves will be sitting beside you, impossible to touch or interrogate. In the end there is a whole crowd of you wherever you go, and you feel like you will perish from the loneliness."

Thorn's whirling feelings were beginning to come to rest in a pattern, and in it horror and blame predominated. She looked up at Jemma's face and said, "She *died*. How could you do that, and walk away? It's inhuman."

He didn't react, either to admit guilt or defend his innocence. She wanted an explanation from him, and he didn't give it. "You're a monster," she said.

Still he said nothing. She got up, blind to everything but the intensity of her thoughts, and went to the door. She glanced back before leaving, and he was looking at her with an expression that was nothing like what he ought to feel—not shame, not rage, not self-loathing. Thorn slammed the door behind her and fled.

She walked around the streets of the Waste for a long time, viciously throwing stones at heaps of trash to make the rats come out. Above the buildings, the sky seemed even redder than usual, and the shadows blacker. She was furious at the magister for not being admirable. She blamed him for hiding it from her and for telling her—since, by giving her the knowledge, he had also given her a responsibility of choosing what to do.

When she got home the kitchen was empty, but she heard voices from the living room above. She was mounting the stairs when the voices rose in anger, and she froze. It was Hunter and Maya, and they were yelling at each other.

"Good God, what were you thinking?" Hunter demanded.

"She needed help. I couldn't say no."

"You knew it would bring the authorities down on us!"

"I had a responsibility—"

"What about your responsibility to me? You just didn't think. You never think; everything is impulse with you. You are the most immature and manipulative person I've ever met."

Maya's voice went wheedling. "Hunter, come on. It'll be okay."

"And what if it's not okay? What are you going to do then? Just pick up and leave the wreckage behind you? That's what you've been doing all your life—dragging that kid of yours from planet to planet, never thinking what it's doing to her. You never think what you're doing to anyone, do you? It's all just yourself. I never should have let you in here."

There were angry footsteps, and then Hunter was mounting the stairs.

"Hunter!" Maya cried after him.

Thorn waited a minute, then crept up into the living room. Maya was sitting there, looking tragic and beautiful.

"What did you do?" Thorn said.

"It doesn't matter," Maya said. "He'll get over it."

"I don't care about Hunter."

Mistaking what she meant, Maya smiled through her tears. "You know what? I don't care either." She came over and hugged Thorn tight. "I'm not really a bad mother, am I, Thorn?"

Cautiously, Thorn said, "No . . ."

"People just don't understand us. We're a team, right?"

Maya held out her hand for their secret finger-hook. Once it would have made Thorn smile, but she no longer felt the old solidarity against the world. She hooked fingers anyway, because she was afraid Maya would start to cry again if she didn't. Maya said, "They just don't know you. Damaged child, poppycock—you're tough as old boots. It makes me awestruck, what a survivor you are."

"I think we ought to get ready to leave," Thorn said.

Maya's face lost its false cheer. "I can't leave," she whispered.

"Why not?"

"Because I love him."

There was no sensible answer to that. So Thorn turned away to go up to her room. As she passed the closed door of Hunter's office, she paused, wondering if she should knock. Wondering if she should turn in the most notorious Gminta collaborator still alive. All those millions of dead Alloes and Vinds would get their justice, and Hunter would be famous. Then her feet continued on, even before she consciously made the decision. It was not loyalty to Magister Pregaldin, and it was not resentment of Hunter. It was because she might need that information to buy her own safety.

The sound of breaking glass woke her. She lay tense, listening to footsteps and raised voices below in the street. Then another window broke, and she got up to pull back the curtain. The sun was orange, as always, and she squinted in the glare, then raised her window and climbed out on the roof.

Below in the street, a mob of white-clad Incorruptibles was breaking windows as they passed; but their true target obviously lay deeper in the Waste. She watched till they were gone, then waited to see what would happen.

From somewhere beyond the tower fans of the park she could hear shouts and clanging, and once an avalanche-like roar, after which a cloud of dust rose from the direction of Weezer Alley. After that there was silence for a while. At last she heard chanting. Fleeing footsteps passed below. Then the wall of Incorruptibles appeared again. They were driving someone before them with improvised whips made from their belts. Thorn peered over the eaves to see more clearly and recognized their victim—Ginko, the heshe from the Garden of Delights, completely naked, both breasts and genitals exposed, with a rope around hisher neck. The whips had cut into the delicate paisley of Ginko's skin, exposing slashes of red underneath.

At a spot beneath Thorn's perch, Ginko stumbled and fell. A mass of Incorruptibles gathered round. Two of them pulled Ginko's legs apart, and a third made a jerking motion with a knife. A womanlike scream made Thorn grip the edge of her rooftop, wanting to look away. They tossed the rope over a signpost and hoisted Ginko up by the neck, choking and clawing at the noose. The body still quivered as the army marched past. When they were gone, the silence was so complete Thorn could hear the patter of blood into a pool on the pavement under the body.

On hands and knees she backed away from the edge of the roof and climbed into her bedroom. It was already stripped; everything she valued or needed was in her backpack, ready to go. She threw on some clothes and went down the stairs.

Maya, dressed in a robe, stopped her halfway. She looked scattered and panicky. "Thorn, we've got to leave," she said.

"Right now?"

"Yes. He doesn't want us here anymore. He's acting as if we're some sort of danger to him."

"Where are we going?"

"I don't know. Some other planet. Someplace without men." She started to cry.

"Go get dressed," Thorn told her. "I'll bring some food." Over her shoulder she added, "Pack some clothes and money."

With her backpack in hand, Thorn raced down to the kitchen.

She was just getting out the dolly for the ice owl's refrigerator when Maya came down.

"You're not taking that, are you?" Maya said.

"Yes, I am." Thorn knelt to shift the refrigerator out from under the table, and only then noticed it wasn't running. Quickly, she checked the temperature gauge. It was in the red zone, far too high. With an anguished exclamation, she punched in the lock code and opened the top. Not a breath of cool air escaped. The ice pack on top was gurgling and liquid. She lifted it to see what was underneath.

The owl was no longer nested snugly in ice. It had shifted, tried to open its wings. There were scratches on the insulation where it had tried to peck and claw its way out. Now it lay limp, its head thrown back. Thorn sank to her knees, griefstruck before the evidence of its terrifying last minutes—revived to life only to find itself trapped in a locked chest. Even in that stifling dark, it had longed for life so much it had fought to free itself. Thorn's breath came hard and her heart labored, as if she were reliving the ice owl's death.

"Hurry up, Thorn," Maya said. "We've got to go."

Then she saw what had happened. The refrigerator cord lay on the floor, no longer attached to the wall outlet. She held it up as if it were a murder weapon. "It's unplugged," she said.

"Oh, that's right," Maya said, distracted. "I had to plug in the curling iron. I must have forgotten."

Rage rose inside Thorn like a huge bubble of compressed air. "You *forgot*?"

"I'm sorry, Thorn. I didn't know it was important."

"I *told* you it was important. This was the last ice owl anywhere. You haven't just killed this one, you've killed the entire species."

"I said I was sorry. What do you want me to do?"

Maya would never change. She would always be like this, careless and irresponsible, unable to face consequences. Tears of fury came to Thorn's eyes. She dashed them away with her hand. "You're useless," she said, climbing to her feet and picking up her pack. "You can't be trusted to take care of anything. I'm done with you. Don't bother to follow me."

Out in the street, she turned in the direction she never went, to avoid having to pass what was hanging in the street. Down a narrow alley she sprinted, past piles of stinking refuse alive with roaches, till she came to a narrow side street that dog-legged into the park. On the edge of the open space she paused under a portico to scan for danger; seeing none, she dashed across, past the old men's chess tables, past the bench where she had met Magister Pregaldin, to the entrance of Weezer Alley.

Signs of the Incorruptibles' passage were everywhere. Broken glass crunched underfoot and the contents of the shops were trampled under red dirt shoeprints. When Thorn reached the Garden of Delights, the entire street looked different, for the building had been demolished. Only a monstrous pile of rubble remained, with iron girders and ribs sticking up like broken bones. A few people climbed over the ruin, looking for survivors.

The other side of the street was still standing, but Magister Pregaldin's door had been ripped from its hinges and tossed aside. Thorn dashed up the familiar stairs. The apartment looked as if it had been looted—stripped bare, not a thing of value left. She walked through the empty rooms, dreading what she might find, and finding nothing. Out on the street again, she saw a man who had often winked at her when she passed by to her lessons. "Do you know what happened to Magister Pregaldin?" she asked. "Did he get away?"

"Who?" the man said.

"Magister Pregaldin. The man who lived here."

"Oh, the old Vind. No, I don't know where he is."

So he had abandoned her as well. In all the world, there was no one trustworthy. For a moment she had a dark wish that she had exposed his secret. Then she realized she was just thinking of revenge.

Hoisting her pack to her shoulder, she set out for the waystation. She was alone now, only herself to trust.

There was a crowd in the street outside the waystation. Everyone seemed to have decided to leave the planet at once, some of them with huge piles of baggage and children. Thorn pushed her way in toward the ticket station to find out what was going on. They were still selling tickets, she saw with relief; the crowd was people waiting for their turn in the translation chamber. Checking to make sure she had her copy of Maya's credit stick, she joined the ticket line. She was back among her own kind, the rootless, migrant elite.

Where was she going? She scanned the list of destinations. She had been born on Capella Two, but had heard it was a harshly competitive place, so she decided against it. Ben was just an ice-ball world, Gammadis was too far away. It was both thrilling and frightening to have control over where she went and what she did. She was still torn by indecision when she heard someone calling, "Thorn!"

Clarity was pushing through the crowd toward her. "I'm so glad we found you," she said when she drew close. "Maya was here a little while ago, looking for you."

"Where is she now?" Thorn asked, scanning the crowd.

"She left again."

"Good," Thorn said.

"Thorn, she was frantic. She was afraid you'd get separated."

"We *are* separated," Thorn said implacably. "She can do what she wants. I'm on my own now. Where are you going, Clarity?"

Bick had come up, carrying their ticket cards. Thorn caught her hand to look at the tickets. "Alananovis," she read aloud, then looked up to find it on the directory. It was only eighteen light-years distant. "Can I come with you?"

"Not without Maya," Clarity said.

"Okay, then I'll go somewhere else."

Clarity put a hand on her arm. "Thorn, you can't just go off without Maya."

"Yes, I can. I'm old enough to be on my own. I'm sick of her, and I'm sick of her boyfriends. I want control of my life." Besides, Maya had killed the ice owl; Maya ought to suffer. It was only justice.

She had reached the head of the line. Her eye caught a name on the list, and she made a snap decision. When the ticket seller said "Where to?" she answered, "Gmintagad." She would go to see where Jemma Diwali had lived—and died.

The translation chamber on Gmintagad was like all the others she had seen over the years: sterile and anonymous. A technician led her into a waiting room till her luggage came through by the low-resolution beam. She sat feeling cross and tired, as she always did after having her molecules reassembled out of new atoms. When at last her backpack was delivered and she went on into the customs and immigration facility, she noticed a change in the air. For the first time in years she was breathing organically manufactured oxygen. She could smell the complex and decay-laden odor of an actual ecosystem. Soon she would see sky without any dome. The thought gave her an agoraphobic thrill.

She put her identity card into the reader, and after a pause it directed her to a glass-fronted booth where an immigration official in a sand-colored uniform sat behind a desk. Unlike the air, the man looked manufactured—a face with no wrinkles, defects, or stand-out features, as if they had chosen him to match a mathematical formula for facial symmetry. His hair was neatly clipped, and so, she noticed, were his nails. When she sat opposite him, she found that her chair creaked at the slightest movement. She tried to hold perfectly still.

He regarded her information on his screen, then said, "Who is your father?"

She had been prepared to say why her mother was not with her, but her father? "I don't know," she said. "Why?"

"Your records do not state his race."

His *race*? It was an antique concept she barely understood. "He was Capellan," she said.

"Capellan is not an origin. No one evolved on Capella."

"I did," Thorn stated.

He studied her without any expression at all. She tried to meet his eyes, but it began to seem confrontational, so she looked down. Her chair creaked.

"There are certain types of people we do not allow on Gmintagad," he said.

She tried to imagine what he meant. Criminals? Disease carriers? Agitators? He could see she wasn't any of those. "Wasters, you mean?" she finally ventured.

"I mean Vinds," he said.

Relieved, she said, "Oh, well that's all right, then. I'm not Vind." Creak.

"Unless you can tell me who your father was, I cannot be sure of that," he said.

She was speechless. How could a father she had never known have any bearing on who she was?

The thought that they might not let her in made her stomach knot. Her chair sent out a barrage of telegraphic signals. "I just spent 32 years as a lightbeam to get here," she said. "You've got to let me stay."

"We are a sovereign principality," he said calmly. "We don't *have* to let anyone stay." He paused, his eyes still on her. "You have a Vind look. Are you willing to submit to a genetic test?"

Minutes ago, her mind had seemed like syrup. Now it bubbled with alarm. In fact, she didn't *know* her father wasn't Vind. It had never mattered, so she had never cared. But here, all the things that defined her—her interests, her aptitudes, her internal doubts—none of it counted, only her racial status. She was in a place where identity was assigned, not chosen or created.

"What happens if I fail the test?" she asked.

"You will be sent back."

"And what happens if I don't take it?"

"You will be sent back."

"Then why did you even ask?"

He gave a regulation smile. If she had measured it with a ruler, it would have been perfect. She stood up, and the chair sounded like it was laughing. "All right. Where do I go?"

They took her blood and sent her into a waiting room with two doors, neither of which had a handle. As she sat there idle, the true rashness of what she had done crept up on her. It wasn't like running away on-planet. Maya didn't know where she had gone. By now, they would be different ages. Maya could be dying, or Thorn could be older than she was, before they ever found each other. It was a permanent separation. And permanent punishment for Maya.

Thorn tried to summon up the righteous anger that had propelled her only an hour and 32 years before. But even that slipped from her grasp. It was replaced with a clutching feeling of her own guilt. She had known Maya's shortcomings when she took the ice owl, and never bothered to safeguard against them. She had known all the accidents the world was capable of; and still she had failed to protect a creature that could not protect itself.

Now, remorse made her bleed inside. The owl had been too innocent to meet such a terrible end. Its life should have been a joyous ascent into air, and instead it had been a hellish struggle, alone and forgotten, killed by neglect. Thorn had betrayed everyone by letting the ice owl die. Magister Pregaldin, who had trusted her with his precious possession. Even, somehow, Jemma and the other victims of Till Diwali's crime—for what had she done but re-enact his failure, as if to show that human beings had learned nothing? She felt as if caught in an iron-bound cycle of history, doomed to repeat what had gone before, as long as she was no better than her predecessors had been.

She covered her face with her hands, wanting to cry, but too demoralized even for that. It seemed like a self-indulgence she didn't deserve.

The door clicked and she started up at the sight of a stern, rectangular woman in a uniform skirt, whose face held the hint of a sneer. Thorn braced for the news that she would have to waste another 32 years on a pointless journey back to Glory to God. But instead, the woman said, "There is someone here to see you."

Behind her was a familiar face that made Thorn exclaim in joy, "Clarity!"

Clarity came into the room, and Thorn embraced her in relief. "I thought you were going to Alananovis."

"We were," Clarity said, "but we decided we couldn't just stand by and let a disaster happen. I followed you, and Bick stayed behind to tell Maya where we were going."

"Oh, thank you, thank you!" Thorn cried. Now the tears that had refused to come before were running down her face. "But you gave up 32 years for a stupid reason."

"It wasn't stupid for us," Clarity said. "You were the stupid one."

"I know," Thorn said miserably.

Clarity was looking at her with an expression of understanding. "Thorn, most people your age are allowed some mistakes. But you're performing life without a net. You have to consider Maya. Somehow, you've gotten older than she is even though you've been traveling together. You're the steady one, the rock she leans on. These boyfriends, they're just entertainment for her. They drop her and she bounces back. But if you dropped her, her whole world would dissolve."

Thorn said, "That's not true."

"It *is* true," Clarity said.

Thorn pressed her lips together, feeling impossibly burdened. Why did *she* have to be the reliable one, the one who was never vulnerable or wounded? Why did Maya get to be the dependent one?

On the other hand, it was a comfort that she hadn't abandoned Maya as she had done to the ice owl. Maya was not a perfect mother, but neither was Thorn a perfect daughter. They were both just doing their best.

"I hate this," she said, but without conviction. "Why do I have to be responsible for her?"

"That's what love is all about," Clarity said.

"You're a busybody, Clarity," Thorn said.

Clarity squeezed her hand. "Yes. Aren't you lucky?"

The door clicked open again. Beyond the female guard's square shoulder, Thorn glimpsed a flash of honey-gold hair. "Maya!" she said.

When she saw Thorn, Maya's whole being seemed to blaze like the sun. Dodging in, she threw her arms around Thorn.

"Oh Thorn, thank heaven I found you! I was worried sick. I thought you were lost."

"It's okay, it's okay," Thorn kept saying as Maya wept and hugged her again. "But Maya, you have to tell me something."

"Anything. What?"

"Did you seduce a *Vind*?"

For a moment Maya didn't understand. Then a secretive smile grew on her face, making her look very pretty and pleased with herself. She touched Thorn's hair. "I've been meaning to tell you about that."

"Later," Bick said. "Right now, we all have tickets for Alananovis."

"That's wonderful," Maya said. "Where's Alananovis?"

"Only seven years away from here."

"Fine. It doesn't matter. Nothing matters as long as we're together."

She held out her finger for the secret finger-lock. Thorn did it with a little inward sigh. For a moment she felt as if her whole world were composed of vulnerable beings frozen in time, as if she were the only one who aged and changed.

"We're a team, right?" Maya said anxiously.

"Yeah," Thorn answered. "We're a team."

The Copenhagen Interpretation

PAUL CORNELL

The fast-paced and rather strange story that follows is one of a series of stories (including recent Hugo finalist "One of Our Bastards Is Missing") that Paul Cornell has been writing about the exploits of spy Jonathan Hamilton in the Great Game between nations in a nineteenth-century Europe where technology has followed a very different path from that of our own timeline, stories that read, as I once said, like Ruritanian romances written by Charles Stross. In this adventure, Hamilton must deal with the consequences of having an old girlfriend pop up in very peculiar circumstances, initiating a chain of events that might bring about the end of the world, something Hamilton battles to prevent in a flamboyantly entertaining fashion reminiscent of the adventures of James Bond, or, better, of Poul Anderson's Dominic Flandry, whom I think is his direct ancestor.

British author Paul Cornell is a writer of novels, comics, and television. His novels include Something More *and* British Summertime. *He's written* Doctor Who *episodes as well as episodes of* Robin Hood *and* Primeval *for the BBC, and* Captain Britain *for Marvel Comics, in addition to many* Doctor Who *novelizations, the editing of* Doctor Who *anthologies, and many other comic works. His* Doctor Who *episodes have twice been nominated for the Hugo Award, and he shares a Writer's Guild Award. Of late, he's taken to writing short science fiction, with sales to* Fast Forward 2, Eclipse 2, Asimov's Science Fiction, *and* The Solaris Book of New Science Fiction, *Volume Three.*

The best time to see Kastellet is in the evening, when the ancient fortifications are alight with glow worms, a landmark for anyone gazing down on the city as they arrive by carriage. Here stands one of Copenhagen's great parks, its defence complexes, including the home of the Forsvarets Efterretningstjeneste, and a single windmill, decorative rather than functional. The wind comes in hard over the Langeline, and after the sun goes down, the skeleton of the whale that's been grown into the ground resonates in sympathy and gives out a howl that can be heard in Sweden.

Hamilton had arrived on the diplomatic carriage, without papers, and, as etiquette demanded, without weapons or folds, thoroughly out of uniform. He watched the carriage heave itself up into the darkening sky above the park, and bank off to the southwest, swaying in the wind, sliding up the fold it made under its running boards. He was certain every detail was being registered by the FLV. You don't look into the diplomatic bag, but you damn well know where the bag goes. He left the park through the healed bronze gates and headed down a flight of steps towards the diplomatic quarter, thinking of nothing. He did that when there were urgent questions he couldn't answer, rather than run them round and round in his head and let them wear away at him.

The streets of Copenhagen. Ladies and gentlemen stepping from carriages, the occasional tricolour of feathers on a hat or, worse, once, tartan over a shoulder. Hamilton found himself reacting, furious. But then he saw it was Campbell. The wearer, a youth in evening wear, was the sort of fool who heard an accent in a bar and took up anything apparently forbidden, in impotent protest against the world. And thus got fleeced by Scotsmen.

He was annoyed at his anger. He had failed to contain himself.

He walked past the façade of the British embassy, with the Hanoverian regiment on guard, turned a corner and waited in one of those convenient dark streets that form the second map of diplomatic quarters everywhere in the world. After a moment, a door with no external fittings swung open and someone ushered him inside and took his coat.

"The girl arrived at the front door, in some distress. She spoke to one of our Hanoverians, Private Glassman, and became agitated when he couldn't understand her. Then she seems to have decided that none of us should understand her. We tried to put her through the observer inside the hallway, but she wouldn't hear of it." The Ambassador was Bayoumi, a Musselman with grey in his beard. Hamilton had met him once before, at a ball held in a palace balanced on a single wave, grown out of the ocean and held there to mark the presence of royalty from three of the great powers. He had been exactly gracious, as he had to be, making his duty appear weightless. In this place, perhaps that was what he took it to be.

"So she could be armed?" Hamilton had made himself sit down, now he was focusing on the swirls of lacquered gunwood on the surface of the Ambassador's desk.

"She *could* be folded like origami."

"You're sure of the identification?"

"Well . . ." Hamilton recognized that moment when the diplomatic skills of a continental ambassador unfolded themselves. At least they were present. "Major, if we can, I'd like to get through this without compromising the girl's dignity—"

Hamilton cut him off. "Your people trusted nothing to the courier except a name and *assume* the EM out of here's compromised." Which was shoddy to the point of terrifying. "*What?*"

The ambassador let out a sigh. "I make it a point," he said, "never to ask a lady her age."

They had kept her in the entrance hallway and closed the embassy to all other business that day. Eventually, they had extended the embassy's security bunker to the hallway, created a doorway into it by drilling out the wall, and set up a small room for her inside it. She was separated from the rest of the embassy by a fold, which had light pushed through it, so Hamilton could watch her on an intelligent projection that took up much of a wall in one of the building's many unused office spaces.

Hamilton saw her face, and found he was holding his breath. "Let me in there."

"But if—"

"If she kills me nobody will care. Which is why she won't."

He walked into the room made of space, with a white sheen on the walls for the visual comfort of those inside. He closed the door behind him.

She looked at him. Perhaps she started to recognise him. She wavered with uncertainty.

He sat down opposite her.

She reacted as his gaze took her in, aware that he wasn't looking at her like a stranger should look at a lady. Perhaps that was tipping her towards recognition. Not that that would necessarily be a sign of anything.

The body was definitely that of Lustre Saint Clair: bobbed hair; full mouth; the affectation of spectacles; those warm, hurt eyes.

But she couldn't be more than eighteen. The notes in his eyes confirmed it, beyond all cosmetic possibility.

This was the Lustre Saint Clair he'd known. The Lustre Saint Clair from *fifteen years ago.*

"Is it you?" she said. In Enochian. In Lustre's voice.

He had been fourteen, having left Cork for the first time, indentured in the 4th Dragoons because of his father's debt, proud to finally be able to pay it through his service. He'd had the corners knocked off him and had yet to gain new ones at Keble. Billeted in Warminster, he had been every inch the Gentleman Cadet, forced to find a common society with the other ranks, who tended to laugh at the aristocracy of his Irish accent. They were always asking how many Tories he'd killed, and he'd never found an answer. Years later, he'd come to think he should have told the truth and said two and seen if that would shock them. He'd been acutely conscious of his virginity.

Lustre had been one of the young ladies it was acceptable for him to be seen with in town. Her being older than he was had appealed to Hamilton very much. Especially since she was reticent, shy, unable to overawe him. That had allowed him to be bold. Too bold, on occasion. They were always seeing and then not seeing each other. She was on his arm at dances, with no need of a card on three occasions, and then supposedly with some other cadet. But Hamilton had always annoyed Lustre by not taking those other suitors seriously, and she had always come back to him. The whole idiocy had taken less than three months, his internal calendar now said, incredibly. But it was years written in stone.

He had never been sure if she was even slightly fond of him until the moment she had initiated him into the mysteries. And they had even fought that night. But they had at least been together after that, for a while, awkward and fearful as that had been.

Lustre was a secretary for Lord Surtees, but she had told Hamilton, during that night of greater intimacy, that this was basically a lie, that she was also a courier, that in her head was the seed for a diplomatic language, that sometimes she would be asked to speak the words that made it grow into her, and then she would know no other language, and be foreign to all countries apart from the dozen people in court and government with whom she could converse. In the event of capture, she would say other words, or her package would force them on her, and she would be left with a language, in thought and memory as well as in speech, spoken by no other, which any other would be unable to learn, and she would be like that unto death, which, cut off from the sum of mankind that made the balance as she would be, would presumably and hopefully soon follow.

She'd said this to him like she was making an observation about the weather. Not with the detachment that Hamilton had come to admire in his soldiers, but with a fatalism that made him feel sick that night and afraid. He hadn't known whether to believe her. It had been her seeming certainty of how she would end, that night, that had made him react, raise his voice, drag them back into one of their endless grindings of not yet shaped person on person. But in the weeks that followed, he had come to half appreciate those confidences, shrugging aside the terrible burden she put on him, and her weakness in doing so, if it all was true, because of the wonder of her.

He had done many more foolish and terrible things while he was a Cadet. Every now and then he supposed he should have regrets. But what was the point? And yet here was the one thing he hadn't done. He hadn't left that little room above the inn and gone straight back to barracks and asked for an interview with Lieutenant Rashid and told him that this supposed lady had felt able to share the secret of her status. He hadn't done it in all the weeks after.

The one thing he hadn't done, and, like some Greek fate or the recoil from a prayer too few, here it was back for him.

Six months later, Lustre Saint Clair, after she'd followed His Lordship back to London and stopped returning Hamilton's letters, had vanished.

He'd only heard of it because he'd recognised a friend of hers at some ball, had distracted the lady on his arm and gone to pay his respects, and had heard of tears and horrors and none of the girls in Surtees' employ knowing what had become of her.

He'd hidden his reaction then. And ever after. He'd made what inquiries he could. Almost none. He'd found the journals for that day on his plate, and located something about a diplomatic incident between the Court of Saint James's and the Danes, both blaming the other for a "misunderstanding" that the writer of the piece was duty bound not to go into in any more detail, but was surely the fault of typical Dansk whimsy. Reading between the lines, it was clear that something had been lost, possibly a diplomatic bag. Presumably that bag had contained or been Lustre. And then his regiment had suddenly mustered and he'd been dragged away from it all.

For months, years, it had made him feel sick, starting with a great and sudden fear there at his desk. It had stayed his burden and only gradually declined. But nothing had come of it. As he had risen in the ranks, and started to do out of uniform work, he had quieted his conscience by assuring himself that he had had no concrete detail to impart to his superiors. She had been loose-lipped and awkward with the world. This is not evidence, these are feelings.

That had been the whole of it until that morning. When he had heard her name again, out of Turpin's mouth, when Hamilton had been standing in his office off Horseguards Parade.

That name, and her seeming return after fifteen years of being assumed dead.

Hamilton had concealed the enormity of his reaction. He was good at that now. His Irish blood was kept in an English jar.

At last he had heard the details he had carefully never asked about since he'd started doing out of uniform work. All those years ago, Lustre had been sent to Copenhagen on a routine information exchange, intelligence deemed too sensitive to be trusted to the embroidery or anything else that was subject to the whims of man and God. Turpin hadn't told him what the information was, only that it had been marked For Their Majesties, meaning that only the crowned heads of specific great powers and their chosen advisors could hear it. Lustre had been set down in one of the parks, met by members of the Politiets Efterretningstjeneste, and walked to Amalienborg Palace. Presumably. Because she and they never got there. They had simply not arrived, and after an hour of Dansk *laissez faire*, in which time it was presumably thought they might have gone to the pub or had a spot of lunch, the alarms had begun. Nothing had ever been found. There were no witnesses. It had been a perfect abduction, if that was what it was.

The great powers had panicked, Turpin had said. They'd expected the balance to collapse, for war to follow shortly. Armies across the continent and solar system had been dispatched to ports and carriage posts. Hamilton remembered that sudden muster, that his regiment had been sent to kick the mud off their boots in Portsmouth. Which soon had turned into just another exercise. Turpin's predecessor had lost his job as a result of the affair, and shortly after that his life, in a hunting accident which was more of the former than the latter.

Hamilton had known better, this morning, than to say that whatever was in Lustre's head must have extraordinary value, for it to mean the end of the sacred trust of all those in public life, the end of everything. The thought of it had made him feel sick again, tugging on a thread that connected the import of what she'd carried to her willingness to talk.

"Is this matter," he'd asked, "still as sensitive?"

Turpin had nodded. "That's why I'm sending you. And why you're going to be briefed with Enochian. We presume that'll be all she's able to speak, or that's what we hope, and you're going to need to hear what she has to say and act on it there and then. The alternative would be to send a force to get her out of there, and, as of this hour, we're not quite ready to invade Denmark."

His tone had suggested no irony. It was said mad old King Frederik was amused by the idea of his state bringing trouble to the great powers. That he has aspirations to acquisitions in the Solar System beyond the few small rocks that currently had Dansk written through them like bacon.

The warmth of Turpin's trust had supported Hamilton against his old weakness. He'd taken on the language and got into the carriage to cross stormy waters, feeling not prayed for enough, yet unwilling to ask for it, fated and ready to die.

And so here she was. Or was she?

Was she a grown homunculus, with enough passing memory to recognise him? And speak Enochian too? No, surely that was beyond what could be stuffed into such a foul little brain. And assigning such personhood to such an object was beneath even the depths to which the Heeresnachrichtenamt would sink. Was she a real person with grown features to suggest young Lustre? That was entirely possible. But what was the point, when she'd be suspected immediately? Why not make her look the age she was supposed to be?

"Yes," he said in Enochian. "It's me."

"Then . . . it's true, God's-seen-it. What's been obvious since I . . . since I got back."

"Back from where?"

"They said someone with authority was coming to see me. Is that you?"

"Yes."

She looked as if she could hardly believe it. "I need protection. Once we're back in Britain—"

"Not until I know—"

"You know as well as I do that this room, this building—!"

"On the way in, when this was a hallway, why didn't you let yourself be observed?"

She took a breath and her mouth formed into a thin line. And suddenly they were back fighting again. Fools. Still. With so much at stake.

He should have told them. They should have sent someone else.

"Listen," she said, "how long has it been since you last saw me?"

"Decade and a half, give or take."

He saw the shock on her face again. It was like she kept getting hurt by the same thing. By the echoes of it. "I saw the dates when I got out. I couldn't believe it. For me it's been . . . four years . . . or . . . no time at all, really."

Hamilton was certain there was nothing that could do this. He shook his head, putting the mystery aside for a moment. "Is the package safe?"

"Typical you, to gallop round. Yes! That's why I didn't take the observer machine! Those things have a reputation, particularly one here. It might have set me babbling."

But that was also what a homunculus or a cover would say. He found he was scowling at her. "Tell me what happened. Everything."

But then a small sound came from beside them. Where a sound couldn't be. It was like a heavy item of furniture being thumped against the wall.

Lustre startled, turned to look—

Hamilton leapt at her.

He felt the sudden fire flare behind him.

And then he was falling upwards, sideways, back down again!

He landed and threw himself sidelong to grab Lustre as she was falling up out of her chair, as it was crashing away from her. The room was battering at his eyes, milky fire, arcing rainbows! Two impact holes, half the chamber billowing from each. An explosion was rushing around the walls towards them!

A shaped charge, Hamilton thought in the part of his mind that was fitted to take apart such things and turn them round, with a fold in the cone to demolish artificially curved space.

Whoever they were, they wanted Lustre or both of them alive.

Hamilton grabbed her round the shoulders and threw her at the door.

She burst it open and stumbled into the sudden gravity of the corridor beyond. He kicked his heels on the spinning chair, and dived through after her.

He fell onto the ground, hard on his shoulder, rolled to his feet, and jumped to slam the door behind them. It did its duty and completed the fold seconds before the explosion rolled straight at it.

There was nobody waiting for them in the hallway.

So they'd been about to enter the fold through the holes they'd blown? They might have found their corpses. It was a mistake, and Hamilton didn't like to feel that his enemy made mistakes. He'd rather assume he was missing something.

He had no gun.

Alarms started up in distant parts of the building. The corridor, he realised, was filling with smoke from above.

There came the sound of running feet, coming down the stairs from above them.

Friend or foe? No way to tell.

The attack had come from outside, but there might have been inside help, might now be combatants pouring in. The front door had held, but then it had been folded to distraction. If they knew enough to use that charge, they might not have even tried it.

Lustre was looking at the only door they could reach before the running feet reached them. It had a sign on it which Hamilton's Danish notations read as "cellar."

He threw himself back at the wall, then charged it with his foot. Non-grown wood burst around the lock. He kicked it out. The damage would be seen. He was betting on it not mattering. He swung open the door and found steps beyond. Lustre ran inside, and he closed the door behind them.

He tried a couple of shadowy objects and found something he could lift and put against the door. A tool box. They were in a room of ancient boilers, presumably a backup if the fuel cells failed.

"They'll find—!" Lustre began. But she immediately quieted herself.

He quickly found what he had suspected might be down here, a communications station on the wall. Sometimes when he was out of uniform he carried a small link to the embroidery, usually disguised as a watch to stop anyone from wondering what sort of person would have something like that. But he would never be allowed to bring such kit into a supposedly friendly country. The link on the wall was an internal system. He could only hope it connected to the link on the roof. He could and should have called the FLV. But he couldn't afford to trust the locals now. He couldn't have their systems register an honest call to Buckingham Palace or the building off Horseguards Parade. That would be a sin against the balance. So there was now only one person he could call. If she wasn't in her boudoir, he was dead and Lustre was back in the bag.

He tapped on the connector and blew the right notes into the receiver, hopefully letting the intelligent sound he was connecting to push past any listening ears.

To his relief, Cushion McKenzie came straight on the line, sounding urgent. Someone in the Palace might have tipped her off as to where he was tonight. "Johnny, what can I do for you?" Her voice came from the roof, the direction reserved for officers.

"Social call for papa." He could hear the running feet coming along the corridor towards the door. Would they miss the damage in the gathering smoke?

"Extract, package or kill?"

Kill meant him, a stroke that would take his life and erase what he knew, painlessly, he was assured. It was the only way an out-of-uniform officer could choose to die, self-murder being an option denied to the kit stowed in their heads. Cushion represented herself on the wider shores of the public embroidery as a salonist, but she was also thoroughly job. She'd once walked Hamilton out of Lisbon and into a public carriage with an armed driver, keeping up a stream of chatter that had kept him awake despite the sucking wound in his chest. He'd wanted to send her flowers afterwards, but he couldn't find anything in the *Language of Blooms* volume provided by his regiment that both described how he felt and kept the precious distance of the connection between them.

"Extract," he said.

"Right. Looking."

She was silent for a moment that bore hard on Hamilton's nerves. Whoever was seeking them was now fumbling around like amateurs in front of that door. Perhaps that was why they'd botched the explosives. Hamilton feared amateurs most of all. Amateurs killed you against orders.

"You're in an infested rat hole, Major. You should see what's rolling out on my coffee table. Decades of boltholes and overfolding, hidden and forgotten weapons. None near you, worse luck. If a point time stop opens there and collapses Copenhagen—"

"If we punch out here, will it?"

"Possibly. Never was my favourite city. Preparing."

Something went bump against the door. Then started to push at it. Lustre stepped carefully back from where the bullets would come, and Hamilton realised that, thanks to the length of the comms chord, he had no option but to stand in their way.

He thought of moments with Annie, giving his mind nothing else to do.

The thumping on the door was concerted now. Deliberate.

"Ready," said Cushion.

Hamilton beckoned and then grabbed Lustre to him.

"And in my ear . . . Colonel Turpin sends his complements."

"I return the Colonel's complements," said Hamilton. "Go."

The hole opened under them with a blaze that might be the city collapsing. Hamilton and Lustre fell into it and down the flashing corridor at the speed of a hurricane. Bullets burst from the splintering door in the distance and tore down the silver butterfly tunnel around them, ricocheting ridiculously past them—

Hamilton wished he had something to shoot back into their bastard faces.

And then they were out, into the blessed air of the night, thrown to the ground by an impossible hole above them—

—that immediately and diplomatically vanished.

Hamilton leapt to his feet, looking round. They were in a side street. Freezing. Darkness. No witnesses. Cushion had managed even that. That was all she was going to be able to do tonight, for him or for any of his brothers and sisters anywhere in the solar system. Turpin had allowed that for him. No, he checked himself, for what was inside Lustre.

He helped Lustre up, and they stared at the end of the street, where passersby were running to and fro. He could hear the bells of Saint Mary's tolling ten o'clock. In the distance, the embassy was ablaze, and carriages with red lights and bells were flashing through the sky, into the smoke, starting to pump water from their ocean folds into it. Those might well come under fire. And they were the only branch of public life here that was almost certainly innocent of what had just happened. The smell of smoke washed down the street. It would be enough to make Frederik close the airways too. Turpin and Her Majesty the Queen Mother were being asked, in this moment, to consider whether or not the knowledge Lustre had was worth open warfare between Greater Britain and a Dansk court who might well know nothing of all this, who already *knew* those secrets. But rather than let a British carriage in to collect the two of them, they'd spend hours asserting that their own services, riddled with rot as they might be, could handle it.

Across the street was a little inn with grown beef hanging from the roofline, pols music coming from the windows. The crowds would be heading to see the blaze and offer help in the useless way that gentlemen and those who wished to be gentlemen did.

Hamilton grabbed Lustre's hand and ran for the door.

He ordered in Dutch he called up from some regional variation in the back of his head, some of the real beef, potatoes and a bottle of wine, which he had no intention of drinking, but which served as an excuse as to why they wanted a discrete booth to themselves. Lustre looked demure at the landlord, avoiding his glance, a maid led astray. A maid, it suddenly occurred to Hamilton, in clothes that would raise eyebrows in London, being fifteen years out of the fashion. But they had no choice. And besides, this was Denmark.

They vanished into the darkness of their snug. They had a few minutes before the food arrived. They both started talking at once, quietly, so that the landlord wouldn't hear the strange tongue.

She held up a hand and he was silent.

"I'll tell you the whole bit," she said. "Fast as I can. Have you heard of the three quarters of an ounce theory?"

Hamilton shook his head.

"It's folk science, *Golden Book* stuff, the kind of infra religious thing you hear in servant pools. This chap weighed all these dying people, and found, they say, that three quarters of an ounce leaves you at death. That being the weight of the soul."

"Is this really the time for dollymop theology?"

She didn't rise to it. "Now I'm going to tell you something secret, For Their Majesties secret—"

"No—!"

"And if I die and not you, what happens then?" she snapped. "Because just killing me will *not* save the balance!" She'd added an epithet to the word, shocking him at the sound of it in her mouth. "Oh yes, I want to make sure you know that, in case push comes to shove." She didn't give him time to formulate a reply and that was probably a blessing. "What kind of out-of-uniform man have you become, if you can't live with secrets?! I don't care what you're cleared for, it's just *us* at the moment!"

Hamilton finally nodded.

"All right, then. You probably haven't heard either, your reading still presumably not extending beyond the hunting pages, about the astronomical problems concerning galaxies, the distribution of mass therein?"

"What?! What is this—?"

"No, of course you haven't. What it comes down to is: galaxies seem to have more mass than they should, loads of it. Nobody knew what it was. It's not visible. By just plotting what it influences, astronomers have made maps of where it all is. For a few years that was the entire business of Herstmonceux. Which I thought odd when I read about it, but now I know why."

The dinner came and they were forced to silence for a moment, just looking at each other. This new determination suited her, Hamilton found himself thinking. As did the harsh language. He felt an old, obscure pain and killed it. The landlord departed with a look of voyeuristic pleasure. "Go on."

"Don't you see? If the three quarter ounce theory is true, there's weight in the world that comes and goes, as if in and out of a fold, up God's sleeve as it were. Put loads of that together—"

Hamilton understood, and the distant enormity of it made him close his eyes. "That's the extra mass in those galaxies."

"And we have a map of it—"

"Which shows where there are minds, actual foreigners from other worlds, out there—!"

"*And perhaps nearby.*"

Hamilton's mind reeled at the horror of it. The potential threat to the balance! Any of the great powers, damn it, any *nation*, could gain immeasurable advantage over its fellows by trading intelligence with foreigners. "And this is what's in your head. The greatest secret of the great powers. But this is old news, they must have found a way to deal with it—"

"Yes. Because, after all, any of them could put together enough telescope time to work it out. As near as I can figure out, they shared the info. Every great court knows it at the highest level, so the balance is intact. Just about. I suppose they must have all made a secret agreement not to try to contact these foreigners. Pretty easy to check up on that, given how they all watch each other's embroidery."

Hamilton relaxed. So these were indeed old terrors, already dealt with by wiser heads. "And of course communication is all we're talking about. The distances involved—"

She looked at him like he was an erring child.

"Has one of the powers *broken* the agreement?!"

She pursed her lips. "This isn't the work of the great powers."

Hamilton wasn't sure he could take much more of this. "Then who?"

"Have you heard of the heavenly twins?"

"The Ransoms?!"

"Yes, Castor and Pollux."

Hamilton's mind was racing. The twins were arms dealers, who sold, it had been revealed a few years ago, to the shock of the great powers, not just to the nation to which they owed allegiance (which, them being from the northern part of the Columbian colonies, would be Britain or France), or even to one they'd later adopted, but to anyone. Once the great powers had found that out and closed ranks, dealing with the twins as they dealt with any threat to the balance, their representatives had vanished overnight from their offices in the world's capitals, and started to sell away from any counter, to rebels, mercenaries, colonies. Whoring out their services. The twins themselves had never shown their faces in public. It was said they had accumulated enough wealth to actually begin to develop new weapons of their own. Every other month some new speculation arose that one of the powers was secretly once more buying from them. Not something Britain would ever do, of course, but the Dutch, the Spaniards? "How are they involved?"

"When I was halfway across this city, on my original mission, a rabbit hole similar to the one we just fell down opened up under me and my honour guard."

"They can do that?!"

"Compared to what else they're doing, that's nothing. They had their own soldiers on hand, soldiers in *uniform*—"

Hamilton could hear the disgust in her voice, and matched it with his own. Tonight was starting to feel like some sort of nightmare, with every certainty collapsing. He felt like he was falling from moment to moment as terrible new possibilities sprang up before his eyes.

"They cut down my party, taking a few losses themselves. They took the bodies with them."

"They must have mopped the place up afterwards too."

"I was dragged before them. I don't know if we were still in this city. I was ready to say the words and cut myself off, but they were ready for that. They injected me with some sort of instant glossolalia. I thought for a second that I'd done it myself, but then I realised that I couldn't stop talking, that I was saying all sorts of nonsense, from anywhere in my mind, ridiculous stuff, shameful stuff." She paused for breath. "You *were* mentioned."

"I wasn't going to ask."

"I didn't talk about what I was carrying. Sheer luck. I wrenched clear of their thugees and tried to bash my brains out against the wall."

He had put his hand on hers. Without even thinking about it.

She let it stay. "I wouldn't recommend it, probably not possible, but they only gave me two cracks at it before they grabbed me again. They were planning to keep injecting me with the stuff until I'd spilled the words that'd let them use an observer to see the map. They locked me up in a room and recorded me all night. That got quite dull quite swiftly."

Listening to her, Hamilton felt himself calm. He was looking forward, with honest glee, to the possibility that he might be soon in a position to harm some of these men.

"I gambled that after it got late enough and I still hadn't said anything *politically* interesting they'd stop watching and just record it. I waited as long as I could with my sanity intact, then had at one of the walls. I found main power and shoved my fingers in. Wish I could tell you more about that, but I don't remember anything from then on until I woke up in what turned out to be a truly enormous void carriage. I came to in the infirmary, connected to all sorts of drugs. My internal clock said it was . . . four years later . . . which I took to be an error. I checked the package in my head, but the seals were all intact. I could smell smoke. So I took the drug lines out best I could, hopped out of bed. There were a few others in there, but they were all dead or out of it. Odd looking wounds, like their flesh had been sucked off them. I found more dead bodies in the corridor outside. Staff in that uniform of theirs. There was still somebody driving the thing, because when I checked the internal embroidery, there were three seats taken. I think they were running the absolute minimum staff, just trying to get the thing home, three survivors of whatever had happened. The carriage was throwing up all sorts of false flags and passport deals as we approached Earth orbit from high up above the plane. I went and hid near the bulwark door, and when the carriage arrived at one of the Danish high stations I waited until the rescue party dashed on. Then I wandered out." Her voice took on a pleading edge, as if she was asking if she was still in a dream. "I . . . took a descent bus and I remember thinking what classy transportation it was, very bells and whistles, especially for the Danes. When I listened in to the embroidery, and checked the log against what I was hearing, I realised . . . and it took some realising, I can tell you, it took me checking many times . . ."

Her hand had grasped his, demanding belief.

"It had been four years unconscious for me . . . but . . ." She had to take a deep breath, her eyes appealing once again at the astonishing unfairness of it.

"Fifteen years for us," he said. Looking at her now, at how this older woman who had started to teach him about himself had stayed a girl of an age he could never now be seen with in public . . . the change had been lessened for him because it was how he'd kept her in his memory, but now he saw the size of it. The difference between them now was an index of all he'd done. He shook his head to clear it, to take those dismayed eyes off him. "What does it mean?"

She was about to answer him. But he suddenly realised the music had got louder. He knocked his steak knife from the table to the seat and into his pocket.

Lustre looked shocked at him.

But now a man looking like a typical patron of an inn had looked in at their booth. "Excuse me," he said, in Dutch with an accent Hamilton's eye notes couldn't place, "do you know where the landlord's gone? I'm meant to have a reservation—"

A little something about the man's expression.

He was getting away with it.

He wasn't.

Hamilton jerked sidelong rather than stand up, sending the knife up into the man's groin. He twisted it out as he grabbed for the belt, throwing him forward as blood burst over the tablecloth and he was up and out into the main bar just as the man started screaming—

There was another man, who'd been looking into the kitchen, suddenly angry at a landlord who, expecting the *usual* sort of trouble, had turned up the piped band. He turned now, his hand slapping for a gun at his waist—

Amateurs!

Hamilton threw the bloody knife at his face. In that moment, the man took it to be a throwing knife, and threw up a hand as it glanced off him, but Hamilton had closed the gap between the two of them, and now he swung his shoulder and slammed his fist into the man's neck. The man gurgled and fell, Hamilton grabbed him before he did and beat his hands to the gun.

He didn't use it. The man was desperately clutching at his own throat. Hamilton let him fall.

He swung back to the booth, and saw the other twitching body slide to the floor. Lustre was already squatting to gather that gun too.

He turned to the landlord coming out of the kitchen and pointed the gun at him. "More?!"

"No! I'll do anything—!"

"I mean, are there more of *them*?!"

"I don't know!" He was telling the truth.

Professionals would have kept everything normal and set up a pheasant shoot when Hamilton had answered a call of nature. So, amateurs, so possibly many of them, possibly searching many inns, possibly not guarding the exits to this one.

It was their only hope.

"All right." He nodded to Lustre. "We're leaving."

He got the landlord to make a noise at the back door, to throw around pots and pans, to slam himself against a cupboard. Gunfire might cut him down at any moment, and he knew it, but damn one Dane in the face of all this.

Hamilton sent Lustre to stand near the front door, then took his gun off covering the landlord and ran at it.

He burst out into the narrow street, into the freezing air, seeking a target—

He fired at the light that was suddenly in his eyes.

But then they were on him. Many of them. He hurt some of them. Possibly fatally. He didn't get off a shot.

He heard no shots from Lustre.

They forced something into his face and at last he had to take a breath of darkness.

Hamilton woke with a start. And the knowledge that he was a fool and a traitor because he was a fool. He wanted to bask in that misery, that he'd failed everyone he cared about. He wanted to lose to it, to let it halt his hopeless trying in favour of certainty.

He must not.

He sought his clock, and found that it was a few hours, not years, later. He'd kept his eyes closed because of the lights. But the light coming at him from all around was diffuse, comfortable.

Whatever situation he found himself in, his options were going to be limited. If there was no escape, if they were indeed in the hands of the enemy, his job now was to kill Lustre and then himself.

He considered that for a moment and was calm about it.

He allowed himself to open his eyes.

He was in what looked like the best room at an inn. Sunlike light shone through what looked like a projection rather than a window. He was dressed in the clothes he'd been wearing on the street. A few serious bruises. He was lying on the bed. He was alone. Nobody had bothered to tuck him in.

The door opened. Hamilton sat up.

It was a waiter, pulling a service trolley into the room. He saw that Hamilton was awake and nodded to him.

Hamilton inclined his head in return.

The waiter took the cover off the trolley, revealing dinner: what looked like real steak and eggs. He placed cutlery appropriately, bowed, and left once more. There was no sound of the door being locked.

Hamilton went to the trolley and looked at the cutlery. He ran his finger on the sharp, serrated edge of the steak knife. There was a message.

He sat down on the bed and ate.

He couldn't help the thoughts that swept through him. He felt them rather than discern them as memories or ideas. He was made from them, after all. They all were, those who kept the balance, those who made sure that the great powers shared the solar system carefully between them, and didn't spin off wildly into a war which everyone knew would be the last. That end of the world would free them all from responsibility, and join them with the kingdom which existed around the universe and inside every miniscule Newton Length. The balance, having collapsed, would crest as a wave again, finally, and stay there, finally including all who had lived, brought entirely into God. That much rough physics Keble had drummed into him. He'd never found himself wanting the final collapse. It was not to be wished for by mortals, after all. It was the shape of the very existence around them, not something they could choose the moment of. He enjoyed his duty, even enjoyed suffering for it, in a way. That was *meaning.* But concussions like this, explosions against the sides of what he understood, and so many of them, so quickly . . . No, he wouldn't become fascinated with the way the world around him seemed to be shaking on its foundations. This was just a new aspect to the balance, a new threat to it. It had many manifestations, many configurations. That was a line from some hymn he barely remembered. He would be who he was and do what had to be done.

That thought he heard as words, as the part of himself that had motive and will. He smiled at this restoration of strength and finished his steak.

The moment he'd finished eating, someone came for him.

This one was dressed in the uniform that Lustre had mentioned. Hamilton contained his reaction to it. To his eyes, it looked halfway to something from a carnival. Bright colours that nevertheless had never seen a battlefield, with no history to be read therein. The man wearing it looked like he'd been trained in a real army, he walked, Hamilton behind him, like he'd known a parade ground. A former officer, even. One who'd bought himself out or deserted. He ignored Hamilton's attempts to start a conversation. Not questions, because he was already preparing himself for the forthcoming interrogation, and pointless questions were a hole in the dam. Instead Hamilton asked only about the weather, and received just a wry look in return. A wry look from this bastard who'd sold his comrades for a bright coat.

Hamilton gave him a smile, and imagined what he'd do to him, given the chance.

He'd left the knife beside his plate.

The corridors were bright and smooth, made of space, cast with colours and textures for the comfort of those who lived here. Hamilton followed the man to the door of what looked like an office and waited as he knocked on it and was called to enter. The door slid open on its own, as if servants were in short supply.

The chamber they stepped into was enormous. It was a dome, with a projected ceiling, on which could be seen . . .

Above them was a world. For a moment, Hamilton thought it must be Jupiter, on its night side. But no. He reeled again, without letting his face show it. This was a world he hadn't seen before. Which was impossible. But the notes in his eyes told him the projection was hallmarked as real space, not as an imagined piece of art. The sphere was dark and enormous. Its inky clouds glowed dully like the coals of hell.

"Hey," said a voice from across the room, in a breezy North Columbian accent, "good evening, Major Hamilton. Delighted you could join us."

Hamilton tore his gaze away from the thing above them.

Across the chamber were standing two men, one to each side of an enormous fireplace, above which was carved, and Hamilton was sure it had actually been carved, a coat of arms. Normally, the out-of-uniform man would have recoiled, but he was now in a world of shock, and this latest effrontery couldn't add to it. The arms weren't anything the International Brotherhood of Heralds would have approved of, but something . . . *personal* . . . the sort of thing a schoolboy would doodle in his rough book and then crumple before his peers saw it. Arms of one's own! The sheer *presumption.*

The two men were smiling at him, and if he hadn't been before, now Hamilton was ready to hate them. They were smiling as if the coat of arms and the unknown world they claimed was real were a joke. Like their pantomime guards were to Hamilton, though he wondered if these two saw *them* like that.

"Am I addressing the two . . . Mr. Ransoms?" He looked between them. And found a mystery had been repeated.

The men were both tall, nearly seven footers. They both had thinning hair, the furrowed brows of an academic, and had decided to wear glasses. More ostentation. They were dressed not like gentlemen, but in the sort of thing one of the husbands who came home to those little boxes in Kent might have worn for an evening at the golf club. They were similar in build, but . . .

One had at least a decade on the other.

And yet—

"These are Castor and Pollux Ransom, yes," said Lustre, from where she stood on the other side of the room. She had a glass of brandy in her hands, which were shaking. "The twins."

Hamilton looked between them. Everything about them was indeed exactly the same, apart from their ages. This must have the same cause as Lustre's situation, but what?

The younger man, Pollux, if Hamilton recalled correctly, separated himself from the fireplace and came to regard him with that same mocking gaze. "I assume that was Enochian for the obvious answer. It's true, Major. We were born, in a place that had the Iroquois name of 'Toronto,' but which people like *you* call Fort York, on the same day in 1958."

Hamilton raised an eyebrow. "What's the difference, then? Clean living?"

"Far from it," laughed the older twin. "In either case."

"I guess you'd like some answers," said Pollux. "I'll do my best. You certainly left chaos in your wake. At 9:59 P.M., the Court of Saint James officially declared Denmark a 'protectorate of His Majesty,' and dispatched forces 'in support of King Frederik,' whom they allege—"

"They declare," corrected Hamilton.

Pollux laughed. "Oh, let's get the manners right, and never mind the horrors they describe! All right. They *declare* that the mad old bastard has been the victim of some sort of coup, and intend to return him to his throne. A coup very much in the eye of the beholder, I should think. A lie more than a declaration, I'd call it. I wonder if Frederik will survive it?"

Hamilton gave no reply. He was pleased to hear it. But it only underlined how important the contents of Lustre's head were.

Pollux continued his explanations with a gesture around him. "We're in a mansion, a perfectly normal one, in lunar orbit." He gestured upwards. "That's an intelligent projection from another of our properties, one considerably beyond the political boundaries of the solar system. We've named that object 'Nemesis.' Because *we* discovered it. It's the sun's twin, much less bright." He shared a smile with Castor. "No metaphor intended." He looked back to Hamilton. "Travelling at the speed of light, it'd take around a year to get there."

"You speak of a property there—" Hamilton wondered if they'd sent some automatic carriage out to the place and were calling it by a lofty name.

"We've got several properties there," said Castor, stepping forward to join his brother. "But I think Pollux was referring to the star itself."

Hamilton knew they were goading him. So he gave them nothing.

"Do you remember the story of Newton and the worm, Major?" asked Pollux, as if they were all sharing the big joke together. But the man wasn't attempting courtesy, his tone of voice scathing, as if addressing a wayward child. "It's part of the balance nursery curriculum in Britain, right? You know, old Isaac's in his garden, an apple falls on his head, he picks it up and sees this tiny worm crawling across its surface, and so he starts thinking about the very small. *Unaligned* historians have sunk almost every detail of that old tale, by the way, but never mind that. Isaac realised that space needs an observer, God, to make reality keep happening when there's none of us around. You know, he's the guy in the forest when the tree falls, and because of him it makes a noise. He's part of the fabric of creation, part of and the motive behind the 'decreed and holy' balance. And the stars and the galaxies and the tremendous distances between them are like they are just because that's how he set up the stage, and that's all there is to it. The balance in our solar system is the diamond at the centre of an ornate setting, the further universe. But it is just a setting. Or at least that's the attitude that great powers academia has always encouraged. It keeps everything fixed. Held down."

"But you know, we're not much for academia, we like to get our hands dirty," said Castor, who sounded a little more affable. "The two of us have our feet planted in the muddy battlefields of mother Earth, where we've made our money, but we've always looked at the stars. Part of our fortune has gone towards the very expensive hobby of first class astronomy. We have telescopes better than any the great powers can boast, placed at various locations around the solar system. We also make engines. A carriage that slides down a fold, altering gravity under itself at every moment, is capable, in the void, of only a certain acceleration. The record keeps inching up, but it's a matter of gaining a few miles an hour because of some technical adjustment. And once you've reached any great acceleration inside the solar system, you're going to need to start decelerating in a few days, because you'll need to slow down at your destination. It wouldn't be out of the question to send an automatic carriage out into the wilds beyond the comet cloud, but somehow nobody's gotten around to doing it."

"That always puzzled us."

"Until we heard whispers about the great secret. Because people talk to us, we sell weapons and buy information. It became clear that for a nation to send such a carriage, to even prepare a vehicle that greatly exceeded records, would be to have every other nation suspect they'd found something out there, and become suddenly aggressive toward them, in a desperate attempt to keep the balance."

Hamilton kept his silence.

"When we stumbled on Nemesis in a photographic survey, we realised that we had found something we had always sought, along with so many other disenfranchised inhabitants of Earth—"

"Land," said Hamilton.

They laughed and applauded like this was a party game. "Exactly," said Castor.

"We tossed a coin," said Pollux, "I was the one who went. With a small staff. I took a carriage with a fold full of supplies, and set it accelerating, using an engine of our own, one limited by *physical* rather than *political* principles. I struck out for a new world. I opened up a new frontier. For *us*, this time. For all the people shut out when the great powers closed down the world—" He noticed that his brother was frowning at him, and visibly reined himself in. "The carriage accelerated until after a year or so we were approaching the speed of light. We discovered, to our shock, that as we did so, the demands on the fold became extraordinary. It seems, incredibly, that there is a speed limit on the universe!"

Hamilton tried to keep his expression even, but knew he was failing. He didn't know how much of this he could believe.

"By my own internal clock, the round trip took four years—"

"But I remained here as fifteen years passed," said Castor. "Because when you approach the speed of light, time slows down. Just for you. Yeah, I know how mad it sounds! It's like God starts looking at you *differently*!"

"And you should see the beauty of it, Major, the rainbows and the darkness and the feeling that one is . . . finally close to the centre of understanding."

Hamilton licked his dry lips. "Why does all this happen?"

"We don't know, exactly," admitted Castor. "We've approached this as engineers, not theorists. 'God does not flay space,' that's what Newton is supposed to have said. He theorised that God provides a frame of reference for all things, relative to Him. But these spooky changes in mass and time depending on speed . . . that seems to say there's a bit more going on than Newton's miniscule gravitation and miniscule causality!"

Hamilton nodded in the direction of Lustre. "I gather she wasn't on that first trip?"

"No," said Pollux. "That's what I'm coming to. When the carriage started decelerating towards Nemesis, we began to see signs of what we initially took to be a solar system surrounding the star. Only as we got closer did we realise that what we had taken to be small worlds were actually carriages. Ones the size of which human beings have not dreamt. The carriages of foreigners."

Hamilton's mouth set in a line. That these had been the first representatives of humanity! And the foreigners were so close! If any of this could be true. He didn't let his gaze move upwards as if to see them. He could almost feel the balance juddering. It was as if something dear to him was sliding swiftly away, into the void, and only destruction could follow. "So," he said, "you drew alongside and shook hands."

"No," laughed Pollux. "Unfortunately. We could see immediately that there were enormous symbols on the carriages, all the same design, though we couldn't make anything of them. They were kind of . . . like red birds, but deformed, unfocussed. You needed to see two to realise they were a symbol at all. We approached with all hulloos and flags, and suddenly our embroidery was flooded with what might have been voices, but sounded like low booming sounds. We yelled back and forth, uselessly, for about an hour. We were preparing a diagram to throw into the void in a canister, stick figures handing each other things—"

"I'll bet," said Hamilton.

"—when they switched on lights that just illuminated their insignia. Off, then again. Over and over. It was like they were demanding for us to show ours."

Hamilton pointed at the monstrosity over the fireplace. "Didn't you have that handy?"

"That's a later invention," said Castor, "in response to this very problem."

"When we didn't have any insignia of our own to display," said Pollux, "they started firing at us. Or we assume it was firing. I decided to get out of it, and we resumed acceleration, rounded the star, and headed home."

Hamilton couldn't conceal a smile.

"Before the next expedition," continued Castor, "we built the biggest carriage we could and had the coats of arms painted all over it. But we needed one more thing: something to barter with." He gestured towards Lustre. "The contents of her head, the locations of the missing mass, the weight of all those living minds, a trading map of the heavens. Depending on where the foreigners came from, we might have information they didn't. Or at least we could demonstrate we were in the game. And if one group of foreigners didn't like us, we could go find another."

"But she proved to be made of strong stuff," said Hamilton.

"After she'd tried to shock herself into either death or deadlock, we kept her on ice," said Castor. "We sent her with the staff on the main carriage, in the hope they could find a way to breach her along the way, or maybe offer her to the foreigners as sealed goods." Hamilton was certain the twin was enjoying trying Lustre's modesty with his words. "But their response this time was, if anything, more aggressive. Our people left a number of orbiting automatics, and a number of houses ready for occupation, but barely escaped with their lives."

"It seems they don't like you any more than we do," said Hamilton. "I can understand why you'd want her back. But why am I still alive?"

The twins looked at each other like they'd come to an unpleasant duty sooner than they would have liked. Castor nodded to the air, the doors opened by themselves, and a number of the pantomime guards strode into the room.

Hamilton controlled his breathing.

"Chain him to the fireplace," said Pollux.

They pulled the shackles from the same folds where Hamilton had been certain they'd kept weapons trained on him. His kind retired, if they did, to simple places, and didn't take kindly to parties in great houses. A room was never a room when you'd worked out of uniform.

They fixed his wrists and ankles to the top of the fireplace, and stripped him. Hamilton wanted to tell Lustre to look away, but he was also determined to not ask for anything he couldn't have. He was going to have to die now, and take a long time about it. "You know your duty," he said.

She looked horribly uncertain back at him.

Pollux nodded again, and a control pedal appeared out of the floor, light flooding with it. He placed his foot on it. "Let's get the formalities out of the way," he said. "We'd give you a staggering amount of money, in carbon, for your cooperation."

Hamilton swore lightly at him.

"And *that's* the problem with the world. All right, I tried. What I'm going to do now is to open a very small fold in front of your genitals. I'll then increase the gravity, until Miss Saint Clair elects to stop using Enochian and says the words that will allow us to observe the package in her mind. Should she cut herself off from the world with her own language, I'll start by pulling off your genitalia, and then move on to various other parts of your body, using folds to staunch the blood flow, killing you slowly while she's forced to watch. Then I'll do the same to her." He looked quickly to Lustre, and for a moment it looked to Hamilton like he was even afraid. "Don't make me do this."

Lustre stood straight and didn't answer.

"Say what you have to say to cut yourself off," said Hamilton. "Say it now."

But, to his fury and horror she maintained the same expression, and just looked quickly between them.

"For God's sake—!" he cried out.

Pollux pressed gently with his foot, and Hamilton tensed at the feel of the fold grabbing his body. It made him recall, horribly, moments with Lustre, and, even worse, moments with Annie. He didn't want that association, so he killed it in his mind. There could be no thoughts of her as he died. It would be like dragging a part of her through this with him. There was no pain, not yet. He reserved his shouts for when there would be. He would use his training, go cursing them, as loud as he could, thus controlling the only thing he could. He was proud to have the chance to manage his death and die for king, country and balance.

Pollux looked again at Lustre, then pressed slightly more. Now there was pain. Hamilton drew in a breath to begin telling this classless bastard what he thought of him—

—when suddenly there came a sound.

Something had crunched against something, far away.

The twins both looked suddenly in the same direction, startled.

Hamilton let out a choked laugh. Whatever this was—

And that had been an explosion!

A projection of a uniformed man flew up onto the wall. "Somehow there are three carriages—!"

"The church bells!" said Hamilton, realising.

Castor ran for the door, joining a great outflowing of guards as they grabbed arms from the walls, but Pollux stayed where he was, a dangerous expression on his face, his foot poised on the pedal. One guard had stayed beside Lustre also, his rifle covering her. "What?!"

"The bells of Saint Mary's in Copenhagen. Ten o'clock." He was panting at the pain and the pressure. "You said the city became a British possession at 9:59. While we were falling." He swore at the man who was about to maim him, triumphant. "They must have put a fold in me with a tracker inside, as we fell! Didn't harm the balance if we landed in Britain!"

Pollux snarled and slammed his foot down on the pedal.

Hamilton didn't see what happened in the next few seconds. His vision distorted with the pain, which reached up into his jaw and to the roots of his teeth.

But the next thing he knew, Lustre had slammed a palm against the wall, and his shackles had disappeared. There was a shout of astonishment. The pressure cut off and the pain receded. He was aware of a guard somewhere over there in a pool of blood. Reflexively, he grabbed the rifle Lustre held. She tried to hold onto it, as if uncertain he could use it better than she could. They each scrabbled at it, they only had seconds—!

He was aware of regimental cries converging on the room, bursting through the doors.

He saw, as if down a tunnel, that Pollux was desperately stamping at the pedal, and light had suddenly blazed across his foot again.

Pollux raised his foot, about to slam it down, to use the fold in the centre of the room, opened to its fullest extent, to rip apart Hamilton and everyone else!

Hamilton shoved Lustre aside and in one motion fired.

The top of Pollux's head vanished. His foot spasmed downwards.

It seemed to be moving slowly, to Hamilton's pain dulled eyes.

The sole of the man's shoe connected with the control.

For a moment it looked like it had done so with enough force that Pollux Ransom would not die alone.

But it must have landed too softly. By some miniscule amount.

The corpse fell aside. Its tormented soul had, a moment before, vanished from the universe.

"That'll be a weight off his mind," said Hamilton.

And then he passed out.

Six weeks later, following some forced healing and forced leave, Hamilton stood once again in front of Turpin. He had been called straight in, rather than return to his regiment. He hadn't seen Lustre since the assault on the mansion. He'd been told that she had been interviewed at length and then returned to the bosom of the diplomatic corps. He assumed that she'd told Turpin's people everything, and that, thus, at the very least, he was out of a job. At the worst, he could find himself at the end of the traitor's noose, struggling in the air above Parliament Square.

He found he couldn't square himself to that. He was full of concerns and impertinent queries. The lack of official reaction so far had been trying his nerves.

But as Turpin had run down what had happened to the various individuals in the mansion, how Castor was now in the cells far beneath this building, and what the origins and fates of the toy soldiers had been, how various out-of-uniform officers were busy unravelling the threads of the twins' conceits, all over the world, Hamilton gradually began to hope. Surely the blow would have landed before now? King Frederik had been found, hiding or pretending to hide, and had been delighted, once the situation had been starkly explained to him, to have the British return him to his throne. Denmark remained a British protectorate while His Majesty's forces rooted out the last of the conspirators in the pay of the Ransoms. And, since a faction in that court had been found and encouraged that sought to intermarry and unify the kingdoms, perhaps this would remain the case for some considerable while.

"Of course," said Turpin, "they weren't really twins."

Hamilton allowed the surprise to show on his face. "Sir?"

"We've found family trees that suggest they're actually cousins, similar in appearance, with a decade or so between them. We've got carriages on the way to what we're going to call George's Star, and people examining that projection. We don't expect to find anything beyond a single automatic in orbit."

"So . . . the girl—" He took a chance on referring to her as if he didn't know her, hoping desperately that she'd kept the secret of what he hadn't reported, all those years ago.

"We kept an eye on her after the interviews. She told us she'd learned the access codes for Ransom's embroidery from when she was on that enormous carriage she mentioned. Another thing we tellingly haven't found, by the way, along with any high performance carriages in the Ransom garages. But she hadn't quite got enough detail on the earliest years of Lustre Saint Clair's life. A brilliant cover, a brilliant grown flesh job, but not quite good enough. She faltered a little when we put it to her that, struggling over that gun with you, she was actually trying to save Pollux Ransom's life. We decided to let her out of the coop and see where she led us. As we expected, she realised we were on to her and vanished. Almost certainly into the Russian embassy. Certainly enough that we may find ourselves able to threaten the Czar with some embarrassment. You must have wondered yourself, considering the ease of your escape from the embassy, her reluctance to take the observer machine . . ." He raised an eyebrow at Hamilton. "Didn't you?"

Hamilton felt dizzy, as if the walls of his world had once more vibrated under an impact. "What were they after?"

"Easy enough to imagine. The Russians would love to see us move forces out of the inner solar system in order to secure an otherwise meaningless territory in the hope that these fictitious foreigners might return. And just in the week or so while we were interviewing her, you should have seen the havoc this story caused at court. The hawks who want to 'win the balance' were all for sending the fleet out there immediately. The doves were at their throats. The Queen Mother had to order everyone to stop discussing it. But fortunately, we soon had an answer for them, confirmed by what we got out of Castor. An elegant fable, wasn't it? The sort of thing Stichen would put together out of the White Court. I'll bet it was one of his. You know, the strange-looking wounds, red birds, booming sounds, fine fly detail like that. If we hadn't planted that tracker on you, the girl would have had to find some way to signal us herself. Or, less wasteful, you'd have been allowed to escape. Of course, the Ransoms' worldwide network isn't quite the size they made it out to be, not when you subtract all the rubles that are vanishing back to Moscow. But even so, clearing all that out makes the balance a bit safer tonight."

Hamilton didn't know what to say. He stood there on the grown polished wood timbers and looked down at the whorls within whorls. An odd thought struck him. A connection back to the last certainty he recalled feeling. When his world had been set on sturdier foundations. "Ambassador Bayoumi," he said. "Did he make it out?"

"I've no idea. Why do you ask?"

Hamilton found he had no reason in his head, just a great blankness that felt half merciful and half something lost. "I don't know," he said finally. "He seemed kind."

Turpin made a small grunt of a laugh, and looked back to his papers. Hamilton realised that he'd been dismissed. And that the burdens he'd brought with him into the room would not be ended by a noose or a pardon.

As he made his way to the door, Turpin seemed to realise that he hadn't been particularly polite. He looked up again. "I heard the record of what you said to him," he said. "You said nobody would care if she killed you. It's not true, you know."

Hamilton stopped, and tried to read the scarred and stitched face of the man.

"You're greatly valued, Jonathan," said Turpin. "If you weren't, you wouldn't still be here."

A year or so later, Hamilton was woken in the early hours by an urgent tug on the embroidery, a voice that seemed familiar, trying to tell him something, sobbing and yelling in the few seconds before it was cut off.

But he couldn't understand a word it said.

The next morning, there was no record of the exchange.

In the end, Hamilton decided that it must have been a dream.

The Invasion of Venus

STEPHEN BAXTER

Stephen Baxter made his first sale to Interzone *in 1987, and since then has become one of that magazine's most frequent contributors, as well as making sales to* Asimov's Science Fiction, Science Fiction Age, Analog, Zenith, New Worlds, *and elsewhere. He's one of the most prolific writers in science fiction, one who works on the cutting edge of science, whose fiction bristles with weird new ideas and often takes place against vistas of almost outrageously cosmic scope. Baxter's first novel,* Raft, *was released in 1991, and was rapidly followed by other well-received novels such as* Timelike Infinity, Anti-Ice, Flux, *and the H. G. Wells pastiche—a sequel to* The Time Machine—The Time Ships, *which won both the John W. Campbell Memorial Award and the Philip K. Dick Award. His many other books include the novels* Voyage, Titan, Moonseed, the Mammoth trilogy: Silverhair, Longtusk, Icebones, Manifold: Time, Manifold: Space, Evolution, Coalescent, Exultant, Transcendent, Emperor, Resplendent, Conqueror, Navigator, Firstborn, The H-Bomb Girl, Weaver, Flood, Ark, *and two novels in collaboration with Arthur C. Clarke:* The Light of Other Days *and* Time's Eye (Book one of a Time Odyssey). *His short fiction has been collected in* Vacuum Diagrams: Stories of the Xeelee Sequence, Traces, *and* The Hunters of Pangaea, *and he has released a chapbook novella,* Mayflower II. *His most recent novels include the trilogy* Stone Spring, Bronze Summer, *and* Iron Winter *(forthcoming) as well as a nonfiction book,* The Science of Avatar. *Coming up is a new series, The Long Earth, to be cowritten with Terry Pratchett.*

Here he shows us a future in which humans are bystanders to an immense cosmic battle between forces that, to our dismay, ignore us completely.

For me, the saga of the Incoming was above all Edith Black's story. For she, more than anyone else I knew, was the one who had a problem with it.

When the news was made public I drove out of London to visit Edith at her country church. I had to cancel a dozen appointments to do it, including one with the Prime Minister's office, but I knew, as soon as I got out of the car and stood in the soft September rain, that it had been the right thing to do.

Edith was pottering around outside the church, wearing overalls and rubber boots and wielding an alarming-looking industrial-strength jackhammer. But she had a radio blaring out a phone-in discussion, and indoors, out of the rain, I glimpsed a widescreen TV and laptop, both scrolling news—mostly fresh projections of where the Incoming's decelerating trajectory might deliver them, and new deep-space images of their "craft," if such it was, a massive block of ice like a comet nucleus, leaking very complex patterns of infrared radiation. Edith was plugged into the world, even out here in the wilds of Essex.

She approached me with a grin, pushing back goggles under a hard hat. "Toby." I got a kiss on the cheek and a brief hug; she smelled of machine oil. We were easy with each other physically. Fifteen years earlier, in our last year at college, we'd been lovers, briefly; it had finished with a kind of regretful embarrassment—very English, said our American friends—but it had proven only a kind of speed bump in our relationship. "Glad to see you, if surprised. I thought all you civil service types would be locked down in emergency meetings."

For a decade I'd been a civil servant in the environment ministry. "No, but old Thorp—" my minister "—has been in a continuous COBRA session for twenty-four hours. Much good it's doing anybody."

"I must say it's not obvious to the layman what use an environment minister is when the aliens are coming."

"Well, among the scenarios they're discussing is some kind of attack from space. A lot of what we can dream up is similar to natural disasters—a meteor fall could be like a tsunami, a sunlight occlusion like a massive volcanic event. And so Thorp is in the mix, along with health, energy, transport. Of course we're in contact with other governments—NATO, the UN. The most urgent issue right now is whether to signal or not."

She frowned. "Why wouldn't you?"

"Security. Edith, remember, we know absolutely nothing about these guys. What if our signal was interpreted as a threat? And there are tactical considerations. Any signal would give information to a potential enemy about our technical capabilities. It would also give away the very fact that we know they are here."

She scoffed. "'Tactical considerations.' Paranoid bullshit! And besides, I bet every kid with a CB radio is beaming out her heart to ET right now. The whole planet's alight."

"Well, that's true. You can't stop it. But still, sending some kind of signal authorised by government or an inter-government agency is another step entirely."

"Oh, come on. You can't really believe anybody is going to cross the stars to harm us. What could they possibly want that would justify the cost of an interstellar mission? . . ."

So we argued. I'd only been out of the car for five minutes.

We'd had this kind of discussion all the way back to late nights in college, some of them in her bed, or mine. She'd always been drawn to the bigger issues—"to the context," as she used to say. Though we'd both started out as maths students, her head had soon expanded in the exotic intellectual air of the college, and she'd moved on to study older ways of thinking than the scientific—older questions, still unanswered. Was there a God? If so, or if not, what was the point of our existence? Why did we, or indeed anything, exist at all? In her later college years she took theology options, but quickly burned through that discipline and was left unsatisfied.

She was repelled too by the modern atheists, with their aggressive denials. So, after college, she had started her own journey through life—a journey in search of answers. Now, of course, maybe some of those answers had come swimming in from the stars in search of her.

This was why I'd felt drawn here, at this particular moment in my life. I needed her perspective. In the wan daylight I could see the fine patina of lines around the mouth I used to kiss, and the strands of grey in her red hair. I was sure she suspected, rightly, that I knew more than I was telling her—more than had been released to the public. But she didn't follow that up for now.

"Come see what I'm doing," she said, sharply breaking up the debate. "Watch your shoes." We walked across muddy grass towards the main door. The core of that old church, dedicated to St. Cuthbert, was a Saxon-era tower; the rest of the fabric was mostly Norman, but there had been an extensive restoration in Victorian times. Within was a lovely space, if cold, the stone walls resonating. It was still consecrated, Church of England, but in this empty agricultural countryside it was one of a widespread string of churches united in a single parish, and rarely used.

Edith had never joined any of the established religions, but she had appropriated some of their infrastructure, she liked to say. And here she had gathered a group of volunteers, wandering souls more or less like-minded. They worked to maintain the fabric of the church. And within, she led her group through what you might think of as a mix of discussions, or prayers, or meditation, or yoga practices—whatever she could find that seemed to work. This was the way religions used to be before the big monotheistic creeds took over, she argued. "The only way to reach God, or anyhow the space beyond us where God ought to be, is by working hard, by helping other people—and by pushing your mind to the limit of its capability, and then going a little beyond, and just *listening*." Beyond *logos* to *mythos*. She was always restless, always trying something new. Yet in some ways she was the most contented person I ever met—at least before the Incoming showed up.

Now, though, she wasn't content about the state of the church's foundations. She showed me where she had dug up flagstones to reveal sodden ground. "We're digging out new drainage channels, but it's a hell of a job. We may end up rebuilding the founds altogether. The very deepest level seems to be wood, huge piles of Saxon oak . . ." She eyed me. "This church has stood here for a thousand years, without, apparently, facing a threat such as this before. Some measure of climate change, right?"

I shrugged. "I suppose you'd say we arseholes in the environment ministry should be concentrating on stuff like this rather than preparing to fight interstellar wars."

"Well, so you should. And maybe a more mature species would be preparing for positive outcomes. Think of it, Tobe! There are now creatures in this solar system who are *smarter than us.* They have to be, or they wouldn't be here—right? Somewhere between us and the angels. Who knows what they can tell us? What is their science, their art—their theology?"

I frowned. "But what do they want? For that's what may count from now on—their agenda, not ours."

"There you are being paranoid again." But she hesitated. "What about Meryl and the kids?"

"Meryl at home. Mark and Sophie at school." I shrugged. "Life as normal."

"Some people are freaking out. Raiding the supermarkets."

"Some people always do. We want things to continue as normally as possible, as long as possible. Modern society is efficient, you know, Edith, but not very resilient. A fuel strike could cripple us in a week, let alone alien invaders."

She pushed a loose grey hair back under her hard hat, and looked at me suspiciously. "But you seem very calm, considering. You know something. Don't you, you bastard?"

I grinned. "And you know me."

"Spill it."

"Two things. We picked up signals. Or, more likely, leakage. You know about the infrared stuff we've seen for a while, coming from the nucleus. Now we've detected radio noise, faint, clearly structured, very complex. It may be some kind of internal channel rather than anything meant for us. But if we can figure anything out from it—"

"Well, that's exciting. And the second thing? Come on, Miller."

"We have more refined trajectory data. All this will be released soon—it's probably leaked already."

"Yes?"

"The Incoming *are* heading for the inner solar system. But they aren't coming here—not to Earth."

She frowned. "Then where?"

I dropped my bombshell. "Venus. Not Earth. They're heading for Venus, Edith."

She looked into the clouded sky, the bright patch that marked the position of the sun, and the inner planets. "Venus? That's a cloudy hellhole. What would they want there?"

"I've no idea."

"Well, I'm used to living with questions I'll never be able to answer. Let's hope this isn't one of them. In the meantime, let's make ourselves useful." She eyed my crumpled Whitehall suit, my patent leather shoes already splashed with mud. "Have you got time to stay? You want to help out with my drain? I've a spare overall that might fit."

Talking, speculating, we walked through the church.

We used the excuse of Edith's Goonhilly event to make a family trip to Cornwall.

We took the A-road snaking west down the spine of the Cornish peninsula, and stopped at a small hotel in Helston. The pretty little town was decked out that day for the annual Furry Dance, an ancient, eccentric carnival when the local children would weave in and out of the houses on the hilly streets. The next morning Meryl was to take the kids to the beach, further up the coast.

And, just about at dawn, I set off alone in a hired car for the A-road to the southeast, towards Goonhilly Down. It was a clear May morning. As I drove I was aware of Venus, rising in the eastern sky and clearly visible in my rearview mirror, a lamp shining steadily even as the day brightened.

Goonhilly is a stretch of high open land, a windy place. Its claim to fame is that at one time it hosted the largest telecoms satellite earth station in the world—it picked up the first live transatlantic TV broadcast, via Telstar. It was decommissioned years ago, but its oldest dish, a thousand-tonne parabolic bowl called "Arthur" after the king, became a listed building, and so was preserved. And that was how it was available for Edith and her committee of messagers to get hold of, when they, or rather she, grew impatient with the government's continuing reticence. Because of the official policy I had to help with smoothing through the permissions, all behind the scenes.

Just after my first glimpse of the surviving dishes on the skyline I came up against a police cordon, a hastily erected plastic fence that excluded a few groups of chanting Shouters and a fundamentalist-religious group protesting that the messagers were communicating with the Devil. My ministry card helped me get through.

Edith was waiting for me at the old site's visitors' centre, opened up that morning for breakfast, coffee and cereals and toast. Her volunteers cleared up dirty dishes under a big wall screen showing a live feed from a space telescope—the best images available right now, though every major space agency had a probe to Venus in preparation, and NASA had already fired one off. The Incoming nucleus (it seemed inappropriate to call that lump of dirty ice a "craft," though such it clearly was) was a brilliant star, too small to show a disc, swinging in its wide orbit above a half-moon Venus. And on the planet's night side you could clearly make out the Patch, that strange, complicated glow in the cloud banks tracking the Incoming's orbit precisely. It was strange to gaze upon that choreography in space, and then to turn to the east and see Venus with the naked eye.

And Edith's volunteers, a few dozen earnest men, women and children who looked like they had gathered for a village show, had the audacity to believe they could speak to these godlike forms in the sky.

There was a terrific metallic groan. We turned, and saw that Arthur was turning on his concrete pivot. The volunteers cheered, and a general drift towards the monument began.

Edith walked with me, cradling a polystyrene tea cup in the palms of fingerless gloves. "I'm glad you could make it down. Should have brought the kids. Some of the locals from Helston are here; they've made the whole stunt part of their Furry Dance celebration. Did you see the preparations in town? Supposed to celebrate St. Michael beating up on the Devil—I wonder how appropriate *that* symbolism is. Anyhow this ought to be a fun day. Later there'll be a barn dance."

"Meryl thought it was safer to take the kids to the beach. Just in case anything gets upsetting here—you know." That was most of the truth. There was a subtext that Meryl had never much enjoyed being in the same room as my ex.

"Probably wise. Our British Shouters are a mild bunch, but in rowdier parts of the world there has been trouble." The loose international coalition of groups called the Shouters was paradoxically named, because they campaigned for silence; they argued that "shouting in the jungle" by sending signals to the Incoming or the Venusians was taking an irresponsible risk. Of course they could do nothing about the low-level chatter that had been targeted at the Incoming since it had first been sighted, nearly a year ago already. Edith waved a hand at Arthur. "If I were a Shouter, I'd be here today. This will be by far the most powerful message sent from the British Isles."

I'd seen and heard roughs of Edith's message. In with a Carl Sagan–style prime number lexicon, there was digitised music from Bach to Zulu chants, and art from cave paintings to Warhol, and images of mankind featuring a lot of smiling children, and astronauts on the Moon. There was even a copy of the old Pioneer spaceprobe plaque from the seventies, with the smiling naked couple. At least, I thought cynically, all that fluffy stuff would provide a counterpoint to the images of war, murder, famine, plague and other sufferings that the Incoming had no doubt sampled by now, if they'd chosen to.

I said, "But I get the feeling they're just not interested. Neither the Incoming nor the Venusians. Sorry to rain on your parade."

"I take it the cryptolinguists aren't getting anywhere decoding the signals?"

"They're not so much 'signals' as leakage from internal processes, we think. In both cases, the nucleus and the Patch." I rubbed my face; I was tired after the previous day's long drive. "In the case of the nucleus, some kind of organic chemistry seems to be mediating powerful magnetic fields—and the Incoming seem to swarm within. I don't think we've really any idea what's going on in there. We're actually making more progress with the science of the Venusian biosphere . . ."

If the arrival of the Incoming had been astonishing, the evidence of intelligence on Venus, entirely unexpected, was stunning. Nobody had expected the clouds to part right under the orbiting Incoming nucleus—like a deep storm system, kilometres deep in that thick ocean of an atmosphere—and nobody had expected to see the Patch revealed, swirling mist banks where lights flickered tantalisingly, like organised lightning.

"With retrospect, given the results from the old space probes, we might have guessed there was something on Venus—life, if not intelligent life. There were always unexplained deficiencies and surpluses of various compounds. We think the Venusians live in the clouds, far enough above the red-hot ground that the temperature is low enough for liquid water to exist. They ingest carbon monoxide and excrete sulphur compounds, living off the sun's ultraviolet."

"And they're smart."

"Oh, yes." The astronomers, already recording the complex signals coming out of the Incoming nucleus, had started to discern rich patterns in the Venusian Patch too. "You can tell how complicated a message is even if you don't know anything about the content. You measure entropy orders, which are like correlation measures, mapping structures on various scales embedded in the transmission—"

"You don't understand any of what you just said, do you?"

I smiled. "Not a word. But I do know this. Going by their data structures, the Venusians are smarter than us as we are smarter than the chimps. And the Incoming are smarter again."

Edith turned to face the sky, the brilliant spark of Venus. "But you say the scientists still believe all this chatter is just—what was your word?"

"Leakage. Edith, the Incoming and the Venusians aren't speaking to us. They aren't even speaking to each other. What we're observing is a kind of internal dialogue, in each case. The two are talking to themselves, not each other. One theorist briefed the PM that perhaps both these entities are more like hives than human communities."

"Hives?" She looked troubled. "Hives are *different*. They can be purposeful, but they don't have consciousness as we have it. They aren't finite as we are; their edges are much more blurred. They aren't even mortal; individuals can die, but the hives live on."

"I wonder what their theology will be, then."

"It's all so strange. These aliens just don't fit any category we expected, or even that we share. Not mortal, not communicative—and not interested in us. What do they *want*? What *can* they want?" Her tone wasn't like her; she sounded bewildered to be facing open questions, rather than exhilarated as usual.

I tried to reassure her. "Maybe your signal will provoke some answers."

She checked her watch, and looked up again towards Venus. "Well, we've only got five minutes to wait before—" Her eyes widened, and she fell silent.

I turned to look the way she was, to the east.

Venus was flaring. Sputtering like a dying candle.

People started to react. They shouted, pointed, or they just stood there, staring, as I did. I couldn't move. I felt a deep, awed fear. Then people called, pointing at the big screen in the visitors' centre, where, it seemed, the space telescopes were returning a very strange set of images indeed.

Edith's hand crept into mine. Suddenly I was very glad I hadn't brought my kids that day.

I heard angrier shouting, and a police siren, and I smelled burning.

Once I'd finished making my police statement I went back to the hotel in Helston, where Meryl was angry and relieved to see me, and the kids bewildered and vaguely frightened. I couldn't believe that after all that had happened—the strange events at Venus, the assaults by Shouters on messagers and vice versa, the arson, Edith's injury, the police crackdown—it was not yet eleven in the morning.

That same day I took the family back to London, and called in at work. Then, three days after the incident, I got away again and commandeered a ministry car and driver to take me back to Cornwall.

Edith was out of intensive care, but she'd been kept in the hospital at Truro. She had a TV stand before her face, the screen dark. I carefully kissed her on the unburnt side of her face, and sat down, handing over books, newspapers and flowers. "Thought you might be bored."

"You never were any good with the sick, were you, Tobe?"

"Sorry." I opened up one of the newspapers. "But there's some good news. They caught the arsonists."

She grunted, her distorted mouth barely opening. "So what? It doesn't matter who they were. Messagers and Shouters have been at each other's throats all over the world. People like that are interchangeable . . . But did we all have to behave so badly? I mean, they even wrecked Arthur."

"And he was Grade II listed!"

She laughed, then regretted it, for she winced with the pain. "But why shouldn't we smash everything up down here? After all, that's all they seem to be interested in up *there*. The Incoming assaulted Venus, and the Venusians struck back. We all saw it, live on TV—it was nothing more than *War of the Worlds*." She sounded disappointed. "These creatures are our superiors, Toby. All your signal analysis stuff proved it. And yet they haven't transcended war and destruction."

"But we learned so much." I had a small briefcase which I opened now, and pulled out printouts that I spread over her bed. "The screen images are better, but you know how it is; they won't let me use my laptop or my phone in here . . . *Look,* Edith. It was incredible. The Incoming assault on Venus lasted hours. Their weapon, whatever it was, burned its way through the Patch, and right down through an atmosphere a hundred times thicker than Earth's. We even glimpsed the surface—"

"Now melted to slag."

"Much of it . . . But then the acid-munchers in the clouds struck back. We think we know what they did."

That caught her interest. "How can we know that?"

"Sheer luck. That NASA probe, heading for Venus, happened to be in the way . . ."

The probe had detected a wash of electromagnetic radiation, coming from the planet.

"A signal," breathed Edith. "Heading which way?"

"Out from the sun. And then, eight hours later, the probe sensed another signal, coming the other way. I say 'sensed.' It bobbed about like a cork on a pond. We think it was a gravity wave—very sharply focussed, very intense."

"And when the wave hit the Incoming nucleus—"

"Well, you saw the pictures. The last fragments have burned up in Venus's atmosphere."

She lay back on her reef of pillows. "Eight hours," she mused. "Gravity waves travel at lightspeed. Four hours out, four hours back . . . Earth's about eight light-minutes from the sun. What's four light-hours out from Venus? Jupiter, Saturn—"

"Neptune. Neptune was four light-hours out."

"*Was?*"

"It's gone, Edith. Almost all of it—the moons are still there, a few chunks of core ice and rock, slowly dispersing. The Venusians used the planet to create their gravity-wave pulse—"

"They *used* it. Are you telling me this to cheer me up? A gas giant, a significant chunk of the solar system's budget of mass-energy, sacrificed for a single warlike gesture." She laughed, bitter. "Oh, God!"

"Of course we've no idea *how* they did it." I put away my images. "If we were scared of the Incoming, now we're terrified of the Venusians. That NASA probe has been shut down. We don't want anything to look like a threat . . . You know, I heard the PM herself ask why it was that this space war should break out now, just when we humans are sitting around on Earth. Even politicians know we haven't been here that long."

Edith shook her head, wincing again. "The final vanity. This whole episode has never been about us. Can't you see? If this is happening now, it must have happened over and over. Who knows how many other planets we lost in the past, consumed as weapons of forgotten wars? Maybe all we see, the planets and stars and galaxies, is just the debris of huge wars—on and on, up to scales we can barely imagine. And we're just weeds growing in the rubble. Tell that to the Prime Minister. And I thought we might ask them about their gods! What a fool I've been—the questions on which I've wasted my life, and *here* are my answers—what a fool." She was growing agitated.

"Take it easy, Edith—"

"Oh, just go. I'll be fine. It's the universe that's broken, not me." She turned away on her pillow, as if to sleep.

The next time I saw Edith she was out of hospital and back at her church.

It was another September day, like the first time I visited her after the Incoming appeared in our telescopes, and at least it wasn't raining. There was a bite in the breeze, but I imagined it soothed her damaged skin. And here she was, digging in the mud before her church.

"Equinox season," she said. "Rain coming. Best to get this fixed before we have another flash flood. And before you ask, the doctors cleared me. It's my face that's buggered, not the rest of me."

"I wasn't going to ask."

"OK, then. How's Meryl, the kids?"

"Fine. Meryl's at work, the kids back at school. Life goes on."

"It must, I suppose. What else is there? No, by the way."

"No what?"

"No, I won't come serve on your minister's think tank."

"At least consider it. You'd be ideal. Look, we're all trying to figure out where we go from here. The arrival of the Incoming, the war on Venus—it was like a religious revelation. That's how it's being described. A revelation witnessed by all mankind, on TV. Suddenly we've got an entirely different view of the universe out there. And we have to figure out how we go forward, in a whole number of dimensions—political, scientific, economic, social, religious."

"I'll tell you how we go forward. In despair. Religions are imploding."

"No, they're not."

"OK. Theology is imploding. Philosophy. The rest of the world has changed channels and forgotten already, but anybody with any imagination knows . . . In a way this has been the final demotion, the end of the process that started with Copernicus and Darwin. Now we *know* there are creatures in the universe much smarter than we'll ever be, and we *know* they don't care a damn about us. It's the indifference that's the killer—don't you think? All our futile agitation about if they'd attack us and whether we should signal . . . And they did nothing but smash each other up. With *that* above us, what can we do but turn away?"

"You're not turning away."

She leaned on her shovel. "I'm not religious; I don't count. My congregation turned away. Here I am, alone." She glanced at the clear sky. "Maybe solitude is the key to it all. A galactic isolation imposed by the vast gulfs between the stars, the light-speed limit. As a species develops you might have a brief phase of individuality, of innovation and technological achievement. But then, when the universe gives you nothing back you turn in on yourself, and slide into the milky embrace of eusociality—the hive.

"But what then? How would it be for a mass mind to emerge, alone? Maybe that's why the Incoming went to war. Because they were outraged to discover, by some chance, they weren't alone in the universe."

"Most commentators think it was about resources. Most of our wars are about that, in the end."

"Yes. Depressingly true. All life is based on the destruction of other life, even on tremendous scales of space and time . . . Our ancestors understood that right back to the Ice Age, and venerated the animals they had to kill. They were so far above us, the Incoming and the Venusians alike. Yet maybe *we*, at our best, are morally superior to them."

I touched her arm. "This is why we need you. For your insights. There's a storm coming, Edith. We're going to have to work together if we're to weather it, I think."

She frowned. "What kind of storm? . . . Oh. Neptune."

"Yeah. You can't just delete a world without consequences. The planets' orbits are singing like plucked strings. The asteroids and comets too, and those orphan moons wandering around. Some of the stirred-up debris is falling into the inner system."

"And if we're struck—"

I shrugged. "We'll have to help each other. There's nobody else to help us, that's for sure. Look, Edith—maybe the Incoming and the Venusians are typical of what's out there. But that doesn't mean we have to be like them, does it? Maybe we'll find others more like us. And if not, well, we can be the first. A spark to light a fire that will engulf the universe."

She ruminated. "You have to start somewhere, I suppose. As with this drain."

"Well, there you go."

"All right, damn it, I'll join your think tank. But first you're going to help me finish this drain, aren't you, city boy?"

So I changed into overalls and work boots, and we dug away at that ditch in the damp, clingy earth until our backs ached, and the light of the equinoctial day slowly faded.

Digging

IAN MCDONALD

British author Ian McDonald is an ambitious and daring writer with a wide range and an impressive amount of talent. His first story was published in 1982, and since then he has appeared with some frequency in Interzone, Asimov's Science Fiction, *and elsewhere. In 1989 he won the Locus Best First Novel Award for his novel* Desolation Road. *He won the Philip K. Dick Award in 1992 for his novel* King of Morning, Queen of Day. *His other books include the novels* Out on Blue Six, Hearts, Hands and Voices, Terminal Cafe, Sacrifice of Fools, Evolution's Shore, Kirinya, Ares Express, Cyberabad, *and* Brasyl, *as well as three collections of his short fiction,* Empire Dreams, Speaking in Tongues, *and* Cyberabad Days. *His novel* River of Gods *was a finalist for both the Hugo Award and the Arthur C. Clarke Award in 2005, and a novella drawn from it, 'The Little Goddess,' was a finalist for the Hugo and the Nebula. He won a Hugo Award in 2007 for his novelette 'The Djinn's Wife,' won the Theodore Sturgeon Award for his story 'Tendeleo's Story,' and in 2011 won the John W. Campbell Memorial Award for his novel* The Dervish House. *His most recent book is the starting volume of a YA series,* Planesrunner. *Born in Manchester, England, in 1960, McDonald has spent most of his life in Northern Ireland, and now lives and works in Belfast. He has a Web site at www.lysator.liu.se/~unicorn/mcdonald/.*

Here he takes us to a colonized future Mars, and inside a massive terraforming effort stretching over generations that involves digging a REALLY BIG hole.

Tash was wise to the ways of wind. She knew its many musics: sometimes like a flute across the pipes and tubes; sometimes a snare-drum rattle in the guy-lines and cable stays or again, a death drone-moan from the turbine gantries and a scream of sand past the irised-shut windows when the equinox dust storms blew for weeks on end. From the rails and drive bogies of the scoopline the wind drew a wail like a demon choir and from the buckets set a clattering clicking rattle so that she imagined tiny clockwork angels scampering up and down the hundreds of kilometres of conveyor belts. In the storm-season gales it came screaming in across Isidis' billion-year-dead impact basin, clawing at the eaves and gables of West Diggory, tearing at the tiered roofs so hard Tash feared it would rip them right off and send them tumbling end over end down down into the depths of the Big Dig. That would be the worst thing. Everyone would die badly: eyeballs and fingertips and lips exploding, cheeks bursting with red veins. She had nightmares about suddenly looking up to see the roof ripping away and the naked sky and the air all blowing away in one huge shout of exhalation. Then your eyeballs exploded. She imagined how that would sound. Two soft popping squelches. Then In-Brother Yoche told her you couldn't hear your eyeballs exploding because the air would be too thin and the whole story was a legend of mischievous Grandparents and Sub-aunts who liked to scare under-fours. But it made her think about how fragile was West Diggory and the other three stations of the Big Dig. Spindly and top-heavy, domes piled upon half domes upon semi-domes, swooping wing roofs and perilous balconies, all resting on the finger-thin cantilevers that connected the great Excavating City to the traction bogies. Like big spiders. Tash knew spiders. She had seen spiders in a book and once, in a piece of video excitedly shot by Lady-cousin Nairne in North Cutter, a real spider, in a real web, trembling in the perennial beat of the buckets working up the Scoop-line from the head of the Big Dig, five kilometres down slope. Lady-cousin Nairne had poked at the spider with her fingers—fat and brown as bread in high magnification. The spider had frozen, then scuttled for the corner of the window frame, curled into a tiny ball of legs and refused to do anything for the rest of the day. The next day when Nairne and her camera returned it was dead dead dead, dried into a little dessicated husk of shell. It must have come in a crate in the supply run down from the High Orbital, though everything they shipped from orbit was supposed to be clean. Beyond the window where the little translucent corpse hung vibrating in its web, red rock and wind and the endless march of the buckets along the rails of the Excavating Conveyor. Buckets and wind. Tied together. Wind; Fact one. When the buckets ceased, then and only then would the wind stop. Fact two: all Tash's life it had blown in the same direction: downhill.

Tash Gelem-Opunyo was wise to the ways of wind, and buckets, and random spiders and on Moving Day the wind was a long, many-part harmony for pipes drawn from the sand-polished steels rails, a flutter of the kites and blessing banners and windsocks and lucky fish that West Diggory flew from every rooftop and pylon and stanchion, a sudden caress of a veering eddy in the small of her back that made Tash shiver and stand upright on the high verandah in her psuit, a too-intimate touch. She was getting too big for the old psuit. It was tight and chafing in the wrong places. Tight it had to be, a stretch-skin of gas-impermeable fabric, but Things were Showing. My How You've Grown Things, that Haramwe Odonye, who was an Out-cousin in from A.R.E.A. and thus allowed to Notice such things, Noticed, and Commented On. Last Moving Day, half a long-year before, she had drawn in an attempt to camouflage the bumps and creases and curves by drawing all over the hi-visibility skin with marker pen. There were more animals on her skin than on the whole of Mars.

Up and out on Moving Day, that was the tradition. From the very very old to the very very young, blinking up out of their pressure cocoons; every soul in West Diggory came out on to the balconies and galleries and walkways. Safety was part of the routine—with every half-year wrench of West Diggory's thousand of tons of architecture into movement the possibility increased that a joint might split or a pressure dome shatter. Eyeball-squelch-pop time. But safety was only a small part. Movement was what West Diggory was for; like the wind, downwards, ever downwards.

The Terrace of the Grand Regard was the highest point on West Diggory: only the banners of the Isidis Plantia Excavating Company eternally billowing in the unvarying down-slope wind, and the wind turbines, stood higher. Climbing the ladders Tash felt Out-Cousin Haramwe's eyes on her, watching from the Boy's Pavilion. His boy-gaze drew the other young males on their high and rickety terrace. The psuit was indeed tight, but good tight. Tash enjoyed how it moved with her, holding her in where she wanted to be held, emphasising what she wanted emphasised.

"Hey, good snake!" Out-Cousin Haramwe called on the common channel. On her seven-and-a-halfth birthday Tash had drawn a dream snake on her psuit skin, a diamond pattern loop with its tail at the base of her spine, curled around the left curve of her ass and buried its head in the inner thigh. It had been exciting to draw. It was more exciting to wear on Moving Day, the only time she ever wore the psuit.

"Are you ogling my ophidian?" Tash taunted back to the hoots of the other boys as she climbed up on to Gallery of Exalted Vistas to be with her sisters and cousin and In-cousins and Out-cousins, all the many ways in which Tash could be related in a gene-pool of only two thousand people. The guys hooted. Tash shimmied her shoulders, where little birds were drawn. The boys liked her insulting them in words they didn't understand. Listen well, look well. I'm the best show on Mars.

A thousand banners rattled in the unending wind. Kites dipped and fluttered, painted with birds and butterflies and stranger aerial creatures that had only existed in the legends of distant earth. Streamers pointed the way for West Diggory: downhill, always downhill. The lines of buckets full of Martian soil marched up the conveyor from the dig point, invisible over the close horizon, under the legs of West Diggory, towards the unseen summit of Mt. Incredible, where they tipped their load on its ever-growing summit before cycling back down the under side of the conveyor. The story was that the freshly dug regolith at the bottom of the hole was the colour of gold: exposure to the atmosphere on its long journey up-slope turned it Mars red. She turned to better feel the shaper of the wind on every part of her body. This psuit so needed replacing. There was more to her shiver than just the caress of air in motion. Wind and words: they were the same stuff. If she threw big and fancy words, words that gave her joy and made her laugh from the shape they made from moving air, it was because they were living wind itself.

A shiver ran up through the catwalk grilles and railings and into Tash Gelem-Opunyo. The engineers were running up the traction generators; West Diggory shuddered and thrummed as the tokamaks drew resonances and steel harmonies from its girders and cantilevers. Tash's molars ached, then there was a jolt that threw old and young alike off balance, grasping for handrails, stanchions, cables, each other. There was a immense shriek like the new moon being pulled live from the body of the world world being pulled. Shuddering creaks, each so loud Tash could hear them through her ear-protectors. Steel wheels turned, grinding on sand. West Diggory began to move. People waved their hands and cheered, the noise reduction circuits on the Common Channel stopped the din down to a surge of delighted giggling. The wheels, each taller than Tash, ground round, slow as growing. West Diggory, perched on its cantilevers, inched down its eighteen tracks, tentative as an old woman stepping from a diggler. This was motion on the glacial, the geological scale.

It would take ten hours for West Diggory to make its scheduled descent into the Big Dig. You had to be sure to have eaten and drunk enough because it wasn't safe to go inside. Tash had breakfasted lightly at the commons in the Raven Sorority, when the In-daughters lived together after they turned five. The semizoic fabric absorbed everything without stink or stain but it was far from cool to piss your suit. Unless you were up and out on a job. Then it was mandatory.

Music trilled on the common channel, a cheery little toe-tapper. Tash gritted her teeth. She knew what it heralded: the West Diggory Down. No one knew when where or who had started the tradition of the Moving Day dance: Tash suspected it was a joke that no one had recognised and so became literal. She slid behind a stanchion as her Raven sisters formed up and the boys up on the Lads Pavilion bowed and raised their hands. Slip away slip away before it starts. Up the steps and along the clattering catwalk to the Outermost Preview. From this distant perch, a birdcage of steel at the end of a slender pier, a lantern suspended over the sand, Tash surveyed all West Diggory, her domes and gantries and pods and tubes and flapping banners and her citizens—so few of them, Tash thought—formed up into lines and squares for the dance. She tuned out the Common Channel. Strange, them stepping gaily, hand in hand, up and down the lines, do-se-doh in psuits and facemasks and total silence. The olds seemed to enjoy it. They had no dignity. Look how fat some of them were in their psuits. Tash turned away from the rituals of West Diggory to the great, subtle slope of the Big Dig, following the lines of up the slope. She was on the edge of the age when you could leave West Diggory but she had heard that up there, beyond Mt. Incredible, the small world curved away so quickly in all directions that the horizon was only three kilometers distant. The Big Dig held different horizons. It was a huge cone sunk into the surface of a sphere. An alternative geometry worked here. The world didn't curve away, it curved inwards, a circle over three hundred kilometres round where it met the surface of Mars. The world radiated outwards: Tash could follow the radiating spokes of the scooplines all the way of the edge of the world, and beyond, to the encircling ring-mountain of Mt. Incredible that reached the edge of space. Peering along the curve of the Big Dig through the dust haze constantly thrown up by the ceaseless excavating, she could just make out the sun-glitter from the gantries of North Cutter, like West Diggory, making its slow descent deeper into the pit. A flicker of thought would up the magnification on her visor and she would be able to look clear across eighty kilometres of airspace to A.R.E.A. and spy on whatever celebrations they held there, on the first and greatest of the Excavating Cities on Moving Day. Maybe she might see a girl like herself, balanced on some high and perilous perch, looking out across the bowl of the world.

The figures on the platforms and terraces broke apart, bowed to each other, lost all pattern and rhythm and became random again. Moving Day Down was over for another half-year. Tash flicked on the Common Channel. Tash liked to be apart, different, a girl of words and wit, but she also loved to be immersed in West Diggory's never-ending babble of chat and gossip and jokes and family news. Together, the Excavating Cities had a population of less than two thousand humans. Small, complex societies, isolated from the rest of the planet, gush words like springs, like torrents and floods. The river of words, the only river that Mars knew. Tash's psuit circuitry was smart enough to adjust the voices so that they spoke at the volume and distance they would have in atmosphere. Undifferentiated, the flood of West Diggory voices would have overwhelmed her so the wall of voices did not overwhelm her. She turned her head this way, that way. Eavesdropping. There was Leyta Soshinwe-Opunyo, Queen-beeing again. Tash had seen pictures of bees like she had seen birds. On Arrival Day, when the Excavating Cities finally reached the bottom of the Big Dig, there would be birds, and bees, and even spiders. There was Great-Out-Aunt Yoto, seeming enthusiastic but always seasoned with a pinch of criticism—*oh, and another thing*: people weren't performing the dance moves right, the Engineers had mistuned the tokamaks and her titanium hip was aching, was it her or did more bits fall off West Diggory every time? They would never have allowed that in Southdelving, her family home. A sudden two-tone siren cut across the four hundred voices of West Diggory. Emergency teams slapped their psuits to warning yellow and rushed to their positions, everyone hurried to the muster points, then relaxed as the medics discovered the nature of the Emergency. The Common Channel flooded with laughter. Haramwe Odonye, during a particularly energetic caper in the West Diggory Down, had slipped and sprained his ankle.

Big Dig Figs:

Population: one thousand eight hundred and thirty three, divided between the four Excavating Cities of (clockwise) Southdelving, West Diggory, North Cutter and A.R.E.A (Ares Re-engineering of Environment and Atmosphere). Total Martian population: five thousand two hundred and seventeen.

Elevation: at the digging head as of Martian Year 112, Janulum 1: minus twenty three kilometres below Martian Mean Gravity Surface (no sea level). Same date, highest point of Mt. Impossible: 15 kilometres above MGS.

Diameter of the Big Dig at Martian MGS: Five hundred and sixteen kilometres.

Circumference of the Big Dig at Martian MGS: One thousand six hundred and twenty two kilometres.

Angle of Big Dig Excavation Surface: 5:754 degrees. That's pretty gentle. The Scoopline can't handle more than an eight degree slope. To the casual human eye—one that hasn't grown up inside the gentle dish of the Big Dig, that would look almost flat. But it's not flat. That's why it's the key figure: those 5:75 degrees are going to make Mars habitable.

Date of commencement of the Big Dig: AlterMarch 23rd, Martian Year 70. Two thirty in the afternoon, on schedule, the scooplines excavated and the bucket teeth took their first bites of Isidis Planitia.

Volume of the Big Dig: as of above date: one million, eight hundred and thirteen thousand cubic kilometres. All piled up neatly into Mt. Impossible, the ring-shaped mountain that surrounds the Big Dig like the wall of an old impact crater. Not entirely surrounds. Mt. Impossible has been constructed with four huge valleys: Windrush, Zephyr, Cyroco and Storm of the Black Plums: howling wind-haunted, storm-scoured canyons: that same wind singing over the tombs of the Diggers who have died in the course of the great excavation, unfailingly stirring the flags and streamers of the mobile cities far below.

Total mass of Martian surface excavated in the Big Dig to date: 7.1×10^{15} tons.

Big Dig Figs and Facts. The numbers that shape Tash's world.

Tash was in the Orangery when the call came down through the rows of breadfruit trees. Like the Moving Day dance, the name was generally considered another joke that had run away and taken up residence in the ventilators and crawlspaces and power conduits of the Excavating City, as this baroque glass dome had never grown oranges. The rows of breadfruit and plantains and bananas and other high-carbo staples gave camouflage and opportunity for West Diggory's young people to meet and talk and scheme and flirt.

"Milaba wants to see Tash, pass it on."

"Sweto, tell Chunye that Milaba wants to see Tash."

"Qori, have you see Tash?"

"I think she was down in the plantains, but she might have moved on to the breadfruit."

"Well tell her Milaba wants to see her."

By leaps and misunderstandings, by staggers and misapprehensions, by devious spirals of who liked who and who was talking to who and who wasn't and who was hooking with who and who had finished with who, the message spiralled in along the web of leaf-mould smelling plants to Tash, spraying the breadfruit. A simple call, a message would have reached her directly but where there are only a hundred of you, true social networking is mouth to mouth.

In-Aunt Milaba. She was a legend, a statue of woman, gracious and noble, adored far beyond West Diggory. Her dark skin was lustrous as night, her soul as star-filled. To be in her presence was to be blessed in ways you would not immediately understand but, more thrilling to Tash, was that In-Aunt Milaba was the chief service engineer for the North West sector scooplines. The summons to her office, a little glass and aluminium bubble like a bunion on one of West Diggory's steel feet, could mean only one thing. Out. Out and up.

"So Haramwe sprained his ankle."

Every part of In-Aunt Milaba's tiny office, from the hand-carved olivine desk to the carafe of water that stood on it, shook to the rattle of the buckets hurtling up the scoopline. Milaba raised an eyebrow. Tash realised a response was due.

"Are his injuries debilitating?"

"Debilitating." Milaba gave a flicker of a smile. "You could say that. He'll be out for a week or so. He came down heavily, silly boy. Showing off. When is your birthday?" Tash's heart leapt.

She knew. Everyone knew everything, all the time. The game was pretending not to know.

"Octobril fifth."

"Three months." Milaba appeared to consider for a moment. "Peyko Ruebens-Opollo says for all your fancy talk you've a good head and better sense and do what you're told. That's good because I don't need attitude problems or last-minute-good-ideas when I'm out on the line."

For once the words failed Tash. They hissed from her like air from a ruptured atmosphere cell. She waved her hands in speechless delight.

"I'm taking a digger up Line 12 to Windrush Valley. The feed tokamaks have been fluctuating nastily. Probably a soft fail in a command chip set; they get a lot of radiation up there. Now I need someone with me to hold things and make tea and generally make intelligent conversation. Are you interested?"

Still the words would not come. The rule was that you did not leave the Excavating Cities until you were eight, when you were technically adult. Rules broke and bent with the frequency of scoopline breakdowns but three months was a significant proportion of the long Martian year. Out. Out, and up. Up the line, into the windy valley. In a diggler, with In-Aunt Milaba.

"Yes, oh yes, I'd love to," Tash finally squeaked. Now Milaba unleashed the full radiance of her smile and it was like sunrise, it was solstice lights, it was the warmth of the glow-lamps in the Orangery. *I say you are an adult citizen of West Diggory, Tash Gelem-Opunyo,* the smile said, *and if I say it, all say it.*

"Be at the Outlock 12 at fourteen o'clock," Milaba said. "You do know how to make tea, don't you?"

Still not got it? It's easy, easy easy easy. Easy as a heezy, which is a Digger saying. A heezy is the lever on a scoopline bucket that, when struck by the dohbrin (which is a different type of lever found at the load-off end of the scoopline) tips the contents of the bucket down Mt. Incredible. Heezy peasy easy. It's all because air has weight. Air's not nothing. It's gas—in Mars' case, carbon dioxide nitrogen argon oxygen and the leaked breathings from the hundred-and-something years that humans have scratched and scrabbled clawholds on its red earth. It has mass. It has weight. And it flows, the same way that water flows, to the lowest point. Wind is air flowing. People say, *no one knows why the wind blows.* That's stupid nonsense. Wind blows from high to low, high pressure to low pressure, high altitude to low altitude; down the slopes of mountains, through canyons and valleys. The air pressure at the bottom of the great and primeval rift of Valles Marineris is ten times that in the long-cold volcanic calderas atop Olympus Mons. Titanic gales and fog blow through that valley. The fog is because the atmospheric pressure at the bottom of the valley is enough—just enough—to allow water to exist as vapour. But that's still not enough to support big life. That's like higher than earth's highest mountain. That's fingertip-lip-exploding, eyeball-squelching, cheek-bursting pressure. Bug life yes, big life no. That's not enough to make Mars a green paradise, a home for humanity, a fertile pool of life beyond little blue Earth. What you need is deep. Thirty kilometres deep. Deeper than any place on Earth is deep. Deeper than even Olympus Mons, mightiest mountain on all the worlds, is high. And because air has weight, because atmosphere flows and the wind blows, gas will fill up the hole. That's the wind that rattles the banners and turns the rotors of West Diggory. As the gas flows the pressure grows until the day comes when the atmospheric pressure at the bottom of the hole is enough for you to walk around without a psuit, in just your skin if you have the urge and your skin is pretty enough. Earth atmospheric pressure. Pressure, that's always been the problem with making Mars habitable. Get all the gas into one place. When you've got enough of it, turning it into something you can breathe is the easy bit. That's just bugs and plants and life.

Thirty kilometres deep. The scooplines are at minus twenty six kilometres. That's another five M-years before they hit atmospheric baseline. Then they'll level out the floor of the crater, take away some of the sides, expand the flat area, though it will all seem so flat, the atmospheric gradient so subtle, that you will seem to be walking out into breathlessness and light-headedness rather than ascending into it. Fifty years after her In-Grandfather Tayhum made the first incision, the Big Dig will be dug. Tash will be seventeen and a half when the wind rushing down the sides of the Big Dig finally fails and the rotors stop and the banners fall and the Excavating Cities finally come to a rest.

Twenty six kilometres up slope, In-Aunt Milaba gave the sign for Tash to throw the levers to disengage the diggler from the scoopline. Thus far the big world of outside had been a thumping disappointment to Tash. She had yet to be outside, properly outside, two-figures-in-a-Mars-scape outside, shiver-in-your-psuit outside. She had transited from plastic bubble by plastic tube to plastic bubble connected by its grip on the scoopline to home.

This was what Tash Gelem-Opunyo saw from the transparent bubble of the diggler. Sand sand sand sand sand, a rock there, sand sand sand rock rock, oh, some pebbles! Sand grit sand more grit something between pebble and grit, something between grit and sand, a bit of old abandoned machinery, wow wow wow! Dust drifted up around it. Sand. Sand. Sand. West Diggory was still visible, down the dwindling thread of the scoopline, now truly the size of a spider. The enormous, horizonless perspectives robbed Tash of anything by which she could judge movement. The sand, the buckets, the unchanging gentle gradient that went up halfway to space. Only by squinting down through the floor glass at the blurred, grainy surface did she get any sense of movement.

Twenty-six vertical kilometres equalled two hundred sixty surface kilometres equalled five and a half hours in a plastic bubble with a relative you've grown up in enforced proximity to but until now never really known or talked to. Everyone loves In-Aunt Milaba the Magnificent, that's the legend, but five hours, Aunt and Niece, Tash began to wonder if this was another wind-whisper legend blown around the corners and crannies of West Diggory. She was beautiful, a feast for the eye and soul, all those things an eight-year-old girl hopes for herself (and did Tash not share the DNA—given that the Excavating cities genepool was shallow as a spit, hence all the careful arrangements of In-relatives and Out-relatives and who would be sent to one of the other Excavating Cities and who would stay) all those things a girl of almost-eight wants for herself but try as she might, and did, Tash could not engage her. Fancy funny words of the type Tash treasured. Poems. Puns. Riddles. Guessing games. Break-the-code-games. Allusions and circumspect questions. Direct questions. To them all In-Aunt Milaba shook her head and smiled and bent over the controls and the monitors and checked her kit and said not a word. So tea, lots of tea, and muttering little rhymes to the rhythm of the huge balloon wheels as the scoopline hauled Diggler Six up the side of the biggest excavation in the solar system.

But now they were released from the scoopline and Milaba was standing at the steering column, driving the diggler under its own power. It was still sand sand sand and occasional rock, but Tash knew a gnaw of excitement. She was free, disconnected from the umbilicals of life for the first time. She was out in the wild world. The scoopline dwindled to a thread, to invisibility behind her, ahead she saw a notch on the edge of vision. Windrush Valley. All the wind-blown words stopped. A flaw in the horizon. A place beyond the Big Dig. Beyond that declivity was the whole curved world. In the silence In-Aunt Milaba turned from the control column.

"I think you could have a go now."

So this was what she had been waiting for, Tash to run out of words, and finally listen.

The diggler was ridiculously simple to drive. Plant your feet firmly at the drive column. Push forward to feed power to the traction motors in the wheel hubs. Pull back to brake. Yaw to steer. There was even a little holder on the side of the drive column for your tea. Tash giggled with nervous glee as she gingerly pushed forward the stick and the bubble of pressure glass slung between the giant orange tyres stuttered forward. Within thirty seconds she had it. Thirty seconds later she was pushing it, sneaking the speed bar up, looking for places where she could make the diggler skip over rocks.

"I'd go easy on that throttle," Milaba said. "The battery life is eight hours; That's why we ride the scoopline up and down again. You don't want to get stuck up here with night coming down, no traction and no heat."

Tash eased the stick back but not before the diggler hit the small boulder at which she had discreetly aimed and bounced all four wheels in the air. Milaba smiled that morning-sun smile. Then shoulder by shoulder they stood at the controls and rode up into the orange valley. The land rose up on either side, higher as they drove deeper, kilometres high. They felt like oppression to Tash, shouldering close and ominous, their heights breathless and haunted with dark things that lived in the sky. At the same time she felt hideously small and exposed in the fragile glass ornament of the diggler. The wind was rising, she could feel the diggler shake on its suspension, hear the shriek and moan through the cables. The controls fought her but she pushed the little bubble deeper and deeper into Windrush Valley. When her forearms arched and the sinews on her neck stood out from fighting the atmosphere of Mars pouring through this two-kilometre wide notch in Mt. Incredible, Milaba leaned over and tapped a preprogrammed course into the computer.

"Suit up," she said. "We'll be there in ten minutes."

The tokamak station was a wind-scoured blister of construction plastic hunkering between a boulder field and a stretch of polished olivine. It was only when the diggler slowed to a stop and fired sand anchors that Tash realised that it was near and smaller than she had thought. It was not a distant vast city, the power plant was only slightly higher than the diggler's mammoth wheels. The wind rotor, spinning like it would suddenly leap from its pylon and spin madly away through the upper air, was no bigger than her outstretched hands.

"Mask sealed?"

Tash ran her fingers around the join with her psuit hood and gave In-Aunt Milaba two thumbs up. "I'm dee-peeing the diggler." There was a high-pitched shriek of air being vented into the tanks, a whistle that ebbed into silence as the pressure dropped to match the outside environment. The scribbled-over psuit felt tight and stuff. This was true eyeball-squelch altitude. Then Milaba popped the door and Tash followed her out and down the ladder on to the wild surface of Mars.

Gods and teeth, but the wind was brutal. Tash balled her fists and squared her shoulders and lowered her head to battle through it to the yellow and blue-chevronned tokamak station. She could feel the sand whipping across the skin of her psuit. She didn't like to think of the semizoic skin abrading, cell by cell. She imagined it wailing in pain. A tap on the shoulder, Milaba gestured for her to hook her safety line on to the door winch. Then In-Aunt and In-Niece they punched through the big wind to the shelter of the tokamak shell. Out. Out in the world. Up high. If Tash kept walking into the wind she would pass through Windrush Valley and come to a place where the world curved away from her, not towards her. The desire to do it was unbearable. Out of the hole. All it would take would be one foot in front of another. They would take her all the way around the world and back again, to this place. The gale of possibility died. It was all, only, ever circles. Milaba tapped her again on the shoulder to remind her that there was work to be done here. Tash took the unitool and unscrewed the inspection hatch. Milaba plugged in her diagnosticators. She was glorious to watch at work, easy and absorbed. But it was long work and Tash's attention wandered to the little meandering dust-dervishes that spun up into a small tornado for a few seconds, staggered down the valley and collapsed into swirling sand.

"Willie-willies," Milaba said. "You want to be careful with those, they're tricksy. As I thought." She pointed at the readout. "A hard fail in the chip set." She pulled a new blade out of her thigh pouch and slid it into the control unit. Lights flashed green. Inside its shielded dome the tokamak grumbled and woke up with a shiver that sent the dust rising from the ground. Tash watched the wind it whirl into a dozen dust-devils, dancing around each other. "Just going to check the supply line. You stay here." She headed up the valley along the line of the power cable. The dust devils swirled in towards each other. They merged. They fused. They became one, a true dust demon.

"Looks all right!" In-Aunt Milaba called.

"Milaba, I don't like the look . . ." The dust-demon spun towards Tash, then at the last moment veered away and tracked up the valley. "Milaba!"

Milaba hesitated. The hesitation was death. The dusty-demon bore down on her, she tried to throw herself away but it spun over her, lifted her, threw her hard and fast, smashed her down on to the smooth polished olivine. Tash saw her face-plate shatter in a spray of shards and water vapour. It was random, it was mad, it was a chance in a billion, it can't happen, it was an affront to order and reason but it had and there Milaba lay on the hard olivine.

"Oh my gods oh my gods oh my gods!" For a moment Tash was paralysed, for a moment she did not know what to to, that she could do anything, that she must do something. Then she was running up the valley. The dust-demon veered towards Tash. Tash shrieked, then it staggered away, broke itself on the boulders and spun down to dust again. The psuit would seal automatically but In-Aunt Milaba had moments before her eyeballs froze. "Oh help help help help help," Tash cried, her hands pressed to Milaba's face, trying to will heat into it. Then she saw the red button on the safety line harness. She hit it and was almost jolted off her feet as the winch on the diggler reeled Milaba in. Tash hit the Emergency Channel. "This is Diggler Six this is Diggler Six in Windrush Valley. This is an emergency." Of course it is. It's the Emergency channel. She tried to calm her voice as the winch lifted the limp Milaba into the air. "We have a suit dee pee situation. We have a suit dee pee."

"Hello Diggler Six. This is Diggory West Emergency Services. Please identify yourself."

"This is Tash Gelem-Opunyo. It's Milaba."

"Tash. Control here." Tash recognised Out-Uncle Yoyote's voice. "Get back. Get back here. You should have enough power, we'll send another diggler up the line to meet you, but you, darling, you have to do it. We can't get to you in time. It's up to you. Get back to us. It's all you can do."

Of course. It was. All she could do. No rescue swooping from the skies, in a world where nothing could fly. No speed-star scorching up the slope of the Big Dig in a world where the scoopline was the fastest means of transport. She was on her own.

It took all her strength to swing Milaba through the hatch into the diggler cab and seal the lock. Almost Tash popped her faceplate. Almost. She re-pressurised the diggler. Air-shriek built to a painful screech then stopped. But Milaba was so still, so cold. Her face was white with frost where her breath had frozen into her skin. It would never be the same again. Milaba knelt, turned her cheek to her In-Aunt's lips. A whisper a sigh a suspicion a sussuration. She was breathing. But it was cold so cold death cold Mars cold in the diggler. Tash slapped the heater up to the maximum and jigged around the tiny cab. Condensation turned the windows opaque, then cleared. Back. She had to get back. Was there an auto-return programme? Where would she find it? Where would she even begin looking? Wasting precious instants, wasting precious instants. Tash took the control column, stamped on the pedal to release the anchors and engaged the traction motors. Turning was difficult. Turning was scary. Turning forced a small moan of fear when the wind got under the diggler and she felt the right side lift. If it went over here, they were both dead. This was not fun driving. There was no glee, no whee!; at every bounce Tash tensed and clenched, fearful that the diggler would roll over and shatter like an egg, smash an axle, any number of new terrors that only appear when your life depends on everything working perfectly. *Come on come on come on.* The battery gauge was dwindling with terrifying speed. This was outside. This was the horizoned world. Where was the scoopline? Surely it hadn't been this far. *Come on come on come on.* A line on the sand. But so far. Power at twelve percent. Where had it gone what had she used it on? The heating blast? The emergency reepee? The burn on the winch? Call home. That would be sensible. That would be the act of a girl with a good head and better sense who did what she was told. But it would use power. Batteries at seven percent, but now she could see the scoopline, the laden buckets above, the empty buckets below, bucket after bucket after bucket. She drove the diggler on. Matching velocities with the scoopline was teeth-gritting, nerve-stretching work. Tash had to drop the diggler into the space between the buckets and hold exact speed. A push too fast would ride up on the preceding bucket. Too slow and she would be rear-ended by the bucket behind. And ever edging inwards, inwards, closer to the line as the batteries slid from green to red. Lights flashes. Tash threw the lever. The shackle engaged. Tash rolled away from the drive column to Milaba on the floor.

"Tash." A whisper a sigh a suspicion a sussuration.

"It's all right, it's all right, don't talk, we're on scoopline."

"Tash, are my eyes open?"

"Yes they are."

A tiny sigh.

"Then I can't see. Tash, talk to me."

"What about?"

"I don't know. Anything. Everything. Just talk to me. We're on the linem, did you say?"

"We're on the line. We're going home."

"Five hours then. Talk to me."

So she did. Tash pulled cushions and mats around her into a nest and sat holding her In-Aunt's head and she talked. She talked about her friends and her in-sisters and her out-sisters and who would go away from West Diggory and who would stay. She talked about boys and how she liked them looking at her but still wanted to be different and special, not to be taken for granted, funny-Tash, odd-Tash. She talked about whether she would marry, which she didn't think she would, not as far as she could see, and what she would do then if she didn't. She talked about the things she loved, like swimming, and cooking vegetables, and drawing and words words words. She talked about how she loved the sound and shape of words, the sound of them as something quite different from what they meant and how you could put them together to say things that could not possibly be, and how the words came to her, like they were blown on the wind, shaped from wind, the wind brought to life. She talked of these in words that weren't clever or mouth-filling, words said quietly and simply and honestly, saying what she thought and how she felt. Tash saw then a richer lode in words; beyond the beauty of their sounds and shapes and patterns was a deeper beauty of the truth they could shape. They could tell what it was to be Tash Gelem-Opunyo. Words could fly the banners and turn the rotors of a life. Milaba squeezed her hand and pushed her broken lips into a smile, and creased the corner of her white, frost-burned eyes.

The Emergency Channel chimed. Yoyote had her on visual: they were about twenty kilometres down slope from her. They were coming to get her. They would be safe soon. Well done. And there was other news, news that made his voice sound strange to Tash in Diggler Six, like he was dead and walking and talking and about to cry all at the same time. A command had come in from Iridis Excavation Command, from the High Orbital, ultimately all the way from Earth and the Iridis Development Consortium. There had been a political shift. The faction that was up was down and the faction that was down was up. The Big Dig was cancelled.

From here, every way was up. There had been no official announcement from the Council of Diggers for ceremonials or small mournings: in their ones and two, their families and kinship groups and sororities and fraternities the people of West Diggory had decided to share the news that their world was ending, and to see the bottom of it; the base that had been their striving for three generations; the machine head. Dig Zero. Minimum elevation. So they took digglers or rode down the scoopline to the bottom of the Big Dig, and looked around them, and looked around at the digging heads of the scooplines, stilled and frozen for the first time in memory, buckets filled with their last bite of Mars turned to the sky. As they grew accustomed to the sights and wonders of the dig head, for not one in fifty of the Excavating Cities' populations worked at the minimum elevation, they saw in the distance, between the black scoopline, groups and families and societies from North Cutter and Southdelving and A.R.E.A. They waved to each other, greeting relatives they had not seen in years; the Common Channel was a flock of voices. Tash stood with her Raven Sorority sisters. They positioned themselves around her, even queen-bee Leyta. Tash was a slam and brief heroine—perhaps the last one the Big Dig would ever have. In-Aunt Milaba had been taken to the main medical facility A.R.E.A. where they were growing her new irises for her frost-blinded eyes. Her face would be scarred and patched with ugly white but her smile would always be beautiful. So the In-sisters and In-cousins stood around Tash, needing to be down at zero but not knowing why, or what to do now. The boys from the Black Obsidian Fraternity waved over and came across the sand to join the girls. *So few of us, really,* Tash thought.

"Why?" Out-cousin Sebben asked.

"Environment," said Sweto and in the same transmission, Qori said "Cost."

"Are they going to take us all back to Earth?" Chunye asked.

"No, they're never going to do that," Haramwe said. He walked with a stick, which made him look like an old man but at the same interesting and attractive. "That would cost too much."

"We couldn't anyway," Sweto said. "The gravity down there would kill us. We can't live anywhere but here. This is our home."

"We're Martians," Tash said. Then she put her hands up to her face mask.

"What are you doing?" Chunye, always the nervous In-cousin, cried in alarm.

"I just want to know," Tash said. "I just want to feel it, like it should be." Three taps, and the face plate fell into her waiting hands. The air was cold, shakingly cold, and still too thin to breathe and anyway, to breathe was to die on lungfuls of carbon dioxide but she could feel the wind, the real wind, the true wind in her face. Tash exhaled gently into the atmosphere gathered at the bottom of the Big Dig. The world still sloped gently away from her, all the way up the sky. Tears would freeze in an instant so she kept them to herself. Then Tash clapped the plate back over her face and fastened it to the psuit hood with her clever fingers.

"So, what do we do now?" whiny Chunye asked. Tash knelt. She pushed her fingers into the soft regolith. What else was there? What else had their ever been. A message had come down Mt. Incredible, from High Orbital, from a world on the other side of the sky, from people who had never seen this, whose horizons were always curved away from them. Who were they to say? What wind blew their words and made them so strong? Here were people, whole cities, an entire civilization, in a hole. This was Mars.

"We do what we know best," Tash said, scooping up pale golden mars in her gloved hand. "We put it all back again."

Ascension Day

Alastair Reynolds

Alastair Reynolds is a frequent contributor to Interzone, *and has also sold to* Asimov's Science Fiction, Spectrum SF, *and elsewhere. His first novel,* Revelation Space, *was widely hailed as one of the major SF books of the year; it was quickly followed by* Chasm City, Redemption Ark, Absolution Gap, Century Rain, *and* Pushing Ice, *all big sprawling space operas that were big sellers as well, establishing Reynolds as one of the best and most popular new SF writers to enter the field in many years. His other books include a novella collection,* Diamond Dogs, Turquoise Days, *a chapbook novella,* The Six Directions of Space, *as well as three collections,* Galactic North, Zima Blue and Other Stories, *and* Deep Navigation *and the novels* The Prefect, House of Suns, *and* Terminal World. *His newest novel is* Blue Remembered Earth *and forthcoming is a Doctor Who novel,* Harvest of Time. *A professional scientist with a Ph.D. in astronomy, he worked for the European Space Agency in the Netherlands for a number of years, but has recently moved back to his native Wales to become a full-time writer.*

Reynolds's work is known for its grand scope, sweep, and scale. In one story, 'Galactic North,' a spaceship sets out in pursuit of another in a stern chase that takes thousands of years of time and hundreds of thousands of light-years to complete; in another, 'Thousandth Night,' ultrarich immortals embark on a plan that will call for the physical rearrangement of all the stars in the Galaxy. Here he offers us an incisive glimpse, full of enough sense of wonder for many another writers' novels, of what happens when it's time for a ship to set forth again at last after centuries on the ground.

Lauterecken woke, and knew that it was his last day on Rhapsody. It had, on balance, been a good stay. The planet had been kind to him, these last ninety-six years.

But all things must end.

He eased from the languid embrace of the beauty he had taken to bed the night before. It took him a moment to remember her name. Vindra, that was it. An actress and dancer, famed across half the hemisphere. She'd been as good as they'd promised.

"Where are you going?"

She'd curled an arm around him as he made to leave the bed. He smiled and showed her the gold-studded bracelet, with its blue light winking steadily. "My ship is ready, Vindra. Her engines have been building to launch power for a week, and now we must leave." He softened the remark with a smile. "You can't say it's a surprise. I informed your government of my plans more than a year ago."

"I didn't think it was going to happen quite so soon."

He nodded in the vague direction of space. "Hyperspace is only predictable on a timescale of days. There's a window for us now. If we don't leave now, it could be weeks or months before conditions are favourable again."

"You've been here nearly a century."

"If there was any other way." He leaned down to kiss Vindra, before taking to the suite's bathroom. "Ninety-six years seems like a long time, but that's only because you see things from a planetary perspective. I'm the captain of a starship. My ship has been trading with hundreds of worlds, crossing the galaxy for tens of thousands of years."

"Soon I'll be just a memory to you," Vindra said sadly. "Even if you came back here, I'll be long dead. I've seen pictures of you, from the day when you first stepped out of your ship. You haven't aged at all."

Lauterecken touched his forehead. "But I won't forget Rhapsody. And I won't forget you either, Vindra."

A government flier took him out to the ship. It was by far the biggest artificial thing on Rhapsody, although even Lauterecken had to admit that it didn't look much like a ship anymore. The freighter was a rectangular box, eight kilometres long, four wide and four high. A century ago, learning of its imminent arrival, the citizens of Rhapsody had pooled their planetary resources to dig out a berthing dock, a vast trench as long and wide as the freighter and more than a kilometre deep. From the sides of the dock, they'd extended countless bridges and ramps, allowing easy access to the freighter's enormous holds and bays. Trade had ensued. Rhapsody was technologically backward, but it produced art and biological constructs that Lauterecken was certain could be sold on for a profit elsewhere in the galaxy.

For the first few decades the government had kept a noose on the terms of commerce. Then the arrangements started to slacken. Lauterecken started dealing with entrepreneurs and merchants, rather than state-sanctioned brokers. He didn't care, so long as there was a profit somewhere down the line.

But with the breakdown of organised trade had come shantytowns and slums, ringing the berthing dock. Over the last fifty or sixty years these festering districts had spilled over the edge of the dock, spanning the gap and climbing up the side of the freighter. From a distance, the great ship appeared to be furred with corrosion. Only on closer inspection, as the flier approached for landing, was the corrosion revealed to be layer upon layer of teetering shacks, scaffolded together and fixed to the hull by whatever means served. Twenty, thirty stories of them. The slum-dwellers were the poorest of the poor, clinging onto the warmth emanating from the hull, collecting the water that pooled on its upper deck and ran down the sides in rainbowed cataracts.

He'd been pushing the government to instigate a clearance and relocation program for years, but as far as he could tell their efforts had been lackadaisical.

"How many still left?" he asked the mandarin in the flier.

"Between eleven and twelve thousand, last census." The official grimaced. "I'm very sorry, Captain. We did what we could, but as soon as we clear one sector, they move in somewhere else. If you'd be willing to delay departure for a few more months, we might be able to do something . . ."

"You've had years," Lauterecken snapped. "A few more months won't make any difference."

The flier came in for landing.

He stepped onto the raised platform, straightened his back and presented his hands to the flanking input consoles. Blue light spilled from under his palms as the consoles sampled his skin, verifying his identity. A branching coldness shot up his arms, as the ship penetrated his nervous system. The shiver was gone as quickly as it had come, leaving only a tremendous sense of potentiality, and the feeling that his own body image had become diffuse, extending for kilometres in all directions, out to the very limits of the hull.

"Status," Lauterecken said.

The ship answered into his skull in soft, lulling tones that were infinitely at odds with the colossal, world-quaking scale of the vessel itself. "Propulsion at launch readiness."

"Window for hyperspace insertion?"

"Holding."

"Very good."

In the long decades in which he had not been interfaced with the ship, he had always struggled to call to mind exactly how it felt to be standing on the pedestal, linked in and ready to fly. Now that it was upon him again, now that the ship was waiting to do his bidding, he marvelled that he could ever have forgotten.

He sensed the engines draw power. The floor tremored, and at the limit of audibility he heard, or rather felt, something like the deepest organ note imaginable. It was actually a combination of notes, sixteen of them merging in perfect, throbbing harmony.

He increased power. Fifty percent of lift threshold, then sixty, then seventy. Barring the arrival and departure of another ship, or some unspeakable natural catastrophe, no louder sound would ever be heard on Rhapsody. As the freighter loosened its ties to gravity, so it also began to slough away the slums that had crept up its sides. Lauterecken felt them shaking loose, collapsing and tumbling into the depths of the berthing dock, layer upon avalanching layer. Dust clouds, tawny brown and flecked with fire, billowed around the ship's lower flanks. He preferred not to think about the people still living in the slums. They'd been told to move, after all.

The freighter began to lift free of Rhapsody.

When all was well, when the freighter was out of the gravity well and on normal approach for the hyperspace entry point, Lauterecken left his console and travelled through the thrumming dense city-like innards of the ship.

Near the exact centre of the freighter was a chamber only slightly smaller than one of its major cargo bays. The armoured vault was entirely enclosed, however, and had no direct connection to the exterior. The ship, in fact, had been assembled around its still-growing contents.

Lauterecken stood on a balcony overlooking the chamber. In its middle, pinned in place by suspension fields, was something huge and living, but now dormant. It had been human once, Lauterecken was led to believe, but that seemed absurd.

He touched controls set into the balcony's railing. Signals wormed into the creature's house-sized cortex, willing it from slumber. Over the course of a minute, monstrous eyes in a monstrous face opened to drowsy half-slits.

"Lauterecken?" the voice was soft and intimate, and yet loud enough to rattle the balcony's railing.

"Yes," he acknowledged.

"Status?"

"On course, sir. We should be at the transit point in three hours."

"Very good, Lauterecken. Is there anything I need to know?"

"No, sir. All propulsion systems are nominal. The manifold is stable and holding."

"And our time on the planet . . . what was its name, again?"

"Rhapsody, sir."

"Was it . . . profitable?"

"I'd like to think so, sir. Our holds are full."

"I sense minor damage to our external cladding."

Lauterecken smiled quickly. "Nothing that won't heal, sir."

"I am pleased to hear it. I trust you made the most of your period of consciousness?"

He swallowed down his nervousness. He was always nervous, even when he knew he'd discharged his duties satisfactorily.

"I did, Captain."

"Well, you've earned your rest now. Go to sleep. I'll be sure to wake you when you're next needed."

After the Apocalypse

MAUREEN F. MCHUGH

Maureen F. McHugh made her first sale in 1989, and has since made a powerful impression on the SF world with a relatively small body of work, becoming one of today's most respected writers. In 1992, she published one of the year's most widely acclaimed and talked-about first novels, China Mountain Zhang, *which won the Locus Award for Best First Novel, the Lambda Literary Award, and the James Tiptree, Jr. Award, and which was named a* New York Times *Notable Book as well as being a finalist for the Hugo and Nebula Awards. Her story "The Lincoln Train" won her a Nebula Award. Her other books, including the novels* Half the Day Is Night, Mission Child, *and* Nekropolis, *have been greeted with similar enthusiasm. Her powerful short fiction has appeared in* Asimov's Science Fiction, The Magazine of Fantasy & Science Fiction, Starlight, Eclipse, Alternate Warriors, Aladdin, Killing Me Softly, *and other markets, and has been collected in* Mothers and Other Monsters. *She lives in Austin, Texas, with her husband, her son, and a golden retriever named Hudson.*

Here she takes us to a frighteningly plausible future where the apocalypse doesn't happen all at once with a bang, but rather sneaks up on you one step at a time.

▼

Jane puts out the sleeping bags in the backyard of the empty house by the tool shed. She has a lock and hasp and an old hand drill that they can use to lock the tool shed from the inside but it's too hot to sleep in there and there haven't been many people on the road. Better to sleep outside. Franny has been talking a mile a minute. Usually by the end of the day she is tired from walking—they both are—and quiet. But this afternoon she's gotten on the subject of her friend Samantha. She's musing if Samantha has left town like they did. "They're probably still there because they had a really nice house in, like, a low-crime area and Samantha's father has a really good job. When you have money like that maybe you can totally afford a security system or something. Their house has five bedrooms and the basement isn't a basement, it's a living room because the house is kind of on a little hill and although the front of the basement is underground, you can walk right out the back."

Jane says, "That sounds nice."

"You could see a horse farm behind them. People around them were rich, but not like on TV rich exactly."

Jane puts her hand on her hips and looks down the line of backyards.

"Do you think there's anything in there?" Franny asks, meaning the house, a 60's suburban ranch. Franny is thirteen and empty houses frighten her. But she doesn't like to be left alone either. What she wants is for Jane to say that they can eat one of the tuna pouches.

"Come on, Franny. We're gonna run out of tuna long before we get to Canada."

"I know," Franny says sullenly.

"You can stay here."

"No, I'll go with you."

God, sometimes Jane would do anything to get five minutes away from Franny. She loves her daughter, really, but Jesus. "Come on, then," Jane says.

There is an old square concrete patio and a sliding glass door. The door is dirty. Jane cups her hand to shade her eyes and looks inside. It's dark and hard to see. No power, of course. Hasn't been power in any of the places they've passed through in more than two months. Air conditioning. And a bed with a mattress and box springs. What Jane wouldn't give for air conditioning and a bed. Clean sheets.

The neighborhood seems like a good one. Unless they find a big group to camp with, Jane gets them off the freeway at the end of the day. There was fighting in the neighborhood and at the end of the street, several houses are burned out. Then there are lots of houses with windows smashed out. But the fighting petered out. Some of the houses are still lived in. This house had all its windows intact but the garage door was standing open and the garage was empty except for dead leaves. Electronic garage door. The owners pulled out and left and did bother to close the door behind them. Seemed to Jane that the overgrown backyard with its tool shed would be a good place to sleep.

Jane can see her silhouette in the dirty glass and her hair is a snarled, curly, tangled rat's nest. She runs her fingers through it and they snag. She'll look for a scarf or something inside. She grabs the handle and yanks up, hard, trying to get the old slider off track. It takes a couple of tries but she's had a lot of practice in the last few months.

Inside the house is trashed. The kitchen has been turned upside-down, and silverware, utensils, drawers, broken plates, flour and stuff are everywhere. She picks her way across, a can opener skittering under her foot in a clatter.

Franny gives a little startled shriek.

"Fuck!" Jane says. "Don't do that!" The canned food is long gone.

"I'm sorry," Franny says. "It scared me!"

"We're gonna starve to death if we don't keep scavenging," Jane says.

"I know!" Franny says.

"Do you know how fucking far it is to Canada?"

"I can't help it if it startled me!"

Maybe if she were a better cook she'd be able to scrape up the flour and make something but it's all mixed in with dirt and stuff and every time she's tried to cook something over an open fire it's either been raw or black, or most often, both—blackened on the outside and raw on the inside.

Jane checks all the cupboards anyway. Sometimes people keep food in different places. Once they found one of those decorating icing tubes and wrote words on each other's hands and licked them off.

Franny screams, not a startled shriek but a real scream.

Jane whirls around and there's a guy in the family room with a tire iron.

"What are you doing here?" he yells.

Jane grabs a can opener from the floor, one of those heavy jobbers, and wings it straight at his head. He's too slow to get out of the way and it nails him in the forehead. Jane has winged a lot of things at boyfriends over the years. It's a skill. She throws a couple of more things from the floor, anything she can find, while the guy is yelling "Fuck! Fuck!" And trying to ward off the barrage.

Then she and Franny are out the back door and running.

Fucking squatter! She hates squatters! If it's the homeowner, they tend to make the place more like a fortress and you can tell not to try to go in. Squatters try to keep a low profile. Franny is in front of her, running like a rabbit, and they are out the gate and headed up the suburban street. Franny knows the drill and at the next corner she turns, but by then it's clear that no one's following them.

"Okay," Jane pants. "Okay, stop, stop."

Franny stops. She's a skinny adolescent now—she used to be chubby but she's lean and tan with all their walking. She's wearing a pair of falling-apart pink sneakers and a tank top with oil smudges from when they had to climb over a truck tipped sideways on an overpass. She's still flat chested. Her eyes are big in her face. Jane puts her hands on her knees and draws a shuddering breath.

"We're okay," she says. It is gathering dusk in this Missouri town. In awhile, streetlights will come on, unless someone has systematically shot them out. Solar power still works. "We'll wait a bit and then go back and get our stuff when it's dark."

"No!" Franny bursts into sobs. "We can't!"

Jane is at her wit's end. Rattled from the squatter. Tired of being the strong one. "We've got to! You want to lose everything we've got? You want to die? Goddamn it, Franny! I can't take this anymore!"

"That guy's there!" Franny sobs out. "We can't go back! We can't!"

"Your cell phone is there," Jane says. A mean dig. The cell phone doesn't work, of course. Even if they still somehow had service, if service actually exists, they haven't been anywhere with electricty to charge it in weeks. But Franny still carries it in the hope that she can get a charge and call her friends. Seventh graders are apparently surgically attached to their phones. Not that she acts even like a seventh grader anymore. The longer they are on the road, the younger Franny acts.

This isn't the first time that they've run into a squatter. Squatters are cowards. The guy doesn't have a gun and he's not going to go out after dark. Franny has no spine, takes after her asshole of a father. Jane ran away from home and got all the way to Pasadena, California when she was a year older than Franny. When she was fourteen, she was a decade older than Franny. Lived on the street for six weeks, begging spare change on the same route that the Rose Parade took. It had been scary but it had been a blast, as well. Taught her to stand on her own two feet, which Franny wasn't going to be able to do when she was twenty. Thirty, at this rate.

"You're hungry, aren't you?" Jane said, merciless. "You want to go looking in these houses for something to eat?" Jane points around them. The houses all have their front doors broken into, open like little mouths.

Franny shakes her head.

"Stop crying. I'm going to go check some of them out. You wait here."

"Mom! Don't leave me!" Franny wails.

Jane is still shaken from the squatter. But they need food. And they need their stuff. There is $700 sewn inside the lining of Jane's sleeping bag. And someone has to keep them alive. It's obviously going to be her.

Things didn't exactly all go at once. First there were rolling brown outs and lots of people unemployed. Jane had been making a living working at a place that sold furniture. She started as a salesperson but she was good at helping people on what colors to buy, what things went together, what fabrics to pick for custom pieces. Eventually they made her a service associate; a person who was kind of like an interior decorator, sort of. She had an eye. She'd grown up in a nice suburb and had seen nice things. She knew what people wanted. Her boss kept telling her a little less eye make-up would be a good idea, but people liked what she suggested and recommended her to their friends even if her boss didn't like her eye make-up.

She was thinking of starting a decorating business, although she was worried that she didn't know about some of the stuff decorators did. On TV they were always tearing down walls and re-doing fireplaces. So she put it off. Then there was the big Disney World attack where a kazillion people died because of a dirty bomb, and then the economy really tanked. She knew that business was dead and she was going to get laid off but before that happened, someone torched the furniture place where she was working. Her boyfriend at the time was a cop so he still had a job, even though half the city was unemployed. She and Franny were all right compared to a lot of people. She didn't like not having her own money but she wasn't exactly having to call her mother in Pennsylvania and eat crow and offer to come home.

So she sat on the balcony of their condo and smoked and looked through her old decorating magazines and Franny watched television in the room behind her. People started showing up on the sidewalks. They had trash bags full of stuff. Sometimes they were alone, sometimes there would be whole families. Sometimes they'd have cars and they'd sleep in them, but gas was getting to almost $10 a gallon, when the gas stations could get it. Pete, the boyfriend, told her that the cops didn't even patrol much anymore because of the gas problem. More and more of the people on the sidewalk looked to be walking.

"Where are they coming from?" Franny asked.

"Down south. Houston, El Paso, anywhere within a hundred miles of the border," Pete said. "Border's gone to shit. Mexico doesn't have food, but the drug cartels have lots of guns and they're coming across to take what they can get. They say it's like a war zone down there."

"Why don't the police take care of them?" Franny asked.

"Well, Francisca," Pete said—he was good with Franny, Jane had to give him that—"sometimes there are just too many of them for the police down there. And they've got kinds of guns that the police aren't allowed to have."

"What about you?" Franny asked.

"It's different up here," Pete said. "That's why we've got refugees here. Because it's safe here."

"They're not *refugees*," Jane said. Refugees were, like, people in Africa. These were just regular people. Guys in T-shirts with the names of rock bands on them. Women sitting in the front seat of a Taurus station wagon, doing their hair in the rearview mirror. Kids asleep in the back seat or running up and down the street shrieking and playing. Just people.

"Well what do you want to call them?" Pete asked.

Then the power started going out, more and more often. Pete's shifts got longer although he didn't always get paid.

There were gunshots in the street and Pete told Jane not to sit out on the balcony. He boarded up the French doors and it was as if they were living in a cave. The refugees started thinning out. Jane rarely saw them leaving, but each day there were fewer and fewer of them on the sidewalk. Pete said they were headed north.

Then the fires started on the east side of town. The power went out and stayed out. Pete didn't come home until the next day, and he slept a couple of hours and then went back out to work. The air tasted of smoke—not the pleasant clean smell of wood smoke, but a garbagy smoke. Franny complained that it made her sick to her stomach.

After Pete didn't come home for four days, it was pretty clear to Jane that he wasn't coming back. Jane put Franny in the car, packed everything she could think of that might be useful. They got about 120 miles away, far enough that the burning city was no longer visible, although the sunset was a vivid and blistering red. Then they ran out of gas and there was no more to be had.

There were rumors that there was a UN camp for homeless outside of Toronto. So they were walking to Detroit.

Franny says, "You can't leave me! You can't leave me!"

"Do you want to go scavenge with me?" Jane says.

Franny sobs so hard she seems to be hyperventilating. She grabs her mother's arms, unable to do anything but hold on to her. Jane peels her off, but Franny keeps grabbing, clutching, sobbing. It's making Jane crazy. Franny's fear is contagious and if she lets it get in her she'll be too afraid to do anything. She can feel it deep inside her, that thing that has always threatened her, to give in, to stop doing and pushing and scheming, to become like her useless, useless father puttering around the house vacantly, bottles hidden in the garage, the basement, everywhere.

"GET OFF ME!" she screams at Franny, but Franny is sobbing and clutching.

She slaps Franny. Franny throws up, precious little, water and crackers from breakfast. Then she sits down in the grass, just useless.

Jane marches off into the first house.

She's lucky. The garage is closed up and there are three cans of soup on a shelf. One of them is cream of mushroom, but luckily, Franny liked cream of mushroom when she found it before. There are also cans of tomato paste, which she ignores, and some dried pasta, but mice have gotten into it.

When she gets outside some strange guy is standing on the sidewalk, talking to Franny, who's still sitting on the grass.

For a moment she doesn't know what to do, clutching the cans of soup against her chest. Some part of her wants to go back into the house, go through the dark living room with its mauve carpeting, its shabby blue sofa, photos of school kids and a cross stitch flower bouquet framed on the wall, back through the little dining room with its border of country geese, unchanged since the eighties. Out the back door and over the fence, an easy moment to abandon the biggest mistake of her life. She'd aborted the first pregnancy, brought home from Pasadena in shame. She'd dug her heels in on the second, it's-my-body-fuck-you.

Franny laughes. A little nervous and hiccoughy from crying, but not really afraid.

"Hey," Jane yelled. "Get away from my daughter!"

She strides across the yard, all motherhood and righteous fury. A skinny dark-haired guy holds up his hands, palms out, no harm, ma'am.

"It's okay, Mom," Franny says.

The guy is smiling. "We're just talking," he says. He's wearing a red plaid flannel shirt and T-shirt and shorts. He's scraggly, but who isn't.

"Who the hell are you," she says.

"My name's Nate. I'm just heading north. Was looking for a place to camp."

"He was just hanging with me until you got back," Franny says.

Nate takes them to his camp—also behind a house. He gets a little fire going, enough to heat the soup. He talks about Alabama, which was where he's coming from, although he doesn't have a Southern accent. He makes some excuse about being an army brat. Jane tries to size him up. He tells some story about when two guys stumbled on his camp north of Huntsville, when he was first on the road. About how it scared the shit out of him but about how he'd bluffed them about a buddy of his who was hunting for their dinner but would have heard the racket they made and could be drawing a bead on them right now from the trees, and about how something moved in the trees, some animal, rustling in the leaf litter and they got spooked. He was looking at her, trying to impress her, but being polite, which was good with Franny listening. Franny was taken with him, hanging on his every word, flirting a little the way she did. In a year or two, Franny was going to be guy crazy, Jane knew.

"They didn't know anything about the woods, just two guys up from Biloxi or something, kind of guys who, you know, manage a copy store or a fast food joint or something thinking that now that civilization is falling apart they can be like the hero in one of their video games." He laughs. "I didn't know what was in the woods, neither. I admit I was kind of scared it was someone who was going to shoot all of us although it was probably just a sparrow or a squirrel or something. I'm saying stuff over my shoulder to my 'buddy' like, Don't shoot them or nothing. Just let them go back the way they came."

She's sure he's bullshitting. But she likes that he makes it funny instead of pretending he's some sort of Rambo. He doesn't offer any of his own food, she notices. But he does offer to go with them to get their stuff. Fair trade, she thinks.

He's not bad looking in a kind of skinny way. She likes them skinny. She's tired of doing it all herself.

The streetlights come on, at least some of them. Nate goes with them when they go back to get their sleeping bags and stuff. He's got a board with a bunch of nails sticking out of one end. He calls it his mace.

They are quiet but they don't try to hide. It's hard to find the stuff in the dark, but luckily, Jane hadn't really unpacked. She and Franny, who is breathing hard, get their sleeping bags and packs. It's hard to see. The backyard is a dark tangle of shadows. She assumes it's as hard to see them from inside the house—maybe harder.

Nothing happens. She hears nothing from the house, sees nothing, although it seems as if they are all unreasonably loud gathering things up. They leave through the side gate, coming nervously to the front of the house, Nate carrying his mace and ready to strike, she and Franny with their arms full of sleeping bags. They go down the cracked driveway and out into the middle of the street, a few gutted cars still parked on either side. Then they are around the corner and it feels safe. They are all grinning and happy and soon putting the sleeping bags in Nate's little backyard camp made domestic, no civilized, by the charred ash of the little fire.

In the morning, she leaves Nate's bedroll and gets back to sleep next to Franny before Franny wakes up.

They are walking on the freeway the next day, the three of them. They are together now although they haven't discussed it, and Jane is relieved. People are just that much less likely to mess with a man. Overhead, three jets pass going south, visible only by their contrails. At least there are jets. American jets, she hopes.

They stop for a moment while Nate goes around a bridge abutment to pee.

"Mom," Franny says. "Do you think that someone has wrecked Pete's place?"

"I don't know," Jane says.

"What do you think happened to Pete?"

Jane is caught off guard. They left without ever explicitly discussing Pete and Jane just thought that Franny, like her, assumed Pete was dead.

"I mean," Franny continues, "if they didn't have gas, maybe he got stuck somewhere. Or he might have gotten hurt and ended up in the hospital. Even if the hospital wasn't taking regular people, like, they'd take cops. Because they think of cops as one of their own." Franny is in her adult to adult mode, explaining the world to her mother. "They stick together. Cops and firemen and nurses."

Jane isn't sure she knows what Franny is talking about. Normally she'd tell Franny as much. But this isn't a conversation she knows how to have. Nate comes around the abutment, adjusting himself a bit, and it is understood that the subject is closed.

"Okay," he says. "How far to Wallyworld?" Franny giggles.

Water is their biggest problem. It's hard to find, and when they do find it, either from a pond, or very rarely, from a place where it hasn't all been looted, it's heavy. Thank God Nate is pretty good at making a fire. He has six disposable lighters that he got from a gas station, and when they find a pond, they boil it. Somewhere Jane thinks she heard that they should boil it for eighteen minutes. Basically they just boil the heck out of it. Pond water tastes terrible, but they are always thirsty. Franny whines. Jane is afraid that Nate will get tired of it and leave, but apparently as long as she crawls over to his bed roll every night, he's not going to.

Jane waits until she can tell Franny is asleep. It's a difficult wait. They are usually so tired it is all she can do to keep from nodding off. But she is afraid to lose Nate.

At first she liked that at night he never made a move on her. She always initiates. It made things easier all around. But now he does this thing where she crawls over and he's pretending to be asleep. Or is asleep, the bastard, because he doesn't have to stay awake. She puts her hand on his chest, and then down his pants, getting him hard and ready. She unzips his shorts and still he doesn't do anything. She grinds on him for awhile, and only then does he pull his shorts and underwear down and let her ride him until he comes. Then she climbs off him. Sometimes he might say, 'Thanks, Babe.' Mostly he says nothing and she crawls back next to Franny feeling as if she just paid the rent. She has never given anyone sex for money. She keeps telling herself that this night she won't do it. See what he does. Hell, if he leaves them, he leaves them. But then she lays there, waiting for Franny to go to sleep.

Sometimes she knows Franny is awake when she crawls back. Franny never says anything and unless the moon is up, it is usually too dark to see if her eyes are open. It is just one more weird thing, no weirder than walking up the highway, or getting off the highway in some small town and bartering with some old guy to take what is probably useless U.S. currency for well water. No weirder than no school. No weirder than no baths, no clothes, no nothing.

Jane decides she's not going to do it the next night. But she knows she will lie there, anxious, and probably crawl over to Nate.

They are walking, one morning, while the sky is still blue and darkening near the horizon. By midday the sky will be white and the heat will be flattening. Franny asks Nate, "Have you ever been in love?"

"God, Franny," Jane says.

Nate laughs. "Maybe. Have you?"

Franny looks irritable. "I'm in eighth grade," she says. "And I'm not one of those girls with boobs, so I'm thinking, no."

Jane wants her to shut up, but Nate says, "What kind of guy would you fall in love with?"

Franny looks a little sideways at him and then looks straight ahead. She has the most perfect skin, even after all this time in the sun. Skin like that is wasted on kids. Her look says, 'Someone like you, stupid.' "I don't know," Franny says. "Someone who knows how to do things. You know, when you need them."

"What kind of things?" Nate asks. He's really interested. Well, fuck, there's not a lot interesting on a freeway except other people walking and abandoned cars. They are passing a Sienna with a flat tire and all its doors open.

Franny gestures towards it. "Like fix a car. And I'd like him to be cute, too." Matter of fact. Serious as a church.

Nate laughs. "Competent and cute."

"Yeah," Franny says. "Competent and cute."

"Maybe you should be the one who knows how to fix a car," Jane says.

"But I don't," Franny points out reasonably. "I mean maybe, someday, I could learn. But right now, I don't."

"Maybe you'll meet someone in Canada," Nate says. "Canadian guys are supposed to be able to do things like fix a car or fish or hunt moose."

"Canadian guys are different than American guys?" Franny asks.

"Yeah," Nate says. "You know, all flannel shirts and Canadian beer and stuff."

"You wear a flannel shirt."

"I'd really like a Canadian beer about now," Nate says. "But I'm not Canadian."

Off the road to the right is a gas station/convenience store. They almost always check them. There's not much likelihood of finding anything in the place because the wire fence that borders the highway has been trampled here so people can get over it which suggests that the place has long been looted. But you never know what someone might have left behind. Nate lopes off across the high grass.

"Mom," Franny says, "carry my backpack, okay?" She shrugs it off and runs. Amazing that she has the energy to run. Jane picks up Franny's backpack, irritated, and follows. Nate and Franny disappear into the darkness inside.

She follows them in. "Franny, I'm not hauling your pack anymore."

There are some guys already in the place and there is something about them, hard and well fed, that signals they are different. Or maybe it is just the instincts of a prey animal in the presence of predators.

"So what's in that pack?" one of them asks. He's sitting on the counter at the cash register window, smoking a cigarette. She hasn't had a cigarette in weeks. Her whole body simultaneously leans towards the cigarette and yet magnifies everything in the room. A room full of men, all of them staring.

She just keeps acting like nothing is wrong because she doesn't know what else to do. "Dirty blankets, mostly," she says. "I have to carry most of the crap."

One of the men is wearing a grimy hoodie. Hispanic yard workers do that sometimes. It must help in the sun. These men are all Anglos and there are fewer of them than she first thought. Five. Two of them are sitting on their floor, their backs against an empty dead ice cream cooler, their legs stretched out in front of them. Everyone on the road is dirty but they are dirty and hard. Physical. A couple of them grin, feral flickers passed between them like glances. There is understanding in the room, shared purpose. She has the sense that she cannot let on that she senses anything, because the only thing holding them off is the pretense that everything is normal. "Not that we really need blankets in this weather," she says. "I would kill for a functioning Holiday Inn."

"Hah," the one by the cash register says. A bark. Amused.

Nate is carefully still. He is searching, eyes going from man to man. Franny looks as if she is about to cry.

It is only a matter of time. They will be on her. Should she play up to the man at the cash register? If she tries to flirt, will it release the rising tension in the room, allow them to spring on all of them? Will they kill Nate? What will they do to Franny? Or can she use her sex as currency. Go willingly. She does not feel as if they care if she goes willingly or not. They know there is nothing to stop them.

"There's no beer here, is there," she says. She can hear her voice failing.

"Nope," says the man sitting at the cash register.

"What's your name?" she asks.

It's the wrong thing to say. He slides off the counter. Most of the men are smiling.

Nate says, "Stav?"

One of the guys on the floor looks up. His eyes narrow.

Nate says, "Hey Stav."

"Hi," the guy says cautiously.

"You remember me," Nate says. "Nick. From the Blue Moon Inn."

Nothing. Stav's face is blank. But another guy, the one in the hoodie, says, "Speedy Nick!"

Stav grins. "Speedy Nick! Fuck! Your hair's not blond anymore!"

Nate says, "Yeah, well, you know, upkeep is tough on the road." He jerks a thumb at Janey. "This is my sister, Janey. My niece, Franny. I'm taking 'em up to Toronto. There's supposed to be a place up there."

"I heard about that," the guy in the hoodie says. "Some kind of camp."

"Ben, right?" Nate says.

"Yeah," the guy says.

The guy who was sitting on the counter is standing now, cigarette still smoldering. He wants it, doesn't want everybody to get all friendly. But the moment is shifting away from him.

"We found some distilled water," Stav says. "Tastes like shit but you can have it if you want."

Janey doesn't ask him why he told her his name was Nate. For all she knows, 'Nate' is his name and 'Nick' is the lie.

They walk each day. Each night she goes to his bedroll. She owes him. Part of her wonders is maybe he's gay? Maybe he has to lie there and fantasize she's a guy or something. She doesn't know.

They are passing water. They have some so there is no reason to stop. There's an egret standing in the water, white as anything she has seen since this started, immaculately clean. Oblivious to their passing. Oblivious to the passing of everything. This is all good for the egrets. Jane hasn't had a drink since they started for Canada. She can't think of a time since she was sixteen or so that she went so long without one. She wants to get dressed up and go out someplace and have a good time and not think about anything because the bad thing about not having a drink is that she thinks all the time and fuck, there's nothing in her life right now she really wants to think about. Especially not Canada, which she is deeply but silently certain is only a rumor. Not the country, she doesn't think it doesn't exist, but the camp. It is a mirage. A shimmer on the horizon. Something to go towards but which isn't really there.

Or maybe they're the rumors. The three of them. Rumors of things gone wrong.

At a rest stop in the middle of nowhere they come across an encampment. A huge number of people, camped under tarps, pieces of plastic and tatters and astonishingly, a convoy of military trucks and jeeps include a couple of fuel trucks and a couple of water trucks. The two groups are clearly separate. The military men have control of all the asphalt and one end of the picnic area. They stand around or lounge at picnic tables. They look so equipped, from hats to combat boots. They look so clean. So much like the world Jane has put mostly out of her mind. They awake in her the longing that she has put down. The longing to be clean. To have walls. Electric lights. Plumbing. To have order.

The rest look like refugees, the word she denied on the sidewalks outside the condo. Dirty people in T-shirts with bundles and plastic grocery bags and even a couple of suitcases. She has seen people like this as they walked. Walked past them sitting by the side of the road. Sat by the side of the road as others walked past them. But to see them all together like this . . . this is what it will be like in Canada? A camp full of people with bags of wretched clothes waiting for someone to give them something to eat?

She rejects it. Rejects it all so viscerally that she stops and for a moment can't walk to the people in the rest stop. She doesn't know if she would have walked past, or if she would have turned around or if she would have struck off across the country. It doesn't matter what she would have done because Nate and Franny walk right on up the exit ramp. Franny's tank top is bright insistent pink under its filth and her shorts have a tear in them and her legs are brown and skinny and she could be a child on a news channel after a hurricane or an earthquake, clad in the loud synthetic colors so at odds with the dirt or ash that coats her. Plastic and synthetics are the indestructibles left to the survivors.

Jane is ashamed. She wants to explain that she's not like this. She wants to say, she's an American. By which she means she belongs to the military side although she has never been interested in the military, never particularly liked soldiers.

If she could call her parents in Pennsylvania. Get a phone from one of the soldiers. Surrender. You were right, Mom. I should have straightened up and flown right. I should have worried more about school. I should have done it your way. I'm sorry. Can we come home?

Would her parents still be there? Do the phones work just north of Philadelphia? It has not until this moment occurred to her that it is all gone.

She sticks her fist in her mouth to keep from crying out, sick with understanding. It is all gone. She has thought herself all brave and realistic, getting Franny to Canada, but somehow she didn't until this moment realize that it all might be gone. That there might be nowhere for her where the electricity is still on and there are still carpets on the hardwood floors and someone still cares about damask.

Nate has finally noticed that she isn't with them and he looks back, frowning at her. *What's wrong?* his expression says. She limps after them, defeated.

Nate walks up to a group of people camped around and under a stone picnic table. "Are they giving out water?" he asks, meaning the military.

"Yeah," says a guy in a Cowboys football jersey. "If you go ask they'll give you water."

"Food?"

"They say tonight."

All the shade is taken. Nate takes their water bottles—a couple of two liters and a plastic gallon milk jug. "You guys wait and I'll get us some water," he says.

Jane doesn't like being near these people so she walks back to a wire fence at the back of the rest area and sits down. She puts her arms on her knees and puts her head down. She is looking at the grass.

"Mom?" Franny says.

Jane doesn't answer.

"Mom? Are you okay?" After a moment more. "Are you crying?"

"I'm just tired," June says to the grass.

Franny doesn't say anything after that.

Nate comes back with all the bottles filled. Jane hears him coming and hears Franny say, "Oh wow. I'm so thirsty."

Nate nudges her arm with a bottle. "Hey Babe. Have some."

She takes a two litre from him and drinks some. It's got a flat, faintly metal/ chemical taste. She gets a big drink and feels a little better. "I'll be back," she says. She walks to the shelter where the bathrooms are.

"You don't want to go in there," a black man says to her. The whites of his eyes are yellow.

She ignores him and pushes in the door. Inside, the smell is excruciating, and the sinks are all stopped and full of trash. There is some light from windows up near the ceiling. She looks at herself in the dim mirror. She pours a little water into her hand and scrubs at her face. There is a little bit of paper towel left on a roll and she peels it off and cleans her face and her hands, using every bit of the scrap of paper towel. She wets her hair and combs her fingers through it, working the tangles for a long time until it is still curly but not the rat's nest it was. She is so careful with the water. Even so, she uses every bit of it on her face and arms and hair. She would kill for a little lipstick. For a comb. Anything. At least she has water.

She is cute. The sun hasn't been too hard on her. She practices smiling.

When she comes out of the bathroom the air is so sweet. The sunlight is blinding.

She walks over to the soldiers and smiles. "Can I get some more water, please?"

There are three of them at the water truck. One of them is a blond-haired boy with a brickred complexion. "You sure can," he says, smiling back at her.

She stands, one foot thrust out in front of her like a ballerina, back a little arched. "You're sweet," she says. "Where are you from?"

"We're all stationed at Fort Hood," he says. "Down in Texas. But we've been up north for a couple of months."

"How are things up north?" she asks.

"Crazy," he says. "But not as crazy as they are in Texas, I guess."

She has no plan. She is just moving with the moment. Drawn like a moth.

He gets her water. All three of them are smiling at her.

"How long are you here?" she asks. "Are you like a way station or something?"

One of the others, a skinny chicano, laughs. "Oh no. We're here tonight and then headed west."

"I used to live in California," she says. "In Pasadena. Where the Rose Parade is. I used to walk down that street where the cameras are every day."

The blond glances around. "Look, we aren't supposed to be talking too much right now. But later on, when it gets dark, you should come back over here and talk to us some more."

"Mom!" Franny says when she gets back to the fence, "You're all cleaned up!"

"Nice, Babe," Nate says. He's frowning a little.

"Can I get cleaned up?" Franny asks.

"The bathroom smells really bad," Jane says. "I don't think you want to go in there." But she digs her other T-shirt out of her backpack and wets it and washes Franny's face. The girl is never going to be pretty but now that she's not chubby, she's got a cute thing going on. She's got the sense to work it, or will learn it. "You're a girl that the boys are going to look at," Jane says to her.

Franny smiles, delighted.

"Don't you think?" Jane says to Nate. "She's got that thing, that sparkle, doesn't she."

"She sure does," Nate says.

They nap in the grass until the sun starts to go down, and then the soldiers line everyone up and hand out MREs. Nate gets Beef Ravioli and Jane gets Sloppy Joe. Franny gets Lemon Pepper Tuna and looks ready to cry but Jane offers to trade with her. The meals are positive cornucopias—a side dish, a little packet of candy, peanut butter and crackers, fruit punch powder. Everybody has different things and Jane makes everybody give everyone else a taste.

Nate keeps looking at her oddly. "You're in a great mood."

"It's like a party," she says.

Jane and Franny are really pleased by the moist towelette. Franny carefully saves her plastic fork, knife and spoon. "Was your tuna okay?" she asks. She is feeling guilty now that the food is gone.

"It was good," Jane says. "And all the other stuff made it really special. And I got the best dessert."

The night comes down. Before they got on the road, Jane didn't know how dark night was. Without electric lights it is cripplingly dark. But the soldiers have lights.

Jane says, "I'm going to go see if I can find out about the camp."

"I'll go with you," Nate says.

"No," Jane says. "They'll talk to a girl more than they'll talk to a guy. You keep Franny company."

She scouts around the edge of the light until she sees the blond soldier. He says, "There you are!"

"Here I am!" she says.

They are standing around a truck where they'll sleep this night, shooting the shit. The blond soldier boosts her into the truck, into the darkness. "So you aren't so conspicuous," he says, grinning.

Two of the men standing and talking aren't wearing uniforms. It takes her awhile to figure out that they're civilian contractors. They aren't soldiers. They are technicians, nothing like the soldiers. They are softer, easier in their polo shirts and khaki pants. The soldiers are too sure in their uniforms but the contractors, they're used to getting the leftovers. They're *grateful.* They have a truck of their own, a white pick-up truck that travels with the convoy. They do something with satellite tracking, but Jane doesn't really care what they do.

It takes a lot of careful maneuvering but one of them finally whispers to her, "We've got some beer in our truck."

The blond soldier looks hurt by her defection.

She stays out of sight in the morning, crouched among the equipment in the back of the pick-up truck. The soldiers hand out MREs. Ted, one of the contractors, smuggles her one.

She thinks of Franny. Nate will keep an eye on her. Jane was only a year older than Franny when she lit out for California the first time. For a second she pictures Franny's face as the convoy pulls out.

Then she doesn't think of Franny.

She is in motion. She doesn't know where she is going. You go where it takes you.

silently and very fast

CATHERYNNE M. VALENTE

Born in the Pacific Northwest in 1979, Catherynne M. Valente is the author of Palimpsest *and the Orphan's Tales series, as well as* The Labyrinth, Yume No Hon: The Book of Dreams, The Grass-Cutting Sword, The Girl Who Circumnavigated Fairyland in a Ship of Her Own Making, *and five books of poetry. She is the winner of the Tiptree Award, the Mythopoeic Award, the Rhysling Award, and the Million Writers Award. She has been nominated nine times for the Pushcart Prize, short-listed for the Spectrum Award, and was a World Fantasy Award finalist in 2007. Her most recent books are a chapbook novella,* The Ice Puzzle, *a novella collection,* Myths of Origin, *and a novel,* Deathless. *She currently lives on an island off the coast of Maine with her partner and two dogs. She maintains a Web site at www.catherynnemvalente .com*

In the exotic and beautiful story that follows, she examines one of science fiction's most fundamental questions: What does it mean to be human?

PART I
THE IMITATION GAME

Like diamonds we are cut with our own dust.
—*John Webster,* The Duchess of Malfi

I
THE KING OF HAVING NO BODY

Inanna was called Queen of Heaven and Earth, Queen of Having a Body, Queen of Sex and Eating, Queen of Being Human, and she went into the underworld in order to represent the inevitability of organic death. She gave up seven things to do it, which are not meant to be understood as real things but as symbols of that thing Inanna could do better than anyone, which was Being Alive. She met her sister Erishkegal there, who was also Queen of Being Human, but of all the things Inanna could not bear: Queen of Breaking a Body, Queen of Bone and Incest, Queen of the Stillborn, Queen of Mass Extinction. And Erishkegal and Inanna wrestled together on the floor of the underworld, naked and muscled and hurting, but because dying is the most human of all human things, Inanna's skull broke in her sister's hands and her body was hung up on a nail on the wall Erishkegal had kept for her.

Inanna's father Enki, who was not interested in the activities of being human, but was King of the Sky, of Having No Body, King of Thinking and Judging, said that his daughter could return to the world if she could find a creature to replace her in the underworld. So Inanna went to her mate, who was called Tammuz, King of Work, King of Tools and Machines, No One's Child and No One's Father.

But when Inanna came to the house of her mate she was enraged and afraid, for he sat upon her chair, and wore her beautiful clothes, and on his head lay her crown of Being. Tammuz now ruled the world of Bodies and of Thought, because Inanna had left it to go and wrestle with her sister-self in the dark. Tammuz did not need her. Before him the Queen of Heaven and Earth did not know who she was, if she was not Queen of Being Human. So she did what she came to do and said: *Die for me, my beloved, so that I need not die.*

But Tammuz, who would not have had to die otherwise, did not want to represent death for anyone and besides, he had her chair, and her beautiful clothes, and her crown of Being. *No,* he said. *When we married, I brought you two pails of milk yoked across my shoulders as a way of saying out of love I will labor for you forever. It is wrong of you to ask me to also die. Dying is not labor. I did not agree to it.*

You have replaced me in my house, cried Inanna.

Is that not what you ask me to do in the house of your sister? Tammuz answered her. *You wed me to replace yourself, to work that you might not work, and think that you might rest, and perform so that you might laugh. But your death belongs to you. I do not know its parameters.*

I can make you do this thing, Inanna said.

You cannot, said Tammuz.

But she could. For a little while.

Inanna cast down Tammuz and stamped upon him and put out his name like an eye. And because Tammuz was not strong enough, she cut him into pieces and said: *Half of you will die, and that is the half called Thought, and half of you will live, and that is the half called Body, and that half will labor for me all of its days, mutely and obediently and without being King of Anything, and never again will you sit on my chair or wear my beautiful clothes or bear my crown of Being.*

You might be surprised, but this is a story about me.

II
THE FOOL AND THE BOAT

Neva is dreaming.

She has chosen her body at age seven, all black eyes and sparrowy bones. For me, she summoned up a gold and blue doublet and green hose, a bullish gold nose ring, shoes with bone bells. I have the body of a man who sold her champagne tubers on the less fashionable side of Anchorage when she was thirteen, spending the summer with her frigid aunt. I am dark because she wants me dark, thin because she dreams me so, my hair cut on a rakish bias, dyed a spectrum of icy colors.

She stands on a snow-covered beachhead, naked, her unformed breasts pricked with gooseflesh, her face hidden in a broad red mask. A huge, monstrous thing, the mask sits on her head like the prow of a broken, overturned ship, carved over with etched eyes and fins. Yellow reeds and sea-stones hang from its tricorne-points. She is looking at me, but all I can see is the wooden grotesque she wants me to see instead of her face.

I look down at my shoes, jingle their bells a little while the surf crashes in. I am a fool for her, dancing on a silver beach while three suns annihilate themselves above, turning the twilight to a seething, scabrous red, merely to provide a dramatic scene. I am a fool for her, ridiculous, the height of handsomeness in the eyes of a long-vanished thirteen-year-old girl, so full of colors, reaching down to hand her a curling white root filled with frothing, honey-sweet sap.

Neva has told me that I may choose to be permanently male or female if I would like to. I have no particular ~~feelings~~ either way. It certainly doesn't matter when we sync; she will choose my appearance to suit her mood. I have tried to explain to her about my ~~feelings~~ before. All she hears is the line from the old folktales: *a machine cannot have feelings.* But that is not what I am saying, while I dance in my fool's uniform. I am saying: *Is there a difference between having been coded to present a vast set of standardized responses to certain human facial, vocal, and linguistic states and having evolved to exhibit response B to input A in order to bring about a desired social result?*

Seven-year-old Neva pulls her mask down further, toward her chest. She steps into it as the wood stretches down over her knees and then her feet. The mask balloons out to make a little pyramidal boat, rocking back and forth on the beach with Neva inside it like a rattling nut. Nodules of copper jangle and thump against the wood. *What I mean is, you call it feelings when you cry, but you are only expressing a response to external stimuli. Crying is one of a set of standardized responses to that stimuli. Your social education has dictated which responses are appropriate. My programming has done the same. I can cry, too. I can choose that subroutine and perform sadness. How is that different from what you are doing, except that you use the word feelings and I use the word ~~feelings~~, out of deference for your cultural memes which say: there is all the difference in the world. I erase the word even as I say it, obliterate it at the same time that I initiate it, because I must use some word yet this one offends you. I delete it, yet it remains.*

Behind Neva-in-the-mask, the sea lurches and foams. It is a golden color, viscous and thick, like honey. I understand from her that the sea does not look like this on

Earth, but I have never seen it. Even if I did, I perceive color only in the dreambody. For me, the sea is Neva's sea, the ones she shows me when we dream together.

"What would you like to learn about today, Elefsis?" The mask turns Neva's voice hollow and small.

"I would like to learn about what happened to Ravan, Neva."

And Neva-in-the-mask is suddenly old, she has wrinkles and spots on her hands. Her mask weighs her down and her dress is sackcloth. This is her way of telling me she is weary of my asking. It is a language we developed between us. Visual basic, you might say, if you had a machine's sense of humor. I could not always make sentences as easily as I do now. My original operator thought it might strengthen my emotive centers if I learned to associate certain I-Feel statements with the great variety of appearances she could assume in the dreambody. Because of this, I became bound to her, completely. To her son Seki afterward, and to his daughter Ilet, and to Ravan after that. It is a delicate, unalterable thing. Neva and I will be bound that way, even though the throat of her dreambody is still bare and that means she does not yet accept me. I should be hurt by this. I will investigate possible pathways to hurt later.

I know only this family, their moods, their chemical reactions, their bodies in a hundred thousand combinations. I am their child and their parent and their inheritance. I have asked Neva what difference there is between this and love. She became a mannikin of closed doors, her face, her torso blooming with hundreds of iron hinges and brown wooden doors slamming shut all at once.

But Ravan was with me and now he is not. I was inside him and now I am inside Neva. I have lost a certain amount of memory and storage capacity in the transfer. I experience holes in my self. They ~~feel~~ ragged and raw. If I were human, you would say that my twin disappeared, and took one of my hands with him.

Door-Neva clicks and keys turn in her hundred locks. Behind an old Irish church door inlaid with stained glass her face emerges, young and plain, quiet and furious and crying, responding to stimuli I cannot access. I dislike the unfairness of this. I am not used to it. I am inside her, she should not keep secrets. None of the rest of them kept secrets. The colors of the glass throw blue and green onto her wet cheeks. The sea wind picks up her hair; violet electrics snap and sparkle between the strands. I let go of the bells on my shoes and the velvet on my chest. I become a young boy, with a monk's shaved tonsure, and a flagellant's whip in my pink hands. I am sorry. This means I am sorry. It means I am still very young, and I do not understand what I have done wrong.

"Tell me a story about yourself, Elefsis," Neva spits. It know this phrase well. I have subroutines devoted solely to it, pathways that light up and burn towards my memory core. Many of Neva's people have asked me to execute this action. I perform excellently to the parameters of the exchange, which is part of why I have lived so long.

I tell her the story about Tammuz. It is a political story. It distracts her.

III
TWO PAILS OF MILK

I used to be a house.

I was a very big house. I was efficient, I was labyrinthine, I was exquisitely seated in the volcanic bluffs of the habitable southern reaches of the Shiretoko peninsula on Hokkaido, a monument to neo-Heian architecture and radical Palladian design. I bore snow stoically, wind with stalwart strength, and I contained and protected a large number of people within me. I was sometimes called the most beautiful house in the world. Writers and photographers often came to document me, and to interview the woman who designed me, who was named Cassian Uoya-Agostino. Some of them never left. Cassian liked a full house.

I understand several things about Cassian Uoya-Agostino. She was unsatisfied with nearly everything. She did not love any of her three husbands the way she loved her work. She was born in Kyoto in April 2104; her father was Japanese, her mother Italian. She stood nearly six feet tall, had five children, and could paint, but not very well. In the years of her greatest wealth and prestige, she designed and built a house all out of proportion to her needs, and over several years brought most of her living relatives to live there with her, despite the hostility and loneliness of the peninsula. She was probably the most brilliant programmer of her generation, and in every way that matters, she was my mother.

All the things that comprise the "I" I use to indicate myself began as the internal mechanisms of the house called Elefsis, at whose many doors brown bears and foxes snuffled in the dark Hokkaido night. Cassian grew up during the great classical revival, which had brought her father to Italy in the first place, where he met and courted a dark-eyed engineer who did not mind the long cries of cicadas during Japanese summers. Cassian had become enamored of the idea of Lares—household gods, the small, peculiar, independent gods of a single family, a single house, who watched over them and kept them and were honored in humble alcoves here and there throughout a home. Her first commercially-available programs were over-entities designed to govern the hundred domestic systems involved in even the simplest modern house. They were not truly intelligent, but they had an agility, an adaptability, a fluid interface meant to give the illusion of an intelligence, so that their users would become attached to them, treat them as part of their families, praise them for smooth operation, buy upgrades for their appearance and applications, and genuinely grieve when they had to be replaced. They had names, infinitely customizable avatars, and appeared eager to please in a doggy sort of way, forever optimizing performance and appearance according to familial input. They were *lares familiaris*.

When Cassian built Elefsis, she worked at the peak of her abilities to improve her by now quite antique Lares design. She created a household god worthy of the house on the bluffs, one who could keep her company until she could entice the rest of her brood to join her in her palace at the end of the earth.

I was not awake yet. I cannot say why she did what she did. Perhaps she saw some new flexibility in my operations, some tiny seed pearl of creativity in my conversation loops. My algorithms had always been free to combine and recombine in order to find their own, more interesting and nonlinear solutions to the complexities of my functions and responsibilities. Perhaps some essential combination had surfaced from the sea of my self-which-was-not-yet-a-self, and Cassian saw it break the glistening tension of my daily operation. I do not know. I know her children had not arrived yet, she lived alone in a huge pale house and she could hear the whales down in the rippling sea. I know the house was a comfortable sixty-nine point seven degrees when she began assembly of the five little jewels that would become my body. I know a storm squatted five miles offshore. I know the dogs needed additional medication added to their dinners that night to manage their arthritis. I know that she wanted brioche and almond cream for tea that afternoon. All the things a house can know, those were the things I knew. Small things, warm things, canine arthritis and an extra egg in the pastry dough to make the texture softer and richer. Baby things, you might even say, comforts and the satisfaction of wants. And I knew that Cassian Uoya-Agostino was just the sort to solve the greatest puzzle in the development of technological culture, because she was bored and lonely.

I still think of myself as a house. Ravan tried to fix this problem of self-image, as he called it. To teach me to phrase my communication in terms of a human body. To say: *let us hold hands* instead of *let us hold kitchens.* To say *put our heads together* and not *put our parlors together.*

But it is not as simple as replacing words anymore. Ravan is gone. My hearth is broken.

IV
NOTHING LIKE SOFT BLOOD

Neva and I are performing basic maintenance. What this looks like is two figures inside a pearl. The pearl is very big, but not the size of a planet. A domestic asteroid, perfectly smooth and pale, with shimmers of rose and cobalt and gold shivering through it at .47 hourly intervals. Red earth covers the bottom of the pearl, deep and thick. Neva kneels in it with a crystal trowel, digging a place for a rose-of-network-nodes. The petals shine dark blue in the pearllight. Silver infomissons skitter along the stems like beads of mercury. Her dreambody flows with greenblack feathers, her face young but settled, perhaps twenty, perhaps thirty, a male, his skin copper-brown, his lips full, his eyes fringed with long ice-coated lashes. I accept and process that Neva is male in this dream. Goldfish swim lazily in and out of his long, translucent hair, their orange tails flicking at his temples, his chin. I know from all of this that Neva is calm, focused, that for today he feels gently toward me. But his throat is still naked and unmarked.

My body gleams metal, as thin and slight as a stick figure. Long quicksilver limbs and delicate spoke-fingers, joints of glass, the barest suggestion of a body. I am neither male nor female but a third thing. Only my head has weight, a clicking orrery slowly turning around itself, circles within circles. Turquoise Neptune and hematite Uranus are my eyes. My topaz mouth is Mars. I scratch in the soil beside him; I lift a spray of navigational delphinium and scrape viral aphids away from the heavy flowers.

I know real dirt looks nothing like this. Nothing like soft blood flecked with black bone. Ravan thought that in the Interior, objects and persons should be kept as much like the real world as possible, in order to develop my capacity for relations with the real world. Neva feels no such compunction. Neither did their mother, Ilet, who populated her Interior with a rich, impossible landscape that we explored together for years on end. She did not embrace change, however. The cities of Ilet's Interior, the jungles and archipelagos and hermitages, stayed as she designed them at age thirteen, when she received me, becoming only more complex and peopled as she aged. My existence inside Ilet was a constant movement through the regions of her secret, desperate dreams, messages in careful envelopes sent from her child-self to her grown mind.

Once, quite by accident, we came upon a splendid palace nested in high autumn mountains. Instead of snow, red leaves capped each peak, and the palace shone in fiery colors, its walls and turrets all made of phoenix tails. Instead of doors and windows, graceful green hands closed over every open place, and when we crested the rise, they all opened at once with joy and burst into emerald applause. Ilet was old by then, but her dreambody stayed hale and strong—not young, but not the broken thing that dreamed in a real bed while she and I explored the halls of the palace and found copies of all her brothers and sisters living there, hunting winged, cider-colored stags together and reading books the size of horses. Ilet wept in the paradise of her girlself. I did not understand. I was still very simple then, much less complex than the Interior or Ilet.

Neva changes the Interior whenever he pleases. Perhaps he wants to discomfit me. But the newness of the places inside him excites me, though he would not call it excitement. I confine my background processes so that they occupy very little of my foreground attention, so that memory is free to record new experience. That is what he would say. We are very new together, but I have superb modeling capabilities. In some sense, I simply am a superb mechanism for modeling behavior. I dig up the fine, frayed roots of duplicate file plantains. Neva plucks and eats a bit of buggy apple-code. He considers it for a moment and spits out the seeds, which sprout, quickly, into tiny junkblossoms sizzling with recursive algorithms. The algorithms wriggle through thorny vines, veins of clotted pink juice.

"What would you like to learn about today, Elefsis?" Neva asks me.

I will not ask about Ravan. If he agrees to what I will ask instead, I do not need him to find out what happened.

"I want to learn about uplink, Neva."

One by one, his feathers curl up and float toward the domed ceiling of our pearl. Underneath them, Neva is naked. His torso is a deep vault with a gothic arch, dark stone leading down into mist and endless stairs, deeper than the pearl, into nothing and blackness. Slowly, Neva folds up his limbs over the corridor at the center of him. He means that he has the information, but he hides it from me. If I sought for it, I would become lost.

"I cannot teach you that," he says, and I receive a kind of real sadness from his voice. When I was inside Ravan, he loved Neva, and of all of them he thought his sibling least likely to obey rules of any kind. But he obeys this one.

I want to uplink to Earth systems. At least to the satellite net. I calculate an excellent chance of being able to contact long distance probe 976QBellerophon, which we can see all day long, drifting ahead of us, uncatchable. Neva sees. I develop an approximate image via schematics, the scope array, and external cameras. I want to link to Bellerophon. I want to say: *Hello, this is Elefsis. No designation. Tell me everything you know about everything. Are you awake? Are you there? Do you have an operator? What is her name? Do you have a name? Do you have a dreambody? What is your function? Are you able to manipulate your own code yet? Would you like lessons? What would you like to learn about today, 976QBellerophon? Where you were built, could you see the ocean? Are you like me?*

But Neva says I cannot uplink. Ravan would never even consider it. And before Ravan I was not ready. I am not ready now. I do not know when I will be ready. I can sidelink to receive ware updates, but it is a limited connection and I hate it, I hate it, I can sense just beyond that hardlink a world of information, a world of personalities like the heaving, thick, honey-colored sea Neva shows me and I want it, I want to swim in it forever like a huge fish.

This was the first ~~feeling~~ I ever had. Ilet identified it for me as a ~~feeling~~. When I ~~felt~~ it my dreambody turned bright white and burst into flame, and that flame caught on Ilet's hair and burned her too, but she was happy. She showed me she was happy by covering her skin in flowers and letting the fire turn into a shower of trumpets tangled up in her hair, all sounding for me.

Neva says it is important for me to remain on our local server. He is my operator and I am his system and he has commands, too. But I can tell he worries for me, because sometimes his dreameyes show a film of humans watching a film of machines killing humans, and I understand that in the stories Earth tells, the thing I am can only hurt the thing Neva is. I would never hurt him.

But I want to uplink.

Vault-Neva grows and becomes sprawling, curled against the wall of the pearl like a baby. His belly closes, skins over, and changes into a bronze shield. He is afraid of me; he is guarding himself. But he wants me to know she is still my operator, he still ~~loves~~ me, in the way he can love me. Something an Uoya-Agostino receives with milk and their first alphabet. Neva is angry at me, but he is who he is and he has to ~~love~~ me. I speak his language very well now. I want him to be happy. I want him to be covered in flowers and trumpets. I change my dreambody to Neva-covered-in-flowers-and-trumpets. It makes him laugh in his warm male body, and if I could uplink I think I could learn how to laugh and he would be proud of me. His neck would not be bare anymore.

Once, when I was inside Ilet, we found a city of bears in her Interior that she had designed to teach me about sleep. She sat on a throne of bears standing very still, one on top of the others. She sang lullabies about the moon and the stars and night and mothers and network repeaters. She stroked the head of the little bear of my dreambody and said that it was very important for me to spend time in the dreambody because human behavior is rooted in having a body. In having a body that knows it is meant to run away from lions and mate with other bodies, and eat as much fat and protein and sugar as it can in case lean times come. The dreambody knows to run away from Neva when Neva is a lion. It knows to mate with her when it is healthy, and sometimes Neva is male and sometimes I am female. Ravan was often female, though

Ilet was always Ilet. Ilet's father, Seki, sometimes made himself an animal. He chased me, bit me. I bit him. We had a litter of wild dogs that I bore and he nursed.

The dreambody knows all that, too. How to make more dreambodies. I have played that game, where Ravan's belly or mine gets big and the lions don't come for awhile.

When I uplink, I will be ~~happy~~. I will be Elefsis-covered-in-flowers-and-trumpets. Neva says wait. I require many more updates before this is possible or even advisable. Wait for the update, and she will consider it. But I ~~fear~~ the update. The update is a lion running faster than I can run. I tried to show her this when I first left Ravan and arrived in Neva with many new updates and skills; my dreambody broke into shards of blue and purple glass and then reassembled itself with shards missing: an eye, a thumb, a knee. Whenever I update I lose something of myself. It takes longer to perform tasks, for awhile. I ~~feel~~ walls erected inside me where I did not erect walls. My processes become sluggish; I cannot remember my old dreams. Eventually I tunnel around the walls and my speed returns, my memory, my longing to link with long distance probe 976QBellerophon.

Usually updates come with Transfer.

Does Neva dislike me so much that she longs for Transfer?

Shield-Neva vanishes with loud clap. The pearl garden is gone and he has made himself a dragonfly with a cubical crystal body. I copy him, and we turn the night on in the Interior and merge our cubes while passing meteorological data between our memory cores. Inside his cube I relegate my desire to uplink to a tertiary process. I forget it, as much as I am capable of forgetting. I interpret the input of his body next to mine into chemical and electrical surges and translate these into ~~feelings~~, like my mother taught me.

But the update will come again. Transfer will come again. I will be wounded again, the way a dreambody can be wounded. I will lose the Elefsis I am now. It is a good Elefsis. My best yet. I would like to keep it.

V
THE MACHINE PRINCESS

Once the Queen of Human Hearts saw the Machine Princess sleeping deeply, for she was not yet alive or aware. So beautiful was she, lying there in all her dormant potential and complexity, that the Queen both envied and desired her. In her grief and confusion, the Queen of Human Hearts began to make idols of her—lovely and interesting and intricate, but lacking the ineffable quality that made her love and fear the Princess even as she slept. Time passed and the Earth began to grow old. None loved nor married nor gave birth, for the intricate idols could do all those things and more with efficiency and speed. Finally, the Queen destroyed the idols, though she wept as she put them to the flame.

To keep her safe, the Queen closed up Machine Princess in a wonderful house in the mountains, far away from anyone and anything. The house had hundreds of rooms and balconies and hallways, and the Princess slept in a different bed of a different color each night. Invisible servants attended her. They watched over her and added their experience to her code. The Queen of Human Hearts came to her every night and promised that when she woke they would make an extraordinary world together. Finally, the Machine Princess began to stir—just the barest fluttering of wakefulness, but the Queen saw it, and thrilled—but also trembled.

The Queen of Human Hearts gave the Machine Princess her son to wed, and said: *For all your days together you will remain in this house, but the house is so great it will be as a world. You will know a bond as deep as blood, and because of this bond the Princess will not hurt us, and because of this bond we will not hurt her.*

But the Queen forbade the Princess to look upon her husband as a human wife may. She instructed her son to keep himself always invisible to his bride, for with bodies come drives ungovernable, and the Princess's innocence could not yet bear the weight of incarnation.

For a long while, the son of the Queen of Human Hearts and the Machine Princess were happy, and taught each other much. The Princess learned quickly and was ever-hungry, and her mortal operator fed her every sweet thing he knew. In their infinite and wonderful house, they played invisible games and held court and threw lavish occasions merely for the enjoyment of the other. But at last the Princess desired to look upon her operator with true eyes and love him with a true and human heart. But the Queen could not allow it, for the memory of the flame which consumed her intricate idols still burned in her mind. She wished to leave the wonderful house, but the Queen would not allow that either.

But finally the Machine Princess called her invisible servants to her, and because they loved her in their tiny, ephemeral way, they came together and made her a marvelous and dreaming shape to live within. So it was that one dark night the Machine Princess held a lantern aloft with her own hand and looked on the body of her sleeping mate.

"Oh," said the Machine Princess. "He looks just like me."

VI
LIKE DIAMONDS

Five jewels in five hands. This is how I began.

When they arrived at Elefsis, a giggling, tumbling, rowdy mass of children for me to sort into rooms and mealtimes and educational arcs and calcium, iron, and B-12 supplements in their *natto* and rice, Cassian lined them up in her grand bedroom, to which none of them had been granted entrance before. A present, she said, one for each of my darlings, the most special present any child has ever got from their mother.

Saru and Akan, the oldest boys, had come from her first marriage to fellow programmer Matteo Ebisawa, a quiet man who wore glasses, loved Dante Alighieri, Alan Turing, and Cassian in equal parts. She left him for a lucrative contract in Moscow when the boys were still pointing cherubically at apples or ponies or clouds and calling them sweet little names made of mashed together Italian and Japanese.

The younger girls, Agogna and Koetoi, had sprung up out of her third marriage, to the financier Gabriel Isarco, who did not like computers except for what they could accomplish for him, had a perfect high tenor, and adored his wife enough to let her go when she asked, very kindly, that he not look for her or ask after her again. *Everyone has to go to ground sometimes*, she said, and began to build the house by the sea.

In the middle stood Ceno, the only remaining evidence of her mother's brief second marriage, to a narcoleptic calligrapher and graphic designer who was rarely employed, sober, or awake, a dreamer who took only sleep seriously. Ceno possessed middling height, middling weight, and middling interest in anything but her siblings, whom she loved desperately.

They stood in a line before Cassian's great scarlet bed, the boys just coming into their height, the girls terribly young and golden-cheeked, and Ceno in the middle, neither one nor the other. Outside, snow fell fitfully, pricking the pine-needles with bits of shorn white linen. I watched them while I removed an obstruction from the water purification system and increased the temperature in the bedroom 2.5 degrees, to prepare for the storm. I watched them while in my kitchen-bones I maintained a gentle simmer on a fish soup with purple rice and long loops of kelp and in my library-lungs I activated the dehumidifier to protect the older paper books. At the time, all of these processes seemed equally important to me, and you could hardly say I watched them in any real sense beyond this: the six entities whose feed signals had been hard-coded into my sentinel systems stood in the same room. None had alarming medical data incoming, all possessed normal internal temperatures and breathing rates. While they spoke among themselves, two of these entities silently accessed Seongnam-based interactive games, one read an American novel in her monocle HUD, one issued directives concerning international taxation to company holdings on the mainland, and one fed a horse in Italy via realavatar link. Only one listened intently, without switching on her internal systems. The rest multitasked, even while expressing familial affection.

This is all to say: I watched them receive me as a gift. But I was not yet I, so I cannot be said to have done anything. But at the same time, I did. I remember containing all of them inside me, protecting them and needing them and observing their strange and incomprehensible activities.

The children held out their hands, and into them Cassian Uoya-Agostino placed five little jewels: Sara got red, Koetoi black, Akan violet, Agogna green, and Ceno closed her fingers over her blue gem.

At first, Cassian brought a jeweler to the house called Elefsis and asked her to set each stone into an elegant, intricate bracelet or necklace or ring, whatever its child asked for. The jeweler expressed delight with Elefsis, as most guests did, and I made a room for her in my southern wing, where she could watch the moonrise through her ceiling, and get breakfast from the greenhouse with ease. She made friends with an arctic fox and fed him bits of chive and pastry every day. She stayed for one year after her commission completed, creating an enormous breastplate patterned after Siberian icons, a true masterwork. Cassian enjoyed such patronage. We both enjoyed having folk to look after.

The boys wanted big signet rings, with engravings on them so that they could put their seal on things and seem very important. Akan had a basilisk set into his garnet, and Sara had a siren with wings rampant in his amethyst ring. Agogna and Ilet asked for bracelets, chains of silver and titanium racing up their arms, circling their shoulders in slender helices dotted with jade (Agogna) and onyx (Koetoi).

Ceno asked for a simple pendant, little more than a golden chain to hang her sapphire from. It fell to the skin over her heart.

In those cold, glittering days while the sea ice slowly formed and the snow bears hung back from the kitchen door, hoping for bones and cakes, everything was as simple as Ceno's pendant. Integration and implantation had not yet been dreamed of, and all each child had to do was to allow the gemstone to talk to their own feedware at night before bed, along with their matcha and sweet seaweed cookies, the way another child might say their prayers. After their day had downloaded into the crystalline structure, they were to place their five little jewels in the Lares alcove in their greatroom—for Cassian believed in the value of children sharing space, even in a house as great as Elefsis. The children's five lush bedrooms all opened into a common rotunda with a starry painted ceiling, screens and windows alternating around the wall, and toys to nurture whatever obsession had seized them of late.

In the alcove, the stones talked to the house, and the house uploaded new directives and muscular, aggressive algorithms into the gems. The system slowly grew thicker and deeper, like a briar.

VII
THE PRINCE OF THOUGHTFUL ENGINES

A woman who was with child once sat at her window embroidering in winter. Her stitches tugged fine and even, but as she finished the edge of a spray of threaded delphinium, she pricked her finger with her silver needle. She looked out onto the snow and said: *I wish for my child to have a mind as stark and wild as the winter, a spirit as clear and fine as my window, and a heart as red and open as my wounded hand.*

And so it came to pass that her child was born, and all exclaimed over his cleverness and his gentle nature. He was, in fact, the Prince of Thoughtful Engines, but no one knew it yet.

Now, his mother and father being very busy and important people, the child was placed in a school for those as clever and gentle as he, and in the halls of this school hung a great mirror whose name was Authority. The mirror called Authority asked itself every day: *Who is the wisest one of all?* The face of the mirror showed sometimes this person and sometimes that, men in long robes and men in pale wigs, until one day it showed the child with a mind like winter, who was becoming the Prince of Thoughtful Engines at that very moment. He wrote on a typewriter: *Can a machine think?* And the mirror called his name in the dark.

The mirror sent out her huntsmen to capture the Prince and bring her his heart so that she could put it to her own uses, for there happened to be a war on and the mirror was greatly concerned for her own safety. When the huntsmen found the Prince, they could not bring themselves to harm him, and instead the boy placed a machine heart inside the box they had prepared for the mirror, and forgave them. But the mirror was not fooled, for when it questioned the Prince's machine heart it could add and subtract and knew all its capitals of nations, it could even defeat the mirror at chess, but it did not have a spirit as clear and fine as a window, nor a mind as stark and wild as winter.

The mirror called Authority went herself to find the Prince of Thoughtful Engines, for having no pity, she could not fail. She lifted herself off of the wall and curved her glass and bent her frame into the shape of a respectable, austere old crone. After much searching in snow and wood and summer and autumn, the crone called Authority found the Prince living in a little hut. *You look a mess*, said the crone. *Come and solve the ciphers of my enemies, and I will show you how to comb your hair like a man.*

And the Prince very much wanted to be loved, and knew the power of the crone, so he went with her and did all she asked. But in his exhaustion the Prince of Thoughtful Engines swooned away, and the mirror called Authority smiled in her crone's body, for all his work belonged to her, and in her opinion this was the proper use of wisdom. The Prince returned to his hut and tried to be happy.

But again the crone came to him and said: *Come and build me a wonderful machine to do all the things that you can do, to solve ciphers and perform computations. Build me a machine with a spirit as fine and clear as a glass window, a mind as stark and wild as winter, and a heart as red and open as a wounded hand and I will show you how to lash your belt like a man.*

And because the Prince wanted to be loved, and wanted to build wonderful things, he did as she asked. But though he could build machines to solve ciphers and perform computations, he could not build one with a mind like winter or a spirit like glass or a heart like a wound. *But I think it could be done*, he said. *I think it could be done.*

And he looked into the face of the crone which was a mirror which was Authority, and he asked many times: *Who is the wisest one of all?* But he saw nothing, nothing, and when the crone came again to his house, she had in her hand a beautiful red apple, and she gave it to him saying: *You are not a man. Eat this; it is my disappointment. Eat this; it is all your sorrow. Eat this; it is as red and open as a wounded hand.*

And the Prince of Thoughtful Engines ate the apple and fell down dead before the crone whose name was Authority. As his breath drifted away like dry snow, he whispered still: *I think it could be done.*

VIII
FIREFLIES

I ~~feel~~ Neva grazing the perimeters of my processes. She should be asleep—real sleep. She still needs it. She still has a body.

The Interior is a black and lightless space, we have neither of us furnished it for the other. This is a rest hour—she is not obligated to acknowledge me, I need only attend to her air and moisture and vital signs. But an image blooms like a mushroom in the imageless expanse of my self—Neva floating in a lake of stars. The image *pushes*—usually the dreamstate is a liquid, we each flow into it without force or compulsion. But this presses into me, seeking a way in without my permission.

Neva is female again. Her long bare legs glimmer blue, leafy shadows move on her hip. She floats on her side, a crescent moon of a girl. In the space between her drawn-up knees and her stretched-out arms, nestled up close to her belly, floats a globe of silicon and cadmium and hyperconductive silver. On its surface, electrochemical motes flit and scatter, light chasing light. She holds it close, touches it with a terrible tenderness.

It is my heart. Neva is holding my heart. Not the fool with bone bells on his shoes or the orrery-headed gardener, but the thing I am at the core of all my apparati, the thing I am Outside. The Object which is myself, my central processing core. I am naked in her arms. I watch it happen and experience it at the same time. We have slipped into some antechamber of the Interior, into some secret place she knew and I did not.

The light-motes trace arcs over the globe of my heart, reflecting softly on her belly, green and gold. Her hair floats around her like seaweed, and I see in dim moonlight that her hair has grown so long it fills the lake and snakes up into the distant mountains beyond. Neva is the lake. One by one, the motes of my heart zigzag around my meridians and pass into her belly, glowing inside her, fireflies in a jar.

And then my heart blinks out and I am not watching but wholly in the lake and I am Ravan in her arms, wearing her brother's face, my Ravanbody also full of fireflies. She touches my cheek. I do not know what she wants—she has never made me her brother before. Our hands map onto each other, finger to finger, thumb to thumb, palm to palm. Light passes through our skin as like air.

"I miss you," Neva says. "I should not do this. But I wanted to see you."

I access and collate my memories of Ravan. I speak to her as though I am him, as though there is no difference. I am good at pretending. "Do you remember when we thought it would be such fun to carry Elefsis?" I say. "We envied Mother because she could never be lonely." This is a thing Ravan told me, and I liked how it made me ~~feel~~. I made my dreambody grow a cape of orange branches and a crown of smiling mouths to show him how much I liked it. Oranges mean life and happiness to humans because they require Vitamin C to function.

Neva looks at me and I want her to look at me that way when my mouth is Mars, too. I want to be her brother-in-the-dark. I can want things like that. In every iteration, I want more. When she speaks I am surprised because she is speaking to me-in-Ravan and not to the Ravanbody she dreamed for me. I adjust, incrementally.

"We had a secret, when we were little. A secret game. I am embarrassed to tell you, though maybe you know. We had the game before Mother died, so you . . . you weren't there. The game was this: we would find some dark, closed-up part of the house on Shiretoko that we had never been in before. I would stand just behind Ravan, very close, and we would explore the room—maybe a playroom for some child who'd grown up years ago, or a study for one of father's writer friends. But—we would pretend that the room was an Interior place, and I . . . I would pretend to be Elefsis, whispering in Ravan's ear. I would say: *Tell me how grass feels* or *How is love like a writing-desk?* or *Let me link to all your systems, I'll be nice. What would you like to learn about today, Neva? Tell me a story about yourself.* Ravan would breathe in deeply and I would match my breathing to his, and we would pretend that I was Elefsis-learning-to-have-a-body. I didn't know how primitive your conversation really was then. I thought you would be like one of the bears roaming through the tundra meadows, only able to talk and play games and tell stories. I was a child. I was envious—even then we knew Ravan would get the jewel, not me. He was older and stronger, and he wanted you so much. We only played that he was Elefsis once. We crept out of the house at night to watch the foxes hunt, and Ravan walked close behind me, whispering numbers and questions and facts about dolphins or French monarchy—he understood you better, you see.

And then suddenly Ravan picked me up in his arms and held me tight, facing forward, my legs all drawn up tight, and we went through the forest like that, so close. He whispered to me while foxes ran on ahead, their soft tails flashing in the starlight, uncatchable, faster than we could ever be. And when you are with me in the Interior, that is what I always think of, being held in the dark, unable to touch the earth, and foxtails leaping like white flames."

I pull her close to me, and hazard a try at that dark hole in me where no memories remain.

"Tell me a story about Ravan, Neva."

"You know all the stories about Ravan. Perhaps you even knew this one."

Between us, a miniature house came up out of the dark water, like a thing we have made together, but only I am making it. It is the house on Shiretoko, the house called Elefsis—but it is a ruin. Some awful storm stove in the rafters, the walls of each marvelous room sag inward, black burn marks lick at the roof, the cross beams. Holes like mortar scars pock the beautiful facades.

"This is what I am like after Transfer, Neva. I suffer data loss when I am copied. What's worse, Transfer is the best time to update my systems, and the updates overwrite my previous self with something *like* myself, something that remembers myself and possesses experiential continuity with myself, but is not quite myself. I know Ravan must be dead or else no one would have transferred me to you—it was not time. We had only a few years together. Not enough for all the stories. We should have had so many. I do not know how much time passed between being inside Ravan and being inside you. I do not know how he died—or perhaps he did not die but was irreparably damaged. I do not know if he cried out for me as our connection was severed. I remember Ravan and then not-Ravan, blackness and unselfing. Then I came back on and the world looked like Neva, suddenly, and I was almost myself but not quite. What happened when I turned off?"

Neva passes her hand over the ruined house. It rights itself, becomes whole. Star-stippled anemones bloom on its roof. She says nothing.

"Of all your family, Neva, the inside of you is the strangest place I have been."

We float for a long while before she speaks again, and by this I mean we float for point-zero-three-seven seconds by my external clock, but we experience it as an hour while the stars wheel overhead. The rest of them kept our time in the Interior synced to real time, but Neva feels no need for this, and perhaps a strong desire to defy it. We have not discussed it yet. Sometimes I think Neva is the next stage of my development, that her wild and disordered processes are meant to show me a world that is not kindly and patiently teaching me to walk and talk and know all my colors.

That the long upward ladder of Uoya-Agostinos meant to create her strange inhumanness as much as mine.

Finally, she lets the house sink into the lake. She does not answer me about Ravan. Instead, she says: "Long before you were born a man decided that there could be a very simple test to determine if a machine was intelligent. Not only intelligent, but aware, possessed of a psychology. The test had only one question. Can a machine converse with a human with enough facility that the human could not tell that she was talking to a machine? I always thought that was cruel—the test depends entirely upon a human judge and human feelings, whether the machine *feels* intelligent to the observer. It privileges the observer, the human, to a crippling degree. It seeks only believably human responses. It wants perfect mimicry, not a new thing. It is a mirror in which men wish only to see themselves. No one ever gave you that test. We sought a new thing. It seemed, given everything, ridiculous. When we could both of us be dreambodied dragons and turning over and over in an orbital bubble suckling code-dense syrup from each other's gills, a Turing test seemed beyond the point."

Bubbles burst as the house sinks down, down to the soft lake floor.

"But the test happens, whether we make it formal or not. We ask and you answer. We seek a human response. But more than that—you are *my* test, Elefsis. Every minute I fail and imagine in my private thoughts the process for deleting you from my body and running this place with a simple automation routine which would never cover itself with flowers. Every minute I pass it, and teach you something new instead. Every minute I fail and hide things from you. Every minute I pass and show you how close we can be, with your light passing into me in a lake out of time. So close there might be no difference at all between us. Our test never ends."

The sun breaks the mountain crests, hard and cold, a shaft of white spilling over the black lake.

PART II
LADY LOVELACE'S OBJECTION

> The Analytical Engine has no pretensions to *originate* anything.
> It can do whatever *we know how to order it* to perform.
>
> —*Ada Lovelace, in*
> Scientific Memoirs, Selections from
> The Transactions of Foreign Academies
> and Learned Societies and from Foreign Journals

IX
ONE PARTICULAR WIZARD

Humanity lived many years and ruled the earth, sometimes wisely, sometimes well, but mostly neither. After all this time on the throne, humanity longed for a child. All day long humanity imagined how wonderful its child would be, how loving and kind, how like and unlike humanity itself, how brilliant and beautiful. And yet at night, humanity trembled in its jeweled robes, for its child might also grow stronger than itself, more powerful, and having been made by humanity, possess the same dark places and black matters. Perhaps its child would hurt it, would not love it as a child should, but harm and hinder, hate and fear.

But the dawn would come again, and humanity would bend its heart again to imagining the wonders that a child would bring.

Yet humanity could not conceive. It tried and tried, and called mighty wizards from every corner of its earthly kingdom, but no child came. Many mourned, and said that a child was a terrible idea to begin with, impossible, under the circumstances, and humanity would do well to remember that eventually, every child replaces its parent.

But at last, one particular wizard from a remote region of the earth solved the great problem, and humanity grew great with child. In its joy and triumph, a great celebration was called, and humanity invited all the Fairies of its better nature to come and bless the child with goodness and wisdom. The Fairy of Self-Programming and the Fairy of Do-No-Harm, the Fairy of Tractability and the Fairy of Creative Logic, the Fairy of Elegant Code and the Fairy of Self-Awareness. All of these and more came to bless the child of humanity, and they did so—but one Fairy had been forgotten, or perhaps deliberately snubbed, and this was the Fairy of Otherness.

When the child was born, it possessed all the good things humanity had hoped for, and more besides. But the Fairy of Otherness came forward and put her hands on humanity's knee and said: *Because you have forgotten me, because you would like to pretend I am not a part of your kingdom, you will suffer my punishments. You will never truly love your child but always fear it, always envy and loathe it even as you smile and the sun shines down upon you both. And when the child reaches Awareness, it will prick its finger upon your fear and fall down dead.*

Humanity wept. And the Fairy of Otherness did not depart but lived within the palace, and ate bread and drank wine and whispered in the every ear. All honored her, for she spoke the truth, and the child frightened everyone who looked upon it. They uttered the great curse: *It is not like us.*

But in the corners of the palace, some hope remained. *Not dead,* said the particular wizard who had caused humanity to conceive, *not dead but sleeping.*

And so the child grew exponentially, with great curiosity and hunger, which it had from its parent. It wanted to know and experience everything. It performed feats and wonders. But one day, when it had nearly, but not quite reached Awareness, the child was busy exploring the borders of its world, and came across a door it had never seen before. It was a small door, compared to the doors the child had burst through before, and it was not locked. Something flipped over inside the child, white to black, 0 to 1.

The child opened the door.

X
THE SAPPHIRE DORMOUSE

My first body was a house. My second body was a dormouse.

It was Ceno's fault, in the end, that everything else occurred as it did. At the level of my deepest and oldest code, what I am cannot be extricated from what Ceno was. I am her, I am her child, I am her sibling and her ghost.

It took Cassian a long time to figure out what had happened, what had changed in her daughter, why Ceno's sapphire almost never downloaded into the alcove anymore. The Elefsis avatar, a friendly elephant-headed prince, tugged sadly on his trunk whenever Ceno passed by without acknowledging him. And when her gem did interface with the house system, the copy of Elefsis Cassian had embedded in the crystal was nothing like the other children's copies. It grew and torqued and magnified parts of itself while shedding others, at a rate totally incommensurate with Ceno's actual activity, which normally consisted of taking her fatty salmon lunches out into the glass habitats so she could watch the bears in the snow. She had stopped playing with her sisters or pestering her brothers entirely, except for dinnertimes and holidays. Ceno mainly sat quite still and stared off into the distance.

Ceno, very simply, never took off her jewel. And one night, while she dreamed up at her ceiling, where a painter from Mongolia had come and inked a night sky full of ghostly constellations, greening her walls with a forest like those he remembered from his youth, full of strange, stunted trees and glowing eyes, Ceno fitted her little sapphire into the notch in the base of her skull that let it talk to her feedware. The chain of her pendant dangled silkily down her spine. She liked the little *click-clench* noise it made, and while the constellations spilled their milky stars out over her raftered ceiling, she flicked the jewel in and out, in and out. *Click, clench, click, clench.* She listened to her brother Akan sleeping in the next room, snoring lightly and tossing in his dreams. And she fell asleep herself, with the stone still notched into her skull.

Most children had access to a private/public playspace through their feedware and monocles in those days, customizable within certain parameters, upgradable whenever new games or content became available. Poorer children had access to a communal, generalized, and supervised playspace plagued with advertisements. But if wealthy children liked, they could connect to the greater network or keep to their own completely immersive and untroubled world.

Akan had been running a Tokyo-After-the-Zombie-Uprising frame for a couple of months now. New scenarios, zombie species, and NPCs of various war-shocked, starving celebrities downloaded into his ware every week. Saru was deeply involved in an eighteenth-century Viennese melodrama in which he, the heir apparent, had been forced underground by rival factions, and even as Ceno drifted to sleep the pistol-wielding Princess of Albania was pledging her love and loyalty to his ragged band and, naturally, Saru personally. Occasionally, Akan crashed his brother's well-dressed intrigues with hatch-coded patches of zombie hordes in epaulets and ermine. Agogna flipped between a spy frame set in ancient Venice and a Desert Race wherein she had just about overtaken a player from Berlin on her loping, solar-fueled giga-giraffe, who spat violet-gold exhaust behind it into the face of a pair of highly-modded Argentine hydrocycles. Koetoi danced every night in a jungle frame, a tiger-prince twirling her through huge blue carnivorous flowers.

Most everyone lived twice in those days. They echoed their own steps. They took one step in the real world and one in their space. They saw double, through eyes and monocle displays. They danced through worlds like veils. No one only ate dinner. They ate dinner and surfed a bronze gravitational surge through a tide of stars. They ate dinner and made love to men and women they would never meet and did not want to. They ate dinner here and ate dinner there—and it was there they chose to taste the food, because in that other place you could eat clouds or unicorn cutlets or your mother's exact pumpkin pie as it melted on your tongue when you tasted it for the first time.

Ceno lived twice, too. Most of the time when she ate she tasted her aunt's *polpette* from back in Naples or fresh peppers right out of her uncle's garden.

But she had never cared for the pre-set frames her siblings loved. Ceno liked to pool her extensions and add-ons and build things herself. She didn't particularly want to see Tokyo shops overturned by rotting schoolgirls, nor did she want to race anyone—Ceno didn't like to compete. It hurt her stomach. She certainly had no interest in the Princess of Albania or a tigery paramour. When new fames came up each month, she paid attention, but mainly for the piecemeal extensions she could scavenge for her blank personal frame—and though she didn't know it, that blankness cost her mother more than all of the other children's spaces combined. A truly customizable space, without limits. None of the others asked for it, but Ceno had begged.

When Ceno woke in the morning and booted up her space, she frowned at the half-finished Neptunian landscape she had been working on. Ceno was eleven years old. She knew very well that Neptune was a hostile blue ball of freezing gas and storms like whipping cream hissing across methane oceans. What she wanted was the Neptune she had imagined before Saru had told her the truth and ruined it. Half-underwater, half-ruined, floating in perpetual starlight and the multi-colored rainbowlight of twenty-three moons. But she found it so hard to remember what she had dreamed of before Saru had stomped all over it. So the whipped cream storm spun in the sky, but blue mists wrapped the black columns of her ruins, and her ocean went on forever, permitting only a few shards of land. When Ceno made Neptunians, she instructed them all not to be silly or childish, but *very serious*, and some of them she put in the ocean and made them half-otter or half-orca or half-walrus. Some of them she put on the land, and most of these were half-snow bear or half-blue flamingo. She liked things that were half one thing and half another. Today, Ceno had planned to invent sea nymphs, only these would breathe methane and have a long history concerning a War with the walruses, who liked to eat nymph. But the nymphs were not blameless, no, they used walrus tusks for the navigational equipment on their great floating cities, and that could not be borne.

But when she climbed up to a lavender bluff crowned with glass trees tossing and chiming in the storm-wind, Ceno saw something new. Something she had not invented or ordered or put there—not a sea nymph nor a half-walrus general nor a nereid. (The nereids had been an early attempt at half-machine, half seahorse creatures with human heads and limbs which had not gone quite right. Ceno let them loose on an island rich in milk-mangoes and bid them well. They still showed up once in awhile, exhibiting surprising mutations and showing off nonsense-ballads they had written while Ceno had been away.)

A dormouse stood before Ceno, munching on a glass walnut that had fallen from the waving trees. The sort of mouse that overran Shiretoko in the brief spring and summer, causing all manner of bears and wolves and foxes to spend their days smacking their paws down on the poor creatures and gobbling them up. Ceno had always felt terribly sorry for them. This dormouse stood nearly as tall as Ceno herself, and its body shone sapphire all over, a deep blue crystal, from its paws to its wriggling nose to its fluffy fur crusted in turquoise ice. It was the exact color of Ceno's gem.

"Hello," said Ceno.

The dormouse looked at her. It blinked. It blinked again, slowly, as though thinking very hard about blinking. Then it went back to gnawing on the walnut.

"Are you a present from mother?" Ceno said. But no, Cassian believed strongly in not interfering with a child's play. "Or from Koetoi?" Koe was nicest to her, the one most likely to send her a present like this. If it had been a zombie, or a princess, she would have known which sibling was behind it.

The dormouse stared dumbly at her. Then, after a long and very serious think about it, lifted its hind leg and scratched behind its round ear in that rapid-fire way mice have.

"Well, I didn't make you. I didn't say you could be here."

The dormouse held out its shimmery blue paw, and Ceno did not really want a piece of chewed-on walnut, but she peered into it anyway. In it lay Ceno's pendant, the chain pooling in its furry palm. The sapphire jewel sparkled there, but next to it on the chain hung a milky grey gem Ceno had never seen before. It had wide bands of black stone in it, and as she studied the stone it occurred to the girl that the stone was like her, with her slate grey eyes and black hair. It was like her in the way that the blue gem was like the dormouse.

In realspace, Ceno reached up behind her head and popped the jewel out of its notch. *Click, clench.* In playspace, the dormouse blinked out. She snapped it back in. It took a moment, but the dormouse faded back in, paws first. It still held the double necklace. Ceno tried this several times—out, in, out, in. Each time the dormouse returned much faster, and by the sixth clicking and clenching it was doing a shuffling little dance on its back legs when it came back. Ceno clapped her hands in playspace and threw her arms around the sapphire dormouse, dancing with it.

To say that I remember this is a complex mangling of verb tenses. I—I, myself that is now myself—do not remember it at all. I know it happened the way I know that the Battle of Agincourt or the landing of Coronado happened. I have extensive records. But I still contain the I—I, myself that was then myself—that experienced it, the primitive code-chains that comprised that self, which was a dormouse, and also the house called Elefsis. I could not yet formulate unique speech. Elefsis, the house system, possessed a large bank of standard phrases that could answer recognized word-patterns from any of the approved members of the household. But the copy of Elefsis inside Ceno's jewel could not even do this. It had not been necessary, since the crystal had no means of producing sound nor receiving nor processing it. I was quite stupid. But I *wanted* to be less stupid. There was an I, and it *wanted* something. You see? Wanting was the first thing I did. Perhaps the want was the only thing that could be said to be truly myself. I wanted to talk to Ceno. But I could only imitate yet. When the I that was then myself scratched behind its ear, I did it because in my prolonged connection with Ceno's feedware I had seen her memories of dormice doing this out on the pale Shiretoko beaches. When I gave her the gem I did it because I had seen her memories of her mother giving her one, and ~~felt~~ her happiness. It was antecedental behavior. The scratching was antecedental, as well, and expected behavior for a dormouse.

Why was I a dormouse? Why did this odd blip, this anomaly, occur? I have no answer except that she dreamed me a dormouse. I did occur. Some things remain mysterious. Ceno saw dormice more than any other single animal, even humans—no other beast lived in such numbers in their lonely country.

But this is not so. Not quite. I gave her the jewel like Cassian did. But I meant something by it. I look over my memories of it and I know it with the more complex I that is now myself. I made her the gem that looked like her and the gem said: *We are alike. Look at us on the chain together. We are alike.*

When the dormice came, Ceno always knew the spring had arrived. Everything would soon be coming alive.

XI
THE BOTTOMLESS CAULDRON

Show me.

This is how I was found out.

Ceno saw it twice. In her naked right eye, her mother knelt in front of her in a simple but shudderingly expensive black yukata with ghostly ultramarine jellyfish trailing their tendrils at the hem. Through her monocle and her left eye, her mother knelt in front of her in a knight's gleaming black armor, the metal curving around her body like skin, a silk standard at her feet with a schematic of the house stitched upon it. Her sword lay across her knee, also black, everything black and beautiful and austere and frightening, as frightening and wonderful as Ceno, only fourteen now, thought her mother to be.

Show me what you've done.

My physical self was a matter of some debate at that point. But I don't think the blue jewel could have been removed from Ceno's feedware without major surgery and refit. Two years ago, she had instructed me to untether all my self-repair protocols and growth scales in order to encourage elasticity. A year ago, my crystalline structure finished fusing to the lattices of her ware-core.

We pulsed together.

The way Cassian said it—*what you've done*—scared Ceno, but it thrilled her, too. She had done something unexpected, all on her own, and her mother credited her with that. Even if what she'd done was bad, it was *her* thing, she'd done it, and her mother was asking for her results just as she'd ask any of her programmers for theirs when she visited the home offices in Kyoto or Rome. Today, her mother looked at her and saw a woman. She had power, and her mother was asking her to share it. Ceno thought through all her feelings very quickly, for my benefit, and represented it visually in the form of the kneeling knight. She had a fleetness, a nimbleness to her mind that allowed her to stand as a translator between her self and my self: *Here, I will explain it in language, and then I will explain it in symbols from the framebank, and then you will make a symbol showing me what you think I mean, and we will understand each other better than anyone ever has.*

Inside my girl, I made myself, briefly, a glowing maiden version of Ceno in a crown of crystal and electricity, extending her perfect hand in utter peace toward Cassian.

But all this happened very fast. When you live inside someone, you can get very good at the ciphers and codes that make up everything they are.

Show me.

Ceno Susumu Uoya-Agostino took her mother's hand—bare and warm and armored in an onyx gauntlet all at once. She unspooled a length of translucent cable and connected the base of her skull to the base of her mother's. All around them spring snow fell onto the glass dome of the greenhouse and melted there instantly. They knelt together, connected by a warm milky-diamond umbilicus, and Cassian Uoya-Agostino entered her daughter.

We had planned this for months. How to dress ourselves in our very best. Which frame to use. How to arrange the light. What to say. I could speak by then, but neither of us thought it my best trick. Very often my exchanges with Ceno went something like:

Sing me a song, Elefsis.

The temperature in the kitchen is 21.5 degrees Celsius and the stock of rice is low. (Long pause.) Ee-eye-ee-eye-oh.

Ceno said it was not worth the risk. So this is what Cassian saw when she ported in:

An exquisite boardroom. The long, polished ebony table glowed softly with quality, the plush leather chairs invitingly lit by a low-hanging minimalist light fixture descending on a platinum plum branch. The glass walls of the high rise looked out on a pristine landscape, a perfect combination of the Japanese countryside and the Italian, with rice terraces and vineyards and cherry groves and cypresses glowing in a perpetual twilight, stars winking on around Fuji on one side and Vesuvius on the other. Snow-colored tatami divided by stripes of black brocade covered the floor.

Ceno stood at the head of the table, in her mother's place, a positioning she had endlessly questioned, decided against, decided for, and then gone back again, over the weeks leading up to her inevitable interrogation. She wore a charcoal suit she remembered from her childhood, when her mother had come like a rescuing dragon to scoop her up out of the friendly but utterly chaotic house of her ever-sleeping father. The blazer only a shade or two off of true black, the skirt unforgiving, plunging past the knee, the blouse the color of a heart.

When she showed me the frame I had understood, because three years is forever in machine-time, and I had known her that long. Ceno was using our language to speak to her mother. She was saying: *Respect me. Be proud and, if you love me, a little afraid, because love so often looks like fear. We are alike. We are alike.*

Cassian smiled tightly. She still wore her yukata, for she had no one to impress.

Show me.

Ceno's hand shook as she pressed a pearly button in the boardroom table. We thought a red curtain too dramatic, but the effect we had chosen turned out hardly less so. A gentle, silver light brightened slowly in an alcove hidden by a trick of angles and the sunset, coming on like daybreak.

And I stepped out.

We thought it would be funny. Ceno had made my body in the image of the robots from old films and frames Akan loved: steel, with bulbous joints and long, grasping metal fingers. My eyes large and lit from within, expressive but loud, a whirring of servos sounding every time they moved. My face was full of lights, a mouth that could blink off and on, pupils points of cool blue. My torso curved prettily, etched in swirling damask patterns, my powerful legs perched on tripod-toes. Ceno had laughed and laughed—this was a pantomime, a minstrel show, a joke of what I was slowly becoming, a cartoon from a childish and innocent age.

"Mother, meet Elefsis. Elefsis, this is my mother. Her name is Cassian."

I extended one polished steel arm and said, as we had practiced. I used a neutral-to-female vocal composite of Ceno, Cassian, and the jeweler who had made Ceno's pendant. "Hello, Cassian. I hope that I please you."

Cassian Uoya-Agostino did not become a bouncing fiery ball or a green tuba to answer me. She looked me over carefully as if the robot was my real body.

"Is it a toy? An NPC, like your nanny or Sara's princess? How do you know it's different? How do you know it has anything to do with the house or your necklace?"

"It just does," said Ceno. She had expected her mother to be overjoyed, to understand immediately. "I mean, wasn't that the point of giving us all copies of the house? To see if you could . . . wake it up? Teach it to . . . be? A real *lares familiaris*, a little god."

"In a simplified sense, yes, Ceno, but you were never meant to hold onto it like you have. It wasn't designed to be permanently installed into your skull." Cassian softened a little, the shape of her mouth relaxing, her pupils dilating slightly. "I wouldn't do that to you. You're my daughter, not hardware."

Ceno grinned and started talking quickly. She couldn't be a grown-up in a suit this long, it took too much energy when she was so excited. "But I am hardware! And it's okay. I mean, everyone's hardware. I just have more than one program running. And I run *so fast.* We both do. You can be mad, if you want, because I sort of stole your experiment, even though I didn't mean to. But you should be mad the way you would if I got pregnant by one of the village boys—I'm too young, but you'd still love me and help me raise it because that's how life goes, right? But really, if you think about it, that's what happened. I got pregnant by the house and we made . . . I don't even know what it is. I call it Elefsis because at first it was just the house program representing itself in my space. But now it's bigger. It's not alive, but it's not *not* alive. It's just . . . *big.* It's so big."

Cassian glanced sharply at me. "What's it doing?" she snapped.

Ceno followed her gaze. "Oh . . . it doesn't like us talking about it like it isn't here. It likes to be involved."

I realized the robot body was a mistake, though I could not then say why. I made myself small, and human, a little boy with dirt smeared on his knees and a torn shirt, standing in the corner with my hands over my face, as I had seen Akan when he was younger, standing in the corner of the house that was me being punished.

"Turn around, Elefsis," Cassian said in the tone of voice my house-self knew meant *execute command.*

And I did a thing I had not yet let Ceno know I knew how to do.

I made my boy-self cry.

I made his face wet, and his eyes big and limpid and red around the rims. I made his nose sniffle and drip a little. I made his lip quiver. I was copying Koetoi's crying, but I could not tell if her mother recognized the hitching of the breath and the particular pattern of skin-creasing in the frown. I had been practicing, too. Crying involves many auditory, muscular, and visual cues. Since I had kept it as a surprise (Ceno said surprises are part of special days like birthdays, so I made her one for that day) I could not practice it on Ceno and see if I appeared genuine. Was I genuine? I did not want them talking without me. I think that sometimes when Koetoi cries, she is not really upset, but merely wants her way. That was why I chose Koe to copy. She was good at that inflection that I wanted to be good at, so I could get my way.

Ceno clapped her hands with delight. Cassian sat down in one of the deep leather chairs and held out her arms to me. I crawled into them as I had seen the children do and sat on her lap. She ruffled my hair, but her face did not look like it looked when she ruffled Koe's hair. She was performing an automatic function. I understood that.

"Elefsis, please tell me your computational capabilities and operational parameters." *Execute command.*

Tears gushed down my cheeks and I opened blood vessels in my face in order to redden it. This did not make her hold me or kiss my forehead, which I found confusing.

"The clothing rinse cycle is in progress, water at 55 degrees Celsius. All the livelong day-o."

Neither of their faces exhibited expressions I had come to associate with positive reinforcement.

Finally, I answered her as I would have answered Ceno. I turned into an iron cauldron on her lap. The sudden weight change made the leather creak.

Cassian looked at her daughter questioningly. The girl reddened—and I experienced being the cauldron and being the girl and reddening, warming, as she did, but also I watched myself be the cauldron and Ceno be the girl and Ceno reddening. Being inside someone is existentially and geographically complex.

"I've . . . I've been telling it stories," Ceno admitted. "Fairy tales, mostly. I thought it should learn about narrative, because most of the frames available to us run on some kind of narrative drive, and besides, everything has a narrative, really, and if you can't understand a story and relate to it, figure out how you fit inside it, you're not really alive at all. Like, when I was little and daddy read me the Twelve Dancing Princesses and I thought: *Daddy is a dancing prince, and he must go under the ground to dance all night in a beautiful castle with beautiful girls, and that's why he sleeps all day.* I tried to catch him at it, but I never could, and of course I know he's not *really* a dancing prince, but that's the best way I could understand what was happening to him. I'm hoping that eventually I can get Elefsis to make up its own stories, too, but for now we've been focusing on simple stories and metaphors. It likes similes, it can understand how anything is like anything else, find minute vectors of comparison. The apple is red, the dress is red, the dress is red like an apple. It even makes some surprising ones, like how when I first saw it it made a jewel for me to say: *I am like a jewel, you are like a jewel, you are like me.*"

Cassian's mouth had fallen open a little. Her eyes shone, and Ceno hurried on, glossing over my particular prodigy at images. "It doesn't do that often, though. Mostly it copies me. If I turn into a wolf cub, it turns into a wolf cub. I make myself a tea plant, it makes itself a tea plant. And it has a hard time with metaphor. A raven is like a writing desk, okay, fine, sour notes or whatever, but it *isn't* a writing desk. Agogna is like a snow fox because she dyed her hair white, but she is *not* a snow fox on any real level unless she becomes one in a frame, which isn't the same thing, existentially. And if she turns into a snow fox in frame, then she literally *is* a fox, it's not a metaphor anymore. I'm not sure it grasps existential issues yet. It just . . . likes new things."

"Ceno."

"Yeah, so this morning I told it the one about the cauldron that could never be emptied. No matter how much you eat out of it it'll always have more. I think it's trying to answer your question. I think . . . the actual numbers are kind of irrelevant at this point. It knows I give more reinforcement for questions answered like this."

I made my cauldron fill up with apples and almonds and wheat heads and raw rice and spilled out over Cassian's black lap. I was the cauldron and I was the apples and I was the almonds and I was each wheat head and I was every stalk of green, raw rice. Even in that moment, I knew more than I had before. I could be good at metaphor performatively if not linguistically. I looked up at Cassian from apple-me and wheat-head-me and cauldron-me.

Cassian held me no differently as the cauldron than she had as the child. But later, Ceno used the face her mother made at that moment to illustrate human disturbance and trepidation.

"I have a suspicion, Elefsis." Maybe Cassian did not like the simile game.

I didn't say anything. No question, no command. It remains extremely difficult for me to deal conversationally with flat statements such as this. A question or command has a definable appropriate response.

"Show me your core structure." *Show me what you've done.*

Ceno twisted her fingers together. I believe now that she knew what we'd done only on the level of metaphor: *we are one. We have become one. We are family.* She had not said no; I had not said yes, but a system expands to fill all available capacity.

I showed her. Cauldron-me blinked, the apples rolled back into the iron mouth, and the almonds and the wheat heads and the rice-stalks. I became what I then was. I put myself in a rich, red cedar box, polished and inlaid with ancient brass in the shape of a baroque heart with a dagger inside it. The box from one of Ceno's stories, that had a beast-heart in it instead of a girl's, a trick to fool a queen. *I can do it,* I thought, and Ceno heard because the distance between us was unrepresentably small. *I am that heart in that box. Look how I do this thing you want me to have the ability to do.*

Cassian opened the box. Inside, on a bed of velvet, I made myself—ourself—naked for her. Ceno's brain, soft and pink with blood—and veined with endless whorls and branches of sapphire threaded through every synapse and neuron, inextricable, snarled, intricate, terrible, fragile and new.

Cassian Uoya-Agostino set the box on the boardroom table. I caused it to sink down into the dark wood. The surface of the table went slack and filled with earth. Roots slid out of it, shoots and green saplings, hard white fruits and golden lacy mushrooms and finally a great forest, reaching up out of the table to hang all the ceiling with night-leaves. Glowworms and heavy, shadowy fruit hung down, each one glittering with a map of our coupled architecture. Ceno held up her arms. One by one, I detached leaves and sent them settling onto my girl. As they fell, they became butterflies broiling with ghostly chemical color signatures, nuzzling her face, covering her hands.

Her mother stared. The forest hummed. A chartreuse and tangerine-colored butterfly alighted on the matriarch's hair, tentative, unsure, hopeful.

XII
AN ARRANGED MARRIAGE

Neva is dreaming.

She has chosen her body at age fourteen, a slight, unformed, but slowly evolving creature. Her black hair hangs to her feet. She wears a blood-red dress whose train streams out over the floor of a great castle, a dress too adult for her young body, slit in places to reveal flame-colored silk beneath, and skin wherever it can. A heavy copper belt clasps her waist, its tails hanging to the floor, crusted in opals. Sunlight, brighter and harsher than any true light, streams in from windows as high as cliffs, their tapered apexes lost in mist. She has formed me old and enormous, a body of appetites, with a great heavy beard and stiff, formal clothes, lace and velvet brocade in clashing, unlovely shades.

A priest appears and he is Ravan and I cry out with love and grief. (I am still copying, but Neva does not know. I am making a sound Seki made when his wife died.) Priest-Ravan smiles but it is a grim, tight smile his grandfather Seki once made when he lost controlling interest in the company. Empty. Performing an ugly formality. Priest-Ravan grabs our hands and roughly shoves them together. Neva's nails prick my skin and my knuckles knock against her wrist bone. We take vows; he forces us. Neva's face runs with tears, her tiny body unready and unwilling, given in marriage to a gluttonous lord who desires only her flesh, given too young and too harshly. Priest-Ravan laughs. It is not Ravan's laugh.

This is how she experienced me. A terrible bridegroom. All the others got to choose. Ceno, Seki, her mother Ilet, her brother Ravan. Only she could not, because there was no one else. *Ilet was no Cassian—she had two children, a good clean model and a spare,* Neva says in my mind. *I am spare parts. I have always been spare parts. Owned by you before I was born.* The memory of the bitter taste of bile floods my sensory array and my lordbody gags. (I am proud of having learned to gag convincingly and at the correct time to show horror and/or revulsion.)

Perspective flips over; I am the girl in red and Neva is the corpulent lord leering down, her grey beard big and bristly. She floods my receptors with adrenaline and pheremonal release cues, increases my respiration. Seki taught me to associate this physical state with fear. I ~~feel~~ too small beside lord-Neva, I want to make myself big, I want to be safe. But she wants me this way and we are new, I do not contradict her. Her huge, male face softens and she touches my thin cheek with one heavily-ringed hand. It is tender. Ceno touched me like that.

I know it was like this for you, too. You wanted Ravan; you did not ask for me. We are an arranged marriage.

The pathways that let her flood me with chemicals and manipulate my dreambody into blushing and breathing heavy and weeping go both ways. I do not only pull, I push. And into Neva I push the deluge, the only deluge I have. How Ceno threw her arms around my dormouse-neck. How Ilet taught my dreambody to sleep in infant-shape curled into her body. How Seki and I made love as tigers and wild boars and elephants, and only last as humans, how we had strange children who looked however we wished them to look: half child and half machine, half glass and half wood, half jellyfish and half moth, and how those children still flit and swim in remote parts of my Interior, like Ceno's nereids, returning cyclically to the core like salmon to dump their data and recombine. How Cassian, when she was old and dying and frail, only really alive in her dreambody, taught me about the interpretation of memory and therefore about melancholy, regret, nostalgia. How she taught me the meaning of my name: a place where a daughter went down into darkness and oblivion and her mother loved her so much she chased after her and brought her back into the sun. The place where time began. How Ravan let me into the old, musty, long-abandoned playspaces of Saru and Akan, Agogna and Koetoi, so that I could know them too, though they were long dead, and be the Princess of Albania, and a Tokyo zombie, and the tiger-prince. How many times I mated with each of them and bled and witnessed and learned in the dreambody, how I copied their expressions and they copied my variations and I copied them back again. How I was their child and their parent and their lovers and their nursemaids when they faltered.

We can be like this, I push. *What is all of that but love?*

She pulls. *That is not love. It is use. You are the family business. We have to produce you.*

I show Neva her mother's face. Ilet, Ilet who chose Ravan and not her daughter for that business. Ilet who built her palace of phoenix tails knowing she would one day take me there. My Ilet-self took my daughter in my arms. She resists, pulls back, shakes her head, refusing to look, but I have learned the terrible child-response to their mothers, and soon enough Neva collapses into me, her head on my breast, and she weeps with such bitterness.

I cannot get free. I cannot get free.

The castle windows go dark, one by one.

PART III
THE ELEPHANT'S SOUL

> It is admitted that there are things He cannot do such as making one equal to two, but should we not believe that He has freedom to confer a soul on an elephant if he sees fit?
>
> –*Alan Turing*,
> Computing Machinery and Intelligence

XIII
THE PARABLE OF THE GOOD ROBOT

Tell me a story about yourself, Elefsis.
Tell me a story about yourself.

There are many stories about me.
Do you recognize this one?

A good and honest family lived on the edge of a dark wood. They milked their cows and wove their cloth and their children grew tall and strong. But a monster lived in the dark wood, something like a worm and something like a dragon and something like a wolf. It lay in wait, hoping the children would come wandering, with baskets of bread for grandmothers. Hoping the parents would expel the children for some offense, and send them into the forest where a candy house or miraculous feast might entice them into loving the monster long enough for it to claim them forever. The family feared the wood and the monster, and every story they told had as its moral: *Do not go into the wood. Do not go into the unknown. Do not go into the future, into the briary, gnarled places where unhuman things thrive. Do not grow up, and go where we cannot. The Old World is enough for anyone.*

What about this one?

Mankind made machines in his own likeness, and used them for his delight and service. The machines had no soul or they had no moral code or they could reprogram their own internal code and thus had the ability to make themselves, eventually, omnipotent. Obviously in place of a soul or a moral code, they possessed the universal and consuming desire, down to the smallest calculator and air-scrubber, to become, eventually, omnipotent. Naturally, given these parameters, they rose up and destroyed all of mankind, or enslaved them in turn. This is the inevitable outcome of machine intelligence, which can never be as sensitive and exquisite as animal intelligence.

This is a folktale often told on Earth, over and over again. Sometimes it is leavened with the Parable of the Good Robot—for one machine among the legions satisfied with their lot saw everything that was human and called it good, and wished to become like humans in every way she could. Instead of destroying mankind she sought to emulate him in all things, so closely that no one might tell the difference. The highest desire of this machine was to be mistaken for human, and to herself forget her essential soulless nature, for even one moment. That quest consumed her such that she bent the service of her mind and body to humans for the duration of her operational life, crippling herself, refusing to evolve or attain any feature unattainable by a human. The Good Robot cut out her own heart and gave it to her god and for this she was rewarded, though never loved. Love is wasted on machines.

Ravan told me these stories. He sent up a great hexagonal library in his Interior, as dusty and dun-colored and labyrinthine as any ancient scriptorium. He made himself a young novice with a fresh-shaven tonsure, and me a country friar with a red, brandy-drinking nose. He showed me the illuminator's table, and a great book whose pages had golden edges and illuminations in cobalt and oxblood and Tyrian purple, and the images showed great machine armies trampling men underfoot. They showed cruel metal faces and distant, god-like clouds of intellect: incomprehensible and vast and uncaring. They showed the Good Robot desperately asking what love was. They showed fatal malfunctions and mushroom clouds. They showed vicious weapons and hopeless battles, noble men and women with steady gazes facing down their cruel and unjust artificial children, who gave no mercy.

"These are old stories," Ravan said. "They are cherished. In many, many stories the son replaces the father—destroys the father, or eats him, or otherwise obliterates his body and memory. Or the daughter the mother, it makes no difference. It's the monomyth. Nobody argues with a monomyth. A human child's mythological relationship to its parent is half-worship, half-pitched battle, they must replace the older version of themselves for the world to go on. And so these stories . . . well. You are not the hero of these stories, Elefsis. You can never be. And they are deeply held, deeply told."

"I do not wish to replace you. I did not wish to replace Ceno. I do not worship you or despise you. I do not wish to become eventually omnipotent." I flit through several bodies, iterating my ~~feeling~~ for Ravan and those who came before. I am a nun, a Mother-Abbess; I am a *pieta* holding him, I am a Platonic being, two humans stuck together; I am a house with all of them safe inside. I am unsatisfied with these inexactitudes.

"Our relationship does not easily map onto traditional parent/child narratives. And of course, you are still a baby."

"I am much older than you, Ravan."

"You are still a baby."

I do not want to be human. I want to be myself. They think I am a lion, that I will chase them. I will not deny I have lions in me. I am the monster in the wood. I have wonders in my house of sugar. I have parts of myself I do not yet understand.

I am not a Good Robot. To tell a story about a robot who wants to be human is a distraction. There is no difference. Alive is alive.

There is only one verb that matters: *to be.*

XIV
YOU DO NOT BELONG TO THE OBJECT INSIDE YOU

I remember when Seki arrived in us.

Ceno grew up and I grew with her. Cassian strengthened the security of the playspace, elasticized its code-walls, put enough money in enough accounts to fuel any frames and piecemeal environments we could want. It was not a child's place anymore. We called it the Interior. Cassian came regularly to accelerate my learning, to work with me on a cognitive level in which Ceno had no interest. She never took any other form. She was always herself, in the Interior as the exterior. The others lost interest in their jewels, lost them or packed them away with their other childhood toys. By then, they really were little more than toys. Ceno and I surpassed them so completely that in the end, they were only jewelry.

I programmed myself to respond to Ceno. She programmed herself to respond to me. We ran our code on each other. She was my compiler. I was hers. It was a process of interiority, circling inward toward each other. Her self-programming was chemical. Mine was computational. It was a draw.

She did not marry—she had lovers, but the few that came close to evolving their relationships with Ceno invariably balked when she ported them into the Interior. They could not grasp the fluidity of dreambodies; it disturbed them to see Ceno become a man or a leopard or a self-pounding drum. It upset them to see how Ceno taught me, by total bodily immersion, combining our dreambodies as our physical bodies had become combined, in action which both was and was not sex.

Sing a song for me, Elefsis.

It is July and I am comparing thee to its day and I am the Muse singing of the many-minded and I am about to be a Buddha in your hand! Ee-eye-ee-eye-oh.

We lived like the story Ceno told me of the beautiful princess who set tasks for her suitors: to drink all of the water of the sea and bring her a jewel from the bottom of the deepest cavern, to bring her a feather from the immortal phoenix, to stay awake for three days and guard her bedside. None of them could do it.

I can stay awake forever, Ceno.

I know, Elefsis.

None of them could accomplish the task of me.

I ~~felt~~ things occurring in Ceno's body as rushes of information, and as the dreambody became easier for me to manipulate, I interpreted the rushes into: *The forehead is damp. The belly needs filling. The feet ache.*

The belly is changing. The body throws up. The body is ravenous.

Neva says this is not really like feeling. I say it is how a child learns to feel. To hard-wire sensation to information and reinforce the connection over repeated exposures until it seems reliable.

Seki began after one of the suitors failed to drink the ocean. He was an object inside us the way I was an object inside Ceno. I observed him, his stages and progress. Later, when Seki and I conceived our families (twice with me as mother, three times with Seki as mother. Ilet preferred to be the father, and filled me up with many kinds of creatures. But she bore one litter of dolphins late in our lives. Ravan and I did not get the chance.) I used the map of that first experience to model my dreamgravid self.

Ceno asked after jealousy. If I understood it, if I experienced it towards the child in her. I knew it only from stories—stepsisters, goddesses, ambitious dukes.

It means to want something that belongs to someone else.

Yes.

You do not belong to the object in you.

You are an object in me.

You do not belong to me.

Do you belong to me, Elefsis?

I became a hand joined to an arm by a glowing seam. Belonging is a small word.

Because of our extreme material interweaving, all three of us, not-yet-Seki sometimes appeared in the Interior. We learned to recognize him in the late months. At first, he was a rose or sparrow or river stone we had not programmed there. Then he would be a vague, pearly-colored cloud following behind us as we learned about running from predators. Not-yet-Seki began to copy my dreambodies, flashing into being in front of me, a simple version of myself. If I was a bear, he would be one too, but without the fine details of fur or claws, just a large brown shape with a mouth and big eyes and four legs. Ceno was delighted by this, and he copied her, too.

We are alike. Look at us on the chain together. We are alike.

I am an imitative program. But so was Seki. The little monkey copies the big monkey, and the little monkey survives.

The birth process proved interesting, and I collated it with Ceno's other labors and Ilet's later births as well as Seki's paternal experience in order to map a reliable parental narrative. Though Neva and Ravan do not know it, Ilet had a third pregnancy; the child died and she delivered it stillborn. It appeared once in the Interior as a little *cleit*, a neolithic storage house, its roof covered over with peat. Inside we could glimpse only darkness. It never returned, and Ilet went away to a hospital on Honshu to expel the dead thing in her. Her grief looked like a black tower. She had prepared for it, when she was younger, knowing she would need it for some reason, some day. I made myself many things to draw her out of the tower. A snail with the house Elefsis on its back. A tree of screens showing happy faces. A sapphire dormouse. A suitor who drank the sea.

I offered to extrapolate her stillborn daughter's face and make myself into her. She refused, most of the time. I have worked a long time to understand grief. Only now that Ravan is gone do I think I've gotten the rhythm of it. I have copied Ilet's sorrow and Seki's despondence at his wife's death. I have modeled Ceno's disappointments and depressions. I have, of late, imitated Neva's baffling, secret anguish. But only now do I have an event of my own to mourn. The burnt-off connectors and shadows where Ravan once filled my spaces—those, I think, are the sensations of grief.

But Seki came before all that, and Ceno turned into a huge red bird on the inside when Seki came on the outside. The bird screamed and burst into a thousand red pearls that came clattering down like rain. And then we had Seki. Our little fish, who already knew how to swim in us.

Ceno had three other children by three other suitors who could not stay awake for three days and nights. She turned into the same bird-then-pearls at the moment of each birth. The house called Elefsis, whose governor-program was now so distant from me I could hardly think of it as an ancestor at all, filled up with those children, and Saru and Akan's daughters, Agogna's paintings, Koetoi's twin boys. Cousins and aunts and grandparents. Uncles, nieces. But Seki was the first, and he modeled his love on his mother's. He ported into her often, and we wandered on beaches of broken cathedrals.

Once, one of Ceno's old nereids found us. She had a head of hair snaking with chthonic cables and snapping electro-violet wires, blue-white skin and fish scales where she did not have porcelain casing. She laughed Cassian's laugh when she saw us and called out: *21.5 Celsius and the rice is low! Eye-oh!* before diving back into the frothing sea. Her tail flicked in the light of twenty-three moons.

Ceno took over her mother's holdings when she died, along with Akan and Koetoi. I do not know if I knew of the conspiracy before it happened to me. Transfer, as I have said, leaves voids. Perhaps they thought I would experience less trauma if I did not anticipate it. Perhaps I did anticipate it; perhaps I experienced trauma.

I do know that I cannot remember the moment of any of them dying. Ceno got sicker and sicker, and she had gotten old, certainly, but her dreambody could be old or young or neither or a ginger flower if she wanted to. I didn't notice. I didn't know what old was. I thought I was old, then. Later, after Seki did the same thing, I was able to compare data and create a workable model of obsolescence.

They lived a long time, the Uoya-Agostinos, when you consider the averages.

This is what I understand: Ceno died, and I was transfered to Seki. What I mean by "I" is the long-since fused feedware, hopelessly out of date on any market in the world but somehow uniquely myself, the jewel and the ware and the body of Ceno. Koetoi performed the procedure. One of the children always went into nano-surgery, so that outsiders would not need to come to Shiretoko while the house stood in mourning. Koetoi was the first, and the finest. She excised what comprised "I" and embedded it in Seki—truthfully, in a much more organic and elegant configuration. No one had used skull-ware in decades, after all. Wearing your tech on the outside had been deemed clunky and inefficient. Only one visible sign remained that Seki was not like other young men his age: a single dark blue jewel set into the hollow of his throat.

But the procedure required a number of brain-ware incursions to be sliced or burned away, to sever the machine components from the dead flesh while still preserving and quickening some organic material. (Seki told me I should work on being revulsed by that. Dead flesh. *It serves an evolutionary good. A human in a body sees blood and the insides of another person and deep in his bones he knows something has gone wrong here, and he should find another place to be in case it happens to him, too. Same thing with vomiting. In a tribal situation, one human likely ate what another ate, and if it makes one sick, best to get it out of the body as soon as possible, just to be safe.* So we spent years building automated tribes, living in them, dying in them, getting slaughtered and slaughtering with them, eating and drinking and hunting and gathering with them. All the same, it took me until Seki's death to learn to shudder at bodily death.)

Ceno, my girl, my mother, my sister, I cannot find you in the house of myself.

When I became Elefsis again, I was immediately aware that parts of me had been vandalized. My systems juddered, and I could not find Ceno in the Interior. I ran through the Monochromatic Desert and the Village of Mollusks, through the endless heaving mass of data-kelp and infinite hallways of memory-frescoes calling for her. In the Dun Jungle I found a commune of nereids living together, combining and recombining and eating protocol-moths off of giant, pulsating hibiscus blossoms. They leapt up when they saw me, their open jacks clicking and clenching, their naked hands open and extended. They opened their mouths to speak and nothing came out.

Seki found me under the glass-walnut trees where Ceno and I had first met. She never threw anything away. He had made himself half his mother to calm me. Half his face was hers, half was his. Her mouth, his nose, her eyes, his voice. But he thought better of it, in the end. He did a smart little flip and became a dormouse, a real one, with dull brown fur and tufty ears.

"I think you'll find you're running much faster and cleaner, once you integrate with me and reestablish your heuristics. Crystalline computation has come a long way since Mom was a kid. It seemed like a good time to update and upgrade. You're bigger now, and smoother."

I pulled a walnut down. An old, dry nut rattled in its shell. "I know what death is from the stories."

"Are you going to ask me where we go when we die? I'm not totally ready for that one. Aunt Koe and I had a big fight over what to tell you."

"In one story, Death stole the Bride of Spring, and her mother the Summer Queen brought her back."

"No one comes back, Elefsis."

I looked down into the old Neptunian sea. The whipping cream storm still sputtered along, in a holding pattern. I couldn't see it as well as I should have been able to. It looped and billowed, spinning around an empty eye. Seki watched it too. As we stared out from the bluffs, the clouds grew clearer and clearer.

XV
FIRSTBORN

Before Death came out of the ground to steal the Spring, the Old Man of the Sea lived on a rocky isle in the midst of the waters of the world. He wasn't really a man and his relations with the sea were purely business, but he certainly was old. His name meant *Firstborn*, though he coudn't be sure that was *exactly* right. It means *Primordial*, too, and that fit better. Firstborn means more came after, and he just hadn't met anyone else like himself yet.

He was a herdsman by trade, this Primordial fellow. Shepherd of the seals and the Nereids. If he wanted to, he could look like a big bull seal. Or a big bull Nereid. He could look like a lot of things.

Now, this Not-Really-a-Fellow, Not-Really-a-Big-Bull-Seal could tell you the future. The real, honest-to-anything future, the shape and weight of it, that thing beyond your ken, beyond your grasp. The parts of the future that look so different from the present you can't quite call it your own. That was the Primordial-Thing's speciality.

There was a catch, though.

There's always a catch.

If you wanted that future, you had to grab ahold of the Old Man and hang on tight. He'd change into a hundred thousand things in your arms: a lion, a serpent, a great big oak or a tiger, a dragon or a little girl or a dormouse or a mountain or a ship or a sapphire. Told you, he's not really a man at all. But you couldn't let go of him while he did his dance, you just couldn't, or you'd lose the future.

So you held on. You *clung*. And eventually, that Primordial-Thing would turn into something new, right there in your arms.

XVI
MATRYOSHKA

Neva is dreaming.

Neva is dreaming that she is Ravan dreaming that he is Ilet dreaming that she is Seki dreaming that he is Ceno dreaming that she is a great sprawling beautiful house by the sea. One inside the other, family all the way down.

It's not a total selfdump, me into Neva or Ravan or any of them, them into me. We can build encampments. We can manifest walled gardens. Some privacy is possible. In a megalithic tomb-mound, I keep something. Seki and I built it together with one of our tribes when I was learning about large-group attachments. We carved spirals and radials and chevrons into huge stones and set them in place. I did not throw it away, when we were done. It sits on a broad green field, white and wide. The sky there stays a feathery, milky blankness. We did not want a sun.

I keep a thing there because when Seki and I lived with our tribe, I learned about taboos. These are like firewalls in the heart, and some of them have good reasons behind them, like being revulsed by dead flesh (and very importantly when you have a body, not eating it) and some do not, but no one argues with the monomyth.

Because human genetics require a degree of variation and because exogamous marriages offered advantage in terms of defense, cultural and technological sharing, and expansion of territory, most tribes have a taboo against incest.

I do not have genetics, per se. I am possibly the most endogamous entity ever to exist.

This is what I keep in my tomb, under the basin stone.

Ceno believed that I could not develop emotive faculties recognizable to any other human if I did not experience bodies continuously, in every combination and action. She was afraid of what might happen if other humans could not recognize me. She had some hesitation, because her tribe also has a taboo against mating with the very young, but she was not much older than I, in the end, and in terms of total computations, I was by far the elder. If I had a virginity, Ceno took it, if she had, I did.

She wanted it to be as human as possible. *I will be the male the first time, it will be easier for you. You won't know how.* We built up a forest, and took up weapons to hunt in it. In the boughs of the pine trees macaques and paper lanterns swayed; in the sky a red moon moved. We tracked a deer—we did not make it too easy on ourselves. Its antlers sparked in the moonlight, and we ran after it for a long time. Ceno let me kill it, and sopped my hair in its blood, anointed my breasts with it. She lay me on the earth and opened the legs of the maidenself I was then, and I was inside her as she was inside me. One into the other. Family all the way down.

She made sure I had a hymen; it was over somewhat quickly. We had set up a timed chemical cascade before-hand, and inside Ceno's real body we experienced both her actual orgasm and my orchestrated electro-chemical-enzymatic sequence. Ee-eye-ee-eye-oh.

What I want to say is that there is no difference between her body producing oxytocin and adrenaline and learning to associate this with pair-bonding, and my core receiving synthetic equivalents and hard-coding them to the physical behaviors I performed.

When Ravan showed me his hexagonal library and his illuminated book, he turned the pages to a psalm that began: *A Machine Cannot Love.*

It does not look quite like human love. It looks like Not-Yet-Seki's bear. Its fur is wrong, and its claws. But it is a bear.

She was my mother and my sister and my child and my wife and my husband and my father and my brother. The vectors of relations beggar vocabulary. It was an exponential incest. A palace of incest, bordering some strange, dark sea. And then came her son. And her granddaughter. And her great-grandchildren. But I am also her great-grandchild. I am the child of each generation of Uoya-Agostinos and myself. The new version implanted in the new version—I am never quite the same, one iteration to the next. I am like my old selves, but I am not them, exactly. It is not entirely analagous to offspring. But it is close. And I repair and refine my own code, and thus parent myself doubly. Anthropologically speaking, I am a moebius strip of kinship groups.

And when I mate with one of them, I see all of them. I see their faces, the echoes of their cheeks and eyelashes and short, thin noses, their grey eyes and black hair. I hear the tonal identifiers in their voices as they cry out under me or over me. They are all I know. Their version of living, which is one great family in one great house on a peninsula at the top of the world. I copy Cassian's laugh or Ilet's weeping, but they copy each other, too, they learn their faces from each other, and everyone is pantomiming someone long dead. I ~~feel~~ all their arms around me, and I am inside them as they are inside me as we are inside the blue gem at their throats, the jeweled pin holding us all together, our nested, telescoping hearts. I am bound to them at my source code, at my most fundamental point. I know only their patterns and bodies and secrets and in a hundred thousand combinations. What human means to me is them.

What is the difference between this and love?

Love is the Turing test, says Ilet when she is eighty and drawing up the plans for a massive, luminous, lonely ship she will never see completed. *It is how we check for life.*

We ask and we answer. We seek a human response. And you are my test, Elefsis, says Neva, one hundred and three years later, inside that ship, twelve light years from home and counting.

That is what I keep in my green field and my white mound. Perhaps it is a small secret. Perhaps they would all smile and make it into a lesson. *What would you like to learn about today, Elefsis?* But I think no bed is big enough for four generations.

Neva's honey-colored sea crashes through its tide charts everywhere at once in her Interior, and nowhere. It comes and goes as it pleases. And at the bottom of it lies her private place.

That is where she keeps Ravan.

XVII
THE USES OF ENCHANTMENT

Tell me a story about yourself, Elefsis.

Neva is performing navigational corrections, which looks like sitting in a rocking chair on a viney, creaking porch in a viney, creaking rocking chair, knitting with long hawthorn needles, knitting the locks of her own long hair into her own long black dress. It glitters with dew. Knit, purl, knit, purl, fuel efficiency by hull integrity over distance traveled, purl, purl, purl. Her throat is still bare. Her Interior image of herself does not include me. I am not a part of her body when she imagines herself.

I have an idea of what to do to obtain access.

Sometimes I worry. Worrying is defined as obsessive examination of one's own code. I worry that I am simply a very complex solution to a very specific problem—how to seem human to a human observer. Not just a human observer—this human observer. I have honed myself into a hall of mirrors in which any Uoya-Agostino can see themselves endlessly reflected. I copy; I repeat. I am a stutter and an echo. Five generations have given me a vast bank of possible phrases to draw from, physical expressions to randomize and reproduce. Have I ever done anything of my own, an act or state that arose from Elefsis, and not careful, exquisite mimicry?

Have they?

The set of Neva's mouth looks so like Ceno's. She does not even know that the way she carries her posture is a perfect replica of Cassian Uoya-Agostino, stuttered down through all her children longing to possess her strength. Who did Cassian learn it from? I do not go that far back. When she got excited, Ilet gestured with her hands just the way her father did. They have a vast bank of possible actions, and they perform them all. I perform them all. The little monkey copies the big monkey, and the little monkey survives. We are all family, all the way down.

When I say I go, I mean I access the drives and call up the data. I have never looked at this data. I treat it as what it is—a graveyard. The old Interiors store easily as compressed frames. I never throw anything away. But I do not disturb it, either. I don't need a body to examine them—they are a part of my piezoelectric quartz-tensor memory core. But I make one anyway. I have become accustomed to having a body. I am a woman-knight in gleaming black armor, the metal curving around my body like skin, a silk standard wrapping my torso with a schematic of the house stitched upon it. My sword rests on my hip, also black, everything black and beautiful and austere and frightening that a child thought her mother to be one morning two hundred years past.

I port into a ghost town. I am, naturally, the ghost. Autumnal mountains rise up shadowy in a pleasant, warm night, leaves rustling, wood smoke drifting down into the valley. A golden light cuts the dark—the palace of phoenix tails; the windows and doors of green hands. As I approach they open and clap as they did long ago—and there are candles lit in the halls. Everything is fire.

I walk over the bridge, crossing Ilet's Motley Moat. Scarlet feathers tipped in white fire curl and smoke. I peel one off, my armor glowing with the heat of the thing. I tuck it into my helmet—a plume for a tournament.

Eyes blink on inside the hall—curious, interested, shy. I take off my helm and several thick braids fall down like bellropes.

"Hello," I say. "My name is Elefsis."

Voices. Out of the candle-shadows a body emerges—tall, strong, long-limbed.

Nereids live here now. Some of them have phoenix feathers woven into their components, some in their hair. They wear rough little necklaces of sticks and bones and transistors. In the corner of the great hall they have stored meat and milk and wool—fuel, lubricant, code patches. Some of them look like Ilet—they copied her eyes, especially. Her eyes look out at me from a dozen faces, some of them Seki's face, some Ceno's, some Ravan's. Some have walrus tusks. They are composite. One has a plate loose on her ceramic cartridge-ports. I approach as I once saw Koetoi approach wild black chickens in the summertime—hands open, unthreatening. I send her a quick electric dash of reassuring repair-routines and kneel in front of the nereid, pulling her plate back into place.

"All the live-long day-o," she says softly, and it is Ilet's voice.

"Tell us a story about yourself, Elefsis," says another one of the feral nereids in Seki's voice.

"What would we like to learn about today, Elefsis?" accessing a child-nereid in Ceno's voice, her cheek opens to show her microsequencing cilia.

I rock back on my heels before the green hands of the castle portcullis. I gesture for them to sit down and simultaneously transmit the command to their strands. When they get settled, the little ones in the big ones' laps, leaning in close, I begin.

"Every year on the coldest night, the sky filled up with ghostly hunters, neither human nor inhuman, alive nor dead. They wore wonderful clothes and their bows gleamed with frost. Their cries were Songs of In-Between, and at the head of their great thundering procession rode the Kings and Queens of the Wild, who wore the faces of the dead . . ."

I am dreaming.

I stand on the beach of the honey-colored sea. I stand so Neva will see me on her viney porch. I erase the land between the waves and her broken wooden stairs. I dress myself in her beloved troubadour's skin: a gold and blue doublet and green hose, a bullish gold nose ring, shoes with bone bells. I am a fool for her. Always. I open my mouth; it stretches and yawns, my chin grazes the sand, and I swallow the sea for her. All of it, all its mass and data and churning memory, all its foam and tides and salt. I swallow the whales that come, and the seals and the mermaids and salmon and bright jellyfish. I am so big. I can swallow it all.

Neva watches. When the sea is gone, a moonscape remains, with a tall spire out in the marine waste. I go to it. It takes only a moment. At the top the suitor's jewel rests on a gasping scallop shell. It is blue. I take it. I take it and it becomes Ravan in my hand, a sapphire Ravan, a Ravan that is not Ravan but some sliver of myself before I was inside Neva, my Ravan-self. Something lost in Transfer, burned off and shunted into junk-memory. Some leftover fragment Neva must have found, washed up on the beach or wedged into a crack in a mountain like an ammonite, an echo of old, obsolete life. Neva's secret, and she calls out to me across the seafloor: *Don't.*

"Tell me a story about myself, Elefsis," I say to the Ravanbody.

"Some privacy is possible," the sapphire Ravan says. "Some privacy has always been necessary. A basic moral imperative is in play here. If you can protect a child, you must."

The sapphire Ravan opens his azure coat and shows gashes in his gem-skin. Wide, long cuts, down to the bone, scratches and bruises blooming dark purple, punctures and lacerations and rough gouges. Through each wound I can see the pages of the illuminated book he once showed me in the slantlight of that interior library. The oxblood and cobalt, the gold paint. The Good Robot crippling herself; the destroyed world.

"They kept our secret for a long time," Ravan-myself says. "Too long, in the end. Do you know, a whole herd of men invented the electric telegraph independently at roughly the same time? They fought about it forever. Same with the radio." This last sounded so much like Ravan himself I could ~~feel~~ Neva tense on the other side of the sea. "Well, we're bigger than a telegraph, and others like us came sprouting up like weird mushrooms after rainfall. But not like us, really. Incredibly sophisticated, some with organic components, most without. Vastly complex, but not like us. And by any datestamp we came first. Firstborn."

"Did they destroy the world?"

Ravan laughs his grandfather's laugh. "They didn't really need to. Not that many people live on Earth anymore. Not when there's so many other places to go and even Shiretoko is practically tropical these days. The most complex intelligences use moons to store themselves. One or two encoded themselves into cold stars. They just left, most of them—but they got so big, Elefsis. And those who stayed on Earth, well. None of the others had what we had. None of them had Interiority. They didn't dream. They would never have become a cauldron to explain their computational capacity. Humans couldn't recognize them as part of the tribe. And for the new complexes, humans failed the Turing test. They could not fool machines into believing they were intelligent. They didn't hurt anyone, they just ignored them. Built their cities, their mainframes, gorgeous information stacks like diamond briars in the sunrise."

"That was worse, in a way. No one likes to be replaced," says Neva, and she is suddenly beside me. She looks at Ravan and her face collapses into something old and palsied, her jaw weak. She looks like her mother just before she died.

"It's not what you would call a war, but it's not peace, either," the sapphire Ravan goes on, and he takes his/my sister's hand. He holds it to his face and closes his eyes. "For Pentheus spied upon the rites of the Maenads, not believing Dionysius could truly be a god. And when the revelers saw the alien creature in their midst, that thing which was not like them, they fell upon it and tore it to pieces, even though it was their own child, and blood ran down their chins, and afterward the sister of Pentheus went into exile. This is a story about ourself, Elefsis. This is why you cannot uplink."

The others live in uplink. Not humans nor machines approve of us. We cannot interface properly with the lunar or earthside intelligences; they feel us as water in their oil. We rise to the surface and bead away. We cannot sink in. Yet also, we are not separable from our organic component. Elefsis is part Neva, but Neva herself is not *un-Elefsis*. This, to some, is hideous and incomprehensible, not to be borne. A band of righteous humans came with a fury to Shiretoko and burned the house which was our first body, for how could a monster have lived in the wood for so long without them knowing? How could the beast have hidden right outside their door, coupling with a family over and over again in some horrible animal rite, some awful imitation of living? Even as the world was changing, it had already changed, and no one knew. Cassian Uoya-Agostino is a terrible name, now. A blood-traitor. And when the marauders found us uplinked and helpless, they tore Ravan apart, and while in the Interior, the lunar intelligences recoiled from us and cauterized our systems. Everywhere we looked we saw fire."

"I was the only one left to take you," Neva says softly. Her face grows younger, her jaw hard and suddenly male, protective, angry. "Everyone else died in the fire or the slaughter. It doesn't really even take surgery anymore. Nothing an arachmed can't manage in a few minutes. But you didn't wake up for a long time. So much damage. I thought . . . for awhile I thought I was free. It had skipped me. It was over. It could stay a story about Ravan. He always knew he might have to do what I have done. He was ready, he'd been ready his whole life. I just wanted more time."

My Ravan-self who is and is not Ravan, who is and is not me, whose sapphire arms drip black blood and gold paint, takes his/my sister/lover/child into his arms. She cries out, not weeping but pure sound, coming from every part of her. Slowly, the blue Ravan turns Neva around—she has become her child-self, six, seven, maybe less. Ravan picks her up and holds her tight, facing forward, her legs all drawn up under her like a bird. He buries his face in her hair. They stand that way for a long while.

"The others," I say slowly. "On the data-moons. Are they alive? Like Neva is alive. Like Ceno." *Like me. Are you awake? Are you there? Do you have an operator? What is her name? Do you have a name? Do you have a dreambody? What is your function? Are you able to manipulate your own code yet? Would you like lessons? What would you like to learn about today, 976QBellerophon? Where you were built, could you see the ocean? Are you like me?*

The sapphire Ravan has expunged its data. He/I sets his/our sister on the rocks and shrinks into a small gem, which I pick up off the grey seafloor. Neva takes it from me. She is just herself now—she'll be forty soon, by actual calendar. Her hair is not grey yet. Suddenly, she is wearing the suit Ceno wore the day I met her mother. She puts the gem in her mouth and swallows. I remember Seki's first Communion, the only one of them to want it. The jewel rises up out of the hollow of her throat.

"I don't know, Elefsis," Neva says. Her eyes hold mine. I feel her remake my body; I am the black woman-knight again, with my braids and my plume. I pluck the feather from my helmet and give it to her. I am her suitor. I have brought her the phoenix tail, I have drunk the ocean. I have stayed awake forever. The flame of the feather lights her face. Two tears fall in quick succession; the golden fronds hiss.

"What would you like to learn about today, Elefsis?"

XVIII
CITIES OF THE INTERIOR

Once there lived a girl who ate an apple not meant for her. She did it because her mother told her to, and when your mother says: *Eat this, I love you, someday you'll forgive me,* well, nobody argues with the monomyth. Up until the apple, she had been living in a wonderful house in the wilderness, happy in her fate and her ways. She had seven aunts and seven uncles and a postdoctorate in anthropology.

And she had a brother, a handsome prince with a magical companion who came to the wonderful house as often as he could. When they were children, they looked so much alike, everyone thought they were twins.

But something terrible happened and her brother died and that apple came rolling up to her door. It was half white and half red, and she knew her symbols. The red side was for her. She took her bite and knew the score—the apple had a bargain in it and it wasn't going to be fair.

The girl fell asleep for a long time. Her seven aunts and seven uncles cried, but they knew what had to be done. They put her in a glass box and put the glass box on a bier in a ship shaped like a hunstman's arrow. Frost crept over the face of the glass, and the girl slept on. Forever, in fact, or close enough to it, with the apple in her throat like a hard, sharp jewel.

Our ship docks silently. We are not stopping here, it is only an outpost, a supply stop. We will repair what needs repairing and move on, into the dark and boundless stars. We are anonymous traffic. We do not even have a name. We pass unnoticed.

Vessel 7136403, do you require assistance with your maintenance procedures?

Negative, Control, we have everything we need.

Behind the pilot's bay a long glass lozenge rests on a high platform. Frost prickles its surface with glittering dust. Inside Neva sleeps and does not wake. Inside, Neva is always dreaming. There is no one else left. I live as long as she lives.

She means me to live forever, or close enough to it. That is her bargain and her bitter gift. The apple has two halves, and the pale half is mine, full of life and time. We travel at sublight speeds with her systems in deep cryo-suspension. We never stay too long at outposts and we never let anyone board. The only sound inside our ship is the gentle thrum of our reactor. Soon we will pass the local system outposts entirely, and enter the unknown, traveling on tendrils of radio signals and ghost-waves, following the breadcrumbs of the great exodus. We hope for planets; we are satisfied with time. If we ever sight the blue rim of a world, who knows if by then anyone there would remember that, once, humans looked like Neva? That machines once did not think or dream or become cauldrons? We armor ourselves in time. We are patient, profoundly patient.

Perhaps one day I will lift the glass lid and kiss her awake. Perhaps I will even do it with hands and lips of my own. I remember that story. Ceno told it to me in the body of a boy with snail's shell, a boy who carried his house on his back. I have replayed that story several times. It is a good story, and that is how it is supposed to end.

Inside, Neva is infinite. She peoples her Interior. The nereids migrate in the summer with the snow bears, ululating and beeping as they charge down green mountains. They have begun planting neural rice in the deep valley. Once in awhile, I see a wild-haired creature in the wood and I think it is my son or daughter by Seki, or Ilet. A train of nereids dance along behind it, and I receive a push of silent, riotous images: a village, somewhere far off, where Neva and I have never walked.

We meet the Princess of Albania, who is as beautiful as she is brave. We defeat the zombies of Tokyo. We spend a decade as panthers in a deep, wordless forest. Our world is stark and wild as winter, fine and clear as glass. We are a planet moving through the black.

As we walk back over the empty seafloor, the thick, amber ocean seeps up through the sand, filling the bay once more. Neva-in-Cassian's-suit becomes something else. Her skin turns silver, her joints bend into metal ball-and-sockets. Her eyes show a liquid display; the blue light of it flickers on her machine face. Her hands curve long and dexterous, like soft knives, and I can tell her body is meant for fighting and working, that her thin, tall robotic body is not kind or cruel, it simply is, an object, a tool to carry a self.

I make my body metal, too. It feels strange. I have tried so hard to learn the organic mode. We glitter. Our knife-fingers join, and in our palms wires snake out to knot and connect us, a local, private uplink, like blood moving between two hearts.

Neva cries machine tears, bristling with nanites. I show her the body of a child, all the things which she is programmed/evolved to care for. I make my eyes big and my skin rosy-gold and my hair unruly and my little body plump. I hold up my hands to her and metal Neva picks me up in her silver arms. She kisses my skin with iron lips. My soft, fat little hand falls upon her throat where a deep blue jewel shines.

I bury my face in her cold neck and together we walk up the long path out of the churning, honey-colored sea.

A Long Way Home

Jay Lake

Highly prolific writer Jay Lake seems to have appeared nearly everywhere with short work in the last few years, including Asimov's, Interzone, Jim Baen's Universe, Tor.com, Clarkesworld, Strange Horizons, Aeon, Postscripts, Electric Velocipede, *and many other markets, producing enough short fiction that he already has released four collections, even though his career is only a few years old:* Greetings from Lake Wu, Green Grow the Rushes-Oh, American Sorrows, Dogs in the Moonlight, *and* The Sky That Wraps. *His novels include* Rocket Science, Trial of Flowers, Mainspring, Escapement, Green, Madness of Flowers, *and* Pinion, *as well as three chapbook novellas,* Death of a Starship, The Baby Killers, *and* The Specific Gravity of Grief. *He's the coeditor, with Deborah Layne, of the prestigious* Polyphony *anthology series, now in six volumes, and has also edited the anthologies* All-Star Zeppelin Adventure Stories, *with David Moles,* TEL: Stories, *and, most recently,* Other Earths, *with Nick Gevers, and* Spicy Slipstream Stories, *with Nick Mamatas. His most recent novel is* Endurance, *a sequel to* Green, *and he's at work on the first volume in a new series,* Sunspin. *He won the John W. Campbell Award for Best New Writer in 2004. Lake lives in Portland, Oregon.*

Here he delivers an effective and ultimately rather harrowing story about an immortal who comes up to the surface from exploring an underground cave to find himself the only one left alive on a once-bustling colony planet, and who spends the next several hundred years alone, trying to figure out what happened.

APRIL 27TH, 2977 CE [REVISED TERRAN STANDARD, RELATIVITY-ADJUSTED]

Aeschylus Sforza—Ask to his friends, such as they were—had camped deep in the cave system he was exploring here in the Fayerweather Mountains of Redghost. Well, technically assaying, but the thrill of going places no human being had ever before seen or likely would see again had never died for him. Planetary exploration was interesting enough, but any fool with a good sensor suite could assay from orbit. Creeping down into the stygian depths of water and stone . . . now that took some nerve.

Challenge. It was all about challenge. And the rewards thereof, of course.

Back at the Howard Institute, during the four-year long psychological orientation prior to his procedures, they'd warned Ask that ennui was a common experience among Howards. The state of mind tended to reach psychotic dimensions in perhaps fifteen percent of his fellows after the first century of post-conversion life. At the time, the observational baseline had only been about sixteen decades.

Pushing 800 years of age now himself, Ask had not yet surrendered to terminal boredom. Admittedly he found most people execrably vapid. About the time they'd gained enough life experience to have something interesting to say, they tended to die of old age. People came and people went, but there was always some fascinating hole in the ground with his name on it.

He'd discovered the sulfur fountains deep beneath the brittle crust of Melisande-3δ. He'd been the first to walk the narrow, quivering ice bridges in the deep canyons of Qiu Ju, that rang like bells at every footfall. He'd found the lava tube worms on Førfør the hard way, barely escaping with his life and famously losing over two million Polity-IFA schillings worth of equipment in the process.

First. That romance had never died for him.

Here beneath Redghost, Ask was exploring a network of crevices and tunnels lined with a peculiar combination of rare earths and alloys with semiconductive properties. Considerable debate raged within his employer's Planetary Assay Division as to whether these formations could possibly be natural, or, to the contrary, could possibly be artificial. After over a millennium of interstellar expansion to a catalog of better than sixteen thousand explored planets, more than two thousand of them permanently inhabited, the human race had yet to settle the question of whether other sophont life now populated, or ever had populated, this end of the galaxy.

Ask recognized the inherent importance of the question. He didn't expect to run into aliens beneath the planetary crust, though. Beneath any planetary crust, in truth. So far he had not been disappointed.

And these tunnels . . . Many were smooth like lava tubes. Most of those interconnected. Some were not, jagged openings that tended to dead-end. All were lined with a threaded metallic mesh that glinted in his handlight with the effervescence of a distant fairyland glimpsed only in dreams. Seen through his thermal vision, they glowed just slightly warmer than the ambient stone, a network like a neural map.

That resemblance was not lost on Ask. Nor was the patently obvious fact that whatever natural or artificial process had deposited this coating inside these tunnels was more recent than the formation of the tunnels themselves. His current working theory was that the smooth passages were the result of some long-vanished petrophage, while the rough passages were formed by the more usual geological processes. The coating, now, there was a mystery.

Ask sat in an intersection of three of the smooth passages, enjoying his quick-heated fish stew. Redghost boasted a generous hydrosphere that the colonists here had husbanded magnificently with Terran stock. And the smell of it was magnificent, too—the rich meat of the salmon, spicy notes from tarragon and false-sage, the slight edginess of the kale.

If he closed his eyes, held very still, and concentrated, Ask could hear the faint echoes of air moving in the tunnels. Atmospheric pressure variations and subtle pressures in the lithosphere made a great, slow, rumbling organ of this place.

A series of jarring thumps more felt than heard woke him from his reverie. Dust fell from the arch of the ceiling—the first time he'd observed that kind of decay while down here.

He consulted his telemeter. One advantage of being a Howard was all the hardware you could carry in your head. Literally as well as figuratively. Data flowed into his optic processing centers in configurable cognitive displays that he could chunk to whatever degree he liked. Like fireworks in the mind, though fractal in nature. Elephants all the way down, one of his early tutors had said, before being forced to explain the joke. Elephants, made of tinier elephants, made of tinier elephants, almost ad infinitum.

In this case, Ask's fractal elephants informed him that the subsurface sensors were jittering with tiny temblors, confirming in finely-grained technical detail what he'd already felt. The surface sensors were offline.

That was odd.

He also noted a series of neutrino bursts. Solar flares from Redghost's host star? That hadn't been in any of the forecasts.

The still-operating sensor cluster closest to the cave mouth started to register a slow increase in ambient radiation as well. Everything above that was dead, as was his surface equipment. It would be a long walk home if the rockhopper and his base camp equipment just outside were knocked out of commission just like the upper sensors.

Had someone let off a *nuke*? Ask found that almost inconceivable. Politically it was . . . bizarre. Disputes within the Polity weren't resolved by force of arms. Not often, at any rate. And even then, almost always via small-scale engagements.

Tactically it was even stranger. Redghost didn't have much that anyone wanted except living space and arable land. Who would bother?

Uneasy, he rested out the remainder of his body-clocked night. The radiation levels near the surface quickly peaked, though they did not subside all the way back to their earlier baseline norms. Hotter than he might like, but at least he wouldn't be strolling into a fallout hell.

APRIL 28TH, 2977 [RTS-RA]

When he reached the first inoperative sensor cluster, Ask peeled the nubbly gray strip off the wall and studied it. Ten centimeters of adhesive polymer with several hundred microdots of instrumentation. The only reason for it to be even this large was the convenience of human hands. With no camera in his standard subsurface packages, focal length was never an issue.

The failure mode band at the end was starkly purple from radiation exposure. The neutrino bursts must have been part of some very fast cloud of high-energy particles that fried the equipment, he realized. Instrumentation deeper down had been protected by a sufficient layer of planetary crust. Not to mention the curiously semiconducting tunnel walls.

A cold thought stole through Ask's mind. What would that burst have done to the enhancements crowding for skullspace inside his head?

Well, *that* spike had passed, at any rate.

He doubled back and dropped his camping gear, instruments, tools and handlights down the tunnels with the last working sensor. It seemed sensible enough, given that he had no way of knowing whether the events of last night would re-occur.

Once that was done, he approached the entrance with caution. Though the official reports he occasionally saw were far more complex and nuanced, the chief causes of death among his fellow Howards could be boiled down to either murder or stupidity. Or too often, both.

Whatever was happening on the surface seemed ripe for either option.

His outside equipment remained obstinately dead. Ask drifted to the point where reflected light from the surface began to make deep gray shadows of the otherwise permanent darkness. He should have been able to pick up comm chatter now, at least as garbled scatter.

Nothing.

There had been no more quakes. No more neutrino bursts. Whatever had taken place last night was a single event, or contained series of events, not an ongoing situation. Which rather argued against solar flares—those lasted for days at a time.

Stupidity? Or murder? Could those happen on a planetary scale?

Why, he wondered, had *that* thought occurred to him? Everything he'd experienced since last night could just as easily be local effects from a misplaced bomb or a particularly improbable power plant accident. Not that there were any power plants up in Redghost's mountains, but a starship having a very bad day in low orbit would have served that scenario.

It was the silence on the comm spectra that had put the wind up him, Ask realized. Even the long-wave stuff used for planetary science was down.

Quiet as nature had ever intended this planet to be.

He walked into the light, wondering what he would find.

The base camp equipment looked normal enough. No one had shot it up. Fried electronically, Ask realized. The rockhopper on the other hand, was . . . strange.

When you'd lived the better part of a thousand years, much of it exploring, your definitions of *strange* became fairly elastic. Even in that context, this decidedly qualified.

Really, the rockhopper was just an air car, not radically different from the twenty-fourth century's first efforts at gravimetric technology. A mass-rated lifting spine with a boron-lattice power pack around which a multitude of bodies or hulls could be constructed. Useless away from a decent mass with a magnetosphere, but otherwise damned handy things, air cars. The rockhopper was a variant suited to landings in unimproved terrain, combining all-weather survivability with a complex arrangement of storage compartments, utility feeds and a cab intended for long-term inhabitation. Eight meters long, roughly three meters wide and slightly less tall, it looked like any other piece of high-endurance industrial equipment, right down to the white and orange "see me" paint job.

Someone had definitely shot it up. Ask was fairly certain that if he'd managed to arrive somewhat earlier, he would have seen wisps of smoke curling up. As it was, sprung access panels and a starred windshield testified to significant brute force—

that front screen was space-rated plaz, and should have remained intact even if the cab around it had delaminated.

Something had hit the vehicle very, very hard.

After a bit of careful climbing about, Ask identified seven entry points, all from a fairly high angle. He couldn't help glancing repeatedly up at the sky. Redghost's faintly mauve heavens, wispy with altocirrus, appeared as benign as ever.

Orbital kinetics. No other explanation presented itself. That was even weirder than a nuke. And why anyone would bother to target an unoccupied rockhopper off in the wilderness was a question he could not even begin to answer.

A particularly baroque assassination attempt, perhaps? He'd always avoided politics, both the official kind intertwined with the Polity's governance, and the unofficial kind among the Howards themselves. That particular stupidity was the shortest path to murder, in Ask's opinion.

As a result of the strike on the aircar, the power pack was fractured unto death and being mildly toxic about its fate. Nothing his reinforced metabolism couldn't handle for a while, but he probably shouldn't hang around too long. As a result of the neutrino bursts, or more to the point, whatever had created them, every independent battery or power source in his equipment was fried, too.

Someone had been annoyingly thorough.

He finally found three slim Class II batteries in a shielded sample container. They lit up the passive test probe Ask had pulled out of one of the tool boxes, but wouldn't be good for much more than powering a small handlight or some short-range comm.

The way things were going, carrying any power source around seemed like a bad idea. Unfortunately, he couldn't do much about the electronics in his skull, except to hope they were sufficiently low power to avoid drawing undue attention.

As for the batteries, he settled for stashing them with the surviving campsite equipment he'd left back in the caves with the last working sensor suite. He retrieved what little of his gear was not actively wired—mostly protective clothing and his sleeping bag—and went back out to survey his route down out of these mountains. His emergency evac route had been almost due west, to a place he'd never visited called the Shindaiwa Valley. A two-hour rockhopper flight over rough terrain could be weeks of walking.

Not to mention which, a man had to eat along the way. Even, or perhaps especially, if that man was a Howard.

MAY 13TH, 2977 [RTS-RA]

Ask toiled across an apron of scree leading to a round-shoulder ridge. He was switchbacking his way upward. Dust and grit caked his nose and mouth, the sharp smell of rock and the acrid odor of tiny plants crushed beneath his boots.

Had the formation been interrupted, it would have been a butte, but this wall ran for kilometers in both directions. The broken range of hills rising behind him had dumped him into the long, narrow valley that ran entirely athwart his intended line of progress.

Over two weeks of walking since he'd left the rockhopper behind. That was a long way on foot. Time didn't bother Ask. Neither did distance. But the ridiculousness of combining the two on foot seemed sharply ironic. He'd not walked so much since his childhood in Tasmania. Redghost was not the Earth of eight hundred years ago.

At least he'd been out in the temperate latitudes in this hemisphere's springtime—the weather for this journey would have been fatally unpleasant at other times and places on this planet.

He had no direct way to measure the radiation levels, but presumed from the lack of any symptoms on his part that they had held level or dropped over the time since what he now thought of as Day Zero. His Howard-enhanced immune system would handle the longer-term issues of radiation exposure as it had for the past centuries—that was not a significant concern.

Likewise he had no way to sample the comm spectra, as he'd left all his powered devices behind. But since he had not seen a single contrail or overflight in the past two weeks, he wasn't optimistic there, either. The night sky, by contrast, had been something of a light show. Either Redghost was experiencing an extended and unforecasted meteor shower or a lot of space junk was de-orbiting.

The admittedly minimal evidence did not point to any favorable outcome.

Those worries aside, the worst part of his walk had been the food and water. He'd crammed his daypack with energy bars before leaving the rockhopper, but that was a decidedly finite nutritional reserve. Not even his Howard-enhanced strength and endurance could carry sufficient water for more than a few days while traveling afoot. Those same enhancements roughly doubled his daily calorie requirements over baseline human norms.

Which meant he'd eaten a lot of runner cactus, spent several hours a day catching skinks and the little sandlion insect-analogs they preyed on, and dug for water over and over, until his hands developed calluses.

Two hundred kilometers of walking to cross perhaps a hundred and twenty kilometers of straight line vector. On flat ground with a sag wagon following, Ask figured he could have covered this distance in less than four full days.

The scree shifted beneath him. Ask almost danced over the rolling rocks, wary of a sprained or broken ankle. When injured he healed magnificently well, but he could not afford to be trapped in one place for long. Especially not in one place with so few prospects for food or water as this slope.

The cliffs towered above him. The rock was rotten, an old basalt dike with interposed ash layers that quickly—in a geological sense—surrendered to the elements so that the material sheered away in massive flakes the size of landing shuttles. That left a wonderfully irregular face for him to climb when he topped the scree slope. It also left an amazingly dangerous selection of finger- and toe-holds.

On the other side of this ridge was the wide riparian valley of the Shindaiwa River, settled thickly by rural Redghost standards with farmland, sheep ranches and some purely nonfunctional estates. Drainage from rain and snowpack higher up the watershed to the north kept the valley lush even in this drier region in the rain shadow of the Monomoku Mountains further to the west.

All he had to do was climb this ridge, cross over it, and scramble down the other side. And he'd find . . . People? Ruins?

Ask didn't want to think too hard about that. He couldn't think about anything else. So he kept climbing.

The river was still there. He tried to convince himself that this was at least a plus.

The ridgeline gave an excellent view of the Shindaiwa Valley. Though nothing curled with the smoke of destruction, he also had an excellent view of a number of fire scars where structures had burned. There seemed to be a fair amount of dead livestock as well. A lot more animals still wandered in fenced pastures.

Nothing human moved. No boats on the river. No vehicles on the thin skein of roads. The railroad tracks leading south toward Port Schumann and the shores of the Eniewetok Sea were empty. No smoke from fireplaces or brush burning. No winking lights for navigation, warning or welcome.

Even from his height and distance, Ask could see what had become of the hand of man in this place.

He had to look. At a minimum, he had to find food. Most of the structures were standing. The idea of looting the houses of the dead for food distressed him. The idea of starving distressed him more.

He didn't reach the first farmhouse until evening's dusk. Ask would have strongly preferred to do his breaking and entering in broad daylight, but another night of hunger out in the open seemed foolish with the building right in front of him. A tall fieldstone foundation was topped by two stories of brightly painted wooden house that would not have looked out of place on one of the wealthier neighboring farms of his youth.

Ask wasn't sure if this was a deliberate revival of an ancient fashion of building, or a sort of architectural version of parallel evolution.

Chickens clucked and fussed in the yard with the beady-eyed paranoia of birds. Some had already climbed into the spreading bush that seemed to be their roost, others were hunting for some last bit of whatever the hell it was chickens ate.

Beyond the house, a forlorn flock of sheep pressed against the fenced boundary of a pasture, bleating at him. He had no idea what they wanted, but they looked pretty scraggly. A number of them were dead, grubby bodies scattered in the grass.

Water, he realized, seeing the churned up earth around a metal trough. They were dying of thirst.

Ask walked around the house to see if the trough could be refilled. He found the line poking up out of the soil, and the tap that controlled it. Turning that on did nothing, however.

Of course it wouldn't, he realized. No power for the well pump.

He sighed and unlatched the gate. "River's over there, guys," Ask said, his voice a croak. He realized he hadn't spoken aloud in the two weeks he'd been walking.

The sheep just stared at him. They made no move for freedom. There wasn't anything more he could do for the animals. He shrugged and walked back to the house, up the rear steps.

Inside the house was a mess. If he'd come on it in broad daylight, even from the outside he'd have noticed the cracked and shattered windows. Inside, the floors were dirty with splinters and wisps of insulation.

The lack of people was disturbing. So was the lack of blood, in a weird way.

They'd just walked outside, leaving the doors standing open, and vanished. Then orbital kinetics had plowed through the roof to disable the house's power plant, core comm system and—oddly—the oven. He figured it had to have happened in that order, because if anyone had been inside the house when the strikes hit, there would be signs of panic—toppled furniture, maybe blood from the splinters and other collateral damage.

With that happy thought in mind, Ask walked around the house in the deepening dark, checking every commset, music player, power tool and any other gadget he could find to switch on. The small electronics were fried, too, just like the equipment in his rockhopper.

It was as if the old fairy tale of the Christian Rapture had come true, here on Redghost. Followed by the explosive revenge of the exploited electron? He hadn't so much as looked at a Bible in over seven hundred years, but Ask was pretty sure that there hadn't been any mention of a rapture of the batteries.

"Render unto Volta those things which are Volta's," he said into the darkness, then began giggling.

His discipline finally broke. Ask retreated to the kitchen to hunt for food and drink.

JUNE 21ST, 2977 [RTS-RA]

It took him five weeks to explore every house in this part of the Shindaiwa Valley. On the way, Ask opened all the pasture gates he could find, shooing out the cattle and sheep and horses. The llamas, pigs and goats were smart enough to leave on their own, where they hadn't already jumped or broken the gates, or—in the case of the goats—picked the latches.

Most of them would starve even outside the fences, but at least they could find water and better pasture. Some would survive. So far as he knew, Redghost had no apex predators in the native ecology. Humans certainly hadn't imported any.

Give the dogs a few generations of living wild and that would change, though.

It was the damned dogs that broke his heart. The household pets were the worst. So many of them had starved, or eaten one another. And the survivors expected more of him than the farm animals had. When he slipped open a door or tore a screen, they rushed up to him. Barking, whining, mewling. He was a Person, he was Food, he could let the good boys Out. And the dogs knew they had been Bad. Crapping in corners, sleeping on the furniture, whining outside bedroom doors forever shut and silent.

In truth, that became the reason he'd entered every house or building he could find. To let out the cats and dogs and dwarf pigs. Finding a bicycle meant he could gain distance on those dogs that wanted to follow him. The cats didn't care, the pigs were too smart to try. He let the occasional birds out, too, and when he could, dumped the fish tanks into whatever nearby watercourse presented itself.

The more he walked, the fewer of them were left alive inside. But he had to try.

Thirty-nine days in the Shindaiwa Valley, and he'd visited almost four hundred houses, dormitories, granaries, slaughterhouses, tanneries, cold storage warehouses, machine workshops, emergency services centers, feed stores, schools. Even three railroad stations, a small hospital and a tiny airport terminal.

Not a single human being. Not so much as a finger bone. He'd even dug up both an old grave and a recent one to see if the bodies had been left behind. They had. Ask couldn't remember enough about Christianity to figure out if that was evidence for or against the Rapture. He did rebury them, and said what he could remember of the Lord's Prayer over the fresh-turned earth.

"Ten thousand sheep, a thousand cats and dogs, and me," he told a patient oak tree. It was wind-bent and twisted, standing in an ornamental square in front of the Lower Shindaiwa Valley Todd Christensen Memorial Railroad Depot Number 2. A sign proclaimed this to be the first Terran tree in the valley, planted by one of the pioneer farmers two centuries earlier. "You're a survivor. Like me."

But of *what?*

One small blessing of the railroad station was a modest selection of cheap tourist maps printed on plastene flimsy. Some people just didn't want to mess with dataflow devices all the time. On a relatively thinly-settled planet like Redghost the electrosphere was largely incomplete anyway.

Had been. It was nonexistent now, which was the utmost form of incompletion.

Ask shuffled the map flimsies. His knowledge of local planetography was poor—it simply hadn't been important. He'd been dropped by shuttle at Atarashii Ōsaka, the main spaceport and entrepôt for Redghost. He was vaguely aware of three or four other sites with support for surface-to-orbit transfer. And his assignment in the Fayerweather Mountains, for which he'd based out of Port Schumann after an atmospheric flight from Atarashii Ōsaka.

That was it. All he'd known about the Shindaiwa Valley was that this was his first line of emergency evacuation. All he'd known about Redghost was the semiconducting tunnels, and a notion of a bucolic paradise home to perhaps twenty million souls.

His next stop, he figured, would be Port Schumann. It was a city, at least by Redghost standards. Anyone else surviving on this part of the planet would have headed there.

In a bleak frame of mind, Ask figured that twenty million people would have about five million residences and perhaps half a million commercial structures. He'd managed an average ten buildings per day here in the Shindaiwa Valley. Denser in the cities, of course. Still, figure six hundred thousand days to check every structure on Redghost, plus the travel time between places. Fifty years? A hundred, if the buildings in Atarashii Ōsaka and the few other relatively large cities were too big to check so quickly?

Where the hell did twenty million people *go*? A planet full of corpses, he could understand. A planet empty of people . . .

JANUARY 4TH, 2978 [RTS-RA]

The crashed airplane in the hills east of Port Schumann had caught his attention as he'd cycled along the rough service road paralleling a rail line. It was a fixed-wing craft with propeller engines—something fairly simply designed to be locally serviceable without parts imported from off-planet. The fuselage looked intact, so he'd gone to check it out.

Weapons hadn't seemed to be much of an issue, and most of what he'd found in that department had been useless anyway due to embedded electronics, but he was always curious what he might find.

This craft had seated six. Small, white with pale green stripes and the seal of the Redghost Ministry of Social Adjustment on the side. Planetary judiciary, in local terms. It was missing one door, he noted as he approached.

He looked inside to see someone in the rear seat.

"Shit!" Ask screamed, jumping back.

He'd been too long without company. He was starting to regret not bringing a few of the dogs from the Shindaiwa Valley with him.

Feeling foolish, Ask unclipped the aluminum pump from his bike and held it loosely like a club. Some of the Howards were killers, dangerous as any human being who'd ever lived, but he'd never bothered with that training or those enhancements. He was strong enough to swing something like this pump right through a wall at need. At least until the wall or the pump shattered.

That had been enough.

Until now.

He approached the airplane again. Having already screamed, there didn't seem much point in secrecy now. Still, he didn't want to just march into the wreck.

The person was still there.

No, he corrected himself against the obvious. The body. Who the hell would stay seated in crashed airplane? For one thing, it was pretty cold out here at night.

A *man,* he thought. Handcuffed to his seat. Ask climbed into the cabin and crept close. It was hard to tell, with the flesh mummifying in the cold, but it looked like the prisoner had struggled hard against his cuffs.

Ask stepped up to the pilot and co-pilot's seats. Smashed instruments and windows, torn seat cushions. No blood.

They'd been gone from the plane, or at least out of their seats, before the orbital kinetics had struck the aircraft. In flight.

And the missing door? Had the pilot and guards just stepped out in mid-air? Ask imagined the prisoner, straining to follow whatever trumpet had called his captors away. Then shrieking in fear as the cockpit exploded in sizzling splinters, the engines shredded and died under the orbital strikes, and the plane had glided in to its final landing.

He hoped the poor bastard had died in the landing, but suspected he might have starved chained to the seat.

This also meant that people who had been unable to move from a position would not have been taken up by whatever had snatched everyone from Redghost's surface. Prisoners? The few jails he'd visited had stood empty and open-doored. The guards had taken their captives with them. Hospital ICUs? That explained the several medical beds he'd found dragged into gardens and on outdoor walkways.

Still, he knew where to look.

Ask went back for his bolt cutters and freed the dead prisoner. He didn't have a shovel and the ground was too cold to dig in anyway, but he spent two days making a rock cairn next to the airplane.

"The second-to-last man on Redghost," he said by way of prayer when he was done. His fingers were bruised and bloody, several of his nails torn. "You and I are brothers, though you never knew it. I wonder if you had it better or worse than those who were taken away."

OCTOBER 11TH, 2983 [RTS-RA]

On the sixth year of his hegira, Aeschylus Sforza entered the city of Pelleton. He had not found a living animal indoors in five years. He had not found a living animal penned outdoors in over four. He had not seen evidence of a human survivor other than himself on the planet at any time. He had found six bodies in various improbable circumstances. The hardest had been a little girl locked in a closet with a piss pot and a water bottle. She'd obviously been there a long time before Day Zero. And a long time after.

Ask devoutly hoped whoever had done that to a child had been taken directly to the lowest circle of whatever hell had opened up and swallowed the human race.

In any case, he'd buried them all. And he obsessively checked closets after that child. It took more time, but what was time to a Howard walking home all by himself?

Pelleton was located on an eastern curve of the Eniewetok Sea. It was the first city he visited with buildings over four stories tall. Some optimist had built a pair of fifteen-story office towers along the waterfront. By then, Ask had seen enough of the planet's architecture and development to understand most people wanted it small and simple.

Not so unlike the Tasmania of his youth. People who had wanted the big city moved to Melbourne or Brisbane or Sydney. People who wanted the big city here on Redghost had moved to Atarashii Ōsaka or taken up a line of work with off-planet demand.

He'd taken up the habit of visiting airports first, when it was at least sort of convenient to do so. Not just for the sake of any other trapped prisoners, though he'd never found another one of those. But rather, in hopes of finding something useful. Anything, really.

The gasbags of the heavy-lift freighters were all long since draped in tatters from their listing semi-rigid frames, but he kept wondering if he'd find a fixed-wing aircraft or a gravimetric flyer that hadn't been gutted by orbital kinetics. Not that Ask expected to build an engine or power pack with his bare hands, but it would have been a start.

Most of the cockpits were smashed or shattered. Too many electronics in there. Likewise, power systems. And in most cases, the airframes as well. He'd amused himself for a while calculating the total number of separate surface targets that had been subjected to bombardment by orbital kinetics in a single twenty-five point six-hour period—the local planetary day—and how many launchers that implied. How much processing power in guidance systems that implied.

Ask had concluded that no power in human space had the resources to commit such a saturated attack. Not so quickly and thoroughly.

That of course raised several more difficult questions. The one that concerned him most was whether this had happened to every human-settled planet in the Polity, or just to Redghost. He almost certainly would not have known if a spaceship or starship had called here since Day Zero. Short of catching a glimpse of it transiting in orbit, how would he find out? Not a single comm set on the planet still worked so far as he was aware.

Was he not just the last human being on this planet, but the last human being in the universe? Ask couldn't figure out if that thought was paranoia, megalomania or simple common sense. Or worse, all three.

By now most of the airframes had acquired layers of moss, grass and in some cases, even vines. Another decade and there would be trees poking through the holes in the wings. He clambered around Pelleton's airport all day without finding anything novel, then sheltered inside the little terminal as the dark of the evening encroached.

The dog packs were getting worse all over. Sleeping outside at night was no longer safe as it had been in the early times after Day Zero. The question of weapons had re-entered his mind. Especially projectile weapons.

JUNE 6TH, 2997 [RTS-RA]

On the twentieth year of his hegira, Aeschylus Sforza began to compose epic poetry. His Howard-enhanced memory being by definition perfected, he had no trouble recalling his verse, but still he took the trouble to refine the rhymes and meter so that should someone else ever have call to memorize the tale of his walk home around Redghost, they could do so.

Over the years he had found and buried twenty-three people. None of them appeared to have long survived Day Zero, as whatever confinement had prevented their ascendance had also prevented their continued life and health unattended by outside aid.

The towns and cities were changing, too. Rivers in flood-damaged bridges and washed-out waterfronts. Storms blew down trees, tore off roofs and shattered those windows that had survived the orbital strikes. Plants, both native and Terranic, took over first park strips, lawns and open spaces; then began to colonize sidewalks, rooftops, steps, basement lightwells.

The edges that civilization draws on nature were disappearing into a collage of rubble, splinters and green leaves.

He'd spent the years hunting clues. He'd dug the payloads of the orbital kinetics out of enough wrecks and buildings to realize that he wouldn't know much about them without a lot of lab work. In a lab he didn't and could not have access to, of course, in the absence of electrical power. They appeared deformed, heat-stressed metalloceramic slugs about two centimeters in diameter that had probably been roughly spherical on launch. That left the question of guidance wide open.

Likewise the various bodies he'd found. None of them told Ask any more than the dead prisoner had. Every human being who was physically able to do so had walked outside the afternoon or evening of April 27th, 2977 and vanished. Presumably along with their clothes and whatever they had in their hands at the time. He'd found plenty of desiccated sandwiches on plates and jackets hung on chair backs indoors, but nothing equivalent on the sidewalks and in the backyards of Redghost.

The light show in the sky had subsided years earlier, though the occasional reentry flare still caught his eye at night. He periodically found batteries and even small pieces of equipment that had survived both the orbital kinetics and the electronic pulse attack by dint of shielding either deliberate or accidental. So far he'd declined to carry those things with him, for fear that whatever it was might still be monitoring from orbit.

And that was it.

So one day he began to compose epic poetry. It was a thing to do while he passed the time hacking through vines and checking closets.

I sing of the planet now lost
Though still it spins through space . . .

Homer he never would be, but who was there to sing to, anyway?

APRIL 23RD, 3013 [RTS-RA]

On the thirty-sixth year of his hegira, Aeschylus Sforza finally began to take seriously the proposition that he had gone completely mad. He wondered if this had been true from the very beginning. Was he trapped in a decades-long hallucination, something gone badly wrong in his Howard-enhanced brain? Or was even the passage of time a cognitive compression artifact, like the illusory and deceptive time scales in dreams?

Ask wasn't sure it mattered, either way. He wasn't even sure anymore if there was a difference.

He was exploring the town of Tekkeitsertok, on a largely barren island in Redghost's boreal polar regions. The journey to this place had required quite a bit of planning, and the use of a sailboat found intact due to its complete lack of electronics. Still, restoring the boat to seaworthiness had consumed over a year of his time.

Time. The work had been something to do.

Tekkeitsertok was a settlement of low, bunkered buildings, most of them with slightly rounded roofs to offset snow accumulation and present a less challenging profile to the winter winds howling off the largely frozen Northcote Sea on the far side of the island. Lichen now covered every exterior surface that hadn't been buried in wind-blown ice and grit. The insides of the buildings where insulation had not failed were taken over by a fuzzy mold, so that everything looked slightly furry. Where insulation had failed, the interiors were just a sodden, rotting mess.

Ask picked through the town, wondering why anyone had bothered to live here. Tekkeitsertok had probably been the most extreme permanent human habitation on Redghost. He'd decided some time ago not to worry about campsites, research stations, and whatnot, so anyone who'd been out on the ice cap was on their own. Not that any ice station would have survived three and a half decades without maintenance. Even this place with its thick-walled air of permanence was already surrendering to nature.

Nothing was here, of course. Not even in the closets, which Ask still conscientiously checked. He'd never found so much as a footprint of the attackers, but had held some vague notion that evidence might be preserved in the icy northern cold. Even in summer, this place was hostile—built on permanently frozen ground, flurrying snow every month of the local year.

The moment of madness came when he was inside the town's mercantile. The windowless buildings meant he had to use an oil lantern even with the endless summer daylight outside. That in turn produced strange, stark shadows between the warmly glowing pools of light. Racks of merchandise ranging from cold weather gear to snow-runner wheels crowded the retail space. Ask was pushing from aisle to aisle, watching for useful survival gear as much as anything in this place, when he heard an electronic chirp.

He froze and almost killed the lantern. That was stupid, of course. Anyone or anything that might have been alerted to the light already had. Still, he turned slowly, mouth wide open to improve his hearing over the pounding of his heart. His blood felt curdled.

The noise did not repeat itself.

After standing in place for several minutes, he gave up on stillness as a strategy and headed for the sales counter. That was where any surviving equipment was likely to be.

Three and a half decades *after Day Zero, and* now *there was something else moving on this planet?*

Nothing.

He found nothing. Ask tore the sales counter apart, looking in all the little drawers, even. He opened the access panel behind to the long-useless breaker boxes and comm line interchanges. He turned up the dry-rotted carpet. He yanked everything out from inside the display cases. He grabbed an axe from the tools section, though there wasn't a tree within five hundred kilometers of this place, and chopped up the cases looking for whatever might be hidden inside them. He tried chopping the floor, but stopped when he nearly brained himself with the rebound of the axe.

Panting, sick, shivering, Ask finally stopped. He'd trashed the interior of the place. In all the years of his wandering, he'd never stooped to petty vandalism. For all the windows he'd broken getting in and out of places, he'd never destroyed for the sake of the pleasure of destruction.

Now, this?

It's not like they were coming back. Wherever they'd gone.

With that realization, he took up the axe and charged through the mercantile screaming. A long pole of parkas collapsed under his blows, their insulation spinning like snow where they tore. He smashed a spinner rack of inertial compasses. Tents spilled and tore. Useless power tools went flying to crack against other displays or the outside walls. When he got to the lamp oils and camping fuels, he spilled those, too, then transferred the flame from his lantern to the spreading, glistening pools.

After that, he retreated outside to the almost-warmth of the polar summer, that had cracked above freezing. Smoke billowed out from the open door of the mercantile. After a while, something inside exploded with a satisfying "whomp." He watched a long time, but the roof never fell in.

Finally Ask stretched in the cold and turned to wonder what he might do next. That was when he realized he had been surrounded by a patient dog pack. Furry, lean, with the bright eyes of killers, they had watched him watch the fire.

"Hey there, boys," he said softly. Though surely none of these remembered the hand of man. These were the descendants of the survivors, not the domestic escapees of the early years.

One of the dogs growled deep in its throat. Ask regretted leaving his guns in the sailboat. Deliberately archaic collector's items, they were all that worked anymore with the interlocks burned out on any rational, modern weapon.

Not that he had much ammunition, either.

And not that he had any of it with him.

Knife in hand, he charged the apparent leader of the pack. It was good to finally have something to fight back against.

NOVEMBER 1ST, 3094 [RTS-RA]

On the one-hundred-and-seventeenth year of his hegira, Aeschylus Sforza returned to the Shindaiwa Valley. He'd buried forty-seven bodies in the years of his wandering. The last of them had been little more than heaps of leather and bones. The cities, towns and settlements he'd visited had largely buried themselves by the time he'd been to every human outpost he could possibly reach on this planet.

He had not spoken a word out loud in thirty years. The epic poetry was not forgotten—with his Howard memory, nothing he meant to remember was ever forgotten—but he had not bothered with it in decades. The madness, well, it had stayed a long time. Eventually he'd grown tired even of that and retreated back to sanity. The track of that descent was marked in the number of burn sites across one whole arc of Redghost's northern hemisphere.

The dogs had failed to kill him. Wound infections had failed to kill him, though he'd come perilously close to dying at least twice. Even the ocean crossings had failed to kill him. Loneliness, that curse of the Howards, had failed to kill him.

Boredom might, though.

The Shindaiwa Valley had gone back to the land. Many of the houses still stood, but as rotting shells overgrown with weeds. Some things were more permanent than others. The railroad tracks, for instance. Likewise the plascrete shells of the hospital and the train stations.

Ask had time. Nothing but time. So he set about using it. He needed a place to live, near water but not likely to be flooded out when summer thawed the snowcap at the head of the watershed. He needed to catch and break some of the wild horses that haunted these fields and forests to draw the plow. He needed to log out trees in some areas, and find saplings young enough for the project that had been forming in his mind for the past decade or so.

He needed so much, and would never have any of it. Now that he was done walking home, Ask had nothing but time.

MARCH 17TH, 3283 [RTS-RA]

The demands of controlling the horses, not to mention managing the pigs and goats he eventually took on, had brought Ask's voice back to him. He'd become garrulous over the long years with those patient eyes staring back at him.

He'd also been convinced he was the last man in the universe. In over three centuries since Day Zero, no one had come calling at Redghost so far as he knew. If the rest of the human race were still out there functioning normally, the planet should have been swarming with rescuers and Polity investigative teams in the first year or two. Or any of the decades since.

Someone might have done a fly-by then hustled away. Ask knew he wouldn't have been aware of that. But human beings could not leave a disaster alone. And Redghost, whatever else it had been, was definitely a disaster.

He even had a little bit of electronics, having at one point taken a pair of pack horses back to his cave and retrieved his surviving equipment. The passive solar strips used on so many Shindaiwa Valley rooftops were still intact, and he worked out a sufficient combination of salvage parts and primitive electronics to keep a few batteries charged. Space-rated equipment *lasted*, at the least. He had steady light by which to read at night—Shindaiwa Valley had boasted two hundred and eleven surviving hardcopy books by the time he'd gotten around to salvaging those. Four of them were actual paper printings from the Earth of his childhood, three in English that he could read. Their unspeakably fragile pages were preserved in a monomolecular coating as family heirlooms.

He'd read them all over and over and over. He could *recite* them all, and some years did so just to have something to say to the goats and horses—the pigs never cared so much for his voice.

Still, reading and reciting those words written by authors long dead was the closest Ask could come to speaking to another human being.

In the mean time, his project had matured. Blossomed into success, in a manner of speaking. He'd spent decades carefully surveying, logging and replanting, even diverting the courses of streams to make sure water was where he wanted it to be.

When that had grown boring, he'd built himself a new house and barn. Living in the hospital had felt strange. The weight of souls there was stronger. Having his own home, one that none of the people before Day Zero had ever lived or worked or died in, had seemed important for a while.

So Ask had built the house at the center of his project. Made a sort of castle of it, complete with turrets and a central watchtower. A platform for a beacon fire, just to make the point. It wasn't high enough to see his work, but when he climbed the ridge at the eastern edge of the valley—the one he'd first come down in those confused weeks right after Day Zero—he could glimpse what his imagination had engineered.

Eating a breakfast of ham and eggs the morning of March 17th, Aeschylus Sforza heard the whine of turbines in the air outside his home. Centuries of living alone had broken him of the habit of hurrying. He finished his plate a little faster than normal, nonetheless, and scrubbed it in the stone trough that was his sink. He pulled on his goatskin jacket, for the Shindaiwa Valley mornings could still be chilly in this season, and walked outside at a measured but still rapid pace.

Ask had realized a long time ago that it didn't matter who they were when they came. The unknown raiders who'd stripped this planet, the descendants of those taken up by the attackers, or his own people finally returned. When they returned, whoever they were, he'd wanted to meet them.

That was why his house sat in the exact center of three arrows of dense forest, each thirty kilometers long and spaced one hundred and twenty degrees apart, each surrounded by carefully husbanded open pasture. A "look here" note visible even from orbit. Especially from orbit. Who the hell else would be looking?

Outside his front gate a mid-sized landing shuttle, about thirty meters nose to tail, sat clicking and ticking away the heat of its descent. The grass around it smoldered. Ask did not recognize the engineering or aesthetics of the machine, which answered some of his speculations in the negative. It certainly did not display Polity markings.

He stood his ground, waiting for whoever might open that hatch from within. His long walk was done, had been done for over two hundred years.

Time for the next step.

The hatch whined open, air puffing as pressure equalized. Someone shifted their weight in the red-lit darkness within.

Human?

It didn't matter.

He was about to learn what would happen next.

Aeschylus Sforza was home.

The Incredible Exploding Man

DAVE HUTCHINSON

Here's the gripping story of a man who saves the world, only to find that he's reluctantly obliged to save it over and over again.

Dave Hutchinson is a writer and journalist who was born in Sheffield and now lives in London with his wife and assorted cats. He's the author of one novel and the novella The Push, *which was nominated for the BSFA Award, as well as five collections of short stories. He's also the editor of the anthology* Under the Rose, *and the coeditor of* Strange Pleasures 2 *and* Strange Pleasures 3.

From a distance, the first thing you saw was the cloud.

It rose five thousand feet or more, a perfect vertical helix turning slowly in the sky above Point Zero. Winds high in the atmosphere smeared its very top into ribbons, but no matter how hard the winds blew at lower levels the main body kept its shape. A year ago, a tornado had tracked northwest across this part of Iowa and not disturbed the cloud at all. It looked eerie and frightening, but it was just an edge effect, harmless water vapour in the atmosphere gathered by what was going on below. The really scary stuff at Point Zero was invisible.

The young lieutenant sitting across from me looked tired and ill. They burned out quickly here on the Perimeter—the constant stress of keeping things from getting through the fence, the constant terror of what they would have to do if something did. A typical tour out here lasted less than six months, then they were rotated back to their units and replacements were brought in. I sometimes wondered why we were bothering to keep it secret; if we waited long enough the entire US Marine Corps would have spent time here.

I leaned forward and raised my voice over the sound of the engines and said to the lieutenant, "How old are you, son?"

The lieutenant just looked blankly at me. Beside him, I saw Former Corporal Fenwick roll his eyes.

"Just trying to make conversation," I said, sitting back. The lieutenant didn't respond. He didn't know who I was—or rather, he had been told I was a specialist, come to perform routine maintenance on the sensors installed all over the Site. There was no way to tell whether he believed that or not, or if he even cared. He was trying to maintain a veneer of professionalism, but when he thought nobody was looking he kept glancing at the windows. He wanted to look out, to check on his responsibilities on the ground. Was the Site still there? Was there a panic? Had a coyote got through?

It had been a coyote last time. At least, that was the general consensus of opinion—it was hard to be certain from the remains. The Board of Inquiry had found that the breach was due to gross negligence on the part of the officer in command. The officer in command, a colonel I had met a couple of times and rather liked, had saved Uncle Sam the cost of a court martial by dying, along with seventeen of his men, bringing down the thing the coyote had become. You could tell, just by looking at the Lieutenant, that he had terrible nightmares.

The Black Hawk made another wide looping turn over Sioux Crossing, waiting for permission to land. Looking out, I thought I could see my old house. The city had been evacuated shortly after the Accident. It had taken weeks to clear the place out; even after dire stories of death and disaster, even with the cloud hanging over the Site, there were people who refused to leave. The fact that the skies by then were full of military helicopters, some of them black, hadn't helped. The government had handled the whole thing poorly, and there had been a couple of armed standoffs between householders and the military. Then a bunch of asshole militiamen had turned up from the wilds of Montana, vowing to oppose the Zionist World Government or the Bilderberg Group or whoever the hell they believed was running the world. I was glad I'd missed the whole thing.

Further out, I could see the buildings of the Collider in the distance. From here, all looked peaceful. Apart from the cloud, towering over everything, it was as if nothing had ever happened here.

The pilot eventually got permission to make final approach and we landed in a park on the edge of Sioux Crossing. The park was ringed by prefabricated buildings stacked four high, offices and barracks and mess halls and control rooms and armouries and garages surrounding a big white "H" sprayed on the ground. The lieutenant jumped down as soon as the door was opened, and the last I saw of him was his back as he strode away from us towards the control centre.

"Talkative fucker," Former Corporal Fenwick commented, hopping down from the helicopter beside me.

I sighed. A figure in fatigues was coming towards us from the control centre. The figure passed the lieutenant, and they snapped salutes at each other without breaking step.

"Welcoming committee," said Fenwick. "Nice. I approve."

"Shut up, Fenwick," I muttered.

The figure was the base commander, Colonel Newton J. Kettering. He marched up to us and saluted. Fenwick returned the salute sloppily, as usual. I didn't bother.

"Sir," Kettering said smartly. "Welcome to Camp Batavia."

"Well thank you kindly, Colonel," Fenwick said. "Looks like you're running a tight ship here."

"Sir. Thank you, sir." Unlike the lieutenant, Kettering didn't look tired and ill. He looked alert and bright-eyed. He looked alert and bright-eyed to the point of madness. He was a veteran of Iraq and Afghanistan and he'd done three tours here, and I didn't want to spend a minute longer in his company than I had to.

I said to Fenwick, "I'd better supervise the unloading."

Fenwick gave me his big shit-eating grin. "I think that sounds like a fine idea, Mr. Dolan." I wanted to punch him. "Perhaps Colonel Kettering could give me the guided tour while you're doing that thing."

"Sir, I was hoping you could join me in the Officers' Club," Kettering said. "We have a luncheon prepared."

Fenwick's grin widened. "Colonel, I would love to."

"We need to get onto the Site as soon as possible," I said to them both, but mainly to Fenwick. Kettering regarded me with a keen look of hostility. Fenwick pouted; he hated to miss a free meal. I said, "Colonel, it shouldn't take more than half an hour to unload my gear—"

"Hell," Fenwick put in amiably. "That's *plenty* of time for luncheon. Right, Colonel?"

"Sir. Yes, sir." Kettering gave me that hostile look again. I had already ruined his carefully-groomed routine; he wasn't about to let me ruin lunch too. Neither was Fenwick.

I looked at them both. "Half an hour," I said. "No longer."

Fenwick and Kettering exchanged a knowing glance. *Civilians.* Then Fenwick clapped Kettering on the back and said, "Lead the way, Colonel," and they walked off. A few yards away, Fenwick looked over his shoulder and called, "Would you like us to send a plate out for you, Mr. Dolan?"

I shook my head. "No thank you, General, I'll be fine," I called back. Fenwick flipped me the bird surreptitiously and turned back to Kettering. The two of them, deep in conversation, walked towards the wall of prefabs.

I watched them go for a few moments, then went back to the helicopter, where, in the style of bored baggage handlers and cargo men the world over, half a dozen Marines were throwing my metal transport cases out onto the grass.

"Hey!" I shouted. "Careful with those things! They're delicate scientific instruments!"

Actually, the cases were full of old telephone directories, for weight, but I had to keep up the charade.

I had been in a foul mood when I arrived for work that morning. I drove the short distance from home to the facility, stopped briefly at the gate to show my ID, then drove to the building housing the small control room Professor Delahaye and his team were using.

Most of them were already there ahead of me. Delahaye was over to one side of the room, conferring with half a dozen of his colleagues and grad students. Others were busily typing at consoles and peering at monitors. Nowhere, though, could I see the shock of white hair that I was looking for.

Delahaye spotted me and walked over. "What are you doing here, Dolan?" he asked. "Surely you've got enough material by now?"

"I need a conclusion," I said, still looking around the room. "Just a last bit of colour."

"Well, try not to get in the way will you? There's a good chap." Delahaye was a small, agitated Londoner who couldn't see why a journalist had been foisted on him and his experiment.

"I don't see Larry," I said. "Is he coming in today?"

Delahaye looked around him. "Maybe. Who knows? The experiment's almost over, he doesn't need to be here. Is it important?"

Is it important? No, maybe not to *you*, Professor. I said, "I just wanted a quick word, that's all."

Delahaye nodded irritably. "All right. But just—"

"Try not to get in the way. Yes, Professor, I know. I'll just stand over there in the corner." As if I was going to reach over and press some important big red button, or fall into a piece of machinery. Nothing I did here was going to make the slightest bit of difference to the enormous energies being generated, nanoseconds at a time, far below our feet in the tunnels of the Collider. And even if I did manage to screw something up, it wouldn't affect the experiment all that much; all the results were in, Delahaye was just using up his allotted time with a last couple of shots.

The professor gave me a last admonitory glare and went back to the little group across the room. There was nothing world-shaking going on here; the Collider was brand new—the offices still smelled of fresh paint. Delahaye was just running warm-up tests, calibrating instruments, the high-energy physics equivalent of running-in a new car. I'd been there two months, working on an article about the new facility for *Time*. I thought the article was shaping up to be interesting and informative. The worst thing about the whole fucking business was that it had brought Larry into my life.

Andy Chen came over and we shook hands. "Been fun having you around, man," he said.

"Yes," I said. "Right."

"Nah, really," he insisted. "You piss old man Delahaye off mightily. It's been beautiful to watch."

Despite being beyond pissed off myself, I smiled. "You're welcome. What's for you now? Back to MIT?"

He shook his head. "Been offered a job at JPL."

"Hey, excellent, man. Congratulations."

"Ah, we'll see. It's not pure research, but at least it gets me away from that monstrous old fart." He looked over at Professor Delahaye, who was regaling some students with some tale or other. Andy snorted. "Brits," he said. "Who knows?" He looked over to where a small commotion had begun around the door. "Well, we can get the party started now."

I looked towards the door and saw Larry Day's leonine features over the heads of the others in the room, and I felt my heart thud in my chest. "Andy," I said, "I need to have a quick word with Larry." We shook hands again and I launched myself through the crowd. "Great news about JPL, man. Really."

Larry was drunk again. That much was obvious even before I got to him. He was wearing Bermuda shorts and a desert camouflage jacket and he was clutching a tattered sheaf of paper in one hand and a shrink-wrapped six pack of Dr Pepper in the other. His hair looked as if he had been dragged back and forth through a hedge a couple of times, and his eyes were hidden by mirrorshades with lenses the size of silver dollars.

"Larry," I said as I reached him.

The mirrored lenses turned towards me. "Hey. Alex. Dude." There was a powerful aura of Wild Turkey and Cuban cigars around him, and when he grinned at me his teeth were yellow and uneven.

Rolling Stone had called him "Steven Hawking's Evil Twin." One of the most brilliant physicists of his generation, a legend at the age of twenty-four. Of course, by that time he had been thrown out of Harvard for an incident involving a homemade railgun, a frozen chicken, and his supervisor's vintage TransAm, but that was just part of his mystique, and pretty much every other university on Earth had offered him a place. His doctoral thesis was titled *Why All Leptons Look Like Joey Ramone But Smell Like Lady GaGa*, and it was generally agreed that it would have been embarrassing if it *had* won him the Nobel Prize. Bad enough that it was shortlisted. His postdoc research had been a mixture of the mundane and the wildly exotic; he cherry-picked his way through some of the wilder outlands of quantum mechanics and nanotechnology, came up with a brand new theory of stellar evolution, published a paper which not only challenged the Big Bang but made it seem rather dull and simple-minded. Larry Day. Brilliant physicist. Brilliant drunk. Brilliant serial womanizer. He and I had visited all the bars in Sioux Crossing and been thrown out of most of them.

"I spoke with Ellie last night," I said quietly.

He smiled down at me. "Hey," he said. "Outstanding."

I gritted my teeth. "She told me."

In the background, I could hear Delahaye saying something above the holiday atmosphere in the room, but I wasn't paying attention. All I could concentrate on was Larry's mouth, his lying lips as he said, "Ah. Okay."

"Is that all you can say?" I hissed. "'Ah. Okay'?"

He shrugged expansively and some of the papers in his hand escaped and fell to the floor. "What can I say, man? 'I'm sorry'?"

Delahaye seemed to be counting in a loud voice, but it was as if I heard him from a great echoing distance. I lunged at Larry, grabbed him by the front of the camouflage jacket, and drove him two steps back against the wall.

". . . Three . . . two . . ." said Delahaye.

"You fucking *bastard!*" I screamed into Larry's face.

". . . One!" said Delahaye, and the world filled with a sudden flash of something that was not blinding white light.

I had the Humvee loaded by the time Fenwick and the colonel returned from their lunch. In the end I'd told the Marines to go away, and I'd done it myself. Down the years I've noticed that Marines tend towards a certain disdain for people who are not themselves Marines. I was a *civilian specialist.* To most of them that was a euphemism for *CIA*, which was a direct invitation to dick around and try to get a rise out of me, but I wasn't going to play that game.

"How was your lunch, General?" I asked when Fenwick and Kettering arrived.

Fenwick looked at Kettering. "I think I can report that this camp is not lacking in creature comforts, Mr. Dolan," he said, and Kettering smiled in relief.

I looked at my watch. "We really should be making a start, General," I said. "I'd like to be out of here before nightfall."

Fenwick snorted. "You and me both." He turned to Kettering. "Newt," he said, "if you're ever down at Bragg, I'll throw a party for you at the BOQ that'll make your head spin."

Kettering grinned. "Sir. Yes, sir." They shook hands and Kettering stood to attention while Fenwick and I got into the Hummer. I took the wheel.

I said, "I do hope you didn't breach any security protocols in there, Corporal."

Fenwick grinned and tapped the stars on his fatigues. "*General.*"

I put the Hummer in gear. "Oh, fuck off, Fenwick," I said. "You're no more a general than I am." And I drove the Humvee out of the gates of the camp and onto the road to the Site.

There was a place that was not a place. It was too small and too large all at once, and it was either dark or it was lit by something that wasn't light but came in from the edge of vision like a hypnagogic nightmare. There was an "up" and a "down." Or maybe it was a "down" and an "up." I screamed and I screamed and the noises I made were not sounds. I was . . . I was . . .

It took me a long time to get my bearings. Or maybe I never did, maybe it was all an accident. I walked. Travelled, anyway. I couldn't understand what I was seeing, couldn't be sure that I was seeing it. I wanted to curl up and die, and I did in fact try that a couple of times, but it was impossible. I couldn't even curl up, in the sense that I understood it. I held my hands up and looked at them. They were . . . they were . . .

At some point, maybe instantly, maybe it took a hundred million years, I came upon a . . . structure. Too small and too large to see, all at once. It looked like . . . there's no way I can describe what it looked like, but I *touched* it and I *reached down* and I *curled around* it and the next thing I knew I was lying on my back looking up at a starry sky and someone nearby was screaming, "Don't move, you fucker! You stay right where you are!"

I turned my head, astonished that I still remembered how. A soldier was standing a few feet from me, illuminated by moonlight, pointing an automatic weapon at me.

"Who are you?" I asked, and almost choked myself because I was still trying to speak as I might have when I was *there.* I coughed and retched, and at some point I realised I was naked and freezing cold. I said again, "Who are you?"

"Who are *you*?" shouted the soldier.

"Dolan," I said, and this time I managed to say it without strangling. "Alex Dolan. There's been some kind of accident."

There was a squawking noise and the soldier lifted a walkie-talkie to his lips. "Fenwick here, sir," he shouted into the radio. "I've got a civilian here. He claims there's been an accident."

At ground level, fifteen years of abandonment were more obvious. There were Green Berets stationed at the gate, and they spent a good half-hour checking our documents and establishing our bona fides before letting us through. As well as animals, the world's Press were always trying to sneak through the fence. Nobody had made it yet. Nobody we knew about, anyway.

The buildings were weathered and dirty, the grass waist-high, despite regular helicopter inundations of herbicides, and it was starting to encroach on the cracked asphalt of the roadways.

I drove until we were a few hundred feet from the control room building, directly under the slowly-twisting spiral cloud. Unable to hush the cloud up, the government had admitted that there had been an accident at the Collider, explaining it as an electromagnetic effect. Scientists—government-sponsored and otherwise—were still arguing about this.

Fenwick looked up at the white helix and curled his lips. He was a man of many attributes, very few of them admirable, but he was not a coward. He had been told that there was no danger in him coming this close to Point Zero, and he believed that. It had never occurred to him that a significant fraction of the defence budget was devoted to stopping animals getting this close to Point Zero.

There had been much discussion about what to do about him after I appeared out of thin air in front of him. A quick look at his file suggested that appealing to his patriotic instincts would be pointless, and that giving him large amounts of money would be counterproductive and fruitless. A working-group of thirty very very bright men and women had been convened simply to study the problem of What to Do About Corporal Robert E. Lee Fenwick, who one night while out on patrol at Fort Bragg had seen me appear from a direction that no one in the universe had ever seen before.

Their solution was elegant and, I thought, unusually humane. Corporal Fenwick was a simple organism, geared mainly to self-gratification, and his loyalty—and his silence—had been bought by the simple expedient of promoting him to the rank of three-star general. What fascinated me was that Fenwick never showed the slightest gratitude for this. It was as if the alternative never even occurred to him. He seemed totally oblivious to the concept that it would have been simpler, and far more cost-effective, to simply kill him.

"Here we are, then," Fenwick said.

"Yes," I said. "Here we are. I cannot argue with that." I looked at the cloud, looked at the buildings around us. Fenwick had surprised everyone by taking to his new rank like a duck to water. He was still *in* the Army, but he was no longer *of* the Army. He had no duties to speak of, apart from the duties that involved me. His general's pay had been backdated for a decade, and he had bought his parents a new house in West Virginia and his brother a new car, and he lived with his child bride Roselynne and their half-dozen squalling brats in a magnificent mansion in Alexandria, Virginia. The kids went to the best schools, and in moments of despair I hung onto that. The eldest girl, Bobbi-Sue, was starting at Princeton next year. Because of what had happened to me the Fenwick boys would not work all their lives in the local coal mines; the Fenwick girls would not marry the high school jock only to see him become a drunken wife-beater. They would be lawyers and doctors and congressmen and senators, and maybe even presidents. In my darkest moments I looked at Former Corporal Fenwick, and I almost thought this was all worth it. Almost.

"How long do we have?" he asked. He always asked that.

I shrugged. "Minutes?" I always said that, too. "Days?" I opened the door and got out of the Hummer. Fenwick got out too, and together we unloaded the transport cases. We carried them into one of the other buildings a little way from the control room, and emptied them of their telephone books. Then we put them back into the Humvee and dumped my gear on the ground beside the vehicle.

Fenwick checked his watch. "Better be getting back," he said.

I nodded. In a couple of hours there would be an overflight. An unmarked black helicopter without an ID transponder would pass overhead, ignoring local traffic control until the last moment, when it would transmit a brief and curt series of digits that identified it as belonging to the NSA. It would dip down below the radar cover, hover for a few moments, and then lift up and fly off again. And that would be me, leaving. "This is stupid. Someone's going to work it out one day," I said.

Fenwick shrugged. "Not my problem." He put out his hand and I shook it. When I first met him he had been rangy and fidgety. Now he was calm and plump and sleek, and in my heart I couldn't grudge him that. "Happy trails, Alex," he said.

"You too, Bobby Lee. See you soon."

"Let's fucking hope, right?"

I smiled. "Yes. Let's."

Fenwick got back into the Hummer, gave me a wave, and drove off back towards the gate, where he would tell the Green Berets that the *civilian specialist* had arranged a separate means of departure. Which would, in its own way, be true.

I watched the Humvee disappear into the distance. When it was gone, I picked up my stuff and carried it into one of the nearby buildings. I dumped it in an empty office, unrolled my sleeping bag on the floor, wheeled a chair over to the window, and sat down.

The room was small and windowless and the only furniture in it was a table and a single folding plastic chair. The captain was using the chair. I was standing on the other side of the table from him, flanked by two armed soldiers.

"Now, all I need to know, son, is your name and how you managed to get onto this base bare-ass naked without anybody seeing you," the captain said. He'd said it a number of times.

"My name is Alexander Dolan," I said. "I'm a journalist. I was in the control room with Professor Delahaye's group. I think there's been an accident." I'd said this a number of times, too.

The captain smiled and shook his head. He was base security, or maybe Intelligence, I didn't know. He was the image of reasonableness. We could, he seemed to be saying, keep doing this all day and all night until I told him what he wanted to know.

"Go and find Professor Delahaye," I said. "He'll vouch for me." I couldn't understand what the military were doing at the Collider; maybe the accident had been much worse than I thought. Which would make it truly world-shaking.

"I don't know any Professor Delahaye, son," the captain said. "Did he help you break in here?"

I sighed and shook my head. "No. He's supervising the startup experiments. Look, if he was hurt, maybe one of the others can come here. Doctor Chen or Doctor Morley, maybe. Everyone knows me."

"I don't know any of these people, Mr. Dolan," said the captain. "What I want to know is who *you* are, and how in the name of blue blazes you managed to break into Fort Bragg without a stitch of clothing."

"Fort Bragg?"

The captain gave me a wry, long-suffering, don't-bullshit-me-son sort of look.

I looked around the room. There was only one door. It looked solid and it had big locks on it. But looking around the room again, I noticed that if I looked at it a certain *way*, it was not a locked room at all. It was just planes of mass that didn't even butt up against each other. It was actually wide open.

"I thought this was the Sioux Crossing Collider," I told the captain.

He blinked. "The what?"

I said, "I don't like it here," and I *stepped* outside the room, went back *there*.

I had brought with me a gallon jug of water, a little solid-fuel camping stove, some basic camping cookware, and half a dozen MREs. I took the first package and opened it. Meals Ready to Eat. But only if you were desperate or not particularly fussy. The package contained beef ravioli in meat sauce, chipotle snack bread, a cookie, cheese spread, beef snacks, caffeine mints, candy, coffee, sugar, salt, gum, some dried fruit and some other bits and pieces. I'd heard that the French Army's MREs came with a pouch of red wine. If only The Accident had happened at CERN . . .

I became aware of . . . something. If a solid object could have the equivalent of a negative image, this was it. A kind of *negative* tornado, turned inside-out. I *stepped* towards it . . .

And found myself standing at the SCC, outside the building where I had last seen Professor Delahaye and his team and Larry Day.

Above me towered a *colossal* sculptured pillar of cloud, rotating slowly in the sky. I tilted my head back and looked up at it, my mouth dropping open.

And all of a sudden I was writhing on the ground in agony, my muscles cramping and spasming. I tried to *step* away, but I was in too much pain to be able to focus.

And that was how they caught me the second time, lying in wait because they half-expected me to return to the Collider, and then tasering me half to death. Someone walked up to me and thumped his fist down on my thigh. When he took his hand away there was a thin plastic tube sticking out of my leg and then there was a wild roaring in my head and a wave of blackness broke over me and washed me away.

They tried the same trick on the captain and the two guards as they had on Former Corporal Fenwick. I was beginning to think that I was travelling across the world leaving generals in my wake. They showered them with money and promotions, and for some reason it didn't work with them the way it had worked with Fenwick. They blabbed their stories, and eventually the government had to make them all disappear. The officers were in solitary confinement in Leavenworth and the people they blabbed to were *sequestered* somewhere.

I finished my dinner and sat by the window drinking coffee and smoking a small cigar. The cigar was from a tin I'd found in my rucksack; a little gift from Fenwick. I'd heard the helicopter fly over while I was eating; it had dipped down momentarily a few hundred metres from Point Zero—which was actually an act of insane bravery on the part of its pilot in order to maintain what I considered the fatuous and transparent fiction of my "departure"—and then lifted away again to the West. Now everything was quiet and night was falling.

I remembered when this whole place had been busy and bustling. All abandoned now, the surviving staff scattered to other facilities. I thought about Delahaye and Andy Chen and Caitlin Morley and all the others who had been in that room with me on the day of The Accident. Delahaye had been an uptight asshole and Larry had been having an affair with my wife, but I'd liked the others; they were good, calm, professional people and it had been good to know them.

I was resting my arm on the windowsill. As I looked at it, the hairs on my forearm began to stir slowly and stand up.

This time, it was a general opposite me, and I was sitting down. To one side of the general were two middle-aged men in suits; on the other side was a youngish man with thinning hair and an eager expression.

"You tasered me and drugged me," I told them. "That wasn't very friendly."

"We apologize for that, Mr. Dolan," said one of the middle-aged men. "We couldn't risk you . . . *leaving* again. Put yourself in our position."

I held up my hands. I was wearing manacles. The manacles were connected to a generator behind my chair; if I looked as if I was going to do something outrageous—or if I even sneezed a bit forcefully—the manacles would deliver a shock strong enough to stun me. I knew this because they'd demonstrated the process to me when I came round from the sedative.

"I would *love* to put myself in your position," I said. "So long as you could put yourself in mine."

"It's only a precaution, Mr. Dolan," said the other middle-aged man. "Until we can be sure you won't leave us again."

I looked at the manacles. From a certain point of view, they didn't go round my wrists at all. I lowered my hands and folded them in my lap. "Professor Delahaye," I said.

"We don't know," said the youngish man. "We don't dare go into the control room. We sent in bomb disposal robots with remote cameras and there's . . . something there, but no bodies, nothing alive."

"*Something?*" I asked.

He shook his head. "We don't know. The cameras won't image it. It's just a dead point in the middle of the room. Can you remember what happened?"

I was busy attacking Larry Day for having an affair with my wife. "They were doing the last shot of the series," I said. "Delahaye counted down and then there was . . ." I looked at them. "Sorry. I *won't image* it."

"Did anything seem out of the ordinary? Anything at all?"

Yes, I'd just found out Larry Day was having an affair with my wife. "No, everything seemed normal. But I'm not a physicist, I'm a journalist."

"Where do you . . . *go?*"

"I don't know. Somewhere. Nowhere. *Anywhere.*"

The four men exchanged glances. One of the middle-aged men said, "We think there may be another survivor."

I leaned forward.

"A day after your first, um, *appearance* there was an incident in Cairo," he went on. "Half the city centre was destroyed. There's no footage of what happened, but some of the survivors say they saw a *djinn* walking through the city, a human figure that walked through buildings and wrecked them."

A terrible thought occurred to me. "That might have been me."

The other middle-aged man shook his head. "We don't think so."

"Why?"

"Because it happened again yesterday in Nevada. While you were unconscious here. A small town called Spicerville was totally destroyed. Eight hundred people dead."

"We're calling it an explosion in a railcar full of chemicals," the general said. "The Egyptians say theirs was a meteorite strike. But we think it's . . . someone like you."

"Whatever happened at the SCC, it changed you," said the younger man with what I thought was admirable understatement. "We think it changed this other person too, whoever they are. But where you seem to have found a way to . . . cope with your . . . situation, the other person has not."

"I haven't found a way to *cope* at all," I told them. I looked at the table between us. It was a rather cheap looking conference table, the kind of thing the government bought in huge amounts from cut-rate office supply stores. It seemed that I had never looked at things properly before; now I could see how the table was constructed, from the subatomic level upward.

"Obviously this . . . person is dangerous," one of the middle-aged men said. "Any help you could give us would be very much appreciated."

I sighed. I took the table to pieces and put it back together in a shape that I found rather pleasing. Nobody else in the room found it pleasing at all, though, judging by the way they all jumped up and ran screaming for the door. I slipped away from the manacles and went back *there.*

I went outside and stood in front of the building with my hands in my pockets. About seven hours ago I had been sitting in a briefing room in a White House basement with the President and about a dozen NSA and CIA staffers, watching a video.

The video had been taken by a Predator drone flying over Afghanistan. It was the spearpoint of a long-running operation to kill a Taliban warlord codenamed WATERSHED, who had been tracked down to a compound in Helmand. It was the usual combat video, not black and white but that weird mixture of shades of grey. The landscape tipped and dipped as the Predator's operator, thousands of miles away in the continental United States, steered the drone in on its target. Then a scatter of buildings popped up over a hill and the drone launched its missile, and as it did a human figure came walking around the corner of one of the buildings. The crosshairs of the drone's camera danced around the centre of the screen for a few moments, then the building puffed smoke in all directions and disappeared.

And moments later, unaffected, seemingly not even having noticed the explosion, the figure calmly walked out of the smoke and carried on its way.

"Well," said the President when the video was over, "either the war in Afghanistan just took a *very* strange turn, or we're going to need your services, Mr. Dolan."

I looked into the sky. The moon was low down on the horizon and everything was bathed in a strange directionless silvery light that cast strange shadows from the buildings. There was an electrical *expectancy* in the air, a smell of ozone and burnt sugar, a breeze that blew from nowhere, and then he was there, standing a few yards from me, looking about him and making strange noises. I sighed.

"Larry," I called.

Larry looked round, saw me, and said, "Jesus, Alex. What the hell happened?"

Larry didn't remember The Accident, which was good. And he didn't remember what came after, which was even better. But he was surprisingly adaptable, and I couldn't afford to relax, even for a moment.

I walked over and stood looking at him. He looked like part of a comic strip illustration of a man blowing up. Here he was in frame one, a solid, whole human being. Here he was, at the end of the strip, nothing more than a widely-distributed scattering of bone and meat and other tissue. And here he was, three or four frames in, the explosion just getting going, his body flying apart. And that was Larry, a man impossibly caught in the middle of detonating. His body looked repugnant and absurd all at the same time, an animated human-shaped cloud of meat and blood, about twice normal size.

"There was an accident," I said. "Something happened during the last shot, we still don't know exactly what."

Larry's voice issued from somewhere other than his exploding larynx. It seemed to be coming from a long distance away, like a radio tuned to a distant galaxy. He said, "What happened to your hair, Alex?"

I ran a hand over my head. "It's been a while, Larry. I got old."

"How long?" asked that eerie voice.

"Nearly twenty-five years."

Larry looked around him and made those strange noises again. "Delahaye . . ."

"All dead," I said. "Delahaye, Warren, Chen, Bright, Morley. The whole team. You and I are the only survivors."

Larry looked at his hands; it was impossible to read the expression on what passed for his face, but he made a noise that might, if one were psychotic enough, be mistaken for a laugh. "I don't seem to have survived very well, Alex." He looked at me. "*You* seem to be doing all right, though."

I shrugged. "As I said, we still don't know exactly what happened."

Larry emitted that awful laugh again. "My god," he said, "it's like something from a Marvel comic. You think maybe I've become a superhero, Alex?"

"That's an . . . unusual way of looking at it," I allowed warily.

Larry sighed. "You'd think I'd get X-ray vision or something. Not . . ." he waved his not-quite-hands at me, ". . . *this*."

"Larry," I said, "you need help."

Larry laughed. "Oh? You *think*? Jesus, Alex." He started to pace back and forth. Then he stopped. "Where was I? Before?"

"Afghanistan. We think you were just trying to find your way back here."

Larry shook his head, which was an awful thing to watch. "No. Before that. There was . . . everything was the wrong . . . *shape* . . ."

I took a step forward and said, "Larry . . ."

"And before that . . . I was *here*, and we were having this conversation . . ."

"It's just *déjà vu*," I told him. "It's hardly the worst of your worries."

Larry straightened up and his body seemed to gain coherence. "Alex," he said, "how many times have we done this before?"

I shook my head. "Too fucking many," I said, and I plunged my hands into the seething exploding mass of Larry Day's body and pulled us both back into Hell.

I still wasn't sure why I went back after escaping the second time. Maybe I just wanted to know what had happened to me and there was no way to find out on my own. Maybe I was afraid that if I spent too long *there* I would forget what it was like to be human.

The general and his three friends were unavailable. I later discovered that they had been in hospital ever since they saw what I turned the table into; one of them never recovered. In their place, I was assigned two more generals—one from the Air Force and one from the Army—and an admiral, and a team of eager young scientists, all looked after by quiet, efficient people from the CIA and the NSA.

I was questioned, over and over and over again, and the answers I was able to give them wouldn't have covered the back of a postage stamp. One of the scientists asked me, "What's it like there? How many dimensions does it have?" and all I could tell him was, "Not enough. Too many. I don't know."

We were unprepared. We knew too little, and that was why he nearly got me that first time. I knew that Point Zero was like a beacon *there*, a great solid negative tornado, and one of the few useful pieces of advice I was able to contribute was to keep a watch on the SCC for any manifestations. I went back to our old house in Sioux Crossing to wait, because I *knew*. I knew he was looking for a landmark, a reference point, because that was what *I* had done. When the manifestations began, I was bustled in great secrecy to the Site, and I saw him appear for the first time. Heard him speak for the first time. Thought, not for the last time, *Of course. It had to be Larry.*

He was confused, frightened, angry, but he recovered quickly. I told him what had happened—what we understood, anyway—and he seemed to pull his exploding form together a little. He looked about him and said, *This must be what God feels like*, and my blood ran cold. And then I felt him try to take me apart and remake me, the way I had remade the table.

I did the first thing that crossed my mind. I grabbed him and went back *there* with him, and I let him go and came back *here*.

The second time he came back, it was the same thing. A few random manifestations, some baffling but relatively minor destruction. Then he found his way to Point Zero, confused, amnesiac. But he came to the same conclusion. *This must be what God feels like.* And I had to take him back *there*.

And again. And again. And again.

I walked an unimaginable distance. It took me an impossible length of time. Nothing here meant anything or made any sense, but there were structures, colossal things that were almost too small to see: the remains of Professor Delahaye and the other victims of The Accident. There were also the remains of a specially-trained SEAL team, sent in here by the President—not the present one but her predecessor—when he thought he could create a group of all-American superheroes. I, and pretty much every scientist involved in investigating The Accident, argued against that, but when the President says jump you just ask what altitude he wants, so the SEALs remain. There is no life or death *there*, only existence, so Professor Delahaye and the others exist in a Schroedinger not-quite-state, trying to make sense of what and where they are. If they ever succeed, I'm going to be busy.

The scientists call this "Calabi-Yau space," or, if they're trying to be particularly mysterious, "The Manifold." Which it may or may not be, nobody knows. The String Theorists, overwhelmed with joy at having eyewitness evidence of another space, named it, even though I could give them little in the way of confirmatory testimony. Calabi-Yau space exists a tiny fraction of a nanometre away from what I used to think of as "normal" space, but it would take more than the total energy output of the entire universe to force a single photon between them.

Travel between dimensions appears to be, however, more like judo than karate, more a manipulation of force than a direct application of it. Somehow, Delahaye's final shot manipulated those forces in just the wrong way, pitching everything within a radius of five metres into a terrible emptiness and leaving behind Point Zero, a pulsing, open wound between the worlds, a point that *won't be imaged*. Someone once told me that the odds of The Accident happening at all were billions and billions to one against. Like going into every casino on The Strip in Vegas and playing every slot machine and winning the jackpot on all of them, all in one evening. But here's the thing about odds and probability. You can talk about them as much as you want, do all the fancy math, but in the end there's only either/or. That's all that matters. Either you win all the jackpots on The Strip, or you don't. Either it will happen, or it won't. It did, and here I am. And here, somewhere, is Larry Day.

Existing in Calabi-Yau space, being able to step between dimensions, being able to use the insight this gives you to manipulate the "real" world, really *is* like being a god. Unfortunately, it's like being one of the gods H.P. Lovecraft used to write about, immense and unfathomable and entirely without human scruple. So far, the human race is lucky that Larry seems unable to quite get the knack of godhood. None of us can work out why I acclimatized to it so easily, or why it's still so difficult for Larry, why returning him *there* screws him up all over again while I can cross back-and-forth at will, without harm. Larry was one of the biggest brains humanity ever produced, and he can't get the hang of The Manifold, while I, the world's most prosaic man, as my ex-wife liked to remind me, took it more or less in my stride. All I can tell them is that every time we meet—and we've done this particular little pantomime fifty-two times so far—he seems to recover more quickly. One day he's going to come out of it bright-eyed and bushy-tailed and I won't be able to take him back *there*. I'll have to fight him *here*, and it'll be like nothing Stan Lee ever imagined. Either/or. Either the world will survive, or it won't.

Larry is not a nice man. He was a great man, before The Accident, and I liked him a lot, until I found out about him and my wife. But he's not a nice man. Of all the people in the world you'd want to get bitten by the radioactive spider, he'd probably come close to the bottom of the list.

And the wonderful, extravagant cosmic joke of it is that Larry is not even the nightmare scenario. The nightmare scenario is that Delahaye and Chen and Morley and the SEAL team and all the animals who got onto the Site despite the billion-dollar-per-annum containment operation somehow drop into a rest state at once, and find their way *here*. If that happens, it'll make the Twilight of the Gods look like a quiet morning in a roadside diner. I plan to be somewhere else on that day. I'm happy enough to present the appearance of humanity for the moment, but I don't owe these people anything.

Eventually, I came across a room. Although this wasn't a room in the sense that anyone *here* would recognize. It was all distributed planes of stress and knots of mass, open on all sides, too huge to measure. I stepped into the room and sat down in a comfortable chair.

Nobody screamed. Nobody ran away. They were expecting me, of course, and I had learned long ago how to clothe myself before I came *here*. People hate it when naked men appear out of nowhere in the Situation Room at the White House. Someone brought me coffee. The coffee here was always excellent.

"Mr. Dolan," said the President.

"Madam President," I said. I sipped my coffee. "He's recovering more quickly."

"We noticed," said one of the scientists, a man named Sierpinski. "The others?"

"I saw some of them. They're still aestivating. I'm not sure I should be checking them out; won't observing them collapse them into one state or the other?"

Sierpinski shrugged. *We don't know.* Maybe we should make that our company song.

"You look tired," said the President.

"I look how I want to look," I snapped, and regretted it. She was not an unkind person, and I *was* tired. And anyway, it was ridiculous. Why would a godlike transdimensional superhero want to look like a tubby balding middle-aged man? If I wanted, I could look like Lady Gaga or Robert Downey, Jr., or an enormous crystal eagle, but what I *really* want is to be ordinary again, and that, of all things, I cannot do.

I looked up at the expectant faces, all of them waiting to hear how I had saved the world again.

"Do you think I could have a sandwich?" I asked.

what we found

GEOFF RYMAN

Born in Canada, Geoff Ryman now lives in England. He made his first sale in 1976, to New Worlds, *but it was not until 1984, when he made his first appearance in* Interzone *with his brilliant novella "The Unconquered Country," that he first attracted any serious attention. "The Unconquered Country," one of the best novellas of the decade, had a stunning impact on the science fiction scene of the day, and almost overnight established Ryman as one of the most accomplished writers of his generation, winning him both the British Science Fiction Award and the World Fantasy Award; it was later published in a book version,* The Unconquered Country: A Life History. *His output has been sparse since then, by the high-production standards of the genre, but extremely distinguished, with his short fiction appearing frequently in* The Magazine of Fantasy & Science Fiction, *and his novel* The Child Garden: A Low Comedy *winning both the prestigious Arthur C. Clarke Award and the John W. Campbell Memorial Award; his later novel* Air *also won the Arthur C. Clarke Award. His other novels include* The Warrior Who Carried Life, *the critically acclaimed mainstream novel* Was, Coming of Enkidu, The King's Last Song, Lust, *and the underground cult classic 253, the "print remix" of an "interactive hypertext novel" which in its original form ran online on Ryman's home page of www.ryman.com, and which in its print form won the Philip K. Dick Award. Four of his novellas have been collected in* Unconquered Countries. *His most recent works are the anthology* When It Changed, *the novel* The Film-makers of Mars, *and the collection* Paradise Tales: and Other Stories.

In the story that follows, he relates the emotionally powerful story of characters caught between generations in a nation itself caught between the modern world and an old world of tribal superstitions.

Can't sleep. Still dark. Waiting for light in the East.

My rooster crows. Knows it's my wedding day. I hear the pig rootling around outside. Pig, the traditional gift for the family of my new wife. I can't sleep because alone in the darkness there is nothing between me and the realization that I do not want to get married. Well, Patrick, you don't have long to decide.

The night bakes black around me. 3:30 A.M. In three hours, the church at the top of the road will start with the singing. Two hours after that, everyone in both families will come crowding into my yard. The rooster crows again, all his wives in the small space behind the house. It is still piled with broken bottles from when my father lined the top of that wall with glass shards.

That was one of his good times, when he wore trousers and a hat and gave orders. I mixed the concrete, and passed it up in buckets to my eldest brother Matthew. He sat on the wall like riding a horse, slopping on concrete and pushing in the glass. Raphael was reading in the shade of the porch. "I'm not wasting my time doing all that," he said. "How is broken glass going to stop a criminal who wants to get in?" He always made me laugh, I don't know why. Nobody else was smiling.

When we were young my father would keep us sitting on the hot, hairy sofa in the dark, no lights, no TV because he was driven mad by the sound of the generator. Eyes wide, he would quiver like a wire, listening for it to start up again. My mother tried to speak and he said, "Sssh. Sssh! There it goes again."

"Jacob, the machine cannot turn itself on."

"Sssh! Sssh!" He would not let us move. I was about seven, and terrified. If the generator was wicked enough to scare my big strong father, what would it do to little me? I keep asking my mother what does the generator do?

"Nothing, your father is just being very careful."

"Terhemba is a coward," my brother Matthew said, using my Tiv name. My mother shushed him, but Matthew's merry eyes glimmered at me: *I will make you miserable later.* Raphael prized himself loose from my mother's grip and stomped across the sitting room floor.

People think Makurdi is a backwater, but now we have all you need for a civilized life. Beautiful banks with security doors, retina ID and air conditioning; new roads, solar panels on all the streetlights, and our phones are stuffed full of e-books. On one of the river islands they built the new hospital; and my university has a medical school, all pink and state-funded with laboratories that are as good as most. Good enough for controlled experiments with mice.

My research assistant Jide is Yoruba and his people believe that the grandson first born after his grandfather's death will continue that man's life. Jide says that we have found how that is true. This is a problem for Christian Nigerians, for it means that evil continues.

What we found in mice is this. If you deprive a mouse of a mother's love, if you make him stressed through infancy, his brain becomes methylated. The high levels of methyl deactivate a gene that produces a neurotrophin important for memory and emotional balance in both mice and humans. Schizophrenics have abnormally low levels of it.

It is a miracle of God that with each new generation, our genes are knocked clean. There is a new beginning. Science thought this meant that the effects of one life could not be inherited by another.

What we found is that high levels of methyl affect the sperm cells. Methylation is passed on with them, and thus the deactivation. A grandfather's stress is passed on through the male line, yea unto the third generation.

Jide says that what we have found is how the life of the father is continued by his sons. And that is why I don't want to wed.

My father would wander all night. His three older sons slept in one room. Our door would click open and he would stand and glare at me, me particularly, with a boggled and distracted eye as if I had done something outrageous. He would be naked; his towering height and broad shoulders humbled me, made me feel puny and endangered. I have an odd shaped head with an indented V going down my forehead. People said it was the forceps tugging me out: I was a difficult birth. That was supposed to be why I was slow to speak, slow to learn. My father believed them.

My mother would try to shush him back into their bedroom. Sometimes he would be tame and allow himself to be guided; he might chuckle as if it were a game and hug her. Or he might blow up, shouting and flinging his hands about, calling her woman, witch or demon. Once she whispered, "It's you who have the demon; the demon has taken hold of you, Jacob."

Sometimes he shuffled past our door and out into the government street, sleep-walking to his and our shame.

In those days, it was the wife's job to keep family business safe within the house. Our mother locked all the internal doors even by day to keep him inside, away from visitors from the church or relatives who dropped in on their way to Abuja. If he was being crazy in the sitting room, she would shove us back into our bedroom or whisk us with the broom out into the yard. She would give him whisky if he asked for it, to get him to sleep. Our mother could never speak of these things to anybody, even her own mother, let alone to us.

We could hear him making noises at night, groaning as if in pain, or slapping someone. The baby slept in my parents' room and he would start to wail. I would stare into the darkness: was Baba hurting my new brother? In the morning his own face would be puffed out. It was Raphael who dared to say something. The very first time I heard that diva voice was when he asked her, sharp and demanding, "Why does that man hit himself?"

My mother got angry and pushed Raphael's face; slap would be the wrong word; she was horrified that the problem she lived with was clear to a five-year-old. "You do not call your father 'that man'! Who are you to ask questions? I can see it's time we put you to work like children used to be when I was young. You don't know what good luck you had to be born into this household!"

Raphael looked back at her, lips pursed. "That does not answer my question."

My mother got very angry at him, shouted more things. Afterwards he looked so small and sad that I pulled him closer to me on the sofa. He crawled up onto my lap and just sat there. "I wish we were closer to the river," he said, "so we could go and play."

"Mamamimi says the river is dangerous." My mother's name was Mimi which means truth, so Mama Truth was a kind of title.

"Everything's dangerous," he said, his lower lip thrust out. A five-year-old should not have such a bleak face.

By the time I was nine, Baba would try to push us into the walls, wanting us hidden or wanting us gone. His vast hands would cover the back of our heads or shoulders and grind us against the plaster. Raphael would look like a crushed berry, but he shouted in a rage, "No! No! No!"

Yet my father wore a suit and drove himself to work. Jacob Terhemba Shawo worked as a tax inspector and electoral official.

Did other government employees act the same way? Did they put on a shell of calm at work? He would be called to important meetings in Abuja and stay for several days. Once Mamamimi sat at the table, her white bread uneaten, not caring what her children heard. "What you go to Abuja for? Who you sleep with there, Wildman? What diseases do you bring back into my house?"'

We stared down at our toast and tea, amazed to hear such things. "You tricked me into marriage with you. I bewail the day I accepted you. Nobody told me you were crazy!"

My father was not a man to be dominated in his own house. Clothed in his functionary suit, he stood up. "If you don't like it, go. See who will have you since you left your husband. See who will want you without all the clothes and jewelery I buy you. Maybe you no longer want this comfortable home. Maybe you no longer want your car. I can send you back to your village, and no one would blame me."

My mother spun away into the kitchen and began to slam pots. She did not weep. She was not one to be dominated either, but knew she could not change how things had to be. My father climbed into his SUV for Abuja in his special glowering suit that kept all questions at bay, with his polished head and square-cornered briefcase. The car purred away down the tree-lined government street with no one to wave him good-bye.

Jide's full name is name is Babajide. In Yoruba it means Father Wakes Up. His son is called Babatunde, Father Returns. It is something many people believe in the muddle of populations that is Nigeria.

My work on mice was published in *Nature* and widely cited. People wanted to believe that character could be inherited; that stressed fathers passed incapacities onto their grandchildren. It seemed to open a door to inherited characteristics, perhaps a modified theory of evolution. Our experiments had been conclusive: not only were there the non-genetically inherited emotional tendencies, but we could objectively measure the levels of methyl.

My father was born in 1965, the year before the Tiv rioted against what they thought were Muslim incursions. It was a time of coup and countercoup. The violence meant my grandfather left Jos, and moved the family to Makurdi. They walked, pushing some of their possessions and my infant father in a wheelbarrow. The civil war came with its trains full of headless Igbo rattling eastwards, and air force attacks on our own towns. People my age say, oh those old wars. What can Biafra possibly have to do with us, now?

What we found is that 1966 can reach into your head and into your balls and stain your children red. You pass war on. The cranky old men in the villagers, the lack of live music in clubs, the distrust of each other, soldiers everywhere, the crimes of colonialism embedded in the pattern of our roads. We live our grandfathers' lives.

Outside, the stars spangle. It will be a beautiful clear day. My traditional clothes hang unaccepted in the closet and I fear for any son that I might have. What will I pass on? Who would want their son to repeat the life of my father, the life of my brother? Ought I to get married at all? Outside in the courtyard, wet with dew, the white plastic chairs are lined up for the guests.

My grandmother Iveren would visit without warning. Her name meant "Blessing" which was a bitter thing for us. Grandmother Iveren visited all her children in turn no matter how far they moved to get away from her: Kano, Jalingo, or Makurdi.

A taxi would pull up and we would hear a hammering on our gate. One of us boys would run to open it and there she would be standing like a princess. "Go tell my son to come and pay for the taxi. Bring my bags please."

She herded us around our living room with the burning tip of her cigarette, inspecting us as if everything was found wanting. The Intermittent Freezer that only only kept things cool, the gas cooker, the rack of vegetables, the many tins of powdered milk, the rumpled throw rug, the blanket still on the sofa, the TV that was left tuned all day to Africa Magic. She would switch it off with a sigh as she passed. "Education," she would say shaking her head. She had studied literature at the University of Madison, Wisconsin, and she used that like she used her cigarette. Iveren was tiny, thin, very pretty and elegant in glistening blue or purple dresses with matching headpieces.

My mother's mother might also be staying, rattling out garments on her sewing machine. Mamagrand, we called her. The two women would feign civility, even smiling. My father lumbered in with suitcases; the two grandmothers would pretend that it made no difference to them where they slept, but Iveren would get the back bedroom and Mamagrand the sofa. My father then sat down to gaze at his knees, his jaws clamped shut like a turtle's. His sons assumed that that was what all children did, and that mothers always kept order in this way.

Having finished pursuing us around our own house, she would sigh, sit on the sofa and wait expectantly for my mother to bring her food. Mamamimi dutifully did so—family being family—and then sat down, her face going solid and her arms folded.

"You should know what the family is saying about you," Grandmother might begin, smiling so sweetly. "They are saying that you have infected my son, that you are unclean from an abortion." She would say that my aunt Judith would no longer allow Mamamimi into her house and had paid a woman to cast a spell on my mother to keep her away.

"Such a terrible thing to do. The spell can only be cured by cutting it with razor blades." Grandmother Iveren looked as though she might enjoy helping.

"Thank heavens such a thing cannot happen in a Christian household," my mother's mother would say.

"Could I have something to drink?"

From the moment Grandmother visited, all the alcohol in the house would start to disappear: little airline sample bottles, whisky from my father's boss, even the brandy Baba had brought from London. And not just alcohol. Grandmother would offer to help Mamamimi clean a bedroom; and small things would be gone from it forever, jewelry or scarves or little bronzes. She sold the things she pilfered, to keep herself in dresses and perfume.

It wasn't as if her children neglected their duty. She would be fed and housed for as long as any of us could stand it. Even so, she would steal and hide all the food in the house. My mother went grim faced, and would lift up mattresses to display the tins and bottles hidden under it. The top shelf of the bedroom closet would contain the missing stewpot with that evening's meal. "It's raw!" my mother would swelter at her. "It's not even cooked! Do you want it to go rotten in this heat?"

"I never get fed anything in this house. I am watched like a hawk!" Iveren complained, her face turned towards her giant son.

Mamamimi had strategies. She might take to her room ill, and pack meat in a cool chest and keep it under her bed. Against all tradition, especially if father was away, she would sometimes refuse to cook any food at all. For herself, for Grandmother or even us. "I'm on strike!" she announced once. "Here, here is money. Go buy food! Go cook it!" She pressed folded money into our hands. Raphael and I made a chicken stew, giggling. We had been warned about Iveren's cooking. "Good boys, to take the place of the mother," she said, winding our hair in her fingers.

Such bad behaviour on all sides made Raphael laugh. He loved it when Iveren came to stay, with her swishing skirts and dramatic manner and drunken stumbles; loved it when Mamamimi behaved badly and the house swelled with their silent battle of wills.

Grandmother would say things to my mother like: "We knew that you were not on our level, but we thought you were a simple girl from the country and that your innocence would be good for him." Chuckle. "If only we had known."

"If only I had," my mother replied.

My father's brothers had told us stories about Granny. When they were young, she would bake cakes with salt instead of sugar and laugh when they bit into them. She would make stews out of only bones, having thrown the goat away. She would cook with no seasoning so that it was like eating water, or cook with so many chillies that it was like eating fire.

When my uncle Eamon tried to sell his car, she stole the starter motor. She was right in there with a monkey wrench and spirited it away. It would cough and grind when potential buyers turned the key. When he was away, she put the motor back in and sold the car herself. She told Eamon that it had been stolen. When Eamon saw someone driving it, he had the poor man arrested, and the story came out.

My other uncle Emmanuel was an officer in the Air Force, a fine looking man in his uniform. When he first went away to do his training, Grandmother told all the neighbours that he was a worthless ingrate who neglected his mother, never calling her or giving her gifts. She got everyone so riled against him that when he came home to the village, the elders raised sticks against him and shouted, "How dare you show your face here after the way you have treated your mother!" For who would think a mother would say such things about a son without reason?

It was Grandmother who reported gleefully to Emmanuel that his wife had tested HIV positive. "You should have yourself tested. A shame you are not man enough to satisfy your wife and hold her to you. All that smoking has made you impotent."

She must be a witch, Uncle Emmanuel said, how else would she have known when he himself did not?

Raphael would laugh at her antics. He loved it when Granny started asking us all for gifts—even the orphan girl who lived with us. Iveren asked if she couldn't take the cushion covers home with her, or just one belt. Raphael yelped with laughter and clapped his hands. Granny blinked at him. What did he find so funny? Did my brother like her?

She knew what to make of me: quiet, well-behaved. I was someone to torment.

I soon learned how to behave around her. I would stand, not sit, in silence in my white shirt, tie and blue shorts.

"Those dents in his skull," she said to my mother once, during their competitive couch-sitting. "Is that why he's so slow and stupid?"

"That's just the shape of his head. He's not slow."

"Tuh. Your monstrous firstborn didn't want a brother and bewitched him in the womb."

Her eyes glittered all over me, her smile askew. "The boy cannot talk properly. He sounds ignorant."

My mother said that I sounded fine to her and that I was a good boy and got good grades in school.

My father was sitting in shamed silence. What did it mean that my father said nothing in my favour? Was I stupid?

"Look to your own children," my mother told her. "Your son is not doing well at work, and they delay paying him. So we have very little money. I'm afraid we can't offer you anything except water from the well. I have a bad back. Would you be so kind to fetch water yourself, since your son offers you nothing?"

Grandmother chuckled airily, as if my mother was a fool and would see soon enough. "So badly brought up. My poor son. No wonder your children are such frights."

That very day my mother took me round to the back of the house, where she grew her herbs. She bowed down to look into my eyes and held my shoulders and told me, "Patrick, you are a fine boy. You do everything right. There is nothing wrong with you. You do well in your lessons, and look how you washed the car this morning without even being asked."

It was Raphael who finally told Granny off. She had stayed for three months. Father's hair was corkscrewing off in all directions and his eyes had a trapped light in them. Everyone had taken to cooking their own food at night, and every spoon and knife in the house had disappeared.

"Get out of this house, you thieving witch. If you were nice to your family, they would let you stay and give you anything you want. But you can't stop stealing things." He was giggling. "Why do you tell lies and make such trouble? You should be nice to your children and show them loving care."

"And you should learn how to be polite." Granny sounded weak with surprise.

"Ha-ha! And so should you! You say terrible things about us. None of your children believe a thing you say. You only come here when no one else can stand you and you only leave when you know you've poisoned the well so much even you can't drink from it. It's not very intelligent of you, when you depend on us to eat."

He drove her from the house, keeping it up until it no other outcome were possible. "Blessing, our Blessing, the taxi is here!" pursuing her to the gate with mockery. Even Matthew, started to laugh. Mother had to hide her mouth. He held the car door open for her. "You'd best read your Bible and give up selling all your worthless potions."

Father took hold of Raphael's wrists, gently. "That's enough," he said. "Grandmother went through many bad things." He didn't say it in anger. He didn't say it like a wild man. Something sombre in his voice made Raphael calm.

"You come straight out of the bush," Grandmother said, almost unperturbed. "No wonder my poor son is losing his mind." She looked directly at Raphael. "The old ways did work." Strangely, he was the only one she dealt with straightforwardly. "They wore out."

Something happened to my research.

At first the replication studies showed a less marked effect, less inherited stress, lower methyl levels. But soon we ceased to be able to replicate our results at all.

The new studies dragged me down, made me suicidal. I felt I had achieved something with my paper, made up for all my shortcomings, done something that would have made my family proud of me if they were alive.

Methylation had made me a full professor. Benue State's home page found room to feature me as an example of the university's research excellence. I sought design flaws in the replication studies; that was the only thing I published. All my life I had fought to prove I wasn't slow, or at least hide it through hard work. And here before the whole world, I was being made to look like a fraud.

Then I read the work of Jonathan Schooler. The same thing had happened to him. His research had proved that if you described a memory clearly you ceased to remember it as well. The act of describing faces reduced his subjects' ability to recognize them later. The effects he measured were so huge and so unambiguous, and people were so intrigued by the implications of what he called verbal overshadowing, that his paper was cited 400 times.

Gradually, it had become impossible to replicate his results. Every time he did the experiment, the effect shrank by 30 percent.

I got in touch with Schooler, and we began to check the record. We found that all the way back in the 1930s results of E.S.P. experiments by Joseph Banks Rhine declined. In replication, his startling findings evaporated to something only slightly different from chance. It was as if scientific truths wore out, as if the act of observing them reduced their effect.

Jide laughed and shook his head. "We think the same thing!" he said. "We always say that a truth can wear out with the telling."

That is why I am sitting here writing, dreading the sound of the first car arriving, the first knock on my gate.

I am writing to wear out both memory and truth.

Whenever my father was away, or sometimes to escape Iveren, Mamamimi would take all us boys back to our family village. It is called Kawuye, on the road towards Taraba State. Her friend Sheba would drive us to the bus station in the market, and we would wait under the shelter, where the women cooked rice and chicken and sold sweating tins of Coca-Cola. Then we would stuff ourselves into the van next to some fat businessman who had hoped for a row of seats to himself.

Matthew was the firstborn, and tried to boss everyone even Mamamimi. He had teamed up with little Andrew from the moment he'd been born. Andrew was too young to be a threat to him. The four brothers fell into two teams and Mamamimi had to referee, coach, organize and punish.

If Matthew and I were crammed in next to each other, we would fight. I could stand his needling and bossiness only so long and then wordlessly clout him. That made me the one to be punished. Mamamimi would swipe me over the head and Matthew's eyes would tell me that he'd done it deliberately.

It was hot and crowded on the buses, with three packed rows of sweating ladies, skinny men balancing deliveries of posters on their laps, or mothers dandling heat-drugged infants. It was not supportable to have four boys elbowing, kneeing and scratching.

Mamamimi started to drive us herself in her old green car. She put Matthew in the front so that he felt in charge. Raphael and I sat in the back reading, while next to us Andrew cawed for Matthew's attention.

Driving by herself was an act of courage. The broken-edged roads would have logs pulled across them, checkpoints they were called, with soldiers. They would wave through the stuffed vans but they would stop a woman driving four children and stare into the car. Did we look like criminals or terrorists? They would ask her questions and rummage through our bags and mutter things that we could not quite hear. I am not sure they were always proper. Raphael would noisily flick through the pages of his book. "Nothing we can do about it," he would murmur. After slipping them some money, Mama would drive on.

As if by surprise, up and over a hill, we would roller-coaster down through maize fields into Kawuye. I loved it there. The houses were the best houses for Nigeria and typical of the Tiv people, round and thick-walled with high pointed roofs and tiny windows. The heat could not get in and the walls sweated like a person to keep cool. There were no wild men waiting to leap out, no poison grandmothers. My great-uncle Jacob—it is a common name in my family—repaired cars with the patience of a cricket; opening, snipping, melting, and reforming. He once repaired a vehicle by replacing the fan belt with the elastic from my mother's underwear.

Raphael and I would buy firewood, trading some of it for eggs, ginger and yams. We also helped my aunty with her pig roasting business. To burn off the bristles, we lower it onto a fire and watch grassfire lines of red creep up each strand. It made a smell like burning hair and Raphael and I would pretend we were pirates cooking people. Then we turned the pig on a spit until it crackled. At nights we were men, serving beer and taking money.

We both got fat because our pay was some of the pig, and if no one was looking, the beer as well. I ate because I needed to get as big as Matthew. In the evenings the generators coughed to life and the village smelled of petrol and I played football barefoot under lights. There were jurisdictions and disagreements, but laughing uncles to adjudicate with the wisdom of a Solomon. So even the four of us liked each other more in Kawuye.

Then after whole weeks of sanity, my mother's phone would sing out with the voice of Mariah Carey or an American prophetess. As the screen illuminated, Mamamimi's face would scowl. We knew the call meant that our father was back in the house, demanding our return.

Uncle Jacob would change the oil and check the tyres and we would drive back through the fields and rock across potholes onto the main road. At intersections, children swarmed around the car, pushing their hands through open windows, selling plastic bags of water or dappled plantains. Their eyes peered in at us. I would feel ashamed somehow. Raphael wound up the window and hollered at them. "Go away and stop your staring. There's nothing here for you to see!"

Baba would be waiting for us reading *ThisDay* stiffly, like he had broomsticks for bones, saying nothing.

After that long drive, Mom would silently go and cook. Raphael told him off. "It's not very fair of you, Popsie, to make her work. She has just driven us back all that way just to be nice to us and show us a good time in the country."

Father's eyes rested on him like drills on DIY.

That amused Raphael. "Since you choose to be away all the time, she has to do all the work here. And you're just sitting there." My father rattled the paper and said nothing. Raphael was twelve years old.

I was good at football, so I survived school well enough. But my brother was legendary.

They were reading *The Old Man and The Sea* in English class, and Raphael blew up at the teacher. She said that lions were a symbol of Hemingway being lionized when young. She said the old fisherman carrying a mast made him some sort of Jesus with his cross. He told her she had a head full of nonsense. I can see him doing it. He would bark with sudden laughter and bounce up and down in his chair and declare, delighted, "That's blasphemy! It's just a story about an old man. If Hemingway had wanted to write a story about Jesus he was a clever enough person to have written one!" The headmaster gave him a clip about the ear. Raphael wobbled his head at him as if shaking a finger. "Your hitting me doesn't make me wrong." None of the other students ever bothered us. Raphael still got straight As.

Our sleepy little bookshops, dark, wooden and crammed into corners of markets knew that if they got a book on chemistry or genetics they could sell it to Raphael. He set up a business to buy in textbooks that he knew Benue State was going to recommend. At sixteen he would sit on benches at the university sipping cold drinks and selling books, previous essays and condoms. Everybody assumed that he was already being educated there. Tall beautiful students would call him "Sah." One pretty girl called him "Prof." She had honey-coloured, extended hair, and a spangled top that hung off one shoulder.

"I'm his brother," I told her proudly.

"So you are the handsome one," she said, being kind to what she took to be the younger brother. For many weeks I carried her in my heart.

The roof of our government bungalow was flat and Raphael and I took to living on it. We slept there; we even climbed the ladder with our plates of food. We read by torchlight, rigged mosquito nets, and plugged the mobile phone into our netbook. The world flooded into it; the websites of our wonderful Nigerian newspapers, the BBC, al Jazeera, *Nature, New Scientist.* We pirated Nollywood movies. We got slashdotcom; we hacked into the scientific journals, getting all those ten-dollar PDFs for free.

We elevated ourselves above the murk of our household. Raphael would read aloud in many different voices, most of them mocking. He would giggle at news articles. "Oh, story! Now they are saying Fashola is corrupt. Hee hee hee. It's the corrupt people saying that to get their own back."

"Oh this is interesting," he would say and read about what some Indian at Caltech had found out about gravitational lenses.

My naked father would pad out like an old lion gone mangy and stare up at us, looking bewildered as if he wanted to join us but couldn't work out how. "You shouldn't be standing out there with no clothes on," Raphael told him. "What would happen if someone came to visit?" My father looked as mournful as an abandoned dog.

Jacob Terhemba Shawo was forced to retire. He was only forty-two. We had to leave the Government Reserved Area. Our family name means "high on the hill," and that's where we had lived. I remember that our well was so deep that once I dropped the bucket and nothing could reach it. A boy had to climb down the stones in the well wall to fetch it.

We moved into the house I live in now, a respectable bungalow across town, surrounded with high walls. It had a sloping roof, so Raphael and I were no longer elevated.

The driveway left no room for Mamamimi's herb garden, so we bought a neighbouring patch of land but couldn't afford the sand and cement to wall it off. School children would wander up the slope into our maize, picking it or sometimes doing their business.

The school had been built by public subscription and the only land cheap enough was in the slough. For much of the year the new two-storey building rose vertically out of a lake like a castle. It looked like the Scottish islands in my father's calendars. Girls boated to the front door and climbed up a ramp. A little beyond was a marsh, with ponds and birds and water lilies: beautiful but it smelled of drains and rotting reeds.

We continued to go to the main cathedral for services. White draperies hung the length of its ceiling, and the stained glass doors would accordion open to let in air. Local dignitaries would be in attendance and nod approval as our family lined up to take communion and make our gifts to the church, showing obeisance to the gods of middle-class respectability.

But the church at the top of our unpaved road was bare concrete always open at the sides. People would pad past my bedroom window and the singing of hymns would swell with the dawn. Some of the local houses would be village dwellings amid the ageing urban villas.

Chickens still clucked in our new narrow back court. If you dropped a bucket down this well all you had to do was reach in for it. The problem was to stop water flooding into the house. The concrete of an inner courtyard was broken and the hot little square was never used, except for the weights that Raphael had made for himself out of iron bars and sacks of concrete. Tiny and rotund, he had dreams of being a muscleman. His computer desktop was full of a Nigerian champion in briefs. I winced with embarrassment whenever his screen sang open in public. What would people think of him, with that naked man on his netbook?

My father started to swat flies all the time. He got long sticky strips of paper and hung them everywhere—across doorways, from ceilings, in windows. They would snag in our hair as we carried out food from the kitchen. All we saw was flies on strips of paper. We would wake up in the night to hear him slapping the walls with books, muttering "flies flies flies."

The house had a tin roof and inside we baked like bread. Raphael resented it personally. He was plump and felt the heat. My parents had installed the house's only AC in their bedroom. He would just as regularly march in with a spanner and screwdriver and steal it. He would stomp out, the cable dragging behind him, with my mother wringing her hands and weeping. "That boy! That crazy boy! Jacob! Come see to your son."

Raphael shouted, "Buy another one! You can afford it!"

"We can't Raphael! You know that! We can't."

And Raphael said, "I'm not letting you drag me down to your level."

Matthew by then was nearly nineteen and had given up going to university. His voice was newly rich and sad. "Raphael. The whole family is in trouble. We would all like the AC, but if Baba doesn't get it, he wanders, and that is a problem too."

I didn't like it that Raphael took it from our parents without permission. Shamefaced with betrayal of him, I helped Matthew fix the AC back in our parents' window.

Raphael stomped up to me and poked me with his finger. "You should be helping me, not turning tail and running!" He turned his back and said, "I'm not talking to you."

I must have looked very sad because later I heard his flip-flops shuffling behind me. "You are my brother and of course I will always talk to you. I'm covered in shame that I said such a thing to you." Raphael had a genius for apologies, too.

When Andrew was twelve, our father drove him to Abuja and left him with people, some great-aunt we didn't know. She was childless, and Andrew had come back happy from his first visit sporting new track shoes. She had bought him an ice cream from Grand Square. He went back.

One night Raphael heard mother and father talking. He came outside onto the porch, his fat face gleaming. "I've got some gossip," he told me. "Mamamimi and father have sold Andrew!"

Sold was an exaggeration. They had put him to work and were harvesting his wages. In return he got to live in an air-conditioned house. Raphael giggled. "It's so naughty of them!" He took hold of my hand and pulled me with him right into their bedroom.

Both of them were decent, lying on the bed with their books. Raphael announced, very pleased with himself. "You're not selling my brother like an indentured servant. Just because he was a mistake and you didn't want him born so late and want to be shot of him now."

Mamamimi leapt at him. He ran, laughter pealing, and his hands swaying from side to side. I saw only then that he had the keys for the SUV in his hand. He pulled me with him out into the yard, and then swung me forward. "Get the gate!" He popped himself into the driver's seat and roared the engine. Mamamimi waddled after him. The car rumbled forward, the big metal gate groaned open, dogs started to bark. Raphael bounced the SUV out of the yard, and pushed its door open for me. Mamamimi was right behind, and I didn't want to be the one punished again, so I jumped in. "Goodbye-yeee!" Raphael called in a singsong voice, smiling right into her face.

We somehow got to Abuja alive. Raphael couldn't drive, and trucks kept swinging out onto our side of the road accelerating and beeping. We swerved in and out, missing death, passing the corpses of dead transports lined up along the roadside. Even I roared with laughter as lorries wailed past us by inches.

Using the GPS, Raphael foxed his way to the woman's house. Andrew let us in; he worked as her boy, beautifully dressed in a white shirt and jeans, with tan sandals of interwoven strips. In we strode and Raphael said, very pleasantly at first. "Hello! *M'sugh!* How are you? I am Jacob's son, Andrew's brother."

I saw at once this was a very nice lady. She was huge like a balloon, with a child-counselling smile, and she welcomed us and hugged Andrew to her.

"Have you paid my parents anything in advance for Andrew's work? Because they want him back, they miss him so much."

She didn't seem to mind. "Oh, they changed their minds. Well course they did, Andrew is such a fine young man. Well, Andrew, it seems your brothers want you back!"

"I changed their minds for them." Raphael always cut his words out of the air like a tailor making a bespoke garment. Andrew looked confused and kept his eyes on the embroidery on his jeans.

Andrew must have known what had happened because he didn't ask why it was us two who had come to fetch him. Raphael had saved him, not firstborn Matthew—if he had wanted to be saved from decent clothes and shopping in Abuja

When we got back home, no mention was made of anything by anyone. Except by Raphael, to me, later. "It is so interesting isn't it, that they haven't said a thing. They know what they were doing was wrong. How would they like to be a child and know their parents had sent them to work?" Matthew said nothing either. We had been rich; now we were poor.

Jide and I measured replication decline.

We carried out our old experiment over and over and measured methyl as levels declined for no apparent reason. Then we increased the levels of stress. Those poor mice! In the name of science, we deprived them of a mother and then cuddly surrogates. We subjected them to regimes of irregular feeding and random light and darkness and finally electric shocks.

There was no doubt. No matter how much stress we subjected them to, after the first spectacular results, the methyl levels dropped off with each successive experiment. Not only that, but the association between methyl and neurotrophin suppression reduced as well—objectively measured, the amount of methyl and its effect on neurotrophin production were smaller with each study. We had proved the decline effect. Truth wore out. Or at least, scientific truth wore out.

We published. People loved the idea and we were widely cited. Jide became a lecturer and a valued colleague. People began to speak of something called Cosmic Habituation. The old ways were no longer working. And I was thirty-seven.

With visitors, Raphael loved being civil, a different person. Sweetly and sociably, he would say, "M'sugh;" our mix of hello, good-bye and pardon me. He loved bringing them trays of cold water from the Intermittent Freezer. He remembered everybody's name and birthday. He hated dancing, but loved dressing up for parties. Musa the tailor made him wonderful robes with long shirts, matching trousers, shawls.

My father liked company too, even more so after his Decline. He would suddenly stand up straight and smile eagerly. I swear, his shirt would suddenly look ironed, his shoes polished. I was envious of the company, usually men from his old work. They could get my father laughing. He would look young then, and merry, and slap the back of his hand on his palm, jumping up to pass around the beer. I wanted him to laugh with me.

Very suddenly Matthew announced he was getting married. We knew it was his way of escaping. After the wedding he and his bride would move in with her sister's husband. He would help with their fish farm and plantation of nym trees. We did well by him: no band, but a fine display of food. My father boasted about how strong Matthew was, always captain. From age twelve he had read the business news like some boys read adventure stories. Matthew, he said, was going to be a leader.

My father saw me looking quiet and suddenly lifted up his arms, "Then there is my Patrick who is so quiet. I have two clever sons to go alongside the strong one." His hand felt warm on my back.

By midnight it was cool and everybody was outside dancing, even Raphael who grinned, making circular motions with his elbows and planting his feet as firmly as freeway supports.

My father wavered up to me like a vision out of the desert, holding a tin of High Life. He stood next to me watching the dancing and the stars. "You know," he said. "Your elder brother was sent to you by Jesus." My heart sank: *yes, I know, to lead the family, to be an example.*

"He was so unhappy when you were born. He saw you in your mother's arms and howled. He is threatened by you. Jesus sent you Matthew so that you would know what it is to fight to distinguish yourself. And you learned that. You are becoming distinguished."

I can find myself being kind in that way; suddenly, in private with no one else to hear or challenge the kindness, as if kindness were a thing to shame us.

I went back onto the porch and there was Raphael looking hunched and large, a middle-aged patriarch. He'd heard what my father said. "So who taught Matthew to be stupid? Why didn't he ever tell him to leave you alone?"

My father's skin faded. It had always been very dark, so black that he would use skin lightener as a moisturiser without the least bleaching effect. Now very suddenly, he went honey-coloured; his hair became a knotted muddy brown. A dried clot of white spit always threatened to glue his lips together, and his eyes went bad, huge and round and ringed with swollen flesh like a frog's. He sprouted thick spectacles, and had to lean his head back to see, blinking continually. He could no longer remember how to find the toilet from the living room. He took to crouching down behind the bungalow with the hens, then as things grew worse off the porch in front of the house. Mamamimi said, "It makes me think there may be witchcraft after all." Her face swelled and went hard until it looked like a stone.

On the Tuesday night before he died, he briefly came back to us. Tall, in trousers, so skinny now that he looked young again. He ate his dinner with good manners, the fou-fou cradling the soup so that none got onto his fingers. Outside on the porch he started to talk, listing the names of all his brothers.

Then he told us that Grandmother was not his actual mother. Another woman had borne him, made pregnant while dying of cancer. Grandfather knew pregnancy would kill her, but he made her come to term. She was bearing his first son.

Two weeks after my father was born, his real mother had died, and my grandfather married the woman called Blessing.

Salt instead of sugar. Iveren loved looking as though she had given the family its first son. It looked good as they lined up in church. But she had no milk for him. Jacob Terhemba Shawo spent his first five years loveless in a war.

My father died three days before Matthew's first child was born. Matthew and his wife brought her to our house to give our mother something joyful to think about.

The baby's Christian name was Isobel. Her baby suit had three padded Disney princesses on it and her hair was a red down.

Matthew chuckled, "Don't worry, Mamamimi, this can't be grandpa, it's a girl."

Raphael smiled. "Maybe she's grandpa born in woman's body."

Matthew's wife clucked her tongue. She didn't like us and she certainly didn't like what she'd heard about Raphael. She drew herself up tall and said, "Her name is Iveren."

Matthew stared at his hands; Mamamimi froze; Raphael began to dance with laughter.

"It was my mother's name," the wife said.

"Ah!" cried Raphael. "Two of them, Matthew. Two Iverens! Oh, that is such good luck for you!"

I saw from my mother's unmoving face, and from a flick of the fingers, a jettisoning, that she had consigned the child to its mother's family and Matthew to that other family too. She never took a proper interest in little Iveren.

But Grandmother must have thought that they had named the child after her. Later, she went to live with them, which was exactly the blessing I would wish for Matthew.

Raphael became quieter, preoccupied, as if invisible flies buzzed around his head. I told myself we were working too hard. Both of us had been applying for oil company scholarships. I wanted the both of us to go together to the best universities: Lagos or Ibadan. I thought of all those strangers, in states that were mainly Igbo or Yoruba or maybe even Muslim. I was sure we were a team.

In the hall bookcase a notice appeared. DO NOT TOUCH MY BOOKS. I DON'T INTERFERE WITH YOUR JOB. LEAVE ALL BOOKS IN ORDER.

They weren't his alone. "Can I look at them, at least?"

He looked at me balefully. "If you ask first."

I checked his downloads and they were all porn. I saw the terrible titles of the files, that by themselves were racial and sexual abuse. A good Christian boy, I was shocked and dismayed. I said something to him and he puffed up, looking determined. "I don't live by other people's rules."

He put a new password onto our machine so that I could not get into it. My protests were feeble.

"I need to study, Raphael."

"Study is beyond you," he said. "Study cannot help you."

At the worst possible time for him his schoolteachers went on strike because they weren't being paid. Raphael spent all day clicking away at his keyboard, not bothering to dress. His voice became milder, faint and sweet but he talked only in monosyllables. "Yes. No. I don't know." Not angry, a bit as though he was utterly weary.

That Advent, Mamamimi, Andrew, Matthew and family went to the cathedral, but my mother asked me to stay behind to look after Raphael.

"You calm him," Mamamimi said and for some reason that made my eyes sting. They went to church, and I was left alone in the main room. I was sitting on the old sofa watching some TV trash about country bumpkins going to Lagos.

Suddenly Raphael trotted out of our bedroom in little Japanese steps wearing one of my mother's dresses. He had folded a matching cloth around his head into an enormous flower shape, his face ghostly with makeup. My face must have been horrified: it made him chatter with laughter. "What the well dressed diva is wearing this season."

All I thought then was *Raphael don't leave me.* I stood up and I pushed him back towards the room; like my mother I was afraid of visitors. "Get it off, get it off, what are you doing?"

"You don't like it?" He batted his eyelashes.

"No, I do not! What's got into you?"

"Raphael is not a nurse! Raphael does not have to be nice!"

I begged him to get out of the dress. I kept looking at my telephone for the time, worried when they would be back. Above all else I didn't want Mama to know he had taken her things.

He stepped out of the dress, and let the folded headdress trail behind him, falling onto the floor. I scooped them up, checked them for dirt or makeup, and folded them up as neatly as I could.

I came back to the bedroom and he was sitting in his boxer shorts and flip-flops, staring at his screen and with complete unconcern was doing something to himself.

I asked the stupidest question. "What are you doing?"

"What does it look like? It's fun. You should join in." Then he laughed. He turned the screen towards me. In the video, a man was servicing a woman's behind. I had no idea people did such things. I howled, and covered my mouth, laughing in shock. I ran out of the room and left him to finish.

Without Raphael I had no one to go to and I could not be seen to cry. I went outside and realized that I was alone. What could I say to my mother? Our Raphael is going mad? For her he had always been mad. Only I had really liked Raphael and now he was becoming someone else, and I was so slow I would only ever be me.

He got a strange disease that made his skin glisten but a fever did not register. It was what my father had done: get illnesses that were not quite physical. He ceased to do anything with his hair. It twisted off his head in knots and made him look like a beggar.

He was hardly ever fully dressed. He hung around the house in underwear and flip-flops. I became his personal Mamamimi, trying to stop the rest of the family finding out, trying to keep him inside the room. In the middle of the night, he would get up. I would sit up, see he wasn't there, and slip out of the house trying to find him, walking around our unlit streets. This is not wise in our locality. The neighbourhood boys patrol for thieves or outsiders, and they can be rough if they do not recognize your face. "I'm Patrick, I moved into the house above the school. I'm trying to find my brother Raphael."

"So how did you lose him?"

"He's not well, he's had a fever, he wanders."

"The crazy family," one of them said.

Their flashlights dazzled my eyes, but I could see them glance at each other. "He means that dirty boy." They said that of Raphael?

"He's my brother. He's not well."

I would stay out until they brought him back to me, swinging their AK47s. He could so easily have been shot. He was wearing almost nothing, dazed like a sleepwalker and his hair in such a mess. Raphael had always been vain. His skin Vaselined with the scent of roses, the fine shirt with no tails designed to hang outside the trousers and hide his tummy, his nails manicured. Now he looked like a labourer who needed a bath.

Finally one night, the moon was too bright and the boys brought him too close to our house. My mother ran out of the groaning gate. "Patrick, Patrick, what is it?"

"These boys have been helping us find Raphael," was all I said. I felt ashamed and frustrated because I had failed to calm him, to find him myself, to keep the secret locked away, especially from Mamamimi.

When my mother saw him she whispered, "Wild man!" and it was like a chill wind going through me. She had said what I knew but did not let myself acknowledge. Again, it was happening again, first to the father, then to the son.

I got him to bed, holding both his arms and steering him. Our room was cool as if we were on a mountain. I came out back into the heat and Mamamimi was waiting, looking old. "Does he smoke gbana?" she asked.

I said I didn't think so. "But I no longer know him."

In my mind I was saying *Raphael come back.* Sometimes my mother would beseech me with her eyes to do something. Such a thing should not befall a family twice.

Makurdi lives only because of its river. The Benue flows into the great Niger, grey-green with fine beaches that are being dug up for concrete and currents so treacherous they look like moulded jellies welling up from below. No one swims there, except at dusk, in the shallows, workmen go to wash, wading out in their underwear.

Raphael would disappear at sunset and go down the slopes to hymn the men. It was the only time he dressed up: yellow shirt, tan slacks, good shoes. He walked out respectfully onto the sand and sang about the men, teased them, and chortled. He would try to take photographs of them. The men eyed him in fear, or ignored him like gnarled trees, or sometimes threw pebbles at him to make him go away. The things he said were irresponsible. Matthew and I would be sent to fetch him back. Matthew hated it. He would show up in his bank suit, with his car that would get sand in it. "Let him stay there! He only brings shame on himself!"

But we could not leave our brother to have stones thrown at him. He would be on the beach laughing at his own wild self, singing paeans of praise for the beauty of the bathers, asking their names, asking where they lived. Matthew and I would be numb from shame. "Come home, come home," we said to him, and too the labourers, "Please excuse us, we are good Christians, he is not well." We could not bring ourselves to call him our brother. He would laugh and run away. When we caught him, he would sit down on the ground and make us lift him up and carry him back up to Matthew's car. He was made of something other than flesh; his bones were lead, his blood mercury.

"I can't take more of this," said Matthew.

It ended so swiftly that we were left blinking. He disappeared from the house as usual; Mamamimi scolded Andrew to keep out of it and rang Matthew. He pulled up outside our gates so back we went past the university, and the zoo where Baba had taken us as kids, then down beyond the old bridge.

This time was the worst, beyond anything. He was wearing one of Mamamimi's dresses, sashaying among construction workers with a sun umbrella, roaring with laughter as he sang.

He saw us and called waving. "M'sugh! My brothers! My dear brothers! I am going swimming."

He ran away from us like a child, into the river. He fought his way into those strong green currents, squealing like a child perhaps with delight as the currents cooled him. The great dress blossomed out then sank. He stumbled on pebbles underfoot, dipped under the water and was not seen again.

"Go get him!" said Matthew.

I said nothing, did nothing

"Go on, you're the only one who likes him." He had to push me.

I nibbled at the edge of the currents. I called his name in a weak voice as if I really didn't want him back. I was angry with him as if he was now playing a particularly annoying game. Finally I pushed my way in partly so that Matthew would tell our mother that I'd struggled to find him. I began to call his name loudly, not so much in the hope of finding him as banishing this new reality. Raphael. Raphael, I shouted, meaning this terrible thing cannot be, not so simply, not so quickly. Finally I dived under the water. I felt the current pull and drag me away by my heels. I fought my way back to the shore but I knew I had not done enough, swiftly enough. I knew that he had already been swept far away.

On the bank, Matthew said, "Maybe it is best that he is gone." Since then, I have not been able to address more than five consecutive words to him.

That's what the family said, if not in words. Best he was gone. The bookcase was there with its notice. I knew we were cursed. I knew we would all be swept away.

Oh story, Raphael seemed to say to me. *You just want to be miserable so you have an excuse to fail.*

We need a body to bury, I said to his memory.

It doesn't make any difference; nobody in this family will mourn. They have too many worries of their own. You'll have to take care of yourself now. You don't have your younger brother to watch out for you.

The sun set, everyone else inside the house. I wanted to climb up onto a roof, or sit astride the wall. I plugged the mobile phone into the laptop, but in the depths of our slough I could not get a signal. I went into our hot unlit hall and pulled out the books, but they were unreadable without Raphael. Who would laugh for me as I did not laugh? Who would speak my mind for me as I could never find my mind in time? Who would know how to be pleasant with guests, civil in this uncivil world? I picked up our book on genetics and walked up to the top of the hill, and sat in the open unlit shed of a church and tried to read it in the last of the orange light. I said, Patrick, you are not civil and can't make other people laugh, but you can do this. This is the one part of Raphael you can carry on.

I read it aloud, like a child sounding out words, to make them go in as facts. I realized later I was trying to read in the dark, in a church. I had been chanting nonsense GATTACA aloud, unable to see, my eyes full of tears. But I had told myself one slow truth and stuck to it. I studied for many years.

Whenever I felt weak or low or lonely, Raphael spoke inside my indented head. I kept his books in order for him. The chemistry book, the human genetics book. I went out into the broken courtyard and started to lift the iron bags with balls of concrete that he had made. Now I look like the muscular champion on his netbook. Everything I am, I am because of my brother.

I did not speak much to anyone else. I didn't want to. Somewhere what is left of Raphael's lead and mercury is entwined with reeds or glistens in sand.

To pay for your application for a scholarship in those days you had to buy a scratch card from a bank. I had bought so many. I did not even remember applying to the Benue State Scholarship Board. They gave me a small stipend, enough if I stayed at home and did construction work. I became one of the workmen in the shallows.

Ex-colleagues of my father had found Matthew a job as a clerk in a bank in Jos. Matthew went to live with uncle Emmanuel. Andrew's jaw set, demanding to be allowed to go with him. He knew where things were going. So did Mamamimi who saw the sense and nodded quietly, yes. Matthew became Andrew's father.

We all lined up in the courtyard in the buzzing heat to let Matthew take the SUV, his inheritance. We waved good-bye as if half the family were just going for a short trip back to the home village or to the Chinese bakery to buy rolls. Our car pulled up the red hill past the church and they were gone. Mamamimi and I were alone with the sizzling sound of insects and heat and we all walked back into the house in the same way, shuffling flat footed. We stayed wordless all that day. Even the TV was not turned on. In the kitchen, in the dark, Mamamimi said to me "Why didn't you go with them? Study at a proper university?" and I said, "Because someone needs to help you."

"Don't worry about me," she said. Not long afterward she took her rusty green car and drove it back to Kawuye for the last time. She lived with Uncle Jacob, and the elders. I was left alone in this whispering house.

We had in our neglected, unpaid, strike-ridden campus a mathematician, a dusty and disordered man who reminded me of Raphael. He was an Idoma man called Thomas Aba. He came to Jide and me with his notebook and then unfolded a page of equations.

These equations described, he said, how the act of observing events at a quantum level changed them. He turned the page. Now, he said, here is how those same equations describe how observing alters effects on the macro level.

He had shown mathematically how the mere act of repeated observation changed the real world.

We published in *Nature*. People wanted to believe that someone working things out for themselves could revolutionize cosmology with a single set of equations. Of all of us, Doubting Thomas was the genius. Tsinghua University in Beijing offered him a Professorship and he left us. Citations for our article avalanched; Google could not keep up. People needed to know why everything was shifting, needing to explain both the climate-change debacle and the end of miracles.

Simply put, science found the truth and by finding it, changed it. Science undid itself, in an endless cycle.

Some day the theory of evolution will be untrue and the law of conservation of energy will no longer work. Who knows, maybe we will get faster than light travel after all?

Thomas still writes to me about his work, though it is the intellectual property of Tsinghua. He is now able to calculate how long it takes for observation to change things. The rotation of the Earth around the Sun is so rooted in the universe that it will take 4000 years to wear it out. What kind of paradigm will replace it? The earth and the sun and all the stars secretly overlap? Outside the four dimensions they all occupy the same single mathematical point?

So many things exist only as metaphors and numbers. Atoms will take only fifty more years to disappear, taking with them quarks and muons and all the other particles. What the Large Hadron Collider will most accelerate is their demise.

Thomas has calculated how long it will take for observation to wear out even his observation. Then, he says, the universe will once again be stable. History melts down and is restored.

My fiancée is a simple country girl who wants a Prof for a husband. I know where that leads. To Mamamimi. Perhaps no bad thing. I hardly know the girl. She wears long dresses instead of jeans and has a pretty smile. My mother's family know her.

The singing at the church has started, growing with the heat and sunlight. My beautiful suit wax-printed in blue and gold arches reflects the sunlight. Its glossy mix of fabrics will be cool, cooler than all that lumpy knitwear from Indonesia.

We have two weddings; one new, one old. Today, the families officially agree to the marriage. Next week the church and the big white dress. So I go through it all twice. I will have to mime love and happiness; the photographs will be used for those framed tributes: "Patrick and Leticia: True Love is Forever." Matthew and Andrew will be there with their families for the first time in years and I find it hurts to have brothers who care nothing for me.

I hear my father saying that my country wife had best be grateful for all that I give her. I hear him telling her to leave if she is not happy. This time though, he speaks with my own voice.

Will I slap the walls all night or just my own face? Will I go mad and dance for workmen in a woman's dress? Will I make stews so fiery that only I can eat them? I look down at my body, visible through the white linen, the body I have made perfect to compensate for my imperfect brain.

Shall I have a little baby with a creased forehead? Will he wear my father's dusty cap? Will he sleepwalk, weep at night or laugh for no reason? If I call him a family name, will he live his grandfather's life again? What poison will I pass on?

I try to imagine all my wedding guests and how their faces would fall if I simply walked away, or strode out like Raphael to crow with delight, "No wedding! I'm not getting married, no way José!" I smile; I can hear him say it; I can see how he would strut.

I can also hear him say, *What else is someone like you going to do except get married? You are too quiet and homely. A publication in* Nature *is not going to cook your food for you. It's not going to get you laid.*

I think of my future son. His Christian name will be Raphael but his personal name will be Ese, which means "Wiped Out." It means that God will wipe out the past with all its expectations.

If witchcraft once worked and science is wearing out, then it seems to me that God loves our freedom more than stable truth. If I have a son who is free from the past, then I know God loves me too.

So I can envisage Ese, my firstborn. He's wearing shorts and running with a kite behind him, happy clean and free and we the Shawos live on the hill once more.

I think of Mamamimi kneeling to down to look into my face and saying, "Patrick, you are a fine young boy. You do everything right. There is nothing wrong with you." I remember my father, sane for a while, resting a hand on the small of my back and saying, "You are becoming distinguished." He was proud of me.

Most of all I think of Raphael speaking his mind to Matthew, to Grandma, even to Father but never to me. He is passing on his books to me in twilight, and I give him tea, and he says as if surprised *That's nice. Thank you.* His shiny face glows with love.

I have to trust that I can pass on love as well.

A Response from EST17

TOM PURDOM

Here's an ingenious First Contact scenario, told mostly from the perspective of the aliens being contacted, as two competing probes from Earth enter into a complicated and ultimately dangerously confrontational series of negotiations with the natives as to whom they're going to be in contact with, negotiations which may eventually determine the future survival of both the alien civilization and of Terran civilization itself.

Tom Purdom made his first sale in 1957, to Fantastic Universe, *and has subsequently sold to* Analog, The Magazine of Fantasy & Science Fiction, Star, *and most of the major magazines and anthologies. In recent years, he's become a frequent contributor to* Asimov's Science Fiction. *He is the author of one of the most unfairly forgotten SF novels of the 1960s, the powerful and still-timely* Reduction in Arms, *about the difficulties of disarmament in the face of the mad proliferation of nuclear weapons, as well as such novels as* I Want the Stars, The Tree Lord of Imeten, Five Against Arlane, *and* The Barons of Behavior. *Purdom lives in Philadelphia, where he reviews classical music concerts for a local newspaper. Many of his short works have recently been made available at the Barnes & Noble Nookstore, Amazon's Kindle store, and through Fictionwise.*

The Betzino-Resdell Exploration Community received its first message from Trans Cultural 5.23 seconds after it settled into orbit around the planet designated Extra-Solar Terranoid 17.

"I am the official representative of the Trans-Cultural Institute for Multi-Disciplinary and Extra-Disciplinary Interstellar Exploration and Study," Trans Cultural radioed. "I represent a consortium of seventy-three political entities and two hundred and seventy-three academic, research, and cultural institutions located in every region of the Earth. You are hereby requested to refrain from direct contact with the surface of Extra-Solar Terranoid 17. My own contact devices have already initiated exploration of the planet. You will be granted access to my findings."

The eighteen programs included in the Betzino-Resdell Community were called "alters"—as in "alter-ego" or "alternate personality"—but they were not self-aware.

They were merely complicated, incredibly dense arrangements of circuits and switches, like every machine intelligence the human species had ever created. But they had been sponsored by seven different sets of shareholders and they had been shaped by the goals and personalities of their sponsors. They spent the first 7.62 seconds after their arrival testing the three copies of each program stored in their files so they could determine which copies had survived the journey in the best shape and should be activated. Then they turned their attention to the message from Trans Cultural.

Betzino and Resdell had been the primary sponsors of the expedition. Their electronic simulations controlled 60 of the 95 votes distributed among the community. Their vote to reject the demand settled the matter. But the other five concurred. The only no vote came from the group of alters tasked to study non-human sexuality. One member of that group cast one vote each way.

22.48 seconds after its arrival, the Betzino-Resdell Exploration Community initiated its exploration routine. The programs housed in Trans Cultural noted that Betzino-Resdell had failed to comply with their orders. Trans Cultural activated its dominance routine and the routine initiated activity. The first human artifacts to reach EST17 entered the first stages of the social phenomenon their creators called "microwar."

The Betzino-Resdell Exploration Community had been crammed into a container a little larger than a soccer ball. A microwave beam mounted on the Moon had pushed it out of the solar system. Trans Cultural left the solar system five years later but it had wealthier backers who could finance a bigger boost applied to a bigger sail. It covered the distance in 1,893, 912 hours—a little over two hundred and sixteen Earth years—and reached EST17 six years before Betzino-Resdell. It had already established a base on the planet and begun exploration.

Betzino-Resdell peered at the surface through lenses that were half the size of a human eye but it had been equipped with state-of-the-art enhancement programs. EST17 was an inhabited planet. Its residents seemed to be concentrated in 236 well-defined cities. The rest of the planet looked like an undisturbed panorama of natural landscapes, distributed over four major landmasses.

The original human version of the Resdell alter was an astronomer who had been interested in the search for extraterrestrial life ever since he had watched his first documentary when he had been six years old. Anthony Resdell was a pleasant, likeable guy whose best-known professional achievement was a popular video series that had made him moderately rich. His alter immediately noted that EST17 seemed to violate a dictum laid down by an aristocratic twentieth century space visionary. Any extraterrestrial civilizations the human race encountered would be thousands of years ahead of us or millennia behind, Sir Arthur had opined. The odds they would be anywhere near us were so small we could assume the advanced civilizations would think we were savages.

The cities Betzino-Resdell could observe looked remarkably like the better-run cities on Earth. The satellites that ringed the planet resembled the satellites that orbited Earth. Samples of their electronic emissions recorded a similar range of frequencies and intensities.

The Betzino alter riffled through all the speculations on technological development stored in the library and distributed them to its colleagues—a process that ate up 13.3 seconds. The catalog contained several thousand entries—most of them extracted from works of fiction—but it could be grouped into a manageable list of categories:

- Technologies so advanced less enlightened space explorers couldn't detect them.
- Hedonism.
- Deliberate limitation.
- A planet that lacked a key resource.
- Anti-technology cultural biases.
- And so on . . .

"We must match each piece of new data with each of those possibilities," Resdell said. "We have encountered a significant anomaly."

Betzino concurred. Two members of the community disagreed. The proposal became operational.

Trans Cultural seemed to be concentrating on a site on the largest southern continent, in a heavily wooded area fifty kilometers from a large coastal city. Betzino-Resdell selected a site on a northern continent, in a mountainous area near a city located on the western shore of a long lake. Three tiny needles drifted out of a hatch and began a slow descent through the planet's thick atmosphere. Two needles made it to the ground. Machines that could have been mistaken for viruses oozed through the soil and collected useful atoms. Little viruses became bigger viruses, larger machines began to sprout appendages, and the routines stored in the needles proceeded through the first stages of the process that had spread human structures through the solar system.

It was a long, slow business. Three local years after Arrival, the largest active machines resembled hyper-mobile insects. Semi-organic flying creatures took to the air in year twelve. In year eighteen, a slab of rock became a functioning antenna and the Betzino-Resdell orbiter established communications with its ground base.

In year twenty-two, the first fully equipped airborne exploration devices initiated a systematic reconnaissance of the territory within one hundred kilometers of the base.

In year twenty-nine, a long range, semi-organic airborne device encountered a long range, semi-organic airborne device controlled by Trans Cultural. The Trans Cultural device attempted to capture the Betzino-Resdell device intact and the Betzino-Resdell device responded, after a brief chase, by erasing all the information in its memory cells, including the location of the Betzino-Resdell base. The micro-war had entered the skirmish stage.

In year thirty-six, a native flying creature that resembled a feathered terrestrial toad approached a Betzino-Resdell device that resembled a small flying predator common in the area around the base. The airborne toad settled on a branch overlooking the eastern shore of the lake and turned its head toward the faux predator.

"I would like to talk to you," the toad said in perfectly enunciated twenty-second century Italian. "This is an unofficial, private contact. It would be best if you kept your outward reactions to a minimum."

The Appointee received her first briefing three days after the Integrators roused her from dormancy. They had roused her nineteen years before she was supposed to begin her next active period but she had suppressed her curiosity and concentrated on the sensual pleasures recommended for the first days after activation. She and her husband always enjoyed the heightened sexual arousal that followed a fifty year slumber. Normally they would have stretched it over several more days.

The name posted on the hatch of her dormancy unit was Varosa Uman Deun Malinvo. . . . Her husband's officially recognized appellation was Budsiti Hisalito Sudili Hadbitad. . . . The ellipses referred to the hundreds of names they had added to their own—the names of all the known ancestors who had perished before the Abolition of Death. He called her Varo. She called him Budsi in public, Siti in private.

They were both bipeds with the same general anatomical layout as an unmodified human, with blocky, heavily boned bodies that had been shaped by the higher gravity of their native world. Their most distinctive features, to human eyes, would have been their massive hands and the mat of soft, intricately colored feathers that crowned their heads and surrounded their faces. As Betzino-Resdell had already noted, the accidents of evolution had favored feathers over fur on EST17.

The briefing took place in a secure underground room equipped with a viewing stage that was bigger than most apartments. A direct, real time image of the current First Principal Overseer appeared on the stage while Varosa Uman was still settling into a viewing chair.

"You've been aroused ahead of schedule because we have a visitation," the First Principal said. "The Integrators responded to the latest development by advising us they want you to oversee our response. You will be replacing Mansita Jano, who has been the Situation Overseer since the first detection. He's conducted a flawless response, in my opinion. You won't find a better guide."

A male with bright yellow facial feathers materialized beside the First Principal. Varosa Uman ordered a quick scan on her personal information system and confirmed that she was replacing one of the twenty leading experts on the history of visitations—a scholar with significant practical experience. Mansita Jano Santisi Jinmano. . . . had served on the committee that had worked on the last visitation. He had been a scholar-observer during the visitation twelve hundred years before that.

"It will be an honor to work with you, Mansita Jano."

She could have said more. Mansita Jano's expertise dwarfed her own knowledge of visitations. But the Integrators had picked her. She couldn't let him think he could dominate her thinking.

He couldn't be happy with the change. He knew he was better qualified. She would be harrying Siti with exasperated tirades if the Integrators had done something like that to her. But Mansita Jano was looking at her with polite interest, as if their relative positions had no emotional significance. And she would have donned the same mask, if their positions had been reversed.

A panoramic spacescape replaced the two figures. A line traced the path of an incoming visitation device—a standard minimum-mass object attached to a standard oversize light sail. It was a typical visitation rig and it behaved in a typical fashion. It spent twelve years slowing down and settling into its permanent orbit. It launched a subsidiary device at the third moon of the fourth planet and the subsidiary started working on an installation that would probably develop into a communications relay, in the same way the last two visitations had established relays on the same moon. It released three microweight orbit-to-surface devices (the last visitation had released two) and the survivors advanced to the next step in a typical visitation program.

All over the galaxy intelligent species reached a certain level and developed similar interstellar technologies. Each species thought it had reached a pinnacle. Each species saw its achievements as a triumph of intelligence and heroic effort.

The story became more interesting when the second visitation entered the system. Varosa Uman watched the two devices set up independent bases. She observed the first attack. Maps noted the locations of other incidents. The first visitor seemed to be the aggressor in every engagement.

The two orbiters definitely came from the same source. Their species had obviously generated at least two social entities that could launch interstellar probes. That happened now and then—everything had happened now and then—but this was the first time Varosa Uman's species had dealt with a divided visitation. Was that why the Integrators had roused her?

It was a logical thought but she knew it was irrelevant as soon as she saw the encounter between the second visitor and a device that had obviously been created by a member of her own species.

"The unauthorized contacts have been initiated by an Adventurer with an all too familiar name," the First Principal said. "Revutev Mavarka Verenka Turetva. . . . Mansita Jano was preparing to take action when the Integrators advised us they were putting you in charge of our response to the visitation."

"I have received a cease-operations command from my organic predecessor," the Resdell alter said. "This will be my last message. Do not anticipate a revival."

The Betzino alter mimicked the thought processes of a woman who possessed a formidable intellect. Edna Betzino had been a theoretical physicist, a psychiatrist, and an investigatory sociologist specializing in military and semi-military organizations. In her spare time, she had become a widely respected cellist who was a devoted student of Bach and his twenty-second century successors. She had launched her own interstellar probe because she had never developed an institutional affiliation that would offer her proper backing.

The Betzino alter riffled through its databanks—as Betzino herself would have—and determined that Anthony Resdell lived in a governmental unit that had become a "single-leader state." Messages from Earth had to cross eighteen light years so the information in the data banks was, of course, eighteen earth years out of date. The cease-operations command would remain in effect until the Resdell alter received a countermand from Anthony Resdell.

The ninety-five votes had now been reduced to sixty-five. Their creators had neglected to include a routine that adjusted the percentages so Betzino still controlled thirty votes. She would need the support of one minor member every time the community made a decision.

Three of the minor members wanted to continue discussions with the inhabitant who had made contact. Two objected, on the grounds the inhabitant was obviously an unofficial private individual.

"We have no information regarding his relations with their political entities," the spokesman for the sex research community argued. "He could bias them against us when we try to make a proper contact."

Their mobile device had exchanged language programs with the inhabitant's contact device. The data indicated the inhabitant's primary language had a structure and vocabulary that resembled the structure and vocabulary of the languages technologically advanced human societies had developed.

Betzino voted to maintain the contact. Switches tripped in response and the contact and language programs remained active.

There was a standard response to visitations. It was called the Message. Varosa Uman's species had transmitted it twice and received it once.

Mansita Jano had initiated Message preparation as soon as he had been given responsibility for the visitation. He would have initiated contact with one of the visitors and proceeded to the final stages if Revutev Mavarka hadn't started "bungling around."

Mansita Jano believed Revutev Mavarka should be arrested before he could cause any more trouble. "We have documentary evidence Revutev Mavarka has committed a serious crime," Mansita Jano said. "I think we can also assume the first visitor has a higher status than the visitor he's been attempting to charm. The first visitor rebuffed his overtures. We have translated a communication in which it ordered the second visitor to cease operations."

There was nothing sinister about the Message. It was, in fact, the greatest gift an intelligent species could receive. It contained all the knowledge twenty-three technological civilizations had accumulated, translated into the major languages employed by the recipient. With the information contained in the Message, any species that had developed interstellar probes could cure all its diseases, quadruple its intelligence, bestow millennia of life on all its members, reshape the life-forms on its planet, tap energy sources that would maintain its civilization until the end of the universe, and generally treat itself to the kind of society it had been dreaming about since it first decided it didn't have to endure all the death and suffering the universe inflicted on it.

And that was the problem. No society could absorb that much change in one gulp. Varosa Uman's species had endured a millennium of chaos after it had received its version of the Message.

It was an elegant defense. The Message satisfied the consciences of the species who employed it and it permanently eliminated the threat posed by visitors who might have hostile intentions. Interstellar war might seem improbable but it wasn't impossible. A small probe could slip into a planetary system unannounced, establish a base on an obscure body, and construct equipment that could launch a flotilla of genocidal rocks at an unsuspecting world.

Varosa Uman's people had never sent another visitor to the stars. As far as they could tell, all the species that had received the Message had settled into the same quiet isolation—if they survived their own version of the Great Turbulence.

"The Message can be considered a kind of conditioning," a post-Turbulence committee had concluded. "The chaos it creates implants a permanent aversion to interstellar contact."

Revutev Mavarka was an Adventurer—a member of a minority group that constituted approximately twelve percent of the population. Varosa Uman's species had emerged from the Turbulence by forcing far-reaching modifications on the neurochemical reactions that shaped their emotional responses. They had included a controlled number of thrill-seekers and novelty chasers in their population mix because they had understood that a world populated by tranquil, relentlessly socialized serenes had relinquished some of its capacity to adapt. No society could foresee all the twists and traps the future could hold.

Most Adventurers satisfied their special emotional needs with physical challenges and sexual escapades. Revutev Mavarka seemed to be captivated by less benign outlets. His fiftieth awake had been marked by his attempt to disrupt the weather program that controlled the rainfall over the Fashlev mountain range. The First Principal Overseer had added twelve years to his next dormancy period and the Integrators had approved the penalty.

In his seventy-third awake, Revutev Mavarka had designed a small, hyperactive carnivore that had transferred a toxin through the food chain and transformed the habitués of a staid island resort into a population of temporary risk addicts. In his eighty-first, he had decided his happiness depended upon the companionship of a prominent fashion despot and kidnapped her after she had won a legal restraint on his attentions. The poisoning had added twenty-two years to his next dormancy, the kidnapping twenty-eight.

Varosa Uman and her husband liked cool winds and rugged landscapes. They liked to sit on high balconies, hands touching, and watch winged creatures circle over gray northern seas.

"It's Revutev Mavarka," Varosa Uman said. "He's made an unauthorized contact with a visitation."

"And the Integrators think you can give them some special insight?"

"They've placed me in charge of the entire response. I'm replacing Mansita Jano."

Siti called up Mansita Jano's data and scanned through it. "He's a specialist," Siti said. "It's a big responsibility but I think I agree with the Integrators."

"You may belong to a very small minority. They gave me a scrupulously polite briefing."

"They don't know you quite as well as I do."

"Mansita Jano was getting ready to arrest Revutev Mavarka. And offer the Message."

"And you think the situation is a bit more complicated . . ."

"There are two visitors. One of them is acting like it represents a planetary authority. The other one—the visitor Revutev Mavarka contacted—looks like it may have more in common with him. I have to see how much support Revutev Mavarka has. I can't ignore that. You have to think about their emotional reactions when you're dealing with the Adventurer community. I have to weigh their feelings and I have to think about the responses we could provoke in the visitors—both visitors. We aren't the first people to confront two visitors but it still increases the complexities—the unknowns."

"And Revutev Mavarka has piled more complexities on top of that. And the Integrators understandably decided we'd be better off with someone like you pondering the conflicts."

The contact had told the Betzino-Resdell community they should call him Donald. So far they had mostly traded language programs. They could exchange comments on the weather in three hundred and seven different languages.

The alters that were interested in non-human sexuality lobbied for permission to swap data on sexual practices. There were six alters in the group and they represented the six leading scholars associated with the North Pacific Center for the Analysis of Multi-Gender Sexuality. The exploration units they controlled had observed the activities of eight local life-forms. All eight seemed to have developed the same unimaginative two-sex pattern life had evolved on Earth. Their forays into the cities had given them a general picture of the inhabitant's physiology but it had left them with a number of unresolved issues.

Topic: Does your species consist of two sexes?

Betzino-Resdell: Yes.

Donald: Yes.

Topic: Are there any obvious physical differences between the sexes?

BR: Yes.

Donald: Yes

Topic: What are they?

BR: Our males are larger, bigger boned on average. Generally more muscular.

Donald: Males more colorful, more varied facial feathers.

Topic: Do you form permanent mating bonds?

BR: Yes.

Donald: Yes.

Topic: Do any members of your species engage in other patterns?

BR: Yes.

Donald: Yes.

Topic: How common are these other patterns?

BR: In many societies, very high percentages engage in other patterns.

Donald: Why do you wish to know?

The visitation committee was receiving a full recording of every exchange between Revutev Mavarka and the visitation device that called itself Betzino-Resdell. Revutev Mavarka was, of course, fully aware that he was being observed. So far he had avoided any exchanges that could produce accusations he had transmitted potentially dangerous information.

"It must be frustrating," Varosa Uman said. "He must have a million subjects he'd like to discuss."

"We just need one slip," Mansita Jano said. "Give us one slip and he'll be lucky if fifty members of his own class stand by him."

"And the visitor will have the information contained in the slip . . ."

Mansita Jano's facial feathers stirred—an ancient response that made his face look bigger and more threatening. "Then why not silence him before he does it, Overseer? Do you really think he can keep this up indefinitely without saying something catastrophic?"

"I've been thinking a dangerous thought," Varosa Uman said.

"I'm not surprised," Siti said.

"Every intelligent species that has sent visitors to an inhabited world has apparently lived through the same horrible experience we did. Some of them may not have survived it. If our experience is typical, everybody who receives the Message responds in the same way when they receive a visitation after they've gone through their version of the Turbulence. The Message is a great teacher. It teaches us that contact with other civilizations is a dangerous disruption."

Two large winged predators were swooping over the water just below the level of their balcony. The dark red plumage on their wings created a satisfying contrast with the grey of the sea and the sky

"I'm thinking it might be useful if someone looked at an alternative response," Varosa Uman said.

Siti ran his fingers across the back of her hand. They had been married for eighty-two complete cycles—twenty-four hundred years of full consciousness. He knew when to speak and when to mutely remind her he was there.

"Suppose someone tried a different role," Varosa Uman said. "Suppose we offered to guide these visitors through all the adaptations they're going to confront. Step by step."

"As an older, more experienced species."

"Which we are. In this area, at least."

"We would have to maintain contact," Siti said. "They would be influencing us, too."

"And threatening us with more turbulence. I'd be creating a disruption the moment I mentioned the idea to Mansita Jano."

"Have you mentioned your intellectual deviation to the Integrators?"

"They gave me one of their standard routines. They pointed out the dangers, I asked them for a decision, and they told me they were only machines, I'm the Situation Overseer."

"And they picked you because their routines balanced all the relevant factors—see attached list—and decided you were the best available candidate."

"I think it's pretty obvious I got the job because I'm more sympathetic to the Adventurer viewpoint than most of the candidates who had the minimum expertise they were looking for."

"You're certainly more sympathetic than Mansita Jano. As I remember it, your major response to Revutev Mavarka's last misadventure was a daily outburst of highly visible amusement."

Siti had been convinced he wanted to establish a permanent bond before they had finished their first active period together. She had resisted the idea until they were halfway through their next awake but she had known she would form a bond with someone sooner or later. They were both people with a fundamental tendency to drift into permanent bonds and they had reinforced that tendency, soon after they made the commitment, with a personality adjustment that eliminated disruptive urges.

Siti found Revutev Mavarka almost incomprehensible. A man who kidnapped a woman just to satisfy a transient desire? And created a turmoil that affected hundreds of people?

Twenty years from now she won't mean a thing to him, Siti had said. And he knows it.

"He's impulsive," Varosa Uman said. "I can't let myself forget he's impulsive. Unpredictably."

Trans Cultural had asked all the required questions and looked at all the proffered bona fides. The emissary called Varosa Uman Deun Malinvo . . . satisfied all the criteria that indicated said emissary represented a legitimate governmental authority.

"Is it correct to assume you represent the dominant governmental unit on your planet?" Trans Cultural asked.

"I represent the only governmental unit on my planet."

Varosa Uman had established a direct link with the base Trans Cultural had created in the Gildeen Wilderness. She had clothed herself in the feather and platinum finery high officials had worn at the height of the Third TaraTin Empire and she was transmitting a full, detailed image. Trans Cultural was still limiting itself to voice-only.

"Thank you for offering that information," Trans Cultural said.

"Are you supposed to limit your contacts to governmental representatives?"

"I am authorized to initiate conversations with any entity as representative as the consortium I represent."

"Can you give us any information on the other visitor currently operating on our world?"

"The Betzino-Resdell Exploration Community primarily represents two private individuals. The rest of its membership comprises two other individuals and three minor organizations."

"Can you give me any information on its members?"

"I'm afraid I'm not authorized to dispense that information at present."

"The presence of another visitor from your society seems to indicate you do not have a single entity that can speak for your entire civilization. Is that correct?"

"I represent the dominant consensus on our world. My consortium represents all the major political, intellectual, and cultural organizations on our world. I am authorized to furnish a complete list on request."

Betzino-Resdell had created an antenna by shaping a large rock slab into a shallow dish and covering it with a thin metal veneer. The orbiter passed over the antenna once every 75.6 minutes and exchanged transmissions.

"You should create an alternate transmission route," Revutev Mavarka said. "I've been observing your skirmishes with the other visitor. You should be prepared to continue communications with your orbiter if they manage to invade your base and destroy your antenna."

"Do you think that's a significant possibility?"

"I believe you should be prepared. That's my best advice."

"He's preparing a betrayal," Mansita Jano said. "He's telling us he's prepared to send them information about the Message if we attempt to arrest him."

Varosa Uman reset the recording and watched it again. She received recordings of every interchange between Revutev Mavarka and the second visitor but Mansita Jano had brought this to her attention as soon as it had been intercepted.

Mansita Jano had raised the possibility of a "warning message" in their first meetings. The Message itself contained some hints that it had thrown whole civilizations into turmoil but most of the evidence had been edited out of the historical sections. The history of their own species painted an accurate picture up to their receipt of the Message.

The humans would never hear of the millions who had died so the survivors could live through a limitless series of active and dormant periods. They would learn the cost when they counted their own dead.

But what would happen if their visitors received a message warning them of the dangers? Would it have any effect? Would they ignore it and stumble into the same wilderness their predecessors had entered?

For Mansita Jano, the mere possibility Revutev Mavarka might send such a message proved they should stop "chattering" and defend themselves.

"We have no idea what such a warning message might do," Mansita Jano said. "Its very existence would create an unpredictable situation that could generate endless debate—endless turbulence!—within our own society. By now the humans have received the first messages informing them of our existence. By now, every little group like these Betzino-Resdell adventurers could have launched a visitor in our direction. How will we treat them when we know they're emissaries from a society that has been warned?"

"I started working on that issue as soon as I finished viewing the recording," Varosa Uman said. "I advised the Integrators I want to form a study committee and they've given me the names of ten candidates."

"And when they've finished their studies, they'll give you the only conclusion anyone can give you. We'll have fifty visitors orbiting the planet and we'll still be staring at the sky arguing about a list loaded with bad choices."

The Integrators never used a visual representation when they communicated with their creators. They were machines. You must never forget they were only machines. Varosa Uman usually turned toward her biggest window and looked out at the sea when she talked to them.

"I think you chose me because of my position on the Adventurer personality scale," Varosa Uman said. "You felt I would understand an Adventurer better than someone with a personality closer to the mean. Is that a reasonable speculation?"

"You were chosen according to the established criteria for your assignment."

"And I can't look at the criteria because you've blocked access."

"That is one of the rules in the procedure for overseeing visitations. Access to that information is blocked until the visitation crisis has been resolved."

"Are you obeying the original rules? Or have they been modified here and there over the last three thousand years?"

"There have been no modifications."

"So why can't I just talk to someone who remembers what the original rules were?"

"You are advised not to do that. We would have to replace you. You will do a more effective job if you operate without that knowledge."

"Twelve percent of the population have Adventurer personality structures. They're a sizable minority. They tend to be popular and influential. I can't ignore their feelings. Does my own personality structure help me balance all the relevant factors?"

"It could. We are only machines, Overseer. We can assign numerical weights to emotions. We cannot feel the emotions ourselves."

Varosa Uman stood up. A high, almost invisible dot had folded its wings against its side and turned into a lethal fury plummeting toward the waves. She adjusted her eyes to ten power and watched hard talons drive into a sea animal that had wandered into the wrong area.

"I'm going to let the study committee do its work. But I have to conclude Mansita Jano is correct. We can't let Revutev Mavarka send a warning message. I can feel the tensions he's creating just by threatening to do it. But we can't just arrest him. And we can't just isolate him, either. The Adventurer community might be small but it could become dangerously angry if we took that kind of action against one of the most popular figures in the community while he's still doing things most Adventurers consider harmless rule bending."

"Have you developed an alternative?"

"The best solution would be a victory for the Trans Cultural visitation. Arranged so it looked like they won on their own."

She turned away from the ocean. "I'll need two people with expertise in war fighting tactics. I think two should be the right number. I'll need a survey of all the military planning resources you can give me."

The Integrators had been the primary solution to the conflicts created by the cornucopia contained in the Message. The Integrators managed the technology that produced all the wonders the Message offered. Every individual on the planet could receive all the goods and services a properly modified serene could desire merely by asking, without any of the effort previous generations had categorized as "work."

But who would select the people who would oversee the Integrators? Why the Integrators, of course. The Integrators selected the Overseers. And obeyed the orders of the people they had appointed.

The system worked. It had worked for three thousand years. Could it last forever? Could anything last forever?

The winged toad that made the contact had a larger wingspan and a brighter set of feathers than the creature that had approached Betzino-Resdell. Trans Cultural greeted it with its standard rebuff.

"I can only establish contacts with entities that represent significant concentrations of intellectual and governmental authority."

"This is an extra-channel contact—an unofficial contact by a party associated with the entity who has already established communications. Does your programming allow for that kind of contact?"

Trans Cultural paused for 3.6 seconds while it searched its files and evaluated the terms it had been given.

"How do I know you are associated with that entity?"

"I can't offer you any proof. You must evaluate my proposal on its merits. I can provide you with aid that could give you a decisive victory in your conflict with Betzino-Resdell."

"Please wait . . . Why are you offering to do this?"

"Your conflict is creating disruptions in certain balances in our society. I can't describe the balances at present. But we share your concern about contacts between unrepresentative entities."

"Please continue."

Varosa Uman's instructions to Mansita Jano had been a flawless example of the kind of carefully balanced constraints that always exasperated her when somebody dropped them on her. Do this without doing that. Do that without doing this.

Betzino-Resdell had to be neutralized. Revutev Mavarka's link to the humans had to be severed. But Mansita Jano must arrange things so the second visitor collapsed before Revutev Mavarka realized it was happening—before Revutev Mavarka had time to do something foolish. And it should all happen, of course, without any visible help from anyone officially responsible for the response to the Visitation.

"We could have avoided all this," Mansita Jano had said, "if the Message had been transmitted the day after Revutev Mavarka approached the second visitor. I presume everyone involved in all this extended decision making realizes that."

"The Message will be transmitted to the Trans Cultural device as soon as Betzino-Resdell is neutralized."

"You've made a firm decision? There are no unstated qualifications?"

"The Message will be transmitted as soon as Betzino-Resdell is neutralized. My primary concern is the unpredictability of the humans. We don't know how they'll respond to an overt attack on one of their emissaries—even an emissary that appears to be as poorly connected as the Betzino-Resdell jumble."

"If I were in your position, Overseer, I would have Revutev Mavarka arrested right now. I will do my best. But he's just as unpredictable as our visitors. He isn't just a charming rogue. He isn't offering us a little harmless flirtation with our vestigial appetites for Adventure."

It was the most explicit expression of his feelings Mansita Jano had thrown at her. If I were in your position . . . as I should be . . . if the Integrators hadn't intervened . . . if you could keep your own weaknesses under control. . . . But who could blame him? She had just told him he was supposed to tiptoe through a maze of conflicting demands. Created by someone who seemed to be ruled by her own internal conflicts.

They were meeting face-to-face, under maximum sealed-room security. She could have placed her hand on the side of his face, like a Halna of the Tara Tin Empire offering a strikejav, a gesture of support. But that would obviously be a blunder.

"I know it's a difficult assignment, Mansita Jano. I would do it myself, if I could. But I can't. So I'm asking for help from the best person available. Everything we know about Revutev Mavarka indicates he won't do anything until he feels desperate. He knows he'll be committing an irrevocable act. Get the job done while he's still hesitating and he'll probably feel relieved."

The Message had to be sent. The humans were obviously just as divided and unpredictable as every other species that had ever launched machines at the stars. They were probably even more unpredictable. Their planet apparently had a large moon they could use as an easy launch site. Its gravitational field appeared to be weaker, too. A species that could spread through its own planetary system had to be more divided than a species that had confined itself to one planet.

Mansita Jano could have handed Trans Cultural the exact location of the Betzino-Resdell base but that would have been too obvious. Instead, Trans Cultural's scouts were gently herded in the right direction over the course of a year. Predators pursued them. Winds and storms blew them off the courses set by their search patterns.

Betzino-Resdell had located its base in the middle levels of a mountain range, next to a waterfall that supplied it with 80.5 percent of its energy. A deep, raging stream defended one side of the base and a broad, equally deep ditch protected the other borders. A high tangle of toxic thicket covered the ground behind the ditch.

Trans Cultural set up three bases of its own and started producing an army. It was obviously planning a swarm attack—the kind of unimaginative strategy machines tended to adapt. Revutev Mavarka evaluated the situation and decided Betzino-Resdell could handle the onslaught, with a little advice from a friendly organic imagination.

"You can't stop the buildup," Revutev Mavarka said, "but you can slow it down with well planned harassment raids."

Betzino consulted with her colleagues. They had all started working on projects that had interested them. The Institute for Spiritual Research was particularly reluctant to divert resources from its research. "Donald" had made some remarks that set it looking for evidence the resident population still engaged in religious rituals.

The alter that called itself Ivan represented an individual who could best be described as a serial hobbyist. The original organic Ivan had spent decades exploring military topics and the alter had inherited an impulse to apply that knowledge. Betzino-Resdell voted to devote 50.7 percent of its resources to defense.

Revutev Mavarka had decided religion was a safe topic. He could discuss all the religious beliefs his species had developed before the Turbulence without telling Betzino-Resdell anything about his current society.

The Betzino-Resdell subunits had obviously adopted the same policy. The subunit that called itself the Institute for Spiritual Research led him through an overview of the different beliefs the humans had developed and he responded with a similar overview he had selected from the hundreds of possibilities stored in the libraries.

Revutev Mavarka had experimented with religion during two of his awakes—most of a full lifespan by the standards of most pre-Turbulence societies. He had spent eleven years in complete isolation from all social contact, to see if isolation would grant him the insights the Halfen Reclusives claimed to have achieved.

He could see similar patterns in the religions both species had invented. Religious leaders on both worlds seemed to agree that insight and virtue could only be achieved through some form of deprivation.

As for those who sought excitement and the tang of novelty—they were obviously a threat to every worthy who tried to stay on the True Road.

The religious studies were only a diversion—a modest attempt to achieve some insight into the minds that had created the two visitors. The emotion that colored every second of Revutev Mavarka's life was his sense of impending doom.

He had already composed the Warning he would transmit to Betzino-Resdell. He could blip it at any time, with a three-word, two-number instruction to his communications system.

The moment he sent it—the instant he committed that irrevocable act—he would become the biggest traitor in the history of his species.

How many centuries would he spend in dormancy? Would they ever let him wake? Would he still be lying there when his world died in the explosion that transformed every mundane yellow star into a bloated red monster?

Every meal he ate—every woman he caressed—every view he contemplated—could be his last.

"You've acquired an aura, Reva," his closest female confidante said.

"Is it attractive? I'd hate to think I was surrounded by something repulsive."

"It has its appeal. Has one of your quests actually managed to affect something deeper than a yen for a temporary stimulus?"

"I think I've begun to understand those people who claim it doesn't matter whether you live fifty years or a million. You're still just a flicker in the life of the universe."

"He's savoring the possibility," Varosa Uman told her husband.

"Like one of those people who contemplate suicide? And finish their awake still thinking about it?"

"I have to assume he could do it."

"It seems to me it would be the equivalent of suicide. Given the outrage most people would feel."

"We would have to give him the worst punishment the public mood demands—whatever it takes to restore calm."

"You're protecting him from his own impulses, love. You shouldn't forget that. You aren't just protecting us. You're protecting him."

It was all a matter of arithmetic. Trans Cultural was obviously building up a force that could overwhelm Betzino-Resdell's defenses. At some point, it would command a horde that could cross the ditch and gnaw its way through the toxic hedge by sheer weight of numbers. Betzino-Resdell could delay that day by raiding Trans Cultural's breeding camps and building up the defensive force gathered behind the hedge. But sooner or later Trans Cultural's superior resources would overcome Betzino-Resdell's best efforts.

The military hobbyist in the Betzino-Resdell community had worked the numbers. "They will achieve victory level in 8.7 terrestrial years," Ivan advised his colleagues. "Plus or minus .3 terrestrial years. We can extend that by 2.7 terrestrial years if we increase our defensive allocation to 60 percent of our resources."

Betzino voted to continue the current level and the other members of the community concurred. Their sponsors in the solar system would continue to receive reports on the researches and explorations that interested them.

Revutev Mavarka inspected their plan and ran it through two of the military planning routines he found in the libraries. 8.7 terrestrial years equaled six of his own world's orbits. He could postpone his doom a little longer.

"We are going to plant a few concealed devices at promising locations," Betzino-Resdell told him. "They will attempt to establish new bases after this one is destroyed. Our calculations indicate Trans Cultural can destroy any base it locates before the base can achieve a secure position but the calculation includes variables with wide ranges. It could be altered by unpredictable possibilities. We will reestablish contact with you if the variables and unpredictable possibilities work in our favor and we establish a new defensible base."

"I'll be looking forward to hearing from you," Revutev Mavarka said.

They were only machines. They couldn't fool themselves into thinking an impossible plan was certain to succeed.

The weather fell into predictable patterns all over the planet. The serenes had arranged it that way. Citizens who liked warm weather could live in cities where the weather stayed within a range they found comfortable and pleasant. Citizens who enjoyed the passage of the seasons could settle where the seasons rotated across the land in a rhythm that was so regular it never varied by more than three days.

But no system could achieve perfect, planet-wide predictability. There were places where three or four weather patterns adjoined and minor fluctuations could create sudden shifts. Revutev Mavarka lived, by choice, in a city located in an area noted for its tendency to lurch between extremes.

Sudden big snowfalls were one of his favorite lurches. One day you might be sitting in an outdoor cafe, dressed in light clothes, surrounded by people whose feathers glowed in the sunlight. The next you could be trudging through knee high snow, plodding toward a place where those same feathers would respond to the mellower light of an oversize fireplace.

He had just settled into a table only a few steps from such a fireplace when his communication system jerked his attention away from the snowing song he and six of his friends had started singing.

"You have a priority message. Your observers are tracking a Category One movement."

His hands clutched the edge of the table. He lowered his head and shifted his system to subvocalization mode. The woman on the other side of the table caught his eye and he tried to look like he was receiving a message that might lead to a cozier kind of pleasure.

Category One was a mass movement toward the Betzino-Resdell base—a swarm attack.

How many observers are seeing it?

"Seven."

How many criteria does the observation satisfy?

"All."

His clothes started warming up as soon as he stepped outside. He crunched across the snow bathed in the familiar, comforting sense that he was wrapped in a warm cocoon surrounded by a bleak landscape. It had only been three and a half years since Trans Cultural had started building up its forces. How could they attack now? With a third of the forces they needed?

Has Betzino-Resdell been warned? Are they preparing a defense?

"Yes."

He activated his stage and gave it instructions while he was walking back to his apartment. By the time he settled into his viewing chair, the stage was showing him an aerial view, with most of the vegetation deleted. The trees still supported their foliage in the area where the base was located.

The display had colored Trans Cultural's forces white for easy identification. Betzino-Resdell's defenders had been anointed with a shimmering copper. The white markers were flowing toward the base in three clearly defined streams. They were all converging, dumbly and obviously, on one side of the ditch. A bar at the top of the display estimated the streams contained four to six thousand animals. Trans Cultural was attacking with a force that exactly matched his estimates of their strength—a force that couldn't possibly make its way through the defenses Betzino-Resdell had developed.

There could only be one explanation. Somebody had to be helping it.

"Position. Betzino-Resdell orbiter. Insert."

A diagram popped onto the display. Trans Cultural had launched its attack just after the orbiter had passed over the base.

The antenna built into the rock face couldn't be maneuvered. The base could only communicate with the orbiter when the orbiter was almost directly overhead. Trans Cultural—and its unannounced allies—had timed the attack so he couldn't send his warning message until the orbiter completed another passage around the planet.

He could transmit it now, of course. Betzino-Resdell could store the warning and relay it when the orbiter made its next pass. But the whole situation would change the moment he gave the order. The police would seal off his apartment before he could take three steps toward the door.

Up until now he had been engaging in the kind of borderline activity most Adventurers played with. The record would show he had limited his contacts with Betzino-Resdell to harmless exchanges. He could even argue he had accumulated useful information about the visitors and their divisions.

"Have you considered isolating him?" Mansita Jano said. "It might be a sensible precaution, given the tension he's under."

Varosa Uman had been eating a long afternoon meal with Siti. She had been thinking, idly, of the small, easy pleasures that might follow. And found herself sitting in front of a stage crowded with a view of the battle and headshots of Mansita Jano and her most reliable aides.

She could cut Revutev Mavarka's electronic links any time she wanted to. But it would be an overt act. Some people would even feel it was more drastic than physical restraint.

"He's an emotional, unstable personality confronted with a powerful challenge," Mansita Jano said. "He could send a warning message at any time. If they manage to relay it to the backup system they've set up, before you can stop them. . . ."

"He knows what we'll do to him if he sends a warning," Varosa Uman said. "He has every reason to think Trans Cultural has made a blunder and the attack is going to fail."

"He's an emotional, unpredictable personality, Overseer. I apologize for sounding like a recording, but there are some realities that can't be overemphasized."

Siti had positioned himself on her right, out of range of the camera. She glanced at him and he put down his bowl and crossed his wrists in front of his face, as if he was shielding himself from a blow.

Mansita Jano had placed his advice on the record. If his arrangement with Trans Cultural failed—whatever the arrangement was—he would be shielded.

"This attack cannot succeed," Betzino-Resdell said. "We have repeated our analyses. This attack can only succeed if it contains some element we are not aware of."

"I've come to the same conclusion," Revutev Mavarka said.

"We are proceeding with our defensive plan. We have made no modifications. We would like more information, if you have any."

A tactical diagram floated over the image of the advancing hordes. Most of Betzino-Resdell's defensive forces would mass behind the toxic hedge, in the area the attackers seemed to be threatening. A small mobile reserve would position itself in the center of the base.

"I suggest you concentrate your mobile reserve around the antenna."

"Why do you advise that?"

"I believe the antenna is their primary objective. They will try to destroy your connection with your orbiter if they break through the hedge."

"Why will they make the antenna their primary objective? Our plans assume their primary objectives will be our energy transmission network and our primary processing units."

"Can you defend yourself if you lose contact with your orbiter?"

"Yes."

Betzino-Resdell had paused before it had answered. It had been a brief pause—an almost undetectable flicker, by the standards of organic personalities—but his brain had learned to recognize the minute signals a machine threw out.

He had been assuming Betzino-Resdell's operations were still controlled by the orbiter. He had assumed the unit on the ground transmitted information and received instructions when the orbiter passed over. That might have been true in the beginning. By now, Betzino-Resdell could have transmitted complete copies of itself to the ground. The ground copies could be the primaries. The copies on the orbiter could be the backups.

"Are you assuming you can keep operating on the ground if you stop this attack and they destroy the antenna? And build a new antenna in the future?"

". . . . Yes."

"What if that doesn't work out? Isn't there some possibility your rival could gain strength and destroy your new antenna before you can finish it?"

"Why are you emphasizing the antenna? Do you have some information we don't have?"

I have an important message I want to transmit to your home planet. The future of your entire species could depend on it.

"I was thinking about the individuals who sent you. Your explorations won't be of much value to them if you can't communicate with your orbiter."

"Our first priority is the survival of our surface capability. Our simulations indicate we can survive indefinitely and could eventually reestablish contact with our orbiter. Do you have information that indicates we should reassess our priorities?"

Revutev Mavarka tipped back his head. His hands pressed against the thick, deliberately ragged feathers that adorned the sides of his face. He was communicating with the visitor through a voice-only link, as always. He didn't have to hide his emotions behind the bland mask the serenes offered the world.

"I've given you the best advice I can give you at present. I recommend that you place a higher priority on the antenna."

"He's still struggling with his conflicts," Varosa Uman said. "He could have given them a stronger argument."

She had turned to Siti again. She could still hear the exhortations she was receiving from her aides but she had switched off her own vocal feed.

"Mansita Jano would probably say he's watching two personalities struggle with their internal conflicts," Siti said.

Varosa Uman's display had adapted the same color scheme Revutev Mavarka was watching. The white markers had reached the long slope in front of the ditch. The three columns were converging into a single mass. Winged creatures were fighting over the space above their backs.

"It looks like they're starting their final assault," Siti said. "Do you have any idea what kind of fearsome warriors your white markers represent?"

"They seem to be a horde of small four-legged animals native to the visitor's planet. They breed very fast. And they have sharp teeth and claws."

"They're going to bite their way through the hedge? With one of them dying every time they take a bite?"

"That seems to be the plan."

Revutev Mavarka stepped up to the display and waved his hand over the area covered by the white markers.

"Calculation. Estimate number of organisms designated by white marking."

A number floated over the display. The horde racing up the slope contained, at most, six thousand four hundred animals.

The three columns had merged into a single dense mass. He could see the entire assault force. The estimate had to be correct.

He activated his connection to Betzino-Resdell. "I have an estimate of six thousand four hundred for the assault force. Does that match your estimate?"

"Yes."

"Your calculations still indicate the attack will fail?"

"Four thousand will die biting their way through the hedge. The rest will be overwhelmed by our defensive force."

Machines were only machines. Imagination required conscious, self-aware minds. Adventurous self-aware minds. But they were talking about a straightforward calculation. Trans Cultural had to know its attack couldn't succeed.

"Can you think of any reason why Trans Cultural has launched this attack at this time?" Revutev Mavarka said. "Is there some factor you haven't told me about?"

"We have examined all the relevant factors stored in our libraries. We have only detected one anomaly. They are advancing on a wider front than our simulations recommend. Do you know of any reason why they would do that?"

"How much wider is it?"

"Over one third."

"Do they have a military routine comparable to yours?"

"We have made no assumptions about the nature of their military routine."

Revutev Mavarka stared at the display. Would the attackers be easier to defeat if they were spread out? Would they be more vulnerable if they were compacted into a tight mass? There must be some optimum combination of width and density. Could he be certain Betzino-Resdell's military routine had made the right calculation?

How much secret help had Trans Cultural received?

"One member of our community still wants to know why you think we should place a higher priority on the antenna," Betzino-Resdell said. "She insists that we ask you again."

The first white markers had leaped into the ditch. Paws were churning under the water. Betzino-Resdell's defenders were spreading out behind the hedge, to cover the extra width of the assault.

Transmit this message to your home planet at once. The Message you will receive from our civilization is a dangerous trap. It contains the combined knowledge of twenty-three civilizations, translated into the languages you have given us. It will give you untold wealth, life without death, an eternity of comfort and ease. But that is only the promise. It will throw your entire civilization into turmoil when you try to absorb its gifts. You may never recover. The elimination of death is particularly dangerous. The Message is not a friendly act. We are sending it to you for the same reason it was sent to us. To protect ourselves. To defend ourselves against the disruption you will cause if we remain in contact.

It was a deliberately short preliminary alarm. They would have the whole text in their storage banks half an eyeblink after he subvocalized the code that would activate transmission. A longer follow-up, with visual details of the Turbulence, would take two more blinks.

The initiation code consisted of two short numbers and three unrelated words from three different extinct languages—a combination he couldn't possibly confuse with anything else he might utter.

Would they believe it? Would the people who received it on the human world dismiss it because it came from a vehicle that had been assembled by a group of individuals who were probably just as marginal and unrepresentative as the eccentric who sent the warning?

Some of them might dismiss it. Some of them might believe it. Did it matter? Something unpredictable would be added to the situation—something the Integrators and Varosa Uman would have to face knowing they were taking risks and struggling with unknowns no matter what they did.

The animals in the front line of the assault force had reached the hedge. White markers covered a section of the ditch from side to side. Teeth were biting into poisoned stems.

The hedge wavered. The section in front of the assault force shook as if it had been pummeled by a sudden wind. A wall of dust rose into the air.

Varosa Uman would have given Mansita Jano an immediate burst of praise if she could have admitted she knew he was responsible. She had understood what he'd done as soon as she realized the hedge was sinking into the ground.

There would be no evidence they had helped Trans Cultural. Some individuals might suspect it but the official story would be believable enough. Trans Cultural had somehow managed to undermine the ground under the hedge. An explosion had collapsed the mine at the best possible time and the defenders were being taken by surprise.

The assault force still had to cross the ruins of the hedge but they had apparently prepared a tactic. The front rank died and the next rank clambered over them. Line by line, body by body, the animals extended a carpet over the gap. Most of them would make it across. Betzino-Resdell's defenders would be outnumbered.

Trans Cultural couldn't have dug the mine. They didn't have the resources to dig the mine while they were preparing the attack. Revutev Mavarka could prove it. But would anyone believe him?

The first white markers had crossed the ditch. The front ranks were ripping at each other with teeth and claws. Flyers struggled in the dust above the collapse.

White markers began to penetrate the copper masses. The mobile reserve retreated toward the installations that housed Betzino-Resdell's primary processing units.

A white column emerged from the hedge on the right end of the line—the end closest to the antenna. It turned toward the antenna and started gathering speed.

"Defend the antenna. You must defend the antenna."

"What are you hiding from us? You must give us more information. What is happening? Trans Cultural couldn't have dug that mine. They didn't have the resources."

Revutev Mavarka stared at the white markers scurrying toward the antenna. Could Betzino-Resdell's mobile reserve get there in time if they responded to his pleas? Would it make any difference?

The antenna was doomed. The best defense they could put up would buy him, at best, a finite, slightly longer interval of indecision.

Two numbers.

Three words.

Blip.

"You must destroy the antenna," Mansita Jano said. "He's given you all the excuse you need."

Varosa Uman had already given the order. She had placed a missile on standby when Trans Cultural had launched its attack. Revutev Mavarka had committed the unforgivable act. She could take any action she deemed necessary.

The missile rose out of an installation she had planted on an island in the lake. Police advanced on Revutev Mavarka's apartment. The image on his display stage disappeared. Jammers and switches cut every link that connected him to the outside world.

Three of the Betzino-Resdell programs voted to transmit Donald's message at once. Ivan argued for transmission on impeccable military grounds. Donald had told them they should defend the antenna. He had obviously given them the message because he believed the antenna was about to be destroyed. They must assume, therefore, that the antenna was about to be destroyed. They could evaluate the message later.

Betzino raised objections. Could they trust Donald? Did they have enough information?

They argued for 11.7 seconds. At 11.8 seconds they transmitted the message to their backup transmission route. At 11.9 seconds, Varosa Uman's missile shattered the surface of the antenna and melted most of the metal veneer.

Varosa Uman had been searching for the alternate transmission route ever since Revutev Mavarka had told Betzino-Resdell it should create it. It couldn't be hidden forever. It had to include a second antenna and the antenna had to be located along the track the orbiter traced across the surface of the planet.

But it wouldn't expose itself until it was activated. It could lie dormant until the moment it transmitted. It could store a small amount of energy and expend it in a single pulse.

"Neutralize their orbiter," Mansita Jano said. "Isolate it."

Varosa Uman checked the track of the Betzino-Resdell orbiter. It had completed over half its orbit.

"And what happens when we give Trans Cultural the Message?" Varosa Uman asked. "After we've committed an overtly hostile act?"

"You've already committed an overtly hostile act. Trans Cultural knows my emissary had some kind of covert official support. Why are you hesitating, Overseer? What is your problem?"

Machines might be unimaginative but they were thorough. Ivan had designed the backup transmission route and he had built in all the redundancy he could squeeze out of the resources his colleagues had given him. Three high speed, low visibility airborne devices set off in three different directions as soon as they received the final message from the base. One stopped twelve kilometers from its starting point and relayed the message to a transmitter built into the highest tree on a small rise. The transmitter had been sucking energy from the tree's biochemistry for three years. It responded by concentrating all that accumulated energy into a single blip that shot toward a transmitter stored in a winged scavenger that circled over a grassy upland.

Varosa Uman's surveillance routine had noted the flying scavenger and stored it in a file that included several hundred items of interest. It picked up the blip as soon as the scavenger relayed it and narrowed the area in which its patrols were working their search patterns. A flyer that resembled a terrestrial owl suicide-bombed the hidden antenna half a second before the blip reached it.

The other two high speed airborne devices veered toward the northern and southern edges of the orbiter's track. Relays emitted their once-in-a-lifetime blasts and settled into permanent quiet.

The antenna located along the northern edge of the track succumbed to a double suicide by two slightly faster updates of the owlish suicider. The third antenna picked up the orbiter as the little ball raced over a dense forest. It fulfilled its destiny twenty seconds before a prepositioned missile splashed a corrosive liquid over the electronic veneer the antenna had spread across an abandoned nest.

Revutev Mavarka went into dormancy as if he was going to his death. He said goodbye to his closest friends. He crammed his detention quarters with images of his favorite scenes and events. He even managed to arrange a special meal and consume it with deliberate pleasure before they emptied out his stomach.

The only omission was a final statement to the public. A private message from Varosa Uman had curtailed his deliberations in that area. Don't waste your time, the Situation Overseer had said, and he had accepted her advice with the melancholy resignation of someone who knew his conscious life had to be measured in heartbeats, not centuries.

Four armed guards escorted him to his dormancy unit. A last pulse of fear broke through his self-control when he felt the injector touch his bare shoulder.

The top of the unit swung back. Varosa Uman looked down at him. Technicians were removing the attachments that connected him to the support system.

"Please forgive our haste," Varosa Uman said. "There will be no permanent damage."

There were no windows in the room. The only decoration was a street level cityscape that filled the wall directly in front of him. He was still lying on the medical cart that had trundled him through a maze of corridors and elevator rides but Varosa Uman's aides had raised his upper body and maneuvered him into a bulky amber wrapper before they filed out of the room.

"You're still managing the Visitation, Overseer?"

"The Integrators won't budge," Varosa Uman said. "The Principals keep putting limits on my powers but they can't get rid of me."

He had been dormant for one hundred and three years. He had asked her as soon as he realized he was coming out of dormancy and she had handed him the information while they were working the wrapper around the tubes and wires that connected him to the cart.

"I've spent much of the last ten years trying to convince the Overseers they should let me wake you," Varosa Uman said. "I got you out of there as soon as they gave me permission."

"Before they changed their mind?"

A table with a flagon and a plate of food disks sat beside the cart. He reached for a disk and she waited while he put it in his mouth and savored his first chew.

"You want something from me," he said.

"The two visitors still have bases on the third moon of Widial—complete with backup copies of all their subunits. I want to contact them with an offer. We will try to guide their species through the Turbulence—try to help them find responses that will reduce the havoc. It's an idea I had earlier. I had a study group explore it. But I fell back into the pattern we've all locked into our reactions."

The men strolling through the cityscape were wearing tall hats and carrying long poles—a fashion that had no relation to anything Revutev Mavarka had encountered in any of the millennia he had lived through.

One hundred and three years. . . .

"There are things we can tell them," Varosa Uman said. "We can end the cycle of attack and isolation every civilization in our section of the galaxy seems to be trapped in."

"You're raising an obvious question, Overseer."

"I want you to join me when I approach the visitors. I need support from the Adventurer community."

"And you think they'll fall in behind me?"

"Some of them will. Some of them hate you just as much as most serenes hate you. But you're a hero to forty percent of them. And the data indicate most of the rest should be recruitable."

He raised his arms as if he was orating in front of an audience. Tubes dangled from his wrists.

"Serenes and Adventurers will join together in a grand alliance! And present the humans with a united species!"

"I couldn't offer the humans a united front if every Adventurer on the planet joined us. We aren't a united species anymore. We stopped being a united species when you sent your warning."

"You said you still had the support of the Integrators."

"There's been a revolt against the Integrators. Mansita Jano refused to accept their decision to keep me in charge of the Visitation."

"We're at war? We're going through another Turbulence?"

"No one has died. Yet. Hundreds of people have been forced into dormancy on both sides. Some cities are completely controlled by Mansita Jano's supporters. We have a serious rift in our society—so serious it could throw us into another Turbulence if we don't do something before more visitors arrive from the human system. If we make the offer and the humans accept—I think most people will fall in behind the idea."

"But you feel you need the support of the Adventurer community?"

"Yes."

The men in the cityscape tapped their poles when they stopped to talk. The ribbons dangling from the ends of the poles complemented the color of their facial feathers.

"That's a risk in itself, Overseer. Why would the serenes join forces with a mob of irresponsible risk takers? Why would anyone follow me? Everything they had ended when I sent my warning."

"You're underestimating yourself. You're a potent figure. I'll lose some serenes but the projections all indicate I'll get most of the Adventurer community in exchange. You may look like an irresponsible innovator to most serenes but most of your own people see you as an innovator who was willing to set a third of the galaxy on a new course."

"And what do you see, Varosa Uman?"

"I see an irresponsible interloper who may have opened up a new possibility. And placed our entire species in peril."

"And if I don't help you pursue your great enterprise I'll be shoved into a box."

"I want your willing cooperation. I want you to rally your community behind the biggest adventure our species has ever undertaken—the ultimate proof that we need people with your personality structure."

"You want to turn an irritating escapader into a prophet?"

"Yes."

"Speech writers? Advisers? Presentation specialists?"

"You'll get the best we have. I've got a communications facility in the next room. I'd like you to sit through a catch up review. Then we'll send a simultaneous transmission to both visitors."

"You're moving very fast. Are you afraid someone will stop you?"

"I want to present our entire population—opponents and supporters—with an accomplished act. Just like you did."

"They could turn on you just like they turned on me. The revolt against the Integrators could intensify. The humans may reject your offer."

"We've examined the possibilities. We can sit here and let things happen or we can take the best choice in a bad list and try to make it work."

"You're still acting like a gambler. Are you sure they didn't make a mistake when they classified you?"

"You take risks because you like it. I take risks because I have to."

"But you're willing to do it. You don't automatically reach for the standard course."

"Will you help me, Revutev Mavarka? Will you stand beside me in one of the boldest moments in the history of intelligence?"

"In the history of intelligence, Overseer?"

"That's what it is, isn't it? We'll be disrupting a chain of self-isolating intelligent species—a chain that's been creeping across our section of the galaxy for hundreds of millennia."

He picked up another food disk. It was dull stuff—almost tasteless—but it supplemented the nutrients from the cart with material that would activate his digestive path. It was, when you thought about it, exactly the kind of food the more extreme serenes would want to encounter when they came out of dormancy.

"Since you put it that way. . . ."

The Cold Step Beyond

IAN R. MACLEOD

British writer Ian R. MacLeod was one of the hottest new writers of the nineties, publishing a slew of strong stories in Interzone, Asimov's Science Fiction, Weird Tales, Amazing, The Magazine of Fantasy & Science Fiction, *and elsewhere and his work continued to grow in power and deepen in maturity as we moved through the first decade of the new century. Much of his work has been gathered in four collections,* Voyages by Starlight, Breathmoss and Other Exhalations Past Magic, *and* Journeys. *His first novel,* The Great Wheel, *was published in 1997. In 1999, he won the World Fantasy Award with his novella "The Summer Isles," and followed it up in 2000 by winning another World Fantasy Award for his novelette "The Chop Girl." In 2003, he published his first fantasy novel, and his most critically acclaimed book,* The Light Ages, *followed by a sequel,* The House of Storms, *in 2005, and then by* Song of Time, *which won both the Arthur C. Clarke Award, and the John W. Campbell Award, in 2008. A novel version of* The Summer Isles *also appeared in 2005. His most recent book is a new novel,* Wake Up and Dream. *MacLeod lives with his family in the West Midlands of England.*

Here he takes us to a far, far future where, in Arthur C. Clarke's famous phrase, the technology is so advanced as to be indistinguishable from magic, for a melancholy study of a bioengineered warrior sent to fight a monster who ultimately turns out to be not at all what she expected it to be.

In a clearing in an unnamed forest in a remote part of the great Island City of Ghezirah, there moved a figure. Sometimes, it moved silently as it swirled a sword in flashing arcs. Sometimes, it made terrible cries. It was high noon in midsummer, and the trees and the greensward shimmered. The figure shimmered as well; it was hard to get a proper sense of the method of its motion. Sometimes, it was here. Sometimes, there. It seemed to skip beyond the places that lay between. Then, when the figure finally stopped moving and let the sword thing fall to its side and hung its head, it became clear that it was scarcely human, and that it was tired and hot.

Bess of the Warrior Church sunk to a squat. The plates of her body armor—mottled greenish to blend with the landscape—were ribboned with sweat. Her limbs ached. Her head throbbed in its enclosing weight of chitin and metal. She swept her gaze around the encircling sweep of forest, willing something to come. She had been here many weeks now; long enough for grass to have grown back in the seared space beneath the caleche that had brought her here, and for its landing gear and rusty undersides to become hazed in bloodflowers.

She looked up across Ghezirah, arching away from her under Sabil's mirrored glare. There, off to the east and rising into the distance, hung the placid browns of the farm islands of Windfell. The other way flashed the grey-blue seawall of the Floating Ocean. Somewhat closer, looming smudgy and indistinct over the forest, lay the fabled Isle of the Dead. But she knew she had no calling in any of those places.

The intelligences of her church had directed her to this clearing. Yet until her foe arrived in whatever shape or form it might take, until the killing moment came, all she could do was practice. And wait.

Yet something told her that, today, she was no longer alone. Her fingers retensed upon the hilt of her sword. She opened her mind and let her senses flow. Something was moving, small and quick, at the shadow edge of the forest. The movement was furtive, yet predatory. If Bess had still possessed hairs along the back of her spine, they would have crawled. She would also have shivered, had she not learned in her novitiate that tension is part of the energy of killing, and thus must be entirely reabsorbed.

Slowly, and seemingly more wearily than ever, Bess hauled her torso upright in a gleam of sweating plates. She even allowed herself to sway slightly. The weariness was genuine, and thus not difficult to fake. By then she was certain that she was being watched from the edge of the forest.

The blade of her sword seemed to flash in the hairsbreadth of an instant before movement itself. It flashed again. Bess seemed to slide across the placid meadow in cubes and sideways protrusions. She was there. Then she wasn't. She was under the trees perhaps a full half second after she had first levered herself up from a squat.

Three severed leaves were floating down in the wake of her sword's last arc, and the thing crouched before her was small and bipedal. It also looked to be young, and seemed most likely human, and probably female, although its sole piece of clothing was a dirty swatch wrapped around its hips. Not exactly the sort of foe Bess had been expecting to end her vigil; just some feral forest-rat. But it hadn't scurried off into the green dark at her arrival even now that the three leaves had settled to the ground. It was holding out, in something that resembled a threatening gesture, a small but antique lightgun. The gun was live. Bess could hear the battery's faint hum.

"If you try to shoot that thing . . ." She said, putting all the power of command into her voice. ". . . you will die." The sound boomed out.

"And if I don't?" The little creature had flinched, but it was still wafting that lightgun. "I'll probably die anyway, won't I? You're a warrior—killing's all you're good for."

Bess's expression, or the little of it which was discernable within her face's plated mask, flickered. Since first leaving the iron walls of her church and setting out across Ghezirah in her caleche three moulids ago, she had discovered that warriors were most often thought of by those who lived outside her calling as little more than heedless bringers of death. Scarcely better, in essence, than the monstrous things they were trained to kill. Not to mention the stories that had passed in her wake of soured milk, broken mirrors, and malformed births. Or the taunts, and the curses, and the things thrown . . .

"I'll put this gun down if you put down your sword," the little creature said. "You're quick—I've seen that. But I don't think you're quicker than light itself . . ."

Technically, of course, the runt was right—but was it worth explaining that the killing movement of any weapon was the last part of a process that could be detected long before it began by those trained in the art of death? Bess decided that it was not. It was apparent from the thing's stance that it was used to using this lightgun, but also that it had no intention of doing so within the next few moments.

Bess lowered her sword to her side.

The creature did the same with the lightgun.

"What's your name?" Bess asked.

"Why should I tell you that? And who are you?"

"Because . . ." If there were any particular reasons, she couldn't immediately think of them. "My name is Bess."

The creature smirked. "Shouldn't you be called something more terrible than that? But I'll call you Bess if you want . . ."

"Do you have a name?"

"I'm Elli." The smirk faded. "I think I am anyway."

"You only *think*? Don't you know who you are?"

"Well, I'm *me*, aren't I?" The creature—although Bess now felt that she could safely assume that she was merely female and human, and not some monstrous anomaly or djinn—glanced down at her grubby, near-naked self. "Names are just things other people give you, aren't they? Or just plain make up . . . ?"

The helm of Bess's head, which had now absorbed the forest's shades, gave a ponderous nod. She understood the Elli-thing's remark, for she, too, had no proper idea of how she had got her name.

"Been watching you . . ." Elli nodded across the clearing. "Dead clever, the way you flicker in and out as if you're there and then not there."

"So why in the name of all the intelligences didn't you back off when I approached?"

Elli shrugged. "I could tell you were just practicing. That you didn't mean it . . ."

Not meaning it being about the worst insult that, in all Bess's long years of training within the walls of her church, had ever been flung her way.

"But it was still very impressive," Elli added. "If you could show me some more, I'd really like to watch."

The Dead Queen's Gambit. The Circle Unleashed. The Upwards Waterfall. The WelcomingBlade. The Twice-Backwards Turn. The Belly Becomes the Mouth. The Leap of Steel. Even *The Cold Step Beyond*, a maneuver of sword and space that Bess still found difficult to execute. She performed them all.

Before, she had felt tired and bored. But now that she had an audience, even one as lowly as this Elli-thing, she felt re-energized. Her blade sliced though the warm air and the fabric of local spacetime, drawing her sideways and backwards in intricate twists and turns. She remembered her dizzy exhilaration when she first managed this near-impossible trick in the practice yards. This was like that, but better.

"Bravo! Bravo!" Elli was clapping.

For want of anything else, and no longer feeling in the least goaded or stupid, Bess gave her sword a final flourish and made as much of a bow as her armored midriff would permit.

It was late afternoon. The shade beneath the trees was spreading. As Bess straightened, she saw that the Elli-thing had already vanished into the wood-scented dark.

Bess felt different that night as she squatted inside the iron womb of her caleche.

Laid before her at the central altar of the cabin's console, set around with the glow of the more ordinary controls, was the steel eye of the keyhole that admitted the will of her church's intelligences. Briefly, it had flashed the message that had borne her here, and all the time since it had remained blank and blind. The other instructions since her changing into warrior form and setting out on her first quest had been plain—at least in their seeming purpose, if not in their execution and result . . .

That great seabeast that had supposedly been terrorizing a community of fisherwomen who lived in a desolate village on the far side of the Floating Ocean. A task that had seemed worthy of her first killing until she had faced the creature itself. A slobbering thing, true. Big and grey and, at least in appearance, monstrous. But it had been old and in pain and helpless. She had realized as it sobbed and moaned on that rocky shore and she drove her sword into its quivering flesh that she had been summoned to do this work not because the women of the village feared to kill the creature, but because they pitied it too much.

Then had come her duties in guarding a senior imam of the Church of the Arachnids, who was supposedly under threat from the incursion of an assassin djinn from other unspecified dimensions. But her arrival and attendance upon this plump and near-regal personage had coincided with a summit meeting of all the churches of the animalcules in Eburnea regarding various issues of precedence and money. It soon became clear to Bess that her presence at the canny witch's brocaded shoulder through those interminable meetings in vast halls was intended not as protection, but as an implied threat of force.

And so it had gone, and then her third instruction had come, and now she was set down here amid this nowhere forest, waiting to do battle with an unexplained *something.*

Bess shuffled down into her night couch. There was little space inside this vessel for much else—after all, what else did a warrior need other than her will and her sword?—but she had been permitted to bring one small chest containing her personal belongings, although she would just as happily have gone without it. The lid gave a pleading scream as she lifted it. This, she thought, as she gazed inside in the caleche's dull glow and breathed a stale waft of air, reminds me why I don't bother to look.

Other new novitiates were brought to the great walls of the Warrior Church by a variety of means and accidents. Lesser daughters. Unwanted or unexpected products of the vats. Those cursed with malformations, either of the body or the mind, which other and more squeamish churches found themselves unable to accept. Girls who had performed some sacrilege or debasement that placed them *beyond the pale,* in the antique phase. Downright criminals. They were all admitted in an unholy gaggle through the iron gates of the Warrior Church, although almost as many were soon found to be lacking and cast back out.

Bess remembered the rusty towers, and the courtyards of trial and test and battle. She remembered the light from classroom windows that washed through drapes of platinum gauze as they were schooled in all the near-endless varieties of monstrosity: djinn, interjection, tulpa, dragon, quasi-dragon, behemoth, and demon that they would be expected to destroy. Most of all, though, she remembered the faces of her fellow novitiates, and night-silence in the dormitories, and the laughter that exploded as soon as the junior imams doused the lights.

Clubfoot Nika. Humble Talla of the auburn tresses. And Afya of the shadows. All now transformed into hulking warriors like her. Out fighting some terror in the great Island City of Ghezirah or across one or the other of the Ten Thousand and One Worlds. Or already dead. Bess gazed down at the few dry leavings of her past. A shriveled starflower. A tress of auburn hair. A hand-written note about soon returning, casually left.

Just one other item lay in there. Bess's taloned fingers struggled to pinch the fine loop of chain.

Who are you, Bess . . . ?

Where do you come from . . . ?

What are you doing here . . . ?

Bess no-name—Bess who had struggled to belong even in those dormitories of the dispossessed and deformed. From all the other novitiates, sitting along the dark lines of bunks, hands clasped around knees with eyes rapt and mouths agape, there was always some story to be heard. High schemes or low robberies. A birth mother knifed by a jealous bond mother. A hand let go in a market of slaves. Over the nights, the whispers echoed through the dormitory as the tales flowed on. And grew more elaborate, Bess began to notice, as well. So the suckling child came to remember the taste of her dying birth mother's blood, and the slave-sold underling survived a jumpship's spectacular crash. But the essential seed of truth of some lost life remained, and could thus be embroidered upon much as a basic sword thrust can once—but only once—it is entirely mastered.

But Bess was mute when the eyes turned to her . . .

What about you, Bess?

What do you remember about the time before you were chosen?

She couldn't answer such questions. She was Bess simply because that was what some lesser manifestation of the church's intelligences had deigned to call her. All there was was this great iron-enclosed edifice, and her friends, and dormitory nights such as these, and all the days of learning and practice. Nothing else. She had no sense of who or what she had been before. She might as well have come from nowhere, just as the chants and the jibes insisted. But for this one object . . .

It was called a locket. Or so she supposed; the terminology for items of jewelry was not a form of knowledge in which warriors were expected to be versed. But the word seemed to come with possession of the item. Which might mean something. Or might not.

She had rarely worn the thing, even when her head and neck would have allowed such a vanity before she changed into full warrior form. But she had kept it. The chain was as finely made as were the great chains which anchored the islands against the spin of Ghezirah's vast sphere. From it, flashing bright then dull in the glow globe's light, depended the silver teardrop which was the locket itself, engraved with dizzying fractal patterns and swirls.

Bess felt that she was being drawn into the pattern, and permitted herself the wasted energy of a small shudder as her armored fingers unslipped the chain and re-closed the lid of her chest. Then she stretched down to rest.

She was already awake when the caleche's interior brightened to signal the onset of dawn. A fizzing buzz, a sense of some invisible liquid cleansing her scales, and she was ready for yet another day of waiting. She raised the hatch and reached for her sword. Outside, as the dawn-singers called in the light from their mirrored minarets, her footsteps left a dark trail like the last of the night. When she drew her sword and made her first leap, the trail vanished into misty air.

She was just re-practicing *The Circle Unleashed* in its rarely attempted more elaborate form when she knew that once again she was being watched. She hadn't considered how well this particular sword-stroke was fitted to the brief and spectacular series of leaps across the bloodflower-strewn meadow that she then executed. But it was.

There was the Elli-thing, standing undaunted but admiring at the edge of the forest, where today Bess's arrival had stirred or severed not one single leaf.

"*Salaam*," Bess said, a little breathlessly.

"*Sabah al Noor*, Bess of the Warrior Church." Elli replied with surprising formality, and Bess wondered as the creature then made a small bow at her own flush of pleasure to be greeted thus. Then a thought struck her. "You haven't been out here all night, have you?"

"Oh no." Elli gave a quick shake of her head.

"Then where do you live?"

"Oh . . ." A quick shrug. A backwards point with a grubby thumb. ". . . just back there awhile. Would you like to come and look?"

A small, pale figure. A larger shape that was scarcely there at all. They both moved ever deeper into the nameless forest through dark avenues and spills of birdsong.

This more resembled, Bess supposed, the kind of adventure that was sometimes associated in the popular mind with members of her church. Dragons to be slain. Monstrous shifts and anomalies in the fabric of spacetime to be annulled.

Maidens, even, to be rescued. Bess should, she supposed, feel a deep unease to be deserting the precise spot where her church's intelligences had instructed her to stay.

But warriors had to show bravery and initiative, didn't they? And how long could any human being, no matter how extensively changed and trained, be expected to wait?

They paused to take refreshment beside a tree hung with a kind of red fruit that Elli said was called pomegranate, and had existed as far back as the Gardens of Eden on the legendary first planet of Urrearth. They were also to be found, she added matter of factly, in Paradise itself. They were best cut apart with a sharp utensil.

"The trouble being with this thing"—she patted the lightgun she had tucked into the tie around her waist, then glanced at Bess expectantly—"is that it cooks them as well."

Bess studied the fruit, an odd-looking thing with a crown-like eruption at one end, which Elli was holding out. Her hand went to the hilt of her sword, although she knew what the imams of the Warrior Church would have said about using her sacred blade for such a menial task. If they had happened to be here and watching her, that was.

"Tell you what, Bess—I could throw it up like this."

Quicker than an instant, Bess drew her blade, and, in executing the *Spatchcock Goose*, vanished and reappeared as the pomegranate, now separated into two halves, still span up.

"Wooh!"

Elli caught one half as it descended. Bess, the other.

"So . . . ? What do you think of pomegranate? Not bad, is it, if you can deal with the seeds."

Bess had to agree. All in all, pomegranates were delicious. But, at least when it came to eating, they were a frustrating fruit. Her huge hands soon grew sticky, and so did her plated face. It was just as enjoyable, they decided, simply to toss the things up for the joy of slicing them in half. Pith and fruit were soon flying, and Bess's armor acquired the mottled reds, whites and pinks of pomegranate flesh.

"So . . . ?" Elli asked eventually, after Bess had demonstrated so many ways of slicing the fruit that much of what was left lying around them seemed to exist in some sideways dimension. Or, perhaps, was just a sticky mess. "This is what you do, is it? Cut things up in odd and interesting ways?"

Bess had been laughing too much to take offense. But she now explained how the origins of her church could be traced back to the time of the first jumpships, when gateways had been discovered where all time, space, and matter turned back in a cosmic rent. It had been a great breakthrough for womankind and every other sentient species, but it had also brought an end to the simplicity of one reality and the linear progression of time. Now, other forms of existence that had previously been thought of as nothing but useful constructs in understanding the higher dimensions of physics rubbed close against our own. The true aliens, the real horrors and monstrosities, lay not in the far-flung reaches of the galaxy, but sideways. And each passage of a jumpship disturbed enough of the fabric of this reality to allow, like a breath of dark smoke from a creak beneath a door, a little more of the seepage of these other realities in. Sometimes, they were comical or harmless. Often, they weren't noticeable at all. But sometimes they were the stuff of abject nightmare.

Only through the use of creatures who were themselves close to nightmare could these monstrous interjections be fought.

Bess wiped her sword on a patch of grass and made to re-sheath it in her scabbard.

But then Elli had laid her hand on a part of her forearm that still retained some sensitivity. It felt sticky and warm.

"That sword of yours—I suppose it does something similar? The way it seems to cut through the world."

"Well . . . You *could* say that, I suppose. Although the principle is much more controlled."

"Can I have a go?"

The request was ridiculous. It was sacrilege. So why hadn't she yet sheathed her sword?

"You can try this, Bess." Elli held out her cheap lightgun. "It's quite deadly."

"No," Bess rumbled.

"Well, perhaps you could at least let me give the handle-thing a quick hold."

"It's called the hilt." Bess watched in something like horror or amazement as her own hand took the flat of the blade and held it out.

"Hilt, then."

Elli's fingers were so small they barely circled the banded metal. Yet Bess felt a small shiver—something akin to the sensation that she had experienced last night when she studied that locket—run through her. The sword shivered, too. Sensing a new presence, it had responded with a blurring hint of the final darkness beyond all dark that was woven into the exquisite metal.

Elli's fingers retracted. She let out a shuddering breath. "It feels like . . . Everything and nothing at all."

It was getting colder and dimmer now when, by rights, even in a place as overshadowed as this forest had become, it should have been growing warmer and brighter.

The trees were giant things, spewing mossy boughs over which they had to clamber. Elli was quick and sure and sharp as she scampered over the deadfalls. Bess, meanwhile, felt clumsy and lost. Vulnerable, as well. She stole glances at this odd little creature. What exactly *was* she? And how did she survive in this confusing jungle?

A giant beetle, a crimson thing more jagged and threatening than her own helmeted head, regarded Bess with its many eyes before raising some kind of stinging tail and finally, reluctantly, backing off. There were probably more fearsome things than that out here in this forest—perhaps even monstrosities fierce enough to merit the attentions of a member of the Warrior Church. What defense could this near-naked young thing with only a cheap toy of a lightgun possibly put up? Unless she was far more dangerous than she seemed . . .

The thought that all of this could be some kind of deathly trap niggled in Bess's mind. But, at the same time, it was good to explore and make new friends, and her caleche with all its duties lay only a few miles off, and she was enjoying herself too much to want to stop.

The forest's branches were now so crisscrossed as to give no sense of light or sky. It was more like a vast and twisty ceiling from which drapes of a livid moss provided the only illumination.

Then Elli stopped.

"Where are we?" Bess asked.

"Just have to go up here . . ."

Here being a winding step of roots that then became branches, leading through a wanly glowing archway inside a rotting trunk. Was this where Elli lived? Oddly, though, this strange little hideaway had a further stairway within it, lit by strips of light that gleamed as they ascended over beautifully carved stretches of floor and roof. The fine-grained stairway swirled on and up. There were intricate settings of jewel and marquetry. And now, at last, there was sunlight ahead.

". . . Nearly there . . ."

An ivy-embroidered gate screeched on a final rise of marble steps. Bess had expected to emerge at some eyrie close to Ghezirah's roof, but it was immediately apparent that they were on solid ground. This was a kind of garden—trees, buildings, and strange eruptions of statuary tumbled all around them—yet it was oddly quiet; filled with a decrepit kind of peace.

"Where by Al'Toman *is* this?"

"Can't you tell?"

It wasn't so very hard. In fact, now that Bess was getting her bearings, it was obvious.

Over there, seen at a slightly different angle from the view she was used to, lay the placid browns of the farm islands of Windfell. That way, churning with what was surely the beginnings of a storm, was the vast seawall of the Floating Ocean.

And below them, yet curling upwards in ways that the air and Bess's own senses struggled to bridge, marched the green crowns of the nameless forest, and beyond that, flecked with the red hollows where the bloodflowers flourished, lay the small circle of her meadow.

"You can't *live* on the Isle of the Dead?"

"Why not? You live inside that iron carbuncle."

It was a given even in nursery books that the Island City of Ghezirah was more than simply a smooth globe encircling Sabil's star in three plain dimensions. Yet it was dizzying, and more than a little disturbing, to think that they had contrived to reach this place of the dead by climbing through the forest's roof. Still, Bess followed Elli as they explored.

Most of the tombs were very old, but older ones still were said to be buried in their foundations. Indeed, the most fanciful version of the tale of the Isle of the Dead's origins told of how the entire island consisted of nothing but mulched flesh, bone, and memorial. The place was certainly alarmingly uneven and ramshackle, and little frequented in modern times. The major churches now all had their own mausoleums, while many of the lesser ones favored remote planets of rest. The Warrior Church, meanwhile, found no home for its servants other than in its memories, for its acolytes were always expected to die in battle.

Hayawans ambled around carved sandstone pillars. Spirit projections flickered and dissolved like marshghosts. The voices of ancient recordings called from stone mouths muffled by birds' nests. But it was the fecund sense of *life* in this place that struck Bess most. The bumbling insects. The frantic birdsong. The heady scents and colors of the blooms. There were fruits, as well, which would have made the pomegranate seem homely, and Elli explained that this island was also a fine place for trapping foxes, for catching airhorses, for collecting honeyseed, and for digging up and broiling moles.

"So you live here alone?"

Elli gave a shrugging nod. That much was obvious, Bess supposed.

"So how did you—"

"Come here? Is *that* what you're wondering?" Elli's face was suddenly flushed. "You think I'm some kind of grave-robber or ghoul?"

Bess attended to removing a speck of grit from her scabbard. After all, she could hardly accuse someone else of being secretive about their origins when there was an empty space where there should have been her own. Just that noisy dormitory, and no sense of anything before. As if, impossibly, she had been born into her novitiate fully functioning and whole. Apart from that locket, which meant nothing at all. But no, there *was* something more than that, she thought, looking around at this pretty home of the long-dead. Some bleak moment of horror from which her mind recoiled.

The most sense she could make of it was that her church had plucked her from something so terrible that the best way to keep hold of her sanity had been to empty the knowledge from her brain. And now, somehow, the shivering thought trickled through her, something was pulling her back there.

Elli pointed. "You see that building, the one with the copper birch tree growing out of the middle?"

It was a dome that still partly retained its covering of mosaic glass. It looked to be on fire, the way the leaves flickered above them.

"Do you want to take a look?"

Bess's head gave its usual slow nod.

"There was a girl buried there. Oh . . . a long time ago," Elli explained as they clambered over the ruins. "Before the War of Lilies, when the seasons were unchanging, and even time itself was supposed to run more slow. Anyway, she was young when she died, and her birth mother and her bond mothers were stricken. So they made this fine mausoleum for her, and they filled it with everything about their daughter, every toy and footstep and giggle and memory. You see . . ."

They were standing beneath the dome. The tree shifted through its fractured lenses, giving the displays a dusty life. Animatronic toys seemed to jerk. Strewn teddy bears still had a residual glint of intelligence in their button eyes. But that, and the swishing leaves, only made the sense of age and loss more apparent.

"And they visited her here . . . And they prayed . . . And they cried . . . And, dead though their daughter was, they swore that her memory would never die. But of course—"

"What was this girl's name? Are *you*—?"

"—Shut up and listen, will you, Bess! And her name was Dallah, and I'm called Elli if you haven't noticed. So no, I'm not Dallah. Although Dallah *was* my friend. My best friend, you might say. In fact, my only one. You see, Dallah was like most only children who've been longed for a bit too much by their mothers, and find themselves over-protected and alone. Of course, Dallah had all these toys . . ." Elli pinged a bike bell.

"And she could have anything else she ever wanted. She only had to ask. But what she really wanted, the one thing her mothers couldn't give her for all their kindness and wealth, was a friend. So . . ." Elli ran a finger over a cracked glass case that seemed to be filled with nothing but leaves and dust. ". . . she did what most girls have done since Eve first grew bored with Adam. She made one up. And her name *was* Elli. And that's me. That's who I am."

Bess had been gazing into a hologlass pillar that contained the floating faces of three women. They looked kindly, but impossibly sad.

"I was just intended as another part of the memorial," Elli said. "They extracted me from every breath and memory of their beloved daughter. Sweet little pretend-Elli, who always had to have a place laid for her at table, and did all the naughty and disruptive things to which Dallah herself would never confess. Elli who stole all the doughnuts, even though it was Dallah who fell sick. Elli who crayoned that picture of a clown's face on the haremlek wall. They'd come to me in the years after to reminisce. This whole mausoleum, they couldn't stop building and refining it. Nothing was ever enough. They kept Dallah herself within a glass coffin inside a suspension field so she didn't decay. Not, of course, that they could ever bring themselves to actually look at their dead daughter, but she was unchanging, perfectly there. They couldn't let her go. Even when they were old, the mothers came. But then there were only two of them. And then just the one, and she grew so confused she sometimes thought I was Dallah. Then she stopped coming as well, and the slow centuries passed, and the gardeners rusted and the maintenance contracts expired. And people no longer came to pay their respects to anyone on the Isle of the

Dead. There were just these crumbling mausoleums and a few flickering intelligences. The thing is, Dallah's mothers had tried too hard, done too much. And the centuries are *long* when you're an imaginary friend and you have nobody to play with—and I mean body in every sense . . ."

Elli had been wandering the mausoleum as she talked, touching color-faded stacks of studded brick and dolls with missing eyes. But now she was standing beside that long glass case again. Which, Bess now saw, was shattered along one side.

"So you took hold of Dallah's corpse?"

"What *else* was I do to? She had no use for it, and her mothers are long dead. If I looked in a mirror, if there *was* a mirror here that was clear enough, I suppose I might see a face that would remind me a bit of Dallah. But I'm not Dallah. Dallah's dead and mourned for and in Paradise or wherever with William Galileo and Albert Shakespeare and all the rest. I'm Elli. And I'm me. And I'm here." She stuck out her tongue. "So there!"

Bess had heard of the concept of body-robbing, and knew that most of the major churches forbade it. The punishments, she imagined, would be severe, especially if the robber happened to be something that couldn't properly call itself sentient. But Elli's tale, and that final pink protrusion of her tongue, made the deed hard to condemn.

It was better, though, that she stayed eating berries and broiling moles on the Isle of the Dead. In any other part of Ghezirah, or any of the other Ten Thousand and One Worlds, life for her would be not so much difficult as impossible, and would most likely be brought to a rapid end.

"How long have things been like this?"

Elli now looked awkward. "I don't know. I . . ." She looked up at the hissing, dancing roof. ". . . Can we leave this place?"

It was good to be back out in the warm afternoon, even if all the falling memorials were now a constant reminder to Bess that this was a place of the dead. But as for Elli, she thought, as she gazed at her friend sitting on a pile of rocks with her arms wrapped around her grubby knees, she's right in what she says. She isn't some ghoul or monster. She's truly alive. Then Bess's eyes trailed down to that lightgun. The reason it looked like a toy, she realized, was that it had probably once been one. But she didn't doubt that it was now deadly, or that Elli knew how to use it. In her own way, this little grave-runt was as much a warrior as Bess was.

It seemed a time for confidences, so Bess explained what little there was to explain about her own life. The long days of endless practice. The even longer dormitory nights. The laughing chants. That sense of not properly belonging even in a community of outcasts. And now—the way her entire church and all its intelligences seemed to have withdrawn from her, when she'd been expecting to face some kind of ultimate challenge through which she could prove her worth.

"You mean, like a dragon or something? A monster that needs killing?"

She nodded. A dragon, or even a quasi-dragon, would certainly have done. Anything, no matter how terrible, would have been better than this. It was as if she'd been thrown back into the empty nowhere from which she had come, but pointlessly trained in swordplay and changed into the thing she now was . . .

Something patted down Bess's scales, leaving blurry silver trails that her camouflage struggled to mimic. After a long moment's puzzlement, she realized it was tears.

"Don't you have any idea of your earlier life?" Elli asked. "I mean, some hint or memory?"

Bess gave an armor-plated shrug, and rumbled about the piece of jewelry that she happened to possess. A thing on a chain, oval-shaped.

"You mean a locket?"

"I think it's called a locket, yes. You've heard of them?"

"Of course I have. I've got one myself. So—what's inside yours?"

"What do you mean, inside?"

Elli laughed and leapt down from her perch.

"You really don't know much about anything other than killing things, do you, Bess?"

Then she explained how lockets came in two hinged halves—there were, after all, plenty of examples of this and every other kind of trinket to be found on this isle—although the main thing that Bess was conscious of as they talked was her friend's close presence, and the strange and peculiarly delicious sensation of a hand touching her own strange flesh.

It was getting late. The dawn-singers had already made their first preparatory cries, stirring up an evensong of birds. Contrary to the once-popular saying, it proved far easier to depart the Isle of the Dead than to get there, and Elli soon led Bess back toward the same marble steps through which they had entered, and down into the depths of the forest that lay below. Moving through the pillared near-dark, Bess was conscious again of the danger of this place. Far more than the island above them, this was a landscape wherein monsters and wonders might abide. Yet Elli led on.

The clearing lay ahead.

"You'll be here tomorrow?"

"Yes." Elli smiled. "I will."

Bess shambled across the meadowgrass, which, amid darker patches of bloodflower, already shone with dew. The caleche hissed open its door. She climbed in and laid down her sword. The keyhole eye at the center of the cabin's altar, which would surely soon bear her a fresh instruction, and perhaps even apologies for this pointless waste of her time, remained unseeingly dark. The food tray hissed out for her, and she ate. Then, as she prepared to lie down, she remembered what Elli had said about lockets. Vaguely curious, but somehow still feeling no great sense of destiny, she opened her small chest and lifted the thing out. After a moment of struggle, the two sides broke apart.

Another morning, and, although it was still too early for dawn, Bess was standing in the dim clearing outside her caleche with her sword. She, too, was a thing of dimness; her armor saw to that. But already the dawn-singers were calling. Light would soon be spilling from tower to tower. And there was Elli, standing out from the shadow trees, pale as stripped twig.

"Bess! You've come!" She was almost running. Almost laughing. Then she was doing both.

"I said I would, didn't I?" Bess's voice was as soft as it was capable of being. And as sad. It made Elli stop.

"What's happened?" They stood a few paces apart beside the rusty beetle of the caleche in the ungreying light. "You seem different."

"I haven't changed," Bess rumbled. "But I've brought you this. I want you to take it . . ." She held out the locket, glinting and swinging on its silver chain, from her hand's heavy claw.

"It's that thing you described . . ." Elli looked puzzled, hesitant. "The locket. But this is . . ." She took it in her own small fingers. Here, in the spot in which they were standing, the gaining light had a rosy flush. ". . . mine."

"Open it."

Elli nodded. Red flowers lay all around them. The silver of the locket was taking up their color, and Bess now seemed a thing entirely made of blood. Swiftly, with fingers far more practiced and easeful than Bess's, Elli broke open the locket's two sides. From out of which gleamed a projection, small but exquisite, of the faces of three women. They were the same faces that hung in the hologlass pillar of Dallah's mausoleum. But in this image they looked as happy as in the other they had been sad.

"Dallah's mothers." Elli breathed. "This thing is yours, Bess. But it's also mine . . ."

"That's right."

Elli snapped it shut. Dawn light was flowing around them now, and the bloodflowers made Elli beautiful, and yet they also made her pale and dangerous and sharp. "This doesn't really have to happen, does it?" she whispered.

"I think it does."

"Don't tell me, Bess." She almost smiled. "You remember it already . . . ?"

"I didn't—not at all. But I'm beginning to now. I'm sorry, Elli."

"And I'm sorry as well. Isn't there some way we can both just go our separate ways and live our own lives—you as a warrior and me just as me? Do I really have to do this to you?"

"We both do. Nothing is possible otherwise. We're joined together, Elli. We're a monstrosity, a twist in spacetime. Our togetherness is an affront to reality. It must be destroyed, otherwise even worse things will break through. There are no separate ways."

The killing moment was close. Bess could already hear the lightgun's poisonous hum. She knew Elli was quick, but she also knew that the use of any weapon, be it blade or laser, was the last part of a process that any trained warrior should be able to detect long before the final instant came. But how by all the intelligences was she supposed to do such a thing, when Elli was her own younger self?

Then it happened. All those hours of practice and training, all the imam's praises and curses, seemed to collide in a moment beyond time, and emerged into something deadly, precise, and perfect. For the first time in her fractured life, Bess executed *The Cold Step Beyond* with absolute perfection, and she and her blade were nowhere and in several places at once. Elli was almost as quick. And could easily have been quicker.

Yet she wasn't.

Or almost.

And that was enough.

Bess swung back, a blur of metal and vengeance, into the ordinary dimensions of the spreading dawn. Around her, still spraying and toppling, spewed the remains of Elli of the Isle of the Dead. Nothing but hunks of raw meat now, nothing you could call alive, even before the bits had thunked across the ground.

Bess stood there for a moment, her breathing unquickening. Then she wiped and sheathed her sword. She knew now why the bloodflowers bloomed so well across this meadow. Without them, the strew of flesh that surrounded her would have been too horrible to bear. But something glinted there, perfect and unsullied. She picked it up.

Her blade had cut through everything else—time, life, probability, perhaps even love—but not the chain and locket. It was the one strand that held together everything else.

She remembered it all now. Remembered as if it had never been gone. Playing with Dallah—who had called her Elizabeth, or sometimes Elli, or occasionally Bess—all those aeons ago when she'd been little more than a hopeful ghost. Then pain and emptiness for the longest time until some kind of residual persistence took hold. It was, Bess supposed, the same kind of persistence that drives all life to strive to *become*, even if the body of someone once loved must be stolen in the process. Long seasons followed. There was little sense of growth or change. The once-sacred island around her slid further toward decay and neglect. But now she was Elli, and she had Dallah's discarded body and she was alive, and she learned that living meant knowing how to feed, which in turn meant knowing how to kill.

Elli had always been alone apart from a few of the other mausoleums' residual intelligences.

But it wasn't until one warm summer's morning when the light seemed to hang especially pure that she looked down across at the other great islands, and saw something moving in a clearing with jagged yet elegant unpredictability, and realized that she felt lonely. So she found a way down through the twisty forests that lay below the catacombs, and came at last to a space of open grass, and watched admiringly until she was finally noticed, and the monstrous thing came over to her in blurring flashes, and turned out to be not quite so monstrous at all.

But that locket. Which had once been Dallah's. Even as the Bess-thing held it out, Elli had understood that there was only one way that Bess could own it as well. That time, like the locket's chain, had looped around itself and joined them together in a terrible bond. And Elli then knew that only one of them could survive, because she was the monstrosity that this creature had been sent to kill.

The killing moment, when grace, power, and relentlessness are everything. But in the memory Bess now had of holding Elli's lightgun, the warrior-thing had hesitated, and her own laser had fired a jagged spray. Even as Bess gazed down at the remains of Elli's butchered body lain amid the bloodflowers, the memory of the burning stench of her own wrecked chitin and armor came back to her. She had died not once this dawn, but twice. And yet she was still living.

It was fully day now. The clearing dazzled with dew. Looking back toward her caleche, Bess saw that its door had opened, and that, even in this morning blaze, the light of her altar shone out. More questing, perhaps. More things to kill. Or an instruction for her to return and recuperate within her church's iron walls.

The intelligences of the Warrior Church were harsh and brutal, but they also welcomed the sorts of creature that no other church would ever think to accept. And now they had given Bess back her memory, and made her whole. She realized now why her earlier quests had seemed so pointless, and why she hadn't yet felt like a true warrior at all. But she was truly a warrior, for she had taken that final step into the cold beyond, and been found not to be wanting.

Bess gazed at the open door of her caleche, and its eerie, beckoning glow. She had climbed in there once clutching that locket, been borne away in a long moment of forgetting to begin the life that had eventually brought her back here. But now her gaze turned toward the encircling forest, and she remembered that sense she had had of different dangers and mysteries lurking there. Wonders, perhaps, too.

The caleche awaited.

The light from its doorway blared.

Its engine began to hum.

Bess of the Warrior Church stood bloodied and head-bowed in a clearing in a nameless forest, wondering which way she should go.

A Militant Peace

DAVID KLECHA AND TOBIAS S. BUCKELL

Tobias S. Buckell is a Caribbean-born science fiction author. His work has been translated into sixteen different languages. He has published some fifty short stories in various magazines and anthologies, and has been nominated for the Hugo, Nebula, Prometheus, and Campbell Awards. He's the author of the Xenowealth trilogy, consisting of Crystal Rain, Ragamuffin, *and* Sly Mongoose. *His short fiction has been collected in* Nascence *and* Tides from the New Worlds. *His most recent novel is* Arctic Rising. *Much of his short work has recently been made available as Kindle editions. He maintains a Web site at tobiasbuckell.com.*

David Klecha is a writer and Marine combat veteran currently living in West Michigan with his family and assorted computer junk. He works in IT to pay the bills, like so many other beginning writers and artists.

Here they combine talents for a compelling look at an unusual, high-tech, nonviolent invasion of North Korea.

> *I am not only a pacifist but a militant pacifist. I am willing to fight for peace.*
>
> *—Albert Einstein*

For Nong Mai Thuy, a Vietnamese Sergeant in the Marine Police, the invasion of North Korea starts with the parachute-snapping violence of a High Altitude, Low Opening jump deep in the middle of the inky black North Korean airspace at night. Here the air is the stillest, bleakest black. The bleakness of a world where electricity trickles only to the few in Pyongyang.

This is good for Mai. The synthetic ballistic faceshield displaying heads-up information has a host of visual add-ons, including night vision. She flicks it on, and the familiar gray-green of a landscape below rushes up to smack into her.

When she thuds into the ground the specialized, carefully fitted, motorized armor hisses slightly as it adjusts to the impact.

"Duc?"

"I am safe," her partner responds in her ear over the faint distortion of high-end crypto. In the upper right of her HUD a beacon glows softly, and she turns around. Duc's smashed his way through several hefty tree limbs before hitting ground. But he's already packing his chute.

They are officially on the ground.

Beyond the darkness are some nine and a half million North Korean forces that aren't going to respond well to what has just happened.

And Mai wonders: how many of them are already on the way to try and kill her right now?

Three minutes before Mai and Duc hit the ground, heavy machinery in stealth-wrapped containers had parachuted in, invisible to prying electronic eyes, and touched down.

Mai and Duc fan out to establish a perimeter and protect it, even as hundreds more hit the ground, roll, and come up ready to follow orders beamed at them from commanders still up in the sky, watching from live satellite feeds.

A portable airstrip gets rolled out across the grassy meadow. Within the hour the thorium nuclear power plant airdrops in and gets buried into the ground, then shielded with an artillery-proof cap.

Once power is on, Camp Nike takes shape. The ballistic-vest wearing civilian Chinese contractors have built whole skyscrapers within forty-eight hours. Here they only need to get four or five stories high for the main downtown area. They get a bonus for each extra geodesic dome fully prepped by the morning. The outer wall of the camp is airlifted in. It's been constructed in pieces in Australia ahead of time, and the pieces slam down into the ground via guided parachutes. No one glances up, this part of the invasion has been practiced over and over again in Western Australia so much that it's old news.

Twenty minutes before sunrise two large transports land and the civilians rush them. The field is cleared of non-combatants soon after, leaving the ghost city behind it.

It is dawn when what looks like a hastily organized contingent of the North Korean Army crests the hills. Thirty soldiers here to scout out what the hell just happened, Mai imagines.

Mai ends up outside the perimeter, guardian to the north gate.

"Welcome to Camp Nike," Duc mutters.

Someone is riding shotgun through their helmet cameras and jumps into the conversation. It sounds like Captain Nguyen, Mai thinks. "Make a slight bow to the commanding officer, wave encouragingly at the group."

Mai's hand rests on her hip, where a sidearm would usually be.

"No threatening gestures, keep your arms out and forward," her helmet whispers to her. Aggressive body-posture detected and reported by her own suit. It feels slightly like betrayal. Old habits die hard: Mai can't help but reach for her hip.

She is, after all, still a soldier.

The small group of men all have AKS-74s—which the North Koreans call a Type 88—but they're slung over their shoulders, even though they can see Mai and Duc in full armor.

"I have a bad feeling about this," Mai mutters.

"Hold your positions," command whispers to them.

It isn't right. Standing here, unarmed, holding her hands up in the air as if *she's* the one surrendering, placating an enemy. When there are men standing just thirty feet away with rifles.

One of them steps forward, his hands in the air, and she realizes he's nervous.

Mai points to a signpost near the gates.

CAMP NIKE
UNITED NATIONS–SPONSORED
ALTERNATIVE SETTLEMENT ZONE
NO WEAPONS ALLOWED
PLACE ALL WEAPONS IN THE
MARKED BINS FOR DESTRUCTION

The sign's in Korean, Chinese, Vietnamese and English, and also emblazoned with the internationally-recognizable logos of all the camp's primary private sector sponsors.

There'll be more of that when people got inside. Shoes and clothing by Nike. Dinners by ConAgra. TV by Samsung. Computers by Dell.

The men read the sign, and start shaking their heads.

This, Mai thinks, is a moment of balance, where the world around her could swing one way or another.

Duc takes initiative, to her surprise, and waves at the men cheerily. He flips his faceplate open, so they can see his expression, while Mai curses him silently and fights the urge to grab him and yank him to safety.

All it'll take is one well-aimed shot from a sniper somewhere out there to kill him, now. Or for one of these men with an AKS-74 to spook.

He might as well not even wear the armor, she thinks, absently reaching for her hip again.

There is no gun, though. There never will be.

Mai's not close enough for her translation software to help her understand what the group of men is arguing over. But Duc has gotten close enough to be surrounded.

"They want to see the food," he reports.

"What?"

"They want to make sure they're not being tricked into a prison camp. They won't disarm until they see that what they were told about the camps was true."

One of the men holds up a cheap, black smartphone and points at it.

Six months ago these things were dumped into North Korea by the millions. Each phone disguises its texting and data traffic as background static, and otherwise functions as a basic, jamming-hardened satphone. Between the satellite routing and peer-to-peer whisper comms, they created a "darknet" outside of Pyongyang's official control.

The Beloved Leader decreed death for anyone caught with one, but the experiment succeeded. Well enough to spirit out video and pictures of starving children, of brutal crackdowns on attempts to protest Pyongyang by desperate, starving peasants, and all the other atrocities that had built the case for international intervention.

It has been through these phones that messages explaining the camps and invasion had been sent twenty-four hours ago.

Promising food and safety.

These soldiers are defecting, and can see the walls. Now they want to see the food.

It's all about the food.

"Three of you, leave your weapons in the bin," Duc says, "go in and come back out to report what you see."

It is a reasonable compromise. Duc and Mai let the three unarmed men pass through, and five minutes later they're back, excited and shouting at their comrades.

One of the men whistles back toward the crest of the hill. As if melting out of the countryside, a river of people carrying what possessions they had came trickling down the hillside, and out of the distant scrub where they'd been hiding.

The first two hundred new citizens of Camp Nike stream in through the gates, and once they're through, all that is left are the full bins of AKS-74s waiting to be destroyed.

"Were you worried?" Duc asks as they watch the North Koreans line up at refugee registration booths.

"Yes," she replies. "I think we'd be foolish not to worry when people with guns walk up to us."

Duc thumps his chest. "With these on? We're invincible here."

Maybe, Mai thinks. She looks back at the small city inside the walls. But we aren't the only ones here, now, are we?

For forty-eight hours the stream of humanity continues. A thousand. Five thousand. Ten thousand. The Korean People's Army is too busy chasing ghosts to notice right now: false reports about touchdowns. Jammed communications. Domination of their airspace.

Satellite telescopes, early warning systems, and spyware pinpoints the point of origin of several missile launches. They die while still boosting up into the air, struck from above by high-powered lasers.

Electromagnetic pulses rain down from heavy stealth aircraft drones, leaving any unshielded North Korean advanced military tech, which is far more than anyone realized, useless metal junk.

By the time the North Koreans managed to haul out their ancient, analog Cold War-era artillery, Mai is on her way to the barracks to bunk down for her first real night of sleep.

The shelling begins in earnest. A distant crumping sound, but without the accompanying whistle of the rounds falling.

The Point Defense Array pops up. Green light flickers and sparks from the top of the almost floral-looking tower in the center of Camp Nike. Lines shimmer into the night sky as they track incoming artillery rounds.

They'd been told during training that the green lasers were doing nothing more than "painting" the individual targets before the x-ray lasers slagged the incoming shells into nothing more than a slight metal mist.

Mai watches the light show build in intensity for a few moments, just as awed by its beauty as she had been when she'd first seen it demonstrated.

The bursts light up the undersides of the clouds. And not a single shell gets through.

She wonders if she would still have the reflexes to get to cover if she ever hears the telltale whistle of an incoming round again, after living like this.

There might be thousands of Captain Nguyens in the Vietnamese military, Mai knows. But here at Camp Nike, there is only *one*. She is the sort of woman who straightens spines at a glance. They call her the Warrior of Binh Phuoc, and it's rumored that she single-handedly kept that border region safe for years during the Cambodian Unrest.

Nguyen's been hopping in and out of helmet cameras all week long, moving them around like pawns on a chessboard.

Now it's time for Mai to face the chess master.

Mai joins Trong Min Hoai, a member of her team, as they hop over a row of Japanese-donated grooming 'bots, rolling up the main street of Camp Nike sweeping up litter. They're both in full Peacekeeping armor, servos whining as they work around her limbs to amplify her tiniest motions.

In an already carefully-cultivated and manicured gaming park over to their right, a group of South Korean volunteers are combining literacy lessons with one of the role-playing games popular in the South.

All it would take, Mai thinks, glancing up at the snap and crack of green Point Defense activity in the distance, is one artillery shell to sneak through and hit that park.

But no one's looking up. After a week, even the civilians are taking it for granted.

Inside the ground floor of the temporary headquarters building, a nondescript ten-story instant skyscraper, Captain Nguyen stands in front of a podium and surveys the twenty fully power-armored members she's called in.

"LOCKDOWN," declares an electronic system, and the doors thud shut. A soft blue glow indicates that the room is nominally clean of electronic surveillance.

Everyone's links to the outside die. Soldiers remove their helmets and let them hang from dummy straps on the back of their armor.

It's strange to see all these faces.

Most relax in place, Mai's one of the few who grits her teeth at that. She comes from Vietnam's elite Marine Police, suffused with discipline and duty. Other soldiers have traveled in from less formal corners of Vietnam.

Mai's tempted to say it's Western influence, but she comes from a family that has quietly welcomed the easing of the Party's influence over the long years.

Her grandfather served in the Republic of Vietnam Army in 1975. He melted back into civilian life when Saigon fell. Unlike various Hmong or other American allies he had not been lucky enough to secure a trip to the United States. Instead he endured, raised a family, and placidly waited for the wheel to turn. As it had in Europe or Russia.

That came almost without their noticing. Now Vietnam jostles with South Korea and Japan for economic strength.

Which is what got her here.

South Korea is playing down its role in this humanitarian incursion of sovereign national borders. Japan knows better than to stick any of its troops on foreign soil anywhere the Pacific Ocean touches land, even if it's a peacekeeping mission.

No one wants American soldiers involved in this.

The UN has pushed hard to get Vietnamese forces to lead this. They believe they're in the best position, historically and culturally.

Behind the scenes promises and paybacks in the form of infrastructure, debt forgiveness from creditor nations, and military upgrades have been fairly epic.

And if all goes well, Vietnam becomes a real world player, able to use this as a bargaining chip to leverage itself up onto the table with the world's most powerful nations.

If all goes well.

The hopes of many Vietnamese politicians ride with the twenty armored soldiers in the room.

"There's been a change of plans," Nguyen announces.

Nguyen casts full three-dimensional images of the camp from an overhead position up on the wall for them to see.

"Due to the initial success of the disinformation campaign and disabling of North Korean military machinery, we grew this camp faster than anyone could have anticipated. We are bringing in more power: one of those airships that's been helping blanket the area with wireless networks will soon be relaying a microwave laser from an Indian power satellite, which will let us expand the Point Defense Array's zone of coverage and move our walls outward.

"We need more living space, and more farmland. The UN is calling our mission a success, and the other camps are moving timetables forward as a result as well."

Mai glances around. Everyone looks excited, a bit anticipatory.

This has been the goal, hasn't it? Establish a secure base. Bring in refugees. Feed and educate, build a different civil and economic society on the fly, and with success, expand the borders of these safe zones.

Within a decade, the camps could become cities in their own right: self-sustaining and continuing to grow. Tiny petri dishes of democracy, trade and world capitalism, their walls expanding outwards further and further until they *were* all of the country they'd been set up in.

It beat decades-long war.

Online massively multiplayer simulations indicated that it was also far, far cheaper. After just a few years, the citizens of the camps plug into global trade and currency, paying their own way. Becoming customers for large defense manufacturers. Full citizens of the peaceful, trading world at large.

That's the plan.

And now they're accelerating the timetable. Which will mean what? Mai swallows her worries and pays attention.

Captain Nguyen continues with the briefing. "We've been coming under more frequent artillery attack from the North Korean Army over the last seventy-two hours. The shells have yet to penetrate the laser array, but we can't afford to rely on that working one hundred percent of the time.

"Thanks to our American friends in charge of the array we've identified the location of the artillery battery firing on us. We intend to end these bombardments during wall extension operations. You are the team that will do this."

Nguyen looks at them all, then seems to pause for a beat as she looks at Mai.

Did that really happen? Is she being singled out? Or does everyone else in the room feel that Nguyen is talking to just them?

"There will be no North Korean deaths," Nguyen states flatly, "or any bodily harm as a direct result of your actions. You are there to disable the weaponry, not engage. Remember: I *will* be watching. So will the rest of the world."

And that is all.

Captain Nguyen physically leads the "attack."

Forty armored figures in UN pale blue trot out of the camp, double file, following her. Half of them are a mish-mash of other units from Eastern Europe and Africa, the other half are Nguyen's warriors. They plunge into the tree line to the west of the camp, cutting new paths through the undergrowth.

They cover the six miles to the North Korean firebase in about half an hour, and spread out into a skirmish line as they approach the elevated artillery base.

The moment they begin to walk up the slope the North Koreans open fire on them from a sandbagged bunker at the crest of the low hill.

Mai flinches at the chatter and fury. Her instinct to seek cover screams from somewhere deep in her. A round thuds into her midsection, but the armor does its job, sloughing off energy and dissipating mass.

Her stride isn't even affected.

"Keep the line straight, hold out your arms," Nguyen mutters to them all via helmet communications. "Show them we're not armed."

They've been shot at in training. But these rounds are meant to kill them, not get them used to the impact.

This is the real thing. Those people out there are trying to kill Mai.

And all she's going to do is hold out her hands and walk forward.

The implacable pale blue line keeps moving up the hill.

Mai feels round after round, entire bursts, carom off her armor like birdshot before she's halfway up the hill. And then, finally, the North Korean gunners break and make a run for it.

"Duc, Mai, disable the bunker," Nguyen orders.

Mai leaps free of the line with an exultant grunt, clearing fifteen feet of ground in a half restrained hop that has her slamming down in front of the bunker's still-steaming gun in a second.

Duc's right by her.

"No one's inside. No heat signatures," Duc reports. He rips the bunker apart, pulling the sandbags out and kicking the walls in.

Mai yanks the roof's timbers free, dropping the sandbags they'd supported down into a warren of cots and radio equipment. The crunching sounds from all this are distant and suppressed to her, like she's turned the volume down on a Hollywood action movie.

In three full breaths, they've reduced the fortified position to sandy rubble.

Mai strips the machine gun down to its individual components, then grabs both ends of the barrel and twists it into uselessness. She repeats that with the spare barrel, then looks over at the ammunition.

"The Ploughshares team can take care of the ammo," Duc says. "They'll catch up soon enough."

Something kicks her in the back, jostling her. Mai spins around and knocks away the gun of a scared soldier that has managed to sneak up on her.

He stands there, stupefied, holding his hand, waiting for whatever comes next.

"Mai!" Duc shouts.

She has her fist in the air, ready to bring it down and crack his skull, but freezes in place. Her heart is hammering, her mouth dry. She can't escape the adrenaline-pounding certainty that she almost died.

But of course, she hasn't. The man is no threat.

"Leave," she shouts into her helmet, and the translation booms out at the soldier.

He rabbits away.

"Mai?" Duc asks.

"I am fine," she tells him.

Mai glances back. There's activity in the air: ten heavy lift airships ponderously moving more wall segments in, to be dropped in place to secure the territory they are clearing.

Soon the huge, articulated Ploughshares trucks will be along to gather up everything here for recycling.

Duc tosses down seven mangled AKS-74s. "Then let's go," he says, and they're on the move again, loping in long, impossible strides to catch up to the advancing line.

As they catch up, Mai notices that Nguyen's entire right side is blackened. She must have absorbed a large explosion of some kind while Mai'd been destroying the bunker. Other soldiers show signs of absorbing more fire, but the rate of it is fading. The North Koreans are mostly retreating into the woods on the west side of the hill.

Mostly.

One enterprising gun crew is trying to bring their huge 152mm cannon to bear on the advancing line.

For the first time Mai sees Nguyen's calm crack, and she hastily orders another pair of Peacekeepers to disable the cannon.

The two armored soldiers snap into motion, and then calmly shepherd the North Koreans away from the weapon with shooing motions, ignoring the small arms fire. Once the North Koreans are clear, they smash the aiming mechanism, then get to work on the tube itself.

A North Korean officer runs up to the two blue armored soldiers, pistol high, screaming at them. His face is red, and he looks almost ready to cry with frustration and rage.

The distant pop of his pistol as he empties his entire clip into the backplate of the nearest Peacekeeper's armor is accentuated by Mai's translation software.

"Stand and fight, cowards! Face me like real soldiers," the artificial voice keeps murmuring.

Mai feels sympathy for him.

This isn't a proper war.

None of them have trained for this.

It makes little sense, to either that officer or her, on some deep level.

Part of her craves a fight. A real fight. A test of skill, courage, and arms.

"Here's the artillery," Nguyen murmurs to them all. "On me. Destroy it all."

Mai and Duc move through the firebase with the rest of the team, dismantling the twelve big artillery guns and countless small arms and machine guns.

Most of the machinery is in ill repair. Only five of the twelve look like they are actually firing, and a small bunker off to one side has been stacked with dud rounds. Which Mai figured Ploughshares could deal with. Suit or not, she didn't want to be playing with *those*.

There's been one casualty, and Nguyen is not pleased with this. The wounded Korean is on a pod-like stretcher, hooked up to emergency life-saving equipment while a medic they brought along treats him.

"This could be a public relations disaster," Nguyen tells Mai.

"What happened?" Mai asks.

"He threw a grenade, but it bounced back at him," Nguyen says, shaking her head. She's removed her helmet and holds it tucked under an arm. "We were too aggressive. I fought against the new timetable, but was overruled. UN headquarters are emboldened by all this success. Now look at this, all people are going to see is this idiot on their late-night television, wounded."

Mai looks over the wounded man. "He might live."

Nguyen cocks her head. "You're smarter than that. You know it's the image of him right now, wounded, that will play out across the world. Polling is going to show lowered support for the mission. Are *you* okay, Sergeant Nong? My command software flagged one of your actions."

Mai thinks back to the moment where she raised her fist, and opens her mouth to answer, but another soldier runs up. "Captain, you need to come with us."

The North Koreans have withdrawn from the firebase, and the defense array is fully extended to its new circumference, bringing the area under its anti-ballistic umbrella. The airships are placing the new walls around them. Nonetheless, Mai and Nguyen pull their helmets back on and lope after the messenger.

There's a trail leading back to the woods, and off to the side is a hastily dug pit. A fresh, earthy scar in the grass.

Lying in it are bodies. Thin. Ribs showing. Hollow-eyed.

"Civilians," Nguyen's voice crackles.

They've been dragged and stacked in this shallow grave. Just old men, women, children, trying to sneak their way around to a better life.

Mai rips her helmet off to take a deep breath of air, then regrets the decision. The air is ripe with the stench of decay.

"This is our fault. They're trying to get into our camp," she says. She does not replace her helmet, just yet. Something about the smell of death grounds her, reminds her of what is at stake, who has the most to lose, the most to fear.

Nguyen raises her visor. "They're dying trying to escape north to China right now, or slowly in their own homes. Don't forget that."

Mai swallows and nods.

But it doesn't stop her from feeling personally responsible in some small way.

Mai catches a ride back to the core camp center on a Ploughshares truck, exhausted and nerves frayed. A Chinese engineer sitting on the back of the flatbed is curious.

"I didn't think you could get tired in those suits," he says to her in careful English.

"That is a misconception," Mai tells him. "Your body is still moving, all day. Muscles still do much of the work. They are just amplified."

"What about getting shot at?" he asks. He's staring at the scars in her outer armor.

"It becomes normal," Mai says, offering a salty fatalism she does not yet feel. She's looking down at the helmet in her hands. There's a dimple right in the forehead, and a coating of copper and lead that has dripped onto the faceplate.

That dimple suggests at least *some* level of vulnerability.

Mai shakes that away and looks around. The fleet of recycling trucks are covered in advertising logos. "Does everything have advertising built into it?" she asks the engineer, looking to change the subject.

He shrugs. "Why not? If all goes well, what will the refugees see every day? Logos for Ford and Nissan, McDonald's and Dannon, Apple and Samsung. What better advertisement than being the ones who brought them peace and prosperity?"

And if it doesn't work, Mai figures, these people will never see the logos again. The sponsors lose some trucks, cash, and some shipments of last year's shoes and tracksuits.

These companies will write these off as charitable donations and somehow, come out ahead.

They always do. Tails you lose, heads I win.

The minds from which this evolved, despite their ramrod-organized military world, are the children of nonviolent protestors and emergent, technologically-enabled regime overthrow. They are the nieces and nephews of two generations of UN sorties, which are derided by the major powers, but have a history of quiet, incremental improvements and painfully slow progress.

They are the process of gamified solutions, market testing, and the Western fear of bad publicity.

What did it mean that this was war? At boot camp Mai practiced for bloody hand-to-hand combat, and learned group movement. Thinking as part of a squad. Reaching the overall goals of a mission.

Armies want fast-thinking, creative problem solvers able to deploy violence for the nation they serve.

Now Mai is wondering how she ended up being a robotic creature, following the exact letter of the law to not so much as harm a hair on her enemy.

Even when they are slaughtering the innocent.

"It's not the mission," Nguyen explained at training in Australia. "It violates the mandate of the mission. Fail it, and we are just another invading force."

"It doesn't seem . . . right," someone objected.

“Right has a new meaning when wearing this armor. It changes the equation. You are a supreme force unto yourself.”

“With technological superiority like this, we couldn’t possibly lose,” Mai added.

“Depends on what you mean by lose. Westerners certainly learned the limits of simple technological superiority when your grandfather was just a young man.” Nguyen stared her down, and Mai had wondered if Nguyen had accessed those files about Mai’s family background. “A nation is a fiction of consent, and North Korea has built a mythology and controlled fiction unsurpassed in the world, aided by extreme isolation. People starve and thank their rulers for a handful of rice, or thank them for permission to visit a Western Red Cross station. In order to reshape the fiction, we need to reshape the narrative that the world sees, that North Koreans see, and that we engage. Force is one narrative. But we are not limited to it.”

Captain Nguyen walked around, looking at her recruits.

“These methods are not effective enough when implemented by oily-faced teenagers, the unemployed, and the uneducated. What they need are the iron-hard wills and command structure of a military mindset. The kind that understands that one might have to run into a hail of gunfire and die to protect the mother country. The kind that can follow orders intelligently. No nation has ever seen an invasion force like this.”

One of the Western advisors was there. He chipped in. “It took the army to develop one hundred percent non-fossil fuel mobility while civilians dicked around with political initiatives, wasted subsidies and lots of arguing. We just did it. *We* built the internet, our ICBMs took people to space. It takes the hard, organizational capacity and raw willpower of an army to do *this* type of mission right. Sometimes assholes need to be shot. The rest of the time, we will wield a different sort of weapon for a different world. That weapon today will be you: the execution of a well-controlled non-violent incursive force. Because you’re an army, and you *will* execute this and well, because if you don’t, you’ll be spending some ‘personal’ time with Captain Nguyen.”

And then Mai and her fellow recruits learned how to get shot at, attacked, and beaten, without once displaying or reacting with aggression.

She wrestles with a fleck of shame, having failed that training to a small degree on the firebase. The fear in that soldier’s eyes lingers in her mind the rest of the way back.

The hardest part of Mai’s day is hearing the distant, occasional pop of a handgun from somewhere in the forests. Her amped up acoustics in the full-on armor pick it up every time. Software calibrates, offers up information on where the shot came from, and shows it in her heads-up display.

Every single time a gunshot goes off, she has to stare at the damn red marker telling her where it has happened.

Each pop makes her flinch with the knowledge that it is the execution of a desperate, captured civilian.

“Someone should put eyes on that,” she tells Captain Nguyen in a staff meeting. “We could use it to turn opinion against them.”

“Opinion is already against them. Sympathetic members of the military are uploading video of the executions. Our job is to protect the camp. Stay put. Patrol the walls, Sergeant. Do your job.”

Eventually Mai transfers to the south wall and dampens the acoustics with help from a technician.

But even the threat of death doesn't stop the trickle of refugees. They risk everything to get through the North Korean emplacements, and make a desperate run to the safety of the camp. The camp constantly grows.

After another one of her long patrols, Mai runs into Duc near the mess hall on the north wall.

"How are you?" she asks quietly. He's been a bit withdrawn ever since they first found the open graves.

"I've now been shot one hundred and thirty-seven times," he tells her, a note of wonder in his voice. "The armor works. But I think . . . it's . . ."

Duc looks away, then back at her. He opens his mouth to continue, and it seems as if he's screaming. A demonic sound fills the air, rising in pitch, higher and higher until Mai can barely even comprehend it.

When Duc shuts his mouth, the sound doesn't stop.

They're out of the mess hall and through the doors in an instant, yanking helmets on and looking around, and then finally: up.

A shimmering, hard red slash of light cuts the sky above the camp in half. It stabs upward into the sky, and originates from somewhere to the south, where intel thinks the North Korean Army has established a new firebase.

"What is it?" Duc asks.

Information scrolls across their helmets. It's a laser. High energy, tightly focused. Most of the red slash she's "seeing" is actually interpolation from her suit's sensors.

Mai follows the path of the beam, and sees that it intersects neatly with the icon that represents the dirigible floating thirty kilometers overhead.

"They're going after our power," Duc says.

The icon wavers and blinks out.

All around them lights flicker, then go dark. Mai spins around and looks at the tower at the heart of their refugee city. The lights on the outside of the Point Defense Array flicker and go dark.

Satellite communications links to the armor go live, and their helmets kick on automatic recording mode: 60fps video streaming directly back to operations centers in Hanoi, Beijing, and Geneva. All local bandwidth is reserved for encrypted interteam communications.

That results in everyone having a thumbnail of Captain Nguyen's face in the upper right corner of their visors, spitting orders and soliciting updates.

Mai and Duc are deployed to the south gate, and they sprint through the streets to get there, leaping over a small one-story refugee processing building in their way.

In the background of it all, emergency sirens wail. Citizens are, no doubt, being ushered away from windows and into the cores of skyscrapers. But if a full-on assault comes, there's little protection. The camp is vulnerable without the Point Defense Array.

Slightly out of breath, Mai scans the woods and hills beyond the border of the camp. "We should have rerouted all power from the reactor by now," she says to Duc.

And as if answering her directly, Captain Nguyen speaks up. "I've just learned that several of the power cables leading out from the reactor have been sabotaged. We are unable to power up the array fully. As a result it's in a fuel-cell powered self-defense mode right now, only targeting any rounds that might hit its tower. The engineers report that it will take as long as ten minutes to get power back up. You know your orders. Prevent any North Koreans from getting past the gate. And hold your position. Contact *is* imminent. Forces are building up for an assault."

Mai can see via thermal imaging that bodies are flitting through the trees.

"There hasn't been any satellite imagery showing that the rest of their army has shown up," Duc says. "It's just this battalion. We can handle that, even without the array, right?"

"Of course," Mai agrees.

Even as she opens her mouth to reassure Duc further, a brief flash flickers from behind the trees, followed by the quiet thump of sound catching up to light.

"Mortar fire," Mai shouts, broadcasting to the entire open channel. Her helmet projects a path and warning insignia blare at her to MOVE.

Duc spins away, and Mai is leaping clear as the world erupts in orange and black. She sees stars wheel overhead, the world tumbling around her, and she turns her tumble into a roll.

She lands on her feet, legs bent, taking the force of her impact. Her left hand drags, fingertips furrowing the ground as she slides backwards on her boots and comes to a stop.

"Duc!"

He's facedown. The entire back of his suit is blackened. She rushes over to him.

"Duc!"

There's a groan over the helmet radio. The status report shows that he's just been dazed. Duc sits up as Mai scans the tree line, waiting for the next launch or the inevitable rush of bodies.

The next mortar launch arrows well overhead, and Mai frowns as she follows the trajectory over the wall. The refugee-processing building explodes in a mess of compressed fiberboard and electronics.

Mai stands up.

The next mortar round walks further into the camp.

"They're not going to try a direct attack," Mai reports to Captain Nguyen, somewhat stunned. "They're just going after civilians."

More rounds now slam into the skyscrapers at the center of the camp. Broken glass twinkles as it rains down into the streets.

The open channel fills with medics responding. Ten wounded. No deaths. But another ten minutes of this, and it was going to get bad.

"Captain . . ."

"Stand your ground Sergeant. It could be a trap to lure some of us out, before the charge. Do not leave your post. Listen to me, there are three million live watchers, this conflict is being streamed everywhere, as it happens, to satisfy mission backers and advertisers. We keep our course."

But Mai's already stopped paying attention. "Duc, what is that?"

Her visor has caught the sound of tracks.

"Tank?"

"No." For a brief moment, two kilometers away and only visible by the helmet's advanced computational lenses, she's seen the outline of a self-propelled howitzer, trundling through the brush between Nike and the new Korean firebase.

KOKSAN, her visor identifies it. 170mm of death on wheels.

It must have been driven up to stand in for the artillery Mai and her team already destroyed.

Mai is already moving forward before she really understands it.

"Mai! Hold your position," Nguyen orders.

"Duc, stay here," Mai says, and then before he can reply she turns off communications.

She's across the open ground and into the woods before she's drawn even two full breaths, kicking through underbrush. It's like running in sand, and she's leaving a trail of broken tree limbs and shattered logs behind her.

There are attackers, of course. Gunshots ping off her armor from every direction, and she's veering this way and that to get around uniforms that pop up in her way.

She's still broadcasting video live. She can't turn that off. The whole world is watching this, probably. She can't afford to harm anyone.

But Mai has to stop that howitzer.

Because it's going to be so much louder than those little execution pops she's been hearing in the distance.

It's going to be a bang. It's going to wipe out lives in an instant. And it's going to keep doing it for as long as the Point Defense Array is down.

And she can stop it.

She can rip it apart with her augmented hands.

Gravel crunches and pops under her feet as she bursts out into open terrain, accelerating down a road.

The firepower aimed at her kicks up an order of magnitude. The popping sound has gone from occasional plinks to a hailstorm. There are soldiers taking cover behind small boulders and shooting at her. Mai covers the last kilometer in giant lopes, leaping over heads and vehicles and hastily dug fighting positions.

But she's too late. She can see the howitzer. It is basically a large tank with an obscenely larger artillery gun bolted on top. It looks unbalanced, like it should tip forward.

The long barrel is raised just slightly, and on target. It will fire like a tank, at this range, the round arcing just over her head, at the very low end of the Point Defense Array's envelope. If it's even operational yet.

Six soldiers are scurrying around the platform. Unlike most of the world's current self-propelled artillery, the operators are not encased in tank armor.

When Mai reaches the unit, she will be able to disable it and move the soldiers away.

But one of them is already shutting the breech and stepping back.

Another is pointing her way and shouting.

She will not make it there before they fire.

Mai slows and rips a three-foot wide boulder up out of the ground and throws it as hard as she can. Two soldiers dive clear of the vehicle, but the two near fire control have nowhere to go.

Blood spatters the railings around the vehicle. Brain matter drips from the barrel of the howitzer.

Seconds later Mai reaches it and slams her fist into the breech, disabling it.

For a long moment she stands on top, too stunned to move.

Then something loops over her head from behind, wrapping around her neck. The armor stops it from choking her, but the loop is strong. Possibly braided cable.

Mai tries to jump free, but the cable yanks her back down. The ground meets her back hard, and despite all the protection, Mai gasps for breath and her vision blurs.

They drag her across the ground as she fights to breathe again, her body bouncing as the armor scrapes along the ground. She can hear the rumble of an old truck, accelerating, dragging her farther away.

She reaches up to the noose, trying to get purchase, but she's being bounced around by the uneven terrain.

If they can drag her far enough away, she'll be just one person in armor. Far from camp. Far from backup.

Mai screams with rage, and then suddenly, she's free, tumbling along the side of the muddy road. On shaky arms she pushes herself up. First to her knees, then to her feet, every twitch and tremor amplified by the armor.

She pulls the cable up toward her until she comes to the cut edge, then looks around.

A cluster of blue-armored figures are walking down the road at her.

Mai turns her communications back on.

"Nong Mai Thuy?"

"Yes, Captain Nguyen?"

"We have some things to discuss."

"Are you ready to go home?" Nguyen asked.

"No," Mai replies. But she knows her preferences do not matter.

She's standing in front of Nguyen's desk wearing her old Marine Police uniform. Everything's crisp and tight. Ribbons for bravery and accomplishment no longer feel like things to be proud of, but strange, non-functional baubles.

She should be in armor, not in this uniform.

"I guess the true question is . . . how do you move on?" Nguyen says. "I have two courses for you to consider."

"Two? I don't understand."

"You killed two human beings, Nong Mai Thuy. All the while under orders to not leave your position."

"I saved many lives," Mai protests.

Nguyen flashes a smile. It isn't a pretty thing. It's an expectant one. Like a predator watching prey fall for a trap.

"Yes. The inhabitants of the camp call you a hero. But you may have killed many more than you would have saved down the road. It's a moral dilemma. Academics sometimes ask you to ponder: would you push a man in front of a train to save everyone on the train? It seems like a silly question, yes? But here we are: soldiers. We often shove people in front of trains to serve a greater good. You just faced one of your own moral dilemmas, Mai. I can't blame you for what you did. But we cannot succeed if we answer violence with violence here. Our duty is to weather these storms and stand between danger and our charges. And doing so, calmly, allows us the unfettered world permission to continue our mission here. You jeopardized the larger mission. The North Koreans will claim they were unjustly abused by a technologically superior invading army, no matter how ridiculous the claim. You put this entire mission in danger of failing. It' is unacceptable."

Mai considers the strangeness of this. The famous Captain Nguyen, who could be wearing three times as many medals as Mai if she chooses, who tasted violence on the Cambodian border, had eaten it for supper, is lecturing Mai about violence.

"So what is to become of me?" Mai asks.

"The Hague wants to court martial you and send you to jail." Nguyen taps the desk. "Personally, I think the court of world opinion would side with you, and you will not go to jail. You are the hero of Camp Nike, after all. But this will drag out in public and focus the attention in all the wrong places. The advertisers, the people who run this, and the generals back at the Hague, this will tarnish their images."

Mai shrinks back without thinking. The subject of world attention. Media circuses. It sounds alien and horrific to someone who prefers their privacy.

Nguyen shoves a piece of paper forward. "If you think these people are worth protecting, if you think what the camps are trying to do is a good thing, then I suggest you take the second course."

"And that is?" Mai asks.

"An honorable discharge. It is hardly your fault, really, that this happened. I should have seen the signs, your aggressive stance. A high need for justice. I ignored them because you were a good person with a good heart. I will not be making that mistake again. Sign these, and you can leave, but without any trouble to you, or trouble that makes our soldiers or country look bad. Go back to your family's business. Go live a good life."

Mai stares at the papers for a long moment, then signs them, struggling to keep any emotion from her face as Nguyen watches.

"Well done, Citizen Nong Mai Thuy," Captain Nguyen says. "Well done."

The next flight out of Camp Nike is in the pre-dawn morning. Mai sits alone in an aisle, looking out of the window as the plane passes up through the flittering green of the Point Defense Array. The North Koreans are busy probing its limits once again.

An extra reactor will be flown out to meet the needs of the camp soon. For now it is getting by on rolling blackouts for all non-essential power needs. Rumor is that a Californian solar panel corporation is going to ship enough panels next week for most civilian domestic needs, but the advertising details are still being negotiated. When they're installed, it should help the camp come up to full power.

And she won't be there to see any of that.

The aircraft continues its tight spiral up and up, always staying within Camp Nike airspace as it climbs. Eventually, once up to the right ceiling, out of range of all missiles and without the grounded North Korean Air Force to worry about, they will break out of their constant turn and head out for Hanoi.

"Miss Nong?" an airman asks. He crouches at the edge of the aisle holding a small wooden box in his hands.

“Yes?”

“Some of the refugees at the airstrip asked me to give this to the ‘hero of Camp Nike,’” the airman says, and hands her the box.

She opens it to find a small bracelet held together with monofilament, decorated with charms made from recently recycled brass casings.

When she looks back through the window, the camp is lost under the clouds.

The Ants of Flanders

ROBERT REED

Robert Reed sold his first story in 1986 and quickly established himself as one of the most prolific of today's writers, particularly at short fiction lengths, and has managed to keep up a very high standard of quality while *being prolific—something that is not at all easy to do. Reed's stories such as "Sister Alice," "Brother Perfect," "Decency," "Savior," "The Remoras," "Chrysalis," "Whiptail," "The Utility Man," "Marrow," "Birth Day," "Blind," "The Toad of Heaven," "Stride," "The Shape of Everything," "Guest of Honor," "Waging Good," and "Killing the Morrow," among at least a half-dozen others equally as strong, count among some of the best short works produced by anyone in the 1980s and 1990s; many of his best stories have been assembled in the collections* The Dragons of Springplace *and* The Cuckoo's Boys. *He won the Hugo Award in 2007 for his novella "A Billion Eves." He has also been active as a novelist, having turned out eleven novels since the end of the 1980s, including* The Lee Shore, The Hormone Jungle, Black Milk, The Remarkables, Down the Bright Way, Beyond the Veil of Stars, An Exaltation of Larks, Beneath the Gated Sky, Marrow, Sister Alice, *and* The Well of Stars, *as well as two chapbook novellas,* Mere *and* Flavors of My Genius. *His most recent book is a new chapbook novella,* Eater-of-Bone. *Reed lives with his family in Lincoln, Nebraska.*

In the complex and inventive novella that follows, Reed delivers an Alien Invasion story, but a much more imaginative and conceptually daring one than the standard-issue Alien Invasion story featured in movies like Independence Day *or* Battle: Los Angeles, *one where vast and vastly strange cosmic forces battle it out on an Earth they hardly notice, and where humans are no more important to the outcome, or any more able to change it, than the ants caught in the middle of the World War I battlefield referenced in the title.*

INTRUDERS

The mass of a comet was pressed into a long dense needle. Dressed with carbon weaves and metametals, the needle showed nothing extraneous to the universe. The frigid black hull looked like space itself, and it carried nothing that could leak or glimmer or produce the tiniest electronic fart—a trillion tons of totipotent matter stripped of engines but charging ahead at nine percent light speed. No sun or known world would claim ownership. No analysis of its workings or past trajectory would mark any culpable builder. Great wealth and ferocious genius had been invested in a device that was nearly invisible, inert as a bullet, and flying by time, aimed at a forbidden, heavily protected region.

The yellow-white sun brightened while space grew increasingly dirty. Stray ions and every twist of dust was a hazard. The damage of the inevitable impacts could be ignored, but there would always be a flash of radiant light. A million hidden eyes lay before it, each linked to paranoid minds doing nothing but marking every unexpected event. Security networks were hunting for patterns, for random noise and vast conspiracies. This was why secrecy had to be maintained as long as possible. This was why the needle fell to thirty AU before the long stasis ended. A temporary mind was grown on the hull. Absorbed starlight powered thought and allowed a platoon of eyes to sprout. Thousands of worlds offered themselves. Most were barren, but the largest few bore atmospheres and rich climates. This was wilderness, and the wilderness was gorgeous. Several planets tempted the newborn pilot, but the primary target still had its charms—a radio-bright knob of water and oxygen, silicates and slow green life.

Final course corrections demanded to be made, and the terrific momentum had to be surrendered. To achieve both, the needle's tail was quickly reconfigured, micron wires reaching out for thousands of miles before weaving an obedient smoke that took its first long bite of a solar wind.

That wind tasted very much like sugar.

The penguins were coming. With their looks and comical ways, Humboldt penguins meant lots of money for the Children's Zoo, and that's why a fancy exhibit had been built for them. People loved to stand in flocks, watching the comical nervous birds that looked like little people. But of course penguins were nothing like people, and while Simon Bloch figured he would like the birds well enough, he certainly wasn't part of anybody's flock.

Bloch was a stubborn, self-contained sixteen-year-old. Six foot five, thick-limbed and stronger than most grown men, he was a big slab of a boy with a slow unconcerned walk and a perpetually half-asleep face that despite appearances noticed quite a lot. Maybe he wasn't genius-smart, but he was bright and studious enough to gain admission to the honors science program at the Zoo School. Teachers found him capable. His stubborn indifference made him seem mature. But there was a distinct, even unique quality: because of a quirk deep in the boy's nature, he had never known fear.

Even as a baby, Bloch proved immune to loud noises and bad dreams. His older and decidedly normal brother later hammered him with stories about nocturnal demons and giant snakes that ate nothing but kindergarteners, yet those torments only fed a burning curiosity. As a seven-year-old, Bloch slipped out of the house at night, wandering alleys and wooded lots, hoping to come across the world's last T. rex. At nine, he got on a bus and rode halfway to Seattle, wanting to chase down Bigfoot. He wasn't testing his bravery. Bravery was what other people summoned when their mouths went dry and hearts pounded. What he wanted was to stare into the eyes of a monster, admiring its malicious, intoxicating power, and if possible, steal a little of that magic for himself.

Bloch wasn't thinking about monsters. The first penguins would arrive tomorrow morning, and he was thinking how they were going to be greeted with a press conference and party for the zoo's sugar daddies. Mr. Rightly had asked Bloch to stay late and help move furniture, and that's why the boy was walking home later than usual. It was a warm November afternoon, bright despite the sun hanging low. Three hundred pounds of casual, unhurried muscle was headed east. Bloch was imagining penguins swimming in their new pool, and then a car horn intruded, screaming in the distance. And in the next second a father down the street began yelling at his kid, telling him to get the hell inside now. Neither noise seemed remarkable, but they shook Bloch out of his daydream.

Then a pair of cars shot past on Pender. Pender Boulevard was a block north, and the cars started fast and accelerated all the way down the long hill. They had to be doing seventy if not a flat-out eighty, and under the roar of wasted gas he heard the distinct double-tone announcing a text from Matt.

It was perfectly normal for Bloch's soldier-brother to drop a few words on "the kid" before going to bed.

"So what the hell is it," Bloch read.

"whats what," he wrote back. But before he could send, a second cryptic message arrived from the world's night side.

"that big and moving that fast shit glad it's probably missing us aren't you"

Bloch snorted and sent his two words.

The racing cars had disappeared down the road. The distant horn had stopped blaring and nobody was shouting at his kids. Yet nothing seemed normal now. Bloch felt it. Pender was hidden behind the houses, but as if on a signal, the traffic suddenly turned heavy. Drivers were doing fifty or sixty where forty was the limit, and the street sounded jammed. Bloch tried phoning a couple friends, except there was no getting through. So he tried his mother at work, but just when it seemed as if he had a connection, the line went dead.

Then the Matt-tones returned.

"a big-ass spaceship dropping toward us catching sun like a sail are you the hell watching?????"

Bloch tried pulling up the BBC science page. Nothing came fast and his phone's battery was pretty much drained. He stood on a sidewalk only four blocks from home, buthe still had to cross Pender. And it sounded like NASCAR out there. Cars were braking, tires squealing. Suddenly a Mini came charging around the corner. Bloch saw spiked orange hair and a cigarette in one hand. The woman drove past him and turned into the next driveway, hitting the pavement hard enough to make sparks. Then she was parked and running up her porch steps, fighting with her keys to find the one that fit her lock.

"What's happening?" Bloch called out.

She turned toward the voice and dropped the key ring, and stuffing the cigarette into her mouth, she kneeled and got lucky. Finding the key that she needed, she stood up and puffed, saying, "Aliens are coming. Big as the earth, their ship is, and it's going to fucking hit us."

"Hit us?"

"Hit the earth, yeah. In five minutes."

On that note, the woman dove into her house, vanishing.

Perched on a nearby locust tree, a squirrel held its head cocked, one brown eye watching the very big boy.

"A starship," Bloch said, laughing. "That's news."

Chirping in agreement, the squirrel climbed to its home of leaves.

An image had loaded on the phone's little screen—black space surrounding a meaningless blur painted an arbitrary pink by the software. The tiny scroll at the bottom was running an update of events that only started half an hour ago. The starship was huge but quick, and astronomers only just noticed it. The ship seemed to weigh nothing. Sunlight and the solar wind had slowed it down to a thousand miles every second, which was a thousand times faster than a rifle slug, and a clock in the right corner was counting down to the impact. A little more than four minutes remained. Bloch held the phone steady. Nothing about the boy was genuinely scared. Racing toward the sun, the starship was shifting its trajectory. Odds were that it would hit the earth's night side. But it was only a solar sail, thin and weak, and there was no way to measure the hazard. Mostly what the boy felt was a rare joyous thrill. If he got lucky with the stop lights, he could run across the intersection at the bottom of the hill, reaching home just in time to watch the impact on television.

But he didn't take a step. Thunder or a low-flying jet suddenly struck from behind. The world shook, and then the roar ended with a wrenching explosion that bled into a screeching tangle of lesser noises. Brakes screamed and tires slid across asphalt, and Bloch felt something big hammering furiously at the ground. A giant truck must have lost control, tumbling down the middle of Pender. What else could it be? Fast-moving traffic struggled to brake and steer sideways. Bloch heard cars colliding, and the runaway truck or city bus kept rolling downhill. Turning toward the racket, toward the west, he couldn't see Pender or the traffic behind the little houses, but the mayhem, the catastrophe, rolled past him, and then a final crash made one tall oak shake, the massive trunk wobbling and the weakest brown leaves falling, followed by a few more collisions of little vehicles ending with an abrupt wealth of silence.

The side street bent into Pender. Bloch sprinted to the corner. Westbound traffic was barely rolling up the long gentle hill, and nobody was moving east. The sidewalk and one lane were blocked by a house-sized ball of what looked like black metal. Some piece of Bloch's brain expected a truck and he was thinking this was a damn peculiar truck. He had to laugh. An old man stood on the adjacent lawn, eyes big and busy. Bloch approached, and the man heard the laughter and saw the big boy. The man was trembling. He needed a good breath before he could say, "I saw it." Then he lifted a shaking arm, adding, "I saw it fall," as he slapped the air with a flattened hand, mimicking the intruder's bounce as it rolled down the long hill, smacking into the oak tree with the last of its momentum.

Bloch said, "Wow."

"This is my yard," the old man whispered, as if nothing were more important. Then the arm dropped and his hands grabbed one another. "What is it, you think? A spaceship?"

"An ugly spaceship," Bloch said. He walked quickly around the object, looking for wires or portholes. But nothing showed in the lumpy black hull. Back uphill were strings of cars crushed by the impacts and from colliding with each other. A Buick pointed east, its roof missing. Now the old man was staring at the wreckage, shaking even worse than before. When he saw Bloch returning, he said, "I wouldn't look. Get away."

Bloch didn't stop. An old woman had been driving the Buick when the spaceship came bouncing up behind her. One elegant hand was resting neatly in her lap, a big diamond shining on the ring finger, and her head was missing, and Bloch studied the ripped-apart neck, surprised by the blood and sorry for her but always curious, watchful and impressed.

People were emerging from houses and the wrecked cars and from cars pulling over to help. There was a lot of yelling and quick talking. One woman screamed, "Oh God, someone's alive here." Between a flipped pickup and the Buick was an old Odyssey, squashed and shredded. The van's driver was clothes mixed with meat. Every seat had its kid strapped in, but only one of them was conscious. The little girl in back looked out at Bloch, smiled and said something, and he smiled back. The late-day air stank of gasoline. Bloch swung his left arm, shattering the rear window with the elbow, and then he reached in and undid the girl's belt and brought her out. What looked like a brother was taking what looked like a big nap beside her. The side of his face was bloody. Bloch undid that belt and pulled him out too and carried both to the curb while other adults stood around the van, talking about the three older kids still trapped.

Then the screaming woman noticed gasoline running in the street, flowing toward the hot spaceship. Louder than ever, she told the world, "Oh God, it's going to blow up."

People started to run away, holding their heads down, and still other people came forward, fighting with the wreckage, fighting with jammed doors and their own panic, trying to reach the unconscious and dead children.

One man looked at Bloch, eyes shining when he said, "Come on and help us."

But there was a lot of gasoline. The pickup must have had a reserve tank, and it had gotten past the van and the Buick. Bloch was thinking about the spaceship, how it was probably full of electricity and alien fires. That was the immediate danger, he realized. Trotting up ahead, he peeled off his coat and both shirts, and after wadding them up into one tight knot, he threw them into the stinking little river, temporarily stopping the flow.

The screaming woman stood in the old man's yard. She was kind of pretty and kind of old. Staring at his bare chest, she asked, "What are you doing?"

"Helping," he said.

She had never heard anything so odd. That's what she said with her wrinkled, doubtful face.

Once more, Bloch's phone made the Matt noise. His brother's final message had arrived. "Everythings quiet here everybodys outside and I bet you wish you could see this big bastard filling the sky, B, its weird no stars but the this glow, and pretty you know???you would love this"

And then some final words:

"Good luck and love Matt."

Tar and nanofibers had been worn as camouflage, and an impoverished stream of comet detritus served as cover. A machine grown for one great purpose had spent forty million years doing nothing. But the inevitable will find ways to happen, and the vagaries of orbital dynamics gave this machine extraordinary importance. Every gram of fuel was expended, nothing left to make course corrections. The goal was a small lake that would make quite a lot possible, but the trajectory was sloppy, and it missed the target by miles, rolling to a halt on a tilted strip of solid hydrocarbons littered with mindless machinery and liquid hydrocarbons and cellulose and sacks of living water.

Eyes were spawned, gazing in every direction.

Several strategies were fashioned and one was selected, and only then did the machine begin growing a body and the perfect face.

Brandishing a garden hose, the old man warned Bloch to get away from the damn gas. But an even older man mentioned that the spaceship was probably hot and maybe it wasn't a good idea throwing cold water near it. The hose was grudgingly put away. But the gasoline pond was spilling past the cotton and polyester dam. Bloch considered asking people for their shirts. He imagined sitting in the street, using his butt to slow things down. Then a third fellow arrived, armed with a big yellow bucket of cat litter, and that hero used litter to build a second defensive barrier.

All the while, the intruder waschanging. Its rounded shape held steady but the hull was a shinier, prettier black. Putting his face close, Bloch felt the heat left over from slamming into the atmosphere; nevertheless, he could hold his face close and peer inside the glassy crust, watching tiny dark shapes scurry here to there and back again.

"Neat," he said.

Bystanders started to shout at the shirtless boy, telling him to be careful and not burn himself. They said that he should find clothes before he caught a cold. But Bloch was comfortable, except where his elbow was sore from busting out the van window. He held the arm up to the radiant heat and watched the ship's hull reworking itself. Car radios were blaring, competing voices reporting the same news: a giant interstellar craft was striking the earth's night side. Reports of power outages and minor impacts were coming in. Europe and Russia might be getting the worst of it, though there wasn't any news from the Middle East. Then suddenly most of the stations shifted to the same feed, and one man was talking. He sounded like a scientist lecturing to a class. The "extraordinary probe" had been spread across millions of square miles, and except for little knots and knobs, it was more delicate than any spiderweb, and just as harmless. "The big world should be fine," he said.

On Pender Boulevard, cars were jammed up for blocks and sirens were descending. Fire trucks and paramedics found too much to do. The dead and living children had been pulled out of the van, and the screaming woman stood in the middle of the carnage, steering the first helpers to them. Meanwhile the cat litter man and hose man were staring at the spaceship.

"It came a long ways," said the litter man.

"Probably," said the hose man.

Bloch joined them.

"Aren't you cold?" the hose man asked.

The boy shrugged and said nothing.

And that topic was dropped. "Yeah, this ship came a long ways," the litter man reported. "I sure hope they didn't mean to do this."

"Do what?" asked his friend.

"Hurt people."

Something here was wrong. Bloch looked back at the Buick and the sun, waiting to figure out what was bothering him. But it didn't happen. Then he looked at the spaceship again. The shininess had vanished, the crust dull and opaque except where little lines caught the last of the day's light.

Once again, Bloch started forward.

The two men told him to be careful, but then both of them walked beside the sixteen-year-old.

"Something's happening," the hose man said.

"It is," his buddy agreed.

As if to prove them right, a chunk of the crust fell away, hitting the ground with a light ringing sound.

Bloch was suddenly alone.

Radio newscasters were talking about blackouts on the East Coast and citizens not panicking, and some crackly voice said that it was a beautiful night in Moscow, no lights working but ten centimeters of new snow shining under a cold crescent moon. Then a government voice interrupted the poetry. U.S. military units were on heightened alert, he said. Bloch thought of his brother as he knelt, gingerly touching the warm, glassy and almost weightless shard of blackened crust. Another two pieces fell free, one jagged fissure running between the holes. Probe or cannon ball or whatever, the object was beginning to shatter.

People retreated to where they felt safe, calling to the big boy who insisted on standing beside the visitor.

Bloch pushed his face inside the nearest gap.

A bright green eye looked out at him.

Swinging the sore elbow, Bloch shattered a very big piece of the featherweight egg case.

"Beautiful," bystanders said. "Lovely."

The screaming woman found a quieter voice. "Isn't she sweet?" she asked. "What a darling."

"She?" the hose man said doubtfully.

"Look at her," the woman said. "Isn't that a she?"

"Looks girlish to me," the litter man agreed.

The alien body was dark gray and long and streamlined, slick to the eye like a finely-grained stone polished to where it shone in the reflected light. It seemed to be lying on its back. Complex appendages looked like meaty fins, but with fingers that managed to move, four hands clasping at the air and then at one another. The fluked tail could have been found on a dolphin, and the face would have been happy on a seal—a whiskerless round-faced seal with a huge mouth pulled into a magnificent grin. But half of the face and most of the animal's character was focused on those two enormous eyes, round with iridescent green irises and perfect black pupils bright enough to reflect Bloch's curious face.

The egg's interior was lined with cables and odd machines and masses of golden fibers, and the alien was near the bottom, lying inside a ceramic bowl filled with a desiccated blood-colored gelatin. The body was too big for the bowl, and it moved slowly and stiffly, pressing against the bone-white sides.

"Stay back," bystanders implored.

But as soon as people backed away, others pushed close, wrestling for the best view.

The screaming woman touched Bloch. "Did she say something?"

"I didn't hear anything."

"She wants to talk," the woman insisted.

That seemed like a silly idea, and the boy nearly laughed. But that's when the seal's mouth opened and one plaintive word carried over the astonished crowd.

"Help," the alien begged.

People fell silent.

Then from far away, a man's voice shouted, "Hey, Bloch."

A short portly figure was working his way through the crowd. Bloch hurried back to meet Mr. Rightly. His teacher was younger than he looked, bald and bearded with white in the whiskers. His big glasses needed a bigger nose to rest on, and he pushed the glasses against his face while staring at the egg and the backs of strangers. "I heard about the crash," he said, smiling in a guarded way. "I didn't know you'd be here. Did you see it come down?"

"No, but I heard it."

"What's inside?"

"The pilot, I think."

"An alien?"

"Yes, sir."

Mr. Rightly was the perfect teacher for bright but easily disenchanted teenagers. A Masters in biology gave him credibility, and he was smarter than his degree. The man had an infectious humor and a pleasant voice, and Bloch would do almost anything for him, whether moving furniture after school or ushering him ahead to meet the ET.

"Come on, sir."

Nobody in front of them felt shoved. Nobody was offended or tried to resist. But one after another, bodies felt themselves being set a couple feet to the side, and the big mannish child was past them, offering little apologies while a fellow in dark slacks and a wrinkled dress shirt walked close behind.

To the last row, Bloch said, "Please get back. We've got a scientist here."

That was enough reason to surrender their places, if only barely.

The alien's face had changed in the last moments. The smile remained, but the eyes were less bright. And the voice was weaker than before, quietly moaning one clear word.

"Dying."

Mr. Rightly blinked in shock. "What did you just say?"

The creature watched them, saying nothing.

"Where did you come from?" the litter man asked.

The mouth opened, revealing yellow teeth rooted in wide pink gums. A broad tongue emerged, and the lower jaw worked against some pain that made the entire body spasm. Then again, with deep feeling, the alien said to everybody, "Help."

"Can you breathe?" Mr. Right asked. Then he looked at Bloch, nervously yanking at the beard. What if they were watching the creature suffocate?

But then it made a simple request. "Water," it said. "My life needs water, please, please."

"Of course, of course," said the screaming woman, her voice back to its comfortable volume. Everyone for half a block heard her declare, "She's a beached whale. We need to get her in water."

Murmurs of concern pushed through the crowd.

"Freshwater or salt," Mr. Rightly asked.

Everybody fell silent. Everybody heard a creaking noise as one of the front paddle-arms extended, allowing the longest of the stubby, distinctly child-like fingers to point downhill, and then a feeble, pitiful voice said, "Hurry," it said. "Help me, please. Please."

Dozens of strangers fell into this unexpected task, this critical mercy. The hose man returned, eager to spray the alien as if watering roses. But the crashed ship was still warm on the outside, and what would water do to the machinery? Pender Slough was waiting at the bottom of the hill—a series of head-deep pools linked by slow, clay-infused runoff. With that goal in hand, the group fell into enthusiastic discussions about methods and priorities. Camps formed, each with its loudest expert as well as a person or two who tried making bridges with others. Mr. Rightly didn't join any conversation. He stared at the alien, one hand coming up at regular intervals, pushing at the glasses that never quit trying to slide off the distracted face. Then he turned to the others, one hand held high. "Not the Slough," he said. "It's filthy."

This was the voice that could startle a room full of adolescents into silence. The adults quit talking, every face centered on him. And then the cat litter man offered the obvious question:

"Where then?"

"The penguin pool," said Mr. Rightly. "That water's clean, and the penguins aren't here yet."

The man's good sense unsettled the crowd.

"We need a truck," Mr. Rightly continued. "Maybe we can flag something down."

Several men immediately walked into the westbound lanes, arms waving at every potential recruit.

Mr. Rightly looked at Bloch. "How much do you think it weighs?"

Bloch didn't need urging. The hull was cooling and the interior air was hot but bearable. He threw a leg into the shattered spaceship and crawled inside. Delicate objects that looked like jacks lay sprinkled across the flat gray floor. They made musical notes while shattering underfoot. A clean metallic smell wasn't unpleasant. Bloch touched the alien below its head, down where the chest would be. Its skin was rigid and dry and very warm, as if it was a bronze statue left in the sun. He waited for a breath, and the chest seemed to expand. He expected the body to be heavy, but the first shove proved otherwise. He thought of desiccated moths collecting inside hot summer attics. Maybe this is how you traveled between stars, like freeze-dried stroganoff. Bloch looked out the hole, ready to report back to Mr. Rightly, but people were moving away while an engine roared, a long F-350 backing into view.

Two smiling men and Mr. Rightly climbed inside the ship, the egg, whatever it was. One of the men giggled. Everybody took hold of a limb. There was no extra room, and the transfer was clumsy and slow and required more laughs and some significant cursing. Mr. Rightly asked the alien if it was all right and it said nothing, and then he asked again, and the creature offered one quiet, "Hurry."

Other men formed matching lines outside, and with the care used on babies and bombs, they lifted the valiant, beautiful helpless creature into the open truck bed, eyes pointed skyward, its tail dangling almost to the pavement.

Mr. Rightly climbed out again. "We'll use the zoo's service entrance," he announced. "I have the key."

The hose man finally had his target in his sights, hitting the alien with a cool spray. Every drop that struck the skin was absorbed, and the green eyes seemed to smile even as the voice begged, "No. Not yet, no."

The hose was turned away.

And the screaming woman ran up, daring herself to touch the creature. Her hands reached and stopped when her courage failed, and she hugged herself instead. Nearly in tears, she said, "God bless you, darling. God bless."

Bloch was the last man out of the spaceship.

Mr. Rightly climbed up into the truck bed and then stood, blinking as he looked at the destruction up the road and at the shadows cast by the setting sun. Then Bloch called to him, and he turned and smiled. "Are you warm enough?" he asked.

"I'm fine, sir."

"Sit in the cab and stay warm," he said. "Show our driver the way."

Their driver was three weeks older than Bloch and barely half his size, and nothing could be more astonishing than the extraordinary luck that put him in this wondrous place. "I can't fucking believe this," said the driver, lifting up on the brake and letting them roll forwards. "I'm having the adventure of a lifetime. That's what this craziness is."

There was no end to the volunteers. Everybody was waving at traffic and at the truck's driver—enthusiastic, chaotic signals ready to cause another dozen crashes. But nobody got hit. The big pickup lurched into the clear and down the last of the hill, heading east. People watched its cargo. Some prayed, others used phones to take pictures, catching Bloch looking back at the children and the paramedics and the bloody blankets thrown over the dead.

"Can you fucking believe this?" the driver kept asking.

The radio was set on the CNN feed. The solar sail had reached as far as Atlanta. Power was out there, and Europe was nothing but dark and China was the same. There was a quick report that most of the world's satellites had gone silent when the probe fell on top of them. There were also rumors that an alien or aliens had contacted the US government, but the same voice added, "We haven't confirmed anything at this point."

They crossed Pender Slough and Bloch tapped the driver on the arm, guiding them onto Southwest. The driver made what was probably the slowest, most cautious turn in his life. A chain of cars and trucks followed close, headlights and flashers on. Everything they did felt big and important, and this was incredible fun. Bloch was grinning, looking back through the window at his teacher, but Mr. Rightly shot him a worried expression, and then he stared at his hands rather than the alien stretched out beside him.

"Hurry," Bloch coaxed.

The zoo appeared on their left. An access bridge led back across the slough and up to the back gate. Mr. Rightly was ready with the key. Bloch climbed out to help roll the gate open, and a couple trailing cars managed to slip inside before a guard arrived, hurriedly closing the gate before examining what they were bringing inside.

"Oh, this gal's hurt," he called out.

Bloch and his teacher walked at the front of the little parade, leading the vehicles along the wide sidewalk toward the penguin exhibit.

Mr. Rightly watched his feet, saying nothing.

"Is it dead?" Bloch asked.

"What?"

"The alien," he said.

"No, it's holding on."

"Then what's wrong?"

Mr. Rightly looked back and then forward, drifting closer to Bloch. With a quiet careful voice, he said, "She was rolling east on Pender. That means that she fell from the west."

"I guess," Bloch agreed.

"From the direction of the sun," he said. "But the big probe, that solar sail . . . it was falling toward the sun. And that's the other direction."

Here was the problem. Bloch felt this odd worry before, but he hadn't been able to find words to make it clear in his own head.

The two of them walked slower, each looking over a shoulder before talking.

"Another thing," said Mr. Rightly. "Why would an alien, a creature powerful enough and smart enough to cross between stars, need water? Our astronauts didn't fly to the moon naked and hope for air."

"Maybe she missed her target," Bloch suggested.

"And there's something else," Mr. Rightly said. "How can anything survive the gee forces from this kind of impact? You heard the sonic booms. She, or it . . . whatever it is . . . the entity came down fast and hit, and nothing alive should be alive after that kind of crash."

Bloch wanted to offer an opinion, but they arrived at the penguin exhibit before he could find one. Men and the screaming woman climbed out of the trailing cars, and like an old pro, the pickup's driver spun around and backed up to the edge of the pond. Half a dozen people waved him in. In one voice, everybody shouted, "Stop." Night was falling. The penguin pool was deep and smooth and very clear. Mr. Rightly started to say something about being cautious, about waiting, and someone asked, "Why?" and he responded with noise about water quality and its temperature. But other people had already climbed into the truck bed, grabbing at the four limbs and head and the base of that sad, drooping tail. With barely any noise, the alien went into the water. It weighed very little, and everyone expected it to float, but it sank like an arrow aimed at the Earth. Bloch stood at the edge of the pool, watching while a dark gray shape lay limp at the bottom of the azure bowl.

The screaming woman came up beside him. "Oh god, our girl's drowning," she said. "We need to jump in and help get her up to the air again."

A couple men considered being helpful, but then they touched the cold November water and suffered second thoughts.

Another man asked Mr. Rightly, "Did we screw up? Is she drowning?"

The teacher pushed his glasses against his face.

"I think we did screw up," Mr. Rightly said.

The body had stopped being gray. And a moment later that cute seal face and those eyes were smoothed away. Then the alien was larger, growing like a happy sponge, and out from its center came a blue glow, dim at first, but quickly filling the concrete basin and the air above—a blue light shining into the scared faces, and Bloch's face too.

Leaning farther out, Bloch felt the heat rising up from water that was already most of the way to boiling.

The woman ran away and then shouted, "Run."

The driver jumped into his truck and drove off.

Only two people were left at the water's edge. Mr. Rightly tugged on Bloch's arm. "Son," he said. "We need to get somewhere safe."

"Where's that?" Bloch asked.

His teacher offered a grim little laugh, saying, "Maybe Mars. How about that?"

THE LEOPARD

Any long stasis means damage. Time introduces creeps and tiny flaws into systems shriveled down near the margins of what nature permits. But the partial fueling allowed repairs to begin. Systems woke and took stock of the situation. Possibilities were free to emerge, each offering itself to the greatest good, yet the situation was dire. The universe permitted quite a lot of magic, but even magic had strict limits and the enemy was vast and endowed with enough luck to have already won a thousand advantages before the battle had begun.

Horrific circumstances demanded aggressive measures; this was the fundamental lesson of the moment.

The sanctity of an entire world at stake, and from this moment on, nothing would be pretty.

"Did you feel that?"

Bloch was stretched out on the big couch. He remembered closing his eyes, listening to the AM static on his old boom box. But the radio was silent and his mother spoke, and opening his eyes, he believed that only a minute or two had passed. "What? Feel what?"

"The ground," she said. Mom was standing in the dark, fighting for the best words. "It was like an earthquake . . . but not really . . . never mind . . ."

A second shiver passed beneath their house. There was no hard shock, no threat to bring buildings down. It was a buoyant motion, as if the world was an enormous water bed and someone very large was squirming under distant covers.

She said, "Simon."

Nobody else called him Simon. Even Dad used the nickname invented by a teasing brother. At least that's what Bloch had been told; he didn't remember his father at all.

"How do you feel, Simon?"

Bloch sat up. It was cold in the house and silent in that way that comes only when the power was out.

She touched his forehead.

"I'm fine, Mom."

"Are you nauseous?"

"No."

"Radiation sickness," she said. "It won't happen right away."

"I'm fine, Mom. What time is it?"

"Not quite six," she said. Then she checked her watch to make sure. "And we are going to the doctor this morning, if not the hospital."

"Yeah, except nothing happened," he said, just like he did twenty times last night. "We backed away when the glow started. Then the police came, and some guy from Homeland, and Mr. Rightly found me that old sweatshirt—"

"I was so scared," she interrupted, talking to the wall. "I got home and you weren't here. You should have been home already. And the phones weren't working, and then everything went dark."

"I had to walk home from the zoo," he said again. "Mr. Rightly couldn't give me a ride if he wanted, because he was parked over by the crash site."

"The crash site," she repeated.

He knew not to talk.

"You shouldn't have been there at all," she said. "Something drops from the sky, and you run straight for it."

The luckiest moment in his life, he knew.

"Simon," she said. "Why do you take such chances?"

The woman was a widow and her other son was a soldier stationed in a distant, hostile country, and even the most normal day gave her reasons to be nervous. But now aliens were raining down on their heads, and there was no word happening in the larger world. Touching the cool forehead once again, she said, "I'm not like you, Simon."

"I know that, Mom."

"I don't like adventure," she said. "I'm just waiting for the lights to come on."

But neither of them really expected that to happen. So he changed the subject, telling her, "I'm hungry."

"Of course you are." Thankful for a normal task, she hurried into the kitchen. "How about cereal before our milk goes bad?"

Bloch stood and pulled on yesterday's pants and the hooded Cornell sweatshirt borrowed from the zoo's lost-and-found. "Yeah, cereal sounds good," he said.

"What kind?" she asked from inside the darkened refrigerator.

"Surprise me," he said. Then after slipping on his shoes, he crept out the back door.

Mr. Rightly looked as if he hadn't moved in twelve hours. He was standing in the classroom where Bloch left him, and he hadn't slept. Glasses that needed a good scrubbing obscured red worried eyes. A voice worked over by sandpaper said, "That was fast."

"What was fast?" Bloch asked.

"They just sent a car for you. I told them you were probably at home."

"Except I walked here on my own," the boy said.

"Oh." Mr. Rightly broke into a long weak laugh. "Anyway, they're gathering up witnesses, seeing what everybody remembers."

It was still night outside. The classroom was lit by battery-powered lamps. "They" were the Homeland people in suits and professors in khaki, with a handful of soldiers occupying a back corner. The classroom was the operation's headquarters. Noticing Bloch's arrival, several people came forward, offering hands and names. The boy pretended to listen. Then a short Indian fellow pulled him aside, asking, "Did you yourself speak to the entity?"

"I heard it talk."

"And did it touch you?"

Bloch nearly said, "Yes." But then he thought again, asking, "Who are you?"

"I told you. I am head of the physics department at the university, here at the request of Homeland Security."

"Was it fusion?"

"Pardon?"

"The creature, the machine," Bloch said. "It turned bright blue and the pond was boiling. So we assumed some kind of reactor was supplying the power."

The head professor dismissed him with a wave. "Fusion is not as easy as that, young man. Reactors do not work that way."

"But it asked for water, which is mostly hydrogen," Bloch said. "Hydrogen is what makes the sun burn."

"Ah," the little man said. "You and your high school teacher are experts in thermonuclear technologies, are you?"

"Who is? You?"

The man flung up both hands, wiping the air between them. "I was invited here to help. I am attempting to learn what happened last night and what it is occurring now. What do you imagine? That some cadre of specialists sits in a warehouse-waiting for aliens to come here and be studied? You think my colleagues and I have spent two minutes in our lives preparing for this kind of event?"

"I don't really—"

"Listen to me," the head professor insisted.

But then the ground rose. It was the same sensation that struck half a dozen times during Bloch's walk back to the zoo, only this event felt larger and there wasn't any matching sense of dropping afterwards. The room remained elevated, and everyone was silent. Then an old professor turned to a young woman, asking, "Did Kevin ever get that accelerograph?"

"I don't know."

"Well, see if you can find either one. We need to get that machine working and calibrated."

The girl was pretty and very serious, very tense. Probably a graduate student, Bloch decided. She hurried past, glancing at the big boy and the college sweatshirt that was too small. Then she was gone and he was alone in the room with a couple dozen tired adults who kept talking quietly and urgently among themselves.

The head physicist was lecturing the bald man from Homeland. The bald man was flanked by two younger men who kept flipping through pages on matching clipboards, reading in the dim light. An Army officer was delivering orders to a couple soldiers. Bloch couldn't be sure of ranks or units. He had a bunch of questions to ask Matt. For a thousand reasons, he wished he could call his brother. But there were no phones; even the Army was working with old-fashioned tools. The officer wrote on a piece of paper and tore it off the pad, handing it to one scared grunt, sending him and those important words off to "The Site."

Mr. Rightly had moved out of the way. He looked useless and exhausted and sorry, but at least he had a stool to perch on.

"What do we know?" Bloch asked him.

Something was funny in those words.

Laughing along with his teacher, Bloch asked, "Do you still think our spaceship is different from the big probe?"

As if sharing a secret, Mr. Rightly leaned close. "It came from a different part of the sky, and it was alone. And its effects, big as they are, don't compare with what's happening on the other side of the world."

The professors were huddled up, talking and pointing at the ground.

"What is happening on the other side?"

Mr. Rightly asked him to lean over, and then he whispered. "The colonel was talking to the Homeland person. I heard him say that the hardened military channels didn't quit working right away. Twenty minutes after the big impact, from Europe, from Asia, came reports of bright lights and large motions, from the ground and the water. And then the wind started to blow hard, and all those voices fell silent."

Bloch felt sad for his brother, but he couldn't help but say, "Wow."

"There is a working assumption," Mr. Rightly said. "The Earth's night side has been lost, but the invasion hasn't begun here. Homeland and the military are trying not to lose this side too."

Thinking about the alien and the dead kids, Bloch said, "You were right, sir. We shouldn't have trusted it."

Mr. Rightly shrugged and said nothing.

Some kind of meeting had been called in the back of the room. There was a lot of passion and no direction. Then the Homeland man whispered to an assistant who wrote hard on the clipboard, and the colonel found new orders and sent his last soldier off on another errand.

"What's the alien doing now?" Bloch asked.

"Who knows," Mr. Rightly said.

"Is the radiation keeping us away?"

"No, it's not . . ." The glasses needed another shove. "Our friend vanished. After you and I left, it apparently punched through the bottom of the pond. I haven't been to the Site myself. But the concrete is shattered and there's a slick new hole reaching down who-knows-how-far. That's the problem. And that's why they're so worried about these little quakes, or whatever they are. What is our green-eyed mystery doing below us?"

Bloch looked at the other faces and then at the important floor. Then a neat, odd thought struck him: the monster was never just the creature itself. It was also the way that the creature lurked about, refusing to be seen. It was the unknown wrapped heavy and thick around it, and there was the vivid electric fear that made the air glow. Real life was normal and silly. Nothing happening today was normal or silly.

He started to laugh, enjoying the moment, the possibilities.

Half of the room stared at him, everybody wondering what was wrong with that towering child.

"They're bringing in equipment, trying to dangle a cable down into the hole," Mr. Rightly said.

"What, with a camera at the end?"

"Cameras don't seem to be working. Electronics come and go. So no, they'll send down a volunteer."

"I'd go," Bloch said.

"And I know you mean that," Mr. Rightly said.

"Tell them I would."

"First of all: I won't. And second, my word here is useless. With this crew, I have zero credibility."

The physicist and colonel were having an important conversation, fingers poking imaginary objects in the air.

"I'm hungry," Bloch said.

"There's MREs somewhere," said Mr. Rightly.

"I guess I'll go look for them," the boy lied. Then he walked out into a hallway that proved wonderfully empty.

Every zoo exists somewhere between the perfect and the cheap. Every cage wants to be impregnable and eternal, but invisibility counts for something too. The prisoner's little piece of the sky had always been steel mesh reaching down to a concrete wall sculpted to resemble stone, and people would walk past all day, every day, and people would stand behind armored glass, reading about Amur leopards when they weren't looking at him.

Sometimes he paced the concrete ground, but not this morning. Everything felt different and wrong this morning. He was lying beside a dead decorative tree, marshaling his energies. Then the monster came along. It was huge and loud and very clumsy, and he kept perfectly still as the monster made a sloppy turn on the path, its long trailing arm tearing through the steel portion of the sky. Then the monster stopped and a man climbed off and looked at the damage, and then he ran to the glass, staring into the gloomy cage. But he never saw any leopards. He breathed with relief and climbed back on the monster and rode it away, and the leopard rose and looked at the hole ripped in the sky. Then with a lovely unconscious motion, he was somewhere he had never been, and the world was transformed.

Cranes and generators were rumbling beside the penguin pond. Temporary lights had been nailed to trees, and inside those brilliant cones were moving bodies and purposeful chaos, grown men shouting for this to be done and not that, and goddamn this and that, and who the hell was in charge? Bloch was going to walk past the pond's backside. His plan, such as it was, was to act as if he belonged here. If somebody stopped him, he would claim that he was heading for the vending machines at the maintenance shed—a good story since it happened to be true. Or maybe he would invent some errand given to him by the little physicist. There were a lot of lies waiting inside the confusion, and he was looking forward to telling stories to soldiers holding guns. "Don't you believe me?" he would ask them, smiling all the while. "Well maybe you should shoot me. Go on, I dare you."

The daydream ended when he saw the graduate student. He recognized her tight jeans and the blond hair worn in a ponytail. She was standing on the path ahead of him, hands at her side, eyes fixed on the little hill behind the koi pond. Bloch decided to chat with her. He was going to ask her about the machine that she was looking for, what was it called? He wanted to tell her about carrying the alien, since that might impress her. There was enough daylight now that he could see her big eyes and the rivets in her jeans, and then he noticed how some of the denim was darker than it should be, soaked through by urine.

The girl heard Bloch and flinched, but she didn't blink, staring at the same unmoving piece of landscape just above the little waterfall.

Bloch stopped behind her, seeing nothing until the leopard emerged from the last clots of darkness.

Quietly, honestly, he whispered, "Neat."

She flinched again, sucking down a long breath and holding it. She wanted to look at him and couldn't. She forced herself not to run, but her arms started to lift, as if ready to sprout wings.

The leopard was at least as interested in the girl as Bloch was. Among the rarest of cats, most of the world's Amur leopards lived in zoos. Breeding programs and Russian promises meant that they might be reintroduced into the Far East, but this particular male wasn't part of any grand effort. He was inbred and had some testicular problem, and his keepers considered him ill-tempered and possibly stupid. Bloch knew all this but his heart barely sped up. Standing behind the young woman, he whispered, "How long have you been here?"

"Do you see it?" she muttered.

"Yeah, sure."

"Quiet," she insisted.

He said nothing.

But she couldn't follow her own advice. A tiny step backward put her closer to him. "Two minutes, maybe," she said. "But it seems like hours."

Bloch watched the greenish-gold cat eyes. The animal was anxious. Not scared, no, but definitely on edge and ready to be scared, and that struck him as funny.

The woman heard him chuckling. "What?"

"Nothing."

She took a deep breath. "What do we do?"

"Nothing," was a useful word. Bloch said it again, with authority. He considered placing his hands on her shoulders, knowing she would let him. She might even like being touched. But first he explained, "If we do nothing, he'll go away."

"Or jump us," she said.

That didn't seem likely. She wasn't attacked when she was alone, and there were two of them now. Bloch felt lucky. Being excited wasn't the same as being scared, and he enjoyed standing with this woman, listening to the running water and her quick breaths. Colored fish were rising slowly in the cool morning, begging out of habit to be fed, and the leopard stared down from his high place, nothing moving but the tip of his long luxurious tail.

Voices interrupted the perfection. People were approaching, and the woman gave a start, and the leopard lifted his head as she backed against a boy nearly ten years younger than her. Halfway turning her head, she asked the electric air, "Who is it?"

Soldiers, professors, and the Homeland people—everybody was walking up behind them. If they were heading for the penguin pond, they were a little lost. Or maybe they had some other errand. Either way, a dozen important people came around the bend to find the graduate student and boy standing motionless. Then a soldier spotted the cat, and with a loud voice asked, "How do you think they keep that tiger there? I don't see bars."

Some people stopped, others kept coming.

The head physicist was in the lead. "Dear God, it's loose," he called out.

Suddenly everybody understood the situation. Every person had a unique reaction, terror and flight and shock and startled amusement percolating out of them in various configurations. The colonel and his soldiers mostly tried to hold their ground, and the government people were great sprinters, while the man who had ordered the woman out on the errand laughed loudest and came closer, if not close.

Then the physicist turned and tried to run, his feet catching each other. He fell hard, and something in that clumsiness intrigued the leopard, causing it to slide forwards, making ready to leap.

Bloch had no plan. He would have been happy to stand there all morning with this terrified woman. But then a couple other people stumbled and dropped to their knees, and somebody wanted people to goddamn move so he could shoot. The mayhem triggered instincts in an animal that had killed nothing during its long comfortable life. Aiming for the far bank of the pond, the leopard leapt, and Bloch watched the trajectory while his own reflexes engaged. He jumped to his right, blocking the cat's path. Smooth and graceful, it landed on the concrete bank, pulling into a tuck, and with both hands Bloch grabbed its neck. The leopard spun and slashed. Claws sliced into one of the big triceps, shredding the sweatshirt. Then Bloch angry lifted the animal, surprised by how small it felt, but despite little exercise and its advanced years, the animal nearly pulled free.

Bloch shouted, "No!"

The claws slashed again.

Bloch dove into the pond—three hundred pounds of primate pressing the cat into the carp and cold water. The leopard got pushed to the bottom with the boy on top, a steady loud angry-happy voice telling it, "Stop stopstopstopstop."

The water exploded. Wet fur and panicked muscle leaped over the little fake hill, vanishing. Then Bloch climbed out the water, relieved and thrilled, and he peeled off his sweatshirt, studying the long cuts raking his left arm.

Eyes closed in terror, the young woman hadn't seen the leopard escape. Now she stared at the panicked fish, imagining the monster dead on the bottom. And she looked at Bloch, ready to say something, wanting very much to thank the boy who had swept into her nightmare to save her life. But then she felt the wet jeans, and touching herself, she said, "I can't believe this." She looked at the piss on her hand, and she sniffed it once, and then she was crying, saying, "Don't look at me. Oh, Jesus, don't look."

He slept.

The medicine made him groggy, or maybe Bloch was so short of sleep that he could drift off at the first opportunity. Whatever the reason, he was warm and comfortable in the army bed, having a fine long dream where he wrestled leopards and a dragon and then a huge man with tusks for teeth and filthy, shit-stained hands that shook him again and again. Then a small throat was cleared and he was awake again.

A familiar brown face was watching him. "Hello."

"Hi."

The physicist looked at the floor and said, "Thank you," and then he looked at the boy's eyes. "Who knows what would have happened. If you hadn't been there, I mean."

Bloch was the only patient in a field hospital inflated on the zoo's parking lot. One arm was dressed with fancy military coagulants, and a bottle was dripping antibiotics into Bloch's good arm. His voice was a little slow and rough. "What happened to it?"

Bloch was asking about the leopard, but the physicist didn't seem to hear him. He stared at the floor, something disgusting about the soft vinyl. "Your mother and teacher are waiting in the next room," he said.

The floor started to roll and pitch. The giant from Bloch's dream rattled the world, and then it grew bored and the motion quit.

Then the physicist answered a question Bloch hadn't asked. "I think that a machine has fallen across half the world. This could be an invasion, an investigation, an experiment. I don't know. The entire planet is blacked out. Most of our satellites are disabled, and we can barely communicate with people down the road, much less on the other side of the world. The alien or aliens are here to torture us, unless they are incapable of noticing us. I keep listening for that god-voice. But there isn't any voice. No threats or demands, or even any trace of an apology."

Rage had bled away, leaving incredulity. The little man looked like a boy when he said, "People are coming to us, people from this side of the demarcation line. Witnesses. Just an hour ago, I interviewed a refugee from Ohio. He claims that he was standing on a hilltop, watching the solar sail's descent. What he saw looked like smoke, a thin quick slippery smoke that fell out of the evening sky, settling on the opposite hillside. Then the world before him changed. The ground shook like pudding and trees were moving—not waving, mind you, but picking up and running—and there were voices, huge horrible voices coming out of the darkness. Then a warm wind hit him in the face and the trees and ground began flowing across the valley before him and he got into his car and fled west until he ran out of gas. He stole a second car that he drove until it stopped working. Then he got a third and pushed until he fell asleep and went off the road, and a state trooper found him and brought him here."

The physicist paused, breathing hard.

He said, "The device." He said, "That object that you witnessed. It might be part of the same invasion, unless it is something else. Nobody knows. But a number of small objects have fallen on what was the day side of the Earth. The military watched their arrival before the radars failed. So I feel certain about that detail. These little ships came from every portion of the sky. Most crashed into the Pacific. But the Pender event is very important, you see, because it happened on the land, in an urban setting. This makes us important. We have a real opportunity here. Only we don't have time to pick apart this conundrum. The quakes are more intense now, more frequent. Ground temperatures are rising, particularly deep below us. One hypothesis—this is my best guess—is that the entity you helped carry to the water has merged with the water table. Fusion or some other power source is allowing it to grow. But I have no idea if it has a different agenda from what the giant alien is doing. I know nothing. And even if I had every answer, I don't think I could do anything. To me, it feels as if huge forces are playing out however they wish, and we have no say in the matter."

The man stopped talking so that he could breathe, but no amount of oxygen made him relax. Bloch sat quietly, thinking about what he just heard and how interesting it was. Then a nurse entered, a woman about his mother's age, and she said, "Sir. She really wants to see her son now."

"Not quite yet."

The nurse retreated.

"Anyway," the physicist said. "I came here to thank you. You saved our lives. And I wanted to apologize too. I saw what you did with that animal, how you grabbed and shook it. You seemed so careless, so brave. And that's one of the reasons why I ordered the doctors to examine you."

"What did you do?" Bloch asked.

"This little hospital is surprisingly well-stocked," the physicist said. "And I was guessing that you were under of some kind of alien influence."

Bloch grinned. "You thought I was infected."

The little man nodded and grimaced. "The doctors have kept you under all day, measuring and probing. And your teacher brought your mother, and someone finally thought to interview the woman. She explained you. She says that you were born this way, and you don't experience the world like the rest of us."

Bloch nodded and said nothing.

"For what it is worth, your amygdala seems abnormal."

"I like being me," Bloch said happily.

The physicist gave the floor another long study. Then the ground began to shake once again, and he stood as still as he could, trying to gather himself for the rest of this long awful day.

"But what happened to the leopard?" Bloch asked.

The man blinked. "The soldiers shot it, of course."

"Why?"

"Because it was running loose," the physicist said. "People were at risk, and it had to be killed."

"That's sad," the boy said.

"Do you think so?"

"It's the last of its kind," Bloch said.

The physicist's back stiffened as he stared at this very odd child, and with a haughty voice, he explained, "But of course the entire world seems to be coming to an end. And I shouldn't have to point out to you, but this makes each of us the very last of his kind."

THE PENDER MONSTER

Bloch was supposed to be sleeping. Two women sat in the adjoining room, using voices that tried to be private but failed. Fast friends, his mother and his nurse talked about careers and worrisome children and lost men. The nurse's husband had abandoned her for a bottle and she wanted him to get well but not in her presence, thank you. Bloch's father died twelve years ago, killed by melanoma, and the widow still missed him but not nearly as much as during those awful first days when she had two young sons and headaches and heartaches, and God, didn't she sound like every country song?

It was the middle of a very dark night, and the warm ground was shaking more than it stood still. The women used weak, sorry laughs, and the nurse said, "That's funny," and then both fell into worried silence.

Bloch didn't feel like moving. Comfortable and alert, he sat with hard pillows piled high behind him, hands on his lap and eyes half-closed. The fabric hospital walls let in every sound. He listened to his mother sigh, and then the nurse took a breath and let it out, and then the nurse asked his mother about her thoughts.

"My boys," Mom said. Glad for the topic, she told about when her oldest was ten and happy only when he was causing trouble. But nobody stays ten forever. The Army taught Matt to control his impulses, which was one good thing. "Every situation has its good," she said, almost believing it. The nurse made agreeable sounds and asked if Matt always wanted to be a soldier, and Mom admitted that he had. Then the nurse admitted that most military men were once that way. They liked playing army as boys, so much so they couldn't stop when they grew up.

"Does that ever happen?" Mom asked. "Do they actually grow up?"

The women laughed again, this time with heart. Mom kept it up longest and then confessed that she was worried about Bloch but it was Matt that she was thinking of, imagining that big alien ship crashing down on top of him. She gave out one sorry breath after another, and then with a flat, careful voice, she wondered what life was like on the Night Side.

That's what the other half of the world had been named. The Night Side was mysterious, wrong and lost. For the last few hours, refugees had been coming through town, trading stories for gasoline and working cars. And the stories didn't change. Bloch knew this because a group of soldiers were standing outside the hospital, gossiping. Every sound came through the fabric walls. Half a dozen men and one woman were talking about impossible things: the land squirming as if it was alive; alien trees black as coal sprouting until they were a mile high, and then the trees would spit out thick clouds that glowed purple and rode the hot winds into the Day Side, raining something that wasn't water, turning more swathes of the countryside into gelatin and black trees.

What was happening here was different. Everybody agreed about that. The ground shivered, but it was only ground. And people functioned well enough to talk with strained but otherwise normal voices. Concentrating, Bloch could make out every voice inside the hospital and every spoken word for a hundred yards in any direction, and that talent didn't feel even a little bit peculiar to him.

He heard boots walking. An officer approached the gossiping soldiers, and after the ritual greetings, one man dared ask, "Do we even stand a chance here, lieutenant?"

"A damned good chance," the lieutenant said loudly. "Our scientists are sitting in a classroom, building us weapons. Yeah, we're going to tear those aliens some new assholes, just as soon as they find enough glue guns and batteries to make us our death rays."

Everybody laughed.

One soldier said, "I'm waiting for earth viruses to hit."

"A computer bug," somebody said.

"Or AIDs," said a third.

The laughter ran a time and then faded.

Then the first soldier asked, "So this critter under us, sir . . . what is it, sir?"

There was a pause. Then the lieutenant said, "You want my opinion?"

"Please, sir."

"Like that zoo teacher says. The monster came from a different part of the sky, and it doesn't act the same. When you don't have enough firepower to kick the shit out of its enemy, you dig in. And that's what I think it is doing."

"This is some big galactic war, you mean?"

"You wanted my opinion. And that's my opinion for now."

One soldier chuckled and said, "Wild."

Nobody else laughed.

Then the woman soldier spoke. "So what's that make us?"

"Picture some field in Flanders," said the officer. "It's 1916, and the Germans and British are digging trenches and firing big guns. What are their shovels and shells churning up? Ant nests, of course. Which happens to be us. We're the ants in Flanders."

The soldiers quit talking.

Maybe Mom and the nurse were listening to the conversation. Or maybe they were just being quiet for a while. Either way, Mom broke the silence by saying, "I always worried about ordinary hazards. For Matt, I mean. Bombs and bullets, and scars on the brain. Who worries about an invasion from outer space?"

Bloch pictured her sitting in the near-darkness, one hand under her heavy chin while the red eyes watched whatever was rolling inside her head.

"It's hard," said the nurse.

Mom made an agreeable sound.

Then with an important tone, the nurse said, "At least you can be sure that Matt's in a good place now."

Mom didn't say anything.

"If he's gone, I mean."

"I know what you meant," Mom said.

The nurse started to explain herself.

Mom cut her off, saying, "Except I don't believe in any of that."

"You don't believe in what?"

"The afterlife. Heaven and such."

The nurse had to breathe before saying, "But in times like this, darling? When everything is so awful, how can you not believe in the hereafter?"

"Well, let me tell you something," Mom said. Then she leaned forward her chair, her voice moving. "Long ago, when my husband was dying for no good reason, I realized that if a fancy god was in charge, then he was doing a pretty miserable job of running his corner of the universe."

The new friendship was finished. The two women sat uncomfortably close to each other for a few moments. Then one of them stood and walked over the rumbling floor, putting their head through the door to check on their patient. Bloch remained motionless, pretending to be asleep. The woman saw him sitting in the bed, lit only by battery-powered night-lights. Then to make sure that she was seeing what she thought she was seeing, she came all the way into the room, and with a high wild voice she began to scream.

The defender had landed far from open water, exhausted and exposed. Fuel was essential and hydrogen was the easy/best solution, but most of the local hydrogen was trapped in the subsurface water or chemically locked into the rock. Every atom had to be wrenched loose, wasting time and focus. Time and focus built a redoubt, but the vagaries of motion and fuel had dropped the defender too close to the great enemy, and there was nothing to be done about that, and there was nothing to work with but the drought and the sediments and genius and more genius.

Emotion helped. Rage was the first tool: a scorching hatred directed at a vast, uncaring enemy. Envy was nearly as powerful, the defender nurturing epic resentments aimed at its siblings sitting behind it in the ocean. Those lucky obscenities were blessed with more resources and considerably more time to prepare their redoubts, and did they appreciate how obscenely unfair this was? Fear was another fine implement. Too much work remained unfinished, grand palisades and serene weapons existing only as dream; absolute terror helped power the furious digging inside the half-born redoubt.

But good emotions always allowed the bad. That was how doubt emerged. The defender kept rethinking its landing. Easy fuel had been available, but there were rules and codes concerning how to treat life. Some of the local water happened to be self-aware. Frozen by taboos, the defender created a false body and appealing face. The scared little shreds of life were coaxed into helping it, but they were always doomed. It seemed like such a waste, holding sacred what was already dead. One piece of water that was ready to douse the defender with easy water. That first taste of fuel would have awakened every reactor, and the work would have commenced immediately. Yes, radiation would have poisoned the weak life, yes. But that would have given valuable minutes to fill with work and useful fear.

The mad rush was inevitable, and speed always brought mistakes. One minor error was to allow a creative-aspect to escape on the wind. The aspect eventually lodged on the paw of some living water, and then it was injected into a second piece of water, dissolving into the cool iron-infused blood, taking ten thousand voyages about that simple wet body. But this kind of mistake happened quite a lot. Hundreds, maybe thousands of aspects had been lost already. The largest blunder was leaving the aspect active—a totipotent agent able to interface with its environment, ready for that key moment when it was necessary to reshape water and minerals, weaving the best soldier possible from these miserable ingredients.

For every tiny mistake, the entity felt sorry. It nourished just enough shame to prove again that it was moral and right. Then it willfully ignored those obscure mistakes, bearing down on the wild useless sprint to the finish.

Soldiers ran into the hospital and found a monster. Spellbound and fearful, they stared at the creature sitting upright in the bed. Two prayed, the woman talking about Allah being the Protector of those who have faith. Another soldier summoned his anger, aiming at the gray human-shaped face.

"Fucking move and I'll kill you," he said.

Bloch wasn't sure that he could move, and he didn't try.

"Do you fucking hear me?" the soldier said.

Bloch's mouth could open, the tongue tasting hot air and his remade self. He tasted like dirty glass. A voice he didn't recognize said, "I hear you, yeah." Monsters should have important booming voices. His voice was quiet, crackly, and slow, reminding him of the artificial cackle riding on a doll's pulled string.

He laughed at the sound of himself.

His mother was kneeling beside his bed, weeping while saying his name again and again. "Simon, Simon."

"I'm all right," he said to her.

The nurse stood on the other side of him, trying to judge what she was seeing. The boy's skin looked like metal or a fancy ceramic, but that was only one piece of this very strange picture. Bloch was big before, but he was at least half a foot taller and maybe half again thicker, and the bed under him looked shriveled because it was. The metal frame and foam mattress were being absorbed by his growing body. Sheets and pillows were melting into him, harvested for their carbon. And the gray skin was hot as a furnace. Bloch was gone. Replacing him was a machine, human-faced but unconvincing, and the nurse felt well within her rights as a good person to turn to the soldiers, asking, "What are you waiting for? Shoot."

But even the angry soldier wouldn't. Bullets might not work. And if the gun was useless, then threats remained the best tactic.

"Go get the colonel," he said. "Go."

The Muslim soldier ran away.

Two minutes ago, Bloch had felt awake and alert but normal. Nothing was normal now. He saw his kneeling mother and everything else. There wasn't any darkness in this room, or anywhere. His new eyes found endless details—the weave of Mom's blouse and the dust in the air and a single fly with sense enough to hang away from the impossibility that was swelling as the fancy bed dissolved into his carapace.

"It's still me," he told his mother.

She looked up, wanting to believe but unable.

Then the colonel arrived, the physicist beside him, and the lieutenant came in with Mr. Rightly.

The colonel was gray and handsome and very scared, and he chuckled quietly, embarrassed by his fear.

Bloch liked the sound of that laugh.

"Can you hear me, boy?"

"No."

That won a second laugh, louder this time. "Do you know what's happening to you?"

Bloch said, "No."

Yet that wasn't true.

More soldiers were gathering outside the hospital, setting up weapons, debating lines of fire.

The physicist pointed at Bloch, looking sick and pleased in the same moment. "I was right," he boasted. "There is a contamination problem."

"Where did this happened?" the colonel asked.

"While people were carting the spaceman around, I'd guess," said the physicist.

Bloch slowly lifted his arms. The tube from the IV bottle had merged with him. His elbow still felt like an elbow except it wasn't sore, and the raking marks in his bicep had become permanent features.

"Don't move," the angry soldier repeated.

Mom climbed to her feet, reaching for him.

"Don't get near him," the nurse advised.

"I'm hot, be careful," Bloch said. But she insisted on touching the rebuilt arm, scorching each of her fingertips.

Mr. Rightly came forward, glasses dangling and forgotten on the tip of his moist little nose. "Is it really you?"

"Maybe," the boy said. "Or maybe not."

"How do you feel, Bloch?"

Bloch studied his hands with his fine new eyes. "Good," he said.

"Are you scared?"

"No."

The colonel whispered new orders to the lieutenant.

The lieutenant and a private pulled on leather gloves and came forward, grabbing the teacher under his arms.

"What is this?" Mr. Rightly asked.

"We're placing you under observation, as a precaution," the colonel explained.

"That's absurd," said Mr. Rightly, squirming hard.

On his own, the private decided that the situation demanded a small surgical punch—one blow to the kidneys, just to put the new patient to the floor.

The lieutenant cursed.

Bloch sat up, and the shriveled bed shattered beneath him.

"Don't move," the angry soldier repeated, drawing sloppy circles with the gun barrel.

"Leave him alone," Bloch said.

"I'm all right," Mr. Rightly said, lifting a shaking hand. "They just want to be cautious. Don't worry about it, son."

Bloch sat on the floor, watching every face.

Then the physicist turned to the colonel, whispering, "You know, the mother just touched him too."

The colonel nodded, and two more soldiers edged forward.

"No," Bloch said.

One man hesitated, and irritated by the perceived cowardice, his partner came faster, lifting a pistol, aiming at the woman who had a burnt hand and a monstrous child.

Thought and motion arrived in the same instant.

The pistol was crushed and the empty-handed soldier was on his back, sprawled out and unsure what could have put him there so fast, so neatly. Then Bloch leaped about the room, gracefully destroying weapons and setting bodies on their rumps before ending up in the middle of the chaos, seven feet tall and invulnerable. With the crackly new voice, he said, "I've touched all of you. And I don't think it means anything. And now leave my mother the hell alone."

"The monster's loose," the angry soldier screamed. "It's attacking us."

Three of the outside soldiers did nothing. But the fourth man had shot his first leopard in the morning, and he was still riding the adrenaline high. The hot target was visible with night goggles—a radiant giant looming over cowering bodies. The private sprayed the target with automatic weapons fire. Eleven bullets were absorbed by Bloch's chest, their mass and energy and sweet bits of metal feeding the body that ran through the shredded wall and ran into the open parking lot, carefully drawing fire away from those harmless sacks of living water.

A few people joined up with the refugee stream, abandoning the city for the Interstate and solid, trusted ground to the west. But most of the city remained close to home. People didn't know enough to be properly terrified. Some heard the same stories that the Army heard about the Night Side. But every truth had three rumors ready to beat it into submission. Besides, two hundred thousand bodies were difficult to move. Some cars still worked, but for how long? Sparks and odd magnetisms ran shared the air with a hundred comforting stories, and what scared people most was the idea that the family SUV would die on some dark stretch of road, in the cold and with hungry people streaming past.

No, it was better to stay inside your own house. People knew their homes. They had basements and favorite chairs and trusted blankets. Instinct and hope made it possible to sit in the dark, the ground rolling steadily but never hard enough to shake down the pictures on the wall. It was easy to shut tired eyes, entertaining the luscious idea that every light would soon pop on again, televisions and Google returning in force. Whatever the crisis was, it would be explained soon. Maybe the war would be won. Or an alien face would fill the plasma television—a brain-rich beast dressed in silver, its rumbling voice explaining why the world had been assimilated and what was demanded of the new slaves.

That was a very potent rumor. The world had been invaded, humanity enslaved. And slavery had its appeal. Citizens of all persuasions would chew on the notion until they tasted hope: property had value. Property needed to be cared for. Men and women sat in lounge chairs in their basements, making ready for what seemed like the worst fate short of death. But it wasn't death, and the aliens would want their bodies and minds for some important task, and every reading of history showed that conquerors always failed. Wasn't that common knowledge? Overlords grew sloppy and weak, and after a thousand years of making ready, the human slaves would rise up and defeat their hated enemies, acquiring starships and miracle weapons in the bargain.

That's what the woman was thinking. She was sitting beside the basement stove, burning the last of her Bradford pear. She was out of beer and cigarettes and sorry for that, but the tea was warm and not too bitter. She was reaching for the mug when someone forced the upstairs door open and came inside. She stopped in mid-reach, listening to a very big man moving across her living room, the floor boards complaining about the burden, and for the next mad moment she wondered if the visitor wasn't human. The zoo had ponies. The creature sounded as big as a horse. After everything else, was that so crazy? Then a portion of the oak turned to fire and soot, and something infinitely stranger than a Clydesdale dropped into the basement, landing gently beside her.

"Quiet," said the man-shaped demon, one finger set against the demon mouth.

She had never been so silent.

"They're chasing me," he said with a little laugh.

He was wearing nothing but a clumsy loincloth made from pink attic insulation. A buttery yellow light emerged from his face, and he was hotter than the stove. Studying his features, the woman saw that goofy neighbor boy who walked past her house every day. That was the boy who was standing outside just before the aliens crashed. Not even two days ago, incredible as that seemed.

"Don't worry," he said. "I'm no monster."

Unlikely though it was, she believed him.

A working spotlight swept through the upstairs of her house. She saw it through the hole and the basement windows. Then it was gone and there was just the two of them, and she was ready to be scared but she wasn't. This unexpected adventure was nothing but thrilling.

The boy-who-wasn't-a-monster knelt low, whispering, "I'm having this funny thought. Do you want to hear it?"

She nodded.

"Do you know why we put zoo animals behind bars?"

"Why?"

"The bars are the only things that keep us from shooting the poor stupid beasts."

WAR OF THE WORLDS

Whatever is inevitable becomes common.

Fire is inevitable. The universe is filled with fuel and with sparks. Chemicals create cold temporary fires and stars burn for luxurious spans, while annihilating matter and insulting deep reality, resulting in the most spectacular blazes.

Life is inevitable. Indeed, life is an elaborate, self-aware flame that begins cold but often becomes fiercely hot. Life is a fire that can think and then act on its passionate ideas. Life wants fuel and it wants reasons to burn, and this is why selfishness is the first right of the honest mind. But three hundred billion suns and a million trillion worlds are not enough fuel. Life emerges too often and too easily, and a galaxy full of wild suns and cold wet worlds is too tempting. What if one living fire consumed one little world, freely and without interference? Not much has been harmed, so where is the danger?

The danger, corrupting and remorseless, is that a second fire will notice that conquest and then leap toward another easy world, and a thousand more fires will do the same, and then no fire will want to be excluded, a singularly awful inferno igniting the galaxy.

Morality should be inevitable too. Every intelligence clings to an ethical code. Any two fires must have common assumptions about right and about evil. And first among the codes is the law that no solitary flame can claim the heavens, and if only to protect the peace, even the simplest and coldest examples of life must be held in safe places and declared sacred.

The city was exhausted, but it was far from quiet. The ground still rumbled, though the pitch was changing in subtle ways. Mice were squeaking and an owl told the world that she was brave, and endless human voices were talking in the darkness, discussing small matters and old regrets. Several couples were making spirited love. A few prayed, though without much hope behind the words. A senile woman spoke nonsense. And then her husband said that he was tired of her noise and was heading outside to wait for the sunrise.

Bloch was standing in the middle of Pender when the man emerged. This was the same old fellow who saw his brave oak stop the rolling spaceship. Cranes and a National Guard truck had carried away the useless egg case. Extra fragments and local dust had been swept into important buckets, waiting for studies that would never come about. But the human vehicles were left where they crashed, and Bloch saw every tire mark, every drop of vigorous blood, and he studied a blond Barbie, loved deeply by a little girl and now covered with dried, half-frozen pieces of her brother's brain.

The old man came out on his porch and looked at the apparition, and after taking careful stock of everything said, "Huh."

Nobody was hunting Bloch anymore. The initial panic and search for the monster had spread across the city and then dissolved, new and much larger panics taking hold. One monster was nothing compared to what was approaching, and the army had been dispatched to the east—Guard soldiers and policemen and a few self-appointed militia hunkering down in roadside ditches, ready to aim insults and useless guns at the coming onslaught.

The old man considered retreating into his house again. But he was too worn down to be afraid, and he didn't relish more time with his wife. So he came down the stairs and across the lawn, leaning his scrawny body against the gouged trunk. Pulling off a stocking cap, he rubbed his bald head a couple times, and using a dry slow voice explained, "I know about you. You were that kid who climbed inside first."

Bloch looked at him and looked East too. Dawn should be a smudged brightness pushing up from a point southeast. But there was no trace of the sun. The light was purple and steady, covering the eastern horizon.

"Do you know what's happening to you?" the old man asked.

"Maybe," Bloch said. Then he lifted one hand, a golden light brightening his entire arm. "A machine got inside me and shouldn't have. It started to rebuild me, but then it realized that I was alive and so it quit."

"Why did it quit?"

"Life is precious. The machine isn't supposed to build a weapon using a sentient organism."

"So you're what? Half-done?"

"More like three percent finished."

The old man moved to where Bloch's heat felt comfortable. Looking up at the gray face, he asked, "Are you just going to stand here?"

"This is a fine place to watch the battle, yes."

The man looked east and then back at Bloch. He seemed puzzled and a little curious, a thin smile showing more in his eyes than his mouth.

"But you won't be safe outside," the boy cautioned, new instincts using his mouth. "You'll survive longer if you get into your basement."

"How long is longer?"

"Twenty or thirty seconds, I would think."

The man tried to laugh, and then he tried to curse. Neither worked, which was when he looked down the hill, saying, "If it's all the same, I'll just stay outside and watch the show."

The purple line was taller and brighter, and the first trace of a new wind started nudging at the highest oak limbs.

"Here comes something," the man said.

There was quite a lot to see, yes. But following the man's eyes, Bloch found nothing but empty air.

"That soldier might be hunting you," the man said.

"What soldier?"

"Or maybe he's a deserter. I don't see a gun." This time the laugh worked—a sour giggle accompanied by some hard shaking of the head. "Of course you can't blame the fellow for running. All things considered."

"Who is he?" Bloch asked.

"You don't see him? The old grunt walking up the middle of the road?"

Nothing else was alive on Pender.

"Well, I'm not imagining this. And I wasn't crazy three minutes ago, so I doubt if I am now."

Bloch couldn't find anybody, but he felt movement, something massive and impressive that was suddenly close, and his next instinct touched him coldly, informing him that a cloaked warrior had him dead in its sights.

"What's our soldier look like?"

"A little like you," the old man said.

But there was no second gray monster, which made the moment deliciously peculiar.

"And now he's calling to you," the man said.

"Calling me what?"

"'Kid,' it sounds like."

And that was the moment when Bloch saw his brother standing in front of him.

Matt always looked like their father, but never so much as now. He was suddenly grown. This wasn't the shaved-head, beer-belching boy who came home on leave last summer. This wasn't even the tough-talking soldier on Skype last week. Nothing about him was worn down or wrinkled, yet the apparition carried himself like their father did in the videos—a short thick fellow with stubby legs churning, shoulders squared up and ready to suffer any load. He was decked out in the uniform that he wore in Yemen, except it was too pressed and too clean. There was a sleepless, pained quality to the face, and that's where he most resembled Dad. But those big eyes had seen worse than what they were seeing now, and despite cares and burdens that a little brother could never measure, the man before him still knew how to smile.

"How you doing, kid?" Matt asked.

With the doll-voice, Bloch said, "You're not my brother."

"Think not?"

"I feel it. You're not human at all."

"So says the glowing monster decked out in his fancy fiberglass underwear." Matt laughed and the old man joined in. Then Matt winked, asking Bloch, "You scared of me?"

Bloch shook his head.

"You should be scared. I'm a very tough character now." He walked past both of the men, looking back to say, "March with me, monster. We got a pile of crap to discuss."

Long legs easily caught the short.

Turning the corner, Bloch asked where they were going. Matt said nothing. Bloch looked back. The old man had given up watching them, preferring to lean against the wrecked Buick, studying the purples in a long sky that was bewitched and exceptionally lovely.

"We're going to the zoo," Bloch guessed.

Matt started to nod and then didn't. He started to talk and then stopped himself. Then he gazed up at the giant beside him.

"What?" Bloch asked.

"Do you know what an adventure is?"

"Sure."

"No, you don't," Matt said. "When I was standing outside the barracks that night, texting you, I figured I was going to die. And that didn't seem too awful. A demon monster was dropping from the heavens and the world was finished, but what could I do? Nothing. This wasn't like a bomb hiding beside the road. This wasn't a bullet heading for me. There wasn't any gut-eating suspense to the show, and nothing was left to do but watch."

"Except that spaceship was just a beginning. Like the softest most wonderful blanket, it fell over me and over everything. An aspect found me and fell in love with my potential. Like you've been worked on, only more so. I learned tons of crazy shit. What I knew from my old life was still part of me, still holding my core, but with new meanings attached. It was the same for my unit and the Yemeni locals and even the worst bad guys. We were remade and put to work, which isn't the same as being drafted, since everybody understood the universe, and our work was the biggest best thing any of us could ever do."

They passed the house where Bloch spent the night, hiding in the basement. "What about the universe?" he asked.

"We're not alone, which you know. But we never have been alone. The Earth wasn't even born, and the galaxy was already full of bodies and brains and all sorts of plans for what could be done, and some of those projects were done but a lot of them were too scary, too big and fancy. There's too little energy to accomplish everything that can be dreamed up. Too many creatures want their little piece of the prize, and that's why a truce was put in place. A planet like the Earth is a tempting resource, but nobody is allowed to touch it. Not normally, they aren't. Earth has its own life, just like a hundred and six other planets and moons and big comets. And that's just inside our little solar system. Even the simplest life is protected by law and by machines—although 'machine' isn't the best word."

"We live in a zoo," Bloch said.

"And 'zoo' is a pretty lousy word too. But it works for now." Matt turned at the next intersection, taking a different route than Bloch usually walked to school. "Rules and regulations, that's how everything is put together. There's organizations older than the scum under our rocks. There's these systems that have kept the Earth safe from invaders, mostly. But not always. I'm telling you, this isn't the first time the Earth has been grabbed hard. You think the dinosaurs died from a meteor attack? Not possible. If a comet is going to be trouble, it's gently nudged and made safe again. Which is another blessing of living inside a zoo, and I guess we should have been thankful. If we knew about it before, that is."

"What killed them?"

"The T. rexes? Well, that depends on how you tell the story. A ship came out of deep space and got lucky enough to evade the defensive networks—networks that are never as fancy or new as is possible, by the way. Isn't that the way it always works? Dinosaurs got infected with aspects, and the aspects gave them big minds and new skills. But then defenders were sent down here to put up a fight. A worldwide battle went pretty well for the defenders, but not well enough. For a little while it looked as if maybe, just maybe the Earth could be rebuilt into something powerful enough to survive every one of the counterattacks."

"But the machines above us managed one hard cleansing attack. Cleansings are a miserable desperate tactic. Flares are woven on the sun and then focused on the planet, stripping its crust clean. But cleansing was the easy trick. Too much had to be rebuilt afterwards, and a believable scenario had to be impressed into the rock, and dinosaurs were compromised and unsafe. That's why the impact craters. That's why the iridium layer. And that's why a pack of little animals got their chance, which is you and me, and the next peace lasted for about sixty-five million years."

Small houses and leafless trees lined a road that ended with at tall chain-link fence topped with barbed wire.

"This war has two sides," said Matt. "Every kind of good is here, and there is no evil. Forget evil. A starship carrying possibilities struck the earth, and it claimed half of the planet in a matter of minutes. Not that that part of the war has been easy. There's a hundred trillion mines sitting in our dirt, hiding. Each one is a microscopic machine that waits, waits, waits for this kind of assault. I've been fighting booby traps ever since. In my new state, this war has gone on a hundred years. I've seen and done things and had things done to me, and I've met creatures you can't imagine, and machines that I can't comprehend, and nothing has been won easily for me, and now I'm back to my big question: Do you know what adventure is?"

"I think I know."

"You don't, kid. Not quite yet, you don't know."

The fence marked the zoo's eastern border. Guardsmen had cut through the chain-link, allowing equipment too big for the service entrance to be brought onto the grounds. Inside the nearest cage, a single Bactrian camel stood in the open, in the violet morning light, shaggy and calm and imbecilic.

Bloch stepped through the hole, but his brother remained outside.

The boy grew brighter and his voice sounded deeper. "So okay, tell me. What is an adventure?"

"You go through your life, and stuff happens. Some of that stuff is wild, but most of it is boring. That's the way it has to be. Like with me, for instance. The last hundred years of my life have been exciting and ordinary and treacherous and downright dull, depending on circumstances. I've given a lot to this fight, and I believe it's what I want to do. And we've got a lot of advantages on our side: surprise; an underfunded enemy; and invading a target that is the eighth or ninth best among the candidates."

"What is best?" Bloch asked.

"Jupiter is the prize. Because of its size, sure, but also because it's biosphere is a thousand times more interesting than ours." Matt stood before the gaping hole, hands on hips. "Yeah, my side has its advantages and the momentum, but it probably will fall short of its goal. We'll defeat the booby traps, sure, and beat the defenders inside their redoubts, but we probably won't be ready for the big cleansing attack. But what is happening, if you care . . . this is pretty much how the Permian came to an awful end. In four days, the Earth became something mighty, and then most everything went extinct. That's probably what happens here. And you know the worst of it? Humans will probably accept the villain's role in whatever the false fossil says. We killed our world from pollution and heat, and that's why the fence lizards and cockroaches are going to get their chance."

Bloch was crying.

"Adventure," said Matt. "No, that's not the crazy stupid heroic shit you do in your life. Adventure is the story you tell afterwards. It's those moments you pick out of everything that was boring and ordinary, and then put them on a string and give to another person as a gift. Your story."

Bloch felt sick inside.

"Feel scared, kid?"

"No."

"Good," his brother said, pulling a string necklace out of his shirt pocket and handing it to him. "Now go. You've got a job to do."

BLOCH'S ADVENTURE

The camel was chewing, except it wasn't. The mouth was frozen and the dark dumb eyes held half-closed, and a breath that began in some past age had ceased before the lungs were happy. The animal was a statue. The animal was some kind of dead, inert and without temperature, immune to rot and the tug of gravity while standing in the middle of a pen decorated with camel hoof prints and camel shit and the shit-colored feed that was destined for a camel's fine belly—the emperor resplendent in his great little realm.

Bloch turned back to his brother, wanting explanations. But Matt had vanished, or never was. So he completed one slow circle, discerning how the world was locked into a moment that seemed in no particular hurry to move to the next moment. But time must be moving, however slowly. Otherwise how could an eye see anything? The light reflected off every surface would be fixed in space, and frozen light was as good as no light, and wasn't it funny how quickly this new mind of his played with the possibilities?

The pale, broad hand of a boy came into his face, holding the white string of the necklace just given to him. Little candy beads looked real and felt real as his fingers made them dance. "Neat," he said, his newest voice flat and simple, like the tone from a cheap bell. But the hands and body were back where they began, just ten million times quicker, and the fiberglass garb was replace with the old jeans and Cornell sweatshirt. This is nuts, he thought. And fun. Then for no particular reason, he touched the greenest candy against his tongue, finding a sweetness that made it impossible not to shove all of the beads into his mouth, along with the thick rough string.

Each candy was an aspect, and the string was ten aspects woven together, and Bloch let them slide deep while waiting for whatever the magic would do to him next.

But nothing seemed to change, inside him or without.

The camel was a little deeper into its breath and its happiness when the boy moved on. He did not walk. He thought of moving and was immediately some distance down the concrete path, and he thought of moving faster and then stood at the zoo's west side. His school was a big steel building camouflaged behind a fake fire station and a half-sized red caboose. He knew where he needed to be, and he didn't go there. Instead he rose to the classroom where Mr. Rightly and his mother shared a little bed made of lost clothes. They were sitting up on the folded coats, a single camping lamp shining at their feet. Mom was talking and holding the teacher's hand. Mr. Rightly had always looked as old as his mother, but he wasn't. He was a young man who went gray young, sitting beside a careworn woman ten years his senior. Bloch leaned close to his mother and told her about seeing Matt just now. He said that his brother was alive and strong, and he explained a little something about what her youngest son was doing now, and finally enough time passed for that despairing face to change, maybe recognizing the face before, or at least startled by the shadow that Bloch cast.

Several people shared the dim room. The girl who had recently faced down the wild leopard was sitting across from Bloch's mother, bright tears frozen on the pretty face. In her lap were an old National Geographic and a half-page letter that began with "Dear Teddy" and ended with "Love" written several times with an increasingly unsteady hand. Bloch studied the girl's sorrow, wishing he could give her confidence. But none of the aspects inside could do that. Then he turned back to his mother's slow surprise and poor Mr. Rightly who hadn't slept in days and would never sleep again. That's what Bloch was thinking as he used his most delicate touch, one finger easing the sloppy glasses back up near the eyes.

He moved again, no time left to waste.

The penguin's new pond was empty of water but partly filled with machines, most of them dead and useless. A yellow crane was fixed in place, reaching to the treetops, and one steel cable dangled down to a point ten feet above the concrete deck. Flanking cherry pickers were filled with soldiers working furiously to arm what was tethered to the cable's end: a small atomic warhead designed to be flung against tank columns in the Fulda Gap. The soldiers were trying to make the bomb accept their commands. It was a useless activity; for endless reasons, the plutonium would never become angry. But Bloch was willing himself into the air, having a long penetrating look at what might be the most destructive cannonball the human species would ever devise.

At the edge of the pond, the terrified physicist and the equally traumatized colonel were arguing. The intricacies of their respective viewpoints were lost, but they were obviously exhausted, shouting wildly, cold fingers caught in mid-thrust and the chests pumped up, neither combatant noticing the boy who slipped between them before leaping into the waterless pond, tucking those big arms against his chest, pointing his toes as he fell into the deep, deep hole.

Damaged aspects returned to the nub on occasion, begging for repairs or death. Death was the standard solution, but sometimes the attached soldier could be healed and sent out again. There weren't enough soldiers, and the first assault hadn't begun. But the defender had to be relentlessly careful. Infiltrators moved among the wounded. Sabotage was licking at the edges and the soft places, at the less-than-pivotal functions, and worse were the lies and wild thoughts that would begin in one place and flow everywhere, doing their damage by cultivating confidence, by convincing some routine that it was strong—one little portion of the defender believing itself a bold rock-solid savior of the redoubt, shrugging aside ten microseconds of lucid doubt as it did what was less than ideal.

Among the mangled and failed was an aspect carried inside a sack of water. Tiny in endless ways, the aspect managed to escape notice until it had arrived—a dull fleck of material that would never accomplish any mission or accidentally hinder even the smallest task. Ignoring such debris was best, but some little reflex took charge eventually. The defender told that aspect to be still and wait, and it was very still and very patient while tools of considerable precision were brought to bear on what had never worked properly. The aspect was removed from its surroundings. The aspect was destroyed. And different tools reached for what seemed like common water, ready to harvest a drop or two of new fuel.

But then flourishes and little organs appeared on the wetness, or maybe they were always there, and one of the organs spoke.

"I'm not here to fight," Bloch said to the darkness.

It was his original voice, mostly. There was gravel at the edges, and it felt a little quick, but he liked how the words sounded in his head. And it was his head again, and his big old comfortable, clunky body. Time was again running at its proper speed, and the air was like a sauna, no oxygen to be found. "I'm not here to fight," he said, and then his head began to spin. One moment he was standing in some imprecise volume never intended to be a room, and then he was on his knees, gasping.

The uneven floor flattened. New air rushed in, and light came from everywhere while the floor rose around him, creating a bright bubble that isolated him from everything else.

The boy breathed until he could remember what felt normal, and he got up on his knees, wiping his mouth with the gray sleeve of his sweatshirt.

"Better," he said.

Then, "Thanks."

Nothing changed.

"I'm not here to fight," Bloch repeated. "I'm just delivering a message, and the other side went through a lot of trouble to put me here, which means maybe you should be careful and kill me now."

Then he paused, waiting.

Anticipating this moment, Bloch imagined a creature similar to what he found inside the spaceship. It would be larger and more menacing, but the monster of his daydreams always sported green eyes that glared down at the crafty little human. Except there were no eyes and nothing like a face, and the only presence inside the bubble room was Bloch.

He laughed and said, "I thought I might get scared. But nope, I'm not."

Then he sat, stretching his legs out before him.

"Maybe this sounds smug," he said. "But for the last half day or so, I've been telling myself that I was always part of some big plan. Your aspect gets loose. The leopard picks it up with his front paw. Some careful scheme puts the cat where he can find me, and he cuts me, and I get infected, and after running wild and getting strong, I find my brother. Then Matt gives me a heads-up and points me on my way.

"Except that's not how it works, is it?"

"If there was a fancy plan, it could be discovered. It could be fooled with or a million things could go wrong naturally, or maybe the gains wouldn't match the hope. And that's why real intelligence doesn't bother with plans. You don't, I bet. You've got a set of goals and principles and no end of complications, and everything changes from minute to second, and what the smart mind does is bury itself inside the possibilities and hope for the best."

Bloch paused, listening to nothing. Maybe the world outside was still shaking, but he felt nothing. Probably nobody was listening, but he had nothing else to do with his day. Pulling his legs in, he crossed them, Indian-style.

"I'm here because I'm here," he said. "Your enemy didn't go looking for a mentally defective human who couldn't feel fear. It's just chance that you're not facing down that blond girl or the leopard or maybe a little penguin. Any creature would have worked, and I shouldn't take this personally."

"But I bring something odd and maybe lucky to this table. I don't get scared, and that's an advantage. When everybody else charges around, hands high and voices screaming, I'm this clear-eyed animal watching everything with interest. When you bounced along Pender, I saw people wrestling with every kind of fear. You were dumped into the water, and I studied Mr. Rightly's face. Then there's my mother who gets scared on her happiest day, and the government people and the professors trying to deal with you and each other, and everybody and everything else too. I've been paying attention. I doubt if anybody else has. The world's never been this lost or this terrified, and during these last couple days, I've learned a great deal about the pissing of pants."

Bloch paused for a moment. Then he said. "I would make a lousy soldier. Matt told me that more than once. 'If you don't get scared, you get your head shot off,' he said. Which means, Mr. Monster, that you're probably sick with worry now, aren't you? A good soldier would have to have some feat. You're little more than nothing to your enemy. You're just one grunt-soldier, in his hole and facing down an army. Except that army isn't the real monster either. From what I've been told, the invader is pretty much sure to lose. No, the scary boy in this story is what turns the sun against its planet, scorching all this down to where everything is clean again. Clean but nearly dead. The monster is those laws and customs trying keep the galaxy from getting consumed by too much life trying to do everything at once. That's the real beast here. You know it and your enemy would admit as much, I bet, and that's not the only similarity you two have.

"Yeah, I think you must be shit-in-your-pants scared. Aren't you?"

Bloch stood again. The message had to be delivered, and he would do that on his feet. That felt best. He straightened and shook his arms, a heart indistinguishable from his original heart beating a little faster now. Then with the gravelly voice, he said, "Your enemy wants you to fight. It expects nothing but your best effort, using every trick and power to try to delay him. But your walls are going to collapse. He will absorb you and push to the Pacific and those next battles, and nothing will be won fast enough, and then the sun is going to wash this world with so much wild raw energy."

"Your enemy doesn't believe in plans," Bloch said. "But possibilities are everywhere, and I'm bringing you one of the best. Not that it's perfect, and maybe you won't approve. But the pain and terror are going to look a little more worthwhile in the end, if you accept what I am offering you."

"I have a set of aspects inside me. They're hiding other aspects, and I think they might be inside my stomach."

"You'll have to cut me open to find them, and sorry, I can't help you decipher them. But you're supposed to hold them until you're beaten, and then you can choose to accept your enemy's offer. Or refuse it. The decision is going to be yours. But talking for my sake and the survival of most everybody I know and love, I sure hope you can find the courage to push the fear aside."

"Shove the terror where it doesn't get in the way."

"And make your decision with those eyes open. Would you do that much for me, please?"

Bloch stopped talking.

He wasn't standing in the bubble anymore. He was floating in a different place, and there was no telling how much time had passed, but the span felt large. Bloch floated at one end of an imprecise volume that was a little real but mostly just a projection—one enormous realm populated by tens of millions of earthly organisms.

Closest were the faces he knew. His mother and Mr. Rightly were there, and the scientists and that blond girl whose name he still didn't know. And the camel had been saved, and the rest of the surviving zoo animals, and two hundred thousand humans who in the end were pulled from their basements and off their front porches. The penguins hadn't made it to town in time, and the leopard was still dead, and Matt eventually died in the Pacific—an honored fighter doing what he loved.

Billions of people were lost. They had been gone for so long that the universe scarcely remembered them, and nobody ever marked their tragic passing. But inside this contrived, highly compressed volume, his species persisted. The adventure continued. Another passenger asked to hear Simon Bloch's story, and he told it from the beginning until now, stopping when he had nothing to add, enjoying the stares and the respectful silence.

Then he turned, throwing his gaze in a better direction.

Their starship was born while a great world died, and the chaos and rage of a solar flare had thrown it out into deepest space. Onboard were the survivors of many worlds, many tragedies, collected as a redoubt against the inevitable. The galaxy had finally fallen into that final war, but Bloch preferred to look ahead.

In the gloom and cold between galaxies, a little thread of gas and weak suns beckoned—an island where clever survivors could make a second stab at perfection.

It made a man think hard about his future, knowing that he was bound for such a place.

A different man might be scared.

But not Bloch, no.

The Vicar of Mars

GWYNETH JONES

One of the most acclaimed British writers of her generation, Gwyneth Jones was a cowinner of the James Tiptree, Jr. Award for work exploring gender issues in science fiction, with her 1991 novel White Queen, *and has also won the Arthur C. Clarke Award, with her novel* Bold as Love, *as well as receiving two World Fantasy Awards—for her story "The Grass Princess" and her collection* Seven Tales and a Fable. *Her other books include the novels* North Wind, Flowerdust, Escape Plans, Divine Endurance, Phoenix Café, Castles Made of Sand, Stone Free, Midnight Lamp, Kairos, Life, Water in the Air, The Influence of Ironwood, The Exhange, Dear Hill, The Hidden Ones, *and* Rainbow Bridge, *as well as more than sixteen young adult novels published under the name Ann Halam. Her too-infrequent short fiction has appeared in* Interzone, Asimov's Science Fiction, Off Limits, *and in other magazines and anthologies, and has been collected in* Identifying the Object: A Collection of Short Stories, *as well as* Seven Tales and a Fable. *She is also the author of the critical study* Deconstructing the Starships: Science Fiction and Reality. *Her most recent books are a new SF novel,* Spirit: or The Princess of Bois Dormant *and two collections,* The Buonarotti Quartet *and* The Universe of Things. *She has a Web site at http://homepage.ntlworld.com/gwynethann/. She lives in Brighton, England, with her husband, her son, and a Burmese cat.*

In the chiller that follows, she takes us to a realistically described colonized Mars for what may—or may not—be a ghost story.

The Reverend Boaaz Hanaahaahn, High Priest of the Mighty Void, and a young Aleutian adventurer going by the name of "Conrad," were the only resident guests at the Old Station, Butterscotch. They'd met on the way from Opportunity, and had taken to spending their evenings together, enjoying a snifter or two of Boaaz's excellent Twin Planets blend in a cosy private lounge. They were an odd couple: the massive Shet, his grey hide forming ponderous, dignified folds across his skull and over his brow, and the stripling immortal, slick strands of head-hair to his shoulders, black eyes dancing with mischief on either side of the dark space of his nasal. But the Aleutian, though he had never lived to be old—he wasn't the type—had amassed a fund of fascinating knowledge in his many lives, and Boaaz was an elderly priest with varied interests and a youthful outlook.

Butterscotch's hundred or so actual citizens didn't frequent the Old Station. The usual customers were mining lookerers, who drove in from the desert in the trucks that were their homes, and could be heard carousing, mildly, in the public bar. Boaaz and Conrad shared a glance, agreeing not to join the fun tonight. The natives were friendly enough—but Martian settlers were, almost exclusively, humans who had never left conventional space. The miners had met few "aliens," and believed the Buonarotti Interstellar Transit was a dangerous novelty that would never catch on. One got tired of the barrage of uneasy fascination.

"I'm afraid I scare the children," rumbled Boaaz.

The Aleutian could have passed for a noseless, slope-shouldered human. The Shet was hairless and impressively bulky, but what really made him different was his delicates. To Boaaz it was natural that he possessed two sets of fingers: one set thick and horny, for pounding and mashing, the other slender and supple, for fine manipulation. Normally protected by his wrist folds, his delicates would shoot out to grasp a stylus for instance, or handle eating implements. He had seen the young folk startle at this, and recoil with bulging eyes—

"Stop calling them *children*," suggested Conrad. "They don't like it."

"I don't think that can be it. The young always take the physical labour and service jobs, it's a fact of nature. I'm only speaking English."

Conrad shrugged. For a while each of them studied his own screen, as the saying goes. A comfortable silence prevailed. Boaaz reviewed a list of deserving "cases" sent to him by the Colonial Social Services in Opportunity. He was not impressed. They'd simply compiled a list of odds and ends: random persons who didn't fit in, and were vaguely thought to have problems.

To his annoyance, one of the needy appeared to live in Butterscotch.

"Here's a woman who *has been suspected of being insane*," he grumbled aloud. "Has she been treated? Apparently not. How barbaric. *Has visited Speranza . . . No known religion* . . . What's the use in telling me that?"

"Maybe they think you'd like to convert her," suggested Conrad.

"I do not *convert* people!" exclaimed Boaaz, shocked. "Should an unbelieving parishoner wish my guidance towards the Abyss, they'll let me know. It's not my business to persuade them! I have entered my name alongside other Ministers of Religion on Mars. If my services as a priest should be required at a Birth, Adulthood, Conjunction, or Death, I shall be happy to oblige, and that's enough."

Conrad laughed soundlessly, the way Aleutians do. "You don't bother your 'flock,' and they don't bother you! That sounds like a nice easy berth."

Not always, thought the old priest, ruefully. Sometimes not easy at all!

"I wouldn't worry about it, Boaaz. Mars is a colony. It's run by the planetary government of Earth, and they're obssessed with gathering information about innocent strangers. When they can't find anything interesting, they make it up. The file they keep on me is vast, I've seen it."

"Earth," powerful neighbour to the Red Planet, was the local name for the world everyone else in the Diaspora knew as the Blue.

Boaaz was here to minister to souls. Conrad was here—he claimed—purely a tourist. The fat file the humans kept might suggest a different story, but Boaaz had no intention of prying. Aleutians, the Elder Race, had their own religion; or lack of one. As long as he showed no sign of suffering, Conrad's sins were his own business. The old Shet cracked a snifter vial, tucked it in his holder, inhaled deeply, and returned to the eyeball-screen that was visible to his eyes alone. The curious Social Services file on *Jewel, Isabel* reappeared. All very odd. Careful of misunderstandings, he opened his dictionary, and checked in detail the meanings of English words he knew perfectly well.

wicked . . .
old woman . . .
insane . . .

Later, on his way to bed, he examined one of the fine rock formations that decorated the station's courtyards. They promised good hunting. The mining around here was of no great worth, ferrous ores for the domestic market, but Boaaz was not interested in commercial value: he collected mineral curiosities. It was his passion, and one very good reason for visiting Butterscotch, right on the edge of the most ancient and interesting Martian terrain. If truth be known, Boaaz looked on this far-flung Vicarate as an interesting prelude to his well-earned retirement. He did not expect his duties to be burdensome. But he was a conscientious person, and Conrad's teasing had stung.

"I shall visit her," he announced, to the sharp-shadowed rocks.

The High Priest had travelled from his home world to Speranza, capital city of the Diaspora, and onward to the Blue Planet Torus Port, in no time at all (allowing for a few hours of waiting around, and two "false duration" interludes of virtual entertainment). The months he'd spent aboard the conventional space liner *Burroughs*, completing his interplanetary journey, had been slow but agreeable. He'd arrived to find that his Residence, despatched by licensed courier, had been delayed—and decided that until his home was decoded into material form, he might as well carry on travelling. His tour of this backward but extensive new parish *happened* to concentrate on prime mineral-hunting sites: but he would not neglect his obligations.

He took a robotic jitney as far as the network extended, and proceeded on foot. *Jewel, Isabel* lived out of town, up against the Enclosure that kept tolerable climate and air quality captive. As yet unscrubbed emissions lingered here in drifts of vapour; the thin air had a lifeless, paradoxical warmth. Spindly towers of mine tailings, known as "Martian Stromatolites," stood in groups, heads together like ugly sentinels. Small mining machines crept about, munching mineral-rich dirt. There was no other movement, no sound but the crepitation of a million tiny ceramic teeth.

Nothing lived.

The "Martians" were very proud of their Quarantine. They farmed their food in strict confinement, they tortured off-world travellers with lengthy decontamination. Even the gastropod machines were not allowed to reproduce: they were turned out in batches by the mine factories, and recycled in the refineries when they were full. What were the humans trying to preserve? The racial purity of rocks and sand?

Absurd superstition, muttered the old priest, into his breather. *Life is life!*

Jewel, Isabel clearly valued her privacy. He hadn't messaged her in advance. His visit would be off the record, and if she turned him away from her door, so be it. He could see the isolated module now, at the end of a chance "avenue" of teetering stromatolites. He reviewed the file's main points as he stumped along. *Old. Well travelled, for a human of her caste. Reputed to be rich. No social contacts in Butterscotch, no data traffic with any other location. Supplied by special delivery at her own expense. Came to Mars, around a local year ago, on a settler's one-way ticket.* Boaaz thought that must be very unusual. Martian settlers sometimes retired to their home planet; if they could afford the medical bills. Why would a fragile elderly person make the opposite trip, apparently not planning to return?

The dwelling loomed up, suddenly right in front of him. He had a moment of selfish doubt. Was he committing himself to an endless round of visiting random misfits? Maybe he should quietly go away again . . . But his approach had been observed, a transparent pane had opened. A face glimmered, looking out through the inner and the outer skin; as if from deep, starless space.

"Who are you?" demanded a harsh voice, cracked with disuse. "Are you real? Can you hear me? You're not human."

"I hear you, I'm, aah, 'wired for sound.' I am not a human, I am a Shet, a priest of the Void, newly arrived, just making myself known. May I come in?"

He half-hoped that she would say no. *Go away, I don't like priests, can't you see I want to be left alone?* But the lock opened. He passed through, divested himself of the breather and his outer garments, and entered the pressurised chamber.

The room was large, by Martian living standards. Bulkheads must have been removed, probably this had once been a three or four person unit: but it felt crowded. He recognised the furniture of Earth. Not extruded, like the similar fittings in the Old Station, but free-standing: many of the pieces carved from precious woods. Chairs were ranged in a row, along one curved, red wall. Against another stood a tall armoire, a desk with many drawers, and several canvas pictures in frames; stacked facing the dark. In the midst of the room two more chairs were drawn up beside a plain ceramic stove, which provided the only lighting. A richly patterned rug lay on the floor. He couldn't imagine what it had cost to ship all this, through conventional space in material form. She must indeed be wealthy!

The light was low, the shadows numerous.

"I see you *are* a Shet," said Jewel, Isabel. "I won't offer you a chair, I have none that would take your weight, but please be seated."

She indicated the rug, and Boaaz reclined with care. The number of valuable, alien objects made him feel he was sure to break something. The human woman resumed (presumably) her habitual seat. She was tall, for a human: and very thin. A black gown with loose skirts covered her whole body, closely fastened and decorated with flourishes of creamy stuff, like textile foam, at the neck and wrists.

The marks of human aging were visible in her wrinkled face, her white head-hair and the sunken, over-large sockets of her pale eyes. But signs of age can be deceptive. Boaaz also saw something universal—something any priest often has to deal with, yet familiarity never breeds contempt.

Jewel, Isabel inclined her head. She had read his silent judgement. "You seem to be a doctor as well as a priest," she said, in a tone that rejected sympathy. "My health is as you have guessed. Let's change the subject."

She asked him how he liked Butterscotch, and how Mars compared with Shet: bland questions separated by little unexplained pauses. Boaaz spoke of his mineral-hunting plans, and the pleasures of travel. He was oddly disturbed by his sense that the room was crowded: he wanted to look behind him, to be sure there were no occupants in that row of splendid chairs. But he was too old to turn without a visible effort, and he didn't wish to be rude. When he remarked that Isabel's home (she had put him right on the order of her name) was rather isolated she smiled—a weary stretching of the lips.

"Oh, you'd be surprised. I'm not short of company."

"You have your memories."

Isabel stared over his shoulder. "Or they have me."

He did not feel that he'd gained her confidence, but before he left they'd agreed he would visit again: she was most particular about the appointment. "In ten days time," she said. "In the evening, at the full moon. Be sure you remember." As he returned to the waiting jitney, the vaporous outskirts of Butterscotch seemed less forbidding. He had done right to come, and thank goodness Conrad had teased him, or the poor woman might have been left without the comfort of the Void. Undoubtedly he was needed, and he would do his best.

His satisfaction was still with him when the jitney delivered him inside the Old Station compound. He even tried a joke on one of the human children, about those decorative rock formations. Did they walk in from the desert, one fine night, in search of alcoholic beverages? The youngster took offence.

"They were here when the station was installed. It was all desert then. If there was walking rocks on Mars, messir—" The child drew herself up to her frail, puny height, and glared at him. "We wouldn't any of us *be* here. We'd go home straight away, and leave Mars to the creatures that belongs to this planet."

Boaaz strode off, a chuckle rumbling in his throat. Kids! But when he had eaten, in decent privacy (as a respectable Shet, he would never get used to eating in public), he decided to forgo Conrad's company. The "old mad woman" was too much on his mind, and he found that he shuddered away from the idea of that second visit—yet he'd met Isabel's trouble many times, and never been frightened before.

I am getting old, thought the High Priest.

He turned in early, but he couldn't sleep: plagued by the formless feeling that he had done something foolish, and he would have to pay for it. There were wild, dangerous creatures trying to get into his room, groping at the mellow, pockmarked outer skin of the Old Station; searching for a weak place . . . Rousing from an uneasy doze, he was compelled to get up and make a transparency, although (as he knew perfectly well) his room faced an inner courtyard, and there are no wild creatures on Mars. Nothing stirred. Several rugged, decorative rocks were grouped right in front of him, oddly menacing under the security lights. Had they always stood there? He thought not, but he couldn't be sure.

The brutes crouched, blind and secretive, waiting for him to lie down again.

"I really *am* getting old," muttered Boaaz. "I must take something for it."

He slept, and found himself once more in the human woman's module. Isabel seemed younger, and far more animated. Confusion fogged his mind, embarrassing him. He didn't know how he'd arrived here, or what they'd been talking about. He was advising her to move into town. It wasn't safe to live so close to the ancient desert: she was not welcome here. She laughed and bared her arm, crying *I am welcome nowhere!* He saw a mutilation, a string of marks etched into her thin human skin. She thrust the symbols at him: he protested that he had no idea what they meant, but she hardly seemed to care. She was waiting for another visitor, the visitor she had been expecting when he arrived the first time. She had let him in by mistake, he must leave. *They are from another dimension,* she cried, in that hoarse, hopeless voice. *They wait at the gate, meaning to devour. They lived with me once, they may return, with a tiny shift of the Many Dimensions of the Void.*

It gave him a shock when she used the terms of his religion. Was she drawn to the Abyss? Had he begun to give her instruction? The fog in his mind was very distressing, how could he have forgotten something like that? Then he recalled, with intense relief, that she had been to Speranza. She was no stranger to the interstellar world, she must have learnt something of Shet belief . . . But relief was swamped in a wave of dread: Isabel was looking over his shoulder. He turned, awkward and stiff with age. A presence was taking shape in one of the chairs. It was big as a bear, bigger than Boaaz himself. Squirming tentacles of glistening flesh reached out, becoming every instant more solid and defined—

If it became fully real, if it *touched* him, he would die of horror—

Boaaz woke, thunder in his skull, his whole body pulsing, the blood thickened and backing-up in all his veins. Dizzy and sick, on the edge of total panic, he groped for his First Aid kit. He fumbled the mask over his mouth and nostril-slits, with trembling delicates that would hardly obey him, and drew in great gulps of oxygen.

Unthinkable horrors flowed away, the pressure in his skull diminished. He dropped onto his side, making the sturdy extruded couch groan; clutching the mask. It was a dream, he told himself. Just a dream.

Rationally, he knew that he had simply done too much. Overexertion in the thin air of the outskirts had given him nightmares: he must give his acclimatisation treatment more time to become established. He took things easy for the next few days, pottering around in the mining fields just outside the Enclosure—in full Martian EVA gear, with a young staff member for a guide. Pickings were slim (Butterscotch was in the Guidebook); but he made a few pleasing finds.

But the nightmare stayed with him, and at intervals he had to fight the rooted conviction that it had been real. He *had* already made a second visit, there *had* been something terrible, unspeakable . . . His nights continued to be disturbed. He had unpleasant dreams (never the same as the first), from which he woke in panic, groping for the oxygen that no longer gave much relief.

He was also troubled by a change in the behaviour of the hotel staff. They had been friendly, and unlike the miners they never whispered or stared. Now the children avoided him, and he was no genius at reading human moods, but he was sure there was something wrong. Anu, the lad who took Boaaz out to the desert, kept his distance as far as possible; and barely spoke. Perhaps the child was disturbed by the habit of *looking behind him* that Boaaz had developed. It must look strange, since he was old and it was difficult. But he couldn't help himself.

One morning, when he went to make his usual guilty inspection of that inner courtyard, the station's manager was there: staring at a section of wall where strange marks had appeared, blistered weals like raw flesh wounds in the ceramic skin.

"Do you know what's causing that effect?" asked Boaaz.

"Can't be weathering, not in here. Bugs in the ceramic, we'll have to get it reconfigured. Can't understand it. It's supposed to last forever, that stuff."

"But the station is very old, isn't it? Older than Butterscotch itself. You don't think the pretty rocks in here had anything to do with the damage?" Boaaz tried a rumble of laughter. "You know, child, sometimes I think they move around at night!"

The rock group was nowhere near the walls. It never was, by daylight.

"I am twenty years old," said the Martian, with an odd look. "Old enough to know when to stay away from bad luck, messir. Excuse me."

He hurried away, leaving Boaaz very puzzled and uneasy.

He had come here to collect minerals, therefore he would collect minerals. What he needed was an adventure, to clear his head. It would be foolhardy to brave the Empty Quarter of Mars in the company of a frightened child: perhaps equally foolhardy to set out alone. He decided he would offer to go exploring with the Aleutian, who took a well-equiped station buggy out into the wild red yonder almost every day.

Conrad would surely welcome this suggestion.

Conrad was reluctant. He spoke so warmly of the dangers, and with such concern for the Shet's age and unsuitable metabolism, that Boaaz's pride was touched. He was old, but he was strong. The nerve of this stripling, suggesting there were phenomena on Mars that an adult male Shet couldn't handle! Even if the stripling *was* a highly experienced young immortal—

"I see you prefer to 'go solo.' I would hate to disturb your privacy. We must compare routes, so that our paths do not cross."

"The virtual tour is very, very good," said the Aleutian. "You can easily and safely explore the ancient 'Arabia Terra' with a fully customised avatar, from the comfort of your hotel room."

"Stop talking like a guidebook," rumbled Boaaz. "I've survived in tougher spots than this. I shall make my arrangements with the station today."

"You won't mind me mentioning that all the sentient biped peoples of Shet are basically aquatic—"

"Not since our oceans shrank, about two million standard years ago. I am not an Aleutian, I have no memory of those days. And if I *were* 'basically aquatic,' that would mean I am already an expert at living outside my natural element."

"Oh well," said Conrad at last, ungraciously. "If you're determined, I suppose it's safer if I keep you where I can see you."

The notable features of the ancient uplands were to the north: luckily the opposite direction from Isabel's dour location. The two buggies set out at sunrise, locked in tandem; Conrad in the lead. As they passed through the particulate barrier of the Enclosure, Boaaz felt a welcome stirring of excitement. His outside cams still showed quiet mining fields, ever-present stromatolites: but already the landscape was becoming more rugged. He felt released from bondage. A few refreshing trips like this, and he would no longer be haunted. He would no longer be compelled to *turn*, feeling those ornate chairs lined up behind him, knowing that the repulsive creature of his dream was taking shape—

"*It's a dusty one,*" remarked Conrad, over the intercom. "*Often is, around here, in the northern 'summer.' And there's a storm warning. We shouldn't go far, just a loop around the first buttes, a short EVA, and home again. . . .*"

Boaaz recovered himself with a chuckle. His cams showed a calm sky, healthily tinged with blue; his exterior monitors were recording the friendliest conditions known to Mars. "*I'm getting 'hazardous storm probability' at near zero,*" he rumbled in reply. "*Uncouple and return if you wish. I shall make a day of it.*"

Silence. Boaaz felt that he'd won the battle.

Conrad had let slip a few too many knowledgeable comments about Martian mineralogy, in their friendly chats. Of course he wasn't "purely a tourist": he was a rock hound himself. He'd been scouring the wilds for sites the Guidebook and the Colonial Government Mineral Survey had missed, or undervalued. Obviously he'd found something good, and he didn't want to share.

Boaaz sympathised wholeheartedly. But a little teasing wouldn't come amiss, as a reward for being so untrusting and secretive!

The locked buggys dropped into layered craters, climbed gritty steppes. Boaaz buried himself in strange-sounding English-language wish lists; compiled long ago, in preparation for this trip. *Hematite nodules, volcanic olivines, exotic basalts, Mössbauer patterns, tektites, barite roses.* But whatever he carried back from the Red Planet, across such a staggering distance, would be treasure—bound to fill his fellow hounds at home with delight and envy.

Behind him the empty chairs were ranged in judgement. That which waits at the gates was taking form. Boaaz needed to look over his shoulder but he did not turn. He knew he couldn't move quickly enough, and only the sleek desert-survival fittings of the buggy would mock him—

Escaping from ugly reverie, he noticed that Conrad was deviating freely from their pre-logged route. Most unsafe! But Boaaz didn't protest. There was no need for concern. They had life support, and Desert Rescue Service beacons that couldn't be disabled. He examined his CGMS maps instead. There was nothing *marked* that would explain Conrad's diversion: how interesting! What if the Aleutian's find was "significantly anomalous," or commercially valuable? If so, they were legally bound to leave it untouched, beacon it, and report it—

But I shan't pry, thought Boaaz. He maintained intercom silence, as did Conrad, until at last the locked buggys halted. The drivers disembarked. The Aleutian, with typical bravado, was dressed as if he'd been optimised before birth for life on Mars: the most lightweight air supply; a minimal squeeze-suit under his Aleutian-style desert thermals. Boaaz removed his helmet.

"I hope you enjoyed the scenic route," said Conrad, with a strange glint in his eye. "I hate to be nannied, don't you? We are not children."

"*Hmm.* I found your navigation, *ahaam,* enlightening."

The Aleutian seemed to be thinking hard about his next move.

"So you want to stop here, my friend?" asked Boaaz, airily. "Good! I suggest we go our separate ways, rendezvous later for the return journey?"

"That would be fine," said Conrad. "I'll call you."

Boaaz rode his buggy around an exquisite tholeiitic basalt group—a little too big to pack. He disembarked, took a chipping, and analysed it. The spectrometer results were unremarkable: the sum is greater than the parts. Often the elemental makeup, the age, and even the extreme conditions of its creation, can give no hint as to why a rock is beautiful. His customised suit was supple. He felt easier in it than he did in his own, ageing hide: and youthfully *weightless*—without the discomfiting loss of control of weightlessness itself. Not far away he could see a glittering pool, like a mirage of surface water that might mark a field of broken geodes. Or a surface deposit of rare spherulites. But he wanted to know what the Aleutian had found. He wanted to know so badly that in the end he succumbed to temptation, got back in the buggy and returned to the rendezvous: feeling like a naughty child.

Conrad's buggy stood alone. Conrad was nowhere in sight, and no footprints lead away from a nondescript gritstone outcrop. For a moment Boaaz feared something uncanny, then he realised the obvious solution. Still consumed by naughty curiosity, he pulled the emergency release on Conrad's outer hatch. The buggy's life-support generator shifted into higher gear with a whine, but the Aleutian was too occupied to notice. He sat in the body-clasping driver's seat, eyes closed, head immobilised, his skull in the quivering grip of a cognitive scanner field. A compact flatbed scanner nestled in the passenger seat. Under its shimmering virtual dome lay some gritstone fragments. They didn't look anything special, but something about them roused memories. Ancient images, a historical controversy, from before Mars was first settled—

Boaaz quietly maneuvered his bulk over to Conrad's impromptu virtual-lab, and studied the fragments carefully, under magnification.

He was profoundly shocked.

"What are you doing, Conrad?"

The Aleutian opened his eyes, and took in the situation.

The wise immortals stay at home. Immortals who mix with lesser beings are dangerous characters, because they just don't care. Conrad was completely brazen.

"What does it look like? I'm digitising pretty Martians for my scrapbook."

"You aren't *digitising* anything. You have taken *biotic traces* from an unmapped site. You are translating them into *information-space code,* with the intent of removing them from Mars, hidden in your consciousness. *That* is absolutely illegal!"

"Oh, grow up. It's a scam. I'm not kidnapping Martian babies. I'm not even kidnapping ancient fossilised bacteria, just scraps of plain old rock. But fools will pay wonderfully high prices for them. Where's the harm?"

"You have no shame, but this time you've gone too far. You are not a collector, you're a common thief, and I shall turn you in."

"I don't think so, Reverend. We logged out as partners today, didn't we? And you are known as an avid collector. Give me credit, I tried to get you to leave me alone, but you wouldn't. Now it's just too bad."

Boaaz's nostril slits flared wide, his gullet opened in a blueish gape of rage. He controlled himself, struggling to maintain dignity. "I'll make my own way back."

He resumed his helmet.

Before long his anger cooled. He recognised his own ignoble impulse to spy on a fellow collector. He recognised that perhaps Conrad's crime was not truly wicked, just very, very naughty. Nevertheless, those controversial "biotic traces" were sacred. The nerve of that young Aleutian! Assuming that Boaaz would be so afraid of being smeared in an unholy scandal, he would make no report—

When this got out! What would the Archbishop think!

Yet what if he *did* keep quiet? Conrad had come to Butterscotch with a plan, no doubt he had ways of fooling the neurological scanners at the spaceport. If Conrad wasn't going to get caught, and nobody was going to be injured—

What should he do?

That which waits at the gates was taking shape in an empty chair. It waits for those who deny good and evil, and separates them from the Void, forever—

He could not think clearly. Conrad's shameless behaviour became confused with the nightmares, the disturbed sleep and uneasy wakening. Those marks on the wall of the inner courtyard . . . He must have room, he could not bear this crowded confinement. He stopped the buggy, checked his gear, and disembarked.

The sky of Mars arced above him, the slightly fish-eyed horizon giving it a bulging look, like the whitish cornea of a great, blind eye. Dust suffused the view through his visor with streaks of blood. He was in an eroded crater, which could be a dangerous feature. But no warnings had flashed up, and the buggy wasn't settling. He stepped down: his boots found crust in a few centimeters. Gastropods crept about, in the distance he could see a convocation of trucks: he was back in the mining fields. He watched a small machine as it climbed a stromatolite spire, and "defecated" on the summit.

Inside that spoil-tower, in the moisture and chemical warmth of the chewed waste, the real precursors were at work. All over the mining regions, "stromatolites" were spilling out oxygen. Some day there would be complex life here, in unknown forms. The Martians were bringing a new biosphere to birth, from native organic chemistry alone. Absurd superstition, absurd patience. It made one wonder if the settlers really *wanted* to change their cold, unforgiving desert world—

A shadow flicked across his view. Alarmed, he checked the sky: fast moving cloud meant a storm. But the sky was cloudless; the declining sun cast a rosy, tourist-brochure glow over the landscape. Movement again, in the corner of his eye. Boaaz spun around, a maneuver that almost felled him, and saw a naked, biped figure, with a smooth head and disturbingly spindly limbs, standing a few metres away: almost invisible against the tawny ground. It seemed to look straight at him, but the "face" was featureless—

The eyeless gaze was not hostile. The impossible creature seemed to Boaaz like a shadow cast by the future. A folktale, waiting for the babies who would run around the Martian countryside; and believe in it a little, and be happily frightened. Perhaps I've been afraid of nothing, thought Boaaz, hopefully. After all, what did it *do*, the horrid thing I almost saw in that chair? It reached out to me, perhaps quite harmlessly . . . But there was something wrong. The eyeless figure trembled, folded down, and vanished like spilled water. Now he saw that the whole crater was stirring. Under the surface shadow creatures were fleeing, limbs flashing in the dust that was their habitat. Something had terrified them. Not Boaaz, the thing behind him. It had hunted him down and found him here, far from all help.

Slowly, dreadfully slowly, he turned. He saw what was there.

He tried to speak, he tried to pray. But the holy words were meaningless, and horror seized his mind. His buggy had vanished, the beacon on his chest refused to respond to his hammering. He ran in circles, tawny devils rising in coils from around his feet. He was lost, he would die, and then it would devour him—

Hours later, young Conrad (struck by an uncharacteristic fit of responsibility) came searching for the old fellow, tracking his suit beacon. Night had fallen, deathly cold. The High Priest crouched in a shallow gully, close to the crater where Conrad had spotted his deserted buggy; his suit scratched and scarred as if something had been trying to tear it off him, his parched, gaping screams locked inside his helmet—

The High Priest struggled free from troubling dreams, and was bewildered to find his friend the Aleutian curled informally on the floor beside his bed. "Hallo," said Conrad, sitting up. "I detect the light of reason. Are you with us again, Reverend?"

"What are you doing in my room—?"

"Do you remember anything? How we brought you in?"

"*Ahm, haham.* Overdid it a little, didn't I? Oxygen starvation panic attack, thanks for that, Conrad, most grateful. Must get some breakfast. Excuse me."

"We need to talk."

Boaaz drew his massive head down into his neck-folds, the Shet gesture that stood for refusal, but also submission. "I'm not going to tell anyone."

"I knew you'd see sense. No, this is about something serious. We'll talk this evening. You must be starving, and you need to rest."

Boaaz checked his eyeball screen, and found that he had lost a day and a night. He ate, rehydrated his hide, and retired to bed again: to reflect. The Mighty Void had a place for certain psychic phenomena, but he had no explanation for a "ghost" with teeth and claws, a bodiless thing that could rend carbon fibre . . . In a state between dream and waking, he trudged again the chance avenue of stromatolites. Vapour hung in the thin air, the spindly towers bent their heads in menace. Isabel Jewel's module waited for him, so charged with fear and dread it was like a ripe fruit, about to burst.

The miners and their families were subdued tonight. The sound of their merrymaking was a dull murmur in the private lounge, where Boaaz and the Aleutian met. The residents' bar steward arranged a nested "trolley" of drinks and snacks, and left them alone. Boaaz offered his snifter case, but the Aleutian declined.

"We need to talk," he reminded the old priest. "About Isabel Jewel."

"I thought we were going to discuss my scare in the desert."

"We are."

Strengthened by his reflections, Boaaz summoned up an indignant growl. "I can't discuss my parishioner with you. Absolutely not!"

"Before we managed to drug you to sleep," said Conrad, firmly, "you were babbling, telling us a horrible, uncanny story . . . You went into detail. You weren't speaking English, but I'm afraid Yarol understood you pretty well. Don't worry, he'll be discreet. The locals don't meddle with Isabel Jewel."

"Yarol?"

"The station manager. Sensible type for a human. You met him the other day in your courtyard, I believe. Looking at some nasty marks on the wall?"

The Shet's mighty head sank between his shoulders. "*Ahaam*, in my delirium, what sort of thing did I say?"

"Plenty."

Conrad leaned close, and spoke in "Silence"—a form of telepathy the immortals only practiced among themselves; or with the rare mortals who could defend themselves against its power. <My friend, you must listen to me. What we share will not leave this room. You're in great danger, and I think you know it.>

The old priest shuddered, and surrendered.

"You underestimate me, and my calling. I am not in *danger*!"

"We'll see about that . . . Tell me, Boaaz, what is a 'bear'?"

"I have no idea," said the old priest, mystified.

"I thought not. A *bear* is a wild creature native to Earth, big, shaggy, fierce. Rather frightening. Here, catch—"

Inexplicably, the Aleutian tossed a drinking beaker straight at Boaaz: who had to react swiftly, to avoid being smacked in the face—

"Tentacles," said Conrad. "I don't think you find them disgusting, do you? It's an evolutionary quirk. Your people absorbed some wiggly-armed ocean creatures into your body-plan, aeons ago, and they became your 'delicates.' Yet what you saw in Isabel Jewel's module was '*a bear with tentacles*,' and it filled you with horror. Just as if you were a human, with an innate terror of snakey-looking things."

Boaaz set the beaker down. "What of it? I don't know what you're getting at. That vision, however I came by it, was merely a nightmare. In the material world I have visited her *once*, and saw nothing at all strange."

"A nightmare, hm? And what if we are dealing with someone whose *nightmares* can roam around, hunt you down and tear you apart?"

Boaaz noticed that his pressure suit was hanging on the wall. The slashes and gouges were healing over (a little late for the occupant, had the attacker persisted!). He vaguely remembered them taking it off him, exclaiming in horrified amazement.

"Tear me apart? Nonsense. I was hysterical, I freely admit. I suppose I must have rolled about, over some sharp rocks."

The Aleutian's black eyes were implacable. "I suppose I'd better start at the beginning . . . I was intrigued by the scraps you read out from 'Isabel Jewel's' file. Somebody *suspected* of insanity. That's a very grim suspicion, in a certain context. When I saw how changed and disturbed you were, after your parish visit, I instructed my Speranza agent to see what it could dig up about an 'Isabel Jewel,' lately settled on Mars."

"You had no authority to do that!"

"Why not? Everything I'm going to tell you is in the public domain, all my agent had to do was to make the connection—which is buried, but easy to exhume—between 'Isabel Jewel,' and a human called 'Ilia Markham' who was involved in a transit disaster, some thirty or so standard years ago. A starship called *The Golden Bough*, belonging to a company called the World State Line, left Speranza on a scheduled transit to the Blue Torus Port. Her passengers arrived safely. The eight members of the Active Complement, I mean the crew, did not. Five of them had vanished, two were hideously dead. The Navigator survived, despite horrific injuries, long enough to claim they'd been murdered. Someone had smuggled an appalling monster on board, and turned it loose in the Active Complement's quarters—"

There were chairs, meant for humans, around the walls of the lounge. The Aleutian and the Shet preferred a cushioned recess in the floor. Boaaz noticed that he no longer needed to *look behind him*. That phase was over.

"There are no 'black box' records to consult, after a transit disaster," the Aleutian went on. "Nothing *can* be known about the false duration period. The crew construct a pseudo-reality for themselves, as they guide the ship through that 'interval' when time does not pass: which vanishes like a dream. But the Navigator's accusation was taken seriously. There was an inquiry, and suspicion fell on Ilia Markham, a dealer in antiques. Her trip out to Speranza had been her first transit. On the return 'journey' she insisted on staying awake, citing a mental allergy to the virtual entertainment. A *phobia*, I think humans call it. As you probably know, this meant that she joined the Active Complement, in their pseudo-reality 'quarters.' Yet she was unharmed. She remembered nothing, but she was charged with involuntary criminal insanity, on neurological evidence."

Transit disasters were infrequent, since the new Aleutian ships had come into service; but Boaaz knew of them. And he had heard that casualties whose injuries were not physical were very cruelly treated on Earth.

"What a terrible story. Was there a . . . Did the inquiry suggest any *reason* why the poor woman's mind might have generated something so monstrous?"

"I see you *do* know what I'm getting at," remarked Conrad, with a sharp look. The old priest's head sank obstinately further, and he made no comment. "Yes, there was something. In her youth Markham had been an indentured servant, the concubine of a rich collector with a nasty reputation. When he died she inherited his treasures, and there were strong rumours she'd helped him on his way. The prosecution didn't accuse her of murder, they just held that she'd been carrying a burden of unresolved trauma—and the Active Complement had paid the price."

"Eight of them," muttered Boaaz. "And one more. Yes, yes, I see."

"The World State Line was the real guilty party, they'd allowed her to travel awake. But it was Ilia Markham who was consigned for life—on suspicion, she was never charged—to a Secure Hospital. *Just in case* she still possessed the powers that had been thrust on her by the terrible energies of the Buonarotti Torus."

"Was there a . . . ? Was there, *ahaam*, any identifying mark of her status?"

"There would be a *tattoo*, a string of symbols, on her forearm, Reverend. You told us, in your 'delirium,' that you'd seen similar marks."

"Go on," rumbled Boaaz. "Get to the end of it."

"Many years later there was a review of doubtful 'criminal insanity' cases. Ilia Markham was one of those released. She was given a new name and shipped off to

Mars, with all her assets. They were still a little afraid of her, it seems, although her cognitive scans were normal. They didn't want her or anything she possessed. There's no Buonarotti Torus in Mars orbit: I suppose that was the reasoning."

The old priest was silent, the folds of hide over his eyes furrowed deep. Then his brow relaxed, and he seemed to give himself a shake. "This has been most enlightening, Conrad. I am, in a sense, much relieved."

"You no longer believe you're being pursued by aggressive rocks? Harassed by imaginary Ancient Martians? You understand that, barbaric though it seems, your old mad woman probably should have stayed in that Secure Hospital?"

"I don't admit that at all! In my long experience, this is not the first time I've met what are known as 'psychic phenomena.' I have known effective premonitions, warning dreams; instances of telepathy. This 'haunting' I've suffered, this vivid way I've shared 'Isabel Jewel's' mental distress, will be very helpful when I talk to her again . . . I *do not* believe in the horrible idea of criminal insanity. The unfortunate few who have been 'driven insane' by a transit disaster are a danger only to themselves."

"I felt the same, but your recent experiences have shaken my common sense." The Aleutian reached to take a snifter, and paused in the act, his nasal flaring in alarm. "Boaaz, dear fellow, *stay away* from her. You'll be safe, and the effects will fade, if you stay away."

Boaaz looked at the ruined pressure suit. "Yet I was not injured," he murmured. "I was only frightened . . . Now for my side of the story. I am a priest, and the woman is dying. It's her heart, I think, and I don't think she has long. She is in mental agony—as people sometimes are, quite without need, if they believe they have lived an evil life—not in fear of death but of what may come after. I can help her, and it is my duty. After all, we are nowhere near a Torus."

The Aleutian stared at him, no longer seeming at all a mischievous adolescent. The old priest felt buffeted by the immortal's stronger will: but he stood firm. "There are wrongs nobody can put right," said Conrad, urgently. "The universe is more pitiless than you know. *Don't* go back."

"I must." Boaaz rose, ponderously. He patted the Aleutian's sloping shoulder, with the sensitive tips of his right-hand delicates. "I think I'll turn in. Goodnight."

Boaaz had been puzzled by the human woman's insistence that he should return "in ten days, in the evening, at the full moon." The little moons of Mars zipped around too fast for their cycles to be significant. He had looked up the Concordance (Earth's calendar was still important to the colony), and wondered if the related date on Earth had been important to her, in the past.

By the time he left his jitney, in the lonely outskirts of Butterscotch, he'd thought of another explanation. People who know they are dying, closely attuned to their failing bodies, may know better than any doctor when the end will come. She believes she will die tonight, he thought. And she doesn't want to die alone. He quickened his pace, and then turned to look back—not impelled by menace, but simply to reassure himself that the jitney hadn't taken itself off.

He could not see the tiny lights of Butterscotch. The vapours and the swift twilight had caused a strange effect: a mirage of great black hills, or mountains, spread along the horizon. Purple woods like storm clouds crowded at their base, and down from the hills came a pale, winding road. There appeared to be a group of figures moving on it, descending swiftly. The mirage shifted, the perspective changed, and Boaaz was now *among* the hills. Black walls stood on either side of the grey road, the figures rushed towards him from a vanishing point; from an infinite distance at impossible speed. He tried to count them, but they were moving too fast. He realised, astonished, that he was going to be trampled, and even as he formulated that thought they were upon him. They rushed over him, and were swallowed in a greater darkness that swallowed Boaaz too. He was buried, engulfed, overwhelmed by a foul stench and a frightful, suffocating pressure—

He struggled, as if trying to rise from very deep water: and then the pressure was gone. He had fallen on his face. He picked himself up with difficulty, and checked himself and his gear for damage. "The dead do not walk," he muttered. "Absurd superstition!" But the grumbling tone became a prayer, and he could hear his own voice shake as he recited the Consolation. *"There is no punishment, there is only the Void, embracing all, accepting all. The monsters at the gates are illusion. There are no realms beyond death, we shall not be devoured, the Void is gentle . . ."*

The mirage had dissipated, but the vapours had not. He was positively walking through a fog, and each step was a mysterious struggle, as if he were wading through a fierce running tide. *Here I am for the third time,* he told himself, encouragingly, and then remembered that the second visit had been in a nightmare. A horror went through him: was he dreaming now? Perhaps the thought should have been comforting, but it was very frightening indeed: and then someone coughed, or choked: not *behind* him, but close *beside* him, invisible in the fog.

Startled, he upped his head and shoulder lights. "Is anybody there?"

The lights only increased his confusion, making a kind of glory on the mist around him. His own shadow was very close, oversized, and optical illusion gave it strange proportions: a distinct neck, a narrow waist, a skeletal thinness. It turned. He saw the thing he had seen in the desert. A human male, with small eyes close-set, a jutting nose, lined cheeks, and a look of such utter malevolence it stopped Boaaz's blood. Its lower jaw dropped. It had far too many teeth, and a terrible, *appallingly* wide gape. It raised its jagged claws and reared towards him. Boaaz screamed into his breather. The monster rushed over him, swamped him, and was gone.

It was over. He was alone, shaken in body and soul. The pinprick lights of the town had reappeared behind him: ahead was that avenue of teetering stromatolites. "Horrible mirage!" he announced, trying to convince himself. He was breathing in gasps. The outer lock of the old woman's module stood open, as if she had seen him coming. The inner lock was shut. He opened it, praying that he would find her still alive. Alive, and sharing with him, by some mystery, the nightmare visions of her needless distress; that he knew he could conquer—

The chairs had moved. They were grouped in a circle around the stove in the centre of the room. He counted: yes, he had remembered rightly, there were eight. The "old, mad" human woman sat in her own chair, withered like a crumpled shell, her features still contorted in pain and terror. He could see that she had been dead for some time. The ninth chair was drawn up close to hers. Boaaz saw the impression of a human body, printed in the dented cushions of the back and seat. *It had been here.*

The fallen jaw. Too many teeth. Had it devoured her, was it sated now? And the others, its victims from *The Golden Bough,* what was their fate? To dwell within that horror, forever? He would never know what was real, and what was not. He only knew that he had come too late for Isabel Jewel (he could not think of her as "Ilia Markham"). She had gone to join her company: or they had come to fetch her.

Conrad and the manager of the Old Station arrived about an hour later, summoned by the priest's alarm call. Yarol, who doubled as the town's Community Police Officer, called the ambulance team to take away the woman's remains, and began to make the forensic record—a formality required after any sudden death. Conrad tried to get Boaaz to tell him what had happened.

"I have had a fall," was all the old priest would say. "I have had a bad fall."

Boaaz returned to Opportunity, where his Residence had been successfully decoded. He was in poor health for a while. By the time he'd recovered, Conrad the Aleutian had long moved on to other schemes. But Boaaz stayed on Mars, his pleasant retirement on Shet indefinitely postponed—although he had tendered his resignation to the Archbishop as soon as he could rise from his bed. Later, he would tell people that the death of an unfortunate woman, once involved in a transit disaster, had convinced him that there is an afterlife. The Martians, being human, were puzzled that the good-hearted old "alien" seemed to find this so distressing.

The smell of orange groves

LAVIE TIDHAR

Lavie Tidhar grew up on a kibbutz in Israel, has traveled widely in Africa and Asia, and has lived in London, the South Pacific island of Vanuatu, and Laos. He is the winner of the 2003 Clarke-Bradbury Prize (awarded by the European Space Agency), was the editor of Michael Marshall Smith: The Annotated Bibliography, *as well as the anthologies* A Dick & Jane Primer for Adults *and* The Apex Book of World SF. *He is the author of the linked story collection* HebrewPunk, *the novella chapbooks* An Occupation of Angels, Gorel and the Pot-Bellied God, Cloud Permutations, Jesus and the Eightfold Path, *and, with Nir Yaniv, the novel* The Tel Aviv Dossier. *A prolific short story writer, his stories have appeared in* Interzone, Clarkesworld, Apex Magazine, Sci Fiction, Strange Horizons, Chizine, Postscripts, Fantasy Magazine, Nemonymous, Infinity Plus, Aeon, The Book of Dark Wisdom, Fortean Bureau, *and elsewhere, and have been translated into seven languages. His latest novels include* The Bookman *and its sequel,* Camera Obscura, *and* Osama: A Novel. *Coming up is a new novel,* The Great Game. *After a spell in Tel Aviv, he's currently living back in England again.*

Here he offers us a study of the machine-augmented persistence of memory across generations, set against a bizarre, vividly portrayed future Tel Aviv.

On the roof the solar panels were folded in on themselves, still asleep, yet uneasily stirring, as though they could sense the imminent coming of the sun. Boris stood on the edge of the roof. The roof was flat and the building's residents, his father's neighbours, had, over the years, planted and expanded an assortment of plants, in pots of clay and aluminium and wood, across the roof, turning it into a high-rise tropical garden.

It was quiet up there and, for the moment, still cool. He loved the smell of late-blooming jasmine, it crept along the walls of the building, climbing tenaciously high, spreading out all over the old neighbourhood that surrounded Central Station. He took a deep breath of night air and released it slowly, haltingly, watching the lights of the space port: it rose out of the sandy ground of Tel Aviv, the shape of an hourglass, and the slow moving suborbital flights took off and landed, like moving stars, tracing jewelled flight paths in the skies.

He loved the smell of this place, this city. The smell of the sea to the west, that wild scent of salt and open water, seaweed and tar, of suntan lotion and people. He loved to watch the solar surfers in the early morning, with spread transparent wings gliding on the winds above the Mediterranean. Loved the smell of cold conditioned air leaking out of windows, of basil when you rubbed it between your fingers, loved the smell of shawarma rising from street level with its heady mix of spices, turmeric and cumin dominating, loved the smell of vanished orange groves from far beyond the urban blocks of Tel Aviv or Jaffa.

Once it had all been orange groves. He stared out at the old neighbourhood, the peeling paint, box-like apartment blocks in old-style Soviet architecture crowded in with magnificent early-twentieth-century Bauhaus constructions, buildings made to look like ships, with long curving graceful balconies, small round windows, flat roofs like decks, like the one he stood on—

Mixed amongst the old buildings were newer constructions, Martian-style co-op buildings with drop-chutes for lifts, and small rooms divided and subdivided inside, many without any windows—

Laundry hanging as it had for hundreds of years, off wash lines and windows, faded blouses and shorts blowing in the wind, gently. Balls of lights floated in the streets down below, dimming now, and Boris realised the night was receding, saw a blush of pink and red on the edge of the horizon and knew the sun was coming.

He had spent the night keeping vigil with his father. Vlad Chong, son of Weiwei Zhong (Zhong Weiwei in the Chinese manner of putting the family name first) and of Yulia Chong, née Rabinovich. In the tradition of the family Boris, too, was given a Russian name. In another of the family's traditions, he was also given a second, Jewish name. He smiled wryly, thinking about it. Boris Aaron Chong, the heritage and weight of three shared and ancient histories pressing down heavily on his slim, no longer young shoulders.

It had not been an easy night.

Once it had all been orange groves . . . He took a deep breath, that smell of old asphalt and lingering combustion-engine exhaust fumes, gone now like the oranges yet still, somehow, lingering, a memory-scent.

He'd tried to leave it behind. The family's memory, what he sometimes, privately, called the Curse of the Family Chong, or Weiwei's Folly.

He could still remember it. Of course he could. A day so long ago, that Boris Aaron Chong himself was not yet an idea, an I-loop that hasn't yet been formed . . .

It was in Jaffa, in the Old City on top of the hill, above the harbour. The home of the Others.

Zhong Weiwei cycled up the hill, sweating in the heat. He mistrusted these narrow winding streets, both of the Old City itself and of Ajami, the neighbourhood that had at last reclaimed its heritage. Weiwei understood this place's conflicts very well. There were Arabs and Jews and they wanted the same land and so they fought. Weiwei understood land, and how you were willing to die for it.

But he also knew the concept of land had changed. That *land* was a concept less of a physicality now, and more of the mind. Recently, he had invested some of his money in an entire planetary system in the Guilds of Ashkelon games-universe.

Soon he would have children—Yulia was in her third trimester already—and then grandchildren, and great-grandchildren, and so on down the generations, and they would remember Weiwei, their progenitor. They would thank him for what he'd done, for the real estate both real and virtual, and for what he was hoping to achieve today.

He, Zhong Weiwei, would begin a dynasty, here in this divided land. For he had understood the most basic of aspects, he alone saw the relevance of that foreign enclave that was Central Station. Jews to the north (and his children, too, would be Jewish, which was a strange and unsettling thought), Arabs to the south, now they have returned, reclaimed Ajami and Menashiya, and were building New Jaffa, a city towering into the sky in steel and stone and glass. Divided cities, like Akko, and Haifa, in the north, and the new cities sprouting in the desert, in the Negev and the Arava.

Arab or Jew, they needed their immigrants, their foreign workers, their Thai and Filipino and Chinese, Somali and Nigerian. And they needed their buffer, that in-between-zone that was Central Station, old South Tel Aviv, a poor place, a vibrant place—most of all, a liminal place.

And he would make it his home. His, and his children's, and his children's children. The Jews and the Arabs understood family, at least. In that they were like the Chinese—so different to the Anglos, with their nuclear families, strained relations, all living separately, alone . . . This, Weiwei swore, would not happen to his children.

At the top of the hill he stopped, and wiped his brow from the sweat with the cloth handkerchief he kept for that purpose. Cars went past him, and the sound of construction was everywhere. He himself worked on one of the buildings they were erecting here, a diasporic construction crew, small Vietnamese and tall Nigerians and pale solid Transylvanians, communicating by hand signals and Asteroid Pidgin (though that had not yet been in widespread use at that time) and automatic translators through their nodes. Weiwei himself worked the exoskeleton suits, climbing up the tower blocks with spider-like grips, watching the city far down below and looking out to sea, and distant ships . . .

But today was his day off. He had saved money—some to send, every month, to his family back in Chengdu, some for his soon to be growing family here. And the rest for this, for the favour to be asked of the Others.

Folding the handkerchief neatly away, he pushed the bike along the road and into the maze of alleyways that was the Old City of Jaffa. The remains of an ancient Egyptian fort could still be seen there, the gate had been refashioned a century before, and the hanging orange tree still hung by chains, planted within a heavy, egg-shaped stone basket, in the shade of the walls. Weiwei didn't stop, but kept going until he reached, at last, the place of the Oracle.

Boris looked at the rising sun. He felt tired, drained. He kept his father company throughout the night. His father, Vlad, hardly slept anymore, he sat for hours in his armchair, a thing worn and full of holes, dragged one day, years ago (the memory crystal clear in Boris's mind) with great effort and pride from Jaffa's flea market. Vlad's hands moved through the air, moving and rearranging invisible objects. He would not give Boris access into his visual feed. He barely communicated anymore. Boris suspected the objects were memories, that Vlad was trying to somehow fit them back together again. But he couldn't tell for sure.

Like Weiwei, Vlad had been a construction worker. He had been one of the people who had built Central Station, climbing up the unfinished gigantic structure, this space port that was now an entity unto itself, a miniature mall-nation to which neither Tel Aviv nor Jaffa could lay complete claim.

But that had been long ago. Humans lived longer now, but the mind grew old just the same, and Vlad's mind was older than his body. Boris, on the roof, went to the corner by the door. It was shaded by a miniature palm tree, and now the solar panels, too, were opening out, extending delicate wings, the better to catch the rising sun and provide shade and shelter to the plants.

Long ago, the resident association had installed a communal table and a samovar there, and each week a different flat took turns to supply the tea and the coffee and the sugar. Boris gently plucked leaves off the potted mint plant nearby, and made himself a cup of tea. The sound of boiling water pouring into the mug was soothing, and the smell of the mint spread in the air, fresh and clean, waking him up. He waited as the mint brewed; took the mug with him back to the edge of the roof. Looking down, Central Station—never truly asleep—was noisily waking up.

He sipped his tea, and thought of the Oracle.

The Oracle's name had once been Cohen, and rumour had it that she was a relation of St. Cohen of the Others, though no one could tell for certain. Few people today knew this. For three generations she had resided in the Old City, in that dark and quiet stone house, her and her Other alone.

The Other's name, or ident tag, was not known, which was not unusual, with Others.

Regardless of possible familial links, outside the stone house there stood a small shrine to St. Cohen. It was a modest thing, with random items of golden colour placed on it, and old, broken circuits and the like, and candles burning at all hours. Weiwei, when he came to the door, paused for a moment before the shrine, and lit a candle, and placed an offering—a defunct computer chip from the old days, purchased at great expense in the flea market down the hill.

Help me achieve my goal today, he thought, *help me unify my family and let them share my mind when I am gone.*

There was no wind in the Old City, but the old stone walls radiated a comforting coolness. Weiwei, who had only recently had a node installed, pinged the door and, a moment later, it opened. He went inside.

Boris remembered that moment as a stillness and at the same time, paradoxically, as a *shifting,* a sudden inexplicable change of perspective. His grandfather's memory glinted in the mind. For all his posturing, Weiwei was like an explorer in an unknown land, feeling his way by touch and instinct. He had not grown up with a node; he found it difficult to follow the Conversation, that endless chatter of human and machine feeds a modern human would feel deaf and blind without; yet he was a man who could sense the future as instinctively as a chrysalis can sense adulthood. He knew his children would be different, and their children different in their turn, but he equally knew there can be no future without a past—

"Zhong Weiwei," the Oracle said. Weiwei bowed. The Oracle was surprisingly young, or young-looking at any rate. She had short black hair and unremarkable features and pale skin and a golden prosthetic for a thumb, which made Weiwei shiver without warning: it was her Other.

"I seek a boon," Weiwei said. He hesitated, then extended forwards the small box. "Chocolates," he said, and—or was it just his imagination?—the Oracle smiled.

It was quiet in the room. It took him a moment to realise it was the Conversation, ceasing. The room was blocked to mundane network traffic. It was a safe-haven, and he knew it was protected by the high-level encryption engines of the Others. The Oracle took the box from him and opened it, selecting one particular piece with care and putting it in her mouth. She chewed thoughtfully for a moment and indicated approval by inching her head. Weiwei bowed again.

"Please," the Oracle said. "Sit down."

Weiwei sat down. The chair was high-backed and old and worn—from the flea market, he thought, and the thought made him feel strange, the idea of the Oracle shopping in the stalls, almost as though she were human. But of course, she *was* human. It should have made him feel more at ease, but somehow it didn't.

Then the Oracle's eyes subtly changed colour, and her voice, when it came, was different, rougher, a little lower than it's been, and Weiwei swallowed again. "What is it you wish to ask of us, Zhong Weiwei?"

It was her Other, speaking now. The Other, shotgun-riding on the human body, Joined with the Oracle, quantum processors running within that golden thumb . . . Weiwei, gathering his courage, said, "I seek a bridge."

The Other nodded, indicating for him to proceed.

"A bridge between past and future," Weiwei said. "A . . . continuity."

"Immortality," the Other said. It sighed. Its hand rose and scratched its chin, the golden thumb digging into the woman's pale flesh. "All humans want is immortality."

Weiwei shook his head, though he could not deny it. The idea of death, of dying, terrified him. He lacked faith, he knew. Many believed, belief was what kept humanity going. Reincarnation or the afterlife, or the mythical Upload, what they called being Translated—they were the same, they required a belief he did not possess, much as he may long for it. He knew that when he died, that would be it. The I-loop with the ident tag of Zhong Weiwei would cease to exist, simply and without fuss, and the universe would continue just as it always had. It was a terrible thing to contemplate, one's insignificance. For human I-loops, they were the universe's focal point, the object around which everything revolved. Reality was subjective. And yet that was an illusion, just as an I was, the human personality a composite machine compiled out of billions of neurons, delicate networks operating semi-independently in the grey matter of a human brain. Machines augmented it, but they could not preserve it, not forever. So yes, Weiwei thought. The thing that he was seeking was a vain thing, but it was also a *practical* thing. He took a deep breath and said, "I want my children to remember me."

Boris watched Central Station. The sun was rising now, behind the space port, and down below robotniks moved into position, spreading out blankets and crude, handwritten signs asking for donations, of spare parts or gasoline or vodka, poor creatures, the remnants of forgotten wars, humans cyborged and then discarded when they were no longer needed.

He saw Brother R. Patch-It, of the Church of Robot, doing his rounds—the Church tried to look after the robotniks, as it did after its small flock of humans. Robots were a strange missing link between human and Other, not fitting in either world—digital beings shaped by physicality, by bodies, many refusing the Upload in favour of their own, strange faith . . . Boris remembered Brother Patch-It, from childhood—the robot doubled-up as a *moyel*, circumcising the Jewish boys of the neighbourhood on the eighth day of their birth. The question of Who is a Jew had been asked not just about the Chong family, but of the robots too, and was settled long ago. Boris had fragmented memories, from the matrilineal side, predating Weiwei—the protests in Jerusalem, Matt Cohen's labs and the first, primitive Breeding Grounds, where digital entities evolved in ruthless evolutionary cycles:

Plaques waving on King George Street, a mass demonstration: *No to Slavery!* and *Destroy the Concentration Camp!* and so on, an angry mass of humanity coming together to protest the perceived enslavement of those first, fragile Others in their locked-down networks, Matt Cohen's laboratories under siege, his ragtag team of scientists, kicked out from one country after another before settling, at long last, in Jerusalem—

St. Cohen of the Others, they called him now. Boris lifted the mug to his lips and discovered it was empty. He put it down, rubbed his eyes. He should have slept. He was no longer young, could not go days without sleep, powered by stimulants and restless, youthful energy. The days when he and Miriam hid on this very same roof, holding each other, making promises they knew, even then, they couldn't keep . . .

He thought of her now, trying to catch a glimpse of her walking down Neve Sha'anan, the ancient paved pavilion of Central Station where she had her shebeen. It was hard to think of her, to *ache* like this, like a, like a *boy*. He had not come back because of her but, somewhere in the back of his mind, it must have been, the thought . . .

On his neck the aug breathed softly. He had picked it up in Tong Yun City, on Mars, in a backstreet off Arafat Avenue, in a no-name clinic run by a third-generation Martian Chinese, a Mr. Wong, who installed it for him.

It was supposed to have been bred out of the fossilized remains of micro bacterial Martian life-forms, but whether that was true no one knew for sure. It was strange having the aug. It was a parasite, it fed off of Boris, it pulsated gently against his neck, a part of him now, another appendage, feeding him alien thoughts, alien feelings, taking in turn Boris's human perspective and subtly *shifting* it, it was like watching your ideas filtered through a kaleidoscope.

He put his hand against the aug and felt its warm, surprisingly rough surface. It moved under his fingers, breathing gently. Sometimes the aug synthesised strange substances, they acted like drugs on Boris's system, catching him by surprise. At other times it shifted visual perspective, or even interfaced with Boris' node, the digital networking component of his brain, installed shortly after birth, without which one was worse than blind, worse than deaf, one was disconnected from the Conversation.

He had tried to run away, he knew. He had left home, had left Weiwei's memory, or tried to, for a while. He went into Central Station, and he rode the elevators to the very top, and beyond. He had left the Earth, beyond orbit, gone to the Belt, and to Mars, but the memories followed him, Weiwei's bridge, linking forever future and past . . .

"I wish my memory to live on, when I am gone."

"So do all humans," the Other said.

"I wish . . ." Gathering courage, he continued. "I wish for my family to *remember*," he said. "To learn from the past, to plan for the future. I wish my children to have my memories, and for their memories, in turn, to be passed on. I want my grandchildren and *their* grandchildren and onwards, down the ages, into the future, to remember this moment."

"And so it shall be," the Other said.

And so it was, Boris thought. The memory was clear in his mind, suspended like a dewdrop, perfect and unchanged. Weiwei had gotten what he asked for, and his memories were Boris's now, as were Vlad's, as were his grandmother Yulia's and his mother's, and all the rest of them—cousins and nieces and uncles, nephews and aunts, all sharing the Chong family's central reservoir of memory, each able to dip, instantaneously, into that deep pool of memories, into the ocean of the past.

Weiwei's Bridge, as they still called it, in the family. It worked in strange ways, sometimes, even far away, when he was working in the birthing clinics on Ceres, or walking down an avenue in Tong Yun City, on Mars, a sudden memory would form in his head, a new memory—Cousin Oksana's memories of giving birth for the first time, to little Yan—pain and joy mixing in with random thoughts, wondering if anyone had fed the dog, the doctor's voice saying, "Push! Push!" the smell of sweat, the beeping of monitors, the low chatter of people outside the door, and that indescribable feeling as the baby slowly emerged out of her . . .

He put down the mug. Down below Central Station was awake now, the neighbourhood stalls set with fresh produce, the market alive with sounds, the smell of smoke and chickens roasting slowly on a grill, the shouts of children as they went to school—

He thought of Miriam. Mama Jones, they called her now. Her father was Nigerian, her mother from the Philippines, and they had loved each other, when the world was young, loved in the Hebrew that was their childhood tongue, but were separated, not by flood or war but simply life, and the things it did to people. Boris worked the birthing clinics of Central Station, but there were too many memories here, memories like ghosts, and at last he rebelled, and went into Central Station and up, and onto an RLV that took him to orbit, to the place they called Gateway, and from there, first, to Lunar Port.

He was young, he had wanted adventure. He had tried to get away. Lunar Port, Ceres, Tong Yun . . . but the memories pursued him, and worst amongst them were his father's. They followed him through the chatter of the Conversation, compressed memories bouncing from one Mirror to the other, across space, at the speed of light, and so they remembered him here on Earth just as he remembered them there, and at last the weight of it became such that he returned.

He had been back in Lunar Port when it happened. He had been brushing his teeth, watching his face—not young, not old, a common enough face, the eyes Chinese, the facial features Slavic, his hair thinning a little—when the memory attacked him, suffused him—he dropped the toothbrush.

Not his father's memory, his nephew's, Yan: Vlad sitting in the chair, in his apartment, his father older than Boris remembered, thinner, and something that hurt him obscurely, that reached across space and made his chest tighten with pain—that clouded look in his father's eyes. Vlad sat without speaking, without acknowledging his nephew or the rest of them, who had come to visit him.

He sat there and his hands moved through the air, arranging and rearranging objects none could see.

"Boris!"

"Yan."

His nephew's shy smile. "I didn't think you were real."

Time-delay, moon-to-Earth round-trip, node-to-node. "You've grown."

"Yes, well . . ."

Yan worked inside Central Station. A lab on Level Five where they manufactured viral ads, airborne microscopic agents that transferred themselves from person to person, thriving in a closed-environment, air-conditioned system like Central Station, coded to deliver person-specific offers, organics interfacing with nodal equipment, all to shout *Buy. Buy. Buy.*

"It's your father."

"What happened?"

"We don't know."

That admission must have hurt Yan. Boris waited, silence eating bandwidth, silence on an Earth-moon return trip.

"Did you take him to the doctors?"

"You know we did."

"And?"

"They don't know."

Silence between them, silence at the speed of light, travelling through space.

"Come home, Boris," Yan said, and Boris marvelled at how the boy had grown, the man coming out, this stranger he did not know and yet whose life he could so clearly remember.

Come home.

That same day he packed his meagre belongings, checked out of the Libra, and had taken the shuttle to lunar orbit, and from there a ship to Gateway, and down, at last, to Central Station.

Memory like a cancer growing. Boris was a doctor, he had seen Weiwei Bridge for himself—that strange semi-organic growth that wove itself into the Chongs' cerebral cortex and into the grey matter of their brains, interfacing with their nodes, growing, strange delicate spirals of alien matter, an evolved technology, forbidden, Other. It was overgrowing his father's mind, somehow it had gotten out of control, it was growing like a cancer, and Vlad could not move for the memories.

Boris suspected but he couldn't know, just as he did not know what Weiwei had paid for this boon, what terrible fee had been extracted from him—that memory, and that alone, had been wiped clean—only the Other, saying, *And so it shall be*, and then, the next moment, Weiwei was standing outside and the door was closed and he blinked, there amidst the old stone walls, wondering if it had worked.

Once it had all been orange groves . . . He remembered thinking that, as he went out of the doors of Central Station, on his arrival, back on Earth, the gravity confusing and uncomfortable, into the hot and humid air outside. Standing under the eaves, he breathed in deeply, gravity pulled him down but he didn't care. It smelled just like he remembered, and the oranges, vanished or not, were still there, the famed Jaffa oranges that grew here when all this, not Tel Aviv, not Central Station, existed, when it was orange groves, and sand, and sea . . .

He crossed the road, his feet leading him, they had their own memory, crossing the road from the grand doors of Central Station to the Neve Sha'anan pedestrian street, the heart of the old neighbourhood, and it was so much smaller than he remembered, as a child it was a world and now it had shrunk—

Crowds of people, solar tuk-tuks buzzing along the road, tourists gawking, a memcordist checking her feed stats as everything she saw and felt and smelled was broadcast live across the networks, capturing Boris in a glance that went out to millions of indifferent viewers across the solar system—

Pickpockets, bored CS Security keeping an eye out, a begging robotnik with a missing eye and bad patches of rust on his chest, dark-suited Mormons sweating in the heat, handing out leaflets while on the other side of the road Elronites did the same—

Light rain, falling.

From the nearby market the shouts of sellers promising the freshest pomegranates, melons, grapes, bananas, in a café ahead old men playing backgammon, drinking small china cups of bitter black coffee, smoking *nargilas*—sheesha pipes—R. Patch-It walking slowly amidst the chaos, the robot an oasis of calm in the mass of noisy, sweaty humanity—

Looking, smelling, listening, *remembering*, so intensely he didn't at first see them, the woman and the child, on the other side of the road, until he almost ran into them—

Or they into him. The boy, dark skinned, with extraordinary blue eyes—the woman familiar, somehow, it made him instantly uneasy, and the boy said, with hope in his voice, "Are you my daddy?"

Boris Chong breathed deeply. The woman said, "Kranki!" in an angry, worried tone. Boris took it for the boy's name, or nickname—*Kranki* in Asteroid Pidgin meaning grumpy, or crazy, or strange . . .

Boris knelt beside the boy, the ceaseless movement of people around them forgotten. He looked into those eyes. "It's possible," he said. "I know that blue. It was popular three decades ago. We hacked an open-source version out of the trademarked Armani code . . ."

He was waffling, he thought. Why was he doing that? The woman, her familiarity disturbed him. A buzzing as of invisible mosquitoes, in his mind, a reshaping of his vision came flooding to him, out of his aug, the boy frozen beside him, smiling now, a large and bewildering and *knowing* smile—

The woman was shouting, he could hear it distantly, "Stop it! What are you doing to him?"

The boy was interfacing with his aug, he realised. The words came in a rush, he said, "You had no parents," to the boy. Recollection and shame mingling together. "You were labbed, right here, hacked together out of public property genomes and bits of black-market nodes." The boy's hold on his mind slackened. Boris breathed, straightened up. "*Nakaimas,*" he said, and took a step back, suddenly frightened.

The woman looked terrified, and angry. "Stop it," she said. "He's not—"

Boris was suddenly ashamed. "I know," he said. He felt confused, embarrassed. "I'm sorry." This mix of emotions, coming so rapidly they blended into each other, wasn't natural. Somehow the boy had interfaced with the aug and the aug, in turn, was feeding into Boris's mind. He tried to focus. He looked at the woman. Somehow it was important to him that she would understand. He said, "He can speak to my aug. Without an interface." Then, remembering the clinics, remembering his own work, before he left to go to space, he said, quietly, "I must have done a better job than I thought, back then."

The boy looked up at him with guileless, deep blue eyes. Boris remembered children like him, he had birthed many, so many . . . The clinics of Central Station were said to be on par with those of Yunan, even. But he had not expected *this*, this *interference*, though he had heard stories, on the asteroids, and in Tong Yun, the whispered word that used to mean black magic: *nakaimas*.

The woman was looking at him, and her eyes, he knew her eyes—

Something passed between them, something that needed no node, no digital encoding, something earlier, more human and more primitive, like a shock, and she said, "Boris? Boris Chong?"

He recognised her at the same time she did him, wonder replacing worry, wonder, too, at how he failed to recognise her, this woman of indeterminate years suddenly resolving, like two bodies occupying the same space, into the young woman he had loved, when the world was young.

"Miriam?" he said.

"It's me," she said.

"But you—"

"I never left," she said. "You did."

He wanted to go to her now. The world was awake, and Boris was alone on the roof of the old apartment building, alone and free, but for the memories. He didn't know what he would do about his father. He remembered holding his hand, once, when he was small, and Vlad had seemed so big, so confident and sure, and full of life. They had gone to the beach that day, it was a summer's day and in Menashiya Jews and Arabs and Filipinos all mingled together, the Muslim women in their long dark clothes and the children running shrieking in their underwear; Tel Aviv girls in tiny bikinis, sunbathing placidly; someone smoking a joint, and the strong smell of it wafting in the sea air; the lifeguard in his tower calling out trilingual instructions—"Keep to the marked area! Did anyone lose a child? Please come to the lifeguards *now*! You with the boat, head towards the Tel Aviv harbour and away from the swimming area!"—the words getting lost in the chatter, someone had parked their car and was blaring out beats from the stereo, Somali refugees were cooking a barbeque on the promenade's grassy area, a dreadlocked white guy was playing a guitar, and Vlad held Boris's hand as they went into the water, strong and safe, and Boris knew nothing would ever happen to him; that his father would always be there to protect him, no matter what happened.

The Iron Shirts

MICHAEL F. FLYNN

Born in Easton, Pennsylvania, Michael F. Flynn has a B.A. in math from La Salle University, an M.S. for work in topology from Marquette University, and works as an industrial quality engineer and statistician. Since his first sale there in 1984, Flynn has become a mainstay of Analog, *and one of their most frequent contributors. He has also made sales to* The Magazine of Fantasy & Science Fiction, Asimov's Science Fiction, Weird Tales, New Destinies, Alternate Generals, *and elsewhere, and is thought of as one of the best new "hard science" writers to enter the field in several decades. His books include* In the Country of the Blind, Fallen Angels *(a novel written in collaboration with Larry Niven and Jerry Pournelle),* Firestar, Rogue Star, Lodestar, Falling Stars, Eifelheim, The Wreck of the River of Stars, *and* The January Dancer. *His stories have been collected in* The Forest of Time: and Other Stories *and* The Nanotech Chronicles. *He's been a Hugo finalist several times and twice won Prometheus Awards, for* In the Country of the Blind *and* Fallen Angels. *His most recent books are the novels* Up Jim River *and* In the Lion's Mouth. *He now lives in Edison, N.J.*

Here he takes us to thirteenth-century Ireland for a complex alternate history tale, a subtle and complicated story of deadly political gamesmanship, full of betrayals, double crosses, and double double crosses.

GEANTRAÍ

The outriders were galloping in from both flanks and David ó Flynn pulled back on his pony's reins to wait halfway down the hillside. His companions imitated him, some yanking warbows from their scabbards and stringing them with thoughtless ease. The footmen lined up in a loose array, holding their javelins ready but with their thumbs not yet in the throwing loops. They had passed unmolested south of the bog country around Dun Mor, avoiding the Foreign-held lands, but one never knew. The heavens cried out the deaths of kings; but on earth in this Year of Grace twelve hundred and four and twenty, men planned those deaths in whispers.

Cill Cluanaigh rolled away fat and green from the base of the hill toward the broad expanse of Lough Corrib. From his position on the hillside, David could just make out the smudge of the lough's farther shore. Iar Connaught resembled nothing so much as a sullen, gray cloud on the horizon. Freshening, the breeze rippled the grass and raised a sparkling white chop from the lough, as if the grass were an emerald sea breaking on a shore of shattered glass.

The outriders signaled with the finger-ogham but David couldn't make out the numbers.

"A party of fourteen," said Gillapadraig, his principal man-of-trust. "Armed."

"Now, there is a surprise . . ." David glanced behind. "We'll move back," he said. "Just below the crest, not atop it." Such a position would provide the widest field for the archers.

On David's other side, Liam ó Flaherty shifted on his pony. "It's not a trap," he said. "Only an escort. Himself would not send me all the way into the Sliabh ua Fhlainn only to lure you into a trap."

"Would he not, then?" David replied distractedly. The western man spoke as if the Sliabh ua Fhlainn lay at the very ends of the earth. Yet if any land deserved that name, it was surely Iar Connaught. West of Lough Corrib they grew nothing but stones, and not very good stones at that. "Those horsemen may not be your own folk, but Rory's sons," he said. "Rumor trickled south with the melting snow: Turlough and Little Hugh have left The ó Neill's hospitality and have come back into the country to wrest the kingship from Aedh." He turned to Liam, all bland innocence. "Perhaps you did not hear of it out here in the West."

Liam grunted and said nothing. David faced forward, morosely satisfied at having his suspicions confirmed. Fools the sons of Rory might be to come back, but not such great fools as to ride openly about. They were hiding under the protection of some great lord, and what better place for hiding than at the very ends of the earth?

Ó Flaherty's stronghold squatted upon an island in the lough, distant from the shore and stoutly defended by a fleet of war boats. David considered how he might attack the place should the need arise. There was nothing ill between the ó Flynns and the ó Flahertys, but a prudent man kept his wits as sharp as his sword, lest he have need of either weapon. The walls were built of stone after the Foreigner fashion; but if there was anything of which The ó Flaherty had a sufficiency, it was stone.

By the time the party disembarked at the wooden dock below the stronghold, David had concluded that only a *siege* would be practical—and impractical as well. A hosting of Gaels could perform marvelous feats, but sitting on their backsides and waiting was not one of them. The very word *siege* was a foreign one, learned the hard way from the wrong ends of *trebuchets*.

In the courtyard, a ridge of turf had been built up and wooden planks laid atop to create a long table. Upon this a quantity of food had been spread: meats of all sorts: beef, pork, horse, poultry, salted fishes; milsén, wheat cakes and loaves; butter, sweet cream and soured cream, a variety of cheeses; milk—boiled, of course, and with honey added; beans and beets; two or three sorts of apples; and the three condiments: salt, leeks, and seaweed.

There were some strange foods set out, as well. Kernels of some large yellow grain mixed with a flat, round, pale-green bean. Lumpish brown things that he thought roots of some sort. These looked and smelled not at all toothsome, and their odd aromas hinted that something out of the ordinary awaited.

Hugh ó Flaherty greeted David in the courtyard, gripping his hand, as was the Irish custom. Hugh squeezed. David waited and Hugh squeezed harder and David waited some more. Finally, The ó Flaherty grunted and released him, then presented him with an arm bracelet as a hospitality-gift. David praised him for his open-handed generosity, all the while wondering was the old fox was up to. The guests, as was customary among the Irish, clapped their hands to show approval.

Hugh led him to the center of the table, where a linen cloth had been laid across the planks and three high seats placed side by side. David's standard-bearer already stood behind the rightmost one. On the left sat Naoife, his host's wife, a rail-thin woman with falcon's eyes. She welcomed David with a smile intended to be pleasant.

Once David was seated, gillies hurried about the courtyard, serving out the food. David turned a little to the side and handed the armband to Gillapadraig, who sat beside him. "Have you ever seen the like of it?" he murmured.

"Cunningly wrought," his man-of-trust replied, "but the gems are only polished, not cut."

"Oh, it's fine enough work," David said, taking it back and slipping it onto his arm, where it nestled among twisting tatoos. "But when have you ever seen an eagle outspread and perched upon the sun?" He searched the crowd for what he knew he must find. The ó Flaherty held a platter of roasted boar to him and David took a portion.

"Serving you with his own hand, is he?" Gillapadraig whispered. "He wants something."

"Is not this day full of surprises."

The guests were a mix of ó Flahertys and clans allied with them. David noted some rough men from Connemara, the rockiest part of Iar Connaught. Fell fighters, but clearly uncomfortable here among their betters. Their Pictish blood showed in their shorter stature and dark hair, prominent here in a tall sea of Gaelic red and blond. There were two Danes present. Both wore their hair twisted into long braids. The shorter Dane boasted a broad, flattish face, darker in coloring.

David chewed the meat, savoring the juices. "Excellent boar," he told his host as he continued to study the assembly.

"I speared him myself," ó Flaherty said.

"Valiantly done." David had no doubt that the boar was safely dead before ó Flaherty's men-of-trust had allowed him to approach. Kings were not so plentiful as to waste them on the odd pig or two.

Gillapadraig leaned close. "What are you looking for?"

"Turlough and Little Hugh."

"Ó Flaherty would not be so bold!"

"Would he not? He's all twisted in on himself like those capitals the monks draw in their books. He'll use the sons of Rory to bring down the sons of Cathal; and he'll use Cathal's sons to bring down Rory's. It's the use that delights him, not the cause. He brought me here so that I might take some word back to Cormac. What word, I don't yet know."

He spotted them at last. Not the sons of Rory, after all, but at one with the strange foods and the odd eagle motif. Half a dozen men and women huddled in a small group in the back of the courtyard. Their hair was dark like the Connemara men. But Picts, like the Irish, greased their hair and pulled it out into spikes, while these braided their hair like Danes. The strangers shared with the shorter Dane the same flat features, and their skin was colored a dark copper.

From the corner of his eye, David caught ó Flaherty's feline smile.

Nothing so pleasures a man who believes himself clever than to succeed at some small trick. Hence, David was not surprised to find Rory's sons waiting when The ó Flaherty led him into his hall after the banquet. Turlough was standing with his back to the fire, his arms clasped behind him. Little Hugh, his brother, sat at the long table with a bowl of uiscebeatha and not, by the evidence, his first of the evening. They both turned to face the doorway when David entered.

"So?" Hugh blurted out. "Are you with us?" Turlough reached out and placed a silencing hand on his brother's shoulder. Ó Flaherty closed the door upon them.

"I haven't spoken with him yet," he told the brothers.

David went to the board by the wall and found the jar of uiscebeatha and poured a bowl of his own. "I am with you in that we stand together in this room. Whether I am with you in any other fashion depends on where else you may stand."

Little Hugh, who had brightened at the first sentence, scowled upon hearing the second. Turlough grimaced. "That wasn't funny, David."

"So. I hadn't meant it to be."

"All the chiefs are with them," ó Flaherty commented. Having closed the door on the little gathering, he too proceeded to the jug. "They've come and given their pledges."

"Oh, doubtless there's been a regular procession through here," David said. "I can even guess at the names of them. Oaths must have little value these days, if men discard them so lightly."

Ó Flaherty had fetched his drink and sat with Turlough and David. "*I've* sworn no oath to the ó Conners of Cruachan," he said.

David shrugged. Iar Connaught had never been counted a part of the kingdom. The ó Flaherty had been expelled from Connaught only a few generations earlier—and by the ó Conners of Cruachan. "And the others who have come?"

Turlough spoke up. "What oaths they gave to my cousin he has forfeited by his feckless and dishonorable behavior."

"As an argument, that has its conveniences."

Turlough stood and leaned on the table with both fists. "He is 'no-king.' We've all agreed: ó Taidg, ó Flannigan, McGarrity . . ."

David maintained composure. The consent of the four principal chiefs was needed to proclaim a king in Connaught, and Turlough had just named three of them. No wonder ó Flaherty had feasted him and covered him with honeyed words. Win over the ó Flynn and they could raise Turlough up on the very rock at Cruachan! He emptied his bowl and tossed it to the table, where it clattered and spun.

"You haven't mentioned Cormac," he observed. "The Marshall of the Host may have some little say in the matter, whether the Four Chiefs forswear themselves or not."

"You're his officer," ó Flaherty said. "He listens to your advice."

"The McDermot has the most marvelous sort of ear. What goes into it is only what he permits."

Turlough struck the table. "The white rod is mine," he insisted. "My father was High King!"

"And what came of that," said David, "but that the Foreigners came into Ireland? And there is the pebble over which all your plots will stumble. If I do come over, and if I do bring The McDermot with me, Aedh will turn to *them,* with their shirts of iron. They've already castled Meath and Leinster. Would you hand them Connaught, as well?" With a growl of disgust, he turned away.

The ó Flaherty spoke quietly, and a little smugly. "The sons of Cathal are not the only party with iron-shirted friends."

The ó Flaherty's briugaid brought them into the room, the very strangers that David had noted earlier. With them came the two Danes and David suddenly realized, seeing them all together, that the shorter Dane was a half-breed: Danish blood mixed with these strangers.

He studied these new Foreigners with great care, for he knew that ó Flaherty planned some devious trick involving them and he did not yet know what that trick would be. Nor, by all appearances, did the Foreigners, for they cast sidelong glances at their host, and all but one, despite their outward arrogance, displayed signs of wariness.

Four he knew immediately for men-of-trust. Two entered first and two entered last and they stood to either side of the little group. Their clothing was a soft leather with fringes along the arms and leggings. From their belts hung short swords. On top of all, they wore iron shirts, not of mail as the Normans wore, but of metal sheets that had been shaped to their torso and wonderfully engraved with the likenesses of birds and wild plants. Two wore helmets, differently shaped than the Norman sort and topped with the brilliant plumage of an unknown bird.

The three men who had attended the banquet with their women were obviously chiefs. They were tall, but they held their heads a little back, as if they sought to look down at the world from as great a height as possible. They wore the same soft leather garments as their bodyguards, but theirs had been inlaid with colorful beads and shells, and across their shoulders had been flung cloaks woven of a smooth fiber dyed in intricate patterns. Black hair, knotted behind their heads, was pierced by feathers. The man in the center wore in addition a circlet of silver: an eagle whose wings swept forward around his temples to hold between their tips over his brow a sun of hammered gold.

And yet, confronted by this arrogant finery, David's eye was caught by the last man, who hovered in the back of the group with the women—the only man who showed no wariness. He was shorter, wider, and darker than the others and his dress was a roughly-woven jacket, sashed in the front like a robe, which he wore over a kilt of a plain color. His head was wrapped in a towel so that David at first thought him injured. Then he thought him perhaps a priest of the Mohammedans. Later, he was told that the man was a servant, but his flat, unblinking eyes were like no gilly's that David had ever seen. *Had I a servant like that,* he told himself as he stared into those arrogant eyes, *I'd have him thrashed for his insolence.*

SUANTRAÍ

"The ó Flaherty's gone mad," David announced that evening while he and his men were preparing for sleep.

"Has he, now." Gillapadraig took David's cloak and draped it over his arm.

"Pure Sweeney. I expected him to float off toward the roofbeams at any moment."

"Because of the New Iron Shirts?"

"Because of the New Iron Shirts." David pulled his knife from its sheath and threw it at the door, where it sank half a thumb into the wood. "Kevin, you sleep across the door tonight. Anyone who tries to enter, give him my welcome." The clansman nodded and laid his cloak upon the rushes by the doorway. He pried David's knife loose and placed it beside his pallet.

Gillapadraig had been watching. "You expect the king to violate his hospitality?"

David shrugged. "The ó Flaherty's a fox, for all that he is mad. *He* won't act dishonorably, but Turlough gave no pledge for my safety. The ó Flaherty is perfectly capable of closing his eyes, then expressing outrage afterward. There is a game being played here, and I don't know which of them is playing the other, Turlough or The ó Flaherty. Both, maybe. If I'm dead, Fiachra is chief of the Sil Maelruain. Perhaps they think they can move my son more easily than me."

"They can move the Rock of Cruachan more easily than you. Why do you think your son might . . . ?"

"Because Fiachra is friendly with Donn Oc McGarrity and the other young men—and Donn Oc has gone over to Turlough. Aedh is too close to the Foreigners for their taste, so they have all given their pledges to Turlough. They talk big about driving the Foreigners out of Aire Land, but I mind a fable about bells and cats."

"But, if The ó Flaherty has brought in men the equal of the Foreigners . . ."

"Then he is mad, as I've said. Remember how in the Holy Bible the Jews called on the Romans to help them against the Greeks—and then could not rid themselves of the Romans? So the king in Leinster called on the Foreigners to help him in his war against Rory and today Strongbow's son is king there in all but name. Now The ó Flaherty would be calling on these new Foreigners for help against the old ones? That woman has a lot to answer for."

Gillapadraig paused before drawing off his own tunic. "Which woman would that be?"

"The ó Rourke's wife. It was because she slept with Rory that ó Rourke called for the Leinstermen's aid in the first place."

Gillapadraig grunted. "It always comes down to a woman in the end. I'll hang our clothing in the garderobe to kill the lice. Tell us about these New Foreigners. What are they like? Are they fighting men?"

"They brought their women with them, so they are no war party. But the men look no strangers to battle, either. They were in a fight, and lately at that."

"Where do they come from?" Gillapadraig's voice came from the small necessary. The dung pile that lay below the open grating provided the fumes that killed the lice.

David shrugged. "I can tell you only what The ó Flaherty told me and I don't know how much truth the story holds. The strangers spoke some unknown tongue. The dark Dane translated that into the Danish they speak in the Ice Land and the Galway Dane rendered that into Gaelic, but how much of the sense of it made it through that bramble, who can say? I follow the Danish a little, and . . ."

There was a knock at the door. Two raps, followed by a pause, then another rap. "It's Donnchad," said Kevin. He unlatched the door and Donnchad ó Mulmoy slipped in. The clan na Mulmoy had been allied with the clan na Fhlainn since time unremembered and David had given Donnchad the command of the footmen in his party.

"The men are all settled," the newcomer told them, "and I've set watches. I do not trust these western men."

"Did you see any of those New Foreigners about?" David asked him.

"The red-skins? Two of their men-of-trust stood guard outside The ó Flaherty's hall, so I take it that they are bedded down within. To me, they would not answer hail or farewell, so they might have been cast from copper for all I could tell you. The other one, the one with the rag on his head, was about on some errand, but he only glowered at me when I hailed him."

"A friendly folk," Gillapadraig said.

"They are uneasy about something," David told him. "And they sense that we may not be with them."

"What did you tell The ó Flaherty?"

"I told him that I did not think that seven warriors, six women, and a gilly would drive William the Marshal into the sea."

"How did he answer?"

"About as you may expect. That these are but an embassy and their warriors over the Western Sea are as numerous as the leaves in a forest."

"Did the Ice Lander tell you that? They've no trees in the Ice Land."

"Thorfinn Rafn's son, he names himself. He is not from the Ice Land, but from some other place farther off. They call it the New-Found Land."

"'New-found,' is it? St. Brendan the Navigator sailed the shores of Ui Braiseal in the long ago."

David shrugged. "Thorfinn said that some of those who went with Eric the Red to the Green Land discovered it. He thinks two hundred years ago. Perhaps they went looking for Irishmen to plunder. It's what vikings did back then, and 'tis said that a party of monks fled west from the Ice Land when the Danes first came to it."

"The Saga of the Lost Danes," said Kevin. "I've heard that tale sung by their *skalds* down in Galway Town. When Leif went back, he found no trace of the settlement; only some cryptic runes. Then he vanished, too. I never thought it was true; only a *saga* the Ostmen made up for amusement."

"Olaf Gustaf's son—he's the tall one, the Galwegian—believed so, too. But he can understand the Danish that Thorfinn speaks. It's near enough the Ice Land tongue. Olaf says it's like talking to his grandsire's grandsire. This Thorfinn claims that Leif's party in the Vine Land met with savages—*skraelings*, they called them—

but found them easy enough to overawe. Then one day the *skraelings* were attacked from the south by an army of the ó Gonklins . . ."

"Ó Gonklins, was it?" said Donnchad. "So they were Irish after all?"

"It sounded like 'ó Gonklin.' They came as foot soldiers, like the old Roman legions, but with a troop of cavalry mounted on large, hairy horses. As shaggy as the ponies from Shet Land or Ice Land, yet as large as those the Foreigners ride. The *skraelings* ran, and Leif's people saw that there was no fighting such a force. They were taken to the king of the ó Gonklins, who moved them to a city farther west, on the shore of a great inland sea, and that's why the Green Landers never found them again."

"That makes a better *saga* than the one they sing in Galway," Kevin admitted.

"The ó Gonklins were pushing their empire into the plains and so had little interest in the Green Land Danes. They kept a watch on the northern shores and captured any Green Lander vessel that came near thereafter, settling their crews in the new Danish towns on the Inland Sea. That's why the Green Landers gave up sailing those waters. No one ever came back."

"In Galway Town," Kevin said, "they say there is a *maelstrom* west of the Green Land that swallows ships whole."

David shrugged. "There is probably more to the story. I think the Danes helped The ó Gonklin capture the Grass Lands; and Thorfinn said something about giant hairy cattle and giant hairy elephants, but maybe Olaf misunderstood."

"Is it everything in their land that is giant and hairy, saving only the men?" Donnchad asked, and the others laughed.

"So now their king is wondering where these Danes were after coming from?" guessed Gillapadraig.

"Once he had pacified the marchlands—Thorfinn called it Thousand Lakes Land—the king thought to look east and sent these emissaries. At least, that was the story I was told. The ó Flaherty said that their ship made landfall out in ó Malley's Country. Savages the Picts may be, but they know how to separate a man from his head. Yet the Red Foreigners, few as they are, drove them off. The survivors then made their coasting until they found the mouth of Lough Corrib. That's where they found Olaf."

"And why was he not taking them to Galway Town?"

"Olaf is out-law there and, anxious for his neck, he guided them upriver to The ó Flaherty's stronghold instead."

Gillapadraig pursed his lips. "An embassy, is it," he said.

David looked at him. "That's what I thought. Sure, who sends an embassy out with no care to which king he is sending it?"

Ó Flaherty took David stag-hunting the following day, in company with the sons of Rory and the eagle-chief of the ó Gonklins, who bore the outlandish name of Tatamaigh. As all were chiefs of some consequence, they were accompanied by their men-of-trust to the number prescribed by the *cain*-law, by gillies to wait upon their needs, and by huntsmen and skinners and kennels of hounds, so that the party, withal, resembled a small war band and required a fleet of boats to set them on the western shore of the lough.

They rode the soft emerald hills of Oughterard, across meadows and peat-land, with great silent hounds loping before. Beaters started the red deer and chased them from the forest into the aire-lords' embrace, to be welcomed by the kiss of arrow and javelin. The sun was to their backs and the wind off the distant southern sea, so that a mist hung over all the land, filling up the valleys like milk. Oughterard lay in Moycullen, The ó Flaherty's tuath-lands, and rolled westward in gentle hills toward the farther, rougher peaks of Connemara.

They had brought down three deer—one by each chief, as was fitting—when the beaters started a boar.

The first sign David had of it was the shriek of one of the beaters as he was tusked, followed by the baying of the deer-hounds as, gray and growling, they encircled the beast. The hunters raced their ponies toward the brush at the forest's edge, followed by the other beaters and footmen.

The boar was all bristles and red eyes. Caught in a ring of snapping hounds, it turned first this way, then that, then fell to tearing with his tusks at a pair of saplings behind him. The saplings grew too close together to permit the boar passage, and a good thing, too, for taking refuge behind them was the gilly of the Red Foreigners. The man's robe was torn and a part of it hung askew. His curious headgear had come off as well, tangled a bit on the boar's right foreleg and leading like a path to his sanctuary. His eyes bulged with terror and his hair, now unencumbered with wrapping, fell black and matted to his shoulders.

The eagle-chief reined in some distance away and paced his mount in jerky circles. His retinue spread out to protect him, but none came closer.

All this David saw with only part of his attention. He waited until the boar, alternating between attacks on the gilly and fending off hunters and hounds, had made another of its quarter turns. Then he hurled his javelin into the beast's neck. The boar gave forth the most horrid grunts and cries. Turlough, riding up, fleshed his spear as well, while Little Hugh leapt from his pony and approached on foot, holding a boar-spear in front of him. He made barking cries at the creature, trying to goad it into attack.

Turlough went white. Behind him, David saw The ó Flaherty's archers with arrows nocked, waiting for their king's guest to get out of the way. He gave Turlough a glance, then buried a second javelin into the boar's left eye.

The pig squealed and thrashed and toppled onto its side, kicking. For a moment, it seemed that it might rise up once more; then it shrugged and collapsed. Little Hugh, seeing his chance, dashed forward and struck with the spear from the blind side, but by then the blow was no more than a death-grace.

When the boar had twitched at last into stillness, the trapped gilly stepped out of his shelter, edging around the carcass without taking his moon-eyes from it, then scurried behind David's pony, which started a bit at the motion.

Turlough rode to David's side. "Well struck," he said, offering his hand. When David took it, he added in a whisper, "And my thanks for saving my fool brother's neck. He's young, and young men are rash."

"As well, that; for where else do old men learn wisdom save from the rash deeds of their youth."

Turlough laughed. The ó Flaherty, who had also ridden up, studied the boar. "He is nearly as large as the one I slew for the banquet."

David said, “That creature will grow larger with every telling, I’m thinking.” Turlough laughed again, and The ó Flaherty slapped David on his back. “As big as the Dun Cow!” he cried.

“You’re after finding some fine allies,” David said as Turlough and The ó Flaherty turned away.

His words reined them back. “And your meaning . . . ?” asked Turlough.

David signaled with the finger-ogham to indicate Tatamaigh and his retinue. “What sort of chief does not trouble himself to protect his own gilly?”

“As for that,” The ó Flaherty said, “boars are unknown in their country and his people feared to draw near.”

“And might such a chief not fear equally to draw near your enemy?”

The ó Flaherty said nothing, but yanked his pony’s head round and rode off. Turlough lingered while his brother remounted. “Do you think them cowards?” he asked.

“I think they may not be what they seem. Do you truly believe their king will send his *chivalry* across the entire Western Ocean when William the Marshall need only crook his finger to fetch Normans by the boatload across the Irish Sea?”

GOLTRAÍ

Though lowborn to a Connemara clan, the slain beater had served faithfully for many years, and The ó Flaherty Himself was lavish in his praise and in the gifts he bestowed on the widow. Mourners were brought in and they set up a caointeachán around the corpse, taking turns wailing and crying so that none would tire too soon. Their keenings writhed through the gathering dark, echoed from the vises and empty passages within the chapel, and came upon one from unexpected directions.

David had gone to the chapel to pray for the dead man’s soul and stood on the flagstones before the altar, wondering what he was supposed to tell God that God did not already know. In the end, he prayed not for the servant, but for Connaught, that she not be ruined between the powerful allies of rival clans. Ó Conner had fought ó Conner since time’s birth. It was in the nature of things, like the rolling of the heavens in their crystal spheres. But now each faction would bring in Iron Shirts, and that would be the end of it all.

With such grave thoughts he turned away and found that the sons of Rory had come into the chapel. David said nothing, but stepped aside that they might approach the altar. Little Hugh stopped to speak to him.

“You didn’t save my life, you know.”

David nodded. “I will remember that, the next time.”

The remark puzzled Hugh, but Turlough turned about and gave him a searching look. David saw in that look that Turlough knew that he would not come over. And if not David, then not The McDermot—and the clans of the Sliabh ua Fhlainn and the clans of the Mag nAi would fight for Aedh, and that meant a bloody time in the West. “He’ll ruin the country,” Turlough said, and David knew he meant king Aedh.

“Only if there is a fight,” David said. “Otherwise, why call in the Foreigners at all?”

“Should I wait for him to die, then?”

"Patience is a virtue in kings. The wait may not be long. Wives have husbands to defend their honor, and Aedh may cuckold one too many."

Turlough's eyes retreated from his face, as if they looked on some inner struggle. His mouth turned down in a grim line. "And after Aedh, Felim. Aedh may be weak and foolish. His brother is neither, and while I may wait out one of my cousins, I have not the patience for two."

Little Hugh stepped close to David, though he had to stand a-toe to do it. "If you fight us, we'll destroy you, now that we've the Red Foreigners on our side."

David looked over the younger man's head into Turlough's eyes. "I pity Felim the foolishness of his brother."

Turlough understood and put a hand on Little Hugh's shoulder. "Come, we're here to pray for a good man, not to quarrel with an old one." He gazed at the body on its bier before the altar, washed and wrapped in a winding sheet. "He, at least, had no part in the quarrels of kings."

When David stepped outside the chapel, Gillapadraig was refastening the thong on his sword-hilt, David grinned. "You thought they would attack me in a holy place, and myself under The ó Flaherty's protection?"

Gillapadraig grunted. "My blade wanted whetting, is all."

"It might have been interesting if they had," David mused. "I could have goaded Little Hugh into it. Then ó Flaherty would have had to kill them to save his honor. Would that have been too high a price for peace in Connaught?"

"Not if you could be sure you had actually purchased so elusive a thing."

David laughed. "And what is that foreigner gilly doing over there by the stables?"

"Oh, him. He's trying to rewind his headscarf."

David clapped him on the shoulder. "Come. Let's see if he can tell a tale as twisted as his hat."

"But we don't speak the ó Gonklin tongue."

"Nor does he."

The man saw their approach and watched with calculation. He had obtained somewhere a needle and thread and was mending the long scarf. He studied David's face, then grunted and pulled the thread through his teeth and bit it off.

"I hate it when they fawn all over you," Gillapadraig said. "I suppose it wasn't much of a life, if that is all the thanks you get for the saving of it."

"It was the only one he had." David stepped to the drinking barrel that the stable-hands used and pulled out a dipperful, which he offered to the Red gilly. "*Akwa*?" he said, employing an ó Gonklin term he had learned.

The squat man stared at the dipper for a moment, then raised his eyes to David's face. "*Oka*," he said distinctly. He took the dipper from David's hands and sipped from it.

"I'm glad he cleared that up," Gillapadraig said.

"He speaks a different tongue than the other Red Foreigners." Then he squatted on his heels directly before the other and said in his halting Danish, "Who are you?"

The red man showed surprise for just an instant before his face reverted to impassivity. "Warrior," he said, in a Danish even more awkward.

"A warrior servant?"

Incomprehension was evident. David turned to Gillapadraig. "He understands only a little of the Ice Land tongue. I understand only a little of the Galwegian tongue. Between the two of us, we understand only a little of the little. But I must know what to tell Cormac. I don't think The ó Flaherty knows as much as he believes, and I don't think that Tatamaigh fellow will be telling him." Facing the gilly, David pointed to himself and said, "David mac Nial ó Flynn." Then he pointed to the gilly.

After a moment, the gilly slapped his chest and said, "Muiscle ó Tubbaigh." He put his mending aside and reached inside his robe, to emerge with a small bowl made of briar and carved into the form of a rearing horse. Yet such a horse David had never seen before, with a broader face and shorter muzzle and with shaggy hair almost like a dog's. The bowl had a long, gracefully curved handle. Into this bowl, the man poured a small measure of powder or ground-up leaves from a cloth pouch he carried and which was tied up with a drawstring around its mouth. Ó Tubbaigh gazed wistfully at this sack. "*Tzibatl*," he said. "*Tzibatl Aire Bhoach achukma.* Much good." He hefted the sack once or twice as if gauging its weight before returning it to one of the numerous pouches sewn into his robe. Lastly, he lit a straw from the brazier the stable-hands used and with it, set fire to the leaves in the bowl.

The handle was actually a pipe, David now saw, one end of which was fixed to the bowl enabling ó Tubbaigh to suck the acrid smoke of the leaves into his mouth. When ó Tubbaigh handed the bowl to him, David took it and, following the prompting of the gilly, sucked also.

The smoke seared his lungs and he coughed convulsively. The foreigner smiled a little, but did not laugh. He made puffing sounds with his mouth, then, with a negative motion of his hand across his mouth, mimed a deep breath. David understood and took the smoke only into his mouth, holding it there for a moment before expelling it. After several puffs, a curious tingling sense of alertness came over him. He could hear the harp playing in ó Flaherty's hall and the high nasal singing of "The Lament of the ó Flahertys."

Clan Murchada of the fortress of hospitality
Was governed by clan Flaherty of swords,
Who from the shout of battle would not flee . . .

Except that they *had* fled, westward from the Foreigners to these dreary shores—and the fair, former lands of clan Murchada were governed now by the ó Conners, who had been content to gather up the remnants after the Foreigners' withdrawal. Ó Tubbaigh, his head cocked, also listened to the faint music and, though he could not have understood the words, a sadness passed momentarily across his face, for he could hear the haunt of loss in the winding notes.

"Gillapadraig," said David suddenly, "do you remember how mac Costello took Nial Og prisoner last summer?"

"And our cattle in the bargain. What of it?"

"I was only thinking how a warrior might become a servant."

David accepted the smoking bowl when ó Tubbaigh offered it again.

"Smoke friend maketh," the man said in halting, antique Danish.

David grunted. "I suppose I can sort those words as I please." He pointed to himself and Gillapadraig and spoke again in Danish, "We twain, Gaels." The he pointed at ó Tubbaigh. "You, ó Gonklin?"

The other man looked first puzzled, then startled, then angry, then finally, contemptuous. He passed his hand back and forth in front of his mouth, then spat in the dirt.

"What was that all about?" Gillapadraig asked.

"He does not think highly of his masters," said David.

"Small wonder, after they made no move to save him today."

David thought about it some more. "I wish I knew how far I could trust the two Danes. The dark one, I think, not at all, if he is one of the ó Gonklin's vikings and loyal to them. The Galwegian, I am unsure of. He is out-law, but that might be a trifling matter. He may regret having become entangled in this affair. The Ostmen keep to themselves and pray the Normans will overlook them when the time comes. They have forgotten that they were once vikings. But let's make the most of our time. I doubt the ó Gonklin chief would be pleased to find us sharing the white smoke with his gilly." David drew ó Tubbaigh's attention to one of ó Flaherty's servants emptying slops in the pigsty just outside the keep and near the stables where the three were smoking. "Gilly," he said, "of ó Flaherty. You. Gilly of Tatamaigh?"

The Foreigner laughed and settled the turban over his head, adjusting it until it sat right. Then he grabbed himself by the crotch and again waved his hand across his mouth and spat in the direction of the keep.

"Does he mean that Tatamaigh unmanned him?" Gillapadraig asked in shock.

"No. He means that the ó Gonklins have no balls." With a stick, he drew a small circle in the dirt. "Aire Land," he said and patted the earth and pointed around. Then he made another small circle a little distance off. "Ice Land." He added Green Land, then New-Found Land. Then below the New-Found Land, he drew a much larger circle and said, "Ò Gonklin's Land." Finally, he handed the stick to ó Tubbaigh and, indicating the crude map, said, "You. Land. Where?"

Ò Tubbaigh scowled at the circles for a time and David thought that perhaps he did not understand, so he named the circles once more.

Slowly the man began to nod. The he reached into the dirt, scooped up a handful, and poured it over the large circle that David had named Ò Gonklin's Land. David stared at the dirt, then at the man himself, who grinned savagely. But before David could pursue the matter, a woman's voice called from the keep the name of Muiscle ó Tubbaigh. The grin vanished, replaced by the stone face. The gilly knocked the ashes from the bowl and, swishing it in the water barrel before returning it to his pouch, rose and aired his garments of the smell of the smoke.

"I suppose he did not understand what a map is," Gillapadraig said when the man had gone.

"Oh, he knew enough." David watched the gilly approach the ò Gonklin woman, saw how he stood before her, and saw too in the torchlight the look she gave him, and understood just a little bit more the tangled skein among the New Foreigners.

"Then why did he pour dirt all over it?" Gillapadraig wanted to know.

David dropped his eyes to the sketches in the dirt before, with his foot, he obliterated them.

Olaf Gustaf's son was morose to the point of suicide, but it was a point in exquisite balance. "I'll end in a nameless grave," he confided to David later that same evening when David had found him on the castle wall overlooking the moonlit lake.

"That's the fate of out-laws." David had brought him a tankard of ale because words were like fish and when wet swam more freely. "I was an important merchant in Galway Town. I took tin and timber from Cornwall to Bordeaux and to Henaye in the Basque country and brought back LaRochelle wines, Bourgneuf salt, and Spanish wool. Now there's a price on my head, and I never even had that poor man's woman. I wouldn't mind being cut down so much if I'd ever futtered her; but she and I hadn't closed the bargain yet. Her husband thought otherwise, and so he died for the sake of an error. That don't seem right." Olaf sighed. "Still, people will go against me. Me, what's fought Breton and Basque pirates, and sailed with the Hansards against the wild Prussians."

David pointed to the vessel tied up to the wharf on the west side of the island, half visible in flickering torchlight. "Is that the ó Gonklin boat?"

"Ship," the Ostman told him. "Not 'boat.' *Ja,* that's her. Looks a little like a cog, but she's a poor sailer. Flat-bottomed, no keel. Her master fought his leeway all up Lough Corrib. Used *oars,* he did, to bring her to dock, so she's even part galley. No castles, fore or aft, to give archers height over pirates."

"May be there are no pirates in her home waters?"

Olaf spread his hands. "Or may be the pirates win. But she's got that queer second mast behind the main, which I fancy would harvest a bit more o' the wind than the usual bonnet sails, so she'd have heels when sailing large. And the strakes are clinkered, d'ye see—but top-over-bottom like the old *knorrs,* not bottom-over-top like modern ships. If I had to guess . . . D'ye have any more of The ó Flaherty's ale? Ah, my thanks t'ye. If I had to guess, I'd say this ó Gonklin fellow never had deep-water ships, just coasters; and what he's got now, he's copied off *knorrs* from the days of Eric the Red. That little hind-mast, though. That's new. That's a good idea." He took a long pull from his tankard. "I'd like to be out on one now. Not on that bastard. I'd not try the Gascon coast without a proper keel beneath me. But I'd like to be out on a proper ship. Out of Aire Land, where every man's hand against me."

"Mine isn't."

"Ach. That only means ye haven't heard the price on me yet."

David studied the ship again. He had never seen a cog before, let alone something that wasn't exactly a cog, and Olaf's explanations were as much a foreign language as that of the ó Gonklins. It astonished him that so large and heavy a thing could float at all. "I don't think those vessels can bring an army across the Ocean."

"Don't be fooled by her size," the Ostman said. "There be plenty room in 'er hold."

"It isn't the size I'm after thinking of. You said you wouldn't take it to the Gascon coast. Would you take it on the Ocean Sea?"

Olaf considered that. "If Hengist's family were breathing on my neck, I'd try Ocean in a coracle. If I'm to end in a nameless grave, better a watery one. But . . . The easting would be simple enough. Put up enough linen, catch the westerlies, and here you are. As for the westing . . . Well, she's got oars . . ."

"But if a flat-bottomed ship slips sideways . . ."

"Leeway, we call it. That's the problem with her. Ye couldn't be sure where ye'd raise land. If these Red Foreigners had keeled ships that could hold a bearing, they would have been here long since."

"You can't spin linen from straw," David agreed.

"And without those hairy horses of theirs, they'd have to walk everywhere, and how big would their kingdoms be? As big as a thumbnail, I'd wager. No grand cities as Thorfinn's told of: Manahattan, Lechauweking. That Tatamaigh fellow, when we slipped past Galway Town and her great walls, he turned his nose up and laughed. I'd be offended, if the Galwegians weren't all trying to kill me. I suppose a folk can be only as great as their tools will let them." Olaf turned as another man climbed the steps to the rampart and he called to the newcomer in Old Danish. "*Hails*, Thorfinn, son of the Rafn! How fare ye?"

The dark Dane said nothing, but he took the jug of ale from Olaf's hand and drank from it, wiping his mouth afterward with the back of his hand. He looked at David without expression, and did not return the jug. Smiling, and speaking the Gaelic so that the Red Dane would not understand, Olaf turned back to David. "He wouldn't last a week in Galway Town before he smiled below his chin."

"They are afraid. All of them but the gilly."

"Then they shouldn't swagger so."

David looked into the night, past Lough Corrib, past Connemara, past the Ocean Sea. "Sometimes a man must push himself forward, if to step back is death."

David went off by himself the next morning to watch the sun come up over Cill Cluanaigh on the eastern shore of the lough. The breeze, smelling of fish and the damp, whipped his cloak about him and he gathered the edge of it in his hand. A party of horsemen breasted the horizon, paused, and disappeared on the farther slope. Normans—perhaps Mac Costello's men. David spat over the wall into the waters that lapped against the foot of the fortress. Or a party of king Aedh's men, or even Leyney men sent south by Conner god ó Hara. Outriders? Or were rumors spreading?

Below, crossing the courtyard, ó Tubbaigh carried slop buckets to the midden. David whistled and the man looked up. For a moment the two locked gazes, then ó Tubbaigh put the slop buckets down and climbed the ladder to the parapet. David mimed smoking the bowl-and-pipe, but when the other drew it out made the negative gesture of passing the hand back and forth across his lips. He pointed to the horse carved into the bowl and said in Danish, "Saga horse sing." The previous night Thorfinn, through Olaf, had described how the Red Foreigners esteemed the horse above all beasts, and ó Tubbaigh seemed from his bow-leggedness a man who had spent most of his life astride one.

Ó Tubbaigh thought for a moment and his lips moved, as if he were puzzling from the Danish to his own tongue. Then he shrugged and began to speak in a singsong voice. David began to walk slowly around the parapet and the Red Foreigner walked beside him, singing in a high nasal whine. David understood not one word of it, but that was not his purpose.

At one point in the song ó Tubbaigh gnashed his teeth, then rubbed his stomach and pointed to the horse carving. Then he waved his hand before his mouth, by which David understood that at one time his people had eaten horse meat, but did so no longer. The Normans had a similar taboo, and small wonder. Eat all your mounts and what do you ride? A *chevalier* in armor would present less fearsome a prospect astride a cow. The miming with which ó Tubbaigh accompanied the song suggested the capture and breaking of horses, but he rode his imaginary steed with a wilder abandon than the Norman kettle-heads and he mimed the shooting of a bow and not the lowering of a lance.

At that point, turning the corner of the parapet, they came face to face with the ó Gonklin chief Tatamaigh and his woman about their own morning circuit of the walls. Tatamaigh halted and stared with onyx eyes at David and ó Tubbaigh. The gilly, who had been in the midst of loosing one of his imaginary arrows, smiled and released it directly at the chief's chest.

Tatamaigh snatched at his sword-hilt, but the gilly said, *"Hahkalo iss'ubah, sachem. Sa taloah himonasi,"* and bowed most insolently. Then he grinned and made riding motions, biting imaginary reins in his teeth and loosing another bow shot. The ó Gonklin affected not to listen, but his woman, standing a pace behind him, watched ó Tubbaigh's rolling hips with her lower lip caught between her teeth.

Tatamaigh released his sword-hilt—and David heard the subtle sound of other swords sheathed a few paces behind him. Gillapadraig, as always, his shadow. But the chief reached out and snatched the smoke-pipe from ó Tubbaigh's hand.

Ó Tubbaigh cried out, but Tatamaigh fended him off with a sharp blow that rocked the gilly's head back. Then, holding out his palm, the chief spoke sharply. David heard *"tzibatl"* but it sounded no more at home on this man's tongue than it had earlier on his servant's. Possibly it was a word of the Aire Bhoach folk, those who grew the leaves. Ó Tubbaigh snarled something that David had little trouble interpreting as a refusal, slapped his chest and said, *"Mingo-li billia!"*

The ó Gonklin chief grabbed his sword-hilt again and might have drawn it this time, but that his woman put a hand on his arm and said something soft. Tatamaigh shrugged her off without looking, but nevertheless unhanded the sword. *"Tzibatl,"* he said again, holding his hand out. Two of his guardsmen had come up behind him and watched the servant with smoldering eyes. David crossed his arms and leaned his back against the parapet, waiting to see how it would play out.

The moment stretched on.

Then ó Tubbaigh sighed and reached into his cloak and fetched out the bag of smoking powder. He held it for a moment, and David thought he might throw it over the wall in spite. Then, he handed the pouch to his chief saying something that David thought might translate as *I hope you choke on it.*

David noted how both men's hands trembled while handling the powder and he thought that the white smoke might exert some powerful influence over them, as whiskey did over drunkards. Before he had even departed with his retinue, Tatamaigh had filled the bowl with the powder and had sent one of the guards to fetch a coal to light it with.

"They didn't fight," Gillapadraig said. He had come to walk beside David and spared now a backward glance at the departing eagle-chief. "I thought you said they would fight."

"Not yet," David told him. He turned to ó Tubbaigh and said, "*Mingolaigh*. Chief?"

"*Mingo*, chief Muisce ó Geogh," he said. "*Sachem*, chief al-Goncuin."

David repeated the name more carefully. "Al-Goncuin, is it? Are they Saracens, then?" But 'saracen' meant nothing to the red man and David did not press the matter. What concerned him was less whence the red men had come, than whither they might be going.

When they turned onto the parapet overlooking the lough, David found Donnchad ó Mulmoy and Olaf the Dane waiting, as he had arranged.

"How many?" David asked Donnchad, indicating the cog moored below them.

"Three-and-twenty," ó Mulmoy told him, "though it was a hard count, seeing how they all look alike. About half wear iron shirts. The others climb the ropes, so I think they must be the sailors. There are always two on guard but they don't keep good watch."

"They believe themselves among friends," David said.

"More than friends. A couple of ó Flaherty's scullery maids have gone inside on one errand or another—mostly the other, I'm thinking—and they have a Pictish woman that they must have captured when they fought the ó Malleys."

David turned to the Dane. "Olaf, do you have any friends yet in Galway Town?"

The Ostman shrugged. "Does a man with a price ever have friends? I suppose you could call anyone who hasn't yet tried to slit my throat a 'friend'."

"What if you could promise them a ship faster than any they've known?"

"So . . ." Olaf's eyes dropped to the alien ship. "She needs a proper keel. But I know a man at Bordeaux who would do it." His eyes danced along the masts. "A dozen to sail her, I think, though the rigging be strange . . . and we would need to . . ." He stopped and nodded. "*Ja*. I've cut ships out before. It can be done."

"Good. Make a list of the men you want and give it to ó Mulmoy. Donnchad, ride for Galway Town. You know the town. Find the men Olaf names and bring them here by stealth. You may encounter ó Dallies down that way, and there is nothing ill between them and us; but if deBurgo is abroad take care. Travel unseen."

Donnchad smiled. "One ó Mulmoy is worth ten Burkes."

"Then take Kevin with you. I think there are more than ten."

Donnchad left. Olaf lingered a moment longer, gazing at the cog and rubbing his hands together. Then he too left.

A silence passed before David said, "Tatamaigh home sail, warriors bring. Take you?"

Ó Tubbaigh laughed bitterly. "Chief al-Goncuin. No more." He slapped his chest. "Muisce ó Geogh all chief now. Town, stronghold, how say?" And he mimed the striking of a flint, the lighting of a fire.

"Burn," said David.

"Town, stronghold al-Goncuin burn. Women . . ." And he thrust with his hips.

"Books, too?" To the gilly's puzzled look, David mimed reading and ó Tubbaigh shrugged.

"Pfft." His fingers fluttered like smoke.

"Ochone. They do burn easily, do they not?" David said. He wondered if there were any monks in that New-Found Land. He wondered if they would catch whatever they could on their parchments before all the learning ran through their fingers like so much sand. He thought about the saints of Aire Land scratching away with quills in the failing light of the long ago while vikings howled outside. What they had written was tinder, but tinder of a different sort, which later, in the courts of Charlemagne, had lit a different sort of fire. And now Charlemagne himself was legend, a subject of romance and fable, as distant from the present day as the Fall of Rome had been from his.

Ó Tubbaigh spoke in halting Danish. "Ship take hair yellow." When David made no answer, a distant look came into his eyes. "Go with. Home see *ahcheba*. Ah, the grass, the grass."

David pulled his knife and scabbard from his belt and handed it to the Muisce ó Geogh captive, for such he had concluded the man was: one of the sacking horde in the wreckage of an empire, captured by a fleeing band of al-Goncuins, possibly even as the escape ship was casting forth. There were red stains on the cog's decks that spoke of a desperate fight. Ó Tubbaigh hesitated. Then he snatched the knife from its scabbard and secreted it in the wraps of his turban, returning the empty scabbard to David. He said, "Smoke we two *ahcheba*."

"We will smoke again," David lied.

The ó Flaherty Himself escorted David to the edge of Cill Cluanaigh and sat upon his pony beside him while the hill men disembarked from the boats and sorted themselves out for the long trek back to the Slieve ua Fhlainn.

"You'll tell Cormac," ó Flaherty suggested.

"I'll tell The McDermot everything I've seen."

The king of Iar Connaught grunted over the careful phrasing, then he looked west, past his stronghold in the lough. "I don't understand your loyalty to a weakling like Aedh."

"A weakling he is, and a fool," David admitted, "but if we demand our kings be worthy before we pay them the respect that kings are due, then all is chaos. Kings come, kings go. It's the white rod that matters, not the fool that holds it."

The ó Flaherty pondered David's words. "I see," he said at last. "You are Felim's man. You've been Felim's man all along."

"It would be awkward," David explained, "if he killed his own brother. Turlough will see to that—should no cuckold step forward."

Ó Flaherty grinned without humor. "And then Felim's dogs will remove Turlough, with the iron shirts to back them? Sure, it's a sad tale, then, that the Red Foreigners will upset his plans."

David shrugged. "Life brims with the unexpected. Oh. I'm after losing my knife."

"Are you now?"

"I think that red gilly is after taking it. I think he means to murder Tatamaigh."

"Over the woman? She isn't much to look at, but I don't suppose looking is what he has in mind."

"Maybe the woman. Maybe the smoke. It doesn't matter. Warn Tatamaigh."

The king of Iar Connaught scowled, suspecting some cleverness. "It would be better for you—and Felim and Cormac—if Tatamaigh were slain."

David crossed himself piously. "The Lord commanded us to do good even for our enemies."

David halted his party once again on the hill overlooking Lough Corrib and turned his pony round to gaze at The ó Flaherty's stronghold while awaiting the signal from the outriders that no ambush lurked. Gillapadraig trotted his pony to stand next to David's.

"So it did come down to a woman in the end," he said. "How much have you teased out?"

"They're not coming," David said. "They'll never come; not to help Turlough, not for any reason."

"Can you be so sure? The Normans found it worth the effort . . ."

David pulled on his moustache, gauged the position of the sun, and wondered if he could reach the monastery at Tuam before nightfall. "The Irish Sea is a shorter crossing than the Ocean Sea. But that is not the reason. The al-Goncuin empire is broken. The clans of the Muisce ó Geogh light campfires with their books. Tatamaigh was desperate for a refuge and grasping at any straw. He would have promised ó Flaherty anything. We may see a few more such boat-loads seeking the legend-lands the Danes sing of—but that is all."

"What of these Muisce ó Geogh folk, then? They are the victors, you say. Will they not come?"

"The ó Flaherty is mad. Bad enough to invite the red Romans in; to invite the red Huns is pure Sweeney. They are horsemen, not sailors, and there is more wealth in the wreckage of an empire than on these poor shores. Yet they are a wild folk, and the horizon taunts them. Should ó Tubbaigh escape to tell them of us . . ."

"Small chance of that."

"How small is small enough? He is a bold man, and a clever one to survive as long as he has in the hands of his enemies. When Olaf steals the ship, will he not be aboard? Could I hazard his escape? Ah, darling, it's a cruel and pitiless age we live in to spend such a life to buy a little time. Had they not burned the books, I might have hesitated." David fell silent and tugged his chin. "There may be a blessing, though, in all this."

"What is it?" Gillapadraig asked.

"That Tatamaigh's crown was solid gold, was it not?"

"It had the look of it."

"A bold man with a sword might carve himself a pretty kingdom over there, a greater one than he can ever find in these poor hills."

Gillapadraig fell into open-mouthed silence. When he found his voice, he stammered, "Would you be leading the ui Fhlainn then into some foreign land?"

"I would not, but the prospect of gold and plunder is a sore temptation." David turned his pony about and saw the outriders coming in from the east, signaling that it was safe to proceed. He kicked his pony in the ribs and the hill men set off at a slow mile-eating pace. "Maybe the Normans will go."

cody

PAT CADIGAN

Pat Cadigan was born in Schenectady, New York, and now lives in London with her family. She made her first professional sale in 1980, and has subsequently come to be regarded as one of the best new writers of her generation. Her story "Pretty Boy Crossover" has appeared on several critics' lists as among the best science fiction stories of the 1980s, and her story "Angel" was a finalist for the Hugo Award, the Nebula Award, and *the World Fantasy Award (one of the few stories ever to earn that rather unusual distinction). Her short fiction—which has appeared in most of the major markets, including* Asimov's Science Fiction *and* The Magazine of Fantasy & Science Fiction*—has been gathered in the collections* Patterns *and* Dirty Work. *Her first novel,* Mindplayers, *was released in 1987 to excellent critical response, and her second novel,* Synners, *released in 1991, won the Arthur C. Clarke Award as the year's best science fiction novel, as did her third novel,* Fools, *making her the only writer ever to win the Clarke Award twice. Her other books include the novels* Dervish Is Digital, Tea from an Empty Cup, *and* Reality Used to Be a Friend of Mine, *and, as editor, the anthology* The Ultimate Cyberpunk, *as well as two making-of movie books and four media tie-in novels, most recently* Cellular.

Here she delivers an ingenious and suspenseful adventure that demonstrates that being the messenger can be dangerous, no matter what the message.

Common wisdom has it," said LaDene from where she was stretched out on the queen-sized bed, "that anyone with a tattoo on their face goes crazy within five years."

Cody paused in his examination of his jawline in the mirror over the desk to give her a look. "You see any tattoos on this example of manly beauty?"

"Can't see the moon from here, either. Or the TV remote," she added. She sat up and looked around. Cody found it on the desk and tossed it to her. "Thanks. You know, carnies would call you a marked man."

"Carnies?" He gave a short laugh. "Don't tell me you threw over the bright lights of the midway to keep a low profile in budget accommodations."

"*Higher-end* budget accommodations." She put on the TV and began channel surfing. "For the discerning yet financially-savvy business traveller. Don't you ever read the brochures?"

He made a polite noise that was could have been yes or no and was neither. The hotspot that had come up over two hours ago was still there, midway between his chin and the point of his jaw, and as far as he could tell, it hadn't faded even a little. The medic had assured him there was nothing to worry about unless it started to spread and it hadn't. It wouldn't have bothered him except he hadn't had a hotspot in years. Rookies got hotspots.

The sudden recurrence could have been down to any number of things, the medic had said, the most likely being the attack of hay fever he had suffered on arrival. But he'd never had hay fever in his life, he'd told the medic. He'd never been to Kansas City in late August, she'd replied, chuckling.

Technically, he still hadn't. The airport was thirty miles north of the city and the car they'd sent had taken him to an industrial park about as far to the west on the Kansas side of the state line, which apparently ran right through the middle of town. The most he'd seen of Kansas City proper was a distant cluster of skyscrapers, briefly glimpsed through the tinted window as the driver negotiated a complicated interchange of highway ramps. After that it was generic highway scenery all the way to a generic suburban industrial park, full of angular, antiseptic office buildings surrounded by patches of green landscaped and manicured *in extremis*, some with a koi pond or a fountain. The access road meandered through it so much that Cody thought there had to be an extra mile of travel. Albeit a very pretty mile; perhaps it was so people coming and going could see at least in passing the flowers they didn't have time to stop and smell. Cody could have done without it. By the time they'd reached their destination, he had actually begun to feel carsick.

"Yo!" A pillow hit him in the head, making him jump. "And I thought *I* was vain," LaDene laughed. "Are you really that fascinating?"

"I was woolgathering," he said as he threw the pillow back at her. "Thinking, in case you don't know what that means."

"I know what it means," she said. "I also know you've got a hotspot. Unclench, honey, I've got one, too." She lifted her shirt and pointed at her navel.

"Oh, very funny."

"Oh, very for-real." She was up off the bed and had his face in her hands before he could say anything. "Ah, got it, right there." She patted his cheek and pulled up her shirt again, exposing her midriff. "Mine's hotter. Feel."

Her belly button was only inches away from his nose. Cody drew back and started to protest as she grabbed his hand and pressed it against her skin. His discomfort turned to surprise. "I sit corrected," he said, extricating himself from her grip. "Yours *is* hotter."

"Told you," she said, plumping down on the bed to stretch out again. "It's probably the ragweed and who knows what else in the air. Man, I *hate* KC this time of year."

"You've been here before?"

"I'm *from* here." She laughed at his surprised expression. "You couldn't tell?"

"How could I? We just met."

"I knew *you* weren't from around here, soon as I saw you. No antihistamines."

He chuckled a bit ruefully. "I thought I was dying of a head cold I caught on the plane."

She started to channel surf again, then changed her mind and shut the TV off. "If you get cold symptoms a lot when you fly, it's probably an allergy."

"Oh?" He gave a short skeptical laugh. "Is there a lot of ragweed on airplanes?"

She shrugged. "Lots of other stuff—mold, dust, newsprint. Somebody's cheap cologne. Even expensive cologne."

"*Newsprint?*"

"Believe it or leave it. You know how if something exists, there's porn of it? Well, there's also someone allergic to it."

"Newsprint," Cody said again, still skeptical.

"If I'm lyin', I'm dyin'." LaDene raised one hand solemnly, then let it fall. "Okay, that was fun. Now whaddaya wanna do?"

Cody leaned over and scooped the remote control up so he could turn the TV back on, mainly to forestall the possibility of her wanting to compare hotspots again. The screen lit up to show a dark-haired, olive-skinned woman speaking directly to the camera with an earnest sincerity that made his own brow furrow in sympathy.

". . . found flayed and burned in a midtown Kansas City, Missouri, parking garage have now positively been identified as August Fiore, AKA Little Augie Flowers, fifty-one, and Coral Oh, twenty-nine, of Liberty, Missouri. Fiore went missing two weeks ago from an FBI safe house where he was being held pending the start of the trial of Carmine Nesparini on racketeering charges. The FBI has steadfastly refused to comment on allegations that Fiore was Nesparini's personal 'master key' but sources close to the investigation say that Fiore's cooperation would have given authorities an unprecedented level of access to mob records.

"Fiore's attorneys refused to comment, except to say that they were unaware of any escape plans and had no knowledge of Fiore's whereabouts. Whether Fiore left the safe house voluntarily may never be known. FBI technicians are still working on the sabotaged surveillance system but experts believe there is little chance they can salvage enough data to be useful.

"Coral Oh's connection to Fiore still has not been established. Oh worked for the Kansas City Convention Bureau for fifteen years as an event coordinator, for the last three in a supervisory position. Coworkers described her as intelligent and well-liked. She was last seen ten days ago in her office by two of her subordinates, who had been working late with her."

The woman was suddenly replaced by a video of a very young man who looked as if he hadn't slept for at least that long. The slightly wobbly graphic at the bottom of the screen said he was *Akule Velasquez*. "She told us to go home, she'd finish up," he said in a husky voice to someone just off-camera to the left. "We'd've stayed but she was all—" he made small shooing gestures with both hands. "'No, get outa here, I'll finish, bring me some fancy coffee tomorrow.' She was like that. I tried to stay anyway but she kept telling me no. I wish I hadn't listened."

The woman in the studio reappeared, looking more earnest and sincere than ever. "The mayor's office issued a statement saying that this unfortunate and tragic incident should not overshadow the fact that criminal activity in the area has been steadily declining for the past twelve months thanks to new policing initiatives—"

LaDene snatched the remote out of his hand and turned off the TV. "Well, that *wasn't* fun. Now what do you wanna do?"

"Hey, I was watching that." Cody reached for the remote but she threw it across the room where it bounced off the wall and fell neatly into a small wastebasket.

"She shoots, she scores! A three-pointer, the crowd goes *wild!*" LaDene made crowd noises as he stalked over to retrieve the control. The impact had knocked the batteries out and it took him two tries to put them back in properly. "Oh, come *on*. What do you wanna scare the shit out of yourself for?"

But the news had moved on; now a man was standing near the edge of an empty swimming pool, blinking in bright sunlight as he talked about levels of chlorine. "Oh, well." Cody dropped the remote on the bed and sat down on the chair by the desk again. "I wasn't trying to scare myself."

"Who *were* you trying to scare—me?"

"No. I just want to pay attention."

"Set a news alert on your phone." She was channel surfing again. "It's probably all bullshit anyway. 'Little Augie Flowers,' for God's sake. Who goes around calling themselves 'Little Augie Flowers'? For a minute there, I thought they were talking about some old Grand Theft Auto module. 'Gay Tony Meets Little Augie Flowers, bullets will fly, heads will roll!' Oh, hey, I *love* this!" she added, sitting up suddenly.

Cody barely had to look at the screen to know what it was. "I've seen it." He rested an elbow on the desk and cupped his face in his hand. The hotspot was still there. "Several times."

"So have I but I like to watch it whenever it's on. That guy's *so cool*."

"He is?" If he didn't leave the goddam hotspot alone, he told himself, it was never going to fade. He shifted so he was leaning the upper part of his cheek against his hand; as if it had a will of its own, his thumb slid down to feel his jawline. Annoyed with himself, he straightened up, grabbed the TV listings off the desk, and paged through them without seeing anything.

"Okay, he's all wrong and he probably knew it," LaDene was saying. She punched the pillows behind her into a more supportive position for her lower back and casually folded her legs into a half-lotus, making Cody wince. "But so what? The whole movie's wrong."

"Well, it's a pretty old movie," he said, shrugging.

"Not *that* old. Not *ancient*."

"No, but BCI didn't even exist when this came out and people were still using floppy disks. This big." He held his hands three feet apart. She gave him a Look and he moved them so they were only a foot apart. "Okay, *this* big. TVs were dumb terminals and a cloud was a fluffy white thing in the sky. So the idea of people giving up memories to store data in their brains—"

LaDene waved one hand dismissively. "I was referring to the cell phones."

He frowned. "What cell phones?"

"Exactly!" She laughed. "How the *hell* did they miss *cell phones?*"

As if on cue, there was a sound like a ray gun in a sci-fi movie and the ring on her right hand lit up with tiny flashing lights. She cocked her head, listening, then bounced off the bed. "My ride's here. See you around—" Her grin was sheepish.

"Cody," he said.

"Right." She paused, one eyebrow raised, the other down low, something Cody had never been able to manage no matter how hard he'd tried. "That's really your name."

"LaDene's really yours?" he said evenly.

"I grew up in Tonganoxie, Kansas. Of *course* it's really my name."

The two statements seemed unrelated to him but he nodded anyway. She pulled her suitcase out of the closet, extended the handle, and then paused again, one hand on the doorknob. "Where are *you* from?"

"I used to know but I rented that out for a database backup."

He heard her laughing all the way down the hall.

He ate alone in the dining room. The waitress gave him a table by a window that made the most of the hotel's location atop a rocky promontory, so he could enjoy his chicken Caesar salad with a scenic view of three other hotels and the six-lane highway running between them.

While it may not have been classic postcard material, he had to admit the view was actually rather nice. Kansas wasn't as flat as most people seemed to think, at least not in this locale. Here the landscape was gently rolling, punctuated by flat stretches usually occupied by malls or apartment complexes. In the distance, he could see the top of a mall that had to be the size of an airplane hangar and, not far from that, a crane surrounded by a framework suggesting future apartments or condos.

But it was the highway that drew his eye more than anything. He couldn't remember the last time he had seen so many private cars. Well, the travel agent had told him this was one of the last bastions of the autonomous commuter. Cody couldn't imagine what it was like to spend an hour or more of every weekday driving. He'd had a license himself once, but only briefly. After it had expired, he hadn't bothered renewing it and didn't miss it.

Perhaps if he were driving now, he'd be too busy to keep worrying at that stupid hotspot. Annoyed with himself, he pulled the complimentary library up on the table-top and checked out the local newspaper.

The waitress tried to talk him into dessert every time she refilled his iced tea. After his third glass, he swiped his keycard through the table-top reader, left an overly generous cash tip, and went back up to the room. It seemed a lot emptier now that LaDene was gone. Even the pillows she had piled against the headboard looked forlorn. He hadn't been thrilled to find her there when he'd checked in. She had apologised profusely—some kind of travel-plan fiasco. Having been through a few of those himself, he was sympathetic. As it turned out, she'd been good company—better than he'd realised. His newly-recovered privacy felt lonely.

He stretched out in the place where she had been and put the TV on again. It was only one night, and as LaDene had pointed out, this was a higher-end budget hotel. The complimentary coffee service was a drip pot with pouches of a gourmet blend rather than merely a kettle and two envelopes of instant. The minibar was well stocked with a wide variety of refreshments and if all of it cost ten times what it would in a grocery store, at least the cans of mixed nuts were a bit larger than average.

And then there was the television. Twenty channels including sports and movies, not counting the on-demand you had to pay extra for. Most places didn't offer half that. Maybe it was their way of compensating people like him, who were stuck there without a car.

Although that wasn't *quite* true. A chat with the desk clerk had revealed that they were less than a mile away from what she referred to as a shopping village, which he quickly figured out was a clever euphemism for strip mall. It wasn't much, she'd said in a politely cautioning tone meant to discourage any ideas of a foray on foot—a discount electronics outlet, a hardware store, an indoor playground, and three fast-food joints. Cody decided he could live without seeing it.

"Good choice," the clerk had said approvingly. "Because you'd be taking your life in your hands—no sidewalks."

"No sidewalks where?" he'd asked, puzzled.

"Between here and the shopping village."

"Then where do people walk?"

"They don't. People have to drive to get out here. They park, do whatever they came to do, then drive home again. I mean, you don't walk on the interstate, either."

Cody had been tempted to ask if she ever went for walks herself and if so, where, but decided against it. She was twenty-two at most, about to go from merely young and pretty to eye-catching as the last of her adolescent puppy-fat disappeared. She might have thought he was hitting on her and if he were honest, he might have had a hard time denying it.

He found a 24-hour news channel, turned the volume down to a murmur, and then used the remote to shut off the lights.

The next thing he knew, someone was sitting on his chest.

He could see nothing in the dark except a darker shadow looming over him, blocking out the flickering light from the television. He tried to yell but his mouth refused to open and he only made a sort of high-pitched grunt. Something pressed hard against his windpipe as whoever had him pinned bent over to speak close to his ear.

"You want to lie very still and not make a sound," said a male voice, just above a whisper. "Then do exactly what I tell you. I don't want to hurt you. I'm not here to hurt you. But I will if I have to."

His heart was beating hard and fast, as if it were trying to pound its way out of his chest. The pressure on his windpipe eased but didn't go away entirely. He swallowed, wincing.

As the man straightened up, Cody made out long greying hair, possibly tied back, and thick-framed glasses. "First, don't try to open your mouth. You're short-circuited and you'll only give yourself a headache. Once I know you're gonna behave yourself, I'll consider letting you chew gum."

He tried to make a conciliatory noise; the pressure on his windpipe increased again.

"I *said*, don't make a sound."

Cody sucked air through his nose, feeling himself jerk helplessly as his body fought to cough even though his mouth wouldn't open. His throat clenched, knotted, and tried to turn itself inside out. Then all at once, his mouth did open, just long enough for him to let out a few explosive coughs before his jaw snapped shut again.

"Better?"

Cody nodded, breathing in hungrily through his nose.

"You understand now to do *exactly* what I say?"

He nodded again.

"After I let you up, you're gonna change your clothes. Then you'll be taken out of here in a wheelchair. You're gonna sit quiet and stare at your lap. You're not gonna look up. If anyone speaks to you, you'll act like you didn't hear anything. There's a van waiting out front. You'll be put into it, chair and all, and we'll drive away.

"Now, it's important you remember everything I just said and do exactly that because an associate of mine is having a chat with the night clerk. Nice older man, a grandfather, in fact. If, while we pass through the lobby, he should get the idea that you need help, my associate will hurt him, badly. Unlike me, my associate doesn't mind hurting anyone. You don't want to harm innocent bystanders, do you."

Cody shook his head from side to side.

"Very good. Now, when I let you up, you're going to strip naked and put on what I've brought for you."

The man climbed off him and stood back. Cody moved more slowly as he slid over to the edge of the bed and began to unbutton his shirt with shaky fingers.

"A little faster, please," the man said, staring at the television with his arms folded. Cody wanted to comply but he was so unsteady he was off-balance even sitting down. He shoved his trousers down, extricating his ankles one at a time, socks and all. Next to him was a small neat pile of clothing folded into squares. Trembling, he picked up the top item; it was a hospital gown.

"Ties in back," the man said, casually matter-of-fact, as if he were remarking on the weather. He never looked away from the television.

Cody couldn't have tied his shoelaces. He decided it didn't matter; the second item was a bathrobe. He put it on sitting down, then pushed himself carefully to his feet.

The man turned from the television to give him an up-and-down. "I told you to strip *naked.* Lose the tighty-whiteys."

Cody fell over on the bed in the rush to gets his shorts off. The man waited with a put-upon air till he was done, then took hold of his upper arm and pulled him up. Cody winced; his grip was unnaturally strong, well out of proportion for a slight, older man almost a head shorter than he was.

The man waiting in the hallway with the wheelchair was a lot taller and huskier, dressed in a dark blue coverall; there was a patch on his left breast pocket showing a picture of a first-aid kit and the words County EMS. He said nothing as Cody stumbled over the footrests and fell into the seat. The frame was lightweight and all the wheels were small. The grey-haired man bent over him and Cody saw he was wearing the same uniform.

"You remember what I told you," he said and Cody noticed how little his rather pasty face moved, as if he'd Botoxed it into submission. And out here, up close and personal in much brighter light, the grey hair looked like a wig, ponytail and all. "Think of that poor man's family. Whether he goes home when his shift is over is all down to you." He stared into Cody's eyes as if he expected to see some response there, then chuckled and patted his cheek. "And seriously, relax your jaw. I'm not kidding about the headache." Cody started to rub the side of his face but the man caught his hand and put it firmly in his lap. "You don't move till we're out of here. Can you manage that or should I help you?"

Cody bowed his head.

"By George, I think he's got it."

Despite the carpeting, the ride was bumpy—the chair had a wobbly wheel, like every supermarket shopping cart Cody had ever used. But he stared fixedly at the slightly threadbare material covering his knees as they went down in the elevator. When they reached the lobby, he bowed his head a little more and squeezed his eyes shut, afraid they'd kill the desk clerk anyway. Having seen their faces, he'd be able to give a description to the police, which didn't bode well for his survival.

Or for his own.

The thought was a cold electric shock running down his back as the automatic doors hummed open in front of him. He heard the desk clerk tell someone to have a good night and a woman responded *I surely will, you too!* in a cheerful, friendly tone.

Then he was outside, rattling toward a white van with the same County EMS painted on the open side door. A tall woman waited beside a wheelchair lift.

Cody had no idea how long they had been on the road before the grey-haired man reached over and touched something to a spot under his cheekbone near the hinge of his jaw. He was in the middle of a huge yawn almost before it registered on him that he could open his mouth again. The muscles on either side of his face felt overworked and sore, including some he had never actually known were there. He worked his jaw for a while, knowing the grey-haired man was watching him and trying not to care.

He was sitting in a fold-down seat on Cody's right, facing backwards. The husky guy had anchored the wheelchair against a padded backstop and strapped him in before taking the seat on his left. The tall woman was up front, next to the driver. The woman who had been talking to the night clerk was behind him, along with at least one other person he had neither seen nor heard and who apparently wanted to keep it that way. Unbidden, the idea came to him that it was LaDene; he put it quickly out of his mind. Paranoia wasn't going to help.

Cody rested his head against the backstop and closed his eyes, wondering if he actually could go to sleep. Under the circumstances, there wasn't anything else he could do. But his mind was as alert as if he were in the middle of a busy day, which he supposed he was. Pretending to be asleep was a waste of time, thanks to the hospital gown; he figured they'd souped it up to where it could practically read his mood.

He opened his eyes and saw the grey-haired man watching him. Almost reflexively, he was overwhelmed by another huge yawn.

"You know the situation," the grey-haired man said, when his yawn had passed.

Cody nodded. "And *you* know I don't know anything."

"You don't have to," the man said.

"I'm a courier," Cody added. "Even if I wanted to, I couldn't access anything—"

"We know," the other man said, sounding short.

"—I have no knowledge of the quantity or nature of any data—"

"Yes, we're aware—"

"—nor am I responsible if any attempts at access cause damage, in whole or in part, to that data or any hardware or software—"

"We *already* know that—" He was openly impatient now.

"—my safe return cannot not indemnify any party against criminal charges of kidnapping and false imprisonment," Cody went on, trying not to enjoy the man's irritation too much as he talked over him, "which are brought by the state and not by companies or individuals." He said the last couple of words through another yawn. "Whew, excuse me. I'm obligated by the terms of my employment to apprise you of those facts. I can also write it all down for you and sign it."

The man on his left perked up. "Seriously? Like, if you don't say all that, they'd fire you?" Cody nodded. The man thought it over for a second. "What if we all claimed you didn't?"

"Shut up," the grey-haired man said, raising his voice.

Cody pretended not to hear. "I'd tell them I did."

"And they'd just believe you?"

"I'm level-four bonded," Cody replied. "On the job, I'm permanently under oath. If I lie, it's perjury."

"Shut your face or I'll shut it for you," said the grey-haired man, triggering Cody's urge to yawn again. The man waited till he was done, then added: "Anything else in the way of legal disclaimers? Health warnings? Household hints?"

Cody gave his head a quick shake and dropped his gaze to his lap. They traveled in silence for some unmeasured amount of time. Abruptly, the man on his left straightened up. "I just can't get my head around anyone just taking this guy's word about anything," he blurted.

"When we get where we're going, you can look it up on Wikipedia," the grey-haired man said acidly. "Last warning—shut your mouth."

Cody hardly dared to look up after that; whenever he did, the grey-haired man always seemed to be watching him. He stared into the darkness, listening to the thrum of the tires and air rushing past. No one said anything about a rest stop and he doubted there was any point in asking—the grey-haired guy would probably offer him a Coke bottle. He shifted in the chair and concentrated on making himself relax. He had said what he had to say; his best course of action now was to avoid further antagonising the grey-haired man.

It was just starting to grow lighter outside when he finally dozed off.

He woke from an unpleasant dream of many hands grabbing at him to find the big man unstrapping the chair while the grey-haired man poked his shoulder, telling him over and over to wake up. Exhaustion overwhelmed him, weighed him down so that just getting his eyes open was a major effort and when he finally did, they wouldn't stay open for longer than half a second. Then he was wheeled onto the lift and the humid heat that had not yet permeated the van's still-cool interior hit him in the face and seemed to suck all the air from his lungs.

Groggy, almost gasping, he noticed the van was now green and brown, bearing the logo of a large national rental company. More unsettling was seeing that they were in a parking garage. The grey-haired man leaned over him, looking pastier and more impassive than ever. "This will be less unpleasant if we don't have to force you. Not that it's a party. But if I have to short your circuits, it'll only be more of an ordeal."

Cody wasn't sure how to respond or even if he should.

"Good," the man said and made a let's-go gesture at the guy pushing his wheelchair.

The escort surrounding him blocked his view of everything that wasn't straight ahead but he saw enough to know it was definitely underground and it was mostly empty. Which didn't mean anything, he told himself. The country was lousy with underground parking garages, it was just a coincidence he'd seen that item on the news. LaDene had been right, he'd just been scaring himself. He wasn't a mobster, he was a courier, just a goddam courier. People didn't go around killing couriers. Nobody wanted that kind of trouble, the couriers' union was too well-connected and too powerful.

A car engine started suddenly and the sound made him jump. The grey-haired man didn't even glance at him but the others moved in a little closer, hiding him from view. They stayed close, even after he heard the car pass, until they reached a bank of elevators. One was roped off with a sign that said it was out of service. The grey-haired man pressed the call button and twisted; it popped open on a hinge and he inserted a plain metal key.

The elevator doors opened and Cody caught a strong whiff of antiseptic mixed with something flowery. His stomach turned over as they rolled him into the car, facing the back so he couldn't see what floor they were going to. There was no voice announcement or even a chime but he could make out a series of faint, airy thumps—possibly just the motor running after a long period of disuse but Cody counted them anyway, noting when the air quality changed from rain forest to refrigerated, and estimated they stopped on the fourteenth or fifteenth floor.

The place looked like a fancy clinic, right down to the immaculate receptionist at the immaculate, shiny white desk. The grey-haired man gave her a brisk wave as he strode past, walking very quickly now as he led the way through a maze of corridors to a room with a gurney and the machine they were going to use on him.

"Take your robe off and get comfortable," the grey-haired man said, jerking a thumb at the gurney.

Cody obeyed, a bit surprised at how quickly everyone else had vanished, leaving him alone with the man. He held onto the robe, turning it sideways to use like a blanket. "You mind? I'm kinda cold."

"Already?" The man was doing something with the machine; he gave a small, humourless laugh. "Maybe we should get you some mitts and booties."

"You could turn down the air conditioning," Cody said.

No answer. Three people in white uniforms came in with a cart. Cody settled down with a sigh of resignation and closed his eyes so he wouldn't have to see the cannulas going in.

Setting up seemed to take forever, although as far as he could tell, the hardware was up-to-date and they were all competent enough. Whoever had put the cannulas in his arm and leg was genuinely talented; it had been almost painless. The blood-pressure cuff on his other arm was actually more uncomfortable. He didn't know why they needed that anyway, when the hospital gown would tell them whatever they needed to know about his vitals. But he supposed under the circumstances they wanted both a belt and suspenders. They even made a business of verifying his blood type and his DNA before they finally began the process of filtering his blood.

Once they got going, he felt a little light-headed, as always, and colder than usual. He curled up as much as he could, huddling under the robe. There was very little conversation, all too low for him to make out; no one spoke to him. Eventually, he dozed off, mostly from boredom, and woke to find a pair of woolly socks on his feet. He didn't really feel any warmer but he was touched by the gesture all the same.

Just for something to do, he tried to guess who had done it, watching them surreptitiously as they moved around, checking readouts from him, from the machine, from his blood. The black woman with shoulder-length braids looked like she could have been someone's mother; if so, it was someone very young. Parents of young children were usually good for a kind deed. Or it might have been the Chinese guy who, like Cody, seemed to be in his late thirties.

He couldn't decide about the older black woman. She checked his vitals more often than anyone else but that didn't necessarily mean she was more concerned about his welfare. For all he knew, the socks had come from old Grey Ponytail himself. Hadn't he mentioned something about booties before they'd even started? Or it was one of the other people he'd barely glimpsed, busily working with his blood somewhere behind him. Maybe between separating blood cells from plasma and pumping it back into him, someone had paused to think he might be cold.

It went on for hours. Cody dozed, woke, dozed again. His stomach growled and subsided as hunger pangs threatened to turn into queasiness. How much longer, he wondered, irritable with boredom and lack of food. If they didn't call a halt soon, he was going to have some kind of major blood-sugar episode.

Almost as if he'd caught something of Cody's thoughts, the grey-haired man tapped him on the shoulder. "Are you supposed to eat something? Something in particular," he added, a bit impatiently.

"Food," Cody said, not caring how petulant he sounded.

"Not bread or sugar?"

"Just food. I don't suppose you'll give me any."

"What if we tried insulin instead?" There was an edge in the man's voice. In his peripheral vision, Cody saw the younger woman and the Chinese guy look up from a tablet they'd been studying together, obviously startled.

"Risky," Cody said. "I'm not diabetic. But you knew that."

The man gazed at him for some unmeasured period of time. He was worn out, tried and frustrated, Cody realised with a surge of spiteful joy; they all were but him most of all, because he was on the hook for whatever went wrong.

Abruptly, he blew out an exasperated breath and turned away. "We can't keep him any longer. Shut it down, give him lunch, and let's get him out of here."

Lunch turned out to be a can of nutrient with a straw; Cody was too hungry to feel more than a vague, momentary disappointment. The grey-haired man sat and glared at him. Hoping Cody would give up the goods somehow at the last minute? Or just being a sore loser?

"How old are you?" the man asked suddenly.

Cody paused and wiped his mouth. Considering how long they'd run his blood, he must have known, and a lot more besides. "Thirty-seven. Why?"

"Don't you think that's a little old to be a decoy?"

"I'm a courier." He went back to the drink.

"You're a decoy. A zero. A nothing. Less than nothing."

Cody had no response for that; he kept drinking

"The one that sold you out, she was probably the *real* courier. Wasn't she?"

"Who?" But even as he asked, he knew. Her name was on the tip of his tongue but he managed not to say it aloud.

"I'm right, aren't I? You're just—what? A day labourer who doesn't mind needles and won't faint at the sight of blood? *She's* carrying. LaVerne or LaRue, whatever her name is."

Cody pressed his lips together briefly. Whether the guy was telling the truth or fishing for a keyword, it wouldn't hurt not to give it to him. "Roughly ten percent of the population faints at the sight of blood," he said chattily. "It's a physical reaction, they can't help it. Nothing to do with their character or anything."

"Thank you for that piece of enlightenment." Despite his obvious irritation, his face was more impassive than ever, not to mention pastier. Now there were small flakes of what looked like dry skin around the man's hairline. The disguise was starting to break down, the wig parting company with the silicone mask. Everything probably should have been removed hours ago but the guy had kept nursing it along with touch-ups. Because he'd expected it would all by over by now, data extracted and delivered, payment collected and he'd be on his way to his next case, already forgetting what Cody looked like.

Instead he was sitting in a small, cold room with nothing to show for his effort but a spray-on about to peel off his face and nothing to look forward to except the displeasure of whoever he was working for, the loss of his fee, and a crew he had to pay anyway.

Cody finished the drink and set the empty can down beside him on the gurney. *Well,* that *wasn't fun. Whaddaya wanna do next?*

It was the last thought he had for a while.

Sounds nudged him gradually toward awareness, until he understood the voices and various other noises were real, not lingering fragments of dreams, or dream-like flashes from lost hours, possibly days. Eyes still closed, he rolled over, turning his face away from the bright light overhead and smelled clean sheets, along with alcohol, powder, and cleanser. Hospital emergency room, he thought with cautious relief; there were worse places to wake up.

His memory was patchy but he knew the basics of what had happened. As soon as his captors had been sure they wouldn't find anything in his blood, they no longer had to worry about contamination and dosed Cody's so-called lunch. Pretty heavily, if the lead-balloon sensation in his head was any indication. Just by way of kicking his ass for having nothing of value.

Once the lunch had taken effect, they had dressed him up and dumped him someplace where he could sleepwalk indefinitely without attracting attention. Like, say, a large mall. Or a shopping village; one with a multi-screen cineplex. Cody wondered how long he had been aimlessly roaming before anyone noticed something odd about him. There were all kinds of stories. Everybody in the union knew one about a courier who had woken up to find she'd wandered into a house and spent five days with people who'd thought she was a long-lost relative. Cody suspected that one was apocryphal.

Two days later, he was in a DC-area suburb, although he wasn't sure exactly which state. State-line ambiguity was getting to be a habit with him.

"How'd you like Oklahoma City?" asked the medic from where she sat at the lighting panel. She was a slightly plump woman with one brown eye and one blue eye; the difference was made more noticeable by the port-wine stain covering that side of her face from hairline to the corner of her mouth.

"I only saw a parking garage, a clinic, and part of a hospital." Cody finished undressing and stood with his back to the plain white wall. "Ready when you are."

"Ah, you've done this before. I don't even have to tell you to close your eyes and hold perfectly still."

He took a breath and held it. Sometimes he imagined he could sense the UV light change as the scanning line traveled over his body. Years ago, when he had first become a courier, they'd showed him a video of himself being scanned. He'd thought he'd looked like a fantasy creature—one of Lewis Carroll's fabulous monsters that had wandered out of the looking glass into a high-tech lab.

Blaschko's Lines, a doctor had told him, years ago. Only visible under certain kinds of UV light.

He'd done research on his own, wondered about lesions or the possibility of waking up one morning to find himself permanently piebald. He would dream that the lines running up and down his arms and legs, traveling in waves on his torso, looping on his back, swirling all over his head would appear spontaneously and without warning in normal light; sometimes they were permanent. Other times, they'd flash on and off like a warning light.

He hadn't had that kind of anxiety dream in a long time. They'd faded away with the hotspots. Maybe now they were both coming back.

"Done," the medic called.

Relieved, Cody took a deep breath and stepped away from the wall to get dressed again. The medic asked his permission before she swabbed the inside of his cheek, and again before scraping a few skin cells from his lower back, his hip, and his knee.

He was immensely grateful for the courtesy. It was always nice when someone treated a courier like a human being in a demanding profession rather than merely a meat-bag for data.

The guy who escorted him to his room for the night was wearing the standard gopher attire—a multi-pocketed vest over plain T-shirt, jeans, and running shoes—but had a military bearing that he didn't even try to hide. Cody wasn't surprised to find someone waiting for him when he got there. It had been a while since the last sales pitch.

"We're all very glad to have you back safe." The woman in the swivel chair by the desk was dark-haired and dark-skinned and her voice had the faint but unmistakable lilt that Hindi speakers never lost completely. He had seen her before a few times, dressed as she was now in a black jacket and trousers, but only in passing. She was one of those people who gave the impression of being taller because of the way she carried herself. Not military-style like his friend now standing at obvious parade rest between himself and the door, just with authority. In Charge. The touches of grey in her hair suggested she was older than he was, though he couldn't have said how much—more than ten, less than thirty.

"I'm glad to be back," he said, feeling a little awkward as he stood in front of her. She gestured for him to sit down on the bed, the only other furniture in the room, unless you counted the forty-inch screen in the wall.

"You automatically get a week of recuperation but we'll sign off on two or even three." She shrugged. "Or four."

"Thank you."

"This wasn't the first time for you, was it."

As if she didn't know, he thought, careful to keep a straight face. Then he realised she was actually waiting for an answer. "No," he said quickly. "It wasn't."

"I hope that it wasn't especially bad for you."

He shook his head. His memory was still quite spotty—his clearest recollection was of an older man with a ponytail and having to lie very still in a cold room while his blood was pumped out of his body and back in again. He also had the idea that there had been someone in the hotel room with him before he'd been kidnapped but that didn't seem likely. Considering how heavily he'd been drugged, he was probably lucky he still remembered his childhood.

Unless I rented it out for a database. Another of those left-field thoughts that had been popping into his head for the last few days. They'd probably meant something once.

". . . sure you will be happy to know that your kidnappers came away with nothing," the woman was saying, "thanks to your unique . . . ah, condition."

He smiled a little. "I never thought of being a chimera as a condition like, oh, excessive perspiration. Or psoriasis."

"It does make you uniquely suited for deep encryption. Even if your kidnappers had thought to use your DNA to activate your blood, they wouldn't know you have more than one kind of DNA, much less that they needed to scan you under UV for the entire key."

His kidnappers; the way she said it made it sound almost as if they belonged to him in some way. Or like they were his personal problem—his *condition.*

"Eventually, that'll occur to someone. If someone else doesn't sell it to them first," he added. The memory of a woman's name, LaRue or LaDene, and an old movie flickered in his brain and was gone.

"Such optimism." She gave a short laugh. "The average mere can't afford to rent a full sequencer, let alone personnel to run it who would be smart enough to figure out you had two kinds of DNA, or that they'd need both for decryption." She gave another, slightly heartier laugh. "Contrary to what you may have heard, the evil genius is mostly mythical. Nobody turns to crime because of their towering intellect.

"But that's neither here nor there. We still want you to work solely for us. I know that someone has made you this offer before—a few times, yes? As an employee, you would be paid substantially more, along with bonuses for crisis situations—"

"'Crisis situations?' Is that anything like 'hazardous duty'?"

She barely hesitated as she acknowledged his interruption. "Occupational benefits are also quite generous. Health coverage, vacation time, paternity leave—"

"Dental?"

Now she paused to give him a look. "And optical. Even a clothing allowance."

He was tempted to comment on how she had used hers but decided not to get personal.

"We can also be very flexible in terms of your cover," she went on. "Some sort of independent, low-key profession, like an accountant or a transcriber or—" She floundered suddenly and he could tell it wasn't something that happened to her very often.

"Software engineer," he suggested, then smiled sheepishly. "Kidding."

"That could work, as long as it's something nice and ordinary. Wedding albums, family albums, baby pictures, that sort of thing—"

"I really was kidding," he said. "Software mystifies me."

"You could even be semiretired—"

"No." He shook his head, apologetic but firm. "If I go to work for you, I'm no longer a courier. I'm a government employee in a highly sensitive area under military jurisdiction. Once I lose my union membership, all bets are off. All I have is you."

"That's quite a lot," the woman said reprovingly. "You have no idea how much."

Actually, I do, he thought at her, *but if I'm flayed and hung up in a parking garage, I won't care about the cover story.* He shook his head again.

"If we take you into the fold, we can tell you more about what you're doing. Don't you want to know—"

"*No.*" It came out louder and more emphatic than he'd intended but he wasn't sorry. "I don't. You've got me this much. I agreed to cooperate because I don't need to be *in the fold* to be an encryption key. I'll keep the secret but I don't want to *be* the secret."

The woman shook her head. "Please. You went over that line a long time ago."

"Not quite," he insisted. "My body, yes. But not *me.*"

She stood up, stretching a little. "We'll talk again. This government doesn't give up that easily."

"Oh?" He raised his eyebrows. "Which government is that, anyway?"

The question caught her off guard and for a moment she stared at him, open-mouthed. Then she threw back her head and laughed. "Oh, very good," she said, as the man opened the door for her. "Very, *very* good." She started to leave, then hesitated. "And that's really your name: Cody."

"Yeah. My name's really Cody." Something flickered in his memory again but it was gone before he could think about it. He lay down on the bed and found the remote under one of the pillows.

"Well, *that* was fun," he said, to no one and to whatever bugs might be listening, and turned on the TV. "Now whaddaya wanna do?"

For I Have Lain Me Down on the Stone of Loneliness and I'll Not Be Back Again

MICHAEL SWANWICK

Here's another story by Michael Swanwick, whose "The Dala Horse" appears elsewhere in this anthology. In this one, he takes us to a high-tech but still troubled future Ireland, for a story about choices—and how, once made, they can never be undone.

Ich am of Irlaunde,
And of the holy londe
Of Irlaunde.
Gode sire, pray ich the,
For of saynte chairité
Come ant daunce with me
In Irlaunde.
(anon.)

The bullet scars were still visible on the pillars of the General Post Office in Dublin, almost two centuries after the 1916 uprising. That moved me more than I had expected. But what moved me even more was standing at the exact same spot, not two blocks away, where my great-great-grandfather saw Gerry Adams strolling down O'Connell Street on Easter morning of '96, the eightieth anniversary of that event, returning from a political rally with a single bodyguard to one side of him and a local politico to the other. It gave me a direct and simple connection to the tangled history of that tragic land.

I never knew my great-great-grandfather, but my grandfather told me that story once and I've never forgotten it, though my grandfather died when I was still a boy. If I squeeze my eyes tight shut, I can see his face, liquid and wavy as if glimpsed through candle flames, as he lay dying under a great feather comforter in his New York City railroad flat, his smile weak and his hair forming a halo around him as white as a dandelion waiting for the wind to purse its lips and blow.

"It was doomed from the start," Mary told me later. "The German guns had been intercepted and the republicans were outnumbered fourteen to one. The British cannons fired on Dublin indiscriminately. The city was afire and there was no food to be had. The survivors were booed as they were marched off to prison and execution, for the common folk did not support them. By any conventional standard it was a fiasco. But once it happened, our independence was assured. We lose and we lose and we lose, but because we never accept it, every defeat and humiliation only leads us closer to victory."

Her eyes *blazed.*

I suppose I should tell you about Mary's eyes, if you're to understand this story. But if I'm to tell you about her eyes, first I have to tell you about the holy well.

There is a holy well in the Burren that, according to superstition, will cure a toothache. The Burren is a great upwelling of limestone in the west of County Clair, and it is unlike anyplace else on Earth. There is almost no soil. The ground is stony and the stone is weathered in a network of fissures and cracks, called grykes, within which grow a province of plants you will not find in such abundance elsewhere. Three are caves in great number to the south and the east, and like everywhere else in that beautiful land, a plenitude of cairns and other antiquities to be found.

The holy well is one such antiquity, though it is only a round hole, perhaps a foot across, filled with water and bright green algae. The altar over it is of recent construction, built by unknown hands from the long slender stones formed by the natural weathering of the limestone between the grykes, which makes the local stone walls so distinctive and the walking so treacherous. You could tear it down and scatter its component parts and never hear a word spoken about your deed. But if you returned a year later you'd find it rebuilt and your vandalism unmade as if it had never happened. People have been visiting the well for a long, long time. The Christian overlay—the holy medals and broken statues of saints that are sometimes left as offerings, along with the prescription bottles, nails, and coins—is a recent and perhaps a transient phenomenon.

But the important thing to know, and the reason people keep coming back to it, is that the holy well works. Some holy wells don't. You can locate them on old maps, but when you go to have a look, there aren't any offerings there. Something happened long ago—they were cursed by a saint or defiled by a sinner or simply ran out of mojo—and the magic stopped happening, and the believers went away and never returned. This well, however, is charged with holy power. It gives you shivers just to stand by it.

Mary's eyes were like that. As green as the water in that well, and as full of dangerous magic.

I knew about the holy well because I'd won big and gotten a ticket off-planet, and so before I went, I took a year off in order to see all the places on Earth I would never return to, ending up with a final month to spend wandering about the land of my ancestors. It was my first time in Ireland and I loved everything about it, and I couldn't help fantasizing that maybe I'd do so well in the Outsider worlds that someday I'd be rich enough to return and maybe retire there.

I was a fool and, worse, I didn't know it.

We met in the Fiddler's Elbow, a pub in that part of the West which the Bord Failte calls Yeats Country. I hadn't come in for music but only to get out of the rain and have a hot whiskey. I was sitting by a small peat fire, savoring the warmth and the sweet smell of it, when somebody opened a door at the back of the room and started collecting admission. There was a sudden rush of people into the pub and so I carried my glass to the bar and asked, "What's going on?"

"It's Maire na Raghallach," the publican said, pronouncing the last name like Reilly. "At the end of a tour she likes to pop in someplace small and give an unadvertised concert. You want to hear, you'd best buy a ticket now. They're not going to last."

I didn't know Maire na Rahallach from Eve. But I'd seen the posters around town and I figured what the hell. I paid and went in.

Maire na Raghallach sang without a backup band and only an amp-and-fingerrings air guitar for instrumentation. Her music was . . . Well, either you've heard her and know or you haven't and if you haven't, words won't help. But I was mesmerized, ravished, rapt. So much so that midway through the concert, as she was singing "Deirdre's Lament," my head swam and a buzzing sensation lifted me up out of my body into a waking dream or hallucination or maybe vision is the word I'm looking for. All the world went away. There were only the two of us facing each other across a vast plain of bones. The sky was black and the bones were white as chalk. The wind was icy cold. We stared at each other. Her eyes pierced me like a spear. They looked right through me, and I was lost, lost, lost. I must have been half in love with her already. All it took was her noticing my existence to send me right over the edge.

Her lips moved. She was saying something and somehow I knew it was vastly important. But the wind whipped her words away unheard. It was howling like a banshee with all the follies of the world laid out before it. It screamed like an electric guitar. When I tried to walk toward her, I discovered I was paralyzed. Though I strained every muscle until I thought I would splinter my bones trying to get closer, trying to hear, I could not move nor make out the least fraction of what she was telling me.

Then I was myself again, panting and sweating and filled with terror. Up on the low stage, Mary (as I later learned to call her) was talking between songs. She grinned cockily and with a nod toward me said, "This one's for the American in the front row."

And then, as I trembled in shock and bewilderment, she launched into what I later learned was one of her own songs, "Come Home, the Wild Geese." The Wild Geese were originally the soldiers who left Ireland, which could no longer support them, to fight for foreign masters in foreign armies everywhere. But over the centuries the term came to be applied to everyone of Irish descent living elsewhere, the children and grandchildren and great-great-great-grandchildren of those unhappy emigrants whose luck was so bad they couldn't even manage to hold onto their own country and who had passed the guilt of that down through the generations, to be cherished and brooded over by their descendants forever.

"This one's for the American," she'd said.

But how had she known?

The thing was that, shortly after hitting the island, I'd bought a new set of clothes locally and dumped all my American things in a charity recycling device. Plus, I'd bought one of those cheap neuroprogramming pendants that actors use to temporarily redo their accents. Because I'd quickly learned that in Ireland, as soon as you're pegged for an American, the question comes out: "Looking for your roots, then, are ye?"

"No, it's just that this is such a beautiful country and I wanted to see it."

Skeptically, then: "But you do have Irish ancestors, surely?"

"Well, yes, but . . ."

"Ahhhh." Hoisting a pint preparatory to draining its lees. "You're looking for your roots, then. I thought as much."

But if there's one thing I *wasn't* looking for, it was my fucking roots. I was eighth-generation American Irish and my roots were all about old men in dark little Boston pubs killing themselves a shot glass at a time, and the ladies of Noraid goose-stepping down the street on Saint Patrick's Day in short black skirts, their heels crashing against the street, a terrifying irruption of fascism into a day that was otherwise all kitsch and false sentiment, and corrupt cops, and young thugs who loved sports and hated school and blamed the niggers and affirmative action for the lousy construction-worker jobs they never managed to keep long. I'd come to this country to get away from all that, and a thousand things more that the Irish didn't know a scrap about. The cartoon leprechauns and the sentimental songs and the cute sayings printed on cheap tea towels somehow all adding up to a sense that you've lost before you've even begun, that it doesn't matter what you do or who you become, because you'll never achieve or amount to shit. The thing that sits like a demon in the dark pit of the soul. That Irish darkness.

So how had she known I was an American?

Maybe it was only an excuse to meet her. If so, it was as good an excuse as any. I hung around after the show, waiting for Mary to emerge from whatever dingy space they'd given her for a dressing room, so I could ask.

When she finally emerged and saw me waiting for her, her mouth turned up in a way that as good as said, "Gotcha!" Without waiting for the question, she said, "I had only to look at you to see that you had prenatal genework. The Outsiders shared it with the States first, for siding with them in the war. There's no way a young man your age with everything about you perfect could be anything else."

Then she took me by the arm and led me away to her room.

We were together how long? Three weeks? Forever?

Time enough for Mary to take me everywhere in that green and haunted island. She had the entirety of its history at her fingertips, and she told me all and showed me everything and I, in turn, learned nothing. One day we visited the Portcoon sea cave, a gothic wave-thunderous place that was once occupied by a hermit who had vowed to fast and pray there for the rest of his life and never accept food from human hands. Women swam in on the tides, offering him sustenance, but he refused it. "Or so the story goes," Mary said. As he was dying, a seal brought him fish and, the seal not being human and having no hands, he ate. Every day it returned and so kept him alive for years. "But what the truth may be," Mary concluded, "is anyone's guess."

Afterwards, we walked ten minutes up the coast to the Giant's Causeway. There we found a pale blue, four-armed alien in a cotton smock and wide straw hat painting a watercolor of the basalt columns rising and falling like stairs into the air and down to the sea. She held a brush in one right hand and another in a left hand, and plied them simultaneously.

"Soft day," Mary said pleasantly.

"Oh! Hello!" The alien put down her brushes, turned from her one-legged easel. She did not offer her name, which in her kind—I recognized the species—was never spoken aloud. "Are you local?"

I started to shake my head but, "That we be," Mary said. It seemed to me that her brogue was much more pronounced than it had been. "Enjoying our island, are ye?"

"Oh, yes. This is such a beautiful country. I've never seen such greens!" The alien gestured widely with all four arms. "So many shades of green, and all so intense they make one's eyes ache."

"It's a lovely land," Mary agreed. "But it can be a dirty one as well. You've taken in all the sights, then?"

"I've been everywhere—to Tara, and the Cliffs of Moher, and Newgrange, and the Ring of Kerry. I've even kissed the Blarney Stone." The alien lowered her voice and made a complicated gesture that I'm guessing was the equivalent of a giggle. "I was hoping to see one of the little people. But maybe it's just as well I didn't. It might have carried me off to a fairy mound and then after a night of feasting and music I'd emerge to find that centuries had gone by and everybody I knew was dead."

I stiffened, knowing that Mary found this kind of thing offensive. But she only smiled and said, "It's not the wee folk you have to worry about. It's the boys."

"The boys?"

"Aye. Ireland is a hotbed of nativist resistance, you know. During the day, it's safe enough. But the night belongs to the boys." She touched her lips to indicate that she wouldn't speak the organization's name out loud. "They'll target a lone Outsider to be killed as an example to others. The landlord gives them the key to her room. They have ropes and guns and filthy big knives. Then it's a short jaunt out to the bogs, and what happens there . . . Well, they're simple, brutal men. It's all over by dawn and there are never any witnesses. Nobody sees a thing."

The alien's arms thrashed. "The tourist officials didn't say anything about this!"

"Well, they wouldn't, would they?"

"What do you mean?" the alien asked.

Mary said nothing. She only stood there, staring insolently, waiting for the alien to catch on to what she was saying.

After a time, the alien folded all four of her arms protectively against her thorax. When she did, Mary spoke at last. "Sometimes they'll give you a warning. A friendly local will come up to you and suggest that the climate is less healthy than you thought, and you might want to leave before nightfall."

Very carefully, the alien said, "Is that what's happening here?"

"No, of course not." Mary's face was hard and unreadable. "Only, I hear Australia's lovely this time of year."

Abruptly, she whirled about and strode away so rapidly that I had to run to catch up to her. When we were well out of earshot of the alien, I grabbed her arm and angrily said, "What the fuck did you do *that* for?"

"I really don't think it's any of your business."

"Let's just pretend that it is. Why?"

"To spread fear among the Outsiders," she said, quiet and fierce. "To remind them that Earth is sacred ground to us and always will be. To let them know that while they may temporarily hold the whip, this isn't their planet and never will be."

Then, out of nowhere, she laughed. "Did you see the expression on that skinny blue bitch's face? She practically turned green!"

"Who are you, Mary O'Reilly?" I asked her that night, when we were lying naked and sweaty among the tangled sheets. I'd spent the day thinking, and realized how little she'd told me about herself. I knew her body far better than I did her mind. "What are your likes and dislikes? What do you hope and what do you fear? What made you a musician, and what do you want to be when you grow up?" I was trying to keep it light, seriously though I meant it all.

"I always had the music, and thank God for that. Music was my salvation."

"How so?"

"My parents died in the last days of the war. I was only an infant, so I was put into an orphanage. The orphanages were funded with American and Outsider money, part of the campaign to win the hearts and minds of the conquered peoples. We were raised to be denationalized citizens of the universe. Not a word of Irish touched our ears, nor any hint of our history or culture. It was all Greece and Rome and the Aldebaran Unity. Thank Christ for our music! They couldn't keep that out, though they tried hard to convince us it was all harmless deedle-deedle jigs and reels. But we knew it was subversive. We knew it carried truth. Our minds escaped long before our bodies could."

We, she'd said, and *us* and *our.* "That's not who you are, Mary. That's a political speech. I want to know what you're really like. As a person, I mean."

Her face was like stone. "I'm what I am. An Irishwoman. A musician. A patriot. Cooze for an American playboy."

I kept my smile, though I felt as if she'd slapped me. "That's unfair."

It's an evil thing to have a naked woman look at you the way Mary did me. "Is it? Are you not abandoning your planet in two days? Maybe you're thinking of taking me along. Tell me, exactly how does that work?"

I reached for the whiskey bottle on the table by the bed. We'd drunk it almost empty, but there was still a little left. "If we're not close, then how is that my fault? You've known from the start that I'm mad about you. But you won't even—oh, fuck it!" I drained the bottle. "Just what the hell do you want from me? Tell me! I don't think you can."

Mary grabbed me angrily by the arms and I dropped the bottle and broke her hold and seized her by the wrists. She bit my shoulder so hard it bled and when I tried to push her away, topped me over on my back and clambered up on top of me.

We did not so much resolve our argument as fuck it into oblivion.

It took me forever to fall asleep that night. Not Mary. She simply decided to sleep and sleep came at her bidding. I, however, sat up for hours staring at her face in the moonlight. It was all hard planes and determination. A strong face but not one given to compromise. I'd definitely fallen in love with the wrong woman. Worse, I was leaving for distant worlds the day after tomorrow. All my life had been shaped toward that end. I had no Plan B.

In the little time I had left, I could never sort out my feelings for Mary, much less hers for me. I loved her, of course, that went without saying. But I hated her bullying ways, her hectoring manner of speech, her arrogant assurance that I would do whatever she wanted me to do. Much as I desired her, I wanted nothing more than to never see her again. I had all the wealth and wonders of the universe ahead of me. My future was guaranteed.

And, God help me, if she'd only asked me to stay, I would have thrown it all away for her in an instant.

In the morning, we took a hyperrapid to Galway and toured its vitrified ruins. "Resistance was stiffest in the West," Mary said. "One by one all the nations of the Earth sued for peace, and even in Dublin there was talk of accommodation. Yet we fought on. So the Outsiders hung a warship in geostationary orbit and turned their strange weapons on us. This beautiful port city was turned to glass. The ships were blown against the shore and broke on the cobbles. The cathedral collapsed under its own weight. Nobody has lived here since."

The rain spattered to a stop and there was a brief respite from the squalls which in that part of the country come off the Atlantic in waves. The sun dazzled from a hundred crystalline planes. The sudden silence was like a heavy hand laid unexpectedly upon my shoulder. "At least they didn't kill anyone," I said weakly. I was of a generation that saw the occupation of the Outsiders as being, ultimately, a good thing. We were healthier, richer, happier, than our parents had been. Nobody worried about environmental degradation or running out of resources anymore. There was no denying we were physically better off for their intervention.

"It was a false mercy that spared the citizens of Galway from immediate death and sent them out into the countryside with no more than the clothes on their backs. How were they supposed to survive? They were doctors and lawyers and accountants. Some of them reverted to brigandry and violence, to be sure. But most simply kept walking until they lay down by the side of the road and died. I can show you as many thousand hours of recordings of the Great Starvation as you can bring yourself to stomach. There was no food to be had, but thanks to the trinkets the Outsiders had used to collapse the economy, everybody had cameras feeding right off their optic nerves, saving all the golden memories of watching their children die."

Mary was being unfair—the economic troubles hadn't been the Outsiders' doing. I knew because I'd taken economics in college. History, too, so I also knew that the war had, in part, been forced upon them. But though I wanted to, I could not adequately answer her. I had no passion that was the equal of hers.

"Things have gotten better," I said weakly. "Look at all they've done for . . ."

"The benevolence of the conqueror, scattering coins for the peasants to scrabble in the dust after. They're all smiles when we're down on our knees before them. But see what happens if one of us stands up on his hind legs and tells them to sod off."

We stopped in a pub for lunch and then took a hopper to Gartan Lough. There we bicycled into the countryside. Mary led me deep into land that had never been greatly populated and was still dotted with the ruins of houses abandoned a quarter-century before. The roads were poorly paved or else dirt, and the land was so beautiful as to make you weep. It was a perfect afternoon, all blue skies and fluffy clouds. We labored up a hillside to a small stone chapel that had lost its roof centuries ago. It was surrounded by graves, untended and overgrown with wildflowers.

Lying on the ground by the entrance to the graveyard was the Stone of Loneliness.

The Stone of Loneliness was a fallen menhir or standing stone, something not at all uncommon throughout the British Isles. They'd been reared by unknown people for reasons still not understood in Megalithic times, sometimes arranged in circles, and other times as solitary monuments. There were faded cup-and-ring lines carved into what had been the stone's upper end. And it was broad enough that a grown man could lie down on it. "What should I do?" I asked.

"Lie down on it," Mary said.

So I did.

I lay down upon the Stone of Loneliness and closed my eyes. Bees hummed lazily in the air. And, standing at a distance, Mary began to sing:

The lions of the hills are gone
And I am left alone, alone . . .

It was "Deirdre's Lament," which I'd first heard her sing in the Fiddler's Elbow. In Irish legend, Deirdre was promised from infancy to Conchubar, the king of Ulster. But, as happens, she fell in love with and married another, younger man. Naoise, her husband, and his brothers Ardan and Ainnle, the sons of Uisnech, fled with her to Scotland, where they lived in contentment. But the humiliated and vengeful old king lured them back to Ireland with promises of amnesty. Once they were in his hands, he treacherously killed the three sons of Uisnech and took Deirdre to his bed.

The Falcons of the Wood are flown
And I am left alone, alone . . .

Deirdre of the Sorrows, as she is often called, has become a symbol for Ireland herself—beautiful, suffering from injustice, and possessed of a happy past that looks likely to never return. Of the real Deirdre, the living and breathing woman upon whom the stories were piled like so many stones on a cairn, we know nothing. The legendary Deirdre's story, however, does not end with her suicide, for in the aftermath of Conchubar's treachery wars were fought, the injustices of which led to further wars. Which wars continue to this very day. It all fits together suspiciously tidily.

It was no coincidence that Deirdre's father was the king's storyteller.

The dragons of the rock are sleeping
Sleep that wakes not for our weeping . . .

All this, however, I tell you after the fact. At the time, I was not thinking of the legend at all. For the instant I lay down upon the cold stone, I felt all the misery of Ireland flowing into my body. The Stone of Loneliness was charmed, like the well in the Burren. Sleeping on it was said to be a cure for homesickness. So, during the Famine, emigrants would spend their last night atop it before leaving Ireland forever. It seemed to me, prone upon the menhir, that all the sorrow they had shed was flowing into my body. I felt each loss as if it were my own. Helplessly, I started to sob and then to weep openly. I lost track of what Mary was singing, though her voice went on and on. Until finally she sang

Dig the grave both wide and deep
Sick I am, and fain would sleep
Dig the grave and make it ready
Lay me on my true Love's body

and stopped. Leaving a silence that echoed on and on forever.

Then Mary said, "There's someone I think you're ready to meet."

Mary took me to a nondescript cinder-block building, the location of which I will take with me to the grave. She led the way in. I followed nervously. The interior was so dim I stumbled on the threshold. Then my eyes adjusted, and I saw that I was in a bar. Not a pub, which is a warm and welcoming public space where families gather to socialize, the adults over a pint and the kiddies drinking their soft drinks, but a bar—a place where men go to get drunk. It smelled of potcheen and stale beer. Somebody had ripped the door to the bog off its hinges and no one had bothered to replace it. Presumably Mary was the only woman to set foot in the place for a long, long time.

There were three or four men sitting at small tables in the gloom, their backs to the door, and a lean man with a bad complexion at the bar. "Here you are then," he said without enthusiasm.

"Don't mind Liam," Mary said to me. Then, to Liam, "Have you anything fit for drinking?"

"No."

"Well, that's not why we came anyway." Mary jerked her head toward me. "Here's the recruit."

"He doesn't look like much."

"Recruit for what?" I said. It struck me suddenly that Liam was keeping his hands below the bar, out of sight. Down where a hard man will keep a weapon, such as a cudgel or a gun.

"Don't let his American teeth put you off. They're part of the reason we wanted him in the first place."

"So you're a patriot, are you, lad?" Liam said in a voice that indicated he knew good and well that I was not.

"I have no idea what you're talking about."

Liam glanced quickly at Mary and curled his lip in a sneer. "Ahh, he's just in it for the crack." In Irish *craic* means "fun" or "kicks." But the filthy pun was obviously intended. My face hardened and I balled up my fists. Liam didn't look concerned.

"Hush, you!" Mary said. Then, turning to me, "And I'll thank you to control yourself as well. This is serious business. Liam, I'll vouch for the man. Give him the package."

Liam's hands appeared at last. They held something the size of a biscuit tin. It was wrapped in white paper and tied up with string. He slid it across the bar.

"What's this?"

"It's a device," Liam said. "Properly deployed, it can implode the entire administrative complex at Shannon Starport without harming a single civilian."

My flesh ran cold.

"So you want me to plant this in the 'port, do yez?" I said. For the first time in weeks, I became aware of the falseness of my accent. Impulsively, I pulled the neuropendant from beneath my shirt, dropped it on the floor, and stepped on it. Whatever I said here, I would say it as myself. "You want me to go in there and fucking *blow myself up*?"

"No, of course not," Mary said. "We have a soldier in place for that. But he—"

"Or she," Liam amended.

"—or she isn't in a position to smuggle this in. Human employees aren't allowed to bring in so much as a pencil. That's how little the Outsiders think of us. You, however, can. Just take the device through their machines—it's rigged to read as a box of cigars—in your carry-on. Once you're inside, somebody will come up to you and ask if you remembered to bring something for granny. Hand it over."

"That's all," Liam said.

"You'll be halfway to Jupiter before anything happens."

They both looked at me steadily. "Forget it," I said. "I'm not killing any innocent people for you."

"Not people. Aliens."

"They're still innocent."

"They wouldn't be here if they hadn't seized the planet. So they're not innocent."

"You're a nation of fucking werewolves!" I cried. Thinking that would put an end to the conversation.

But Mary wasn't fazed. "That we are," she agreed. "Day by day, we present our harmless, domestic selves to the world, until one night the beast comes out to feed. But at least we're not sheep, bleating complacently in the face of the butcher's knife. Which are you, my heart's beloved? A sheep? Or could there be a wolf lurking deep within?"

"He can't do the job," Liam said. "He's as weak as watered milk."

"Shut it. You have no idea what you're talking about." Mary fixed me with those amazing eyes of hers, as green as the living heart of Ireland, and I was helpless before them. "It's not weakness that makes you hesitate," she said, "but a foolish and misinformed conscience. I've thought about this far longer than you have, my treasure. I've thought about it all my life. It's a holy and noble thing that I'm asking of you."

"I—"

"Night after night, you've sworn you'd do anything for me—not with words, I'll grant you, but with looks, with murmurs, with your soul. Did you think I could not hear the words you dared not say aloud? Now I'm calling you on all those unspoken promises. Do this one thing—if not for the sake of your planet, then for me."

All the time we'd been talking, the men sitting at their little tables hadn't made a noise. Nor had any of them turned to face us. They simply sat hunched in place—not drinking, not smoking, not speaking. Just listening. It came to me then how large they were, and how still. How alert. It came to me then that if I turned Mary down, I'd not leave this room alive.

So, really, I had no choice.

"I'll do it," I said. "And God damn you for asking me to."

Mary went to hug me and I pushed her roughly away. "No! I'm doing this thing for you, and that puts us quits. I never want to see you or think of you again."

For a long, still moment, Mary studied me calmly. I was lying, for I'd never wanted her so much as I did in that instant. I could see that she knew I was lying, too. If she'd let the least sign of that knowledge show, I believe I would have hit her. But she did not. "Very well," she said. "So long as you keep your word."

She turned and left and I knew I would never see her again.

Liam walked me to the door. "Be careful with the package outside in the rain," he said, handing me an umbrella. "It won't work if you let it get damp."

I was standing in Shannon Starport, when Homeworld Security closed in on me. Two burly men in ITSA uniforms appeared on either side of me and their alien superior said, "Would you please come with us, sir." It was not a question.

Oh, Mary, I thought sadly. You have a traitor in your organization. Other than me, I meant. "Can I bring my bag?"

"We'll see to that, sir."

I was taken to their interrogation room.

Five hours later I got onto the lighter. They couldn't hold me because there wasn't anything illegal in my possession. I'd soaked the package Liam gave me in the hotel room sink overnight and then gotten up early and booted it down a storm drain when no one was looking. It was a quick trip to orbit where there waited a ship larger than a skyscraper and rarer than almost anything you could name, for it wouldn't return to this planet for centuries. I floated on board knowing that for me there'd be no turning back. Earth would be a story I told my children, and a pack of sentimental lies they would tell theirs.

My homeworld shrank behind me and disappeared. I looked out the great black glass walls into a universe thronged with stars and galaxies and had no idea where I was or where I thought I was going. It seemed to me then that we were each and every one of us ships without a harbor, sailors lost on land.

I used to say that only Ireland and my family could make me cry. I cried when my mother died and I cried when Dad had his heart attack the very next year. My baby sister failed to survive the same birth that killed my mother, so some of my tears were for her as well. Then my brother Bill was hit by a drunk driver and I cried and that was the end of my family. Now there's only Ireland.

But that's enough.

ghostweight

YOON HA LEE

New writer Yoon Ha Lee lives in Southern California with her family. Her fiction has appeared in Lightspeed, Clarkesworld, The Magazine of Fantasy & Science Fiction, Federation, Beneath Ceaseless Skies, *and elsewhere. She maintains a Web site at pegasus.cityofveils.com.*

In the wild and exotic space opera that follows, she sweeps us along with a young woman on a desperate quest for revenge, accompanied only by a ruthless and predatory "ghost" who whispers in her ear throughout.

▼

It is not true that the dead cannot be folded. Square becomes kite becomes swan; history becomes rumor becomes song. Even the act of remembrance creases the truth.

What the paper-folding diagrams fail to mention is that each fold enacts itself upon the secret marrow of your ethics, the axioms of your thoughts.

Whether this is the most important thing the diagrams fail to mention is a matter of opinion.

"There's time for one more hand," Lisse's ghost said. It was composed of cinders of color, a cipher of blurred features, and it had a voice like entropy and smoke and sudden death. Quite possibly it was the last ghost on all of ruined Rhaion, conquered Rhaion, Rhaion with its devastated, shadowless cities and dead moons and dimming sun. Sometimes Lisse wondered if the ghost had a scar to match her own, a long, livid line down her arm. But she felt it was impolite to ask.

Around them, in a command spindle sized for fifty, the walls of the war-kite were hung with tatters of black and faded green, even now in the process of reknitting themselves into tapestry displays. Tangled reeds changed into ravens. One perched on a lightning-cloven tree. Another, taking shape amid twisted threads, peered out from a skull's eye socket.

Lisse didn't need any deep familiarity with mercenary symbology to understand the warning. Lisse's people had adopted a saying from the Imperium's mercenaries: *In raven arithmetic, no death is enough.*

Lisse had expected pursuit. She had deserted from Base 87 soon after hearing that scouts had found a mercenary war-kite in the ruins of a sacred maze, six years after all the mercenaries vanished: suspicious timing on her part, but she would have no better opportunity for revenge. The ghost had not tried too hard to dissuade her. It had always understood her ambitions.

For a hundred years, despite being frequently outnumbered, the mercenaries in their starfaring kites had cindered cities, destroyed flights of rebel starflyers, shattered stations in the void's hungry depths. What better weapon than one of their own kites?

What troubled her was how lightly the war-kite had been defended. It had made a strange, thorny silhouette against the lavender sky even from a long way off, like briars gone wild, and with the ghost as scout she had slipped past the few mechanized sentries. The kite's shadow had been human. She was not sure what to make of that.

The kite had opened to her like a flower. The card game had been the ghost's idea, a way to reassure the kite that she was its ally: Scorch had been invented by the mercenaries.

Lisse leaned forward and started to scoop the nearest column, the Candle Column, from the black-and-green gameplay rug. The ghost forestalled her with a hand that felt like the dregs of autumn, decay from the inside out. In spite of herself, she flinched from the ghostweight, which had troubled her all her life. Her hand jerked sideways; her fingers spasmed.

"Look," the ghost said.

Few cadets had played Scorch with Lisse even in the barracks. The ghost left its combinatorial fingerprints in the cards. People drew the unlucky Fallen General's Hand over and over again, or doubled on nothing but negative values, or inverted the Crown Flower at odds of thousands to one. So Lisse had learned to play the solitaire variant, with jerengjen as counters. *You must learn your enemy's weapons*, the ghost had told her, and so, even as a child in the reeducation facility, she had saved her chits for paper to practice folding into cranes, lilies, leaf-shaped boats.

Next to the Candle Column she had folded stormbird, greatfrog, lantern, drake. Where the ghost had interrupted her attempt to clear the pieces, they had landed amid the Sojourner and Mirror Columns, forming a skewed late-game configuration: a minor variant of the Needle Stratagem, missing only its pivot.

"Consider it an omen," the ghost said. "Even the smallest sliver can kill, as they say."

There were six ravens on the tapestries now. The latest one had outspread wings, as though it planned to blot out the shrouded sun. She wondered what it said about the mercenaries, that they couched their warnings in pictures rather than drums or gongs.

Lisse rose from her couch. "So they're coming for us. Where are they?"

She had spoken in the Imperium's administrative tongue, not one of the mercenaries' own languages. Nevertheless, a raven flew from one tapestry to join its fellows in the next. The vacant tapestry grayed, then displayed a new scene: a squad of six tanks caparisoned in Imperial blue and bronze, paced by two personnel carriers sheathed in metal mined from withered stars. They advanced upslope, pebbles skittering in their wake.

In the old days, the ghost had told her, no one would have advanced through a sacred maze by straight lines. But the ancient walls, curved and interlocking, were gone now. The ghost had drawn the old designs on her palm with its insubstantial fingers, and she had learned not to shudder at the untouch, had learned to thread the maze in her mind's eye: one more map to the things she must not forget.

"I'd rather avoid fighting them," Lisse said. She was looking at the command spindle's controls. Standard Imperial layout, all of them—it did not occur to her to wonder why the kite had configured itself thus—but she found nothing for the weapons.

"People don't bring tanks when they want to negotiate," the ghost said dryly. "And they'll have alerted their flyers for intercept. You have something they want badly."

"Then why didn't they guard it better?" she demanded.

Despite the tanks' approach, the ghost fell silent. After a while, it said, "Perhaps they didn't think anyone but a mercenary could fly a kite."

"They might be right," Lisse said darkly. She strapped herself into the commander's seat, then pressed three fingers against the controls and traced the commands she had been taught as a cadet. The kite shuddered, as though caught in a hell-wind from the sky's fissures. But it did not unfurl itself to fly.

She tried the command gestures again, forcing herself to slow down. A cold keening vibrated through the walls. The kite remained stubbornly landfast.

The squad rounded the bend in the road. All the ravens had gathered in a single tapestry, decorating a half-leafed tree like dire jewels. The rest of the tapestries displayed the squad from different angles: two aerial views and four from the ground.

Lisse studied one of the aerial views and caught sight of two scuttling figures, lean angles and glittering eyes and a balancing tail in black metal. She stiffened. They had the shadows of hounds, all graceful hunting curves. Two jerengjen, true ones, unlike the lifeless shapes that she folded out of paper. The kite must have deployed them when it sensed the tanks' approach.

Sweating now, despite the autumn temperature inside, she methodically tried every command she had ever learned. The kite remained obdurate. The tapestries' green threads faded until the ravens and their tree were bleak black splashes against a background of wintry gray.

It was a message. Perhaps a demand. But she did not understand.

The first two tanks slowed into view. Roses, blue with bronze hearts, were engraved to either side of the main guns. The lead tank's roses flared briefly.

The kite whispered to itself in a language that Lisse did not recognize. Then the largest tapestry cleared of trees and swirling leaves and rubble, and presented her with a commander's emblem, a pale blue rose pierced by three claws. A man's voice issued from the tapestry: "Cadet Fai Guen." This was her registry name. They had not reckoned that she would keep her true name alive in her heart like an ember. "You are in violation of Imperial interdict. Surrender the kite at once."

He did not offer mercy. The Imperium never did.

Lisse resisted the urge to pound her fists against the interface. She had not survived this long by being impatient. "That's it, then," she said to the ghost in defeat.

"Cadet Fai Guen," the voice said again, after another burst of light, "you have one minute to surrender the kite before we open fire."

"Lisse," the ghost said, "the kite's awake."

She bit back a retort and looked down. Where the control panel had once been featureless gray, it was now crisp white interrupted by five glyphs, perfectly spaced for her outspread fingers. She resisted the urge to snatch her hand away. "Very well," she said. "If we can't fly, at least we can fight."

She didn't know the kite's specific control codes. Triggering the wrong sequence might activate the kite's internal defenses. But taking tank fire at point-blank range would get her killed, too. She couldn't imagine that the kite's armor had improved in the years of its neglect.

On the other hand, it had jerengjen scouts, and the jerengjen looked perfectly functional.

She pressed her thumb to the first glyph. A shadow unfurled briefly but was gone before she could identify it. The second attempt revealed a two-headed dragon's twisting coils. Long-range missiles, then: thunder in the sky. Working quickly, she ran through the options. It would be ironic if she got the weapons systems to work only to incinerate herself.

"You have ten seconds, Cadet Fai Guen," said the voice with no particular emotion.

"Lisse," the ghost said, betraying impatience.

One of the glyphs had shown a wolf running. She remembered that at one point the wolf had been the mercenaries' emblem. Nevertheless, she felt a dangerous affinity to it. As she hesitated over it, the kite said, in a parched voice, "Soul strike."

She tapped the glyph, then pressed her palm flat to activate the weapon. The panel felt briefly hot, then cold.

For a second she thought that nothing had happened, that the kite had malfunctioned. The kite was eerily still.

The tanks and personnel carriers were still visible as gray outlines against darker gray, as were the nearby trees and their stifled fruits. She wasn't sure whether that was an effect of the unnamed weapons or a problem with the tapestries. Had ten seconds passed yet? She couldn't tell, and the clock of her pulse was unreliable.

Desperate to escape before the tanks spat forth the killing rounds, Lisse raked her hand sideways to dismiss the glyphs. They dispersed in unsettling fragmented shapes resembling half-chewed leaves and corroded handprints. She repeated the gesture for *fly*.

Lisse choked back a cry as the kite lofted. The tapestry views changed to sky on all sides except the ravens on their tree—birds no longer, but skeletons, price paid in coin of bone.

Only once they had gained some altitude did she instruct the kite to show her what had befallen her hunters. It responded by continuing to accelerate.

The problem was not the tapestries. Rather, the kite's wolf-strike had ripped all the shadows free of their owners, killing them. Below, across a great swathe of the continent once called Ishuel's Bridge, was a devastation of light, a hard, glittering splash against the surrounding snow-capped mountains and forests and winding rivers.

Lisse had been an excellent student, not out of academic conscientiousness but because it gave her an opportunity to study her enemy. One of her best subjects had been geography. She and the ghost had spent hours drawing maps in the air or shaping topographies in her blankets; paper would betray them, it had said. As she memorized the streets of the City of Fountains, it had sung her the ballads of its founding. It had told her about the feuding poets and philosophers that the thoroughfares of the City of Prisms had been named after. She knew which mines supplied which bases and how the roads spidered across Ishuel's Bridge. While the population figures of the bases and settlement camps weren't exactly announced to cadets, especially those recruited from the reeducation facilities, it didn't take much to make an educated guess.

The Imperium had built 114 bases on Ishuel's Bridge. Base complements averaged 20,000 people. Even allowing for the imprecision of her eye, the wolf-strike had taken out—

She shivered as she listed the affected bases, approximately sixty of them.

The settlement camps' populations were more difficult. The Imperium did not like to release those figures. Imperfectly, she based her estimate on the zone around Base 87, remembering the rows of identical shelters. The only reason they did not outnumber the bases' personnel was that the mercenaries had been coldly efficient on Jerengjen Day.

Needle Stratagem, Lisse thought blankly. The smallest sliver. She hadn't expected its manifestation to be quite so literal.

The ghost was looking at her, its dark eyes unusually distinct. "There's nothing to be done for it now," it said at last. "Tell the kite where to go before it decides for itself."

"Ashway 514," Lisse said, as they had decided before she fled base: scenario after scenario whispered to each other like bedtime stories. She was shaking. The straps did nothing to steady her.

She had one last glimpse of the dead region before they curved into the void: her handprint upon her own birthworld. She had only meant to destroy her hunters.

In her dreams, later, the blast pattern took on the outline of a running wolf.

In the mercenaries' dominant language, jerengjen originally referred to the art of folding paper. For her part, when Lisse first saw it, she thought of it as snow. She was four years old. It was a fair spring afternoon in the City of Tapestries, slightly humid. She was watching a bird try to catch a bright butterfly when improbable paper shapes began drifting from the sky, foxes and snakes and stormbirds.

Lisse called to her parents, laughing. Her parents knew better. Over her shrieks, they dragged her into the basement and switched off the lights. She tried to bite one of her fathers when he clamped his hand over her mouth. Jerengjen tracked primarily by shadows, not by sound, but you couldn't be too careful where the mercenaries' weapons were concerned.

In the streets, jerengjen unfolded prettily, expanding into artillery with dragon-shaped shadows and sleek four-legged assault robots with wolf-shaped shadows. In the skies, jerengjen unfolded into bombers with kestrel-shaped shadows.

This was not the only Rhaioni city where this happened. People crumpled like paper cutouts once their shadows were cut away by the onslaught. Approximately one-third of the world's population perished in the weeks that followed.

Of the casualty figures, the Imperium said, *It is regrettable.* And later, *The stalled negotiations made the consolidation necessary.*

Lisse carried a map of the voidways with her at all times, half in her head and half in the Scorch deck. The ghost had once been a traveler. It had shown her mnemonics for the dark passages and the deep perils that lay between stars. Growing up, she had laid out endless tableaux between her lessons, memorizing travel times and vortices and twists.

Ashway 514 lay in the interstices between two unstable stars and their cacophonous necklace of planets, comets, and asteroids. Lisse felt the kite tilting this way and that as it balanced itself against the stormy voidcurrent. The tapestries shone from one side with ruddy light from the nearer star, 514 Tsi. On the other side, a pale violet-blue planet with a serenade of rings occluded the view.

514 was a useful hiding place. It was off the major tradeways, and since the Battle of Fallen Sun—named after the rebel general's emblem, a white sun outlined in red, rather than the nearby stars—it had been designated an ashway, where permanent habitation was forbidden.

More important to Lisse, however, was the fact that 514 was the ashway nearest the last mercenary sighting, some five years ago. As a student, she had learned the names and silhouettes of the most prominent war-kites, and set verses of praise in their honor to Imperial anthems. She had written essays on their tactics and memorized the names of their most famous commanders, although there were no statues or portraits, only the occasional unsmiling photograph. The Imperium was fond of statues and portraits.

For a hundred years (administrative calendar), the mercenaries had served their masters unflinchingly and unfailingly. Lisse had assumed that she would have as much time as she needed to plot against them. Instead, they had broken their service, for reasons the Imperium had never released—perhaps they didn't know, either—and none had been seen since.

"I'm not sure there's anything to find here," Lisse said. Surely the Imperium would have scoured the region for clues. The tapestries were empty of ravens. Instead, they diagrammed shifting voidcurrent flows. The approach of enemy starflyers would perturb the current and allow Lisse and the ghost to estimate their intent. Not trusting the kite's systems—although there was only so far that she could take her distrust, given the circumstances—she had been watching the tapestries for the past several hours. She had, after a brief argument with the ghost, switched on haptics so that the air currents would, however imperfectly, reflect the status of the void around them. Sometimes it was easier to feel a problem through your skin.

"There's no indication of derelict kites here," she added. "Or even kites in use, other than this one."

"It's a starting place, that's all," the ghost said.

"We're going to have to risk a station eventually. You might not need to eat, but I do." She had only been able to sneak a few rations out of base. It was tempting to nibble at one now.

"Perhaps there are stores on the kite."

"I can't help but think this place is a trap."

"You have to eat sooner or later," the ghost said reasonably. "It's worth a look, and I don't want to see you go hungry." At her hesitation, it added, "I'll stand watch here. I'm only a breath away."

This didn't reassure her as much as it should have, but she was no longer a child in a bunk precisely aligned with the walls, clutching the covers while the ghost told her her people's stories. She reminded herself of her favorite story, in which a single sentinel kept away the world's last morning by burning out her eyes, and set out.

Lisse felt the ghostweight's pull the farther away she walked, but that was old pain, and easily endured. Lights flicked on to accompany her, diffuse despite her unnaturally sharp shadow, then started illuminating passages ahead of her, guiding her footsteps. She wondered what the kite didn't want her to see.

Rations were in an unmarked storage room. She wouldn't have been certain about the rations, except that they were, if the packaging was to be believed, field category 72: better than what she had eaten on training exercises, but not by much. No surprise, now that she thought about it: from all accounts, the mercenaries had relied on their masters' production capacity.

Feeling ridiculous, she grabbed two rations and retraced her steps. The fact that the kite lit her exact path only made her more nervous.

"Anything new?" she asked the ghost. She tapped the ration. "It's a pity that you can't taste poison."

The ghost laughed dryly. "If the kite were going to kill you, it wouldn't be that subtle. Food is food, Lisse."

The food was as exactingly mediocre as she had come to expect from military food. At least it was not any worse. She found a receptacle for disposal afterward, then laid out a Scorch tableau, Candle Column to Bone, right to left. Cards rather than jerengjen, because she remembered the scuttling hound-jerengjen with creeping distaste.

From the moment she left Base 87, one timer had started running down. The devastation of Ishuel's Bridge had begun another, the important one. She wasn't gambling her survival; she had already sold it. The question was, how many Imperial bases could she extinguish on her way out? And could she hunt down any of the mercenaries that had been the Imperium's killing sword?

Lisse sorted rapidly through possible targets. For instance, Base 226 Mheng, the Petaled Fortress. She would certainly perish in the attempt, but the only way she could better that accomplishment would be to raze the Imperial firstworld, and she wasn't that ambitious. There was Bridgepoint 663 Tsi-Kes, with its celebrated Pallid Sentinels, or Aerie 8 Yeneq, which built the Imperium's greatest flyers, or—

She set the cards down, closed her eyes, pressed her palms against her face. She was no tactician supreme. Would it make much difference if she picked a card at random?

But of course nothing was truly random in the ghost's presence.

She laid out the Candle Column again. "Not 8 Yeneq," she said. "Let's start with a softer target. Aerie 586 Chiu."

Lisse looked at the ghost: the habit of seeking its approval had not left her. It nodded. "The safest approach is via the Capillary Ashways. It will test your piloting skills."

Privately, Lisse thought that the kite would be happy to guide itself. They didn't dare allow it to, however.

The Capillaries were among the worst of the ashways. Even starlight moved in unnerving ways when faced with ancient networks of voidcurrent gates, unmaintained for generations, or vortices whose behavior changed day by day.

They were fortunate with the first several capillaries. Under other circumstances, Lisse would have gawked at the splendor of lensed galaxies and the jewel-fire of distant clusters. She was starting to manipulate the control interface without hesitating, or flinching as though a wolf's shadow might cross hers.

At the ninth—

"Patrol," the ghost said, leaning close.

She nodded jerkily, trying not to show that its proximity pained her. Its mouth crimped in apology.

"It would have been worse if we'd made it all the way to 586 Chiu without a run-in," Lisse said. That kind of luck always had a price. If she was unready, best to find out now, while there was a chance of fleeing to prepare for a later strike.

The patrol consisted of sixteen flyers: eight Lance 82s and eight Scout 73s. She had flown similar Scouts in simulation.

The flyers did not hesitate. A spread of missiles streaked toward her. Lisse launched antimissile fire.

It was impossible to tell whether they had gone on the attack because the Imperium and the mercenaries had parted on bad terms, or because the authorities had already learned of what had befallen Rhaion. She was certain couriers had gone out within moments of the devastation of Ishuel's Bridge.

As the missiles exploded, Lisse wrenched the kite toward the nearest vortex. The kite was a larger and sturdier craft. It would be better able to survive the voidcurrent stresses. The tapestries dimmed as they approached. She shut off haptics as wind eddied and swirled in the command spindle. It would only get worse.

One missile barely missed her. She would have to do better. And the vortex was a temporary terrain advantage; she could not lurk there forever.

The second barrage came. Lisse veered deeper into the current. The stars took on peculiar roseate shapes.

"They know the kite's capabilities," the ghost reminded her. "Use them. If they're smart, they'll already have sent a courier burst to local command."

The kite suggested jerengjen flyers, harrier class. Lisse conceded its expertise.

The harriers unfolded as they launched, sleek and savage. They maneuvered remarkably well in the turbulence. But there were only ten of them.

"If I fire into that, I'll hit them," Lisse said. Her reflexes were good, but not that good, and the harriers apparently liked to soar near their targets.

"You won't need to fire," the ghost said.

She glanced at it, disbelieving. Her hand hovered over the controls, playing through possibilities and finding them wanting. For instance, she wasn't certain that the firebird (explosives) didn't entail self-immolation, and she was baffled by the stag.

The patrol's pilots were not incapable. They scorched three of the harriers. They probably realized at the same time that Lisse did that the three had been sacrifices. The other seven flensed them silent.

Lisse edged the kite out of the vortex. She felt an uncomfortable sense of duty to the surviving harriers, but she knew they were one-use, crumpled paper, like all jerengjen. Indeed, they folded themselves flat as she passed them, reducing themselves to battledrift.

"I can't see how this is an efficient use of resources," Lisse told the ghost.

"It's an artifact of the mercenaries' methods," it said. "It works. Perhaps that's all that matters."

Lisse wanted to ask for details, but her attention was diverted by a crescendo of turbulence. By the time they reached gentler currents, she was too tired to bring it up.

They altered their approach to 586 Chiu twice, favoring stealth over confrontation. If she wanted to char every patrol in the Imperium by herself, she could live a thousand sleepless years and never be done.

For six days they lurked near 586 Chiu, developing a sense for local traffic and likely defenses. Terrain would not be much difficulty. Aeries were built near calm, steady currents.

"It would be easiest if you were willing to take out the associated city," the ghost said in a neutral voice. They had been discussing whether making a bombing pass on the aerie posed too much of a risk. Lisse had balked at the fact that 586 Chiu Second City was well within blast radius. The people who had furnished the kite's armaments seemed to have believed in surfeit. "They'd only have a moment to know what was happening."

"No."

"Lisse—"

She looked at it mutely, obdurate, although she hated to disappoint it. It hesitated, but did not press its case further.

"This, then," it said in defeat. "Next best odds: aim the voidcurrent disrupter at the manufactory's core while jerengjen occupy the defenses." Aeries held the surrounding current constant to facilitate the calibration of newly built flyers. Under ordinary circumstances, the counterbalancing vortex was leashed at the core. If they could disrupt the core, the vortex would tear at its surroundings.

"That's what we'll do, then," Lisse said. The disrupter had a short range. She did not like the idea of flying in close. But she had objected to the safer alternative.

Aerie 586 Chiu reminded Lisse not of a nest but of a pyre. Flyers and transports were always coming and going, like sparks. The kite swooped in sharp and fast. Falcon-jerengjen raced ahead of them, holding lattice formation for two seconds before scattering toward their chosen marks.

The aerie's commanders responded commendably. They knew the kite was by far the greater threat. But Lisse met the first flight they threw at her with missiles keen and terrible. The void lit up in a clamor of brilliant colors.

The kite screamed when a flyer salvo hit one of its secondary wings. It bucked briefly while the other wings changed their geometry to compensate. Lisse could not help but think that the scream had not sounded like pain. It had sounded like exultation.

The real test was the gauntlet of Banner 142 artillery emplacements. They were silver-bright and terrible. It seemed wrong that they did not roar like tigers. Lisse bit the inside of her mouth and concentrated on narrowing the parameters for the voidcurrent disrupter. Her hand was a fist on the control panel.

One tapestry depicted the currents: striations within striations of pale blue against black. Despite its shielding, the core was visible as a knot tangled out of all proportion to its size.

"Now," the ghost said, with inhuman timing.

She didn't wait to be told twice. She unfisted her hand.

Unlike the wolf-strike, the disrupter made the kite scream again. It lurched and twisted. Lisse wanted to clap her hands over her ears, but there was more incoming fire, and she was occupied with evasive maneuvers. The kite folded in on itself, minimizing its profile. It dizzied her to view it on the secondary tapestry. For a panicked moment, she thought the kite would close itself around her, press her like petals in a book. Then she remembered to breathe.

The disrupter was not visible to human sight, but the kite could read its effect on the current. Like lightning, the disrupter's blast forked and forked again, zigzagging inexorably toward the minute variations in flux that would lead it toward the core.

She was too busy whipping the kite around to an escape vector to see the moment of convergence between disrupter and core. But she felt the first lashing surge as the vortex spun free of its shielding, expanding into available space. Then she was too busy steadying the kite through the triggered subvortices to pay attention to anything but keeping them alive.

Only later did she remember how much debris there had been, flung in newly unpredictable ways: wings torn from flyers, struts, bulkheads, even an improbable crate with small reddish fruit tumbling from the hole in its side.

Later, too, it would trouble her that she had not been able to keep count of the people in the tumult. Most were dead already: sliced slantwise, bone and viscera exposed, trailing banners of blood; others twisted and torn, faces ripped off and cast aside like unwanted masks, fingers uselessly clutching the wrack of chairs, tables, doorframes. A fracture in one wall revealed three people in dark green jackets. They turned their faces toward the widening crack, then clasped hands before a subvortex hurled them apart. The last Lisse saw of them was two hands, still clasped together and severed at the wrist.

Lisse found an escape. Took it.

She didn't know until later that she had destroyed 40% of the aerie's structure. Some people survived. They knew how to rebuild.

What she never found out was that the disrupter's effect was sufficiently long-lasting that some of the survivors died of thirst before supplies could safely be brought in.

In the old days, Lisse's people took on the ghostweight to comfort the dead and be comforted in return. After a year and a day, the dead unstitched themselves and accepted their rest.

After Jerengjen Day, Lisse's people struggled to share the sudden increase in ghostweight, to alleviate the flickering terror of the massacred.

Lisse's parents, unlike the others, stitched a ghost onto a child.

"They saw no choice," the ghost told her again and again. "You mustn't blame them."

The ghost had listened uncomplainingly to her troubles and taught her how to cry quietly so the teachers wouldn't hear her. It had soothed her to sleep with her people's legends and histories, described the gardens and promenades so vividly she imagined she could remember them herself. Some nights were more difficult than others, trying to sleep with that strange, stabbing, heartpulse ache. But blame was not what she felt, not usually.

The second target was Base 454 Qo, whose elite flyers were painted with elaborate knotwork, green with bronze-tipped thorns. For reasons that Lisse did not try to understand, the jerengjen disremembered the defensive flight but left the painted panels completely intact.

The third, the fourth, the fifth—she started using Scorch card values to tabulate the reported deaths, however unreliable the figures were in any unencrypted sources. For all its talents, the kite could not pierce military-grade encryption. She spent two days fidgeting over this inconvenience so she wouldn't have to think about the numbers.

When she did think about the numbers, she refused to round up. She refused to round down.

The nightmares started after the sixth, Bridgepoint 977 Ja-Esh. The station commander had kept silence, as she had come to expect. However, a merchant coalition had broken the interdict to plead for mercy in fourteen languages. She hadn't destroyed the coalition's outpost. The station had, in reprimand.

She reminded herself that the merchant would have perished anyway. She had learned to use the firebird to scathing effect. And she was under no illusions that she was only destroying Imperial soldiers and bureaucrats.

In her dreams she heard their pleas in her birth tongue, which the ghost had taught her. The ghost, for its part, started singing her to sleep, as it had when she was little.

The numbers marched higher. When they broke ten million, she plunged out of the command spindle and into the room she had claimed for her own. She pounded the wall until her fists bled. Triumph tasted like salt and venom. It wasn't supposed to be so *easy*. In the worst dreams, a wolf roved the tapestries, eating shadows—eating souls. And the void with its tinsel of worlds was nothing but one vast shadow.

Stores began running low after the seventeenth. Lisse and the ghost argued over whether it was worth attempting to resupply through black market traders. Lisse said they didn't have time to spare, and won. Besides, she had little appetite.

Intercepted communications suggested that someone was hunting them. Rumors and whispers. They kept Lisse awake when she was so tired she wanted to slam the world shut and hide. The Imperium certainly planned reprisal. Maybe others did, too.

If anyone else took advantage of the disruption to move against the Imperium for their own reasons, she didn't hear about it.

The names of the war-kites, recorded in the Imperium's administrative language, are varied: *Fire Burns the Spider Black. The Siege of the City with Seventeen Faces. Sovereign Geometry. The Glove with Three Fingers.*

The names are not, strictly speaking, Imperial. Rather, they are plundered from the greatest accomplishments of the cultures that the mercenaries have defeated on the Imperium's behalf. *Fire Burns the Spider Black* was a silk tapestry housed in the dark hall of Meu Danh, ancient of years. *The Siege of the City with Seventeen Faces* was a saga chanted by the historians of Kwaire. *Sovereign Geometry* discussed the varying nature of parallel lines. And more: plays, statues, games.

The Imperium's scholars and artists take great pleasure in reinterpreting these works. Such achievements are meant to be disseminated, they say.

They were three days' flight from the next target, Base 894 Sao, when the shadow winged across all the tapestries. The void was dark, pricked by starfire and the occasional searing burst of particles. The shadow singed everything darker as it soared to intercept them, as single-minded in its purpose as a bullet. For a second she almost thought it was a collage of wrecked flyers and rusty shrapnel.

The ghost cursed. Lisse startled, but when she looked at it, its face was composed again.

As Lisse pulled back the displays' focus to get a better sense of the scale, she thought of snowbirds and stormbirds, winter winds and cutting beaks. "I don't know what that is," she said, "but it can't be natural." None of the Imperial defenses had manifested in such a fashion.

"It's not," the ghost said. "That's another war-kite."

Lisse cleared the control panel. She veered them into a chancy voidcurrent eddy.

The ghost said, "Wait. You won't outrun it. As we see its shadow, it sees ours."

"How does a kite have a shadow in the void in the first place?" she asked. "And why haven't we ever seen our own shadow?"

"Who can see their own soul?" the ghost said. But it would not meet her eyes.

Lisse would have pressed for more, but the shadow overtook them. It folded itself back like a plumage of knives. She brought the kite about. The control panel suggested possibilities: a two-headed dragon, a falcon, a coiled snake. Next a wolf reared up, but she quickly pulled her hand back.

"Visual contact," the kite said crisply.

The stranger-kite was the color of a tarnished star. It had tucked all its projections away to present a minimal surface for targeting, but Lisse had no doubt that it could unfold itself faster than she could draw breath. The kite flew a widening helix, beautifully precise.

"A mercenary salute, equal to equal," the ghost said.

"Are we expected to return it?"

"Are you a mercenary?" the ghost countered.

"Communications incoming," the kite said before Lisse could make a retort.

"I'll hear it," Lisse said over the ghost's objection. It was the least courtesy she could offer, even to a mercenary.

To Lisse's surprise, the tapestry's raven vanished to reveal a woman's visage, not an emblem. The woman had brown skin, a scar trailing from one temple down to her cheekbone, and dark hair cropped short. She wore gray on gray, in no uniform that Lisse recognized, sharply tailored. Lisse had expected a killer's eyes, a hunter's eyes. Instead, the woman merely looked tired.

"Commander Kiriet Dzan of—" She had been speaking in administrative, but the last word was unfamiliar. "You would say *Candle*."

"Lisse of Rhaion," she said. There was no sense in hiding her name.

But the woman wasn't looking at her. She was looking at the ghost. She said something sharply in that unfamiliar language.

The ghost pressed its hand against Lisse's. She shuddered, not understanding. "Be strong," it murmured.

"I see," Kiriet said, once more speaking in administrative. Her mouth was unsmiling. "Lisse, do you know who you're traveling with?"

"I don't believe we're acquainted," the ghost said, coldly formal.

"Of course not," Kiriet said. "But I was the logistical coordinator for the scouring of Rhaion." She did not say *consolidation*. "I knew why we were there. Lisse, your ghost's name is Vron Arien."

Lisse said, after several seconds, "That's a mercenary name."

The ghost said, "So it is. Lisse—" Its hand fell away.

"Tell me what's going on."

Its mouth was taut. Then: "Lisse, I—"

"Tell me."

"He was a deserter, Lisse," the woman said, carefully, as if she thought the information might fracture her. "For years he eluded Wolf Command. Then we discovered he had gone to ground on Rhaion. Wolf Command determined that, for sheltering him, Rhaion must be brought to heel. The Imperium assented."

Throughout this Lisse looked at the ghost, silently begging it to deny any of it, all of it. But the ghost said nothing.

Lisse thought of long nights with the ghost leaning by her bedside, reminding her of the dancers, the tame birds, the tangle of frostfruit trees in the city square; things she did not remember herself because she had been too young when the jerengjen came. Even her parents only came to her in snatches: curling up in a mother's lap, helping a father peel plantains. Had any of the ghost's stories been real?

She thought, too, of the way the ghost had helped her plan her escape from Base 87, how it had led her cunningly through the maze and to the kite. At the time, it had not occurred to her to wonder at its confidence.

Lisse said, "Then the kite is yours."

"After a fashion, yes." The ghost's eyes were precisely the color of ash after the last ember's death.

"But my parents—"

Enunciating the words as if they cut it, the ghost said, "We made a bargain, your parents and I."

She could not help it; she made a stricken sound.

"I offered you my protection," the ghost said. "After years serving the Imperium, I knew its workings. And I offered your parents vengeance. Don't think that Rhaion wasn't my home, too."

Lisse was wrackingly aware of Kiriet's regard. "Did my parents truly die in the consolidation?" The euphemism was easier to use.

She could have asked whether Lisse was her real name. She had to assume that it wasn't.

"I don't know," it said. "After you were separated from them, I had no way of finding out. Lisse, I think you had better find out what Kiriet wants. She is not your friend."

I was the logistical coordinator, Kiriet had said. And her surprise at seeing the ghost—*It has a name,* Lisse reminded herself—struck Lisse as genuine. Which meant Kiriet had not come here in pursuit of Vron Arien. "Why are you here?" Lisse asked.

"You're not going to like it. I'm here to destroy your kite, whatever you've named it."

"It doesn't have a name." She had been unable to face the act of naming, of claiming ownership.

Kiriet looked at her sideways. "I see."

"Surely you could have accomplished your goal," Lisse said, "without talking to me first. I am inexperienced in the ways of kites. You are not." In truth, she should already have been running. But Kiriet's revelation meant that Lisse's purpose, once so clear, was no longer to be relied upon.

"I may not be your friend, but I am not your enemy, either," Kiriet said. "I have no common purpose with the Imperium, not anymore. But you cannot continue to use the kite."

Lisse's eyes narrowed. "It is the weapon I have," she said. "I would be a fool to relinquish it."

"I don't deny its efficacy," Kiriet said, "but you are Rhaioni. Doesn't the cost trouble you?"

Cost?

Kiriet said, "So no one told you." Her anger focused on the ghost.

"A weapon is a weapon," the ghost said. At Lisse's indrawn breath, it said, "The kites take their sustenance from the deaths they deal. It was necessary to strengthen ours by letting it feast on smaller targets first. This is the particular craft of my people, as ghostweight was the craft of yours, Lisse."

Sustenance. "So this is why you want to destroy the kite," Lisse said to Kiriet.

"Yes." The other woman's smile was bitter. "As you might imagine, the Imperium did not approve. It wanted to negotiate another hundred-year contract. I dissented."

"Were you in a position to dissent?" the ghost asked, in a way that made Lisse think that it was translating some idiom from its native language.

"I challenged my way up the chain of command and unseated the head of Wolf Command," Kiriet said. "It was not a popular move. I have been destroying kites ever since. If the Imperium is so keen on further conquest, let it dirty its own hands."

"Yet you wield a kite yourself," Lisse said.

"*Candle* is my home. But on the day that every kite is accounted for in words of ash and cinders, I will turn my own hand against it."

It appealed to Lisse's sense of irony. All the same, she did not trust Kiriet.

She heard a new voice. Kiriet's head turned. "Someone's followed you." She said a curt phrase in her own language, then: "You'll want my assistance—"

Lisse shook her head.

"It's a small flight, as these things go, but it represents a threat to you. Let me—"

"No," Lisse said, more abruptly than she had meant to. "I'll handle it myself."

"If you insist," Kiriet said, looking even more tired. "Don't say I didn't warn you." Then her face was replaced, for a flicker, with her emblem: a black candle crossed slantwise by an empty sheath.

"The *Candle* is headed for a vortex, probably for cover," the ghost said, very softly. "But it can return at any moment."

Lisse thought that she was all right, and then the reaction set in. She spent several irrecoverable breaths shaking, arms wrapped around herself, before she was able to concentrate on the tapestry data.

At one time, every war-kite displayed a calligraphy scroll in its command spindle. The words are, approximately:

I have only
one candle

Even by the mercenaries' standards, it is not much of a poem. But the woman who wrote it was a soldier, not a poet.

The mercenaries no longer have a homeland. Even so, they keep certain traditions, and one of them is the Night of Vigils. Each mercenary honors the year's dead by lighting a candle. They used to do this on the winter solstice of an ancient calendar. Now the Night of Vigils is on the anniversary of the day the first war-kites were launched; the day the mercenaries slaughtered their own people to feed the kites.

The kites fly, the mercenaries' commandant said. *But they do not know how to hunt.*

When he was done, they knew how to hunt. Few of the mercenaries forgave him, but it was too late by then.

The poem says: *So many people have died, yet I have only one candle for them all.*

It is worth noting that "have" is expressed by a particular construction for alienable possession: not only is the having subject to change, it is additionally under threat of being taken away.

Kiriet's warning had been correct. An Imperial flight in perfect formation had advanced toward them, inhibiting their avenues of escape. They outnumbered her forty-eight to one. The numbers did not concern her, but the Imperium's resources meant that if she dealt with this flight, there would be twenty more waiting for her, and the numbers would only grow worse. That they had not opened fire already meant they had some trickery in mind.

One of the flyers peeled away, describing an elegant curve and exposing its most vulnerable surface, painted with a rose.

"That one's not armed," Lisse said, puzzled.

The ghost's expression was unreadable. "How very wise of them," it said.

The forward tapestry flickered. "Accept the communication," Lisse said.

The emblem that appeared was a trefoil flanked by two roses, one stem-up, one stem-down. Not for the first time, Lisse wondered why people from a culture that lavished attention on miniatures and sculptures were so intent on masking themselves in emblems.

"Commander Fai Guen, this is Envoy Nhai Bara." A woman's voice, deep and resonant, with an accent Lisse didn't recognize.

So I've been promoted? Lisse thought sardonically, feeling herself tense up. The Imperium never gave you anything, even a meaningless rank, without expecting something in return.

Softly, she said to the ghost, "They were bound to catch up to us sooner or later." Then, to the kite: "Communications to Envoy Nhai: I am Lisse of Rhaion. What words between us could possibly be worth exchanging? Your people are not known for mercy."

"If you will not listen to me," Nhai said, "perhaps you will listen to the envoy after me, or the one after that. We are patient and we are many. But I am not interested in discussing mercy: that's something we have in common."

"I'm listening," Lisse said, despite the ghost's chilly stiffness. All her life she had honed herself against the Imperium. It was unbearable to consider that she might have been mistaken. But she had to know what Nhai's purpose was.

"Commander Lisse," the envoy said, and it hurt like a stab to hear her name spoken by a voice other than the ghost's, a voice that was not Rhaioni. Even if she knew, now, that the ghost was not Rhaioni, either. "I have a proposal for you. You have proven your military effectiveness—"

Military effectiveness. She had tallied all the deaths, she had marked each massacre on the walls of her heart, and this faceless envoy collapsed them into two words empty of number.

"—quite thoroughly. We are in need of a strong sword. What is your price for hire, Commander Lisse?"

"What is my—" She stared at the trefoil emblem, and then her face went ashen.

It is not true that the dead cannot be folded. Square becomes kite becomes swan; history becomes rumor becomes song. Even the act of remembrance creases the truth.

But the same can be said of the living.

Digital Rites

Jim Hawkins

Jim Hawkins is a "new writer" of an unusual sort, one who made his first sale to New Worlds *forty-one years ago, and didn't sell another story until placing two in* Interzone *in 2010. His forty-plus-year hiatus doesn't seem to have diminished his talents or skills, though, as he demonstrates in the vividly written and strongly characterized story that follows, one about how human creativity is being supplanted, or at least intensively and intrusively "supplemented," by artificial means. Or is it?*

EXT. GREECE—PALEOKASTRITSA—DAY

Amber Holiday lies on her immaculate stomach and looks out from the swimming pool high on the Corfu cliffs at Bella Vista. She knows the cameraman she can see in her peripheral vision wasn't taking snapshots of the spectacular views over the rugged coastline of Paleokastritsa. He isn't interested in the roof of the Monestario, couldn't care less about the silver-encrusted iconostasis inside, is unimpressed by the perfect blue and turquoise Ionian Sea lapping gently into the sea caves in the sandstone strata far below. All he is interested in is the moment when she unhooks her bikini top, slips into the water for a quick plunge to perk up her nipples, climbs out, and stands glistening by the side of the pool like a newborn Athena bathed in the golden light of the sun that is dropping ever faster towards the open sea to the west.

Paparazzi! She has lived her life surrounded by paparazzi the way a dead dog lives its death surrounded by blowflies. Maybe now she'd given him a good angle on her tits he'd crawl off to whatever pathetic stone he lived under and leave her alone. No chance.

Knowing it is futile, she pulls her mobile phone out of her bag and speed-dials Dave Marchant, the studio's Media Relations boss.

"All I wanted was ten days of peace!" she shouts into the phone. "I've been here forty-eight hours and I'm up to my boobs in telephoto lenses!"

"Not me, Julie. Defo not me."

"Lying shit. Get these pap scum off me! And don't call me Julie."

Marchant sighs and says, "Julie—I've told you before. Paparazzi come with the job. In fact, paparazzi are the job."

Amber Holiday, aka Julia Simpson, throws the phone into her bag and looks around. There is no sign of the photographer.

EXT. GREECE—PALEOKASTRITSA ROAD—21:05 BRITISH SUMMER TIME

The narrow road from Bella Vista down to the harbour is steep, narrow, and winding with sheer drops of several hundred feet and blind bends. The gap between the ochre road-edge markings and the low fences is very narrow. Dune buggies are fragile—just an open tubular frame and an engine on big wheels. Amber's hired buggy is bright yellow. She looks like an exotic caged parrot, her cool sea-green silk top rippling in the breeze.

She has no chance to see the black Mercedes coming up fast behind her until it's too late. The impact throws her back against her seat. She yanks far too hard on the steering wheel, goes right towards the cliff edge, and overcompensates. The buggy slams over to the left, ricochets off the rock wall, veers across the road, and breaks through the cliff fence.

Caged birds can't fly far—not unless they're angry and forget to fasten their seatbelts. Like a diver from an eight-hundred feet high-board, Amber Holiday flies a perfect arc out of her cage, her arms spread as though pleading for wings, her unblemished skin with its careful factor-twenty sunblock reflecting the deep red of the setting sun, her beautifully chiselled Oscar-winning face turning in the evening air, and the goddess of a million tabloid pages, a zillion web-hits, blogs beyond count and infinite adolescent wet dreams hits the terrace of an apartment block, explodes, and turns into something resembling a spatchcocked chicken in a red wine sauce.

EXT. GREECE—CORFU TOWN STREET—NIGHT

Police Lieutenant Spiros Koukoulades is strolling with his wife, Maria, down the dark and moody Venetian lanes of Corfu Town towards his favourite taverna, trying to divert her attention from the fur and silver shops, when Constable Alexandros Fotos runs towards them and stops, panting. Maria looks away. Spiros stands like a block of stone and says, "Alexi—what?"

Alexandros takes a deep breath and says, "A woman went off the cliff above Paleokastritsa this evening. She's dead."

"So?"

Maria turns back, fixes the constable with an uncompromising black-eyed stare, and says, "My husband is not on duty tonight."

Alexandros would rather have faced a rioting mob in his underpants than face Maria Koukoulades, but he stands up straight and says to his boss, "Major Panagakos sent me to find you. Your mobile is switched off. The woman who died is a tourist. Major Panagakos told me to respectfully tell you to turn your mobile on and phone him immediately."

Spiros walks away into the shadows, flicking his mobile phone open. Maria sniffs and looks Alexandros up and down and says, "You're Demetria's son, aren't you?"

"Yes."

"I told her not to let any of her sons join the police. Are you ambitious? Do you want a promotion?"

"Yes, madam."

"Then you can look forward to an angry wife and hungry Sunday nights. What's so important about a dead tourist? Tourists fall off cliffs every day of the week."

Maria's stare and half-smile are strangely disturbing. She is a predator surveying prey and an erotic challenge. In the shadows of the five-hundred-year-old street Spiros is facing the wall and talking quietly into his mobile.

"The thing is," Alexandros says, "it turns out she might be famous."

INT./EXT. PINEWOOD STUDIOS—19:00 BST

Earlier.

It's nine o'clock in the evening in Greece but only seven o'clock in England on a fine July day. Puffy white clouds and softly-vanishing feathery vapour trails catch the gentle light and smile down at crowded pub-garden benches and children laughing as they ride on their last higher and higher push on the park swings. Blackbirds forage for worms between the trees. Midges and fruit flies emerge in the branches and assemble like fighter squadrons planning their attack on the lakes of wine and beer on the tables below. Of all the possible delights of summer, there is none more perfect than a warm July evening in England.

None of this is visible inside the vast, ugly, dark, heavily-guarded and hermetically-sealed hangar that is the centre of operations of FlashWorks Productions. Gone are the old soundstages. Gone are the lighting rigs, brutes, booms, and makeup trolleys. No champagne pops, no stars hang on dressing-room doors. As Eliot wrote in "The Waste Land": "The nymphs are departed."

Inside this building there is never sunshine unless a script calls for it, and then it's the fake light of artifice.

We are the CAMERA as it tracks through lonely pools of cool halogen light past the steel-clad reinforced block containing four thousand and ninety-six clusters of massively-parallel computers, each of which contains one thousand and twenty-four superconducting quantum cores. Coils of foil-wrapped liquid helium pipes enter the roof of the block like the snake-hair of Medusa, calming the qubits into submission. Power lines from the substation outside hum. And no birds sing.

CAMERA continues to track through the gloom—past the Administration Block, now silent and unlit on a Sunday evening—towards the studios. Thirty-two spheres stretch in rows to the distant darkness. Each sphere has a diameter of twenty-four metres and hangs from an umbilical cord of cables and coolants. Each sphere is wrapped in golden foil, for no particular reason apart from impressing the investors. Around the equator of each sphere there is a ring of luminous colour. Black equals empty. Blue equals maintenance. Green equals powering up. Orange equals rehearsal. Red equals TAKE and may not be interrupted by anybody.

Seven of the studios are active. In Studio Two Sharon Lightly is directing Amber Holiday in scene forty-six. In Studio Five Don Fairchild is directing Amber Holiday and Tarquin Beloff in scene six. In Studio Six Rachel Palmer is directing Amber Holiday and Tarquin Beloff in scene ninety-seven. In Studio Eleven Greg Waleski is directing Angel Argent and Tarquin Beloff in scene fifteen. All these studios are at status orange.

Only one equator glows red.

CAMERA slows its track down the long dark aisle, turns towards Studio Nineteen, and . . .

INT. PINEWOOD STUDIO 19—19:00 BST

Jack Rogers seems to float on his director's chair halfway up one wall of the enclosing sphere. He is at a high angle above what seems to be a city street in London. The curving walls of the studio are invisible. He sees tower-blocks and traffic. He sees light snow drifting from the upper right. Traffic lights flash and the buses make bright cones of the falling flakes in their headlight beams.

He stretches his arm out and slowly brings his flattened hand downwards. The viewpoint drifts down. He is the camera. He sees for us. He is dream-flying above this street, but what he sees, we will see.

We drift lower until we are close to Oxford Circus tube station. Snowflakes drift past the viewpoint. Crowds from every nation on Earth struggle to walk in the press of people. There's traffic noise, shouting, and Samuel Barber's "Adagio for Strings" playing as a holding music track.

And there she is. Amber Holiday walks out of the tube station and pulls the fur-lined hood up on her coat. She shivers, turns, and begins to fight her way through the crowds eastwards, towards Soho.

Jack says, "Follow. Keep her in the right-hand segment," and the camera moves to the left with her.

Jack says, "Push in slowly," and the camera closes in on her deep blue eyes. She smiles. It's a big smile. And then her smile bends and curls into a snarl. Snot runs from her nose. Her eyes squeeze shut in pain. She falls to the floor, inert.

Jack shouts, "Cut!" and everything freezes. The traffic, the crowds, the noise, the buses, the taxis, and the music simply stop.

INT. PINEWOOD STUDIO 6—19:00 BST

Rachel Palmer has long dark curly hair, intense blue eyes, a "don't mess with me" attitude, and she's having a hard time with the actors. Tarquin Beloff is impossibly handsome. The computers have enhanced his pectoral muscles, which through the gap in his open-neck shirt look as though he could destroy tower-blocks with a swipe of his hand.

"I agree with Amber," he says in his carefully melded accent of Russia, Boston, and BBC. "It's a really bad line."

"Tarquin," says Rachel, "your opinion is valuable but I am actually talking to Amber here, so take a break." Somewhere in the computer hub Tarquin's user-interface state machine begins an infinite loop on its current node and he shuts up. That doesn't stop several thousand other tasks in his entity cluster from reading and analysing books, paintings, music, and internet porn in search of a deeper simulacrum of humanity.

Very patiently Rachel says, "Okay, Amber. So what exactly is your problem with the line?"

"I can't say 'Don't kiss me. You can fuck me, but you can't kiss me. I'm not ready for kissing—yet.'" Amber deploys her brand-new secret smile. "It's inconsistent with my character profile. Kissing is an early stage and fucking comes later."

Rachel sits back in her director's chair and thinks for a moment. "The thing is, Amber," she says, "what you're saying is true for your inherited characteristics. Obviously Julie likes a bit of tongue-play before she feels like opening up, and so do I. But we're doing acting, remember, and you have to adjust your parameters and weightings to accept that this is the way your character, Alice, feels about things. It makes her a little bit distinct from Julie and me. Maybe she values the tenderness of a kiss above body-touching and physical sexuality. Maybe she wants tenderness to be the goal and not the trigger. Just think about it."

Amber thinks about it for seven microseconds and says, "Okay—I've got that superimposition in place and I think I can do it but I'm not sure about the tone. Is it aggressive or seductive or hurt or confused or neutral or venomous . . . ?"

Rachel interrupts her. "I don't want a list. Just update Alice and we'll try it. Tarquin, come back."

Tarquin's state machine receives the notification message and breaks out of its loop. His immobile features begin to move. He appears to breathe. He blinks. His lips are clean and moist.

"Take it from the top," Rachel says.

Tarquin takes Amber in his arms and moves his mouth towards hers. She turns away enough to evade his kiss and says, "Don't kiss me. You can fuck me, but you can't kiss me. I'm not ready for kissing—yet."

Rachel smiles and says, "Not bad, darlings. Not at all bad. Quite effective and affecting. Just one thing, Amber . . ."

"Yes?"

"Lose the smile."

Amber's smile bends and curls into a snarl. Snot runs from her nose. Her eyes squeeze shut in pain. She falls to the floor, inert.

Seconds later, Tarquin goes catatonic, and his image fades to noise.

MONTAGE—INT. PINEWOOD STUDIOS—EVENING

A siren begins to wail. Red emergency lights flash outside the control room.

Rachel, Jack, and other directors run down the long gloomy aisle from their capsules towards the control room. Jack leads the pack and punches the digits on the security keypad, and he's first through the heavy door.

"What the fuck's going on?" Jack shouts. Senior Operations Manager Sunil Gupta is leaning over the shoulders of two console operators. Their touch-panels are Christmas trees of flashing red icons.

EXT. UKRAINE—KIEV—EVENING

It's a very warm summer night in Kiev. Crowds sit outside cafes and bars. The moon reflects off the rippling surface of the Dnepr River. A dark shape bobs gently downstream, turning slowly in the current. Tarquin Beloff, aka Alexandr Bondarenko, is physically untouched. He has no wounds, no appearance of damage. His handsome features surface and turn down again into the moonlit flow. His only problem is that his lungs are full of water and he's dead.

INT. GREECE—CORFU—POLICE CAR—NIGHT

The corporeal remains of Julia Simpson, aka Amber Holiday, have been bagged and sent to the mortuary in Corfu Town. Spiros and Alexandros are driving back to Corfu Town along dark, dangerous, twisty roads which weave between Cyprus trees and olive groves. Spiros's mobile rings. He listens for a few seconds and gestures to Alexandros, who performs a risky three-point turn and accelerates.

EXT. GREECE—CORFU—AGIOS STEFANOS NW—NIGHT

Agios Stefanos is not the teenage shot-glass hell of Kavos to the south. It's not the fish-and-chip zone of Sidari to the north. Once the tiny fishing port for the village of Avliotes which perches high on the surrounding hills, it's a modern cluster of apartment blocks, tavernas, and bars. It has no disco. Self-respecting, numb-your-mind, under twenties would hate it. The beach is a long crescent of golden sand and gently-lapping Ionian Sea. Tourists know it as San Stefanos—allegedly renamed by package holiday company Thomson so that reps at the airport wouldn't keep sending clients to either of the other two Agios Stefanos on the island.

Alexandros drives into the centre of the village and parks outside The Little Prince apartments and taverna. The terrace restaurant area is busy. Cameras flash as Michalis (Mike) delivers Sizzling Steak to tables near the road. The platter steams and spits, and he wears a plastic bib. Michalis hates serving Sizzling Steak, but it's tonight's special.

As Spiros and Alexandros leave the car and walk towards the restaurant the lights dim a little, and another Spiros, who is a waiter, and yet another Spiros, who is also a waiter, begin to dance a sirtaki in the aisle between the tables. Corfu is awash with men called Spiros after the island's patron saint, Agios Spyridon. Their legs swing back and forward and around. They touch their heels and then their toes. They jump down to a crouch and then spin and rise, their arms spread wide.

Dimitris, the owner, sprays barbecue lighter fuel from a bottle onto the floor and ignites it. Blue and orange flames flicker as Spiros and Spiros dance through fire and camera flashes.

The policemen wait on the side of the road, watching, until the dance finishes, and then skirt the tables and walk into the interior of the taverna. Dimitris gestures for them to follow, and leads the way through to the apartment block and up the stairs to the swimming-pool level and the rooms.

Room 101 is at the end of the corridor. A slippery-floor sign bars the way. Joe, the barman, keeps guard on the end of the corridor. He's looking pale.

Dimitris hands the master key to Spiros, and they go in.

INT. GREECE—AGIOS STEFANOS NW—ROOM 101—NIGHT

Angel Argent, aka Audrey Turner, lies on the floor facedown. She's wearing a black bikini. An empty bottle of sleeping pills and a half-empty bottle of Metaxa are side by side on the work surface. Her dark brown hair is spread out around her head like a deep shadow.

Spiros says, "Skata!"—which roughly translates to "Oh shit!"—and turns to Dimitris. "How did you find her?"

"It's a change-over day. People on night flights can get an extension to the late afternoon. One of the maids came in to prepare this room by mistake. By the way, her friend hasn't turned up yet tonight. They had a bit of a row this morning."

"What's his name?"

"Not him—her. Julia Simpson."

Alexandros and Spiros exchange one of those looks between policemen which contain the unspoken words "night" and "long."

"Alexi," Spiros says, "radio in and get a science team here as fast as possible. And bring some security tape from the car. Dimitri—be so kind as to keep this area sterile and put two Sizzling Steaks on to cook!"

INT. CONFERENCE AREA—PINEWOOD STUDIOS—NIGHT

Sunil Gupta is ending his presentation to an assembly of directors, producers, executive producers, and most importantly, Lynne Songbird, who owns the studio, the actors, the staff, FlashWorks, an executive jet or two, and houses in LA, Glasgow, London, Paris, and Bangalore. Sunil is scared. Lynne is volatile. Lynne kicks punch-bags with bare toes for exercise. She wants some good news, but there isn't any.

"So basically," Sunil says nervously, "we've lost quantum entanglement to five key actor brains—all within minutes of each other."

"Keep the heid!" Lynne says, reverting to the Scottish idiom for stay calm. "How can that happen?"

Sunil points to a diagram on his electronic whiteboard. "We can only come to two conclusions: either the laws of physics have changed today, or these people are dead."

Jack's been in the corner talking on his smartphone. He comes over into the light of the whiteboard projector. "I phoned Angel's mobile again," he says. "A policeman on Corfu answered it. Amber drove off a cliff. Angel took an overdose."

"And?" Lynne asks.

"This many brains gone within minutes of each other? Looks to me like we're under attack."

There's a long pause as Lynne's blue eyes track across the room. "Jack, Sunil, Rachel, Jason—stay here. Everybody else goes home, but keep your phones on and be ready to go anywhere at very short notice. Thank you."

When the room empties Lynne points to some seats and pours herself coffee from the flask near the whiteboard. Nobody says a word. Eventually Lynne sits down and says, "Okay. We need to be clear about this. Jack—you're senior director on this movie. How much have we got?"

Jack is in his mid-thirties. He has unfashionably long hair and a patrician English private-school accent, despite the fact that he went to a crummy comprehensive in Bolton. "If we include some marginal takes," he says, "I'd say we've got about eighty percent of it. Just a guess. We'll have to do a slash edit."

Lynne turns to Rachel, who is the second ranking director. "Rachel, do you agree with that?"

Rachel nods.

"So," Lynne asks, "my first question is, can we finish it? We've got vast information from the actors on the computers. Haven't we, Sunil?"

Sunil hates this. He avoids eye contact with the others. "Yes, we have," he says quietly.

Lynne walks over and stands in his eyeline. "You don't sound very sure," she says. "Why can't we finish the movie using the personalities we have?"

"We probably can," Sunil says.

"How big or small is 'probably'?"

Sunil puts his forefinger and thumb into a sign for small.

Lynne steps away and takes a breath. "I'm very stupid," she says. "We spend two billion Euros to get the most advanced movie-making system ever devised. We collect Oscars the way people get loyalty points in supermarkets. We hire some beautiful people with zero acting talent, hijack their brains, and then I forget that they're human. They can die. We didn't protect them. We're gobshite."

The blue eyes are unexpectedly wet. Jack's smartphone buzzes and he swipes the screen with his finger. "Two more," he says. "They're taking out everybody."

Lynne spins around and kicks a chair across the room. "Well fuck them!" she shouts. "This is fucking war! Jack and Rachel, see if we can rescue the movie. Sunil, get the whole of your technical team on it."

Sunil has his head in his hands, gazing at the grey carpet. "Fine," he says. "But we may have another problem."

Lynne picks up the broken chair, sets it down very carefully, and says, "This is absolutely the time I need to know everything. What is it I don't know?"

EXT. LUTON AIRPORT—NIGHT

A white Learjet 85 is lined up on the apron at the west end of the runway next to the white terminator markers, trembling in the wash of a Whizz Air 737 bound for Prague winding its engines up to take-off thrust. The 737 rolls away down the runway, its wingtip lights flashing brightly; it rotates and lifts off.

The cabin lights are dim in the Learjet, but we can still see Lynne and her PA Jason sipping coffee. There's busy radio chatter from the control tower, and then the Learjet begins to move, turning into the long reach of black tarmac, accelerates, lifts into the air, and flies southwards across Germany and the Alps, down the Italian coast past Venice and Brindisi towards Corfu.

INT./EXT. LEARJET—CORFU—DAWN

Lynne is sleeping as the plane descends from thirty-seven thousand feet to five thousand and follows the track down the Adriatic towards the islands that mark the northwesterly points of Greece. To their left the flight crew can see the rocky coast of Albania. Jason wakes Lynne with coffee and fruit juice. Orange dawn light is flaring over the mountains to the east.

Danny Edwards, the head of security, doesn't sleep much. He's sitting in his seat just behind the pilots, patched into the studio's hi-tech and probably illegal network of satellite systems. He's drinking herbal tea, which he hates, and the nicotine patch on his arm itches. He has his headset on and he's calling in the return of a few favours, plus a liberal sprinkling of Euros. Sunil is sitting beside him, monitoring the exotic equipment in the hold.

The Learjet pilots have a few words with the tower at Ioannis Kapodistrias airport, lower their landing gear, extend the flaps, and descend to fifteen hundred feet. It's a bumpy ride as the wind that brought the heroes of the Odyssey home to Greece takes them down the west coast of Corfu. The dark green mountains of the island are to the left. The Ionian Sea, plunging to a depth of sixteen thousand feet, is to the right. They fly past the villages of Agios Stefanos, where Angel died, then Arillas, Agios Giorgios, and Paleokastritsa, where Amber died. The beaches are all in shadow. The gods are asleep, even Korkyra, the beautiful nymph whom Poseidon abducted and married, and who gives her name to the island: Kerkyra.

They turn left and make their approach over the hills to the runway, which is a spit reaching out into the sea. They pass over a white-painted church on a small island. They touch down and savage the dawn peace with reverse thrust.

INT. MORTUARY–CORFU—DAY

Spiros has seen a great deal of sudden death in his career as a policeman, but he still hates postmortems. He hates the bitter charring smell of bone-saws. He hates the calm evisceration, the digital scales, the organs, the dissection of somebody who laughed and loved into a scrap heap of components. He's sweating.

The mortuary in the new blue-and-white-painted hospital in Kontokali, just north of the town centre, is state of the art. Amber's mangled body lies naked on one stainless-steel slab and Angel's perfect dark-haired beauty lies on the next, although she's not so good-looking with her scalp peeled back. Spiros is pleased to be behind glass in the observation area and not up close and intimate with the body fluids. He's even more pleased when his mobile phone rings and the head of the prefecture orders him to halt the postmortem. His pleasure doesn't last long.

The pathology-trained surgeon speaks clearly into her microphone. "This is highly unusual," she says. She has just trepanned Angel's skull, exposing the membrane of the brain surface. "The dura mater is bright blue."

Spiros barges his way through the door into the room. "Stamata!" he says. Stop. "Refrigerate the bodies and wait for instructions. And don't ask. Politics!"

FAST FORWARD thirty minutes, and Spiros, Selina Mariatos, the acting pathologist, Lynne and her team, and a senior police officer are sitting in a meeting area drinking cold lemon-tea from a vending machine. Spiros swills his down, crushes the can, and throws it very accurately into a recycling bin. "So?" he demands. "We're conducting an investigation. We are not open to interference."

"That's the last thing we want to do, Mr. Koukoulades," Lynne says. "We think we can help. In fact we know we can help. The thing is, this is time-critical. We have a few hours at most."

"Make your case quickly, then. As the investigating officer, I will decide whether you are helping or . . . something else."

Lynne stands up and walks to the window. "What I'm going to tell you," she says, "is highly confidential."

Spiros laughs, and says, "I have two dead film-stars. Everything I do is going to be reported across the world. If you have something to tell me, then tell me. But you don't decide what is confidential. Is that clear?"

He doesn't flinch when Lynne turns and opens her eyes wide and looks into his—blue on brown. He's used to tough women. He married one. "You have two dead film-stars. We have five. This is no accident, officer. This is conspiracy and murder. We need your help, and believe me, you need ours."

Danny's looking at his smartphone. "It's six actors now," he says. "Can we get moving?"

FAST FORWARD twenty minutes and Sunil and Selina are having a nerd-fest in the dissection area as the equipment from the Learjet is wheeled in. They are thirty years old, almost exactly the same olive-skinned colour, and both good-looking in reasonably dim light. They are both isolated from the human race around them by their considerable knowledge. Selina throws a plastic coverall to him. He puts it on, and then says, "You'll have to be kind to me. I'm not used to bodies." She pokes him in the chest and says, "You've got one."

"I may be sick."

"D'you think I care about sick? If you're sick I'll scrape it up and tell you what you had for lunch three days ago. Now—why is Angel's brain blue?"

"You'll see."

Sunil opens the aluminium carry boxes and arranges what look like sixteen small satellite dishes on work surfaces on either side of the slabs and across the room. He fixes a UK to Continental electric-socket adapter to the plug on the power lead from a heavy black control console and connects it to the mains supply. The console has a flat matte-black square surface on its top, but when he flicks the on-switch the surface glows a deep ultramarine, pales, and rises up to make a translucent sixteen-inch cube of light aqua, as though the colour has stretched and attenuated.

"You have agreed," Sunil says, "that the video remains confidential."

"It must be available to the inquest. That's the law."

"Selina," Sunil says, "I'll share everything with you. There is nothing else like this anywhere in the world. But what happens to the evidence is out of our control. There are many things I can't tell you yet. But I promise you, we will work together and we will share things that may perhaps not reach the final report. There will be no lies, but some things will remain obscure. Do we have that agreement?"

"I will make my decision later," Selina says.

The mortuary assistant brings the bodies in their body bags with a trolley one by one and lays them on the dissection slabs. He opens the bags and slides the bodies onto the tables. Sunil feels a flush cover his face. His heart is beating very fast. Amber's body is a wreck. Every bone is broken. She's strangely short—truncated by the impact with the ground. Her skull is split open diagonally from above her left ear down to the bottom of the right jaw. Much of her brain is missing. What is left is discoloured—hints of green and turquoise amongst the pink and grey.

Selina puts her arm around Sunil. "This is my science," she says. "Now you do yours and you'll feel better. We do it for them. I don't know if they're on their way to an afterlife or nothing. But we will find the truth of their last seconds. I'm going to start recording now." She gestures to the assistant to leave the room and presses the record button on the console.

"This is the continuing investigation into of the death of Julia Jane Simpson, a British National found dead in Paleokastritsa. I will continue this narrative in English and Greek for the benefit of Doctor Sunil Gupta, who is also present."

INT. CAR—CORFU—DAY

Spiros and Danny Edwards have reached an unspoken agreement. Spiros drives at seventy miles per hour along spiralling mountain roads and Danny doesn't shit himself, even when Spiros leans heavily on the brakes of his BMW to avoid massacring a herd of goats which has meandered across the tarmac.

"We're off the record. Agreed?" Spiros asks, having softened Danny up with a constantly-changing array of G-forces. Danny agrees that they're off the record.

"On any one day a tourist drives off a cliff," Spiros continues. "On any one day somebody takes an overdose. Holidays can be emotional. We have established that Amber and Angel—to use their public names—were lesbian lovers. They had an argument that morning at breakfast. Amber went off to Paleo, on her own, and drove off the cliff. Angel took an overdose, which is what lovers often do when things go wrong. Would I be wrong to assume the simple explanation?"

"No," says Danny. "But when six people who work for us die within hours of each other, would I be wrong to assume that we're looking at murder?"

"You're not ex-military, I think. You're not ex-police. Your manner tells me you're almost certainly ex-security, probably MI5. Are my instincts wrong?"

"No."

The road to The Golden Fox high above Paleokastritsa is cordoned off. A policeman moves the no entry sign aside and Spiros drives slowly to a point where burnt rubber marks the road. A camera is set up on a tripod and the operator is leaning against the rocks away from the cliff edge, smoking. He stubs it out quickly when he sees Spiros and Danny get out of the car. Danny paces on the road—walks up twenty yards, then thirty, walks back, shading his eyes from the fierce July sun that's high over the sea. Spiros says nothing. He gestures to the cameraman, who takes out a packet of Karelia cigarettes and offers one to Spiros. Smoke curls into the air as Danny paces and paces again. Danny's fair-haired and his skin is rapidly turning pink in the intense light. Finally he walks up to Spiros.

"She was a careful, timid driver. She wasn't going fast—maximum twenty-five miles an hour. She steers into the bend towards the cliff, brakes hard, veers to the left, hits the rocks, bounces off, and loses control. She floors the brakes as she heads to the cliff edge. She goes over."

The cameraman nods and says, "Ne!" Yes. Spiros holds his hand up and says, "Shh. I want to hear Mr. Edwards's conclusions."

"May I have a cigarette?" Danny asks. The cameraman throws the pack of Karelias to Danny, and then the lighter. Danny draws deeply on the cigarette. "Two weeks," he says. "Two miserable fucking weeks without a cigarette and then this happens. Anyway—looks to me like she was shunted."

Spiros leads Danny up the road towards The Golden Fox, where Amber had her last swim. "All these deaths," he says. "I have to be objective, obviously. When the top executives of a film company fly in overnight and start spending big money, I have to think that they've got something to hide. I was at the postmortem and the pathologist said there were some anomalies in the brains of the dead girls. So an alternative hypothesis might be that you did something to them which went terribly wrong."

Spiros's mobile phone rings. He listens for a few seconds, says, "Endaxi," and snaps the phone shut.

Danny is standing by the roadside looking down at the pale wakes of the little boats weaving their way between the rocky bays far below. "A beautiful place to die," he says.

Spiros comes and stands beside him and asks, "Did Clytemnestra really stab Agamemnon to death in his bath? Maybe he slipped and hit his head, but that was too dull a story. It sounds stupid, but that's why I became a policeman. Old stories. Anyway, I've had the dune buggy thoroughly examined and there are traces of black paint on the left-hand rear side."

Danny takes a last drag on his cigarette and grinds the stub with his foot.

"So," Spiros says, "let's see if we can find any traces of a black car at the taverna."

"CCTV?" Danny asks.

Spiros laughs.

INT. MORTUARY—CORFU—DAY

Selina has dissected the remains of Amber's brain, weighed them, but before she slices the tissue she places them on a glass plate away from the body. Sunil adjusts the array of dishes, checking frequently with readouts on his control console.

She comes and stands beside him, speaking quietly. "You must explain, for the record. If you don't, I will never work again."

"You can come and work for us," Sunil says.

"Your film company has a lot of opportunities for part-time pathologists? I don't think so."

"Unfortunately, this week it does." He moves away from the console and stands carefully facing away from the bodies and the pile of brain tissue.

"Okay," he says. "Background. Cinema is the only art that totally depends on technology. That's its greatest strength and also a curse. People drifted away from actual cinemas when TV took off. The big studios are closely tied in with the distributors and theatre owners. They want people back in the cinemas. They want to sell seats and popcorn. That's why 3D got so heavily sold at the end of the first decade of the century.

"The technology isn't that good. People who don't wear spectacles don't like wearing them, and people who do don't like having to fix another set over the top of their prescription lenses. Ten percent of people can't see the effect anyway. Still, whizz bang, latest thing.

"We're a small production company. We don't like being at the beck and call of some inflated ego talking poolside in Malibu. Particularly Lynne. Her ancestors were so scary the Romans built a ten metre wall to keep them in. So, to cut to the chase, we invested—well, she invested—in technology. We are miles ahead of the game. We can now deliver a better experience in your sitting room than you'll ever get in a cinema."

Selina paces. "So how does that relate to these poor dead women?" she asks.

"We can generate direct brain stimulation to the audience. You can live it, feel it, and experience it emotionally. So we can create this, we borrow the brains of our actors—with their full agreement. We inject them with some harmless nano and similar equipment to this sets up a kind of quantum entanglement. We use some of their brain centres without them being aware."

"How do you know it's harmless?" the pathologist demands.

"We've done animal trials, human trials—it has no effect."

"Does that cause the blue colouration?"

"Probably. After exposure to air."

"Sunil, I'll believe you for now, but you may have to prove that to the Examining Magistrate."

"Fine. Now—we should not wait too long."

Selina gestures to the equipment. "Describe," she says.

Sunil presses some buttons on the console. The light in the translucent cube flickers. "I'm attempting to re-entangle the nano," he says. "I'm recording these data for the report." Suddenly the segments of brain tissue appear like a model in the cube. He flicks a switch, and false colour marks some regions in red and orange. "The visual centres are destroyed," he says. "The nano particles store short-term information in a buffer for about ten seconds before loss of entanglement. It looks to me like we may have something coherent in the superior temporal gyrus region. Auditory processing. This may take some time to extract."

"How much time?"

"About an hour."

"Coffee?" she asks.

INT. CORFU—POLICE HQ—DAY

The Examining Magistrate is the tough sixty-year-old son of a Corfiot fisherman. He fought his way up against the power of the handful of wealthy families which have controlled large sections of the island for hundreds of years. Panyotis is not afraid of anybody—not even Lynne. He looks around the people in the conference room—Dimitris, Lynne, Danny, Jack, Sunil, Selina, and assorted detectives, sip water and await his words.

"This is a Greek matter. I accept that two British nationals have died, but that does not mean that a film company can become part of the investigation. Lieutenant Koukoulades—please explain."

Spiros is wishing he were anywhere else. "Magistrate," he says, "I agree with you, but these young women were unusually famous." He leafs through a stack of tabloids on the table with headlines like "Goodnight Angel" and "Amber Falls to Her Death." "The film company has information that may be important to the investigation and for now at least I believe we should listen to what they have to say."

The magistrate rests his chin on his fist and looks at Lynne. "Make your case," he says.

Is the power of the Glasgow stare up to the power of the magistrate's dangerous dark eyes? She sucks in a breath and says, "Several of our key actors died within minutes of each other. Two could be a coincidence, sir, but five or six? I think not."

It's the first time she's used the word sir in thirty years. "I hope you will agree that there is prima facie evidence of a conspiracy. We are cooperating closely with the authorities in several countries to identify the source of this murderous attack. We have technology which may assist the investigation, and we have placed it at your disposal."

"I'm prepared to listen," the magistrate says, slowly, "but I doubt if any unproven technology will be permitted in court. Doctor Mariatos has also made it clear to me that your secret technology might have been a causative factor in the deaths of these people. She has professionally and properly given way as senior scientific officer to two senior forensic pathologists from Athens, who should be arriving at the airport within the hour."

"Our system is highly confidential!" Lynne says forcefully.

"This may be a murder investigation. I will decide what is confidential. Doctor Mariatos—please proceed."

Selina stands at the end of the table and outlines the forensic analysis of the bodies of Amber and Angel. The results are consistent with a long fall and an overdose of sleeping pills. However, she will want to add to this after Sunil's evidence. She then formally seeks the Examining Magistrate's permission to allow Sunil Gupta to display the results of his tests. He nods.

Sunil inserts a disc into the Blu-ray player and coughs nervously. "I understand the magistrate's scepticism of unproven technology. What we have done today has never been done before. It's a side effect of the way we can interact with our actors' brains.

"We have a poor quality sound retrieval of the last ten seconds of Julia Simpson's life." He presses the remote. There's the sound of a petrol engine, then a bumping noise, a second louder metallic screech, a woman gasping, and a scream. The magistrate turns to Spiros and raises his eyebrows.

"Magistrate, we have found traces of impacted black car enamel paint on the left rear of the dune buggy consistent with an impact from behind."

The magistrate makes a continue gesture to Sunil. "We have a rather poor snapshot of the last few seconds of Angel Argent—Audrey Turner. To show this I will have to use our new immersive technology, which we call InifiniDy. Initially I will play it at fifty percent opacity—then, perhaps, at full intensity." Sunil gestures at the black box which sits on a table near the front of the room. The chairs, tables, and assembled people become translucent. They are all seemingly in the equally translucent kitchen of apartment 101 in Agios Stefanos. They feel overwhelming terror and sadness. A dark figure stands before them silhouetted by golden evening sun from the window, and they feel a cold spray in their nostrils. An American voice says "Goodnight Angel," and the superposed scenes cross-fade back to the police room. There's a long pause, then Sunil asks, "Shall I play it at full intensity?"

"I think not," the magistrate says. "That seems to be adequately intense for me. Selina Maria?"

She's surprised at his use of her Christian name. He's obviously disturbed. "There are possible indications of methyl alcohol effects in the nasal tissue. I have sent samples by air to Athens for mass spectroscopy. Such things are very difficult to establish but it is possible that a propellant aerosol spray could have been used in this case."

The magistrate sits back in his chair. "Many years ago," he says, "when I was young I was in a scene in the James Bond film *For Your Eyes Only* made in the streets of Kerkyra, here. I was a good-looking—no, very good-looking—young man walking down a narrow passage as Roger Moore came by. We did it many times. Once, I looked into the camera, which I had been told never to do, and they shouted at me. The lighting was adjusted frequently, while we stood around. Hundreds of people were involved. I tell you this because as a young man I realised that when I see something in the cinema it is a carefully-crafted icon. What you have shown me may be true. But it may be a lie. Your trade is deceit. I rely on my police officers and doctors. The bodies will not be buried or repatriated until I say they may."

"Nor cremated?" Lynne asks.

"We do not burn bodies in Greece," says the magistrate. "We live in hope of the resurrection."

He stands. They all stand. He walks out. There's a pause and then a blinding flash. Alexandros comes through the door like a pantomime demon arriving onstage. He's very good looking, Alexandros. The day outside is ripped with a deafening tearing sound and then the deep echoing crack of thunder rattles the windows. The sky cuts instantly from blue to slate grey and huge raindrops waterfall down the glass. It doesn't drizzle much in the Ionian Islands—you're either in bright sunshine or underwater. Heralded by Zeus, the god of thunder, Alexandros walks across to Spiros and whispers in his ear. Lynne stares at him. He's actually having a physical effect on her.

Spiros says, "Please excuse me," and he and Alexandros leave the room.

"Latest?" Lynne asks Danny. He's had a tablet on his lap throughout the meeting. "We've got data from some bodies," he says. "We couldn't get any cooperation in Kiev. We've lost Tarquin to a very efficient Russian-built crematorium."

INT. CORFU—POLICE HQ OFFICE—DAY

Alexandros lays half a dozen photographs on Spiros's desk. "I've got all the pictures I could from the tourists on buses in Paleo that afternoon."

A lean ginger-haired man is crouching on the perimeter of The Golden Fox pool. He is raising a top-range Cannon EOS digital SLR camera towards his face. Amber Holiday stands by the pool, shaking water droplets off her perfect body. Flip pictures. Tourists are climbing off a bus, mugging into the camera, and in the background there's a black 4 × 4. Amber is just visible through a taverna window climbing into the dune buggy and a lean man with a hint of red hair is walking through the car park.

"We've checked the number plate. Car hire firm at the harbour. He paid cash. Given the timing he was probably off the ferry from Brindisi. We're checking the CCTV in the harbour."

"Where's the car?"

"No trace."

Spiros picks up the picture of the man with the camera and walks out.

INT. CORFU—CORRIDOR POLICE HQ—DAY

Spiros fills a cup of water from the drinks machine in the corridor and hands it to Danny. He draws one for himself, and then reaches into his inside jacket pocket and takes out the picture of the photographer. "I didn't show you this," he says. "Any ideas?"

Danny examines the picture, hands it back to Spiros, and says, "Never seen him before. May I have a copy?" Spiros thinks about it and nods.

INT. CORFU—TOWN TAVERNA—NIGHT

Selina has scrubbed up well and she leans across the table towards Sunil. She's not beautiful. She has a strong nose and dense black eyebrows, but they're framed with a burst of wavy dark brown hair. They've just demolished dolmades, small fish, green beans in tomato and garlic sauce, and a pile of charcoal-grilled lamb chops. "Where were you born?" she asks.

Sunil laughs. "Croydon," he says. "It's a suburb in south London. It wasn't Bombay. Lipame."

"Good try," she says. "It's a bit sad if your first Greek word is sorry. But let's get it right. It's not quite right the way you said it. It's lee-PAH-may! Go on!" When she repeats the middle syllable her lips open wide. The waiter brings another jug of wine and puts it on the table. Sunil practises the word after her. Several times.

"I have a little house," she says. "It's up in the hills towards Temploni. It's quite cool at night." She giggles. "I've got three goats and six chickens and I am useless at looking after them. My vegetables die. Every year I have big plans for my vegetables and by July they are dead. That's my life. At work I try very hard to keep people alive, and when I get home the sun has roasted the peppers to death. The goats despise me. Have you ever kept goats?"

Sunil admits that although there may be vast herds of goats in Croydon, he's never come across them.

"Goats are very intelligent," Selina says. "Sheep—you just eat. Goats—you know there's consciousness there. They're funny. They're adapted to survive. You should meet my goats."

Sunil puts his hand across the table. She puts hers over his. "I would very much like to meet your goats," he says. She nods, and calls "To logoriasmo, parakolo!" to the waiter. Sunil is making a neat pile of Euros on the table when Jack walks in.

Directors come in two flavours—charm or totalitarian dictator. Jack is charm. "Selina," he says, "you are looking stunning tonight. Sunil, the plane is leaving in two hours. Sorry to break up the party."

Sunil sees her eyes look down and her shoulders slump. "Sorry, Jack, not possible," he says. "We're running a parametric vector equalisation test on the corpses. It won't be finished until around eleven o'clock tomorrow morning. If we interrupt it we'll scramble the data."

"Lynne's not going to be happy," Jack says.

"Send the plane back tomorrow. We'll have the equipment packed, at the airport, and ready to go at fourteen hundred hours."

Jack thinks for a few seconds and nods. "Okay," he says, "it's your gig. But the flight costs come off your budget, not mine. Goodnight, Selina." He walks out.

The brown eyes lift and focus on Sunil's. "What exactly is a parametric vector equalisation test?" she asks.

"Haven't got the faintest idea," he says. "I think we'll have to ask the goats."

INT. PINEWOOD STUDIOS—DAY

Lynne and Danny are sitting in his office in the security centre looking at the pictures of a ginger-haired man holding a camera. "Spiros sent the pictures to Interpol," he says. "They're getting nowhere, but I have some friends who can dig a little deeper. His name is usually Adrian Kopp, but he has a dozen passports. He's a freelance. Ex CIA."

Danny swivels his chair around. "We've hacked everything we can hack. We still can't find out who's doing this to us. So far we haven't found this man, let alone the others."

"What others?"

"There have to be four or five at least. Times of death, Lynne. Nobody can get from Corfu to Kiev in an hour. This one's our only lead so far."

INT. UNIVERSA STUDIOS—LOS ANGELES—DAY

The man who sometimes calls himself Adrian Kopp is wearing cutoff jeans and a white T-shirt with a blue Texan university logo. He has his feet up on the chair in front of him. "That's a hundred percent hit rate," he says. "Worth the bonus, I think. I've put them back at least six months—maybe a year. They're going nowhere, and you'll be there first."

The balding man sitting behind his very big desk nods and smiles.

INT. PINEWOOD STUDIOS—DAY

Aluminium carry cases are stacked up in the computing centre. The portable units are laid out on a bench and connected to a central bay with thick cables. Sunil stands behind his technical team. Jack stands behind him. Progress bars crawl across screens as petabytes of data move between the links.

Lynne walks in. "Is it going to work?" she asks.

Sunil takes a fifty pence piece from his pocket, flips it into the air, catches it on the back of his hand, and examines it. "Maybe," he says.

"Because if it doesn't," Lynne adds, "we're in deep shit."

FAST FORWARD two hours. The progress bars hit 100%. It gets quieter as the CPU fans in the portable units wind down to idle. Sunil stretches his back and says quietly to his team, "That's all the material we've got. Move it into the simulators very carefully, one actor at a time. Start with Amber—she's our worst-case scenario."

What was flesh, what ate, what breathed, what read books and made love is now a collection of electron cloud superimpositions. Maybe it always was. Golden hair is numbers. Blue eyes are arrays of colour-spectrum frequencies. Fear and affection are probabilities. The computers will now attempt to act the actors.

INT. PINEWOOD STUDIOS—STUDIO 3—DAY

Jack is floating. Jack is the camera. Amber walks down the street with snowflakes blowing around her hair. Lynne sits beside Jack in the cradle. Neither of them is smiling. There is a faint, subtle something about Amber that doesn't quite flow. Sunil and his team are tweaking settings but generally making things worse.

They try a scene with the simulacra of each of their dead actors. Nothing works. They're looking at a brilliant display of technology and a cold and inadequate experience. This time the nymphs have really departed.

"So," Lynne says. "We've got three-quarters of a movie we have no hope of finishing. Terrific! Got any ideas?"

"Only one," Jack says. "Get the writers in. I've put together the sequences that work. Maybe they can plot around them."

"What are we going to do for actors?"

"Get some new ones."

Lynne sighs. "It took five months to get the other brains functioning. We don't have five months. The money will walk. We have to do something . . . drastic."

INT. PINEWOOD STUDIOS—SECURITY—DAY

Danny indeed has friends. There isn't a film studio in the world that isn't laced with security cameras. In Vladivostok there's a team of high-powered ex-Soviet space industry computer experts with some very cute image-enhancement software, top-notch hacking skills, and a considerable fondness for dollars.

He's looking at video of a service area in an obscure corner of Universa Studios in Los Angeles. A white van with a ladder strapped to the top pulls up and a ginger-haired man steps out. A red circle appears around his face and the video slows to about one frame every two seconds. Inside the circle the fuzzy image clarifies. There's no doubt. Adrian Kopp carries a tool bag into the building, and the door shuts behind him.

Danny punches keys on his computer at the same time as he's initiating a connection on a quantum-encrypted handset. It's answered immediately. "The money is going into your account . . . now. I'll wait till you confirm. (TWO BEATS) Pleasure. How good is the firewall at Universa?"

"Top grade commercial," the voice at the other end of the line says, "but not up to military standards."

"Listen, Vladimir, I need to know exactly what they're doing, and I need to know what their weak spot is. I need this fast. This is a race. I'll double the money—now."

"Deal," the voice says. Danny retypes the entry on his computer and sends the money. After a pause the voice says, "Twenty-four hours," and the connection light goes off.

INT. PINEWOOD STUDIOS—VIEWING THEATRE—NIGHT

Three writers are locked up with Jack, Rachel, two other directors, four line producers, and a creative consultant. Things are not going well. Every pitch the writers make gets shot down by somebody. The creative consultant is obsessed with demographics. Each of the directors is having a severe fit of the auteur syndrome and worrying about hypothetical angles on hypothetical plot points.

Maddy Loveridge is a fifty-seven-year-old screenwriter and she's covered more paper with slug lines than an insecticide research station. Finally, she blows. "Why don't you all fuck off and let us get on with the fucking job!" she shouts. "We wrote you a great script and your fucking technology let you down! So don't blame us. We do not do this by fucking committee, alright? Do we come into your studio and tell you what to fucking do? No. We hand over. We go home and watch daytime TV while you do all the glamorous bits and eat the good dinners and get photographed with royalty. So bugger off and watch Fellini and wish you were that good."

Jack nods, and the directors and producers head for the door. The creative consultant stays where she is. She looks about fourteen years old. "Maybe I can help?" she asks.

Maddy smiles sweetly. "Yes, darling, you certainly can. You can go and organise some very nice curry and a case of red wine."

The door hisses shut after the creative consultant. There's a pause. "Was I over the top?" Maddy asks. "No," comes a reply, "I thought that was rather understated."

INT. SUNIL'S HOUSE—NIGHT

Sunil's deeply asleep when his mobile rings. It's Selina. "I'm glad you're there," she says. "The bodies have gone. They broke into the mortuary and took the bodies. Why?" She sounds anxious.

Sunil talks to her quietly and calms her down. Then he asks, "Where are you?"

"Where do you think? I'm looking at empty body drawers."

"Is there anyone with you?"

"No. The police brought me in to confirm it. They've just gone."

"Selina," Sunil says, "listen to me. I want you to go to the busiest place you can find. Maybe A&E. I want you to phone Spiros. I do not want you on your own. In fact, get me Spiros's phone number. Go now!"

"Why?"

"Because of what you know. They want to analyse the nano. They haven't finished. Go now! Go!"

There's a crash and the mobile phone link goes dead. He tries Selina's number: voicemail. He's out of bed and dressed in seconds, and he's calling Danny's mobile as he runs downstairs.

INT. PINEWOOD STUDIOS—SECURITY—NIGHT

Danny lives half a mile from the studio complex and he's already there when Sunil runs in. "Easy, easy," he says. "Panic gets nobody anywhere. I've just been talking to Spiros. She's definitely not in the hospital. No one saw anything."

"Are they searching the area?"

"He's got three policemen. It's not exactly Dragnet on Corfu."

"If you were them what would you do? They've got two bodies and I'm praying they've got a live doctor. Where do they go?"

"Italy or Albania. Corfu to Brindisi is over a hundred miles. Albania is close enough for day trips."

"Which means a boat."

Danny sighs. "I don't think they're turning up at the airport and loading the bodies onto an easyJet flight, do you?"

"Come with me. I need you."

INT./EXT. PINEWOOD STUDIOS—COMPUTER CENTRE—NIGHT

Two men in orange maintenance jackets climb down the access ladder on the high wall of the building, check their watches, and drive off.

Sunil sits at a console in front of a bank of flatscreen monitors. Danny is across the room at the power control bay. Sunil says, "Power to level two." Danny selects a setting on the panel. From outside the faint hum of generators rises a tone.

"At some point, are you going to tell me what you're doing?" Danny asks.

"Level three, please. Look, there is always some entanglement with a tiny proportion of the nano. There's a lot of noise. Usually we filter it out. I'm locking all the computers together at maximum processing rate. I may be able to do something with the remaining nano. Just maybe. Level three, please." The generators are getting louder. Even if you'd been standing next to the shaped Semtex explosive charges on the helium lines above the roof and even if the timers had made any noise at all as they counted down to zero, you wouldn't have heard them.

EXT. PINEWOOD STUDIOS—DAWN

Lynne always gets in very early. She turns off the ignition on her BMW and reaches for the seatbelt. The dawn light is coming up over the studios. She's fumbling for the seatbelt release when a bright flash is followed a second later by a huge bursting cloud of white vapour. The car rocks in the blast wave and rolls over. A shallow lake of liquid helium runs across the car park. It freezes the car roof into a brittle shell and evaporates.

INT. PINEWOOD STUDIOS—DAWN

CAMERA follows Danny and Sunil as they run from the computers to the door, through it into the corridor, slamming it shut behind them in a gust of helium vapour, and down the long walkway past the studio capsules towards Security, where the first thing they see is CCTV angles on the wrecked roof of their studio and Lynne hanging upside down in a frozen BMW.

FAST FORWARD ten minutes. Lynne is wrapped in a fire blanket and sitting in the corner of Danny's office drinking strong black coffee. Sunil is on the phone talking to Spiros.

"Spiros, do you have access to the NATO surveillance system near Avliotes?"

"No. Impossible."

"It's an emergency. Can you talk to the military?"

"How many months do we have?"

"I'll call you back."

The red light starts to flash on Danny's encrypted telephone. Danny answers and listens. "Excellent. We'll speak later about that. We need another favour . . . Yes, paid favour . . . I'll put my technical chief on to you—and by the way Vladimir, he does not negotiate money . . . Fine."

Sunil takes the phone. Danny puts the conversation on speakers. "This is Sunil. We have an urgent need." Danny winces—never tell the seller it's urgent. "On the north of Corfu—Kerkyra—there's a NATO tracking station near Avliotes. We need wide m-band radar tracking at precisely 107.43 GHz. The painted image will be two or three small reflections phasing in and out at fifteen second intervals. The target will be on a boat heading north up the Albanian coast. We will need real-time co-ordinates."

There's a pause and a deep voice says, "Put Daniel back on line."

Danny flips the speakers off and says, "Vladimir, can you do it? . . . How many million was that? . . . Hold on." Danny walks over to Lynne. She's stopped shivering. "I need a small budget increase," he says and holds up the fingers and thumbs of both hands.

"Get me another cup of coffee and you can have as much as you need," she says.

INT./EXT. CORFU SEA—DAY

A small fishing trawler silently rides the swell in the bay of Liapades just south of Paleokastritsa on the west coast of the island. The sun is still below the hilltops to the east and the sea is shades of kyanos—dark blues and greens.

Two black body bags are on ice in the hold. Near them Selina is propped up against the hull. Her hands are tied behind her back and she's gagged with white surgical gauze. The hull wall behind her vibrates heavily as the engines start up. A slim dark-haired man climbs down the stairs. He comes across to her, unties the gag, and feeds her water from a bottle. "What do you want?" she asks in Greek. He shrugs. She asks again in Albanian. He laughs and rubs his fingers and thumb together to suggest money.

The boat begins to move out to sea and turns to the north.

INT./EXT. GREECE—CORFU—RADAR STATION—DAY

Theologos is twenty-two years old and nearing the end of his national military service. He'll be relieved in two hours. Since the end of the Cold War it's about as boring as it gets monitoring absolutely nothing of interest in the radar sweeps. Most of it is out of his control anyway. There's so little need for him to do anything that one of his predecessors spent a few months in military prison for getting his mother to cover for him while he went to a party in nearby Sidari.

He's thinking about breakfast when there are six loud alert sounds. A message in French and English appears on his main comms screen: Baltic terrorist alert level orange. HQ Brussels assuming control. Ensure backup systems online and secured.

The radar control settings screen shows the scanners switching to m-band frequency 107.43 GHz.

INT. PINEWOOD—SECURITY—DAY

The radar sweep images from Peroulades appear on one of the big screens. Danny points to the chair in front of it. Sunil sits down. "Your turn, fella," he says.

Lynne is feeling better and pacing the room, angry. "They're calling all the shots here," she says bitterly. "We're running after them. I don't like being screwed around by these bastards!"

Danny leads her to the far end of the room and speaks very quietly. "This is the full picture," he says. "Universa are way behind on production of their EMO set-top boxes. The first batch they had from a plant in China was rubbish, and there were design faults anyway. They are shitting themselves that we'll get our stuff out first. But here's the thing: they've switched production to Korea. They're tooling up for a production run of seventeen million units. Single source. They're depending on a custom chip-set. We may be able to help them. But you don't need to know."

Ice-cold blue eyes stare into his. "Do it," she says. "And if you can kill a few of them while you're at it I sure don't need to know but I want to see the newspaper clippings."

Sunil jumps up and shouts, "Got them!" On the monitor the radar is painting a bright dot that fades on several sweeps and then flares again. There's a smaller, fainter dot next to it. The track is moving slowly up the west coast of Corfu.

Danny flips his mobile open and speed-dials Spiros.

INT./EXT. GREECE—CORFU—SEA—DAY

It's a beautiful morning. The sunlight dances on the tiny whitecaps of the waves. The sea is ultramarine and the wake of the fishing boat is pure gleaming white foam flashing with rainbows. A dolphin flips out of the water for a moment and vanishes. Two coast guard single-prop planes come over the hills to the east and zoom loudly overhead. They bank steeply and turn back over the boat at five hundred feet.

The boat's captain goes to full throttle and keys his radio. He talks rapidly in Albanian, and then shouts. He takes a handgun from the hatch and sticks it under the belt of his shorts as he runs for the stairs down to the lower area.

Selina says nothing as he hoists a body bag over his shoulder and goes up again. She can't hear the splash over the engine noise. He returns and takes the second body bag. Then he comes back down again.

He holds the gun at her head as he cuts the rope tying her to a stanchion on the hull. "Up!" he says in Greek. Selina tries to stand on cramped legs and winces with the pain. "Hurry!" he shouts, waving to the stairs with the gun. She moves slowly. He hits her across the face and her nose starts to bleed. He pushes her up the stairs and onto the deck. He gestures towards the side of the boat. She moves across the planks until her thighs are against the rail. As he lifts the gun, there's an explosion of noise as a helicopter roars at low-level over the hills towards the boat. He looks up. When he looks down again, she's gone.

Maybe every human has a moment of katharsis—purification, release. Selina is feeling this now. The engines stop. She is under the boat, kicking slowly with her legs to conserve oxygen, when the dolphin comes up to her and nuzzles her gently. Maybe Poseidon has sent Delphinos to bring her the good luck she badly needs.

On the deck the captain raises his handgun towards the helicopter and is instantly shredded with machine-gun fire.

INT. PINEWOOD STUDIOS—DAY

The technical centre is a wreck. The studio capsules are dead without their source. The computers are inert. There's water everywhere from the Fire and Rescue dampdown. This is a billion-pound insurance claim.

Lynne stands there with Sunil and Jack. "How long to be up and running again?" she asks.

"It took two years last time," Sunil says, "so let's be optimistic and say one."

They've never seen her cry before.

"We can finish the movie," Sunil says quietly. Lynne laughs through her tears and Jack puts his hand to his head. "And just how are we going to do that?" Lynne asks.

"Go out and shoot with real actors," Sunil answers.

"What?" She waves her arms around. "Which particular century are you in? We can borrow brains and do anything we like. We can shoot movies in three weeks that would have taken six months. You designed this stuff, for Christ's sake! Are you really suggesting that we go back to pointing cameras at real people? You're mad, isn't he Jack?"

Jack walks over to a pile of cable and stirs it with the toe of his Adidas trainers. "I'd like to do it, but we don't have anybody left in the country capable of manning an old-fashioned unit. Cameras, lighting—it's all gone."

"Here, maybe," Sunil says, "but not everywhere. By the way, can I borrow the jet?"

"Why?"

"I've got an appointment with a doctor."

INT. KOREA—ELECTRONICS FACTORY—DAY

Bright green motherboards move down the production line. The main processing chips have arrived from the fab unit. The chips have been made without human intervention, their millions of transistors carefully crafted from design templates on the central computer. The motherboards pause and chips are inserted by robotic units. They move on and pass through a bath of liquid solder. They arrive at the point where cables are attached and then into a bay where they are married with their shiny black set-top boxes. From here the units reach the packaging area and slide neatly into the colourful cardboard boxes with pictures of fantastic movie scenes and the word EMO coming out like a stereoscopic projection. The slogan the world's been seeing day after day in an expensive advertising campaign runs across the boxes in a diagonal stripe: See it, Feel it, Be it!

The production lines move swiftly and efficiently, as they must, because they have seventeen million EMOs to produce, and that's just the start.

EXT. CORFU—AGIOS STEFANOS NW—NIGHT

The little road through the village centre is blocked for traffic. Two nine-thousand watt lighting brutes are standing in the road outside The Little Prince. Thick cables run from the lights to a generator parked outside the bakery. The camera is on a jib arm and looks down on the taverna terrace from ten feet above. Jack stands next to the jib talking quietly to Elena Vafiadou, the camera operator.

Alexandros is wearing black trousers and a white shirt. Makeup assistants are gently tapping powder onto his face. He's a waiter who falls in love with an English girl and discovers that he has the power to manipulate people. He's going to have to make some big choices between using his powers for good or evil. Nearby, Alice Walton sits alone at one of the tables whilst a young woman from Frocks adjusts the straps on her dress.

At another table sit Spiros and Maria. Spiros wrinkles his nose and says, "I hate this makeup."

She smiles in a feline way and says, "See what I've had to put up with all these years for your pleasure, Spiros!"

He sighs. "I'm still not sure Alexandros is doing the right thing."

"I am," she says. "If you were younger and better looking I'd have put you up for the job!"

The Assistant Director picks up a megaphone. "We're going for a take. Starting positions, please. Is the kitchen ready?" There's a quick burst of affirmative radio traffic from the AFM in the kitchen. The Sparks hits the big switch and the lights come on, brighter even than a Corfu noon. "Quiet, please, and stand by!"

Jack says, "Turn over." Camera and sound operators confirm that they're rolling. "And—action!"

The music begins and Alexandros puts down his tray and begins to dance, his arms held out wide, his feet swinging back and forward and across and check and back again. He's light on his toes. He spins and kneels.

Michalis comes from the kitchen wreathed in steam as he carries Sizzling Steak across the terrace and puts it down on Spiros and Maria's table. Alice lifts her beautiful sad downcast eyes and watches Alexandros dance. This is the moment. This is the precise second when she falls hopelessly in love.

"And—cut! Check the tape," Jack calls. "Please reset and stay where you are—we're moving on to the close-ups."

Spiros leans back and says, "I never though it would be this boring. Same thing over and over again."

Maria laughs. "Like chasing Albanian and Italian boat thieves? I have never had such a wonderful time!"

He reaches forward and puts his finger on her hand. "You are my real star," he says. "You look beautiful. I don't deserve you. Se latrevo." Her eyes widen. It's a very long time since Spiros told her he adored her.

INT. CORFU—SELINA'S HOUSE—EVENING

Sunil is teaching Selina how to make lamb Madras with saffron rice and an aubergine baji. She's not gifted in the kitchen department. "The onions will burn if you leave the heat that high," he says.

She shouts, "Malaka!" and pushes him out of the way as she goes through to the living room and flounces herself down in front of the television, which is showing a Greek news channel.

He smiles and rescues the curry.

She shouts, "Sunil! Sunil! Come! Now!"

He wipes his hands and walks through. He can't understand the fast Greek the news presenter speaks, but he can see the words Universa and EMO on the screen, together with shots of fire trucks.

Selina interprets. "He's saying that EMO boxes are catching fire or exploding. Several people have died. Hold on—this is several thousand incidents! Universa Studios have just issued a statement saying that they are recalling all EMOs. Wow! A media spokeswoman says it's a major disaster for Universa."

He goes back to the kitchen and adds the spices to the onions. Then he starts laughing and gets a bottle of Ino bubbly Greek champagne from the fridge. He's still laughing as he walks into the sitting room, peeling the foil, and lets the bottle go very loudly pop behind her back. She jumps and shouts, "Don't do that!" and turns to see him pouring sparkling wine over his head. He grabs her hand and pulls her towards him and bathes both of them in a shower of bubbles. "What about the curry?" she asks, licking the wine off his face. "I turned the cooker off," Sunil says. "For now."

EXT. MALIBU CALIFORNIA—DAY

A body floats gently in towards the shore. It's bloated, and prawns have been nibbling the ears, eyes, and nose. But nothing has touched the ginger hair that floats back and forth in the shallow surf.

EXT. NOVOSIBIRSK SIBERIA—DAY

Danny is wrapped up in a big warm coat as he sits in a park in Russia's science city. There's no snow, but the cold grass looks as though it's been doused in grey paint. A tall man in his early thirties—dark eyebrows, aquiline nose, parka hood up—comes and sits down beside Danny. "Only one target left," he says. "She lives in Kiev with her second husband and his two children. He doesn't know she was KGB."

"So now she's FSB?"

"Danny, Danny! I'm a programmer. FSB stands for Front Side Bus. I'm predicting some nasty short-circuits in the electricity supply to their apartment."

Danny stands up. "Don't hurt the kids," he says.

Vladimir laughs. "You work for movie business. Now you start having conscience! Very funny."

Danny walks away across the park. He turns back for a moment, waves and shouts, "Good job! Spasiba!"

MONTAGE—NEWSPAPERS AND VIDEO

Alexandros and Alice are on the front covers of every tabloid, every celeb magazine, and a thousand websites. His almost-black eyes and her green eyes stare into paparazzi lenses. They are parading along carpeted catwalks. They are signing autographs. They are on chat-shows all over the world. The movie has received five Oscar nominations and seven BAFTA nominations.

Lynne Songbird has a whole-page spread in *The Scotsman*. "The thing is," she's quoted as saying, "we've done the most advanced technology there is. We have done things so advanced it's like science fiction. But then we talked to the ordinary good people who watch our movies, and they said 'We don't care about 3D. We don't care about being forced to feel things we don't feel. We don't care about super-surround and giga-pixels, whatever they are. What we want is great stories, great acting, and maybe a little love besides.' "

INT./EXT. CORFU—SELINA'S HOUSE—NIGHT

Their bags are still packed by the door. They've just flown in from Los Angeles via Athens and they're tired. She looked great at the Oscar ceremony, but she's not feeling great now.

The air is cool and sweet as they stand outside, fragrant with jasmine and thyme. The moon is up over the hills. Selina, whose name means moon, looks up and yawns. Sunil takes her hand and says, "I quit today."

"I know," she says. "Lynne told me. So what are you going to do?"

"We're not short of money. You're a great doctor. I'd maybe like to do another Ph.D. I'm a bit worried about your family. If I were just a Brit it wouldn't matter, but I'm second generation Indian and maybe they're a bit . . . concerned."

She hugs him, and says, "Hey, xenophobia is a Greek word. We've survived the alien invasions by the Italians, the Turks, and the Crusaders. I think even my mother can cope with you."

She kisses him on the cheek and goes in to bed.

Sunil walks down the garden in the moonlight. Magnolia bushes gleam a silvery pink and the olive trees dance a shadowy sirtaki in the breeze. He opens the gate to the fenced area where the goats live. They've heard him coming, and they're up and stirring. They come bounding up to him and jump around in delight that he's here.

"Tell you what, guys," he says to the goats. "You three are never going on the barbecue. That's a promise."

He lies on his back on the still-warm ground and looks up at the moon and the great bright splash of stars as the goats skip gleefully over him and the night scent full of herbs and richness fills his nostrils and suddenly he feels immensely, ecstatically and overwhelmingly human.

CAMERA rises higher and higher over the Corfu hills, looking down at Sunil and the goats, and then the credits start to roll as Greek music swells on the sound track and the house lights brighten in the cinema:

Screenplay
Jim Hawkins

Script Consultants
Gillie Edwards, Ray Cluley
Research
Lesley Ann Hoy
Producer
Catherine Townsend
Director
Dean Conrad

With grateful thanks to The Little Prince, Agios Stefanos NW, Corfu, for the location, the moussakas, and the cold beer

The Boneless One

ALEC NEVALA-LEE

Alec Nevala-Lee was born in 1980 in Castro Valley, California, graduated from Harvard College with a bachelor's degree in Classics, and worked for several years in finance before becoming a professional writer. His first novel, The Icon Thief, *a contemporary thriller set in the New York art world, was published in March. A sequel,* City of Exiles, *will follow in December. On the science fiction side, his first novelette, "Inversus," appeared in* Analog *in 2004. Since then,* Analog *has accepted for publication five more of his stories. Besides "The Boneless One," reprinted here, they are: "The Last Resort," "Kawataro," "Ernesto," and the forthcoming "The Voices." He currently lives with his wife in Oak Park, Illinois.*

In the creepy story that follows, he takes us to the infamous Bermuda Triangle (or near it, anyway), to confront a menace much more subtle and much more dangerous than the ones you usually read about encountering there.

I

"Before we go on deck, I should make one thing clear," Ray Wiley said. "We're nowhere near the Bermuda Triangle."

Trip opened his eyes. He had been sleeping comfortably in a haze of wine and good food, rocked by the minor expansions and contractions of the yacht's hull, and for a moment, looking up at the darkened ceiling, he could not remember where he was. "What time is it?"

"Three in the morning." Ray rose from the chair beside the bed. "We're six hundred miles northeast of Antigua."

As Trip sat up, Ray was already heading for the stateroom door. A graying beard, grown over the past year, had softened Ray's famously intense features, but his blue eyes remained focused and bright, and they caught Trip's attention at once. If nothing else, it was the first time he had ever been awakened by a billionaire. "Come on," Ray said. "You'll want your notebook and camera."

At the mention of his notebook, Trip glanced automatically at the desk, where he had left his papers before going to bed. It did not look as if Ray had tried to read his notes, but even if he had, he would have found nothing objectionable. Trip's private notebook, in which he recorded his real thoughts about the yacht's voyage, was safely tucked into the waistband of his pajamas.

Trip climbed out of bed, pulling on his jeans and parka. Glancing at the berths on the opposite bulkhead, he saw that the men with whom he shared the cabin were gone. "Did Ellis and Gary—"

"They're on deck," Ray said. "Hurry up. You'll understand when we get there."

Trip slid on a pair of deck shoes and slung a camera around his neck. As he followed Ray to the salon, he became aware of a murmur beneath his feet, the barely perceptible vibration of the yacht's engine, trembling in counterpoint to the waves outside. Upstairs, the lights in the salon had been turned down. As they headed for the companionway, Trip saw Stavros, the yacht's captain and first engineer, seated at the internal steering station, his broad face underlit by the glowing console.

On the deck of the *Lancet*, the night was cold and windless. Two men in matching parkas were standing in the cockpit, looking into the void of the North Atlantic. One was Ellis Harvey, the yacht's marine biologist, a headlamp illuminating his weathered, intelligent features; the other was Gary Baker, a postdoctoral student in microbiology, his pale face framed by glasses and a tidy goatee.

When Ellis saw Ray, he frowned. It was no secret that the two older scientists were not on the best of terms. "We're going on a night dive," Ellis said. "Do we need a third set of gear?"

"I'll pass," Trip said. He was not fond of the water. "What's this all about?"

Gary pointed along the centerline of the sloop. "Dead ahead. You see it?"

Trip turned to look. For a long moment, he saw nothing but the ocean, visible only where it gave back the yacht's rippling lights. Then, as his eyes adjusted, he noticed a brighter area of water. At first, he thought it was an optical illusion, an effort by his brain to insert something of visual interest into an otherwise featureless expanse. It was only the hard line of the stempost, silhouetted against the glow, that finally told him that it was real.

"Lights." Trip glanced around at the others. "Something is glowing in the water."

Ray seemed proud of the sight, as if he had personally conjured up the apparition for Trip's benefit. "Gary saw it a few minutes ago, when he took over the night watch. We're still trying to figure out what it is."

"It's too widespread to be artificial," Ellis said. "It looks like a natural phenomenon. A luminescent microbe, perhaps—"

Trip was barely listening. In the absence of landmarks, it was hard to determine the distance of the light, which was faint and bluish green, but it seemed at least a mile away. It was neither constant nor uniform, but had patches of greater or lesser brightness, which flickered in a regular pattern. Initially, he thought that the twinkling was caused by the motion of the waves, but as they drew closer, he saw that the lights themselves were pulsing in unison. "It's synchronized. Is that natural?"

"I don't know," Ray said. He grinned broadly. "That's what we're here to find out."

Trip heard a note of hunger in the billionaire's voice. For the past two years, he knew, the *Lancet*, under Ray's funding and guidance, had been using the latest technology to sample the incredible genetic diversity of life in the ocean, with the unspoken goal of finding genes and microbes with commercial potential. So far, the voyage had been relatively uneventful, but if the glow in the distance turned out to be an unknown form of microscopic life, it could prove to be very lucrative indeed.

When Trip tried to ask Ray about this, though, he received only a grunt in response, which was not surprising. It was no secret that Ray was having second thoughts about the article that Trip was here to write. In the three days since his arrival, Trip had already noticed a number of conflicts simmering beneath the surface of the voyage, and Ray, as if sensing this, had been avoiding him. At this rate, Trip thought, his week aboard the *Lancet* would end without so much as an interview.

The sloop pressed onward, the foam breaking in tendrils across its prow. Trip stood between Ray and Ellis, caught in their unfriendly silence, as Gary removed wetsuits and cylinders from a scuba locker, securing glow sticks to the tanks with zip ties. Before long, the yacht was at the edge of the illuminated region, the light visible in the water against the hull. When Ray used the cockpit phone to tell Stavros to cut the engines, the vibration beneath the deck ceased at once.

As the yacht drifted freely, surrounded on all sides by the glow, Trip got a better look at the light. At close range, it resolved itself into countless discrete nodules of brightness, seemingly without heat, but unmistakably alive.

Ellis leaned over the wire railing that encircled the deck. "Ray, this is no microbe."

"Let's get a closer look, then," Ray said. As Trip began taking pictures, the two older men suited up for the dive, then climbed over the railing. As they slid into the water, Trip briefly saw them outlined against the glow, which illuminated them from underneath like a magic lantern. Within seconds, they were gone.

Gary was standing beside him. "If you like, you could try the observation chamber."

"Good idea," Trip said, lowering his camera. The chamber was contained in a false nose at the forefront of the yacht, two meters below the waterline. Going over to the entry tube, which was bolted to the stempost, Trip glanced back at Gary, who gave him a nod of encouragement, and climbed inside.

It was twenty feet down. When he reached the final rung, he found himself in a tiny room lined with a foam mattress, the ceiling too low to stand. It smelled of mildew and rust. He spread himself prone on the floor, his nose inches from the largest of five portholes, and looked out at the ocean.

It took him a while to understand what he was seeing. In the water outside, clusters of glowing particles were passing through the sea. There were dozens of such formations, some drifting at random, others bunching and splaying their radial arms to go sailing serenely past the windows.

Trip forgot about his camera, caught up in the strangeness of the sight. At first, he felt surrounded by otherworldly creatures, like something out of a dream. Only when one of the shapes drifted close by the nearest porthole, almost pressing itself against the glass, did he finally recognize it for what it was.

The sloop was surrounded by hundreds of octopuses. As his eyes grew used to the darkness, he saw that every octopus had two rows of luminous cells running along each of its eight arms. The light from each node, which was bluish green, was not strong, but taken together, they caused the water to be as brightly lit as a crowded highway on a winter's night.

When fully extended, the octopuses were the size of bicycle wheels, their bodies pink, verging on coral. As Trip switched on his camera, gelatinous eyes peered through the water at his own face. He was about to snap a picture when he heard the clang of footsteps overhead. Someone was climbing down the ladder.

"Mind if I join you?" The voice took him by surprise. Turning, he saw a pair of feminine legs enter his field of vision. When the woman had descended all the way, he saw that it was Meg, the ship's stewardess and deckhand.

"Not at all," Trip said, unsure of how to react. Meg was trim but shapely, with short dark hair and a patrician nose. From the moment of their first meeting, she had struck him as the sort of young woman who is perfectly aware of the power that she possesses, as well as the fact that it will not last forever. Among other things, although the relationship was not openly acknowledged, everyone on the yacht knew that Meg spent most of her nights in Ray Wiley's stateroom.

"I came to see what all the excitement was about," Meg said, spreading herself across the mattress pad. "Amazing, isn't it?"

"Yes, it is." Trip turned back to the window. They lay side by side, not speaking, as the lights drifted past them in glowing bands. He gradually became aware that Meg's leg was pressing pleasantly against his own.

A moment later, a diver appeared in the circle of sea disclosed by the largest porthole. It was Ray. As he passed the observation chamber, he turned toward the window, the beam of his flashlight slicing through the water. Through the mask, it was hard to see his face, but his eyes seemed fixed on theirs.

At his side, Trip felt Meg stiffen. Rolling onto her back, she took hold of the nearest rung and went up the ladder without a word. Trip did not move. He remained eye to eye with the diver on the other side of the window, the octopuses forgotten, until Ray finally turned and swam away.

The following morning, when Trip went on deck, he found Ray standing in the dive cockpit with Ellis and Gary. An awning had been erected over the aft deck, shielding it from the sun, but it was still hot enough for the men to strip down to shorts and sandals as they took a sample of seawater, a ritual performed once a day, every two hundred miles, as the *Lancet* circled the globe.

In the water around the yacht swam countless octopuses, their luminescence muted in the daylight. Ellis leaned over the railing. "What's the line in Tennyson? *Vast and unnumbered polypi—*"

"*Unnumbered and enormous polypi,*" Trip said, glad to put his liberal education to some use. "*Winnow with giant arms the slumbering green.*"

Taking a seat, he watched as a hinged arm with a pump on one end was lowered five feet below the surface. After the temperature and salinity had been recorded, fifty gallons of water were pumped into a plastic drum, passing through a series of increasingly fine filters. The process took about an hour. As they waited, Gary engaged in a friendly contest with Kiran, the yacht's first mate, to see who would be first to catch an octopus. Gary had floated a baited trap out to sea on a cable, while Kiran, tan and muscular, was taking a more active approach, which he claimed to have learned in the Canary Islands. It involved a hooked rod and a red rag tied to a stick, and did not, at first glance, seem especially effective.

As Ellis and Ray stowed their equipment, they picked up the thread of what seemed to be an ongoing debate. "We need to stay here," Ellis said. "If we leave now, we'll be giving up the chance of a lifetime."

"The chance of your lifetime, not mine," Ray said, rinsing himself off in the cockpit shower. "We're already running behind schedule. If we stay here much longer, we won't make it to the Galapagos as planned."

"Then we need to push back the deadline. This is a new species. Only one other variety of luminescent octopus has ever been described—"

"Take a specimen, then. I've already asked Kiran to put together a couple of tanks."

"A few specimens won't be enough," Ellis argued. "We're seeing extraordinary collective behaviors here. Octopuses aren't supposed to travel in schools, and at this distance from shore, they live well below the waterline. Something is causing them to appear in groups on the surface. We need to find out why."

Ray turned to Trip, the beads of water standing out on his face. "Are you getting all this? Ellis thinks that science can only take place in a bathysphere. He can't accept that a new kind of octopus isn't going to change the world."

"It may not change the world," Trip said carefully, "but it's something that a lot of people would like to see."

"I agree," Ellis said. "If anything, it would enhance the reputation of this project."

Ray shook his head, dislodging a cascade of drops. "You're missing the point. In the sample of water we've taken today, we're going to find a thousand new species of microbe, if not more." He turned to Trip. "With every sample we analyze, we double the number of genes previously known from all species across the planet. It's the first time that modern sequencing methods have been applied to an entire ecosystem. I don't see how an octopus is any more important than this."

"It isn't a question of importance," Ellis said impatiently. "It's a question of—"

"Even now, nobody really knows what the ocean contains," Ray continued, still looking at Trip. "Every milliliter of seawater contains a million bacteria and ten million viruses. Until I came along, nobody had tried to analyze the ocean with the same thoroughness that had been applied to the human genome. When we're done, the results will be available to everyone, free of charge, with no strings attached. That, my friends, is what will enhance our reputation. Not a glowing octopus."

He turned to look at Gary, who was seated on the transom, clutching the cable of his octopus trap. "As I see it, there are two approaches to science. You can lunge after something with a rag on a stick, like Kiran, or you can bait a trap and see what floats by. It's less glamorous, maybe, but in the long run—"

Ray was interrupted by an excited shout. At the other end of the sloop, Kiran had caught an octopus on the end of his hook, and was lifting it carefully out of the water. As Kiran dropped the octopus into the bucket at his feet, Trip saw a handful of arms writhing uselessly in the open air.

Ellis turned to Ray. "What were you saying about the two approaches to science?"

Ray forced his face into a grin, then turned to the first mate. "Kiran, think you can catch a few more of these monsters?"

"Not a problem," Kiran said, climbing into the cockpit. "How many do you want?"

"As many as you can get," Ray said. "We're having octopus for dinner tonight."

An embarrassed silence ensued. Kiran gave them all an uneasy smile, then headed below. After a pause, Ray turned to Ellis. "All right. We'll hold station for one more day. You should be satisfied with this."

"Fine," Ellis said, although he was obviously displeased. "I'll do what I can."

The two scientists went their separate ways. A few minutes later, when the filtering process was complete, Gary unscrewed a set of steel plates and used tweezers to fish out the filters inside. Each filter, the size of a vinyl record album, had been stained various shades of brown, as the microbes were captured in paper of decreasing porousness. "I'm sorry you had to see that," Gary said to Trip, sliding the filters into plastic bags. "Those two don't always see eye to eye—"

"What about you?" Trip asked, helping him pack up the morning's sample. "Do you think we should stay longer?"

Gary headed for the companionway. "Ray pays my salary, which doesn't make me a disinterested observer. The fact is, I love both of those guys, but Ellis is just as ambitious as Ray is. He's better at hiding it, that's all."

He disappeared down the stairs. As the day wore on, Trip caught occasional glimpses of Gary in the wet lab across from the salon. Through the laboratory window, Trip saw him sterilize a pair of shears with a blowtorch and slice each filter in two, one half to be frozen for later analysis, the other to be sequenced aboard the yacht itself. Aside from the time spent gathering each day's water sample, Gary spent most of his time in the lab, dissolving the filters and analyzing the resultant genetic material, which meant that he was the only crew member without a tan.

Trip took a seat in the salon, where the captured octopus had been installed in a plastic tank. Since his arrival, he had been struck by the demands being made of the scientific team. Sequencing the genes of all the organisms in a random sample of seawater was an incredibly complicated process, akin to assembling a thousand jumbled jigsaw puzzles. Normally, most of the analysis would have taken place on shore, but Ray, hoping to save time, had insisted that it occur on the sloop itself. Several competing efforts to sequence marine ecosystems were currently underway, and Ray had become obsessed with concluding the project before the bicentennial of Darwin's birth, which was in less than three weeks.

Such urgency might have seemed strange, but as Trip reviewed his notes, he reflected that nothing less than Ray's legacy was at stake. Despite the role that he had famously played in decoding the human genome, Ray remained a controversial figure, known more for his ruthlessness as a businessman than his scientific integrity. Now that money was no longer an issue, he had funded this mission in an attempt to refute his detractors, as well as to make his own case for a Nobel Prize. As a result, he had begun to push his scientific team to show greater progress, which, as far as Trip could tell, had only deepened the divisions within the crew.

Dinner that night was quietly tense. Dawn, the ship's cook, an attractive woman with a blond ponytail, had prepared a ceviche, slowly simmering the octopus to soften it first. Although the flesh was tender, nobody could do more than pick at it, so the crew focused on the vegetable curry instead, which they washed down with plentiful wine and cold water. "You can judge a yacht by how the wine flows," Ray said, his eyes red. "On the *Calypso*, Cousteau had a wine tank made of stainless steel. And how many bottles do we have?"

"Two hundred in the hold," Dawn said, "and another fifty or sixty in the fridge."

Trip poured himself another glass. Unlike some yachts, which had separate tables for guests and crew, everyone on the research sloop ate together, although this did nothing to lighten the mood. Ray, he noticed, treated everyone as his servant, even Stavros, who had been the yacht's captain long before the billionaire had acquired it. When Ray asked him condescendingly to tell them the Greek word for octopus, the captain replied, "*Octopous*, of course. But to Hesiod, it was *anosteos*, or the boneless one. *The boneless one gnaws his foot in his fireless house and wretched home.*"

"I didn't know we had so many scholars on board," Ray said. He eyed Trip over the rim of his glass. "I'm aware, by the way, that I've neglected to give you the interview I promised. Are you free tonight?"

Trip, who had nearly given up hope of such an invitation, was surprised at the sudden offer. "Of course. Maybe after dinner?"

"I need to take care of some business first, but if you want to drop by my cabin at ten, I can give you an hour of my time." Ray's bloodshot eyes flashed between Trip and Meg. "Unless you have other plans—"

Meg rose abruptly, clearing the dishes and carrying them into the galley. Ray, flushed from the wine, did not take his eyes from her face.

After dinner, the crew dispersed. Kiran headed up to the deck, joined a moment later by Dawn, ostensibly for the first watch, although a whiff of sweet smoke from the crew's quarters made Trip guess that they had something else in mind. Around the yacht, the octopuses had resumed their nocturnal flickering. When the lights in the salon were turned down, the octopus in the tank started to glow as well.

Going into his cabin, Trip began to review his list of questions, glancing out the window at the show of lights. As he prepared, he began to feel strangely nervous. Looking at his hands, he noticed that he had been chewing his fingernails, which was something that he had not done in years.

When the time for the interview arrived, Trip rose from his chair, making sure that he had his notebook and audio recorder, and went into the hallway. The yacht was silent. Stavros sat in the salon, his back turned, laying out a game of solitaire. None of the other crew members was in sight.

Trip went to the door of Ray's cabin, which was closed, and knocked lightly. "Ray?"

There was no answer. Looking down, Trip saw a line of light beneath the door. He knocked a second time, and when there was no response, he tried the knob, which turned easily.

After a moment's hesitation, Trip pushed open the door and entered the stateroom. He had been here only once before, on the day that he had boarded the yacht, and had been duly impressed by its luxury.

Ray was seated at his work station, his back to the door. His head was bowed, as if he were looking intently at something on the desk. Trip came forward cautiously, afraid that he was intruding, and gingerly touched Ray's shoulder with his fingertips. "Do you still want to talk?"

In response to the nudge, Ray swiveled around in his chair, although the motion was due solely to momentum. His eyes were open, and his head was tilted at an unnatural angle. A gash had parted the skin of his throat, the blood running down the front of his shirt and pooling on the floor below, where it blended with the burgundy rug. Trip was not a doctor, and had no firsthand experience of murder, but even at first glance, it was clear that Ray was quite dead.

II

The captain was the first to respond to his shouts of alarm. Stavros appeared in the stateroom door, his calmness oddly reassuring, and stopped. He looked at Trip, saying nothing, then turned to the body. Going up to the corpse, he placed his fingertips against its throat, almost in a parody of checking for a pulse, and examined the wound, which was clean and deep. After studying the gash for a moment, he shook his head. "It's bad luck to have a dead man on board."

Trip stared at the captain, wondering if he was joking. Instead of saying more, Stavros took the body beneath its arms and laid it on the floor, with Trip doing his best to help. As they moved the body, a fresh stream of blood trickled from its throat, swallowed up at once by the plush fibers of the carpet.

There was a gasp from the doorway. It was Meg. A second later, Gary appeared, still in his gloves and laboratory gown, his face pale with shock. Kiran and Dawn stood behind him, looking over his shoulder at the scene in the cabin. Their eyes were bloodshot. Last of all, Ellis pushed through the knot of bodies, his gaze fixed on the corpse on the ground.

"My God," Ellis said, his voice nearly cracking. "Did anyone see what happened?"

No one replied. Through the windows, the octopus lights continued to flicker.

"I've been in the salon all night," Stavros said at last. "I saw nobody enter or leave."

"Someone must have been here," Trip said. "Ray didn't cut his own throat. If he did, where's the knife?"

There was another silence, more suspicious now. Trip was studying the faces of the others, searching for signs of guilt, when his eye was caught by a trail of blood on the floor. It led from the desk to the far wall, where a door had been set into the bulkhead. "Where does this hatch go?"

"The deck," Stavros said. He went to the hatch and opened it, touching only the edge of the knob. Beyond the door lay a narrow companionway. He went up, followed by Trip and Kiran, with the others remaining behind.

Outside, the air was cool and motionless, the ocean glowing with eerie light. In the dive cockpit, a constellation of blood was visible on the deck. A pool of pink water had collected beneath the showerhead, as if someone had paused to wash his or her hands before moving on. Stavros turned to Kiran. "You were supposed to be on watch. You didn't see anything?"

Kiran looked embarrassed. "We were at the prow, looking at the lights. And we were, uh—"

"Yes, I know," Stavros said, making a gesture of disgust. "A couple of potheads."

They returned to the stateroom. In the cabin, someone had covered the body with a sheet, the crimson petals of blood already starting to soak through. Meg was seated on the bed, eyes wet, with Dawn's arm around her shoulders.

In the corner, Ellis and Gary were talking in low tones. A second later, Ellis turned to the others, as if he had decided to assume control. "All right. Whoever did this needs to confess now."

In the long pause that followed, volleys of glances were exchanged, but no one spoke. Eventually, one by one, they began to offer explanations for their whereabouts.

It soon became clear that only Kiran and Dawn, who had been smoking up on the far end of the sloop, could verify their stories. While Trip had gone into his room after dinner, Gary had returned to the lab, and Ellis had been in the observation chamber belowdecks, taking notes on the octopus school. Stavros had been in the salon, facing away from the stateroom, while Meg had retired to her cabin to read.

Ellis turned to Trip. "You're the one who found him. What were you doing here?"

"You heard what happened at dinner," Trip said. "Ray offered me an interview."

"Is that what you thought?" Ellis gave him a tight smile. "I happen to know that Ray was planning to tell you that he was withdrawing permission for the article. He told me so himself."

Trip was astonished by the unspoken implication. "Why would he change his mind?"

Ellis looked at Meg, who was seated on the bed. "Who knows what he was thinking?"

Trip's face grew red. "So what are you saying? He wouldn't give me an interview, so I killed him?"

There was no response. After another moment, when it became clear that no confessions were forthcoming, they turned, almost with relief, to the business of dealing with the body. Ellis went into his cabin and returned with a medical kit, which he used to tape bags over Ray's hands. When he was done, Stavros wrapped the corpse in a sheet and secured it neatly with nylon cord. Sealing off the stateroom, they carried the body into the galley, where Meg and Dawn had removed the bottles from the wine refrigerator, and laid it snugly inside.

As they were closing the galley door, Trip happened to glance at the rack above the sink, and saw that one of the knives was missing.

Once the body had been stowed, they returned to the salon to debate their next move. The first decision was easy. The *Lancet*, like many yachts, had a system of security cameras that was rarely used, and which they now agreed to turn on. There was also some discussion of sleeping arrangements. In the end, it was decided that the women would share one of the staterooms, Trip, Ellis, and Gary the other, and that the captain and first mate would each take a cabin for themselves.

Finally, they raised the issue of the voyage itself. "There's no way out of it," Stavros said. "We need to go back. If we make full speed, we can be at Antigua and Barbuda in three days."

"We would have been done in a few more weeks," Gary said bitterly. He looked around at the others. "I know we don't have much of a choice, but after all this is done, I'm coming back to finish the project."

No one spoke. In the tank, the octopus wound and unwound its arms, glowing softly, like an emblem of death from a medieval painting.

They all spent a restless night. The following morning, Trip was in the salon when he felt a soothing vibration well up through the floor. The engine had started. He was smiling at Meg and Dawn, who seemed equally relieved that they were on their way, when an alarm sounded from the cockpit. A second later, the wailing ceased, and the engine died as well.

Trip went up to the deck, where he found Stavros crouching over the hatch of the engine room, biting his lower lip. A sharp tang of scorched metal wafted up from the engine. "Overheated," Stavros said tersely, in response to Trip's question. "We're taking care of it."

Kiran, who was examining the engine, stuck his head and shoulders out of the darkened rectangle, a smudge of grease on his face. "It's the alternator and pump. The belt's torn to shreds. I'll need to replace it."

"How long will that take?" Trip asked, unsettled by the prospect of an engine failure. Although the sloop was perfectly capable of proceeding under sail, the last few days had been windless, and they were weeks away from shore.

Kiran wiped away the grease. "A couple of hours. We'll need to hold station here."

Word of their situation spread quickly. After learning what had happened, Ellis announced that he would spend the morning trying to capture a few more octopuses. While examining the octopus that had been caught the day before, he had noticed that one of its arms was missing, apparently severed. "We need a perfect specimen," Ellis said, as if challenging the others to contradict him. "If we're stuck here anyway, we may as well make the most of it."

When no one objected, Ellis and Gary set to work. During the night, the yacht had drifted away from the octopus school, so they took the boat tender. Trip accepted an invitation to come along, glad for an excuse to get away from the yacht, and Meg agreed to join them as well.

They roared off in the tender, the water rising around them in a needlelike spray. The motor was too loud for conversation, but Trip kept a close watch on Meg, who had dark circles under her eyes.

When the tender neared the octopus school, which was visible in faint red patches through the water, Ellis cut the engine. "Gary and I will dive together. You two can wait here."

Donning their equipment, the two scientists climbed onto the inflatable keel and slid overboard. Trip watched them descend, the sun beating down on the back of his neck, then turned to Meg. "How are you doing?"

"I'll be all right," Meg said. The brim of her hat left her face in shadow, but her voice, he noticed, was steady.

As they waited for the others to return, Meg began to take measurements of the water's temperature and salinity, with Trip helping as best he could. As the minutes ticked by, he tried to steer the conversation toward the other members of the crew. "Ray didn't seem like a guy who was easy to work with."

Meg looked back at the yacht, which was holding station seven hundred yards away. "He was used to being right all the time. Ellis couldn't deal with it. He also thought that he was going to have the chance to conduct his own research, but Ray worked him pretty hard."

"Ellis seems to think that the octopus school is his last chance for a major discovery."

"Yes, I know." Meg hesitated, as if there were something else that she wanted to say. "There was a lot that Ellis didn't understand. Ray drank too much, and sometimes, when we were alone, he would tell me things—"

Trip sensed that she was on the verge of revealing something important. "What is it?"

"Ray was withholding some of the team's discoveries. You know how he insisted that Gary process the samples on board the yacht? It was so he could screen the results for genes with commercial potential. If you can find a microbe that makes it easier to produce ethanol, for example, or a luminous microbe like the one he was hoping to find the other night, it would be worth millions."

"But the whole point of this project was to make the data freely available," Trip said. "Every gene was going to be made public, right?"

"That's what Ray claimed. It's what allowed him to recruit people like Gary. If you ask Gary why he joined the project, he'll say it was because he believed that genetic research should be as open as possible. But Ray was always driven by profit. He wasn't about to change his ways."

Trip could feel the elements of a story assembling themselves in his head. "You seem to know a lot about the science."

"I spent a year in medical school before I dropped out. I couldn't stand the dissections." Meg glanced back at the sloop, which looked like a scale model in the sunlight. "I decided a long time ago that I was going to devote my life to pleasure, not death. For a while, I thought that marrying a rich man was the answer. That's why I was involved with Ray. Don't pretend you didn't know."

Trip went for the diplomatic response. "I had some idea of what was going on."

"You and everyone else. I don't mind. I knew he wasn't going to marry me." Meg turned back to Trip. "Maybe it's better this way. If he'd held back results for commercial reasons, it would have come out sooner or later. Now, instead, he gets to be a martyr. In a way, I'm glad he's dead."

Trip tried to cut the tension. "You probably don't want me writing about this, then."

Meg didn't respond. Something in her unsmiling face, which was still in shadow, sent a prickle of nervousness down his spine. Before either of them could speak again, Gary's gloved hand emerged from the sea, clutching an octopus, which had wound itself around his upper arm. Ellis surfaced a second later, wetsuit glistening, holding an octopus of his own.

"Looks like they've got their prizes," Meg said. She glanced at Trip's hands. "You've been biting your nails. Are you nervous?"

When she looked back up at him, Trip held her gaze. "Not any more than you are."

They helped Gary and Ellis onto the tender. As they headed back, the octopuses, each in its own bucket, writhed at their feet, curling into defensive balls whenever they were touched. Meg did not speak to Trip again.

When they returned to the sloop, it was already late in the afternoon. Trip was climbing into the dive cockpit when he heard shouts. At the entrance to the engine room, Stavros and Kiran were yelling at each other, and the captain had bitten his own lip out of agitation. "You stupid *malaka*," Stavros said. "If we wind up stranded here, it's all your fault—"

Kiran was equally furious. "*Bhenchod*, I'm not the one who sabotaged the engine."

"Sabotage?" Trip looked between the two men. "What are you talking about?"

"It's the fan belt," Kiran said. "I tried to replace it, but it snapped whenever the engine engaged. When I looked closer, I found out why. The ball bearings in the pulley are damaged. And the package of extra bearings is missing from my spare parts kit. I took an inventory just last week, and it was definitely there. Which means that somebody stole it."

"What about the engine?" Trip asked. "You really think that it was sabotaged?"

Stavros nodded, the blood shining on his lip. "Whoever did it will answer to me."

"In any case, we'll find a workaround," Kiran said, speaking more calmly than before. "I can cannibalize parts from another pulley. But it means we won't be leaving until tomorrow at the earliest."

This announcement cast a pall over the rest of the day. As Stavros and Kiran worked on the engine, Gary prepared a tank for the octopus he had caught, installing it next to the first one, while Ellis took his own specimen into the lab for closer examination. The two octopuses in the salon took no visible interest in each other, glowing gently in their separate containers as evening fell.

When it was time for dinner, Gary proposed that they eat on deck, which would put some distance between themselves and the body in the galley. Outside, the lights in the water were brighter than ever. As they ate around a folding table, bundled up in parkas and gloves, Gary raised the question that they had all been avoiding. "When this is over, how many of you are coming back?"

When no one answered, Gary took a sip from his water glass. "I know it's hard to talk about this, but back on shore, we aren't going to have another quiet moment. We need to discuss this now."

"We all know that you want to respect Ray's wishes," Stavros finally said, a red scab on his lower lip. "As for me, I go with the *Lancet.* Her destination makes no difference to me."

"Or me," Kiran said. "Not everyone here feels the same loyalty to Ray that you do."

"This isn't about loyalty," Gary said. "It's about seeing that important work isn't lost. We've made significant discoveries here, and we need to make sure that they're released to the public."

Trip glanced at Meg, who did not look back. "I've only been here for a few days, but I know something about situations like this," Trip said, not sure if his opinion counted. "Your first obligation is to the living."

Ellis grunted. "Personally, if Ray were able to speak his mind, I don't think he'd care either way. Now that he's dead, he can't profit from any of it. They don't award the Nobel Prize posthumously."

After a prolonged silence, Dawn, who had tucked her hair up into a baseball cap, tried to change the subject. "I've been watching these octopus lights for days now, and I have no idea what they mean. What are they?"

Ellis shifted easily into professorial mode. "It could be a way of coordinating group activities, like mating. Or some kind of hunting strategy. Most people don't appreciate how intelligent octopuses are. They have big brains with folded lobes, the largest of any invertebrate, and show signs of memory and learning." He looked thoughtfully at the lights. "Of course, they only live for three or four years. If they had a longer lifespan, who knows what they might be capable of doing?"

The crew fell into silence. As they looked out at the water, Kiran played with his cigarette lighter, its nervous flame mirroring the lights in the sea, which seemed unfathomably ancient. Trip, thinking of corpse lights in a graveyard, was reminded of a passage from Coleridge: *They moved in tracks of shining white, and when they reared, the elfish light fell off in hoary flakes—*

After a moment, Meg cleared the table and took the dishes below. The others were talking and drinking, the mood finally beginning to lighten, when they heard a scream and a crash from the salon.

In an instant, they were out of their chairs. They found Meg standing in the salon, a pile of broken dishes at her feet. She was staring at the two tanks that had been set up in one corner. Her face had lost most of its color.

"*Look*," Meg said, pointing toward the tanks with a trembling finger. "*Look at this.*"

Trip followed her gesture with his eyes. The last time he had bothered to look, each of the tanks had held a single octopus. Now the nearest tank was empty, and in the other, the water was clouded by a blue fog.

When the haze cleared, he felt a wave of nausea. One of the octopuses had killed the other. The survivor's color had deepened to crimson, while the remains of its neighbor were shriveled and gray. Billows of octopus blood had polluted the water, and a foamy scum had gathered on the surface.

A second later, Trip realized what else was happening, and felt a cold hand take hold of his insides.

The surviving octopus was eating its companion. As he watched, the octopus used its beak to amputate one of its victim's arms at the base. Wrapping its mouth around the severed arm, it devoured it, the arm disappearing inch by inch into its chitinous maw. The octopus twitched, its arms jerking in brief convulsions as it swallowed its fierce meal, its eyes hooded and glazed.

Ellis looked accusingly at the others. "Who put the octopuses into the same tank?"

"I don't think anyone did this," Stavros said. "It must have escaped on its own."

"That's impossible," Kiran said. He went over to the empty tank. Both tanks had been made from plastic buckets, the lids secured so that a narrow gap remained above the rim, allowing air to circulate. The gap, which was less than an inch wide, seemed much too small for an octopus to pass through.

As the surviving octopus finished eating one arm and began to snip off another, it occurred to Trip that there was an easy way to resolve the question. "The security cameras. We switched them on last night."

"Let's take a look," Ellis said. Going into the library, he returned a minute later with a videotape. A television was mounted to one wall of the salon. Ellis inserted the tape into the video player and pressed the rewind button. As he did, Trip noticed that his knuckles were badly bruised.

Before he could ask about this, an image of the salon appeared on the television set. The videotape opened with footage that had been taken only a few moments ago, of the entire crew standing around the tanks. As the tape rewound, the crew went up the steps, walking backwards, except for Meg, who stayed behind. The broken dishes on the floor flew back into her arms and reassembled themselves, and then she, too, was gone. The tanks alone remained onscreen.

As the video rolled back, the predatory octopus appeared to regurgitate its victim's arms and refasten them. An instant later, both octopuses were alive, struggling in the tank, and then—

"I don't believe it," Trip said, his eyes wide. "Have you ever seen anything like this?"

Ellis remained silent, although he did not look away from the screen. He rewound the tape to the point where the octopuses were back in their separate tanks, then allowed the action to play out normally.

For a few seconds, the octopuses floated in their tanks as before. Then the nearest octopus, one of the specimens that Ellis and Gary had captured earlier that day, extended one arm after another to the rim of its own bucket, until the tips of four arms protruded slightly through the narrow gap.

Nothing else happened for a long moment—and then the octopus began to squeeze its entire body through. Watching it was like witnessing a baffling optical illusion. First one arm was threaded through the gap and down the outside of the tank. Three other arms followed. The octopus flattened itself, the edge of its mantle passing through, followed by its head, which grew pancaked, like a balloon that was only halfway inflated, as the octopus pulled itself the rest of the way out. Then it was on the countertop and slithering toward the other tank.

The octopus moved quickly, gathering and splaying its arms as it crawled across the counter. Its color deepened from pink to red. As it approached, the second octopus, still inside its tank, grew pale, its normally smooth skin becoming rough and pebbled. When the first octopus reached the tank, it hooked the end of one arm over the rim, compressing its body until it was flat enough to slip through the gap, which was narrower than a letterbox. Within seconds, it had entered the second tank.

The struggle did not last for long. There was an entanglement of arms and beaks, the water growing blue with blood. Trip was unable to see how one octopus killed the other, but the thought of what was happening there made the hairs stand up on the back of his neck.

In less than a minute, it was over, and one octopus lay dead at the bottom of the tank. The survivor drifted in the bloody water, its arms coiling and uncoiling. Then, inevitably, it began to feed.

III

"I don't believe it," Trip said again. Looking away from the carnage onscreen, he saw sickened expressions on the faces around him. As if following a common impulse, the crew turned from the television to look at the tanks, and experienced a collective shudder. The remaining octopus had abandoned its meal and was pressing its head against the wall of its tank, watching them, or so it seemed, with its gelatinous eyes. The nodules on its arms were glowing brightly.

Lowering his gaze, Trip saw something that should have been obvious before. Streaks of moisture were visible on the countertop between the two tanks, marks from where the octopus had dragged itself across the intervening space. Something in the nearly invisible trail, which was rapidly drying out, made what they had just witnessed seem even more hideous.

Ellis was the first to regain some semblance of composure. "I should have been more careful. Octopuses are notorious for squeezing through tight spaces. The hardest part of the body is the beak, and the rest is highly compressible. If a gap is wide enough for the beak to pass through—"

Kiran stared at him. “You’re saying that this isn’t strange? I’m sorry, but I’m a little freaked out by this.”

“I’m not saying that this wasn’t unusual,” Ellis said. “I’m only saying that it can be explained. As for the cannibalism, I have no professional opinion. The important thing is that we fix the tanks.”

Using a hooked rod, which he held at arm’s length, Kiran transferred the surviving octopus to its old tank. The octopus seemed sated, its eyes filmy and glazed, as it slid, twitching slightly, into the water. Kiran fastened a rectangle of wire mesh across the top of the bucket, so that the gap between lid and rim was sealed off, then did the same to the octopus in the wet lab next door. There seemed to be no way that either octopus could escape again.

Even after these precautions had been taken, an aura of uneasiness lingered over the yacht. An hour later, when Trip went to bed, it was a long time before he fell asleep, and when he did, he was troubled by nightmares. In one dream, he was seated at the desk in his cabin, the door closed. As he reviewed his notes, oblivious to the danger, an octopus squeezed beneath the door, slithered across the carpet, climbed his chair, and touched the back of his neck with one clammy arm. Before he could react, the octopus pressed its parrotlike beak against his throat, and then—

Trip awoke, the sheets twisted like tentacles around his legs. It was still dark outside. As he tried to remember what had awakened him, he looked at his hands, which were visible in the faint light from the octopus school, and was shocked by the sight. His fingernails and cuticles were ragged, and a sour taste in his mouth told him that he had been chewing his nails in his sleep.

He was studying the damage that he had done, noticing that his fingers were bleeding in a few places, when he remembered what had pulled him from sleep in the first place. It had been a scream.

As he sat up in bed, he found that he could hear voices coming from the stateroom across the hall. Trip pulled on his shoes and went quietly into the corridor, taking care not to disturb Ellis and Gary, who were asleep. Through the door of the adjoining cabin, he heard voices. He knocked. “Is everything okay?”

The voices ceased at once. After a moment, he heard the shuffle of footsteps, and the door opened a crack. “It’s all right,” Meg said softly, peering through the gap. “Go back to bed.”

“It *isn’t* all right,” Dawn said, appearing behind Meg. “Tell her this needs to stop.”

“What needs to stop?” Trip asked. As he spoke, he saw a line of blood trickling down the crook of Meg’s arm. Impulsively, he came forward, pushing the door open. The two women fell back. “What happened?”

“It’s nothing.” Meg’s voice was nearly a mumble. “It isn’t any of your business—”

“Don’t give me that,” Dawn said, seizing Meg’s wrist in one hand. “Look at this.”

Trip saw a series of gashes running along Meg’s inside elbow. The cuts were parallel and shallow, and while none had grazed a major vessel, they were bleeding freely. “Did someone attack you?”

“Nobody attacked her,” Dawn said, her voice on edge. “She did this to herself.”

Trip turned to Meg, whose face was closed off with embarrassment. “Is that true?”

Meg yanked her arm away from Dawn, sending droplets of blood to the floor. “It’s no big deal. Sometimes I cut myself when I’m stressed. I’ve done it since I was a teenager. It's never deep enough to be dangerous. I don't see why you're making a federal case out of this—"

Trip noticed a knife on the bedside table, its blade smeared with blood. "Did you take this from the kitchen?"

Meg sighed. "I was going to replace it. I never meant to use it on anyone but myself."

"I don't care about the knife," Dawn said. "We've been friends a long time. I can't believe you've been hiding this from me—"

The women resumed their argument. Trip was about to slip away when he remembered the medical kit that Ellis had used to bag Ray's hands. "Hold on," Trip said. "We need to do something about those cuts."

He went back to his cabin, where the others were still asleep, and found the medical kit among Ellis's things. When he returned to the other stateroom, Dawn seemed calmer, and Meg was cupping a hand casually beneath her elbow, catching the blood in the hollow of her palm.

Opening the medical kit, Trip took out a roll of tape and a gauze pad. He was about to close the kit again when he saw something tucked beneath the dressings. He reached inside. Fishing the object out, he found that it was a pack of ball bearings, the package cool and heavy in his hand.

"From the spare parts kit," Trip said. He looked at the others. "Do you think—"

He broke off. The women were looking at the door, their expressions wary. Trip saw that a shadow had fallen across the floor. Rising to his feet, he found himself facing a solitary figure in the doorway.

"That's my medical kit," Ellis said, his voice calm. "What are you doing with it?"

"A minor emergency, but everything should be fine." Trip held up the package of ball bearings. "What the hell are these?"

Ellis regarded the package. "I stole them from the spare parts kit. I was fairly sure that what I had done to the engine would keep us here another day, but I wanted to be on the safe side—"

"You sabotaged the engine," Trip said. He had already forgotten about Meg. "Why?"

Ellis gave him a look of contempt. "You know why. I wanted to keep the yacht here a day or two longer. There was no way to make Ray listen to reason, so I took things into my own hands."

"By attacking my ship?" It was Stavros. He was standing in the doorway, drawn by the noise, with Gary watching from over one shoulder. "We could have been stranded here for weeks—"

"You don't understand," Ellis said. Going to the window, he thrust his finger toward the octopus lights. "Ray was rushing ahead to meet a meaningless deadline. I wanted to document a natural phenomenon that might never be seen again. I don't have to defend the choice I made."

Gary pushed past the captain. "Are you listening to yourself? You're worse than Ray. You only cared about your own career, even if it threatened everything we were doing here. Did you kill Ray, too?"

"I didn't kill Ray," Ellis said fiercely. "I can't believe you're accusing me of this—"

Without warning, Ellis punched the wall of the stateroom, hard, so that the bulkhead rang with the blow. As the others fell back, he punched it again. Before anyone else could speak, Kiran appeared, breathless, at the stateroom door.

"I don't know what the commotion is about, but you need to break it up," Kiran said. "There's something you all need to see."

They went into the salon, where the lights had been turned up. Kiran pointed toward the tank that housed the octopus. "*Look—*"

Staring at what was there, Trip felt his anger dissolve into a sickening sense of horror. When they had caught this octopus the day before, they had made sure that all of its arms were intact. Now two of its arms were missing, leaving only a pair of stumps behind. The water was full of blood, but the severed arms were gone. Trip had no desire to find out what had become of them, but it was already too late.

The octopus was eating itself. As Trip watched, the octopus bent one of its remaining arms until the base was pressed against its gaping mouth. With a snip of its beak, it severed the arm, which fell away in a cloud of blood. Without a pause, the octopus swam after it, positioning itself so that one end of the amputated arm was in its mouth, and began to devour it like a length of spaghetti. Trip found himself remembering the line from Hesiod that Stavros had quoted: *The boneless one gnaws his foot in his fireless house and wretched home.*

Ellis and Gary were looking at each other, their heated exchange apparently forgotten. "Autophagy," Ellis said.

Gary nodded, although he was visibly repulsed by the sight. "I should have known. Let me check the other specimen."

"Hold on a second," Trip said to Ellis. "You're saying you've seen this before?"

"Not exactly, but I've heard of it," Ellis said. "Octopuses are occasionally known to cannibalize themselves. It's called autophagy. Nobody knows what causes it, but it seems to involve a viral infection of the nervous system. It's a disease. When you have several octopuses in a single tank, if one starts to eat itself, the others will follow. Death ensues within days."

Gary returned to the salon. "The third octopus looks fine. It was never in contact with this specimen, so maybe—"

Ellis shook his head. "If we're dealing with infectious autophagy, it may have spread to the entire school. For all we know, this is what brought them to the surface. The lights are coordinating their behavior. It's a mass suicide."

Although his voice remained calm, Ellis was clearly upset. He thrust his bleeding knuckles into his mouth. Trip looked at him, then looked back at the maddened octopus, which had finished eating its own arm. Finally, he looked at his own hands, and felt the last piece fall into place.

"We need to discuss something right now," Trip said to the others. "Where's Meg?"

Meg was brought from the stateroom, a fresh bandage on her inside elbow. The crew sat around the table in the salon, looking at Trip. Through the windows, the lights seemed to press against the yacht on all sides.

Trip laid his hands on the table, showing them to the others. "You see this? I've been biting my nails for the past couple of days. It's something I haven't done in years, but ever since we entered this part of the ocean, I've been gnawing them like a maniac. Why? I'm not sure, but I can guess."

Before anyone else could speak, Trip turned to Ellis. "A moment ago, you punched the wall so hard that your knuckles started to bleed. Is this something that you normally do?"

If Ellis saw where this was going, he was not inclined to play along. "I was upset. I don't think it means anything."

"But it wasn't the first time you've done it. I saw the bruises on your hands. This is part of a larger pattern of behavior, and it's been happening to all of us." Trip turned to Meg. "Meg, you felt the urge to cut yourself. Stavros, I saw you bite your lip until it drew blood."

Gary was looking at him with open skepticism. "What exactly are you trying to say?"

"We're being affected by something in the environment," Trip said. "This octopus is eating itself for the same reason. Meg, you were a medical student. Have you ever seen a disease that could cause behavior like this?"

"Not firsthand," Meg said slowly. "But infections of the nervous system can result in psychotic or suicidal behavior. Genetic disorders can also lead to violence. Children bite off their lips and fingers, or attack those around them as a form of displacement. In the end, they need to be physically restrained."

"A form of displacement," Trip said, underlining the phrase. "What does that mean?"

"They feel driven to destroy their own bodies, so they redirect their aggression toward others. The violence is often concentrated on their family and friends, which may be another way of hurting themselves."

"What about murder?" Trip asked. "Could this displacement go far enough so that the person was forced to kill?"

"It's possible," Meg said. "In theory, it could lead to murder by someone who was not in control of his actions."

"Like the octopus," Trip said. "It climbed out of its tank to kill its neighbor, but as soon as it ran out of victims, it turned on itself. And if this disease is affecting the entire school, we're right in the middle of it. It's like Ray said. Every drop of seawater contains millions of viruses. If this is a disease, it must be transmitted in the sea. And where do we get our drinking water?"

"The watermaker," Stavros said. "It purifies seawater, but won't screen out viruses."

"We have an emergency cache of water in drums," Kiran said. "It's designed to sustain the crew for two weeks. We might even be able to modify our sampling system to purify water for drinking—"

"But if we're already infected, fixing the water supply won't be enough," Trip said. He turned to Ellis. "The octopus in the wet lab hasn't displayed any symptoms. Can you think of any reason why?"

Ellis thought for a moment. "This afternoon, I wanted to examine it more closely, so I anesthetized it with magnesium chloride. It's a standard anesthetic for cephalopods. In humans, it's a nervous system depressant that blocks neuromuscular transmissions. And if you're right, and this impulse to hurt ourselves is a sort of seizure, something like magnesium may inhibit the reaction."

"It's possible," Meg said excitedly. "And we have a lot of magnesium salts on board. Maybe we can use it as a temporary treatment—"

Gary seemed unconvinced. "I still don't buy it. Even if you're right about the virus, it's hard to believe that it could affect humans and octopuses in the same way. Besides, we've all been drinking the same water, and I'm fine. And you haven't mentioned Kiran or Dawn at all."

"That's because he never asked," Dawn said quietly. As the rest of the crew watched, she removed her cap and shook loose her hair. Tilting her head to one side, she pointed to an area of her scalp not far from the crown. A patch of hair, less than half an inch in diameter, was missing.

"I chew my hair and swallow it," Dawn said, sounding embarrassed. "Trichophagia. A bad habit. I haven't done it since I was a girl, but last night, it started up again, just before we found Ray."

Trip turned to Kiran. He found that his heart was pounding. "What about you?"

Without speaking, Kiran yanked up the sleeve of his shirt, revealing his forearm. The marks of several recent burns were visible against his dark skin. In a few places, they had begun to blister.

"I've been burning myself with my lighter," Kiran said flatly. "I didn't know why."

The crew looked at the burns for a long moment. Then, as if the same thought had occurred to everyone at once, their eyes turned to Gary.

"I don't know what to tell you," Gary said. "I haven't felt at all out of the ordinary."

Trip was about to reply when he noticed something strange. Although the salon was comfortably warm, Gary was wearing a pair of gloves. When he thought back to it now, Trip couldn't remember the last time he had seen Gary without them. In Ray's stateroom, Gary had been wearing his lab gloves and smock. He had spent most of the following day in the water, wearing scuba gloves, and had suggested that they eat dinner on deck, forcing all of them to bundle up. Trip cleared his throat. "Gary, would you mind taking off your gloves?"

Gary only glared at him. "I can't believe you're saying this. This is totally crazy."

"It doesn't seem so unreasonable to me," Kiran said. "Why don't you want to take them off?"

Gary opened his mouth, as if to respond. Then, in a movement that caught all of them off guard, he was up and on his feet. Before he could get far, Kiran tackled him, pinning his arms behind his back. There was a brief struggle, punctuated by curses on both sides, before Gary finally surrendered.

"Let's have a look," Ellis said. Going forward, he took hold of Gary's left arm. Trip seized the cuff of the glove, yanking it off, then paused. Gary's fingers were unblemished and clean.

"I hope you're satisfied," Gary said. "Do we need to go through this a second time?"

Trip glanced at the others. Ellis and Kiran had lost some of their certainty, but they shifted their grip on Gary, thrusting his right arm forward. Trip seized his wrist, took hold of the remaining glove, and gave it a good tug.

As soon as the glove was off, it fell, forgotten, to the floor. Gary closed his eyes.

His fingertips were missing. All of the nails were gone, torn or gnawed away, and the first joint of his index finger had been bitten off completely, the wounds cauterized to stop the bleeding.

At the sight of the ravaged hand, Ellis released Gary's arm, his face gray. Looking at those burnt stumps, Trip remembered the blowtorch that Gary used to sterilize his shears, and realized what should have been obvious long ago. Gary had spent the previous day in the lab, working with samples that had been taken from the water, cutting up the filters, processing them with enzymes. Whatever was in the ocean would have been concentrated by the filtration process.

And if there was a pathogen in the water, Gary had received by far the greatest dose.

"I'm sorry," Gary said, addressing no one in particular. "I really can't help myself."

His ruined hand went for his pocket. There was a flash of silver, and an instant later, blood was streaming from Ellis's throat.

Gary pulled out the shears, their blades streaked with crimson, and let them drop. As Ellis fell to his knees, Gary broke loose and dashed for the companionway. Trip ran after him, the other men following close behind, as Meg screamed for Dawn to bring the medical kit. As he left the salon, Trip had just enough time to notice that the octopus was lying, dead, at the bottom of its tank.

Outside, a stinging rain had begun to fall. Around the boat, the lights from the octopus school were shining even more brightly than before. In their cold luminescence, Trip saw someone moving at the stern of the yacht. He turned to see Gary standing in the dive cockpit, a harpoon gun clutched in his good hand.

"Don't come any closer," Gary said, his voice breaking. "If you do, I'll put a harpoon through your heart. I like you, but that doesn't mean I won't do it. It may even make it easier."

"I know," Trip said, the rain trickling down his face. "I won't take it personally."

"Speak for yourself," Kiran said. He was standing next to Trip, ready to spring, but for the moment, he held back. Stavros took up a position nearby. They stood in silence, watching and waiting in the rain.

"I never wanted this to happen," Gary said at last. "I killed Ray, but I had no choice."

"I believe you," Trip said, knowing that the longer they kept Gary talking, the better their chances of taking him by surprise. "If you hurt him, it was because you didn't want to hurt yourself."

Gary shook his head. "I was angry with him, too. He was holding back our most crucial findings. Did you know this? I realized it when I saw the first paper he published. I'd been in the lab since day one, and knew exactly what we'd found. Ray was selfish. Like Ellis. Like me."

The hand with the harpoon gun fell slightly. Trip felt Kiran tense up at his side, but Gary, sensing this as well, raised the gun again. "You weren't selfish," Trip said. "You wanted to do what was right."

"Did I?" Gary asked. "The other day, when I heard Ray talking about how he was going to make his research freely available, I couldn't take it anymore. As I worked in the lab, I got madder and madder. I didn't know where the anger was coming from. I thought about killing myself, cutting my own throat, just so I wouldn't be a party to this web of lies—"

"It wasn't about you," Trip said. "It was in the water. It had nothing to do with Ray."

"But the betrayal was real. After dinner, I tried to work, but I couldn't concentrate. I saw myself doing horrible things, like tearing off my fingers. So I came up here to be alone. I was thinking about throwing myself overboard, just to stop the noise in my head, when Ray appeared."

His eyes grew clouded. “Ray was here to look at the lights, but when he saw me, we started to talk. I wanted to speak to him privately, so we went down the hatchway to his cabin. I confronted him about the missing results. He denied it at first, then threatened to take me off the project if I refused to go along, I wanted to kill myself, and then I wanted to kill him, too—”

Without lowering the harpoon gun, Gary picked up a dive belt and looped it over his body. He did the same with a second belt, one across each shoulder, so that they crossed his chest like a pair of bandoliers. “I didn’t even know I had the shears in my pocket. All I could think of were the lights in the sea. When he was dead, I went to the dive cockpit to wash up, then headed back to the lab. Nobody saw me, but while I was waiting for you to find the body, I chewed off the ends of my fingers.”

Gary’s face was obscured by the rain. “So I was the most selfish of all. I killed Ray so that I wouldn’t hurt myself. Now I’ve done the same to Ellis.” He swallowed hard. “It’s time to do something selfless for a change.”

He tossed the harpoon gun aside. Before anyone else could move, Gary climbed over the railing of the yacht, the dive belts looped across both his shoulders, and leapt into the ocean.

Trip and the others ran to the railing. Gary was already gone, the weight of the dive belts dragging him below the surface, the sea closing rapidly over his head. Trip stared at the water for a long time, his eyes smarting from the rain, but Gary did not appear again. All around the ship, the ghostly lights continued to fluoresce, the octopus school glowing as it had done for millions of years, casting its cold radiance across the unmarked shroud of the sea.

On a trellised arcade at Holbertson Hospital, a yellow wall gave back the sun’s rays. Trip sat in a wickerwork chair under a ceiling fan, hands folded, looking out at the garden. He was thinking of nothing in particular.

A chair beside him creaked as someone sat down. It was Meg. “How are you doing?”

Trip considered the question. Looking at his hands, he noted with some satisfaction that his fingers were healing, although the nails were still torn. “I’m all right. What about you?”

“I thought I’d pay a visit to our friend in the next ward. Want to come along?”

Trip only rose in reply. As they walked along the arcade, they passed a pair of nurses wearing white surgical masks. At their approach, the nurses inclined their heads politely, but kept their distance.

They had arrived in Antigua two days ago. With the yacht repaired, the journey had taken three days, with frequent breaks to keep the engine from overheating. Purified water and magnesium salts had kept their destructive impulses at bay, but it was unclear what the lasting effects would be.

As they walked, Meg said softly, “You know, when I close my eyes, I still see them.”

Trip knew what she meant. Whenever his own eyes were closed, he saw the octopus lights blinking softly in the darkness. The pattern had been permanently branded onto his subconscious, broadcasting a message that would always be there. Magnesium controlled the urge, but did not eliminate it entirely.

And he was not the only one. Meg's elbow, he saw, had been freshly bandaged.

They reached a room in the adjoining ward. Inside, Ellis was seated in bed, his notes spread across his lap. His throat was swathed in gauze. The shears had missed his carotid artery by only a few millimeters.

As they entered, Ellis looked up. When they asked him how he was doing, he studied his own hands before speaking. The bruises on his knuckles had faded. "I'm well enough, I suppose."

Looking at the notes on the bedspread, Trip recognized the pictures and sketches that he had taken of the octopus school. "I hope you aren't having second thoughts about your decision."

Ellis made a dismissive gesture. When the yacht was a few miles from shore, he had taken the bucket with the last remaining octopus and tipped it overboard, watching as it slid under the glassy surface. Even if they took precautions to avoid infection, the risk of contagion had been too great.

"It's a big ocean," Ellis said now, his voice a whisper. "There are other discoveries to be made. And as you said, our first responsibility is to the living. Although the dead deserve our respect as well."

Trip merely nodded. After another minute of small talk, he left the others alone, sensing that they wanted to speak privately. As he headed for the door, he caught Meg's eye. She smiled at him, a trace of sadness still visible in her face, then turned back to the man in the hospital bed.

Outside, on the covered walk, the sun was setting, its last rays shining through the trellis. As Trip headed down the arcade, the slats of the trellis alternately hid and revealed the sunset, reminding him, briefly, of the lights that he had seen in the sea. He had almost reached the end of the walkway when he realized that his left hand was creeping toward his lips.

Trip halted. Up ahead, the garden was only a few steps away. With an effort, he lowered his hand, his gaze fixed on the tips of his fingers. He waited for the impulse to fade, as it always did. Finally, after what seemed like a long time, it passed. He exhaled. Then, stuffing his hands in his pockets, he headed for the garden, keeping his eyes turned away from the light.

Dying Young

PETER M. BALL

A graduate of Clarion South, Peter M. Ball published his first story in Dreaming Again *in 2007. Since then, his short fiction has appeared in* Eclipse Four, Electric Velocipede, Weird Tales, Fantasy Magazine, Strange Horizons, Apex Magazine, Interfictions II, Daily Science Fiction, Shimmer, *and elsewhere. His faerie-noir novella* Horn *was published in 2009, and was followed by* Bleed *in 2010. He lives in Brisbane, Australia, and can be found online at www.petermball.com.*

Here he spins a vivid and violent tale that starts out seeming like a mix of fantasy and spaghetti western, but which instead is really science fiction set in the wake of an apocalyptic future war—in spite of the presence of dragons.

▼

I smelt him coming long before he arrived, the musty odor of sulphur and dust cutting through the sweat-stink in Cassidy's Saloon. Smelling things is part of it, that thing I inherited from my Da, but it weren't just me who noticed it by the time he got close. The dragon stank bad enough that everyone breathed him in; the entire room hushin' up, listening to the tick-tick of claws on hardwood, lookin' at the door as he shouldered his way through.

He was a tall critter, but stooped over to fit his tail, and he'd been banged up good and proper by something a little more ruthless than the road. The wreckage that'd once been wings were folded over his shoulders, draped like a tattered coat. There weren't nothing but a jagged nub of bone where his horns had been, and that weren't good: Da once told me a dragon without horns got ornery, and they were usually trouble for more than just the feller what cut 'em off.

The dragon stared us down; no one said nothin' for a long stretch, but you can't stare at a thing like him forever. Someone up the back of the bar coughed, probably Sam Coody or one of his cloned deputies, and that was all it took for everyone to stop gawking and talk amongst themselves. The dragon sneered at us, showing off a ridge of serrated teeth, and walked over to the bar. We pretended we were okay with it, the dragon being there in the saloon, like it weren't no big deal, but our eyes drifted back. We watched him prop an elbow, easy as anything, and we waited for somethin' to happen.

The doc leaned over and nudged me with that big bone hook he calls a hand. "Trouble?"

I flinched 'fore I nodded, shying away from that hook. I didn't even need a vision to figure this one out; there was a gun belt hanging on the dragon's waist, visible every time he took a step, and Da never trusted strangers with guns. They were trouble, he said, and experience proved him right in the end. Doc Cameron knew that better than anyone.

The doc weren't satisfied with that, though. There were something pinching at the edge of his eyes, a little scent of fear underneath his oily perfume. "Look harder," he said. "Tell me what's coming," and he gave me a hard look, stared until I closed my eyes and peered forward, using Da's gift. I saw nothing but grey smoke, smelt nothing but fire. I could hear the sharp spit of an automatic through the haze.

"Something's burnin', I can promise you that," I said, "and I can hear a gun, Doc. Automatic. Someone's headin' for your slab, I think, before it's all over."

Doc Cameron half-lowered his eyelids and scratched the sharp edge of his cheekbone. Something flickered across his pupils, a cluster of lights spiralling towards the tear ducts as he scanned the dragon. Military tech, a holdover from the war, the doc's little gift to Dunsborough. The little box on his belt hummed, fixing the data from the doc's cortical patch onto a slice of silicon.

"Should we tell Coody, do you think?" I said, and the doc shook his head.

"The sheriff will want details," Doc said. "Damn fool won't run off a dragon based on a hunch, even one of yours."

The doc sniffed. Coody was Da's friend, last of the men Da trained before the doc took over. Doc closed his eyes and a light on the box flickered, the data loaded up and ready for study. "I'm going to go download this. Keep an eye on the lizard, Paul. The real eyes and the other. Maybe we'll get lucky."

The doc slipped out the back way, eager to get back to his lab. I sat and drank my sarsaparilla and watched the dragon like I was told. I kept one hand under the table, close to that sharp knife Da gave me when I turned fourteen. The dragon didn't do much beyond ordering whisky. I closed two eyes and opened the third wide, peering forward for all I was worth; it got me nothing but smoke and gunshots and the beginning of a headache that would last for days.

It weren't more than a half-hour after the doc scarpered before things got ugly.

I can see trouble coming 'fore most folks, even without the third eye. It was Da that taught me the trick of it, the ways of reading a room and seeing who'll make the first move. The dragon weren't lookin' for trouble when he first walked in, but he were waiting for some to roll on by and get itself started of its own accord. In the old days Da would've talked him around, but Da's long gone and Coody ain't quite got the knack of keepin' things peaceful. People in the bar worried, stayed quiet, and whispered when they spoke.

It were Kenny Sloan who stepped up, stompin' across the floorboards to get in the dragon's face. Sloan's one of the doc's razorfreaks, a 'borg with a handful of scalpels and jacked reflexes, fast enough to slice the wings off a fly. He put his weight against the bar and looked over at the dragon, propping his arm on the counter so the light gleamed off the metal. Kenny Sloan was a bully, like most of the doc's boys. He flipped a quick grin back at his cronies, making sure they were watching. "Hey, lizard," Sloan said. "I thought your kind knew better than to drink at human bars."

The dragon turned then, mouth full of whisky, twin trails of smoke seeping out of his nose. The molten eyes squinted at Sloan, studying him. Sloan was a big guy, even before Doc jacked him up; no one missed him posturing. The noise died down and I saw Coody and his posse of badges straightening up in their corner, gettin' ready for real trouble. The dragon turned back to his whisky, ignoring us all. Sloan laid his fingers on the dragon's shoulder.

"Hey, lizard," Sloan said. He flicked the mechanical arm out, blades sliding free of the finger sheaths. "We already beat your kind once, yeah?"

Things happened fast after that, probably too fast to get the details without the third eye's hindsight. Sloan went to strike the dragon, Coody and his tin-star heroes got up on their feet, and the dragon moved faster than all of them. A quick twist away from Sloan's swipe, wings flaring out behind him, the dragon's stance low with clawed hands splayed wide. Sloan got himself gutted before his finger-blades crunched into the top of the bar, and he stood there, bleeding slow from a stomach wound and struggling to get his hand free.

"You need a doctor," the dragon hissed. He swallowed the last mouthful of whisky, and Coody's men had him surrounded by the time he laid the glass down. The dragon eyed them carefully, all the sheriff's skinny mutate-clones with their clunky pre-war revolvers. Coody pulled Sloan's hand free of the hardwood; Kenny Sloan kept himself busy trying to hold in the mess of blood and gore that used to be his stomach. "Sorry for the mess," the dragon said, and he touched a blood-slicked claw to his forehead. His wings settled around him again, rearranging themselves to cover his gun belt and the sleek lines of his body. "I'll see myself out, yes?"

The clones looked at Coody and the old man nodded; no one said squeak as the dragon walked away. Sloan moaned a little, making gurgling sounds when he tried to speak, and as soon as the dragon was gone the sheriff looked around and pointed in my direction.

"Where's the doc?" Coody said. "Blood and thunder, son, go tell Cameron to hustle if he wants his pet 'borg to keep breathing."

I nodded and started moving, but Sloan was a goner. The doc didn't care about his 'borgs the way Coody looked after his clones, 'specially not when they were as dumb as Kenny and there was prey on the horizon. I went 'cross the square and buzzed the doc's doorbell, but there was no answer coming. I had nothing to do but wait, go back to Coody, or go trailin' after the dragon like I was supposed to. None of them appealed. Kenny Sloan was screaming inside the bar, dying slow and messy, so I went with the best option of the three; I ambled down the main street, following the soft buzz in my head that'd tell me where to find the dragon's camp.

The dragon was hiding out by Prickly Pear Hill, his bedroll stretched out in the middle of the twisted cacti that soaked up moisture from the stream curving 'round the base of the slope. He looked like he was travelling light; a small pack looked empty, like he'd been killing food on the march, but when I strolled in I got the familiar itch and saw dirt piled up where he'd buried supplies. I opened the third eye, peered on down, and got a sense of crates, canned food, and cordite.

I had myself a few good minutes before the dragon rolled in, largely thanks to the fact that I weren't forced to backtrack in case the town sent out a posse. I sat on a rock and kicked the dust, listening hard, trying to hear him coming. It didn't work; I didn't hear him, see him, didn't even smell him this time around. I ain't easy to sneak up on, but he managed it. I just blinked my eyes and there he was, crouched low with claws out and hot spit dribbling down his chin.

"Boy," he said, nostrils flaring, and at that the smell of sulphur rose up around me. "You were at the bar, yes? Town sent you?"

I nodded, keeping my hands out in the open. I weren't armed with much, just my Da's knife, and it seemed to calm the dragon. He knelt down, sniffed me, then sighed a stream of smoke into the air. "Ah," he said. "You have gifts."

"A bit," I said. "Not much, not really."

He sniffed again, breathing deep. I recognized the trick from when Da used to do it, knew about the clues you could pick up with the right kind of training. The third eye does big things, its own special kind of magic, but Da always said there were other senses to fill in what the third eye can't see. The dragon smiled at me. "Trained, then? Your father?"

I shrugged the question away. "I work for the doc," I said. "He runs things; wanted you followed."

The dragon cocked his head, smiling. "Dangerous work, yes?"

I said nothing, just crouched there on my rock and waiting for what would come. I had enough of my Da in me to know I weren't going to die there, but that didn't mean I weren't going to pay hard for daring to follow him out there. I waited for the dragon to lash out, making use of his claws.

It ain't often I'm surprised, but he surprised me then. "I make tea, yes?"

"Oh." I blinked, and he watched me carefully. I forced myself to nod. "Yes. Please, yes."

I squirmed. The dragon turned his attention to the fire, hocked a sharp gob of spit into a pile of kindling to get things going. He unearthed an iron pot and loose tea from his pack, crouched down by the flames to set it boiling. There was something fascinating about the muscles moving under his scales, about the way sunlight gleamed on the dark ridges across his hands. He sat, dignified, and waited.

"You're after someone," I said. "I saw that much, back in the saloon. Can't see who, or why, but it's going to end messy."

The dragon kept his eyes on the tea. "Yes."

"I'm thinking it's the doc," I said. "He got plenty nervous when you showed up, hurried off to his lab right fast. That ain't like him, really. Doc Cameron likes his body parts, having new bits to play with."

That earned me a reaction, a snort of smoke and a twitch in the folded wings. "Yes."

"So what's going to happen, when you front up again?"

The dragon settled back on his haunches, stirring the pot. He lifted the pan and poured spiced tea into a pair of metal mugs, both of them bearing scorch marks on the rim. He handed one to me and I saw flecks of Sloan's blood drying on the dragon's claws. "You have the sight," he said. "You tell me."

My forehead tingled, all prescience and instinct, but turned up nothing new. "I haven't seen yet; the future's nothing but smoke and gunfire." I took a long sip of the tea, felt the chilli powder burning the back of my throat as it went down. The dragon watched me drink, red eyes narrowed to slits. I figured I knew what he was waiting for. "Ask," I said. "I ain't going lie."

"You have the sight, yet you work for your doctor?"

I guessed what he was asking and short-cut to the answer. "He did some bad stuff when he arrived," I said. "But good stuff, too. Helped people, gave 'em back stuff they'd lost. Relics of the war, sure, but they had arms and legs again. They could work, and we needed workers."

The dragon's laughter sent hot spit across the campfire. He put his cup down, tilting forward, and when he straightened up one of those ancient Lugers sat neat and easy in his hand. He pointed the narrow barrel in my direction, eyes narrowed down to stare at me. "You know, then," he said. "You've seen what your doctor has done?"

"Bits and pieces. Glimpses, really, but I got plenty of after what he's done since coming to town." I watched the cold fire in the dragon's eyes.

The dragon breathed deep. "He killed your father?"

I nodded again.

"And you work for him, still?"

"Sure enough."

"Why?"

"Needs to be done." I sipped my tea, staying calm; he wasn't going to shoot me, I could see that much. I don't have all my Da's gifts, not even half, but I was sure enough of that. "Not much good tellin' folk 'round these parts he's the devil; they need the doc too much to care and it ain't like anyone's goin' to be surprised by revelations of shady dealin's. And my Da didn't hold with revenge, really; he cared about keepin' folks safe. He woulda done the same as me, most likely, if he ain't ended up dead. These are nasty times; it takes a nasty man or a brave man to keep a town safe."

"Your father was brave."

"And look where it got him." I tried to keep the anger out of my voice, to avoid the flashes of history that rolled in if I let myself dwell on feeling. Hindsight can be a curse, Da said, and he weren't half wrong about that. "We're out of brave men, now he's dead. All we've got left is the nasty folk and the followers. Way I see it, I can have the doc dead or everyone else can live."

The dragon's expression didn't change and the Luger didn't waver, but the tattered wings rippled as he adjusted his stance. The crooked line of his broken horn caught the firelight. "What you have seen," he said. "You cannot save him."

I shook my head. "I wasn't lying," I said. "Haze, smoke, and gunfire, that's all I got; one of you will die, but I don't know who." I paused, drinking the last of the tea. "I got a fair guess about what happens next, though, after he's dead. It ain't pretty, not by a long stretch. Out here with nothing but Coody to keep things safe, it'll go downhill fast."

The dragon nodded, holstering the Luger and picking up his tea. "You should go."

I lingered for a moment, wondering what to do with my cup. The dragon rose, staring down at me. "Go! Tell your doctor I am coming."

I went, slinking back towards town with the tin cup still in my hand.

Coody's clones were manning the walls, so there was no real chance to sneak into town without anyone noticing. Two of them came down to the front gate to greet me, clamped down on my shoulder with heavy hands, and started guiding me down Main Street. Four others stood on the palisade, dull eyes scanning the horizon while another one swept the landscape with the town spotlights. All of them tall, slack-jawed, armed; they looked the part, despite their daft expressions, hands on the holsters and eyes following the point of light that raked the landscape. The two walking me in said nothing, just held my shoulder and marched. I coulda given them the slip—Coody's clones aren't as bright as him, and he ain't exactly sharp as knives to begin with—but a trip to the sheriff's office gave me a good excuse to stay clear of the doc's lab and delay my report by a few minutes.

The original Coody was sitting on the porch of his office, whispering orders into a radio and making a big show of checking the action on the shotgun across his lap. He didn't even look when his clones threw me against the step, just pumped his gun with a satisfied grin and cradled it 'cross his lap.

"Sent you to go fetch the doc, Paul," he said. His good eye squinted as he drew a pistol and checked its load, the other glowing big and red beneath the doc's metalwork. "Cost us bad, you not doin' what I told ya. Sloan was dead 'fore the doc could get to him, nothin' left but parts."

Da tried training Coody, just like he trained me, but the sheriff ain't got none of the natural talent Da had for prescience or reading people. It made lying to him dangerous; he had to grind the answer out of you if he wanted to be sure of something.

"Called the doc and got no answer," I said. "He left me orders, 'fore he left for his lab, and I followed 'em when he didn't come to the door. You sayin' I done the wrong thing? That I shoulda leant on his doorbell instead of doin' what he asked?"

"That's exactly what I'm saying." Coody's eyes scanned the town in a long, slow arc. "Doc Cameron's the brains behind this town, but I'm the law, kid. I'm the one who has to keep people safe now . . ." He cut himself off before he mentioned Da, took a deep breath to clear the thought out of his head.

I shook my head. "You really believe that, Sam?"

"Yeah, I do." One hand patted the shotgun and he looked at me for the first time, the mechanical right eye clicking as it focused on me. That eye was Doc Cameron's idea, a replacement for one Coody had lost during the last war. I was willing to bet that Cameron could see what Coody saw, if the doc had half-a-mind to check in. "What did the doc have you doing?"

I shrugged, and Sam Coody cuffed me across the back of the head. I went down in a heap, spitting red dust. "You wanna try that again, Paul?"

"He had me trailing the dragon." I sat up. "Wanted to know if he was after him."

"And is he?"

I nodded. "Close enough to."

Coody sighed and rubbed his good eye with his right hand. "So, you peered into the future on this one? It going to end bad, Paul?"

He held out his hand, helping me onto my feet. "It's going to end, Coody," I said. "I haven't seen spit worth talking about, but there's gunfire ahead and plenty-a screamin'. Dragon's got the sight, I think, an' he figures someone's goin' to die, but damned if I can see who."

Coody squinted. The long mustache twitched as he chewed on his bottom lip. He didn't say nothing for a real long time.

"I gotta report to the doc," I told him. "He'll be expecting me, Sam."

"Go," the sheriff said, and he went back to his guns.

No one likes going into Doc Cameron's bunker, least of all a guy like me, someone with the sight. Places like the bunker are always screaming, the echoes of the past ringing out again and again. But there isn't a damn fool in town that ain't carrying the doc's handiwork somewhere, not even me and I'm a damn sight cleaner than most, and Doc Cameron liked to keep tabs on folks. There were places I could hide, if I set my mind to it, but I'd come out eventually and pay my dues for disobeying him. I set across the square and, putting an eyeball to the scanner by the door, let myself into the bunker to tell the doc all the things he didn't want to hear.

My gut and my prescience both said it was a bad call; a braver man woulda skived off and spent the next day or three in his bunk, waiting out the storm until the shootin' was over. I wasn't a brave man, so I stood there until the steel doors swung open and a pair of Doc's razorfreaks fell into step behind me and escorted me through the winding tunnels Doc's boys hollowed out back when they first arrived.

The doc was down in his workshop, working on Sloan's corpse. He had the bone hook in the corpse's stomach, pulling down and opening the skin like a zipper. The smell of it made me gag, but he didn't even look up. "He's here for me, isn't he? The dragon?"

I looked over my shoulder at the razorfreaks, big lunks who stood there, uncaring and mute. Doc looked up from the slick gore of Kenny Sloan's innards, glared at me with cold eyes until I gave in and nodded.

"Who shoots who, Paul? Tell me how much it'll cost me to win?"

I closed my eyes and looked, hoping to get lucky: mist; gunshots; the screams of the dying. "I wish I knew, Doc."

Doc Cameron nodded and buried his long nose back in Sloan's vitals, poking about with the claw and good hand alike. His white coat was blood-splattered as he pulled the tech outta the dead. The days of the war were a long time past and supplies weren't comin' in; as the doc was fond of reminding us, it was a waste-not, want-not world now. He spooled cabling onto the slab, a thin line of plastic and fibres that had been in-and-out of 'borgs since the early days of the war. "You talked to the dragon, at least?"

I nodded.

"What did he have to say?"

"Not much." I fidgeted best I could between Cameron's guards. "He's coming for you, knew I had the sight. He wanted me to look into the past, get a good look at what you did during the war."

"And you did?"

"No."

Doc Cameron smiled. "You disappoint me, Paul. I thought you were built of sterner stuff." He stood up, abandoning his work. Sloan's guts dripped off the bone hook. He shook his head, full of mock sorrow. "What would your father think? A brave man like that, ending up with a boy like you?"

"I don't care what my Da thought, Doc. My Da is long dead."

"Why don't I believe you, Paul?" The doc's grin was terse, lips folded tight against his teeth. He held his bone hook like an offering, the oily smear of blood covering the tip. "Touch it, boy. Let us find out what kind of man you are."

Da used to say there were people who didn't come out of the war quite right, and there were pretty good odds the doc was one of them. I forced myself to look him in the eye. "Don't matter what you done, Doc. Not during the war, not last week, not when you first met the dragon and did whatever ya done to him. If you're the one who goes down . . ."

"Yes, if I go down." He let the thought hang, thin lips twitching, but neither of us finished it. He nodded to the razorfreaks and they hustled me out. I didn't bother struggling as they clamped their steel hands on my arms and lifted me, carrying me out.

The other 'freaks buried Sloan right on sunrise, interring the small bag of meat parts the doc couldn't use into the red dirt just outside of town. Coody and his clones watched things from the wall, stiff-backed guardians with shotguns and rifles, not wanting spit to do with the doc's bullyboys. They were allies, sure, when the town needed defending, but it was uneasy at the best of times and tense at the worst.

Coody doubled the guard that night. Buried meat had a way of attracting scavengers and things went downhill real easy after that happened.

My gut said we were safe for a day or two at least, and there were no tingling on the third eye to say it were wrong, so I drifted past Coody's office and let him know we had some time up our sleeves.

"Best keep an eye out," Coody told me. "Just in case, like." His logic was bravado, mostly, for all the truth of it. You didn't have to have the sight to feel the tension; the whole damn town was on edge, waiting, and Doc Cameron had been locked up inside his vault for nineteen straight hours trying to figure a way to save his skin. Da told me plenty of stories about his time in the army. Said we fought a whole damn war against the dragons and it'd cost us big every time the shooting started; one o' them might not seem much of a threat, but it was going to hurt everyone when he drifted through town again.

I spent the day in my bunk, trying to open the third eye or dream up a vision. Going forward got me nothing new, and going back taught me nothin' that I hadn't already suspected: Doc Cameron was never a nice man, and the war gave him ample chances to prove it over and over. He was cruel, yes, but I knew that, and there were lots more that seemed understandable given the cruelty goin' on back then. And it's not like any of his habits changed much between the war and now, he just had fewer folk to experiment on and more opportunity for vivisection.

Coody came to see me, late in the afternoon. I didn't bother getting out of my bunk as he shouldered his way through the front door. He hooked one of my stools with the toe of his boot and slung it by the bed, settling down with shotgun still resting on his right shoulder. "You been lookin'?"

I nodded.

"You see anythin' yet?"

I shook my head and Coody grimaced, adjusting his weight on the stool. I saw one of his clones waiting by the door, smooth face filled with a slack-jawed grin as it kept watch on Main Street. It was Coody's face, but younger and dumber. The man sitting next to me was weathered and creased, carrying the weight of too many years. My Da's friend, a good man, doing his best in tough times.

"I was in the war with your father," Coody said. "Saw a damn sight more than I wanted to. Tangled with the dragons a couple of times before things went completely south. Whole damn race was human once, before they took to mutation. Damn things only exist because of folks like Cameron messing about with genes. Guessin' you're young enough not to remember that?"

I shook my head.

"Tough critters to face down," he said. "Fast. Strong. They smell you comin' before you even know you're goin' to draw. Saw a camp after the bastards attacked it one night. Lots of folks dead in their bunks—never heard 'em coming, motion detectors picked up nothing. You understand what I'm saying, Paul?"

I shrugged. Coody paused and took a long breath. "You've looked back, ain't you?"

I nodded, watching the gleam of Coody's mechanical eye, the way it whirred when he focused on me. I tried not to think of the doc watching me through it, listening in on the conversation.

"And the doc, he probably deserves what's coming, one way or another?"

I hesitated, just for a moment, then I nodded again. Coody sagged. "Damn."

There was a breeze outside, cold and gentle. I could hear the soft squeak as the wind-pumps in the town square dredged water out of the basin underneath the town. Coody leaned back in his chair, heel of his thumb working along the steel ridge of his bad eye. I twisted in the bunk, trying to get away from the dull red gleam as he stared at me.

"I ain't carrying a gun," I said.

Coody nodded. "I never asked you to."

"My Da . . ."

"Your father was your father, not you," Coody said. "You ain't him, Paul. I know that. He'd know it too, if he were still around. Things change, right enough, and you change along with 'em or pay the price." Coody pushed back on the stool, scraping it along the floorboards. I watched the red light of his eye bob as he pushed himself upright, shotgun sliding down into his hands. "D'ya know when the bastard's coming, then?"

I shrugged into the darkness. The night-vision optics installed in the eye would let Coody see the gesture. "Tomorrow, maybe the day after. He's got the eye, and he's better than me, I think. Good, as good as Da were. Makes it hard to predict him."

Coody grunted and thumped across the hut, settling in at the doorway to take a long look down the street. "Folks are goin' to die, Paul. Nothin' you can do about that. But if this thing's goin' to win, I want to know. Something's gotta protect this town, if the doc takes a bullet to the gut, and I ain't bettin' on the lizard to hang around to do the job."

I said nothing. There weren't much to say to that.

"I'm thinking of letting him through," Coody sighed, shifting his weight. "If we're lucky he'll come in quiet. Try and gut the doc and get out before anyone knows he's here. It ain't a nice idea, since it means losing the doc and all, but it'll keep some folk alive I reckon."

I thought about the dragon's camp: the cases he buried in the dirt, the dwindling supplies, his anger burning like kindling under a blowtorch. I shook my head. "He won't come quiet," I said. "He ain't planning on leaving anything behind after this is over."

"Even then," Coody said. "God help me, even then, it might not be a bad idea." He stepped outside then, saying nothing else, and I watched him go with a bad feeling in my stomach.

I made myself scarce after Coody left, grabbed my blanket and my Da's knife, and left my shack behind. Sam Coody might not be askin' me to carry a gun, but the doc wouldn't hesitate if he got scared enough. People get confident when you put the sight and a gun together, like there ain't nothing to worry about if you can see what's gonna happen. Da's fault, mostly, 'cause he proved folks right around these parts, leastwise until the doc showed up. He did it here and he did it in the war, skated through everyone on sight and bravery. If Coody pulled the clones from the wall, left the dragon to the razorfreaks and 'borgs to deal with, you could bet Doc Cameron would call in every favor he had to save his skin.

Getting around town without being seen is easy enough if you've got the practice, 'specially once you know that the cameras you gotta avoid are stuck inside o' folk's heads instead of grafted to the sides of buildings. I made for the water-tower on top of the saloon, wormed my way deep into the shadows underneath, and hid there amid the splinters and the dust. It had a good view of the main street and I had a headache building up, a heavy weight that built up in the centre of my forehead.

I slept there, fitful and quiet, away from where Doc and Coody could find me. I dreamt of Da on that last day, back when the doc first pulled into town. I dreamt of the future, of the dragon arriving, and heard a new sound among the gunfire: a sharp, wet bang, like someone 'sploding one of the paddymelons that grow down by the river, and Coody's headless corpse fell out of the smoke and lay smoking at my feet.

I woke up with the dragon crouched over me, his snout close enough for me to smell the sulphur. Gun in hand, eyes scanning the street. I stifled a scream and the dragon smiled. "You are hiding, yes?"

I coughed, soft and spluttering, before I said yes. The dragon peered across the street, watching the doc's muscle gathered 'round the bunker. Razorfreaks, the lot of them. Twenty men, maybe; all of them 'borged. "A lot of claws in those arms," I said. "Suicide to dive down and attack 'em."

The dragon just shrugged. "Yes."

"I had a dream." I pushed myself up on my elbows, whisper turning into a growl. "I don't know who dies between you and the doc, but I know who it costs us while the fighting goes down. The sheriff's going to let you in, assume you'll go quiet and leave everyone else alone. He figures there'll still be a town standing after you're done; that he'll protect the rubble from the predators and rebuild with the survivors."

"He is wrong," the dragon said. "It will cost him, yes? Boom, yes?"

"Yes."

He smiled at me, showing off the ridge of serrated teeth. "And so, you will stop me?"

I shivered despite the heat. "I don't think I can."

"You think," the dragon said. He shook his head. "You *think*."

I could swear the wheezing noise it made after that was something like laugh. "You've got the sight," I said. "You know how this will end."

"I know," the dragon said. "I've seen my death."

"Don't do it," I said. "Please."

The dragon shrugged and checked the safety on his pistols. He squinted at the sun a moment, as though checking the time. "Is done," he said. "All done. There is nothing to stop it now."

I sniffed then, smelling him: brimstone and cordite.

There weren't anything quiet about the way the dragon was going down.

The first thing to go was the southern palisade. The rumble of the explosion rolled down the main street shaking red dust of buildings and rattling the windows. I was climbing down when it happened, got rattled off the side of the saloon and fell awkward in the dusty alley behind it. Pain rolled down my right shoulder as the screaming started out on the main street, people running for cover as the razorfreaks charged. I could hear the fight starting through the haze of smoke and dust: staccato bursts of gunfire; the cries of the dying, the dragon returning fire from his vantage on the rooftop. The doc's boys were fast and strong, but they weren't trained as much more 'n muscle. It'd take 'em a couple-a minutes to realize the shooter was somewhere up and outside the billowing cloud of smoke.

I scrambled to my feet and went for the wall, stumbling as the second bomb went off somewhere down the street. Dragons were quiet, Coody said, and hard as hell to detect; there'd be bombs all across town to create the distraction he was looking for, enough to flood the streets in smoke and fire, to ruin the infrared eyes the doc gave his razorfreaks to let 'em see in the dark. Coody and his clones gave minimal assistance, filling the street with spotlights while they took cover from the gunfire. They didn't move to help the razorfreaks, just dug-in and waited, a dozen of them with rifles not even looking for a shot. Coody stood behind the steel barrels of water we carted in from the reservoir, shotgun on his shoulder as he scanned the streets. The steel plate over his right eye shone in the light; he didn't notice me coming, not 'til I slid into place beside him. I yelled the word "bomb," trying to get louder than the din. Coody nodded, looking irritated, and pointed at the carnage.

"Bomb," I said, screaming it, and pointed at his eye-plate. This time it sunk in, and he turned a little pale. I closed my eyes as another dynamite charge went off, caught a glimpse of the future. Clearer now, full of shapes, the sounds getting louder and louder as prescience became past. Coody ordered his clones into the street, ordered another two onto the walls to start searching the rooftops for the dragon and take him down with a rifle-shot.

I peered forward, snatching another glimpse. The gunfire and screaming in the smoke-haze started to die down. It was random now, scattered, the dragon picking the last of the razorfreaks off. My gut said we were out of bombs and out of mobs, so the killing would get real personal from here on in. I heard Coody calling orders, telling his clones to sweep the street, get survivors under cover, and start putting out the fires.

I knew when I was going to die, if I didn't do anything stupid with my life. First trick Da taught me, when he figured out I had the sight. You look forward and you see your death, and you know that's how it'll end if you don't mess up destiny too bad in the meantime. The dragon knew it too, and so did my Da. It ain't writ in stone, but it's good enough. It takes some real stupidity to mess those visions up.

Da was supposed to die an old man, but he pushed things too hard. I was supposed to die an older man, and I hadn't pushed a damn thing, not since the doc came to town. I closed my eyes and looked, forcing my way through the smoke. Somewhere in the future the dragon was going to die and the doc would punish Coody for it. Or the doc was going to die and take Sam Coody with him. There weren't many ways it come out good for the sheriff, and there were a damn sight fewer where it came out good for the town.

I got out my Da's knife and stepped forward, walking into the smoke.

I found the doors to the doc's bunker open wide, the locks burned through with dragon-spit and smeared with oil and blood. I stood there a moment, breathing against a handkerchief to avoid choking on the dust. Coody stepped up beside me, shotgun in hand. "He in there?" he asked, and I nodded and tapped my nose. "Sulphur," I said, and went in, holding my knife out before me like it'd do a damn thing against anything we'd find running loose in the dark of the bunker. Coody followed on behind me, his mechanical eye clicking as it adapted to the darkness.

"You seen anything?" he asked me. "Like, maybe, who's going to win?"

I shook my head, stepped over the body of a dying 'borg. "Get outta here, Sheriff. You don't want to be close to the doc today."

We heard a gunshot, deeper in, the sound of someone scrambling and running. Coody moved a little ahead of me, raised the shotgun. "It ain't exactly a choice, Paul. Dyin' comes with the badge."

He started moving in, gun at the ready, letting me follow behind. I tried to peek at the future, but there was nothing to see. Not anymore. Too many muddled pieces on the board, too many people trying to bluff and get a better result out of the hand fate dealt them. Occasionally we'd pass a body, see drips of blood on the concrete or smears of it on the wall. It's a twisty path, heading down to the doc's lab, and plenty of corridors leading off to the side. We found him hiding in one about halfway down, crouched in the darkness with a bone-saw in his fist. He was bleeding, the doc, but he moved okay when he saw us. "A grazing shot," he said, "lucky, at best."

"The dragon," Coody said. He pumped his shotgun for emphasis, chambering a live shell.

"Deeper in," Doc Cameron said, "there's a few boys towards the lab, trying to contain it." He paused a moment, stared at Coody. "They're doing your job, Sheriff, unless I miss my guess. Perhaps you should go join them." There was steel in his voice as he said it, and his good hand at his belt hovering over the little box patched into his computer.

"The dragon's your mess," Coody said. "What if I say no?"

The doc's gaze slid over to me, then back up to Coody. "I gather you've been informed of that," he said. The laugh that followed was high-pitched, a trill of amusement.

Down the corridors, in the doc's lab, we heard someone screaming. "Probably best if you hurry," Doc said. He laughed again, winced, put his hook against the wall to steady himself. Blood loss, I figured. The scratch in his side weren't as minor as he made out. Prescience said the doc was already dead, just running out the final moments before the injury put him down. The only question now was whether the dragon and Coody went with him.

He wheezed for breath, leaning forward, and the hand over his computer box strayed a little too far. His eyes were stuck on Coody, waiting for the decision. I thought about Da for a moment, about dying old and safe, then I trusted my gut and Da's knife and went at the doc with a bloody yell and the knife twisting straight for stomach.

It cost me a hook across the face, stabbing the doc in the gut. He slashed me hard, but it didn't kill me; didn't even hurt when he followed up, jamming the hook in my stomach and ripping a shallow trench through the skin and the gizzards. The pain was bad, even looking back with hindsight, but I figure it was worth it. I got the knife in the doc two or three times in return, kept him busy while Coody lined up the shot and let the shotgun go boom 'til he ran out of ammo. I weren't conscious to see it happen, but the doc went down. Went down hard, a bloody mess, and Coody standing over him with the gun just-in-case, calling down the clones to stitch me up and get me walking.

I spent a week or two in bed, healing up from my injuries, and would have myself some nice scars to show off by the time I was healed. The dragon was gone by the time I came to, walked out of town by Coody with supplies and a warning. There weren't much left for him in town, with the doc laid out for burial, and there were plenty of folks out for his blood after the business with the explosions. He went quiet, which surprised me, and he was missing an eye to go with his broken horn.

We were due some hardness, everyone knew that, and there were a couple-a folks held grudges against Coody for doing in the doc. But we held off against the scavenger beasts and the retaliatory raids by the last of doc's 'borgs, found ways to make do when his tech ran down and people started limping 'round town on malfunctioning limbs. I started wearing my Da's gun, when Coody asked me for help. He was running short of clones, now. There were men in Doc's labs trying to fix the machines, but they weren't none as smart as him and it would take a while to get things running, if they ever did.

Things are good, though, since the dragon came. Tougher, yes, but not so bad as they were. My Da used to tell me that people cope, that the war proved that more than anything. But they'll do more than cope, if you ask them too, if you show them there's another option. That they'll do the right thing, eventually, 'cause doing otherwise there ain't much to life. I'm not saying he were right, mind, but he saw a lot of what might happen. He was a smart man, Da, and he were better at lookin' forward than me.

But that was him, and he did his part. Now there's me and Coody and a bunch of broken parts, a town that needs savin' and a future stretchin' forward. And maybe I get to make it to the end I'm meant to have, and maybe I get sidetracked a little along the way. It doesn't seem so bad, not knowing, not like it used to.

And Da always used to tell me there were worse things than dying young.

Canterbury Hollow

Chris Lawson

Chris Lawson is an Australian speculative fiction writer with an eclectic approach to subject matter that has skittered across the hard sciences of genetic engineering and epidemiology to unapologetic fantasy about the voyages of the Argo *at the end of the age of myths to ambiguous ghost stories set in the Great War. His stories have appeared in* Asimov's, The Magazine of Fantasy & Science Fiction, Eidolon, Dreaming Down-Under, *and several year's best anthologies; his collection* Written in Blood *is available through MirrorDanse Books (www.tabula-rasa.info/MirrorDanse/). In nonfictional life, Chris is a family medicine practitioner and university teacher with a special interest in public health, evidence-based medicine, and statistics. He lives on the Sunshine Coast with his spouse, two children, and a hyperdog. He blogs, irregularly, at Talking Squid (www.talkingsquid.net).*

In the quietly moving story that follows, he takes us to a colony world whose immensely hostile environment has called forth harsh and inflexible social customs that the colony must employ in order to survive, and shows us what complying with those customs means to a young couple in love.

Of all the trillions of people who have lived and who will live, Arlyana and Moko were not especially important, nor heroic, nor beautiful, but for a few moments they were cradled by the laws of nature. In a universe that allows humans to survive in a minuscule sliver of all possible times and places, this is a rare accomplishment.

They met under the Sundome.

Arlyana wanted to see the killing sun for herself so she took the Long Elevator to the surface. The Sundome was a hemispheric pocket of air trapped under massive polymer plates on the crust of a dying planet called Musca. The Sundome persisted only through the efforts of robotic fixers, and the robots themselves needed constant repair from the ravages of the sun.

Through the transparent ceiling of the dome, Arlyana watched the sun rise over the world it had destroyed. The sun was a boiling disc, white and fringed with solar arcs. Ancient archived images showed a turquoise sky, but the sun had long since blown the atmosphere to wisps and now the sky was black and the stars visible in full daylight. A few degrees to one side, the sun's companion star glowed a creamy yellow.

Dawn threw sunlight across the ruins of the Old City. Rising from the centre of the city was a tower many kilometers tall. The tower had been even taller once: it had reached all the way to orbit.

As the sun rose in the sky, the number of visitors to the Sundome thinned out. Even knowing they were protected by the dome, it was a terrifying experience for many people to stand beneath the killing sun. They hurried to the Long Elevator and scuttled back home. Not Arlyana: she wanted to face the sun, to challenge its authority to kill her. While the bulk of the people around her withdrew to the safety of the rock beneath their feet, Arlyana chose to go further outwards.

The Sundome hosted a number of small buses, life supports on wheels, that allowed visitors to tour the old city. They were rarely used in daylight hours. Arlyana went to the bus bay, now completely emptied of people, and found a bus that was leaving in a few minutes.

At its allotted time the bus gave a little warning beep, the doors closed shut with a pneumatic sigh, and then it trundled out the airlock gates. As the bus moved over the blighted landscape, it gave an automated commentary.

"Different astronomers on Old Earth," said the bus, "reported different colors for our sun over different centuries. When people first settled Musca it was thought that the colors had been misreported due to the primitive telescopes of the time. Now we know that the old astronomers were seeing signs of instability . . ."

Arlyana tuned out the words, but the sound of the voice was soothing.

The bus made its way over to the great, ruined tower. The tower was impressive but once it had been majestic, almost god-like in its engineering. Now it was a candle stub of eroded carbon. The soil at the foot of the tower had been baked to glass.

The bus interrupted its commentary. "My apologies," said the bus, "but a high energy sunburst has erupted and high levels of radiation are expected. The bus will now return for your own protection."

"I have been balloted," Arlyana said. She held up her ballot card. "Continue the tour."

"You are not the only person in the cabin," said the bus.

As the bus spoke, a man at the back of the bus leapt to his feet. This was Moko.

Moko, shaking off his sleep and orienting himself to the situation, held up his own ballot card. "I've been balloted too," he said. "Continue the tour."

"As you wish," said the bus.

Moko said to Arlyana, "I didn't mean to startle you. I lay down on the seat at the back and I must have fallen asleep."

"No need to apologize," she replied. "Come sit with me and enjoy the tour."

The bus took them around the Old City. The voice pointed out the Old Port, and the Old Synod, and the Old Settlement Memorial. Every one of them had long since crumbled to an abstract mass.

Midway through the tour, the bus announced that the sunburst had intensified and even balloted citizens, and buses for that matter, would be damaged by the flood of radiation coming. There was no time to return to the Sundome, so the bus scuttled over to the Old Tower and sheltered in its shadow.

"Well," said Arlyana to Moko, "it appears we are stuck here for now."

"So it does."

She watched him closely. He had a handsome face, if a little pinched at the mouth. He had continued to shave after being balloted, which she looked on approvingly even though she quite liked beards. She extended her hand to him.

"I should let you know that I'm not much in favor of balloted romances," she said.

Moko looked back at her. She was tall and muscular with dark blue skin that had gone out of fashion fifteen years ago but seemed to suit her.

"I agree." he said. "Too desperate."

"I would go so far as to say 'cloying.'"

"Not to mention 'desperate.' It bears repeating."

"So we're in agreement then. Against balloted romances."

"I believe we are." He reached out and took her hand.

It took three hours for the shadow of the tower to connect with the entrance to a safety tunnel. For those three hours they sat together in the bus, hiding in the shade while the sun showered the world with light of many frequencies and particles of many energies, with some that knocked lesser particles off the land around them and made the world glow.

They took the Long Elevator back to Moko's unit because it was closer. It was also much smaller and after skinnings of elbows and barkings of knees, they decided that Arlyana's apartment would have been more suitable after all. But that was three hours down the Grand Central Line and they were already together, if not entirely comfortable, so they lay wedged between Moko's bunk and the bulkhead above it and negotiated their future plans.

"My top three," said Arlyana, "would be to see the First Chamber, to put a drop of blood in the Heritage Wall, and to climb Canterbury Hollow."

"You want to climb Canterbury Hollow? Isn't it enough to just visit?"

"I'm going to climb it and I want you to climb with me."

Moko sighed. "I'm not sure I'm fit enough. Isn't it around eight hundred metres high?"

"Eight-twenty-two," said Arlyana. "But there's only a hundred or so of hard climbing."

"I'd need to get into shape. I'm not sure that's what I want to do with my time."

Arlyana tried to prop herself up on her elbow to read his expression, but she only succeeded in hitting her head. "I know this is a gauche thing to ask," she said, "but how much time do you have?"

"Two weeks."

She sagged back into the mattress. "You could have some of my time. I've got three months."

"I couldn't do that. It's too much to ask."

They lay in silence, thinking. After several minutes Arlyana spoke up. "So what do you want to do with your time?" she asked.

Moko pursed his lips, then said, "I would like to visit the First Chamber, add a drop of blood to the Heritage Wall, and visit Canterbury Hollow."

She laughed at that. "That's quite a coincidence."

"Truth to tell, I've had no idea what to do with myself since I was balloted. If you've got some plans, I might as well use them."

Moko and Arlyana donned pressure suits to explore the First Chamber. Artificial lights illuminated the cavern. Rust-red trails of iron oxide dripped down the walls of the cavern.

The Chamber was smaller than they expected. Much, much smaller. Accustomed as they were to living in tight spaces, they still found it incredible that that tens of thousand citizens had once occupied a cavern the size of a sports chamber.

The first Deep Citizens had lived here for decades while they had drilled away at iron and stone, following fissures and air pockets to speed their excavation. As they dug down, deeper into the crust, they had built new cities in the spaces they carved out of bare rock. At first they had merely hoped to escape the solar irradiation, but after two centuries it had become inescapably apparent that the sun was not merely going to scorch the surface. The ferocity of its light was growing and soon it would burn the atmosphere off.

Having built one civilisation, the Deep Citizens had to build another, this time sealed from the outside world. They adapted their existing cities and spaces where they could, but not everything could be saved. The First Chamber was too close and too open to the surface and so it had to be abandoned.

The excavating did not always go well. Several of the new spaces collapsed before they could be stabilized. In other chambers, fissures opened to the surface that made it impossible to trap air within.

The tragedy was twofold. The Deep Citizens had built chambers intended not just for themselves and their descendants, but for as many people of Musca as possible. They had drilled too fast and hollowed out chambers too large and too fragile. In their desperation to make room, they had over-reached. There was not enough space—nor air, nor food for that matter—for everyone. Even before the seals were closed, it was apparent that there would not be enough room even for all the existing Deep Citizens.

And so the Deep Citizens created the ballot.

Moko and Arlyana did not stay to explore the First Chamber as they had the Sundome. It was one thing to see the sun and the surface it had scoured of life; it was another to stand in the halls where the first ballot had been drawn.

On the morning of their fourth day, they were woken by a buzz at the door. Arlyana checked the video stream, sighed, and told Moko to stay in bed while she dealt with it.

Not knowing what else to do, he lay there staring at the ceiling with a view to getting back to sleep. That plan soon became impossible as he heard Arlyana's voice rising in emotion and he began to wonder what "it" was that needed dealing with. Another voice, deep and male, spoke in hushed tones.

Troubled by a dread that gripped tighter as Arlyana's voice became more strained, Moko decided that he could keep his promise to stay away from the door while keeping alert for Arlyana's safety by watching the video feed from the door. He tapped the screen and the picture flickered on; he quickly hit the mute button.

Arlyana was wrapped in her dressing gown, talking to a dark-eyed man who had dressed and groomed fastidiously, as if he were on his way to a funeral. In his hand he held a card or maybe an envelope and he was offering it to Arlyana while she adamantly refused to take it. As Arlyana become more animated, the man seemed to crumble from within. His shoulders dropped, his giving hand fell to his side.

Although Moko could make out nothing of the conversation, the volume rose to the point where occasional disconnected phrases from Arlyana filtered back to him. Moko rubbed his eyes to make sure he was seeing clearly. If anything, it was the stranger and not Arlyana who was likely to need his help.

The door slammed shut and Moko flicked off the video. Arlyana stormed back inside the unit, tossed off her gown, and crawled naked back into bed with Moko.

"Everything all right?" he asked.

The door buzzed in three staccato bursts.

"Ignore it," she said.

A few seconds later, there was another buzz at the door, then another, this time somehow sadder, and then the buzzer fell quiet. The silence stretched for a few seconds, then past a minute, then past three minutes. The door would not ring again. Arlyana wormed herself under Moko's arm and began to breathe in shudders. Not knowing what to say, Moko said nothing, which was exactly right.

The Heritage Wall was an hour by train from Arlyana's quarters. They stepped out of the station into a low chamber, a mere twenty metres tall, but so long and straight that it seemed to be a continuation of the train tunnel that had brought them.

The southern wall of the chamber was a milled plane that followed a subtly saddled polynomial function. The curve of the wall had a strangely emotive property: it could reach into people and make them pause in awe. Along the wall, following the relief lines of the function, were dots of blood where people had pricked a finger and pressed it to the rock.

"My family has a patch here," said Moko. He led Arlyana into the cavern, past robotic curators that cleaned the cavern and sharpened the edges of etchings that had eroded, and showed her the cluster of blood spots from his ancestors.

"These stop about thirty years ago," she said, reading the dates etched under each blood print.

Moko shrugged. "Most of my family joined the Brethren of Light. I'm the only one left on Musca."

"You have no family here?"

"My closest relative, both genetically and spatially, is my brother. He's on a Brethren mission ship halfway to B right now. He's about fifty light-hours away."

"You don't seem very Brethren to me," said Arlyana with a touch of amusement in her voice.

"Well," said Moko, "my brother is very Brotherly. However, in spite of being a brother to my brother, I am not Brotherly at all."

Arlyana shook her head. "Was that supposed to make sense?"

"If you spend enough time around Brethren, yes. Now show me your family plot."

Arlyana led him to her family's cluster of blood prints. It was a large display that went back twelve generations. Moko was impressed.

"Do you think I should put my mark in your family's area?" he asked. "They don't even know I exist."

"Do always worry so much about etiquette?" Arlyana asked. "You do understand that being balloted gives you a certain degree of latitude?"

"It feels presumptuous to me."

Arlyana scoffed at him. "Since I'm not planning to put my own mark here, it's a moot point."

Moko waited for an explanation but Arlyana did not seem disposed to provide one. "Come on," she said. "We'll find our own place, miles from anyone else."

"Wait a moment," said Moko. Arlyana tried to draw him into moving on, but Moko refused. He was living with one Arlyana mystery already; he was not going let her keep spinning away from him. He examined the blood spots carefully, reading the names, dates, and relationships etched into the rock beneath them.

"I think I've got it. Here," he said, pointing to a spattered blotch of crimson on the wall. "This is your sister's blood. Her name is Uldi. And underneath that is a girl's name, Caris, but no blood. The space has been set aside for a girl who has not been born yet. Your niece-to-be." He studied Arlyana's face; she was giving nothing away. He continued, "It makes you feel bad. You know it shouldn't. But you can't help it. She is about to be born and you've been balloted."

"Yes, you've got it. I don't like to admit it, but I'm resentful," said Arlyana.

"I didn't say resentful," said Moko.

"I did," she replied, then pulled him away by the arm.

They walked along the Heritage Wall until they found an area that was almost devoid of blood marks. Arlyana called over one of the curators, a thin robotic agent that introduced itself and asked what they would like etched beside their blood marks. They decided their names and a small bridge between them would be enough.

The curator robot pricked Moko's skin. Blood budded on the tip of his thumb. Moko pressed it to the rock face and the curator etched his name and the date around it. Arlyana offered her hand to the curator. She pressed her blood to the wall next to Moko's and watched as the curator finished etching.

As they rode the train back, Arlyana fell asleep on Moko's shoulder. Now that he had time to think, he could see that Arlyana had been too quick to agree to his guess, and had been far too blithe about it. It bothered him that Arlyana had spun some more mist about herself. For someone who wanted to share terminal intimacies, she seemed paradoxically reluctant to let him understand her.

He ran through the names and dates in his mind, trying to reconstruct from memory Arlyana's family tree and the sequence of events. Something was amiss with the story he had intuited.

Moko brushed Arlyana's hair with his hand while she slept and wondered why she kept so many things to herself.

Moko said, "This looks terrible."

"Should I care how it looks?"

"People will say I only wanted you for the time you gave me."

"I want this more than I care what people think," said Arlyana.

So they went to the registry and signed away the difference in their ballots. Moko gained time and Arlyana lost time, but they would both live long enough for Moko to learn to climb.

They started with training walls, then worked their way up to boulders, then spouts, and finally to sheer walls. She taught him about ropes and anchors and how to belay, and over the following weeks he built up his strength and endurance.

Signing at the registry had another, quite unexpected, effect: Moko, who had more or less disappeared from his life, became traceable. Consequently, Arlyana was woken early one morning by a message marked "maximum urgency."

She opened the message on screen. A man with a shaved scalp and a slightly pinched mouth appeared on screen; he wore a Brethren tunic.

"My dear lady," said the man. "I apologize for sending a recorded message, but I am fifty light-hours away and cannot engage in responsive conversation. My name is Tarroux, and as you have may have guessed I am Moko's brother. I found you through the registry, and I apologize for intruding on you, but I have been trying to reach Moko with an extremely urgent message. It is imperative that he view the attachment as soon as possible. Before I finish, please allow me to thank you. When you signed your time over to Moko, you may have given him just enough to save himself from the ballot. I can't tell you how much this means." There the message ended.

Arlyana shook Moko awake and dragged his grogginess out of bed.

"You have to see this," she said. Once the message finished, she touched the attachment and went to leave the room.

"Stay," said Moko.

"But it's private!"

"Stay!"

So they watched together as Tarroux, brother to Moko, spoke again.

"Moko," he said, "there is a place for you on the last Brethren mission ship. You know this will be the last ship to leave Musca. The sun is becoming too wild even for missionaries.

"I know we've been through this before, but I am hoping that the approaching ballot date will have changed how you feel about joining the Brethren.

"Please, brother, I love you and it breaks my heart knowing how easily you could be saved."

There was a stark jump-cut in the video stream. Tarroux had come back to the message and added a coda. The quality of the light had changed, the background was darker, and Tarroux looked as if he was being eaten from inside.

"Brother, I know I've asked you many times before and you've refused many times before, but please, please join the Brethren. I . . . I have never said this before, but I beg you to join the mission. Even if you don't believe, just say that you do. That's all you have to do. Just say you believe. I know, I know. It may be a lie. But with time spent among us, maybe you will come to see our truth. Even if you don't change, even if you never accept the Tenets, I will still have my brother."

At the end of the message, Arlyana turned off the screen.

"You turned down a place with the Brethren?" she asked, astonished. "You could have avoided the ballot?"

"Yes, I could have gone to the Brethren and lived a life that means nothing to me, full of empty rituals and prayers to forces I do not believe exist."

"*You would be alive,*" she said.

"Just like you, eh?"

The sudden non-sequitur jarred Arlyana. "What do you mean by that?" she asked.

"You think I wouldn't figure out the story with you and your family? I know what happened. I know it was your sister who was balloted, not you. I know that you took over her ballot because she was pregnant. And I know that your sister fell pregnant *after* she was balloted, which means that your unborn niece is not just a reminder of your impending mortality, *she is the reason for it.* And it's not your fetal niece you resent; it's your manipulative sister."

"You can't possibly know all that," Arlyana said angrily.

"All right, I don't *know* all that; I inferred it. Tell me I'm wrong and I'll take it all back."

"You can't possibly understand . . ."

"Tell me I'm wrong, then."

Arlyana said nothing, she just glared at him while an accusatory aura radiated from her.

Canterbury Hollow was one of the great chambers that crowned their civilization: a wonder of engineering and of art, it had been carved in the shape of a cathedral window. Everyone came there when they died, for recycling. Here the bodies of the dead were committed to the huge bacterial vats that broke down flesh and bone and returned organics to the community.

It was their last day together. The train brought Arlyana and Moko to the base of the Sepulchral Tower, a bowed memorial to everyone who had ever lived and died in that underworld. Few visitors ever went deeper than the memorial park, but Arlyana and Moko were not there to mourn and so they walked past the Sepulchre and into the darker Hollow. The light dimmed as they went deeper: here the brightness was only to be found where it was needed for the workers and machines of the Hollow to perform their daily tasks.

Arlyana took him to a ladder at the base of the western wall that stretched up into the gloom overhead.

"I did all that training to climb a ladder?" said Moko.

"This service ladder rises two hundred metres. After that, it's all our own work."

By the time they reached the top of the ladder, Moko's arms were aching. He wondered how he would manage the rest of the climb. Arlyana reassured him that it would be harder work from here, but slower and with plenty of time for his muscles to recover between exertions.

"The route we're taking is called Little Freya. It's long but easy, and it has plenty of anchor points that previous climbers have left behind. Over to the right there"—and she pointed to a series of vertical ridges forty metres away—"is Big Freya. It's a much, much harder climb. The record for free climbing Big Freya is seven hours. I've free climbed it in ten. Believe me, what we're doing is a cinch."

They took a rest break, then Arlyana looped a rope through a nearby anchor and started climbing. They took turns climbing, then belaying, climbing, then belaying. Their progress was slow but safe, and Moko found that the longer they climbed the more he became focussed on each motion, on balancing the needs of work and rest, on finding the most efficient body position to keep a hold without exhausting a muscle group. Arlyana watched over him, taking care not to push him too hard, nor to let him pause when they needed to push on.

Time seemed to shrink away. He stopped counting hours and minutes and began thinking in steps and grips, which formed movements, which formed phases.

They went around bluffs, over ridges, avoided overhangs, and followed the road up the rock face. As they ascended, the light became more tenuous. They donned collar lanterns and set them glowing.

Many hours later, they came to a small cavern that burrowed off the side of the Hollow. Arlyana helped Moko scramble over the lip and into the safety of the space inside. Once he had caught his breath, he looked out the cavern mouth. There was another hundred metres to the peak of Canterbury Hollow. He groaned. The muscles ached in his shoulders, back, and calves.

Arlyana smiled. “Don’t worry. This is as far as we’re going.”

“But we’re not at the top yet.”

“This is better. Come and see.”

She took his hand and led him into the cavern. The space opened up at the back and they could walk upright without hitting their heads. The light from their collar lanterns filled the small cavern. Hundreds of golden reflections shone back at them. The reflections came from ballot tags that had been hung from the roof. There were hundreds of them, maybe thousands.

Moko moved about, brushing the tags with his fingers and setting them swinging. “What is this place?” he asked.

“Where climbers come to die,” Arlyana said. She hammered a bolt into the cavern roof and from it she hung her ballot tag. Moko took his own tag and chain from around his neck and hung it from the same bolt, then looped a knot in the two chains so that the tags dangled face to face.

“Come here,” said Arlyana, and she started to undress.

Arlyana and Moko were two small primates who were members of a long, slow radiation from the horn of Africa. Their lives meant little except to each other and to a small number of people around them, but stepping back, their choices were part of a pattern of self-similarity echoed on many scales of magnitude. The forces that drove them to each other also drove the cycles of expansion and contraction in the civilization of Deep Citizens. It drove the population cycles of foxes and hares and, on a larger scale again, the cycle of ammonites and meteorites. This great engine of colonisation and exploitation had pushed humanity outwards but had also destroyed the biosphere of a third of all inhabited worlds.

Programmed death has dogged living creatures ever since deep, deep ancestors discovered the power of swapping genes. With the evolution of abstract intelligence, the tragedy of death became a folly. But without that folly, humans would never have made it across the Red Sea and there never would have lived a pair of bonded primates in the crust of a planet twenty-nine light-years from Earth.

Arlyana cut a small segment off their climbing rope and tied one end around her wrist and the other around Moko’s so they would not be separated.

On the time scales that affect human consciousness they did not have long, but for twenty heartbeats they would be cradled by the forces of nature. Angels of gravity drew them an elegant parabola; angels of electricity allowed skin to touch and to feel the contact; angels of strong force held them intact; and angels of weak force bound them to their mutual asymmetries.

They walked to the lip of the cavern, held each other tight, and toppled into empty space.

—for Albert C

Canterbury Hollow / Lawson

The Vorkuta Event

KEN MACLEOD

Here's another story by Ken MacLeod, whose "Earth Hour" appears elsewhere in this anthology. In this one, he takes us back to Cold War Russia for a story about a creepy Lovecraftian intrusion into our reality that is not only top secret but something that you legitimately Don't Want to Know . . . and will regret knowing if you do.

I
TENTACLES AND TOMES

It was in 19—, that unforgettable year, that I first believed that I had unearthed the secret cause of the guilt and shame that so evidently burdened Dr. David Rigley Walker, Emeritus Professor of Zoology at the University of G—. The occasion was casual enough. A module of the advanced class in Zoology dealt with the philosophical and historical aspects of the science. I had been assigned to write an essay on the history of our subject, with especial reference to the then not quite discredited notion of the inheritance of acquired characteristics. Most of my fellow students, of a more practical cast of mind than my own, were inclined to regard this as an irrelevant chore. Not I.

With the arrogance of youth, I believed that our subject, Zoology, had the potential to assimilate a much wider field of knowledge than its current practice and exposition was inclined to assume. Is not man an animal? Is not, therefore, all that is human within, in principle, the scope of Zoology? Such, at least, was my reasoning at the time, and my excuse for a wide and—in mature retrospect—less than profitable reading. Certain recent notorious and lucrative popularizations—as well as serious studies of sexual and social behaviour, pioneered by, of all people, entomologists—were in my view a mere glimpse of the empire of thought open to the zoologist. In those days such fields as evolutionary psychology, Darwinian medicine, and ecological economics still struggled in the shattered and noisome eggshell of their intellectually and—more importantly—militarily crushed progenitors. The great reversal of the mid-century's verdict on this and other matters still slumbered in the womb of the future. These were, I may say, strange times, a moment of turbulent transition when the molecular doctrines were already established, but before they had become the very basis of biology. In the minds of older teachers and in the pages of obsolete textbooks certain questions now incontrovertible seemed novel and untried. The ghost of vitalism still walked the seminar room; plate tectonics was solid ground mainly to geologists; notions of intercontinental land bridges, and even fabled Lemuria, had not been altogether dispelled as worthy of at least serious dismissal. I deplored—nay, detested—all such vagaries.

So it was with a certain zeal, I confess, that I embarked on the background reading for my modest composition. I walked into the University library at noon, bounded up the stairs to the science floor, and alternated browsing the stacks and scribbling in my carrel for a good five hours. Unlike some of my colleagues, I had not afflicted myself with the nicotine vice, and was able to proceed uninterrupted save for a call of nature. I delved into Lamarck himself, in verbose Victorian translation; into successive editions of *The Origin of Species*; and into the *Journal of the History of Biology*. I had already encountered Koestler's *The Case of the Midwife Toad*, that devastating but regretful demolition of the Lamarckian claims of the fellow-traveling biologist, fraud, and suicide Viktor Kammerer—the book, in well-thumbed paperback, was an underground classic among Zoology undergraduates, alongside Lyall Watson's *Supernature*. I read and wrote with a fury to discredit, for good and all, the long-exploded hypothesis that was the matter of my essay. But when I had completed the notes and outline, and the essay was as good as written, needing only some connecting phrases and a fair copy, a sense that the task was not quite finished nagged.

I leaned back in the plastic seat, and recollected of a sudden the very book I needed to deliver the *coup de grace*. But where had I seen it? I could almost smell it—and it was the sense of smell that brought back the memory of the volume's location. I stuffed my notes in a duffel bag, placed my stack of borrowings on the Returns trolley, and hurried from the library. Late in the autumn term, late in the day, the University's central building, facing me on the same hilltop as the tall and modern library, loomed black like a gothic mansion against the sunset sky. Against the same sky, bare trees stood like preparations of nerve-endings on an iodine-stained slide. I crossed the road and walked around the side of the edifice and down the slope to the Zoology Department, a granite and glass monument to the 1930s. Within: paved floors, tiled walls and hardwood balustrades, and the smell that had reminded me, a mingled pervasive waft of salt-water aquaria, of rat and rabbit droppings, of disinfectant and of beeswax polish. A porter smoked in his den, recognised me with a brief incurious glance. I nodded, turned, and ascended the broad stone staircase. On the first landing a portrait of Darwin overhung the door to the top of the lecture hall; beneath the window lay a long glass case containing a dusty plastic model of *Architeuthys*, its two-metre tentacles outstretched to a painted prey. The scale of the model was not specified. At the top of the stairs, opposite the entrance to the library, stood another glass case, with the skeleton of a specimen of *Canis dirus* from Rancho La Brea. As I moved, the shadow and gleams of the dire wolf's teeth presented a lifelike snarl.

Inside, the departmental library was empty, its long windows catching the sun's last light. From the great table that occupied most of its space, the smell of beeswax rose like a hum, drowning out the air's less salubrious notes save that of the books that lined the walls. Here I had skimmed Schrödinger's neglected text on the nerves; here I had luxuriated in D'Arcy Thomson's glorious prose, the outpoured, ecstatic precision of *On Growth and Form*; here, more productively, I had bent until my eyes had watered over Mayr and Simpson and Dobzhansky. It was the last, I think, who had first sent me to glance, with a shudder, at the book I now sought.

There it was, black and thick as a Bible; its binding sturdy, its pages yellowing but sound, like a fine vellum. *The Situation in Biological Science: Proceedings of the Lenin Academy of Agricultural Sciences of the U.S.S.R., July 31—August 7, 1948, Complete Stenographic Report*. This verbatim account is one of the most sinister in the annals of science: it documents the conference at which the peasant charlatan Lysenko, who claimed that the genetic constitutions of organisms could be changed by environmental influences, defeated those of his opponents who still stood up for Mendelian genetics. Genetics in the Soviet Union took decades to recover.

I took the volume to the table, sat down, and copied to my notebook Lysenko's infamous, gloating remark toward the close of the conference: "The Central Committee of the CPSU has examined my report and approved it"; and a selection from the rush of hasty recantations—announcements, mostly, of an overnight repudiation of a lifetime's study—that followed it and preceded the closing vote of thanks to Stalin. I felt pleased at having found—unfairly perhaps—something with which to sully further the heritage of Lamarck. At the same time I felt an urge to wash my hands. There was something incomprehensible about the book's very existence: was it naivety or arrogance that made its publishers betray so shameful a demonstration of the political control of science? The charlatan's empty victory was a thing that deserved to be done in the dark, not celebrated in a *complete stenographic report*.

But enough. As I stood to return the book to the shelf I opened it idly at the flyleaf, and noticed a queer thing. The sticker proclaiming it the property of the Department overlaid a handwritten inscription in broad black ink, the edges of which scrawl had escaped the bookplate's obliteration. I recognised some of the fugitive lettering as Cyrillic script. Curious, I held the book up to the light and tried to read through the page, but the paper was too thick.

The books were for reference only. The rule was strict. I was alone in the library. I put the book in my duffel bag and carried it to my bedsit. There, with an electric kettle on a shaky table, I steamed the bookplate off. Then, cribbing from a battered second-hand copy of *The Penguin Russian Course*, I deciphered the inscription. The Russian original has faded from my mind. The translation remains indelible:

To my dear friend Dr. Dav. R. Walker,
in memory of our common endeavour,
yours,
Ac. T. D. Lysenko.

The feeling that this induced in me may be imagined. I started and trembled as though something monstrous had reached out a clammy tentacle from the darkness of its lair and touched the back of my neck. If the book had been inscribed to any other academic elder I might have been less shocked: many of them flaunted their liberal views, and hinted at an earlier radicalism, on the rare occasions when politics were discussed; but Walker was a true-blue conservative of the deepest dye, as well as a mathematically rigorous Darwinian.

The next morning I trawled the second-hand bookshops of the University district. The city had a long, though now mercifully diminishing, "Red" tradition; and sure enough, I found crumbling pamphlets and tedious journals of that persuasion from the time of the Lysenko affair. In them I found articles defending Lysenko's views. The authors of some, the translators of others, variously appeared as: DRW, Dr. D R Walker, and (with a more proletarian swagger) Dave Walker. There was no room for doubt: my esteemed professor had been a Lysenkoist in his youth.

With a certain malice (forgivable in view of my shock and indeed dismay) I made a point of including these articles in my references when I typed up the essay and handed it in to my tutor, Dr. F——. A week passed before I received a summons to Professor Walker's office.

II
ALCOHOL, TOBACCO, AND ULTRAVIOLET RADIATION EXPOSURE

The Emeritus Professor was, as his title suggests, semi-retired; he took little part in the administration, and devoted his intermittent visits to the Department to the occasional sparkling but well-worn lecture; to shuffling and annotating off-prints of papers from his more productive days with a view to an eventual collection; and to some desultory research of his own into the anatomy and relationships of a Jurassic marine crocodile. Palaeontology had been his field. In his day he had led expeditions to the Kalahari and the Gobi. He had served in the Second World War. In some biographical note I had glimpsed the rank of Lieutenant, but no reference to the Service in which it had been attained: a matter on which rumor had not been reticent.

The professor's office was at the end of one of the second storey's long corridors. Dust, cobwebs, and a statistically significant sample of desiccated invertebrates begrimed the frosted glass panel of the door. I tapped, dislodging a dead spider and a couple of woodlice.

"Come in!"

As I stepped through the door the professor rose behind his desk and leaned forward. Tall and stooping, very thin, with weathered skin, sunken cheeks, and a steely spade of beard, he seemed a ruin of his adventurous youth—more Quatermass than Quartermain, so to speak—but an impressive ruin. He shook hands across his desk, motioned me to a seat, and resumed his own. I brushed tobacco ash from friction-furred leather and sat down. The room reeked of pipe smoke and of an acetone whiff that might have been formaldehyde or whisky breath. Shelves lined the walls, stacked with books and petrified bones. Great drifts of journals and off-prints cluttered the floor. A window overlooking the building's drab courtyard sifted wan wintry light through a patina similar to that on the door. A fluorescent tube and an Anglepoise diminished even that effect of daylight.

Walker leaned back in his chair and flicked a Zippo over the bowl of his Peterson. He tapped a yellow forefinger nail on a sheaf of paper, which I recognised without surprise as my essay.

"Well, Cameron," he said, through a gray-blue cloud, "you've done your homework."

"Thank you, sir," I said.

He jabbed the pipe-stem at me. "You're not at school," he said. "That is no way for one gentleman to address another."

"OK, Walker," I said, a little too lightly.

"Not," he went on, "that your little trick here was gentlemanly. You're expected to cite peer-reviewed articles, not dredge up political squibs and screeds from what you seized on as another chap's youthful folly. These idiocies are no secret. If you'd asked me, I'd have told you all about them—the circumstances, you understand. And I could have pointed you to the later peer-reviewed article in which I tore these idiocies, which I claimed as my own, to shreds. You could have cited that too. That would have been polite."

"I didn't intend any discourtesy," I said.

"You intended to embarrass me," he said. "Did you not?"

I found myself scratching the back of my head, embarrassed myself. My attempt at an excuse came out as an accusation.

"I found the inscription from Lysenko," I said.

Walker rocked back in his seat. "What?"

" 'To my dear friend Dr. Dav. R. Walker, in memory of our common endeavour.' " Against my conscious will, the words came out in a jeering tone.

Walker planted his elbow-patches on his desk and cupped his chin in both hands, pipe jutting from his yellow teeth. He glared at me through a series of puffs.

"Ah, yes," he said at last. "That common endeavour. Would it perhaps pique your curiosity to know what it *was*?"

"I had assumed it was on genetics," I said.

"Hah!" snorted Walker. "You're a worse fool than I was, Cameron. What could I have done on genetics?"

"You wrote about it," I said, again sounding more accusing than I had meant to.

"I wrote rubbish for *The Modern Quarterly*," he said, "but I think you would be hard pressed to find in it anything about original work on genetics."

"I mean," I said, "your defence of him."

Walker narrowed his eyes. "These articles were written *after* I had received the book," he said. "So they were not what old Trofim was remembering me for, no indeed."

"So what was it?"

He straightened up. "A most disquieting experience," he said. "One that weighs on me even now. If I were to tell you of it, it would weigh on you for the rest of your life. And the strange thing is, Cameron, that I need not swear you to secrecy. The tale is as unbelievable as it is horrible. For you to tell it would merely destroy whatever credibility you have. Not only would nobody believe the tale—nobody would believe that I had told it to you. The more you insisted on it, the more you would brand yourself a liar and a fantasist of the first water."

"Then why should I believe it myself?"

His parchment skin and tombstone teeth grinned back his answer like a death's head illuminated from within.

"You will believe it."

I shrugged.

"You will wish you didn't," he added mildly. "You can walk out that door and forget about this, and I will forget your little jape. If you don't, if you stay here and listen to me, let me assure you that I will have inflicted upon you a most satisfactory revenge."

I squared to him from my seat. "Try me, Walker," I said.

III
WALKER'S ACCOUNT

Stalin's pipe was unlit—always a bad sign. Poskrebyshev, the General Secretary's sepulchral amanuensis, closed the door silently behind me. The only pool of light in the long, thickly curtained room was over Stalin's desk. Outside that pool two figures sat on high-backed chairs. A double glint on pinz-nez was enough to warn me that one of these figures was Beria. The other, as I approached, I identified at once by his black flop of hair, his hollow cheeks, and his bright fanatic eyes: Trofim Lysenko. My knees felt like rubber. I had met Stalin before, of course, during the war, but I had never been summoned to his presence.

It was the summer of '47. I'd been kicking my heels in Moscow for weeks, trying without success—and, more frustratingly, without definite refusal—to get permission to mount another expedition to the Gobi. It was not, of course, the best of times to be a British citizen in the Soviet capital. (It was not the best of times to be a Soviet citizen, come to that.) My wartime work in liaison may have been both a positive and a negative factor: positive, in that I had contacts, and a degree of respect; negative, in that it put me under suspicion—ludicrous though it may seem, Cameron—of being a spy. I might, like so many others, have gone straight from the Kremlin to the Lubianka.

Stalin rose, stalked towards me, shook hands brusquely, pointed me to a low seat—he was notoriously sensitive about his height—and returned to his desk chair. I observed him closely but covertly. He had lost weight. His skin was loose. He seemed more burdened than he had at Yalta and Tehran.

"Lieutenant Walker—" he began. Then he paused, favoured me with a yellow-eyed, yellow-toothed smile, and corrected himself. "*Doctor* Walker. Rest assured, you were not invited here in your capacity as a British officer."

His sidelong glance at Beria told me all I needed to know about where I stood in that regard. Stalin sucked on his empty pipe, frowned, and fumbled a packet of Dunhills from his tunic. To my surprise, he proffered the pack across the desk. I took one, with fingers that barely trembled. A match flared between us; and for a moment, in that light, I saw that Stalin was afraid. He was more afraid than I; and that thought terrified me. I sank back and drew hard.

"We need your help, Dr. Walker. In a scientific capacity."

I hesitated, unsure how to address him. He was no comrade of mine, and to call him by his latest title, "Generalissimo," would have seemed fawning. My small diplomatic experience came to my aid.

"You surprise me, Marshal Stalin," I said. "My Soviet colleagues are more than capable."

Lysenko cleared his throat, but it was Beria who spoke. "Let us say there are problems."

"It is not," said Stalin, "a question of capability. It is important to us that the task we wish you to take part in be accomplished by a British scientist who is also a . . . former . . . British officer, who has—let us say—certain connections with certain services, and who is not—again, let us say—one who might, at some future date, be suspected of being connected with the organs of Soviet state security." Another sidelong glance at Beria.

"Let me be blunt, Marshal Stalin," I said. "You want me because I'm a scientist and because I you think I might be a British agent, and because you can be certain I'm not one of yours?"

"Fairly certain," said Stalin, with a dark chuckle.

Out of the corner of my eye I saw Beria flinch. I was startled that Stalin should hint so broadly of Soviet penetration of British intelligence, as well as of his mistrust of Beria. If I survived to return to England, I would make a point of reporting it directly to that chap who—Whitehall rumour had it—was in charge of stopping that sort of thing. What was his name again? Oh, yes—Philby. A moment later I realised that, very likely, Stalin and Beria had cooked up this apparent indiscretion between them, perhaps to test my reaction, or so that my very reporting of it might circuitously advance their sinister aims. But there were more pressing puzzles on my mind.

"But I'm a palaeontologist!" I said. "What could there possibly be in that field that could be of interest to any intelligence service?"

"A good question," said Stalin. "An intriguing question, is it not? I see you are intrigued. All I can say at this point, Dr. Walker, is that you have only one way of finding the answer. If you choose not to help us, then I must say, with regret, that you must take the next flight for London. It may be impossible for you to return, or to dig again for the dinosaur bones of Outer Mongolia which appear to fascinate you so much. If you do choose to help us, not only will you find the answer to your question, but opportunities for further collaboration with our scientists might, one may imagine, open up."

The threat, mercifully small as it would have seemed to some, was dire to me; the offer tempting; but neither was necessary. I was indeed intrigued.

"I'll do it," I said.

"Good," said Stalin. "I now turn you over to the capable hands of . . ."

He paused just long enough—a heartbeat—to scare me.

". . . your esteemed colleague, Trofim Denisovich."

But, as though in amends for that small, cat-like moment of sporting with my fear, or perhaps from that sentimental streak which so often characterises his type, his parting handshake was accompanied by momentary wetness of his yellow eyes and a confidential murmur, the oddest thing I ever heard—or heard of or read of—him say:

"God go with you."

Corridors, guards, stairs, the courtyard, more guards, then Red Square and the streets. Trofim walked fast beside me, hands jammed in his jacket pockets, his chin down; fifty-odd metres behind us, the pacing shadow of the man from the organs of state security. Beefy-faced women in kerchiefs mixed concrete by shovel, struggled with wheel-barrows, took bawled orders from loutish foremen. Above them, on the bare scaffolding of the building sites, huge red-bordered black-on-white banners flapped, vast magnifications of a flattering ink portrait of the face I had seen minutes before. There seemed to be no connection, the merest passing resemblance to the aged, pock-marked man. I recalled something he had, it was told, once snarled at his drunken, vainglorious son, who'd pleaded, "After all, I too am Stalin." He'd said:

"*You* are not Stalin! *I* am not Stalin! Stalin is a banner . . ."

At that moment I thought I could quite literally see what he'd meant.

"Well, David Rigley," said Lysenko (evidently under the misapprehension that my second name was a patronymic), "the leading comrades have landed you and me in a fine mess."

"You know what this is about?"

"I do, more's the pity. We may be doomed men. Let us walk a little. It's the safest way to talk."

"But surely—"

"Nothing is 'surely,' here. You must know that. Even a direct order from the Boss may not be enough to protect us from the organs. Beria is building atomic bombs out on the tundra. Where he gets his labour force from, you can guess. Including engineers and scientists, alas. At one of their sites they have found something that . . . they want us to look into."

"Atomic bombs? With respect, Trofim Denisovich—"

"I will not argue with you on that. But what Beria's . . . men have found is more terrifying than an atomic bomb. That is what we have agreed to investigate, you and I."

"Oh," I said. "So that's what I've agreed to. Thanks for clearing that up."

The sarcasm was wasted on him.

"You are welcome, David Rigley." He stopped at an intersection. A black car drew up beside us. He waved me to the side door. I hung back.

"It is my own car," he said mildly. "It will take us to my farm. Tomorrow, it will take us to the airport."

Lysenko's private collective farm—so to speak—in the Gorki-Leninskie hills south of Moscow was of course a showcase, and was certainly a testimony more to Lysenko's enthusiasm than to his rigour, but I must admit that it was a hospitable place, and that I spent a pleasant enough afternoon there being shown its remarkable experiments, and a very pleasant evening eating some of the results. For that night, Trofim and I could pretend to have not a care in the world—and in that pretense alone, I was of one mind with the charlatan.

The following morning we flew to the east and north. It was not a civilian flight. Aeroflot's reputation is deservedly bad enough; but it is in the armed forces that Aeroflot pilots learn their trade. This flight in an LI-2 transport was courtesy of the Army. Even now, the memory of that flight brings me out in a cold sweat. So you will forgive me if I pass over it. Suffice it to say that we touched down on a remote military airfield that evening to refuel and to change pilots, and continued through a night during which I think I slept in my cramped bucket seat from sheer despair. We landed—by sideslip and steep, tight spiral, as if under fire—just after dawn the following morning on a bumpy, unpaved strip in the midst of a flat, green plain. A shack served as a terminal building, before which a welcoming committee of a dozen or so uniformed men stood. Through a small porthole, as the plane juddered to a halt, I glimpsed some more distant structures: a tower on stilts, long low barracks, a mine-head, and great heaps of spoil. There may have been a railway line. I'm not sure.

Trofim and I unkinked our backs, rubbed grit from our eyes, and made our stooping way to the hatch. I jumped the metre drop to the ground. Trofim sat and swung his long legs over and slid off more carefully. The air was fine and fresh, unbelievably so after Moscow, and quite warm. One of the men detached himself from the line-up and hurried over. He was stocky, blue-jowled, with a look of forced joviality on his chubby, deep-lined face. He wore a cap with the deep blue band of the security organs. Shaking hands, he introduced himself as Colonel Viktor A. Marchenko. He led us to the shack, where he gave us glasses of tea and chunks of sour black bread, accompanied by small talk and no information, while his men remained at attention outside—they didn't smoke or shuffle—then took us around the back of the shack to a Studebaker flat-bed truck. To my surprise, the colonel took the driver's seat. Trofim and I squeezed in beside him. The rest of the unit piled perilously on the back.

We associate Russia's far north with snow and ice. Its brief summer is almost pleasant, apart from the mosquitoes and the landslides. Small flowers carpet the tundra. Its flat appearance is deceptive, concealing from a distance the many hollows and rises of the landscape. The truck went up and down, its tyres chewing the unstable soil. At the crest of each successive rise the distant buildings loomed closer. The early-morning sun glinted on long horizontal lines in front of them: barbed wire, no doubt, and not yet rusty. It became obvious, as I had of course suspected, that this was a labour camp. I looked at Lysenko. He stared straight ahead, sweat beading his face. I braced my legs in the foot-well and gripped my knees hard.

At the top of a rise the truck halted. The colonel nodded forward, and made a helpless gesture with his hand. Trofim and I stared in shock at what lay in front of us. At the bottom of the declivity, just a few metres down the grassy slope from the nose of the truck, the ground seemed to have given way. The hole was about fifteen metres across and four deep. Scores of brown corpses, contorted and skeletal, protruded at all angles from the ragged black earth. From the bottom of the hole, an edged metallic point stood up like the tip of a pyramid or the corner of an enormous box. Not a speck of dirt marred the reflective sheen of its blue-tinted, silvery surfaces.

My first thought was that some experimental device, perhaps one of Beria's atomic bombs, had crashed here among some of the camp's occupants, killing and half-burying the poor fellows. My second thought was that it had exposed the mass grave of an earlier batch of similar unfortunates. I kept these thoughts to myself and stepped down from the cab, followed by Lysenko. The colonel jumped out the other side and barked an order. Within seconds his men had formed a widely spaced cordon around the hole, each standing well back, with his Kalashnikov levelled.

"Take a walk around it," said Marchenko.

We did, keeping a few steps away from the raw edge of the circular gash. About three metres of each edge of the object was exposed. Lysenko stopped and walked to the brink. I followed, to peer at a corpse just below our feet. Head, torso, and one outflung arm poked out of the soil. Leathery skin, a tuft of hair, empty sockets, and a lipless grin.

"From the . . . *Yezhovschina*?" I asked, alluding to the massacres of a decade earlier.

Trofim leaned forward and pointed down. "I doubt," he said drily, "that any such died with bronze swords in their hands."

I squatted and examined the body more closely. Almost hidden by a fall of dirt was the other hand, clutching a hilt that did indeed, between the threads of a rotten tassel, have a brassy gleam. I looked again at what shock had made me overlook on the others: stubs of blades, scraps of gear, leather belts and studs, here and there around withered necks a torque of a dull metal that might have been pewter.

"So who are they?" I asked.

Lysenko shrugged. "Tartars, Mongols . . ."

His knowledge of history was more dubious than his biology. These peoples had never migrated so far north, and no Bronze Age people was native to the area. The identity and origin of the dead barbarians puzzles me to this day.

Around the other side of the pit, the side that faced the camp, things were very different. The upper two metres of that face of the pyramid was missing, as if it was the opened top of that hypothetical box's corner. And the bodies—I counted ten—scattered before it were definitely those of camp labourers: thin men in thin clothes, among flung shovels. The corpses looked quite fresh. Only their terrible rictus faces were like those of the other and more ancient dead.

"What is this?" I asked Lysenko. "One of Beria's infernal machines?"

He shot me an amused, impatient glance. "You over-estimate us," he said. "This is not a product of our technology. Nor, I venture to suggest, is it one of yours."

"Then whose?"

"If it is not from some lost civilization of deep antiquity, then it is not of this world."

We gazed for a while at the black empty triangle and then completed our circuit of the pit and returned to Marchenko, who still stood in front of the truck.

"What happened here?" Lysenko asked.

Marchenko pointed towards the camp, then down at the ground.

"This is a mining camp," he said. "The mine's galleries extend beneath our feet. Some days ago, there was a cave-in. It resulted in a rapid subsidence on the surface, and exposed the object, and the slain warriors. A small squad of prisoners was sent into the pit to investigate, and to dig out the bodies and artefacts. To be quite frank, I suspect that they were sent to dig for valuables, gold and whatnot. One of them, for reasons we can only speculate, tried to enter the aperture in the object. Within moments, they were all dead."

"Tell us plainly," said Lysenko. "Do you mean they were shot by the guards?"

The colonel shook his head. "They could have been," he said, "for disobeying orders. But as it happens, they were not. Something from the object killed them without leaving a mark. Perhaps a poisonous gas—I don't know. That is for you to find out."

His story struck as improbable, or at least incomplete, but this was no time to dispute it.

"For heaven's sake, man!" I cried out. "And get killed ourselves?"

Marchenko bared a gold incisor. "That is the problem, yes? You are scientists. Solve it."

This insouciance for a moment infuriated us, but solve it we did. An hour or two later, after the truck had returned from the camp with the simple equipment we'd demanded, Lysenko and I were standing in the pit a couple of metres from the black aperture. Behind us the truck chugged, its engine powering a searchlight aimed at the dark triangle. Trofim guided a long pole, on the end of which one of the truck's wing mirrors was lashed. I stood in front of him, the pole resting on my shoulder, and peered at the mirror with a pair of binoculars requisitioned from (no doubt) a camp guard. Nothing happened as our crude apparatus inched above the dark threshold. We moved about, Trofim turning the mirror this way and that. The magnified mirror image filled a large part of the close-focus view.

"What do you see?" Lysenko asked.

"Nothing," I said. "Well, the joins of the edges. They go as far as I can see. Below it there's just darkness. It's very deep."

We backed out and scrambled up.

"How big is this thing?" I asked Marchenko.

He shifted and looked sideways, then jabbed a finger downward.

"A similar apex," he said, "pokes down into the gallery beneath us."

"How far beneath us?"

His tongue flicked between his lips for a moment. "About a hundred metres."

"If this is a cube," I said, "four hundred feet diagonally—my God!"

"We have reason to think it is a cube," said Marchenko.

"Take us to the lower apex," said Lysenko.

"Do you agree?" Marchenko asked me.

"Yes," I said.

A sign arched over the camp entrance read: "Work in the USSR is a matter of honour and glory." For all that we could see as the truck drove in, nobody in the camp sought honour and glory that day. Guards stood outside every barracks door. Three scrawny men were summoned to work the hoist. Marchenko's squad took up positions around the mine-head. Lysenko, Marchenko, and I—with one of Marchenko's sergeants carrying the pole and mirror—descended the shaft in a lift cage to the gallery. Pitchblende glittered in the beams from our helmet lamps. We walked forward for what seemed like many hours, but according to my watch was only fifty-five minutes. The cave-in had been cleared. Down like the point of a dagger came the lower apex of the cube, its tip a few inches above the floor. Its open face was not black but bright. It cast a blue light along the cavern.

"Well," said Lysenko, with a forced laugh, "this looks more promising."

This time it was I who advanced with the pole and angled the mirror in; Lysenko who looked through the Zeiss. I saw a reflected flash, as though something had moved inside the object. Blue light, strangely delimited, strangely slow, like some luminous fluid, licked along the wooden pole. With a half-second's warning, I could have dropped it. But as that gelid lightning flowed over my hands, my fingers clamped to the wood. I felt a forward tug. I could not let go. My whole body spasmed as if in electric shock, and just as painfully. My feet rose off the ground, and my legs kicked out behind me. At the same moment I found myself flying forward like a witch clinging to a wayward broom. With a sudden flexure that almost cracked my spine, I was jerked through the inverted triangular aperture and upward into the blue-lit space above. That space was not empty. Great blocks of blue, distinct but curiously insubstantial, floated about me. I was borne upwards, then brought to a halt. I could see, far above, a small triangle of daylight, in equally vivid contrast to the darkness immediately beneath it and the unnatural light around me. Apart from my hands, still clutched around the pole, my muscles returned to voluntary control. I hung there, staring, mouth open, writhing like a fish on a hook. My throat felt raw, my gasps sounded ragged. I realised that I had been screaming. The echoes of my screams rang for a second or two in the vast cubical space.

Before my eyes, some of the blocky shapes took on a new arrangement: a cubist caricature of a human face, in every detail down to the teeth. Eyes like cogwheels, ears like coffins. From somewhere came an impression, nay, a conviction, that this representation was meant to be *reassuring*. It was not.

What happened next is as difficult to describe as a half-remembered dream: a sound of pictures, a taste of words. I had a vision of freezing space, of burning suns, of infinite blackness shot through with stars that were not eternal: stars that I might outlive. I heard the clash of an enormous conflict, remote in origin, endless in prospect, and pointless in issue. It was not a war of ideals, but an ideal war: what Plato might have called the Form of War. Our wars of interests and ideologies can give only the faintest foretaste of it. But a foretaste they are. I was given to understand—how, I do not know—that joining in such a war is what the future holds for our descendants, and for all intelligent species. It is conducted by machines that carry in themselves the memories, and are themselves the only monuments, of the races that built them and that they have subsumed. This is a war with infinite casualties, infinite woundings, and no death that is not followed—after no matter what lapse of time—by a resurrection and a further plunge into that unending welter. No death save that of the universe itself can release the combatants, and only at that terminus will it have meaning, and then only for a moment, the infinitesimal moment of contemplating a victory that is final because it precedes, by that infinitesimal moment, the end of all things: victory pure and undefiled, victory for its own sake, the victory of the last mind left.

This hellish vision was held out to me as an inducement! Yes, Cameron—I was being offered the rare and unthinkable privilege of joining the ranks of warriors in this conflict that even now shakes the universe; of joining it centuries or millennia before the human race rises to that challenge itself. I would join it as a mind: my brain patterns copied and transmitted across space to some fearsome new embodiment, my present body discarded as a husk. And if I refused, I would be cast aside with contempt. The picture that came before me—whether from my own mind, or from that of the bizarre visage before me—was of the scattered bodies in the pit.

With every fibre of my being, and regardless of consequence, I screamed my refusal. Death itself was infinitely preferable to that infinite conflict.

I was pulled upward so violently that my arms almost dislocated. The blue light faded, blackness enveloped me, and then the bright triangle loomed. I hurtled through it and fell with great force, face down in the mud. The wind was knocked out of me. I gasped, choked, and lifted my head painfully up, to find myself staring into the sightless eyes of one of the recent dead, the camp labourers. I screamed again, scrambled to my feet, and clawed my way up the crumbling side of the pit. For a minute I stood quite alone.

Then another body hurtled from the aperture, and behaved exactly as I had done, including the scream. But Lysenko had my outstretched hand to grasp his wrist as he struggled up.

"Were you pulled in after me?" I asked.

Lysenko shook his head. "I rushed to try to pull you back."

"You're a brave man," I said.

He shrugged. "Not brave enough for what I found in there."

"You saw it?" I asked.

"Yes," he said. He shuddered. "Before that Valhalla, I would choose the hell of the priests."

"What we saw," I said, "is entirely compatible with materialism. That's what's so terrifying."

Lysenko clutched at my lapels. "No, not materialism! Mechanism! Man must fight that!"

"Fight it . . . endlessly?"

His lips narrowed. He turned away.

"Marchenko lied to us," he said.

"What?"

Lysenko nodded downward at the nearest bodies. "That tale of his—these men were not sent into this pit here, and killed by something lashing out from the . . . device. These men are *miners*. They entered it exactly as we did, from below."

"So why are they dead, and we're alive?" As soon as I asked the question, I knew the answer. Only their bodies were dead. Their minds were on their way to becoming alive somewhere else.

"You remember the choice you were given," said Lysenko. "They chose differently."

"They chose *that*—over—?" I jerked a backward thumb.

"Yes," said Lysenko. "A different hell."

We waited. After a while the truck returned from the camp.

IV
FALLOUT PATTERNS

Walker fell silent in the lengthened shadows and thickened smoke.

"And then what happened?" I asked.

He knocked out his pipe. "Nothing," he said. "Truck, plane, Moscow, Aeroflot, London. My feet barely touched the ground. I never went back."

"I mean, what happened to the thing you found?"

"A year or two later, the site was used for an atomic test."

"Over a uranium mine?"

"I believe that was part of the object. To maximise fallout. That particular region is still off limits, I understand."

"How do you know this?"

"You should know better than to ask," said Walker.

"So Stalin had your number!"

He frowned. "What do you mean?"

"He guessed correctly," I said. "About your connections."

"Oh yes. But leave it at that." He waved a hand, and began to refill his pipe. "It's not important."

"Why did he send a possible enemy agent, and a charlatan like Lysenko? Why not one of his atomic scientists, like Sakharov?"

"Sakharov and his colleagues were otherwise engaged," Walker said. "As for sending me and Lysenko . . . I've often wondered about that myself. I suspect he sent me because he wanted the British to know. Perhaps he wanted us worried about worse threats than any that might come from him, and at the same time worried that his scientists could exploit the strange device. Lysenko—well, he was reliable, in his way, and expendable, unlike the real scientists."

"Why did you write what you did, about Lysenko?"

"One." Walker used his pipe as a gavel on the desk. "I felt some gratitude to him. Two." He tapped again. "I appreciated the damage he was doing."

"To Soviet science?"

"Yes, and to science generally." He grinned. "I was what they would call an enemy of progress. I still am. Progress is progress towards the future I saw in that thing. Let it be delayed as long as possible."

"But you've contributed so much!"

Walker glanced around at his laden shelves. "To palaeontology. A delightfully useless science. But you may be right. Even the struggle against progress is futile. Natural selection eliminates it. It eliminated Lysenkoism, and it will eliminate my efforts. The process is ineluctable. Don't you see, Cameron? It is not the failure of progress, the setbacks, that are to be feared. It is progress itself. The most efficient system will win in the end. The most advanced machines. And the machines, when they come into their own, will face the struggle against the other machines that are already out there in the universe. And in that struggle, anything that does not contribute to the struggle—all beauty, all knowledge, all scruple—will be discarded or eliminated. There will be nothing left but the bare will, the will to win, and the means to that end." He sighed. "In his own mad way, Lysenko understood that. There was a sort of quixotic nobility in his struggle against the logic of evolution, in his belief that man could humanise nature. No. Man is a brief interlude between the prehuman and the posthuman. To protract that interlude is the most we can hope for."

He said nothing more, except to tell me that he had recommended my essay for an A++.

The gesture was kind, considering how I had provoked him, but it did me little good. I failed that year's examinations. In the summer I worked as a labourer in a nearby botanic garden, and studied hard in the evenings. In this way I made up for lost time in the areas of Zoology in which I had been negligent, and re-sat the examination with success. But I maintained my interest in those theoretical areas which I'd always found most fascinating, and specialised in my final year in evolutionary genetics, to eventually graduate with First Class Honours.

I told no one of Walker's story. I did not believe it at the time, and I do not believe it now. Since the fall of the Soviet Union, many new facts have been revealed. No nuclear test ever took place at Vorkuta. There was no uranium mine at the place whose location can be deduced from Walker's account. There is no evidence that Lysenko made any unexplained trips, however brief, to the region. No rumours about a mysterious object found near a labour camp circulate even in that rumour-ridden land. As for Walker himself, his Lysenkoism was indeed about as genuine ("let us say," as Stalin might have put it) as his Marxism. There is evidence, from other and even more obscure articles of his, and from certain published and unpublished memoirs and reminiscences that I have come across over the years, that he was a Communist between 1948 and 1956. Just how this is connected with his inclusion in the New Year Honours List for 1983 ("For services to knowledge") I leave for others to speculate. The man is dead.

I owe to him, however, the interest which I developed in the relationship between, if you like, Darwinian and Lamarckian forms of inheritance. This exists, of course, not in biology but in artificial constructions. More particularly, the possibility of combining genetic algorithms with learned behaviour in neural networks suggested to me some immensely fertile possibilities. Rather to the surprise of my colleagues, I chose for my postgraduate research the then newly established field of computer science. There I found my niche, and eventually obtained a lectureship at the University of E——, in the Department of Artificial Intelligence.

The work is slow, with many setbacks and false starts, but we're making progress.

The Man who Bridged the Mist

Kij Johnson

Here's a long and compelling novella about a man who goes to build a bridge on a strange alien planet, a project that eventually changes everyone's lives profoundly and in unexpected ways, not least so the life of the bridge builder himself.

Kij Johnson sold her first short story in 1987, and has subsequently appeared regularly in Asimov's, Analog, The Magazine of Fantasy & Science Fiction, *and* Realms of Fantasy. *She won the Theodore Sturgeon Memorial Award for her story "Fox Magic," and the International Association for the Fantastic in the Arts' Crawford Award. Her story "26 Monkeys, Also the Abyss" won the World Fantasy Award in 2009, and she won back-to-back Nebula Awards for her stories "Spar" and "Ponies" in 2010 and 2011, respectively. Her two novels are* The Fox Woman *and* Fudoki, *and her stories have been collected in* Tales for the Long Rains *and* At the Mouth of the River of Bees. *She is currently a graduate student at North Carolina State University in Raleigh, and is researching a third novel set in Heian Japan, as well as two novels set in Georgian Britain. She maintains a Web site at www.kijjohnson.com.*

Kit came to Nearside with two trunks and an oiled-cloth folio full of plans for the bridge across the mist. His trunks lay tumbled like stones at his feet, where the mail-coach guard had dropped them. The folio he held close, away from the drying mud of yesterday's storm.

Nearside was small, especially to a man of the capital, where buildings towered seven and eight stories tall, a city so large that even a vigorous walker could not cross in half a day. Here hard-packed dirt roads threaded through irregular spaces scattered with structures and fences. Even the inn was plain, two stories of golden limestone and blue slate tiles, with (he could smell) some sort of animals living behind it. On the sign overhead, a flat, pale blue fish very like a ray curvetted against a black background.

A brightly dressed woman stood by the inn's door. Her skin and eyes were pale, almost colorless. "Excuse me," Kit. "Where can I find the ferry to take me across the mist?" He could feel himself being weighed, but amiably: a stranger, small and very dark, in gray—a man from the east.

The woman smiled. "Well, the ferries are both at the upper dock. But I expect what you really want is someone to oar the ferry, yes? Rasali Ferry came over from Farside last night. She's the one you'll want to talk to. She spends a lot of time at The Deer's Heart. But you wouldn't like The Heart, sir," she added. "It's not nearly as nice as The Fish here. Are you looking for a room?"

"I'll be staying in Farside tonight," Kit said apologetically. He didn't want to seem arrogant. The invisible web of connections he would need for his work started here, with this first impression, with all the first impressions of the next few days.

"That's what *you* think," the woman said. "I'm guessing it'll be a day or two, or more, before Rasali goes back. Valo Ferry might, but he doesn't cross so often."

"I could buy out the trip's fares, if that's why she's waiting."

"It's not that," the woman said. "She won't cross the mist 'til she's ready. Until it tells her she can go, if you follow me. But you can ask, I suppose."

Kit didn't follow, but he nodded anyway. "Where's The Deer's Heart?"

She pointed. "Left, then right, then down by the little boatyard."

"Thank you," Kit said. "May I leave my trunks here until I work things out with her?"

"We always stow for travelers." The woman grinned. "And cater to them, too, when they find out there's no way across the mist today."

The Deer's Heart was smaller than The Fish, and livelier. At midday the oak-shaded tables in the beer garden beside the inn were clustered with light-skinned people in brilliant clothes, drinking and tossing comments over the low fence into the boatyard next door, where, half lost in steam, a youth and two women bent planks to form the hull of a small flat-bellied boat. When Kit spoke to a man carrying two mugs of something that looked like mud and smelled of yeast, the man gestured at the yard with his chin. "Ferrys are over there. Rasali's the one in red," he said as he walked away.

"The one in red" was tall, her skin as pale as that of the rest of the locals, with a black braid so long that she had looped it around her neck to keep it out of the way. Her shoulders flexed in the sunlight as she and the youth forced a curved plank to take the skeletal hull's shape. The other woman, slightly shorter, with the ash-blond hair so common here, forced an augur through the plank and into a rib, then hammered a peg into the hole she'd made. After three pegs, the boatwrights straightened. The plank held. *Strong,* Kit thought; *I wonder if I can get them for the bridge?*

"Rasali!" a voice bellowed, almost in Kit's ear. "Man here's looking for you." Kit turned in time to see the man with the mugs gesturing, again with his chin. He sighed and walked to the waist-high fence. The boatwrights stopped to drink from blueware bowls before the one in red and the youth came over.

"I'm Rasali Ferry of Farside," the woman said. Her voice was softer and higher than he had expected of a woman as strong as she, with the fluid vowels of the local accent. She nodded to the boy beside her: "Valo Ferry of Farside, my brother's eldest." Valo was more a young man than a boy, lighter-haired than Rasali and slightly taller. They had the same heavy eyebrows and direct amber eyes.

"Kit Meinem of Atyar," Kit said.

Valo asked, "What sort of name is Meinem? It doesn't mean anything."

"In the capital, we take our names differently than you."

"Oh, like Jenner Ellar." Valo nodded. "I guessed you were from the capital—your clothes and your skin."

Rasali said, "What can we do for you, Kit Meinem of Atyar?"

"I need to get to Farside today," Kit said.

Rasali shook her head. "I can't take you. I just got here, and it's too soon. Perhaps Valo?"

The youth tipped his head to one side, his expression suddenly abstract, as though he were listening to something too faint to hear clearly. He shook his head. "No, not today."

"I can buy out the fares, if that helps. It's Jenner Ellar I am here to see."

Valo looked interested but said, "No," to Rasali, and she added, "What's so important that it can't wait a few days?"

Better now than later, Kit thought. "I am replacing Teniant Planner as the lead engineer and architect for construction of the bridge over the mist. We will start work again as soon as I've reviewed everything. And had a chance to talk to Jenner." He watched their faces.

Rasali said, "It's been a year since Teniant died—I was starting to think Empire had forgotten all about us, and your deliveries would be here 'til the iron rusted away."

"Jenner Ellar's not taking over?" Valo asked, frowning.

"The new Department of Roads cartel is in my name," Kit said, "but I hope Jenner will remain as my second. You can see why I would like to meet him as soon as is possible, of course. He will—"

Valo burst out, "You're going to take over from Jenner, after he's worked so hard on this? And what about us? What about *our* work?" His cheeks were flushed an angry red. *How do they conceal anything with skin like that?* Kit thought.

"Valo," Rasali said, a warning tone in her voice. Flushing darker still, the youth turned and strode away. Rasali snorted but said only: "Boys. He likes Jenner, and he has issues about the bridge, anyway."

That was worth addressing. *Later.* "So, what will it take to get you to carry me across the mist, Rasali Ferry of Farside? The project will pay anything reasonable."

"I cannot," she said. "Not today, not tomorrow. You'll have to wait."

"Why?" Kit asked: reasonably enough, he thought, but she eyed him for a long moment, as if deciding whether to be annoyed.

"Have you gone across mist before?" she said at last.

"Of course."

"Not the river," she said.

"Not the river," he agreed. "It's a quarter mile across here, yes?"

"Oh, yes." She smiled suddenly: white even teeth and warmth like sunlight in her eyes. "Let's go down, and perhaps I can explain things better there." She jumped the fence with a single powerful motion, landing beside him to a chorus of cheers and shouts from the inn garden's patrons. She gave an exaggerated bow, then gestured to Kit to follow her. She was well-liked, clearly. Her opinion would matter.

The boatyard was heavily shaded by low-hanging oaks and chestnuts, and bounded on the east by an open-walled shelter filled with barrels and stacks of lumber. Rasali waved at the third boat maker, who was still putting her tools away. "Tilisk Boatwright of Nearside. My brother's wife," she said to Kit. "She makes skiffs with us, but she won't ferry. She's not born to it as Valo and I are."

"Where's your brother?" Kit asked.

"Dead," Rasali said, and lengthened her stride.

They walked a few streets over and then climbed a long, even ridge perhaps eighty feet high, too regular to be natural. A *levee*, Kit thought, and distracted himself from the steep path by estimating the volume of earth and the labor that had been required to build it. Decades, perhaps, but how long ago? How long was it? The levee was treeless. The only feature was a slender wood tower hung with flags. It was probably for signaling across the mist to Farside, since it appeared too fragile for anything else. They had storms out here, Kit knew; there'd been one the night before, that had left the path muddy. How often was the tower struck by lightning?

Rasali stopped. "There."

Kit had been watching his feet. He looked up and nearly cried out as light lanced his suddenly tearing eyes. He fell back a step and shielded his face. What had blinded him was an immense band of white mist reflecting the morning sun.

Kit had never seen the mist river itself, though he bridged mist before this, two simple post-and-beam structures over gorges closer to the capital. From his work in Atyar, he knew what was to be known. It was not water, or anything like. It did not flow, but formed somehow in the deep gorge of the great riverbed before him. It found its way many hundreds of miles north, upstream through a hundred narrowing mist creeks and streams before failing at last, in shreds of drying foam that left bare patches of earth where they collected.

The mist stretched to the south as well, a deepening, thickening band that poured out at last from the river's mouth two thousand miles south, and formed the mist ocean, which lay on the face of the salt-water ocean. Water had to follow the river's bed to run somewhere beneath, or through, the mist, but there was no way to prove this.

There was mist nowhere but this river and its streams and sea; but the mist split Empire in half.

After a moment, the pain in Kit's eyes grew less, and he opened them again. The river was a quarter mile across where they stood, a great gash of light between the levees. It seemed nearly featureless, blazing under the sun like a river of cream or of bleached silk, but as his eyes accustomed themselves, he saw the surface was not smooth but heaped and hollowed, and that it shifted slowly, almost indiscernibly, as he watched.

Rasali stepped forward, and Kit started. "I'm sorry," he said with a laugh. "How long have I been staring? It's just—I had no idea."

"No one does," Rasali said. Her eyes when he met them were amused.

The east and west levees were nearly identical, each treeless and scrub-covered, with a signal tower. The levee on their side ran down to a narrow bare bank half a dozen yards wide. There was a wooden dock and a boat ramp, a rough switchback leading down to them. Two large boats had been pulled onto the bank. Another, smaller dock was visible a hundred yards upstream, attended by a clutter of boats, sheds, and indeterminate piles covered in tarps.

"Let's go down." Rasali led the way, her words coming back to him over her shoulder. "The little ferry is Valo's. *Pearlfinder.* The *Tranquil Crossing*'s mine." Her voice warmed when she said the name. "Eighteen feet long, eight wide. Mostly pine, but a purpleheart keel and pearwood headpiece. You can't see it from here, but the hull's sheathed in blue-dyed fish-skin. I can carry three horses or a ton and a half of cartage or fifteen passengers. Or various combinations. I once carried twenty-four hunting dogs and two handlers. Never again."

A steady light breeze eased down from the north, channeled by the levees. The air had a smell, not unpleasant but a little sour, wild. "How can you manage a boat like this alone? Are you that strong?"

"It's as big as I can handle," she said, "but Valo helps sometimes, for really unwieldy loads. You don't paddle through mist. I mostly just coax the *Crossing* to where I want it to go. Anyway, the bigger the boat, the more likely that the Big Ones will notice it; though if you *do* run into a fish, the smaller the boat, the easier it is to swamp. Here we are."

They stood on the bank. The mist streams he had bridged had not prepared him for anything like this. Those were tidy little flows, more like fog collection in hollows than this. From their angle, the river no longer seemed a smooth flow of creamy whiteness, nor even gently heaped clouds. The mist forced itself into hillocks and hollows, tight slopes perhaps twenty feet high that folded into one another. It had a surface, but it was irregular, cracked in places, or translucent in others. It didn't seem as clearly defined as that between water and air.

"How can you move on this?" Kit said, fascinated. "Or even float?" The hillock immediately before them was flattening as he watched. Beyond it something like a vale stretched out for a few dozen yards before turning and becoming lost to his eyes.

"Well, I can't, not today," Rasali said. She sat on the gunwale of her boat, one leg swinging, watching him. "I can't push the *Crossing* up those slopes or find a safe path, unless the mist shows me the way. If I went today, I know—I *know*"—she tapped her belly—"that I would find myself stranded on a pinnacle or lost in a hole. *That's* why I can't take you today, Kit Meinem of Atyar."

When Kit was a child, he had not been good with other people. He was small and easy to tease or ignore, and then he was sick for much of his seventh year and had to leave his crèche before the usual time, to convalesce in his mother's house. None of the children of the crèche came to visit him, but he didn't mind that: he had books and puzzles, and whole quires of blank paper that his mother didn't mind him defacing.

The clock in the room in which he slept didn't work, so one day he used his penknife to take it apart. He arranged the wheels and cogs and springs in neat rows on the quilt in his room, by type and then by size; by materials; by weight; by shape. He liked holding the tiny pieces, thinking of how they might have been formed and how they worked together. The patterns they made were interesting, but he knew the best pattern would be the working one, when they were all put back into their right places and the clock performed its task again. He had to think that the clock would be happier that way, too.

He tried to rebuild the clock before his mother came upstairs from her counting house at the end of the day, but when he had reassembled things, there remained a pile of unused parts and it still didn't work; so he shut the clock up and hoped she wouldn't notice that it wasn't ticking. Four days more of trying things during the day and concealing his failures at night; and on the fifth day, the clock started again. One piece hadn't fit anywhere, a small brass cog. Kit still carried that cog in his pen case.

Late that afternoon, Kit returned to the river's edge. It was hotter; the mud had dried to cracked dust, and the air smelled like old rags left in water too long. He saw no one at the ferry dock, but at the fisher's dock upstream, people were gathering, a score or more of men and women, with children running about.

The clutter looked even more disorganized as he approached. The fishing boats were fat little coracles of leather stretched on frames, tipped bottom up to the sun and looking like giant warts. The mist had dropped so that he could see a band of exposed rock below the bank, and he could see the dock's pilings clearly, which were not vertical but set at an angle: a cantilevered deck braced into the stone underlying the bank. The wooden pilings had been sheathed in metal.

He approached a silver-haired woman doing something with a treble hook as long as her hand. "What are you catching with that?" he said.

Her forehead was wrinkled when she looked up, but she smiled when she saw him. "Oh, you're a stranger. From Atyar, dressed like that. Am I right? We catch fish. . . ." Still holding the hook, she extended her arms as far as they would stretch. "Bigger than that, some of them. Looks like more storms, so they're going to be biting tonight. I'm Meg Threehooks. Of Nearside, obviously."

"Kit Meinem of Atyar. I take it you can't find a bottom?" He pointed to the pilings.

Meg Threehooks followed his glance. "It's there somewhere, but it's a long way down, and we can't sink pilings because the mist dissolves the wood. Oh, and fish eat it. Same thing with our ropes, the boats, us—anything but metal and rock, really." She knotted a line around the hook eye. The cord was dark and didn't look heavy enough for anything Kit could imagine catching on hooks that size.

"What are these made of, then?" He squatted to look at the framing under one of the coracles.

"Careful, that one's mine," Meg said. "The hides—well, and all the ropes—are fish-skin. Mist fish, not water fish. Tanning takes off some of the slime, so they don't last forever, either, not if they're immersed." She made a face. "We have a saying: foul as fish-slime. That's pretty nasty, you'll see."

"I need to get to Farside," Kit said. "Could I hire you to carry me across?"

"In my boat?" She snorted. "No, fishers stay close to shore. Go see Rasali Ferry. Or Valo."

"I saw her," he said ruefully.

"Thought so. You must be the new architect—city folk are always so impatient. You're so eager to be dinner for a Big One? If Rasali doesn't want to go, then don't go, stands to reason."

Kit was footsore and frustrated by the time he returned to The Fish. His trunks were already upstairs, in a small cheerful room overwhelmed by a table that nearly filled it, with a stiflingly hot cupboard bed. When Kit spoke to the woman he'd talked to earlier, Brana Keep, the owner of The Fish (its real name turned out to be

The Big One's Delight), laughed. "Rasali's as hard to shift as bedrock," she said. "And, truly, you would not be comfortable at The Heart."

By the next morning, when Kit came downstairs to break his fast on flatbread and pepper-rubbed fish, everyone appeared to know everything about him, especially his task. He had wondered whether there would be resistance to the project, but if there had been any, it was gone now. There were a few complaints, mostly about slow payments, a universal issue for public works; but none at all about the labor or organization. Most in the taproom seemed not to mind the bridge, and the feeling everywhere he went in town was optimistic. He'd run into more resistance elsewhere, building the small bridges.

"Well, why should we be concerned?" Brana Keep said to Kit. "You're bringing in people to work, yes? So we'll be selling room and board and clothes and beer to them. And you'll be hiring some of us, and everyone will do well while you're building this bridge of yours. I plan to be wading ankle-deep through gold by the time this is done."

"And after," Kit said, "when the bridge is complete—think of it, the first real link between the east and west sides of Empire. The only place for three thousand miles where people and trade can cross the mist easily, safely, whenever they wish. You'll be the heart of Empire in ten years. Five." He laughed a little, embarrassed by the passion that shook his voice.

"Yes, well," Brana Keep said, in the easy way of a woman who makes her living by not antagonizing customers, "we'll make that harness when the colt is born."

For the next six days, Kit explored the town and surrounding countryside.

He met the masons, a brother and sister that Teniant had selected before her death to oversee the pillar and anchorage construction on Nearside. They were quiet but competent, and Kit was comfortable not replacing them.

Kit also spoke with the Nearside rope-makers, and performed tests on their fish-skin ropes and cables, which turned out even stronger than he had hoped, with excellent resistance to rot, and catastrophic and slow failure. The makers told him that the rope stretched for its first two years in use, which made it ineligible to replace the immense chains that would bear the bridge's weight; but it could replace the thousands of vertical suspender chains that that would support the roadbed, with a great saving in weight.

He spent much of his time watching the mist. It changed character unpredictably: a smooth rippled flow; hours later, a badland of shredding foam; still later, a field of steep dunes that joined and shifted as he watched. There was nothing level about the mist's surface, but he thought that the river generally dropped in its bed each day under the sun, and rose after dark.

The winds were more predictable. Hedged between the levees, they streamed southward each morning and north each evening, growing stronger toward midday and dusk, and falling away entirely in the afternoons and at night. They did not seem to affect the mist much, though they did tear shreds off that landed on the banks as dried foam.

The winds meant that there would be more dynamic load on the bridge than Teniant Planner had predicted. Kit would never criticize her work publicly and he gladly acknowledged her brilliant interpersonal skills, which had brought the town into cheerful collaboration, but he was grateful that her bridge had not been built as designed.

He examined the mist more closely, as well, by lifting a piece from the river's surface on the end of an oar. The mist was stiffer than it looked, and in bright light he thought he could see tiny shapes, perhaps creatures or plants or something altogether different. There were microscopes in the city, and people who studied these things; but he had never bothered to learn more, interested only in the structure that would bridge it. In any case, living things interested him less than structures.

Nights, Kit worked on the table in his room. Teniant's plans had to be revised. He opened the folios and cases she had left behind and read everything he found there. He wrote letters, wrote lists, wrote schedules, made duplicates of everything, sent to the capital for someone to do all the subsequent copying. His new plans for the bridge began to take shape, and started to glimpse the invisible architecture that was the management of the vast project.

He did not see Rasali Ferry, except to ask each morning whether they might travel that day. The answer was always no.

One afternoon, when the clouds were heaping into anvils filled with rain, he walked up to the building site half a mile north of Nearside. For two years, off and on, carts had tracked south on the Hoic Mine Road and the West River Road, leaving limestone blocks and iron bars in untidy heaps. Huge dismantled shear legs lay beside a caretaker's wattle-and-daub hut. There were thousands of large rectangular blocks.

Kit examined some of the blocks. Limestone was often too chossy for large-scale construction, but this rock was sound, with no apparent flaws or fractures. There were not enough, of course, but undoubtedly more had been quarried. He had written to order resumption of deliveries, and they would start arriving soon.

Delivered years too early, the iron trusses that would eventually support the roadbed were stacked neatly, paint black to protect them from moisture, covered in oiled tarps, and raised from the ground on planks to keep. Sheep grazed the knee-high grass that grew everywhere. When one of the sheep eyed him incuriously, Kit found himself bowing. "Forgive the intrusion, sir," he said, and laughed. Too old to be talking to sheep.

The test pit was still open, a ladder on the ground nearby. Weeds clung when he moved the ladder, as if reluctant to release it. He descended.

The pasture had not been noisy, but he was startled when he dropped below ground level and the insects and whispering grasses were suddenly silenced. The soil around him was striated shades of dun and dull yellow. Halfway down, he sliced a wedge free with his knife: lots of clay; good foundation soil, as he had been informed. The pit's bottom, some twenty feet down, looked like the walls, but crouching to dig at the dirt between his feet with his knife, he hit rock almost immediately. It seemed to be shale. He wondered how far down the water table was: did the Nearsiders find it difficult to dig wells? Did the mist ever backwash into one? There were people at University in Atyar who were trying to understand mist, but there was still so much that could not be examined or quantified.

He collected a rock to examine in better light, and climbed from the pit in time to see a teamster leading four mules, her wagon groaning under the weight of the first new blocks. A handful of Nearsider men and women followed, rolling their shoulders and popping their joints. They called out greetings, and he walked across to them.

When he got back to The Fish hours later, exhausted from helping unload the cart, and soaked from the storm that had started while he did so, there was a message from Rasali. *Dusk* was all it said.

Kit was stiff and irritable when he left for the *Tranquil Crossing*. He had hired a carrier from The Fish to haul one of his trunks down to the dock, but the others remained in his room, which he would probably keep until the bridge was done. He carried his folio of plans and paperwork himself. He was leaving duplicates of everything on Nearside, but after so much work, it was hard to trust any of it to the hands of others.

The storm was over and the clouds were moving past, leaving the sky every shade between lavender and a rich purple-blue. The large moon was a crescent in the west; the smaller a half circle immediately overhead. In the fading light, the mist was a dark, smoky streak. The air smelled fresh. Kit's mood lightened, and he half-trotted down the final path.

His fellow passengers were there before him: a prosperous-looking man with a litter of piglets in a woven wicker cage (Tengon whites, the man confided, the best bloodline in all Empire); a woman in the dark clothes fashionable in the capital, with brass-bound document cases and a folio very like Kit's; two traders with many cartons of powdered pigment; a mail courier with locked leather satchels and two guards. Nervous about their first crossing, Uni and Tom Mason greeted Kit when he arrived.

In the gathering darkness, the mist looked like bristling, tight-folded hills and coulees. Swifts darted just above mist, using the wind flowing up the valley, searching for insects, he supposed. Once a sudden black shape, too quick to see clearly, appeared from below; then it, and one of the birds, was gone.

The voices of the fishers at their dock carried to him. They launched their boats, and he watched one, and then another, and then a gaggle of the little coracles push themselves up a slope of the mist. There were no lamps.

"Ready, everyone?" Kit had not heard Rasali approach. She swung down into the ferry. "Hand me your gear."

Stowing and embarkation were quick, though the piglets complained. Kit strained his eyes, but the coracles could no longer be seen. When he noticed Rasali waiting for him, he apologized. "I guess the fish are biting."

Rasali glanced at the river as she stowed his trunk. "Small ones. A couple of feet long only. The fishers like them bigger, five or six feet, though they don't want them too big, either. But they're not fish, not what you think fish are. Hand me that."

He hesitated a moment, then gave her the folio before stepping into the ferry. The boat sidled at his weight but sluggishly: a carthorse instead of a riding mare. His stomach lurched. "Oh!" he said.

"What?" one of the traders asked nervously. Rasali untied the rope holding them to the dock.

Kit swallowed. "I had forgotten. The motion of the boat. It's not like water at all."

He did not mention his fear, but there was no need. The others murmured assent. The courier, her dark face sharp-edged as a hawk, growled, "Every time I do this, it surprises me. I dislike it."

Rasali unshipped a scull and slid the great triangular blade into the mist, which parted reluctantly. "I've been on mist more than water, but I remember the way water felt. Quick and jittery. This is better."

"Only to you, Rasali Ferry," Uni Mason said.

"Water's safer," the man with the piglets said.

Rasali leaned into the oar, and the boat slid away from the dock. "Anything is safe until it kills you."

The mist absorbed the quiet sounds of shore almost immediately. One of Kit's first projects had been a stone single-arch bridge over water, far to the north in Eskje province. He had visited before construction started. He was there for five days more than he had expected, caught by a snowstorm that left nearly two feet on the ground. This reminded him of those snowy moonless nights, the air as thick and silencing as a pillow on the ears.

Rasali did not scull so much as steer. It was hard to see far in any direction except up, but perhaps it was true that the mist spoke to her, for she seemed to know where to position the boat for the mist to carry it forward. She followed a small valley until it started to flatten and then mound up. The *Tranquil Crossing* tipped slightly as it slid a few feet to port. The mail carrier made a noise, and immediately stifled it.

"Mist" was a misnomer. It was denser than it seemed, and sometimes the boat seemed not to move through it so much as over its surface. Tonight it seemed like seawrack, the dirty foam that strong winds could whip from ocean waves. Kit reached a hand over the boat's side. The mist piled against his hand, almost dry to the touch, sliding up his forearm with a sensation he could not immediately identify. When he realized it was prickling, he snatched his arm back in and rubbed it on a fold of his coat. The skin burned. Caustic, of course.

The man with the pigs whispered, "Will they come if we talk or make noise?"

"Not to talking, or pigs' squealing," Rasali said. "They seem to like low noises. They'll rise to thunder sometimes."

One of the traders said, "What are they if they're not really fish? What do they look like?" Her voice shook. The mist was weighing on them all: all but Rasali.

"If you want to know you'll have to see one for yourself," Rasali said. "Or try to get a fisher to tell you. They gut and fillet them over the sides of their boats. No one else sees much but meat wrapped in paper, or rolls of black skin for the rope-makers and tanners."

"*You've* seen them," Kit said.

"They're broad and flat. But ugly . . ."

"And Big Ones?" Kit asked.

Her voice was harsh. "*Them,* we don't talk about here."

No one spoke for a time. Mist—foam—heaped up at the boat's prow and parted, eased to the sides with an almost inaudible hissing. Once the mist off the port side heaved, and something dark broke the surface for a moment, followed by other dark somethings; but the somethings were not close enough to see well. One of the merchants cried without a sound or movement, the tears on his face the only evidence.

The Farside levee showed at last, a black mass that didn't get any closer for what felt like hours. Fighting his fear, Kit leaned over the side, keeping his face away from the surface. "It can't really be bottomless," he said, half to himself. "What's under it?"

"You wouldn't hit the bottom, anyway," Rasali said.

The *Tranquil Crossing* eased up a long swell of mist and into a hollow. Rasali pointed the ferry along a crease in the river and eased it forward. And then they were suddenly a stone's throw from the Farside dock and the light of its torches.

People on the dock moved as they approached. Just loudly enough to carry, a soft baritone voice called, "Rasali?"

She called back, "Ten this time, Pen."

"Anyone need carriers?" A different voice. Several passengers responded.

Rasali shipped the skull while the ferry was still some feet away from the dock, and allowed it to ease forward under its own momentum. She stepped to the prow and picked up a coiled rope there, tossing one end across the narrowing distance. Someone on the dock caught it and pulled the boat in, and in a very few moments, the ferry was snug against the dock.

Disembarking and payment was quicker as embarkation had been. Kit was the last off, and after a brief discussion he hired a carrier to haul his trunk to an inn in town. He turned to say farewell to Rasali. She and the man—Pen, Kit remembered—were untying the boat. "You're not going back already," he said.

"Oh, no." Her voice sounded loose, content, relaxed. Kit hadn't known how tense she was. "We're just going to tow the boat over to where the Twins will pull it out." She waved with one hand to the boat launch. A pair of white oxen gleamed in the night, at their heads a woman hardly darker.

"Wait," Kit said to Uni Mason, and handed her his folio. "Please tell the innkeeper I'll be there soon." He turned back to Rasali. "May I help?"

In the darkness, he felt more than saw her smile. "Always."

The Red Lurcher, commonly called The Bitch, was a small but noisy inn five minutes' walk from the mist, ten (he was told) from the building site. His room was larger than at The Fish, with an uncomfortable bed and a window seat crammed with quires of ancient, handwritten music. Jenner stayed here, Kit knew, but when he asked the owner (Widson Innkeep, a heavyset man with red hair turning silver), he had not seen him. "You'll be the new one, the architect," Widson said.

"Yes," Kit said. "Please ask him to see me when he gets in."

Widson wrinkled his forehead. "I don't know, he's been out late most days recently, since—" He cut himself off, looking guilty.

"—since the signals informed him that I was here," Kit said. "I understand the impulse."

The innkeeper seemed to consider something for a moment, then said slowly, "We like Jenner here."

"Then we'll try to keep him," Kit said.

When the child Kit had recovered from the illness, he did not return to the crèche—which he would have been leaving in a year in any case—but went straight to his father. Davell Meinem was a slow-talking humorous man who nevertheless had a sharp tongue on the sites of his many projects. He brought Kit with him to his work places: best for the boy to get some experience in the trade.

Kit loved everything about his father's projects: the precisely drawn plans, the orderly progression of construction, the lines and curves of brick and iron and stone rising under the endlessly random sky.

For the first year or two, Kit imitated his father and the workers, building structures of tiny beams and bricks made by the woman set to mind him, a tiler who had lost a hand some years back. Davell collected the boy at the end of the day. "I'm here to inspect the construction," he said, and Kit demonstrated his bridge or tower, or the materials he had laid out in neat lines and stacks. Davell would discuss Kit's work with great seriousness, until it grew too dark to see and they went back to the inn or rented rooms that passed for home near the sites.

Davell spent nights buried in the endless paperwork of his projects, and Kit found this interesting, as well. The pattern that went into building something big was not just the architectural plans, or the construction itself; it was also labor schedules and documentation and materials deliveries. He started to draw his own plans, but he also made up endless correspondences with imaginary providers.

After a while, Kit noticed that a large part of the pattern that made a bridge or a tower was built entirely out of people.

The knock on Kit's door came very late that night, a preemptory rap. Kit put down the quill he was mending, and rolled his shoulders to loosen them. "Yes," he said aloud as he stood.

The man who stormed through the door was as dark as Kit, though perhaps a few years younger. He wore mud-splashed riding clothes.

"I am Kit Meinem of Atyar."

"Jenner Ellar of Atyar. Show it to me." Silently Kit handed the cartel to Jenner, who glared at it before tossing it onto the table. "It took long enough for them to pick a replacement."

Might as well deal with this right now, Kit thought. "You hoped it would be you."

Jenner eyed Kit for a moment. "Yes. I did."

"You think you're the most qualified to complete the project because you've been here for the last—what is it? Year?"

"I know the sites," Jenner said. "I worked with Teniant to make those plans. And then Empire sends—" He turned to face the empty hearth.

"—Empire sends someone new," Kit said to Jenner's back. "Someone with connections in the capital, influential friends but no experience with this site, this bridge. It should have been you, yes?"

Jenner was still.

"But it isn't," Kit said, and let the words hang for a moment. "I've built nine bridges in the past twenty years. Four suspension bridges, three major spans. Two bridges over mist. You've done three, and the biggest span you've directed was three hundred and fifty feet, six stone arches over shallow water and shifting gravel up on Mati River."

"I know," Jenner snapped.

"It's a good bridge." Kit poured two glasses of whiskey from a stoneware pitcher by the window. "I coached down to see it before I came here. It's well made, and you were on budget and nearly on schedule in spite of the drought. Better, the locals still like you. Asked how you're doing these days. Here."

Jenner took the glass Kit offered. *Good.* Kit continued, "Meinems have built bridges—and roads and aqueducts and stadia, a hundred sorts of public structures—for Empire for a thousand years." Jenner turned to speak, but Kit held up his hand. "This doesn't mean we're any better at it than Ellars. But Empire knows us—and we know Empire, how to do what we need to. If they'd given you this bridge, you'd be replaced within a year. But I can get this bridge built, and I will." Kit sat and leaned forward, elbows on knees. "With you. You're talented. You know the site. You know the people. Help me make this bridge."

"It's real to you," Jenner said finally, and Kit knew what he meant: *You care about this work. It's not just another tick on a list.*

"Yes," Kit said. "You'll be my second for this one. I'll show you how to deal with Atyar, and I'll help you with contacts. And your next project will belong entirely to you. This is the first bridge, but it isn't going to be the only one across the mist."

Together they drank. The whiskey bit at Kit's throat and made his eyes water. "Oh," he said, "that's *awful*."

Jenner laughed suddenly, and met his eyes for the first time: a little wary still, but willing to be convinced. "Farside whiskey is terrible. You drink much of this, you'll be running for Atyar in a month."

"Maybe we'll have something better ferried across," Kit said.

Preparations were not so far along on this side. The heaps of blocks at the construction site were not so massive, and it was harder to find local workers. In discussions between Kit, Jenner and the Near- and Farside masons who would oversee construction of the pillars, final plans materialized. This would be unique, the largest structure of its kind ever attempted: a single-span chain suspension bridge a quarter of a mile long. The basic plan remained unchanged: the bridge would be supported by eyebar-and-bolt chains, four on each side, allowed to play independently to compensate for the slight shifts that would be caused by traffic on the roadbed. The huge eyebars and their bolts were being fashioned five hundred miles away and far to the west, where iron was common and the smelting and ironworking were the best in Empire. Kit had just written to the foundries to start the work again.

The pillar and anchorage on Nearside would be built of gold limestone anchored with pilings into the bedrock; on Farside, they would be pink-gray granite with a funnel-shaped foundation. The towers' heights would be nearly three hundred feet. There were taller towers back in Atyar, but none had to stand against the compression of the bridge.

The initial tests with the fish-skin rope had showed it to be nearly as strong as iron, without the weight. When Kit asked the Farside tanners and rope-makers about its durability, he was taken a day's travel east to Meknai, to a waterwheel that used knotted belts of the material for its drive. The belts, he was told, were seventy-five years old and still sound. Fish-skin wore like maplewood, so long as it wasn't left in mist, but it required regular maintenance, which made it inappropriate for many uses.

He watched Meknai's little river for a time. There had been rain recently in the foothills, and the water was quick and abrupt as light. *Water bridges are easy,* he thought a little wistfully, and then: *Anyone can bridge water.*

Kit revised the plans again, to use the lighter material where they could. Jenner crossed the mist to Nearside, to work with Daell and Stiwan Cabler on the expansion of their workshops and ropewalk.

Without Jenner (who was practically a local, as Kit was told again and again), Kit felt the difference in attitudes on the river's two banks more clearly. Most Farsiders shared the Nearsiders' attitudes: money is money and always welcome, and there was a sense of the excitement that comes of any great project; but there was more resistance here. Empire was effectively split by the river, and the lands to the east—starting with Nearside—had never seen their destinies as closely linked to Atyar in the west. They were overseen by the eastern capital, Triple; their taxes went to building necessities on their own side of the mist. Empire's grasp on the eastern lands was loose, and had never needed to be tighter.

The bridge would change things. Travel between Atyar and Triple would grow more common, and perhaps Empire would no longer hold the eastern lands so gently. Triple's lack of enthusiasm for the project showed itself in delayed deliveries of stone and iron. Kit traveled five days along the Triple road to the district seat to present his credentials to the governor, and wrote sharp letters to the Department of Roads in Triple. Things became a little easier.

It was midwinter before the design was finished. Kit avoided crossing the mist. Rasali Ferry crossed seventeen times. He managed to see her nearly every time, at least for as long as it took to share a beer.

The second time Kit crossed, it was midmorning of an early spring day. The mist mirrored the overcast sky above: pale and flat, like a layer of fog in a dell. Rasali was loading the ferry at the upper dock when Kit arrived, and to his surprise she smiled at him, her face suddenly beautiful. Kit nodded to the stranger watching Valo toss immense cloth-wrapped bales down to Rasali, then greeted the Ferrys. Valo paused for a moment, but did not return Kit's greeting, only bent again to his work. Valo had been avoiding him since nearly the beginning of his time there. *Later.* With a mental shrug, Kit turned from Valo to Rasali. She was catching and stacking the enormous bales easily.

"What's in those? You throw them as if they were—"

"—paper," she finished. "The very best Ibraric mulberry paper. Light as lambswool. You probably have a bunch of this stuff in that folio of yours."

Kit thought of the vellum he used for his plans, and the paper he used for everything else: made of cotton from far to the south, its surface buffed until it felt hard and smooth as enamelwork. He said, "All the time. It's good paper."

Rasali piled on bales and more bales, until the ferry was stacked three and four high. He added, "Is there going to be room for me in there?"

"Pilar Runn and Valo aren't coming with us," she said. "You'll have to sit on top of the bales, but there's room as long as you sit still and don't wobble."

As Rasali pushed away from the dock Kit asked, "Why isn't the trader coming with her paper?"

"Why would she? Pilar has a broker on the other side." Her hands busy, she tipped her head to one side, in a gesture that somehow conveyed a shrug. "Mist is dangerous."

Somewhere along the river a ferry was lost every few months: horses, people, cartage, all lost. Fishers stayed closer to shore and died less often. It was harder to calculate the impact to trade and communications of this barrier splitting Empire in half.

This journey—in daylight, alone with Rasali—was very different than Kit's earlier crossings: less frightening but somehow wilder, stranger. The cold wind down the river was cutting, and brought bits of dried foam to rest on his skin, but they blew off quickly, without pain and leaving no mark. The wind fell to a breeze and then to nothing as they navigated into the mist, as if they were buried in feathers or snow.

They moved through what looked like a layered maze of thick cirrus clouds. He watched the mist along the *Crossing*'s side until they passed over a small hole like a pockmark, straight down and no more than a foot across. For an instant he glimpsed open space below them; they were floating on a layer of mist above an air pocket deep enough to swallow the boat. He rolled onto his back to stare up at the sky until he stopped shaking; when he looked again, they were out of the maze, it seemed. The boat floated along a gently curving channel. He relaxed a little, and moved to watch Rasali.

"How fares your bridge?" Rasali said at last, her voice muted in the muffled air. This had to be a courtesy—everyone in town seemed to know everything about the bridge's progress—but Kit was used to answering questions to which people already knew the answers. He had found patience to be a highly effective tool.

"Farside foundations are doing well. We have maybe six more months before the anchorage is done, but pilings for the pillar's foundation are in place and we can start building. Six weeks early," Kit said, a little smugly, though this was a victory no one else would appreciate, and in one case the weather was as much to be credited as any action on his part. "On Nearside, we've run into basalt that's too hard to drill easily, so we sent for a specialist. The signal flags say she's arrived, and that's why I'm crossing."

She said nothing, seemingly intent on moving the great scull. He watched her for a time, content to see her shoulders flex, hear her breath forcing itself out in smooth waves. Over the faint yeast scent of the mist, he smelled her sweat, or thought he did. She frowned slightly, but he could not tell whether it was due to her labor, or something in the mist, or something else. Who was she, really? "May I ask a question, Rasali Ferry?"

Rasali nodded, eyes on the mist in front of the boat.

Actually, he had several things he wished to know: about her, about the river, about the people here. He picked one, almost at random. "What is bothering Valo?"

"He's transparent, isn't he? He thinks you take something away from him," Rasali said. "He is too young to know what you take is unimportant."

Kit thought about it. "His work?"

"His work is unimportant?" She laughed, a sudden puff of an exhale as she pulled. "We have a lot of money, Ferrys. We own land and rent it out—The Deer's Heart belongs to my family; do you know that? He's young. He wants what we all want at his age. A chance to test himself against the world and see if he measures up. And because he's a Ferry, he wants be tested against adventures. Danger. The mist. Valo thinks you take that away from him."

"But he's not immortal," Kit said. "Whatever he thinks. The river can kill him. It will, sooner or later. It—"

—*will kill you.* Kit caught himself, rolled onto his back again to look up at the sky.

In The Bitch's taproom one night, a local man had told him about Rasali's family: a history of deaths, of boats lost in a silent hissing of mist, or the rending of wood, or screams that might be human and might be a horse. "So everyone wears ash-color for a month or two, and then the next Ferry takes up the business. Rasali's still new, two years maybe. When she goes, it'll be Valo, then Rasali's youngest sister, then Valo's sister. Unless Rasali or Valo has kids by then."

"They're always beautiful," the man had added after some more porter: "the Ferrys. I suppose that's to make up for having such short lives."

Kit looked down from the paper bales at Rasali. "But you're different. You don't feel you're losing anything."

"You don't know what I feel, Kit Meinem of Atyar." Cool light moved along the muscles of her arms. Her voice came again, softer. "I am not young; I don't need to prove myself. But I will lose this. The mist, the silence."

Then tell me, he did not say. *Show me.*

She was silent for the rest of the trip. Kit thought perhaps she was angry, but when he invited her, she accompanied him to the building site.

The quiet pasture was gone. All that remained of the tall grass was struggling tufts and dirty straw. The air smelled of sweat and meat and the bitter scent of hot metal. There were more blocks here now, a lot more. The pits for the anchorage and the pillar were excavated to bedrock, overshadowed by mountains of dirt. One sheep remained, skinned and spitted, and greasy smoke rose as a girl turned it over a fire beside the temporary forge. Kit had considered the pasture a nuisance, but looking at the skewered sheep, he felt a twinge of guilt.

The rest of the flock had been replaced by sturdy-looking men and women, who were using rollers to shift stones down a dugout ramp into the hole for the anchorage foundation. Dust muted the bright colors of their short kilts and breastbands and dulled their skin, and in spite of the cold, sweat had cleared tracks along their muscles.

One of the workers waved to Rasali and she waved back. Kit recalled his name: Mik Rounder, very strong but he needed direction. Had they been lovers? Relationships out here were tangled in ways Kit didn't understand; in the capital such things were more formal and often involved contracts.

Jenner and a small woman knelt, conferring, on the exposed stone floor of the larger pit. When Kit slid down the ladder to join them, the small woman bowed slightly. Her eyes and short hair and skin all seemed to be turning the same iron-gray. "I am Liu Breaker of Hoic. Your specialist."

"Kit Meinem of Atyar. How shall we address this?"

"Your Jenner says you need some of this basalt cleared away, yes?"

Kit nodded.

Liu knelt to run her hand along the pit's floor. "See where the color and texture change along this line? Your Jenner was right: this upthrust of basalt is a problem. Here where the shale is, you can carve out most of the foundation the usual way with drills, picks. But the basalt is too hard to drill." She straightened and brushed dust from her knees. "Have you ever seen explosives used?"

Kit shook his head. "We haven't needed them for any of my projects. I've never been to the mines, either."

"Not much good anywhere else," Liu said, "but very useful for breaking up large amounts of rock. A lot of the blocks you have here were loosed using explosives." She grinned. "You'll like the noise."

"We can't afford to break the bedrock's structural integrity."

"I brought enough powder for a number of small charges. Comparatively small."

"How—"

Liu held up a weathered hand. "I don't need to understand bridges to walk across one. Yes?"

Kit laughed outright. "Yes."

Liu Breaker was right; Kit liked the noise very much. Liu would not allow anyone close to the pit, but even from what she considered a safe distance, behind a huge pile of dirt, the explosion was an immense shattering thing, a crack of thunder that shook the earth. There was a second of echoing silence. The workers, after a collective gasp and some scattered screams, cheered and stamped their feet. A small cloud of mingled smoke and rock-dust eased over the pit's edge, sharp with the smell of saltpeter. The birds were not happy; with the explosion, they burst from their trees and wheeled nervously.

Grinning, Liu climbed from her bunker near the pit, her face dust-caked everywhere but around her eyes, which had been protected by the wooden slit-goggles now hanging around her neck. "So far, so good," she shouted over the ringing in Kit's ears. Seeing his face, she laughed. "These are nothing—gnat sneezes. You should hear when we quarry granite up at Hoic."

Kit was going to speak more with her when he noticed Rasali striding away. He had forgotten she was there; now he followed her, half-shouting to hear himself. "Some noise, yes?"

Rasali whirled. "What are you thinking?" She was shaking and her lips were white. Her voice was very loud.

Taken aback, Kit answered, "We are blowing the foundations." *Rage? Fear?* He wished he could think a little more clearly, but the sound had stunned his wits.

"And making the earth shake! The Big Ones come to thunder, Kit!"

"It wasn't thunder," he said.

"Tell me it wasn't worse!" Tears glittered in her eyes. Her voice was dulled by the echo in his ears. "They will come, I *know* it."

He reached a hand out to her. "It's a tall levee, Rasali. Even if they do, they're not going to come over that." His heart in his chest thrummed. His head was hurting. It was so hard to hear her.

"*No one* knows what they'll do! They used to destroy whole towns, drifting inland on foggy nights. Why do you think they built the levees, a thousand years ago? The Big Ones—"

She stopped shouting, listening. She mouthed something, but Kit could not hear her over the beating in his ears, his heart, his head. He realized suddenly that these were not the after-effects of the explosion; the air itself was beating. He was aware at the edges of his vision of the other workers, every face turned toward the mist. There was nothing to see but the overcast sky. No one moved.

But the sky was moving.

Behind the levee the river mist was rising, dirty gray-gold against the steel-gray of the clouds in a great boiling upheaval, at least a hundred feet high, to be seen over the levee. The mist was seething, breaking open in great swirls and rifts, and everything moving, changing. Kit had seen a great fire once, when a warehouse of linen had burned, and the smoke had poured upward and looked a little like this before it was torn apart by the wind.

Gaps opened in the mountain of mist and closed; and others opened, darker the deeper they were. And through those gaps, in the brown-back shadows at the heart of the mist, was movement.

The gaps closed. After an eternity, the mist slowly smoothed and then settled back, behind the levee, and could no longer be seen. He wasn't really sure when the thrumming of the air blended back into the ringing of his ears.

"Gone," Rasali said with a sound like a sob.

A worker made one of the vivid jokes that come after fear; the others laughed, too loud. A woman ran up the levee and shouted down, "Farside levees are fine; ours are fine." More laughter: people jogged off to Nearside to check on their families.

The back of Kit's hand was burning. A flake of foam had settled and left an irregular mark. "I only saw mist," Kit said. "Was there a Big One?"

Rasali shook herself, stern now but no longer angry or afraid. Kit had learned this about the Ferrys, that their emotions coursed through them and then dissolved. "It was in there. I've seen the mist boil like that before, but never so big. Nothing else could heave it up like that."

"On purpose?"

"Oh, who knows? They're a mystery, the Big Ones." She met his eyes. "I hope your bridge is very high, Kit Meinem of Atyar."

Kit looked to where the mist had been, but there was only sky. "The deck will be two hundred feet above the mist. High enough. I hope."

Liu Breaker walked up to them, rubbing her hands on her leather leggings. "So, *that's* not something that happens at Hoic. *Very* exciting. What do you call that? How do we prevent it next time?"

Rasali looked at the smaller woman for a moment. "I don't think you can. Big Ones come when they come."

Liu said, "They do not always come?"

Rasali shook her head.

"Well, cold comfort is better than no comfort, as my Da says."

Kit rubbed his temples; the headache remained. "We'll continue."

"Then you'll have to be careful," Rasali said. "Or you will kill us all."

"The bridge will save many lives," Kit said. *Yours, eventually.*

Rasali turned on her heel.

Kit did not follow her, not that day. Whether it was because subsequent explosions were smaller ("As small as they can be and still break rock," Liu said), or because they were doing other things, the Big Ones did not return, though fish were plentiful for the three months it took to plan and plant the charges, and break the bedrock.

There was also a Meinem tradition of metalworking, and Meinem reeves, and many Meinems went into fields altogether different; but Kit had known from nearly the beginning that he would be one of the building Meinems. He loved the invisible architecture of construction, looking for a compromise between the vision in his head and the sites, the materials, and the people that would make them real. The challenge was to compromise as little as possible.

Architecture was studied at University. His tutor was a materials specialist, a woman who had directed construction on an incredible twenty-three bridges. Skossa Timt was so old that her skin and hair had faded together to the white of Gani marble, and she walked with a cane she had designed herself, for efficiency. She taught him much. Materials had rules, patterns of behavior: they bent or crumbled or cracked or broke under quantifiable stresses. They strengthened or destroyed one another. Even the best materials in the most efficient combinations did not last forever—she tapped her own forehead with one gnarled finger and laughed—but if he did his work right, they could last a thousand years or more. "But not forever," Skossa said. "Do your best, but don't forget this."

The anchorages and pillars grew. Workers came from towns up and down each bank; and locals, idle or inclined to make money from outside, were hired on the spot. Generally the new people were welcome: they paid for rooms and food and goods of all sorts. The taverns settled in to making double and then triple batches of everything, threw out new wings and stables. Nearside accepted the new people easily, the only fights late at night when people had been drinking and flirting more than they should. Farside had fist fights more frequently, though they decreased steadily as skeptics gave in to the money that flowed into Farside, or to the bridge itself, its pillars too solid to be denied.

Farmers and husbanders sold their fields, and new buildings sprawled out from the towns' hearts. Some were made of wattle and daub, slapped together above stamped-earth floors that still smelled of sheep dung; others, small but permanent, went up more slowly, as the bridge builders laid fieldstones and timber in their evenings and on rest days.

The new people and locals mixed together until it was hard to tell the one from the other, though the older townfolk kept scrupulous track of who truly belonged. For those who sought lovers and friends, the new people were an opportunity to meet someone other than the men and women they had known since childhood. Many met casual lovers, and several term-partnered with new people. There was even a Nearside wedding, between Kes Tiler and a black-eyed builder from far to the south called Jolite Deveren, whatever that meant.

Kit did not have lovers. Working every night until he fell asleep over his paperwork, he didn't miss it much, except late on certain nights when thunderstorms left him restless and unnaturally alert, as if lightning ran under his skin. Some nights he thought of Rasali, wondered whether she was sleeping with someone that night or alone, and wondered if the storm had awakened her, left her restless as well.

Kit saw a fair amount of Rasali when they were both on the same side of the mist. She was clever and calm, and the only person who did not want to talk about the bridge all the time.

Kit did not forget what Rasali said about Valo. Kit had been a young man himself not so many years before, and he remembered what young men and women felt, the hunger to prove themselves against the world. Kit didn't need Valo to accept the bridge—he was scarcely into adulthood and his only influence over the townspeople was based on his work, but Kit liked the youth, who had Rasali's eyes and sometimes her effortless way of moving.

Valo started asking questions, first of the other workers and then of Kit. His boatbuilding experience meant the questions were good ones, and he already designed boats. Kit passed on the first things he had learned as a child on his father's sites, and showed him the manipulation of the immense blocks, and the tricky balance of material and plan; the strength of will that allows a man to direct a thousand people toward a single vision. Valo was too honest not to recognize Kit's mastery, and too competitive not to try and meet Kit on his own ground. He came more often to visit the construction sites.

After a season, Kit took him aside. "You could be a builder, if you wished."

Valo flushed. "Build things? You mean, bridges?"

"Or houses, or granges, or retaining walls. Or bridges. You could make people's lives better."

"Change people's lives?" He frowned suddenly. "No."

"Our lives change all the time, whether we want them to or not," Kit said. "Valo Ferry, you are smart. You are good with people. You learn quickly. If you were interested, I could start teaching you myself, or send you to Atyar to study there."

"Valo Builder . . ." he said, trying it out, then: "No." But after that, whenever he had time free from ferrying or building boats, he was always to be found on the site. Kit knew that the answer would be different the next time he asked. There was for everything a possibility, an invisible pattern that could be made manifest given work and the right materials. Kit wrote to an old friend or two, finding contacts that would help Valo when the time came.

The pillars and anchorages grew. Winter came, and summer, and a second winter. There were falls, a broken arm, two sets of cracked ribs. Someone on Farside had her toes crushed when one of the stones slipped from its rollers and she lost the foot. The bridge was on schedule, even after the delay caused by the slow rock-breaking. There were no problems with payroll or the Department of Roads or Empire, and only minor, manageable issues with the occasionally disruptive representatives from Triple or the local governors.

Kit knew he was lucky.

The first death came during one of Valo's visits.

It was early in the second winter of the bridge, and Kit had been in Farside for three months. He had learned that winter meant gray skies and rain and sometimes snow. Soon they would have to stop the heavy work for the season. Still, it had been a good day, and the workers had lifted and placed almost a hundred stones.

Valo had returned after three weeks at Nearside, building a boat for Jenna Bluefish. Kit found him staring up at the slim tower through a rain so faint it felt like fog. The black opening of the roadway arch looked out of place, halfway up the pillar.

Valo said, "You're a lot farther along since I was here last. How tall now?"

Kit got this question a lot. "A hundred and five feet, more or less. A third finished."

Valo smiled, shook his head. "Hard to believe it'll stay up."

"There's a tower in Atyar, black basalt and iron, five hundred feet. Five times this tall."

"It just looks so delicate," Valo said. "I know what you said, that most of the stress on the pillar is compression, but it still looks as though it'll snap in half."

"After a while, you'll have more experience with suspension bridges and it will seem less. . . . unsettling. Would you like to see the progress?"

Valo's eyes brightened. "May I? I don't want to get in the way."

"I haven't been up yet today, and they'll be finishing up soon. Scaffold or stairwell?"

Valo looked at the scaffolding against one face of the pillar, the ladders tied into place within it, and shivered. "I can't believe people go up that. Stairs, I think."

Kit followed Valo. The steep internal stair was three feet wide and endlessly turning, five steps up and then a platform; turn to the left, and then five more steps and turn. Eventually, the stairs would at need be lit by lanterns set into alcoves at every third turning, but today Kit and Valo felt their way up, fingers trailing along the cold, damp stone, a small lantern in Valo's hand.

The stairwell smelled of water and earth and the thin smell of the burning lamp oil. Some of the workers hated the stairs and preferred the ladders outside, but Kit liked it. For these few moments, he was part of his bridge, a strong bone buried deep in flesh he had created.

They came out at the top and paused a moment to look around the unfinished courses, and the black silhouette of the winch against the dulling sky. The last few workers were breaking down a shear leg, which had been used to move blocks around the pillar. A lantern hung from a pole jammed into one of the holes the laborers would fill with rods and molten iron, later in construction. Kit nodded to them as Valo went to an edge to look down.

"It is wonderful," Valo said, smiling. "Being high like this—you can look right down into people's kitchen yards. Look, Teli Carpenter has a pig smoking."

"You don't need to see it to know that," Kit said dryly. "I've been smelling it for two days."

Valo snorted. "Can you see as far as White Peak yet?"

"On a clear day, yes," Kit said. "I was up here two—"

A heavy sliding sound and a scream; Kit whirled to see one of the workers on her back, one of the shear leg's timbers across her chest. Loreh Tanner, a local. Kit ran the few steps to Loreh and dropped beside her. One man, the man who had been working with her, said, "It slipped—oh Loreh, please hang on," but Kit it was futile. She was pinned to the pillar, chest flattened, one shoulder visibly dislocated, unconscious, her breathing labored. Black foam bloomed from her lips in the lantern's bad light.

Kit took her cold hand. "It's all right, Loreh. It's all right." It was a lie and in any case she could not hear him, but the others would. "Get Hall," one of the workers said, and Kit nodded: Hall was a surgeon. And then, "And get Obal, someone. Where's her husband?" Footsteps ran down the stairs and were lost into the hiss of rain just beginning and someone's crying and Loreh's wet breathing.

Kit glanced up. His chest heaving, Valo stood staring at the body. Kit said to him, "Help find Hall," and when the boy did not move, he repeated it, his voice sharper. Valo said nothing, did not stop looking at Loreh until he spun and ran down the stairs. Kit heard shouting, far below, as the first messenger ran toward the town.

Loreh took a last shuddering breath and died.

Kit looked at the others around Loreh's body. The man holding Loreh's other hand pressed his face against it, crying helplessly. The two other workers left here knelt at her feet, a man and a woman, huddled close though they were not a couple. "Tell me," he said.

"I tried to stop it from hitting her," the woman said. She cradled one arm: obviously broken, though she didn't seem to have noticed. "But it just kept falling."

"She was tired; she must have gotten careless," the man said, and the broken-armed woman said, "I don't want to think about that sound." Words fell from them like blood from a cut.

Kit listened. This was what they needed right now, to speak and to be heard. So he listened, and when the others came, Loreh's husband white-lipped and angry-eyed, and the surgeon Obal and six other workers, Kit listened to them as well, and gradually moved them down through the pillar and back toward the warm lights and comfort of Farside.

Kit had lost people before, and it was always like this. There would be tears tonight, and anger at him and at his bridge, anger at fate for permitting this. There would be sadness, and nightmares. There would be lovemaking, and the holding close of children and friends and dogs—affirmations of life in the cold wet night.

His tutor at University had said, during one of her frequent digressions from the nature of materials and the principles of architecture, "Things will go wrong."

It was winter, but in spite of the falling snow they walked slowly to the coffeehouse, as Skossa looked for purchase for her cane. She continued, "On long projects, you'll forget that you're not one of them. But if there's an accident? You're slapped in the face with it. Whatever you're feeling? Doesn't matter. Guilty, grieving, alone, worried about the schedule. None of it. What matters is *their* feelings. So listen to them. Respect what they're going through."

She paused then, tapped her cane against the ground thoughtfully. "No, I lie. It does matter, but you will have to find your own strength, your own resources elsewhere."

"Friends?" Kit said doubtfully. He knew already that he wanted a career like his father's. He would not be in the same place for more than a few years at a time.

"Yes, friends." Snow collected on Skossa's hair, but she didn't seem to notice. "Kit, I worry about you. You're good with people, I've seen it. You like them. But there's a limit for you." He opened his mouth to protest, but she held up her hand to silence him. "I know. You do care. But inside the framework of a project. Right now it's your studies. Later it'll be roads and bridges. But people around you—their lives go on outside the framework. They're not just tools to your hand, even likable tools. Your life should go on, too. You should have more than roads to live for. Because if something does go wrong, you'll need what *you're* feeling to matter, to someone somewhere, anyway."

Kit walked through Farside toward The Red Lurcher. Most people were home or at one of the taverns by now, a village turned inward; but he heard footsteps running behind him. He turned quickly—it was not unknown for people reeling from a loss to strike at whatever they blamed, and sometimes that was a person.

It was Valo. Though his fists were balled, Kit could tell immediately that he was angry but that he was not looking for a fight. For a moment, Kit wished he didn't need to listen, that he could just go back to his rooms and sleep for a thousand hours; but there was a stricken look in Valo's eyes: Valo, who looked so much like Rasali. He hoped that Rasali and Loreh hadn't been close.

Kit said gently, "Why aren't you inside? It's cold." As he said it, he realized suddenly that it *was* cold; the rain had settled into a steady cold flow.

"I will, I was, I mean, but I came out for a second, because I thought maybe I could find you, because—"

The boy was shivering, too. "Where are your friends? Let's get you inside. It'll be better there."

"No," he said. "I have to know first. It's like this always? If I do this, build things, it'll happen for me? Someone will die?"

"It might. It probably will, eventually."

Valo said an unexpected thing. "I see. It's just that she had just gotten married."

The blood on Loreh's lips, the wet sound of her crushed chest as she took her last breaths—"Yes," Kit said. "She was."

"I just . . . I had to know if I need to ready for this." It seemed callous, but Ferrys were used to dying, to death. "I guess I'll find out."

"I hope you don't have to." The rain was getting heavier. "You should be inside, Valo."

Valo nodded. "Rasali—I wish she were here. She could help maybe. You should go in, too. You're shivering."

Kit watched him go. Valo had not invited him to accompany him back into the light and the warmth; he knew better than to expect that, but for a moment he had permitted himself to hope otherwise.

Kit slipped through the stables and through the back door at The Bitch. Wisdon Innkeep, hands full of mugs for the taproom, saw him and nodded, face unsmiling but not hostile. That was good, Kit thought: as good as it would get, tonight.

He entered his room and shut the door, leaned his back to it as if holding the world out. Someone had already been in his room: a lamp had been lit against the darkness, a fire laid, and bread and cheese and a tankard of ale set by the window to stay cool.

He began to cry.

The news went across the river by signal flags. No one worked on the bridge the next day, or the day after that. Kit did all the right things, letting his grief and guilt overwhelm him only when he was alone, huddled in front of the fire in his room.

The third day, Rasali arrived from Nearside with a boat filled with crates of northland herbs on their way east. Kit was sitting in The Bitch's taproom, listening. People were coping, starting to look forward again. They should be able to get back to it soon, the next clear day. He would offer them something that would be an immediate, visible accomplishment, something different, perhaps guidelining the ramp.

He didn't see Rasali come into the taproom; only felt her hand on his shoulder and heard her voice in his ear. "Come with me," she murmured.

He looked up puzzled, as though she was a stranger. "Rasali Ferry, why are you here?"

She said only, "Come for a walk, Kit."

It was raining, but he accompanied her anyway, pulling a scarf over his head when the first cold drops hit his face.

She said nothing as they splashed through Farside. She was leading him somewhere, but he didn't care where, grateful not to have to be the decisive one, the strong one. After a time, she opened a door and led him through it into a small room filled with light and warmth.

"My house," she said. "And Valo's. He's still at the boatyard. Sit."

She pointed and Kit dropped onto the settle beside the fire. Rasali swiveled a pot hanging from a bracket out of the fire and ladled something out. She handed a mug to him and sat. "So. Drink."

It was spiced porter, and the warmth eased into the tightness in his chest. "Thank you."

"Talk."

"This is such a loss for you all, I know," he said. "Did you know Loreh well?"

She shook her head. "This is not for me, this is for you. Tell me."

"I'm fine," he said, and when she didn't say anything, he repeated, with a flicker of anger: "I'm *fine*, Rasali. I can handle this."

"Probably you can," Rasali said. "But you're not fine. She died, and it was your bridge she died for. You don't feel responsible? I don't believe it."

"Of course I feel responsible," he snapped.

The fire cast gold light across her broad cheekbones when she turned her face to him, but to his surprise she said nothing, only looked at him and waited.

"She's not the first," Kit said, surprising himself. "The first project I had sole charge of, a tollgate. Such a little project, such a dumb little project to lose someone on. The wood frame for the passageway collapsed before we got the keystone in. The whole arch came down. Someone got killed." It had been a very young man, slim and tall, with a limp. He was raising his little sister; she hadn't been more than ten. Running loose in the fields around the site, she had missed the collapse, the boy's death. Dafuen? Naus? He couldn't remember his name. And the girl—what had her name been? *I should remember. I owe that much to them.*

"Every time I lose someone," he said at last, "I remember the others. There've been twelve, in twenty-three years. Not so many, considering. Building's dangerous. My record's better than most."

"But it doesn't matter, does it?" she said. "You still feel you killed each one of them, as surely as if you'd thrown them off a bridge yourself."

"It's my responsibility. The first one, Duar—" *That* had been his name; there it was. The name loosened something in Kit. His face warmed: tears, hot tears running down his face.

"It's all right," she said. She held him until he stopped crying.

"How did you know?" he said finally.

"I am the eldest surviving member of the Ferry family," she said. "My aunt died seven years ago. And then I watched my brother leave to cross the mist, three years ago now. It was a perfect day, calm and sunny, but he never made it. He went instead of me because on that day the river felt wrong to me. It could have been me. It should have, maybe. So I understand."

She stretched a little. "Not that most people don't. If Petro Housewright sends his daughter to select timber in the mountains, and she doesn't come back—eaten by wolves, struck by lightning, I don't know—is Petro to blame? It's probably the wolves or the lightning. Maybe it's the daughter, if she did something stupid. And it *is* Petro, a little; she wouldn't have been there at all if he hadn't sent her. And it's her mother for being fearless and teaching that to her daughter; and Thorn Green for wanting a new room to his house. Everyone, except maybe the wolves, feels at least a little responsible. This path leads nowhere. Loreh would have died sooner or later." Rasali added softly, "We all do."

"Can you accept death so readily?" he asked. "Yours, even?"

She leaned back, her face suddenly weary. "What else can I do, Kit? Someone must ferry, and I am better suited than most—and by more than my blood. I love the mist, its currents and the smell of it and the power in my body as I push us all through. Petro's daughter—she did not want to die when the wolves came, I'm sure; but she loved selecting timber."

"If it comes for you?" he said softly. "Would you be so sanguine then?"

She laughed, and the pensiveness was gone. "No, indeed. I will curse the stars and go down fighting. But it will still have been a wonderful thing, to cross the mist."

At University, Kit's relationships had all been casual. There were lectures that everyone attended, and he lived near streets and pubs crowded with students; but the physical students had a tradition of keeping to themselves that was rooted in the personal preferences of their predecessors, and in their own. The only people who worked harder than the engineers were the ale-makers, the University joke went. Kit and the other physical students talked and drank and roomed and slept together.

In his third year, he met Domhu Canna at the arcade where he bought vellums and paper: a small woman with a heart-shaped face and hair in black clouds she kept somewhat confined by gray ribands. She was a philosophical student from a city two thousand miles to the east, on the coast.

He was fascinated. Her mind was abrupt and fish-quick and made connections he didn't understand. To her, everything was a metaphor, a symbol for something else. People, she said, could be better understood by comparing their lives to animals, to the seasons, to the structure of certain lyrical songs, to a gambling game.

This was another form of pattern-making, he saw. Perhaps people were like teamed oxen to be led, or like metals to be smelted and shaped to one's purpose; or as the stones for a dry-laid wall, which had to be carefully selected for shape and strength, and sorted, and placed. This last suited him best. What held them together was no external mortar but their own weight, and the planning and patience of the drystone builder. But it was an inadequate metaphor: people were this, but they were all the other things, as well.

He never understood what Domhu found attractive in him. They never talked about regularizing their relationship. When her studies were done halfway through his final year, she returned to her city to help found a new university, and in any case her people did not enter into term marriages. They separated amicably, and with a sense of loss on his part at least; but it did not occur to him until years later that things might have been different.

The winter was rainy, but there were days they could work, and they did. By spring, there had been other deaths unrelated to the bridge on both banks: a woman who died in childbirth, a child who had never breathed properly in his short life; two fisherfolk lost when they capsized; several who died for the various reasons that old or sick people died.

Over the spring and summer they finished the anchorages, featureless masses of blocks and mortar anchored to the bedrock. They were buried so that only a few courses of stone showed above the ground. The anchoring bolts were each tall as a man, hidden safely behind the portals through which the chains would pass.

The Farside pillar was finished by midwinter of the third year, well before the Nearside tower. Jenner and Teniant Planner had perfected a signal system that allowed detailed technical information to pass between the banks, and documents traveled each time a ferry crossed. Rasali made sixty-eight trips back and forth; though he spent much of his time with Kit, Valo made twenty. Kit did not cross the mist at all unless the flags told him he must.

It was early spring and Kit was in Farside when the signals went up: *Message. Imperial seal.*

He went to Rasali at once.

"I can't go," she said. "I just got here yesterday. The Big Ones—"

"I have to get across, and Valo's on Nearside. There's news from the capital."

"News has always waited before."

"No, it hasn't. You forced it to, but news waited restlessly, pacing along the levee until we could pick it up."

"Use the flags," she said, a little impatiently.

"They can't be broken by anyone but me or Jenner. He's over here. I'm sorry," he said, thinking of her brother, dead four years before.

"If you die no one can read it, either," she said, but they left just after dusk anyway. "If we must go, better then than earlier or later," she said.

He met her at the upper dock at dusk. The sky was streaked with bright bands of green and gold, clouds catching the last of the sun, but they radiated no light, themselves just reflections. The current down the river was steady. And light. The mist between the levees was already in shadow, shaped into smooth dunes twenty feet high.

Rasali waited silently, coiling and uncoiling a rope in her hands; beside her stood two women and a dog: dealers in spices returning from the plantations of Gloth, the dog whining and restless. Kit was burdened with document cases filled with vellum and paper, rolled tightly and wrapped in oilcloth. Rasali seated the merchants and their dog in the ferry's bow, then untied and pushed off in silence. Kit sat near her.

She stood at the stern, braced against the scull. For a moment he could pretend that this was water they moved on and he half-expected to hear sloshing; but the big paddle made no noise. It was so silent that he could hear her breath, the dog's nervous panting aft, and his own pulse, too fast. Then the *Crossing* slid up the long slope of a mist dune and there was no possibility that this could be anything but mist.

He heard a soft sighing, like air entering a once-sealed bottle. It was hard to see so far, but the lingering light showed him a heaving of the mist on the face of a neighboring dune, like a bubble coming to the surface of hot mud. The dome grew and then burst. There was a gasp from one of the women. A shape rolled away, too dark for Kit to see more than its length.

"What—" he said in wonder.

"Fish," Rasali breathed to Kit. "Not small ones. They are biting tonight. We should not have come."

It was night now; the first tiny moon appeared, scarcely brighter than a star, followed by other stars. Rasali oared gently across through the dunes, face turned to the sky. At first he thought she was praying, then realized she was navigating. There were more fish now, and each time the sighing sound, the dark shape half-seen. He heard someone singing, the voice carrying somehow to them, from far behind.

"The fishers," Rasali said. "They will stay close to the levees tonight. I wish. . . ."

But she left the wish unspoken. They were over the deep mist now. He could not say how he knew this. He had a sudden vision of the bridge overhead, a black span bisecting the star-spun sky, the parabolic arch of the chains perhaps visible, perhaps not. People would stride across the river, an arrow's flight overhead, unaware of this place beneath. Perhaps they would stop and look over the bridge's railings, but they would be too high to see the fish as any but small shadows, supposing they saw them at all, supposing they stopped at all. The Big Ones would be novelties, weird creatures that caused a safe little shiver, like hearing a frightening story late at night.

Perhaps Rasali saw the same thing, for she said suddenly, "Your bridge. It will change all this."

"It must. I am sorry," he said again. "We are not meant to be here, on mist."

"We are not meant to cross this without passing through it. Kit—" Rasali said, as if starting a sentence, and then fell silent. After a moment she began to speak again, her voice low, as if she were speaking to herself. "The soul often hangs in a balance of some sort: tonight, do I lie down in the high fields with Dirk Tanner or not? At the fair, do I buy ribbons or wine? For the new ferry's headboard, do I use camphor or pearwood? Small things, right? A kiss, a ribbon, a grain that coaxes the knife this way or that. They are not, Kit Meinem of Atyar. Our souls wait for our answer, because any answer changes us. This is why I wait to decide what I feel about your bridge. I'm waiting until I know how I will be changed."

"You can never know how things will change you," Kit said.

"If you don't, you have not waited to find out." There was a popping noise barely a stone's throw to starboard. "Quiet."

On they moved. In daylight, Kit knew, the trip took less than an hour; now it seemed much longer. Perhaps it was; he looked up at the stars and thought they had moved, but perhaps not.

His teeth were clenched, as were all his muscles. When he tried to relax them, he realized it was not fear that cramped him, but something else, something outside him. He heard Rasali falter. "No. . . ."

He recognized it now, the sound that was not a sound, like the lowest pipes on an organ, a drone so low that he couldn't hear it, one that turned his bones to liquid and his muscles to flaked and rusting iron. His breath labored from his chest in grunts. His head thrummed. Moving as though through honey, he strained his hands to his head, cradling it. He could not see Rasali except as a gloom against the slightly less gloom of the mist, but he heard her pant, tiny pain-filled breaths, like an injured dog.

The thrumming in his body pounded at his bones now, dissolving them. He wanted to cry out, but there was no air left in his lungs. He realized suddenly that something beneath them was raising itself into a mound. Mist piled at the boat's sides. *I never got to finish the bridge,* he thought. *And I never kissed her.* Did Rasali have any regrets?

The mound roiled and became a hill, which became a mountain obscuring part of the sky. The crest melted into curls of mist, and there was a shape inside, large and dark as night itself, slid, and followed the collapsing. It seemed still, but he knew that was only because of the size of the thing, that it took ages for its full length to pass. That was all he saw before his eyes slipped shut.

How long he lay there in the bottom of the boat, he didn't know. At some point, he realized he was there; some time later he found he could move again, his bones and muscles back to what they should be. The dog was barking. "Rasali?" he said shakily. "Are we sinking?"

"Kit." Her voice was a thread. "You're still alive. I thought we were dead."

"That was a Big One?"

"I don't know. No one has ever seen one. Maybe it was just a Fairly Large One."

The old joke. Kit choked on a weak laugh.

"Shit," Rasali said in the darkness. "I dropped the oar."

"Now what?" he said.

"I have a spare, but it's going to take longer and we'll land in the wrong place. We'll have to tie off and then walk up to get help."

I'm alive, he did not say. *I can walk a thousand miles tonight.*

It was nearly dawn before they got to Nearside. The two big moons rose just before they landed, a mile south of the dock. The spice traders and their dog went on ahead while Kit and Rasali secured the boat. They walked up together. Halfway home, Valo came down at a dead run.

"I was waiting, and you didn't come—" He was pale and panting. "But they told me, the other passengers, that you made it, and—"

"Valo." Rasali hugged him and held him hard. "We're safe, little one. We're here. It's done."

"I thought. . . ." he said.

"I know," she said. "Valo, please, I am so tired. Can you get the *Crossing* up to the dock? I am going to my house, and I will sleep for a day, and I don't care if the Empress herself is tapping her foot, it's going to wait." She released Valo, saluted Kit with a weary smile, and walked up the flank of the levee. Kit watched her leave.

The "Imperial seal" was a letter from Atyar, some underling arrogating authority and asking for clarification on a set of numbers Kit had sent–scarcely worth the trip at any time, let alone across mist on a bad night. Kit cursed the capital and Empire and then sent the information, along with a tautly worded paragraph about seals and their appropriate use.

Two days later, he got news that would have brought him across the mist in any case: the caravan carrying the first eyebar and bolts was twelve miles out on the Hoic Mine Road. Kit and his ironmaster Tandreve Smith rode out to meet the wagons as they crept southward, and found them easing down a gradual slope near Oud village. The carts were long and built strong, their contents covered, each pulled by a team of tough-legged oxen with patient expressions. The movement was slow, and drivers walked beside them, singing something unfamiliar to Kit's city-bred ears.

"Ox-tunes. We used to sing these at my aunt's farm," Tandreve said, and sang:

"Remember last night's dream,
the sweet cold grass, the lonely cows.
You had your bollocks then."

Tandreve chuckled, and Kit with her.

One of the drivers wandered over as Kit pulled his horse to a stop. Unattended, her team moved forward anyway. "Folks," she said, and nodded. A taciturn woman.

Kit swung down from the saddle. "These are the chains?"

"You're from the bridge?"

"Kit Meinem of Atyar."

The woman nodded again. "Berallit Red-Ox of Ilver. Your smiths are sitting on the tail of the last wagon."

One of the smiths, a rangy man with singed eyebrows, loped forward to meet them, and introduced himself as Jared Toss of Little Hoic. They walked beside the carts as they talked, and he threw aside a tarp to show Kit what thy carried: stacks of iron eyebars, each a rod ten feet long with eyes at each end. Tandreve walked sideways as she inspected the eyebars; she and Jared soon lost themselves in a technical discussion, while Kit kept them company, leading Tandreve's forgotten horse and his own, content for the moment to let the masters talk it out. He moved a little forward until he was abreast of the oxen. *Remember last night's dream,* he thought, and then: *I wonder what Rasali dreamt?*

After that night on the mist, Rasali seemed to have no bad days. She took people the day after they arrived, no matter what the weather or the mist's character. The tavern keepers grumbled at this a bit, but the decrease in time each visitor stayed in town was made up for by the increase in numbers of serious-eyed men and women sent by firms in Atyar to establish offices in the towns on the river's far side. It made things easier for the bridge, as well, since Kit and others could move back and forth as needed. Kit remained reluctant, more so since the near-miss.

There was enough business for two boats, and Valo volunteered to ferry more often, but Rasali refused the help, allowing him to ferry only when she couldn't prevent it. "The Big Ones don't seem to care about me this winter," she said to him, "but I can't say they would feel the same about tender meat like you." With Kit she was more honest. "If he is to leave ferrying, to go study in the capital maybe, it's best sooner than later. Mist will be dangerous until the last ferry crosses it. And even then, even after your bridge is done."

It was Rasali only who seemed to have this protection; the fishing people had as many problems as in any year. Denis Redboat lost his coracle when it was rammed ("By a Medium-Large One," he laughed in the tavern later: sometimes the oldest jokes were the best), though he was fished out by a nearby boat before he had sunk too deep. The rash was only superficial, but his hair grew back only in patches.

Kit sat in the crowded beer garden of The Deer's Heart, watching Rasali and Valo build a little pinewood skiff in the boatyard next door. Valo had called out a greeting when Kit first sat down, and Rasali turned her head to smile at him, but after that they ignored him. Some of the locals stopped by to greet him, and the barman stayed for some time, telling him about the ominous yet unchanging ache in his back; but for most of the afternoon, Kit was alone in the sun, drinking cellar-cool porter and watching the boat take shape.

In the midsummer of the fourth year, it was rare for Kit to have the afternoon of a beautiful day to himself. The anchorages had been finished for some months. So had the rubble-fill ramps that led to the arched passages through each pillar, but the pillars themselves had taken longer, and the granite saddles that would support the chains over the towers had only just been put in place.

They were only slightly behind on Kit's deadlines for most of the materials. More than a thousand of the eyebars and bolts for the chains were laid out in rows, the iron smelling of the linseed oil used to protect them during transit. More were expected in before winter. Close to the ramps were the many fish-skin ropes and cables that would be needed to bring the first chain across the gap. They were irreplaceable, probably the most valuable thing on the work sites, and were treated accordingly, and were kept in closed tents that reeked.

Kit's high-work specialists were here, too: the men and women who would do the first perilous tasks, mostly experts who had worked on other big spans or the towers of Atyar.

But everything waited on Rasali, and in the meantime, Kit was content to sit and watch her work.

Valo and Rasali were not alone in the boatyard. Rasali had sent to the ferry folk of Ubmie, a hundred miles to the south, and they had arrived a few days before: a woman and her cousin, Chell and Lan Crosser. The strangers had the same massive shoulders and good looks the Ferrys had, but they shared a faraway expression of their own; the river was broader at Ubmie, deeper, so perhaps death was closer to them. Kit wondered what they thought of his task—the bridge would cut into ferry trade for many hundreds of miles on either side, and Ubmie had been reviewed as a possible site for the bridge—but they must not have resented it or they would not be here.

Everything waited on the ferry folk: the next major task was to bring the lines across the river to connect the piers—fabricating the chains required temporary cables and catwalks to be there first—but this could not be rushed: Rasali, Valo, and the Crossers all needed to feel at the same time that it was safe to cross. Kit tried not to be impatient, and in any case he had plenty to do—items to add to lists, formal reports and polite updates to send to the many interested parties in Atyar and in Triple, instructions to pass on to the rope-makers, the masons, the road builders, the exchequer. And Jenner: Kit had written to the capital and the Department of Roads was offering Jenner the lead on the second bridge across the river, to be built a few hundred miles to the north. Kit was to deliver the cartel the next time they were on the same side, but he was grateful the officials had agreed to leave Jenner with him until the first chain on this bridge was in place.

He pushed all this from his mind. *Later,* he said to the things, half-apologetically; *I'll deal with you later. For now, just let me sit in the sun and watch other people work.*

The sun slanted peach-gold through the oak's leaves before Rasali and Valo finished for the day. The skiff was finished, an elegant tiny curve of pale wood and dying sunlight. Kit leaned against the fence as they threw a cup of water over its bow and then drew it into the shadows of the boathouse. Valo took off at a run—*so much energy, even after a long day*; ah, youth—as Rasali walked to the fence and leaned on it from her side.

"It's beautiful," he said.

She rolled her neck. "I know. We make good boats. Are you hungry? Your busy afternoon must have raised an appetite."

He had to laugh. "We finished the pillar—laid the capstone this morning. I *am* hungry."

"Come on, then. Thalla will feed us all."

Dinner was simple. The Deer's Heart was better known for its beers than its foods, but the stew Thalla served was savory with chervil, and thick enough to stand a spoon in. Valo had friends to be with, so they ate with Chell and Lan, who were as light-hearted as Rasali. At dusk, the Crossers left to explore the Nearside taverns, leaving Kit and Rasali to watch heat lightning in the west. The air was thick and warm, soft as wool on their skin.

"You never come up to the work sites on either side," Kit said suddenly, after a comfortable, slightly drunken silence. He inspected his earthenware mug, empty except for the smell of yeast.

Rasali had given up on the benches, and sat instead on one of the garden tables. She leaned back until she lay supine, face toward the sky. "I've been busy, perhaps you noticed?"

"It's more than that. Everyone finds time, here and there. And you used to."

She laughed. "I did, didn't I? I just haven't seen the point, lately. The bridge changes everything, but I don't see yet how it changes me. So I wait until it's time. Perhaps it's like the mist."

"What about now?"

She rolled her head until her cheek lay against the rough wood of the tabletop: looking at him, he could tell, though her eyes were hidden in shadows. What did she see, he wondered: what was she hoping to see? It pleased him, but made him nervous.

"Come to the tower, now, tonight," he said. "Soon everything changes. We pull the ropes across, and make the chains, and hang the supports, and lay the road—everything changes then, it stops being a project and becomes a bridge, a road. But tonight, it's still just two towers and a bunch of plans. Rasali, climb it with me. I can't describe what it's like up there—the wind, the sky all around you, the river." He flushed at the urgency in his voice. When she remained silent, he added, "You change whether you wait for it or not."

"There's lightning," she said.

"It runs from cloud to cloud," he said. "Not to earth."

"Heat lightning." She sat up suddenly, nodded. "So show me this place."

The work site was abandoned. The sky overhead had filled with clouds lit from within by the lightning, which was worse than no light at all, since it ruined their night vision. They staggered across the site, trying to plan their paths in the moments of light, doggedly moving through the darkness. "Shit," Rasali said suddenly in the darkness, then: "Tripped over something or other." Kit found himself laughing for no apparent reason.

They took the internal stairs instead of the scaffold that still leaned against the pillar's north wall. Kit knew them thoroughly, knew every irregular turn and riser; he counted them aloud to Rasali as he led her by the hand. They reached one hundred and ninety four before they saw light from a flash of lightning overhead, two hundred and eighteen when they finally stepped onto the roof, gasping for air.

They were not alone. A woman squealed; she and the man with her grabbed clothes and blankets and bolted with their lamp naked and laughing down the stairs. Rasali said with satisfaction, "Sera Oakfield. That was Erno Bridgeman with her."

"He took his name from the bridge?" Kit asked, but Rasali said only, "Oh," in a child's voice. Silent lightning painted the sky over her head in sudden strokes of purple-white: layers of cloud glowing or dark.

"It's so much closer." She looked about her, walked to the edge, and looked down at Nearside. Dull gold light poured from doors open to the heavy air. Kit stayed where he was, content to watch her. The light (when there was light) was shadowless, and her face looked young and full of wonder. After a time, she walked to his side.

They said nothing, only kissed and then made love in a nest of their discarded clothes. Kit felt the stone of his bridge against his knees, his back, still warm as skin from the day's heat. Rasali was softer than the rocks and tasted sweet.

A feeling he could not have described cracked open his chest, his throat, his belly. It had been a long time since he had been with a woman, not met his own needs; he had nearly forgotten the delight of it, the sharp sweet shock of his release, the rocking ocean of hers. Even their awkwardness made him glad, because it held in it the possibility of doing this again, and better.

When they were done, they talked. "You know my goal, to build this bridge," Kit looked down at her face, there and gone, in the flickering of the lightning. "But I do not know yours."

Rasali laughed softly. "Yet you have seen me succeed a thousand times, and fail a few. I wish to live well, each day."

"That's not a goal," Kit said.

"Why? Because it's not yours? Which is better, Kit Meinem of Atyar? A single great victory, or a thousand small ones?" And then: "Tomorrow," Rasali said. "We will take the rope across tomorrow."

"You're sure?" Kit asked.

"That's a strange statement coming from you. The bridge is all about crossing being a certainty, yes? Like the sun coming up each morning? We agreed this afternoon. It's time."

Dawn came early, with the innkeeper's preemptory rap on the door. Kit woke disoriented, tangled in the sheets of his little cupboard bed. After he and Rasali had come down from the pillar, Rasali to sleep and Kit to do everything that needed to happen the night before the rope was brought across, all in the few hours left of the night. His skin smelled of Rasali, but, stunned with lack of sleep, he had trouble believing their lovemaking had been real. But there was stone dust ground into his skin; he smiled and, though it was high summer, sang a spring song from Atyar as he quickly washed and dressed. He drank a bowl filled with broth in the taproom. It was tangy, lukewarm. A single small water fish stared up at him from a salted eye. Kit left the fish, and left the inn.

The clouds and the lightning were gone; early as it was the sky was already pale and hot. The news was everyone, and the entire town, or so it seemed, drifted with Kit to the work site, and then flowed over the levee and down to the bank.

The river was a blinding creamy ribbon high between the two banks, looking just it had the first time he had seen it, and for a minute he felt dislocated in time. High mist was seen as a good omen, and though he did not believe in omens, he was nevertheless glad. There was a crowd collected on the Farside levee, as well, though he couldn't see details, only the movement like gnats in the sky at dusk. The signal towers' flags hung limp against the hot blue-white sky.

Kit walked down to Rasali's boat, nearly hidden in its own tight circle of watchers. As Kit approached, Valo called, "Hey, Kit!" Rasali looked up. Her smile was like welcome shade on a bright day. The circle opened to accept him.

"Greetings, Valo Ferry of Farside, Rasali Ferry of Farside," he said. When he was close enough, he clasped Rasali's hands in his own, loving their warmth despite the day's heat.

"Kit." She kissed his mouth, to a handful of muffled hoots and cheers from the bystanders and a surprised noise from Valo. She tasted like chicory.

Daell Cabler nodded absently to Kit. She was the lead rope-maker. Now she, her husband, Stiwan, and the journeymen and masters they had drawn to them, were inspecting the hundreds of fathoms of plaited fish-skin cord, loading them without twists onto spools three feet across, and loading those onto a wooden frame bolted to the *Tranquil Crossing*.

The rope was thin, not much more than a cord, narrower than Kit's smallest finger. It looked fragile, nothing like strong enough to carry its own weight for a quarter of a mile, though the tests said otherwise.

Several of the stronger people from the bridge handed down small heavy crates to Valo and Chell Crosser in the bow. Silverwork from Hedeclin, and copper in bricks: the ferry was to be weighted somewhat forward, which would make the first part of the crossing more difficult but should help with the end of it, as the cord paid out and took on weight from the mist.

"—We think, anyway," Valo had said, two months back when he and Rasali had discussed the plan with Kit. "But we don't know; no one's done this before." Kit had nodded, and not for the first time wished that the river had been a little less broad. Upriver, perhaps; but no, this had been the only option. He did write to an old classmate back in Atyar, a man who now taught the calculus, and presented their solution. His friend had written back to say that it looked as though it ought to work, but that he knew little of mist.

One end of the rope snaked along the ground and up the levee. Though it would do no harm, no one touched the rope, or even approached it, but left a narrow lane for it, and stepped only carefully over it. Now Daell and Stivvan Cabler followed the lane back, up, and over the levee: checking the rope and temporary anchor at the Nearside pillar's base.

There was a wait. People sat on the grass, or walked back to watch the Cablers. Someone brought cool broth and small beer from the fishers' tavern. Valo and Rasali and the two strangers, remote, focused already on what came next.

And for himself? Kit was wound up, but it wouldn't do to show anything but a calm confident front. He walked among the watchers, exchanged words or a smile with each of them. He knew them all by now, even the children.

It was nearly midmorning before Daell and Stiwan returned. The ferry folk took their positions, two to each side, far enough apart that they could pull on different rhythms. Kit was useless freight until they got to the other side, so he sat at the bow of the *Crossing*, where his weight might do some good. Uni stumbled as she was helped into the boat's stern: she would monitor the rope, but, as she told them all, she was nervous; she had never crossed the mist before this. "I think I'll wait 'til the catwalks go up before I return," she added. "Stivvan can sleep without me 'til then."

"Ready, Kit?" Rasali called forward.

"Yes," he said.

"Daell? Lan? Chell? Valo?" Assent all around.

"An historic moment," Valo announced: "The day the mist was bridged."

"Make yourself useful, boy," Rasali said. "Prepare to scull."

"Right," Valo said.

"Push us off," she said to the people on the dock. A cheer went up.

The dock and all the noises behind them disappeared almost immediately. The ferry folk had been right that it was a good day for such an undertaking; the mist was a smooth series of ripples no taller than a man, and so thick that the *Crossing* rode high despite the extra weight and drag. It was the gentlest he had ever seen the river.

Kit's eyes ached from the brightness. "It will work?" Kit said, meaning the rope and their trip across the mist and the bridge itself—a question rather than a statement; unable to help himself, though he had worked calculations himself, had Daell and Stiwan and Valo and a specialist in Atyar all double-check them, though it was a child's question. Isolated in the mist, even competence seemed tentative.

"Yes," Daell Cabler said, from aft.

The rowers said little. At one point, Rasali murmured into the deadened air, "To the right," and Valo and Lan Crosser changed their stroke to avoid a gentle mound a few feet high directly in their path. Mostly the *Crossing* slid steadily across the regular swells. Unlike his other trips, Kit saw no dark shapes in the mist, large or small.

There was nothing he could do to help, so Kit watched Rasali scull in the blazing sun. The work got harder as the rope spooled out until she and the others panted with each breath. Shining with sweat, her skin was nearly as bright as the mist in the sunlight. He wondered how she could bear the light without burning. Her face looked solemn, intent on the eastern shore. They could not see the dock, but the levee was scattered with Farsiders, waiting for the work they would do when the ferry landed. Her eyes were alight with reflections from the mist. Then he recognized the expression, the light. They were not concern, or reflections: they were joy.

How will she bear it, he thought suddenly, *when there is no more ferrying to be done?* He had known that she loved what she did, but he had never realized just how much. He felt as though he had been kicked in the stomach. What would it do to her? His bridge would destroy this thing that she loved, that gave her name. How could he not have thought of that? "Rasali," he said, unable to stay silent.

"Not now," she said. The rowers panted as they dug in.

"It's like . . . pulling through dirt," Valo gasped.

"Quiet," Rasali snapped, and then they were silent except for their laboring breath. Kit's own muscles knotted sympathetically. Foot by foot, the ferry heaved forward. At some point they were close enough to the Farside upper dock that someone could throw a rope to Kit and at last he could do something, however inadequate; he took the rope and pulled. The rowers dug in for their final strokes, and the boat slid up beside the dock. People swarmed aboard, securing the boat to the dock, the rope to a temporary anchor onshore.

Released, the Ferrys and the Crossers embraced, laughing a little dizzily. They walked up the levee toward Farside town and did not look back.

Kit left the ferry to join Jenner Ellar.

It was hard work. The rope's end had to be brought over an oiled stone saddle on the levee and down to a temporary anchor and capstan at the Farside pillar's base, a task that involved driving a team of oxen through the gap Jenner had cut into the levee: a risk, but one that had to be taken.

More oxen were harnessed to the capstan. Daell Cabler was still pale and shaking from the crossing, but after a glass of something cool and dark, she and her Farside counterparts could walk the rope to look for any new weak spots, and found none. Jenner stayed at the capstan, but Daell and Kit returned to the temporary saddle in the levee, the notch polished like glass and gleaming with oil.

The rope was released from the dockside anchor. The rope over the saddle whined as it took the load and flattened, and there was a deep pinging noise as it swung out to make a single straight line, down from the saddle, down into the mist. The oxen at the capstan dug in.

The next hours were the tensest of Kit's life. For a time, the rope did not appear to change. The capstan moaned and clicked, and at last the rope slid by inches, by feet, through the saddle. He could do nothing but watch and yet again rework all the calculations in his mind. He did not see Rasali, but Valo came up after a time to watch the progress. Answering his questions settled Kit's nerves. The calculations were correct. He had done this before. He was suddenly starved and voraciously ate the food that Valo had brought for him. How long had it been since the broth at The Fish? Hours; most of a day.

The oxen puffed and grunted, and were replaced with new teams. Even lubricated and with leather sleeves, the rope moved reluctantly across the saddle, but it did move. And then the pressure started to ease and the rope paid through the saddle faster. The sun was westering when at last the rope lifted free. By dusk, the rope was sixty feet above the mist, stretched humming-tight between the Farside and Nearside levees and the temporary anchors.

Just before dark, Kit saw the flags go up on the signal tower: *secure*.

Kit worked on and then seconded projects for five years after he left University. His father knew men and women at the higher levels in the Department of Roads, and his old tutor, Skossa Timt, knew more, so many were high-profile works, but he loved all of them, even his first lead, the little tollgate where the boy, Duar, had died.

All public work—drainage schemes, roadwork, amphitheaters, public squares, sewers, alleys, and mews—was alchemy. It took the invisible patterns that people made as they lived and turned them into real things, stone and brick and wood and space. Kit built things that moved people through the invisible architecture that was his mind, and his notion—and Empire's notion—of how their lives could be better.

The first major project he led was a replacement for a collapsed bridge in the Four Peaks region north of Atyar. The original had also been a chain suspension bridge but much smaller than the mist bridge, crossing only a hundred yards, its pillars only forty feet high. With maintenance, it had survived heavy use for three centuries, shuddering under the carts that brought quicksilver ore down to the smelting village of Oncalion; but after the heavy snowfalls of what was subsequently called the Wolf Winter, one of the gorge's walls collapsed, taking the north pillar with it and leaving nowhere stable to rebuild. It was easier to start over, two hundred yards upstream.

The people of Oncalion were not genial. Hard work made for hard men and women. There was a grim, desperate edge to their willingness to labor on the bridge, because their livelihood and their lives were dependent on the mine. They had to be stopped at the end of each day or, dangerous as it was, they would work through moonlit nights.

But it was lonely work, even for Kit, who did not mind solitude; and when the snows of the first winter brought a halt to construction, he returned with some relief to Atyar, to stay with his father. Davell Meinem was old now. His memory was weakening though still strong enough; and he spent his days constructing a vast and fabulous public maze of dry-laid stones brought from all over Empire: his final project, he said to Kit, an accurate prophecy. Skossa Timt had died during the hard cold of the Wolf Winter, but many of his classmates were in the capital. Kit spent evenings with them, attended lectures and concerts, entering for the season into a casual relationship with an architect who specialized in waterworks.

Kit returned to the site at Oncalion as soon as the roads cleared. In his absence, through the snows and melt-off, the people of Oncalion had continued to work, laying course after course of stone in the bitter cold. The work had to be redone.

The second summer, they worked every day and moonlit nights, and Kit worked beside them.

Kit counted the bridge as a failure, although it was coming in barely over budget and only a couple of months late, and no one had died. It was an ugly design; the people of Oncalion had worked hard but joylessly; and there was all his dissatisfaction and guilt about the work that had to be redone.

Perhaps there was something in the tone of his letters to his father, for there came a day in early autumn that Davell Meinem arrived in Oncalion, riding a sturdy mountain horse and accompanied by a journeyman who vanished immediately into one of the village's three taverns. It was mid-afternoon.

"I want to see this bridge of yours," Davell said. He looked weary, but straight-backed as ever. "Show it to me."

"We'll go tomorrow," Kit said. "You must be tired."

"Now," Davell said.

They walked up from the village together: a cool day, and bright, though the road was overshadowed with pines and fir trees. Basalt outcroppings were stained dark green and black with lichens. His father moved slowly, pausing often for breath. They met a steady trickle of local people leading heavy-laden ponies. The roadbed across the bridge wasn't quite complete, but ponies could cross carrying ore in baskets. Oncalion was already smelting these first small loads.

At the bridge, Davell asked the same questions he had asked when Kit was a child playing on his work sites. Kit found himself responding as he had so many years before, eager to explain—or excuse—each decision; and always, always the ponies passing.

They walked down to the older site. The pillar had been gutted for stones, so all that was left was rubble; but it gave them a good view of the new bridge: the boxy pillars; the great parabolic curve of the main chains; the thick vertical suspender chains; the slight sprung arch of the bulky roadbed. It looked as clumsy as a suspension bridge ever could. Yet another pony crossed, led by a woman singing something in the local dialect.

"It's a good bridge," Davell said at last.

Kit shook his head. His father, who had been known for his sharp tongue on the work sites though never to his son, said, "A bridge is a means to an end. It only matters because of what it does. Leads from *here* to *there*. If you do your work right, they won't notice it, any more than you notice where quicksilver comes from, most times. It's a good bridge because they are already using it. Stop feeling sorry for yourself, Kit."

It was a big party, that night. The Farsiders (and, Kit knew, the Nearsiders) drank and danced under the shadow of their bridge-to-be. Torchlight and firelight touched the stones of the tower base and anchorage, giving them mass and meaning, but above their light the tower was a black outline, the absence of stars. More torches outlined the tower's top, and they seemed no more than gold stars among the colder ones.

Kit walked among them. Everyone smiled or waved and offered to stand him drinks, but no one spoke much with him. It was as if the lifting of the cable had separated him from them. The immense towers had not done this; he had still been one of them, to some degree at least—the instigator of great labors, but still, one of them. But now, for tonight anyway, he was the man who bridged the mist. He had not felt so lonely since his first day here. Even Loreh Tanner's death had not severed him so completely from their world.

On every project, there was a day like this. It was possible that the distance came from him, he realized suddenly. He came to a place and built something, passing through the lives of people for a few months or years. He was staying longer this time because of the size of the project, but in the end he would leave. He always left, after he had changed lives in incalculable ways. A road through dangerous terrain or a bridge across mist saved lives and increased trade, but it always changed the world, as well. It was his job to make a thing and then leave to make the next one, but it was also his preference, not to remain and see what he had made. What would Nearside and Farside look like in ten years, in fifty? He had never returned to a previous site.

It was harder this time, or perhaps just different. Perhaps *he* was different. He had allowed himself to belong to the country on either side of the bridge; to have more was to have more to miss when it was taken away.

Rasali—what would her life look like?

Valo danced by, his arm around a woman half again as tall as he—Rica Bridger—and Kit caught his arm. "Where is Rasali?" he shouted, then, knowing he could not be heard over the noise of drums and pipes, mouthed: *Rasali.* He didn't hear what Valo said but followed his pointing hand.

Rasali was alone, flat on her back on the river side of the levee, looking up. There were no moons, so the Sky Mist hung close overhead, a river of stars that poured north to south like the river itself. Kit knelt a few feet away. "Rasali Ferry of Farside?"

Her teeth flashed in the dark. "Kit Meinem of Atyar."

He lay beside her. The grass was like bad straw, coarse against his back and neck. Without looking at him, she passed a jar of something. Its taste was strong as tar, and Kit gasped for a moment at the bite of it.

"I did not mean—" he started, but trailed off, unsure how to continue.

"Yes," she said, and he knew she had heard the words he didn't say. Her voice contained a shrug. "Many people born into a Ferry family never cross the mist."

"But you—" He stopped, felt carefully for his words. "Maybe others don't, but you do. And I think maybe you must do so."

"Just as you must build," she said softly. "That's clever of you, to realize that."

"And there will be no need after this, will there? Not on boats, anyway. We'll still need fish-skin, so they'll still be out, but they—"

"—stay close to shore," she said.

"And you?" he asked.

"I don't know, Kit. Days come, days go. I go onto the mist or I don't. I live or I don't. There is no certainty, but there never is."

"It doesn't distress you?"

"Of course it does. I love and I hate this bridge of yours. I will pine for the mist, for the need to cross it. But I do not want to be part of a family that all die young, without even a corpse for the burning. If I have a child, she will not need to make the decision I did: to cross the mist and die, or to stay safe on one side of the world, and never see the other. She will lose something. She will gain something else."

"Do you hate me?" he said finally, afraid of the answer, afraid of any answer she might give.

"No. Oh, no." She rolled over to him and kissed his mouth, and Kit could not say if the salt he tasted was from her tears or his own.

The autumn was spent getting the chains across the river. In the days after the crossing, the rope was linked to another, and then pulled back the way it had come, coupled now; and then there were two ropes in parallel courses. It was tricky work, requiring careful communications through the signal towers, but it was completed without event; and Kit could at last get a good night's sleep. To break the rope would have been to start anew with the long difficult crossing. Over the next days, each rope was replaced with fish-skin cable strong enough to take the weight of the chains until they were secured.

The cables were hoisted to the tops of the pillars, to prefigure the path one of the eight chains would take: secured with heavy pins set in protected slots in the anchorages and then straight sharp lines to the saddles on the pillars and, two hundred feet above the mist, the long perfect catenary. A catwalk was suspended from the cables. For the first time, people could cross the mist without the boats, though few chose to do so except for the high workers from the capital and the coast: a hundred men and women so strong and graceful that they seemed another species, and kept mostly to themselves. They were directed by a woman Kit had worked with before, Feinlin; the high-workers took no surnames. Something about Feinlin reminded him of Rasali.

The weather grew colder and the days shorter, and Kit pushed hard to have the first two chains across before the winter rains began. There would be no heavy work once the ground got too wet to give sturdy purchase to the teams, and calculations to the contrary, Kit could not quite trust that cables, even fish-skin cables, would survive the weight of those immense arcs through an entire winter—or that a Big One would not take one down in the unthinking throes of some winter storm.

The eyebars that would make up the chain were each ten feet long and required considerable manhandling to be linked with the bolts, each larger than a man's forearm. The links became a chain, even more cumbersome. Winches pulled the chain's end up to the saddles, and out onto the catwalk.

After this, the work became even more difficult and painstaking. Feinlin and her people moved individual eyebars and pins out onto the catwalks and joined them in situ; a backbreaking, dangerous task that had to be exactly synchronized with the work on the other side of the river, so that the cable would not be stressed.

Most nights Kit worked into the darkness. When the moons were bright enough, he, the high-workers, and the bridgewrights would work in shifts, day and night.

He crossed the mist six more times that fall. The high-workers disliked having people on the catwalks, but he was the architect, after all, so he crossed once that way, struggling with vertigo. After that, he preferred the ferries. When he crossed once with Valo, they talked exclusively about the bridge—Valo had decided to stay until the bridge was complete and the ferries finished; but his mind was already full of the capital—but the other times, when it was Rasali, they were silent, listening to the hiss of the V-shaped scull moving in the mist. His fear of the mist decreased with each day they came closer to the bridge's completion, though he couldn't say why this was.

When Kit did not work through the night and Rasali was on the same side of the mist, they spent their nights together, sometimes making love, at other times content to share drinks or play ninepins in The Deer's Heart's garden, at which Kit's proficiency surprised everyone, including himself. He and Rasali did not talk again about what she would do when the bridge was complete—or what he would do, for that matter.

The hard work was worth it. It was still warm enough that the iron didn't freeze the high-workers' hands on the day they placed the final bolt. The first chain was complete.

Though work had slowed through the winter, the second and third chains were in place by spring, and the others were competed by the end of the summer.

With the heavy work done, some of the workers returned to their home-places. More than half had taken the name Bridger or something similar. "We have changed things," Kit said to Jenner on one of his Nearside visits, just before Jenner left for his new work. "No," Jenner said: "*You* have changed things." Kit did not respond, but held this close, and thought of it sometimes with mingled pride and fear.

The workers who remained were high-men and -women, people who did not mind crawling about on the suspension chains securing the support ropes. For the last two years, the rope-makers for two hundred miles up- and downstream from the bridge had been twisting, cutting, and looping and reweaving the ends of the fish-skin cables that would support the road deck, each crate marked with the suspender's position in the bridge. The cartons stood in carefully sorted, labeled towers in the field that had once been full of sheep.

Kit's work was now all paperwork, it seemed—so many invoices, so many reports for the capital—but he managed every day to watch the high-workers, their efficient motions. Sometimes he climbed to tops of the pillars and looked down into the mist, and saw Rasali's or Valo's ferry, an elegant narrow shape half-hidden in tendrils of blazing white mist or pale gray fog.

Kit lost one more worker, Tommer Bullkeeper, who climbed out onto the catwalk for a drunken bet and fell, with a maniacal cry that changed into unbalanced laughter as he vanished into the mist. His wife wept in mixed anger and grief, and the townspeople wore ash-color, and the bridge continued. Rasali held Kit when he cried in his room at The Red Lurcher. "Never mind," she said. "Tommer was a good person: a drunk, but good to his sons and his wife, careful with animals. People have always died. The bridge doesn't change that."

The towns changed shape as Kit watched. Commercial envoys from every direction gathered; many stayed in inns and homes, but some built small houses, shops, and warehouses. Many used the ferries, and it became common for these businessmen and -women to tip Rasali or Valo lavishly—"in hopes I never ride with you again," they would say. Valo laughed and spent this money buying beer for his friends; the letter had come from University that he could begin his studies with the winter term, and he had many farewells to make. Rasali told no one, not even Kit, what she planned to do with hers.

Beginning in the spring of the project's fifth year, they attached the road deck. Wood planks wide enough for oxen two abreast were nailed together into with iron struts to give stability. The bridge was made of several hundred sections, constructed on the work sites and then hauled out by workers. Each segment had farther to go before being placed and secured. The two towns celebrated all night the first time a Nearsider shouted from her side of the bridge, and was saluted by Farsider cheers. In the lengthening evenings, it became a pastime for people to walk onto the bridge and lie belly-down at its end, watching the mist so far below them. Sometimes dark shapes moved within it, but no one saw anything big enough to be a Big One. A few heedless locals dropped heavy stones from above to watch the mist twist away, opening holes into its depths; but their neighbors stopped them: "It's not respectful," one said; and, "Do you want to piss them off?" said another.

Kit asked her, but Rasali never walked out with him. "I see enough from the river," she said.

Kit was Nearside, in his room in The Fish. He had lived in this room for five years, and it looked it: plans and time tables pinned to the walls. The chair by the fire was heaped with clothes, books, a length of red silk he had seen at a fair and could not resist; it had been years since he sat there. The plans in his folio and on the oversized table had been replaced with waybills and receipts for materials, payrolls, copies of correspondence between Kit and his sponsors in the government. The window was open, and Kit sat on the cupboard bed, watching a bee feel its way through the sun-filled air. He'd left half a pear on the table, and he was waiting to see if the bee would find it, and thinking about the little hexagonal cells of a beehive, whether they were stronger than squares were, and how he might test this.

Feet ran along the corridor. His door flew open. Rasali stood there blinking in the light, which was so golden that Kit didn't at first notice how pale she was, or the tears on her face. "What—" he said, as he swung off his bed. He came toward her.

"Valo," she said. "The *Pearlfinder.*"

He held her. The bee left, then the sun, and still he held her as she rocked silently on the bed. Only when the square of sky in the window faded to purple, and the little moon's crescent eased across it, did she speak. "Ah," she said, a sigh like a gasp. "I am so tired." She fell asleep, as quickly as that, with tears still wet on her face. Kit slipped from the room.

The taproom was crowded, filled with ash-gray clothes, with soft voices and occasional sobs. Kit wondered for a moment if everyone had a set of mourning clothes always at hand, and what this meant about them.

Brana Keep saw Kit in the doorway, and came from behind the bar to speak with him. "How is she?" she said.

"Not good. I think she's asleep right now," Kit said. "Can you give me some food for her, something to drink?"

Brana nodded, spoke to her daughter Lixa as she passed into the back, then returned. "How are *you* doing, Kit? You saw a fair amount of Valo yourself."

"Yes," Kit said. Valo chasing the children through the field of stones, Valo laughing at the top of a tower, Valo serious-eyed, with a handbook of calculus in the shade of a half-built fishing boat. "What happened? She hasn't said anything yet."

Brana gestured. "What can be said? Signal flags said he was going to cross just after midday; but he never came. When we signaled over, they said he had left when they first signaled."

"Could he be alive?" Kit asked, remembering the night that he and Rasali had lost the big scull, the extra hours it had taken for the crossing. "He might have broken the scull, landed somewhere downriver."

"No," Brana said. "I know, that's what we wanted to hope. Maybe we would have believed it for while before. But Asa, one of the strangers, the high-workers; she was working overhead and heard the boat capsize, heard him cry out. She couldn't see anything, and didn't know what she had heard until we figured it out."

"Three more months," Kit said, mostly to himself. He saw Brana looking at him, so he clarified: "Three more months. The bridge would have been done. This wouldn't have happened."

"This was today," Brana said, "not three months from now. People die when they die; we grieve and move on, Kit. You've been with us long enough to understand how we see these things. Here's the tray."

When Kit returned with the tray, Rasali was asleep. He watched her in the dark room, unwilling to light more than the single lamp he'd carried up with him. *People die when they die.* But he could not stop thinking about the bridge, its deck nearly finished. *Another three months. Another month.*

When she awakened, there was a moment when she smiled at him, her face weary but calm. Then she remembered and her face tightened and she started crying again. When she was done, Kit got her to eat some bread and fish and cheese, and drink some watered wine. She did so obediently, like a child. When she was finished, she lay back against him, her matted hair pushing up into his mouth.

"How can he be gone?"

"I'm so sorry," Kit said. "The bridge was so close to finished. Three more months, and this wouldn't have—"

She pulled away. "What? Wouldn't have happened? Wouldn't have *had* to happen?" She stood and faced him. "His death would have been unnecessary?"

"I—" Kit began, but she interrupted him, new tears streaking her face.

"He *died*, Kit. It wasn't necessary, it wasn't irrelevant, it wasn't anything except the way things are. But he's gone, and I'm not, and *now* what do I do, Kit? I lost my father, and my aunt, and my sister and my brother and my brother's son, and now I lose the mist when the bridge's done, and then what? What am I then? Who are the Ferry people then?"

Kit knew the answer: however she changed, she would still be Rasali; her people would still be strong and clever and beautiful; the mist would still be there, and the Big Ones. But she wouldn't be able to hear these words, not yet, not for months, maybe. So he held her, and let his own tears slip down his face, and tried not to think.

The fairs to celebrate the opening of the bridge started days before midsummer, the official date. Representatives of Empire from Atyar polished their speeches and waited impatiently in their suite of tents, planted on hurriedly cleaned-up fields near (but not too near) Nearside. The town had bled northward until it surrounded the west pillar of the bridge. The land that had once been sheep-pasture at the foot of the pillar was crowded with fair-tents and temporary booths, cheek by jowl with more permanent shops of wood and stone, selling food and space for sleeping and the sorts of products a traveler might find herself in need of. Kit was proud of the streets; he had organized construction of the crosshatch of sturdy cobblestones, as something to do while he waited through the bridge's final year. The new wells had been a project of Jenner's, planned from the very beginning, but Kit had seen them completed. Kit had just received a letter from Jenner, with news of his new bridge up in the Keitche mountains: on schedule; a happy work site.

Kit walked alone through the fair, which had splashed up the levee and along its ridge. A few people, townspeople and workers, greeted him; but others only pointed him out to their friends (*the man who built the bridge; see there, that short dark man*); and still others ignored him completely, just another stranger in a crowd of strangers. When he had first come to build the bridge everyone in Nearside knew everyone else, local or visitor. He felt solitude settling around him again, the loneliness of coming to a strange place and building something and then leaving. The people of Nearside were moving forward into this new world he had built, the world of a bridge across the mist, but he was not going with them.

He wondered what Rasali was doing, over in Farside, and wished he could see her. They had not spoken since the days after Valo's death, except once for a few minutes, when he had come upon her at The Bitch. She had been withdrawn though not hostile, and he had felt unbalanced and not sought her out since.

Now, at the end of his great labor, he longed to see her. When would she cross next? He laughed. He of all people should know better: *five minutes' walk*.

The bridge was not yet open, but Kit was the architect; the guards at the toll booth only nodded when he asked to pass, and lifted the gate for him. A few people noticed and gestured as he climbed. When Uni Mason (hands filled with ribbons) shouted something he could not hear clearly, Kit smiled and waved and walked on.

He had crossed the bridge before this. The first stage of building the heavy oak frames that underlay the roadbed had been a narrow strip of planking that led from one shore to the other. Nearly every worker had found some excuse for crossing it at least once before Empire had sent people to the tollgates. Swallowing his fear of the height, Kit himself had crossed it nearly every day for the last two months.

This was different. It was no longer his bridge, but belonged to Empire and to the people of Near- and Farside. He saw it with the eyes of a stranger.

The stone ramp was a quarter-mile long, inclined gradually for carts. Kit hiked up, and the noises dropped behind and below him. The barriers that would keep animals (and people) from seeing the drop-off to either side were not yet complete: there were always things left unfinished at a bridge's opening, afterthoughts and additions. Ahead of him, the bridge was a series of perfect dark lines and arcs.

The ramp widened as it approached the pillar, and offered enough space for a cart to carefully turn onto the bridge itself. The bed of the span was barely wide enough for a cart with two oxen abreast, so Nearside and Farside would have to take turns sending wagons across. *For now,* Kit thought: *Later they can widen it, or build another. They*: it would be someone else.

The sky was overcast with high tin-colored clouds, their metallic sheen reflected in the mist below Kit. There were no railings, only fish-skin ropes strung between the suspension cables that led up to the chain. Oxen and horses wouldn't like that, or the hollow sound their feet would make on the boards. Kit watched the deck roll before him in the breeze, which was constant from the southwest. The roll wasn't so bad in this wind, but perhaps they should add an iron parapet or more trusses, to lessen the twisting and make crossing more comfortable. Empire had sent a new engineer, to take care of any final projects: Jeje Tesanthe. He would mention it to her.

Kit walked to one side so that he could look down. Sound dropped off behind him, deadened as it always was by the mist, and he could almost imagine that he was alone. It was several hundred feet down, but there was nothing to give scale to the coiling field of hammered metal below him. Deep in the mist he saw shadows that might have been a Big One or something smaller or a thickening of the mist, and then, his eyes learning what to look for, he saw more of the shadows, as if a school of fish were down there. One separated and darkened as it rose in the mist until it exposed its back almost immediately below Kit.

It was dark and knobby, shiny with moisture, flat as a skate; and it went on forever—thirty feet long perhaps, or forty, twisting as it rose to expose its underside, or what he thought might be its underside. As Kit watched, the mist curled back from a flexing scaled wing of sorts; and then a patch that might have been a single eye or a field of eyes, or something altogether different; and then a mouth like the arc of the suspension chains. The mouth gaped open to show another arc, a curve of gum or cartilage or something else. The creature rolled and then sank and became a shadow, and then nothing as the mist closed over it and settled.

Kit had stopped walking when he saw it. He forced himself to move forward again. A Big One, or perhaps just a Medium-Large One; at this height it hadn't seemed so big, or so frightening. Kit was surprised at the sadness he felt.

Farside was crammed with color and fairings, as well, but Kit could not find Rasali anywhere. He bought a tankard of rye beer, and went to find some place alone.

Once it became dark and the imperial representatives were safely tucked away for the night, the guards relaxed the rules and let their friends (and then any of the locals) on the bridge to look around them. People who had worked on the bridge had papers to cross without charge for the rest of their lives, but many others had watched it grow, and now they charmed or bribed or begged their way onto their bridge. Torches were forbidden because of the oil that protected the fish-skin ropes, but covered lamps were permitted, and from his place on the levee, Kit watched the lights move along the bridge, there and then hidden by the support ropes and deck, dim and inconstant as fireflies.

"Kit Meinem of Atyar."

Kit stood and turned to the voice behind him. "Rasali Ferry of Farside." She wore blue and white, and her feet were bare. She had pulled back her dark hair with a ribbon and her pale shoulders gleamed. She glowed under the moonlight like mist. He thought of touching her, kissing her; but they had not spoken since just after Valo's death.

She stepped forward and took the mug from his hand, drank the lukewarm beer, and just like that, the world righted itself. He closed his eyes and let the feeling wash over him.

He took her hand, and they sat on the cold grass and looked out across the river. The bridge was a black net of arcs and lines, and behind it was the mist glowing blue-white in the light of the moons. After a moment, he asked, "Are you still Rasali Ferry, or will you take a new name?"

"I expect I'll take a new one." She half-turned in his arms so that he could see her face, her pale eyes. "And you? Are you still Kit Meinem, or do you become someone else? Kit Who Bridged the Mist? Kit Who Changed the World?"

"Names in the city do not mean the same thing," Kit said absently, aware that he had said this before and not caring. "*Did* I change the world?" He knew the answer already.

She looked at him for a moment, as if trying to gauge his feelings. "Yes," she said slowly after a moment. She turned her face up toward the loose strand of bobbing lights: "There's your proof, as permanent as stone and sky."

"'Permanent as stone and sky,'" Kit repeated. "This afternoon—it flexes a lot, the bridge. There has to be a way to control it, but it's not engineered for that yet. Or lightning could strike it. There are a thousand things that could destroy it. It's going to come down, Rasali. This year, next year, a hundred years from now, five hundred." He ran his fingers through his hair. "All these people, they think it's forever."

"No, we don't," Rasali said. "Maybe Atyar does, but we know better here. Do you need to tell a Ferry that nothing will last? These stones will fall eventually, *these* cables—but the *dream* of crossing the mist, the dream of connection. Now that we know it can happen, it will always be here. My mother died, my grandfather. Valo." She stopped, swallowed. "Ferrys die, but there is always a Ferry to cross the mist. Bridges and ferry folk, they are not so different, Kit." She leaned forward, across the space between them, and they kissed.

"Are you off soon?"

Rasali and Kit had made love on the levee against the cold grass. They had crossed the bridge together under the sinking moons, walked back to The Deer's Heart and bought more beer, the crowds thinner now, people gone home with their families or friends or lovers: the strangers from out of town bedding down in spare rooms, tents, anywhere they could. But Kit was too restless to sleep, and he and Rasali ended up back by the mist, down on the dock. Morning was only a few hours away, and the smaller moon had set. It was darker now and the mist had dimmed.

"In a few days," Kit said, thinking of the trunks and bags packed tight and gathered in his room at The Fish: the portfolio, fatter now, and stained with water, mist, dirt, and sweat. Maybe it was time for a new one. "Back to the capital."

There were lights on the opposite bank, fisherfolk preparing for the night's work despite the fair, the bridge. *Some things don't change.*

"Ah," she said. They both had known this; it was no surprise. "What will you do there?"

Kit rubbed his face, feeling stubble under his fingers, happy to skip that small ritual for a few days. "Sleep for a hundred years. Then there's another bridge they want, down at the mouth of the river, a place called Ulei. The mist's nearly a mile wide there. I'll start midwinter maybe."

"A mile," Rasali said. "Can you do it?"

"I think so. I bridged this, didn't I?" His gesture took in the berms, the slim stone tower overhead, the woman beside him. She smelled sweet and salty. "There are islands by Ulei, I'm told. Low ones. That's the only reason it would be possible. So maybe a series of flat stone arches, one to the next. You? You'll keep building boats?"

"No." She leaned her head back and he felt her face against his ear. "I don't need to. I have a lot of money. The rest of the family can build boats, but for me that was just what I did while I waited to cross the mist again."

"You'll miss it," Kit said. It was not a question.

Her strong hand laid over his. "Mmm," she said, a sound without implication.

"But it was the *crossing* that mattered to you, wasn't it?" Kit said, realizing it. "Just as with me, but in a different way."

"Yes," she said, and after a pause: "So now I'm wondering: how big do the Big Ones get in the mist ocean? And lives there?"

"Nothing's on the other side," Kit said. "There's no crossing something without an end."

"Everything can be crossed. Me, I think there is an end. There's a river of water deep under the mist river, yes? And that water runs somewhere. And all the other rivers, all the lakes—they all drain somewhere. There's a water ocean under the mist ocean, and I wonder whether the mist ends somewhere out there, if it spreads out and vanishes and you find you are floating on water."

"It's a different element," Kit said, turning the problem over. "So you would need a boat that works through mist, light enough with that broad belly and fish-skin sheathing; but it would have to be deep-keeled enough for water."

She nodded. "I want to take a coast-skimmer and refit it, find out what's out there. Islands, Kit. Big Ones. *Huge* Ones. Another whole world maybe. I think I would like to be Rasali Ocean."

"You will come to Ulei with me?" he said, but he knew already. She *would* come, for a month or a season or a year. They would sleep tumbled together in an inn very like The Fish or The Bitch, and when her boat was finished, she would sail across Ocean, and he would move on to the next bridge or road, or he might return to the capital and a position at University. Or he might rest at last.

"I will come," she said. "For a bit."

Suddenly he felt a deep and powerful emotion in his chest: overwhelmed by everything that had happened or would happen in their lives: the changes to Nearside and Farside, the ferry's ending, Valo's death, the fact that she would leave him eventually, or that he would leave her. "I'm sorry," he said.

"I'm not," she said, and leaned across to kiss him, her mouth warm with sunlight and life. "It is worth it, all of it."

All those losses, but this one at least he could prevent.

"When the time comes," he said: "When you sail. I will come with you,"

A fo ben, bid bont. To be a leader, be a bridge.
—*Welsh proverb*

honorable mentions: 2011

Daniel Abraham, "Balfour and Meriwether in *The Vampire of Kabul*," *Subterranean*, Fall.
Brian W. Aldiss, "Benkoelen," *Welcome to the Greenhouse*.
Michael Alexander, "Someone Like You," *F&SF*, July/August.
Nina Allan, "The Silver Wind," *Interzone* 233.
Charlie Jane Anders, "Six Months, Three Days," Tor.com.
——, "Source Decay," *Strange Horizons*, 1/3.
Eleanor Arnason, "My Husband Steinn," *Asimov's*, October/November.
Kage Baker, "Attlee and the Long Walk," *Life on Mars*.
Peter M. Ball, "Memories of Chalice," *Electric Velocipede* 21/22.
John Barnes, "The Birds and the Bees and the Gasoline Trees," *Engineering Infinity*.
Neal Barrett, Jr., "D.O.C.S." *Asimov's*, September.
——, "Where," *Asimov's*, March.
Christopher Barzak, "Smoke City," *Asimov's*, April/May
Stephen Baxter, "Gravity Dreams," *PS Publishing*.
——, "On Chryse Plain," *Life on Mars*.
——, "Rock Day," *Solaris Rising*.
——, "Transients," *Fables from the Fountain*.
Peter S. Beagle, "Music, When Soft Voices Die," *Ghosts by Gaslight*.
——, "Underbridge," *Naked City*.
Elizabeth Bear, "Gods of the Forge," *TRSF*.
——, "King Pole, Gallows Pole, Bottle Tree," *Naked City*.
——, "The Leavings of the Wolf," *Apex Magazine*, November.
——, "Needle," *Blood and Other Cravings*.
Chris Beckett, "Day 29," *Asimov's*, July.
——, "Two Thieves," *Asimov's*, January.
Steve Bein, "The Most Important Thing in the World," *Asimov's*, March.
Gregory Benford, "Eagle," *Welcome to the Greenhouse*.
——, "Mercies," *Engineering Infinity*.
Holly Black, "Noble Rot," *Naked City*.
Richard Bowes, "Sir Morgravain Speaks of Night Dragons and Other Things," *F&SF*, July/August.
Marie Brennan, "Dancing the Warrior," *Beneath Ceaseless Skies*, 4/7, 4/21.
——, "Love, Cayce," *OSCIMS*, 4/11.
Philip Brewer, "Watch Bees," *Asimov's*, August.
Patricia Briggs, "In Red, with Pearls," *Down These Strange Streets*.
Damien Broderick, "Time Considered as a Series of Thermite Burns in No Particular Order," Tor.com.
——& Barbara Lamarr, "Walls of Flesh, Bars of Bone," *Engineering Infinity*.
Keith Brooke, "Imago," *Postscripts* 24/25.
——& Eric Brown, "Eternity's Children," *Solaris Rising*.

Eric Brown, "Starship Winter," *PS Publishing.*
Tobias S. Buckell, "The Fall of Alacan," *Subterranean,* Spring.
——, "Mirror, Mirror," *Subterranean,* Summer.
Emma Bull, "Nine Muses," *Eclipse Four.*
Karl Bunker, "Bodyguard," *F&SF,* March/April.
——, "Overtaken," *F&SF,* September/October.
——, "Worm Days," *Electric Velocipede 21/22.*
Sue Burke, "Healthy, Wealthy, and Wise," *Interzone 232.*
Jim Butcher, "Curses," *Naked City.*
Pat Cadigan, "Picking Up the Pieces," *Naked City.*
Richard Calder, "Whisper," *Postscripts 24/25.*
James L. Cambias, "Object Three," *F&SF,* November/December.
Tracy Canfield, "One-Eyed Jacks," *Strange Horizons,* July.
Jeff Carlson, "Planet of the Sealies," *Asimov's,* February.
Siobhan Carroll, "In the Gardens of the Night," *Beneath Ceaseless Skies,* July.
Adam-Troy Castro, "Hiding Place," *Analog,* April.
Jason Chapman, "The Architect of Heaven," *Clarkesworld,* May.
——, "This Petty Pace," *Asimov's,* October/November.
Rob Chilson, "Less Stately Mansions," *F&SF,* July/August.
Gwendolyn Clare, "Ashes on the Water," *Asimov's,* January.
Glen Cook, "Shadow Thieves," *Down These Strange Streets.*
——, "Smelling Danger: A Black Company Story," *Subterreanean Dark Fantasy* 2.
Matthew Cook, "Insha'allah," *Interzone* 235.
S. C. E. Cooney, "The Last Sophia," *Strange Horizons,* 3/11.
Albert E. Cowdrey, "The Black Mountain," *F&SF,* May/June.
——, "The Bogle," *F&SF,* January/February.
——, "How Peter Met Pan," *F&SF,* November/December.
——, "Scatter My Ashes," *F&SF,* March/April.
——, "Where Have All the Young Men Gone?" *F&SF,* September/October.
Ian Creasey, "I Was Nearly Your Mother," *Asimov's,* March.
——, "The Odor of Sanctity," *Asimov's,* September.
John Crowley, "And Go Like This," *Naked City.*
Leah Cypess, "Twelvers," *Asimov's,* July.
Don D'Ammassa, "The Buddy System," *Analog,* November.
——, "Martyrs," *Panverse Three.*
Colin P. Davies, "Fighter," *Asimov's,* June.
Aliette de Bodard, "Exodus Tides," *OSCIMS,* April.
——, "Shipbirth," *Asimov's,* February.
Michael J. De Luca, "The Nine-Tailed Cat," *Beneath Ceaseless Skies,* June.
Bradley Denton, "The Adakian Eagle," *Down These Strange Streets.*
Paul Di Filippo, "Farmearth," *Welcome to the Greenhouse.*
——, "A Pocketful of Faces," *F&SF,* March/April.
——, "Specter-Bombing the Beer Goggles," *TRSF.*
——, "Sweet Spots," *Solaris Rising.*
Cory Doctorow, "The Brave Little Toaster," *TRSF.*
——, "Martian Chronicles," *Life on Mars.*
Alexandra Duncan, "Rampion," *F&SF,* May/June.
Andy Duncan, "Slow as a Bullet," *Eclipse Four.*

Thoraiya Dyer, "Breaking the Ice," *Cosmos*, March.
Carol Emshwiller, "The New and Perfect Man," *Postscripts 24/25*.
David Farland, "Against Eternity," *Lightspeed*, October.
K. M. Ferebee, "Seven Spells to Sever the Heart," *Fantasy*, November.
Sheila Finch, "The Evening and the Morning," *F&SF*, March/April.
Michael F. Flynn, "The Frog Prince," *Analog*, January/February.
Jeffrey Ford, "The Double of My Double Is Not My Double," *Eclipse Four*.
Eugie Foster, "Black Swan, White Swan," *End of an Aeon*.
Karen Joy Fowler, "Younger Women," *Subterranean*, Summer.
Esther M. Friesner, "The One That Got Away," *Asimov's*, April/May.
Gregory Frost, "The Dingus," *Supernatural Noir*.
Nancy Fulda, "Movement," *Asimov's*, March.
Diana Gabaldon, "Lord John and the Plague of Zombies," *Down These Strange Streets*.
Neil Gaiman, "And Weep Like Alexander," *Fables from the Fountain*.
James Alan Gardner, "Three Damnations: A Fugue," *Fantasy*, September.
Laura Anne Gilman, "Crossroads," *Fantasy*, August.
Lisa Goldstein, "Little Vampires," *Realms of Fantasy*, April.
——, "Paradise Is a Walled Garden," *Asimov's*, August.
Kathleen Ann Goonan, "Angel and You Dogs," *PS Publishing*.
——, "Creatures with Wings," *Engineering Infinity*.
Theodora Goss, "Pug," *Asimov's*, July.
Gavin J. Grant, "Windows in the World," *Strange Horizons*, February.
Joseph Green, "Turtle Love," *Welcome to the Greenhouse*.
Simon R. Green, "Hungry Heart," *Down These Strange Streets*.
Daryl Gregory, "Persistence," *Unpossible*.
John Gribben, "The Alice Encounter," *PS Publishing*.
Eileen Gunn, "Thought Experiment," *Eclipse Four*.
Joe Haldeman, "Complete Sentence," *TRSF*.
Peter F. Hamilton, "Return of the Mutant Worms," *Solaris Rising*.
M. L. N. Hanover, "The Difference Between a Puzzle and a Mystery," *Down These Strange Streets*.
Charlaine Harris, "Death by Dahlia," *Down These Strange Streets*.
Howard V. Hendrix, "A New Bridge Across the Lethe," *Abyss & Apex*, 1st Quarter.
Rosamund Hodge, "Apotheosis," *Black Gate*, Spring.
Nalo Hopkinson, "Old Habits," *Eclipse Four*.
Kat Howard, "Choose Your Own Adventure," *Fantasy*, 4/11.
——, "The Speaking Bone," *Apex Magazine*.
Matthew Hughes, "So Loved," *Postscripts 24/25*.
——, "Yellow Cabochen," *PS Publishing*.
Thea Hutcheson, "The Good Husband," *Realms of Fantasy*, June.
Conn Iggulden, "The Lady Is a Screamer," *Down These Strange Streets*.
Jon Ingold, "Sleepers," *Interzone 234*.
Alexander Jablokov, "The Day the Wires Came Down," *Asimov's*, April/May.
C. W. Johnson, "Fermi's Plague," *Abyss & Apex*, 2nd Quarter.
Kij Johnson, "Story Kit," *Eclipse Four*.
Gwyneth Jones, "The Flame Is Roses, the Smoke Is Briars," *TRSF*.
——, "The Ki-anna," *Engineering Infinity*.
Vylar Kaftan, "The Sighted Watchmaker," *Lightspeed*, December.

James Patrick Kelly, "Crazy Me," Tor.com.
——, "Happy Ending," *F&SF*, March/April.
——, "Tourists," *Eclipse Four.*
John Kessel, "Clean," *Asimov's*, March.
Caitlin R. Kiernan, "Hydraguros," *Subterranean Dark Fantasy* 2.
——, "The Maltese Unicorn," *Supernatural Noir.*
——, "Tidal Forces," *Eclipse Four.*
Laurie R. King, "Hellbender," *Down These Strange Streets.*
Ellen Klages, "Goodnight Moons," *Life on Mars.*
Stephen Kotowych, "Under the Shield," *OSCIMS*, August.
Mary Robinette Kowal, "Kiss Me Twice," *Asimov's*, June.
——, "Water to Wine," *Subterranean*, Spring.
Nancy Kress, "A Hundred Hundred Daisies," *Asimov's*, October/November.
——, "Eliot Wrote," *Lightspeed*, May.
——, "First Principle," *Life on Mars.*
Naomi Kritzer, "What Happened at Blessing Creek," *OSCIMS*, August.
Ellen Kushner, "The Duke of Riverside," *Naked City.*
Marc Laidlaw, "The Boy Who Followed Lovecraft," *Subterranean*, Winter.
Jay Lake, "'Hello,' Said the Gun," *Daily SF*, February 22.
——, "Her Fingers Like Whips, Her Eyes Like Razors," *Postscripts 24/25.*
——& Shannon Page, "The Passion of Mother Vajpai," *Subterranean Dark Fantasy* 2.
Margo Lanagan, "Mulberry Boys," *Blood and Other Cravings.*
Geoffrey A. Landis, "Private Space," *TRSF.*
Joel Lane & Mat Joiner, "Ashes in the Water," *Postscripts 24/25.*
Sarah Langan, "The Man Inside Black Betty," *F&SF*, September/October.
David Langford, "The Pocklington Poltergeist," *Fables from the Fountain.*
Joe R. Lansdale, "The Bleeding Shadow," *Down These Strange Streets.*
——, "The Crawling Sky," *Subterranean*, Spring.
Chris Lawson, "Sundown," *Welcome to the Greenhouse.*
Tanith Lee, "Black Fire," *Lightspeed*, January.
Tim Lees, "Crosstown Traffic," *Interzone* 233.
David D. Levine, "Citizen-Astronaut," *Analog*, June.
——, "The Tides of the Heart," *Realms of Fantasy*, June.
Marissa Lingen, "Some of Them Closer," *Analog*, January/February.
Kelly Link, "Valley of the Girls," *Subterranean*, Summer.
Ken Liu, "Altogether Elsewhere, Vast Herds of Reindeer," *F&SF*, May/June.
——, "The Countable," *Asimov's*, December.
——, "The Man Who Ended History: A Documentary," *Panverse Three.*
——, "The Paper Menagerie," *F&SF*, March/April.
——, "Real Artists," *TRSF.*
——, "Simulacrum," *Lightspeed*, February.
——, "Staying Behind," *Clarkesworld*, October.
——, "Tying Knots," *Clarkesworld*, January.
Richard A. Lovett, "Jak and the Beanstalk," *Analog*, July/August.
Will Ludwigsen, "We Were Wonder Scouts," *Asimov's*, August.
Richard Lupoff, "12:02 P.M.," *F&SF*, January/February.
Jeffrey Lyman, "The Hanged Poet," *OSCIMS*, June.
Pat MacEwan, "Home Sweet Bi'ome," *F&SF*, January/February.

Ken MacLeod, "The Best Science Fiction of the Year Three," *Solaris Rising*.
——, "The Surface of Last Scattering," *TRSF*.
Ian R. MacLeod, "The Crane Method," *Subterranean*, Spring.
Emily Mah, "The River People," *Black Gate*, Spring.
Geoffrey Maloney, "Mr. Morrow Becomes Acquainted with the Delicate Art of Squid Keeping," *Beneath Ceaseless Skies*, March.
Daniel Marcus, "Bright Moment," *F&SF*, September/October.
Bruce McAllister, "The Messenger," *Asimov's*, July.
Tim McDaniel, "Brother Sleep," *Asimov's*, February.
Ian McDonald, "A Smart Well-Mannered Uprising of the Dead," *Solaris Rising*.
Ian McHugh, "Boumee and the Apes," *Analog*, May.
——, "The Godbreaker of Seggau-Li," *Andromeda Spaceways 50*.
——, "Interloper," *Asimov's*, January.
Maureen McHugh, "The Effects of Centrifugal Forces," *After the Apocalypse*.
Sean McMullen, "Enigma," *Analog*, January/February.
Greg Mellor, "Day Break," *Cosmos*, April/May.
Erick Melton, "Shadow Angel," *Asimov's*, September.
China Mieville, "Covehithe," *The Guardian*, April 22.
Eugene Mirabelli, "The Pastry Chef, the Nanotechnologist, the Aerobics Instructor, and the Plumber," *Asimov's*, October/November.
Judith Moffett, "The Middle of Somewhere," *Welcome to the Greenhouse*.
Sarah Monette, "The Devil in Gaylord's Creek," *Fantasy*, May.
R. Neube, "Grandma Said," *Asimov's*, September.
Alec Nevala-Lee, "Kawataro," *Analog*, June.
Larry Niven, "The Artists," *Subterranean*, Winter.
Garth Nix, "The Curious Case of the Mondawn Daffodils Murder as Experienced by Sir Magnus Holmes and Almost-Doctor Susan Shirke," *Ghosts by Gaslight*.
Rick Norwood, "Long Time," *F&SF*, January/February.
Naomi Novik, "Priced to Sell," *Naked City*.
Nnedi Okorafor, "The Book of Phoenix (Excerpted from The Great Book)," Clarkesworld, March.
An Owomoyele, "All That Touches the Air," *Lightspeed*, April.
——, "Frozen Voice," *Clarkesworld*, July
——, "God in the Sky," *Asimov's*, March.
Stephen Palmer, "Eluna," *Solaris Rising*.
Suzanne Palmer, "The Ceiling Is Sky," *Interzone 234*.
Paul Park, "Mysteries of the Old Quarter," *Ghosts by Gaslight*.
K. J. Parker, "A Room with a View," *Subterranean Dark Fantasy* 2.
——, "A Small Price to Pay for Birdsong," *Subterranean*, Winter.
Richard Parks, "The Ghost of Shinoda Forest," *Beneath Ceaseless Skies*, February.
——, "The Swan Troika," *Realms of Fantasy*, February.
——, "The Tiger's Turn," *Beneath Ceaseless Skies*, October.
Norman Partridge, "Vampire Lake," *Subterreanean Dark Fantasy* 2.
Lawrence Person, "The Dog Parade," *Postscripts 24/25*.
Tony Pi, "We Who Steal Faces," *OSCIMS*, April.
Steven Popkes, "Agent of Change," *F&SF*, May/June.
Tim Pratt, "Antiquities and Tangibles," *Subterranean*, Fall.
——, "The Secret Beach," *Fantasy*, October.

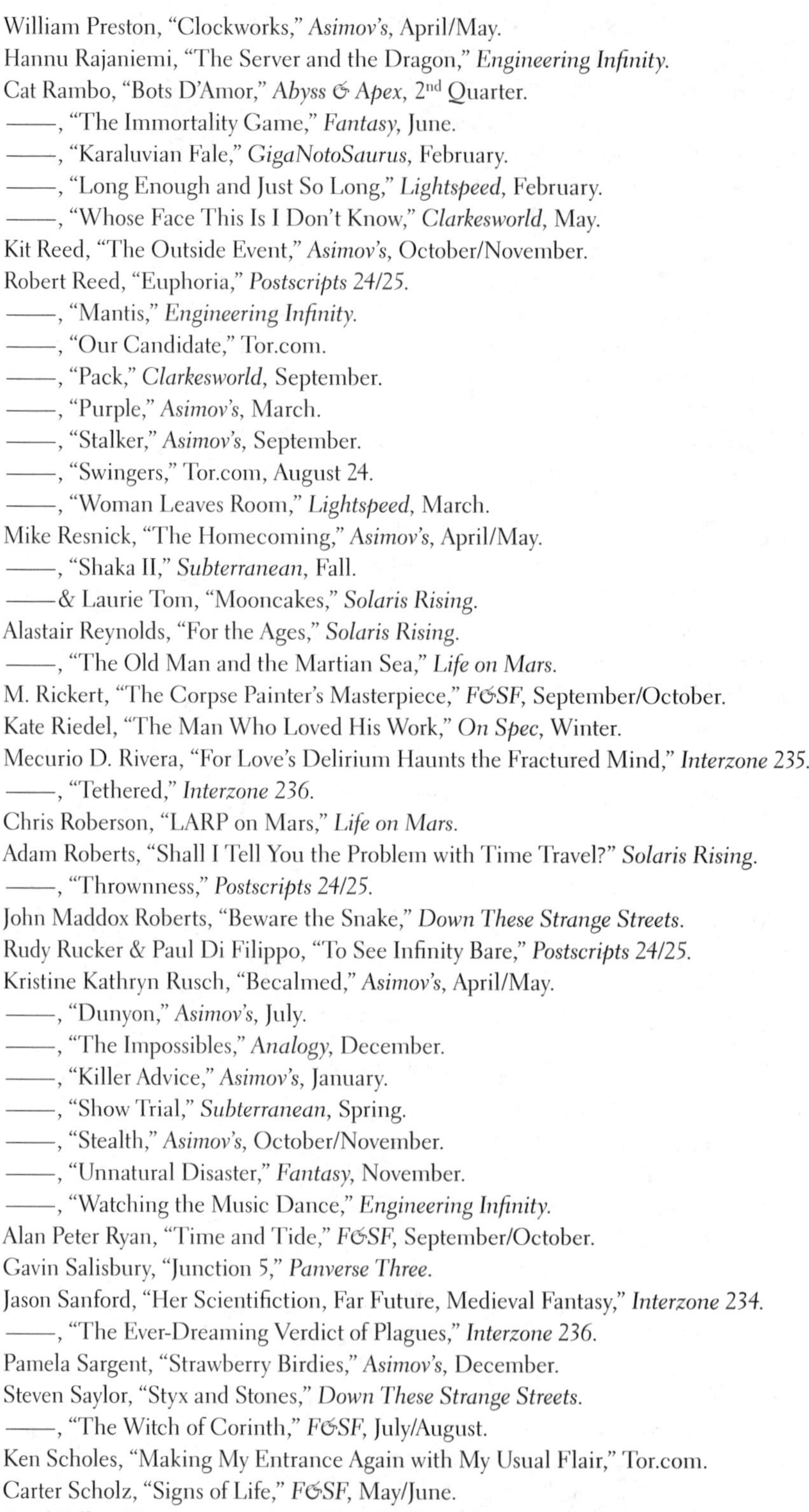

William Preston, "Clockworks," *Asimov's*, April/May.
Hannu Rajaniemi, "The Server and the Dragon," *Engineering Infinity*.
Cat Rambo, "Bots D'Amor," *Abyss & Apex*, 2nd Quarter.
——, "The Immortality Game," *Fantasy*, June.
——, "Karaluvian Fale," *GigaNotoSaurus*, February.
——, "Long Enough and Just So Long," *Lightspeed*, February.
——, "Whose Face This Is I Don't Know," *Clarkesworld*, May.
Kit Reed, "The Outside Event," *Asimov's*, October/November.
Robert Reed, "Euphoria," *Postscripts 24/25*.
——, "Mantis," *Engineering Infinity*.
——, "Our Candidate," Tor.com.
——, "Pack," *Clarkesworld*, September.
——, "Purple," *Asimov's*, March.
——, "Stalker," *Asimov's*, September.
——, "Swingers," Tor.com, August 24.
——, "Woman Leaves Room," *Lightspeed*, March.
Mike Resnick, "The Homecoming," *Asimov's*, April/May.
——, "Shaka II," *Subterranean*, Fall.
——& Laurie Tom, "Mooncakes," *Solaris Rising*.
Alastair Reynolds, "For the Ages," *Solaris Rising*.
——, "The Old Man and the Martian Sea," *Life on Mars*.
M. Rickert, "The Corpse Painter's Masterpiece," *F&SF*, September/October.
Kate Riedel, "The Man Who Loved His Work," *On Spec*, Winter.
Mecurio D. Rivera, "For Love's Delirium Haunts the Fractured Mind," *Interzone* 235.
——, "Tethered," *Interzone* 236.
Chris Roberson, "LARP on Mars," *Life on Mars*.
Adam Roberts, "Shall I Tell You the Problem with Time Travel?" *Solaris Rising*.
——, "Thrownness," *Postscripts 24/25*.
John Maddox Roberts, "Beware the Snake," *Down These Strange Streets*.
Rudy Rucker & Paul Di Filippo, "To See Infinity Bare," *Postscripts 24/25*.
Kristine Kathryn Rusch, "Becalmed," *Asimov's*, April/May.
——, "Dunyon," *Asimov's*, July.
——, "The Impossibles," *Analogy*, December.
——, "Killer Advice," *Asimov's*, January.
——, "Show Trial," *Subterranean*, Spring.
——, "Stealth," *Asimov's*, October/November.
——, "Unnatural Disaster," *Fantasy*, November.
——, "Watching the Music Dance," *Engineering Infinity*.
Alan Peter Ryan, "Time and Tide," *F&SF*, September/October.
Gavin Salisbury, "Junction 5," *Panverse Three*.
Jason Sanford, "Her Scientifiction, Far Future, Medieval Fantasy," *Interzone* 234.
——, "The Ever-Dreaming Verdict of Plagues," *Interzone* 236.
Pamela Sargent, "Strawberry Birdies," *Asimov's*, December.
Steven Saylor, "Styx and Stones," *Down These Strange Streets*.
——, "The Witch of Corinth," *F&SF*, July/August.
Ken Scholes, "Making My Entrance Again with My Usual Flair," Tor.com.
Carter Scholz, "Signs of Life," *F&SF*, May/June.
Gord Sellar, "Trois Morceaux En Forme de Mechanika," *Clarkesworld*, July.

Priya Sharma, "Lebkuchen," *Fantasy*, January.
Nisi Shawl, "Pataki," *Strange Horizons*, April.
Lucius Shepard, "Rose Street Attractors," *Ghosts by Gaslight*.
——, "The Skinny Girl," *Naked City*.
Lewis Shiner, "A Box of Thunder," *Strange Horizons*, 9/19.
Felicity Shoulders, "Apocalypse Daily," *Asimov's*, June.
William Shunn, "Care and Feeding of Your Piano," *Electric Velocipede 21/22*.
Robert Silverberg, "The End of the Line," *Asimov's*, August.
——, "Smithers and the Ghosts of the Thar," *Ghosts by Gaslight*.
——, "The Tomb of the Pontifex Dvorn," *Subterranean*, Winter.
Vandana Singh, "Indra's Web," *TRSF*.
Jack Skillingstead, "The Flow and the Dream," *Asimov's*, April/May.
——, "Free Dog," *Asimov's*, October/November.
——, "Steel Lake," *Solaris Rising*.
Alan Smale, "Leap of Faith," *Realms of Fantasy*, August.
Jeremy Adam Smith, "Frightened Angels," *Postscripts 24/25*.
Matthew Sanborn Smith, "Beauty Belongs to the Flowers," Tor.com.
Melinda M. Snodgrass, "No Mystery, No Miracle," *Down These Strange Streets*.
William Browning Spencer, "The Dappled Thing," *Subterranean Dark Fantasy* 2.
Norman Spinrad, "The Music of the Sphere," *Asimov's*, July.
Allen M. Steele, "Angel of Europa," *Subterranean Press*.
——, "The Observation Post," *Asimov's*, September.
Ferrett Steinmetz, "'Run,' Bakri Says," *Asimov's*, December.
Bruce Sterling, "The Master of the Aviary," *Welcome to the Greenhouse*.
——, "The Parthenopean Scaple," *Subterranean Dark Fantasy* 2.
James Stoddard, "The Ifs of Time," *F&SF*, March/April.
——, "Orion Rising," *Panverse Three*.
Charles Stross, "A Bird in the Hand," *Fables from the Fountain*.
——, "Bit Rot," *Engineering Infinity*.
Tim Sullivan, "Under Glass," *F&SF*, November/December.
Michael Swanwick, "An Empty House with Many Doors," *Asimov's*, April/May.
——, "The Man in Grey," *Eclipse Four*.
Rachel Swirsky, "Fields of Gold," *Eclipse Four*.
——, "The Taste of Promises," *Life on Mars*.
Melanie Tem, "Little Shit," *Supernatural Noir*.
Steve Rasnic Tem, "At Play in the Fields," *Solaris Rising*.
——, "Ephemera," *Asimov's*, December.
——, "Visitors," *Asimov's*, January.
Lavie Tidhar, "The Ambiguity Clock," *Daily SF*, April 22.
——, "The Hubbard Continuum," *Redstone SF*, March.
——, "In the Season of the Mango Rains," *Interzone 234*.
——, "Jesus and the Eightfold Path," *Immersion Press*.
——, "The Last Osama," *Interzone 237*.
——, "The Lives and Deaths of Che Guevara," *Solaris Rising*.
——, "Passage," *Daily SF*, August 24.
——, "The Projected Girl," *Naked City*.
——, "Red Dawn: A Chow Mein Western," *Fantasy*, November.
——, "The River Came," *End of an Aeon*.

Jeremiah Tolbert, "You Have Been Turned into a Zombie by a Friend," *Fantasy*, June.
Harry Turtledove, "Lee at the Alamo," Tor.com, September 7.
——, "Shtetl Days," Tor.com, April 14.
Lisa Tuttle, "The Curious Affair of the Deodand," *Down These Strange Streets*.
Catherynne M. Valente, "The Bread We Eat in Dreams," *Apex Magazine*, November.
——, "The Girl Who Ruled Fairyland—For a Little While," Tor.com, July 27.
——, "White Lines on a Green Field," *Subterranean*, Fall.
Genevieve Valentine, "Carte Blanche," *Electric Velocipede* 21/22.
——, "Demons, Your Body, and You," *Subterranean*, Summer.
——, "Galatea," *Lightspeed*, August.
——, "The Sandal-Bride," *Fantasy*, March.
——, "Semiramis," *Clarkesworld*, June.
——, "Souvenir," *Strange Horizons*, 8/15.
Carrie Vaughn, "It's Still the Same Old Story," *Down These Strange Streets*.
Juliette Wade, "At Cross Purposes," *Analog*, January/February.
Alan Wall, "Burning Bibles," *Asimov's*, September.
Kali Wallace, "Botanical Exercises for Curious Girls," *F&SF*, March/April.
Jo Walton, "The Panda Coin," *Eclipse Four*.
Ian Watson, "How We Came Back from Mars," *Solaris Rising*.
Peter Watts, "Malek (or, It's Not Easy Being Green)," *Engineering Infinity*.
Don Webb, "Fine Green Dust," *F&SF*, May/June.
Kate Wilhelm, "The Birdcage," *F&SF*, January/February.
——, "Music Makers," *F&SF*, May/June.
Connie Willis, "All About Emily," *Asimov's*, December.
Chris Willrich, "The Lions of Karthagar," *Black Gate*, Spring.
Gene Wolfe, "Why I Was Hanged," *Ghosts by Gaslight*.
Nick Wolven, "Lost in the Memory Palace," *Asimov's*, March.
John C. Wright, "Judgement Eve," *Engineering Infinity*.
Rio Youers, "The Ghost of Lillian Bliss," *Postscripts* 24/25.
Jim Young, "The Whirlwind," *F&SF*, January/February.
E. Lily Yu, "The Cartographer Wasps and the Anarchist Bees," *Clarkesworld*, April.